THE GREATEST NOVELS *of* MARK TWAIN

CLASSICS

Reprint 2022

FiNGERPRINT! CLASSICS
An imprint of Prakash Books India Pvt. Ltd.

113/A, Darya Ganj,
New Delhi-110 002
Tel: (011) 2324 7062 – 65, Fax: (011) 2324 6975
Email: info@prakashbooks.com/sales@prakashbooks.com

facebook www.facebook.com/fingerprintpublishing
twitter www.twitter.com/FingerprintP
www.fingerprintpublishing.com

ISBN: 978 93 8881 045 6

Samuel Langhorne Clemens, better known by his pen name Mark Twain, was born in Florida, Missouri, on November 30, 1835, to Jane Lampton and John Marshall Clemens. In 1839, four years after his birth, his family shifted to Hannibal, a developing port city along the banks of River Mississippi, in the slaveholding state of Missouri. This later provided the setting for *The Adventures of Tom Sawyer* and, its sequel, *The Adventures of Huckleberry Finn*.

At the age of thirteen, Twain left school to become a printer's apprentice, after which he joined his elder brother's newspaper as a printer and an editorial assistant. It was here he realised he enjoyed writing. For the next few years, he travelled to various places working as a printer and educating himself in public libraries. When Twain was in his early twenties, he apprenticed as a steamboat pilot and studied the Mississippi. After a couple of years of experience, he gained his pilot's license and worked as a river pilot till 1861.

Twain continued his travels and tried his hand at mining in Virginia City, Nevada, but failed. He then joined the *Territorial Enterprise*, a Virginia City newspaper. His first story, *The Celebrated Jumping Frog of Calaveras County*, was published in 1865 in New York's *The Saturday Press*. With this came his first success as a writer. The story went to be popular, brought him nationwide attention, and was also translated into classic Greek. He earned praise from critics and peers for his wit and satire in prose and speech and became friends with presidents, artists, industrialists, and European royalty.

In 1866, he travelled as a reporter to Sandwich Islands (present-day Hawaii) for *Sacramento Union*. His travelogues became the basis for his first lectures. In 1867, he wrote a popular collection of travel letters during his tour to Europe and Middle East, which were compiled as *The Innocents Abroad*, his first novel, and published in 1869. In 1870-71, he wrote *Roughing It*. Published in 1872, the book was inspired by his experiences in Western America.

Twain married Olivia Langdon in February 1870 after overcoming her father's reluctance. The couple had three daughters—Susy, Clara, and Jean. The Twain family moved to Connecticut in 1873. They stayed there for almost seventeen years, spending their summers at Quarry Farm in Elmira. Most of his classic novels were written during this period.

The Adventures of Tom Sawyer came out in 1876. Set in the fictional town of St. Petersburg, it features Tom Sawyer—one of the best-loved characters in American fiction. From stealing the jam jar and narrowly escaping being hit to accompanying Huckleberry Finn to the graveyard at night, Tom's life is full of escapades. Drawn on Twain's years in Missouri as a child and his experiences as a pilot on the Mississippi, the novel is suggestive of the life in the towns by the Mississippi River. It brings out the inequalities of adult reality from beneath the innocence of childhood.

A Tramp Abroad was published in 1880. *The Prince and the Pauper* was Twain's first attempt at writing historical fiction. It was first published in Canada in 1881 and then in 1882 in the United States. Considered to be Twain's most infamous work, it is the story of two young boys—Tom Candy, a pauper, and Edward Tudor, the Prince of Wales—who are identical in appearance.

Twain's *The Adventures of Huckleberry Finn* was first published in 1884 in the United Kingdom. It was published in the United States in February 1885. Considered the first great American novel by some, it is the story of Huck's adventures in the Mississippi Valley. A direct sequel to *The Adventures of Tom Sawyer*, it traces Huck's moral development. A work of immeasurable richness and complexity, it remains an incomparable adventure story and a classic of American humour, more than a century after its publication.

Between 1885 and 1889, Twain worked on *A Connecticut Yankee in King Arthur's Court*. It was first published in December 1889 in England. A brilliant satire featuring time travel, it reveals the absurdities of the social and political norms of those times.

Twain lost a lot of money through his investments in the typesetting company and publishing house. Both were a failure. In June 1891, he moved to Europe. The family travelled across Europe in the years that followed. In 1893-94, *Pudd'nhead Wilson* was serialized in *The Century Magazine*. It was published as a novel in 1894. Twain was completely bankrupt by this time. His daughter Susy's death in 1896 left him in further despair.

Twain undertook a lot of lecture tours which helped him repay his creditors. By the beginning of the twentieth century, Twain had not only paid off all his debts, but had also become well-known as a writer and humorist. He lost his wife in 1904. In 1906, he began writing his autobiography in the *North American Review*. He also started a club for girls called the Angel Fish and Aquarium Club.

In 1907, Twain was awarded an honorary doctorate in letters by the Oxford University. He died on April 21, 1910, in Redding, Connecticut, after suffering a heart attack. Lauded as the 'greatest American humorist of his age' and called 'the father of American literature' by William Faulkner, Mark Twain continues to remain celebrated more than a century after his death.

Contents

The Adventures of Tom Sawyer (1876)

To

My Wife

This Book

is

Affectionately Dedicated

Preface

Most of the adventures recorded in this book really occurred; one or two were experiences of my own, the rest those of boys who were schoolmates of mine. Huck Finn is drawn from life; Tom Sawyer also, but not from an individual—he is a combination of the characteristics of three boys whom I knew, and therefore belongs to the composite order of architecture.

The odd superstitions touched upon were all prevalent among children and slaves in the West at the period of this story—that is to say, thirty of forty years ago.

Although my book is intended mainly for the entertainment of boys and girls, I hope it will not be shunned by men and women on that account, for part of my plan has been to try to pleasantly remind adults of what they once were themselves, and of how they felt and thought and talked, and what queer enterprises they sometimes engaged in.

The Author
Hartford, 1876

1

"Tom!"

No answer.

"TOM!"

No answer.

"What's gone with that boy, I wonder? You TOM!"

No answer.

The old lady pulled her spectacles down and looked over them about the room; then she put them up and looked out under them. She seldom or never looked *through* them for so small a thing as a boy; they were her state pair, the pride of her heart, and were built for "style," not service—she could have seen through a pair of stove-lids just as well. She looked perplexed for a moment, and then said, not fiercely, but still loud enough for the furniture to hear:

"Well, I lay if I get hold of you I'll—"

She did not finish, for by this time she was bending down and punching under the bed with the broom, and so she needed breath to punctuate the punches with. She resurrected nothing but the cat.

"I never did see the beat of that boy!"

She went to the open door and stood in it and looked out among the tomato vines and "jimpson" weeds that constituted the garden. No Tom. So she lifted up her voice at an angle calculated for distance and shouted:

"Y-o-u-u *Tom*!"

There was a slight noise behind her and she turned just in time to seize a small boy by the slack of his roundabout and arrest his flight.

"There! I might 'a' thought of that closet. What you been doing in there?"

"Nothing."

"Nothing! Look at your hands. And look at your mouth. What *is* that truck?"

"I don't know, aunt."

"Well, *I* know. It's jam—that's what it is. Forty times I've said if you didn't let that jam alone I'd skin you. Hand me that switch."

The switch hovered in the air—the peril was desperate—

"My! Look behind you, aunt!"

The old lady whirled round, and snatched her skirts out of danger. The lad fled on the instant, scrambled up the high board-fence, and disappeared over it.

His Aunt Polly stood surprised a moment, and then broke into a gentle laugh.

Aunt Polly Beguiled

"Hang the boy, can't I never learn anything? Ain't he played me tricks enough like that for me to be looking out for him by this time? But old fools is the biggest fools there is. Can't learn an old dog new tricks, as the saying is. But my goodness, he never plays them alike, two days, and how is a body to know what's coming? He 'pears to know just how long he can torment me before I get my dander up, and he knows if he can make out to put me off for a minute or make me laugh, it's all down again and I can't hit him a lick. I ain't doing my duty by that boy, and that's the Lord's truth, goodness knows. Spare the rod and spile the child, as the Good Book says. I'm a laying up sin and suffering for us both, I know. He's full of the Old Scratch, but laws-a-me! he's my own dead sister's boy, poor thing, and I ain't got the heart to lash him, somehow. Every time I let him off, my conscience does hurt me so, and every time I hit him my old heart most breaks. Well-a-well, man that is born of woman is of few days and full of trouble, as the Scripture says, and I reckon it's so. He'll play hookey this evening,* and I'll just be obleeged to make him work, tomorrow, to punish him. It's mighty hard to make him work Saturdays, when all the boys is having holiday, but he hates work more than he hates anything else, and I've *got* to do some of my duty by him, or I'll be the ruination of the child."

* Southwestern for "afternoon"

Tom did play hookey, and he had a very good time. He got back home barely in season to help Jim, the small coloured boy, saw next-day's wood and split the kindlings before supper—at least he was there in time to tell his adventures to Jim while Jim did three-fourths of the work. Tom's younger brother (or rather half-brother) Sid was already through with his part of the work (picking up chips), for he was a quiet boy, and had no adventurous, troublesome ways.

A Good Opportunity

While Tom was eating his supper, and stealing sugar as opportunity offered, Aunt Polly asked him questions that were full of guile, and very deep—for she wanted to trap him into damaging revealments. Like many other simple-hearted souls, it was her pet vanity to believe she was endowed with a talent for dark and mysterious diplomacy, and she loved to contemplate her most transparent devices as marvels of low cunning. Said she:

"Tom, it was middling warm in school, warn't it?"

"Yes'm."

"Powerful warm, warn't it?"

"Yes'm."

"Didn't you want to go in a-swimming, Tom?"

A bit of a scare shot through Tom—a touch of uncomfortable suspicion. He searched Aunt Polly's face, but it told him nothing. So he said:

"No'm—well, not very much."

The old lady reached out her hand and felt Tom's shirt, and said:

"But you ain't too warm now, though." And it flattered her to reflect that she had discovered that the shirt was dry without anybody knowing that that was what she had in her mind. But in spite of her, Tom knew where the wind lay, now. So he forestalled what might be the next move:

"Some of us pumped on our heads—mine's damp yet. See?"

Aunt Polly was vexed to think she had overlooked that bit of circumstantial evidence, and missed a trick. Then she had a new inspiration:

"Tom, you didn't have to undo your shirt collar where I sewed it, to pump on your head, did you? Unbutton your jacket!"

The trouble vanished out of Tom's face. He opened his jacket. His shirt collar was securely sewed.

"Bother! Well, go 'long with you. I'd made sure you'd played hookey and been a-swimming. But I forgive ye, Tom. I reckon you're a kind of a singed cat, as the saying is—better'n you look. *This* time."

She was half sorry her sagacity had miscarried, and half glad that Tom had stumbled into obedient conduct for once.

But Sidney said:

"Well, now, if I didn't think you sewed his collar with white thread, but it's black."

"Why, I did sew it with white! Tom!"

But Tom did not wait for the rest. As he went out at the door he said:

"Siddy, I'll lick you for that."

In a safe place Tom examined two large needles which were thrust into the lapels of his jacket, and had thread bound about them—one needle carried white thread and the other black. He said:

"She'd never noticed if it hadn't been for Sid. Confound it! sometimes she sews it with white, and sometimes she sews it with black. I wish to geeminy she'd stick to one or t'other—I can't keep the run of 'em. But I bet you I'll lam Sid for that. I'll learn him!"

He was not the Model Boy of the village. He knew the model boy very well though—and loathed him.

Within two minutes, or even less, he had forgotten all his troubles. Not because his troubles were one whit less heavy and bitter to him than a man's are to a man, but because a new and powerful interest bore them down and drove them out of his mind for the time—just as men's misfortunes are forgotten in the excitement of new enterprises. This new interest was a valued novelty in whistling, which he had just acquired from a negro, and he was suffering to practise it undisturbed. It consisted in a peculiar bird-like turn, a sort of liquid warble, produced by touching the tongue to the roof of the mouth at short intervals in the midst of the music—the reader probably remembers how to do it, if he has ever been a boy. Diligence and attention soon gave him the knack of it, and he strode down the street with his mouth full of harmony and his soul full of gratitude. He felt much as an astronomer feels who has discovered a new planet—no doubt, as far as strong, deep, unalloyed pleasure is concerned, the advantage was with the boy, not the astronomer.

The summer evenings were long. It was not dark, yet. Presently Tom checked his whistle. A stranger was before him—a boy a shade larger than himself. A newcomer of any age or either sex was an impressive curiosity in the poor little shabby village of St. Petersburg. This boy was well dressed, too—well dressed on a weekday. This was simply astounding. His cap was a dainty thing, his close-buttoned blue cloth roundabout was new and natty, and so were his pantaloons. He had shoes on—and it was only Friday. He even wore a necktie, a bright bit of ribbon. He had a citified air about him that ate into Tom's vitals. The more Tom stared at the splendid marvel, the higher he turned up his nose at his finery and the shabbier and shabbier his own outfit seemed to him to grow. Neither boy spoke. If one moved, the other moved—but only sidewise, in a circle; they kept face to face and eye to eye all the time. Finally Tom said:

"I can lick you!"

"I'd like to see you try it."

"Well, I can do it."

"No you can't, either."

"Yes I can."

"No you can't."

"I can."

"You can't."

"Can!"

"Can't!"

An uncomfortable pause. Then Tom said:

"What's your name?"

"'Tisn't any of your business, maybe."

"Well I 'low I'll *make* it my business."

"Well why don't you?"

"If you say much, I will."

"Much—much—*much*. There now."

"Oh, you think you're mighty smart, *don't* you? I could lick you with one hand tied behind me, if I wanted to."

"Well why don't you *do* it? You *say* you can do it."

"Well I *will*, if you fool with me."

"Oh yes—I've seen whole families in the same fix."

"Smarty! You think you're *some*, now, *don't* you? Oh, what a hat!"

"You can lump that hat if you don't like it. I dare you to knock it off—and anybody that'll take a dare will suck eggs."

"You're a liar!"

"You're another."

"You're a fighting liar and dasn't take it up."

"Aw—take a walk!"

"Say—if you give me much more of your sass I'll take and bounce a rock off'n your head."

"Oh, of *course* you will."

"Well I *will*."

"Well why don't you *do* it then? What do you keep *saying* you will for? Why don't you *do* it? It's because you're afraid."

"I *ain't* afraid."

"You are."

"I ain't."

"You are."

Another pause, and more eying and sidling around each other. Presently they were shoulder to shoulder. Tom said:

"Get away from here!"

"Go away yourself!"

"I won't."

"I won't either."

So they stood, each with a foot placed at an angle as a brace, and both shoving with might and main, and glowering at each other with hate. But neither could get an advantage. After struggling till both were hot and flushed, each relaxed his strain with watchful caution, and Tom said:

"You're a coward and a pup. I'll tell my big brother on you, and he can thrash you with his little finger, and I'll make him do it, too."

"What do I care for your big brother? I've got a brother that's bigger than he is—and what's more, he can throw him over that fence, too." [Both brothers were imaginary.]

"That's a lie."

"*Your* saying so don't make it so."

Tom drew a line in the dust with his big toe, and said:

"I dare you to step over that, and I'll lick you till you can't stand up. Anybody that'll take a dare will steal sheep."

The new boy stepped over promptly, and said:

"Now you said you'd do it, now let's see you do it."

"Don't you crowd me now; you better look out."

"Well, you *said* you'd do it—why don't you do it?"

"By jingo! for two cents I *will* do it."

The new boy took two broad coppers out of his pocket and held them out with derision. Tom struck them to the ground. In an instant both boys were rolling and tumbling in the dirt, gripped together like cats; and for the space of a minute they tugged and tore at each other's hair and clothes, punched and scratched each other's nose, and covered themselves with dust and glory. Presently the confusion took form, and through the fog of battle Tom appeared, seated astride the new boy, and pounding him with his fists.

"Holler 'nuff!" said he.

The boy only struggled to free himself. He was crying—mainly from rage.

"Holler 'nuff!"—and the pounding went on.

At last the stranger got out a smothered "'Nuff!" and Tom let him up and said:

"Now that'll learn you. Better look out who you're fooling with next time."

The new boy went off brushing the dust from his clothes, sobbing, snuffling, and occasionally looking back and shaking his head and threatening what he would do to Tom the "next time he caught him out." To which Tom responded with jeers, and started off in high feather, and as soon as his back was turned the new boy snatched up a stone, threw it and hit him between the shoulders and then turned tail and ran like an antelope. Tom chased the traitor home, and thus found out where he lived. He then held a position at the gate for some time, daring the enemy to come outside, but the enemy only made faces at him through the window and declined. At last the enemy's mother appeared, and called Tom a bad, vicious, vulgar child, and ordered him away. So he went away; but he said he "'lowed" to "lay" for that boy

He got home pretty late that night, and when he climbed cautiously in at the window, he uncovered an ambuscade, in the person of his aunt; and when she saw the state his clothes were in her resolution to turn his Saturday holiday into captivity at hard labour became adamantine in its firmness.

2

Saturday morning was come, and all the summer world was bright and fresh, and brimming with life. There was a song in every heart; and if the heart was young the music issued at the lips. There was cheer in every face and a spring in every step. The locust-trees were in bloom and the fragrance of the blossoms filled the air. Cardiff Hill, beyond the village and above it, was green with vegetation and it lay just far enough away to seem a Delectable Land, dreamy, reposeful, and inviting.

Tom appeared on the sidewalk with a bucket of whitewash and a long-handled brush. He surveyed the fence, and all gladness left him and a deep melancholy settled down upon his spirit. Thirty yards of board fence nine feet high. Life to him seemed hollow, and existence but a burden. Sighing, he dipped his brush and passed it along the topmost plank; repeated the operation; did it again; compared the insignificant whitewashed streak with the far-reaching continent of unwhitewashed fence, and sat down on a tree-box discouraged. Jim came skipping out at the gate with a tin pail, and singing Buffalo Gals. Bringing water from the town pump had always been hateful work in Tom's eyes, before, but now it did not strike him so. He remembered that there was company at the pump. White, mulatto, and negro boys and girls were always there waiting their turns, resting, trading playthings, quarrelling, fighting, skylarking. And he remembered that although the pump was only a hundred and fifty yards off, Jim never got back with a bucket of water under an hour—and even then somebody generally had to go after him. Tom said:

"Say, Jim, I'll fetch the water if you'll whitewash some."

Jim shook his head and said:

"Can't, Mars Tom. Ole missis, she tole me I got to go an' git dis water an' not stop foolin' roun' wid anybody. She say she spec' Mars Tom gwine to ax me to whitewash, an' so she tole me go 'long an' 'tend to my own business—she 'lowed *she'd* 'tend to de whitewashin'."

"Oh, never you mind what she said, Jim. That's the way she always talks. Gimme the bucket—I won't be gone only a a minute. *She* won't ever know."

"Oh, I dasn't, Mars Tom. Ole missis she'd take an' tar de head off'n me. 'Deed she would."

"*She*! She never licks anybody—whacks 'em over the head with her thimble—and who cares for that, I'd like to know. She talks awful, but talk don't hurt—anyways it don't if she don't cry. Jim, I'll give you a marvel. I'll give you a white alley!"

Jim began to waver.

"White alley, Jim! And it's a bully taw."

"My! Dat's a mighty gay marvel, I tell you! But Mars Tom I's powerful 'fraid ole missis—"

"And besides, if you will I'll show you my sore toe."

Jim was only human—this attraction was too much for him. He put down his pail, took the white alley, and bent over the toe with absorbing interest while the bandage was being unwound. In another moment he was flying down the street with his pail and a tingling rear, Tom was whitewashing with vigor, and Aunt Polly was retiring from the field with a slipper in her hand and triumph in her eye.

But Tom's energy did not last. He began to think of the fun he had planned for this day, and his sorrows multiplied. Soon the free boys would come tripping along on all sorts of delicious expeditions, and they would make a world of fun of him for having to work—the very thought of it burnt him like fire. He got out his worldly wealth and examined it—bits of toys, marbles, and trash; enough to buy an exchange of *work*, maybe, but not half enough to buy so much as half an hour of pure freedom. So he returned his straitened means to his pocket, and gave up the idea of trying to buy the boys. At this dark and hopeless moment an inspiration burst upon him! Nothing less than a great, magnificent inspiration.

He took up his brush and went tranquilly to work. Ben Rogers hove in sight presently—the very boy, of all boys, whose ridicule he had been dreading. Ben's gait was the hop-skip-and-jump—proof enough that his heart was light and his anticipations high. He was eating an apple, and giving a long, melodious whoop, at intervals, followed by a deep-toned ding-dong-dong, ding-dong-dong, for he was personating a steamboat. As he drew near, he slackened speed, took the middle of the street, leaned far over to starboard and rounded to ponderously and with laborious pomp and circumstance—for he was personating the Big Missouri, and considered himself to be drawing nine feet of water. He was boat and captain and engine-bells combined, so he had to imagine himself standing on his own hurricane-deck giving the orders and executing them:

"Stop her, sir! Ting-a-ling-ling!" The headway ran almost out, and he drew up slowly toward the sidewalk.

"Ship up to back! Ting-a-ling-ling!" His arms straightened and stiffened down his sides.

"Set her back on the stabboard! Ting-a-ling-ling! Chow! ch-chow-wow! Chow!" His right hand, meantime, describing stately circles—for it was representing a forty-foot wheel.

"Let her go back on the labboard! Ting-a-ling-ling! Chow-ch-chow-chow!" The left hand began to describe circles.

"Stop the stabboard! Ting-a-ling-ling! Stop the labboard! Come ahead on the stabboard! Stop her! Let your outside turn over slow! Ting-a-ling-ling! Chow-ow-ow! Get out that head-line! *lively* now! Come—out with your spring-line—what're you about there! Take a turn round that stump with the bight of it! Stand by that stage, now—let her go! Done with the engines, sir! Ting-a-ling-ling! *Sh't! s'h't! sh't!*" (trying the gauge-cocks).

Tom went on whitewashing—paid no attention to the steamboat. Ben stared a moment and then said:

"*Hi-Yi! You're* up a stump, ain't you!"

No answer. Tom surveyed his last touch with the eye of an artist, then he gave his brush another gentle sweep and surveyed the result, as before. Ben ranged up alongside of him. Tom's mouth watered for the apple, but he stuck to his work. Ben said:

"Hello, old chap, you got to work, hey?"

Tom wheeled suddenly and said:

"Why, it's you, Ben! I warn't noticing."

"Say—I'm going in a-swimming, I am. Don't you wish you could? But of course you'd druther *work*—wouldn't you? Course you would!"

Tom contemplated the boy a bit, and said:

"What do you call work?"

"Why, ain't *that* work?"

Ain't that Work?

Tom resumed his whitewashing, and answered carelessly:

"Well, maybe it is, and maybe it ain't. All I know, is, it suits Tom Sawyer."

"Oh come, now, you don't mean to let on that you *like* it?"

The brush continued to move.

"Like it? Well, I don't see why I oughtn't to like it. Does a boy get a chance to whitewash a fence every day?"

That put the thing in a new light. Ben stopped nibbling his apple. Tom swept his brush daintily back and forth—stepped back to note the effect—added a touch here and there—criticised the effect again—Ben watching every move and getting more and more interested, more and more absorbed. Presently he said:

"Say, Tom, let *me* whitewash a little."

Tom considered, was about to consent; but he altered his mind:

"No—no—I reckon it wouldn't hardly do, Ben. You see, Aunt Polly's awful particular about this fence—right here on the street, you know—but if it was the back fence I wouldn't mind and *she* wouldn't. Yes, she's awful particular about this fence; it's got to be done very careful; I reckon there ain't one boy in a thousand, maybe two thousand, that can do it the way it's got to be done."

"No—is that so? Oh come, now—lemme just try. Only just a little—I'd let *you*, if you was me, Tom."

"Ben, I'd like to, honest injun; but Aunt Polly—well, Jim wanted to do it, but she wouldn't let him; Sid wanted to do it, and she wouldn't let Sid. Now don't you see how I'm fixed? If you was to tackle this fence and anything was to happen to it—"

"Oh, shucks, I'll be just as careful. Now lemme try. Say—I'll give you the core of my apple."

"Well, here—No, Ben, now don't. I'm afeard—"

"I'll give you *all* of it!"

Tom gave up the brush with reluctance in his face, but alacrity in his heart. And while the late steamer Big Missouri worked and sweated in the sun, the retired artist sat on a barrel in the shade close by, dangled his legs, munched his apple, and planned the slaughter of more innocents. There was no lack of material; boys happened along every little while; they came to jeer, but remained to whitewash. By the time Ben was fagged out, Tom had traded the next chance to Billy Fisher for a kite, in good repair; and when he played out, Johnny Miller bought in for a dead rat and a string to swing it with—and so on, and so on, hour after hour. And when the middle of the afternoon came, from being a poor poverty-stricken boy in the morning, Tom was literally rolling in wealth. He had besides the things before mentioned, twelve marbles, part of a jews-harp, a piece of blue bottle-glass to look through, a spool cannon, a key that wouldn't unlock anything, a fragment of chalk, a glass stopper of a decanter, a tin soldier, a couple of tadpoles, six firecrackers, a kitten with only one eye, a brass doorknob, a dog-collar—but no dog—the handle of a knife, four pieces of orange-peel, and a dilapidated old window sash.

He had had a nice, good, idle time all the while—plenty of company—and the fence had three coats of whitewash on it! If he hadn't run out of whitewash he would have bankrupted every boy in the village.

Tom said to himself that it was not such a hollow world, after all. He had discovered a great law of human action, without knowing it—namely, that in order to make a man or a boy covet a thing, it is only necessary to make the thing difficult to attain. If he had been a great and wise philosopher, like the writer of this book, he would now have comprehended that Work consists of whatever a body is *obliged* to do, and that Play consists of whatever a body is not obliged to do. And this would help him to understand why constructing artificial flowers or performing on a treadmill is work, while rolling ten-pins or climbing Mont Blanc is only amusement. There are wealthy gentlemen in England who drive four-horse passenger-coaches twenty or thirty miles on a daily line, in the summer, because the privilege costs them considerable money; but if they were offered wages for the service, that would turn it into work and then they would resign.

The boy mused awhile over the substantial change which had taken place in his worldly circumstances, and then wended toward headquarters to report.

3

Tom presented himself before Aunt Polly, who was sitting by an open window in a pleasant rearward apartment, which was bedroom, breakfast room, dining room, and library, combined. The balmy summer air, the restful quiet, the odour of the flowers, and the drowsing murmur of the bees had had their effect, and she was nodding over her knitting—for she had no company but the cat, and it was asleep in her lap. Her spectacles were propped up on her grey head for safety. She had thought that of course Tom had deserted long ago, and she wondered at seeing him place himself in her power again in this intrepid way. He said: "Mayn't I go and play now, aunt?"

"What, a'ready? How much have you done?"

"It's all done, aunt."

"Tom, don't lie to me—I can't bear it."

"I ain't, aunt; it *is* all done."

Aunt Polly placed small trust in such evidence. She went out to see for herself; and she would have been content to find twenty per cent. of Tom's statement true. When she found the entire fence white-washed, and not only whitewashed but elaborately coated and recoated, and even a streak added to the ground, her astonishment was almost unspeakable. She said:

"Well, I never! There's no getting round it, you can work when you're a mind to, Tom." And then she diluted the compliment by adding, "But it's powerful seldom you're a mind to, I'm bound to say. Well, go 'long and play; but mind you get back some time in a week, or I'll tan you."

She was so overcome by the splendour of his achievement that she took him into the closet and selected a choice apple and delivered it to him, along with an improving lecture upon the added value and flavor a treat took to itself when it came without sin through virtuous effort. And while she closed with a happy Scriptural flourish, he "hooked" a doughnut.

Then he skipped out, and saw Sid just starting up the outside stairway that led to the back rooms on the second floor. Clods were handy and the air was full of them in a twinkling. They raged around Sid like a hailstorm; and before Aunt Polly could collect her surprised faculties and sally to the rescue, six or seven clods had taken personal effect, and Tom was over the fence and gone. There was a gate, but as a general thing he was too crowded for time to make use of it. His soul was at peace, now that he had settled with Sid for calling attention to his black thread and getting him into trouble.

Tom skirted the block, and came round into a muddy alley that led by the back of his aunt's cow-stable. He presently got safely beyond the reach of capture and punishment, and hastened toward the public square of the village, where two "military" companies of boys had met for conflict, according to previous appointment. Tom was General of one of these armies, Joe Harper (a bosom friend) General of the other. These two great commanders did not condescend to fight in person—that being better suited to the still smaller fry—but sat together on an eminence and conducted the field operations by orders delivered through aides-de-camp. Tom's army won a great victory, after a long and hard-fought battle. Then the dead were counted, prisoners exchanged, the terms of the next disagreement agreed upon, and the day for the necessary battle appointed; after which the armies fell into line and marched away, and Tom turned homeward alone.

After the Battle

As he was passing by the house where Jeff Thatcher lived, he saw a new girl in the garden—a lovely little blue-eyed creature with yellow hair plaited into two long-tails, white summer frock and embroidered pan-talettes. The fresh-crowned hero fell without firing a shot. A certain Amy Lawrence vanished out of his heart and left not even a memory of herself behind. He had thought he loved her to distraction; he had regarded his passion as adoration; and behold it was only a poor little evanescent partiality. He had been months winning her; she had confessed hardly a week ago; he had been the happiest and the proudest boy in the world only seven short days, and here in one instant of time she had gone out of his heart like a casual stranger whose visit is done.

He worshipped this new angel with furtive eye, till he saw that she had discovered him; then he pretended he did not know she was present, and began to "show off" in all sorts of absurd boyish ways, in order to win her admiration. He kept up this grotesque foolishness for some time; but by and by, while he was in the midst of some dangerous gymnastic performances, he glanced aside and saw that the little girl was wending her way toward the house. Tom came up to the fence and leaned on it, grieving, and hoping she would tarry yet awhile longer. She halted a moment on the steps and then moved toward the door. Tom heaved a great sigh as she put her foot on the threshold. But his face lit up, right away, for she tossed a pansy over the fence a moment before she disappeared.

The boy ran around and stopped within a foot or two of the flower, and then shaded his eyes with his hand and began to look down street as if he had discovered something of interest going on in that direction. Presently he picked up a straw and began trying to balance it on his nose, with his head tilted far back; and as he moved from side to side, in his efforts, he edged nearer and nearer toward the pansy; finally his bare foot rested upon it, his pliant toes closed upon it, and he hopped away with the treasure and disappeared round the corner. But only for a minute—only while he could button the flower inside his jacket, next his heart—or next his stomach, possibly, for he was not much posted in anatomy, and not hypercritical, anyway.

He returned, now, and hung about the fence till nightfall, "showing off," as before; but the girl never exhibited herself again, though Tom comforted himself a little with the hope that she had been near some window, meantime, and been aware of his attentions. Finally he strode home reluctantly, with his poor head full of visions.

All through supper his spirits were so high that his aunt wondered "what had got into the child." He took a good scolding about clodding Sid, and did not seem to mind it in the least. He tried to steal sugar under his aunt's very nose, and got his knuckles rapped for it. He said:

"Aunt, you don't whack Sid when he takes it."

"Well, Sid don't torment a body the way you do. You'd be always into that sugar if I warn't watching you."

Presently she stepped into the kitchen, and Sid, happy in his immunity, reached for the sugar bowl—a sort of glorying over Tom which was wellnigh unbearable. But Sid's fingers slipped and the bowl dropped and broke. Tom was in ecstasies. In such ecstasies that he even controlled his tongue and was silent. He said to himself that he would not speak a word, even when his aunt came in, but would sit perfectly still till she asked who did the mischief; and then he would tell, and there would be nothing so good in the world as to see that pet model "catch it." He was so brimful of exultation that he could hardly hold himself when the old lady came back and stood above the wreck discharging lightnings of wrath from over her spectacles. He said to himself, "Now it's coming!" And the next instant he was sprawling on the floor! The potent palm was uplifted to strike again when Tom cried out:

"Hold on, now, what 'er you belting *me* for?—Sid broke it!"

Aunt Polly paused, perplexed, and Tom looked for healing pity. But when she got her tongue again, she only said:

"Umf! Well, you didn't get a lick amiss, I reckon. You been into some other audacious mischief when I wasn't around, like enough."

Then her conscience reproached her, and she yearned to say something kind and loving; but she judged that this would be construed into a confession that she had been in the wrong, and discipline forbade that. So she kept silence, and went about her affairs with a troubled heart. Tom sulked in a corner and exalted his woes. He knew that in her heart his aunt was on her knees to him, and he was morosely gratified by the consciousness of it. He would hang out no signals, he would take notice of none. He knew that a yearning glance fell upon him, now and then, through a film of tears, but he refused recognition of it. He pictured himself lying sick unto death and his aunt bending over him beseeching one little forgiving word, but he would turn his face to the wall, and die with that word unsaid. Ah, how would she feel then? And he pictured himself brought home from the river, dead, with his curls all wet, and his sore heart at rest. How she would throw herself upon him, and how her tears would fall like rain, and her lips pray God to give her back her boy and she would never, never abuse him any more! But he would lie there cold and white and make no sign—a poor little sufferer, whose griefs were at an end. He so worked upon his feelings with the pathos of these dreams, that he had to keep swallowing, he was so like to choke; and his eyes swam in a blur of water, which overflowed when he winked, and ran down and trickled from the end of his nose. And such a luxury to him was this petting of his sorrows, that he could not bear to have any worldly cheeriness or any grating delight intrude upon it; it was too sacred for such contact; and so, presently, when his cousin Mary danced in, all alive with the joy of seeing home again after an age-long visit of one week to the country, he got up and moved in clouds and darkness out at one door as she brought song and sunshine in at the other.

He wandered far from the accustomed haunts of boys, and sought desolate places that were in harmony with his spirit. A log raft in the river invited him, and he seated himself on its outer edge and contemplated the dreary vastness of the stream, wishing, the while, that he could only be drowned, all at once and unconsciously, without undergoing the uncomfortable routine devised by nature. Then he thought of his flower. He got it out, rumpled and wilted, and it mightily increased his dismal felicity. He wondered if she would pity him if she knew? Would she cry, and wish that she had a right to put her arms around his neck and comfort him? Or would she turn coldly away like all the hollow world? This picture brought such an agony of pleasurable suffering that he worked it over and over again in his mind and set it up in new and varied lights, till he wore it threadbare. At last he rose up sighing and departed in the darkness.

About half-past nine or ten o'clock he came along the deserted street to where the Adored Unknown lived; he paused a moment; no sound fell upon his listening ear; a candle was casting a dull glow upon the curtain of a second-storey window. Was the sacred presence there? He climbed the fence, threaded his stealthy way through the plants, till he stood under that window; he looked up at it long, and with emotion; then he laid him down on the ground under it, disposing himself upon his back, with his hands clasped upon his breast and holding his poor wilted flower. And thus he would die—out in the cold world, with no shelter over his homeless head, no friendly hand to wipe the death-damps from his brow, no loving face to bend pityingly over him when the great agony came. And thus *she* would see him when she looked out upon the glad morning, and oh! would she drop one little tear upon his poor, lifeless form, would she heave one little sigh to see a bright young life so rudely blighted, so untimely cut down?

The window went up, a maidservant's discordant voice profaned the holy calm, and a deluge of water drenched the prone martyr's remains!

The strangling hero sprang up with a relieving snort. There was a whiz as of a missile in the air, mingled with the murmur of a curse, a sound as of shivering glass followed, and a small, vague form went over the fence and shot away in the gloom.

Not long after, as Tom, all undressed for bed, was surveying his drenched garments by the light of a tallow dip, Sid woke up; but if he had any dim idea of making any "references to allusions," he thought better of it and held his peace, for there was danger in Tom's eye.

Tom turned in without the added vexation of prayers, and Sid made mental note of the omission.

4

The sun rose upon a tranquil world, and beamed down upon the peaceful village like a benediction. Breakfast over, Aunt Polly had family worship: it began with a prayer built from the ground up of solid courses of Scriptural quotations, welded together with a thin mortar of originality; and from the summit of this she delivered a grim chapter of the Mosaic Law, as from Sinai.

Then Tom girded up his loins, so to speak, and went to work to "get his verses." Sid had learned his lesson days before. Tom bent all his energies to the memorizing of five verses, and he chose part of the Sermon on the Mount, because he could find no verses that were shorter. At the end of half an hour Tom had a vague general idea of his lesson, but no more, for his mind was traversing the whole field of human thought, and his hands were busy with distracting recreations. Mary took his book to hear him recite, and he tried to find his way through the fog:

"Blessed are the—a—a—"

"Poor"—

"Yes—poor; blessed are the poor—a—a—"

"In spirit—"

"In spirit; blessed are the poor in spirit, for they—they—"

"*Theirs*—"

"For *theirs*. Blessed are the poor in spirit, for theirs is the kingdom of heaven. Blessed are they that mourn, for they—they—"

"Sh—"

"For they—a—"

"S, H, A—"

"For they S, H—Oh, I don't know what it is!"

"*Shall!*"

"Oh, *shall!* for they shall—for they shall—a—a—shall mourn—a—a—blessed are they that shall—they that—a—they that shall mourn, for they shall—a—shall *what*? Why don't you tell me, Mary?—what do you want to be so mean for?"

"Oh, Tom, you poor thick-headed thing, I'm not teasing you. I wouldn't do that. You must go and learn it again. Don't you be discouraged, Tom, you'll manage it—and if you do, I'll give you something ever so nice. There, now, that's a good boy."

"All right! What is it, Mary, tell me what it is."

"Never you mind, Tom. You know if I say it's nice, it is nice."

"You bet you that's so, Mary. All right, I'll tackle it again."

And he did "tackle it again"—and under the double pressure of curiosity and prospective gain he did it with such spirit that he accomplished a shining success. Mary gave him a brand-new "Barlow" knife worth twelve and a half cents; and the convulsion of delight that swept his system shook him to his foundations. True, the knife would not cut anything, but it was a "sure-enough" Barlow, and there was inconceivable grandeur in that—though where the Western boys ever got the idea that such a weapon could possibly be counterfeited to its injury is an imposing mystery and will always remain so, perhaps. Tom contrived to scarify the cupboard with it, and was arranging to begin on the bureau, when he was called off to dress for Sunday-school.

Using the "Barlow"

Mary gave him a tin basin of water and a piece of soap, and he went outside the door and set the basin on a little bench there; then he dipped the soap in the water and laid it down; turned up his sleeves; poured out the water on the ground, gently, and then entered the kitchen and began to wipe his face diligently on the towel behind the door. But Mary removed the towel and said:

"Now ain't you ashamed, Tom. You mustn't be so bad. Water won't hurt you."

Tom was a trifle disconcerted. The basin was refilled, and this time he stood over it a little while, gathering resolution; took in a big breath and began. When he entered the kitchen presently, with both eyes shut and groping for the towel with his hands, an honourable testimony of suds and water was dripping from his face.

But when he emerged from the towel, he was not yet satisfactory, for the clean territory stopped short at his chin and his jaws, like a mask; below and beyond this line there was a dark expanse of unirrigated soil that spread downward in front and backward around his neck. Mary took him in hand, and when she was done with him he was a man and a brother, without distinction of colour, and his saturated hair was neatly brushed, and its short curls wrought into a dainty and symmetrical general effect. [He privately smoothed out the curls, with labour and difficulty, and plastered his hair close down to his head; for he held curls to be effeminate, and his own filled his life with bitterness.] Then Mary got out a suit of his clothing that had been used only on Sundays during two years—they were simply called his "other clothes"—and so by that we know the size of his wardrobe. The girl "put him to rights" after he had dressed himself; she buttoned his neat roundabout up to his chin, turned his vast shirt collar down over his shoulders, brushed him off and crowned him with his speckled straw hat. He now looked exceedingly improved and uncomfortable. He was fully as uncomfortable as he looked; for there was a restraint about whole clothes and cleanliness that galled him. He hoped that Mary would forget his shoes, but the hope was blighted; she coated them thoroughly with tallow, as was the custom, and brought them out. He lost his temper and said he was always being made to do everything he didn't want to do. But Mary said, persuasively:

"Please, Tom—that's a good boy."

So he got into the shoes snarling. Mary was soon ready, and the three children set out for Sunday-school—a place that Tom hated with his whole heart; but Sid and Mary were fond of it.

Sabbath-school hours were from nine to half-past ten; and then church service. Two of the children always remained for the sermon voluntarily, and the other always remained too—for stronger reasons. The church's high-backed, uncushioned pews would seat about three hundred persons; the edifice was but a small, plain affair, with a sort of pine board tree-box on top of it for a steeple. At the door Tom dropped back a step and accosted a Sunday-dressed comrade:

"Say, Billy, got a yaller ticket?"

"Yes."

"What'll you take for her?"

"What'll you give?"

"Piece of lickrish and a fish-hook."

"Less see 'em."

Tom exhibited. They were satisfactory, and the property changed hands. Then Tom traded a couple of white alleys for three red tickets, and some small trifle or other for a couple of blue ones. He waylaid other boys as they came, and went on buying tickets of various colours ten or fifteen minutes longer. He entered the church, now, with a swarm of clean and noisy boys and girls, proceeded to his seat and started a quarrel with the first boy that came handy. The teacher, a grave, elderly man, interfered; then turned his back a moment and Tom pulled a boy's hair in the next bench, and was absorbed in his book when the boy turned around; stuck a pin in another boy, presently, in order to hear him say "Ouch!" and got a new reprimand from his teacher. Tom's whole class were of a pattern—restless, noisy, and troublesome. When they came to recite their lessons, not one of them knew his verses perfectly, but had to be prompted all along. However, they worried through, and each got his reward—in small blue tickets, each with a passage of Scripture on it; each blue ticket was pay for two verses of the recitation. Ten blue tickets equalled a red one, and could be exchanged for it; ten red tickets equalled a yellow one; for ten yellow tickets the superintendent gave a very plainly bound Bible (worth forty cents in those easy times) to the pupil. How many of my readers would have the industry and application to memorize two thousand verses, even for a Dore Bible? And yet Mary had acquired two Bibles in this way—it was the patient work of two years—and a boy of German parentage had won four or five. He once recited three thousand verses without stopping; but the strain upon his mental faculties was too great, and he was little better than an idiot from that day forth—a grievous misfortune for the school, for on great occasions, before company, the superintendent (as Tom expressed it) had always made this boy come out and "spread himself." Only the older pupils managed to keep their tickets and stick to their tedious work long enough to get a Bible, and so the delivery of one of these prizes was a rare and noteworthy circumstance; the successful pupil was so great and conspicuous for that day that on the spot every scholar's heart was fired with a fresh ambition that often lasted a couple of weeks. It is possible that Tom's mental stomach had never really hungered for one of those prizes, but unquestionably his entire being had for many a day longed for the glory and the eclat that came with it.

In due course the superintendent stood up in front of the pulpit, with a closed hymn book in his hand and his forefinger inserted between its leaves, and commanded attention. When a Sunday-school superintendent makes his customary little speech, a hymn book in the hand is as necessary as is the inevitable sheet of music in the hand of a singer who stands forward on the platform and sings a solo at a concert—though why, is a mystery: for neither the hymn book nor the sheet of music is ever referred to by the sufferer. This superintendent was a slim creature of thirty-five, with a sandy goatee and short sandy hair; he wore a stiff standing-collar whose upper edge almost reached his ears and whose sharp points curved forward abreast the corners of his mouth—a fence that compelled a straight lookout ahead, and a turning of the whole body when a side view was required; his chin was propped on a spreading cravat which was as broad and as long as a banknote, and had fringed ends; his boot toes were turned sharply up, in the fashion of the day, like sleigh-runners—an effect patiently and laboriously produced by the young men by sitting with their toes pressed against a wall for hours together. Mr. Walters was very earnest of mien, and very sincere and honest at heart; and he held sacred things and places in such reverence, and so separated them from worldly matters, that unconsciously to himself his Sunday-school voice had acquired a peculiar intonation which was wholly absent on weekdays. He began after this fashion:

"Now, children, I want you all to sit up just as straight and pretty as you can and give me all your attention for a minute or two. There—that is it. That is the way good little boys and girls should do. I see one little girl who is looking out of the window—I am afraid she thinks I am out there somewhere—perhaps up in one of the trees making a speech to the little birds. [Applausive titter.] I want to tell you how good it makes me feel to see so many bright, clean little faces assembled in a place like this, learning to do right and be good." And so forth and so on. It is not necessary to set down the rest of the oration. It was of a pattern which does not vary, and so it is familiar to us all.

The latter third of the speech was marred by the resumption of fights and other recreations among certain of the bad boys, and by fidgetings and whisperings that extended far and wide, washing even to the bases of isolated and incorruptible rocks like Sid and Mary. But now every sound ceased suddenly, with the subsidence of Mr. Walters' voice, and the conclusion of the speech was received with a burst of silent gratitude.

A good part of the whispering had been occasioned by an event which was more or less rare—the entrance of visitors: lawyer Thatcher, accompanied by a very feeble and aged man; a fine, portly, middle-aged gentleman with iron-grey hair; and a dignified lady who was doubtless the latter's wife. The lady was leading a child. Tom had been restless and full of chafings and repinings; conscience-smitten, too—he could not meet Amy Lawrence's eye, he could not brook her loving gaze. But when he saw this small newcomer his soul was all ablaze with bliss in a moment. The next moment he was "showing off" with all his might—cuffing boys, pulling hair, making faces—in a word, using every art that seemed likely to fascinate a girl and win her applause. His exaltation had but one alloy—the memory of his humiliation in this angel's garden—and that record in sand was fast washing out, under the waves of happiness that were sweeping over it now.

The visitors were given the highest seat of honour, and as soon as Mr. Walters' speech was finished, he introduced them to the school. The middle-aged man turned out to be a prodigious personage—no less a one than the county judge—altogether the most august creation these children had ever looked upon—and they wondered what kind of material he was made of—and they half wanted to hear him roar, and were half afraid he might, too. He was from Constantinople, twelve miles away—so he had travelled, and seen the world—these very eyes had looked upon the county court house—which was said to have a tin roof. The awe which these reflections inspired was attested by the impressive silence and the ranks of staring eyes. This was the great Judge Thatcher, brother of their own lawyer. Jeff Thatcher immediately went forward, to be familiar with the great man and be envied by the school. It would have been music to his soul to hear the whisperings:

"Look at him, Jim! He's a going up there. Say—look! he's a going to shake hands with him—he *is* shaking hands with him! By jings, don't you wish you was Jeff?"

Mr. Walters fell to "showing off," with all sorts of official bustlings and activities, giving orders, delivering judgments, discharging directions here, there, everywhere that he could find a target. The librarian "showed off"—running hither and thither with his arms full of books and making a deal of the splutter and fuss that insect authority delights in. The young lady teachers "showed off"—bending sweetly over pupils that were lately being boxed, lifting pretty warning fingers at bad little boys and patting good ones lovingly. The young gentlemen teachers "showed off" with small scoldings and other little displays of authority and fine attention to discipline—and most of the teachers, of both sexes, found business up at the library, by the pulpit; and it was business that frequently had to be done over again two or three times (with much seeming vexation). The little girls "showed off" in various ways, and the little boys "showed off" with such diligence that the air was thick with paper wads and the murmur of scufflings. And above it all the great man sat and beamed a majestic judicial smile upon all the house, and warmed himself in the sun of his own grandeur—for he was "showing off," too.

There was only one thing wanting to make Mr. Walters' ecstasy complete, and that was a chance to deliver a Bible-prize and exhibit a prodigy. Several pupils had a few yellow tickets, but none had enough—he had been around among the star pupils inquiring. He would have given worlds, now, to have that German lad back again with a sound mind.

And now at this moment, when hope was dead, Tom Sawyer came forward with nine yellow tickets, nine red tickets, and ten blue ones, and demanded a Bible. This was a thunderbolt out of a clear sky. Walters was not expecting an application from this source for the next ten years. But there was no getting around it—here were the certified checks, and they were good for their face. Tom was therefore elevated to a place with the Judge and the other elect, and the great news was announced from headquarters. It was the most stunning surprise of the decade, and so profound was the sensation that it lifted the new hero up to the judicial one's altitude, and the school had two marvels to gaze upon in place of one. The boys were all eaten up with envy—but those that suffered the bitterest pangs were those who perceived too late that they themselves had contributed to this hated splendour by trading tickets to Tom for the wealth he had amassed in selling whitewashing privileges. These despised themselves, as being the dupes of a wily fraud, a guileful snake in the grass.

The prize was delivered to Tom with as much effusion as the superintendent could pump up under the circumstances; but it lacked somewhat of the true gush, for the poor fellow's instinct taught him that there was a mystery here that could not well bear the light, perhaps; it was simply preposterous that this boy had warehoused two thousand sheaves of Scriptural wisdom on his premises—a dozen would strain his capacity, without a doubt.

Amy Lawrence was proud and glad, and she tried to make Tom see it in her face—but he wouldn't look. She wondered; then she was just a grain troubled; next a dim suspicion came and went—came again; she watched; a furtive glance told her worlds—and then her heart broke, and she was jealous, and angry, and the tears came and she hated everybody. Tom most of all (she thought).

Tom was introduced to the Judge; but his tongue was tied, his breath would hardly come, his heart quaked—partly because of the awful greatness of the man, but mainly because he was her parent. He would have liked to fall down and worship him, if it were in the dark. The Judge put his hand on Tom's head and called him a fine little man, and asked him what his name was. The boy stammered, gasped, and got it out:

"Tom."

"Oh, no, not Tom—it is—"

"Thomas."

"Ah, that's it. I thought there was more to it, maybe. That's very well. But you've another one I daresay, and you'll tell it to me, won't you?"

"Tell the gentleman your other name, Thomas," said Walters, "and say sir. You mustn't forget your manners."

"Thomas Sawyer—sir."

Tom as a Sunday-school Hero

"That's it! That's a good boy. Fine boy. Fine, manly little fellow. Two thousand verses is a great many—very, very great many. And you never can be sorry for the trouble you took to learn them; for knowledge is worth more than anything there is in the world; it's what makes great men and good men; you'll be a great man and a good man yourself, some day, Thomas, and then you'll look back and say, It's all owing to the precious Sunday-school privileges of my boyhood—it's all owing to my dear teachers that taught me to learn—it's all owing to the good superintendent, who encouraged me, and watched over me, and gave me a beautiful Bible—a splendid elegant Bible—to keep and have it all for my own, always—it's all owing to right bringing up! That is what you will say, Thomas—and you wouldn't take any money for those two thousand verses—no indeed you wouldn't. And now you wouldn't mind telling me and this lady some of the things you've learned—no, I know you wouldn't—for we are proud of little boys that learn. Now, no doubt you know the names of all the twelve disciples. Won't you tell us the names of the first two that were appointed?"

Tom was tugging at a button-hole and looking sheepish. He blushed, now, and his eyes fell. Mr. Walters' heart sank within him. He said to himself, it is not possible that the boy can answer the simplest question—why *did* the Judge ask him? Yet he felt obliged to speak up and say:

"Answer the gentleman, Thomas—don't be afraid."

Tom still hung fire.

"Now I know you'll tell me," said the lady. "The names of the first two disciples were—"

"*David And Goliah!*"

Let us draw the curtain of charity over the rest of the scene.

5

About half-past ten the cracked bell of the small church began to ring, and presently the people began to gather for the morning sermon. The Sunday-school children distributed themselves about the house and occupied pews with their parents, so as to be under supervision. Aunt Polly came, and Tom and Sid and Mary sat with her—Tom being placed next the aisle, in order that he might be as far away from the open window and the seductive outside summer scenes as possible. The crowd filed up the aisles: the aged and needy postmaster, who had seen better days; the mayor and his wife—for they had a mayor there, among other unnecessaries; the justice of the peace; the widow Douglass, fair, smart, and forty, a generous, good-hearted soul and well-to-do, her hill mansion the only palace in the town, and the most hospitable and much the most lavish in the matter of festivities that St. Petersburg could boast; the bent and venerable Major and Mrs. Ward; lawyer Riverson, the new notable from a distance; next the belle of the village, followed by a troop of lawn-clad and ribbon-decked young heartbreakers; then all the young clerks in town in a body—for they had stood in the vestibule sucking their cane-heads, a circling wall of oiled and simpering admirers, till the last girl had run their gantlet; and last of all came the Model Boy, Willie Mufferson, taking as heedful care of his mother as if she were cut glass. He always brought his mother to church, and was the pride of all the matrons. The boys all hated him, he was so good. And besides, he had been "thrown up to them" so much. His white handkerchief was hanging out of his pocket behind, as usual on Sundays—accidentally. Tom had no handkerchief, and he looked upon boys who had as snobs.

The Model □oy

The congregation being fully assembled, now, the bell rang once more, to warn laggards and stragglers, and then a solemn hush fell upon the church which was only broken by the tittering and whispering of the choir in the gallery. The choir always tittered and whispered all through service. There was once a church choir that was not ill-bred, but I have forgotten where it was, now. It was a great many years ago, and I can scarcely remember anything about it, but I think it was in some foreign country.

The minister gave out the hymn, and read it through with a relish, in a peculiar style which was much admired in that part of the country. His voice began on a medium key and climbed steadily up till it reached a certain point, where it bore with strong emphasis upon the topmost word and then plunged down as if from a spring-board:

Shall I be car-ri-ed toe the skies, on flow'ry *beds* of ease,
Whilst others fight to win the prize, and sail thro' *blood*-y seas?

He was regarded as a wonderful reader. At church "sociables" he was always called upon to read poetry; and when he was through, the ladies would lift up their hands and let them fall helplessly in their laps, and "wall" their eyes, and shake their heads, as much as to say, "Words cannot express it; it is too beautiful, TOO beautiful for this mortal earth."

After the hymn had been sung, the Rev. Mr. Sprague turned himself into a bulletin board, and read off "notices" of meetings and societies and things till it seemed that the list would stretch out to the crack of doom—a queer custom which is still kept up in America, even in cities, away here in this age of abundant newspapers. Often, the less there is to justify a traditional custom, the harder it is to get rid of it.

And now the minister prayed. A good, generous prayer it was, and went into details: it pleaded for the church, and the little children of the church; for the other churches of the village; for the village itself; for the county; for the State; for the State officers; for the United States; for the churches of the United States; for Congress; for the President; for the officers of the Government; for poor sailors, tossed by stormy seas; for the oppressed millions groaning under the heel of European monarchies and Oriental despotisms; for such as have the light and the good tidings, and yet have not eyes to see nor ears to hear withal; for the heathen in the far islands of the sea; and closed with a supplication that the words he was about to speak might find grace and favour, and be as seed sown in fertile ground, yielding in time a grateful harvest of good. Amen.

There was a rustling of dresses, and the standing congregation sat down. The boy whose history this book relates did not enjoy the prayer, he only endured it—if he even did that much. He was restive all through it; he kept tally of the details of the prayer, unconsciously—for he was not listening, but he knew the ground of old, and the clergyman's regular route over it—and when a little trifle of new matter was interlarded, his ear detected it and his whole nature resented it; he considered additions unfair, and scoundrelly. In the midst of the prayer a fly had lit on the back of the pew in front of him and tortured his spirit by calmly rubbing its hands together, embracing its head with its arms, and polishing it so vigorously that it seemed to almost part company with the body, and the slender thread of a neck was exposed to view; scraping its wings with its hind legs and smoothing them to its body as if they had been coat-tails; going through its whole toilet as tranquilly as if it knew it was perfectly safe. As indeed it was; for as sorely as Tom's hands itched to grab for it they did not dare—he believed his soul would be instantly destroyed if he did such a thing while the prayer was going on. But with the closing sentence his hand began to curve and steal forward; and the instant the "Amen" was out the fly was a prisoner of war. His aunt detected the act and made him let it go.

The minister gave out his text and droned along monotonously through an argument that was so prosy that many a head by and by began to nod—and yet it was an argument that dealt in limitless fire and brimstone and thinned the predestined elect down to a company so small as to be hardly worth the saving. Tom counted the pages of the sermon; after church he always knew how many pages there had been, but he seldom knew anything else about the discourse. However, this time he was really interested for a little while. The minister made a grand and moving picture of the assembling together of the world's hosts at the millennium when the lion and the lamb should lie down together and a little child should lead them. But the pathos, the lesson, the moral of the great spectacle were lost upon the boy; he only thought of the conspicuousness of the principal character before the on-looking nations; his face lit with the thought, and he said to himself that he wished he could be that child, if it was a tame lion.

Now he lapsed into suffering again, as the dry argument was resumed. Presently he bethought him of a treasure he had and got it out. It was a large black beetle with formidable jaws—a "pinchbug," he called it. It was in a percussion-cap box. The first thing the beetle did was to take him by the finger. A natural fillip followed, the beetle went floundering into the aisle and lit on its back, and the hurt finger went into the boy's mouth. The beetle lay there working its helpless legs, unable to turn over. Tom eyed it, and longed for it; but it was safe out of his reach. Other people uninterested in the sermon found relief in the beetle, and they eyed it too. Presently a vagrant poodle dog came idling along, sad at heart, lazy with the summer softness and the quiet, weary of captivity, sighing for change. He spied the beetle; the drooping tail lifted and wagged. He surveyed the prize; walked around it; smelt at it from a safe distance; walked around it again; grew bolder, and took a closer smell; then lifted his lip and made a gingerly snatch at it, just missing it; made another, and another; began to enjoy the diversion; subsided to his stomach with the beetle between his paws, and continued his experiments; grew weary at last, and then indifferent and absent-minded. His head nodded, and little by little his chin descended and touched the enemy, who seized it. There was a sharp yelp, a flirt of the poodle's head, and the beetle fell a couple of yards away, and lit on its back once more. The neighbouring spectators shook with a gentle inward joy, several faces went behind fans and handkerchiefs, and Tom was entirely happy. The dog looked foolish, and probably felt so; but there was resentment in his heart, too, and a craving for revenge. So he went to the beetle and began a wary attack on it again; jumping at it from every point of a circle, lighting with his fore-paws within an inch of the creature, making even closer snatches at it with his teeth, and jerking his head till his ears flapped again. But he grew tired once more, after a while; tried to amuse himself with a fly but found no relief; followed an ant around, with his nose close to the floor, and quickly wearied of that; yawned, sighed, forgot the beetle entirely, and sat down on it. Then there was a wild yelp of agony and the poodle went sailing up the aisle; the yelps continued, and so did the dog; he crossed the house in front of the altar; he flew down the other aisle; he crossed before the doors;

he clamored up the home-stretch; his anguish grew with his progress, till presently he was but a woolly comet moving in its orbit with the gleam and the speed of light. At last the frantic sufferer sheered from its course, and sprang into its master's lap; he flung it out of the window, and the voice of distress quickly thinned away and died in the distance.

By this time the whole church was red-faced and suffocating with suppressed laughter, and the sermon had come to a dead standstill. The discourse was resumed presently, but it went lame and halting, all possibility of impressiveness being at an end; for even the gravest sentiments were constantly being received with a smothered burst of unholy mirth, under cover of some remote pew-back, as if the poor parson had said a rarely facetious thing. It was a genuine relief to the whole congregation when the ordeal was over and the benediction pronounced.

Tom Sawyer went home quite cheerful, thinking to himself that there was some satisfaction about divine service when there was a bit of variety in it. He had but one marring thought; he was willing that the dog should play with his pinchbug, but he did not think it was upright in him to carry it off.

6

Monday morning found Tom Sawyer miserable. Monday morning always found him so—because it began another week's slow suffering in school. He generally began that day with wishing he had had no intervening holiday, it made the going into captivity and fetters again so much more odious.

Tom lay thinking. Presently it occurred to him that he wished he was sick; then he could stay home from school. Here was a vague possibility. He canvassed his system. No ailment was found, and he investigated again. This time he thought he could detect colicky symptoms, and he began to encourage them with considerable hope. But they soon grew feeble, and presently died wholly away. He reflected further. Suddenly he discovered something. One of his upper front teeth was loose. This was lucky; he was about to begin to groan, as a "starter," as he called it, when it occurred to him that if he came into court with that argument, his aunt would pull it out, and that would hurt. So he thought he would hold the tooth in reserve for the present, and seek further. Nothing offered for some little time, and then he remembered hearing the doctor tell about a certain thing that laid up a patient for two or three weeks and threatened to make him lose a finger. So the boy eagerly drew his sore toe from under the sheet and held it up for inspection. But now he did not know the necessary symptoms. However, it seemed well worth while to chance it, so he fell to groaning with considerable spirit.

But Sid slept on unconscious.

Tom groaned louder, and fancied that he began to feel pain in the toe.

No result from Sid.

Tom was panting with his exertions by this time. He took a rest and then swelled himself up and fetched a succession of admirable groans.

Sid snored on.

Tom was aggravated. He said, "Sid, Sid!" and shook him. This course worked well, and Tom began to groan again. Sid yawned, stretched, then brought himself up on his elbow with a snort, and began to stare at Tom. Tom went on groaning. Sid said:

"Tom! Say, Tom!" [No response.] "Here, Tom! TOM! What is the matter, Tom?" And he shook him and looked in his face anxiously.

Tom moaned out:

"Oh, don't, Sid. Don't joggle me."

"Why, what's the matter, Tom? I must call auntie."

"No—never mind. It'll be over by and by, maybe. Don't call anybody."

"But I must! *Don't* groan so, Tom, it's awful. How long you been this way?"

"Hours. Ouch! Oh, don't stir so, Sid, you'll kill me."

"Tom, why didn't you wake me sooner? Oh, Tom, *don't!* It makes my flesh crawl to hear you. Tom, what is the matter?"

"I forgive you everything, Sid. [Groan.] Everything you've ever done to me. When I'm gone—"

"Oh, Tom, you ain't dying, are you? Don't, Tom—oh, don't. Maybe—"

"I forgive everybody, Sid. [Groan.] Tell 'em so, Sid. And Sid, you give my window-sash and my cat with one eye to that new girl that's come to town, and tell her—"

But Sid had snatched his clothes and gone. Tom was suffering in reality, now, so handsomely was his imagination working, and so his groans had gathered quite a genuine tone.

Sid flew downstairs and said:

"Oh, Aunt Polly, come! Tom's dying!"

"Dying!"

"Yes'm. Don't wait—come quick!"

"Rubbage! I don't believe it!"

But she fled upstairs, nevertheless, with Sid and Mary at her heels. And her face grew white, too, and her lip trembled. When she reached the bedside she gasped out:

"You Tom! Tom, what's the matter with you?"

"Oh, auntie, I'm—"

"What's the matter with you—what is the matter with you, child?"

"Oh, auntie, my sore toe's mortified!"

The old lady sank down into a chair and laughed a little, then cried a little, then did both together. This restored her and she said:

"Tom, what a turn you did give me. Now you shut up that nonsense and climb out of this."

The groans ceased and the pain vanished from the toe. The boy felt a little foolish, and he said:

"Aunt Polly, it *seemed* mortified, and it hurt so I never minded my tooth at all."

"Your tooth, indeed! What's the matter with your tooth?"

"One of them's loose, and it aches perfectly awful."

"There, there, now, don't begin that groaning again. Open your mouth. Well—your tooth *is* loose, but you're not going to die about that. Mary, get me a silk thread, and a chunk of fire out of the kitchen."

Tom said:

"Oh, please, auntie, don't pull it out. It don't hurt any more. I wish I may never stir if it does. Please don't, auntie. I don't want to stay home from school."

"Oh, you don't, don't you? So all this row was because you thought you'd get to stay home from school and go a-fishing? Tom, Tom, I love you so, and you seem to try every way you can to break my old heart with your outrageousness." By this time the dental instruments were ready. The old lady made one end of the silk thread fast to Tom's tooth with a loop and tied the other to the bedpost. Then she seized the chunk of fire and suddenly thrust it almost into the boy's face. The tooth hung dangling by the bedpost, now.

But all trials bring their compensations. As Tom wended to school after breakfast, he was the envy of every boy he met because the gap in his upper row of teeth enabled him to expectorate in a new and admirable way. He gathered quite a following of lads interested in the exhibition; and one that had cut his finger and had been a centre of fascination and homage up to this time, now found himself suddenly without an adherent, and shorn of his glory. His heart was heavy, and he said with a disdain which he did not feel that it wasn't anything to spit like Tom

Sawyer; but another boy said, "Sour grapes!" and he wandered away a dismantled hero.

Shortly Tom came upon the juvenile pariah of the village, Huckleberry Finn, son of the town drunkard. Huckleberry was cordially hated and dreaded by all the mothers of the town, because he was idle and lawless and vulgar and bad—and because all their children admired him so, and delighted in his forbidden society, and wished they dared to be like him. Tom was like the rest of the respectable boys, in that he envied Huckleberry his gaudy outcast condition, and was under strict orders not to play with him. So he played with him every time he got a chance. Huckleberry was always dressed in the cast-off clothes of full-grown men, and they were in perennial bloom and fluttering with rags. His hat was a vast ruin with a wide crescent lopped out of its brim; his coat, when he wore one, hung nearly to his heels and had the rearward buttons far down the back; but one suspender supported his trousers; the seat of the trousers bagged low and contained nothing, the fringed legs dragged in the dirt when not rolled up.

Huckleberry came and went, at his own free will. He slept on doorsteps in fine weather and in empty hogsheads in wet; he did not have to go to school or to church, or call any being master or obey anybody; he could go fishing or swimming when and where he chose, and stay as long as it suited him; nobody forbade him to fight; he could sit up as late as he pleased; he was always the first boy that went barefoot in the spring and the last to resume leather in the fall; he never had to wash, nor put on clean clothes; he could swear wonderfully. In a word, everything that goes to make life precious that boy had. So thought every harassed, hampered, respectable boy in St. Petersburg.

Tom hailed the romantic outcast:

"Hello, Huckleberry!"

"Hello yourself, and see how you like it."

"What's that you got?"

"Dead cat."

"Lemme see him, Huck. My, he's pretty stiff. Where'd you get him?"

"Bought him off'n a boy."

"What did you give?"

"I give a blue ticket and a bladder that I got at the slaughterhouse."

"Where'd you get the blue ticket?"

"Bought it off'n Ben Rogers two weeks ago for a hoop-stick."

"Say—what is dead cats good for, Huck?"

"Good for? Cure warts with."

"No! Is that so? I know something that's better."

"I bet you don't. What is it?"

"Why, spunk-water."

"Spunk-water! I wouldn't give a dern for spunk-water."

"You wouldn't, wouldn't you? D'you ever try it?"

"No, I hain't. But Bob Tanner did."

"Who told you so!"

"Why, he told Jeff Thatcher, and Jeff told Johnny Baker, and Johnny told Jim Hollis, and Jim told Ben Rogers, and Ben told a nigger, and the nigger told me. There now!"

"Well, what of it? They'll all lie. Leastways all but the nigger. I don't know *him*. But I never see a nigger that *wouldn't* lie. Shucks! Now you tell me how Bob Tanner done it, Huck."

"Why, he took and dipped his hand in a rotten stump where the rain-water was."

"In the daytime?"

"Certainly."

"With his face to the stump?"

"Yes. Least I reckon so."

"Did he say anything?"

"I don't reckon he did. I don't know."

"Aha! Talk about trying to cure warts with spunk-water such a blame fool way as that! Why, that ain't a-going to do any good. You got to go all by yourself, to the middle of the woods, where you know there's a spunk-water stump, and just as it's midnight you back up against the stump and jam your hand in and say:

'Barley-corn, barley-corn, injun-meal shorts,
Spunk-water, spunk-water, swaller these warts,'

and then walk away quick, eleven steps, with your eyes shut, and then turn around three times and walk home without speaking to anybody. Because if you speak the charm's busted."

"Well, that sounds like a good way; but that ain't the way Bob Tanner done."

"No, sir, you can bet he didn't, becuz he's the wartiest boy in this town; and he wouldn't have a wart on him if he'd knowed how to work spunk-water. I've took off thousands of warts off of my hands that way, Huck. I play with frogs so much that I've always got considerable many warts. Sometimes I take 'em off with a bean."

"Yes, bean's good. I've done that."

"Have you? What's your way?"

"You take and split the bean, and cut the wart so as to get some blood, and then you put the blood on one piece of the bean and take and dig a hole and bury it 'bout midnight at the crossroads in the dark of the moon, and then you burn up the rest of the bean. You see that piece that's got the blood on it will keep drawing and drawing, trying to fetch the other piece to it, and so that helps the blood to draw the wart, and pretty soon off she comes."

"Yes, that's it, Huck—that's it; though when you're burying it if you say 'Down bean; off wart; come no more to bother me!' it's better. That's the way Joe Harper does, and he's been nearly to Coonville and most everywheres. But say—how do you cure 'em with dead cats?"

"Why, you take your cat and go and get in the graveyard 'long about midnight when somebody that was wicked has been buried; and when it's midnight a devil will come, or maybe two or three, but you can't see 'em, you can only hear something like the wind, or maybe hear 'em talk; and when they're taking that feller away, you heave your cat after 'em and say, 'Devil follow corpse, cat follow devil, warts follow cat, I'm done with ye!' That'll fetch *any* wart."

"Sounds right. D'you ever try it, Huck?"

"No, but old Mother Hopkins told me."

"Well, I reckon it's so, then. Becuz they say she's a witch."

"Say! Why, Tom, I *know* she is. She witched pap. Pap says so his own self. He come along one day, and he see she was a-witching him, so he took up a rock, and if she hadn't dodged, he'd a got her. Well, that very night he rolled off'n a shed wher' he was a layin drunk, and broke his arm."

"Why, that's awful. How did he know she was a-witching him?"

"Lord, pap can tell, easy. Pap says when they keep looking at you right stiddy, they're a-witching you. Specially if they mumble. Becuz when they mumble they're saying the Lord's Prayer backards."

"Say, Hucky, when you going to try the cat?"

"Tonight. I reckon they'll come after old Hoss Williams tonight."

"But they buried him Saturday. Didn't they get him Saturday night?"

"Why, how you talk! How could their charms work till midnight?—and *then* it's Sunday. Devils don't slosh around much of a Sunday, I don't reckon."

"I never thought of that. That's so. Lemme go with you?"

"Of course—if you ain't afeard."

"Afeard! 'Tain't likely. Will you meow?"

"Yes—and you meow back, if you get a chance. Last time, you kep' me a-meowing around till old Hays went to throwing rocks at me and says 'Dern that cat!' and so I hove a brick through his window—but don't you tell."

"I won't. I couldn't meow that night, becuz auntie was watching me, but I'll meow this time. Say—what's that?"

"Nothing but a tick."

"Where'd you get him?"

"Out in the woods."

"What'll you take for him?"

"I don't know. I don't want to sell him."

"All right. It's a mighty small tick, anyway."

"Oh, anybody can run a tick down that don't belong to them. I'm satisfied with it. It's a good enough tick for me."

"Sho, there's ticks a plenty. I could have a thousand of 'em if I wanted to."

"Well, why don't you? Becuz you know mighty well you can't. This is a pretty early tick, I reckon. It's the first one I've seen this year."

"Say, Huck—I'll give you my tooth for him."

"Less see it."

Tom got out a bit of paper and carefully unrolled it. Huckleberry viewed it wistfully. The temptation was very strong. At last he said:

"Is it genuwyne?"

Tom lifted his lip and showed the vacancy.

"Well, all right," said Huckleberry, "it's a trade."

Tom enclosed the tick in the percussion-cap box that had lately been the pinchbug's prison, and the boys separated, each feeling wealthier than before.

When Tom reached the little isolated frame school-house, he strode in briskly, with the manner of one who had come with all honest speed. He hung his hat on a peg and flung himself into his seat with business-like alacrity. The master, throned on high in his great splint-bottom arm-chair, was dozing, lulled by the drowsy hum of study. The interruption roused him.

"Thomas Sawyer!"

Tom knew that when his name was pronounced in full, it meant trouble.

"Sir!"

"Come up here. Now, sir, why are you late again, as usual?"

Tom was about to take refuge in a lie, when he saw two long tails of yellow hair hanging down a back that he recognized by the electric sympathy of love; and by that form was *the only vacant place* on the girls' side of the school-house. He instantly said:

"*I stopped to talk with Huckleberry Finn!*"

The master's pulse stood still, and he stared helplessly. The buzz of study ceased. The pupils wondered if this foolhardy boy had lost his mind. The master said:

"You—you did what?"

"Stopped to talk with Huckleberry Finn."

There was no mistaking the words.

"Thomas Sawyer, this is the most astounding confession I have ever listened to. No mere ferule will answer for this offence. Take off your jacket."

The master's arm performed until it was tired and the stock of switches notably diminished. Then the order followed:

"Now, sir, go and sit with the girls! And let this be a warning to you."

Result of Tom's Truthfulness

The titter that rippled around the room appeared to abash the boy, but in reality that result was caused rather more by his worshipful awe of his unknown idol and the dread pleasure that lay in his high good fortune. He sat down upon the end of the pine bench and the girl hitched herself away from him with a toss of her head. Nudges and winks and whispers traversed the room, but Tom sat still, with his arms upon the long, low desk before him, and seemed to study his book.

By and by attention ceased from him, and the accustomed school murmur rose upon the dull air once more. Presently the boy began to steal furtive glances at the girl. She observed it, "made a mouth" at him and gave him the back of her head for the space of a minute. When she cautiously faced around again, a peach lay before her. She thrust it away. Tom gently put it back. She thrust it away again, but with less animosity. Tom patiently returned it to its place. Then she let it remain. Tom scrawled on his slate, "Please take it—I got more." The girl glanced at the words, but made no sign. Now the boy began to draw something on the slate, hiding his work with his left hand. For a time the girl refused to notice; but her human curiosity presently began to manifest itself by hardly perceptible signs. The boy worked on, apparently unconscious. The girl made a sort of non-committal attempt to see, but the boy did not betray that he was aware of it. At last she gave in and hesitatingly whispered:

"Let me see it."

Tom as an Artist

Tom partly uncovered a dismal caricature of a house with two gable ends to it and a corkscrew of smoke issuing from the chimney. Then the girl's interest began to fasten itself upon the work and she forgot everything else. When it was finished, she gazed a moment, then whispered:

"It's nice—make a man."

The artist erected a man in the front yard, that resembled a derrick. He could have stepped over the house; but the girl was not hypercritical; she was satisfied with the monster, and whispered:

"It's a beautiful man—now make me coming along."

Tom drew an hourglass with a full moon and straw limbs to it and armed the spreading fingers with a portentous fan. The girl said:

"It's ever so nice—I wish I could draw."

"It's easy," whispered Tom, "I'll learn you."

"Oh, will you? When?"

"At noon. Do you go home to dinner?"

"I'll stay if you will."

"Good—that's a whack. What's your name?"

"Becky Thatcher. What's yours? Oh, I know. It's Thomas Sawyer."

"That's the name they lick me by. I'm Tom when I'm good. You call me Tom, will you?"

"Yes."

Now Tom began to scrawl something on the slate, hiding the words from the girl. But she was not backward this time. She begged to see. Tom said:

"Oh, it ain't anything."

"Yes it is."

"No it ain't. You don't want to see."

"Yes I do, indeed I do. Please let me."

"You'll tell."

"No I won't—deed and deed and double deed won't."

"You won't tell anybody at all? Ever, as long as you live?"

"No, I won't ever tell *any*body. Now let me."

"Oh, *you* don't want to see!"

"Now that you treat me so, I *will* see." And she put her small hand upon his and a little scuffle ensued, Tom pretending to resist in earnest but letting his hand slip by degrees till these words were revealed: "*I love you.*"

"Oh, you bad thing!" And she hit his hand a smart rap, but reddened and looked pleased, nevertheless.

Just at this juncture the boy felt a slow, fateful grip closing on his ear, and a steady lifting impulse. In that wise he was borne across the house and deposited in his own seat, under a peppering fire of giggles from the whole school. Then the master stood over him during a few awful moments, and finally moved away to his throne without saying a word. But although Tom's ear tingled, his heart was jubilant.

Interrupted Courtship

As the school quieted down Tom made an honest effort to study, but the turmoil within him was too great. In turn he took his place in the reading class and made a botch of it; then in the geography class and turned lakes into mountains, mountains into rivers, and rivers into continents, till chaos was come again; then in the spelling class, and got "turned down," by a succession of mere baby words, till he brought up at the foot and yielded up the pewter medal which he had worn with ostentation for months.

7

The harder Tom tried to fasten his mind on his book, the more his ideas wandered. So at last, with a sigh and a yawn, he gave it up. It seemed to him that the noon recess would never come. The air was utterly dead. There was not a breath stirring. It was the sleepiest of sleepy days. The drowsing murmur of the five and twenty studying scholars soothed the soul like the spell that is in the murmur of bees. Away off in the flaming sunshine, Cardiff Hill lifted its soft green sides through a shimmering veil of heat, tinted with the purple of distance; a few birds floated on lazy wing high in the air; no other living thing was visible but some cows, and they were asleep. Tom's heart ached to be free, or else to have something of interest to do to pass the dreary time. His hand wandered into his pocket and his face lit up with a glow of gratitude that was prayer, though he did not know it. Then furtively the percussion-cap box came out. He released the tick and put him on the long flat desk. The creature probably glowed with a gratitude that amounted to prayer, too, at this moment, but it was premature: for when he started thankfully to travel off, Tom turned him aside with a pin and made him take a new direction.

Tom's bosom friend sat next him, suffering just as Tom had been, and now he was deeply and gratefully interested in this entertainment in an instant. This bosom friend was Joe Harper. The two boys were sworn friends all the week, and embattled enemies on Saturdays. Joe took a pin out of his lapel and began to assist in exercising the prisoner. The sport grew in interest momently. Soon Tom said that they were interfering with each other, and neither getting the fullest benefit of the tick. So he put Joe's slate on the desk and drew a line down the middle of it from top to bottom.

"Now," said he, "as long as he is on your side you can stir him up and I'll let him alone; but if you let him get away and get on my side, you're to leave him alone as long as I can keep him from crossing over."

"All right, go ahead; start him up."

The tick escaped from Tom, presently, and crossed the equator. Joe harassed him awhile, and then he got away and crossed back again. This change of base occurred often. While one boy was worrying the tick with absorbing interest, the other would look on with interest as strong, the two heads bowed together over the slate, and the two souls dead to all things else. At last luck seemed to settle and abide with Joe. The tick tried this, that, and the other course, and got as excited and as anxious as the boys themselves, but time and again just as he would have victory in his very grasp, so to speak, and Tom's fingers would be twitching to begin, Joe's pin would deftly head him off, and keep possession. At last Tom could stand it no longer. The temptation was too strong. So he reached out and lent a hand with his pin. Joe was angry in a moment. Said he:

"Tom, you let him alone."

"I only just want to stir him up a little, Joe."

"No, sir, it ain't fair; you just let him alone."

"Blame it, I ain't going to stir him much."

"Let him alone, I tell you."

"I won't!"

"You shall—he's on my side of the line."

"Look here, Joe Harper, whose is that tick?"

"I don't care whose tick he is—he's on my side of the line, and you sha'n't touch him."

"Well, I'll just bet I will, though. He's my tick and I'll do what I blame please with him, or die!"

A tremendous whack came down on Tom's shoulders, and its duplicate on Joe's; and for the space of two minutes the dust continued to fly from the two jackets and the whole school to enjoy it. The boys had been too absorbed to notice the hush that had stolen upon the school awhile before when the master came tiptoeing down the room and stood over them. He had contemplated a good part of the performance before he contributed his bit of variety to it.

When school broke up at noon, Tom flew to Becky Thatcher, and whispered in her ear:

"Put on your bonnet and let on you're going home; and when you get to the corner, give the rest of 'em the slip, and turn down through the lane and come back. I'll go the other way and come it over 'em the same way."

So the one went off with one group of scholars, and the other with another. In a little while the two met at the bottom of the lane, and when they reached the school they had it all to themselves. Then they sat together, with a slate before them, and Tom gave Becky the pencil and held her hand in his, guiding it, and so created another surprising house. When the interest in art began to wane, the two fell to talking. Tom was swimming in bliss. He said:

"Do you love rats?"

"No! I hate them!"

"Well, I do, too—*live* ones. But I mean dead ones, to swing round your head with a string."

"No, I don't care for rats much, anyway. What I like is chewing-gum."

"O, I should say so! I wish I had some now."

"Do you? I've got some. I'll let you chew it awhile, but you must give it back to me."

That was agreeable, so they chewed it turn about, and dangled their legs against the bench in excess of contentment.

"Was you ever at a circus?" said Tom.

"Yes, and my pa's going to take me again some time, if I'm good."

"I been to the circus three or four times—lots of times. Church ain't shucks to a circus. There's things going on at a circus all the time. I'm going to be a clown in a circus when I grow up."

"O, are you! That will be nice. They're so lovely, all spotted up."

"Yes, that's so. And they get slathers of money—most a dollar a day, Ben Rogers says. Say, Becky, was you ever engaged?"

"What's that?"

"Why, engaged to be married."

"No."

"Would you like to?"

"I reckon so. I don't know. What is it like?"

"Like? Why it ain't like anything. You only just tell a boy you won't ever have anybody but him, ever ever ever, and then you kiss and that's all. Anybody can do it."

"Kiss? What do you kiss for?"

"Why, that, you know, is to—well, they always do that."

"Everybody?"

"Why, yes, everybody that's in love with each other. Do you remember what I wrote on the slate?"

"Ye—yes."

"What was it?"

"I sha'n't tell you."

"Shall I tell *you*?"

"Ye—yes—but some other time."

"No, now."

"No, not now—tomorrow."

"Oh, no, *now*. Please, Becky—I'll whisper it, I'll whisper it ever so easy."

Becky hesitating, Tom took silence for consent, and passed his arm about her waist and whispered the tale ever so softly, with his mouth close to her ear. And then he added:

"Now you whisper it to me—just the same."

She resisted, for a while, and then said:

"You turn your face away so you can't see, and then I will. But you mustn't ever tell anybody—*will* you, Tom? Now you won't, *will* you?"

"No, indeed, indeed I won't. Now, Becky."

He turned his face away. She bent timidly around till her breath stirred his curls and whispered, "I—love—you!"

Then she sprang away and ran around and around the desks and benches, with Tom after her, and took refuge in a corner at last, with her little white apron to her face. Tom clasped her about her neck and pleaded:

"Now, Becky, it's all done—all over but the kiss. Don't you be afraid of that—it ain't anything at all. Please, Becky." And he tugged at her apron and the hands.

By and by she gave up, and let her hands drop; her face, all glowing with the struggle, came up and submitted. Tom kissed the red lips and said:

"Now it's all done, Becky. And always after this, you know, you ain't ever to love anybody but me, and you ain't ever to marry anybody but me, ever never and forever. Will you?"

"No, I'll never love anybody but you, Tom, and I'll never marry anybody but you—and you ain't to ever marry anybody but me, either."

"Certainly. Of course. That's *part* of it. And always coming to school or when we're going home, you're to walk with me, when there ain't anybody looking—and you choose me and I choose you at parties, because that's the way you do when you're engaged."

Vain Pleading

"It's so nice. I never heard of it before."

"Oh, it's ever so gay! Why, me and Amy Lawrence—"

The big eyes told Tom his blunder and he stopped, confused.

"O, Tom! Then I ain't the first you've ever been engaged to!"

The child began to cry. Tom said:

"O, don't cry, Becky, I don't care for her any more."

"Yes, you do, Tom—you know you do."

Tom tried to put his arm about her neck, but she pushed him away and turned her face to the wall, and went on crying. Tom tried again, with soothing words in his mouth, and was repulsed again. Then his pride was up, and he strode away and went outside. He stood about, restless and uneasy, for a while, glancing at the door, every now and then, hoping she would repent and come to find him. But she did not. Then he began to feel badly and fear that he was in the wrong. It was a hard struggle with him to make new advances, now, but he nerved himself to it and entered. She was still standing back there in the corner, sobbing, with her face to the wall. Tom's heart smote him. He went to her and stood a moment, not knowing exactly how to proceed. Then he said hesitatingly:

"Becky, I—I don't care for anybody but you."

No reply—but sobs.

"Becky"—pleadingly. "Becky, won't you say something?"

More sobs.

Tom got out his chiefest jewel, a brass knob from the top of an andiron, and passed it around her so that she could see it, and said:

"Please, Becky, won't you take it?"

She struck it to the floor. Then Tom marched out of the house and over the hills and far away, to return to school no more that day. Presently Becky began to suspect. She ran to the door; he was not in sight; she flew around to the play-yard; he was not there. Then she called:

"Tom! Come back, Tom!"

She listened intently, but there was no answer. She had no companions but silence and loneliness. So she sat down to cry again and upbraid herself; and by this time the scholars began to gather again, and she had to hide her griefs and still her broken heart and take up the cross of a long, dreary, aching afternoon, with none among the strangers about her to exchange sorrows with.

8

Tom dodged hither and thither through lanes until he was well out of the track of returning scholars, and then fell into a moody jog. He crossed a small "branch" two or three times, because of a prevailing juvenile superstition that to cross water baffled pursuit. Half an hour later he was disappearing behind the Douglas mansion on the summit of Cardiff Hill, and the school-house was hardly distinguishable away off in the valley behind him. He entered a dense wood, picked his pathless way to the centre of it, and sat down on a mossy spot under a spreading oak. There was not even a zephyr stirring; the dead noonday heat had even stilled the songs of the birds; nature lay in a trance that was broken by no sound but the occasional far-off hammering of a woodpecker, and this seemed to render the pervading silence and sense of loneliness the more profound. The boy's soul was steeped in melancholy; his feelings were in happy accord with his surroundings. He sat long with his elbows on his knees and his chin in his hands, meditating. It seemed to him that life was but a trouble, at best, and he more than half envied Jimmy Hodges, so lately released; it must be very peaceful, he thought, to lie and slumber and dream forever and ever, with the wind whispering through the trees and caressing the grass and the flowers over the grave, and nothing to bother and grieve about, ever any more. If he only had a clean Sunday-school record he could be willing to go, and be done with it all. Now as to this girl. What had he done? Nothing. He had meant the best in the world, and been treated like a dog—like a very dog. She would be sorry some day—maybe when it was too late. Ah, if he could only die *temporarily*!

But the elastic heart of youth cannot be compressed into one constrained shape long at a time. Tom presently began to drift insensibly back into the concerns of this life again. What if he turned his back, now, and disappeared mysteriously? What if he went away—ever so far away, into unknown countries beyond the seas—and never came back any more! How would she feel then! The idea of being a clown recurred to him now, only to fill him with disgust. For frivolity and jokes and spotted tights were an offense, when they intruded themselves upon a spirit that was exalted into the vague august realm of the romantic. No, he would be a soldier, and return after long years, all war-worn and illustrious. No—better still, he would join the

Indians, and hunt buffaloes and go on the warpath in the mountain ranges and the trackless great plains of the Far West, and away in the future come back a great chief, bristling with feathers, hideous with paint, and prance into Sunday-school, some drowsy summer morning, with a blood-curdling war-whoop, and sear the eyeballs of all his companions with unappeasable envy. But no, there was something gaudier even than this. He would be a pirate! That was it! *now* his future lay plain before him, and glowing with unimaginable splendour. How his name would fill the world, and make people shudder! How gloriously he would go plowing the dancing seas, in his long, low, black-hulled racer, the Spirit of the Storm, with his grisly flag flying at the fore! And at the zenith of his fame, how he would suddenly appear at the old village and stalk into church, brown and weather-beaten, in his black velvet doublet and trunks, his great jack-boots, his crimson sash, his belt bristling with horse-pistols, his crime-rusted cutlass at his side, his slouch hat with waving plumes, his black flag unfurled, with the skull and crossbones on it, and hear with swelling ecstasy the whisperings, "It's Tom Sawyer the Pirate!—the Black Avenger of the Spanish Main!"

Yes, it was settled; his career was determined. He would run away from home and enter upon it. He would start the very next morning. Therefore he must now begin to get ready. He would collect his resources together. He went to a rotten log near at hand and began to dig under one end of it with his Barlow knife. He soon struck wood that sounded hollow. He put his hand there and uttered this incantation impressively:

"What hasn't come here, come! What's here, stay here!"

Then he scraped away the dirt, and exposed a pine shingle. He took it up and disclosed a shapely little treasure-house whose bottom and sides were of shingles. In it lay a marble. Tom's astonishment was boundless! He scratched his head with a perplexed air, and said:

"Well, that beats anything!"

Then he tossed the marble away pettishly, and stood cogitating. The truth was, that a superstition of his had failed, here, which he and all his comrades had always looked upon as infallible. If you buried a marble with certain necessary incantations, and left it alone a fortnight, and then opened the place with the incantation he had just used, you would find that all the marbles you had ever lost had gathered themselves together there, meantime, no matter how widely they had been separated. But now, this thing had actually and unquestionably failed. Tom's whole structure of faith was shaken to its foundations. He had many a time heard of this thing succeeding but never of its failing before. It did not occur to him that he had tried it several times before, himself, but could never find the hiding places afterward. He puzzled over the matter some time, and finally decided that some witch had interfered and broken the charm. He thought he would satisfy himself on that point; so he searched around till he found a small sandy spot with a little funnel-shaped depression in it. He laid himself down and put his mouth close to this depression and called:

"Doodle-bug, doodle-bug, tell me what I want to know! Doodle-bug, doodle-bug, tell me what I want to know!"

The sand began to work, and presently a small black bug appeared for a second and then darted under again in a fright.

"He dasn't tell! So it *was* a witch that done it. I just knowed it."

He well knew the futility of trying to contend against witches, so he gave up discouraged. But it occurred to him that he might as well have the marble he had just thrown away, and therefore he went and made a patient search for it. But he could not find it. Now he went back to his treasure-house and carefully placed himself just as he had been standing when he tossed the marble away; then he took another marble from his pocket and tossed it in the same way, saying:

"Brother, go find your brother!"

He watched where it stopped, and went there and looked. But it must have fallen short or gone too far; so he tried twice more. The last repetition was successful. The two marbles lay within a foot of each other.

Just here the blast of a toy tin trumpet came faintly down the green aisles of the forest. Tom flung off his jacket and trousers, turned a suspender into a belt, raked away some brush behind the rotten log, disclosing a rude bow and arrow, a lath sword and a tin trumpet, and in a moment had seized these things and bounded away, barelegged, with fluttering shirt. He presently halted under a great elm, blew an answering blast, and then began to tiptoe and look warily out, this way and that. He said cautiously—to an imaginary company:

"Hold, my merry men! Keep hid till I blow."

Now appeared Joe Harper, as airily clad and elaborately armed as Tom. Tom called:

"Hold! Who comes here into Sherwood Forest without my pass?"

"Guy of Guisborne wants no man's pass. Who art thou that—that—"

"Dares to hold such language," said Tom, prompting—for they talked "by the book," from memory.

"Who art thou that dares to hold such language?"

"I, indeed! I am Robin Hood, as thy caitiff carcase soon shall know."

"Then art thou indeed that famous outlaw? Right gladly will I dispute with thee the passes of the merry wood. Have at thee!"

They took their lath swords, dumped their other traps on the ground, struck a fencing attitude, foot to foot, and began a grave, careful combat, "two up and two down." Presently Tom said:

"Now, if you've got the hang, go it lively!"

So they "went it lively," panting and perspiring with the work. By and by Tom shouted:

"Fall! fall! Why don't you fall?"

"I sha'n't! Why don't you fall yourself? You're getting the worst of it."

"Why, that ain't anything. I can't fall; that ain't the way it is in the book. The book says, 'Then with one back-handed stroke he slew poor Guy of Guisborne.' You're to turn around and let me hit you in the back."

There was no getting around the authorities, so Joe turned, received the whack and fell.

"Now," said Joe, getting up, "you got to let me kill *you*. That's fair."

"Why, I can't do that, it ain't in the book."

"Well, it's blamed mean—that's all."

"Well, say, Joe, you can be Friar Tuck or Much the miller's son, and lam me with a quarter-staff; or I'll be the Sheriff of Nottingham and you be Robin Hood a little while and kill me."

This was satisfactory, and so these adventures were carried out. Then Tom became Robin Hood again, and was allowed by the treacherous nun to bleed his strength away through his neglected wound. And at last Joe, representing a whole tribe of weeping outlaws, dragged him sadly forth, gave his bow into his feeble hands, and Tom said, "Where this arrow falls, there bury poor Robin Hood under the greenwood tree." Then he shot the arrow and fell back and would have died, but he lit on a nettle and sprang up too gaily for a corpse.

The boys dressed themselves, hid their accoutrements, and went off grieving that there were no outlaws any more, and wondering what modern civilization could claim to have done to compensate for their loss. They said they would rather be outlaws a year in Sherwood Forest than President of the United States forever.

9

At half-past nine, that night, Tom and Sid were sent to bed, as usual. They said their prayers, and Sid was soon asleep. Tom lay awake and waited, in restless impatience. When it seemed to him that it must be nearly daylight, he heard the clock strike ten! This was despair. He would have tossed and fidgeted, as his nerves demanded, but he was afraid he might wake Sid. So he lay still, and stared up into the dark. Everything was dismally still. By and by, out of the stillness, little, scarcely perceptible noises began to emphasize themselves. The ticking of the clock began to bring itself into notice. Old beams began to crack mysteriously. The stairs creaked faintly. Evidently spirits were abroad. A measured, muffled snore issued from Aunt Polly's chamber. And now the tiresome chirping of a cricket that no human ingenuity could locate, began. Next the ghastly ticking of a death-watch in the wall at the bed's head made Tom shudder—it meant that somebody's days were numbered. Then the howl of a far-off dog rose on the night air, and was answered by a fainter howl from a remoter distance. Tom was in an agony. At last he was satisfied that time had ceased and eternity begun; he began to doze, in spite of himself; the clock chimed eleven, but he did not hear it. And then there came, mingling with his half-formed dreams, a most melancholy caterwauling. The raising of a neighbouring window disturbed him. A cry of "Scat! you devil!" and the crash of an empty bottle against the back of his aunt's woodshed brought him wide awake, and a single minute later he was dressed and out of the window and creeping along the roof of the "ell" on all fours. He "meow'd" with caution once or twice, as he went; then jumped to the roof of the woodshed and thence to the ground. Huckleberry Finn was there, with his dead cat. The boys moved off and disappeared in the gloom. At the end of half an hour they were wading through the tall grass of the graveyard.

It was a graveyard of the old-fashioned Western kind. It was on a hill, about a mile and a half from the village. It had a crazy board fence around it, which leaned inward in places, and outward the rest of the time, but stood upright nowhere. Grass and weeds grew rank over the whole cemetery. All the old graves were sunken in, there was not a tombstone on the place; round-topped, worm-eaten boards staggered over the graves, leaning for support and finding none. "Sacred to the memory of" So-and-So had been painted on them once, but it could no longer have been read, on the most of them, now, even if there had been light.

A faint wind moaned through the trees, and Tom feared it might be the spirits of the dead, complaining at being disturbed. The boys talked little, and only under their breath, for the time and the place and the pervading solemnity and silence oppressed their spirits. They found the sharp new heap they were seeking, and ensconced themselves within the protection of three great elms that grew in a bunch within a few feet of the grave.

Then they waited in silence for what seemed a long time. The hooting of a distant owl was all the sound that troubled the dead stillness. Tom's reflections grew oppressive. He must force some talk. So he said in a whisper:

"Hucky, do you believe the dead people like it for us to be here?"

Huckleberry whispered:

"I wisht I knowed. It's awful solemn like, *ain't* it?"

"I bet it is."

There was a considerable pause, while the boys canvassed this matter inwardly. Then Tom whispered:

"Say, Hucky—do you reckon Hoss Williams hears us talking?"

"O' course he does. Least his sperrit does."

Tom, after a pause:

"I wish I'd said Mister Williams. But I never meant any harm. Everybody calls him Hoss."

"A body can't be too partic'lar how they talk 'bout these-yer dead people, Tom."

This was a damper, and conversation died again. Presently Tom seized his comrade's arm and said:

"Sh!"

"What is it, Tom?" And the two clung together with beating hearts.

"Sh! There 'tis again! Didn't you hear it?"

"I—"

"There! Now you hear it."

"Lord, Tom, they're coming! They're coming, sure. What'll we do?"

"I dono. Think they'll see us?"

"O, Tom, they can see in the dark, same as cats. I wisht I hadn't come."

"O, don't be afeard. I don't believe they'll bother us. We ain't doing any harm. If we keep perfectly still, maybe they won't notice us at all."

"I'll try to, Tom, but, Lord, I'm all of a shiver."

"Listen!"

The boys bent their heads together and scarcely breathed. A muffled sound of voices floated up from the far end of the graveyard.

"Look! See there!" whispered Tom. "What is it?"

"It's devil-fire. Oh, Tom, this is awful."

Some vague figures approached through the gloom, swinging an old-fashioned tin lantern that freckled the ground with innumerable little spangles of light. Presently Huckleberry whispered with a shudder:

"It's the devils sure enough. Three of 'em! Lordy, Tom, we're goners! Can you pray?"

"I'll try, but don't you be afeard. They ain't going to hurt us. 'Now I lay me down to sleep, I—'"

"Sh!"

"What is it, Huck?"

"They're *humans*! One of 'em is, anyway. One of 'em's old Muff Potter's voice."

"No—'tain't so, is it?"

"I bet I know it. Don't you stir nor budge. He ain't sharp enough to notice us. Drunk, the same as usual, likely—blamed old rip!"

"All right, I'll keep still. Now they're stuck. Can't find it. Here they come again. Now they're hot. Cold again. Hot again. Red hot! They're p'inted right, this time. Say, Huck, I know another o' them voices; it's Injun Joe."

"That's so—that murderin' half-breed! I'd druther they was devils a dern sight. What kin they be up to?"

The whisper died wholly out, now, for the three men had reached the grave and stood within a few feet of the boys' hiding place.

"Here it is," said the third voice; and the owner of it held the lantern up and revealed the face of young Dr. Robinson.

Potter and Injun Joe were carrying a handbarrow with a rope and a couple of shovels on it. They cast down their load and began to open the grave. The doctor put the lantern at the head of the grave and came and sat down with his back against one of the elm trees. He was so close the boys could have touched him.

"Hurry, men!" he said, in a low voice; "the moon might come out at any moment."

They growled a response and went on digging. For some time there was no noise but the grating sound of the spades discharging their freight of mould and gravel. It was very monotonous. Finally a spade struck upon the coffin with a dull woody accent, and within another minute or two the men had hoisted it out on the ground. They pried off the lid with their shovels, got out the body and dumped it rudely on the ground. The moon drifted from behind the clouds and exposed the pallid face. The barrow was got ready and the corpse placed on it, covered with a blanket, and bound to its place with the rope. Potter took out a large spring-knife and cut off the dangling end of the rope and then said:

"Now the cussed thing's ready, Sawbones, and you'll just out with another five, or here she stays."

"That's the talk!" said Injun Joe.

"Look here, what does this mean?" said the doctor. "You required your pay in advance, and I've paid you."

"Yes, and you done more than that," said Injun Joe, approaching the doctor, who was now standing. "Five years ago you drove me away from your father's kitchen one night, when I come to ask for something to eat, and you said I warn't there for any good; and when I swore I'd get even with you if it took a hundred years, your father had me jailed for a vagrant. Did you think I'd forget? The Injun blood ain't in me for nothing. And now I've *got* you, and you got to *settle*, you know!"

He was threatening the doctor, with his fist in his face, by this time. The doctor struck out suddenly and stretched the ruffian on the ground. Potter dropped his knife, and exclaimed:

"Here, now, don't you hit my pard!" and the next moment he had grappled with the doctor and the two were struggling with might and main, trampling the grass and tearing the ground with their heels. Injun Joe sprang to his feet, his eyes flaming with passion, snatched up Potter's knife, and went creeping, catlike and stooping, round and round about the combatants, seeking an opportunity. All at once the doctor flung himself free, seized the heavy headboard of Williams' grave and felled Potter to the earth with it—and in the same instant the half-breed saw his chance and drove the knife to the hilt in the young man's breast. He reeled and fell partly upon Potter, flooding him with his blood, and in the same moment the clouds blotted out the dreadful spectacle and the two frightened boys went speeding away in the dark.

Presently, when the moon emerged again, Injun Joe was standing over the two forms, contemplating them. The doctor murmured inarticulately, gave a long gasp or two and was still. The half-breed muttered:

"*That* score is settled—damn you."

Then he robbed the body. After which he put the fatal knife in Potter's open right hand, and sat down on the dismantled coffin. Three—four—five minutes passed, and then Potter began to stir and moan. His hand closed upon the knife; he raised it, glanced at it, and let it fall, with a shudder. Then he sat up, pushing the body from him, and gazed at it, and then around him, confusedly. His eyes met Joe's.

"Lord, how is this, Joe?" he said.

"It's a dirty business," said Joe, without moving.

"What did you do it for?"

"I! I never done it!"

"Look here! That kind of talk won't wash."

Potter trembled and grew white.

"I thought I'd got sober. I'd no business to drink tonight. But it's in my head yet—worse'n when we started here. I'm all in a muddle; can't recollect anything of it, hardly. Tell me, Joe—*honest*, now, old feller—did I do it? Joe, I never meant to—'pon my soul and honour, I never meant to, Joe. Tell me how it was, Joe. O, it's awful—and him so young and promising."

"Why, you two was scuffling, and he fetched you one with the headboard and you fell flat; and then up you come, all reeling and staggering like, and snatched the knife and jammed it into him, just as he fetched you another awful clip—and here you've laid, as dead as a wedge till now."

"O, I didn't know what I was a-doing. I wish I may die this minute if I did. It was all on account of the whiskey and the excitement, I reckon. I never used a weepon in my life before, Joe. I've fought, but never with weepons. They'll all say that. Joe, don't tell! Say you won't tell, Joe—that's a good feller. I always liked you, Joe, and stood up for you, too. Don't you remember? You *won't* tell, *will* you, Joe?" And the poor creature dropped on his knees before the stolid murderer, and clasped his appealing hands.

"No, you've always been fair and square with me, Muff Potter, and I won't go back on you. There, now, that's as fair as a man can say."

"O, Joe, you're an angel. I'll bless you for this the longest day I live." And Potter began to cry.

"Come, now, that's enough of that. This ain't any time for blubbering. You be off yonder way and I'll go this. Move, now, and don't leave any tracks behind you."

Potter started on a trot that quickly increased to a run. The half-breed stood looking after him. He muttered:

"If he's as much stunned with the lick and fuddled with the rum as he had the look of being, he won't think of the knife till he's gone so far he'll be afraid to come back after it to such a place by himself—chicken-heart!"

Two or three minutes later the murdered man, the blanketed corpse, the lidless coffin, and the open grave were under no inspection but the moon's. The stillness was complete again, too.

10

The two boys flew on and on, toward the village, speechless with horror. They glanced backward over their shoulders from time to time, apprehensively, as if they feared they might be followed. Every stump that started up in their path seemed a man and an enemy, and made them catch their breath; and as they sped by some outlying cottages that lay near the village, the barking of the aroused watchdogs seemed to give wings to their feet.

"If we can only get to the old tannery before we break down!" whispered Tom, in short catches between breaths. "I can't stand it much longer."

Huckleberry's hard pantings were his only reply, and the boys fixed their eyes on the goal of their hopes and bent to their work to win it. They gained steadily on it, and at last, breast to breast, they burst through the open door and fell grateful and exhausted in the sheltering shadows beyond. By and by their pulses slowed down, and Tom whispered:

"Huckleberry, what do you reckon'll come of this?"

"If Doctor Robinson dies, I reckon hanging'll come of it."

"Do you though?"

"Why, I *know* it, Tom."

Tom thought a while, then he said:

"Who'll tell? We?"

"What are you talking about? S'pose something happened and Injun Joe *didn't* hang? Why, he'd kill us some time or other, just as dead sure as we're a laying here."

"That's just what I was thinking to myself, Huck."

"If anybody tells, let Muff Potter do it, if he's fool enough. He's generally drunk enough."

Tom said nothing—went on thinking. Presently he whispered:

"Huck, Muff Potter don't know it. How can he tell?"

"What's the reason he don't know it?"

"Because he'd just got that whack when Injun Joe done it. D'you reckon he could see anything? D'you reckon he knowed anything?"

"By hokey, that's so, Tom!"

"And besides, look-a-here—maybe that whack done for *him*!"

"No, 'taint likely, Tom. He had liquor in him; I could see that; and besides, he always has. Well, when pap's full, you might take and belt him over the head with a church and you couldn't phase him. He says so, his own self. So it's the same with Muff Potter, of course. But if a man was dead sober, I reckon maybe that whack might fetch him; I dono."

After another reflective silence, Tom said:

"Hucky, you sure you can keep mum?"

"Tom, we *got* to keep mum. You know that. That Injun devil wouldn't make any more of drownding us than a couple of cats, if we was to squeak 'bout this and they didn't hang him. Now, look-a-here, Tom, less take and swear to one another—that's what we got to do—swear to keep mum."

"I'm agreed. It's the best thing. Would you just hold hands and swear that we—"

"O, no, that wouldn't do for this. That's good enough for little rubbishy common things—specially with gals, cuz *they* go back on you anyway, and blab if they get in a huff—but there orter be writing 'bout a big thing like this. And blood."

Tom's whole being applauded this idea. It was deep, and dark, and awful; the hour, the circumstances, the surroundings, were in keeping with it. He picked up a clean pine shingle that lay in the moonlight, took a little fragment of "red keel" out of his pocket, got the moon on his work, and painfully scrawled these lines, emphasizing each slow down-stroke by clamping his tongue between his teeth, and letting up the pressure on the up-strokes.

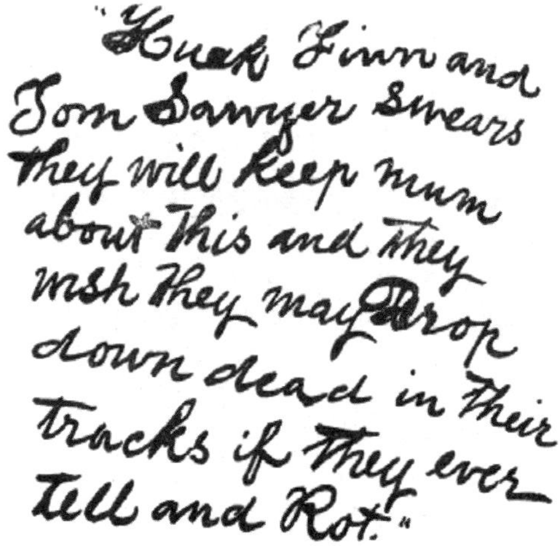

Huckleberry was filled with admiration of Tom's facility in writing, and the sublimity of his language. He at once took a pin from his lapel and was going to prick his flesh, but Tom said:

"Hold on! Don't do that. A pin's brass. It might have verdigrease on it."

"What's verdigrease?"

"It's p'ison. That's what it is. You just swaller some of it once—you'll see."

So Tom unwound the thread from one of his needles, and each boy pricked the ball of his thumb and squeezed out a drop of blood. In time, after many squeezes, Tom managed to sign his initials, using the ball of his little finger for a pen. Then he showed Huckleberry how to make an H and an F, and the oath was complete. They buried the shingle close to the wall, with some dismal ceremonies and incantations, and the fetters that bound their tongues were considered to be locked and the key thrown away.

A figure crept stealthily through a break in the other end of the ruined building, now, but they did not notice it.

"Tom," whispered Huckleberry, "does this keep us from *ever* telling—*always*?"

"Of course it does. It don't make any difference *what* happens, we got to keep mum. We'd drop down dead—don't *you* know that?"

"Yes, I reckon that's so."

They continued to whisper for some little time. Presently a dog set up a long, lugubrious howl just outside—within ten feet of them. The boys clasped each other suddenly, in an agony of fright.

"Which of us does he mean?" gasped Huckleberry.

"I dono—peep through the crack. Quick!"

"No, *you*, Tom!"

"I can't—I can't *do* it, Huck!"

"Please, Tom. There 'tis again!"

"O, lordy, I'm thankful!" whispered Tom. "I know his voice. It's Bull Harbison."*

"O, that's good—I tell you, Tom, I was most scared to death; I'd a bet anything it was a *stray* dog."

The dog howled again. The boys' hearts sank once more.

"O, my! that ain't no Bull Harbison!" whispered Huckleberry. "*Do*, Tom!"

Tom, quaking with fear, yielded, and put his eye to the crack. His whisper was hardly audible when he said:

"O, Huck, *it's a stray dog*!"

"Quick, Tom, quick! Who does he mean?"

"Huck, he must mean us both—we're right together."

---

* If Mr. Harbison owned a slave named Bull, Tom would have spoken of him as "Harbison's Bull," but a son or a dog of that name was "Bull Harbison."

"O, Tom, I reckon we're goners. I reckon there ain't no mistake 'bout where *I'll* go to. I been so wicked."

"Dad fetch it! This comes of playing hookey and doing everything a feller's told *not* to do. I might a been good, like Sid, if I'd a tried—but no, I wouldn't, of course. But if ever I get off this time, I lay I'll just *waller* in Sunday-schools!" And Tom began to snuffle a little.

"*You* bad!" and Huckleberry began to snuffle too. "Consound it, Tom Sawyer, you're just old pie, 'long-side o' what I am. Oh, *lordy*, lordy, lordy, I wisht I only had half your chance."

Tom choked off and whispered:

"Look, Hucky, look! He's got his *back* to us!"

Hucky looked, with joy in his heart.

"Well, he has, by jingoes! Did he before?"

"Yes, he did. But I, like a fool, never thought. Oh, this is bully, you know. *Now* who can he mean?"

The howling stopped. Tom pricked up his ears.

"Sh! What's that?" he whispered.

"Sounds like—like hogs grunting. No—it's somebody snoring, Tom."

"That *is* it! Where 'bouts is it, Huck?"

"I bleeve it's down at 'tother end. Sounds so, anyway. Pap used to sleep there, sometimes, 'long with the hogs, but laws bless you, he just lifts things when *he* snores. Besides, I reckon he ain't ever coming back to this town any more."

The spirit of adventure rose in the boys' souls once more.

"Hucky, do you das't to go if I lead?"

"I don't like to, much. Tom, s'pose it's Injun Joe!"

Tom quailed. But presently the temptation rose up strong again and the boys agreed to try, with the understanding that they would take to their heels if the snoring stopped. So they went tiptoeing stealthily down, the one behind the other. When they had got to within five steps of the snorer, Tom stepped on a stick, and it broke with a sharp snap. The man moaned, writhed a little, and his face came into the moonlight. It was Muff Potter. The boys' hearts had stood still, and their hopes too, when the man moved, but their fears passed away now. They tip-toed out, through the broken weather-boarding, and stopped at a little distance to exchange a parting word. That long, lugubrious howl rose on the night air again! They turned and saw the strange dog standing within a few feet of where Potter was lying, and *facing* Potter, with his nose pointing heavenward.

"O, geeminy, it's *him*!" exclaimed both boys, in a breath.

"Say, Tom—they say a stray dog come howling around Johnny Miller's house, 'bout midnight, as much as two weeks ago; and a whippoorwill come in and lit on the banisters and sung, the very same evening; and there ain't anybody dead there yet."

"Well, I know that. And suppose there ain't. Didn't Gracie Miller fall in the kitchen fire and burn herself terrible the very next Saturday?"

"Yes, but she ain't *dead.* And what's more, she's getting better, too."

"All right, you wait and see. She's a goner, just as dead sure as Muff Potter's a goner. That's what the niggers say, and they know all about these kind of things, Huck."

Then they separated, cogitating. When Tom crept in at his bedroom window the night was almost spent. He undressed with excessive caution, and fell asleep congratulating himself that nobody knew of his escapade. He was not aware that the gently-snoring Sid was awake, and had been so for an hour.

When Tom awoke, Sid was dressed and gone. There was a late look in the light, a late sense in the atmosphere. He was startled. Why had he not been called—persecuted till he was up, as usual? The thought filled him with bodings. Within five minutes he was dressed and downstairs, feeling sore and drowsy. The family were still at table, but they had finished breakfast. There was no voice of rebuke; but there were averted eyes; there was a silence and an air of solemnity that struck a chill to the culprit's heart. He sat down and tried to seem gay, but it was uphill work; it roused no smile, no response, and he lapsed into silence and let his heart sink down to the depths.

After breakfast his aunt took him aside, and Tom almost brightened in the hope that he was going to be flogged; but it was not so. His aunt wept over him and asked him how he could go and break her old heart so; and finally told him to go on, and ruin himself and bring her grey hairs with sorrow to the grave, for it was no use for her to try any more. This was worse than a thousand whippings, and Tom's heart was sorer now than his body. He cried, he pleaded for forgiveness, promised to reform over and over again, and then received his dismissal, feeling that he had won but an imperfect forgiveness and established but a feeble confidence.

He left the presence too miserable to even feel revengeful toward Sid; and so the latter's prompt retreat through the back gate was unnecessary. He moped to school gloomy and sad, and took his flogging, along with Joe Harper, for playing hookey the day before, with the air of one whose heart was busy with heavier woes and wholly dead to trifles. Then he betook himself to his seat, rested his elbows on his desk and his jaws in his hands, and stared at the wall with the stony stare of suffering that has reached the limit and can no further go. His elbow was pressing against some hard substance. After a long time he slowly and sadly changed his position, and took up this object with a sigh. It was in a paper. He unrolled it. A long, lingering, colossal sigh followed, and his heart broke. It was his brass andiron knob!

This final feather broke the camel's back.

11

Close upon the hour of noon the whole village was suddenly electrified with the ghastly news. No need of the as yet un-dreamed-of telegraph; the tale flew from man to man, from group to group, from house to house, with little less than telegraphic speed. Of course the schoolmaster gave holiday for that afternoon; the town would have thought strangely of him if he had not.

A gory knife had been found close to the murdered man, and it had been recognized by somebody as belonging to Muff Potter—so the story ran. And it was said that a belated citizen had come upon Potter washing himself in the "branch" about one or two o'clock in the morning, and that Potter had at once sneaked off—suspicious circumstances, especially the washing which was not a habit with Potter. It was also said that the town had been ransacked for this "murderer" (the public are not slow in the matter of sifting evidence and arriving at a verdict), but that he could not be found. Horsemen had departed down all the roads in every direction, and the Sheriff "was confident" that he would be captured before night.

All the town was drifting toward the graveyard. Tom's heartbreak vanished and he joined the procession, not because he would not a thousand times rather go anywhere else, but because an awful, unaccountable fascination drew him on. Arrived at the dreadful place, he wormed his small body through the crowd and saw the dismal spectacle. It seemed to him an age since he was there before. Somebody pinched his arm. He turned, and his eyes met Huckleberry's. Then both looked elsewhere at once, and wondered if anybody had noticed anything in their mutual glance. But everybody was talking, and intent upon the grisly spectacle before them.

"Poor fellow!" "Poor young fellow!" "This ought to be a lesson to grave robbers!" "Muff Potter'll hang for this if they catch him!" This was the drift of remark; and the minister said, "It was a judgment; His hand is here."

Now Tom shivered from head to heel; for his eye fell upon the stolid face of Injun Joe. At this moment the crowd began to sway and struggle, and voices shouted, "It's him! it's him! he's coming himself!"

"Who? Who?" from twenty voices.

"Muff Potter!"

"Hallo, he's stopped!—Look out, he's turning! Don't let him get away!"

People in the branches of the trees over Tom's head said he wasn't trying to get away—he only looked doubtful and perplexed.

"Infernal impudence!" said a bystander; "wanted to come and take a quiet look at his work, I reckon—didn't expect any company."

The crowd fell apart, now, and the Sheriff came through, ostentatiously leading Potter by the arm. The poor fellow's face was haggard, and his eyes showed the fear that was upon him. When he stood before the murdered man, he shook as with a palsy, and he put his face in his hands and burst into tears.

"I didn't do it, friends," he sobbed; "'pon my word and honour I never done it."

"Who's accused you?" shouted a voice.

This shot seemed to carry home. Potter lifted his face and looked around him with a pathetic hopelessness in his eyes. He saw Injun Joe, and exclaimed:

"O, Injun Joe, you promised me you'd never—"

"Is that your knife?" and it was thrust before him by the Sheriff.

Potter would have fallen if they had not caught him and eased him to the ground. Then he said:

"Something told me 't if I didn't come back and get—" He shuddered; then waved his nerveless hand with a vanquished gesture and said, "Tell 'em, Joe, tell 'em—it ain't any use any more."

Then Huckleberry and Tom stood dumb and staring, and heard the stony-hearted liar reel off his serene statement, they expecting every moment that the clear sky would deliver God's lightnings upon his head, and wondering to see how long the stroke was delayed. And when he had finished and still stood alive and whole, their wavering impulse to break their oath and save the poor betrayed prisoner's life faded and vanished away, for plainly this miscreant had sold himself to Satan and it would be fatal to meddle with the property of such a power as that.

"Why didn't you leave? What did you want to come here for?" somebody said.

"I couldn't help it—I couldn't help it," Potter moaned. "I wanted to run away, but I couldn't seem to come anywhere but here." And he fell to sobbing again.

Injun Joe repeated his statement, just as calmly, a few minutes afterward on the inquest, under oath; and the boys, seeing that the lightnings were still withheld, were confirmed in their belief that Joe had sold himself to the devil. He was now become, to them, the most balefully interesting object they had ever looked upon, and they could not take their fascinated eyes from his face.

They inwardly resolved to watch him nights, when opportunity should offer, in the hope of getting a glimpse of his dread master.

Injun Joe helped to raise the body of the murdered man and put it in a wagon for removal; and it was whispered through the shuddering crowd that the wound bled a little! The boys thought that this happy circumstance would turn suspicion in the right direction; but they were disappointed, for more than one villager remarked:

"It was within three feet of Muff Potter when it done it."

Tom's fearful secret and gnawing conscience disturbed his sleep for as much as a week after this; and at breakfast one morning Sid said:

"Tom, you pitch around and talk in your sleep so much that you keep me awake half the time."

Tom blanched and dropped his eyes.

"It's a bad sign," said Aunt Polly, gravely. "What you got on your mind, Tom?"

"Nothing. Nothing 't I know of." But the boy's hand shook so that he spilled his coffee.

"And you do talk such stuff," Sid said. "Last night you said, 'It's blood, it's blood, that's what it is!' You said that over and over. And you said, 'Don't torment me so—I'll tell!' Tell *what*? What is it you'll tell?"

Everything was swimming before Tom. There is no telling what might have happened, now, but luckily the concern passed out of Aunt Polly's face and she came to Tom's relief without knowing it. She said:

"Sho! It's that dreadful murder. I dream about it most every night myself. Sometimes I dream it's me that done it."

Mary said she had been affected much the same way. Sid seemed satisfied. Tom got out of the presence as quick as he plausibly could, and after that he complained of toothache for a week, and tied up his jaws every night. He never knew that Sid lay nightly watching, and frequently slipped the bandage free and then leaned on his elbow listening a good while at a time, and afterward slipped the bandage back to its place again. Tom's distress of mind wore off gradually and the toothache grew irksome and was discarded. If Sid really managed to make anything out of Tom's disjointed mutterings, he kept it to himself.

It seemed to Tom that his schoolmates never would get done holding inquests on dead cats, and thus keeping his trouble present to his mind. Sid noticed that Tom never was coroner at one of these inquiries, though it had been his habit to take the lead in all new enterprises; he noticed, too, that Tom never acted as a witness—and that was strange; and Sid did not overlook the fact that Tom even showed a marked aversion to these inquests, and always avoided them when he could. Sid marveled, but said nothing. However, even inquests went out of vogue at last, and ceased to torture Tom's conscience.

Every day or two, during this time of sorrow, Tom watched his opportunity and went to the little grated jail-window and smuggled such small comforts through to the "murderer" as he could get hold of. The jail was a trifling little brick den that stood in a marsh at the edge of the village, and no guards were afforded for it; indeed, it was seldom occupied. These offerings greatly helped to ease Tom's conscience.

The villagers had a strong desire to tar-and-feather Injun Joe and ride him on a rail, for body-snatching, but so formidable was his character that nobody could be found who was willing to take the lead in the matter, so it was dropped. He had been careful to begin both of his inquest-statements with the fight, without confessing the grave-robbery that preceded it; therefore it was deemed wisest not to try the case in the courts at present.

12

One of the reasons why Tom's mind had drifted away from its secret troubles was, that it had found a new and weighty matter to interest itself about. Becky Thatcher had stopped coming to school. Tom had struggled with his pride a few days, and tried to "whistle her down the wind," but failed. He began to find himself hanging around her father's house, nights, and feeling very miserable. She was ill. What if she should die! There was distraction in the thought. He no longer took an interest in war, nor even in piracy. The charm of life was gone; there was nothing but dreariness left. He put his hoop away, and his bat; there was no joy in them any more. His aunt was concerned. She began to try all manner of remedies on him. She was one of those people who are infatuated with patent medicines and all new-fangled methods of producing health or mending it. She was an inveterate experimenter in these things. When something fresh in this line came out she was in a fever, right away, to try it; not on herself, for she was never ailing, but on anybody else that came handy. She was a subscriber for all the "Health" periodicals and phrenological frauds; and the solemn ignorance they were inflated with was breath to her nostrils. All the "rot" they contained about ventilation, and how to go to bed, and how to get up, and what to eat, and what to drink, and how much exercise to take, and what frame of mind to keep one's self in, and what sort of clothing to wear, was all gospel to her, and she never observed that her health-journals of the current month customarily upset everything they had recommended the month before. She was as simple-hearted and honest as the day was long, and so she was an easy victim. She gathered together her quack periodicals and her quack medicines, and thus armed with death, went about on her pale horse, metaphorically speaking, with "hell following after." But she never suspected that she was not an angel of healing and the balm of Gilead in disguise, to the suffering neighbours.

The water treatment was new, now, and Tom's low condition was a windfall to her. She had him out at daylight every morning, stood him up in the woodshed and drowned him with a deluge of cold water; then she scrubbed him down with a towel like a file, and so brought him to; then she rolled him up in a wet sheet and put him away under blankets till she sweated his soul clean and "the yellow stains of it came through his pores"—as Tom said.

Yet notwithstanding all this, the boy grew more and more melancholy and pale and dejected. She added hot baths, sitz baths, shower baths, and plunges. The boy remained as dismal as a hearse. She began to assist the water with a slim oatmeal diet and blister-plasters. She calculated his capacity as she would a jug's, and filled him up every day with quack cure-alls.

Tom had become indifferent to persecution by this time. This phase filled the old lady's heart with consternation. This indifference must be broken up at any cost. Now she heard of Pain-killer for the first time. She ordered a lot at once. She tasted it and was filled with gratitude. It was simply fire in a liquid form. She dropped the water treatment and everything else, and pinned her faith to Pain-killer. She gave Tom a teaspoonful and watched with the deepest anxiety for the result. Her troubles were instantly at rest, her soul at peace again; for the "indifference" was broken up. The boy could not have shown a wilder, heartier interest, if she had built a fire under him.

Tom felt that it was time to wake up; this sort of life might be romantic enough, in his blighted condition, but it was getting to have too little sentiment and too much distracting variety about it. So he thought over various plans for relief, and finally hit upon that of professing to be fond of Pain-killer. He asked for it so often that he became a nuisance, and his aunt ended by telling him to help himself and quit bothering her. If it had been Sid, she would have had no misgivings to alloy her delight; but since it was Tom, she watched the bottle clandestinely. She found that the medicine did really diminish, but it did not occur to her that the boy was mending the health of a crack in the sitting-room floor with it.

One day Tom was in the act of dosing the crack when his aunt's yellow cat came along, purring, eyeing the teaspoon avariciously, and begging for a taste. Tom said:

"Don't ask for it unless you want it, Peter."

But Peter signified that he did want it.

"You better make sure."

Peter was sure.

"Now you've asked for it, and I'll give it to you, because there ain't anything mean about me; but if you find you don't like it, you mustn't blame anybody but your own self."

Peter was agreeable. So Tom pried his mouth open and poured down the Pain-killer. Peter sprang a couple of yards in the air, and then delivered a war-whoop and set off round and round the room, banging against furniture, upsetting flowerpots, and making general havoc. Next he rose on his hind feet and pranced around, in a frenzy of enjoyment, with his head over his shoulder and his voice proclaiming his unappeasable happiness. Then he went tearing around the house again spreading chaos and destruction in his path. Aunt Polly entered in time to see him throw a few double summersets, deliver a final mighty hurrah, and sail through the open window, carrying the rest of the flowerpots with him. The old lady stood petrified with astonishment, peering over her glasses; Tom lay on the floor expiring with laughter.

"Tom, what on earth ails that cat?"

"I don't know, aunt," gasped the boy.

"Why, I never see anything like it. What did make him act so?"

"Deed I don't know, Aunt Polly; cats always act so when they're having a good time."

A General Good Time

"They do, do they?" There was something in the tone that made Tom apprehensive.

"Yes'm. That is, I believe they do."

"You *do*?"

"Yes'm."

The old lady was bending down, Tom watching, with interest emphasized by anxiety. Too late he divined her "drift." The handle of the telltale teaspoon was visible under the bed-valance. Aunt Polly took it, held it up. Tom winced, and dropped his eyes. Aunt Polly raised him by the usual handle—his ear—and cracked his head soundly with her thimble.

"Now, sir, what did you want to treat that poor dumb beast so, for?"

"I done it out of pity for him—because he hadn't any aunt."

"Hadn't any aunt!—you numskull. What has that got to do with it?"

"Heaps. Because if he'd had one she'd a burnt him out herself! She'd a roasted his bowels out of him 'thout any more feeling than if he was a human!"

Aunt Polly felt a sudden pang of remorse. This was putting the thing in a new light; what was cruelty to a cat *might* be cruelty to a boy, too. She began to soften; she felt sorry. Her eyes watered a little, and she put her hand on Tom's head and said gently:

"I was meaning for the best, Tom. And, Tom, it *did* do you good."

Tom looked up in her face with just a perceptible twinkle peeping through his gravity:

"I know you was meaning for the best, aunty, and so was I with Peter. It done *him* good, too. I never see him get around so since—"

"O, go 'long with you, Tom, before you aggravate me again. And you try and see if you can't be a good boy, for once, and you needn't take any more medicine."

Tom reached school ahead of time. It was noticed that this strange thing had been occurring every day latterly. And now, as usual of late, he hung about the gate of the schoolyard instead of playing with his comrades. He was sick, he said, and he looked it. He tried to seem to be looking everywhere but whither he really was looking—down the road. Presently Jeff Thatcher hove in sight, and Tom's face lighted; he gazed a moment, and then turned sorrowfully away. When Jeff arrived, Tom accosted him; and "led up" warily to opportunities for remark about Becky, but the giddy lad never could see the bait. Tom watched and watched, hoping whenever a frisking frock came in sight, and hating the owner of it as soon as he saw she was not the right one. At last frocks ceased to appear, and he dropped hopelessly into the dumps; he entered the empty schoolhouse and sat down to suffer. Then one more frock passed in at the gate, and Tom's heart gave a great bound. The next instant he was out, and "going on" like an Indian; yelling, laughing, chasing boys, jumping over the fence at risk of life and limb, throwing handsprings, standing on his head—doing all the heroic things he could conceive of, and keeping a furtive eye out, all the while, to see if Becky Thatcher was noticing. But she seemed to be unconscious of it all; she never looked. Could it be possible that she was not aware that he was there? He carried his exploits to her immediate vicinity; came war-whooping around, snatched a boy's cap, hurled it to the roof of the schoolhouse, broke through a group of boys, tumbling them in every direction, and fell sprawling, himself, under Becky's nose, almost upsetting her—and she turned, with her nose in the air, and he heard her say: "Mf! some people think they're mighty smart—always showing off!"

Tom's cheeks burned. He gathered himself up and sneaked off, crushed and crestfallen.

13

Tom's mind was made up now. He was gloomy and desperate. He was a forsaken, friendless boy, he said; nobody loved him; when they found out what they had driven him to, perhaps they would be sorry; he had tried to do right and get along, but they would not let him; since nothing would do them but to be rid of him, let it be so; and let them blame *him* for the consequences—why shouldn't they? What right had the friendless to complain? Yes, they had forced him to it at last: he would lead a life of crime. There was no choice.

By this time he was far down Meadow Lane, and the bell for school to "take up" tinkled faintly upon his ear. He sobbed, now, to think he should never, never hear that old familiar sound any more—it was very hard, but it was forced on him; since he was driven out into the cold world, he must submit—but he forgave them. Then the sobs came thick and fast.

Just at this point he met his soul's sworn comrade, Joe Harper—hard-eyed, and with evidently a great and dismal purpose in his heart. Plainly here were "two souls with but a single thought." Tom, wiping his eyes with his sleeve, began to blubber out something about a resolution to escape from hard usage and lack of sympathy at home by roaming abroad into the great world never to return; and ended by hoping that Joe would not forget him.

But it transpired that this was a request which Joe had just been going to make of Tom, and had come to hunt him up for that purpose. His mother had whipped him for drinking some cream which he had never tasted and knew nothing about; it was plain that she was tired of him and wished him to go; if she felt that way, there was nothing for him to do but succumb; he hoped she would be happy, and never regret having driven her poor boy out into the unfeeling world to suffer and die.

As the two boys walked sorrowing along, they made a new compact to stand by each other and be brothers and never separate till death relieved them of their troubles. Then they began to lay their plans. Joe was for being a hermit, and living on crusts in a remote cave, and dying, some time, of cold and want and grief; but after listening to Tom, he conceded that there were some conspicuous advantages about a life of crime, and so he consented to be a pirate.

Three miles below St. Petersburg, at a point where the Mississippi River was a trifle over a mile wide, there was a long, narrow, wooded island, with a shallow bar at the head of it, and this offered well as a rendezvous. It was not inhabited; it lay far over toward the further shore, abreast a dense and almost wholly unpeopled forest. So Jackson's Island was chosen. Who were to be the subjects of their piracies was a matter that did not occur to them. Then they hunted up Huckleberry Finn, and he joined them promptly, for all careers were one to him; he was indifferent. They presently separated to meet at a lonely spot on the riverbank two miles above the village at the favourite hour—which was midnight. There was a small log raft there which they meant to capture. Each would bring hooks and lines, and such provision as he could steal in the most dark and mysterious way—as became outlaws. And before the afternoon was done, they had all managed to enjoy the sweet glory of spreading the fact that pretty soon the town would "hear something." All who got this vague hint were cautioned to "be mum and wait."

About midnight Tom arrived with a boiled ham and a few trifles, and stopped in a dense undergrowth on a small bluff overlooking the meeting place. It was starlight, and very still. The mighty river lay like an ocean at rest. Tom listened a moment, but no sound disturbed the quiet. Then he gave a low, distinct whistle. It was answered from under the bluff. Tom whistled twice more; these signals were answered in the same way. Then a guarded voice said:

"Who goes there?"

"Tom Sawyer, the Black Avenger of the Spanish Main. Name your names."

"Huck Finn the Red-Handed, and Joe Harper the Terror of the Seas." Tom had furnished these titles, from his favourite literature.

"'Tis well. Give the countersign."

Two hoarse whispers delivered the same awful word simultaneously to the brooding night:

"*Blood*!"

Then Tom tumbled his ham over the bluff and let himself down after it, tearing both skin and clothes to some extent in the effort. There was an easy, comfortable path along the shore under the bluff, but it lacked the advantages of difficulty and danger so valued by a pirate.

The Terror of the Seas had brought a side of bacon, and had about worn himself out with getting it there. Finn the Red-Handed had stolen a skillet and a quantity of half-cured leaf tobacco, and had also brought a few corn-cobs to make pipes with. But none of the pirates smoked or "chewed" but himself. The Black Avenger of the Spanish Main said it would never do to start without some fire. That was a wise thought; matches were hardly known there in that day. They saw a fire smouldering upon a great raft a hundred yards above, and they went stealthily thither and helped themselves to a chunk. They made an imposing adventure of it, saying, "Hist!" every now and then, and suddenly halting with finger on lip; moving with hands on imaginary dagger-hilts; and giving orders in dismal whispers that if "the foe" stirred, to "let him have it to the hilt," because "dead men tell no tales." They knew well enough that the raftsmen were all down at the village laying in stores or having a spree, but still that was no excuse for their conducting this thing in an unpiratical way.

They shoved off, presently, Tom in command, Huck at the after oar and Joe at the forward. Tom stood amidships, gloomy-browed, and with folded arms, and gave his orders in a low, stern whisper:

"Luff, and bring her to the wind!"

"Aye-aye, sir!"

"Steady, steady-y-y-y!"

"Steady it is, sir!"

"Let her go off a point!"

"Point it is, sir!"

As the boys steadily and monotonously drove the raft toward mid-stream it was no doubt understood that these orders were given only for "style," and were not intended to mean anything in particular.

"What sail's she carrying?"

"Courses, tops'ls, and flying-jib, sir."

"Send the r'yals up! Lay out aloft, there, half a dozen of ye—foretopmaststuns'l! Lively, now!"

"Aye-aye, sir!"

"Shake out that maintogalans'l! Sheets and braces! *now* my hearties!"

"Aye-aye, sir!"

"Hellum-a-lee—hard a port! Stand by to meet her when she comes! Port, port! *Now*, men! With a will! Stead-y-y-y!"

"Steady it is, sir!"

The raft drew beyond the middle of the river; the boys pointed her head right, and then lay on their oars. The river was not high, so there was not more than a two or three mile current. Hardly a word was said during the next three-quarters of an hour. Now the raft was passing before the distant town. Two or three glimmering lights showed where it lay, peacefully sleeping, beyond the vague vast sweep of star-gemmed water, unconscious of the tremendous event that was happening. The Black Avenger stood still with folded arms, "looking his last" upon the scene of his former joys and his later sufferings, and wishing "she" could see him now, abroad on the wild sea, facing peril and death with dauntless heart, going to his doom with a grim smile on his lips. It was but a small strain on his imagination to remove Jackson's Island beyond eye-shot of the village, and so he "looked his last" with a broken and satisfied heart. The other pirates were looking their last, too; and they all looked so long that they came near letting the current drift them out of the range of the island. But they discovered the danger in time, and made shift to avert it. About two o'clock in the morning the raft grounded on the bar two hundred yards above the head of the island, and they waded back and forth until they had landed their freight. Part of the little raft's belongings consisted of an old sail, and this they spread over a nook in the bushes for a tent to shelter their provisions; but they themselves would sleep in the open air in good weather, as became outlaws.

They built a fire against the side of a great log twenty or thirty steps within the sombre depths of the forest, and then cooked some bacon in the frying pan for supper, and used up half of the corn "pone" stock they had brought. It seemed glorious sport to be feasting in that wild, free way in the virgin forest of an unexplored and uninhabited island, far from the haunts of men, and they said they never would return to civilization. The climbing fire lit up their faces and threw its ruddy glare upon the pillared tree-trunks of their forest temple, and upon the varnished foliage and festooning vines.

When the last crisp slice of bacon was gone, and the last allowance of corn pone devoured, the boys stretched themselves out on the grass, filled with contentment. They could have found a cooler place, but they would not deny themselves such a romantic feature as the roasting campfire.

"*Ain't* it gay?" said Joe.

"It's *nuts*!" said Tom. "What would the boys say if they could see us?"

"Say? Well, they'd just die to be here—hey, Hucky!"

"I reckon so," said Huckleberry; "anyways, I'm suited. I don't want nothing better'n this. I don't ever get enough to eat, gen'ally—and here they can't come and pick at a feller and bullyrag him so."

"It's just the life for me," said Tom. "You don't have to get up, mornings, and you don't have to go to school, and wash, and all that blame foolishness. You see a pirate don't have to do *anything*, Joe, when he's ashore, but a hermit *he* has to be praying considerable, and then he don't have any fun, anyway, all by himself that way."

"O yes, that's so," said Joe, "but I hadn't thought much about it, you know. I'd a good deal rather be a pirate, now that I've tried it."

"You see," said Tom, "people don't go much on hermits, nowadays, like they used to in old times, but a pirate's always respected. And a hermit's got to sleep on the hardest place he can find, and put sackcloth and ashes on his head, and stand out in the rain, and—"

"What does he put sackcloth and ashes on his head for?" inquired Huck.

"I dono. But they've *got* to do it. Hermits always do. You'd have to do that if you was a hermit."

"Dern'd if I would," said Huck.

"Well, what would you do?"

"I dono. But I wouldn't do that."

"Why, Huck, you'd *have* to. How'd you get around it?"

"Why, I just wouldn't stand it. I'd run away."

"Run away! Well, you *would* be a nice old slouch of a hermit. You'd be a disgrace."

The Red-Handed made no response, being better employed. He had finished gouging out a cob, and now he fitted a weed stem to it, loaded it with tobacco, and was pressing a coal to the charge and blowing a cloud of fragrant smoke—he was in the full bloom of luxurious contentment. The other pirates envied him this majestic vice, and secretly resolved to acquire it shortly. Presently Huck said:

"What does pirates have to do?"

Tom said:

"Oh they have just a bully time—take ships and burn them, and get the money and bury it in awful places in their island where there's ghosts and things to watch it, and kill everybody in the ships—make 'em walk a plank."

"And they carry the women to the island," said Joe; "they don't kill the women."

"No," assented Tom, "they don't kill the women—they're too noble. And the women's always beautiful, too.

"And don't they wear the bulliest clothes! Oh no! All gold and silver and di'monds," said Joe, with enthusiasm.

"Who?" said Huck.

"Why the pirates."

Huck scanned his own clothing forlornly.

"I reckon I ain't dressed fitten for a pirate," said he, with a regretful pathos in his voice; "but I ain't got none but these."

But the other boys told him the fine clothes would come fast enough, after they should have begun their adventures. They made him understand that his poor rags would do to begin with, though it was customary for wealthy pirates to start with a proper wardrobe.

Gradually their talk died out and drowsiness began to steal upon the eyelids of the little waifs. The pipe dropped from the fingers of the Red-

Handed, and he slept the sleep of the conscience-free and the weary. The Terror of the Seas and the Black Avenger of the Spanish Main had more difficulty in getting to sleep. They said their prayers inwardly, and lying down, since there was nobody there with authority to make them kneel and recite aloud; in truth, they had a mind not to say them at all, but they were afraid to proceed to such lengths as that, lest they might call down a sudden and special thunderbolt from heaven. Then at once they reached and hovered upon the imminent verge of sleep—but an intruder came, now, that would not "down." It was conscience. They began to feel a vague fear that they had been doing wrong to run away; and next they thought of the stolen meat, and then the real torture came. They tried to argue it away by reminding conscience that they had purloined sweetmeats and apples scores of times; but conscience was not to be appeased by such thin plausibilities; it seemed to them, in the end, that there was no getting around the stubborn fact that taking sweetmeats was only "hooking," while taking bacon and hams and such valuables was plain simple stealing—and there was a command against that in the Bible. So they inwardly resolved that so long as they remained in the business, their piracies should not again be sullied with the crime of stealing. Then conscience granted a truce, and these curiously inconsistent pirates fell peacefully to sleep.

14

When Tom awoke in the morning, he wondered where he was. He sat up and rubbed his eyes and looked around. Then he comprehended. It was the cool grey dawn, and there was a delicious sense of repose and peace in the deep pervading calm and silence of the woods. Not a leaf stirred; not a sound obtruded upon great Nature's meditation. Beaded dewdrops stood upon the leaves and grasses. A white layer of ashes covered the fire, and a thin blue breath of smoke rose straight into the air. Joe and Huck still slept.

Now, far away in the woods a bird called; another answered; presently the hammering of a woodpecker was heard. Gradually the cool dim grey of the morning whitened, and as gradually sounds multiplied and life manifested itself. The marvel of Nature shaking off sleep and going to work unfolded itself to the musing boy. A little green worm came crawling over a dewy leaf, lifting two-thirds of his body into the air from time to time and "sniffing around," then proceeding again—for he was measuring, Tom said; and when the worm approached him, of its own accord, he sat as still as a stone, with his hopes rising and falling, by turns, as the creature still came toward him or seemed inclined to go elsewhere; and when at last it considered a painful moment with its curved body in the air and then came decisively down upon Tom's leg and began a journey over him, his whole heart was glad—for that meant that he was going to have a new suit of clothes—without the shadow of a doubt a gaudy piratical uniform. Now a procession of ants appeared, from nowhere in particular, and went about their labours; one struggled manfully by with a dead spider five times as big as itself in its arms, and lugged it straight up a tree-trunk. A brown spotted lady-bug climbed the dizzy height of a grass blade, and Tom bent down close to it and said, "Lady-bug, lady-bug, fly away home, your house is on fire, your children's alone," and she took wing and went off to see about it—which did not surprise the boy, for he knew of old that this insect was credulous about conflagrations, and he had practised upon its simplicity more than once. A tumblebug came next, heaving sturdily at its ball, and Tom touched the creature, to see it shut its legs against its body and pretend to be dead. The birds were fairly rioting by this time. A catbird, the Northern mocker, lit in a tree over Tom's head, and trilled out her imitations of her neighbours in a rapture of enjoyment; then a shrill jay swept down, a flash of blue flame, and stopped on a twig almost within the boy's reach, cocked his head to one side and eyed the strangers with a consuming curiosity; a grey squirrel and a big fellow of the "fox" kind came skurrying along, sitting up at intervals to inspect and chatter at the boys, for the wild things had probably never seen a human being before and scarcely knew whether to be afraid or not. All Nature was wide awake and stirring, now; long lances of sunlight pierced down through the dense foliage far and near, and a few butterflies came fluttering upon the scene.

Tom stirred up the other pirates and they all clattered away with a shout, and in a minute or two were stripped and chasing after and tumbling over each other in the shallow limpid water of the white sandbar. They felt no longing for the little village sleeping in the distance beyond the majestic waste of water. A vagrant current or a slight rise in the river had carried off their raft, but this only gratified them, since its going was something like burning the bridge between them and civilization.

They came back to camp wonderfully refreshed, glad-hearted, and ravenous; and they soon had the campfire blazing up again. Huck found a spring of clear cold water close by, and the boys made cups of broad oak or hickory leaves, and felt that water, sweetened with such a wildwood charm as that, would be a good enough substitute for coffee. While Joe was slicing bacon for breakfast, Tom and Huck asked him to hold on a minute; they stepped to a promising nook in the riverbank and threw in their lines; almost immediately they had reward. Joe had not had time to get impatient before they were back again with some handsome bass, a couple of sun-perch and a small catfish—provisions enough for quite a family. They fried the fish with the bacon, and were astonished; for no fish had ever seemed so delicious before. They did not know that the quicker a fresh-water fish is on the fire after he is caught the better he is; and they reflected little upon what a sauce open-air sleeping, open-air exercise, bathing, and a large ingredient of hunger makes, too.

They lay around in the shade, after breakfast, while Huck had a smoke, and then went off through the woods on an exploring expedition. They tramped gayly along, over decaying logs, through tangled underbrush, among solemn monarchs of the forest, hung from their crowns to the ground with a drooping regalia of grape-vines. Now and then they came upon snug nooks carpeted with grass and jewelled with flowers.

They found plenty of things to be delighted with, but nothing to be astonished at. They discovered that the island was about three miles long and a quarter of a mile wide, and that the shore it lay closest to was only separated from it by a narrow channel hardly two hundred yards wide. They took a swim about every hour, so it was close upon the middle of the afternoon when they got back to camp. They were too hungry to stop to fish, but they fared sumptuously upon cold ham, and then threw themselves down in the shade to talk. But the talk soon began to drag, and then died. The stillness, the solemnity that brooded in the woods, and the sense of loneliness, began to tell upon the spirits of the boys. They fell to thinking. A sort of undefined longing crept upon them. This took dim shape, presently—it was budding homesickness. Even Finn the Red-Handed was dreaming of his doorsteps and empty hogsheads. But they were all ashamed of their weakness, and none was brave enough to speak his thought.

For some time, now, the boys had been dully conscious of a peculiar sound in the distance, just as one sometimes is of the ticking of a clock which he takes no distinct note of. But now this mysterious sound became more pronounced, and forced a recognition. The boys started, glanced at each other, and then each assumed a listening attitude. There was a long silence, profound and unbroken; then a deep, sullen boom came floating down out of the distance.

"What is it!" exclaimed Joe, under his breath.

"I wonder," said Tom in a whisper.

"'Tain't thunder," said Huckleberry, in an awed tone, "becuz thunder—"

"Hark!" said Tom. "Listen—don't talk."

They waited a time that seemed an age, and then the same muffled boom troubled the solemn hush.

"Let's go and see."

They sprang to their feet and hurried to the shore toward the town. They parted the bushes on the bank and peered out over the water. The little steam ferry-boat was about a mile below the village, drifting with the current. Her broad deck seemed crowded with people. There were a great many skiffs rowing about or floating with the stream in the neighbourhood of the ferryboat, but the boys could not determine what the men in them were doing. Presently a great jet of white smoke burst from the ferryboat's side, and as it expanded and rose in a lazy cloud, that same dull throb of sound was borne to the listeners again.

The Search for the Drowned

"I know now!" exclaimed Tom; "somebody's drownded!"

"That's it!" said Huck; "they done that last summer, when Bill Turner got drownded; they shoot a cannon over the water, and that makes him come up to the top. Yes, and they take loaves of bread and put quicksilver in 'em and set 'em afloat, and wherever there's anybody that's drownded, they'll float right there and stop."

"Yes, I've heard about that," said Joe. "I wonder what makes the bread do that."

"Oh it ain't the bread, so much," said Tom; "I reckon it's mostly what they *say* over it before they start it out."

"But they don't say anything over it," said Huck. "I've seen 'em and they don't."

"Well, that's funny," said Tom. "But maybe they say it to themselves. Of *course* they do. Anybody might know that."

The other boys agreed that there was reason in what Tom said, because an ignorant lump of bread, uninstructed by an incantation, could not be expected to act very intelligently when set upon an errand of such gravity.

"By jings, I wish I was over there, now," said Joe.

"I do too" said Huck "I'd give heaps to know who it is."

The boys still listened and watched. Presently a revealing thought flashed through Tom's mind, and he exclaimed:

"Boys, I know who's drownded—it's us!"

They felt like heroes in an instant. Here was a gorgeous triumph; they were missed; they were mourned; hearts were breaking on their account; tears were being shed; accusing memories of unkindness to these poor lost lads were rising up, and unavailing regrets and remorse were being indulged; and best of all, the departed were the talk of the whole town, and the envy of all the boys, as far as this dazzling notoriety was concerned. This was fine. It was worth while to be a pirate, after all.

As twilight drew on, the ferryboat went back to her accustomed business and the skiffs disappeared. The pirates returned to camp. They were jubilant with vanity over their new grandeur and the illustrious trouble they were making. They caught fish, cooked supper and ate it, and then fell to guessing at what the village was thinking and saying about them; and the pictures they drew of the public distress on their account were gratifying to look upon—from their point of view. But when the shadows of night closed them in, they gradually ceased to talk, and sat gazing into the fire, with their minds evidently wandering elsewhere. The excitement was gone, now, and Tom and Joe could not keep back thoughts of certain persons at home who were not enjoying this fine frolic as much as they were. Misgivings came; they grew troubled and unhappy; a sigh or two escaped, unawares. By and by Joe timidly ventured upon a roundabout "feeler" as to how the others might look upon a return to civilization—not right now, but—

Tom withered him with derision! Huck, being uncommitted as yet, joined in with Tom, and the waverer quickly "explained," and was glad to get out of the scrape with as little taint of chicken-hearted home-sickness clinging to his garments as he could. Mutiny was effectually laid to rest for the moment.

As the night deepened, Huck began to nod, and presently to snore. Joe followed next. Tom lay upon his elbow motionless, for some time, watching the two intently. At last he got up cautiously, on his knees, and went searching among the grass and the flickering reflections flung by the campfire. He picked up and inspected several large semi-cylinders of the thin white bark of a sycamore, and finally chose two which seemed to suit him. Then he knelt by the fire and painfully wrote something upon each of these with his "red keel"; one he rolled up and put in his jacket pocket, and the other he put in Joe's hat and removed it to a little distance from the owner. And he also put into the hat certain schoolboy treasures of almost inestimable value—among them a lump of chalk, an India-rubber ball, three fishhooks, and one of that kind of marbles known as a "sure 'nough crystal." Then he tiptoed his way cautiously among the trees till he felt that he was out of hearing, and straightway broke into a keen run in the direction of the sandbar.

15

A few minutes later Tom was in the shoal water of the bar, wading toward the Illinois shore. Before the depth reached his middle he was halfway over; the current would permit no more wading, now, so he struck out confidently to swim the remaining hundred yards. He swam quartering upstream, but still was swept downward rather faster than he had expected. However, he reached the shore finally, and drifted along till he found a low place and drew himself out. He put his hand on his jacket pocket, found his piece of bark safe, and then struck through the woods, following the shore, with streaming garments. Shortly before ten o'clock he came out into an open place opposite the village, and saw the ferryboat lying in the shadow of the trees and the high bank. Everything was quiet under the blinking stars. He crept down the bank, watching with all his eyes, slipped into the water, swam three or four strokes and climbed into the skiff that did "yawl" duty at the boat's stern. He laid himself down under the thwarts and waited, panting.

Presently the cracked bell tapped and a voice gave the order to "cast off." A minute or two later the skiff's head was standing high up, against the boat's swell, and the voyage was begun. Tom felt happy in his success, for he knew it was the boat's last trip for the night. At the end of a long twelve or fifteen minutes the wheels stopped, and Tom slipped overboard and swam ashore in the dusk, landing fifty yards downstream, out of danger of possible stragglers.

He flew along unfrequented alleys, and shortly found himself at his aunt's back fence. He climbed over, approached the "ell," and looked in at the sitting-room window, for a light was burning there. There sat Aunt Polly, Sid, Mary, and Joe Harper's mother, grouped together, talking. They were by the bed, and the bed was between them and the door. Tom went to the door and began to softly lift the latch; then he pressed gently and the door yielded a crack; he continued pushing cautiously, and quaking every time it creaked, till he judged he might squeeze through on his knees; so he put his head through and began, warily.

"What makes the candle blow so?" said Aunt Polly. Tom hurried up. "Why, that door's open, I believe. Why, of course it is. No end of strange things now. Go 'long and shut it, Sid."

Tom disappeared under the bed just in time. He lay and "breathed" himself for a time, and then crept to where he could almost touch his aunt's foot.

"But as I was saying," said Aunt Polly, "he warn't *bad*, so to say—only mischeevous. Only just giddy, and harum-scarum, you know. He warn't any more responsible than a colt. *He* never meant any harm, and he was the best-hearted boy that ever was"—and she began to cry.

"It was just so with my Joe—always full of his devilment, and up to every kind of mischief, but he was just as unselfish and kind as he could be—and laws bless me, to think I went and whipped him for taking that cream, never once recollecting that I throwed it out myself because it was sour, and I never to see him again in this world, never, never, never, poor abused boy!" And Mrs. Harper sobbed as if her heart would break.

"I hope Tom's better off where he is," said Sid, "but if he'd been better in some ways—"

"*Sid!*" Tom felt the glare of the old lady's eye, though he could not see it. "Not a word against my Tom, now that he's gone! God'll take care of *him*—never you trouble *your*self, sir! Oh, Mrs. Harper, I don't know how to give him up! I don't know how to give him up! He was such a comfort to me, although he tormented my old heart out of me, 'most."

"The Lord giveth and the Lord hath taken away—Blessed be the name of the Lord! But it's so hard—Oh, it's so hard! Only last Saturday my Joe busted a firecracker right under my nose and I knocked him sprawling. Little did I know then, how soon—Oh, if it was to do over again I'd hug him and bless him for it."

"Yes, yes, yes, I know just how you feel, Mrs. Harper, I know just exactly how you feel. No longer ago than yesterday noon, my Tom took and filled the cat full of Pain-killer, and I did think the cretur would tear the house down. And God forgive me, I cracked Tom's head with my thimble, poor boy, poor dead boy. But he's out of all his troubles now. And the last words I ever heard him say was to reproach—"

But this memory was too much for the old lady, and she broke entirely down. Tom was snuffling, now, himself—and more in pity of himself than anybody else. He could hear Mary crying, and putting in a kindly word for him from time to time. He began to have a nobler opinion of himself than ever before. Still, he was sufficiently touched by his aunt's grief to long to rush out from under the bed and overwhelm her with joy—and the theatrical gorgeousness of the thing appealed strongly to his nature, too, but he resisted and lay still.

He went on listening, and gathered by odds and ends that it was conjectured at first that the boys had got drowned while taking a swim; then the small raft had been missed; next, certain boys said the missing lads had promised that the village should "hear something" soon; the wise-heads had "put this and that together" and decided that the lads had gone off on that raft and would turn up at the next town below, presently; but toward noon the raft had been found, lodged against the Missouri shore some five or six miles below the village—and then hope perished; they must be drowned, else hunger would have driven them home by nightfall if not sooner. It was believed that the search for the bodies had been a fruitless effort merely because the drowning must have occurred in mid-channel, since the boys, being good swimmers, would otherwise have escaped to shore. This was Wednesday night. If the bodies continued missing until Sunday, all hope would be given over, and the funerals would be preached on that morning. Tom shuddered.

Mrs. Harper gave a sobbing goodnight and turned to go. Then with a mutual impulse the two bereaved women flung themselves into each other's arms and had a good, consoling cry, and then parted. Aunt Polly was tender far beyond her wont, in her goodnight to Sid and Mary. Sid snuffled a bit and Mary went off crying with all her heart.

Aunt Polly knelt down and prayed for Tom so touchingly, so appealingly, and with such measureless love in her words and her old trembling voice, that he was weltering in tears again, long before she was through.

He had to keep still long after she went to bed, for she kept making broken-hearted ejaculations from time to time, tossing unrestfully, and turning over. But at last she was still, only moaning a little in her sleep. Now the boy stole out, rose gradually by the bedside, shaded the candle-light with his hand, and stood regarding her. His heart was full of pity for her. He took out his sycamore scroll and placed it by the candle. But something occurred to him, and he lingered considering. His face lighted with a happy solution of his thought; he put the bark hastily in his pocket. Then he bent over and kissed the faded lips, and straightway made his stealthy exit, latching the door behind him.

He threaded his way back to the ferry landing, found nobody at large there, and walked boldly on board the boat, for he knew she was tenantless except that there was a watchman, who always turned in and slept like a graven image. He untied the skiff at the stern, slipped into it, and was soon rowing cautiously upstream. When he had pulled a mile above the village, he started quartering across and bent himself stoutly to his work. He hit the landing on the other side neatly, for this was a familiar bit of work to him. He was moved to capture the skiff, arguing that it might be considered a ship and therefore legitimate prey for a pirate, but he knew a thorough search would be made for it and that might end in revelations. So he stepped ashore and entered the woods.

He sat down and took a long rest, torturing himself meanwhile to keep awake, and then started warily down the home-stretch. The night was far spent. It was broad daylight before he found himself fairly abreast the island bar. He rested again until the sun was well up and gilding the great river with its splendour, and then he plunged into the stream. A little later he paused, dripping, upon the threshold of the camp, and heard Joe say:

"No, Tom's true-blue, Huck, and he'll come back. He won't desert. He knows that would be a disgrace to a pirate, and Tom's too proud for that sort of thing. He's up to something or other. Now I wonder what?"

"Well, the things is ours, anyway, ain't they?"

"Pretty near, but not yet, Huck. The writing says they are if he ain't back here to breakfast."

"Which he is!" exclaimed Tom, with fine dramatic effect, stepping grandly into camp.

A sumptuous breakfast of bacon and fish was shortly provided, and as the boys set to work upon it, Tom recounted (and adorned) his adventures. They were a vain and boastful company of heroes when the tale was done. Then Tom hid himself away in a shady nook to sleep till noon, and the other pirates got ready to fish and explore.

16

After dinner all the gang turned out to hunt for turtle eggs on the bar. They went about poking sticks into the sand, and when they found a soft place they went down on their knees and dug with their hands. Sometimes they would take fifty or sixty eggs out of one hole. They were perfectly round white things a trifle smaller than an English walnut. They had a famous fried-egg feast that night, and another on Friday morning.

After breakfast they went whooping and prancing out on the bar, and chased each other round and round, shedding clothes as they went, until they were naked, and then continued the frolic far away up the shoal water of the bar, against the stiff current, which latter tripped their legs from under them from time to time and greatly increased the fun. And now and then they stooped in a group and splashed water in each other's faces with their palms, gradually approaching each other, with averted faces to avoid the strangling sprays, and finally gripping and struggling till the best man ducked his neighbour, and then they all went under in a tangle of white legs and arms and came up blowing, sputtering, laughing, and gasping for breath at one and the same time.

When they were well exhausted, they would run out and sprawl on the dry, hot sand, and lie there and cover themselves up with it, and by and by break for the water again and go through the original performance once more. Finally it occurred to them that their naked skin represented flesh-coloured "tights" very fairly; so they drew a ring in the sand and had a circus—with three clowns in it, for none would yield this proudest post to his neighbour.

Next they got their marbles and played "knucks" and "ringtaw" and "keeps" till that amusement grew stale. Then Joe and Huck had another swim, but Tom would not venture, because he found that in kicking off his trousers he had kicked his string of rattlesnake rattles off his ankle, and he wondered how he had escaped cramp so long without the protection of this mysterious charm. He did not venture again until he had found it, and by that time the other boys were tired and ready to rest. They gradually wandered apart, dropped into the "dumps," and fell to gazing longingly across the wide river to where the village lay drowsing in the sun. Tom found himself writing "BECKY" in the sand with his big toe; he scratched it out, and was angry with himself for his weakness. But he wrote it again, nevertheless; he could not help it. He erased it once more and then took himself out of temptation by driving the other boys together and joining them.

But Joe's spirits had gone down almost beyond resurrection. He was so homesick that he could hardly endure the misery of it. The tears lay very near the surface. Huck was melancholy, too. Tom was downhearted, but tried hard not to show it. He had a secret which he was not ready to tell, yet, but if this mutinous depression was not broken up soon, he would have to bring it out. He said, with a great show of cheerfulness:

"I bet there's been pirates on this island before, boys. We'll explore it again. They've hid treasures here somewhere. How'd you feel to light on a rotten chest full of gold and silver—hey?"

But it roused only faint enthusiasm, which faded out, with no reply. Tom tried one or two other seductions; but they failed, too. It was discouraging work. Joe sat poking up the sand with a stick and looking very gloomy. Finally he said:

"O, boys, let's give it up. I want to go home. It's so lonesome."

"Oh no, Joe, you'll feel better by and by," said Tom. "Just think of the fishing that's here."

"I don't care for fishing. I want to go home."

"But, Joe, there ain't such another swimming place anywhere."

"Swimming's no good. I don't seem to care for it, somehow, when there ain't anybody to say I sha'n't go in. I mean to go home."

"O, shucks! Baby! You want to see your mother, I reckon."

"Yes, I *do* want to see my mother—and you would, too, if you had one. I ain't any more baby than you are." And Joe snuffled a little.

"Well, we'll let the crybaby go home to his mother, won't we, Huck? Poor thing—does it want to see its mother? And so it shall. You like it here, don't you, Huck? We'll stay, won't we?"

Huck said, "Y-e-s"—without any heart in it.

"I'll never speak to you again as long as I live," said Joe, rising. "There now!" And he moved moodily away and began to dress himself.

"Who cares!" said Tom. "Nobody wants you to. Go 'long home and get laughed at. Oh, you're a nice pirate. Huck and me ain't cry-babies. We'll stay, won't we, Huck? Let him go if he wants to. I reckon we can get along without him, per'aps."

But Tom was uneasy, nevertheless, and was alarmed to see Joe go sullenly on with his dressing. And then it was discomforting to see Huck eying Joe's preparations so wistfully, and keeping up such an ominous silence. Presently, without a parting word, Joe began to wade off toward the

Illinois shore. Tom's heart began to sink. He glanced at Huck. Huck could not bear the look, and dropped his eyes. Then he said:

"I want to go, too, Tom. It was getting so lonesome anyway, and now it'll be worse. Let's us go, too, Tom."

"I won't! You can all go, if you want to. I mean to stay."

"Tom, I better go."

"Well, go 'long—who's hendering you."

Huck began to pick up his scattered clothes. He said:

"Tom, I wisht you'd come, too. Now you think it over. We'll wait for you when we get to shore."

"Well, you'll wait a blame long time, that's all."

Huck started sorrowfully away, and Tom stood looking after him, with a strong desire tugging at his heart to yield his pride and go along too. He hoped the boys would stop, but they still waded slowly on. It suddenly dawned on Tom that it was become very lonely and still. He made one final struggle with his pride, and then darted after his comrades, yelling:

"Wait! Wait! I want to tell you something!"

They presently stopped and turned around. When he got to where they were, he began unfolding his secret, and they listened moodily till at last they saw the "point" he was driving at, and then they set up a war-whoop of applause and said it was "splendid!" and said if he had told them at first, they wouldn't have started away. He made a plausible excuse; but his real reason had been the fear that not even the secret would keep them with him any very great length of time, and so he had meant to hold it in reserve as a last seduction.

The lads came gaily back and went at their sports again with a will, chattering all the time about Tom's stupendous plan and admiring the genius of it. After a dainty egg and fish dinner, Tom said he wanted to learn to smoke, now. Joe caught at the idea and said he would like to try, too. So Huck made pipes and filled them. These novices had never smoked anything before but cigars made of grapevine, and they "bit" the tongue, and were not considered manly anyway.

Now they stretched themselves out on their elbows and began to puff, charily, and with slender confidence. The smoke had an unpleasant taste, and they gagged a little, but Tom said:

"Why, it's just as easy! If I'd a knowed this was all, I'd a learnt long ago."

"So would I," said Joe. "It's just nothing."

"Why, many a time I've looked at people smoking, and thought well I wish I could do that; but I never thought I could," said Tom.

"That's just the way with me, hain't it, Huck? You've heard me talk just that way—haven't you, Huck? I'll leave it to Huck if I haven't."

"Yes—heaps of times," said Huck.

"Well, I have too," said Tom; "oh, hundreds of times. Once down by the slaughterhouse. Don't you remember, Huck? Bob Tanner was there, and Johnny Miller, and Jeff Thatcher, when I said it. Don't you remember, Huck, 'bout me saying that?"

"Yes, that's so," said Huck. "That was the day after I lost a white alley. No, 'twas the day before."

"There—I told you so," said Tom. "Huck recollects it."

"I bleeve I could smoke this pipe all day," said Joe. "I don't feel sick."

"Neither do I," said Tom. "I could smoke it all day. But I bet you Jeff Thatcher couldn't."

"Jeff Thatcher! Why, he'd keel over just with two draws. Just let him try it once. *He'd* see!"

"I bet he would. And Johnny Miller—I wish could see Johnny Miller tackle it once."

"O, don't I!" said Joe. "Why, I bet you Johnny Miller couldn't any more do this than nothing. Just one little snifter would fetch *him*."

"'Deed it would, Joe. Say—I wish the boys could see us now."

"So do I."

"Say—boys, don't say anything about it, and some time when they're around, I'll come up to you and say, 'Joe, got a pipe? I want a smoke.' And you'll say, kind of careless like, as if it warn't anything, you'll say, 'Yes, I got my *old* pipe, and another one, but my tobacker ain't very good.' And I'll say, 'Oh, that's all right, if it's *strong* enough.' And then you'll out with the pipes, and we'll light up just as ca'm, and then just see 'em look!"

"By jings, that'll be gay, Tom! I wish it was *now*!"

"So do I! And when we tell 'em we learned when we was off pirating, won't they wish they'd been along?"

"O, I reckon not! I'll just *bet* they will!"

So the talk ran on. But presently it began to flag a trifle, and grow disjointed. The silences widened; the expectoration marvellously increased. Every pore inside the boys' cheeks became a spouting fountain; they could scarcely bail out the cellars under their tongues fast enough to prevent an inundation; little overflowings down their throats occurred in spite of all they could do, and sudden retchings followed every time. Both boys were looking very pale and miserable, now. Joe's pipe dropped from his nerveless fingers. Tom's followed. Both fountains were going furiously and both pumps bailing with might and main. Joe said feebly:

"I've lost my knife. I reckon I better go and find it."

Tom said, with quivering lips and halting utterance:

"I'll help you. You go over that way and I'll hunt around by the spring. No, you needn't come, Huck—we can find it."

So Huck sat down again, and waited an hour. Then he found it lonesome, and went to find his comrades. They were wide apart in the woods, both very pale, both fast asleep. But something informed him that if they had had any trouble they had got rid of it.

They were not talkative at supper that night. They had a humble look, and when Huck prepared his pipe after the meal and was going to prepare theirs, they said no, they were not feeling very well—something they ate at dinner had disagreed with them.

About midnight Joe awoke, and called the boys. There was a brooding oppressiveness in the air that seemed to bode something. The boys huddled themselves together and sought the friendly companionship of the fire, though the dull dead heat of the breathless atmosphere was stifling. They sat still, intent and waiting. The solemn hush continued. Beyond the light of the fire everything was swallowed up in the blackness of darkness. Presently there came a quivering glow that vaguely revealed the foliage for a moment and then vanished. By and by another came, a little stronger. Then another. Then a faint moan came sighing through the branches of the forest and the boys felt a fleeting breath upon their cheeks, and shuddered with the fancy that the Spirit of the Night had gone by. There was a pause. Now a weird flash turned night into day and showed every little grass-blade, separate and distinct, that grew about their feet. And it showed three white, startled faces, too. A deep peal of thunder went rolling and tumbling down the heavens and lost itself in sullen rumblings in the distance. A sweep of chilly air passed by, rustling all the leaves and snowing the flaky ashes broadcast about the fire. Another fierce glare lit up the forest and an instant crash followed that seemed to rend the treetops right over the boys' heads. They clung together in terror, in the thick gloom that followed. A few big raindrops fell pattering upon the leaves.

"Quick! boys, go for the tent!" exclaimed Tom.

They sprang away, stumbling over roots and among vines in the dark, no two plunging in the same direction. A furious blast roared through the trees, making everything sing as it went. One blinding flash after another came, and peal on peal of deafening thunder. And now a drenching rain poured down and the rising hurricane drove it in sheets along the ground. The boys cried out to each other, but the roaring wind and the booming thunder-blasts drowned their voices utterly. However, one by one they straggled in at last and took shelter under the tent, cold, scared, and streaming with water; but to have company in misery seemed something to be grateful for. They could not talk, the old sail flapped so furiously, even if the other noises would have allowed them. The tempest rose higher and higher, and presently the sail tore loose from its fastenings and went winging away on the blast. The boys seized each others' hands and fled, with many tumblings and bruises, to the shelter of a great oak that stood upon the riverbank. Now the battle was at its highest. Under the ceaseless conflagration of lightning that flamed in the skies, everything below stood out in clean-cut and shadowless distinctness: the bending trees, the billowy river, white with foam, the driving spray of spume-flakes, the dim outlines of the high bluffs on the other side, glimpsed through the drifting cloud-rack and the slanting veil of rain. Every little while some giant tree yielded the fight and fell crashing through the younger growth; and the unflagging thunder-peals came now in ear-splitting explosive bursts, keen and sharp, and unspeakably appalling. The storm culminated in one matchless effort that seemed likely to tear the island to pieces, burn it up, drown it to the treetops, blow it away, and deafen every creature in it, all at one and the same moment. It was a wild night for homeless young heads to be out in.

But at last the battle was done, and the forces retired with weaker and weaker threatenings and grumblings, and peace resumed her sway. The boys went back to camp, a good deal awed; but they found there was still something to be thankful for, because the great sycamore, the shelter of their beds, was a ruin, now, blasted by the lightnings, and they were not under it when the catastrophe happened.

Everything in camp was drenched, the campfire as well; for they were but heedless lads, like their generation, and had made no provision against rain. Here was matter for dismay, for they were soaked through and chilled. They were eloquent in their distress; but they presently discovered that the fire had eaten so far up under the great log it had been built against (where it curved upward and separated itself from the ground), that a handbreadth or so of it had escaped wetting; so they patiently wrought until, with shreds and bark gathered from the under sides of sheltered logs, they coaxed the fire to burn again. Then they piled on great dead boughs till they had a roaring furnace, and were gladhearted once more. They dried their boiled ham and had a feast, and after that they sat by the fire and expanded and glorified their midnight adventure until morning, for there was not a dry spot to sleep on, anywhere around.

As the sun began to steal in upon the boys, drowsiness came over them, and they went out on the sandbar and lay down to sleep. They got scorched out by and by, and drearily set about getting breakfast. After the meal they felt rusty, and stiff-jointed, and a little homesick once more. Tom saw the signs, and fell to cheering up the pirates as well as he could. But they cared nothing for marbles, or circus, or swimming, or anything. He reminded them of the imposing secret, and raised a ray of cheer. While it lasted, he got them interested in a new device. This was to knock off being pirates, for a while, and be Indians for a change. They were attracted by this idea; so it was not long before they were stripped, and striped from head to heel with black mud, like so many zebras—all of them chiefs, of course—and then they went tearing through the woods to attack an English settlement.

By and by they separated into three hostile tribes, and darted upon each other from ambush with dreadful warwhoops, and killed and scalped each other by thousands. It was a gory day. Consequently it was an extremely satisfactory one.

Terrible Slaughter

They assembled in camp toward suppertime, hungry and happy; but now a difficulty arose—hostile Indians could not break the bread of hospitality together without first making peace, and this was a simple impossibility without smoking a pipe of peace. There was no other process that ever they had heard of. Two of the savages almost wished they had remained pirates. However, there was no other way; so with such show of cheerfulness as they could muster they called for the pipe and took their whiff as it passed, in due form.

And behold, they were glad they had gone into savagery, for they had gained something; they found that they could now smoke a little without having to go and hunt for a lost knife; they did not get sick enough to be seriously uncomfortable. They were not likely to fool away this high promise for lack of effort. No, they practiced cautiously, after supper, with right fair success, and so they spent a jubilant evening. They were prouder and happier in their new acquirement than they would have been in the scalping and skinning of the Six Nations. We will leave them to smoke and chatter and brag, since we have no further use for them at present.

17

But there was no hilarity in the little town that same tranquil Saturday afternoon. The Harpers, and Aunt Polly's family, were being put into mourning, with great grief and many tears. An unusual quiet possessed the village, although it was ordinarily quiet enough, in all conscience. The villagers conducted their concerns with an absent air, and talked little; but they sighed often. The Saturday holiday seemed a burden to the children. They had no heart in their sports, and gradually gave them up.

In the afternoon Becky Thatcher found herself moping about the deserted schoolhouse yard, and feeling very melancholy. But she found nothing there to comfort her. She soliloquized:

"Oh, if I only had a brass andiron-knob again! But I haven't got anything now to remember him by." And she choked back a little sob.

Presently she stopped, and said to herself:

"It was right here. Oh, if it was to do over again, I wouldn't say that—I wouldn't say it for the whole world. But he's gone now; I'll never, never, never see him any more."

This thought broke her down, and she wandered away, with tears rolling down her cheeks. Then quite a group of boys and girls—playmates of Tom's and Joe's—came by, and stood looking over the paling fence and talking in reverent tones of how Tom did so-and-so the last time they saw him, and how Joe said this and that small trifle (pregnant with awful prophecy, as they could easily see now!)—and each speaker pointed out the exact spot where the lost lads stood at the time, and then added something like "and I was a-standing just so—just as I am now, and as if you was him—I was as close as that—and he smiled, just this way—and then something seemed to go all over me, like—awful, you know—and I never thought what it meant, of course, but I can see now!"

Then there was a dispute about who saw the dead boys last in life, and many claimed that dismal distinction, and offered evidences, more or less tampered with by the witness; and when it was ultimately decided who *did* see the departed last, and exchanged the last words with them, the lucky parties took upon themselves a sort of sacred importance, and were gaped at and envied by all the rest. One poor chap, who had no other grandeur to offer, said with tolerably manifest pride in the remembrance:

"Well, Tom Sawyer he licked me once."

But that bid for glory was a failure. Most of the boys could say that, and so that cheapened the distinction too much. The group loitered away, still recalling memories of the lost heroes, in awed voices.

When the Sunday-school hour was finished, the next morning, the bell began to toll, instead of ringing in the usual way. It was a very still Sabbath, and the mournful sound seemed in keeping with the musing hush that lay upon nature. The villagers began to gather, loitering a moment in the vestibule to converse in whispers about the sad event. But there was no whispering in the house; only the funereal rustling of dresses as the women gathered to their seats disturbed the silence there. None could remember when the little church had been so full before. There was finally a waiting pause, an expectant dumbness, and then Aunt Polly entered, followed by Sid and Mary, and they by the Harper family, all in deep black, and the whole congregation, the old minister as well, rose reverently and stood until the mourners were seated in the front pew. There was another communing silence, broken at intervals by muffled sobs, and then the minister spread his hands abroad and prayed. A moving hymn was sung, and the text followed: "I am the Resurrection and the Life."

As the service proceeded, the clergyman drew such pictures of the graces, the winning ways, and the rare promise of the lost lads that every soul there, thinking he recognized these pictures, felt a pang in remembering that he had persistently blinded himself to them always before, and had as persistently seen only faults and flaws in the poor boys. The minister related many a touching incident in the lives of the departed, too, which illustrated their sweet, generous natures, and the people could easily see, now, how noble and beautiful those episodes were, and remembered with grief that at the time they occurred they had seemed rank rascalities, well deserving of the cowhide. The congregation became more and more moved, as the pathetic tale went on, till at last the whole company broke down and joined the weeping mourners in a chorus of anguished sobs, the preacher himself giving way to his feelings, and crying in the pulpit.

There was a rustle in the gallery, which nobody noticed; a moment later the church door creaked; the minister raised his streaming eyes above his handkerchief, and stood transfixed! First one and then another pair of eyes followed the minister's, and then almost with one impulse the congregation rose and stared while the three dead boys came marching up the aisle, Tom in the lead, Joe next, and Huck, a ruin of drooping rags, sneaking sheepishly in the rear! They had been hid in the unused gallery listening to their own funeral sermon!

Aunt Polly, Mary, and the Harpers threw themselves upon their restored ones, smothered them with kisses and poured out thanksgivings, while poor Huck stood abashed and uncomfortable, not knowing exactly what to do or where to hide from so many unwelcoming eyes. He wavered, and started to slink away, but Tom seized him and said:

"Aunt Polly, it ain't fair. Somebody's got to be glad to see Huck."

"And so they shall. I'm glad to see him, poor motherless thing!" And the loving attentions Aunt Polly lavished upon him were the one thing capable of making him more uncomfortable than he was before.

Suddenly the minister shouted at the top of his voice: "Praise God from whom all blessings flow—*sing*!—and put your hearts in it!"

Tom's Proudest Moment

And they did. Old Hundred swelled up with a triumphant burst, and while it shook the rafters Tom Sawyer the Pirate looked around upon the envying juveniles about him and confessed in his heart that this was the proudest moment of his life.

As the "sold" congregation trooped out they said they would almost be willing to be made ridiculous again to hear Old Hundred sung like that once more.

Tom got more cuffs and kisses that day—according to Aunt Polly's varying moods—than he had earned before in a year; and he hardly knew which expressed the most gratefulness to God and affection for himself.

18

That was Tom's great secret—the scheme to return home with his brother pirates and attend their own funerals. They had paddled over to the Missouri shore on a log, at dusk on Saturday, landing five or six miles below the village; they had slept in the woods at the edge of the town till nearly daylight, and had then crept through back lanes and alleys and finished their sleep in the gallery of the church among a chaos of invalided benches.

At breakfast, Monday morning, Aunt Polly and Mary were very loving to Tom, and very attentive to his wants. There was an unusual amount of talk. In the course of it Aunt Polly said:

"Well, I don't say it wasn't a fine joke, Tom, to keep everybody suffering 'most a week so you boys had a good time, but it is a pity you could be so hard-hearted as to let me suffer so. If you could come over on a log to go to your funeral, you could have come over and give me a hint some way that you warn't *dead*, but only run off."

"Yes, you could have done that, Tom," said Mary; "and I believe you would if you had thought of it."

"Would you, Tom?" said Aunt Polly, her face lighting wistfully. "Say, now, would you, if you'd thought of it?"

"I—well, I don't know. 'Twould 'a' spoiled everything."

"Tom, I hoped you loved me that much," said Aunt Polly, with a grieved tone that discomforted the boy. "It would have been something if you'd cared enough to *think* of it, even if you didn't *do* it."

"Now, auntie, that ain't any harm," pleaded Mary; "it's only Tom's giddy way—he is always in such a rush that he never thinks of anything."

"More's the pity. Sid would have thought. And Sid would have come and *done* it, too. Tom, you'll look back, some day, when it's too late, and wish you'd cared a little more for me when it would have cost you so little."

"Now, auntie, you know I do care for you," said Tom.

"I'd know it better if you acted more like it."

"I wish now I'd thought," said Tom, with a repentant tone; "but I dreamt about you, anyway. That's something, ain't it?"

"It ain't much—a cat does that much—but it's better than nothing. What did you dream?"

"Why, Wednesday night I dreamt that you was sitting over there by the bed, and Sid was sitting by the woodbox, and Mary next to him."

"Well, so we did. So we always do. I'm glad your dreams could take even that much trouble about us."

"And I dreamt that Joe Harper's mother was here."

"Why, she was here! Did you dream any more?"

"O, lots. But it's so dim, now."

"Well, *try* to recollect—can't you?"

"Somehow it seems to me that the wind—the wind blowed the—the—"

"Try harder, Tom! The wind did blow something. Come!"

Tom pressed his fingers on his forehead an anxious minute, and then said:

"I've got it now! I've got it now! It blowed the candle!"

"Mercy on us! Go on, Tom—go on!"

"And it seems to me that you said, 'Why, I believe that that door—'"

"Go *on*, Tom!"

"Just let me study a moment—just a moment. Oh, yes—you said you believed the door was open."

"As I'm sitting here, I did! Didn't I, Mary! Go on!"

"And then—and then—well I won't be certain, but it seems like as if you made Sid go and—and—"

"Well? Well? What did I make him do, Tom? What did I make him do?"

"You made him—you—Oh, you made him shut it."

"Well, for the land's sake! I never heard the beat of that in all my days! Don't tell *me* there ain't anything in dreams, any more. Sereny Harper shall know of this before I'm an hour older. I'd like to see her get around *this* with her rubbage 'bout superstition. Go on, Tom!"

"Oh, it's all getting just as bright as day, now. Next you said I warn't *bad*, only mischeevous and harum-scarum, and not any more responsible than—than—I think it was a colt, or something."

"And so it was! Well, goodness gracious! Go on, Tom!"

"And then you began to cry."

"So I did. So I did. Not the first time, neither. And then—"

"Then Mrs. Harper she began to cry, and said Joe was just the same, and she wished she hadn't whipped him for taking cream when she'd throwed it out her own self—"

"Tom! The sperrit was upon you! You was a prophesying—that's what you was doing! Land alive, go on, Tom!"

"Then Sid he said—he said—"

"I don't think I said anything," said Sid.

"Yes you did, Sid," said Mary.

"Shut your heads and let Tom go on! What did he say, Tom?"

"He said—I *think* he said he hoped I was better off where I was gone to, but if I'd been better sometimes—"

"*There*, d'you hear that! It was his very words!"

"And you shut him up sharp."

"I lay I did! There must 'a' been an angel there. There *was* an angel there, somewheres!"

"And Mrs. Harper told about Joe scaring her with a firecracker, and you told about Peter and the Pain-killer—"

"Just as true as I live!"

"And then there was a whole lot of talk 'bout dragging the river for us, and 'bout having the funeral Sunday, and then you and old Miss Harper hugged and cried, and she went."

"It happened just so! It happened just so, as sure as I'm a-sitting in these very tracks. Tom, you couldn't told it more like if you'd 'a' seen it! And then what? Go on, Tom!"

"Then I thought you prayed for me—and I could see you and hear every word you said. And you went to bed, and I was so sorry that I took and wrote on a piece of sycamore bark, 'We ain't dead—we are only off being pirates,' and put it on the table by the candle; and then you looked so good, laying there asleep, that I thought I went and leaned over and kissed you on the lips."

"Did you, Tom, *did* you! I just forgive you everything for that!" And she seized the boy in a crushing embrace that made him feel like the guiltiest of villains.

"It was very kind, even though it was only a—dream," Sid soliloquized just audibly.

"Shut up, Sid! A body does just the same in a dream as he'd do if he was awake. Here's a big Milum apple I've been saving for you, Tom, if you was ever found again—now go 'long to school. I'm thankful to the good God and Father of us all I've got you back, that's long-suffering and merciful to them that believe on Him and keep His word, though goodness knows I'm unworthy of it, but if only the worthy ones got His blessings and had His hand to help them over the rough places, there's few enough would smile here or ever enter into His rest when the long night comes. Go 'long Sid, Mary, Tom—take yourselves off—you've hendered me long enough."

The children left for school, and the old lady to call on Mrs. Harper and vanquish her realism with Tom's marvellous dream. Sid had better judgment than to utter the thought that was in his mind as he left the house. It was this: "Pretty thin—as long a dream as that, without any mistakes in it!"

What a hero Tom was become, now! He did not go skipping and prancing, but moved with a dignified swagger as became a pirate who felt that the public eye was on him. And indeed it was; he tried not to seem to see the looks or hear the remarks as he passed along, but they were food and drink to him. Smaller boys than himself flocked at his heels, as proud to be seen with him, and tolerated by him, as if he had been the drummer at the head of a procession or the elephant leading a menagerie into town. Boys of his own size pretended not to know he had been away at all; but they were consuming with envy, nevertheless. They would have given anything to have that swarthy sun-tanned skin of his, and his glittering notoriety; and Tom would not have parted with either for a circus.

At school the children made so much of him and of Joe, and delivered such eloquent admiration from their eyes, that the two heroes were not long in becoming insufferably "stuck-up." They began to tell their adventures to hungry listeners—but they only began; it was not a thing likely to have an end, with imaginations like theirs to furnish material. And finally, when they got out their pipes and went serenely puffing around, the very summit of glory was reached.

Tom decided that he could be independent of Becky Thatcher now. Glory was sufficient. He would live for glory. Now that he was distinguished, maybe she would be wanting to "make up." Well, let her—she should see that he could be as indifferent as some other people. Presently she arrived. Tom pretended not to see her. He moved away and joined a group of boys and girls and began to talk. Soon he observed that she was tripping gayly back and forth with flushed face and dancing eyes, pretending to be busy chasing schoolmates, and screaming with laughter when she made a capture; but he noticed that she always made her captures in his vicinity, and that she seemed to cast a conscious eye in his direction at such times, too. It gratified all the vicious vanity that was in him; and so, instead of winning him, it only "set him up" the more and made him the more diligent to avoid betraying that he knew she was about. Presently she gave over skylarking, and moved irresolutely about, sighing once or twice and glancing furtively and wistfully toward Tom. Then she observed that now Tom was talking more particularly to Amy Lawrence than to any one else. She felt a sharp pang and grew disturbed and uneasy at once. She tried to go away, but her feet were treacherous, and carried her to the group instead. She said to a girl almost at Tom's elbow—with sham vivacity:

"Why, Mary Austin! you bad girl, why didn't you come to Sunday-school?"

"I did come—didn't you see me?"

"Why no! Did you? Where did you sit?"

"I was in Miss Peters' class, where I always go. I saw *you*."

"Did you? Why, it's funny I didn't see you. I wanted to tell you about the picnic."

"O, that's jolly. Who's going to give it?"

"My ma's going to let me have one."

"O, goody; I hope she'll let *me* come."

"Well, she will. The picnic's for me. She'll let anybody come that I want, and I want you."

"That's ever so nice. When is it going to be?"

"By and by. Maybe about vacation."

"O, won't it be fun! You going to have all the girls and boys?"

"Yes, every one that's friends to me—or wants to be"; and she glanced ever so furtively at Tom, but he talked right along to Amy Lawrence about the terrible storm on the island, and how the lightning tore the great sycamore tree "all to flinders" while he was "standing within three feet of it."

"O, may I come?" said Grace Miller.

"Yes."

"And me?" said Sally Rogers.

"Yes."

"And me, too?" said Susy Harper. "And Joe?"

"Yes."

And so on, with clapping of joyful hands till all the group had begged for invitations but Tom and Amy. Then Tom turned coolly away, still talking, and took Amy with him. Becky's lips trembled and the tears came to her eyes; she hid these signs with a forced gayety and went on chattering, but the life had gone out of the picnic, now, and out of everything else; she got away as soon as she could and hid herself and had what her sex call "a good cry." Then she sat moody, with wounded pride, till the bell rang. She roused up, now, with a vindictive cast in her eye, and gave her plaited tails a shake and said she knew what *she'd* do.

A Flirtation

At recess Tom continued his flirtation with Amy with jubilant self-satisfaction. And he kept drifting about to find Becky and lacerate her with the performance. At last he spied her, but there was a sudden falling of his mercury. She was sitting cosily on a little bench behind the schoolhouse looking at a picture-book with Alfred Temple—and so absorbed were they, and their heads so close together over the book, that they did not seem to be conscious of anything in the world besides. Jealousy ran red-hot through Tom's veins. He began to hate himself for throwing away the chance Becky had offered for a reconciliation. He called himself a fool, and all the hard names he could think of. He wanted to cry with vexation. Amy chatted happily along, as they walked, for her heart was singing, but Tom's tongue had lost its function. He did not hear what Amy was saying, and whenever she paused expectantly he could only stammer an awkward assent, which was as often misplaced as otherwise. He kept drifting to the rear of the schoolhouse, again and again, to sear his eyeballs with the hateful spectacle there. He could not help it. And it maddened him to see, as he thought he saw, that Becky Thatcher never once suspected that he was even in the land of the living. But she did see, nevertheless; and she knew she was winning her fight, too, and was glad to see him suffer as she had suffered.

Becky Retaliates

Amy's happy prattle became intolerable. Tom hinted at things he had to attend to; things that must be done; and time was fleeting. But in vain—the girl chirped on. Tom thought, "Oh, hang her, ain't I ever going to get rid of her?" At last he must be attending to those things—and she said artlessly that she would be "around" when school let out. And he hastened away, hating her for it.

A Sudden Frost

"Any other boy!" Tom thought, grating his teeth. "Any boy in the whole town but that Saint Louis smarty that thinks he dresses so fine and is aristocracy! Oh, all right, I licked you the first day you ever saw this town, mister, and I'll lick you again! You just wait till I catch you out! I'll just take and—"

And he went through the motions of thrashing an imaginary boy—pummeling the air, and kicking and gouging. "Oh, you do, do you? You holler 'nough, do you? Now, then, let that learn you!" And so the imaginary flogging was finished to his satisfaction.

Tom fled home at noon. His conscience could not endure any more of Amy's grateful happiness, and his jealousy could bear no more of the other distress. Becky resumed her picture inspections with Alfred, but as the minutes dragged along and no Tom came to suffer, her triumph began to cloud and she lost interest; gravity and absentmindedness followed, and then melancholy; two or three times she pricked up her ear at a footstep, but it was a false hope; no Tom came. At last she grew entirely miserable and wished she hadn't carried it so far. When poor Alfred, seeing that he was losing her, he did not know how, kept exclaiming: "O, here's a jolly one! look at this!" she lost patience at last, and said, "Oh, don't bother me! I don't care for them!" and burst into tears, and got up and walked away.

Alfred dropped alongside and was going to try to comfort her, but she said:

Counter-irritation

"Go away and leave me alone, can't you! I hate you!"

So the boy halted, wondering what he could have done—for she had said she would look at pictures all through the nooning—and she walked on, crying. Then Alfred went musing into the deserted schoolhouse. He was humiliated and angry. He easily guessed his way to the truth—the girl had simply made a convenience of him to vent her spite upon Tom Sawyer. He was far from hating Tom the less when this thought occurred to him. He wished there was some way to get that boy into trouble without much risk to himself. Tom's spelling-book fell under his eye. Here was his opportunity. He gratefully opened to the lesson for the afternoon and poured ink upon the page.

Becky, glancing in at a window behind him at the moment, saw the act, and moved on, without discovering herself. She started homeward, now, intending to find Tom and tell him; Tom would be thankful and their troubles would be healed. Before she was half way home, however, she had changed her mind. The thought of Tom's treatment of her when she was talking about her picnic came scorching back and filled her with shame. She resolved to let him get whipped on the damaged spelling-book's account, and to hate him forever, into the bargain.

19

Tom arrived at home in a dreary mood, and the first thing his aunt said to him showed him that he had brought his sorrows to an unpromising market:

"Tom, I've a notion to skin you alive!"

"Auntie, what have I done?"

"Well, you've done enough. Here I go over to Sereny Harper, like an old softy, expecting I'm going to make her believe all that rubbage about that dream, when lo and behold you she'd found out from Joe that you was over here and heard all the talk we had that night. Tom, I don't know what is to become of a boy that will act like that. It makes me feel so bad to think you could let me go to Sereny Harper and make such a fool of myself and never say a word."

This was a new aspect of the thing. His smartness of the morning had seemed to Tom a good joke before, and very ingenious. It merely looked mean and shabby now. He hung his head and could not think of anything to say for a moment. Then he said:

"Auntie, I wish I hadn't done it—but I didn't think."

"Oh, child, you never think. You never think of anything but your own selfishness. You could think to come all the way over here from Jackson's Island in the night to laugh at our troubles, and you could think to fool me with a lie about a dream; but you couldn't ever think to pity us and save us from sorrow."

"Auntie, I know now it was mean, but I didn't mean to be mean. I didn't, honest. And besides, I didn't come over here to laugh at you that night."

"What did you come for, then?"

"It was to tell you not to be uneasy about us, because we hadn't got drowned."

"Tom, Tom, I would be the thankfullest soul in this world if I could believe you ever had as good a thought as that, but you know you never did—and I know it, Tom."

"Indeed and 'deed I did, auntie—I wish I may never stir if I didn't."

"O, Tom, don't lie—don't do it. It only makes things a hundred times worse."

"It ain't a lie, auntie; it's the truth. I wanted to keep you from grieving—that was all that made me come."

"I'd give the whole world to believe that—it would cover up a power of sins, Tom. I'd 'most be glad you'd run off and acted so bad. But it ain't reasonable; because, why didn't you tell me, child?"

"Why, you see, when you got to talking about the funeral, I just got all full of the idea of our coming and hiding in the church, and I couldn't somehow bear to spoil it. So I just put the bark back in my pocket and kept mum."

"What bark?"

"The bark I had wrote on to tell you we'd gone pirating. I wish, now, you'd waked up when I kissed you—I do, honest."

The hard lines in his aunt's face relaxed and a sudden tenderness dawned in her eyes.

"*Did* you kiss me, Tom?"

"Why, yes, I did."

"Are you sure you did, Tom?"

"Why, yes, I did, auntie—certain sure."

"What did you kiss me for, Tom?"

"Because I loved you so, and you laid there moaning and I was so sorry."

The words sounded like truth. The old lady could not hide a tremor in her voice when she said:

"Kiss me again, Tom!—and be off with you to school, now, and don't bother me any more."

The moment he was gone, she ran to a closet and got out the ruin of a jacket which Tom had gone pirating in. Then she stopped, with it in her hand, and said to herself:

"No, I don't dare. Poor boy, I reckon he's lied about it—but it's a blessed, blessed lie, there's such a comfort come from it. I hope the Lord—I *know* the Lord will forgive him, because it was such good-heartedness in him to tell it. But I don't want to find out it's a lie. I won't look."

She put the jacket away, and stood by musing a minute. Twice she put out her hand to take the garment again, and twice she refrained. Once more she ventured, and this time she fortified herself with the thought: "It's a good lie—it's a good lie—I won't let it grieve me." So she sought the jacket pocket. A moment later she was reading Tom's piece of bark through flowing tears and saying: "I could forgive the boy, now, if he'd committed a million sins!"

20

There was something about Aunt Polly's manner, when she kissed Tom, that swept away his low spirits and made him lighthearted and happy again. He started to school and had the luck of coming upon Becky Thatcher at the head of Meadow Lane. His mood always determined his manner. Without a moment's hesitation he ran to her and said:

"I acted mighty mean today, Becky, and I'm so sorry. I won't ever, ever do that way again, as long as ever I live—please make up, won't you?"

The girl stopped and looked him scornfully in the face:

"I'll thank you to keep yourself *to* yourself, Mr. Thomas Sawyer. I'll never speak to you again."

She tossed her head and passed on. Tom was so stunned that he had not even presence of mind enough to say "Who cares, Miss Smarty?" until the right time to say it had gone by. So he said nothing. But he was in a fine rage, nevertheless. He moped into the schoolyard wishing she were a boy, and imagining how he would trounce her if she were. He presently encountered her and delivered a stinging remark as he passed. She hurled one in return, and the angry breach was complete. It seemed to Becky, in her hot resentment, that she could hardly wait for school to "take in," she was so impatient to see Tom flogged for the injured spelling-book. If she had had any lingering notion of exposing Alfred Temple, Tom's offensive fling had driven it entirely away.

Poor girl, she did not know how fast she was nearing trouble herself. The master, Mr. Dobbins, had reached middle age with an unsatisfied ambition. The darling of his desires was, to be a doctor, but poverty had decreed that he should be nothing higher than a village schoolmaster. Every day he took a mysterious book out of his desk and absorbed himself in it at times when no classes were reciting. He kept that book under lock and key. There was not an urchin in school but was perishing to have a glimpse of it, but the chance never came. Every boy and girl had a theory about the nature of that book; but no two theories were alike, and there was no way of getting at the facts in the case. Now, as Becky was passing by the desk, which stood near the door, she noticed that the key was in the lock! It was a precious moment. She glanced around; found herself alone, and the next instant she had the book in her hands. The title page—Professor Somebody's *Anatomy*—carried no information to her mind; so she began to turn the leaves. She came at once upon a handsomely engraved and coloured frontispiece—a human figure, stark naked. At that moment a shadow fell on the page and Tom Sawyer stepped in at the door and caught a glimpse of the picture. Becky snatched at the book to close it, and had the hard luck to tear the pictured page half down the middle. She thrust the volume into the desk, turned the key, and burst out crying with shame and vexation.

"Tom Sawyer, you are just as mean as you can be, to sneak up on a person and look at what they're looking at."

Caught in the Act

"How could I know you was looking at anything?"

"You ought to be ashamed of yourself, Tom Sawyer; you know you're going to tell on me, and oh, what shall I do, what shall I do! I'll be whipped, and I never was whipped in school."

Then she stamped her little foot and said:

"*Be* so mean if you want to! I know something that's going to happen. You just wait and you'll see! Hateful, hateful, hateful!"—and she flung out of the house with a new explosion of crying.

Tom stood still, rather flustered by this onslaught. Presently he said to himself:

"What a curious kind of a fool a girl is! Never been licked in school! Shucks! What's a licking! That's just like a girl—they're so thin-skinned and chicken-hearted. Well, of course I ain't going to tell old Dobbins on this little fool, because there's other ways of getting even on her, that ain't so mean; but what of it? Old Dobbins will ask who it was tore his book. Nobody'll answer. Then he'll do just the way he always does—ask first one and then t'other, and when he comes to the right girl he'll know it, without any telling. Girls' faces always tell on them. They ain't got any backbone. She'll get licked. Well, it's a kind of a tight place for Becky Thatcher, because there ain't any way out of it." Tom conned the thing a moment longer, and then added: "All right, though; she'd like to see me in just such a fix—let her sweat it out!"

Tom joined the mob of skylarking scholars outside. In a few moments the master arrived and school "took in." Tom did not feel a strong interest in his studies. Every time he stole a glance at the girls' side of the room Becky's face troubled him. Considering all things, he did not want to pity her, and yet it was all he could do to help it. He could get up no exultation that was really worthy the name. Presently the spelling-book discovery was made, and Tom's mind was entirely full of his own matters for a while after that. Becky roused up from her lethargy of distress and showed good interest in the proceedings. She did not expect that Tom could get out of his trouble by denying that he spilt the ink on the book himself; and she was right. The denial only seemed to make the thing worse for Tom. Becky supposed she would be glad of that, and she tried to believe she was glad of it, but she found she was not certain. When the worst came to the worst, she had an impulse to get up and tell on Alfred Temple, but she made an effort and forced herself to keep still—because, said she to herself, "he'll tell about me tearing the picture sure. I wouldn't say a word, not to save his life!"

Tom took his whipping and went back to his seat not at all broken-hearted, for he thought it was possible that he had unknowingly upset the ink on the spelling-book himself, in some skylarking bout—he had denied it for form's sake and because it was custom, and had stuck to the denial from principle.

A whole hour drifted by, the master sat nodding in his throne, the air was drowsy with the hum of study. By and by, Mr. Dobbins straightened himself up, yawned, then unlocked his desk, and reached for his book, but seemed undecided whether to take it out or leave it. Most of the pupils glanced up languidly, but there were two among them that watched his movements with intent eyes. Mr. Dobbins fingered his book absently for a while, then took it out and settled himself in his chair to read! Tom shot a glance at Becky. He had seen a hunted and helpless rabbit look as she did, with a gun leveled at its head. Instantly he forgot his quarrel with her. Quick—something must be done! done in a flash, too! But the very imminence of the emergency paralyzed his invention. Good!—he had an inspiration! He would run and snatch the book, spring through the door and fly. But his resolution shook for one little instant, and the chance was lost—the master opened the volume. If Tom only had the wasted opportunity back again! Too late. There was no help for Becky now, he said. The next moment the master faced the school. Every eye sank under his gaze. There was that in it which smote even the innocent with fear. There was silence while one might count ten—the master was gathering his wrath. Then he spoke:

"Who tore this book?"

There was not a sound. One could have heard a pin drop. The stillness continued; the master searched face after face for signs of guilt.

"Benjamin Rogers, did you tear this book?"

A denial. Another pause.

"Joseph Harper, did you?"

Another denial. Tom's uneasiness grew more and more intense under the slow torture of these proceedings. The master scanned the ranks of boys—considered a while, then turned to the girls:

"Amy Lawrence?"

A shake of the head.

"Gracie Miller?"

The same sign.

"Susan Harper, did you do this?"

Another negative. The next girl was Becky Thatcher. Tom was trembling from head to foot with excitement and a sense of the hopelessness of the situation.

"Rebecca Thatcher" [Tom glanced at her face—it was white with terror]—"did you tear—no, look me in the face" [her hands rose in appeal]—"did you tear this book?"

A thought shot like lightning through Tom's brain. He sprang to his feet and shouted—"I done it!"

Tom Astonishes the School

The school stared in perplexity at this incredible folly. Tom stood a moment, to gather his dismembered faculties; and when he stepped forward to go to his punishment the surprise, the gratitude, the adoration that shone upon him out of poor Becky's eyes seemed pay enough for a hundred floggings. Inspired by the splendour of his own act, he took without an outcry the most merciless flaying that even Mr. Dobbins had ever administered; and also received with indifference the added cruelty of a command to remain two hours after school should be dismissed—for he knew who would wait for him outside till his captivity was done, and not count the tedious time as loss, either.

Tom went to bed that night planning vengeance against Alfred Temple; for with shame and repentance Becky had told him all, not forgetting her own treachery; but even the longing for vengeance had to give way, soon, to pleasanter musings, and he fell asleep at last with Becky's latest words lingering dreamily in his ear—

"Tom, how *could* you be so noble!"

21

Vacation was approaching. The schoolmaster, always severe, grew severer and more exacting than ever, for he wanted the school to make a good showing on "Examination" day. His rod and his ferule were seldom idle now—at least among the smaller pupils. Only the biggest boys, and young ladies of eighteen and twenty, escaped lashing. Mr. Dobbins' lashings were very vigorous ones, too; for although he carried, under his wig, a perfectly bald and shiny head, he had only reached middle age, and there was no sign of feebleness in his muscle. As the great day approached, all the tyranny that was in him came to the surface; he seemed to take a vindictive pleasure in punishing the least shortcomings. The consequence was, that the smaller boys spent their days in terror and suffering and their nights in plotting revenge. They threw away no opportunity to do the master a mischief. But he kept ahead all the time. The retribution that followed every vengeful success was so sweeping and majestic that the boys always retired from the field badly worsted. At last they conspired together and hit upon a plan that promised a dazzling victory. They swore in the sign-painter's boy, told him the scheme, and asked his help. He had his own reasons for being delighted, for the master boarded in his father's family and had given the boy ample cause to hate him. The master's wife would go on a visit to the country in a few days, and there would be nothing to interfere with the plan; the master always prepared himself for great occasions by getting pretty well fuddled, and the sign-painter's boy said that when the dominie had reached the proper condition on Examination Evening he would "manage the thing" while he napped in his chair; then he would have him awakened at the right time and hurried away to school.

In the fullness of time the interesting occasion arrived. At eight in the evening the schoolhouse was brilliantly lighted, and adorned with wreaths and festoons of foliage and flowers. The master sat throned in his great chair upon a raised platform, with his blackboard behind him. He was looking tolerably mellow. Three rows of benches on each side and six rows in front of him were occupied by the dignitaries of the town and by the parents of the pupils. To his left, back of the rows of citizens, was a spacious temporary platform upon which were seated the scholars who were to take part in the exercises of the evening; rows of small boys, washed and dressed to an intolerable state of discomfort; rows of gawky big boys; snow-banks of girls and young ladies clad in lawn and muslin and conspicuously conscious of their bare arms, their grandmothers' ancient trinkets, their bits of pink and blue ribbon and the flowers in their hair. All the rest of the house was filled with non-participating scholars.

Examination Evening

The exercises began. A very little boy stood up and sheepishly recited, "You'd scarce expect one of my age to speak in public on the stage," etc.—accompanying himself with the painfully exact and spasmodic gestures which a machine might have used—supposing the machine to be a trifle out of order. But he got through safely, though cruelly scared, and got a fine round of applause when he made his manufactured bow and retired.

A little shame-faced girl lisped, "Mary had a little lamb," etc., performed a compassion-inspiring curtsy, got her meed of applause, and sat down flushed and happy.

Tom Sawyer stepped forward with conceited confidence and soared into the unquenchable and indestructible "Give me liberty or give me death" speech, with fine fury and frantic gesticulation, and broke down in the middle of it. A ghastly stage-fright seized him, his legs quaked under him and he was like to choke. True, he had the manifest sympathy of the house but he had the house's silence, too, which was even worse than its sympathy. The master frowned, and this completed the disaster. Tom struggled awhile and then retired, utterly defeated. There was a weak attempt at applause, but it died early.

"The Boy Stood on the Burning Deck" followed; also "The Assyrian Came Down," and other declamatory gems. Then there were reading exercises, and a spelling fight. The meager Latin class recited with honour. The prime feature of the evening was in order, now—original "compositions" by the young ladies. Each in her turn stepped forward to the edge of the platform, cleared her throat, held up her manuscript (tied with dainty ribbon), and proceeded to read, with laboured attention to "expression" and punctuation. The themes were the same that had been illuminated upon similar occasions by their mothers before them, their grandmothers, and doubtless all their ancestors in the female line clear back to the Crusades. "Friendship" was one; "Memories of Other Days"; "Religion in History"; "Dream Land"; "The Advantages of Culture"; "Forms of Political Government Compared and Contrasted"; "Melancholy"; "Filial Love"; "Heart Longings," etc., etc.

A prevalent feature in these compositions was a nursed and petted melancholy; another was a wasteful and opulent gush of "fine language"; another was a tendency to lug in by the ears particularly prized words and phrases until they were worn entirely out; and a peculiarity that conspicuously marked and marred them was the inveterate and intolerable sermon that wagged its crippled tail at the end of each and every one of them. No matter what the subject might be, a brain-racking effort was made to squirm it into some aspect or other that the moral and religious mind could contemplate with edification. The glaring insincerity of these sermons was not sufficient to compass the banishment of the fashion from the schools, and it is not sufficient today; it never will be sufficient while the world stands, perhaps. There is no school in all our land where the young ladies do not feel obliged to close their compositions with a sermon; and you will find that the sermon of the most frivolous and the least religious girl in the school is always the longest and the most relentlessly pious. But enough of this. Homely truth is unpalatable.

Let us return to the "Examination." The first composition that was read was one entitled "Is this, then, Life?" Perhaps the reader can endure an extract from it:

> "In the common walks of life, with what delightful emotions does the youthful mind look forward to some anticipated scene of festivity! Imagination is busy sketching rose-tinted pictures of joy. In fancy, the voluptuous votary of fashion sees herself amid the festive throng, 'the observed of all observers.' Her graceful form, arrayed in snowy robes, is whirling through the mazes of the joyous dance; her eye is brightest, her step is lightest in the gay assembly.

"In such delicious fancies time quickly glides by, and the welcome hour arrives for her entrance into the Elysian world, of which she has had such bright dreams. How fairy-like does everything appear to her enchanted vision! Each new scene is more charming than the last. But after a while she finds that beneath this goodly exterior, all is vanity, the flattery which once charmed her soul, now grates harshly upon her ear; the ballroom has lost its charms; and with wasted health and imbittered heart, she turns away with the conviction that earthly pleasures cannot satisfy the longings of the soul!"

And so forth and so on. There was a buzz of gratification from time to time during the reading, accompanied by whispered ejaculations of "How sweet!" "How eloquent!" "So true!" etc., and after the thing had closed with a peculiarly afflicting sermon the applause was enthusiastic.

Then arose a slim, melancholy girl, whose face had the "interesting" paleness that comes of pills and indigestion, and read a "poem." Two stanzas of it will do:

A MISSOURI MAIDEN'S FAREWELL TO ALABAMA

"Alabama, goodbye! I love thee well!
But yet for a while do I leave thee now!
Sad, yes, sad thoughts of thee my heart doth swell,
And burning recollections throng my brow!
For I have wandered through thy flowery woods;
Have roamed and read near Tallapoosa's stream;
Have listened to Tallassee's warring floods,
And wooed on Coosa's side Aurora's beam.
"Yet shame I not to bear an o'erfull heart,
Nor blush to turn behind my tearful eyes;
'Tis from no stranger land I now must part,
'Tis to no strangers left I yield these sighs.
Welcome and home were mine within this State,
Whose vales I leave—whose spires fade fast from me
And cold must be mine eyes, and heart, and tete,
When, dear Alabama! they turn cold on thee!"

There were very few there who knew what "tete" meant, but the poem was very satisfactory, nevertheless.

Next appeared a dark-complexioned, black-eyed, black-haired young lady, who paused an impressive moment, assumed a tragic expression, and began to read in a measured, solemn tone:

"*A Vision*

"Dark and tempestuous was night. Around the throne on high not a single star quivered; but the deep intonations of the heavy thunder constantly vibrated upon the ear; whilst the terrific lightning revelled in angry mood through the cloudy chambers of heaven, seeming to scorn the power exerted over its terror by the illustrious Franklin! Even the boisterous winds unanimously came forth from their mystic homes, and blustered about as if to enhance by their aid the wildness of the scene.

"At such a time, so dark, so dreary, for human sympathy my very spirit sighed; but instead thereof,

"'My dearest friend, my counsellor, my comforter and guide—
My joy in grief, my second bliss in joy,' came to my side.

She moved like one of those bright beings pictured in the sunny walks of fancy's Eden by the romantic and young, a queen of beauty unadorned save by her own transcendent loveliness. So soft was her step, it failed to make even a sound, and but for the magical thrill imparted by her genial touch, as other unobtrusive beauties, she would have glided away unperceived—unsought. A strange sadness rested upon her features, like icy tears upon the robe of December, as she pointed to the contending elements without, and bade me contemplate the two beings presented."

This nightmare occupied some ten pages of manuscript and wound up with a sermon so destructive of all hope to non-Presbyterians that it took the first prize. This composition was considered to be the very finest effort of the evening. The mayor of the village, in delivering the prize to the author of it, made a warm speech in which he said that it was by far the most "eloquent" thing he had ever listened to, and that Daniel Webster himself might well be proud of it.

It may be remarked, in passing, that the number of compositions in which the word "beauteous" was over-fondled, and human experience referred to as "life's page," was up to the usual average.

Now the master, mellow almost to the verge of geniality, put his chair aside, turned his back to the audience, and began to draw a map of America on the blackboard, to exercise the geography class upon. But he made a sad business of it with his unsteady hand, and a smothered titter rippled over the house. He knew what the matter was, and set himself to right it. He sponged out lines and remade them; but he only distorted them more than ever, and the tittering was more pronounced. He threw his entire attention upon his work, now, as if determined not to be put down by the mirth. He felt that all eyes were fastened upon him; he imagined he was succeeding, and yet the tittering continued; it even manifestly increased. And well it might. There was a garret above, pierced with a scuttle over his head; and down through this scuttle came a cat, suspended around the haunches by a string; she had a rag tied about her head and jaws to keep her from mewing; as she slowly descended she curved upward and clawed at the string, she swung downward and clawed at the intangible air. The tittering rose higher and higher—the cat was within six inches of the absorbed teacher's head—down, down, a little lower, and she grabbed his wig with her desperate claws, clung to it, and was snatched up into the garret in an instant with her trophy still in her possession! And how the light did blaze abroad from the master's bald pate—for the sign-painter's boy had *gilded* it!

That broke up the meeting. The boys were avenged. Vacation had come.

NOTE:—The pretended "compositions" quoted in this chapter are taken without alteration from a volume entitled "Prose and Poetry, by a Western Lady"—but they are exactly and precisely after the schoolgirl pattern, and hence are much happier than any mere imitations could be.

22

Tom joined the new order of Cadets of Temperance, being attracted by the showy character of their "regalia." He promised to abstain from smoking, chewing, and profanity as long as he remained a member. Now he found out a new thing—namely, that to promise not to do a thing is the surest way in the world to make a body want to go and do that very thing. Tom soon found himself tormented with a desire to drink and swear; the desire grew to be so intense that nothing but the hope of a chance to display himself in his red sash kept him from withdrawing from the order. Fourth of July was coming; but he soon gave that up—gave it up before he had worn his shackles over forty-eight hours—and fixed his hopes upon old Judge Frazer, justice of the peace, who was apparently on his deathbed and would have a big public funeral, since he was so high an official. During three days Tom was deeply concerned about the Judge's condition and hungry for news of it. Sometimes his hopes ran high—so high that he would venture to get out his regalia and practice before the looking glass. But the Judge had a most discouraging way of fluctuating. At last he was pronounced upon the mend—and then convalescent. Tom was disgusted; and felt a sense of injury, too. He handed in his resignation at once—and that night the Judge suffered a relapse and died. Tom resolved that he would never trust a man like that again.

The funeral was a fine thing. The Cadets paraded in a style calculated to kill the late member with envy. Tom was a free boy again, however—there was something in that. He could drink and swear, now—but found to his surprise that he did not want to. The simple fact that he could, took the desire away, and the charm of it.

Tom presently wondered to find that his coveted vacation was beginning to hang a little heavily on his hands.

He attempted a diary—but nothing happened during three days, and so he abandoned it.

The first of all the negro minstrel shows came to town, and made a sensation. Tom and Joe Harper got up a band of performers and were happy for two days.

Even the Glorious Fourth was in some sense a failure, for it rained hard, there was no procession in consequence, and the greatest man in the world (as Tom supposed), Mr. Benton, an actual United States Senator, proved an overwhelming disappointment—for he was not twenty-five feet high, nor even anywhere in the neighbourhood of it.

A circus came. The boys played circus for three days afterward in tents made of rag carpeting—admission, three pins for boys, two for girls—and then circusing was abandoned.

A phrenologist and a mesmerizer came—and went again and left the village duller and drearier than ever.

There were some boys-and-girls' parties, but they were so few and so delightful that they only made the aching voids between ache the harder.

Becky Thatcher was gone to her Constantinople home to stay with her parents during vacation—so there was no bright side to life anywhere.

The dreadful secret of the murder was a chronic misery. It was a very cancer for permanency and pain.

Then came the measles.

During two long weeks Tom lay a prisoner, dead to the world and its happenings. He was very ill, he was interested in nothing. When he got upon his feet at last and moved feebly downtown, a melancholy change had come over everything and every creature. There had been a "revival," and everybody had "got religion," not only the adults, but even the boys and girls. Tom went about, hoping against hope for the sight of one blessed sinful face, but disappointment crossed him everywhere. He found Joe Harper studying a Testament, and turned sadly away from the depressing spectacle. He sought Ben Rogers, and found him visiting the poor with a basket of tracts. He hunted up Jim Hollis, who called his attention to the precious blessing of his late measles as a warning. Every boy he encountered added another ton to his depression; and when, in desperation, he flew for refuge at last to the bosom of Huckleberry Finn and was received with a Scriptural quotation, his heart broke and he crept home and to bed realizing that he alone of all the town was lost, forever and forever.

And that night there came on a terrific storm, with driving rain, awful claps of thunder and blinding sheets of lightning. He covered his head with the bedclothes and waited in a horror of suspense for his doom; for he had not the shadow of a doubt that all this hubbub was about him. He believed he had taxed the forbearance of the powers above to the extremity of endurance and that this was the result. It might have seemed to him a waste of pomp and ammunition to kill a bug with a battery of artillery, but there seemed nothing incongruous about the getting up such an expensive thunderstorm as this to knock the turf from under an insect like himself.

By and by the tempest spent itself and died without accomplishing its object. The boy's first impulse was to be grateful, and reform. His second was to wait—for there might not be any more storms.

The next day the doctors were back; Tom had relapsed. The three weeks he spent on his back this time seemed an entire age. When he got abroad at last he was hardly grateful that he had been spared, remembering how lonely was his estate, how companionless and forlorn he was. He drifted listlessly down the street and found Jim Hollis acting as judge in a juvenile court that was trying a cat for murder, in the presence of her victim, a bird. He found Joe Harper and Huck Finn up an alley eating a stolen melon. Poor lads! they—like Tom—had suffered a relapse.

23

At last the sleepy atmosphere was stirred—and vigorously: the murder trial came on in the court. It became the absorbing topic of village talk immediately. Tom could not get away from it. Every reference to the murder sent a shudder to his heart, for his troubled conscience and fears almost persuaded him that these remarks were put forth in his hearing as "feelers"; he did not see how he could be suspected of knowing anything about the murder, but still he could not be comfortable in the midst of this gossip. It kept him in a cold shiver all the time. He took Huck to a lonely place to have a talk with him. It would be some relief to unseal his tongue for a little while; to divide his burden of distress with another sufferer. Moreover, he wanted to assure himself that Huck had remained discreet.

"Huck, have you ever told anybody about—that?"

"'Bout what?"

"You know what."

"Oh—'course I haven't."

"Never a word?"

"Never a solitary word, so help me. What makes you ask?"

"Well, I was afeard."

"Why, Tom Sawyer, we wouldn't be alive two days if that got found out. *You* know that."

Tom felt more comfortable. After a pause:

"Huck, they couldn't anybody get you to tell, could they?"

"Get me to tell? Why, if I wanted that half-breed devil to drownd me they could get me to tell. They ain't no different way."

"Well, that's all right, then. I reckon we're safe as long as we keep mum. But let's swear again, anyway. It's more surer."

"I'm agreed."

So they swore again with dread solemnities.

"What is the talk around, Huck? I've heard a power of it."

"Talk? Well, it's just Muff Potter, Muff Potter, Muff Potter all the time. It keeps me in a sweat, constant, so's I want to hide som'ers."

"That's just the same way they go on round me. I reckon he's a goner. Don't you feel sorry for him, sometimes?"

"Most always—most always. He ain't no account; but then he hain't ever done anything to hurt anybody. Just fishes a little, to get money to get drunk on—and loafs around considerable; but lord, we all do that—leastways most of us—preachers and such like. But he's kind of good—he give me half a fish, once, when there warn't enough for two; and lots of times he's kind of stood by me when I was out of luck."

"Well, he's mended kites for me, Huck, and knitted hooks on to my line. I wish we could get him out of there."

"My! we couldn't get him out, Tom. And besides, 'twouldn't do any good; they'd ketch him again."

"Yes—so they would. But I hate to hear 'em abuse him so like the dickens when he never done—that."

"I do too, Tom. Lord, I hear 'em say he's the bloodiest looking villain in this country, and they wonder he wasn't ever hung before."

"Yes, they talk like that, all the time. I've heard 'em say that if he was to get free they'd lynch him."

"And they'd do it, too."

The boys had a long talk, but it brought them little comfort. As the twilight drew on, they found themselves hanging about the neighbourhood of the little isolated jail, perhaps with an undefined hope that something would happen that might clear away their difficulties. But nothing happened; there seemed to be no angels or fairies interested in this luckless captive.

The boys did as they had often done before—went to the cell grating and gave Potter some tobacco and matches. He was on the ground floor and there were no guards.

His gratitude for their gifts had always smote their consciences before—it cut deeper than ever, this time. They felt cowardly and treacherous to the last degree when Potter said:

"You've been mighty good to me, boys—better'n anybody else in this town. And I don't forget it, I don't. Often I says to myself, says I, 'I used to mend all the boys' kites and things, and show 'em where the good fishin' places was, and befriend 'em what I could, and now they've all forgot old Muff when he's in trouble; but Tom don't, and Huck don't—*they* don't forget him, says I, 'and I don't forget them.' Well, boys, I done an awful thing—drunk and crazy at the time—that's the only way I account for it—and now I got to swing for it, and it's right. Right, and *best*, too, I reckon—hope so, anyway. Well, we won't talk about that. I don't want to make *you* feel bad; you've befriended me. But what I want to say, is, don't *you* ever get drunk—then you won't ever get here. Stand a litter furder west—so—that's it; it's a prime comfort to see faces that's friendly when a body's in such a muck of trouble, and there don't none come here but yourn. Good friendly faces—good friendly faces. Git up on one another's backs and let me touch 'em. That's it. Shake hands—yourn'll come through the bars, but mine's too big. Little hands, and weak—but they've helped Muff Potter a power, and they'd help him more if they could."

Tom went home miserable, and his dreams that night were full of horrors. The next day and the day after, he hung about the courtroom, drawn by an almost irresistible impulse to go in, but forcing himself to stay out. Huck was having the same experience. They studiously avoided each other. Each wandered away, from time to time, but the same dismal fascination always brought them back presently. Tom kept his ears open when idlers sauntered out of the courtroom, but invariably heard distressing news—the toils were closing more and more relentlessly around poor Potter. At the end of the second day the village talk was to the effect that Injun Joe's evidence stood firm and unshaken, and that there was not the slightest question as to what the jury's verdict would be.

Tom was out late, that night, and came to bed through the window. He was in a tremendous state of excitement. It was hours before he got to sleep. All the village flocked to the courthouse the next morning, for this was to be the great day. Both sexes were about equally represented in the packed audience. After a long wait the jury filed in and took their places; shortly afterward, Potter, pale and haggard, timid and hopeless, was brought in, with chains upon him, and seated where all the curious eyes could stare at him; no less conspicuous was Injun Joe, stolid as ever. There was another pause, and then the judge arrived and the sheriff proclaimed the opening of the court. The usual whisperings among the lawyers and gathering together of papers followed. These details and accompanying delays worked up an atmosphere of preparation that was as impressive as it was fascinating.

Now a witness was called who testified that he found Muff Potter washing in the brook, at an early hour of the morning that the murder was discovered, and that he immediately sneaked away. After some further questioning, counsel for the prosecution said—

"Take the witness."

The prisoner raised his eyes for a moment, but dropped them again when his own counsel said—

"I have no questions to ask him."

The next witness proved the finding of the knife near the corpse. Counsel for the prosecution said:

"Take the witness."

"I have no questions to ask him," Potter's lawyer replied.

A third witness swore he had often seen the knife in Potter's possession.

"Take the witness."

Counsel for Potter declined to question him. The faces of the audience began to betray annoyance. Did this attorney mean to throw away his client's life without an effort?

Several witnesses deposed concerning Potter's guilty behavior when brought to the scene of the murder. They were allowed to leave the stand without being cross-questioned.

Every detail of the damaging circumstances that occurred in the graveyard upon that morning which all present remembered so well was brought out by credible witnesses, but none of them were cross-examined by Potter's lawyer. The perplexity and dissatisfaction of the house expressed itself in murmurs and provoked a reproof from the bench. Counsel for the prosecution now said:

"By the oaths of citizens whose simple word is above suspicion, we have fastened this awful crime, beyond all possibility of question, upon the unhappy prisoner at the bar. We rest our case here."

A groan escaped from poor Potter, and he put his face in his hands and rocked his body softly to and fro, while a painful silence reigned in the courtroom. Many men were moved, and many women's compassion testified itself in tears. Counsel for the defence rose and said:

"Your honour, in our remarks at the opening of this trial, we foreshadowed our purpose to prove that our client did this fearful deed while under the influence of a blind and irresponsible delirium produced by drink. We have changed our mind. We shall not offer that plea." [Then to the clerk:] "Call Thomas Sawyer!"

A puzzled amazement awoke in every face in the house, not even excepting Potter's. Every eye fastened itself with wondering interest upon Tom as he rose and took his place upon the stand. The boy looked wild enough, for he was badly scared. The oath was administered.

"Thomas Sawyer, where were you on the seventeenth of June, about the hour of midnight?"

Tom glanced at Injun Joe's iron face and his tongue failed him. The audience listened breathless, but the words refused to come. After a few moments, however, the boy got a little of his strength back, and managed to put enough of it into his voice to make part of the house hear:

"In the graveyard!"

"A little bit louder, please. Don't be afraid. You were—"

"In the graveyard."

A contemptuous smile flitted across Injun Joe's face.

"Were you anywhere near Horse Williams' grave?"

"Yes, sir."

"Speak up—just a trifle louder. How near were you?"

"Near as I am to you."

"Were you hidden, or not?"

"I was hid."

"Where?"

"Behind the elms that's on the edge of the grave."

Injun Joe gave a barely perceptible start.

"Any one with you?"

"Yes, sir. I went there with—"

"Wait—wait a moment. Never mind mentioning your companion's name. We will produce him at the proper time. Did you carry anything there with you."

Tom hesitated and looked confused.

"Speak out, my boy—don't be diffident. The truth is always respectable. What did you take there?"

"Only a—a—dead cat."

There was a ripple of mirth, which the court checked.

"We will produce the skeleton of that cat. Now, my boy, tell us everything that occurred—tell it in your own way—don't skip anything, and don't be afraid."

Tom began—hesitatingly at first, but as he warmed to his subject his words flowed more and more easily; in a little while every sound ceased but his own voice; every eye fixed itself upon him; with parted lips and bated breath the audience hung upon his words, taking no note of time, rapt in the ghastly fascinations of the tale. The strain upon pent emotion reached its climax when the boy said:

"—and as the doctor fetched the board around and Muff Potter fell, Injun Joe jumped with the knife and—"

Crash! Quick as lightning the half-breed sprang for a window, tore his way through all opposers, and was gone!

24

Tom was a glittering hero once more—the pet of the old, the envy of the young. His name even went into immortal print, for the village paper magnified him. There were some that believed he would be President, yet, if he escaped hanging.

As usual, the fickle, unreasoning world took Muff Potter to its bosom and fondled him as lavishly as it had abused him before. But that sort of conduct is to the world's credit; therefore it is not well to find fault with it.

Tom's days were days of splendour and exultation to him, but his nights were seasons of horror. Injun Joe infested all his dreams, and always with doom in his eye. Hardly any temptation could persuade the boy to stir abroad after nightfall. Poor Huck was in the same state of wretchedness and terror, for Tom had told the whole story to the lawyer the night before the great day of the trial, and Huck was sore afraid that his share in the business might leak out, yet, notwithstanding Injun Joe's flight had saved him the suffering of testifying in court. The poor fellow had got the attorney to promise secrecy, but what of that? Since Tom's harassed conscience had managed to drive him to the lawyer's house by night and wring a dread tale from lips that had been sealed with the dismalest and most formidable of oaths, Huck's confidence in the human race was well nigh obliterated.

Tom Dreams

Daily Muff Potter's gratitude made Tom glad he had spoken; but nightly he wished he had sealed up his tongue.

Half the time Tom was afraid Injun Joe would never be captured; the other half he was afraid he would be. He felt sure he never could draw a safe breath again until that man was dead and he had seen the corpse.

Rewards had been offered, the country had been scoured, but no Injun Joe was found. One of those omniscient and awe-inspiring marvels, a detective, came up from St. Louis, moused around, shook his head, looked wise, and made that sort of astounding success which members of that craft usually achieve. That is to say, he "found a clew." But you can't hang a "clew" for murder, and so after that detective had got through and gone home, Tom felt just as insecure as he was before.

The slow days drifted on, and each left behind it a slightly lightened weight of apprehension.

25

There comes a time in every rightly-constructed boy's life when he has a raging desire to go somewhere and dig for hidden treasure. This desire suddenly came upon Tom one day. He sallied out to find Joe Harper, but failed of success. Next he sought Ben Rogers; he had gone fishing. Presently he stumbled upon Huck Finn the Red-Handed. Huck would answer. Tom took him to a private place and opened the matter to him confidentially. Huck was willing. Huck was always willing to take a hand in any enterprise that offered entertainment and required no capital, for he had a troublesome superabundance of that sort of time which is not money. "Where'll we dig?" said Huck.

"O, most anywhere."

"Why, is it hid all around?"

"No, indeed it ain't. It's hid in mighty particular places, Huck—sometimes on islands, sometimes in rotten chests under the end of a limb of an old dead tree, just where the shadow falls at midnight; but mostly under the floor in ha'nted houses."

"Who hides it?"

"Why, robbers, of course—who'd you reckon? Sunday-school sup'rintendents?"

"I don't know. If 'twas mine I wouldn't hide it; I'd spend it and have a good time."

"So would I. But robbers don't do that way. They always hide it and leave it there."

"Don't they come after it any more?"

"No, they think they will, but they generally forget the marks, or else they die. Anyway, it lays there a long time and gets rusty; and by and by somebody finds an old yellow paper that tells how to find the marks—a paper that's got to be ciphered over about a week because it's mostly signs and hy'roglyphics."

"Hyro—which?"

"Hy'roglyphics—pictures and things, you know, that don't seem to mean anything."

The Private Conference

"Have you got one of them papers, Tom?"

"No."

"Well then, how you going to find the marks?"

"I don't want any marks. They always bury it under a ha'nted house or on an island, or under a dead tree that's got one limb sticking out. Well, we've tried Jackson's Island a little, and we can try it again some time; and there's the old ha'nted house up the Still-House branch, and there's lots of dead-limb trees—dead loads of 'em."

"Is it under all of them?"

"How you talk! No!"

"Then how you going to know which one to go for?"

"Go for all of 'em!"

"Why, Tom, it'll take all summer."

"Well, what of that? Suppose you find a brass pot with a hundred dollars in it, all rusty and grey, or rotten chest full of di'monds. How's that?"

Huck's eyes glowed.

"That's bully. Plenty bully enough for me. Just you gimme the hundred dollars and I don't want no di'monds."

"All right. But I bet you *I* ain't going to throw off on di'monds. Some of 'em's worth twenty dollars apiece—there ain't any, hardly, but's worth six bits or a dollar."

"No! Is that so?"

"Cert'nly—anybody'll tell you so. Hain't you ever seen one, Huck?"

"Not as I remember."

"O, kings have slathers of them."

"Well, I don' know no kings, Tom."

"I reckon you don't. But if you was to go to Europe you'd see a raft of 'em hopping around."

"Do they hop?"

"Hop?—your granny! No!"

"Well, what did you say they did, for?"

"Shucks, I only meant you'd *see* 'em—not hopping, of course—what do they want to hop for?—but I mean you'd just see 'em—scattered around, you know, in a kind of a general way. Like that old humpbacked Richard."

"Richard? What's his other name?"

"He didn't have any other name. Kings don't have any but a given name."

"No?"

"But they don't."

"Well, if they like it, Tom, all right; but I don't want to be a king and have only just a given name, like a nigger. But say—where you going to dig first?"

"Well, I don't know. S'pose we tackle that old dead-limb tree on the hill t'other side of Still-House branch?"

"I'm agreed."

So they got a crippled pick and a shovel, and set out on their three-mile tramp. They arrived hot and panting, and threw themselves down in the shade of a neighbouring elm to rest and have a smoke.

"I like this," said Tom.

"So do I."

"Say, Huck, if we find a treasure here, what you going to do with your share?"

"Well, I'll have pie and a glass of soda every day, and I'll go to every circus that comes along. I bet I'll have a gay time."

"Well, ain't you going to save any of it?"

"Save it? What for?"

"Why, so as to have something to live on, by and by."

"O, that ain't any use. Pap would come back to thish-yer town some day and get his claws on it if I didn't hurry up, and I tell you he'd clean it out pretty quick. What you going to do with yourn, Tom?"

"I'm going to buy a new drum, and a sure'nough sword, and a red necktie and a bull pup, and get married."

"Married!"

"That's it."

"Tom, you—why, you ain't in your right mind."

"Wait—you'll see."

"Well, that's the foolishest thing you could do. Look at pap and my mother. Fight! Why, they used to fight all the time. I remember, mighty well."

"That ain't anything. The girl I'm going to marry won't fight."

"Tom, I reckon they're all alike. They'll all comb a body. Now you better think 'bout this awhile. I tell you you better. What's the name of the gal?"

"It ain't a gal at all—it's a girl."

"It's all the same, I reckon; some says gal, some says girl—both's right, like enough. Anyway, what's her name, Tom?"

"I'll tell you some time—not now."

"All right—that'll do. Only if you get married I'll be more lonesomer than ever."

"No you won't. You'll come and live with me. Now stir out of this and we'll go to digging."

They worked and sweated for half an hour. No result. They toiled another half hour. Still no result. Huck said:

"Do they always bury it as deep as this?"

"Sometimes—not always. Not generally. I reckon we haven't got the right place."

Business

So they chose a new spot and began again. The labour dragged a little, but still they made progress. They pegged away in silence for some time. Finally Huck leaned on his shovel, swabbed the beaded drops from his brow with his sleeve, and said:

"Where you going to dig next, after we get this one?"

"I reckon maybe we'll tackle the old tree that's over yonder on Cardiff Hill back of the widow's."

"I reckon that'll be a good one. But won't the widow take it away from us, Tom? It's on her land."

"*She* take it away! Maybe she'd like to try it once. Whoever finds one of these hid treasures, it belongs to him. It don't make any difference whose land it's on."

That was satisfactory. The work went on. By and by Huck said:

"Blame it, we must be in the wrong place again. What do you think?"

"It is mighty curious, Huck. I don't understand it. Sometimes witches interfere. I reckon maybe that's what's the trouble now."

"Shucks! Witches ain't got no power in the daytime."

"Well, that's so. I didn't think of that. Oh, I know what the matter is! What a blamed lot of fools we are! You got to find out where the shadow of the limb falls at midnight, and that's where you dig!"

"Then consound it, we've fooled away all this work for nothing. Now hang it all, we got to come back in the night. It's an awful long way. Can you get out?"

"I bet I will. We've got to do it tonight, too, because if somebody sees these holes they'll know in a minute what's here and they'll go for it."

"Well, I'll come around and maow tonight."

"All right. Let's hide the tools in the bushes."

The boys were there that night, about the appointed time. They sat in the shadow waiting. It was a lonely place, and an hour made solemn by old traditions. Spirits whispered in the rustling leaves, ghosts lurked in the murky nooks, the deep baying of a hound floated up out of the distance, an owl answered with his sepulchral note. The boys were subdued by these solemnities, and talked little. By and by they judged that twelve had come; they marked where the shadow fell, and began to dig. Their hopes commenced to rise. Their interest grew stronger, and their industry kept pace with it. The hole deepened and still deepened, but every time their hearts jumped to hear the pick strike upon something, they only suffered a new disappointment. It was only a stone or a chunk. At last Tom said:

"It ain't any use, Huck, we're wrong again."

"Well, but we *can't* be wrong. We spotted the shadder to a dot."

"I know it, but then there's another thing."

"What's that?".

"Why, we only guessed at the time. Like enough it was too late or too early."

Huck dropped his shovel.

"That's it," said he. "That's the very trouble. We got to give this one up. We can't ever tell the right time, and besides this kind of thing's too awful, here this time of night with witches and ghosts a-fluttering around so. I feel as if something's behind me all the time; and I'm afeard to turn around, becuz maybe there's others in front a-waiting for a chance. I been creeping all over, ever since I got here."

"Well, I've been pretty much so, too, Huck. They most always put in a dead man when they bury a treasure under a tree, to look out for it."

"Lordy!"

"Yes, they do. I've always heard that."

"Tom, I don't like to fool around much where there's dead people. A body's bound to get into trouble with 'em, sure."

"I don't like to stir 'em up, either. S'pose this one here was to stick his skull out and say something!"

"Don't Tom! It's awful."

"Well, it just is. Huck, I don't feel comfortable a bit."

"Say, Tom, let's give this place up, and try somewheres else."

"All right, I reckon we better."

"What'll it be?"

Tom considered a while; and then said:

"The ha'nted house. That's it!"

"Blame it, I don't like ha'nted houses, Tom. Why, they're a dern sight worse'n dead people. Dead people might talk, maybe, but they don't come sliding around in a shroud, when you ain't noticing, and peep over your shoulder all of a sudden and grit their teeth, the way a ghost does. I couldn't stand such a thing as that, Tom—nobody could."

"Yes, but, Huck, ghosts don't travel around only at night. They won't hender us from digging there in the day time."

"Well, that's so. But you know mighty well people don't go about that ha'nted house in the day nor the night."

"Well, that's mostly because they don't like to go where a man's been murdered, anyway—but nothing's ever been seen around that house except in the night—just some blue lights slipping by the windows—no regular ghosts."

"Well, where you see one of them blue lights flickering around, Tom, you can bet there's a ghost mighty close behind it. It stands to reason. Becuz you know that they don't anybody but ghosts use 'em."

"Yes, that's so. But anyway they don't come around in the daytime, so what's the use of our being afeard?"

"Well, all right. We'll tackle the ha'nted house if you say so—but I reckon it's taking chances."

They had started down the hill by this time. There in the middle of the moonlit valley below them stood the "ha'nted" house, utterly isolated, its fences gone long ago, rank weeds smothering the very doorsteps, the chimney crumbled to ruin, the window-sashes vacant, a corner of the roof caved in. The boys gazed awhile, half expecting to see a blue light flit past a window; then talking in a low tone, as befitted the time and the circumstances, they struck far off to the right, to give the haunted house a wide berth, and took their way homeward through the woods that adorned the rearward side of Cardiff Hill.

26

About noon the next day the boys arrived at the dead tree; they had come for their tools. Tom was impatient to go to the haunted house; Huck was measurably so, also—but suddenly said—

"Lookyhere, Tom, do you know what day it is?"

Tom mentally ran over the days of the week, and then quickly lifted his eyes with a startled look in them—

"My! I never once thought of it, Huck!"

"Well, I didn't neither, but all at once it popped onto me that it was Friday."

"Blame it, a body can't be too careful, Huck. We might 'a' got into an awful scrape, tackling such a thing on a Friday."

"*Might*! Better say we *would*! There's some lucky days, maybe, but Friday ain't."

"Any fool knows that. I don't reckon *you* was the first that found it out, Huck."

"Well, I never said I was, did I? And Friday ain't all, neither. I had a rotten bad dream last night—dreampt about rats."

"No! Sure sign of trouble. Did they fight?"

"No."

"Well, that's good, Huck. When they don't fight it's only a sign that there's trouble around, you know. All we got to do is to look mighty sharp and keep out of it. We'll drop this thing for today, and play. Do you know Robin Hood, Huck?"

"No. Who's Robin Hood?"

"Why, he was one of the greatest men that was ever in England—and the best. He was a robber."

"Cracky, I wisht I was. Who did he rob?"

"Only sheriffs and bishops and rich people and kings, and such like. But he never bothered the poor. He loved 'em. He always divided up with 'em perfectly square."

"Well, he must 'a' been a brick."

"I bet you he was, Huck. Oh, he was the noblest man that ever was. They ain't any such men now, I can tell you. He could lick any man in England, with one hand tied behind him; and he could take his yew bow and plug a ten-cent piece every time, a mile and a half."

"What's a *yew* bow?"

"I don't know. It's some kind of a bow, of course. And if he hit that dime only on the edge he would set down and cry—and curse. But we'll play Robin Hood—it's noble fun. I'll learn you."

"I'm agreed."

So they played Robin Hood all the afternoon, now and then casting a yearning eye down upon the haunted house and passing a remark about the morrow's prospects and possibilities there. As the sun began to sink into the west they took their way homeward athwart the long shadows of the trees and soon were buried from sight in the forests of Cardiff Hill.

On Saturday, shortly after noon, the boys were at the dead tree again. They had a smoke and a chat in the shade, and then dug a little in their last hole, not with great hope, but merely because Tom said there were so many cases where people had given up a treasure after getting down within six inches of it, and then somebody else had come along and turned it up with a single thrust of a shovel. The thing failed this time, however, so the boys shouldered their tools and went away feeling that they had not trifled with fortune, but had fulfilled all the requirements that belong to the business of treasure-hunting.

When they reached the haunted house there was something so weird and grisly about the dead silence that reigned there under the baking sun, and something so depressing about the loneliness and desolation of the place, that they were afraid, for a moment, to venture in. Then they crept to the door and took a trembling peep. They saw a weed-grown, floorless room, unplastered, an ancient fireplace, vacant windows, a ruinous staircase; and here, there, and everywhere hung ragged and abandoned cobwebs. They presently entered, softly, with quickened pulses, talking in whispers, ears alert to catch the slightest sound, and muscles tense and ready for instant retreat.

In a little while familiarity modified their fears and they gave the place a critical and interested examination, rather admiring their own boldness, and wondering at it, too. Next they wanted to look upstairs. This was something like cutting off retreat, but they got to daring each other, and of course there could be but one result—they threw their tools into a corner and made the ascent. Up there were the same signs of decay. In one corner they found a closet that promised mystery, but the promise was a fraud—there was nothing in it. Their courage was up now and well in hand. They were about to go down and begin work when—

"Sh!" said Tom.

"What is it?" whispered Huck, blanching with fright.

"Sh! . . . There! . . . Hear it?"

"Yes! . . . Oh, my! Let's run!"

"Keep still! Don't you budge! They're coming right toward the door."

The boys stretched themselves upon the floor with their eyes to knotholes in the planking, and lay waiting, in a misery of fear.

"They've stopped. . . . No—coming. . . . Here they are. Don't whisper another word, Huck. My goodness, I wish I was out of this!"

Two men entered. Each boy said to himself: "There's the old deaf and dumb Spaniard that's been about town once or twice lately—never saw t'other man before."

"T'other" was a ragged, unkempt creature, with nothing very pleasant in his face. The Spaniard was wrapped in a *serape*; he had bushy white whiskers; long white hair flowed from under his sombrero, and he wore green goggles. When they came in, "t'other" was talking in a low voice; they sat down on the ground, facing the door, with their backs to the wall, and the speaker continued his remarks. His manner became less guarded and his words more distinct as he proceeded:

"No," said he, "I've thought it all over, and I don't like it. It's dangerous."

"Dangerous!" grunted the "deaf and dumb" Spaniard—to the vast surprise of the boys. "Milksop!"

This voice made the boys gasp and quake. It was Injun Joe's! There was silence for some time. Then Joe said:

"What's any more dangerous than that job up yonder—but nothing's come of it."

"That's different. Away up the river so, and not another house about. 'Twon't ever be known that we tried, anyway, long as we didn't succeed."

"Well, what's more dangerous than coming here in the daytime!—anybody would suspicion us that saw us."

"I know that. But there warn't any other place as handy after that fool of a job. I want to quit this shanty. I wanted to yesterday, only it warn't any use trying to stir out of here, with those infernal boys playing over there on the hill right in full view."

"Those infernal boys" quaked again under the inspiration of this remark, and thought how lucky it was that they had remembered it was Friday and concluded to wait a day. They wished in their hearts they had waited a year.

The two men got out some food and made a luncheon. After a long and thoughtful silence, Injun Joe said:

"Look here, lad—you go back up the river where you belong. Wait there till you hear from me. I'll take the chances on dropping into this town just once more, for a look. We'll do that 'dangerous' job after I've spied around a little and think things look well for it. Then for Texas! We'll leg it together!"

This was satisfactory. Both men presently fell to yawning, and Injun Joe said:

"I'm dead for sleep! It's your turn to watch."

He curled down in the weeds and soon began to snore. His comrade stirred him once or twice and he became quiet. Presently the watcher began to nod; his head drooped lower and lower, both men began to snore now.

The boys drew a long, grateful breath. Tom whispered:

"Now's our chance—come!"

Huck said:

"I can't—I'd die if they was to wake."

Tom urged—Huck held back. At last Tom rose slowly and softly, and started alone. But the first step he made wrung such a hideous creak from the crazy floor that he sank down almost dead with fright. He never made a second attempt. The boys lay there counting the dragging moments till it seemed to them that time must be done and eternity growing grey; and then they were grateful to note that at last the sun was setting.

Now one snore ceased. Injun Joe sat up, stared around—smiled grimly upon his comrade, whose head was drooping upon his knees—stirred him up with his foot and said:

"Here! *You're* a watchman, ain't you! All right, though—nothing's happened."

"My! have I been asleep?"

"Oh, partly, partly. Nearly time for us to be moving, pard. What'll we do with what little swag we've got left?"

"I don't know—leave it here as we've always done, I reckon. No use to take it away till we start south. Six hundred and fifty in silver's something to carry."

"Well—all right—it won't matter to come here once more."

"No—but I'd say come in the night as we used to do—it's better."

"Yes: but look here; it may be a good while before I get the right chance at that job; accidents might happen; 'tain't in such a very good place; we'll just regularly bury it—and bury it deep."

"Good idea," said the comrade, who walked across the room, knelt down, raised one of the rearward hearth-stones and took out a bag that jingled pleasantly. He subtracted from it twenty or thirty dollars for himself and as much for Injun Joe, and passed the bag to the latter, who was on his knees in the corner, now, digging with his bowie-knife.

The boys forgot all their fears, all their miseries in an instant. With gloating eyes they watched every movement. Luck!—the splendour of it was beyond all imagination! Six hundred dollars was money enough to make half a dozen boys rich! Here was treasure-hunting under the happiest auspices—there would not be any bothersome uncertainty as to where to dig. They nudged each other every moment—eloquent nudges and easily understood, for they simply meant—"Oh, but ain't you glad *now* we're here!"

Joe's knife struck upon something.

"Hello!" said he.

"What is it?" said his comrade.

"Half-rotten plank—no, it's a box, I believe. Here—bear a hand and we'll see what it's here for. Never mind, I've broke a hole."

He reached his hand in and drew it out—

"Man, it's money!"

The two men examined the handful of coins. They were gold. The boys above were as excited as themselves, and as delighted.

Joe's comrade said:

"We'll make quick work of this. There's an old rusty pick over amongst the weeds in the corner the other side of the fireplace—I saw it a minute ago."

He ran and brought the boys' pick and shovel. Injun Joe took the pick, looked it over critically, shook his head, muttered something to himself, and then began to use it. The box was soon unearthed. It was not very large; it was iron bound and had been very strong before the slow years had injured it. The men contemplated the treasure awhile in blissful silence.

"Pard, there's thousands of dollars here," said Injun Joe.

"'Twas always said that Murrel's gang used to be around here one summer," the stranger observed.

"I know it," said Injun Joe; "and this looks like it, I should say."

"Now you won't need to do that job."

The half-breed frowned. Said he:

"You don't know me. Least you don't know all about that thing. 'Tain't robbery altogether—it's *revenge*!" and a wicked light flamed in his eyes. "I'll need your help in it. When it's finished—then Texas. Go home to your Nance and your kids, and stand by till you hear from me."

"Well—if you say so; what'll we do with this—bury it again?"

"Yes. [Ravishing delight overhead.] *No*! by the great Sachem, no! [Profound distress overhead.] I'd nearly forgot. That pick had fresh earth on it! [The boys were sick with terror in a moment.] What business has a pick and a shovel here? What business with fresh earth on them? Who brought them here—and where are they gone? Have you heard anybody?—seen anybody? What! bury it again and leave them to come and see the ground disturbed? Not exactly—not exactly. We'll take it to my den."

"Why, of course! Might have thought of that before. You mean Number One?"

"No—Number Two—under the cross. The other place is bad—too common."

"All right. It's nearly dark enough to start."

Injun Joe got up and went about from window to window cautiously peeping out. Presently he said:

"Who could have brought those tools here? Do you reckon they can be upstairs?"

The boys' breath forsook them. Injun Joe put his hand on his knife, halted a moment, undecided, and then turned toward the stairway. The boys thought of the closet, but their strength was gone. The steps came creaking up the stairs—the intolerable distress of the situation woke the stricken resolution of the lads—they were about to spring for the closet, when there was a crash of rotten timbers and Injun Joe landed on the ground amid the debris of the ruined stairway. He gathered himself up cursing, and his comrade said:

"Now what's the use of all that? If it's anybody, and they're up there, let them *stay* there—who cares? If they want to jump down, now, and get into trouble, who objects? It will be dark in fifteen minutes—and then let them follow us if they want to. I'm willing. In my opinion, whoever hove those things in here caught a sight of us and took us for ghosts or devils or something. I'll bet they're running yet."

Joe grumbled awhile; then he agreed with his friend that what daylight was left ought to be economized in getting things ready for leaving. Shortly afterward they slipped out of the house in the deepening twilight, and moved toward the river with their precious box.

Tom and Huck rose up, weak but vastly relieved, and stared after them through the chinks between the logs of the house. Follow? Not they. They were content to reach ground again without broken necks, and take the townward track over the hill. They did not talk much. They were too much absorbed in hating themselves—hating the ill luck that made them take the spade and the pick there. But for that, Injun Joe never would have suspected. He would have hidden the silver with the gold to wait there till his "revenge" was satisfied, and then he would have had the misfortune to find that money turn up missing. Bitter, bitter luck that the tools were ever brought there!

They resolved to keep a lookout for that Spaniard when he should come to town spying out for chances to do his revengeful job, and follow him to "Number Two," wherever that might be. Then a ghastly thought occurred to Tom.

"Revenge? What if he means *us*, Huck!"

"O, don't!" said Huck, nearly fainting.

They talked it all over, and as they entered town they agreed to believe that he might possibly mean somebody else—at least that he might at least mean nobody but Tom, since only Tom had testified.

Very, very small comfort it was to Tom to be alone in danger! Company would be a palpable improvement, he thought.

27

The adventure of the day mightily tormented Tom's dreams that night. Four times he had his hands on that rich treasure and four times it wasted to nothingness in his fingers as sleep forsook him and wakefulness brought back the hard reality of his misfortune. As he lay in the early morning recalling the incidents of his great adventure, he noticed that they seemed curiously subdued and far away—somewhat as if they had happened in another world, or in a time long gone by. Then it occurred to him that the great adventure itself must be a dream! There was one very strong argument in favour of this idea—namely, that the quantity of coin he had seen was too vast to be real. He had never seen as much as fifty dollars in one mass before, and he was like all boys of his age and station in life, in that he imagined that all references to "hundreds" and "thousands" were mere fanciful forms of speech, and that no such sums really existed in the world. He never had supposed for a moment that so large a sum as a hundred dollars was to be found in actual money in any one's possession. If his notions of hidden treasure had been analyzed, they would have been found to consist of a handful of real dimes and a bushel of vague, splendid, ungraspable dollars.

But the incidents of his adventure grew sensibly sharper and clearer under the attrition of thinking them over, and so he presently found himself leaning to the impression that the thing might not have been a dream, after all. This uncertainty must be swept away. He would snatch a hurried breakfast and go and find Huck.

Huck was sitting on the gunwale of a flatboat, listlessly dangling his feet in the water and looking very melancholy. Tom concluded to let Huck lead up to the subject. If he did not do it, then the adventure would be proved to have been only a dream.

"Hello, Huck!"

"Hello, yourself."

Silence, for a minute.

"Tom, if we'd 'a' left the blame tools at the dead tree, we'd 'a' got the money. Oh, ain't it awful!"

"'Tain't a dream, then, 'tain't a dream! Somehow I most wish it was. Dog'd if I don't, Huck."

"What ain't a dream?"

"Oh, that thing yesterday. I been half thinking it was."

"Dream! If them stairs hadn't broke down you'd 'a' seen how much dream it was! I've had dreams enough all night—with that patch-eyed Spanish devil going for me all through 'em—rot him!"

"No, not rot him. *Find* him! Track the money!"

"Tom, we'll never find him. A feller don't have only one chance for such a pile—and that one's lost. I'd feel mighty shaky if I was to see him, anyway."

"Well, so'd I; but I'd like to see him, anyway—and track him out—to his Number Two."

"Number Two—yes, that's it. I been thinking 'bout that. But I can't make nothing out of it. What do you reckon it is?"

"I dono. It's too deep. Say, Huck—maybe it's the number of a house!"

"Goody! . . . No, Tom, that ain't it. If it is, it ain't in this one-horse town. They ain't no numbers here."

"Well, that's so. Lemme think a minute. Here—it's the number of a room—in a tavern, you know!"

"O, that's the trick! They ain't only two taverns. We can find out quick."

"You stay here, Huck, till I come."

Tom was off at once. He did not care to have Huck's company in public places. He was gone half an hour. He found that in the best tavern, No. 2 had long been occupied by a young lawyer, and was still so occupied. In the less ostentatious house, No. 2 was a mystery. The tavern-keeper's young son said it was kept locked all the time, and he never saw anybody go into it or come out of it except at night; he did not know any particular reason for this state of things; had had some little curiosity, but it was rather feeble; had made the most of the mystery by entertaining himself with the idea that that room was "ha'nted"; had noticed that there was a light in there the night before.

"That's what I've found out, Huck. I reckon that's the very No. 2 we're after."

"I reckon it is, Tom. Now what you going to do?"

"Lemme think."

Tom thought a long time. Then he said:

"I'll tell you. The back door of that No. 2 is the door that comes out into that little close alley between the tavern and the old rattle trap of a brick store. Now you get hold of all the door-keys you can find, and I'll nip all of auntie's, and the first dark night we'll go there and try 'em. And mind you, keep a lookout for Injun Joe, because he said he was going to drop into town and spy around once more for a chance to get his revenge. If you see him, you just follow him; and if he don't go to that No. 2, that ain't the place."

"Lordy, I don't want to foller him by myself!"

"Why, it'll be night, sure. He mightn't ever see you—and if he did, maybe he'd never think anything."

"Well, if it's pretty dark I reckon I'll track him. I dono—I dono. I'll try."

"You bet I'll follow him, if it's dark, Huck. Why, he might 'a' found out he couldn't get his revenge, and be going right after that money."

"It's so, Tom, it's so. I'll foller him; I will, by jingoes!"

"Now you're *talking*! Don't you ever weaken, Huck, and I won't."

28

That night Tom and Huck were ready for their adventure. They hung about the neighbourhood of the tavern until after nine, one watching the alley at a distance and the other the tavern door. Nobody entered the alley or left it; nobody resembling the Spaniard entered or left the tavern door. The night promised to be a fair one; so Tom went home with the understanding that if a considerable degree of darkness came on, Huck was to come and "maow," whereupon he would slip out and try the keys. But the night remained clear, and Huck closed his watch and retired to bed in an empty sugar hogshead about twelve.

Tuesday the boys had the same ill luck. Also Wednesday. But Thursday night promised better. Tom slipped out in good season with his aunt's old tin lantern, and a large towel to blindfold it with. He hid the lantern in Huck's sugar hogshead and the watch began. An hour before midnight the tavern closed up and its lights (the only ones thereabouts) were put out. No Spaniard had been seen. Nobody had entered or left the alley. Everything was auspicious. The blackness of darkness reigned, the perfect stillness was interrupted only by occasional mutterings of distant thunder.

Tom got his lantern, lit it in the hogshead, wrapped it closely in the towel, and the two adventurers crept in the gloom toward the tavern. Huck stood sentry and Tom felt his way into the alley. Then there was a season of waiting anxiety that weighed upon Huck's spirits like a mountain. He began to wish he could see a flash from the lantern—it would frighten him, but it would at least tell him that Tom was alive yet. It seemed hours since Tom had disappeared. Surely he must have fainted; maybe he was dead; maybe his heart had burst under terror and excitement. In his uneasiness Huck found himself drawing closer and closer to the alley; fearing all sorts of dreadful things, and momentarily expecting some catastrophe to happen that would take away his breath. There was not much to take away, for he seemed only able to inhale it by thimblefuls, and his heart would soon wear itself out, the way it was beating. Suddenly there was a flash of light and Tom came tearing by him:

"Run!" said he; "run, for your life!"

He needn't have repeated it; once was enough; Huck was making thirty or forty miles an hour before the repetition was uttered. The boys never stopped till they reached the shed of a deserted slaughterhouse at the lower end of the village. Just as they got within its shelter the storm burst and the rain poured down. As soon as Tom got his breath he said:

"Huck, it was awful! I tried two of the keys, just as soft as I could; but they seemed to make such a power of racket that I couldn't hardly get my breath I was so scared. They wouldn't turn in the lock, either. Well, without noticing what I was doing, I took hold of the knob, and open comes the door! It warn't locked! I hopped in, and shook off the towel, and, *Great Caesar's Ghost!*"

"What!—what'd you see, Tom?"

"Huck, I most stepped onto Injun Joe's hand!"

"No!"

"Yes! He was lying there, sound asleep on the floor, with his old patch on his eye and his arms spread out."

"Lordy, what did you do? Did he wake up?"

"No, never budged. Drunk, I reckon. I just grabbed that towel and started!"

"I'd never 'a' thought of the towel, I bet!"

"Well, I would. My aunt would make me mighty sick if I lost it."

"Say, Tom, did you see that box?"

"Huck, I didn't wait to look around. I didn't see the box, I didn't see the cross. I didn't see anything but a bottle and a tin cup on the floor by Injun Joe; yes, I saw two barrels and lots more bottles in the room. Don't you see, now, what's the matter with that ha'nted room?"

"How?"

"Why, it's ha'nted with whiskey! Maybe *all* the Temperance Taverns have got a ha'nted room, hey, Huck?"

"Well, I reckon maybe that's so. Who'd 'a' thought such a thing? But say, Tom, now's a mighty good time to get that box, if Injun Joe's drunk."

"It is, that! You try it!"

Huck shuddered.

"Well, no—I reckon not."

"And I reckon not, Huck. Only one bottle alongside of Injun Joe ain't enough. If there'd been three, he'd be drunk enough and I'd do it."

There was a long pause for reflection, and then Tom said:

"Lookyhere, Huck, less not try that thing any more till we know Injun Joe's not in there. It's too scary. Now, if we watch every night, we'll be dead sure to see him go out, some time or other, and then we'll snatch that box quicker'n lightning."

"Well, I'm agreed. I'll watch the whole night long, and I'll do it every night, too, if you'll do the other part of the job."

"All right, I will. All you got to do is to trot up Hooper Street a block and maow—and if I'm asleep, you throw some gravel at the window and that'll fetch me."

"Agreed, and good as wheat!"

"Now, Huck, the storm's over, and I'll go home. It'll begin to be daylight in a couple of hours. You go back and watch that long, will you?"

"I said I would, Tom, and I will. I'll ha'nt that tavern every night for a year! I'll sleep all day and I'll stand watch all night."

"That's all right. Now, where you going to sleep?"

"In Ben Rogers' hayloft. He lets me, and so does his pap's nigger man, Uncle Jake. I tote water for Uncle Jake whenever he wants me to, and any time I ask him he gives me a little something to eat if he can spare it. That's a mighty good nigger, Tom. He likes me, becuz I don't ever act as if I was above him. Sometime I've set right down and eat *with* him. But you needn't tell that. A body's got to do things when he's awful hungry he wouldn't want to do as a steady thing."

"Well, if I don't want you in the daytime, I'll let you sleep. I won't come bothering around. Any time you see something's up, in the night, just skip right around and maow."

29

The first thing Tom heard on Friday morning was a glad piece of news—Judge Thatcher's family had come back to town the night before. Both Injun Joe and the treasure sunk into secondary importance for a moment, and Becky took the chief place in the boy's interest. He saw her and they had an exhausting good time playing "hispy" and "gully-keeper" with a crowd of their schoolmates. The day was completed and crowned in a peculiarly satisfactory way: Becky teased her mother to appoint the next day for the long-promised and long-delayed picnic, and she consented. The child's delight was boundless; and Tom's not more moderate. The invitations were sent out before sunset, and straightway the young folks of the village were thrown into a fever of preparation and pleasurable anticipation. Tom's excitement enabled him to keep awake until a pretty late hour, and he had good hopes of hearing Huck's "maow," and of having his treasure to astonish Becky and the picnickers with, next day; but he was disappointed. No signal came that night.

Morning came, eventually, and by ten or eleven o'clock a giddy and rollicking company were gathered at Judge Thatcher's, and everything was ready for a start. It was not the custom for elderly people to mar the picnics with their presence. The children were considered safe enough under the wings of a few young ladies of eighteen and a few young gentlemen of twenty-three or thereabouts. The old steam ferry-boat was chartered for the occasion; presently the gay throng filed up the main street laden with provision-baskets. Sid was sick and had to miss the fun; Mary remained at home to entertain him. The last thing Mrs. Thatcher said to Becky, was—

"You'll not get back till late. Perhaps you'd better stay all night with some of the girls that live near the ferry-landing, child."

"Then I'll stay with Susy Harper, mamma."

"Very well. And mind and behave yourself and don't be any trouble."

Presently, as they tripped along, Tom said to Becky:

"Say—I'll tell you what we'll do. 'Stead of going to Joe Harper's we'll climb right up the hill and stop at the Widow Douglas'. She'll have ice-cream! She has it most every day—dead loads of it. And she'll be awful glad to have us."

"O, that will be fun!"

Then Becky reflected a moment and said:

"But what will mamma say?"

"How'll she ever know?"

The girl turned the idea over in her mind, and said reluctantly:

"I reckon it's wrong—but—"

"But shucks! Your mother won't know, and so what's the harm? All she wants is that you'll be safe; and I bet you she'd 'a' said go there if she'd 'a' thought of it. I know she would!"

The Widow Douglas' splendid hospitality was a tempting bait. It and Tom's persuasions presently carried the day. So it was decided to say nothing to anybody about the night's programme. Presently it occurred to Tom that maybe Huck might come this very night and give the signal. The thought took a deal of the spirit out of his anticipations. Still he could not bear to give up the fun at Widow Douglas'. And why should he give it up, he reasoned—the signal did not come the night before, so why should it be any more likely to come tonight? The sure fun of the evening outweighed the uncertain treasure; and, boy-like, he determined to yield to the stronger inclination and not allow himself to think of the box of money another time that day.

Three miles below town the ferryboat stopped at the mouth of a woody hollow and tied up. The crowd swarmed ashore and soon the forest distances and craggy heights echoed far and near with shoutings and laughter. All the different ways of getting hot and tired were gone through with, and by and by the rovers straggled back to camp fortified with responsible appetites, and then the destruction of the good things began. After the feast there was a refreshing season of rest and chat in the shade of spreading oaks. By and by somebody shouted:

"Who's ready for the cave?"

Everybody was. Bundles of candles were procured, and straightway there was a general scamper up the hill. The mouth of the cave was up the hillside—an opening shaped like a letter A. Its massive oaken door stood unbarred. Within was a small chamber, chilly as an icehouse, and walled by Nature with solid limestone that was dewy with a cold sweat. It was romantic and mysterious to stand here in the deep gloom and look out upon the green valley shining in the sun. But the impressiveness of the situation quickly wore off, and the romping began again. The moment a candle was lighted there was a general rush upon the owner of it; a struggle and a gallant defence followed, but the candle was soon knocked down or blown out, and then there was a glad clamor of laughter and a new chase. But all things have an end. By and by the procession went filing down the steep descent of the main avenue, the flickering rank of lights dimly revealing the lofty walls of rock almost to their point of junction sixty feet overhead. This main avenue was not more than eight or ten feet wide. Every few steps other lofty and still narrower crevices branched from it on either hand—for McDougal's cave was but a vast labyrinth of crooked aisles that ran into each other and out again and led nowhere. It was said that one might wander days and nights together through its intricate tangle of rifts and chasms, and never find the end of the cave; and that he might go down, and down, and still down, into the earth, and it was just the same—labyrinth under labyrinth, and no end to any of them. No man "knew" the cave. That was an impossible thing. Most of the young men knew a portion of it, and it was not customary to venture much beyond this known portion. Tom Sawyer knew as much of the cave as any one.

The procession moved along the main avenue some three-quarters of a mile, and then groups and couples began to slip aside into branch avenues, fly along the dismal corridors, and take each other by surprise at points where the corridors joined again. Parties were able to elude each other for the space of half an hour without going beyond the "known" ground.

By and by, one group after another came straggling back to the mouth of the cave, panting, hilarious, smeared from head to foot with tallow drippings, daubed with clay, and entirely delighted with the success of the day. Then they were astonished to find that they had been taking no note of time and that night was about at hand. The clanging bell had been calling for half an hour. However, this sort of close to the day's adventures was romantic and therefore satisfactory. When the ferryboat with her wild freight pushed into the stream, nobody cared sixpence for the wasted time but the captain of the craft.

Huck was already upon his watch when the ferryboat's lights went glinting past the wharf. He heard no noise on board, for the young people were as subdued and still as people usually are who are nearly tired to death. He wondered what boat it was, and why she did not stop at the wharf—and then he dropped her out of his mind and put his attention upon his business. The night was growing cloudy and dark. Ten o'clock came, and the noise of vehicles ceased, scattered lights began to wink out, all straggling foot-passengers disappeared, the village betook itself to its slumbers and left the small watcher alone with the silence and the ghosts. Eleven o'clock came, and the tavern lights were put out; darkness everywhere, now. Huck waited what seemed a weary long time, but nothing happened. His faith was weakening. Was there any use? Was there really any use? Why not give it up and turn in?

A noise fell upon his ear. He was all attention in an instant. The alley door closed softly. He sprang to the corner of the brick store. The next moment two men brushed by him, and one seemed to have something under his arm. It must be that box! So they were going to remove the treasure. Why call Tom now? It would be absurd—the men would get away with the box and never be found again. No, he would stick to their wake and follow them; he would trust to the darkness for security from discovery. So communing with himself, Huck stepped out and glided along behind the men, cat-like, with bare feet, allowing them to keep just far enough ahead not to be invisible.

They moved up the river street three blocks, then turned to the left up a cross street. They went straight ahead, then, until they came to the path that led up Cardiff Hill; this they took. They passed by the old Welshman's house, halfway up the hill, without hesitating, and still climbed upward. Good, thought Huck, they will bury it in the old quarry. But they never stopped at the quarry. They passed on, up the summit. They plunged into the narrow path between the tall sumach bushes, and were at once hidden in the gloom. Huck closed up and shortened his distance, now, for they would never be able to see him. He trotted along awhile; then slackened his pace, fearing he was gaining too fast; moved on a piece, then stopped altogether; listened; no sound; none, save that he seemed to hear the beating of his own heart. The hooting of an owl came over the hill—ominous sound! But no footsteps. Heavens, was everything lost! He was about to spring with winged feet, when a man cleared his throat not four feet from him! Huck's heart shot into his throat, but he swallowed it again; and then he stood there shaking as if a dozen agues had taken charge of him at once, and so weak that he thought he must surely fall to the ground. He knew where he was. He knew he was within five steps of the stile leading into Widow Douglas' grounds. Very well, he thought, let them bury it there; it won't be hard to find.

Now there was a voice—a very low voice—Injun Joe's:

"Damn her, maybe she's got company—there's lights, late as it is."

"I can't see any."

This was that stranger's voice—the stranger of the haunted house. A deadly chill went to Huck's heart—this, then, was the "revenge" job! His thought was, to fly. Then he remembered that the Widow Douglas had been kind to him more than once, and maybe these men were going to murder her. He wished he dared venture to warn her; but he knew he didn't dare—they might come and catch him. He thought all this and more in the moment that elapsed between the stranger's remark and Injun Joe's next—which was—

"Because the bush is in your way. Now—this way—now you see, don't you?"

"Yes. Well, there *is* company there, I reckon. Better give it up."

"Give it up, and I just leaving this country forever! Give it up and maybe never have another chance. I tell you again, as I've told you before, I don't care for her swag—you may have it. But her husband was rough on me—many times he was rough on me—and mainly he was the justice of the peace that jugged me for a vagrant. And that ain't all. It ain't a millionth part of it! He had me *horsewhipped*!—horsewhipped in front of the jail, like a nigger!—with all the town looking on! *Horsewhipped*!—do you understand? He took advantage of me and died. But I'll take it out of *her*."

"Oh, don't kill her! Don't do that!"

"Kill? Who said anything about killing? I would kill *him* if he was here; but not her. When you want to get revenge on a woman you don't kill her—bosh! you go for her looks. You slit her nostrils—you notch her ears like a sow!"

"By God, that's—"

"Keep your opinion to yourself! It will be safest for you. I'll tie her to the bed. If she bleeds to death, is that my fault? I'll not cry, if she does. My friend, you'll help me in this thing—for *my* sake—that's why you're here—I mightn't be able alone. If you flinch, I'll kill you. Do you understand that?

And if I have to kill you, I'll kill her—and then I reckon nobody'll ever know much about who done this business."

"Well, if it's got to be done, let's get at it. The quicker the better—I'm all in a shiver."

"Do it *now*? And company there? Look here—I'll get suspicious of you, first thing you know. No—we'll wait till the lights are out—there's no hurry."

Huck felt that a silence was going to ensue—a thing still more awful than any amount of murderous talk; so he held his breath and stepped gingerly back; planted his foot carefully and firmly, after balancing, one-legged, in a precarious way and almost toppling over, first on one side and then on the other. He took another step back, with the same elaboration and the same risks; then another and another, and—a twig snapped under his foot! His breath stopped and he listened. There was no sound—the stillness was perfect. His gratitude was measureless. Now he turned in his tracks, between the walls of sumach bushes—turned himself as carefully as if he were a ship—and then stepped quickly but cautiously along. When he emerged at the quarry he felt secure, and so he picked up his nimble heels and flew. Down, down he sped, till he reached the Welshman's. He banged at the door, and presently the heads of the old man and his two stalwart sons were thrust from windows.

"What's the row there? Who's banging? What do you want?"

"Let me in—quick! I'll tell everything."

"Why, who are you?"

"Huckleberry Finn—quick, let me in!"

"Huckleberry Finn, indeed! It ain't a name to open many doors, I judge! But let him in, lads, and let's see what's the trouble."

"Please don't ever tell I told you," were Huck's first words when he got in. "Please don't—I'd be killed, sure—but the widow's been good friends to me sometimes, and I want to tell—I *will* tell if you'll promise you won't ever say it was me."

"By George, he *has* got something to tell, or he wouldn't act so!" exclaimed the old man; "out with it and nobody here'll ever tell, lad."

Three minutes later the old man and his sons, well armed, were up the hill, and just entering the sumach path on tiptoe, their weapons in their hands. Huck accompanied them no further. He hid behind a great bowlder and fell to listening. There was a lagging, anxious silence, and then all of a sudden there was an explosion of firearms and a cry.

Huck waited for no particulars. He sprang away and sped down the hill as fast as his legs could carry him.

30

As the earliest suspicion of dawn appeared on Sunday morning, Huck came groping up the hill and rapped gently at the old Welshman's door. The inmates were asleep, but it was a sleep that was set on a hair-trigger, on account of the exciting episode of the night. A call came from a window:

"Who's there!"

Huck's scared voice answered in a low tone:

"Please let me in! It's only Huck Finn!"

"It's a name that can open this door night or day, lad!—and welcome!"

These were strange words to the vagabond boy's ears, and the pleasantest he had ever heard. He could not recollect that the closing word had ever been applied in his case before. The door was quickly unlocked, and he entered. Huck was given a seat and the old man and his brace of tall sons speedily dressed themselves.

"Now, my boy, I hope you're good and hungry, because breakfast will be ready as soon as the sun's up, and we'll have a piping hot one, too—make yourself easy about that! I and the boys hoped you'd turn up and stop here last night."

"I was awful scared," said Huck, "and I run. I took out when the pistols went off, and I didn't stop for three mile. I've come now becuz I wanted to know about it, you know; and I come before daylight becuz I didn't want to run across them devils, even if they was dead."

"Well, poor chap, you do look as if you'd had a hard night of it—but there's a bed here for you when you've had your breakfast. No, they ain't dead, lad—we are sorry enough for that. You see we knew right where to put our hands on them, by your description; so we crept along on tiptoe till we got within fifteen feet of them—dark as a cellar that sumach path was—and just then I found I was going to sneeze. It was the meanest kind of luck! I tried to keep it back, but no use—'twas bound to come, and it did come! I was in the lead with my pistol raised, and when the sneeze started those scoundrels a-rustling to get out of the path, I sung out, 'Fire boys!' and blazed away at the place where the rustling was. So did the boys. But they were off in a jiffy, those villains, and we after them, down through the woods. I judge we never touched them. They fired a shot apiece as they started, but their bullets whizzed by and didn't do us any harm. As soon as we lost the sound of their feet we quit chasing, and went down and stirred up the constables. They got a posse together, and went off to guard the river bank, and as soon as it is light the sheriff and a gang are going to beat up the woods. My boys will be with them presently. I wish we had some sort of description of those rascals—'twould help a good deal. But you couldn't see what they were like, in the dark, lad, I suppose?"

"Oh yes; I saw them downtown and follered them."

"Splendid! Describe them—describe them, my boy!"

"One's the old deaf and dumb Spaniard that's ben around here once or twice, and t'other's a mean-looking, ragged—"

"That's enough, lad, we know the men! Happened on them in the woods back of the widow's one day, and they slunk away. Off with you, boys, and tell the sheriff—get your breakfast tomorrow morning!"

The Welshman's sons departed at once. As they were leaving the room Huck sprang up and exclaimed:

"Oh, please don't tell *any*body it was me that blowed on them! Oh, please!"

"All right if you say it, Huck, but you ought to have the credit of what you did."

"Oh no, no! Please don't tell!"

When the young men were gone, the old Welshman said:

"They won't tell—and I won't. But why don't you want it known?"

Huck would not explain, further than to say that he already knew too much about one of those men and would not have the man know that he knew anything against him for the whole world—he would be killed for knowing it, sure.

The old man promised secrecy once more, and said:

"How did you come to follow these fellows, lad? Were they looking suspicious?"

Huck was silent while he framed a duly cautious reply. Then he said:

"Well, you see, I'm a kind of a hard lot—least everybody says so, and I don't see nothing agin it—and sometimes I can't sleep much, on account of thinking about it and sort of trying to strike out a new way of doing. That was the way of it last night. I couldn't sleep, and so I come along upstreet 'bout midnight, a-turning it all over, and when I got to that old shackly brick store by the Temperance Tavern, I backed up agin the wall to have another think. Well, just then along comes these two chaps slipping along close by me, with something under their arm, and I reckoned they'd stole it. One was a-smoking, and t'other one wanted a light; so they stopped right before me and the cigars lit up their faces and I see that the big one was the deaf and dumb Spaniard, by his white whiskers and the patch on his eye, and t'other one was a rusty, ragged-looking devil."

"Could you see the rags by the light of the cigars?"

This staggered Huck for a moment. Then he said:

"Well, I don't know—but somehow it seems as if I did."

"Then they went on, and you—"

"Follered 'em—yes. That was it. I wanted to see what was up—they sneaked along so. I dogged 'em to the widder's stile, and stood in the dark and heard the ragged one beg for the widder, and the Spaniard swear he'd spile her looks just as I told you and your two—"

"What! The *deaf and dumb* man said all that!"

Huck had made another terrible mistake! He was trying his best to keep the old man from getting the faintest hint of who the Spaniard might be, and yet his tongue seemed determined to get him into trouble in spite of all he could do. He made several efforts to creep out of his scrape, but the old man's eye was upon him and he made blunder after blunder. Presently the Welshman said:

"My boy, don't be afraid of me. I wouldn't hurt a hair of your head for all the world. No—I'd protect you—I'd protect you. This Spaniard is not deaf and dumb; you've let that slip without intending it; you can't cover that up now. You know something about that Spaniard that you want to keep dark. Now trust me—tell me what it is, and trust me—I won't betray you."

Huck looked into the old man's honest eyes a moment, then bent over and whispered in his ear:

"'Tain't a Spaniard—it's Injun Joe!"

The Welshman almost jumped out of his chair. In a moment he said:

"It's all plain enough, now. When you talked about notching ears and slitting noses I judged that that was your own embellishment, because white men don't take that sort of revenge. But an Injun! That's a different matter altogether."

During breakfast the talk went on, and in the course of it the old man said that the last thing which he and his sons had done, before going to bed, was to get a lantern and examine the stile and its vicinity for marks of blood. They found none, but captured a bulky bundle of—

"Of *what*?"

If the words had been lightning they could not have leaped with a more stunning suddenness from Huck's blanched lips. His eyes were staring wide, now, and his breath suspended—waiting for the answer. The Welshman started—stared in return—three seconds—five seconds—ten—then replied:

"Of burglar's tools. Why, what's the *matter* with you?"

Huck sank back, panting gently, but deeply, unutterably grateful. The Welshman eyed him gravely, curiously—and presently said:

"Yes, burglar's tools. That appears to relieve you a good deal. But what did give you that turn? What were *you* expecting we'd found?"

Huck was in a close place—the inquiring eye was upon him—he would have given anything for material for a plausible answer—nothing suggested itself—the inquiring eye was boring deeper and deeper—a senseless reply offered—there was no time to weigh it, so at a venture he uttered it—feebly:

"Sunday-school books, maybe."

Poor Huck was too distressed to smile, but the old man laughed loud and joyously, shook up the details of his anatomy from head to foot, and ended by saying that such a laugh was money in a-man's pocket, because it cut down the doctor's bill like everything. Then he added:

"Poor old chap, you're white and jaded—you ain't well a bit—no wonder you're a little flighty and off your balance. But you'll come out of it. Rest and sleep will fetch you out all right, I hope."

Huck was irritated to think he had been such a goose and betrayed such a suspicious excitement, for he had dropped the idea that the parcel brought from the tavern was the treasure, as soon as he had heard the talk at the widow's stile. He had only thought it was not the treasure, however—he had not known that it wasn't—and so the suggestion of a captured bundle was too much for his self-possession. But on the whole he felt glad the little episode had happened, for now he knew beyond all question that that bundle was not *the* bundle, and so his mind was at rest and exceedingly comfortable. In fact, everything seemed to be drifting just in the right direction, now; the treasure must be still in No. 2, the men would be captured and jailed that day, and he and Tom could seize the gold that night without any trouble or any fear of interruption.

Just as breakfast was completed there was a knock at the door. Huck jumped for a hiding place, for he had no mind to be connected even remotely with the late event. The Welshman admitted several ladies and gentlemen, among them the Widow Douglas, and noticed that groups of citizens were climbing up the hill—to stare at the stile. So the news had spread.

The Welshman had to tell the story of the night to the visitors. The widow's gratitude for her preservation was outspoken.

"Don't say a word about it, madam. There's another that you're more beholden to than you are to me and my boys, maybe, but he don't allow me to tell his name. We wouldn't have been there but for him."

Of course this excited a curiosity so vast that it almost belittled the main matter—but the Welshman allowed it to eat into the vitals of his visitors, and through them be transmitted to the whole town, for he refused to part with his secret. When all else had been learned, the widow said:

"I went to sleep reading in bed and slept straight through all that noise. Why didn't you come and wake me?"

"We judged it warn't worth while. Those fellows warn't likely to come again—they hadn't any tools left to work with, and what was the use of waking you up and scaring you to death? My three negro men stood guard at your house all the rest of the night. They've just come back."

More visitors came, and the story had to be told and retold for a couple of hours more.

There was no Sabbath-school during day-school vacation, but everybody was early at church. The stirring event was well canvassed. News came that not a sign of the two villains had been yet discovered. When the sermon was finished, Judge Thatcher's wife dropped alongside of Mrs. Harper as she moved down the aisle with the crowd and said:

"Is my Becky going to sleep all day? I just expected she would be tired to death."

"Your Becky?"

"Yes," with a startled look—"didn't she stay with you last night?"

"Why, no."

Mrs. Thatcher turned pale, and sank into a pew, just as Aunt Polly, talking briskly with a friend, passed by. Aunt Polly said:

"Goodmorning, Mrs. Thatcher. Goodmorning, Mrs. Harper. I've got a boy that's turned up missing. I reckon my Tom stayed at your house last night—one of you. And now he's afraid to come to church. I've got to settle with him."

Mrs. Thatcher shook her head feebly and turned paler than ever.

"He didn't stay with us," said Mrs. Harper, beginning to look uneasy. A marked anxiety came into Aunt Polly's face.

"Joe Harper, have you seen my Tom this morning?"

"No'm."

"When did you see him last?"

Joe tried to remember, but was not sure he could say. The people had stopped moving out of church. Whispers passed along, and a boding uneasiness took possession of every countenance. Children were anxiously questioned, and young teachers. They all said they had not noticed whether Tom and Becky were on board the ferryboat on the homeward trip; it was dark; no one thought of inquiring if any one was missing. One young man finally blurted out his fear that they were still in the cave! Mrs. Thatcher swooned away. Aunt Polly fell to crying and wringing her hands.

The alarm swept from lip to lip, from group to group, from street to street, and within five minutes the bells were wildly clanging and the whole town was up! The Cardiff Hill episode sank into instant insignificance, the burglars were forgotten, horses were saddled, skiffs were manned, the ferryboat ordered out, and before the horror was half an hour old, two hundred men were pouring down highroad and river toward the cave.

Tom and Becky stir up the Town

All the long afternoon the village seemed empty and dead. Many women visited Aunt Polly and Mrs. Thatcher and tried to comfort them. They cried with them, too, and that was still better than words. All the tedious night the town waited for news; but when the morning dawned at last, all the word that came was, "Send more candles—and send food." Mrs. Thatcher was almost crazed; and Aunt Polly, also. Judge Thatcher sent messages of hope and encouragement from the cave, but they conveyed no real cheer.

The old Welshman came home toward daylight, spattered with candle-grease, smeared with clay, and almost worn out. He found Huck still in the bed that had been provided for him, and delirious with fever. The physicians were all at the cave, so the Widow Douglas came and took charge of the patient. She said she would do her best by him, because, whether he was good, bad, or indifferent, he was the Lord's, and nothing that was the Lord's was a thing to be neglected. The Welshman said Huck had good spots in him, and the widow said—

"You can depend on it. That's the Lord's mark. He don't leave it off. He never does. Puts it somewhere on every creature that comes from his hands."

Early in the forenoon parties of jaded men began to straggle into the village, but the strongest of the citizens continued searching. All the news that could be gained was that remotenesses of the cavern were being ransacked that had never been visited before; that every corner and crevice was going to be thoroughly searched; that wherever one wandered through the maze of passages, lights were to be seen flitting hither and thither in the distance, and shoutings and pistol-shots sent their hollow reverberations to the ear down the sombre aisles. In one place, far from the section usually traversed by tourists, the names "BECKY & TOM" had been found traced upon the rocky wall with candle-smoke, and near at hand a grease-soiled bit of ribbon. Mrs. Thatcher recognized the ribbon and cried over it. She said it was the last relic she should ever have of her child; and that no other memorial of her could ever be so precious, because this one parted latest from the living body before the awful death came. Some said that now and then, in the cave, a far-away speck of light would glimmer, and then a glorious shout would burst forth and a score of men go trooping down the echoing aisle—and then a sickening disappointment always followed; the children were not there; it was only a searcher's light.

Three dreadful days and nights dragged their tedious hours along, and the village sank into a hopeless stupor. No one had heart for anything. The accidental discovery, just made, that the proprietor of the Temperance Tavern kept liquor on his premises, scarcely fluttered the public pulse, tremendous as the fact was. In a lucid interval, Huck feebly led up to the subject of taverns, and finally asked—dimly dreading the worst—if anything had been discovered at the Temperance Tavern since he had been ill.

"Yes," said the widow.

Huck started up in bed, wild-eyed: "What? What was it?"

"Liquor!—and the place has been shut up. Lie down, child—what a turn you did give me!"

"Only tell me just one thing—only just one—please! Was it Tom Sawyer that found it?"

The widow burst into tears. "Hush, hush, child, hush! I've told you before, you must *not* talk. You are very, very sick!"

Then nothing but liquor had been found; there would have been a great

Tom's Marks

powwow if it had been the gold. So the treasure was gone forever—gone forever! But what could she be crying about? Curious that she should cry.

These thoughts worked their dim way through Huck's mind, and under the weariness they gave him he fell asleep. The widow said to herself:

"There—he's asleep, poor wreck. Tom Sawyer find it! Pity but somebody could find Tom Sawyer! Ah, there ain't many left, now, that's got hope enough, or strength enough, either, to go on searching."

31

Now to return to Tom and Becky's share in the picnic. They tripped along the murky aisles with the rest of the company, visiting the familiar wonders of the cave—wonders dubbed with rather over-descriptive names, such as "The Drawing Room," "The Cathedral," "Aladdin's Palace," and so on. Presently the hide-and-seek frolicking began, and Tom and Becky engaged in it with zeal until the exertion began to grow a trifle wearisome; then they wandered down a sinuous avenue holding their candles aloft and reading the tangled webwork of names, dates, postoffice addresses, and mottoes with which the rocky walls had been frescoed (in candle-smoke). Still drifting along and talking, they scarcely noticed that they were now in a part of the cave whose walls were not frescoed. They smoked their own names under an overhanging shelf and moved on. Presently they came to a place where a little stream of water, trickling over a ledge and carrying a limestone sediment with it, had, in the slow-dragging ages, formed a laced and ruffled Niagara in gleaming and imperishable stone. Tom squeezed his small body behind it in order to illuminate it for Becky's gratification. He found that it curtained a sort of steep natural stairway which was enclosed between narrow walls, and at once the ambition to be a discoverer seized him.

Wonders of the Cave

Becky responded to his call, and they made a smoke-mark for future guidance, and started upon their quest. They wound this way and that, far down into the secret depths of the cave, made another mark, and branched off in search of novelties to tell the upper world about. In one place they found a spacious cavern, from whose ceiling depended a multitude of shining stalactites of the length and circumference of a man's leg; they walked all about it, wondering and admiring, and presently left it by one of the numerous passages that opened into it. This shortly brought them to a bewitching spring, whose basin was incrusted with a frostwork of glittering crystals; it was in the midst of a cavern whose walls were supported by many fantastic pillars which had been formed by the joining of great stalactites and stalagmites together, the result of the ceaseless water-drip of centuries. Under the roof vast knots of bats had packed themselves together, thousands in a bunch; the lights disturbed the creatures and they came flocking down by hundreds, squeaking and darting furiously at the candles. Tom knew their ways and the danger of this sort of conduct. He seized Becky's hand and hurried her into the first corridor that offered; and none too soon, for a bat struck Becky's light out with its wing while she was passing out of the cavern. The bats chased the children a good distance; but the fugitives plunged into every new passage that offered, and at last got rid of the perilous things. Tom found a subterranean lake, shortly, which stretched its dim length away until its shape was lost in the shadows. He wanted to explore its borders, but concluded that it would be best to sit down and rest awhile, first. Now, for the first time, the deep stillness of the place laid a clammy hand upon the spirits of the children. Becky said—

"Why, I didn't notice, but it seems ever so long since I heard any of the others."

"Come to think, Becky, we are away down below them—and I don't know how far away north, or south, or east, or whichever it is. We couldn't hear them here."

Becky grew apprehensive.

"I wonder how long we've been down here, Tom? We better start back."

Attacked by Natives

"Yes, I reckon we better. P'raps we better."

"Can you find the way, Tom? It's all a mixed-up crookedness to me."

"I reckon I could find it—but then the bats. If they put our candles out it will be an awful fix. Let's try some other way, so as not to go through there."

"Well. But I hope we won't get lost. It would be so awful!" and the girl shuddered at the thought of the dreadful possibilities.

They started through a corridor, and traversed it in silence a long way, glancing at each new opening, to see if there was anything familiar about the look of it; but they were all strange. Every time Tom made an examination, Becky would watch his face for an encouraging sign, and he would say cheerily:

"Oh, it's all right. This ain't the one, but we'll come to it right away!"

But he felt less and less hopeful with each failure, and presently began to turn off into diverging avenues at sheer random, in desperate hope of finding the one that was wanted. He still said it was "all right," but there was such a leaden dread at his heart that the words had lost their ring and sounded just as if he had said, "All is lost!" Becky clung to his side in an anguish of fear, and tried hard to keep back the tears, but they would come. At last she said:

"O, Tom, never mind the bats, let's go back that way! We seem to get worse and worse off all the time."

Tom stopped.

"Listen!" said he.

Profound silence; silence so deep that even their breathings were conspicuous in the hush. Tom shouted. The call went echoing down the empty aisles and died out in the distance in a faint sound that resembled a ripple of mocking laughter.

"Oh, don't do it again, Tom, it is too horrid," said Becky.

"It is horrid, but I better, Becky; they might hear us, you know," and he shouted again.

The "might" was even a chillier horror than the ghostly laughter, it so confessed a perishing hope. The children stood still and listened; but there was no result. Tom turned upon the back track at once, and hurried his steps. It was but a little while before a certain indecision in his manner revealed another fearful fact to Becky—he could not find his way back!

"O, Tom, you didn't make any marks!"

"Becky, I was such a fool! Such a fool! I never thought we might want to come back! No—I can't find the way. It's all mixed up."

"Tom, Tom, we're lost! we're lost! We never can get out of this awful place! Oh, why *did* we ever leave the others!"

Despair

She sank to the ground and burst into such a frenzy of crying that Tom was appalled with the idea that she might die, or lose her reason. He sat down by her and put his arms around her; she buried her face in his bosom, she clung to him, she poured out her terrors, her unavailing regrets, and the far echoes turned them all to jeering laughter. Tom begged her to pluck up hope again, and she said she could not. He fell to blaming and abusing himself for getting her into this miserable situation; this had a better effect. She said she would try to hope again, she would get up and follow wherever he might lead if only he would not talk like that any more. For he was no more to blame than she, she said.

So they moved on again—aimlessly—simply at random—all they could do was to move, keep moving. For a little while, hope made a show of reviving—not with any reason to back it, but only because it is its nature to revive when the spring has not been taken out of it by age and familiarity with failure.

By and by Tom took Becky's candle and blew it out. This economy meant so much! Words were not needed. Becky understood, and her hope died again. She knew that Tom had a whole candle and three or four pieces in his pockets—yet he must economise.

By and by, fatigue began to assert its claims; the children tried to pay attention, for it was dreadful to think of sitting down when time was grown to be so precious, moving, in some direction, in any direction, was at least progress and might bear fruit; but to sit down was to invite death and shorten its pursuit.

At last Becky's frail limbs refused to carry her farther. She sat down. Tom rested with her, and they talked of home, and the friends there, and the comfortable beds and, above all, the light! Becky cried, and Tom tried to think of some way of comforting her, but all his encouragements were grown threadbare with use, and sounded like sarcasms. Fatigue bore so heavily upon Becky that she drowsed off to sleep. Tom was grateful. He sat looking into her drawn face and saw it grow smooth and natural under the influence of pleasant dreams; and by and by a smile dawned and rested there. The peaceful face reflected somewhat of peace and healing into his own spirit, and his thoughts wandered away to bygone times and dreamy memories. While he was deep in his musings, Becky woke up with a breezy little laugh—but it was stricken dead upon her lips, and a groan followed it.

"Oh, how *could* I sleep! I wish I never, never had waked! No! No, I don't, Tom! Don't look so! I won't say it again."

"I'm glad you've slept, Becky; you'll feel rested, now, and we'll find the way out."

"We can try, Tom; but I've seen such a beautiful country in my dream. I reckon we are going there."

"Maybe not, maybe not. Cheer up, Becky, and let's go on trying."

They rose up and wandered along, hand in hand and hopeless. They tried to estimate how long they had been in the cave, but all they knew was that it seemed days and weeks, and yet it was plain that this could not be, for their candles were not gone yet. A long time after this—they could not tell how long—Tom said they must go softly and listen for dripping water—they must find a spring. They found one presently, and Tom said it was time to rest again. Both were cruelly tired, yet Becky said she thought she could go a little farther. She was surprised to hear Tom dissent. She could not understand it. They sat down, and Tom fastened his candle to the wall in front of them with some clay. Thought was soon busy; nothing was said for some time. Then Becky broke the silence:

"Tom, I am so hungry!"

Tom took something out of his pocket.

"Do you remember this?" said he.

Becky almost smiled.

"It's our wedding-cake, Tom."

"Yes—I wish it was as big as a barrel, for it's all we've got."

"I saved it from the picnic for us to dream on, Tom, the way grownup people do with wedding-cake—but it'll be our—"

She dropped the sentence where it was. Tom divided the cake and Becky ate with good appetite, while Tom nibbled at his moiety. There was abundance of cold water to finish the feast with. By and by Becky suggested that they move on again. Tom was silent a moment. Then he said:

"Becky, can you bear it if I tell you something?"

Becky's face paled, but she thought she could.

"Well, then, Becky, we must stay here, where there's water to drink. That little piece is our last candle!"

Becky gave loose to tears and wailings. Tom did what he could to comfort her, but with little effect. At length Becky said:

"Tom!"

"Well, Becky?"

"They'll miss us and hunt for us!"

"Yes, they will! Certainly they will!"

"Maybe they're hunting for us now, Tom."

"Why I reckon maybe they are. I hope they are."

"When would they miss us, Tom?"

"When they get back to the boat, I reckon."

"Tom, it might be dark then—would they notice we hadn't come?"

"I don't know. But anyway, your mother would miss you as soon as they got home."

A frightened look in Becky's face brought Tom to his senses and he saw that he had made a blunder. Becky was not to have gone home that night! The children became silent and thoughtful. In a moment a new burst of grief from Becky showed Tom that the thing in his mind had struck hers also—that the Sabbath morning might be half spent before Mrs. Thatcher discovered that Becky was not at Mrs. Harper's.

The children fastened their eyes upon their bit of candle and watched it melt slowly and pitilessly away; saw the half inch of wick stand alone at last; saw the feeble flame rise and fall, climb the thin column of smoke, linger at its top a moment, and then—the horror of utter darkness reigned!

How long afterward it was that Becky came to a slow consciousness that she was crying in Tom's arms, neither could tell. All that they knew was, that after what seemed a mighty stretch of time, both awoke out of a dead stupor of sleep and resumed their miseries once more. Tom said it might be Sunday, now—maybe Monday. He tried to get Becky to talk, but her sorrows were too oppressive, all her hopes were gone. Tom said that they must have been missed long ago, and no doubt the search was going on. He would shout and maybe some one would come. He tried it; but in the darkness the distant echoes sounded so hideously that he tried it no more.

The hours wasted away, and hunger came to torment the captives again. A portion of Tom's half of the cake was left; they divided and ate it. But they seemed hungrier than before. The poor morsel of food only whetted desire.

By and by Tom said:

"*Sh*! Did you hear that?"

Both held their breath and listened. There was a sound like the faintest, far-off shout. Instantly Tom answered it, and leading Becky by the hand, started groping down the corridor in its direction. Presently he listened again; again the sound was heard, and apparently a little nearer.

"It's them!" said Tom; "they're coming! Come along, Becky—we're all right now!"

The joy of the prisoners was almost overwhelming. Their speed was slow, however, because pitfalls were somewhat common, and had to be guarded against. They shortly came to one and had to stop. It might be three feet deep, it might be a hundred—there was no passing it at any rate. Tom got down on his breast and reached as far down as he could. No bottom. They must stay there and wait until the searchers came. They listened; evidently the distant shoutings were growing more distant! a moment or two more and they had gone altogether. The heart-sinking misery of it! Tom whooped until he was hoarse, but it was of no use. He talked hopefully to Becky; but an age of anxious waiting passed and no sounds came again.

The children groped their way back to the spring. The weary time dragged on; they slept again, and awoke famished and woe-stricken. Tom believed it must be Tuesday by this time.

Now an idea struck him. There were some side passages near at hand. It would be better to explore some of these than bear the weight of the heavy time in idleness. He took a kite-line from his pocket, tied it to a projection, and he and Becky started, Tom in the lead, unwinding the line as he groped along. At the end of twenty steps the corridor ended in a "jumping-off place." Tom got down on his knees and felt below, and then as far around the corner as he could reach with his hands conveniently; he made an effort to stretch yet a little farther to the right, and at that moment, not twenty yards away, a human hand, holding a candle, appeared from behind a rock! Tom lifted up a glorious shout, and instantly that hand was followed by the body it belonged to—Injun Joe's! Tom was paralyzed; he could not move. He was vastly gratified the next moment, to see the "Spaniard" take to his heels and get himself out of sight. Tom wondered that Joe had not recognized his voice and come over and killed him for testifying in court.

But the echoes must have disguised the voice. Without doubt, that was it, he reasoned. Tom's fright weakened every muscle in his body. He said to himself that if he had strength enough to get back to the spring he would stay there, and nothing should tempt him to run the risk of meeting Injun Joe again. He was careful to keep from Becky what it was he had seen. He told her he had only shouted "for luck."

But hunger and wretchedness rise superior to fears in the long run. Another tedious wait at the spring and another long sleep brought changes. The children awoke tortured with a raging hunger. Tom believed that it must be Wednesday or Thursday or even Friday or Saturday, now, and that the search had been given over. He proposed to explore another passage. He felt willing to risk Injun Joe and all other terrors. But Becky was very weak. She had sunk into a dreary apathy and would not be roused. She said she would wait, now, where she was, and die—it would not be long. She told Tom to go with the kite-line and explore if he chose; but she implored him to come back every little while and speak to her; and she made him promise that when the awful time came, he would stay by her and hold her hand until all was over.

Tom kissed her, with a choking sensation in his throat, and made a show of being confident of finding the searchers or an escape from the cave; then he took the kite-line in his hand and went groping down one of the passages on his hands and knees, distressed with hunger and sick with bodings of coming doom.

32

Tuesday afternoon came, and waned to the twilight. The village of St. Petersburg still mourned. The lost children had not been found. Public prayers had been offered up for them, and many and many a private prayer that had the petitioner's whole heart in it; but still no good news came from the cave. The majority of the searchers had given up the quest and gone back to their daily avocations, saying that it was plain the children could never be found. Mrs. Thatcher was very ill, and a great part of the time delirious. People said it was heartbreaking to hear her call her child, and raise her head and listen a whole minute at a time, then lay it wearily down again with a moan. Aunt Polly had drooped into a settled melancholy, and her grey hair had grown almost white. The village went to its rest on Tuesday night, sad and forlorn.

Away in the middle of the night a wild peal burst from the village bells, and in a moment the streets were swarming with frantic half-clad people, who shouted, "Turn out! turn out! they're found! they're found!" Tin pans and horns were added to the din, the population massed itself and moved toward the river, met the children coming in an open carriage drawn by shouting citizens, thronged around it, joined its homeward march, and swept magnificently up the main street roaring huzzah after huzzah!

The village was illuminated; nobody went to bed again; it was the greatest night the little town had ever seen. During the first half-hour a procession of villagers filed through Judge Thatcher's house, seized the saved ones and kissed them, squeezed Mrs. Thatcher's hand, tried to speak but couldn't—and drifted out raining tears all over the place.

Aunt Polly's happiness was complete, and Mrs. Thatcher's nearly so. It would be complete, however, as soon as the messenger dispatched with the great news to the cave should get the word to her husband. Tom lay upon a sofa with an eager auditory about him and told the history of the wonderful adventure, putting in many striking additions to adorn it withal; and closed with a description of how he left Becky and went on an exploring expedition; how he followed two avenues as far as his kite-line would reach; how he followed a third to the fullest stretch of the kite-line, and was about to turn back when he glimpsed a far-off speck that looked like daylight; dropped the line and groped toward it, pushed his head and shoulders through a small hole, and saw the broad Mississippi rolling by!

The Escape from the Cave

And if it had only happened to be night he would not have seen that speck of daylight and would not have explored that passage any more! He told how he went back for Becky and broke the good news and she told him not to fret her with such stuff, for she was tired, and knew she was going to die, and wanted to. He described how he laboured with her and convinced her; and how she almost died for joy when she had groped to where she actually saw the blue speck of daylight; how he pushed his way out at the hole and then helped her out; how they sat there and cried for gladness; how some men came along in a skiff and Tom hailed them and told them their situation and their famished condition; how the men didn't believe the wild tale at first, "because," said they, "you are five miles down the river below the valley the cave is in"—then took them aboard, rowed to a house, gave them supper, made them rest till two or three hours after dark and then brought them home.

Before day-dawn, Judge Thatcher and the handful of searchers with him were tracked out, in the cave, by the twine clews they had strung behind them, and informed of the great news.

Three days and nights of toil and hunger in the cave were not to be shaken off at once, as Tom and Becky soon discovered. They were bedridden all of Wednesday and Thursday, and seemed to grow more and more tired and worn, all the time. Tom got about, a little, on Thursday, was downtown Friday, and nearly as whole as ever Saturday; but Becky did not leave her room until Sunday, and then she looked as if she had passed through a wasting illness.

Tom learned of Huck's sickness and went to see him on Friday, but could not be admitted to the bedroom; neither could he on Saturday or Sunday. He was admitted daily after that, but was warned to keep still about his adventure and introduce no exciting topic. The Widow Douglas stayed by to see that he obeyed. At home Tom learned of the Cardiff Hill event; also that the "ragged man's" body had eventually been found in the river near the ferry-landing; he had been drowned while trying to escape, perhaps.

About a fortnight after Tom's rescue from the cave, he started off to visit Huck, who had grown plenty strong enough, now, to hear exciting talk, and Tom had some that would interest him, he thought. Judge Thatcher's house was on Tom's way, and he stopped to see Becky. The Judge and some friends set Tom to talking, and some one asked him ironically if he wouldn't like to go to the cave again. Tom said he thought he wouldn't mind it. The Judge said:

"Well, there are others just like you, Tom, I've not the least doubt. But we have taken care of that. Nobody will get lost in that cave any more."

"Why?"

"Because I had its big door sheathed with boiler iron two weeks ago, and triple-locked—and I've got the keys."

Tom turned as white as a sheet.

"What's the matter, boy! Here, run, somebody! Fetch a glass of water!"

The water was brought and thrown into Tom's face.

"Ah, now you're all right. What was the matter with you, Tom?"

"Oh, Judge, Injun Joe's in the cave!"

33

Within a few minutes the news had spread, and a dozen skiff-loads of men were on their way to McDougal's cave, and the ferryboat, well filled with passengers, soon followed. Tom Sawyer was in the skiff that bore Judge Thatcher.

When the cave door was unlocked, a sorrowful sight presented itself in the dim twilight of the place. Injun Joe lay stretched upon the ground, dead, with his face close to the crack of the door, as if his longing eyes had been fixed, to the latest moment, upon the light and the cheer of the free world outside. Tom was touched, for he knew by his own experience how this wretch had suffered. His pity was moved, but nevertheless he felt an abounding sense of relief and security, now, which revealed to him in a degree which he had not fully appreciated before how vast a weight of dread had been lying upon him since the day he lifted his voice against this bloody-minded outcast.

Injun Joe's bowie-knife lay close by, its blade broken in two. The great foundation-beam of the door had been chipped and hacked through, with tedious labour; useless labour, too, it was, for the native rock formed a sill outside it, and upon that stubborn material the knife had wrought no effect; the only damage done was to the knife itself. But if there had been no stony obstruction there the labour would have been useless still, for if the beam had been wholly cut away Injun Joe could not have squeezed his body under the door, and he knew it. So he had only hacked that place in order to be doing something—in order to pass the weary time—in order to employ his tortured faculties. Ordinarily one could find half a dozen bits of candle stuck around in the crevices of this vestibule, left there by tourists; but there were none now. The prisoner had searched them out and eaten them. He had also contrived to catch a few bats, and these, also, he had eaten, leaving only their claws. The poor unfortunate had starved to death. In one place, near at hand, a stalagmite had been slowly growing up from the ground for ages, builded by the water-drip from a stalactite overhead. The captive had broken off the stalagmite, and upon the stump had placed a stone, wherein he had scooped a shallow hollow to catch the precious drop that fell once in every three minutes with the dreary regularity of a clock-tick—a dessertspoonful once in four and twenty hours. That drop was falling when the Pyramids were new; when Troy fell; when the foundations of Rome were laid; when Christ was crucified; when the Conqueror created the British empire; when Columbus sailed; when the massacre at Lexington was "news." It is falling now; it will still be falling when all these things shall have sunk down the afternoon of history, and the twilight of tradition, and been swallowed up in the thick night of oblivion. Has everything a purpose and a mission? Did this drop fall patiently during five thousand years to be ready for this flitting human insect's need? and has it another important object to accomplish ten thousand years to come? No matter. It is many and many a year since the hapless half-breed scooped out the stone to catch the priceless drops, but to this day the tourist stares longest at that pathetic stone and that slow-dropping water when he comes to see the wonders of McDougal's cave. Injun Joe's cup stands first in the list of the cavern's marvels; even "Aladdin's Palace" cannot rival it.

Injun Joe was buried near the mouth of the cave; and people flocked there in boats and wagons from the towns and from all the farms and hamlets for seven miles around; they brought their children, and all sorts of provisions, and confessed that they had had almost as satisfactory a time at the funeral as they could have had at the hanging.

This funeral stopped the further growth of one thing—the petition to the governor for Injun Joe's pardon. The petition had been largely signed; many tearful and eloquent meetings had been held, and a committee of sappy women been appointed to go in deep mourning and wail around the governor, and implore him to be a merciful ass and trample his duty under foot. Injun Joe was believed to have killed five citizens of the village, but what of that? If he had been Satan himself there would have been plenty of weaklings ready to scribble their names to a pardon-petition, and drip a tear on it from their permanently impaired and leaky water-works.

The morning after the funeral Tom took Huck to a private place to have an important talk. Huck had learned all about Tom's adventure from the

Welshman and the Widow Douglas, by this time, but Tom said he reckoned there was one thing they had not told him; that thing was what he wanted to talk about now. Huck's face saddened. He said:

"I know what it is. You got into No. 2 and never found anything but whiskey. Nobody told me it was you; but I just knowed it must 'a' ben you, soon as I heard 'bout that whiskey business; and I knowed you hadn't got the money becuz you'd 'a' got at me some way or other and told me even if you was mum to everybody else. Tom, something's always told me we'd never get holt of that swag."

"Why, Huck, I never told on that tavern-keeper. *You* know his tavern was all right the Saturday I went to the picnic. Don't you remember you was to watch there that night?"

"Oh yes! Why, it seems 'bout a year ago. It was that very night that I follered Injun Joe to the widder's."

"*You* followed him?"

"Yes—but you keep mum. I reckon Injun Joe's left friends behind him, and I don't want 'em souring on me and doing me mean tricks. If it hadn't ben for me he'd be down in Texas now, all right."

Then Huck told his entire adventure in confidence to Tom, who had only heard of the Welshman's part of it before.

"Well," said Huck, presently, coming back to the main question, "whoever nipped the whiskey in No. 2, nipped the money, too, I reckon—anyways it's a goner for us, Tom."

"Huck, that money wasn't ever in No. 2!"

"What!" Huck searched his comrade's face keenly. "Tom, have you got on the track of that money again?"

"Huck, it's in the cave!"

Huck's eyes blazed.

"Say it again, Tom."

"The money's in the cave!"

"Tom—honest injun, now—is it fun, or earnest?"

"Earnest, Huck—just as earnest as ever I was in my life. Will you go in there with me and help get it out?"

"I bet I will! I will if it's where we can blaze our way to it and not get lost."

"Huck, we can do that without the least little bit of trouble in the world."

"Good as wheat! What makes you think the money's—"

"Huck, you just wait till we get in there. If we don't find it I'll agree to give you my drum and everything I've got in the world. I will, by jings."

"All right—it's a whiz. When do you say?"

"Right now, if you say it. Are you strong enough?"

"Is it far in the cave? I ben on my pins a little, three or four days, now, but I can't walk more'n a mile, Tom—least I don't think I could."

"It's about five mile into there the way anybody but me would go, Huck, but there's a mighty short cut that they don't anybody but me know about. Huck, I'll take you right to it in a skiff. I'll float the skiff down there, and I'll pull it back again all by myself. You needn't ever turn your hand over."

"Less start right off, Tom."

"All right. We want some bread and meat, and our pipes, and a little bag or two, and two or three kite-strings, and some of these new-fangled things they call lucifer matches. I tell you, many's the time I wished I had some when I was in there before."

A trifle after noon the boys borrowed a small skiff from a citizen who was absent, and got under way at once. When they were several miles below "Cave Hollow," Tom said:

"Now you see this bluff here looks all alike all the way down from the cave hollow—no houses, no wood-yards, bushes all alike. But do you see that white place up yonder where there's been a landslide? Well, that's one of my marks. We'll get ashore, now."

They landed.

"Now, Huck, where we're a-standing you could touch that hole I got out of with a fishing-pole. See if you can find it."

Huck searched all the place about, and found nothing. Tom proudly marched into a thick clump of sumach bushes and said:

"Here you are! Look at it, Huck; it's the snuggest hole in this country. You just keep mum about it. All along I've been wanting to be a robber, but I knew I'd got to have a thing like this, and where to run across it was the bother. We've got it now, and we'll keep it quiet, only we'll let Joe Harper and Ben Rogers in—because of course there's got to be a Gang, or else there wouldn't be any style about it. Tom Sawyer's Gang—it sounds splendid, don't it, Huck?"

"Well, it just does, Tom. And who'll we rob?"

"Oh, most anybody. Waylay people—that's mostly the way."

"And kill them?"

A Business Trip

"No, not always. Hive them in the cave till they raise a ransom."

"What's a ransom?"

"Money. You make them raise all they can, off'n their friends; and after you've kept them a year, if it ain't raised then you kill them. That's the general way. Only you don't kill the women. You shut up the women, but you don't kill them. They're always beautiful and rich, and awfully scared. You take their watches and things, but you always take your hat off and talk polite. They ain't anybody as polite as robbers—you'll see that in any book. Well, the women get to loving you, and after they've been in the cave a week or two weeks they stop crying and after that you couldn't get them to leave. If you drove them out they'd turn right around and come back. It's so in all the books."

"Why, it's real bully, Tom. I believe it's better'n to be a pirate."

"Yes, it's better in some ways, because it's close to home and circuses and all that."

By this time everything was ready and the boys entered the hole, Tom in the lead. They toiled their way to the farther end of the tunnel, then made their spliced kite-strings fast and moved on. A few steps brought them to the spring, and Tom felt a shudder quiver all through him. He showed Huck the fragment of candle-wick perched on a lump of clay against the wall, and described how he and Becky had watched the flame struggle and expire.

The boys began to quiet down to whispers, now, for the stillness and gloom of the place oppressed their spirits. They went on, and presently entered and followed Tom's other corridor until they reached the "jumping-off place." The candles revealed the fact that it was not really a precipice, but only a steep clay hill twenty or thirty feet high. Tom whispered:

"Now I'll show you something, Huck."

He held his candle aloft and said:

"Look as far around the corner as you can. Do you see that? There—on the big rock over yonder—done with candle-smoke."

"Tom, it's a *cross*!"

"*Now* where's your Number Two? '*under the cross*,' hey? Right yonder's where I saw Injun Joe poke up his candle, Huck!"

Huck stared at the mystic sign awhile, and then said with a shaky voice:

"Tom, less git out of here!"

"What! and leave the treasure?"

"Yes—leave it. Injun Joe's ghost is round about there, certain."

"No it ain't, Huck, no it ain't. It would ha'nt the place where he died—away out at the mouth of the cave—five mile from here."

"No, Tom, it wouldn't. It would hang round the money. I know the ways of ghosts, and so do you."

Tom began to fear that Huck was right. Misgivings gathered in his mind. But presently an idea occurred to him—

"Looky here, Huck, what fools we're making of ourselves! Injun Joe's ghost ain't a going to come around where there's a cross!"

The point was well taken. It had its effect.

"Tom, I didn't think of that. But that's so. It's luck for us, that cross is. I reckon we'll climb down there and have a hunt for that box."

Tom went first, cutting rude steps in the clay hill as he descended. Huck followed. Four avenues opened out of the small cavern which the great rock stood in. The boys examined three of them with no result. They found a small recess in the one nearest the base of the rock, with a pallet of blankets spread down in it; also an old suspender, some bacon rind, and the well-gnawed bones of two or three fowls. But there was no moneybox. The lads searched and researched this place, but in vain. Tom said:

"He said *under* the cross. Well, this comes nearest to being under the cross. It can't be under the rock itself, because that sets solid on the ground."

They searched everywhere once more, and then sat down discouraged. Huck could suggest nothing. By and by Tom said:

"Looky here, Huck, there's footprints and some candle-grease on the clay about one side of this rock, but not on the other sides. Now, what's that for? I bet you the money *is* under the rock. I'm going to dig in the clay."

"That ain't no bad notion, Tom!" said Huck with animation.

Tom's "real Barlow" was out at once, and he had not dug four inches before he struck wood.

"Hey, Huck!—you hear that?"

Huck began to dig and scratch now. Some boards were soon uncovered and removed. They had concealed a natural chasm which led under the rock. Tom got into this and held his candle as far under the rock as he could, but said he could not see to the end of the rift. He proposed to explore. He stooped and passed under; the narrow way descended gradually. He followed its winding course, first to the right, then to the left, Huck at his heels. Tom turned a short curve, by and by, and exclaimed:

"My goodness, Huck, looky here!"

It was the treasure box, sure enough, occupying a snug little cavern, along with an empty powder-keg, a couple of guns in leather cases, two or three pairs of old moccasins, a leather belt, and some other rubbish well soaked with the water-drip.

"Got it at last!" said Huck, ploughing among the tarnished coins with his hand. "My, but we're rich, Tom!"

"Huck, I always reckoned we'd get it. It's just too good to believe, but we *have* got it, sure! Say—let's not fool around here. Let's snake it out. Lemme see if I can lift the box."

It weighed about fifty pounds. Tom could lift it, after an awkward fashion, but could not carry it conveniently.

"I thought so," he said; "*they* carried it like it was heavy, that day at the ha'nted house. I noticed that. I reckon I was right to think of fetching the little bags along."

The money was soon in the bags and the boys took it up to the cross rock.

"Now less fetch the guns and things," said Huck.

"No, Huck—leave them there. They're just the tricks to have when we go to robbing. We'll keep them there all the time, and we'll hold our orgies there, too. It's an awful snug place for orgies."

"What orgies?"

"I dono. But robbers always have orgies, and of course we've got to have them, too. Come along, Huck, we've been in here a long time. It's getting late, I reckon. I'm hungry, too. We'll eat and smoke when we get to the skiff."

They presently emerged into the clump of sumach bushes, looked warily out, found the coast clear, and were soon lunching and smoking in the skiff. As the sun dipped toward the horizon they pushed out and got under way. Tom skimmed up the shore through the long twilight, chatting cheerily with Huck, and landed shortly after dark.

"Now, Huck," said Tom, "we'll hide the money in the loft of the widow's woodshed, and I'll come up in the morning and we'll count it and divide, and then we'll hunt up a place out in the woods for it where it will be safe. Just you lay quiet here and watch the stuff till I run and hook Benny Taylor's little wagon; I won't be gone a minute."

He disappeared, and presently returned with the wagon, put the two small sacks into it, threw some old rags on top of them, and started off, dragging his cargo behind him. When the boys reached the Welshman's house, they stopped to rest. Just as they were about to move on, the Welshman stepped out and said:

"Hallo, who's that?"

"Huck and Tom Sawyer."

"Good! Come along with me, boys, you are keeping everybody waiting. Here—hurry up, trot ahead—I'll haul the wagon for you. Why, it's not as light as it might be. Got bricks in it?—or old metal?"

"Old metal," said Tom.

"I judged so; the boys in this town will take more trouble and fool away more time hunting up six bits' worth of old iron to sell to the foundry than they would to make twice the money at regular work. But that's human nature—hurry along, hurry along!"

The boys wanted to know what the hurry was about.

"Never mind; you'll see, when we get to the Widow Douglas's."

Huck said with some apprehension—for he was long used to being falsely accused—

"Mr. Jones, we haven't been doing nothing."

The Welshman laughed.

"Well, I don't know, Huck, my boy. I don't know about that. Ain't you and the widow good friends?"

"Yes. Well, she's ben good friends to me, anyway."

"All right, then. What do you want to be afraid for?"

This question was not entirely answered in Huck's slow mind before he found himself pushed, along with Tom, into Mrs. Douglas' drawing room. Mr. Jones left the wagon near the door and followed.

The place was grandly lighted, and everybody that was of any consequence in the village was there. The Thatchers were there, the Harpers, the Rogerses, Aunt Polly, Sid, Mary, the minister, the editor, and a great many more, and all dressed in their best. The widow received the boys as heartily as any one could well receive two such looking beings. They were covered with clay and candle-grease. Aunt Polly blushed crimson with humiliation, and frowned and shook her head at Tom. Nobody suffered half as much as the two boys did, however. Mr. Jones said:

"Tom wasn't at home, yet, so I gave him up; but I stumbled on him and Huck right at my door, and so I just brought them along in a hurry."

"And you did just right," said the widow. "Come with me, boys."

She took them to a bedchamber and said:

"Now wash and dress yourselves. Here are two new suits of clothes—shirts, socks, everything complete. They're Huck's—no, no thanks, Huck—Mr. Jones bought one and I the other. But they'll fit both of you. Get into them. We'll wait—come down when you are slicked up enough."

Then she left.

34

Huck said: "Tom, we can slope, if we can find a rope. The window ain't high from the ground."

"Shucks! what do you want to slope for?"

"Well, I ain't used to that kind of a crowd. I can't stand it. I ain't going down there, Tom."

"Oh, bother! It ain't anything. I don't mind it a bit. I'll take care of you."

Sid appeared.

"Tom," said he, "auntie has been waiting for you all the afternoon. Mary got your Sunday clothes ready, and everybody's been fretting about you. Say—ain't this grease and clay, on your clothes?"

"Now, Mr. Siddy, you jist 'tend to your own business. What's all this blowout about, anyway?"

"It's one of the widow's parties that she's always having. This time it's for the Welshman and his sons, on account of that scrape they helped her out of the other night. And say—I can tell you something, if you want to know."

"Well, what?"

"Why, old Mr. Jones is going to try to spring something on the people here tonight, but I overheard him tell auntie today about it, as a secret, but I reckon it's not much of a secret *now*. Everybody knows—the widow, too, for all she tries to let on she don't. Mr. Jones was bound Huck should be here—couldn't get along with his grand secret without Huck, you know!"

"Secret about what, Sid?"

"About Huck tracking the robbers to the widow's. I reckon Mr. Jones was going to make a grand time over his surprise, but I bet you it will drop pretty flat."

Sid chuckled in a very contented and satisfied way.

"Sid, was it you that told?"

"Oh, never mind who it was. *Somebody* told—that's enough."

"Sid, there's only one person in this town mean enough to do that, and that's you. If you had been in Huck's place you'd 'a' sneaked down the hill and never told anybody on the robbers. You can't do any but mean things, and you can't bear to see anybody praised for doing good ones. There—no thanks, as the widow says"—and Tom cuffed Sid's ears and helped him to the door with several kicks. "Now go and tell auntie if you dare—and tomorrow you'll catch it!"

Some minutes later the widow's guests were at the supper-table, and a dozen children were propped up at little side-tables in the same room, after the fashion of that country and that day. At the proper time Mr. Jones made his little speech, in which he thanked the widow for the honour she was doing himself and his sons, but said that there was another person whose modesty—

And so forth and so on. He sprung his secret about Huck's share in the adventure in the finest dramatic manner he was master of, but the surprise it occasioned was largely counterfeit and not as clamorous and effusive as it might have been under happier circumstances. However, the widow made a pretty fair show of astonishment, and heaped so many compliments and so much gratitude upon Huck that he almost forgot the nearly intolerable discomfort of his new clothes in the entirely intolerable discomfort of being set up as a target for everybody's gaze and everybody's laudations.

The widow said she meant to give Huck a home under her roof and have him educated; and that when she could spare the money she would start him in business in a modest way. Tom's chance was come. He said:

"Huck don't need it. Huck's rich!"

Nothing but a heavy strain upon the good manners of the company kept back the due and proper complimentary laugh at this pleasant joke. But the silence was a little awkward. Tom broke it—

"Huck's got money. Maybe you don't believe it, but he's got lots of it. Oh, you needn't smile—I reckon I can show you. You just wait a minute."

Tom ran out of doors. The company looked at each other with a perplexed interest—and inquiringly at Huck, who was tongue-tied.

"Sid, what ails Tom?" said Aunt Polly. "He—well, there ain't ever any making of that boy out. I never—"

Tom entered, struggling with the weight of his sacks, and Aunt Polly did not finish her sentence. Tom poured the mass of yellow coin upon the table and said:

"There—what did I tell you? Half of it's Huck's and half of it's mine!"

Tom Backs his Statement

The spectacle took the general breath away. All gazed, nobody spoke for a moment. Then there was a unanimous call for an explanation. Tom said he could furnish it, and he did. The tale was long, but brimful of interest. There was scarcely an interruption from any one to break the charm of its flow. When he had finished, Mr. Jones said—

"I thought I had fixed up a little surprise for this occasion, but it don't amount to anything now. This one makes it sing mighty small, I'm willing to allow."

The money was counted. The sum amounted to a little over twelve thousand dollars. It was more than any one present had ever seen at one time before, though several persons were there who were worth considerably more than that in property.

35

The reader may rest satisfied that Tom's and Huck's windfall made a mighty stir in the poor little village of St. Petersburg. So vast a sum, all in actual cash, seemed next to incredible. It was talked about, gloated over, glorified, until the reason of many of the citizens tottered under the strain of the unhealthy excitement. Every "haunted" house in St. Petersburg and the neighbouring villages was dissected, plank by plank, and its foundations dug up and ransacked for hidden treasure—and not by boys, but men—pretty grave, unromantic men, too, some of them. Wherever Tom and Huck appeared they were courted, admired, stared at. The boys were not able to remember that their remarks had possessed weight before; but now their sayings were treasured and repeated; everything they did seemed somehow to be regarded as remarkable; they had evidently lost the power of doing and saying commonplace things; moreover, their past history was raked up and discovered to bear marks of conspicuous originality. The village paper published biographical sketches of the boys.

The Widow Douglas put Huck's money out at six per cent., and Judge Thatcher did the same with Tom's at Aunt Polly's request. Each lad had an income, now, that was simply prodigious—a dollar for every weekday in the year and half of the Sundays. It was just what the minister got—no, it was what he was promised—he generally couldn't collect it. A dollar and a quarter a week would board, lodge, and school a boy in those old simple days—and clothe him and wash him, too, for that matter.

Judge Thatcher had conceived a great opinion of Tom. He said that no commonplace boy would ever have got his daughter out of the cave. When Becky told her father, in strict confidence, how Tom had taken her whipping at school, the Judge was visibly moved; and when she pleaded grace for the mighty lie which Tom had told in order to shift that whipping from her shoulders to his own, the Judge said with a fine outburst that it was a noble, a generous, a magnanimous lie—a lie that was worthy to hold up its head and march down through history breast to breast with George Washington's lauded Truth about the hatchet! Becky thought her father had never looked so tall and so superb as when he walked the floor and stamped his foot and said that. She went straight off and told Tom about it.

Judge Thatcher hoped to see Tom a great lawyer or a great soldier some day. He said he meant to look to it that Tom should be admitted to the National Military Academy and afterward trained in the best law school in the country, in order that he might be ready for either career or both.

Huck Finn's wealth and the fact that he was now under the Widow Douglas' protection introduced him into society—no, dragged him into it, hurled him into it—and his sufferings were almost more than he could bear. The widow's servants kept him clean and neat, combed and brushed, and they bedded him nightly in unsympathetic sheets that had not one little spot or stain which he could press to his heart and know for a friend. He had to eat with a knife and fork; he had to use napkin, cup, and plate; he had to learn his book, he had to go to church; he had to talk so properly that speech was become insipid in his mouth; whithersoever he turned, the bars and shackles of civilization shut him in and bound him hand and foot.

He bravely bore his miseries three weeks, and then one day turned up missing. For forty-eight hours the widow hunted for him everywhere in great distress. The public were profoundly concerned; they searched high and low, they dragged the river for his body. Early the third morning Tom Sawyer wisely went poking among some old empty hogsheads down behind the abandoned slaughterhouse, and in one of them he found the refugee. Huck had slept there; he had just breakfasted upon some stolen odds and ends of food, and was lying off, now, in comfort, with his pipe. He was unkempt, uncombed, and clad in the same old ruin of rags that had made him picturesque in the days when he was free and happy. Tom routed him out, told him the trouble he had been causing, and urged him to go home. Huck's face lost its tranquil content, and took a melancholy cast. He said:

"Don't talk about it, Tom. I've tried it, and it don't work; it don't work, Tom. It ain't for me; I ain't used to it. The widder's good to me, and friendly; but I can't stand them ways. She makes me get up just at the same time every morning; she makes me wash, they comb me all to thunder; she won't let me sleep in the woodshed; I got to wear them blamed clothes that just smothers me, Tom; they don't seem to any air git through 'em, somehow; and they're so rotten nice that I can't set down, nor lay down, nor roll around anywher's; I hain't slid on a cellar-door for—well, it 'pears to be years; I got to go to church and sweat and sweat—I hate them ornery sermons! I can't ketch a fly in there, I can't chaw. I got to wear shoes all Sunday. The widder eats by a bell; she goes to bed by a bell; she gits up by a bell—everything's so awful reg'lar a body can't stand it."

"Well, everybody does that way, Huck."

"Tom, it don't make no difference. I ain't everybody, and I can't *stand* it. It's awful to be tied up so. And grub comes too easy—I don't take no interest in vittles, that way. I got to ask to go a-fishing; I got to ask to go in a-swimming—dern'd if I hain't got to ask to do everything. Well, I'd got to talk so nice it wasn't no comfort—I'd got to go up in the attic and rip out awhile, every day, to git a taste in my mouth, or I'd a died, Tom. The widder wouldn't let me smoke; she wouldn't let me yell, she wouldn't let me gape, nor stretch, nor scratch, before folks—" [Then with a spasm of special irritation and injury]—"And dad fetch it, she prayed all the time! I never see such a woman! I *had* to shove, Tom—I just had to. And besides, that school's going to open, and I'd a had to go to it—well, I wouldn't stand *that*, Tom. Looky-here, Tom, being rich ain't what it's cracked up to be. It's just worry and worry, and sweat and sweat, and a-wishing you was dead all the time.

Now these clothes suits me, and this bar'l suits me, and I ain't ever going to shake 'em any more. Tom, I wouldn't ever got into all this trouble if it hadn't 'a' ben for that money; now you just take my sheer of it along with your'n, and gimme a ten-center sometimes—not many times, becuz I don't give a dern for a thing 'thout it's tollable hard to git—and you go and beg off for me with the widder."

"Oh, Huck, you know I can't do that. 'Tain't fair; and besides if you'll try this thing just a while longer you'll come to like it."

"Like it! Yes—the way I'd like a hot stove if I was to set on it long enough. No, Tom, I won't be rich, and I won't live in them cussed smothery houses. I like the woods, and the river, and hogsheads, and I'll stick to 'em, too. Blame it all! just as we'd got guns, and a cave, and all just fixed to rob, here this dern foolishness has got to come up and spile it all!"

Tom saw his opportunity—

"Lookyhere, Huck, being rich ain't going to keep me back from turning robber."

"No! Oh, good-licks; are you in real dead-wood earnest, Tom?"

"Just as dead earnest as I'm sitting here. But Huck, we can't let you into the gang if you ain't respectable, you know."

Huck's joy was quenched.

"Can't let me in, Tom? Didn't you let me go for a pirate?"

"Yes, but that's different. A robber is more high-toned than what a pirate is—as a general thing. In most countries they're awful high up in the nobility—dukes and such."

"Now, Tom, hain't you always ben friendly to me? You wouldn't shet me out, would you, Tom? You wouldn't do that, now, *would* you, Tom?"

"Huck, I wouldn't want to, and I *don't* want to—but what would people say? Why, they'd say, 'Mph! Tom Sawyer's Gang! pretty low characters in it!' They'd mean you, Huck. You wouldn't like that, and I wouldn't."

Huck was silent for some time, engaged in a mental struggle. Finally he said:

"Well, I'll go back to the widder for a month and tackle it and see if I can come to stand it, if you'll let me b'long to the gang, Tom."

"All right, Huck, it's a whiz! Come along, old chap, and I'll ask the widow to let up on you a little, Huck."

"Will you, Tom—now will you? That's good. If she'll let up on some of the roughest things, I'll smoke private and cuss private, and crowd through or bust. When you going to start the gang and turn robbers?"

"Oh, right off. We'll get the boys together and have the initiation tonight, maybe."

"Have the which?"

"Have the initiation."

"What's that?"

"It's to swear to stand by one another, and never tell the gang's secrets, even if you're chopped all to flinders, and kill anybody and all his family that hurts one of the gang."

"That's gay—that's mighty gay, Tom, I tell you."

"Well, I bet it is. And all that swearing's got to be done at midnight, in the lonesomest, awfulest place you can find—a ha'nted house is the best, but they're all ripped up now."

"Well, midnight's good, anyway, Tom."

"Yes, so it is. And you've got to swear on a coffin, and sign it with blood."

"Now, that's something *like*! Why, it's a million times bullier than pirating. I'll stick to the widder till I rot, Tom; and if I git to be a reg'lar ripper of a robber, and everybody talking 'bout it, I reckon she'll be proud she snaked me in out of the wet."

Conclusion

So endeth this chronicle. It being strictly a history of a *boy*, it must stop here; the story could not go much further without becoming the history of a *man*. When one writes a novel about grown people, he knows exactly where to stop—that is, with a marriage; but when he writes of juveniles, he must stop where he best can.

Most of the characters that perform in this book still live, and are prosperous and happy. Some day it may seem worth while to take up the story of the younger ones again and see what sort of men and women they turned out to be; therefore it will be wisest not to reveal any of that part of their lives at present.

The Prince and The Pauper (1881)

To

Those Good-mannered and Agreeable Children,

Susie and Clara Clemens,

This Book

is

Affectionately Inscribed

By their Father

The quality of mercy . . .
is twice bless'd;
It blesseth him that gives, and him that takes;
'Tis mightiest in the mightiest: it becomes
the throned monarch better than his crown.

—*Merchant of Venice*

I will set down a tale as it was told to me by one who had it of his father, which latter had it of HIS *father, this last having in like manner had it of* HIS *father—and so on, back and still back, three hundred years and more, the fathers transmitting it to the sons and so preserving it. It may be history, it may be only a legend, a tradition. It may have happened, it may not have happened: but it* COULD *have happened. It may be that the wise and the learned believed it in the old days; it may be that only the unlearned and the simple loved it and credited it.*

1

The birth of the Prince and the Pauper

In the ancient city of London, on a certain autumn day in the second quarter of the sixteenth century, a boy was born to a poor family of the name of Canty, who did not want him. On the same day another English child was born to a rich family of the name of Tudor, who did want him. All England wanted him too. England had so longed for him, and hoped for him, and prayed God for him, that, now that he was really come, the people went nearly mad for joy. Mere acquaintances hugged and kissed each other and cried. Everybody took a holiday, and high and low, rich and poor, feasted and danced and sang, and got very mellow; and they kept this up for days and nights together. By day, London was a sight to see, with gay banners waving from every balcony and housetop, and splendid pageants marching along. By night, it was again a sight to see, with its great bonfires at every corner, and its troops of revellers making merry around them. There was no talk in all England but of the new baby, Edward Tudor, Prince of Wales, who lay lapped in silks and satins, unconscious of all this fuss, and not knowing that great lords and ladies were tending him and watching over him—and not caring, either. But there was no talk about the other baby, Tom Canty, lapped in his poor rags, except among the family of paupers whom he had just come to trouble with his presence.

2

Tom's early life

Let us skip a number of years.

London was fifteen hundred years old, and was a great town—for that day. It had a hundred thousand inhabitants—some think double as many. The streets were very narrow, and crooked, and dirty, especially in the part where Tom Canty lived, which was not far from London Bridge. The houses were of wood, with the second story projecting over the first, and the third sticking its elbows out beyond the second. The higher the houses grew, the broader they grew. They were skeletons of strong criss-cross beams, with solid material between, coated with plaster. The beams were painted red or blue or black, according to the owner's taste, and this gave the houses a very picturesque look. The windows were small, glazed with little diamond-shaped panes, and they opened outward, on hinges, like doors.

The house which Tom's father lived in was up a foul little pocket called Offal Court, out of Pudding Lane. It was small, decayed, and rickety, but it was packed full of wretchedly poor families. Canty's tribe occupied a room on the third floor. The mother and father had a sort of bedstead in the corner; but Tom, his grandmother, and his two sisters, Bet and Nan, were not restricted—they had all the floor to themselves, and might sleep where they chose. There were the remains of a blanket or two, and some bundles of ancient and dirty straw, but these could not rightly be called beds, for they were not organised; they were kicked into a general pile, mornings, and selections made from the mass at night, for service.

Bet and Nan were fifteen years old—twins. They were good-hearted girls, unclean, clothed in rags, and profoundly ignorant. Their mother was like them. But the father and the grandmother were a couple of fiends. They got drunk whenever they could; then they fought each other or anybody else who came in the way; they cursed and swore always, drunk or sober; John Canty was a thief, and his mother a beggar. They made beggars of the children, but failed to make thieves of them. Among, but not of, the dreadful rabble that inhabited the house, was a good old priest whom the King had turned out of house and home with a pension of a few farthings, and he used to get the children aside and teach them right ways secretly. Father Andrew also taught Tom a little Latin, and how to read and write; and would have done the same with the girls, but they were afraid of the jeers of their friends, who could not have endured such a queer accomplishment in them.

All Offal Court was just such another hive as Canty's house. Drunkenness, riot and brawling were the order, there, every night and nearly all night long. Broken heads were as common as hunger in that place. Yet little Tom was not unhappy. He had a hard time of it, but did not know it. It was the sort of time that all the Offal Court boys had, therefore he supposed it was the correct and comfortable thing. When he came home empty-handed at night, he knew his father would curse him and thrash him first, and that when he was done the awful grandmother would do it all over again and improve on it; and that away in the night his starving mother would slip to him stealthily with any miserable scrap or crust she had been able to save for him by going hungry herself, notwithstanding she was often caught in that sort of treason and soundly beaten for it by her husband.

"With Any Miserable Crust"

No, Tom's life went along well enough, especially in summer. He only begged just enough to save himself, for the laws against mendicancy were stringent, and the penalties heavy; so he put in a good deal of his time listening to good Father Andrew's charming old tales and legends about giants and fairies, dwarfs and genii, and enchanted castles, and gorgeous kings and princes. His head grew to be full of these wonderful things, and many a night as he lay in the dark on his scant and offensive straw, tired, hungry, and smarting from a thrashing, he unleashed his imagination and soon forgot his aches and pains in delicious picturings to himself of the charmed life of a petted prince in a regal palace. One desire came in time to haunt him day and night: it was to see a real prince, with his own eyes. He spoke of it once to some of his Offal Court comrades; but they jeered him and scoffed him so unmercifully that he was glad to keep his dream to himself after that.

He often read the priest's old books and got him to explain and enlarge upon them. His dreamings and readings worked certain changes in him, by and by. His dream-people were so fine that he grew to lament his shabby clothing and his dirt, and to wish to be clean and better clad. He went on playing in the mud just the same, and enjoying it, too; but, instead of splashing around in the Thames solely for the fun of it, he began to find an added value in it because of the washings and cleansings it afforded.

Tom could always find something going on around the Maypole in Cheapside, and at the fairs; and now and then he and the rest of London had a chance to see a military parade when some famous unfortunate was carried prisoner to the Tower, by land or boat. One summer's day he saw poor Anne Askew and three men burned at the stake in Smithfield, and heard an ex-Bishop preach a sermon to them which did not interest him. Yes, Tom's life was varied and pleasant enough, on the whole.

By and by Tom's reading and dreaming about princely life wrought such a strong effect upon him that he began to *act* the prince, unconsciously. His speech and manners became curiously ceremonious and courtly, to the vast admiration and amusement of his intimates. But Tom's influence among these young people began to grow now, day by day; and in time he came to be looked up to, by them, with a sort of wondering awe, as a superior being. He seemed to know so much! and he could do and say such marvellous things! and withal, he was so deep and wise! Tom's remarks, and Tom's performances, were reported by the boys to their elders; and these, also, presently began to discuss Tom Canty, and to regard him as a most gifted and extraordinary creature. Full-grown people brought their perplexities to Tom for solution, and were often astonished at the wit and wisdom of his decisions. In fact he was become a hero to all who knew him except his own family—these, only, saw nothing in him.

Privately, after a while, Tom organised a royal court! He was the prince; his special comrades were guards, chamberlains, equerries, lords and ladies in waiting, and the royal family. Daily the mock prince was received with elaborate ceremonials borrowed by Tom from his romantic readings; daily the great affairs of the mimic kingdom were discussed in the royal council, and daily his mimic highness issued decrees to his imaginary armies, navies, and viceroyalties.

After which, he would go forth in his rags and beg a few farthings, eat his poor crust, take his customary cuffs and abuse, and then stretch himself upon his handful of foul straw, and resume his empty grandeurs in his dreams.

"Longing for the pork-pies"

And still his desire to look just once upon a real prince, in the flesh, grew upon him, day by day, and week by week, until at last it absorbed all other desires, and became the one passion of his life.

One January day, on his usual begging tour, he tramped despondently up and down the region round about Mincing Lane and Little East Cheap, hour after hour, bare-footed and cold, looking in at cook-shop windows and longing for the dreadful pork-pies and other deadly inventions displayed there—for to him these were dainties fit for the angels; that is, judging by the smell, they were—for it had never been his good luck to own and eat one. There was a cold drizzle of rain; the atmosphere was murky; it was a melancholy day. At night Tom reached home so wet and tired and hungry that it was not possible for his father and grandmother to observe his forlorn condition and not be moved—after their fashion; wherefore they gave him a brisk cuffing at once and sent him to bed. For a long time his pain and hunger, and the swearing and fighting going on in the building, kept him awake; but at last his thoughts drifted away to far, romantic lands, and he fell asleep in the company of jewelled and gilded princelings who live in vast palaces, and had servants salaaming before them or flying to execute their orders. And then, as usual, he dreamed that *he* was a princeling himself.

All night long the glories of his royal estate shone upon him; he moved among great lords and ladies, in a blaze of light, breathing perfumes, drinking in delicious music, and answering the reverent obeisances of the glittering throng as it parted to make way for him, with here a smile, and there a nod of his princely head.

And when he awoke in the morning and looked upon the wretchedness about him, his dream had had its usual effect—it had intensified the sordidness of his surroundings a thousandfold. Then came bitterness, and heartbreak, and tears.

3

Tom's Meeting with the Prince

Tom got up hungry, and sauntered hungry away, but with his thoughts busy with the shadowy splendours of his night's dreams. He wandered here and there in the city, hardly noticing where he was going, or what was happening around him. People jostled him, and some gave him rough speech; but it was all lost on the musing boy. By and by he found himself at Temple Bar, the farthest from home he had ever travelled in that direction. He stopped and considered a moment, then fell into his imaginings again, and passed on outside the walls of London. The Strand had ceased to be a country-road then, and regarded itself as a street, but by a strained construction; for, though there was a tolerably compact row of houses on one side of it, there were only some scattered great buildings on the other, these being palaces of rich nobles, with ample and beautiful grounds stretching to the river—grounds that are now closely packed with grim acres of brick and stone.

Tom discovered Charing Village presently, and rested himself at the beautiful cross built there by a bereaved king of earlier days; then idled down a quiet, lovely road, past the great cardinal's stately palace, toward a far more mighty and majestic palace beyond—Westminster. Tom stared in glad wonder at the vast pile of masonry, the wide-spreading wings, the frowning bastions and turrets, the huge stone gateway, with its gilded bars and its magnificent array of colossal granite lions, and other the signs and symbols of English royalty. Was the desire of his soul to be satisfied at last?

Here, indeed, was a king's palace. Might he not hope to see a prince now—a prince of flesh and blood, if Heaven were willing?

At each side of the gilded gate stood a living statue—that is to say, an erect and stately and motionless man-at-arms, clad from head to heel in shining steel armour. At a respectful distance were many country folk, and people from the city, waiting for any chance glimpse of royalty that might offer. Splendid carriages, with splendid people in them and splendid servants outside, were arriving and departing by several other noble gateways that pierced the royal enclosure.

Poor little Tom, in his rags, approached, and was moving slowly and timidly past the sentinels, with a beating heart and a rising hope, when all at once he caught sight through the golden bars of a spectacle that almost made him shout for joy. Within was a comely boy, tanned and brown with sturdy outdoor sports and exercises, whose clothing was all of lovely silks and satins, shining with jewels; at his hip a little jewelled sword and dagger; dainty buskins on his feet, with red heels; and on his head a jaunty crimson cap, with drooping plumes fastened with a great sparkling gem. Several gorgeous gentlemen stood near—his servants, without a doubt. Oh! he was a prince—a prince, a living prince, a real prince—without the shadow of a question; and the prayer of the pauper-boy's heart was answered at last.

Tom's breath came quick and short with excitement, and his eyes grew big with wonder and delight. Everything gave way in his mind instantly to one desire: that was to get close to the prince, and have a good, devouring look at him. Before he knew what he was about, he had his face against the gate-bars. The next instant one of the soldiers snatched him rudely away, and sent him spinning among the gaping crowd of country gawks and London idlers. The soldier said—

"Mind thy manners, thou young beggar!"

The crowd jeered and laughed; but the young prince sprang to the gate with his face flushed, and his eyes flashing with indignation, and cried out—

"How dar'st thou use a poor lad like that? How dar'st thou use the King my father's meanest subject so? Open the gates, and let him in!"

You should have seen that fickle crowd snatch off their hats then. You should have heard them cheer, and shout, "Long live the Prince of Wales!"

The soldiers presented arms with their halberds, opened the gates, and presented again as the little Prince of Poverty passed in, in his fluttering rags, to join hands with the Prince of Limitless Plenty.

Edward Tudor said—

"Thou lookest tired and hungry: thou'st been treated ill. Come with me."

Half a dozen attendants sprang forward to—I don't know what; interfere, no doubt. But they were waved aside with a right royal gesture, and they stopped stock still where they were, like so many statues. Edward took Tom to a rich apartment in the palace, which he called his cabinet. By his command a repast was brought such as Tom had never encountered before except in books. The prince, with princely delicacy and breeding, sent away the servants, so that his humble guest might not be embarrassed by their critical presence; then he sat near by, and asked questions while Tom ate.

"What is thy name, lad?"

"Tom Canty, an' it please thee, sir."

"'Tis an odd one. Where dost live?"

"In the city, please thee, sir. Offal Court, out of Pudding Lane."

"Offal Court! Truly 'tis another odd one. Hast parents?"

"Parents have I, sir, and a grand-dam likewise that is but indifferently precious to me, God forgive me if it be offence to say it—also twin sisters, Nan and Bet."

"Then is thy grand-dam not over kind to thee, I take it?"

"Neither to any other is she, so please your worship. She hath a wicked heart, and worketh evil all her days."

"Doth she mistreat thee?"

"There be times that she stayeth her hand, being asleep or overcome with drink; but when she hath her judgment clear again, she maketh it up to me with goodly beatings."

A fierce look came into the little prince's eyes, and he cried out—

"What! Beatings?"

"Oh, indeed, yes, please you, sir."

"*Beatings*!—and thou so frail and little. Hark ye: before the night come, she shall hie her to the Tower. The King my father"—

"In sooth, you forget, sir, her low degree. The Tower is for the great alone."

"True, indeed. I had not thought of that. I will consider of her punishment. Is thy father kind to thee?"

"Not more than Gammer Canty, sir."

"Fathers be alike, mayhap. Mine hath not a doll's temper. He smiteth with a heavy hand, yet spareth me: he spareth me not always with his tongue, though, sooth to say. How doth thy mother use thee?"

"She is good, sir, and giveth me neither sorrow nor pain of any sort. And Nan and Bet are like to her in this."

"How old be these?"

"How old be these?"

"Fifteen, an' it please you, sir."

"The Lady Elizabeth, my sister, is fourteen, and the Lady Jane Grey, my cousin, is of mine own age, and comely and gracious withal; but my sister the Lady Mary, with her gloomy mien and—Look you: do thy sisters forbid their servants to smile, lest the sin destroy their souls?"

"They? Oh, dost think, sir, that *they* have servants?"

The little prince contemplated the little pauper gravely a moment, then said—

"And prithee, why not? Who helpeth them undress at night? Who attireth them when they rise?"

"None, sir. Wouldst have them take off their garment, and sleep without—like the beasts?"

"Their garment! Have they but one?"

"Ah, good your worship, what would they do with more? Truly they have not two bodies each."

"It is a quaint and marvellous thought! Thy pardon, I had not meant to laugh. But thy good Nan and thy Bet shall have raiment and lackeys enow, and that soon, too: my cofferer shall look to it. No, thank me not; 'tis nothing. Thou speakest well; thou hast an easy grace in it. Art learned?"

"I know not if I am or not, sir. The good priest that is called Father Andrew taught me, of his kindness, from his books."

"Know'st thou the Latin?"

"But scantly, sir, I doubt."

"Learn it, lad: 'tis hard only at first. The Greek is harder; but neither these nor any tongues else, I think, are hard to the Lady Elizabeth and my cousin. Thou should'st hear those damsels at it! But tell me of thy Offal Court. Hast thou a pleasant life there?"

"In truth, yes, so please you, sir, save when one is hungry. There be Punch-and-Judy shows, and monkeys—oh such antic creatures! and so bravely dressed!—and there be plays wherein they that play do shout and fight till all are slain, and 'tis so fine to see, and costeth but a farthing—albeit 'tis main hard to get the farthing, please your worship."

"Tell me more."

"We lads of Offal Court do strive against each other with the cudgel, like to the fashion of the 'prentices, sometimes."

The prince's eyes flashed. Said he—

"Marry, that would not I mislike. Tell me more."

"We strive in races, sir, to see who of us shall be fleetest."

"That would I like also. Speak on."

"In summer, sir, we wade and swim in the canals and in the river, and each doth duck his neighbour, and splatter him with water, and dive and shout and tumble and—"

"'Twould be worth my father's kingdom but to enjoy it once! Prithee go on."

"We dance and sing about the Maypole in Cheapside; we play in the sand, each covering his neighbour up; and times we make mud pastry—oh the lovely mud, it hath not its like for delightfulness in all the world!—we do fairly wallow in the mud, sir, saving your worship's presence."

"Oh, prithee, say no more, 'tis glorious! If that I could but clothe me in raiment like to thine, and strip my feet, and revel in the mud once, just once, with none to rebuke me or forbid, meseemeth I could forego the crown!"

"And if that I could clothe me once, sweet sir, as thou art clad—just once—"

"Oho, wouldst like it? Then so shall it be. Doff thy rags, and don these splendours, lad! It is a brief happiness, but will be not less keen for that. We will have it while we may, and change again before any come to molest."

A few minutes later the little Prince of Wales was garlanded with Tom's fluttering odds and ends, and the little Prince of Pauperdom was tricked out in the gaudy plumage of royalty. The two went and stood side by side before a great mirror, and lo, a miracle: there did not seem to have been any change made! They stared at each other, then at the glass, then at each other again. At last the puzzled princeling said—

"What dost thou make of this?"

"Ah, good your worship, require me not to answer. It is not meet that one of my degree should utter the thing."

"Then will *I* utter it. Thou hast the same hair, the same eyes, the same voice and manner, the same form and stature, the same face and countenance that I bear. Fared we forth naked, there is none could say which was you, and which the Prince of Wales. And, now that I am clothed as thou wert clothed, it seemeth I should be able the more nearly to feel as thou didst when the brute soldier—Hark ye, is not this a bruise upon your hand?"

"Yes; but it is a slight thing, and your worship knoweth that the poor man-at-arms—"

"Peace! It was a shameful thing and a cruel!" cried the little prince, stamping his bare foot. "If the King—Stir not a step till I come again! It is a command!"

In a moment he had snatched up and put away an article of national importance that lay upon a table, and was out at the door and flying through the palace grounds in his bannered rags, with a hot face and glowing eyes. As soon as he reached the great gate, he seized the bars, and tried to shake them, shouting—

"Open! Unbar the gates!"

The soldier that had maltreated Tom obeyed promptly; and as the prince burst through the portal, half-smothered with royal wrath, the soldier fetched him a sounding box on the ear that sent him whirling to the roadway, and said—

"Take that, thou beggar's spawn, for what thou got'st me from his Highness!"

The crowd roared with laughter. The prince picked himself out of the mud, and made fiercely at the sentry, shouting—

"I am the Prince of Wales, my person is sacred; and thou shalt hang for laying thy hand upon me!"

The soldier brought his halberd to a present-arms and said mockingly—

"I salute your gracious Highness." Then angrily—"Be off, thou crazy rubbish!"

Here the jeering crowd closed round the poor little prince, and hustled him far down the road, hooting him, and shouting—

"Way for his Royal Highness! Way for the Prince of Wales!"

4

The Prince's troubles begin

After hours of persistent pursuit and persecution, the little prince was at last deserted by the rabble and left to himself. As long as he had been able to rage against the mob, and threaten it royally, and royally utter commands that were good stuff to laugh at, he was very entertaining; but when weariness finally forced him to be silent, he was no longer of use to his tormentors, and they sought amusement elsewhere. He looked about him, now, but could not recognize the locality. He was within the city of London—that was all he knew. He moved on, aimlessly, and in a little while the houses thinned, and the passers-by were infrequent. He bathed his bleeding feet in the brook which flowed then where Farringdon Street now is; rested a few moments, then passed on, and presently came upon a great space with only a few scattered houses in it, and a prodigious church. He recognized this church. Scaffoldings were about, everywhere, and swarms of workmen; for it was undergoing elaborate repairs. The prince took heart at once—he felt that his troubles were at an end, now. He said to himself, "It is the ancient Grey Friars' Church, which the king my father hath taken from the monks and given for a home for ever for poor and forsaken children, and new-named it Christ's Church. Right gladly will they serve the son of him who hath done so generously by them—and the more that that son is himself as poor and as forlorn as any that be sheltered here this day, or ever shall be."

He was soon in the midst of a crowd of boys who were running, jumping, playing at ball and leap-frog, and otherwise disporting themselves, and right noisily, too. They were all dressed alike, and in the fashion which in that day prevailed among serving-men and 'prentices*—that is to say, each had on the crown of his head a flat black cap about the size of a saucer, which

* It is most reasonable to regard the dress as copied from the costume of the citizens of London of that period, when long blue coats were the common habit of apprentices and serving-men, and yellow stockings were generally worn; the coat fits closely to the body, but has loose sleeves, and beneath is worn a sleeveless yellow under-coat; around the waist is a red leathern girdle; a clerical band around the neck, and a small flat black cap, about the size of a saucer, completes the costume.—Timbs' Curiosities of London.

was not useful as a covering, it being of such scanty dimensions, neither was it ornamental; from beneath it the hair fell, unparted, to the middle of the forehead, and was cropped straight around; a clerical band at the neck; a blue gown that fitted closely and hung as low as the knees or lower; full sleeves; a broad red belt; bright yellow stockings, gartered above the knees; low shoes with large metal buckles. It was a sufficiently ugly costume.

The boys stopped their play and flocked about the prince, who said with native dignity—

"Good lads, say to your master that Edward Prince of Wales desireth speech with him."

A great shout went up at this, and one rude fellow said—

"Marry, art thou his grace's messenger, beggar?"

The prince's face flushed with anger, and his ready hand flew to his hip, but there was nothing there. There was a storm of laughter, and one boy said—

"Didst mark that? He fancied he had a sword—belike he is the prince himself."

This sally brought more laughter. Poor Edward drew himself up proudly and said—

"I am the prince; and it ill beseemeth you that feed upon the king my father's bounty to use me so."

This was vastly enjoyed, as the laughter testified. The youth who had first spoken, shouted to his comrades—

"Ho, swine, slaves, pensioners of his grace's princely father, where be your manners? Down on your marrow bones, all of ye, and do reverence to his kingly port and royal rags!"

With boisterous mirth they dropped upon their knees in a body and did mock homage to their prey. The prince spurned the nearest boy with his foot, and said fiercely—

"Take thou that, till the morrow come and I build thee a gibbet!"

Ah, but this was not a joke—this was going beyond fun. The laughter ceased on the instant, and fury took its place. A dozen shouted—

"Hale him forth! To the horse-pond, to the horse-pond! Where be the dogs? Ho, there, Lion! ho, Fangs!"

Then followed such a thing as England had never seen before—the sacred person of the heir to the throne rudely buffeted by plebeian hands, and set upon and torn by dogs.

As night drew to a close that day, the prince found himself far down in the close-built portion of the city. His body was bruised, his hands were bleeding, and his rags were all besmirched with mud. He wandered on and on, and grew more and more bewildered, and so tired and faint he could hardly drag one foot after the other. He had ceased to ask questions of anyone, since they brought him only insult instead of information. He kept muttering to himself, "Offal Court—that is the name; if I can but find it before my strength is wholly spent and I drop, then am I saved—for his people will take me to the palace and prove that I am none of theirs, but the true prince, and I shall have mine own again." And now and then his mind reverted to his treatment by those rude Christ's Hospital boys, and he said, "When I am king, they shall not have bread and shelter only, but also teachings out of books; for a full belly is little worth where the mind is starved, and the heart. I will keep this diligently in my remembrance, that this day's lesson be not lost upon me, and my people suffer thereby; for learning softeneth the heart and breedeth gentleness and charity."*

The lights began to twinkle, it came on to rain, the wind rose, and a raw and gusty night set in. The houseless prince, the homeless heir to the throne of England, still moved on, drifting deeper into the maze of squalid alleys where the swarming hives of poverty and misery were massed together.

Suddenly a great drunken ruffian collared him and said—

"A drunken ruffian collared him"

* It appears that Christ's Hospital was not originally founded as a school; its object was to rescue children from the streets, to shelter, feed, clothe them.—Timbs' Curiosities of London.

"Out to this time of night again, and hast not brought a farthing home, I warrant me! If it be so, an' I do not break all the bones in thy lean body, then am I not John Canty, but some other."

The prince twisted himself loose, unconsciously brushed his profaned shoulder, and eagerly said—

"Oh, art *his* father, truly? Sweet heaven grant it be so—then wilt thou fetch him away and restore me!"

"*His* father? I know not what thou mean'st; I but know I am *thy* father, as thou shalt soon have cause to—"

"Oh, jest not, palter not, delay not!—I am worn, I am wounded, I can bear no more. Take me to the king my father, and he will make thee rich beyond thy wildest dreams. Believe me, man, believe me!—I speak no lie, but only the truth!—put forth thy hand and save me! I am indeed the Prince of Wales!"

The man stared down, stupefied, upon the lad, then shook his head and muttered—

"Gone stark mad as any Tom o' Bedlam!"—then collared him once more, and said with a coarse laugh and an oath, "But mad or no mad, I and thy Gammer Canty will soon find where the soft places in thy bones lie, or I'm no true man!"

With this he dragged the frantic and struggling prince away, and disappeared up a front court followed by a delighted and noisy swarm of human vermin.

5

Tom as a Patrician

Tom Canty, left alone in the prince's cabinet, made good use of his opportunity. He turned himself this way and that before the great mirror, admiring his finery; then walked away, imitating the prince's high-bred carriage, and still observing results in the glass. Next he drew the beautiful sword, and bowed, kissing the blade, and laying it across his breast, as he had seen a noble knight do, by way of salute to the lieutenant of the Tower, five or six weeks before, when delivering the great lords of Norfolk and Surrey into his hands for captivity. Tom played with the jewelled dagger that hung upon his thigh; he examined the costly and exquisite ornaments of the room; he tried each of the sumptuous chairs, and thought how proud he would be if the Offal Court herd could only peep in and see him in his grandeur. He wondered if they would believe the marvellous tale he should tell when he got home, or if they would shake their heads, and say his overtaxed imagination had at last upset his reason.

At the end of half an hour it suddenly occurred to him that the prince was gone a long time; then right away he began to feel lonely; very soon he fell to listening and longing, and ceased to toy with the pretty things about him; he grew uneasy, then restless, then distressed. Suppose some one should come, and catch him in the prince's clothes, and the prince not there to explain. Might they not hang him at once, and inquire into his case afterward? He had heard that the great were prompt about small matters. His fear rose higher and higher; and trembling he softly opened the door to the antechamber, resolved to fly and seek the prince, and, through him, protection and release. Six gorgeous gentlemen-servants and two young pages of high degree, clothed like butterflies, sprang to their feet and bowed low before him. He stepped quickly back and shut the door. He said—

"Resolved to fly"

"Oh, they mock at me! They will go and tell. Oh! why came I here to cast away my life?"

He walked up and down the floor, filled with nameless fears, listening, starting at every trifling sound. Presently the door swung open, and a silken page said—

"The Lady Jane Grey."

The door closed and a sweet young girl, richly clad, bounded toward him. But she stopped suddenly, and said in a distressed voice—

"Oh, what aileth thee, my lord?"

Tom's breath was nearly failing him; but he made shift to stammer out—

"Ah, be merciful, thou! In sooth I am no lord, but only poor Tom Canty of Offal Court in the city. Prithee let me see the prince, and he will of his grace restore to me my rags, and let me hence unhurt. Oh, be thou merciful, and save me!"

By this time the boy was on his knees, and supplicating with his eyes and uplifted hands as well as with his tongue. The young girl seemed horror-stricken. She cried out—

"O my lord, on thy knees?—and to *me*!"

Then she fled away in fright; and Tom, smitten with despair, sank down, murmuring—

"There is no help, there is no hope. Now will they come and take me."

Whilst he lay there benumbed with terror, dreadful tidings were speeding through the palace. The whisper—for it was whispered always—flew from menial to menial, from lord to lady, down all the long corridors, from story to story, from saloon to saloon, "The prince hath gone mad, the prince hath gone mad!" Soon every saloon, every marble hall, had its groups of glittering lords and ladies, and other groups of dazzling lesser folk, talking earnestly together in whispers, and every face had in it dismay. Presently a splendid official came marching by these groups, making solemn proclamation—

"IN THE NAME OF THE KING!

Let none list to this false and foolish matter, upon pain of death, nor discuss the same, nor carry it abroad. In the name of the King!"

The whisperings ceased as suddenly as if the whisperers had been stricken dumb.

Soon there was a general buzz along the corridors, of "The prince! See, the prince comes!"

Poor Tom came slowly walking past the low-bowing groups, trying to bow in return, and meekly gazing upon his strange surroundings with bewildered and pathetic eyes. Great nobles walked upon each side of him, making him lean upon them, and so steady his steps. Behind him followed the court-physicians and some servants.

Presently Tom found himself in a noble apartment of the palace and heard the door close behind him. Around him stood those who had come with him. Before him, at a little distance, reclined a very large and very fat man, with a wide, pulpy face, and a stern expression. His large head was very grey; and his whiskers, which he wore only around his face, like a frame, were grey also. His clothing was of rich stuff, but old, and slightly frayed in places. One of his swollen legs had a pillow under it, and was wrapped in bandages. There was silence now; and there was no head there but was bent in reverence, except this man's. This stern-countenanced invalid was the dread Henry VIII. He said—and his face grew gentle as he began to speak—

"How now, my lord Edward, my prince? Hast been minded to cozen me, the good King thy father, who loveth thee, and kindly useth thee, with a sorry jest?"

Poor Tom was listening, as well as his dazed faculties would let him, to the beginning of this speech; but when the words 'me, the good King' fell upon his ear, his face blanched, and he dropped as instantly upon his knees as if a shot had brought him there. Lifting up his hands, he exclaimed—

"Thou the *King*? Then am I undone indeed!"

This speech seemed to stun the King. His eyes wandered from face to face aimlessly, then rested, bewildered, upon the boy before him. Then he said in a tone of deep disappointment—

"Alack, I had believed the rumour disproportioned to the truth; but I fear me 'tis not so." He breathed a heavy sigh, and said in a gentle voice, "Come to thy father, child: thou art not well."

Tom was assisted to his feet, and approached the Majesty of England, humble and trembling. The King took the frightened face between his hands, and gazed earnestly and lovingly into it awhile, as if seeking some grateful sign of returning reason there, then pressed the curly head against his breast, and patted it tenderly. Presently he said—

"Dost not know thy father, child? Break not mine old heart; say thou know'st me. Thou *dost* know me, dost thou not?"

"Yea: thou art my dread lord the King, whom God preserve!"

"True, true—that is well—be comforted, tremble not so; there is none here would hurt thee; there is none here but loves thee. Thou art better now; thy ill dream passeth—is't not so? Thou wilt not miscall thyself again, as they say thou didst a little while agone?"

"I pray thee of thy grace believe me, I did but speak the truth, most dread lord; for I am the meanest among thy subjects, being a pauper born, and 'tis by a sore mischance and accident I am here, albeit I was therein nothing blameful. I am but young to die, and thou canst save me with one little word. Oh speak it, sir!"

"Die? Talk not so, sweet prince—peace, peace, to thy troubled heart—thou shalt not die!"

Tom dropped upon his knees with a glad cry—

"God requite thy mercy, O my King, and save thee long to bless thy land!" Then springing up, he turned a joyful face toward the two lords in waiting, and exclaimed, "Thou heard'st it! I am not to die: the King hath said it!" There was no movement, save that all bowed with grave respect; but no one spoke. He hesitated, a little confused, then turned timidly toward the King, saying, "I may go now?"

"Go? Surely, if thou desirest. But why not tarry yet a little? Whither wouldst go?"

Tom dropped his eyes, and answered humbly—

"Peradventure I mistook; but I did think me free, and so was I moved to seek again the kennel where I was born and bred to misery, yet which harboureth my mother and my sisters, and so is home to me; whereas these pomps and splendours whereunto I am not used—oh, please you, sir, to let me go!"

The King was silent and thoughtful a while, and his face betrayed a growing distress and uneasiness. Presently he said, with something of hope in his voice—

"Perchance he is but mad upon this one strain, and hath his wits unmarred as toucheth other matter. God send it may be so! We will make trial."

Then he asked Tom a question in Latin, and Tom answered him lamely in the same tongue. The lords and doctors manifested their gratification also. The King said—

"'Twas not according to his schooling and ability, but showeth that his mind is but diseased, not stricken fatally. How say you, sir?"

The physician addressed bowed low, and replied—

"It jumpeth with my own conviction, sire, that thou hast divined aright."

The King looked pleased with this encouragement, coming as it did from so excellent authority, and continued with good heart—

"Now mark ye all: we will try him further."

He put a question to Tom in French. Tom stood silent a moment, embarrassed by having so many eyes centred upon him, then said diffidently—

"I have no knowledge of this tongue, so please your majesty."

The King fell back upon his couch. The attendants flew to his assistance; but he put them aside, and said—

"Trouble me not—it is nothing but a scurvy faintness. Raise me! There, 'tis sufficient. Come hither, child; there, rest thy poor troubled head upon thy father's heart, and be at peace. Thou'lt soon be well: 'tis but a passing fantasy. Fear thou not; thou'lt soon be well." Then he turned toward the company: his gentle manner changed, and baleful lightnings began to play from his eyes. He said—

"List ye all! This my son is mad; but it is not permanent. Over-study hath done this, and somewhat too much of confinement. Away with his books and teachers! see ye to it. Pleasure him with sports, beguile him in wholesome ways, so that his health come again." He raised himself higher still, and went on with energy, "He is mad; but he is my son, and England's heir; and, mad or sane, still shall he reign! And hear ye further, and proclaim it: whoso speaketh of this his distemper worketh against the peace and order of these realms, and shall to the gallows! . . . Give me to drink—I burn: this sorrow sappeth my strength. . . . There, take away the cup. . . . Support me. There, that is well. Mad, is he? Were he a thousand times mad, yet is he Prince of Wales, and I the King will confirm it. This very morrow shall he be installed in his princely dignity in due and ancient form. Take instant order for it, my Lord Hertford."

One of the nobles knelt at the royal couch, and said—

"The King's majesty knoweth that the Hereditary Great Marshal of England lieth attainted in the Tower. It were not meet that one attainted—"

"Peace! Insult not mine ears with his hated name. Is this man to live for ever? Am I to be baulked of my will? Is the prince to tarry uninstalled, because, forsooth, the realm lacketh an Earl Marshal free of treasonable taint to invest him with his honours? No, by the splendour of God! Warn my Parliament to bring me Norfolk's doom before the sun rise again, else shall they answer for it grievously!"*

Lord Hertford said—

"The King's will is law;" and, rising, returned to his former place.

Gradually the wrath faded out of the old King's face, and he said—

"Kiss me, my prince. There . . . what fearest thou? Am I not thy loving father?"

---

* The King was now approaching fast towards his end; and fearing lest Norfolk should escape him, he sent a message to the Commons, by which he desired them to hasten the Bill, on pretence that Norfolk enjoyed the dignity of Earl Marshal, and it was necessary to appoint another, who might officiate at the ensuing ceremony of installing his son Prince of Wales.—Hume's History of England, vol. iii. p. 307.

"Thou art good to me that am unworthy, O mighty and gracious lord: that in truth I know. But—but—it grieveth me to think of him that is to die, and—"

"Ah, 'tis like thee, 'tis like thee! I know thy heart is still the same, even though thy mind hath suffered hurt, for thou wert ever of a gentle spirit. But this duke standeth between thee and thine honours: I will have another in his stead that shall bring no taint to his great office. Comfort thee, my prince: trouble not thy poor head with this matter."

"But is it not I that speed him hence, my liege? How long might he not live, but for me?"

"Take no thought of him, my prince: he is not worthy. Kiss me once again, and go to thy trifles and amusements; for my malady distresseth me. I am aweary, and would rest. Go with thine uncle Hertford and thy people, and come again when my body is refreshed."

Tom, heavy-hearted, was conducted from the presence, for this last sentence was a death-blow to the hope he had cherished that now he would be set free. Once more he heard the buzz of low voices exclaiming, "The prince, the prince comes!"

His spirits sank lower and lower as he moved between the glittering files of bowing courtiers; for he recognized that he was indeed a captive now, and might remain for ever shut up in this gilded cage, a forlorn and friendless prince, except God in his mercy take pity on him and set him free.

And, turn where he would, he seemed to see floating in the air the severed head and the remembered face of the great Duke of Norfolk, the eyes fixed on him reproachfully.

His old dreams had been so pleasant; but this reality was so dreary!

6

Tom Receives Instructions

Tom was conducted to the principal apartment of a noble suite, and made to sit down—a thing which he was loth to do, since there were elderly men and men of high degree about him. He begged them to be seated also, but they only bowed their thanks or murmured them, and remained standing. He would have insisted, but his 'uncle' the Earl of Hertford whispered in his ear—

"Prithee, insist not, my lord; it is not meet that they sit in thy presence."

The Lord St. John was announced, and after making obeisance to Tom, he said—

"I come upon the King's errand, concerning a matter which requireth privacy. Will it please your royal highness to dismiss all that attend you here, save my lord the Earl of Hertford?"

Observing that Tom did not seem to know how to proceed, Hertford whispered him to make a sign with his hand, and not trouble himself to speak unless he chose. When the waiting gentlemen had retired, Lord St. John said—

"His majesty commandeth, that for due and weighty reasons of state, the prince's grace shall hide his infirmity in all ways that be within his power, till it be passed and he be as he was before. To wit, that he shall deny to none that he is the true prince, and heir to England's greatness; that he shall uphold his princely dignity, and shall receive, without word or sign of protest, that reverence and observance which unto it do appertain of right and ancient usage; that he shall cease to speak to any of that lowly birth and life his malady hath conjured out of the unwholesome imaginings of o'er-wrought fancy; that he shall strive with diligence to bring unto his memory again those faces which he was wont to know—and where he faileth he shall hold his peace, neither betraying by semblance of surprise or other sign that he hath forgot; that upon occasions of state, whensoever any matter shall perplex him as to the thing he should do or the utterance he should make, he shall show nought of unrest to the curious that look on, but take advice in that matter of the Lord Hertford, or my humble self, which are commanded of the King to be upon this service and close at call, till this commandment be dissolved. Thus saith the King's majesty, who sendeth greeting to your royal highness, and prayeth that God will of His mercy quickly heal you and have you now and ever in His holy keeping."

The Lord St. John made reverence and stood aside. Tom replied resignedly—

"The King hath said it. None may palter with the King's command, or fit it to his ease, where it doth chafe, with deft evasions. The King shall be obeyed."

Lord Hertford said—

"Touching the King's majesty's ordainment concerning books and such like serious matters, it may peradventure please your highness to ease your time with lightsome entertainment, lest you go wearied to the banquet and suffer harm thereby."

Tom's face showed inquiring surprise; and a blush followed when he saw Lord St. John's eyes bent sorrowfully upon him. His lordship said—

"Thy memory still wrongeth thee, and thou hast shown surprise—but suffer it not to trouble thee, for 'tis a matter that will not bide, but depart with thy mending malady. My Lord of Hertford speaketh of the city's banquet which the King's majesty did promise, some two months flown, your highness should attend. Thou recallest it now?"

"It grieves me to confess it had indeed escaped me," said Tom, in a hesitating voice; and blushed again.

At this moment the Lady Elizabeth and the Lady Jane Grey were announced. The two lords exchanged significant glances, and Hertford stepped quickly toward the door. As the young girls passed him, he said in a low voice—

"I pray ye, ladies, seem not to observe his humours, nor show surprise when his memory doth lapse—it will grieve you to note how it doth stick at every trifle."

Meantime Lord St. John was saying in Tom's ear—

"Please you, sir, keep diligently in mind his majesty's desire. Remember all thou canst—*seem* to remember all else. Let them not perceive that thou art much changed from thy wont, for thou knowest how tenderly thy old play-fellows bear thee in their hearts and how 'twould grieve them. Art willing, sir, that I remain?—and thine uncle?"

Tom signified assent with a gesture and a murmured word, for he was already learning, and in his simple heart was resolved to acquit himself as best he might, according to the King's command.

In spite of every precaution, the conversation among the young people became a little embarrassing at times. More than once, in truth, Tom was near to breaking down and confessing himself unequal to his tremendous part; but the tact of the Princess Elizabeth saved him, or a word from one or the other of the vigilant lords, thrown in apparently by chance, had the same happy effect. Once the little Lady Jane turned to Tom and dismayed him with this question—

"Hast paid thy duty to the Queen's majesty today, my lord?"

Tom hesitated, looked distressed, and was about to stammer out something at hazard, when Lord St. John took the word and answered for him with the easy grace of a courtier accustomed to encounter delicate difficulties and to be ready for them—

"He hath indeed, madam, and she did greatly hearten him, as touching his majesty's condition; is it not so, your highness?"

Tom mumbled something that stood for assent, but felt that he was getting upon dangerous ground. Somewhat later it was mentioned that Tom was to study no more at present, whereupon her little ladyship exclaimed—

"'Tis a pity, 'tis a pity! Thou wert proceeding bravely. But bide thy time in patience: it will not be for long. Thou'lt yet be graced with learning like thy father, and make thy tongue master of as many languages as his, good my prince."

"My father!" cried Tom, off his guard for the moment. "I trow he cannot speak his own so that any but the swine that wallow in the styes may tell his meaning; and as for learning of any sort soever—"

He looked up and encountered a solemn warning in my Lord St. John's eyes.

He stopped, blushed, then continued low and sadly: "Ah, my malady persecuteth me again, and my mind wandereth. I meant the King's grace no irreverence."

"We know it, sir," said the Princess Elizabeth, taking her 'brother's' hand between her two palms, respectfully but caressingly; "trouble not thyself as to that. The fault is none of thine, but thy distemper's."

"Thou'rt a gentle comforter, sweet lady," said Tom, gratefully, "and my heart moveth me to thank thee for't, an' I may be so bold."

Once the giddy little Lady Jane fired a simple Greek phrase at Tom. The Princess Elizabeth's quick eye saw by the serene blankness of the target's front that the shaft was overshot; so she tranquilly delivered a return volley of sounding Greek on Tom's behalf, and then straightway changed the talk to other matters.

Time wore on pleasantly, and likewise smoothly, on the whole. Snags and sandbars grew less and less frequent, and Tom grew more and more at his ease, seeing that all were so lovingly bent upon helping him and overlooking his mistakes. When it came out that the little ladies were to accompany him to the Lord Mayor's banquet in the evening, his heart gave a bound of relief and delight, for he felt that he should not be friendless, now, among that multitude of strangers; whereas, an hour earlier, the idea of their going with him would have been an insupportable terror to him.

Tom's guardian angels, the two lords, had had less comfort in the interview than the other parties to it. They felt much as if they were piloting a great ship through a dangerous channel; they were on the alert constantly, and found their office no child's play. Wherefore, at last, when the ladies' visit was drawing to a close and the Lord Guilford Dudley was announced, they not only felt that their charge had been sufficiently taxed for the present, but also that they themselves were not in the best condition to take their ship back and make their anxious voyage all over again. So they respectfully advised Tom to excuse himself, which he was very glad to do, although a slight shade of disappointment might have been observed upon my Lady Jane's face when she heard the splendid stripling denied admittance.

There was a pause now, a sort of waiting silence which Tom could not understand. He glanced at Lord Hertford, who gave him a sign—but he failed to understand that also. The ready Elizabeth came to the rescue with her usual easy grace. She made reverence and said—

"Have we leave of the prince's grace my brother to go?"

Tom said—

"Indeed your ladyships can have whatsoever of me they will, for the asking; yet would I rather give them any other thing that in my poor power lieth, than leave to take the light and blessing of their presence hence. Give ye good den, and God be with ye!" Then he smiled inwardly at the thought, "'Tis not for nought I have dwelt but among princes in my reading, and taught my tongue some slight trick of their broidered and gracious speech withal!"

When the illustrious maidens were gone, Tom turned wearily to his keepers and said—

"May it please your lordships to grant me leave to go into some corner and rest me?"

Lord Hertford said—

"So please your highness, it is for you to command, it is for us to obey. That thou should'st rest is indeed a needful thing, since thou must journey to the city presently."

He touched a bell, and a page appeared, who was ordered to desire the presence of Sir William Herbert. This gentleman came straightway, and conducted Tom to an inner apartment. Tom's first movement there was to reach for a cup of water; but a silk-and-velvet servitor seized it, dropped upon one knee, and offered it to him on a golden salver.

Next the tired captive sat down and was going to take off his buskins, timidly asking leave with his eye, but another silk-and-velvet discomforter went down upon his knees and took the office from him. He made two or three further efforts to help himself, but being promptly forestalled each time, he finally gave up, with a sigh of resignation and a murmured "Beshrew me, but I marvel they do not require to breathe for me also!" Slippered, and wrapped in a sumptuous robe, he laid himself down at last to rest, but not to sleep, for his head was too full of thoughts and the room too full of people. He could not dismiss the former, so they stayed; he did not know enough to dismiss the latter, so they stayed also, to his vast regret—and theirs.

Tom's departure had left his two noble guardians alone. They mused a while, with much head-shaking and walking the floor, then Lord St. John said—

"Plainly, what dost thou think?"

"Plainly, then, this. The King is near his end; my nephew is mad—mad will mount the throne, and mad remain. God protect England, since she will need it!"

"Verily it promiseth so, indeed. But . . . have you no misgivings as to . . . as to . . ."

The speaker hesitated, and finally stopped. He evidently felt that he was upon delicate ground. Lord Hertford stopped before him, looked into his face with a clear, frank eye, and said—

"Speak on—there is none to hear but me. Misgivings as to what?"

"I am full loth to word the thing that is in my mind, and thou so near to him in blood, my lord. But craving pardon if I do offend, seemeth it not strange that madness could so change his port and manner?—not but that his port and speech are princely still, but that they *differ*, in one unweighty trifle or another, from what his custom was aforetime. Seemeth it not strange that madness should filch from his memory his father's very lineaments; the customs and observances that are his due from such as be about him; and, leaving him his Latin, strip him of his Greek and French? My lord, be not offended, but ease my mind of its disquiet and receive my grateful thanks. It haunteth me, his saying he was not the prince, and so—"

"Peace, my lord, thou utterest treason! Hast forgot the King's command? Remember I am party to thy crime if I but listen."

St. John paled, and hastened to say—

"I was in fault, I do confess it. Betray me not, grant me this grace out of thy courtesy, and I will neither think nor speak of this thing more. Deal not hardly with me, sir, else am I ruined."

"I am content, my lord. So thou offend not again, here or in the ears of others, it shall be as though thou hadst not spoken. But thou need'st not have misgivings. He is my sister's son; are not his voice, his face, his form, familiar to me from his cradle? Madness can do all the odd conflicting things thou seest in him, and more. Dost not recall how that the old Baron Marley, being mad, forgot the favour of his own countenance that he had known for sixty years, and held it was another's; nay, even claimed he was the son of Mary Magdalene, and that his head was made of Spanish glass; and, sooth to say, he suffered none to touch it, lest by mischance some heedless hand might shiver it? Give thy misgivings easement, good my lord. This is the very prince—I know him well—and soon will be thy king; it may advantage thee to bear this in mind, and more dwell upon it than the other."

After some further talk, in which the Lord St. John covered up his mistake as well as he could by repeated protests that his faith was thoroughly grounded now, and could not be assailed by doubts again, the Lord Hertford relieved his fellow-keeper, and sat down to keep watch and ward alone. He was soon deep in meditation, and evidently the longer he thought, the more he was bothered. By and by he began to pace the floor and mutter.

"Tush, he *must* be the prince! Will any be in all the land maintain there can be two, not of one blood and birth, so marvellously twinned? And even were it so, 'twere yet a stranger miracle that chance should cast the one into the other's place. Nay, 'tis folly, folly, folly!"

Presently he said—

"Now were he impostor and called himself prince, look you *that* would be natural; that would be reasonable. But lived ever an impostor yet, who, being called prince by the king, prince by the court, prince by all, *denied* his dignity and pleaded against his exaltation? *No*! By the soul of St. Swithin, no! This is the true prince, gone mad!"

7

Tom's First Royal Dinner

Somewhat after one in the afternoon, Tom resignedly underwent the ordeal of being dressed for dinner. He found himself as finely clothed as before, but everything different, everything changed, from his ruff to his stockings. He was presently conducted with much state to a spacious and ornate apartment, where a table was already set for one. Its furniture was all of massy gold, and beautified with designs which well-nigh made it priceless, since they were the work of Benvenuto. The room was half-filled with noble servitors. A chaplain said grace, and Tom was about to fall to, for hunger had long been constitutional with him, but was interrupted by my lord the Earl of Berkeley, who fastened a napkin about his neck; for the great post of Diaperers to the Prince of Wales was hereditary in this nobleman's family. Tom's cupbearer was present, and forestalled all his attempts to help himself to wine. The Taster to his highness the Prince of Wales was there also, prepared to taste any suspicious dish upon requirement, and run the risk of being poisoned. He was only an ornamental appendage at this time, and was seldom called upon to exercise his function; but there had been times, not many generations past, when the office of taster had its perils, and was not a grandeur to be desired. Why they did not use a dog or a plumber seems strange; but all the ways of royalty are strange. My Lord d'Arcy, First Groom of the Chamber, was there, to do goodness knows what; but there he was—let that suffice. The Lord Chief Butler was there, and stood behind Tom's chair, overseeing the solemnities, under command of the Lord Great Steward and the Lord Head Cook, who stood near. Tom had three hundred and eighty-four servants beside these; but they were not all in that room, of course, nor the quarter of them; neither was Tom aware yet that they existed.

All those that were present had been well drilled within the hour to remember that the prince was temporarily out of his head, and to be careful to show no surprise at his vagaries. These 'vagaries' were soon on exhibition before them; but they only moved their compassion and their sorrow, not their mirth. It was a heavy affliction to them to see the beloved prince so stricken.

Poor Tom ate with his fingers mainly; but no one smiled at it, or even seemed to observe it. He inspected his napkin curiously, and with deep interest, for it was of a very dainty and beautiful fabric, then said with simplicity—

"Prithee, take it away, lest in mine unheedfulness it be soiled."

The Hereditary Diaperer took it away with reverent manner, and without word or protest of any sort.

Tom examined the turnips and the lettuce with interest, and asked what they were, and if they were to be eaten; for it was only recently that men had begun to raise these things in England in place of importing them as luxuries from Holland.* His question was answered with grave respect, and no surprise manifested. When he had finished his dessert, he filled his pockets with nuts; but nobody appeared to be aware of it, or disturbed by it. But the next moment he was himself disturbed by it, and showed discomposure; for this was the only service he had been permitted to do with his own hands during the meal, and he did not doubt that he had done a most improper and unprincely thing. At that moment the muscles of his nose began to twitch, and the end of that organ to lift and wrinkle. This continued, and Tom began to evince a growing distress. He looked appealingly, first at one and then another of the lords about him, and tears came into his eyes. They sprang forward with dismay in their faces, and begged to know his trouble. Tom said with genuine anguish—

"I crave your indulgence: my nose itcheth cruelly. What is the custom and usage in this emergence? Prithee, speed, for 'tis but a little time that I can bear it."

None smiled; but all were sore perplexed, and looked one to the other in deep tribulation for counsel. But behold, here was a dead wall, and nothing in English history to tell how to get over it. The Master of Ceremonies was not present: there was no one who felt safe to venture upon this uncharted sea, or risk the attempt to solve this solemn problem. Alas! there was no Hereditary Scratcher. Meantime the tears had overflowed their banks, and begun to trickle down Tom's cheeks. His twitching nose was pleading more urgently than ever for relief. At last nature broke down the barriers of etiquette: Tom lifted up an inward prayer for pardon if he was doing wrong, and brought relief to the burdened hearts of his court by scratching his nose himself.

* It was not till the end of this reign (Henry VIII) that any salads, carrots, turnips, or other edible roots were produced in England. The little of these vegetables that was used was formerly imported from Holland and Flanders. Queen Catherine, when she wanted a salad, was obliged to dispatch a messenger thither on purpose.—Hume's *History of England*, vol. iii. p. 314.

His meal being ended, a lord came and held before him a broad, shallow, golden dish with fragrant rosewater in it, to cleanse his mouth and fingers with; and my lord the Hereditary Diaperer stood by with a napkin for his use. Tom gazed at the dish a puzzled moment or two, then raised it to his lips, and gravely took a draught. Then he returned it to the waiting lord, and said—

"Nay, it likes me not, my lord: it hath a pretty flavour, but it wanteth strength."

This new eccentricity of the prince's ruined mind made all the hearts about him ache; but the sad sight moved none to merriment.

Tom's next unconscious blunder was to get up and leave the table just when the chaplain had taken his stand behind his chair, and with uplifted hands, and closed, uplifted eyes, was in the act of beginning the blessing. Still nobody seemed to perceive that the prince had done a thing unusual.

By his own request our small friend was now conducted to his private cabinet, and left there alone to his own devices. Hanging upon hooks in the oaken wainscoting were the several pieces of a suit of shining steel armour, covered all over with beautiful designs exquisitely inlaid in gold. This martial panoply belonged to the true prince—a recent present from Madam Parr the Queen. Tom put on the greaves, the gauntlets, the plumed helmet, and such other pieces as he could don without assistance, and for a while was minded to call for help and complete the matter, but bethought him of the nuts he had brought away from dinner, and the joy it would be to eat them with no crowd to eye him, and no Grand Hereditaries to pester him with undesired services; so he restored the pretty things to their several places, and soon was cracking nuts, and feeling almost naturally happy for the first time since God for his sins had made him a prince. When the nuts were all gone, he stumbled upon some inviting books in a closet, among them one about the etiquette of the English court. This was a prize. He lay down upon a sumptuous divan, and proceeded to instruct himself with honest zeal. Let us leave him there for the present.

8

The Question of the Seal

About five o'clock Henry VIII awoke out of an unrefreshing nap, and muttered to himself, "Troublous dreams, troublous dreams! Mine end is now at hand: so say these warnings, and my failing pulses do confirm it." Presently a wicked light flamed up in his eye, and he muttered, "Yet will not I die till *He* go before."

His attendants perceiving that he was awake, one of them asked his pleasure concerning the Lord Chancellor, who was waiting without.

"Admit him, admit him!" exclaimed the King eagerly.

The Lord Chancellor entered, and knelt by the King's couch, saying—

"I have given order, and, according to the King's command, the peers of the realm, in their robes, do now stand at the bar of the House, where, having confirmed the Duke of Norfolk's doom, they humbly wait his majesty's further pleasure in the matter."

The King's face lit up with a fierce joy. Said he—

"Lift me up! In mine own person will I go before my Parliament, and with mine own hand will I seal the warrant that rids me of—"

His voice failed; an ashen pallor swept the flush from his cheeks; and the attendants eased him back upon his pillows, and hurriedly assisted him with restoratives. Presently he said sorrowfully—

"Alack, how have I longed for this sweet hour! and lo, too late it cometh, and I am robbed of this so coveted chance. But speed ye, speed ye! let others do this happy office sith 'tis denied to me. I put my Great Seal in commission: choose thou the lords that shall compose it, and get ye to your work. Speed ye, man! Before the sun shall rise and set again, bring me his head that I may see it."

"According to the King's command, so shall it be. Will't please your majesty to order that the Seal be now restored to me, so that I may forth upon the business?"

"The Seal? Who keepeth the Seal but thou?"

"Please your majesty, you did take it from me two days since, saying it should no more do its office till your own royal hand should use it upon the Duke of Norfolk's warrant."

"Why, so in sooth I did: I do remember. . . . What did I with it? . . . I am very feeble. . . . So oft these days doth my memory play the traitor with me. . . . 'Tis strange, strange—"

The King dropped into inarticulate mumblings, shaking his grey head weakly from time to time, and gropingly trying to recollect what he had done with the Seal. At last my Lord Hertford ventured to kneel and offer information—

"Sire, if that I may be so bold, here be several that do remember with me how that you gave the Great Seal into the hands of his highness the Prince of Wales to keep against the day that—"

"True, most true!" interrupted the King. "Fetch it! Go: time flieth!"

Lord Hertford flew to Tom, but returned to the King before very long, troubled and empty-handed. He delivered himself to this effect—

"It grieveth me, my lord the King, to bear so heavy and unwelcome tidings; but it is the will of God that the prince's affliction abideth still, and he cannot recall to mind that he received the Seal. So came I quickly to report, thinking it were waste of precious time, and little worth withal, that any should attempt to search the long array of chambers and saloons that belong unto his royal high—"

A groan from the King interrupted the lord at this point. After a little while his majesty said, with a deep sadness in his tone—

"Trouble him no more, poor child. The hand of God lieth heavy upon him, and my heart goeth out in loving compassion for him, and sorrow that I may not bear his burden on mine old trouble-weighted shoulders, and so bring him peace."

He closed his eyes, fell to mumbling, and presently was silent. After a time he opened his eyes again, and gazed vacantly around until his glance rested upon the kneeling Lord Chancellor. Instantly his face flushed with wrath—

"What, thou here yet! By the glory of God, an' thou gettest not about that traitor's business, thy mitre shall have holiday the morrow for lack of a head to grace withal!"

The trembling Chancellor answered—

"Good your Majesty, I cry you mercy! I but waited for the Seal."

"Man, hast lost thy wits? The small Seal which aforetime I was wont to take with me abroad lieth in my treasury. And, since the Great Seal hath flown away, shall not it suffice? Hast lost thy wits? Begone! And hark ye—come no more till thou do bring his head."

The poor Chancellor was not long in removing himself from this dangerous vicinity; nor did the commission waste time in giving the royal assent to the work of the slavish Parliament, and appointing the morrow for the beheading of the premier peer of England, the luckless Duke of Norfolk.*

9

The River Pageant

At nine in the evening the whole vast river-front of the palace was blazing with light. The river itself, as far as the eye could reach citywards, was so thickly covered with watermen's boats and with pleasure-barges, all fringed with coloured lanterns, and gently agitated by the waves, that it resembled a glowing and limitless garden of flowers stirred to soft motion by summer winds. The grand terrace of stone steps leading down to the water, spacious enough to mass the army of a German principality upon, was a picture to see, with its ranks of royal halberdiers in polished armour, and its troops of brilliantly costumed servitors flitting up and down, and to and fro, in the hurry of preparation.

Presently a command was given, and immediately all living creatures vanished from the steps. Now the air was heavy with the hush of suspense and expectancy. As far as one's vision could carry, he might see the myriads of people in the boats rise up, and shade their eyes from the glare of lanterns and torches, and gaze toward the palace.

A file of forty or fifty state barges drew up to the steps. They were richly gilt, and their lofty prows and sterns were elaborately carved. Some of them were decorated with banners and streamers; some with cloth-of-gold and arras embroidered with coats-of-arms; others with silken flags that had

* The House of Peers, without examining the prisoner, without trial or evidence, passed a Bill of Attainder against him and sent it down to the Commons . . . The obsequious Commons obeyed his (the King's) directions; and the King, having affixed the Royal assent to the Bill by commissioners, issued orders for the execution of Norfolk on the morning of January 29 (the next day).—Hume's *History of England*, vol iii. p 306.

numberless little silver bells fastened to them, which shook out tiny showers of joyous music whenever the breezes fluttered them; others of yet higher pretensions, since they belonged to nobles in the prince's immediate service, had their sides picturesquely fenced with shields gorgeously emblazoned with armorial bearings. Each state barge was towed by a tender. Besides the rowers, these tenders carried each a number of men-at-arms in glossy helmet and breastplate, and a company of musicians.

"A troop of halberdiers appeared in the gateway"

The advance-guard of the expected procession now appeared in the great gateway, a troop of halberdiers. 'They were dressed in striped hose of black and tawny, velvet caps graced at the sides with silver roses, and doublets of murrey and blue cloth, embroidered on the front and back with the three feathers, the prince's blazon, woven in gold. Their halberd staves were covered with crimson velvet, fastened with gilt nails, and ornamented with gold tassels. Filing off on the right and left, they formed two long lines, extending from the gateway of the palace to the water's edge. A thick rayed cloth or carpet was then unfolded, and laid down between them by attendants in the gold-and-crimson liveries of the prince. This done, a flourish of trumpets resounded from within. A lively prelude arose from the musicians on the water; and two ushers with white wands marched with a slow and stately pace from the portal. They were followed by an officer bearing the civic mace, after whom came another carrying the city's sword; then several sergeants of the city guard, in their full accoutrements, and with badges on their sleeves; then the Garter King-at-arms, in his tabard; then several Knights of the Bath, each with a white lace on his sleeve; then their esquires; then the judges, in their robes of scarlet and coifs; then the Lord High Chancellor of England, in a robe of scarlet, open before, and purfled with minever; then a deputation of aldermen, in their scarlet cloaks; and then the heads of the different civic companies, in their robes of state. Now came twelve French gentlemen, in splendid habiliments, consisting of pourpoints of white damask barred with gold, short mantles of crimson velvet lined with violet taffeta, and carnation-coloured *hauts-de-chausses*, and took their way down the steps. They were of the suite of the French ambassador, and were followed by twelve cavaliers of the suite of the Spanish ambassador, clothed in black velvet, unrelieved by any ornament. Following these came several great English nobles with their attendants.'

There was a flourish of trumpets within; and the Prince's uncle, the future great Duke of Somerset, emerged from the gateway, arrayed in a 'doublet of black cloth-of-gold, and a cloak of crimson satin flowered with gold, and ribanded with nets of silver.' He turned, doffed his plumed cap, bent his body in a low reverence, and began to step backward, bowing at each step. A prolonged trumpet-blast followed, and a proclamation, "Way for the high and mighty the Lord Edward, Prince of Wales!" High aloft on the palace walls a long line of red tongues of flame leapt forth with a thunder-crash; the massed world on the river burst into a mighty roar of welcome; and Tom Canty, the cause and hero of it all, stepped into view and slightly bowed his princely head.

He was "magnificently habited in a doublet of white satin, with a front-piece of purple cloth-of-tissue, powdered with diamonds, and edged with ermine. Over this he wore a mantle of white cloth-of-gold, pounced with the triple-feathered crest, lined with blue satin, set with pearls and precious stones, and fastened with a clasp of brilliants. About his neck hung the order of the Garter, and several princely foreign orders;" and wherever light fell upon him jewels responded with a blinding flash. O Tom Canty, born in a hovel, bred in the gutters of London, familiar with rags and dirt and misery, what a spectacle is this!

10

The Prince in the Toils

We left John Canty dragging the rightful prince into Offal Court, with a noisy and delighted mob at his heels. There was but one person in it who offered a pleading word for the captive, and he was not heeded; he was hardly even heard, so great was the turmoil. The Prince continued to struggle for freedom, and to rage against the treatment he was suffering, until John Canty lost what little patience was left in him, and raised his oaken cudgel in a sudden fury over the Prince's head. The single pleader for the lad sprang to stop the man's arm, and the blow descended upon his own wrist. Canty roared out—

"Thou'lt meddle, wilt thou? Then have thy reward."

"A dim form sank to the ground"

His cudgel crashed down upon the meddler's head: there was a groan, a dim form sank to the ground among the feet of the crowd, and the next moment it lay there in the dark alone. The mob pressed on, their enjoyment nothing disturbed by this episode.

Presently the Prince found himself in John Canty's abode, with the door closed against the outsiders. By the vague light of a tallow candle which was thrust into a bottle, he made out the main features of the loathsome den, and also the occupants of it. Two frowsy girls and a middle-aged woman cowered against the wall in one corner, with the aspect of animals habituated to harsh usage, and expecting and dreading it now. From another corner stole a withered hag with streaming grey hair and malignant eyes. John Canty said to this one—

"Tarry! There's fine mummeries here. Mar them not till thou'st enjoyed them: then let thy hand be heavy as thou wilt. Stand forth, lad. Now say thy foolery again, an thou'st not forgot it. Name thy name. Who art thou?"

The insulted blood mounted to the little prince's cheek once more, and he lifted a steady and indignant gaze to the man's face and said—

"'Tis but ill-breeding in such as thou to command me to speak. I tell thee now, as I told thee before, I am Edward, Prince of Wales, and none other."

The stunning surprise of this reply nailed the hag's feet to the floor where she stood, and almost took her breath. She stared at the Prince in stupid amazement, which so amused her ruffianly son, that he burst into a roar of laughter. But the effect upon Tom Canty's mother and sisters was different. Their dread of bodily injury gave way at once to distress of a different sort. They ran forward with woe and dismay in their faces, exclaiming—

"Oh, poor Tom, poor lad!"

The mother fell on her knees before the Prince, put her hands upon his shoulders, and gazed yearningly into his face through her rising tears. Then she said—

"Oh, my poor boy! Thy foolish reading hath wrought its woeful work at last, and ta'en thy wit away. Ah! why did'st thou cleave to it when I so warned thee 'gainst it? Thou'st broke thy mother's heart."

The Prince looked into her face, and said gently—

"Thy son is well, and hath not lost his wits, good dame. Comfort thee: let me to the palace where he is, and straightway will the King my father restore him to thee."

"The King thy father! Oh, my child! unsay these words that be freighted with death for thee, and ruin for all that be near to thee. Shake of this gruesome dream. Call back thy poor wandering memory. Look upon me. Am not I thy mother that bore thee, and loveth thee?"

The Prince shook his head and reluctantly said—

"God knoweth I am loth to grieve thy heart; but truly have I never looked upon thy face before."

The woman sank back to a sitting posture on the floor, and, covering her eyes with her hands, gave way to heart-broken sobs and wailings.

"Let the show go on!" shouted Canty. "What, Nan!—what, Bet! Mannerless wenches! will ye stand in the Prince's presence? Upon your knees, ye pauper scum, and do him reverence!"

He followed this with another horse-laugh. The girls began to plead timidly for their brother; and Nan said—

"An thou wilt but let him to bed, father, rest and sleep will heal his madness: prithee, do."

"Do, father," said Bet; "he is more worn than is his wont. Tomorrow will he be himself again, and will beg with diligence, and come not empty home again."

This remark sobered the father's joviality, and brought his mind to business. He turned angrily upon the Prince, and said—

"The morrow must we pay two pennies to him that owns this hole; two pennies, mark ye—all this money for a half-year's rent, else out of this we go. Show what thou'st gathered with thy lazy begging."

The Prince said—

"Offend me not with thy sordid matters. I tell thee again I am the King's son."

A sounding blow upon the Prince's shoulder from Canty's broad palm sent him staggering into goodwife Canty's arms, who clasped him to her breast, and sheltered him from a pelting rain of cuffs and slaps by interposing her own person. The frightened girls retreated to their corner; but the grandmother stepped eagerly forward to assist her son. The Prince sprang away from Mrs. Canty, exclaiming—

"Thou shalt not suffer for me, madam. Let these swine do their will upon me alone."

This speech infuriated the swine to such a degree that they set about their work without waste of time. Between them they belaboured the boy right soundly, and then gave the girls and their mother a beating for showing sympathy for the victim.

"Now," said Canty, "to bed, all of ye. The entertainment has tired me."

The light was put out, and the family retired. As soon as the snorings of the head of the house and his mother showed that they were asleep, the young girls crept to where the Prince lay, and covered him tenderly from the cold with straw and rags; and their mother crept to him also, and stroked his hair, and cried over him, whispering broken words of comfort and compassion in his ear the while. She had saved a morsel for him to eat, also; but the boy's pains had swept away all appetite—at least for black and tasteless crusts. He was touched by her brave and costly defence of him, and by her commiseration; and he thanked her in very noble and princely words, and begged her to go to her sleep and try to forget her sorrows. And he added that the King his father would not let her loyal kindness and devotion go unrewarded. This return to his 'madness' broke her heart anew, and she strained him to her breast again and again, and then went back, drowned in tears, to her bed.

As she lay thinking and mourning, the suggestion began to creep into her mind that there was an undefinable something about this boy that was lacking in Tom Canty, mad or sane. She could not describe it, she could not tell just what it was, and yet her sharp mother-instinct seemed to detect it and perceive it. What if the boy were really not her son, after all? Oh, absurd! She almost smiled at the idea, spite of her griefs and troubles. No matter, she found that it was an idea that would not 'down,' but persisted in haunting her. It pursued her, it harassed her, it clung to her, and refused to be put away or ignored. At last she perceived that there was not going to be any peace for her until she should devise a test that should prove, clearly and without question, whether this lad was her son or not, and so banish these wearing and worrying doubts. Ah, yes, this was plainly the right way out of the difficulty; therefore she set her wits to work at once to contrive that test. But it was an easier thing to propose than to accomplish. She turned over in her mind one promising test after another, but was obliged to relinquish them all—none of them were absolutely sure, absolutely perfect; and an imperfect one could not satisfy her. Evidently she was racking her head in vain—it seemed manifest that she must give the matter up. While this depressing thought was passing through her mind, her ear caught the regular breathing of the boy, and she knew he had fallen asleep. And while she listened, the measured breathing was broken by a soft, startled cry, such as one utters in a troubled dream. This chance occurrence furnished her instantly with a plan worth all her laboured tests combined. She at once set herself feverishly, but noiselessly, to work to relight her candle, muttering to herself, "Had I but seen him *then*, I should have known! Since that day, when he was little, that the powder burst in his face, he hath never been startled of a sudden out of his dreams or out of his thinkings, but he hath cast his hand before his eyes, even as he did that day; and not as others would do it, with the palm inward, but always with the palm turned outward—I have seen it a hundred times, and it hath never varied nor ever failed. Yes, I shall soon know, now!"

By this time she had crept to the slumbering boy's side, with the candle, shaded, in her hand. She bent heedfully and warily over him, scarcely breathing in her suppressed excitement, and suddenly flashed the light in his face and struck the floor by his ear with her knuckles. The sleeper's eyes sprang wide open, and he cast a startled stare about him—but he made no special movement with his hands.

The poor woman was smitten almost helpless with surprise and grief; but she contrived to hide her emotions, and to soothe the boy to sleep again; then she crept apart and communed miserably with herself upon the disastrous result of her experiment. She tried to believe that her Tom's madness had banished this habitual gesture of his; but she could not do it. "No," she said, "his *hands* are not mad; they could not unlearn so old a habit in so brief a time. Oh, this is a heavy day for me!"

Still, hope was as stubborn now as doubt had been before; she could not bring herself to accept the verdict of the test; she must try the thing again—the failure must have been only an accident; so she startled the boy out of his sleep a second and a third time, at intervals—with the same result which had marked the first test; then she dragged herself to bed, and fell sorrowfully asleep, saying, "But I cannot give him up—oh no, I cannot, I cannot—he *must* be my boy!"

The poor mother's interruptions having ceased, and the Prince's pains having gradually lost their power to disturb him, utter weariness at last sealed his eyes in a profound and restful sleep. Hour after hour slipped away, and still he slept like the dead. Thus four or five hours passed. Then his stupor began to lighten. Presently, while half asleep and half awake, he murmured—

"Sir William!"

After a moment—

"Ho, Sir William Herbert! Hie thee hither, and list to the strangest dream that ever . . . Sir William! dost hear? Man, I did think me changed to a pauper, and . . . Ho there! Guards! Sir William! What! is there no groom of the chamber in waiting? Alack! it shall go hard with—"

"What aileth thee?" asked a whisper near him. "Who art thou calling?"

"Sir William Herbert. Who art thou?"

"I? Who should I be, but thy sister Nan? Oh, Tom, I had forgot! Thou'rt mad yet—poor lad, thou'rt mad yet: would I had never woke to know it again! But prithee master thy tongue, lest we be all beaten till we die!"

The startled Prince sprang partly up, but a sharp reminder from his stiffened bruises brought him to himself, and he sank back among his foul straw with a moan and the ejaculation—

"Alas! it was no dream, then!"

In a moment all the heavy sorrow and misery which sleep had banished were upon him again, and he realised that he was no longer a petted prince in a palace, with the adoring eyes of a nation upon him, but a pauper, an outcast, clothed in rags, prisoner in a den fit only for beasts, and consorting with beggars and thieves.

In the midst of his grief he began to be conscious of hilarious noises and shoutings, apparently but a block or two away. The next moment there were several sharp raps at the door; John Canty ceased from snoring and said—

"Who knocketh? What wilt thou?"

A voice answered—

"Know'st thou who it was thou laid thy cudgel on?"

"No. Neither know I, nor care."

"Belike thou'lt change thy note eftsoons. An thou would save thy neck, nothing but flight may stead thee. The man is this moment delivering up the ghost. 'Tis the priest, Father Andrew!"

"God-a-mercy!" exclaimed Canty. He roused his family, and hoarsely commanded, "Up with ye all and fly—or bide where ye are and perish!"

Scarcely five minutes later the Canty household were in the street and flying for their lives. John Canty held the Prince by the wrist, and hurried him along the dark way, giving him this caution in a low voice—

"Mind thy tongue, thou mad fool, and speak not our name. I will choose me a new name, speedily, to throw the law's dogs off the scent. Mind thy tongue, I tell thee!"

He growled these words to the rest of the family—

"If it so chance that we be separated, let each make for London Bridge; whoso findeth himself as far as the last linen-draper's shop on the bridge, let him tarry there till the others be come, then will we flee into Southwark together."

At this moment the party burst suddenly out of darkness into light; and not only into light, but into the midst of a multitude of singing, dancing, and shouting people, massed together on the river frontage. There was a line of bonfires stretching as far as one could see, up and down the Thames; London Bridge was illuminated; Southwark Bridge likewise; the entire river was aglow with the flash and sheen of coloured lights; and constant explosions of fireworks filled the skies with an intricate commingling of shooting splendours and a thick rain of dazzling sparks that almost turned night into day; everywhere were crowds of revellers; all London seemed to be at large.

John Canty delivered himself of a furious curse and commanded a retreat; but it was too late. He and his tribe were swallowed up in that swarming hive of humanity, and hopelessly separated from each other in an instant. We are not considering that the Prince was one of his tribe; Canty still kept his grip upon him. The Prince's heart was beating high with hopes of escape, now. A burly waterman, considerably exalted with liquor, found himself rudely shoved by Canty in his efforts to plough through the crowd; he laid his great hand on Canty's shoulder and said—

"Nay, whither so fast, friend? Dost canker thy soul with sordid business when all that be leal men and true make holiday?"

"Mine affairs are mine own, they concern thee not," answered Canty, roughly; "take away thy hand and let me pass."

"Sith that is thy humour, thou'lt *not* pass, till thou'st drunk to the Prince of Wales, I tell thee that," said the waterman, barring the way resolutely.

"Give me the cup, then, and make speed, make speed!"

Other revellers were interested by this time. They cried out—

"The loving-cup, the loving-cup! make the sour knave drink the loving-cup, else will we feed him to the fishes."*

So a huge loving-cup was brought; the waterman, grasping it by one of its handles, and with the other hand bearing up the end of an imaginary napkin, presented it in due and ancient form to Canty, who had to grasp the opposite handle with one of his hands and take off the lid with the other, according to ancient custom. This left the Prince hand-free for a second, of course. He wasted no time, but dived among the forest of legs about him and disappeared. In another moment he could not have been harder to find, under that tossing sea of life, if its billows had been the Atlantic's and he a lost sixpence.

He very soon realised this fact, and straightway busied himself about his own affairs without further thought of John Canty. He quickly realised another thing, too. To wit, that a spurious Prince of Wales was being feasted by the city in his stead. He easily concluded that the pauper lad, Tom Canty, had deliberately taken advantage of his stupendous opportunity and become a usurper.

Therefore there was but one course to pursue—find his way to the Guildhall, make himself known, and denounce the impostor. He also made up his mind that Tom should be allowed a reasonable time for spiritual preparation, and then be hanged, drawn and quartered, according to the law and usage of the day in cases of high treason.

---

* The loving-cup, and the peculiar ceremonies observed in drinking from it, are older than English history. It is thought that both are Danish importations. As far back as knowledge goes, the loving-cup has always been drunk at English banquets. Tradition explains the ceremonies in this way. In the rude ancient times it was deemed a wise precaution to have both hands of both drinkers employed, lest while the pledger pledged his love and fidelity to the pledgee, the pledgee take that opportunity to slip a dirk into him!

11

At Guildhall

The royal barge, attended by its gorgeous fleet, took its stately way down the Thames through the wilderness of illuminated boats. The air was laden with music; the river banks were beruffled with joy-flames; the distant city lay in a soft luminous glow from its countless invisible bonfires; above it rose many a slender spire into the sky, incrusted with sparkling lights, wherefore in their remoteness they seemed like jewelled lances thrust aloft; as the fleet swept along, it was greeted from the banks with a continuous hoarse roar of cheers and the ceaseless flash and boom of artillery.

To Tom Canty, half buried in his silken cushions, these sounds and this spectacle were a wonder unspeakably sublime and astonishing. To his little friends at his side, the Princess Elizabeth and the Lady Jane Grey, they were nothing.

Arrived at the Dowgate, the fleet was towed up the limpid Walbrook (whose channel has now been for two centuries buried out of sight under acres of buildings) to Bucklersbury, past houses and under bridges populous with merry-makers and brilliantly lighted, and at last came to a halt in a basin where now is Barge Yard, in the centre of the ancient city of London. Tom disembarked, and he and his gallant procession crossed Cheapside and made a short march through the Old Jewry and Basinghall Street to the Guildhall.

Tom and his little ladies were received with due ceremony by the Lord Mayor and the Fathers of the City, in their gold chains and scarlet robes of state, and conducted to a rich canopy of state at the head of the great hall, preceded by heralds making proclamation, and by the Mace and the City Sword. The lords and ladies who were to attend upon Tom and his two small friends took their places behind their chairs.

At a lower table the Court grandees and other guests of noble degree were seated, with the magnates of the city; the commoners took places at a multitude of tables on the main floor of the hall. From their lofty vantage-ground the giants Gog and Magog, the ancient guardians of the city, contemplated the spectacle below them with eyes grown familiar to it in forgotten generations. There was a bugle-blast and a proclamation, and a fat butler appeared in a high perch in the leftward wall, followed by his servitors bearing with impressive solemnity a royal baron of beef, smoking hot and ready for the knife.

After grace, Tom (being instructed) rose—and the whole house with him—and drank from a portly golden loving-cup with the Princess Elizabeth; from her it passed to the Lady Jane, and then traversed the general assemblage. So the banquet began.

By midnight the revelry was at its height. Now came one of those picturesque spectacles so admired in that old day. A description of it is still extant in the quaint wording of a chronicler who witnessed it:

'Space being made, presently entered a baron and an earl apparelled after the Turkish fashion in long robes of bawdkin powdered with gold; hats on their heads of crimson velvet, with great rolls of gold, girded with two swords, called scimitars, hanging by great bawdricks of gold. Next came yet another baron and another earl, in two long gowns of yellow satin, traversed with white satin, and in every bend of white was a bend of crimson satin, after the fashion of Russia, with furred hats of grey on their heads; either of them having an hatchet in their hands, and boots with *pykes*' (points a foot long), 'turned up. And after them came a knight, then the Lord High Admiral, and with him five nobles, in doublets of crimson velvet, voyded low on the back and before to the cannell-bone, laced on the breasts with chains of silver; and over that, short cloaks of crimson satin, and on their heads hats after the dancers' fashion, with pheasants' feathers in them. These were apparelled after the fashion of Prussia. The torchbearers, which were about an hundred, were apparelled in crimson satin and green, like Moors, their faces black. Next came in a *mommarye.* Then the minstrels, which were disguised, danced; and the lords and ladies did wildly dance also, that it was a pleasure to behold.'

And while Tom, in his high seat, was gazing upon this 'wild' dancing, lost in admiration of the dazzling commingling of kaleidoscopic colours which the whirling turmoil of gaudy figures below him presented, the ragged but real little Prince of Wales was proclaiming his rights and his wrongs, denouncing the impostor, and clamouring for admission at the gates of Guildhall! The crowd enjoyed this episode prodigiously, and pressed forward and craned their necks to see the small rioter. Presently they began to taunt him and mock at him, purposely to goad him into a higher and still more entertaining fury. Tears of mortification sprang to his eyes, but he stood his ground and defied the mob right royally. Other taunts followed, added mockings stung him, and he exclaimed—

"I tell ye again, you pack of unmannerly curs, I am the Prince of Wales! And all forlorn and friendless as I be, with none to give me word of grace or help me in my need, yet will not I be driven from my ground, but will maintain it!"

"Though thou be prince or no prince, 'tis all one, thou be'st a gallant lad, and not friendless neither! Here stand I by thy side to prove it; and mind I tell thee thou might'st have a worser friend than Miles Hendon and yet not tire thy legs with seeking. Rest thy small jaw, my child; I talk the language of these base kennel-rats like to a very native."

The speaker was a sort of Don Caesar de Bazan in dress, aspect, and bearing. He was tall, trim-built, muscular. His doublet and trunks were of rich material, but faded and threadbare, and their gold-lace adornments were sadly tarnished; his ruff was rumpled and damaged; the plume in his slouched hat was broken and had a bedraggled and disreputable look; at his side he wore a long rapier in a rusty iron sheath; his swaggering carriage marked him at once as a ruffler of the camp. The speech of this fantastic figure was received with an explosion of jeers and laughter. Some cried, "'Tis another prince in disguise!" "'Ware thy tongue, friend: belike he is dangerous!" "Marry, he looketh it—mark his eye!" "Pluck the lad from him—to the horse-pond wi' the cub!"

Instantly a hand was laid upon the Prince, under the impulse of this happy thought; as instantly the stranger's long sword was out and the meddler went to the earth under a sounding thump with the flat of it. The next moment a score of voices shouted, "Kill the dog! Kill him! Kill him!" and the mob closed in on the warrior, who backed himself against a wall and began to lay about him with his long weapon like a madman. His victims sprawled this way and that, but the mob-tide poured over their prostrate forms and dashed itself against the champion with undiminished fury.

His moments seemed numbered, his destruction certain, when suddenly a trumpet-blast sounded, a voice shouted, "Way for the King's messenger!" and a troop of horsemen came charging down upon the mob, who fled out of harm's reach as fast as their legs could carry them. The bold stranger caught up the Prince in his arms, and was soon far away from danger and the multitude.

Return we within the Guildhall. Suddenly, high above the jubilant roar and thunder of the revel, broke the clear peal of a bugle-note. There was instant silence—a deep hush; then a single voice rose—that of the messenger from the palace—and began to pipe forth a proclamation, the whole multitude standing listening.

The closing words, solemnly pronounced, were—

"The King is dead!"

The great assemblage bent their heads upon their breasts with one accord; remained so, in profound silence, a few moments; then all sank upon their knees in a body, stretched out their hands toward Tom, and a mighty shout burst forth that seemed to shake the building—

"Long live the King!"

Poor Tom's dazed eyes wandered abroad over this stupefying spectacle, and finally rested dreamily upon the kneeling princesses beside him, a moment, then upon the Earl of Hertford. A sudden purpose dawned in his face. He said, in a low tone, at Lord Hertford's ear—

"Answer me truly, on thy faith and honour! Uttered I here a command, the which none but a king might hold privilege and prerogative to utter, would such commandment be obeyed, and none rise up to say me nay?"

"None, my liege, in all these realms. In thy person bides the majesty of England. Thou art the king—thy word is law."

Tom responded, in a strong, earnest voice, and with great animation—

"Then shall the king's law be law of mercy, from this day, and never more be law of blood! Up from thy knees and away! To the Tower, and say the King decrees the Duke of Norfolk shall not die!"*

The words were caught up and carried eagerly from lip to lip far and wide over the hall, and as Hertford hurried from the presence, another prodigious shout burst forth—

"The reign of blood is ended! Long live Edward, King of England!"

---

* Had Henry VIII survived a few hours longer, his order for the duke's execution would have been carried into effect. 'But news being carried to the Tower that the King himself had expired that night, the lieutenant deferred obeying the warrant; and it was not thought advisable by the Council to begin a new reign by the death of the greatest nobleman in the kingdom, who had been condemned by a sentence so unjust and tyrannical.'—Hume's *History of England*, vol. iii, p. 307.

12

The Prince and His Deliverer

As soon as Miles Hendon and the little prince were clear of the mob, they struck down through back lanes and alleys toward the river. Their way was unobstructed until they approached London Bridge; then they ploughed into the multitude again, Hendon keeping a fast grip upon the Prince's—no, the King's—wrist. The tremendous news was already abroad, and the boy learned it from a thousand voices at once—"The King is dead!" The tidings struck a chill to the heart of the poor little waif, and sent a shudder through his frame. He realised the greatness of his loss, and was filled with a bitter grief; for the grim tyrant who had been such a terror to others had always been gentle with him. The tears sprang to his eyes and blurred all objects. For an instant he felt himself the most forlorn, outcast, and forsaken of God's creatures—then another cry shook the night with its far-reaching thunders: "Long live King Edward the Sixth!" and this made his eyes kindle, and thrilled him with pride to his fingers' ends. "Ah," he thought, "how grand and strange it seems—*I am King*!"

"Our friends threaded their way"

Our friends threaded their way slowly through the throngs upon the bridge. This structure, which had stood for six hundred years, and had been a noisy and populous thoroughfare all that time, was a curious affair, for a closely packed rank of stores and shops, with family quarters overhead, stretched along both sides of it, from one bank of the river to the other. The Bridge was a sort of town to itself; it had its inn, its beer-houses, its bakeries, its haberdasheries, its food markets, its manufacturing industries, and even its church. It looked upon the two neighbours which it linked together—London and Southwark—as being well enough as suburbs, but not otherwise particularly important. It was a close corporation, so to speak; it was a narrow town, of a single street a fifth of a mile long, its population was but a village population and everybody in it knew all his fellow-townsmen intimately, and had known their fathers and mothers before them—and all their little family affairs into the bargain. It had its aristocracy, of course—its fine old families of butchers, and bakers, and what-not, who had occupied the same old premises for five or six hundred years, and knew the great history of the Bridge from beginning to end, and all its strange legends; and who always talked bridgy talk, and thought bridgy thoughts, and lied in a long, level, direct, substantial bridgy way. It was just the sort of population to be narrow and ignorant and self-conceited. Children were born on the Bridge, were reared there, grew to old age, and finally died without ever having set a foot upon any part of the world but London Bridge alone. Such people would naturally imagine that the mighty and interminable procession which moved through its street night and day, with its confused roar of shouts and cries, its neighings and bellowing and bleatings and its muffled thunder-tramp, was the one great thing in this world, and themselves somehow the proprietors of it. And so they were, in effect—at least they could exhibit it from their windows, and did—for a consideration—whenever a returning king or hero gave it a fleeting splendour, for there was no place like it for affording a long, straight, uninterrupted view of marching columns.

Men born and reared upon the Bridge found life unendurably dull and inane elsewhere. History tells of one of these who left the Bridge at the age of seventy-one and retired to the country. But he could only fret and toss in his bed; he could not go to sleep, the deep stillness was so painful, so awful, so oppressive. When he was worn out with it, at last, he fled back to his old home, a lean and haggard spectre, and fell peacefully to rest and pleasant dreams under the lulling music of the lashing waters and the boom and crash and thunder of London Bridge.

In the times of which we are writing, the Bridge furnished 'object lessons' in English history for its children—namely, the livid and decaying heads of renowned men impaled upon iron spikes atop of its gateways. But we digress.

Hendon's lodgings were in the little inn on the Bridge. As he neared the door with his small friend, a rough voice said—

"So, thou'rt come at last! Thou'lt not escape again, I warrant thee; and if pounding thy bones to a pudding can teach thee somewhat, thou'lt not keep us waiting another time, mayhap,"—and John Canty put out his hand to seize the boy.

Miles Hendon stepped in the way and said—

"Not too fast, friend. Thou art needlessly rough, methinks. What is the lad to thee?"

"If it be any business of thine to make and meddle in others' affairs, he is my son."

"'Tis a lie!" cried the little King, hotly.

"Boldly said, and I believe thee, whether thy small headpiece be sound or cracked, my boy. But whether this scurvy ruffian be thy father or no, 'tis all one, he shall not have thee to beat thee and abuse, according to his threat, so thou prefer to bide with me."

"I do, I do—I know him not, I loathe him, and will die before I will go with him."

"Then 'tis settled, and there is nought more to say."

"We will see, as to that!" exclaimed John Canty, striding past Hendon to get at the boy; "by force shall he—"

"If thou do but touch him, thou animated offal, I will spit thee like a goose!" said Hendon, barring the way and laying his hand upon his sword hilt. Canty drew back. "Now mark ye," continued Hendon, "I took this lad under my protection when a mob of such as thou would have mishandled him, mayhap killed him; dost imagine I will desert him now to a worser fate?—for whether thou art his father or no—and sooth to say, I think it is a lie—a decent swift death were better for such a lad than life in such brute hands as thine. So go thy ways, and set quick about it, for I like not much bandying of words, being not over-patient in my nature."

John Canty moved off, muttering threats and curses, and was swallowed from sight in the crowd. Hendon ascended three flights of stairs to his room, with his charge, after ordering a meal to be sent thither. It was a poor apartment, with a shabby bed and some odds and ends of old furniture in it, and was vaguely lighted by a couple of sickly candles. The little King dragged himself to the bed and lay down upon it, almost exhausted with hunger and fatigue. He had been on his feet a good part of a day and a night (for it was now two or three o'clock in the morning), and had eaten nothing meantime. He murmured drowsily—

"Prithee call me when the table is spread," and sank into a deep sleep immediately.

A smile twinkled in Hendon's eye, and he said to himself—

"By the mass, the little beggar takes to one's quarters and usurps one's bed with as natural and easy a grace as if he owned them—with never a by-your-leave or so-please-it-you, or anything of the sort. In his diseased ravings he called himself the Prince of Wales, and bravely doth he keep up the character. Poor little friendless rat, doubtless his mind has been disordered with ill-usage. Well, I will be his friend; I have saved him, and it draweth me strongly to him; already I love the bold-tongued little rascal. How soldier-like he faced the smutty rabble and flung back his high defiance! And what a comely, sweet and gentle face he hath, now that sleep hath conjured away its troubles and its griefs. I will teach him; I will cure his malady; yea, I will be his elder brother, and care for him and watch over him; and whoso would shame him or do him hurt may order his shroud, for though I be burnt for it he shall need it!"

He bent over the boy and contemplated him with kind and pitying interest, tapping the young cheek tenderly and smoothing back the tangled curls with his great brown hand. A slight shiver passed over the boy's form. Hendon muttered—

"See, now, how like a man it was to let him lie here uncovered and fill his body with deadly rheums. Now what shall I do? 'twill wake him to take him up and put him within the bed, and he sorely needeth sleep."

He looked about for extra covering, but finding none, doffed his doublet and wrapped the lad in it, saying, "I am used to nipping air and scant apparel, 'tis little I shall mind the cold!"—then walked up and down the room, to keep his blood in motion, soliloquising as before.

"His injured mind persuades him he is Prince of Wales; 'twill be odd to have a Prince of Wales still with us, now that he that *was* the prince is prince no more, but king—for this poor mind is set upon the one fantasy, and will not reason out that now it should cast by the prince and call itself the king . . . If my father liveth still, after these seven years that I have heard nought from home in my foreign dungeon, he will welcome the poor lad and give him generous shelter for my sake; so will my good elder brother, Arthur; my other brother, Hugh—but I will crack his crown an *he* interfere, the fox-hearted, ill-conditioned animal! Yes, thither will we fare—and straightway, too."

A servant entered with a smoking meal, disposed it upon a small deal table, placed the chairs, and took his departure, leaving such cheap lodgers as these to wait upon themselves. The door slammed after him, and the noise woke the boy, who sprang to a sitting posture, and shot a glad glance about him; then a grieved look came into his face and he murmured to himself, with a deep sigh, "Alack, it was but a dream, woe is me!" Next he noticed Miles Hendon's doublet—glanced from that to Hendon, comprehended the sacrifice that had been made for him, and said, gently—

"Thou art good to me, yes, thou art very good to me. Take it and put it on—I shall not need it more."

Then he got up and walked to the washstand in the corner and stood there, waiting. Hendon said in a cheery voice—

"We'll have a right hearty sup and bite, now, for everything is savoury and smoking hot, and that and thy nap together will make thee a little man again, never fear!"

The boy made no answer, but bent a steady look, that was filled with grave surprise, and also somewhat touched with impatience, upon the tall knight of the sword. Hendon was puzzled, and said—

"What's amiss?"

"Good sir, I would wash me."

"Oh, is that all? Ask no permission of Miles Hendon for aught thou cravest. Make thyself perfectly free here, and welcome, with all that are his belongings."

Still the boy stood, and moved not; more, he tapped the floor once or twice with his small impatient foot. Hendon was wholly perplexed. Said he—

"Bless us, what is it?"

"Prithee pour the water, and make not so many words!"

Hendon, suppressing a horse-laugh, and saying to himself, "By all the saints, but this is admirable!" stepped briskly forward and did the small insolent's bidding; then stood by, in a sort of stupefaction, until the command, "Come—the towel!" woke him sharply up. He took up a towel, from under the boy's nose, and handed it to him without comment. He now proceeded to comfort his own face with a wash, and while he was at it his adopted child seated himself at the table and prepared to fall to. Hendon dispatched his ablutions with alacrity, then drew back the other chair and was about to place himself at table, when the boy said, indignantly—

"Forbear! Wouldst sit in the presence of the King?"

This blow staggered Hendon to his foundations. He muttered to himself, "Lo, the poor thing's madness is up with the time! It hath changed with the great change that is come to the realm, and now in fancy is he *king*!

Good lack, I must humour the conceit, too—there is no other way—faith, he would order me to the Tower, else!"

And pleased with this jest, he removed the chair from the table, took his stand behind the King, and proceeded to wait upon him in the courtliest way he was capable of.

While the King ate, the rigour of his royal dignity relaxed a little, and with his growing contentment came a desire to talk. He said—"I think thou callest thyself Miles Hendon, if I heard thee aright?"

"Yes, Sire," Miles replied; then observed to himself, "If I *must* humour the poor lad's madness, I must 'Sire' him, I must 'Majesty' him, I must not go by halves, I must stick at nothing that belongeth to the part I play, else shall I play it ill and work evil to this charitable and kindly cause."

The King warmed his heart with a second glass of wine, and said—"I would know thee—tell me thy story. Thou hast a gallant way with thee, and a noble—art nobly born?"

"We are of the tail of the nobility, good your Majesty. My father is a baronet—one of the smaller lords by knight service*—Sir Richard Hendon of Hendon Hall, by Monk's Holm in Kent."

"The name has escaped my memory. Go on—tell me thy story."

"'Tis not much, your Majesty, yet perchance it may beguile a short half-hour for want of a better. My father, Sir Richard, is very rich, and of a most generous nature. My mother died whilst I was yet a boy. I have two brothers: Arthur, my elder, with a soul like to his father's; and Hugh, younger than I, a mean spirit, covetous, treacherous, vicious, underhanded—a reptile. Such was he from the cradle; such was he ten years past, when I last saw him—a ripe rascal at nineteen, I being twenty then, and Arthur twenty-two. There is none other of us but the Lady Edith, my cousin—she was sixteen then—beautiful, gentle, good, the daughter of an earl, the last of her race, heiress of a great fortune and a lapsed title. My father was her guardian. I loved her and she loved me; but she was betrothed to Arthur from the cradle, and Sir Richard would not suffer the contract to be broken. Arthur loved another maid, and bade us be of good cheer and hold fast to the hope that delay and luck together would some day give success to our several causes. Hugh loved the Lady Edith's fortune, though in truth he said it was herself he loved—but then 'twas his way, alway, to say the one thing and mean the other. But he lost his arts upon the girl; he could deceive my father, but none else. My father loved him best of us all, and trusted and believed him; for he was the youngest

* He refers to the order of baronets, or baronettes; the *barones minores*, as distinct from the parliamentary barons—not, it need hardly be said, to the baronets of later creation.

child, and others hated him—these qualities being in all ages sufficient to win a parent's dearest love; and he had a smooth persuasive tongue, with an admirable gift of lying—and these be qualities which do mightily assist a blind affection to cozen itself. I was wild—in troth I might go yet farther and say *very* wild, though 'twas a wildness of an innocent sort, since it hurt none but me, brought shame to none, nor loss, nor had in it any taint of crime or baseness, or what might not beseem mine honourable degree.

"Yet did my brother Hugh turn these faults to good account—he seeing that our brother Arthur's health was but indifferent, and hoping the worst might work him profit were I swept out of the path—so—but 'twere a long tale, good my liege, and little worth the telling. Briefly, then, this brother did deftly magnify my faults and make them crimes; ending his base work with finding a silken ladder in mine apartments—conveyed thither by his own means—and did convince my father by this, and suborned evidence of servants and other lying knaves, that I was minded to carry off my Edith and marry with her in rank defiance of his will.

"Three years of banishment from home and England might make a soldier and a man of me, my father said, and teach me some degree of wisdom. I fought out my long probation in the continental wars, tasting sumptuously of hard knocks, privation, and adventure; but in my last battle I was taken captive, and during the seven years that have waxed and waned since then, a foreign dungeon hath harboured me. Through wit and courage I won to the free air at last, and fled hither straight; and am but just arrived, right poor in purse and raiment, and poorer still in knowledge of what these dull seven years have wrought at Hendon Hall, its people and belongings. So please you, sir, my meagre tale is told."

"Thou hast been shamefully abused!" said the little King, with a flashing eye. "But I will right thee—by the cross will I! The King hath said it."

Then, fired by the story of Miles's wrongs, he loosed his tongue and poured the history of his own recent misfortunes into the ears of his astonished listener. When he had finished, Miles said to himself—

"Lo, what an imagination he hath! Verily, this is no common mind; else, crazed or sane, it could not weave so straight and gaudy a tale as this out of the airy nothings wherewith it hath wrought this curious romaunt. Poor ruined little head, it shall not lack friend or shelter whilst I bide with the living. He shall never leave my side; he shall be my pet, my little comrade. And he shall be cured!—ay, made whole and sound—then will he make himself a name—and proud shall I be to say, 'Yes, he is mine—I took him, a homeless little ragamuffin, but I saw what was in him, and I said his name would be heard some day—behold him, observe him—was I right?'"

The King spoke—in a thoughtful, measured voice—

"Thou didst save me injury and shame, perchance my life, and so my crown. Such service demandeth rich reward. Name thy desire, and so it be within the compass of my royal power, it is thine."

This fantastic suggestion startled Hendon out of his reverie. He was about to thank the King and put the matter aside with saying he had only done his duty and desired no reward, but a wiser thought came into his head, and he asked leave to be silent a few moments and consider the gracious offer—an idea which the King gravely approved, remarking that it was best to be not too hasty with a thing of such great import.

Miles reflected during some moments, then said to himself, "Yes, that is the thing to do—by any other means it were impossible to get at it—and certes, this hour's experience has taught me 'twould be most wearing and inconvenient to continue it as it is. Yes, I will propose it; 'twas a happy accident that I did not throw the chance away." Then he dropped upon one knee and said—

"He dropped on one knee"

"My poor service went not beyond the limit of a subject's simple duty, and therefore hath no merit; but since your Majesty is pleased to hold it worthy some reward, I take heart of grace to make petition to this effect. Near four hundred years ago, as your grace knoweth, there being ill blood betwixt John, King of England, and the King of France, it was decreed that two champions should fight together in the lists, and so settle the dispute by what is called the arbitrament of God. These two kings, and the Spanish king, being assembled to witness and judge the conflict, the French champion appeared; but so redoubtable was he, that our English knights refused to measure weapons with him. So the matter, which was a weighty one, was like to go against the English monarch by default. Now in the Tower lay the Lord de Courcy, the mightiest arm in England, stripped of his honours and possessions, and wasting with long captivity. Appeal was made to him; he gave assent, and came forth arrayed for battle; but no sooner did the Frenchman glimpse his huge frame and hear his famous name but he fled away, and the French king's cause was lost. King John restored De Courcy's titles and possessions, and said, 'Name thy wish and thou shalt have it, though it cost me half my kingdom;' whereat De Courcy, kneeling, as I do now, made answer, 'This, then, I ask, my liege; that I and my successors may have and hold the privilege of remaining covered in the presence of the kings of England, henceforth while the throne shall last.' The boon was granted, as your Majesty knoweth; and there hath been no time, these four hundred years, that that line has failed of an heir; and so, even unto this day, the head of that ancient house still weareth his hat or helm before the King's Majesty, without let or hindrance, and this none other may do.* Invoking this precedent in aid of my prayer, I beseech the King to grant to me but this one grace and privilege—to my more than sufficient reward—and none other, to wit: that I and my heirs, for ever, may *sit* in the presence of the Majesty of England!"

"Rise, Sir Miles Hendon, Knight," said the King, gravely—giving the accolade with Hendon's sword—"rise, and seat thyself. Thy petition is granted. Whilst England remains, and the crown continues, the privilege shall not lapse."

His Majesty walked apart, musing, and Hendon dropped into a chair at table, observing to himself, "'Twas a brave thought, and hath wrought me a mighty deliverance; my legs are grievously wearied. An I had not thought of that, I must have had to stand for weeks, till my poor lad's wits are cured." After a little, he went on, "And so I am become a knight of the Kingdom of Dreams and Shadows! A most odd and strange position, truly, for one so matter-of-fact as I. I will not laugh—no, God forbid, for this thing which is so substanceless to me is *real* to him. And to me, also, in one way, it is not a falsity, for it reflects with truth the sweet and generous spirit that is in him." After a pause: "Ah, what if he should call me by my fine title before folk!—there'd be a merry contrast betwixt my glory and my raiment! But no matter, let him call me what he will, so it please him; I shall be content."

* The lords of Kingsale, descendants of De Courcy, still enjoy this curious privilege.

13

The Disappearance of the Prince

A heavy drowsiness presently fell upon the two comrades. The King said—

"Remove these rags."—meaning his clothing.

Hendon disapparelled the boy without dissent or remark, tucked him up in bed, then glanced about the room, saying to himself, ruefully, "He hath taken my bed again, as before—marry, what shall *I* do?" The little King observed his perplexity, and dissipated it with a word. He said, sleepily—

"Thou wilt sleep athwart the door, and guard it." In a moment more he was out of his troubles, in a deep slumber.

"Dear heart, he should have been born a king!" muttered Hendon, admiringly; "he playeth the part to a marvel."

Then he stretched himself across the door, on the floor, saying contentedly—

"I have lodged worse for seven years; 'twould be but ill gratitude to Him above to find fault with this."

He dropped asleep as the dawn appeared. Toward noon he rose, uncovered his unconscious ward—a section at a time—and took his measure with a string. The King awoke, just as he had completed his work, complained of the cold, and asked what he was doing.

"'Tis done, now, my liege," said Hendon; "I have a bit of business outside, but will presently return; sleep thou again—thou needest it. There—let me cover thy head also—thou'lt be warm the sooner."

The King was back in dreamland before this speech was ended. Miles slipped softly out, and slipped as softly in again, in the course of thirty or forty minutes, with a complete second-hand suit of boy's clothing, of cheap material, and showing signs of wear; but tidy, and suited to the season of the year. He seated himself, and began to overhaul his purchase, mumbling to himself—

"A longer purse would have got a better sort, but when one has not the long purse one must be content with what a short one may do—

"'There was a woman in our town,
In our town did dwell—'

"He stirred, methinks—I must sing in a less thunderous key; 'tis not good to mar his sleep, with this journey before him, and he so wearied out, poor chap . . . This garment—'tis well enough—a stitch here and another one there will set it aright. This other is better, albeit a stitch or two will not come amiss in it, likewise . . . *These* be very good and sound, and will keep his small feet warm and dry—an odd new thing to him, belike, since he has doubtless been used to foot it bare, winters and summers the same . . . Would thread were bread, seeing one getteth a year's sufficiency for a farthing, and such a brave big needle without cost, for mere love. Now shall I have the demon's own time to thread it!"

And so he had. He did as men have always done, and probably always will do, to the end of time—held the needle still, and tried to thrust the thread through the eye, which is the opposite of a woman's way. Time and time again the thread missed the mark, going sometimes on one side of the needle, sometimes on the other, sometimes doubling up against the shaft; but he was patient, having been through these experiences before, when he was soldiering. He succeeded at last, and took up the garment that had lain waiting, meantime, across his lap, and began his work.

"The inn is paid—the breakfast that is to come, included—and there is wherewithal left to buy a couple of donkeys and meet our little costs for the two or three days betwixt this and the plenty that awaits us at Hendon Hall—

"'She loved her hus—'

"Body o' me! I have driven the needle under my nail! . . . It matters little—'tis not a novelty—yet 'tis not a convenience, neither. . . . We shall be merry there, little one, never doubt it! Thy troubles will vanish there, and likewise thy sad distemper—

"'She loved her husband dearilee,
But another man—'

"These be noble large stitches!"—holding the garment up and viewing it admiringly—"they have a grandeur and a majesty that do cause these small stingy ones of the tailor-man to look mightily paltry and plebeian—

"'She loved her husband dearilee,
But another man he loved she—'

"Marry, 'tis done—a goodly piece of work, too, and wrought with expedition. Now will I wake him, apparel him, pour for him, feed him, and then will we hie us to the mart by the Tabard Inn in Southwark and—be pleased to rise, my liege!—he answereth not—what ho, my liege!—of a truth must I profane his sacred person with a touch, sith his slumber is deaf to speech. What!"

He threw back the covers—the boy was gone!

He stared about him in speechless astonishment for a moment; noticed for the first time that his ward's ragged raiment was also missing; then he began to rage and storm and shout for the innkeeper. At that moment a servant entered with the breakfast.

"Explain, thou limb of Satan, or thy time is come!" roared the man of war, and made so savage a spring toward the waiter that this latter could not find his tongue, for the instant, for fright and surprise. "Where is the boy?"

In disjointed and trembling syllables the man gave the information desired.

"You were hardly gone from the place, your worship, when a youth came running and said it was your worship's will that the boy come to you straight, at the bridge-end on the Southwark side. I brought him hither; and when he woke the lad and gave his message, the lad did grumble some little for being disturbed 'so early,' as he called it, but straightway trussed on his rags and went with the youth, only saying it had been better manners that your worship came yourself, not sent a stranger—and so—"

"And so thou'rt a fool!—a fool and easily cozened—hang all thy breed! Yet mayhap no hurt is done. Possibly no harm is meant the boy. I will go fetch him. Make the table ready. Stay! the coverings of the bed were disposed as if one lay beneath them—happened that by accident?"

"I know not, good your worship. I saw the youth meddle with them—he that came for the boy."

"Thousand deaths! 'Twas done to deceive me—'tis plain 'twas done to gain time. Hark ye! Was that youth alone?"

"All alone, your worship."

"Art sure?"

"Sure, your worship."

"Collect thy scattered wits—bethink thee—take time, man."

After a moment's thought, the servant said—

"When he came, none came with him; but now I remember me that as the two stepped into the throng of the Bridge, a ruffian-looking man plunged out from some near place; and just as he was joining them—"

"What *then*?—out with it!" thundered the impatient Hendon, interrupting.

"Just then the crowd lapped them up and closed them in, and I saw no more, being called by my master, who was in a rage because a joint that the scrivener had ordered was forgot, though I take all the saints to witness that to blame *me* for that miscarriage were like holding the unborn babe to judgment for sins com—"

"Out of my sight, idiot! Thy prating drives me mad! Hold! Whither art flying? Canst not bide still an instant? Went they toward Southwark?"

"Even so, your worship—for, as I said before, as to that detestable joint, the babe unborn is no whit more blameless than—"

"Art here *yet*! And prating still! Vanish, lest I throttle thee!" The servitor vanished. Hendon followed after him, passed him, and plunged down the stairs two steps at a stride, muttering, "'Tis that scurvy villain that claimed he was his son. I have lost thee, my poor little mad master—it is a bitter thought—and I had come to love thee so! No! by book and bell, *not* lost! Not lost, for I will ransack the land till I find thee again. Poor child, yonder is his breakfast—and mine, but I have no hunger now; so, let the rats have it—speed, speed! that is the word!" As he wormed his swift way through the noisy multitudes upon the Bridge he several times said to himself—clinging to the thought as if it were a particularly pleasing one—"He grumbled, but he *went*—he went, yes, because he thought Miles Hendon asked it, sweet lad—he would ne'er have done it for another, I know it well."

14

'Le Roi Est Mort—Vive Le Roi'

Toward daylight of the same morning, Tom Canty stirred out of a heavy sleep and opened his eyes in the dark. He lay silent a few moments, trying to analyse his confused thoughts and impressions, and get some sort of meaning out of them; then suddenly he burst out in a rapturous but guarded voice—

"I see it all, I see it all! Now God be thanked, I am indeed awake at last! Come, joy! vanish, sorrow! Ho, Nan! Bet! kick off your straw and hie ye hither to my side, till I do pour into your unbelieving ears the wildest madcap dream that ever the spirits of night did conjure up to astonish the soul of man withal! . . . Ho, Nan, I say! Bet!"

A dim form appeared at his side, and a voice said—

"Wilt deign to deliver thy commands?"

"Commands? . . . O, woe is me, I know thy voice! Speak thou—who am I?"

"Thou? In sooth, yesternight wert thou the Prince of Wales; today art thou my most gracious liege, Edward, King of England."

Tom buried his head among his pillows, murmuring plaintively—

"Alack, it was no dream! Go to thy rest, sweet sir—leave me to my sorrows."

Tom slept again, and after a time he had this pleasant dream. He thought it was summer, and he was playing, all alone, in the fair meadow called Goodman's Fields, when a dwarf only a foot high, with long red whiskers and a humped back, appeared to him suddenly and said, "Dig by that stump." He did so, and found twelve bright new pennies—wonderful riches! Yet this was not the best of it; for the dwarf said—

"I know thee. Thou art a good lad, and a deserving; thy distresses shall end, for the day of thy reward is come. Dig here every seventh day, and thou shalt find always the same treasure, twelve bright new pennies. Tell none—keep the secret."

Then the dwarf vanished, and Tom flew to Offal Court with his prize, saying to himself, "Every night will I give my father a penny; he will think I begged it, it will glad his heart, and I shall no more be beaten. One penny every week the good priest that teacheth me shall have; mother, Nan, and Bet the other four. We be done with hunger and rags, now, done with fears and frets and savage usage."

In his dream he reached his sordid home all out of breath, but with eyes dancing with grateful enthusiasm; cast four of his pennies into his mother's lap and cried out—

"They are for thee!—all of them, every one!—for thee and Nan and Bet—and honestly come by, not begged nor stolen!"

The happy and astonished mother strained him to her breast and exclaimed—

"It waxeth late—may it please your Majesty to rise?"

Ah! that was not the answer he was expecting. The dream had snapped asunder—he was awake.

He opened his eyes—the richly clad First Lord of the Bedchamber was kneeling by his couch. The gladness of the lying dream faded away—the poor boy recognized that he was still a captive and a king. The room was filled with courtiers clothed in purple mantles—the mourning colour—and with noble servants of the monarch. Tom sat up in bed and gazed out from the heavy silken curtains upon this fine company.

The weighty business of dressing began, and one courtier after another knelt and paid his court and offered to the little King his condolences upon his heavy loss, whilst the dressing proceeded. In the beginning, a shirt was taken up by the Chief Equerry in Waiting, who passed it to the First Lord of the Buckhounds, who passed it to the Second Gentleman of the Bedchamber, who passed it to the Head Ranger of Windsor Forest, who passed it to the Third Groom of the Stole, who passed it to the Chancellor Royal of the Duchy of Lancaster, who passed it to the Master of the Wardrobe, who passed it to Norroy King-at-Arms, who passed it to the Constable of the Tower, who passed it to the Chief Steward of the Household, who passed it to the Hereditary Grand Diaperer, who passed it to the Lord High Admiral of England, who passed it to the Archbishop of Canterbury, who passed it to the First Lord of the Bedchamber, who took what was left of it and put it on Tom. Poor little wondering chap, it reminded him of passing buckets at a fire.

Each garment in its turn had to go through this slow and solemn process; consequently Tom grew very weary of the ceremony; so weary that he felt an almost gushing gratefulness when he at last saw his long silken hose begin the journey down the line and knew that the end of the matter was drawing near. But he exulted too soon. The First Lord of the Bedchamber received the hose and was about to encase Tom's legs in them, when a sudden flush invaded his face and he hurriedly hustled the things back into the hands of the Archbishop of Canterbury with an astounded look and a whispered, "See, my lord!" pointing to a something connected with the hose. The Archbishop paled, then flushed, and passed the hose to the Lord High Admiral, whispering, "See, my lord!" The Admiral passed the hose to the Hereditary Grand Diaperer, and had hardly breath enough in his body to ejaculate, "See, my lord!" The hose drifted backward along the line, to the Chief Steward of the Household, the Constable of the Tower, Norroy King-at-Arms, the Master of the Wardrobe, the Chancellor Royal of the Duchy of Lancaster, the Third Groom of the Stole, the Head Ranger of Windsor Forest, the Second Gentleman of the Bedchamber, the First Lord of the Buckhounds—accompanied always with that amazed and frightened "See! see!"—till they finally reached the hands of the Chief Equerry in Waiting, who gazed a moment, with a pallid face, upon what had caused all this dismay, then hoarsely whispered, "Body of my life, a tag gone from a truss-point!—to the Tower with the Head Keeper of the King's Hose!"—after which he leaned upon the shoulder of the First Lord of the Buckhounds to regather his vanished strength whilst fresh hose, without any damaged strings to them, were brought.

But all things must have an end, and so in time Tom Canty was in a condition to get out of bed. The proper official poured water, the proper official engineered the washing, the proper official stood by with a towel, and by and by Tom got safely through the purifying stage and was ready for the services of the Hairdresser-royal. When he at length emerged from this master's hands, he was a gracious figure and as pretty as a girl, in his mantle and trunks of purple satin, and purple-plumed cap. He now moved in state toward his breakfast room, through the midst of the courtly assemblage; and as he passed, these fell back, leaving his way free, and dropped upon their knees.

After breakfast he was conducted, with regal ceremony, attended by his great officers and his guard of fifty Gentlemen Pensioners bearing gilt battle-axes, to the throne room, where he proceeded to transact business of state. His 'uncle,' Lord Hertford, took his stand by the throne, to assist the royal mind with wise counsel.

The body of illustrious men named by the late King as his executors appeared, to ask Tom's approval of certain acts of theirs—rather a form, and yet not wholly a form, since there was no Protector as yet. The Archbishop of Canterbury made report of the decree of the Council of Executors concerning the obsequies of his late most illustrious Majesty, and finished by reading the signatures of the Executors, to wit: the Archbishop of Canterbury; the Lord Chancellor of England; William Lord St. John; John Lord Russell; Edward Earl of Hertford; John Viscount Lisle; Cuthbert Bishop of Durham—

Tom was not listening—an earlier clause of the document was puzzling him. At this point he turned and whispered to Lord Hertford—

"What day did he say the burial hath been appointed for?"

"The sixteenth of the coming month, my liege."

"'Tis a strange folly. Will he keep?"

Poor chap, he was still new to the customs of royalty; he was used to seeing the forlorn dead of Offal Court hustled out of the way with a very different sort of expedition. However, the Lord Hertford set his mind at rest with a word or two.

A secretary of state presented an order of the Council appointing the morrow at eleven for the reception of the foreign ambassadors, and desired the King's assent.

Tom turned an inquiring look toward Hertford, who whispered—

"Your Majesty will signify consent. They come to testify their royal masters' sense of the heavy calamity which hath visited your Grace and the realm of England."

Tom did as he was bidden. Another secretary began to read a preamble concerning the expenses of the late King's household, which had amounted to 28,000 pounds during the preceding six months—a sum so vast that it made Tom Canty gasp; he gasped again when the fact appeared that 20,000 pounds of this money was still owing and unpaid;* and once more when it appeared that the King's coffers were about empty, and his twelve hundred servants much embarrassed for lack of the wages due them. Tom spoke out, with lively apprehension—

"We be going to the dogs, 'tis plain. 'Tis meet and necessary that we take a smaller house and set the servants at large, sith they be of no value but to make delay, and trouble one with offices that harass the spirit and shame the soul, they misbecoming any but a doll, that hath nor brains nor hands to help itself withal. I remember me of a small house that standeth over against the fish-market, by Billingsgate—"

A sharp pressure upon Tom's arm stopped his foolish tongue and sent a blush to his face; but no countenance there betrayed any sign that this strange speech had been remarked or given concern.

A secretary made report that forasmuch as the late King had provided in his will for conferring the ducal degree upon the Earl of Hertford and raising his brother, Sir Thomas Seymour, to the peerage, and likewise Hertford's son to an earldom, together with similar aggrandisements to other great servants of the Crown, the Council had resolved to hold a sitting on the 16th of February for the delivering and confirming of these honours, and that meantime, the late King not having granted, in writing, estates suitable to the support of these dignities, the Council, knowing his private wishes in that regard, had thought proper to grant to Seymour '500 pound lands,' and to Hertford's son '800 pound lands, and 300 pound of the next bishop's lands which should fall vacant,'—his present Majesty being willing.†

Tom was about to blurt out something about the propriety of paying the late King's debts first, before squandering all this money, but a timely touch upon his arm, from the thoughtful Hertford, saved him this indiscretion; wherefore he gave the royal assent, without spoken comment, but with much inward discomfort. While he sat reflecting a moment over the ease with which he was doing strange and glittering miracles, a happy thought shot into his mind: why not make his mother Duchess of Offal Court, and

---

* Hume.

† Ib.

give her an estate? But a sorrowful thought swept it instantly away: he was only a king in name, these grave veterans and great nobles were his masters; to them his mother was only the creature of a diseased mind; they would simply listen to his project with unbelieving ears, then send for the doctor.

The dull work went tediously on. Petitions were read, and proclamations, patents, and all manner of wordy, repetitious, and wearisome papers relating to the public business; and at last Tom sighed pathetically and murmured to himself, "In what have I offended, that the good God should take me away from the fields and the free air and the sunshine, to shut me up here and make me a king and afflict me so?" Then his poor muddled head nodded a while and presently drooped to his shoulder; and the business of the empire came to a standstill for want of that august factor, the ratifying power. Silence ensued around the slumbering child, and the sages of the realm ceased from their deliberations.

During the forenoon, Tom had an enjoyable hour, by permission of his keepers, Hertford and St. John, with the Lady Elizabeth and the little Lady Jane Grey; though the spirits of the princesses were rather subdued by the mighty stroke that had fallen upon the royal house; and at the end of the visit his 'elder sister'—afterwards the 'Bloody Mary' of history—chilled him with a solemn interview which had but one merit in his eyes, its brevity. He had a few moments to himself, and then a slim lad of about twelve years of age was admitted to his presence, whose clothing, except his snowy ruff and the laces about his wrists, was of black—doublet, hose, and all. He bore no badge of mourning but a knot of purple ribbon on his shoulder. He advanced hesitatingly, with head bowed and bare, and dropped upon one knee in front of Tom. Tom sat still and contemplated him soberly a moment. Then he said—

"Rise, lad. Who art thou. What wouldst have?"

The boy rose, and stood at graceful ease, but with an aspect of concern in his face. He said—

"Of a surety thou must remember me, my lord. I am thy whipping-boy."

"My *whipping*-boy?"

"The same, your Grace. I am Humphrey—Humphrey Marlow."

Tom perceived that here was someone whom his keepers ought to have posted him about. The situation was delicate. What should he do?—pretend he knew this lad, and then betray by his every utterance that he had never heard of him before? No, that would not do. An idea came to his relief: accidents like this might be likely to happen with some frequency, now that business urgencies would often call Hertford and St. John from his side, they being members of the Council of Executors; therefore perhaps it would be well to strike out a plan himself to meet the requirements of such emergencies. Yes, that would be a wise course—he would practise on this boy, and see what sort of success he might achieve. So he stroked his brow perplexedly a moment or two, and presently said—

"Now I seem to remember thee somewhat—but my wit is clogged and dim with suffering—"

"Alack, my poor master!" ejaculated the whipping-boy, with feeling; adding, to himself, "In truth 'tis as they said—his mind is gone—alas, poor soul! But misfortune catch me, how am I forgetting! They said one must not seem to observe that aught is wrong with him."

"'Tis strange how my memory doth wanton with me these days," said Tom. "But mind it not—I mend apace—a little clue doth often serve to bring me back again the things and names which had escaped me. (And not they, only, forsooth, but e'en such as I ne'er heard before—as this lad shall see.) Give thy business speech."

"'Tis matter of small weight, my liege, yet will I touch upon it, an' it please your Grace. Two days gone by, when your Majesty faulted thrice in your Greek—in the morning lessons—dost remember it?"

"Y-e-s—methinks I do. (It is not much of a lie—an' I had meddled with the Greek at all, I had not faulted simply thrice, but forty times.) Yes, I do recall it, now—go on."

"The master, being wroth with what he termed such slovenly and doltish work, did promise that he would soundly whip me for it—and—"

"Whip *thee*!" said Tom, astonished out of his presence of mind. "Why should he whip *thee* for faults of mine?"

"Ah, your Grace forgetteth again. He always scourgeth me when thou dost fail in thy lessons."

"True, true—I had forgot. Thou teachest me in private—then if I fail, he argueth that thy office was lamely done, and—"

"Oh, my liege, what words are these? I, the humblest of thy servants, presume to teach *thee*?"

"Then where is thy blame? What riddle is this? Am I in truth gone mad, or is it thou? Explain—speak out."

"But, good your Majesty, there's nought that needeth simplifying.—None may visit the sacred person of the Prince of Wales with blows; wherefore, when he faulteth, 'tis I that take them; and meet it is and right, for that it is mine office and my livelihood."*

* James I and Charles II had whipping-boys, when they were little fellows, to take their punishment for them when they fell short in their lessons; so I have ventured to furnish my small prince with one, for my own purposes.

Tom stared at the tranquil boy, observing to himself, "Lo, it is a wonderful thing—a most strange and curious trade; I marvel they have not hired a boy to take my combings and my dressings for me—would heaven they would!—an' they will do this thing, I will take my lashings in mine own person, giving God thanks for the change." Then he said aloud—

"And hast thou been beaten, poor friend, according to the promise?"

"No, good your Majesty, my punishment was appointed for this day, and peradventure it may be annulled, as unbefitting the season of mourning that is come upon us; I know not, and so have made bold to come hither and remind your Grace about your gracious promise to intercede in my behalf—"

"With the master? To save thee thy whipping?"

"Ah, thou dost remember!"

"My memory mendeth, thou seest. Set thy mind at ease—thy back shall go unscathed—I will see to it."

"Oh, thanks, my good lord!" cried the boy, dropping upon his knee again. "Mayhap I have ventured far enow; and yet—"

Seeing Master Humphrey hesitate, Tom encouraged him to go on, saying he was "in the granting mood."

"Then will I speak it out, for it lieth near my heart. Sith thou art no more Prince of Wales but King, thou canst order matters as thou wilt, with none to say thee nay; wherefore it is not in reason that thou wilt longer vex thyself with dreary studies, but wilt burn thy books and turn thy mind to things less irksome. Then am I ruined, and mine orphan sisters with me!"

"Ruined? Prithee how?"

"My back is my bread, O my gracious liege! if it go idle, I starve. An' thou cease from study mine office is gone thou'lt need no whipping-boy. Do not turn me away!"

Tom was touched with this pathetic distress. He said, with a right royal burst of generosity—

"Discomfort thyself no further, lad. Thine office shall be permanent in thee and thy line for ever." Then he struck the boy a light blow on the shoulder with the flat of his sword, exclaiming, "Rise, Humphrey Marlow, Hereditary Grand Whipping-Boy to the Royal House of England! Banish sorrow—I will betake me to my books again, and study so ill that they must in justice treble thy wage, so mightily shall the business of thine office be augmented."

The grateful Humphrey responded fervidly—

"Thanks, O most noble master, this princely lavishness doth far surpass my most distempered dreams of fortune. Now shall I be happy all my days, and all the house of Marlow after me."

Tom had wit enough to perceive that here was a lad who could be useful to him. He encouraged Humphrey to talk, and he was nothing loath. He was delighted to believe that he was helping in Tom's 'cure'; for always, as soon as he had finished calling back to Tom's diseased mind the various particulars of his experiences and adventures in the royal schoolroom and elsewhere about the palace, he noticed that Tom was then able to 'recall' the circumstances quite clearly. At the end of an hour Tom found himself well freighted with very valuable information concerning personages and matters pertaining to the Court; so he resolved to draw instruction from this source daily; and to this end he would give order to admit Humphrey to the royal closet whenever he might come, provided the Majesty of England was not engaged with other people. Humphrey had hardly been dismissed when my Lord Hertford arrived with more trouble for Tom.

He said that the Lords of the Council, fearing that some overwrought report of the King's damaged health might have leaked out and got abroad, they deemed it wise and best that his Majesty should begin to dine in public after a day or two—his wholesome complexion and vigorous step, assisted by a carefully guarded repose of manner and ease and grace of demeanour, would more surely quiet the general pulse—in case any evil rumours *had* gone about—than any other scheme that could be devised.

Then the Earl proceeded, very delicately, to instruct Tom as to the observances proper to the stately occasion, under the rather thin disguise of 'reminding' him concerning things already known to him; but to his vast gratification it turned out that Tom needed very little help in this line—he had been making use of Humphrey in that direction, for Humphrey had mentioned that within a few days he was to begin to dine in public; having gathered it from the swift-winged gossip of the Court. Tom kept these facts to himself, however.

Seeing the royal memory so improved, the Earl ventured to apply a few tests to it, in an apparently casual way, to find out how far its amendment had progressed. The results were happy, here and there, in spots—spots where Humphrey's tracks remained—and on the whole my lord was greatly pleased and encouraged. So encouraged was he, indeed, that he spoke up and said in a quite hopeful voice—

"If your majesty will but tax your memory"

"Now am I persuaded that if your Majesty will but tax your memory yet a little further, it will resolve the puzzle of the Great Seal—a loss which was of moment yesterday, although of none today, since its term of service ended with our late lord's life. May it please your Grace to make the trial?"

Tom was at sea—a Great Seal was something which he was totally unacquainted with. After a moment's hesitation he looked up innocently and asked—

"What was it like, my lord?"

The Earl started, almost imperceptibly, muttering to himself, "Alack, his wits are flown again!—it was ill wisdom to lead him on to strain them"—then he deftly turned the talk to other matters, with the purpose of sweeping the unlucky seal out of Tom's thoughts—a purpose which easily succeeded.

15

Tom as King

The next day the foreign ambassadors came, with their gorgeous trains; and Tom, throned in awful state, received them. The splendours of the scene delighted his eye and fired his imagination at first, but the audience was long and dreary, and so were most of the addresses—wherefore, what began as a pleasure grew into weariness and home-sickness by and by. Tom said the words which Hertford put into his mouth from time to time, and tried hard to acquit himself satisfactorily, but he was too new to such things, and too ill at ease to accomplish more than a tolerable success. He looked sufficiently like a king, but he was ill able to feel like one. He was cordially glad when the ceremony was ended.

The larger part of his day was 'wasted'—as he termed it, in his own mind—in labours pertaining to his royal office. Even the two hours devoted to certain princely pastimes and recreations were rather a burden to him than otherwise, they were so fettered by restrictions and ceremonious observances. However, he had a private hour with his whipping-boy which he counted clear gain, since he got both entertainment and needful information out of it.

The third day of Tom Canty's kingship came and went much as the others had done, but there was a lifting of his cloud in one way—he felt less uncomfortable than at first; he was getting a little used to his circumstances and surroundings; his chains still galled, but not all the time; he found that the presence and homage of the great afflicted and embarrassed him less and less sharply with every hour that drifted over his head.

But for one single dread, he could have seen the fourth day approach without serious distress—the dining in public; it was to begin that day. There were greater matters in the programme—for on that day he would have to preside at a council which would take his views and commands concerning the policy to be pursued toward various foreign nations scattered far and near over the great globe; on that day, too, Hertford would be formally chosen to the grand office of Lord Protector; other things of note were appointed for that fourth day, also; but to Tom they were all insignificant compared with the ordeal of dining all by himself with a multitude of curious eyes fastened upon him and a multitude of mouths whispering comments upon his performance—and upon his mistakes, if he should be so unlucky as to make any.

Still, nothing could stop that fourth day, and so it came. It found poor Tom low-spirited and absent-minded, and this mood continued; he could not shake it off. The ordinary duties of the morning dragged upon his hands, and wearied him. Once more he felt the sense of captivity heavy upon him.

Late in the forenoon he was in a large audience-chamber, conversing with the Earl of Hertford and dully awaiting the striking of the hour appointed for a visit of ceremony from a considerable number of great officials and courtiers.

After a little while, Tom, who had wandered to a window and become interested in the life and movement of the great highway beyond the palace gates—and not idly interested, but longing with all his heart to take part in person in its stir and freedom—saw the van of a hooting and shouting mob of disorderly men, women, and children of the lowest and poorest degree approaching from up the road.

"I would I knew what 'tis about!" he exclaimed, with all a boy's curiosity in such happenings.

"Thou art the King!" solemnly responded the Earl, with a reverence. "Have I your Grace's leave to act?"

"O blithely, yes! O gladly, yes!" exclaimed Tom excitedly, adding to himself with a lively sense of satisfaction, "In truth, being a king is not all dreariness—it hath its compensations and conveniences."

The Earl called a page, and sent him to the captain of the guard with the order—

"Let the mob be halted, and inquiry made concerning the occasion of its movement. By the King's command!"

A few seconds later a long rank of the royal guards, cased in flashing steel, filed out at the gates and formed across the highway in front of the multitude. A messenger returned, to report that the crowd were following a man, a woman, and a young girl to execution for crimes committed against the peace and dignity of the realm.

Death—and a violent death—for these poor unfortunates! The thought wrung Tom's heart-strings. The spirit of compassion took control of him, to the exclusion of all other considerations; he never thought of the offended laws, or of the grief or loss which these three criminals had inflicted upon their victims; he could think of nothing but the scaffold and the grisly fate hanging over the heads of the condemned. His concern made him even forget, for the moment, that he was but the false shadow of a king, not the substance; and before he knew it he had blurted out the command—

"Bring them here!"

Then he blushed scarlet, and a sort of apology sprung to his lips; but observing that his order had wrought no sort of surprise in the Earl or the waiting page, he suppressed the words he was about to utter. The page, in the most matter-of-course way, made a profound obeisance and retired backwards out of the room to deliver the command. Tom experienced a glow of pride and a renewed sense of the compensating advantages of the kingly office. He said to himself, "Truly it is like what I was used to feel when I read the old priest's tales, and did imagine mine own self a prince, giving law and command to all, saying 'Do this, do that,' whilst none durst offer let or hindrance to my will."

Now the doors swung open; one high-sounding title after another was announced, the personages owning them followed, and the place was quickly half-filled with noble folk and finery. But Tom was hardly conscious of the presence of these people, so wrought up was he and so intensely absorbed in that other and more interesting matter. He seated himself absently in his chair of state, and turned his eyes upon the door with manifestations of impatient expectancy; seeing which, the company forbore to trouble him, and fell to chatting a mixture of public business and court gossip one with another.

In a little while the measured tread of military men was heard approaching, and the culprits entered the presence in charge of an under-sheriff and escorted by a detail of the king's guard. The civil officer knelt before Tom, then stood aside; the three doomed persons knelt, also, and remained so; the guard took position behind Tom's chair. Tom scanned the prisoners curiously. Something about the dress or appearance of the man had stirred a vague memory in him. "Methinks I have seen this man ere now . . . but the when or the where fail me."—Such was Tom's thought. Just then the man glanced quickly up and quickly dropped his face again, not being able to endure the awful port of sovereignty; but the one full glimpse of the face which Tom got was sufficient. He said to himself: "Now is the matter clear; this is the stranger that plucked Giles Witt out of the Thames, and saved his life, that windy, bitter, first day of the New Year—a brave good deed—pity he hath been doing baser ones and got himself in this sad case . . . I have not forgot the day, neither the hour; by reason that an hour after, upon the stroke of eleven, I did get a hiding by the hand of Gammer Canty which was of so goodly and admired severity that all that went before or followed after it were but fondlings and caresses by comparison."

Tom now ordered that the woman and the girl be removed from the presence for a little time; then addressed himself to the under-sheriff, saying—

"Good sir, what is this man's offence?"

The officer knelt, and answered—

"So please your Majesty, he hath taken the life of a subject by poison."

Tom's compassion for the prisoner, and admiration of him as the daring rescuer of a drowning boy, experienced a most damaging shock.

"The thing was proven upon him?" he asked.

"Most clearly, sire."

Tom sighed, and said—

"Take him away—he hath earned his death. 'Tis a pity, for he was a brave heart—na—na, I mean he hath the *look* of it!"

The prisoner clasped his hands together with sudden energy, and wrung them despairingly, at the same time appealing imploringly to the 'King' in broken and terrified phrases—

"O my lord the King, an' thou canst pity the lost, have pity upon me! I am innocent—neither hath that wherewith I am charged been more than but lamely proved—yet I speak not of that; the judgment is gone forth against me and may not suffer alteration; yet in mine extremity I beg a boon, for my doom is more than I can bear. A grace, a grace, my lord the King! in thy royal compassion grant my prayer—give commandment that I be hanged!"

Tom was amazed. This was not the outcome he had looked for.

"Odds my life, a strange *boon*! Was it not the fate intended thee?"

"O good my liege, not so! It is ordered that I be *boiled alive*!"*

The hideous surprise of these words almost made Tom spring from his chair. As soon as he could recover his wits he cried out—

"Have thy wish, poor soul! an' thou had poisoned a hundred men thou shouldst not suffer so miserable a death."

The prisoner bowed his face to the ground and burst into passionate expressions of gratitude—ending with—

* In the reign of Henry VIII poisoners were, by Act of Parliament, condemned to be *boiled to death*. This Act was repealed in the following reign.

In Germany, even in the seventeenth century, this horrible punishment was inflicted on coiners and counterfeiters. Taylor, the Water Poet, describes an execution he witnessed in Hamburg in 1616. The judgment pronounced against a coiner of false money was that he should '*be boiled to death in oil*; not thrown into the vessel at once, but with a pulley or rope to be hanged under the armpits, and then let down into the oil *by degrees*; first the feet, and next the legs, and so to boil his flesh from his bones alive.'—Dr. J. Hammond Trumbull's Blue Laws, True and False, p. 13.

"If ever thou shouldst know misfortune—which God forefend!—may thy goodness to me this day be remembered and requited!"

Tom turned to the Earl of Hertford, and said—

"My lord, is it believable that there was warrant for this man's ferocious doom?"

"It is the law, your Grace—for poisoners. In Germany coiners be boiled to death in *oil*—not cast in of a sudden, but by a rope let down into the oil by degrees, and slowly; first the feet, then the legs, then—"

"O prithee no more, my lord, I cannot bear it!" cried Tom, covering his eyes with his hands to shut out the picture. "I beseech your good lordship that order be taken to change this law—oh, let no more poor creatures be visited with its tortures."

The Earl's face showed profound gratification, for he was a man of merciful and generous impulses—a thing not very common with his class in that fierce age. He said—

"These your Grace's noble words have sealed its doom. History will remember it to the honour of your royal house."

The under-sheriff was about to remove his prisoner; Tom gave him a sign to wait; then he said—

"Good sir, I would look into this matter further. The man has said his deed was but lamely proved. Tell me what thou knowest."

"If the King's grace please, it did appear upon the trial that this man entered into a house in the hamlet of Islington where one lay sick—three witnesses say it was at ten of the clock in the morning, and two say it was some minutes later—the sick man being alone at the time, and sleeping—and presently the man came forth again and went his way. The sick man died within the hour, being torn with spasms and retchings."

"Did any see the poison given? Was poison found?"

"Marry, no, my liege."

"Then how doth one know there was poison given at all?"

"Please your Majesty, the doctors testified that none die with such symptoms but by poison."

Weighty evidence, this, in that simple age. Tom recognized its formidable nature, and said—

"The doctor knoweth his trade—belike they were right. The matter hath an ill-look for this poor man."

"Yet was not this all, your Majesty; there is more and worse. Many testified that a witch, since gone from the village, none know whither, did foretell, and speak it privately in their ears, that the sick man *would die by poison*—and more, that a stranger would give it—a stranger with brown hair and clothed in a worn and common garb; and surely this prisoner doth answer woundily to the bill. Please your Majesty to give the circumstance that solemn weight which is its due, seeing it was *foretold*."

This was an argument of tremendous force in that superstitious day. Tom felt that the thing was settled; if evidence was worth anything, this poor fellow's guilt was proved. Still he offered the prisoner a chance, saying—

"If thou canst say aught in thy behalf, speak."

"Nought that will avail, my King. I am innocent, yet cannot I make it appear. I have no friends, else might I show that I was not in Islington that day; so also might I show that at that hour they name I was above a league away, seeing I was at Wapping Old Stairs; yea more, my King, for I could show, that whilst they say I was *taking* life, I was *saving* it. A drowning boy—"

"Peace! Sheriff, name the day the deed was done!"

"At ten in the morning, or some minutes later, the first day of the New Year, most illustrious—"

"Let the prisoner go free—it is the King's will!"

Another blush followed this unregal outburst, and he covered his indecorum as well as he could by adding—

"It enrageth me that a man should be hanged upon such idle, hare-brained evidence!"

A low buzz of admiration swept through the assemblage. It was not admiration of the decree that had been delivered by Tom, for the propriety or expediency of pardoning a convicted poisoner was a thing which few there would have felt justified in either admitting or admiring—no, the admiration was for the intelligence and spirit which Tom had displayed. Some of the low-voiced remarks were to this effect—

"This is no mad king—he hath his wits sound."

"How sanely he put his questions—how like his former natural self was this abrupt imperious disposal of the matter!"

"God be thanked, his infirmity is spent! This is no weakling, but a king. He hath borne himself like to his own father."

The air being filled with applause, Tom's ear necessarily caught a little of it. The effect which this had upon him was to put him greatly at his ease, and also to charge his system with very gratifying sensations.

However, his juvenile curiosity soon rose superior to these pleasant thoughts and feelings; he was eager to know what sort of deadly mischief the woman and the little girl could have been about; so, by his command, the two terrified and sobbing creatures were brought before him.

"What is it that these have done?" he inquired of the sheriff.

"Please your Majesty, a black crime is charged upon them, and clearly proven; wherefore the judges have decreed, according to the law, that they be hanged. They sold themselves to the devil—such is their crime."

Tom shuddered. He had been taught to abhor people who did this wicked thing. Still, he was not going to deny himself the pleasure of feeding his curiosity for all that; so he asked—

"Where was this done?—and when?"

"On a midnight in December, in a ruined church, your Majesty."

Tom shuddered again.

"Who was there present?"

"Only these two, your grace—and *that other*."

"Have these confessed?"

"Nay, not so, sire—they do deny it."

"Then prithee, how was it known?"

"Certain witnesses did see them wending thither, good your Majesty; this bred the suspicion, and dire effects have since confirmed and justified it. In particular, it is in evidence that through the wicked power so obtained, they did invoke and bring about a storm that wasted all the region round about. Above forty witnesses have proved the storm; and sooth one might have had a thousand, for all had reason to remember it, sith all had suffered by it."

"Certes this is a serious matter." Tom turned this dark piece of scoundrelism over in his mind a while, then asked—

"Suffered the woman also by the storm?"

Several old heads among the assemblage nodded their recognition of the wisdom of this question. The sheriff, however, saw nothing consequential in the inquiry; he answered, with simple directness—

"Indeed did she, your Majesty, and most righteously, as all aver. Her habitation was swept away, and herself and child left shelterless."

"Methinks the power to do herself so ill a turn was dearly bought. She had been cheated, had she paid but a farthing for it; that she paid her soul, and her child's, argueth that she is mad; if she is mad she knoweth not what she doth, therefore sinneth not."

The elderly heads nodded recognition of Tom's wisdom once more, and one individual murmured, "An' the King be mad himself, according to report, then is it a madness of a sort that would improve the sanity of some I wot of, if by the gentle providence of God they could but catch it."

"What age hath the child?" asked Tom.

"Nine years, please your Majesty."

"By the law of England may a child enter into covenant and sell itself, my lord?" asked Tom, turning to a learned judge.

"The law doth not permit a child to make or meddle in any weighty matter, good my liege, holding that its callow wit unfitteth it to cope with the riper wit and evil schemings of them that are its elders. The *Devil* may buy a child, if he so choose, and the child agree thereto, but not an Englishman—in this latter case the contract would be null and void."

"It seemeth a rude unchristian thing, and ill contrived, that English law denieth privileges to Englishmen to waste them on the devil!" cried Tom, with honest heat.

This novel view of the matter excited many smiles, and was stored away in many heads to be repeated about the Court as evidence of Tom's originality as well as progress toward mental health.

The elder culprit had ceased from sobbing, and was hanging upon Tom's words with an excited interest and a growing hope. Tom noticed this, and it strongly inclined his sympathies toward her in her perilous and unfriended situation. Presently he asked—

"How wrought they to bring the storm?"

"*By pulling off their stockings*, sire."*

This astonished Tom, and also fired his curiosity to fever heat. He said, eagerly—

"It is wonderful! Hath it always this dread effect?"

"Always, my liege—at least if the woman desire it, and utter the needful words, either in her mind or with her tongue."

Tom turned to the woman, and said with impetuous zeal—

"Exert thy power—I would see a storm!"

There was a sudden paling of cheeks in the superstitious assemblage, and a general, though unexpressed, desire to get out of the place—all of which was lost upon Tom, who was dead to everything but the proposed cataclysm. Seeing a puzzled and astonished look in the woman's face, he added, excitedly—

"Never fear—thou shalt be blameless. More—thou shalt go free—none shall touch thee. Exert thy power."

"Oh, my lord the King, I have it not—I have been falsely accused."

"Thy fears stay thee. Be of good heart, thou shalt suffer no harm. Make a storm—it mattereth not how small a one—I require nought great or harmful, but indeed prefer the opposite—do this and thy life is spared—thou shalt go out free, with thy child, bearing the King's pardon, and safe from hurt or malice from any in the realm."

---

* A woman and her daughter, *nine years old*, were hanged in Huntingdon for selling their souls to the devil, and raising a storm by pulling off their stockings!—Dr. J. Hammond Trumbull's Blue Laws, True and False, p. 20.

The woman prostrated herself, and protested, with tears, that she had no power to do the miracle, else she would gladly win her child's life alone, and be content to lose her own, if by obedience to the King's command so precious a grace might be acquired.

Tom urged—the woman still adhered to her declarations. Finally he said—

"I think the woman hath said true. An' *my* mother were in her place and gifted with the devil's functions, she had not stayed a moment to call her storms and lay the whole land in ruins, if the saving of my forfeit life were the price she got! It is argument that other mothers are made in like mould. Thou art free, goodwife—thou and thy child—for I do think thee innocent. *Now* thou'st nought to fear, being pardoned—pull off thy stockings!—an' thou canst make me a storm, thou shalt be rich!"

The redeemed creature was loud in her gratitude, and proceeded to obey, whilst Tom looked on with eager expectancy, a little marred by apprehension; the courtiers at the same time manifesting decided discomfort and uneasiness. The woman stripped her own feet and her little girl's also, and plainly did her best to reward the King's generosity with an earthquake, but it was all a failure and a disappointment. Tom sighed, and said—

"There, good soul, trouble thyself no further, thy power is departed out of thee. Go thy way in peace; and if it return to thee at any time, forget me not, but fetch me a storm."*

---

* The young King discovered an extreme attachment to his uncle, who was, in the main, a man of moderation and probity.—Hume's *History of England*, vol. iii, p. 324.

But if he (the Protector) gave offence by assuming too much state, he deserves great praise on account of the laws passed this session, by which the rigour of former statutes was much mitigated, and some security given to the freedom of the constitution. All laws were repealed which extended the crime of treason beyond the statute of the twenty-fifth of Edward III; all laws enacted during the late reign extending the crime of felony; all the former laws against Lollardy or heresy, together with the statute of the Six Articles. None were to be accused for words, but within a month after they were spoken. By these repeals several of the most rigorous laws that ever had passed in England were annulled; and some dawn, both of civil and religious liberty, began to appear to the people. A repeal also passed of that law, the destruction of all laws, by which the King's proclamation was made of equal force with a statute.—Ibid. vol. iii. p. 339.

16

The State Dinner

The dinner hour drew near—yet strangely enough, the thought brought but slight discomfort to Tom, and hardly any terror. The morning's experiences had wonderfully built up his confidence; the poor little ash-cat was already more wonted to his strange garret, after four days' habit, than a mature person could have become in a full month. A child's facility in accommodating itself to circumstances was never more strikingly illustrated.

Let us privileged ones hurry to the great banqueting room and have a glance at matters there whilst Tom is being made ready for the imposing occasion. It is a spacious apartment, with gilded pillars and pilasters, and pictured walls and ceilings. At the door stand tall guards, as rigid as statues, dressed in rich and picturesque costumes, and bearing halberds. In a high gallery which runs all around the place is a band of musicians and a packed company of citizens of both sexes, in brilliant attire. In the centre of the room, upon a raised platform, is Tom's table. Now let the ancient chronicler speak:

"A gentleman enters the room bearing a rod, and along with him another bearing a tablecloth, which, after they have both kneeled three times with the utmost veneration, he spreads upon the table, and after kneeling again they both retire; then come two others, one with the rod again, the other with a salt-cellar, a plate, and bread; when they have kneeled as the others had done, and placed what was brought upon the table, they too retire with the same ceremonies performed by the first; at last come two nobles, richly clothed, one bearing a tasting-knife, who, after prostrating themselves three times in the most graceful manner, approach and rub the table with bread and salt, with as much awe as if the King had been present."*

So end the solemn preliminaries. Now, far down the echoing corridors we hear a bugle-blast, and the indistinct cry, "Place for the King! Way for the King's most excellent majesty!" These sounds are momently repeated—they grow nearer and nearer—and presently, almost in our faces, the martial note peals and the cry rings out, "Way for the King!" At this instant the shining

* Leigh Hunt's *The Town*, p. 408, quotation from an early tourist.

pageant appears, and files in at the door, with a measured march. Let the chronicler speak again:—

"First come Gentlemen, Barons, Earls, Knights of the Garter, all richly dressed and bareheaded; next comes the Chancellor, between two, one of which carries the royal sceptre, the other the Sword of State in a red scabbard, studded with golden fleurs-de-lis, the point upwards; next comes the King himself—whom, upon his appearing, twelve trumpets and many drums salute with a great burst of welcome, whilst all in the galleries rise in their places, crying 'God save the King!' After him come nobles attached to his person, and on his right and left march his guard of honour, his fifty Gentlemen Pensioners, with gilt battle-axes."

This was all fine and pleasant. Tom's pulse beat high, and a glad light was in his eye. He bore himself right gracefully, and all the more so because he was not thinking of how he was doing it, his mind being charmed and occupied with the blithe sights and sounds about him—and besides, nobody can be very ungraceful in nicely-fitting beautiful clothes after he has grown a little used to them—especially if he is for the moment unconscious of them. Tom remembered his instructions, and acknowledged his greeting with a slight inclination of his plumed head, and a courteous "I thank ye, my good people."

He seated himself at table, without removing his cap; and did it without the least embarrassment; for to eat with one's cap on was the one solitary royal custom upon which the kings and the Cantys met upon common ground, neither party having any advantage over the other in the matter of old familiarity with it. The pageant broke up and grouped itself picturesquely, and remained bareheaded.

Now to the sound of gay music the Yeomen of the Guard entered, "the tallest and mightiest men in England, they being carefully selected in this regard"—but we will let the chronicler tell about it:—

"The Yeomen of the Guard entered, bareheaded, clothed in scarlet, with golden roses upon their backs; and these went and came, bringing in each turn a course of dishes, served in plate. These dishes were received by a gentleman in the same order they were brought, and placed upon the table, while the taster gave to each guard a mouthful to eat of the particular dish he had brought, for fear of any poison."

Tom made a good dinner, notwithstanding he was conscious that hundreds of eyes followed each morsel to his mouth and watched him eat it with an interest which could not have been more intense if it had been a deadly explosive and was expected to blow him up and scatter him all about the place. He was careful not to hurry, and equally careful not to do anything whatever for himself, but wait till the proper official knelt down and did it for him. He got through without a mistake—flawless and precious triumph.

"He marched away in the midst of his pageant"

When the meal was over at last and he marched away in the midst of his bright pageant, with the happy noises in his ears of blaring bugles, rolling drums, and thundering acclamations, he felt that if he had seen the worst of dining in public it was an ordeal which he would be glad to endure several times a day if by that means he could but buy himself free from some of the more formidable requirements of his royal office.

17

Foo-foo the First

Miles Hendon hurried along toward the Southwark end of the bridge, keeping a sharp look-out for the persons he sought, and hoping and expecting to overtake them presently. He was disappointed in this, however. By asking questions, he was enabled to track them part of the way through Southwark; then all traces ceased, and he was perplexed as to how to proceed. Still, he continued his efforts as best he could during the rest of the day. Nightfall found him leg-weary, half-famished, and his desire as far from accomplishment as ever; so he supped at the Tabard Inn and went to bed, resolved to make an early start in the morning, and give the town an exhaustive search. As he lay thinking and planning, he presently began to reason thus: The boy would escape from the ruffian, his reputed father, if possible; would he go back to London and seek his former haunts? No, he would not do that, he would avoid recapture. What, then, would he do? Never having had a friend in the world, or a protector, until he met Miles Hendon, he would naturally try to find that friend again, provided the effort did not require him to go toward London and danger. He would strike for Hendon Hall, that is what he would do, for he knew Hendon was homeward bound and there he might expect to find him. Yes, the case was plain to Hendon—he must lose no more time in Southwark, but move at once through Kent, toward Monk's Holm, searching the wood and inquiring as he went. Let us return to the vanished little King now.

The ruffian whom the waiter at the inn on the bridge saw 'about to join' the youth and the King did not exactly join them, but fell in close behind them and followed their steps. He said nothing. His left arm was in a sling, and he wore a large green patch over his left eye; he limped slightly, and used an oaken staff as a support. The youth led the King a crooked course through Southwark, and by and by struck into the high road beyond. The King was irritated, now, and said he would stop here—it was Hendon's place to come to him, not his to go to Hendon. He would not endure such insolence; he would stop where he was. The youth said—

"Thou'lt tarry here, and thy friend lying wounded in the wood yonder? So be it, then."

The King's manner changed at once. He cried out—

"Wounded? And who hath dared to do it? But that is apart; lead on, lead on! Faster, sirrah! Art shod with lead? Wounded, is he? Now though the doer of it be a duke's son he shall rue it!"

It was some distance to the wood, but the space was speedily traversed. The youth looked about him, discovered a bough sticking in the ground, with a small bit of rag tied to it, then led the way into the forest, watching for similar boughs and finding them at intervals; they were evidently guides to the point he was aiming at. By and by an open place was reached, where were the charred remains of a farmhouse, and near them a barn which was falling to ruin and decay. There was no sign of life anywhere, and utter silence prevailed. The youth entered the barn, the King following eagerly upon his heels. No one there! The King shot a surprised and suspicious glance at the youth, and asked—

"Where is he?"

A mocking laugh was his answer. The King was in a rage in a moment; he seized a billet of wood and was in the act of charging upon the youth when another mocking laugh fell upon his ear. It was from the lame ruffian who had been following at a distance. The King turned and said angrily—

"He seized a billet of wood"

"Who art thou? What is thy business here?"

"Leave thy foolery," said the man, "and quiet thyself. My disguise is none so good that thou canst pretend thou knowest not thy father through it."

"Thou art not my father. I know thee not. I am the King. If thou hast hid my servant, find him for me, or thou shalt sup sorrow for what thou hast done."

John Canty replied, in a stern and measured voice—

"It is plain thou art mad, and I am loath to punish thee; but if thou provoke me, I must. Thy prating doth no harm here, where there are no ears that need to mind thy follies; yet it is well to practise thy tongue to wary speech, that it may do no hurt when our quarters change. I have done a murder, and may not tarry at home—neither shalt thou, seeing I need thy service. My name is changed, for wise reasons; it is Hobbs—John Hobbs; thine is Jack—charge thy memory accordingly. Now, then, speak. Where is thy mother? Where are thy sisters? They came not to the place appointed—knowest thou whither they went?"

The King answered sullenly—

"Trouble me not with these riddles. My mother is dead; my sisters are in the palace."

The youth near by burst into a derisive laugh, and the King would have assaulted him, but Canty—or Hobbs, as he now called himself—prevented him, and said—

"Peace, Hugo, vex him not; his mind is astray, and thy ways fret him. Sit thee down, Jack, and quiet thyself; thou shalt have a morsel to eat, anon."

Hobbs and Hugo fell to talking together, in low voices, and the King removed himself as far as he could from their disagreeable company. He withdrew into the twilight of the farther end of the barn, where he found the earthen floor bedded a foot deep with straw. He lay down here, drew straw over himself in lieu of blankets, and was soon absorbed in thinking. He had many griefs, but the minor ones were swept almost into forgetfulness by the supreme one, the loss of his father. To the rest of the world the name of Henry VIII brought a shiver, and suggested an ogre whose nostrils breathed destruction and whose hand dealt scourgings and death; but to this boy the name brought only sensations of pleasure; the figure it invoked wore a countenance that was all gentleness and affection. He called to mind a long succession of loving passages between his father and himself, and dwelt fondly upon them, his unstinted tears attesting how deep and real was the grief that possessed his heart. As the afternoon wasted away, the lad, wearied with his troubles, sank gradually into a tranquil and healing slumber.

After a considerable time—he could not tell how long—his senses struggled to a half-consciousness, and as he lay with closed eyes vaguely wondering where he was and what had been happening, he noted a murmurous sound, the sullen beating of rain upon the roof. A snug sense of comfort stole over him, which was rudely broken, the next moment, by a chorus of piping cackles and coarse laughter. It startled him disagreeably, and he unmuffled his head to see whence this interruption proceeded. A grim and unsightly picture met his eye. A bright fire was burning in the middle of the floor, at the other end of the barn; and around it, and lit weirdly up by the red glare, lolled and sprawled the motliest company of tattered gutter-scum and ruffians, of both sexes, he had ever read or dreamed of. There were huge stalwart men, brown with exposure, long-haired, and clothed in fantastic rags; there were middle-sized youths, of truculent countenance, and similarly clad; there were blind mendicants, with patched or bandaged eyes; crippled ones, with wooden legs and crutches; diseased ones, with running sores peeping from ineffectual wrappings; there was a villain-looking pedlar with his pack; a knife-grinder, a tinker, and a barber-surgeon, with the implements of their trades; some of the females were hardly-grown girls, some were at prime, some were old and wrinkled hags, and all were loud, brazen, foul-mouthed; and all soiled and slatternly; there were three sore-faced babies; there were a couple of starveling curs, with strings about their necks, whose office was to lead the blind.

The night was come, the gang had just finished feasting, an orgy was beginning; the can of liquor was passing from mouth to mouth. A general cry broke forth—

"A song! a song from the Bat and Dick and Dot-and-go-One!"

One of the blind men got up, and made ready by casting aside the patches that sheltered his excellent eyes, and the pathetic placard which recited the cause of his calamity. Dot-and-go-One disencumbered himself of his timber leg and took his place, upon sound and healthy limbs, beside his fellow-rascal; then they roared out a rollicking ditty, and were reinforced by the whole crew, at the end of each stanza, in a rousing chorus. By the time the last stanza was reached, the half-drunken enthusiasm had risen to such a pitch, that everybody joined in and sang it clear through from the beginning, producing a volume of villainous sound that made the rafters quake. These were the inspiring words:—

'Bien Darkman's then, Bouse Mort and Ken,
The bien Coves bings awast,
On Chates to trine by Rome Coves dine
For his long lib at last.
Bing'd out bien Morts and toure, and toure,
Bing out of the Rome vile bine,
And toure the Cove that cloy'd your duds,
Upon the Chates to trine.'

(From 'The English Rogue.' London, 1665.)

Conversation followed; not in the thieves' dialect of the song, for that was only used in talk when unfriendly ears might be listening. In the course of it, it appeared that 'John Hobbs' was not altogether a new recruit, but had trained in the gang at some former time. His later history was called for, and when he said he had 'accidentally' killed a man, considerable satisfaction was expressed; when he added that the man was a priest, he was roundly applauded, and had to take a drink with everybody. Old acquaintances welcomed him joyously, and new ones were proud to shake him by the hand. He was asked why he had 'tarried away so many months.' He answered—

"London is better than the country, and safer, these late years, the laws be so bitter and so diligently enforced. An' I had not had that accident, I had stayed there. I had resolved to stay, and never more venture country-wards—but the accident has ended that."

He inquired how many persons the gang numbered now. The 'ruffler,' or chief, answered—

"Five and twenty sturdy budges, bulks, files, clapperdogeons and maunders, counting the dells and doxies and other morts.* Most are here, the rest are wandering eastward, along the winter lay. We follow at dawn."

"I do not see the Wen among the honest folk about me. Where may he be?"

"Poor lad, his diet is brimstone, now, and over hot for a delicate taste. He was killed in a brawl, somewhere about midsummer."

"I sorrow to hear that; the Wen was a capable man, and brave."

"That was he, truly. Black Bess, his dell, is of us yet, but absent on the eastward tramp; a fine lass, of nice ways and orderly conduct, none ever seeing her drunk above four days in the seven."

"She was ever strict—I remember it well—a goodly wench and worthy all commendation. Her mother was more free and less particular; a troublesome and ugly-tempered beldame, but furnished with a wit above the common."

"We lost her through it. Her gift of palmistry and other sorts of fortune-telling begot for her at last a witch's name and fame. The law roasted her to death at a slow fire. It did touch me to a sort of tenderness to see the gallant way she met her lot—cursing and reviling all the crowd that gaped and gazed around her, whilst the flames licked upward toward her face and catched her thin locks and crackled about her old grey head—cursing them! why an' thou should'st live a thousand years thoud'st never hear so masterful a cursing. Alack, her art died with her. There be base and weakling imitations left, but no true blasphemy."

The Ruffler sighed; the listeners sighed in sympathy; a general depression fell upon the company for a moment, for even hardened outcasts like these are not wholly dead to sentiment, but are able to feel a fleeting sense of loss and affliction at wide intervals and under peculiarly favouring circumstances—as in cases like to this, for instance, when genius and culture depart and leave no heir. However, a deep drink all round soon restored the spirits of the mourners.

"Have any others of our friends fared hardly?" asked Hobbs.

"Some—yes. Particularly new comers—such as small husbandmen turned shiftless and hungry upon the world because their farms were taken from them to be changed to sheep ranges. They begged, and were whipped at the cart's tail, naked from the girdle up, till the blood ran; then set in the stocks to be pelted; they begged again, were whipped again, and deprived of an ear; they begged a third time—poor devils, what else could they do?—

* Canting terms for various kinds of thieves, beggars and vagabonds, and their female companions.

and were branded on the cheek with a red-hot iron, then sold for slaves; they ran away, were hunted down, and hanged. 'Tis a brief tale, and quickly told. Others of us have fared less hardly. Stand forth, Yokel, Burns, and Hodge—show your adornments!"

"They were whipped at the cart's tail"

These stood up and stripped away some of their rags, exposing their backs, criss-crossed with ropy old welts left by the lash; one turned up his hair and showed the place where a left ear had once been; another showed a brand upon his shoulder—the letter V—and a mutilated ear; the third said—

"I am Yokel, once a farmer and prosperous, with loving wife and kids—now am I somewhat different in estate and calling; and the wife and kids are gone; mayhap they are in heaven, mayhap in—in the other place—but the kindly God be thanked, they bide no more in *England*! My good old blameless mother strove to earn bread by nursing the sick; one of these died, the doctors knew not how, so my mother was burnt for a witch, whilst my babes looked on and wailed. English law!—up, all, with your cups!—now all together and with a cheer!—drink to the merciful English law that delivered *her* from the English hell! Thank you, mates, one and all. I begged, from house to house—I and the wife—bearing with us the hungry kids—but it was crime to be hungry in England—so they stripped us and lashed us through three towns. Drink ye all again to the merciful English law!—for its lash drank deep of my Mary's blood and its blessed deliverance came quick. She lies there, in the potter's field, safe from all harms. And the kids—well, whilst the law lashed me from town to town, they starved. Drink, lads—only a drop—a drop to the poor kids, that never did any creature harm. I begged again—begged, for a crust, and got the stocks and lost an ear—see, here bides the stump; I begged again, and here is the stump of the other to keep me minded of it. And still I begged again, and was sold for a slave—here on my cheek under this stain, if I washed it off, ye might see the red S the branding-iron left there! A *slave*! Do you understand that word? An English *slave*!—that is he that stands before ye. I have run from my master, and when I am found—the heavy curse of heaven fall on the law of the land that hath commanded it!—I shall hang!"*

A ringing voice came through the murky air—

"Thou shalt *not*!—and this day the end of that law is come!"

All turned, and saw the fantastic figure of the little King approaching hurriedly; as it emerged into the light and was clearly revealed, a general explosion of inquiries broke out—

"Who is it? *What* is it? Who art thou, manikin?"

The boy stood unconfused in the midst of all those surprised and questioning eyes, and answered with princely dignity—

"I am Edward, King of England."

A wild burst of laughter followed, partly of derision and partly of delight in the excellence of the joke. The King was stung. He said sharply—

"Ye mannerless vagrants, is this your recognition of the royal boon I have promised?"

He said more, with angry voice and excited gesture, but it was lost in a whirlwind of laughter and mocking exclamations. 'John Hobbs' made several attempts to make himself heard above the din, and at last succeeded—saying—

"Mates, he is my son, a dreamer, a fool, and stark mad—mind him not—he thinketh he *is* the King."

"I *am* the King," said Edward, turning toward him, "as thou shalt know to thy cost, in good time. Thou hast confessed a murder—thou shalt swing for it."

"*Thou'lt* betray me?—*thou*? An' I get my hands upon thee—"

* So young a King and so ignorant a peasant were likely to make mistakes; and this is an instance in point. This peasant was suffering from this law by anticipation; the King was venting his indignation against a law which was not yet in existence; for this hideous statute was to have birth in this little King's own reign. However, we know, from the humanity of his character, that it could never have been suggested by him.

"Knocking hobbs down"

"Tut-tut!" said the burley Ruffler, interposing in time to save the King, and emphasising this service by knocking Hobbs down with his fist, "hast respect for neither Kings *nor* Rufflers? An' thou insult my presence so again, I'll hang thee up myself." Then he said to his Majesty, "Thou must make no threats against thy mates, lad; and thou must guard thy tongue from saying evil of them elsewhere. *Be king*, if it please thy mad humour, but be not harmful in it. Sink the title thou hast uttered—'tis treason; we be bad men in some few trifling ways, but none among us is so base as to be traitor to his King; we be loving and loyal hearts, in that regard. Note if I speak truth. Now—all together: 'Long live Edward, King of England!'"

"LONG LIVE EDWARD, KING OF ENGLAND!"

The response came with such a thundergust from the motley crew that the crazy building vibrated to the sound. The little King's face lighted with pleasure for an instant, and he slightly inclined his head, and said with grave simplicity—

"I thank you, my good people."

This unexpected result threw the company into convulsions of merriment. When something like quiet was presently come again, the Ruffler said, firmly, but with an accent of good nature—

"Drop it, boy, 'tis not wise, nor well. Humour thy fancy, if thou must, but choose some other title."

A tinker shrieked out a suggestion—

"Foo-foo the First, King of the Mooncalves!"

The title 'took,' at once, every throat responded, and a roaring shout went up, of—

"Long live Foo-foo the First, King of the Mooncalves!" followed by hootings, cat-calls, and peals of laughter.

"Hale him forth, and crown him!"

"Robe him!"

"Sceptre him!"

"Throne him!"

These and twenty other cries broke out at once! and almost before the poor little victim could draw a breath he was crowned with a tin basin, robed in a tattered blanket, throned upon a barrel, and sceptred with the tinker's soldering-iron. Then all flung themselves upon their knees about him and sent up a chorus of ironical wailings, and mocking supplications, whilst they swabbed their eyes with their soiled and ragged sleeves and aprons—

"Throne him"

"Be gracious to us, O sweet King!"

"Trample not upon thy beseeching worms, O noble Majesty!"

"Pity thy slaves, and comfort them with a royal kick!"

"Cheer us and warm us with thy gracious rays, O flaming sun of sovereignty!"

"Sanctify the ground with the touch of thy foot, that we may eat the dirt and be ennobled!"

"Deign to spit upon us, O Sire, that our children's children may tell of thy princely condescension, and be proud and happy for ever!"

But the humorous tinker made the 'hit' of the evening and carried off the honours. Kneeling, he pretended to kiss the King's foot, and was indignantly spurned; whereupon he went about begging for a rag to paste over the place upon his face which had been touched by the foot, saying it must be preserved from contact with the vulgar air, and that he should make his fortune by going on the highway and exposing it to view at the rate of a hundred shillings a sight. He made himself so killingly funny that he was the envy and admiration of the whole mangy rabble.

Tears of shame and indignation stood in the little monarch's eyes; and the thought in his heart was, "Had I offered them a deep wrong they could not be more cruel—yet have I proffered nought but to do them a kindness—and it is thus they use me for it!"

18

The Prince with the Tramps

The troop of vagabonds turned out at early dawn, and set forward on their march. There was a lowering sky overhead, sloppy ground under foot, and a winter chill in the air. All gaiety was gone from the company; some were sullen and silent, some were irritable and petulant, none were gentle-humoured, all were thirsty.

The Ruffler put 'Jack' in Hugo's charge, with some brief instructions, and commanded John Canty to keep away from him and let him alone; he also warned Hugo not to be too rough with the lad.

"Troop of vagabonds set forward"

After a while the weather grew milder, and the clouds lifted somewhat. The troop ceased to shiver, and their spirits began to improve. They grew more and more cheerful, and finally began to chaff each other and insult passengers along the highway. This showed that they were awaking to an appreciation of life and its joys once more. The dread in which their sort was held was apparent in the fact that everybody gave them the road, and took their ribald insolences meekly, without venturing to talk back. They snatched linen from the hedges, occasionally in full view of the owners, who made no protest, but only seemed grateful that they did not take the hedges, too.

By and by they invaded a small farmhouse and made themselves at home while the trembling farmer and his people swept the larder clean to furnish a breakfast for them. They chucked the housewife and her daughters under the chin whilst receiving the food from their hands, and made coarse jests about them, accompanied with insulting epithets and bursts of horse-laughter. They threw bones and vegetables at the farmer and his sons, kept them dodging all the time, and applauded uproariously when a good hit was made. They ended by buttering the head of one of the daughters who resented some of their familiarities. When they took their leave they threatened to come back and burn the house over the heads of the family if any report of their doings got to the ears of the authorities.

About noon, after a long and weary tramp, the gang came to a halt behind a hedge on the outskirts of a considerable village. An hour was allowed for rest, then the crew scattered themselves abroad to enter the village at different points to ply their various trades—'Jack' was sent with Hugo. They wandered hither and thither for some time, Hugo watching for opportunities to do a stroke of business, but finding none—so he finally said—

"I see nought to steal; it is a paltry place. Wherefore we will beg."

"*We*, forsooth! Follow thy trade—it befits thee. But *I* will not beg."

"Thou'lt not beg!" exclaimed Hugo, eyeing the King with surprise. "Prithee, since when hast thou reformed?"

"What dost thou mean?"

"Mean? Hast thou not begged the streets of London all thy life?"

"I? Thou idiot!"

"Spare thy compliments—thy stock will last the longer. Thy father says thou hast begged all thy days. Mayhap he lied. Peradventure you will even make so bold as to *say* he lied," scoffed Hugo.

"Him *you* call my father? Yes, he lied."

"Come, play not thy merry game of madman so far, mate; use it for thy amusement, not thy hurt. An' I tell him this, he will scorch thee finely for it."

"Save thyself the trouble. I will tell him."

"I like thy spirit, I do in truth; but I do not admire thy judgment. Bone-rackings and bastings be plenty enow in this life, without going out of one's way to invite them. But a truce to these matters; *I* believe your father. I doubt not he can lie; I doubt not he *doth* lie, upon occasion, for the best of us do that; but there is no occasion here. A wise man does not waste so good a commodity as lying for nought. But come; sith it is thy humour to give over begging, wherewithal shall we busy ourselves? With robbing kitchens?"

The King said, impatiently—

"Have done with this folly—you weary me!"

Hugo replied, with temper—

"Now harkee, mate; you will not beg, you will not rob; so be it. But I will tell you what you *will* do. You will play decoy whilst *I* beg. Refuse, an' you think you may venture!"

The King was about to reply contemptuously, when Hugo said, interrupting—

"Peace! Here comes one with a kindly face. Now will I fall down in a fit. When the stranger runs to me, set you up a wail, and fall upon your knees, seeming to weep; then cry out as all the devils of misery were in your belly, and say, 'Oh, sir, it is my poor afflicted brother, and we be friendless; o' God's name cast through your merciful eyes one pitiful look upon a sick, forsaken, and most miserable wretch; bestow one little penny out of thy riches upon one smitten of God and ready to perish!'—and mind you, keep you *on* wailing, and abate not till we bilk him of his penny, else shall you rue it."

Then immediately Hugo began to moan, and groan, and roll his eyes, and reel and totter about; and when the stranger was close at hand, down he sprawled before him, with a shriek, and began to writhe and wallow in the dirt, in seeming agony.

"O, dear, O dear!" cried the benevolent stranger, "O poor soul, poor soul, how he doth suffer! There—let me help thee up."

"O noble sir, forbear, and God love you for a princely gentleman—but it giveth me cruel pain to touch me when I am taken so. My brother there will tell your worship how I am racked with anguish when these fits be upon me. A penny, dear sir, a penny, to buy a little food; then leave me to my sorrows."

"A penny! thou shalt have three, thou hapless creature,"—and he fumbled in his pocket with nervous haste and got them out. "There, poor lad, take them and most welcome. Now come hither, my boy, and help me carry thy stricken brother to yon house, where—"

"I am not his brother," said the King, interrupting.

"What! not his brother?"

"Oh, hear him!" groaned Hugo, then privately ground his teeth. "He denies his own brother—and he with one foot in the grave!"

"Boy, thou art indeed hard of heart, if this is thy brother. For shame!—and he scarce able to move hand or foot. If he is not thy brother, who is he, then?"

"A beggar and a thief! He has got your money and has picked your pocket likewise. An' thou wouldst do a healing miracle, lay thy staff over his shoulders and trust Providence for the rest."

But Hugo did not tarry for the miracle. In a moment he was up and off like the wind, the gentleman following after and raising the hue and cry lustily as he went. The King, breathing deep gratitude to Heaven for his own release, fled in the opposite direction, and did not slacken his pace until he was out of harm's reach. He took the first road that offered, and soon put the village behind him. He hurried along, as briskly as he could, during several hours, keeping a nervous watch over his shoulder for pursuit; but his fears left him at last, and a grateful sense of security took their place. He recognized, now, that he was hungry, and also very tired. So he halted at a farmhouse; but when he was about to speak, he was cut short and driven rudely away. His clothes were against him.

He wandered on, wounded and indignant, and was resolved to put himself in the way of like treatment no more. But hunger is pride's master; so, as the evening drew near, he made an attempt at another farmhouse; but here he fared worse than before; for he was called hard names and was promised arrest as a vagrant except he moved on promptly.

The night came on, chilly and overcast; and still the footsore monarch laboured slowly on. He was obliged to keep moving, for every time he sat down to rest he was soon penetrated to the bone with the cold. All his sensations and experiences, as he moved through the solemn gloom and the empty vastness of the night, were new and strange to him. At intervals he heard voices approach, pass by, and fade into silence; and as he saw nothing more of the bodies they belonged to than a sort of formless drifting blur, there was something spectral and uncanny about it all that made him shudder. Occasionally he caught the twinkle of a light—always far away, apparently—almost in another world; if he heard the tinkle of a sheep's bell, it was vague, distant, indistinct; the muffled lowing of the herds floated to him on the night wind in vanishing cadences, a mournful sound; now and then came the complaining howl of a dog over viewless expanses of field and forest; all sounds were remote; they made the little King feel that all life and activity were far removed from him, and that he stood solitary, companionless, in the centre of a measureless solitude.

He stumbled along, through the gruesome fascinations of this new experience, startled occasionally by the soft rustling of the dry leaves overhead, so like human whispers they seemed to sound; and by and by he came suddenly upon the freckled light of a tin lantern near at hand. He stepped back into the shadows and waited. The lantern stood by the open door of a barn. The King waited some time—there was no sound, and nobody stirring. He got so cold, standing still, and the hospitable barn looked so enticing, that at last he resolved to risk everything and enter. He started swiftly and stealthily, and just as he was crossing the threshold he heard voices behind him. He darted behind a cask, within the barn, and stooped down. Two farm-labourers came in, bringing the lantern with them, and fell to work, talking meanwhile. Whilst they moved about with the light, the King made good use of his eyes and took the bearings of what seemed to be a good-sized stall at the further end of the place, purposing to grope his way to it when he should be left to himself. He also noted the position of a pile of horse blankets, midway of the route, with the intent to levy upon them for the service of the crown of England for one night.

By and by the men finished and went away, fastening the door behind them and taking the lantern with them. The shivering King made for the blankets, with as good speed as the darkness would allow; gathered them up, and then groped his way safely to the stall. Of two of the blankets he made a bed, then covered himself with the remaining two. He was a glad monarch, now, though the blankets were old and thin, and not quite warm enough; and besides gave out a pungent horsey odour that was almost suffocatingly powerful.

Although the King was hungry and chilly, he was also so tired and so drowsy that these latter influences soon began to get the advantage of the former, and he presently dozed off into a state of semi-consciousness. Then, just as he was on the point of losing himself wholly, he distinctly felt something touch him! He was broad awake in a moment, and gasping for breath. The cold horror of that mysterious touch in the dark almost made his heart stand still. He lay motionless, and listened, scarcely breathing. But nothing stirred, and there was no sound. He continued to listen, and wait, during what seemed a long time, but still nothing stirred, and there was no sound. So he began to drop into a drowse once more, at last; and all at once he felt that mysterious touch again! It was a grisly thing, this light touch from this noiseless and invisible presence; it made the boy sick with ghostly fears. What should he do? That was the question; but he did not know how to answer it. Should he leave these reasonably comfortable quarters and fly from this inscrutable horror? But fly whither? He could not get out of the barn; and the idea of scurrying blindly hither and thither in the dark, within the captivity of the four walls, with this phantom gliding after him, and visiting him with that soft hideous touch upon cheek or shoulder at every turn, was intolerable. But to stay where he was, and endure this living death all night—was that better? No. What, then, was there left to do? Ah, there was but one course; he knew it well—he must put out his hand and find that thing!

It was easy to think this; but it was hard to brace himself up to try it. Three times he stretched his hand a little way out into the dark, gingerly; and snatched it suddenly back, with a gasp—not because it had encountered anything, but because he had felt so sure it was just *going* to. But the fourth time, he groped a little further, and his hand lightly swept against something soft and warm. This petrified him, nearly, with fright; his mind was in such a state that he could imagine the thing to be nothing else than a corpse, newly dead and still warm. He thought he would rather die than touch it again. But he thought this false thought because he did not know the immortal strength of human curiosity. In no long time his hand was tremblingly groping again—against his judgment, and without his consent—but groping persistently on, just the same. It encountered a bunch of long hair;

he shuddered, but followed up the hair and found what seemed to be a warm rope; followed up the rope and found an innocent calf!—for the rope was not a rope at all, but the calf's tail.

The King was cordially ashamed of himself for having gotten all that fright and misery out of so paltry a matter as a slumbering calf; but he need not have felt so about it, for it was not the calf that frightened him, but a dreadful non-existent something which the calf stood for; and any other boy, in those old superstitious times, would have acted and suffered just as he had done.

The King was not only delighted to find that the creature was only a calf, but delighted to have the calf's company; for he had been feeling so lonesome and friendless that the company and comradeship of even this humble animal were welcome. And he had been so buffeted, so rudely entreated by his own kind, that it was a real comfort to him to feel that he was at last in the society of a fellow-creature that had at least a soft heart and a gentle spirit, whatever loftier attributes might be lacking. So he resolved to waive rank and make friends with the calf.

While stroking its sleek warm back—for it lay near him and within easy reach—it occurred to him that this calf might be utilised in more ways than one. Whereupon he re-arranged his bed, spreading it down close to the calf; then he cuddled himself up to the calf's back, drew the covers up over himself and his friend, and in a minute or two was as warm and comfortable as he had ever been in the downy couches of the regal palace of Westminster.

Pleasant thoughts came at once; life took on a cheerfuller seeming. He was free of the bonds of servitude and crime, free of the companionship of base and brutal outlaws; he was warm; he was sheltered; in a word, he was happy. The night wind was rising; it swept by in fitful gusts that made the old barn quake and rattle, then its forces died down at intervals, and went moaning and wailing around corners and projections—but it was all music to the King, now that he was snug and comfortable: let it blow and rage, let it batter and bang, let it moan and wail, he minded it not, he only enjoyed it. He merely snuggled the closer to his friend, in a luxury of warm contentment, and drifted blissfully out of consciousness into a deep and dreamless sleep that was full of serenity and peace. The distant dogs howled, the melancholy kine complained, and the winds went on raging, whilst furious sheets of rain drove along the roof; but the Majesty of England slept on, undisturbed, and the calf did the same, it being a simple creature, and not easily troubled by storms or embarrassed by sleeping with a king.

19

The Prince with the Peasants

When the King awoke in the early morning, he found that a wet but thoughtful rat had crept into the place during the night and made a cosy bed for itself in his bosom. Being disturbed now, it scampered away. The boy smiled, and said, "Poor fool, why so fearful? I am as forlorn as thou. 'Twould be a sham in me to hurt the helpless, who am myself so helpless. Moreover, I owe you thanks for a good omen; for when a king has fallen so low that the very rats do make a bed of him, it surely meaneth that his fortunes be upon the turn, since it is plain he can no lower go."

He got up and stepped out of the stall, and just then he heard the sound of children's voices. The barn door opened and a couple of little girls came in. As soon as they saw him their talking and laughing ceased, and they stopped and stood still, gazing at him with strong curiosity; they presently began to whisper together, then they approached nearer, and stopped again to gaze and whisper. By and by they gathered courage and began to discuss him aloud. One said—

"He hath a comely face."

The other added—

"And pretty hair."

"But is ill clothed enow."

"And how starved he looketh."

They came still nearer, sidling shyly around and about him, examining him minutely from all points, as if he were some strange new kind of animal, but warily and watchfully the while, as if they half feared he might be a sort of animal that would bite, upon occasion. Finally they halted before him, holding each other's hands for protection, and took a good satisfying stare with their innocent eyes; then one of them plucked up all her courage and inquired with honest directness—

"Who art thou, boy?"

"I am the King," was the grave answer.

The children gave a little start, and their eyes spread themselves wide open and remained so during a speechless half minute. Then curiosity broke the silence—

"The *King*? What King?"

"The King of England."

The children looked at each other—then at him—then at each other again—wonderingly, perplexedly; then one said—

"Didst hear him, Margery?—he said he is the King. Can that be true?"

"How can it be else but true, Prissy? Would he say a lie? For look you, Prissy, an' it were not true, it *would* be a lie. It surely would be. Now think on't. For all things that be not true, be lies—thou canst make nought else out of it."

It was a good tight argument, without a leak in it anywhere; and it left Prissy's half-doubts not a leg to stand on. She considered a moment, then put the King upon his honour with the simple remark—

"If thou art truly the King, then I believe thee."

"I am truly the King."

This settled the matter. His Majesty's royalty was accepted without further question or discussion, and the two little girls began at once to inquire into how he came to be where he was, and how he came to be so unroyally clad, and whither he was bound, and all about his affairs. It was a mighty relief to him to pour out his troubles where they would not be scoffed at or doubted; so he told his tale with feeling, forgetting even his hunger for the time; and it was received with the deepest and tenderest sympathy by the gentle little maids. But when he got down to his latest experiences and they learned how long he had been without food, they cut him short and hurried him away to the farmhouse to find a breakfast for him.

The King was cheerful and happy now, and said to himself, "When I am come to mine own again, I will always honour little children, remembering how that these trusted me and believed in me in my time of trouble; whilst they that were older, and thought themselves wiser, mocked at me and held me for a liar."

The children's mother received the King kindly, and was full of pity; for his forlorn condition and apparently crazed intellect touched her womanly heart. She was a widow, and rather poor; consequently she had seen trouble enough to enable her to feel for the unfortunate. She imagined that the demented boy had wandered away from his friends or keepers; so she tried to find out whence he had come, in order that she might take measures to return him; but all her references to neighbouring towns and villages, and all her inquiries in the same line went for nothing—the boy's face, and his answers, too, showed that the things she was talking of were not familiar to him. He spoke earnestly and simply about court matters, and broke down, more than once, when speaking of the late King 'his father'; but whenever the conversation changed to baser topics, he lost interest and became silent.

The woman was mightily puzzled; but she did not give up. As she proceeded with her cooking, she set herself to contriving devices to surprise the boy into betraying his real secret. She talked about cattle—he showed no concern; then about sheep—the same result: so her guess that he had been a shepherd boy was an error; she talked about mills; and about weavers, tinkers, smiths, trades and tradesmen of all sorts; and about Bedlam, and jails, and charitable retreats: but no matter, she was baffled at all points. Not altogether, either; for she argued that she had narrowed the thing down to domestic service. Yes, she was sure she was on the right track, now; he must have been a house servant. So she led up to that. But the result was discouraging. The subject of sweeping appeared to weary him; fire-building failed to stir him; scrubbing and scouring awoke no enthusiasm. The goodwife touched, with a perishing hope, and rather as a matter of form, upon the subject of cooking. To her surprise, and her vast delight, the King's face lighted at once! Ah, she had hunted him down at last, she thought; and she was right proud, too, of the devious shrewdness and tact which had accomplished it.

Her tired tongue got a chance to rest, now; for the King's, inspired by gnawing hunger and the fragrant smells that came from the sputtering pots and pans, turned itself loose and delivered itself up to such an eloquent dissertation upon certain toothsome dishes, that within three minutes the woman said to herself, "Of a truth I was right—he hath holpen in a kitchen!" Then he broadened his bill of fare, and discussed it with such appreciation and animation, that the goodwife said to herself, "Good lack! how can he know so many dishes, and so fine ones withal? For these belong only upon the tables of the rich and great. Ah, now I see! ragged outcast as he is, he must have served in the palace before his reason went astray; yes, he must have helped in the very kitchen of the King himself! I will test him."

Full of eagerness to prove her sagacity, she told the King to mind the cooking a moment—hinting that he might manufacture and add a dish or two, if he chose; then she went out of the room and gave her children a sign to follow after. The King muttered—

"Another English king had a commission like to this, in a bygone time—it is nothing against my dignity to undertake an office which the great Alfred stooped to assume. But I will try to better serve my trust than he; for he let the cakes burn."

The intent was good, but the performance was not answerable to it, for this King, like the other one, soon fell into deep thinkings concerning his vast affairs, and the same calamity resulted—the cookery got burned. The woman returned in time to save the breakfast from entire destruction; and she promptly brought the King out of his dreams with a brisk and cordial tongue-lashing. Then, seeing how troubled he was over his violated trust, she softened at once, and was all goodness and gentleness toward him.

The boy made a hearty and satisfying meal, and was greatly refreshed and gladdened by it. It was a meal which was distinguished by this curious feature, that rank was waived on both sides; yet neither recipient of the favour was aware that it had been extended. The goodwife had intended to feed this young tramp with broken victuals in a corner, like any other tramp or like a dog; but she was so remorseful for the scolding she had given him, that she did what she could to atone for it by allowing him to sit at the family table and eat with his betters, on ostensible terms of equality with them; and the King, on his side, was so remorseful for having broken his trust, after the family had been so kind to him, that he forced himself to atone for it by humbling himself to the family level, instead of requiring the woman and her children to stand and wait upon him, while he occupied their table in the solitary state due to his birth and dignity. It does us all good to unbend sometimes. This good woman was made happy all the day long by the applauses which she got out of herself for her magnanimous condescension to a tramp; and the King was just as self-complacent over his gracious humility toward a humble peasant woman.

When breakfast was over, the housewife told the King to wash up the dishes. This command was a staggerer, for a moment, and the King came near rebelling; but then he said to himself, "Alfred the Great watched the cakes; doubtless he would have washed the dishes too—therefore will I essay it."

He made a sufficiently poor job of it; and to his surprise too, for the cleaning of wooden spoons and trenchers had seemed an easy thing to do. It was a tedious and troublesome piece of work, but he finished it at last. He was becoming impatient to get away on his journey now; however, he was not to lose this thrifty dame's society so easily. She furnished him some little odds and ends of employment, which he got through with after a fair fashion and with some credit. Then she set him and the little girls to paring some winter apples; but he was so awkward at this service that she retired him from it and gave him a butcher's knife to grind.

Afterwards she kept him carding wool until he began to think he had laid the good King Alfred about far enough in the shade for the present in the matter of showy menial heroisms that would read picturesquely in storybooks and histories, and so he was half-minded to resign. And when, just after the noonday dinner, the goodwife gave him a basket of kittens to drown, he did resign. At least he was just going to resign—for he felt that he must draw the line somewhere, and it seemed to him that to draw it at kitten-drowning was about the right thing—when there was an interruption. The interruption was John Canty—with a peddler's pack on his back—and Hugo.

The King discovered these rascals approaching the front gate before they had had a chance to see him; so he said nothing about drawing the line, but took up his basket of kittens and stepped quietly out the back way, without a word. He left the creatures in an out-house, and hurried on, into a narrow lane at the rear.

20

The Prince and the Hermit

The high hedge hid him from the house, now; and so, under the impulse of a deadly fright, he let out all his forces and sped toward a wood in the distance. He never looked back until he had almost gained the shelter of the forest; then he turned and descried two figures in the distance. That was sufficient; he did not wait to scan them critically, but hurried on, and never abated his pace till he was far within the twilight depths of the wood. Then he stopped; being persuaded that he was now tolerably safe. He listened intently, but the stillness was profound and solemn—awful, even, and depressing to the spirits. At wide intervals his straining ear did detect sounds, but they were so remote, and hollow, and mysterious, that they seemed not to be real sounds, but only the moaning and complaining ghosts of departed ones. So the sounds were yet more dreary than the silence which they interrupted.

It was his purpose, in the beginning, to stay where he was the rest of the day; but a chill soon invaded his perspiring body, and he was at last obliged to resume movement in order to get warm. He struck straight through the forest, hoping to pierce to a road presently, but he was disappointed in this. He travelled on and on; but the farther he went, the denser the wood became, apparently. The gloom began to thicken, by and by, and the King realised that the night was coming on. It made him shudder to think of spending it in such an uncanny place; so he tried to hurry faster, but he only made the less speed, for he could not now see well enough to choose his steps judiciously; consequently he kept tripping over roots and tangling himself in vines and briers.

And how glad he was when at last he caught the glimmer of a light! He approached it warily, stopping often to look about him and listen. It came from an unglazed window-opening in a shabby little hut. He heard a voice, now, and felt a disposition to run and hide; but he changed his mind at once, for this voice was praying, evidently. He glided to the one window of the hut, raised himself on tiptoe, and stole a glance within. The room was small; its floor was the natural earth, beaten hard by use; in a corner was a bed of rushes and a ragged blanket or two; near it was a pail, a cup, a basin, and two or three pots and pans; there was a short bench and a three-legged stool; on the hearth the remains of a faggot fire were smouldering; before a shrine, which was lighted by a single candle, knelt an aged man, and on an old wooden box at his side lay an open book and a human skull. The man was of large, bony frame; his hair and whiskers were very long and snowy white; he was clothed in a robe of sheepskins which reached from his neck to his heels.

"A holy hermit!" said the King to himself; "now am I indeed fortunate."

The hermit rose from his knees; the King knocked. A deep voice responded—

"Enter!—but leave sin behind, for the ground whereon thou shalt stand is holy!"

The King entered, and paused. The hermit turned a pair of gleaming, unrestful eyes upon him, and said—

"Who art thou?"

"I am the King," came the answer, with placid simplicity.

"Welcome, King!" cried the hermit, with enthusiasm. Then, bustling about with feverish activity, and constantly saying, "Welcome, welcome," he arranged his bench, seated the King on it, by the hearth, threw some faggots on the fire, and finally fell to pacing the floor with a nervous stride.

"Welcome! Many have sought sanctuary here, but they were not worthy, and were turned away. But a King who casts his crown away, and despises the vain splendours of his office, and clothes his body in rags, to devote his life to holiness and the mortification of the flesh—he is worthy, he is welcome!—here shall he abide all his days till death come." The King hastened to interrupt and explain, but the hermit paid no attention to him—did not even hear him, apparently, but went right on with his talk, with a raised voice and a growing energy. "And thou shalt be at peace here. None shall find out thy refuge to disquiet thee with supplications to return to that empty and foolish life which God hath moved thee to abandon. Thou shalt pray here; thou shalt study the Book; thou shalt meditate upon the follies and delusions of this world, and upon the sublimities of the world to come; thou shalt feed upon crusts and herbs, and scourge thy body with whips, daily, to the purifying of thy soul. Thou shalt wear a hair shirt next thy skin; thou shalt drink water only; and thou shalt be at peace; yes, wholly at peace; for whoso comes to seek thee shall go his way again, baffled; he shall not find thee, he shall not molest thee."

The old man, still pacing back and forth, ceased to speak aloud, and began to mutter. The King seized this opportunity to state his case; and he did it with an eloquence inspired by uneasiness and apprehension. But the hermit went on muttering, and gave no heed. And still muttering, he approached the King and said impressively—

"'Sh! I will tell you a secret!" He bent down to impart it, but checked himself, and assumed a listening attitude. After a moment or two he went on tiptoe to the window-opening, put his head out, and peered around in the gloaming, then came tiptoeing back again, put his face close down to the King's, and whispered—

"I am an archangel!"

"I will tell you a secret"

The King started violently, and said to himself, "Would God I were with the outlaws again; for lo, now am I the prisoner of a madman!" His apprehensions were heightened, and they showed plainly in his face. In a low excited voice the hermit continued—

"I see you feel my atmosphere! There's awe in your face! None may be in this atmosphere and not be thus affected; for it is the very atmosphere of heaven. I go thither and return, in the twinkling of an eye. I was made an archangel on this very spot, it is five years ago, by angels sent from heaven to confer that awful dignity. Their presence filled this place with an intolerable brightness. And they knelt to me, King! yes, they knelt to me! for I was greater than they. I have walked in the courts of heaven, and held speech with the patriarchs. Touch my hand—be not afraid—touch it. There—now thou hast touched a hand which has been clasped by Abraham and Isaac and Jacob! For I have walked in the golden courts; I have seen the Deity face to face!" He paused, to give this speech effect; then his face suddenly changed, and he started to his feet again saying, with angry energy, "Yes, I am an archangel; *a mere archangel!*—I that might have been pope! It is verily true. I was told it from heaven in a dream, twenty years ago; ah, yes, I was to be pope!—and I *should* have been pope, for Heaven had said it—but the King dissolved my religious house, and I, poor obscure unfriended monk, was cast homeless upon the world, robbed of my mighty destiny!" Here he began to mumble again, and beat his forehead in futile rage, with his fist; now and then articulating a venomous curse, and now and then a pathetic "Wherefore I am nought but an archangel—I that should have been pope!"

So he went on, for an hour, whilst the poor little King sat and suffered. Then all at once the old man's frenzy departed, and he became all gentleness. His voice softened, he came down out of his clouds, and fell to prattling along so simply and so humanly, that he soon won the King's heart completely. The old devotee moved the boy nearer to the fire and made him comfortable; doctored his small bruises and abrasions with a deft and tender hand; and then set about preparing and cooking a supper—chatting pleasantly all the time, and occasionally stroking the lad's cheek or patting his head, in such a gently caressing way that in a little while all the fear and repulsion inspired by the archangel were changed to reverence and affection for the man.

This happy state of things continued while the two ate the supper; then, after a prayer before the shrine, the hermit put the boy to bed, in a small adjoining room, tucking him in as snugly and lovingly as a mother might; and so, with a parting caress, left him and sat down by the fire, and began to poke the brands about in an absent and aimless way. Presently he paused; then tapped his forehead several times with his fingers, as if trying to recall some thought which had escaped from his mind. Apparently he was unsuccessful. Now he started quickly up, and entered his guest's room, and said—

"Thou art King?"

"Yes," was the response, drowsily uttered.

"What King?"

"Of England."

"Of England? Then Henry is gone!"

"Alack, it is so. I am his son."

A black frown settled down upon the hermit's face, and he clenched his bony hands with a vindictive energy. He stood a few moments, breathing fast and swallowing repeatedly, then said in a husky voice—

"Dost know it was he that turned us out into the world houseless and homeless?"

There was no response. The old man bent down and scanned the boy's reposeful face and listened to his placid breathing. "He sleeps—sleeps soundly;" and the frown vanished away and gave place to an expression of evil satisfaction. A smile flitted across the dreaming boy's features. The hermit muttered, "So—his heart is happy;" and he turned away. He went stealthily about the place, seeking here and there for something; now and then halting to listen, now and then jerking his head around and casting a quick glance toward the bed; and always muttering, always mumbling to himself. At last he found what he seemed to want—a rusty old butcher knife and a whetstone. Then he crept to his place by the fire, sat himself down, and began to whet the knife softly on the stone, still muttering, mumbling, ejaculating. The winds sighed around the lonely place, the mysterious voices of the night floated by out of the distances. The shining eyes of venturesome mice and rats peered out at the old man from cracks and coverts, but he went on with his work, rapt, absorbed, and noted none of these things.

At long intervals he drew his thumb along the edge of his knife, and nodded his head with satisfaction. "It grows sharper," he said; "yes, it grows sharper."

He took no note of the flight of time, but worked tranquilly on, entertaining himself with his thoughts, which broke out occasionally in articulate speech—

"His father wrought us evil, he destroyed us—and is gone down into the eternal fires! Yes, down into the eternal fires! He escaped us—but it was God's will, yes it was God's will, we must not repine. But he hath not escaped the fires! No, he hath not escaped the fires, the consuming, unpitying, remorseless fires—and *they* are everlasting!"

And so he wrought, and still wrought—mumbling, chuckling a low rasping chuckle at times—and at times breaking again into words—

"It was his father that did it all. I am but an archangel; but for him I should be pope!"

The King stirred. The hermit sprang noiselessly to the bedside, and went down upon his knees, bending over the prostrate form with his knife uplifted. The boy stirred again; his eyes came open for an instant, but there was no speculation in them, they saw nothing; the next moment his tranquil breathing showed that his sleep was sound once more.

The hermit watched and listened, for a time, keeping his position and scarcely breathing; then he slowly lowered his arms, and presently crept away, saying—

"It is long past midnight; it is not best that he should cry out, lest by accident someone be passing."

He glided about his hovel, gathering a rag here, a thong there, and another one yonder; then he returned, and by careful and gentle handling he managed to tie the King's ankles together without waking him. Next he essayed to tie the wrists; he made several attempts to cross them, but the boy always drew one hand or the other away, just as the cord was ready to be applied; but at last, when the archangel was almost ready to despair, the boy crossed his hands himself, and the next moment they were bound. Now a bandage was passed under the sleeper's chin and brought up over his head and tied fast—and so softly, so gradually, and so deftly were the knots drawn together and compacted, that the boy slept peacefully through it all without stirring.

21

Hendon to the Rescue

The old man glided away, stooping, stealthy, cat-like, and brought the low bench. He seated himself upon it, half his body in the dim and flickering light, and the other half in shadow; and so, with his craving eyes bent upon the slumbering boy, he kept his patient vigil there, heedless of the drift of time, and softly whetted his knife, and mumbled and chuckled; and in aspect and attitude he resembled nothing so much as a grizzly, monstrous spider, gloating over some hapless insect that lay bound and helpless in his web.

After a long while, the old man, who was still gazing—yet not seeing, his mind having settled into a dreamy abstraction—observed, on a sudden, that the boy's eyes were open! wide open and staring!—staring up in frozen horror at the knife. The smile of a gratified devil crept over the old man's face, and he said, without changing his attitude or his occupation—

"Son of Henry the Eighth, hast thou prayed?"

The boy struggled helplessly in his bonds, and at the same time forced a smothered sound through his closed jaws, which the hermit chose to interpret as an affirmative answer to his question.

"Then pray again. Pray the prayer for the dying!"

A shudder shook the boy's frame, and his face blenched. Then he struggled again to free himself—turning and twisting himself this way and that; tugging frantically, fiercely, desperately—but uselessly—to burst his fetters; and all the while the old ogre smiled down upon him, and nodded his head, and placidly whetted his knife; mumbling, from time to time, "The moments are precious, they are few and precious—pray the prayer for the dying!"

The boy uttered a despairing groan, and ceased from his struggles, panting. The tears came, then, and trickled, one after the other, down his face; but this piteous sight wrought no softening effect upon the savage old man.

The dawn was coming now; the hermit observed it, and spoke up sharply, with a touch of nervous apprehension in his voice—

"I may not indulge this ecstasy longer! The night is already gone. It seems but a moment—only a moment; would it had endured a year! Seed of the Church's spoiler, close thy perishing eyes, an' thou fearest to look upon—"

The rest was lost in inarticulate mutterings. The old man sank upon his knees, his knife in his hand, and bent himself over the moaning boy.

Hark! There was a sound of voices near the cabin—the knife dropped from the hermit's hand; he cast a sheepskin over the boy and started up, trembling. The sounds increased, and presently the voices became rough and angry; then came blows, and cries for help; then a clatter of swift footsteps, retreating. Immediately came a succession of thundering knocks upon the cabin door, followed by—

"Hullo-o-o! Open! And dispatch, in the name of all the devils!"

Oh, this was the blessedest sound that had ever made music in the King's ears; for it was Miles Hendon's voice!

The hermit, grinding his teeth in impotent rage, moved swiftly out of the bedchamber, closing the door behind him; and straightway the King heard a talk, to this effect, proceeding from the 'chapel':—

"Homage and greeting, reverend sir! Where is the boy—*my* boy?"

"What boy, friend?"

"What boy! Lie me no lies, sir priest, play me no deceptions!—I am not in the humour for it. Near to this place I caught the scoundrels who I judged did steal him from me, and I made them confess; they said he was at large again, and they had tracked him to your door. They showed me his very footprints. Now palter no more; for look you, holy sir, an' thou produce him not—Where is the boy?"

"O good sir, peradventure you mean the ragged regal vagrant that tarried here the night. If such as you take an interest in such as he, know, then, that I have sent him of an errand. He will be back anon."

"How soon? How soon? Come, waste not the time—cannot I overtake him? How soon will he be back?"

"Thou need'st not stir; he will return quickly."

"So be it, then. I will try to wait. But stop!—*you* sent him of an errand?—you! Verily this is a lie—he would not go. He would pull thy old beard, an' thou didst offer him such an insolence. Thou hast lied, friend; thou hast surely lied! He would not go for thee, nor for any man."

"For any *man*—no; haply not. But I am not a man."

"*What*! Now o' God's name what art thou, then?"

"It is a secret—mark thou reveal it not. I am an archangel!"

There was a tremendous ejaculation from Miles Hendon—not altogether unprofane—followed by—

"This doth well and truly account for his complaisance! Right well I knew he would budge nor hand nor foot in the menial service of any mortal; but, lord, even a king must obey when an archangel gives the word o' command! Let me—'sh! What noise was that?"

All this while the little King had been yonder, alternately quaking with terror and trembling with hope; and all the while, too, he had thrown all the strength he could into his anguished moanings, constantly expecting them to reach Hendon's ear, but always realising, with bitterness, that they failed, or at least made no impression. So this last remark of his servant came as comes a reviving breath from fresh fields to the dying; and he exerted himself once more, and with all his energy, just as the hermit was saying—

"Noise? I heard only the wind."

"Mayhap it was. Yes, doubtless that was it. I have been hearing it faintly all the—there it is again! It is not the wind! What an odd sound! Come, we will hunt it out!"

Now the King's joy was nearly insupportable. His tired lungs did their utmost—and hopefully, too—but the sealed jaws and the muffling sheepskin sadly crippled the effort. Then the poor fellow's heart sank, to hear the hermit say—

"Ah, it came from without—I think from the copse yonder. Come, I will lead the way."

The King heard the two pass out, talking; heard their footsteps die quickly away—then he was alone with a boding, brooding, awful silence.

It seemed an age till he heard the steps and voices approaching again—and this time he heard an added sound—the trampling of hoofs, apparently. Then he heard Hendon say—

"I will not wait longer. I *cannot* wait longer. He has lost his way in this thick wood. Which direction took he? Quick—point it out to me."

"He—but wait; I will go with thee."

"Good—good! Why, truly thou art better than thy looks. Marry I do not think there's not another archangel with so right a heart as thine. Wilt ride? Wilt take the wee donkey that's for my boy, or wilt thou fork thy holy legs over this ill-conditioned slave of a mule that I have provided for myself?—and had been cheated in too, had he cost but the indifferent sum of a month's usury on a brass farthing let to a tinker out of work."

"No—ride thy mule, and lead thine ass; I am surer on mine own feet, and will walk."

"Then, prithee, mind the little beast for me while I take my life in my hands and make what success I may toward mounting the big one."

Then followed a confusion of kicks, cuffs, tramplings and plungings, accompanied by a thunderous intermingling of volleyed curses, and finally a bitter apostrophe to the mule, which must have broken its spirit, for hostilities seemed to cease from that moment.

With unutterable misery the fettered little King heard the voices and footsteps fade away and die out. All hope forsook him, now, for the moment, and a dull despair settled down upon his heart. "My only friend is deceived and got rid of," he said; "the hermit will return and—" He finished with a gasp; and at once fell to struggling so frantically with his bonds again, that he shook off the smothering sheepskin.

And now he heard the door open! The sound chilled him to the marrow—already he seemed to feel the knife at his throat. Horror made him close his eyes; horror made him open them again—and before him stood John Canty and Hugo!

He would have said "Thank God!" if his jaws had been free.

A moment or two later his limbs were at liberty, and his captors, each gripping him by an arm, were hurrying him with all speed through the forest.

22

A Victim of Treachery

Once more 'King Foo-foo the First' was roving with the tramps and outlaws, a butt for their coarse jests and dull-witted railleries, and sometimes the victim of small spitefulness at the hands of Canty and Hugo when the Ruffler's back was turned. None but Canty and Hugo really disliked him. Some of the others liked him, and all admired his pluck and spirit. During two or three days, Hugo, in whose ward and charge the King was, did what he covertly could to make the boy uncomfortable; and at night, during the customary orgies, he amused the company by putting small indignities upon him—always as if by accident. Twice he stepped upon the King's toes—accidentally—and the King, as became his royalty, was contemptuously unconscious of it and indifferent to it; but the third time Hugo entertained himself in that way, the King felled him to the ground with a cudgel, to the prodigious delight of the tribe. Hugo, consumed with anger and shame, sprang up, seized a cudgel, and came at his small adversary in a fury. Instantly a ring was formed around the gladiators, and the betting and cheering began.

But poor Hugo stood no chance whatever. His frantic and lubberly 'prentice-work found but a poor market for itself when pitted against an arm which had been trained by the first masters of Europe in single-stick, quarter-staff, and every art and trick of swordsmanship. The little King stood, alert but at graceful ease, and caught and turned aside the thick rain of blows with a facility and precision which set the motley on-lookers wild with admiration; and every now and then, when his

"Hugo stood no chance"

practised eye detected an opening, and a lightning-swift rap upon Hugo's head followed as a result, the storm of cheers and laughter that swept the place was something wonderful to hear. At the end of fifteen minutes, Hugo, all battered, bruised, and the target for a pitiless bombardment of ridicule, slunk from the field; and the unscathed hero of the fight was seized and borne aloft upon the shoulders of the joyous rabble to the place of honour beside the Ruffler, where with vast ceremony he was crowned King of the Game-Cocks; his meaner title being at the same time solemnly cancelled and annulled, and a decree of banishment from the gang pronounced against any who should thenceforth utter it.

All attempts to make the King serviceable to the troop had failed. He had stubbornly refused to act; moreover, he was always trying to escape. He had been thrust into an unwatched kitchen, the first day of his return; he not only came forth empty-handed, but tried to rouse the housemates. He was sent out with a tinker to help him at his work; he would not work; moreover, he threatened the tinker with his own soldering-iron; and finally both Hugo and the tinker found their hands full with the mere matter of keeping his from getting away. He delivered the thunders of his royalty upon the heads of all who hampered his liberties or tried to force him to service. He was sent out, in Hugo's charge, in company with a slatternly woman and a diseased baby, to beg; but the result was not encouraging—he declined to plead for the mendicants, or be a party to their cause in any way.

Thus several days went by; and the miseries of this tramping life, and the weariness and sordidness and meanness and vulgarity of it, became gradually and steadily so intolerable to the captive that he began at last to feel that his release from the hermit's knife must prove only a temporary respite from death, at best.

But at night, in his dreams, these things were forgotten, and he was on his throne, and master again. This, of course, intensified the sufferings of the awakening—so the mortifications of each succeeding morning of the few that passed between his return to bondage and the combat with Hugo, grew bitterer and bitterer, and harder and harder to bear.

The morning after that combat, Hugo got up with a heart filled with vengeful purposes against the King. He had two plans, in particular. One was to inflict upon the lad what would be, to his proud spirit and 'imagined' royalty, a peculiar humiliation; and if he failed to accomplish this, his other plan was to put a crime of some kind upon the King, and then betray him into the implacable clutches of the law.

In pursuance of the first plan, he purposed to put a 'clime' upon the King's leg; rightly judging that that would mortify him to the last and perfect degree; and as soon as the clime should operate, he meant to get Canty's help, and *force* the King to expose his leg in the highway and beg for alms. 'Clime' was the cant term for a sore, artificially created. To make a clime, the operator made a paste or poultice of unslaked lime, soap, and the rust of old iron, and spread it upon a piece of leather, which was then bound tightly upon the leg. This would presently fret off the skin, and make the flesh raw and angry-looking; blood was then rubbed upon the limb, which, being fully dried, took on a dark and repulsive colour. Then a bandage of soiled rags was put on in a cleverly careless way which would allow the hideous ulcer to be seen, and move the compassion of the passer-by.*

Hugo got the help of the tinker whom the King had cowed with the soldering-iron; they took the boy out on a tinkering tramp, and as soon as they were out of sight of the camp they threw him down and the tinker held him while Hugo bound the poultice tight and fast upon his leg.

"Hugo bound the poultice tight and fast"

The King raged and stormed, and promised to hang the two the moment the sceptre was in his hand again; but they kept a firm grip upon him and enjoyed his impotent struggling and jeered at his threats. This continued until the poultice began to bite; and in no long time its work would have been perfected, if there had been no interruption. But there was; for about this time the 'slave' who had made the speech denouncing England's laws, appeared on the scene, and put an end to the enterprise, and stripped off the poultice and bandage.

* From *The English Rogue*. London, 1665.

The King wanted to borrow his deliverer's cudgel and warm the jackets of the two rascals on the spot; but the man said no, it would bring trouble—leave the matter till night; the whole tribe being together, then, the outside world would not venture to interfere or interrupt. He marched the party back to camp and reported the affair to the Ruffler, who listened, pondered, and then decided that the King should not be again detailed to beg, since it was plain he was worthy of something higher and better—wherefore, on the spot he promoted him from the mendicant rank and appointed him to steal!

Hugo was overjoyed. He had already tried to make the King steal, and failed; but there would be no more trouble of that sort, now, for of course the King would not dream of defying a distinct command delivered directly from head-quarters. So he planned a raid for that very afternoon, purposing to get the King in the law's grip in the course of it; and to do it, too, with such ingenious strategy, that it should seem to be accidental and unintentional; for the King of the Game-Cocks was popular now, and the gang might not deal over-gently with an unpopular member who played so serious a treachery upon him as the delivering him over to the common enemy, the law.

Very well. All in good time Hugo strolled off to a neighbouring village with his prey; and the two drifted slowly up and down one street after another, the one watching sharply for a sure chance to achieve his evil purpose, and the other watching as sharply for a chance to dart away and get free of his infamous captivity for ever.

Both threw away some tolerably fair-looking opportunities; for both, in their secret hearts, were resolved to make absolutely sure work this time, and neither meant to allow his fevered desires to seduce him into any venture that had much uncertainty about it.

Hugo's chance came first. For at last a woman approached who carried a fat package of some sort in a basket. Hugo's eyes sparkled with sinful pleasure as he said to himself, "Breath o' my life, an' I can but put *that* upon him, 'tis good-den and God keep thee, King of the Game-Cocks!" He waited and watched—outwardly patient, but inwardly consuming with excitement—till the woman had passed by, and the time was ripe; then said, in a low voice—

"Tarry here till I come again," and darted stealthily after the prey.

The King's heart was filled with joy—he could make his escape, now, if Hugo's quest only carried him far enough away.

But he was to have no such luck. Hugo crept behind the woman, snatched the package, and came running back, wrapping it in an old piece of blanket which he carried on his arm. The hue and cry was raised in a moment, by the woman, who knew her loss by the lightening of her burden, although she had not seen the pilfering done. Hugo thrust the bundle into the King's hands without halting, saying—

"Now speed ye after me with the rest, and cry 'Stop thief!' but mind ye lead them astray!"

The next moment Hugo turned a corner and darted down a crooked alley—and in another moment or two he lounged into view again, looking innocent and indifferent, and took up a position behind a post to watch results.

The insulted King threw the bundle on the ground; and the blanket fell away from it just as the woman arrived, with an augmenting crowd at her heels; she seized the King's wrist with one hand, snatched up her bundle with the other, and began to pour out a tirade of abuse upon the boy while he struggled, without success, to free himself from her grip.

Hugo had seen enough—his enemy was captured and the law would get him, now—so he slipped away, jubilant and chuckling, and wended campwards, framing a judicious version of the matter to give to the Ruffler's crew as he strode along.

The King continued to struggle in the woman's strong grasp, and now and then cried out in vexation—

"Unhand me, thou foolish creature; it was not I that bereaved thee of thy paltry goods."

The crowd closed around, threatening the King and calling him names; a brawny blacksmith in leather apron, and sleeves rolled to his elbows, made a reach for him, saying he would trounce him well, for a lesson; but just then a long sword flashed in the air and fell with convincing force upon the man's arm, flat side down, the fantastic owner of it remarking pleasantly, at the same time—

"Marry, good souls, let us proceed gently, not with ill blood and uncharitable words. This is matter for the law's consideration, not private and unofficial handling. Loose thy hold from the boy, goodwife."

The blacksmith averaged the stalwart soldier with a glance, then went muttering away, rubbing his arm; the woman released the boy's wrist reluctantly; the crowd eyed the stranger unlovingly, but prudently closed their mouths. The King sprang to his deliverer's side, with flushed cheeks and sparkling eyes, exclaiming—

"Thou hast lagged sorely, but thou comest in good season, now, Sir Miles; carve me this rabble to rags!"

23

The Prince a Prisoner

Hendon forced back a smile, and bent down and whispered in the King's ear—

"Softly, softly, my prince, wag thy tongue warily—nay, suffer it not to wag at all. Trust in me—all shall go well in the end." Then he added to himself: "*Sir* Miles! Bless me, I had totally forgot I was a knight! Lord, how marvellous a thing it is, the grip his memory doth take upon his quaint and crazy fancies! . . . An empty and foolish title is mine, and yet it is something to have deserved it; for I think it is more honour to be held worthy to be a spectre-knight in his Kingdom of Dreams and Shadows, than to be held base enough to be an earl in some of the *real* kingdoms of this world."

The crowd fell apart to admit a constable, who approached and was about to lay his hand upon the King's shoulder, when Hendon said—

"Gently, good friend, withhold your hand—he shall go peaceably; I am responsible for that. Lead on, we will follow."

The officer led, with the woman and her bundle; Miles and the King followed after, with the crowd at their heels. The King was inclined to rebel; but Hendon said to him in a low voice—

"Reflect, Sire—your laws are the wholesome breath of your own royalty; shall their source resist them, yet require the branches to respect them? Apparently one of these laws has been broken; when the King is on his throne again, can it ever grieve him to remember that when he was seemingly a private person he loyally sank the king in the citizen and submitted to its authority?"

"Thou art right; say no more; thou shalt see that whatsoever the King of England requires a subject to suffer, under the law, he will himself suffer while he holdeth the station of a subject."

When the woman was called upon to testify before the justice of the peace, she swore that the small prisoner at the bar was the person who had committed the theft; there was none able to show the contrary, so the King stood convicted. The bundle was now unrolled, and when the contents proved to be a plump little dressed pig, the judge looked troubled, whilst

Hendon turned pale, and his body was thrilled with an electric shiver of dismay; but the King remained unmoved, protected by his ignorance. The judge meditated, during an ominous pause, then turned to the woman, with the question—

"What dost thou hold this property to be worth?"

The woman courtesied and replied—

"Three shillings and eightpence, your worship—I could not abate a penny and set forth the value honestly."

The justice glanced around uncomfortably upon the crowd, then nodded to the constable, and said—

"Clear the court and close the doors."

It was done. None remained but the two officials, the accused, the accuser, and Miles Hendon. This latter was rigid and colourless, and on his forehead big drops of cold sweat gathered, broke and blended together, and trickled down his face. The judge turned to the woman again, and said, in a compassionate voice—

"'Tis a poor ignorant lad, and mayhap was driven hard by hunger, for these be grievous times for the unfortunate; mark you, he hath not an evil face—but when hunger driveth—Good woman! dost know that when one steals a thing above the value of thirteenpence ha'penny the law saith he shall *hang* for it?"

The little King started, wide-eyed with consternation, but controlled himself and held his peace; but not so the woman. She sprang to her feet, shaking with fright, and cried out—

"Oh, good lack, what have I done! God-a-mercy, I would not hang the poor thing for the whole world! Ah, save me from this, your worship—what shall I do, what *can* I do?"

The justice maintained his judicial composure, and simply said—

"Doubtless it is allowable to revise the value, since it is not yet writ upon the record."

"Then in God's name call the pig eightpence, and heaven bless the day that freed my conscience of this awesome thing!"

Miles Hendon forgot all decorum in his delight; and surprised the King and wounded his dignity, by throwing his arms around him and hugging him. The woman made her grateful adieux and started away with her pig; and when the constable opened the door for her, he followed her out into the narrow hall. The justice proceeded to write in his record book. Hendon, always alert, thought he would like to know why the officer followed the woman out; so he slipped softly into the dusky hall and listened. He heard a conversation to this effect—

"It is a fat pig, and promises good eating; I will buy it of thee; here is the eightpence."

"Eightpence, indeed! Thou'lt do no such thing. It cost me three shillings and eightpence, good honest coin of the last reign, that old Harry that's just dead ne'er touched or tampered with. A fig for thy eightpence!"

"Stands the wind in that quarter? Thou wast under oath, and so swore falsely when thou saidst the value was but eightpence. Come straightway back with me before his worship, and answer for the crime!—and then the lad will hang."

"There, there, dear heart, say no more, I am content. Give me the eightpence, and hold thy peace about the matter."

The woman went off crying: Hendon slipped back into the courtroom, and the constable presently followed, after hiding his prize in some convenient place. The justice wrote a while longer, then read the King a wise and kindly lecture, and sentenced him to a short imprisonment in the common jail, to be followed by a public flogging. The astounded King opened his mouth, and was probably going to order the good judge to be beheaded on the spot; but he caught a warning sign from Hendon, and succeeded in closing his mouth again before he lost anything out of it. Hendon took him by the hand, now, made reverence to the justice, and the two departed in the wake of the constable toward the jail. The moment the street was reached, the inflamed monarch halted, snatched away his hand, and exclaimed—

"Idiot, dost imagine I will enter a common jail *alive*?"

Hendon bent down and said, somewhat sharply—

"*Will* you trust in me? Peace! and forbear to worsen our chances with dangerous speech. What God wills, will happen; thou canst not hurry it, thou canst not alter it; therefore wait, and be patient—'twill be time enow to rail or rejoice when what is to happen has happened."*

---

* When Connecticut and New Haven were framing their first codes, larceny above the value of twelve pence was a capital crime in England—as it had been since the time of Henry I. —Dr. J. Hammond Trumbull's Blue Laws, True and False, p. 17.

The curious old book called *The English Rogue* makes the limit thirteen pence ha'penny: death being the portion of any who steal a thing 'above the value of thirteen pence ha'penny.'

24

The Escape

The short winter day was nearly ended. The streets were deserted, save for a few random stragglers, and these hurried straight along, with the intent look of people who were only anxious to accomplish their errands as quickly as possible, and then snugly house themselves from the rising wind and the gathering twilight. They looked neither to the right nor to the left; they paid no attention to our party, they did not even seem to see them. Edward the Sixth wondered if the spectacle of a king on his way to jail had ever encountered such marvellous indifference before. By and by the constable arrived at a deserted market-square, and proceeded to cross it. When he had reached the middle of it, Hendon laid his hand upon his arm, and said in a low voice—

"Bide a moment, good sir, there is none in hearing, and I would say a word to thee."

"My duty forbids it, sir; prithee hinder me not, the night comes on."

"Stay, nevertheless, for the matter concerns thee nearly. Turn thy back a moment and seem not to see: *let this poor lad escape*."

"This to me, sir! I arrest thee in—"

"Nay, be not too hasty. See thou be careful and commit no foolish error,"—then he shut his voice down to a whisper, and said in the man's ear—"the pig thou hast purchased for eightpence may cost thee thy neck, man!"

The poor constable, taken by surprise, was speechless, at first, then found his tongue and fell to blustering and threatening; but Hendon was tranquil, and waited with patience till his breath was spent; then said—

"I have a liking to thee, friend, and would not willingly see thee come to harm. Observe, I heard it all—every word. I will prove it to thee." Then he repeated the conversation which the officer and the woman had had together in the hall, word for word, and ended with—

"There—have I set it forth correctly? Should not I be able to set it forth correctly before the judge, if occasion required?"

The man was dumb with fear and distress, for a moment; then he rallied, and said with forced lightness—

"'Tis making a mighty matter, indeed, out of a jest; I but plagued the woman for mine amusement."

"Kept you the woman's pig for amusement?"

The man answered sharply—

"Nought else, good sir—I tell thee 'twas but a jest."

"I do begin to believe thee," said Hendon, with a perplexing mixture of mockery and half-conviction in his tone; "but tarry thou here a moment whilst I run and ask his worship—for nathless, he being a man experienced in law, in jests, in—"

He was moving away, still talking; the constable hesitated, fidgeted, spat out an oath or two, then cried out—

"Hold, hold, good sir—prithee wait a little—the judge! Why, man, he hath no more sympathy with a jest than hath a dead corpse!—come, and we will speak further. Ods body! I seem to be in evil case—and all for an innocent and thoughtless pleasantry. I am a man of family; and my wife and little ones—List to reason, good your worship: what wouldst thou of me?"

"Only that thou be blind and dumb and paralytic whilst one may count a hundred thousand—counting slowly," said Hendon, with the expression of a man who asks but a reasonable favour, and that a very little one.

"It is my destruction!" said the constable despairingly. "Ah, be reasonable, good sir; only look at this matter, on all its sides, and see how mere a jest it is—how manifestly and how plainly it is so. And even if one granted it were not a jest, it is a fault so small that e'en the grimmest penalty it could call forth would be but a rebuke and warning from the judge's lips."

Hendon replied with a solemnity which chilled the air about him—

"This jest of thine hath a name, in law—wot you what it is?"

"I knew it not! Peradventure I have been unwise. I never dreamed it had a name—ah, sweet heaven, I thought it was original."

"Yes, it hath a name. In the law this crime is called *Non compos mentis lex talionis sic transit gloria mundi*."

"Ah, my God!"

"And the penalty is death!"

"God be merciful to me a sinner!"

"By advantage taken of one in fault, in dire peril, and at thy mercy, thou hast seized goods worth above thirteenpence ha'penny, paying but a trifle for the same; and this, in the eye of the law, is constructive barratry, misprision of treason, malfeasance in office, *ad hominem expurgatis in statu quo*—and the penalty is death by the halter, without ransom, commutation, or benefit of clergy."

"Bear me up, bear me up, sweet sir, my legs do fail me! Be thou merciful—spare me this doom, and I will turn my back and see nought that shall happen."

"Good! now thou'rt wise and reasonable. And thou'lt restore the pig?"

"I will, I will indeed—nor ever touch another, though heaven send it and an archangel fetch it. Go—I am blind for thy sake—I see nothing. I will say thou didst break in and wrest the prisoner from my hands by force. It is but a crazy, ancient door—I will batter it down myself betwixt midnight and the morning."

"Do it, good soul, no harm will come of it; the judge hath a loving charity for this poor lad, and will shed no tears and break no jailer's bones for his escape."

25

Hendon Hall

As soon as Hendon and the King were out of sight of the constable, his Majesty was instructed to hurry to a certain place outside the town, and wait there, whilst Hendon should go to the inn and settle his account. Half an hour later the two friends were blithely jogging eastward on Hendon's sorry steeds. The King was warm and comfortable, now, for he had cast his rags and clothed himself in the second-hand suit which Hendon had bought on London Bridge.

Hendon wished to guard against over-fatiguing the boy; he judged that hard journeys, irregular meals, and illiberal measures of sleep would be bad for his crazed mind; whilst rest, regularity, and moderate exercise would be pretty sure to hasten its cure; he longed to see the stricken intellect made well again and its diseased visions driven out of the tormented little head; therefore he resolved to move by easy stages toward the home whence he had so long been banished, instead of obeying the impulse of his impatience and hurrying along night and day.

When he and the King had journeyed about ten miles, they reached a considerable village, and halted there for the night, at a good inn. The former relations were resumed; Hendon stood behind the King's chair, while he dined, and waited upon him; undressed him when he was ready for bed; then took the floor for his own quarters, and slept athwart the door, rolled up in a blanket.

The next day, and the day after, they jogged lazily along talking over the adventures they had met since their separation, and mightily enjoying each other's narratives. Hendon detailed all his wide wanderings in search of the King, and described how the archangel had led him a fool's journey all over the forest, and taken him back to the hut, finally, when he found he could not get rid of him. Then—he said—the old man went into the bedchamber and came staggering back looking broken-hearted, and saying he had expected to find that the boy had returned and laid down in there to rest, but it was not so. Hendon had waited at the hut all day; hope of the King's return died out, then, and he departed upon the quest again.

"And old Sanctum Sanctorum *was* truly sorry your highness came not back," said Hendon; "I saw it in his face."

"Marry I will never doubt *that*!" said the King—and then told his own story; after which, Hendon was sorry he had not destroyed the archangel.

During the last day of the trip, Hendon's spirits were soaring. His tongue ran constantly. He talked about his old father, and his brother Arthur, and told of many things which illustrated their high and generous characters; he went into loving frenzies over his Edith, and was so glad-hearted that he was even able to say some gentle and brotherly things about Hugh. He dwelt a deal on the coming meeting at Hendon Hall; what a surprise it would be to everybody, and what an outburst of thanksgiving and delight there would be.

It was a fair region, dotted with cottages and orchards, and the road led through broad pasture lands whose receding expanses, marked with gentle elevations and depressions, suggested the swelling and subsiding undulations of the sea. In the afternoon the returning prodigal made constant deflections from his course to see if by ascending some hillock he might not pierce the distance and catch a glimpse of his home. At last he was successful, and cried out excitedly—

"There is the village, my Prince, and there is the Hall close by! You may see the towers from here; and that wood there—that is my father's park. Ah, *now* thou'lt know what state and grandeur be! A house with seventy rooms—think of that!—and seven and twenty servants! A brave lodging for such as we, is it not so? Come, let us speed—my impatience will not brook further delay."

All possible hurry was made; still, it was after three o'clock before the village was reached. The travellers scampered through it, Hendon's tongue going all the time. "Here is the church—covered with the same ivy—none gone, none added." "Yonder is the inn, the old Red Lion—and yonder is the marketplace." "Here is the Maypole, and here the pump—nothing is altered; nothing but the people, at any rate; ten years make a change in people; some of these I seem to know, but none know me." So his chat ran on. The end of the village was soon reached; then the travellers struck into a crooked, narrow road, walled in with tall hedges, and hurried briskly along it for half a mile, then passed into a vast flower garden through an imposing gateway, whose huge stone pillars bore sculptured armorial devices. A noble mansion was before them.

"Welcome to Hendon Hall, my King!" exclaimed Miles. "Ah, 'tis a great day! My father and my brother, and the Lady Edith will be so mad with joy that they will have eyes and tongue for none but me in the first transports of the meeting, and so thou'lt seem but coldly welcomed—but mind it not; 'twill soon seem otherwise; for when I say thou art my ward, and tell them how costly is my love for thee, thou'lt see them take thee to their breasts for Miles Hendon's sake, and make their house and hearts thy home for ever after!"

The next moment Hendon sprang to the ground before the great door, helped the King down, then took him by the hand and rushed within. A few steps brought him to a spacious apartment; he entered, seated the King with more hurry than ceremony, then ran toward a young man who sat at a writing-table in front of a generous fire of logs.

"Embrace me, Hugh," he cried, "and say thou'rt glad I am come again! and call our father, for home is not home till I shall touch his hand, and see his face, and hear his voice once more!"

But Hugh only drew back, after betraying a momentary surprise, and bent a grave stare upon the intruder—a stare which indicated somewhat of offended dignity, at first, then changed, in response to some inward thought or purpose, to an expression of marvelling curiosity, mixed with a real or assumed compassion. Presently he said, in a mild voice—

"Thy wits seem touched, poor stranger; doubtless thou hast suffered privations and rude buffetings at the world's hands; thy looks and dress betoken it. Whom dost thou take me to be?"

"Take thee? Prithee for whom else than whom thou art? I take thee to be Hugh Hendon," said Miles, sharply.

The other continued, in the same soft tone—

"And whom dost thou imagine thyself to be?"

"Imagination hath nought to do with it! Dost thou pretend thou knowest me not for thy brother Miles Hendon?"

An expression of pleased surprise flitted across Hugh's face, and he exclaimed—

"What! thou art not jesting? can the dead come to life? God be praised if it be so! Our poor lost boy restored to our arms after all these cruel years! Ah, it seems too good to be true, it *is* too good to be true—I charge thee, have pity, do not trifle with me! Quick—come to the light—let me scan thee well!"

He seized Miles by the arm, dragged him to the window, and began to devour him from head to foot with his eyes, turning him this way and that, and stepping briskly around him and about him to prove him from all points of view; whilst the returned prodigal, all aglow with gladness, smiled, laughed, and kept nodding his head and saying—

"Go on, brother, go on, and fear not; thou'lt find nor limb nor feature that cannot bide the test. Scour and scan me to thy content, my good old Hugh—I am indeed thy old Miles, thy same old Miles, thy lost brother, is't not so? Ah, 'tis a great day—I *said* 'twas a great day! Give me thy hand, give me thy cheek—lord, I am like to die of very joy!"

He was about to throw himself upon his brother; but Hugh put up his hand in dissent, then dropped his chin mournfully upon his breast, saying with emotion—

"Ah, God of his mercy give me strength to bear this grievous disappointment!"

Miles, amazed, could not speak for a moment; then he found his tongue, and cried out—

"*What* disappointment? Am I not thy brother?"

Hugh shook his head sadly, and said—

"I pray heaven it may prove so, and that other eyes may find the resemblances that are hid from mine. Alack, I fear me the letter spoke but too truly."

"What letter?"

"One that came from over sea, some six or seven years ago. It said my brother died in battle."

"It was a lie! Call thy father—he will know me."

"One may not call the dead."

"Dead?" Miles's voice was subdued, and his lips trembled. "My father dead!—oh, this is heavy news. Half my new joy is withered now. Prithee let me see my brother Arthur—he will know me; he will know me and console me."

"He, also, is dead."

"God be merciful to me, a stricken man! Gone—both gone—the worthy taken and the worthless spared, in me! Ah! I crave your mercy!—do not say the Lady Edith—"

"Is dead? No, she lives."

"Then, God be praised, my joy is whole again! Speed thee, brother—let her come to me! An' *she* say I am not myself—but she will not; no, no, *she* will know me, I were a fool to doubt it. Bring her—bring the old servants; they, too, will know me."

"All are gone but five—Peter, Halsey, David, Bernard, and Margaret."

So saying, Hugh left the room. Miles stood musing a while, then began to walk the floor, muttering—

"The five arch-villains have survived the two-and-twenty leal and honest—'tis an odd thing."

He continued walking back and forth, muttering to himself; he had forgotten the King entirely. By and by his Majesty said gravely, and with a touch of genuine compassion, though the words themselves were capable of being interpreted ironically—

"Mind not thy mischance, good man; there be others in the world whose identity is denied, and whose claims are derided. Thou hast company."

"Ah, my King," cried Hendon, colouring slightly, "do not thou condemn me—wait, and thou shalt see. I am no impostor—she will say it; you shall hear it from the sweetest lips in England. I an impostor? Why, I know this old hall, these pictures of my ancestors, and all these things that are about us, as a child knoweth its own nursery. Here was I born and bred, my lord; I speak the truth; I would not deceive thee; and should none else believe, I pray thee do not *thou* doubt me—I could not bear it."

"I do not doubt thee," said the King, with a childlike simplicity and faith.

"I thank thee out of my heart!" exclaimed Hendon with a fervency which showed that he was touched. The King added, with the same gentle simplicity—

"Dost thou doubt *me*?"

A guilty confusion seized upon Hendon, and he was grateful that the door opened to admit Hugh, at that moment, and saved him the necessity of replying.

"A beautiful lady, richly clothed, followed Hugh"

A beautiful lady, richly clothed, followed Hugh, and after her came several liveried servants. The lady walked slowly, with her head bowed and her eyes fixed upon the floor. The face was unspeakably sad. Miles Hendon sprang forward, crying out—

"Oh, my Edith, my darling—"

But Hugh waved him back, gravely, and said to the lady—

"Look upon him. Do you know him?"

At the sound of Miles's voice the woman had started slightly, and her cheeks had flushed; she was trembling now. She stood still, during an impressive pause of several moments; then slowly lifted up her head and looked into Hendon's eyes with a stony and frightened gaze; the blood sank out of her face, drop by drop, till nothing remained but the grey pallor of death; then she said, in a voice as dead as the face, "I know him not!" and turned, with a moan and a stifled sob, and tottered out of the room.

Miles Hendon sank into a chair and covered his face with his hands. After a pause, his brother said to the servants—

"You have observed him. Do you know him?"

They shook their heads; then the master said—

"The servants know you not, sir. I fear there is some mistake. You have seen that my wife knew you not."

"Thy *wife*!" In an instant Hugh was pinned to the wall, with an iron grip about his throat. "Oh, thou fox-hearted slave, I see it all! Thou'st writ the lying letter thyself, and my stolen bride and goods are its fruit. There—now get thee gone, lest I shame mine honourable soldiership with the slaying of so pitiful a mannikin!"

Hugh, red-faced, and almost suffocated, reeled to the nearest chair, and commanded the servants to seize and bind the murderous stranger. They hesitated, and one of them said—

"He is armed, Sir Hugh, and we are weaponless."

"Armed! What of it, and ye so many? Upon him, I say!"

But Miles warned them to be careful what they did, and added—

"Ye know me of old—I have not changed; come on, an' it like you."

This reminder did not hearten the servants much; they still held back.

"Then go, ye paltry cowards, and arm yourselves and guard the doors, whilst I send one to fetch the watch!" said Hugh. He turned at the threshold, and said to Miles, "You'll find it to your advantage to offend not with useless endeavours at escape."

"Escape? Spare thyself discomfort, an' that is all that troubles thee. For Miles Hendon is master of Hendon Hall and all its belongings. He will remain—doubt it not."

26

Disowned

The King sat musing a few moments, then looked up and said—

"'Tis strange—most strange. I cannot account for it."

"No, it is not strange, my liege. I know him, and this conduct is but natural. He was a rascal from his birth."

"Oh, I spake not of *him*, Sir Miles."

"Not of him? Then of what? What is it that is strange?"

"That the King is not missed."

"How? Which? I doubt I do not understand."

"Indeed? Doth it not strike you as being passing strange that the land is not filled with couriers and proclamations describing my person and making search for me? Is it no matter for commotion and distress that the Head of the State is gone; that I am vanished away and lost?"

"Most true, my King, I had forgot." Then Hendon sighed, and muttered to himself, "Poor ruined mind—still busy with its pathetic dream."

"But I have a plan that shall right us both—I will write a paper, in three tongues—Latin, Greek and English—and thou shalt haste away with it to London in the morning. Give it to none but my uncle, the Lord Hertford; when he shall see it, he will know and say I wrote it. Then he will send for me."

"Might it not be best, my Prince, that we wait here until I prove myself and make my rights secure to my domains? I should be so much the better able then to—"

The King interrupted him imperiously—

"Peace! What are thy paltry domains, thy trivial interests, contrasted with matters which concern the weal of a nation and the integrity of a throne?" Then, he added, in a gentle voice, as if he were sorry for his severity, "Obey, and have no fear; I will right thee, I will make thee whole—yes, more than whole. I shall remember, and requite."

So saying, he took the pen, and set himself to work. Hendon contemplated him lovingly a while, then said to himself—

"An' it were dark, I should think it *was* a king that spoke; there's no denying it, when the humour's upon on him he doth thunder and lighten like your true King; now where got he that trick? See him scribble and scratch away contentedly at his meaningless pot-hooks, fancying them to be Latin and Greek—and except my wit shall serve me with a lucky device for diverting him from his purpose, I shall be forced to pretend to post away tomorrow on this wild errand he hath invented for me."

The next moment Sir Miles's thoughts had gone back to the recent episode. So absorbed was he in his musings, that when the King presently handed him the paper which he had been writing, he received it and pocketed it without being conscious of the act. "How marvellous strange she acted," he muttered. "I think she knew me—and I think she did *not* know me. These opinions do conflict, I perceive it plainly; I cannot reconcile them, neither can I, by argument, dismiss either of the two, or even persuade one to outweigh the other. The matter standeth simply thus: she *must* have known my face, my figure, my voice, for how could it be otherwise? Yet she *said* she knew me not, and that is proof perfect, for she cannot lie. But stop—I think I begin to see. Peradventure he hath influenced her, commanded her, compelled her to lie. That is the solution. The riddle is unriddled. She seemed dead with fear—yes, she was under his compulsion. I will seek her; I will find her; now that he is away, she will speak her true mind. She will remember the old times when we were little playfellows together, and this will soften her heart, and she will no more betray me, but will confess me. There is no treacherous blood in her—no, she was always honest and true.

She has loved me, in those old days—this is my security; for whom one has loved, one cannot betray."

He stepped eagerly toward the door; at that moment it opened, and the Lady Edith entered. She was very pale, but she walked with a firm step, and her carriage was full of grace and gentle dignity. Her face was as sad as before.

Miles sprang forward, with a happy confidence, to meet her, but she checked him with a hardly perceptible gesture, and he stopped where he was. She seated herself, and asked him to do likewise. Thus simply did she take the sense of old comradeship out of him, and transform him into a stranger and a guest. The surprise of it, the bewildering unexpectedness of it, made him begin to question, for a moment, if he *was* the person he was pretending to be, after all. The Lady Edith said—

"Sir, I have come to warn you. The mad cannot be persuaded out of their delusions, perchance; but doubtless they may be persuaded to avoid perils. I think this dream of yours hath the seeming of honest truth to you, and therefore is not criminal—but do not tarry here with it; for here it is dangerous." She looked steadily into Miles's face a moment, then added, impressively, "It is the more dangerous for that you *are* much like what our lost lad must have grown to be if he had lived."

"Heavens, madam, but I *am* he!"

"I truly think you think it, sir. I question not your honesty in that; I but warn you, that is all. My husband is master in this region; his power hath hardly any limit; the people prosper or starve, as he wills. If you resembled not the man whom you profess to be, my husband might bid you pleasure yourself with your dream in peace; but trust me, I know him well; I know what he will do; he will say to all that you are but a mad impostor, and straightway all will echo him." She bent upon Miles that same steady look once more, and added: "If you *were* Miles Hendon, and he knew it and all the region knew it—consider what I am saying, weigh it well—you would stand in the same peril, your punishment would be no less sure; he would deny you and denounce you, and none would be bold enough to give you countenance."

"Most truly I believe it," said Miles, bitterly. "The power that can command one life-long friend to betray and disown another, and be obeyed, may well look to be obeyed in quarters where bread and life are on the stake and no cobweb ties of loyalty and honour are concerned."

A faint tinge appeared for a moment in the lady's cheek, and she dropped her eyes to the floor; but her voice betrayed no emotion when she proceeded—

"I have warned you—I must still warn you—to go hence. This man will destroy you, else. He is a tyrant who knows no pity. I, who am his fettered slave, know this. Poor Miles, and Arthur, and my dear guardian, Sir Richard, are free of him, and at rest: better that you were with them than that you bide here in the clutches of this miscreant. Your pretensions are a menace to his title and possessions; you have assaulted him in his own house: you are ruined if you stay. Go—do not hesitate. If you lack money, take this purse, I beg of you, and bribe the servants to let you pass. Oh, be warned, poor soul, and escape while you may."

Miles declined the purse with a gesture, and rose up and stood before her.

"Grant me one thing," he said. "Let your eyes rest upon mine, so that I may see if they be steady. There—now answer me. Am I Miles Hendon?"

"No. I know you not."

"Swear it!"

The answer was low, but distinct—

"I swear."

"Oh, this passes belief!"

"Fly! Why will you waste the precious time? Fly, and save yourself."

At that moment the officers burst into the room, and a violent struggle began; but Hendon was soon overpowered and dragged away. The King was taken also, and both were bound and led to prison.

27

In Prison

The cells were all crowded; so the two friends were chained in a large room where persons charged with trifling offences were commonly kept. They had company, for there were some twenty manacled and fettered prisoners here, of both sexes and of varying ages—an obscene and noisy gang. The King chafed bitterly over the stupendous indignity thus put upon his royalty, but Hendon was moody and taciturn. He was pretty thoroughly bewildered; he had come home, a jubilant prodigal, expecting to find everybody wild with joy over his return; and instead had got the cold shoulder and a jail. The promise and the fulfilment differed so widely that the effect was stunning; he could not decide whether it was most tragic or most grotesque. He felt much as a man might who had danced blithely out to enjoy a rainbow, and got struck by lightning.

But gradually his confused and tormenting thoughts settled down into some sort of order, and then his mind centred itself upon Edith. He turned her conduct over, and examined it in all lights, but he could not make anything satisfactory out of it. Did she know him—or didn't she know him? It was a perplexing puzzle, and occupied him a long time; but he ended, finally, with the conviction that she did know him, and had repudiated him for interested reasons. He wanted to load her name with curses now; but this name had so long been sacred to him that he found he could not bring his tongue to profane it.

"Chained in a large room"

Wrapped in prison blankets of a soiled and tattered condition, Hendon and the King passed a troubled night. For a bribe the jailer had furnished liquor to some of the prisoners; singing of ribald songs, fighting, shouting, and carousing was the natural consequence. At last, a while after midnight, a man attacked a woman and nearly killed her by beating her over the head with his manacles before the jailer could come to the rescue. The jailer restored peace by giving the man a sound clubbing about the head and shoulders—then the carousing ceased; and after that, all had an opportunity to sleep who did not mind the annoyance of the moanings and groanings of the two wounded people.

During the ensuing week, the days and nights were of a monotonous sameness as to events; men whose faces Hendon remembered more or less distinctly, came, by day, to gaze at the 'impostor' and repudiate and insult him; and by night the carousing and brawling went on with symmetrical regularity. However, there was a change of incident at last. The jailer brought in an old man, and said to him—

"The villain is in this room—cast thy old eyes about and see if thou canst say which is he."

Hendon glanced up, and experienced a pleasant sensation for the first time since he had been in the jail. He said to himself, "This is Blake Andrews, a servant all his life in my father's family—a good honest soul, with a right heart in his breast. That is, formerly. But none are true now; all are liars. This man will know me—and will deny me, too, like the rest."

The old man gazed around the room, glanced at each face in turn, and finally said—

"I see none here but paltry knaves, scum o' the streets. Which is he?"

The jailer laughed.

"Here," he said; "scan this big animal, and grant me an opinion."

The old man approached, and looked Hendon over, long and earnestly, then shook his head and said—

"Marry, *this* is no Hendon—nor ever was!"

"Right! Thy old eyes are sound yet. An' I were Sir Hugh, I would take the shabby carle and—"

The jailer finished by lifting himself a-tip-toe with an imaginary halter, at the same time making a gurgling noise in his throat suggestive of suffocation. The old man said, vindictively—

"Let him bless God an' he fare no worse. An' *I* had the handling o' the villain he should roast, or I am no true man!"

The jailer laughed a pleasant hyena laugh, and said—

"Give him a piece of thy mind, old man—they all do it. Thou'lt find it good diversion."

Then he sauntered toward his ante-room and disappeared. The old man dropped upon his knees and whispered—

"God be thanked, thou'rt come again, my master! I believed thou wert dead these seven years, and lo, here thou art alive! I knew thee the moment I saw thee; and main hard work it was to keep a stony countenance and seem to see none here but tuppenny knaves and rubbish o' the streets. I am old and poor, Sir Miles; but say the word and I will go forth and proclaim the truth though I be strangled for it."

"No," said Hendon; "thou shalt not. It would ruin thee, and yet help but little in my cause. But I thank thee, for thou hast given me back somewhat of my lost faith in my kind."

The old servant became very valuable to Hendon and the King; for he dropped in several times a day to 'abuse' the former, and always smuggled in a few delicacies to help out the prison bill of fare; he also furnished the current news. Hendon reserved the dainties for the King; without them his Majesty might not have survived, for he was not able to eat the coarse and wretched food provided by the jailer. Andrews was obliged to confine himself to brief visits, in order to avoid suspicion; but he managed to impart a fair degree of information each time—information delivered in a low voice, for Hendon's benefit, and interlarded with insulting epithets delivered in a louder voice for the benefit of other hearers.

So, little by little, the story of the family came out. Arthur had been dead six years. This loss, with the absence of news from Hendon, impaired the father's health; he believed he was going to die, and he wished to see Hugh and Edith settled in life before he passed away; but Edith begged hard for delay, hoping for Miles's return; then the letter came which brought the news of Miles's death; the shock prostrated Sir Richard; he believed his end was very near, and he and Hugh insisted upon the marriage; Edith begged for and obtained a month's respite, then another, and finally a third; the marriage then took place by the death-bed of Sir Richard. It had not proved a happy one. It was whispered about the country that shortly after the nuptials the bride found among her husband's papers several rough and incomplete drafts of the fatal letter, and had accused him of precipitating the marriage—and Sir Richard's death, too—by a wicked forgery. Tales of cruelty to the Lady Edith and the servants were to be heard on all hands; and since the father's death Sir Hugh had thrown off all soft disguises and become a pitiless master toward all who in any way depended upon him and his domains for bread.

There was a bit of Andrew's gossip which the King listened to with a lively interest—

"There is rumour that the King is mad. But in charity forbear to say *I* mentioned it, for 'tis death to speak of it, they say."

His Majesty glared at the old man and said—

"The King is *not* mad, good man—and thou'lt find it to thy advantage to busy thyself with matters that nearer concern thee than this seditious prattle."

"What doth the lad mean?" said Andrews, surprised at this brisk assault from such an unexpected quarter. Hendon gave him a sign, and he did not pursue his question, but went on with his budget—

"The late King is to be buried at Windsor in a day or two—the 16th of the month—and the new King will be crowned at Westminster the 20th."

"Methinks they must needs find him first," muttered his Majesty; then added, confidently, "but they will look to that—and so also shall I."

"In the name of—"

But the old man got no further—a warning sign from Hendon checked his remark. He resumed the thread of his gossip—

"Sir Hugh goeth to the coronation—and with grand hopes. He confidently looketh to come back a peer, for he is high in favour with the Lord Protector."

"What Lord Protector?" asked his Majesty.

"His Grace the Duke of Somerset."

"What Duke of Somerset?"

"Marry, there is but one—Seymour, Earl of Hertford."

The King asked sharply—

"Since when is *he* a duke, and Lord Protector?"

"Since the last day of January."

"And prithee who made him so?"

"Himself and the Great Council—with help of the King."

His Majesty started violently. "The *King*!" he cried. "*What* king, good sir?"

"What king, indeed! (God-a-mercy, what aileth the boy?) Sith we have but one, 'tis not difficult to answer—his most sacred Majesty King Edward the Sixth—whom God preserve! Yea, and a dear and gracious little urchin is he, too; and whether he be mad or no—and they say he mendeth daily—his praises are on all men's lips; and all bless him, likewise, and offer prayers that he may be spared to reign long in England; for he began humanely with saving the old Duke of Norfolk's life, and now is he bent on destroying the cruellest of the laws that harry and oppress the people."

This news struck his Majesty dumb with amazement, and plunged him into so deep and dismal a reverie that he heard no more of the old man's gossip. He wondered if the 'little urchin' was the beggar-boy whom he left dressed in his own garments in the palace. It did not seem possible that this could be, for surely his manners and speech would betray him if he pretended to be the Prince of Wales—then he would be driven out, and search made for the true prince. Could it be that the Court had set up some sprig of the nobility in his place? No, for his uncle would not allow that—he was all-powerful and could and would crush such a movement, of course. The boy's musings profited him nothing; the more he tried to unriddle the mystery the more perplexed he became, the more his head ached, and the worse he slept. His impatience to get to London grew hourly, and his captivity became almost unendurable.

Hendon's arts all failed with the King—he could not be comforted; but a couple of women who were chained near him succeeded better. Under their gentle ministrations he found peace and learned a degree of patience. He was very grateful, and came to love them dearly and to delight in the sweet and soothing influence of their presence. He asked them why they were in prison, and when they said they were Baptists, he smiled, and inquired—

"Is that a crime to be shut up for in a prison? Now I grieve, for I shall lose ye—they will not keep ye long for such a little thing."

They did not answer; and something in their faces made him uneasy. He said, eagerly—

"You do not speak; be good to me, and tell me—there will be no other punishment? Prithee tell me there is no fear of that."

They tried to change the topic, but his fears were aroused, and he pursued it—

"Will they scourge thee? No, no, they would not be so cruel! Say they would not. Come, they *will* not, will they?"

The women betrayed confusion and distress, but there was no avoiding an answer, so one of them said, in a voice choked with emotion—

"Oh, thou'lt break our hearts, thou gentle spirit!—God will help us to bear our—"

"It is a confession!" the King broke in. "Then they *will* scourge thee, the stony-hearted wretches! But oh, thou must not weep, I cannot bear it. Keep up thy courage—I shall come to my own in time to save thee from this bitter thing, and I will do it!"

When the King awoke in the morning, the women were gone.

"They are saved!" he said, joyfully; then added, despondently, "but woe is me!—for they were my comforters."

Each of them had left a shred of ribbon pinned to his clothing, in token of remembrance. He said he would keep these things always; and that soon he would seek out these dear good friends of his and take them under his protection.

Just then the jailer came in with some subordinates, and commanded that the prisoners be conducted to the jail-yard. The King was overjoyed—it would be a blessed thing to see the blue sky and breathe the fresh air once more. He fretted and chafed at the slowness of the officers, but his turn came at last, and he was released from his staple and ordered to follow the other prisoners with Hendon.

The court or quadrangle was stone-paved, and open to the sky. The prisoners entered it through a massive archway of masonry, and were placed in file, standing, with their backs against the wall. A rope was stretched in front of them, and they were also guarded by their officers. It was a chill and lowering morning, and a light snow which had fallen during the night whitened the great empty space and added to the general dismalness of its aspect. Now and then a wintry wind shivered through the place and sent the snow eddying hither and thither.

In the centre of the court stood two women, chained to posts. A glance showed the King that these were his good friends. He shuddered, and said to himself, "Alack, they are not gone free, as I had thought. To think that such as these should know the lash!—in England! Ay, there's the shame of it—not in Heathennesse, Christian England! They will be scourged; and I, whom they have comforted and kindly entreated, must look on and see the great wrong done; it is strange, so strange, that I, the very source of power in this broad realm, am helpless to protect them. But let these miscreants look well to themselves, for there is a day coming when I will require of them a heavy reckoning for this work. For every blow they strike now, they shall feel a hundred then."

A great gate swung open, and a crowd of citizens poured in. They flocked around the two women, and hid them from the King's view. A clergyman entered and passed through the crowd, and he also was hidden. The King now heard talking, back and forth, as if questions were being asked and answered, but he could not make out what was said. Next there was a deal of bustle and preparation, and much passing and repassing of officials through that part of the crowd that stood on the further side of the women; and whilst this proceeded a deep hush gradually fell upon the people.

Now, by command, the masses parted and fell aside, and the King saw a spectacle that froze the marrow in his bones. Faggots had been piled about the two women, and a kneeling man was lighting them!

The women bowed their heads, and covered their faces with their hands; the yellow flames began to climb upward among the snapping and crackling faggots, and wreaths of blue smoke to stream away on the wind; the clergyman lifted his hands and began a prayer—just then two young girls came flying through the great gate, uttering piercing screams, and threw themselves upon the women at the stake. Instantly they were torn away by the officers, and one of them was kept in a tight grip, but the other broke loose, saying she would die with her mother; and before she could be stopped she had flung her arms about her mother's neck again. She was torn away once more, and with her gown on fire. Two or three men held her, and the burning portion of her gown was snatched off and thrown flaming aside, she struggling all the while to free herself, and saying she would be alone in the world, now; and begging to be allowed to die with her mother. Both the girls screamed continually, and fought for freedom; but suddenly this tumult was drowned under a volley of heart-piercing shrieks of mortal agony—the King glanced from the frantic girls to the stake, then turned away and leaned his ashen face against the wall, and looked no more. He said, "That which I have seen, in that one little moment, will never go out from my memory, but will abide there; and I shall see it all the days, and dream of it all the nights, till I die. Would God I had been blind!"

Hendon was watching the King. He said to himself, with satisfaction, "His disorder mendeth; he hath changed, and groweth gentler. If he had followed his wont, he would have stormed at these varlets, and said he was King, and commanded that the women be turned loose unscathed. Soon his delusion will pass away and be forgotten, and his poor mind will be whole again. God speed the day!"

That same day several prisoners were brought in to remain over night, who were being conveyed, under guard, to various places in the kingdom, to undergo punishment for crimes committed. The King conversed with these—he had made it a point, from the beginning, to instruct himself for the kingly office by questioning prisoners whenever the opportunity offered—and the tale of their woes wrung his heart. One of them was a poor half-witted woman who had stolen a yard or two of cloth from a weaver—she was to be hanged for it. Another was a man who had been accused of stealing a horse; he said the proof had failed, and he had imagined that he was safe from the halter; but no—he was hardly free before he was arraigned for killing a deer in the King's park; this was proved against him, and now he was on his way to the gallows. There was a tradesman's apprentice whose case particularly distressed the King; this youth said he found a hawk, one evening, that had escaped from its owner, and he took it home with him, imagining himself entitled to it; but the court convicted him of stealing it, and sentenced him to death.

The King was furious over these inhumanities, and wanted Hendon to break jail and fly with him to Westminster, so that he could mount his throne and hold out his sceptre in mercy over these unfortunate people and save their lives. "Poor child," sighed Hendon, "these woeful tales have brought his malady upon him again; alack, but for this evil hap, he would have been well in a little time."

Among these prisoners was an old lawyer—a man with a strong face and a dauntless mien. Three years past, he had written a pamphlet against the Lord Chancellor, accusing him of injustice, and had been punished for it by the loss of his ears in the pillory, and degradation from the bar, and in addition had been fined 3,000 pounds and sentenced to imprisonment for life. Lately he had repeated his offence; and in consequence was now under sentence to lose *what remained of his ears*, pay a fine of 5,000 pounds, be branded on both cheeks, and remain in prison for life.

"These be honourable scars," he said, and turned back his grey hair and showed the mutilated stubs of what had once been his ears.

The King's eye burned with passion. He said—

"None believe in me—neither wilt thou. But no matter—within the compass of a month thou shalt be free; and more, the laws that have dishonoured thee, and shamed the English name, shall be swept from the statute books. The world is made wrong; kings should go to school to their own laws, at times, and so learn mercy."*

28

The Sacrifice

Meantime Miles was growing sufficiently tired of confinement and inaction. But now his trial came on, to his great gratification, and he thought he could welcome any sentence provided a further imprisonment should not be a part of it. But he was mistaken about that. He was in a fine fury when he found himself described as a 'sturdy vagabond' and sentenced to sit two hours in the stocks for bearing that character and for assaulting the master of Hendon Hall. His pretensions as to brothership with his prosecutor, and rightful heirship to the Hendon honours and estates, were left contemptuously unnoticed, as being not even worth examination.

---

* From many descriptions of larceny the law expressly took away the benefit of clergy: to steal a horse, or a hawk, or woollen cloth from the weaver, was a hanging matter. So it was to kill a deer from the King's forest, or to export sheep from the kingdom.—Dr. J. Hammond Trumbull's Blue Laws, True and False, p. 13.

William Prynne, a learned barrister, was sentenced (long after Edward VI.'s time) to lose both his ears in the pillory, to degradation from the bar, a fine of 3,000 pounds, and imprisonment for life. Three years afterwards he gave new offence to Laud by publishing a pamphlet against the hierarchy. He was again prosecuted, and was sentenced to lose what remained of his ears, to pay a fine of 5,000 pounds, to be branded on both his cheeks with the letters S. L. (for Seditious Libeller), and to remain in prison for life. The severity of this sentence was equalled by the savage rigour of its execution.—Ibid. p. 12.

He raged and threatened on his way to punishment, but it did no good; he was snatched roughly along by the officers, and got an occasional cuff, besides, for his irreverent conduct.

The King could not pierce through the rabble that swarmed behind; so he was obliged to follow in the rear, remote from his good friend and servant. The King had been nearly condemned to the stocks himself for being in such bad company, but had been let off with a lecture and a warning, in consideration of his youth. When the crowd at last halted, he flitted feverishly from point to point around its outer rim, hunting a place to get through; and at last, after a deal of difficulty and delay, succeeded. There sat his poor henchman in the degrading stocks, the sport and butt of a dirty mob—he, the body servant of the King of England! Edward had heard the sentence pronounced, but he had not realised the half that it meant. His anger began to rise as the sense of this new indignity which had been put upon him sank home; it jumped to summer heat, the next moment, when he saw an egg sail through the air and crush itself against Hendon's cheek, and heard the crowd roar its enjoyment of the episode. He sprang across the open circle and confronted the officer in charge, crying—

"He confronted the officer in charge"

"For shame! This is my servant—set him free! I am the—"

"Oh, peace!" exclaimed Hendon, in a panic, "thou'lt destroy thyself. Mind him not, officer, he is mad."

"Give thyself no trouble as to the matter of minding him, good man, I have small mind to mind him; but as to teaching him somewhat, to that I am well inclined." He turned to a subordinate and said, "Give the little fool a taste or two of the lash, to mend his manners."

"Half a dozen will better serve his turn," suggested Sir Hugh, who had ridden up, a moment before, to take a passing glance at the proceedings.

The King was seized. He did not even struggle, so paralysed was he with the mere thought of the monstrous outrage that was proposed to be inflicted upon his sacred person. History was already defiled with the record of the scourging of an English king with whips—it was an intolerable reflection that he must furnish a duplicate of that shameful page. He was in the toils, there was no help for him; he must either take this punishment or beg for its remission. Hard conditions; he would take the stripes—a king might do that, but a king could not beg.

But meantime, Miles Hendon was resolving the difficulty. "Let the child go," said he; "ye heartless dogs, do ye not see how young and frail he is? Let him go—I will take his lashes."

"Marry, a good thought—and thanks for it," said Sir Hugh, his face lighting with a sardonic satisfaction. "Let the little beggar go, and give this fellow a dozen in his place—an honest dozen, well laid on." The King was in the act of entering a fierce protest, but Sir Hugh silenced him with the potent remark, "Yes, speak up, do, and free thy mind—only, mark ye, that for each word you utter he shall get six strokes the more."

Hendon was removed from the stocks, and his back laid bare; and whilst the lash was applied the poor little King turned away his face and allowed unroyal tears to channel his cheeks unchecked. "Ah, brave good heart," he said to himself, "this loyal deed shall never perish out of my memory. I will not forget it—and neither shall *they*!" he added, with passion. Whilst he mused, his appreciation of Hendon's magnanimous conduct grew to greater and still greater dimensions in his mind, and so also did his gratefulness for it. Presently he said to himself, "Who saves his prince from wounds and possible death—and this he did for me—performs high service; but it is little—it is nothing—oh, less than nothing!—when 'tis weighed against the act of him who saves his prince from *shame*!"

Hendon made no outcry under the scourge, but bore the heavy blows with soldierly fortitude. This, together with his redeeming the boy by taking his stripes for him, compelled the respect of even that forlorn and degraded mob that was gathered there; and its gibes and hootings died away, and no sound remained but the sound of the falling blows. The stillness that pervaded the place, when Hendon found himself once more in the stocks, was in strong contrast with the insulting clamour which had prevailed there so little a while before. The King came softly to Hendon's side, and whispered in his ear—

"Kings cannot ennoble thee, thou good, great soul, for One who is higher than kings hath done that for thee; but a king can confirm thy nobility to men." He picked up the scourge from the ground, touched Hendon's bleeding shoulders lightly with it, and whispered, "Edward of England dubs thee Earl!"

Hendon was touched. The water welled to his eyes, yet at the same time the grisly humour of the situation and circumstances so undermined his gravity that it was all he could do to keep some sign of his inward mirth from showing outside. To be suddenly hoisted, naked and gory, from the common stocks to the Alpine altitude and splendour of an Earldom, seemed to him the last possibility in the line of the grotesque. He said to himself, "Now am I finely tinselled, indeed! The spectre-knight of the Kingdom of Dreams and Shadows is become a spectre-earl—a dizzy flight for a callow wing! An' this go on, I shall presently be hung like a very maypole with fantastic gauds and make-believe honours. But I shall value them, all valueless as they are, for the love that doth bestow them. Better these poor mock dignities of mine, that come unasked, from a clean hand and a right spirit, than real ones bought by servility from grudging and interested power."

The dreaded Sir Hugh wheeled his horse about, and as he spurred away, the living wall divided silently to let him pass, and as silently closed together again. And so remained; nobody went so far as to venture a remark in favour of the prisoner, or in compliment to him; but no matter—the absence of abuse was a sufficient homage in itself. A late comer who was not posted as to the present circumstances, and who delivered a sneer at the 'impostor,' and was in the act of following it with a dead cat, was promptly knocked down and kicked out, without any words, and then the deep quiet resumed sway once more.

29

To London

When Hendon's term of service in the stocks was finished, he was released and ordered to quit the region and come back no more. His sword was restored to him, and also his mule and his donkey. He mounted and rode off, followed by the King, the crowd opening with quiet respectfulness to let them pass, and then dispersing when they were gone.

Hendon was soon absorbed in thought. There were questions of high import to be answered. What should he do? Whither should he go? Powerful help must be found somewhere, or he must relinquish his inheritance and remain under the imputation of being an impostor besides. Where could he hope to find this powerful help? Where, indeed! It was a knotty question. By and by a thought occurred to him which pointed to a possibility—the slenderest of slender possibilities, certainly, but still worth considering, for lack of any other that promised anything at all. He remembered what old Andrews had said about the young King's goodness and his generous championship of the wronged and unfortunate. Why not go and try to get speech of him and beg for justice? Ah, yes, but could so fantastic a pauper get admission to the august presence of a monarch? Never mind—let that matter take care of itself; it was a bridge that would not need to be crossed till he should come to it. He was an old campaigner, and used to inventing shifts and expedients: no doubt he would be able to find a way. Yes, he would strike for the capital. Maybe his father's old friend Sir Humphrey Marlow would help him—'good old Sir Humphrey, Head Lieutenant of the late King's kitchen, or stables, or something'—Miles could not remember just what or which. Now that he had something to turn his energies to, a distinctly defined object to accomplish, the fog of humiliation and depression which had settled down upon his spirits lifted and blew away, and he raised his head and looked about him. He was surprised to see how far he had come; the village was away behind him. The King was jogging along in his wake, with his head bowed; for he, too, was deep in plans and thinkings. A sorrowful misgiving clouded Hendon's newborn cheerfulness: would the boy be willing to go again to a city where, during all his brief life, he had never known anything but ill-usage and pinching want? But the question must be asked; it could not be avoided; so Hendon reined up, and called out—

"Hendon mounted and rode off with the king"

"I had forgotten to inquire whither we are bound. Thy commands, my liege!"

"To London!"

Hendon moved on again, mightily contented with the answer—but astounded at it too.

"In the midst of a jam of howling people"

The whole journey was made without an adventure of importance. But it ended with one. About ten o'clock on the night of the 19th of February they stepped upon London Bridge, in the midst of a writhing, struggling jam of howling and hurrahing people, whose beer-jolly faces stood out strongly in the glare from manifold torches—and at that instant the decaying head of some former duke or other grandee tumbled down between them, striking Hendon on the elbow and then bounding off among the hurrying confusion of feet. So evanescent and unstable are men's works in this world!—the late good King is but three weeks dead and three days in his grave, and already the adornments which he took such pains to select from prominent people for his noble bridge are falling. A citizen stumbled over that head, and drove his own head into the back of somebody in front of him, who turned and knocked down the first person that came handy, and was promptly laid out himself by that person's friend. It was the right ripe time for a free fight, for the festivities of the morrow—Coronation Day—were already beginning; everybody was full of strong drink and patriotism; within five minutes the free fight was occupying a good deal of ground; within ten or twelve it covered an acre of so, and was become a riot. By this time Hendon and the King were hopelessly separated from each other and lost in the rush and turmoil of the roaring masses of humanity. And so we leave them.

30

Tom's Progress

Whilst the true King wandered about the land poorly clad, poorly fed, cuffed and derided by tramps one while, herding with thieves and murderers in a jail another, and called idiot and impostor by all impartially, the mock King Tom Canty enjoyed quite a different experience.

When we saw him last, royalty was just beginning to have a bright side for him. This bright side went on brightening more and more every day: in a very little while it was become almost all sunshine and delightfulness. He lost his fears; his misgivings faded out and died; his embarrassments departed, and gave place to an easy and confident bearing. He worked the whipping-boy mine to ever-increasing profit.

He ordered my Lady Elizabeth and my Lady Jane Grey into his presence when he wanted to play or talk, and dismissed them when he was done with them, with the air of one familiarly accustomed to such performances. It no longer confused him to have these lofty personages kiss his hand at parting.

"To kiss his hand at parting"

He came to enjoy being conducted to bed in state at night, and dressed with intricate and solemn ceremony in the morning. It came to be a proud pleasure to march to dinner attended by a glittering procession of officers of state and gentlemen-at-arms; insomuch, indeed, that he doubled his guard of gentlemen-at-arms, and made them a hundred. He liked to hear the bugles sounding down the long corridors, and the distant voices responding, "Way for the King!"

He even learned to enjoy sitting in throned state in council, and seeming to be something more than the Lord Protector's mouthpiece. He liked to receive great ambassadors and their gorgeous trains, and listen to the affectionate messages they brought from illustrious monarchs who called him brother. O happy Tom Canty, late of Offal Court!

He enjoyed his splendid clothes, and ordered more: he found his four hundred servants too few for his proper grandeur, and trebled them. The adulation of salaaming courtiers came to be sweet music to his ears. He remained kind and gentle, and a sturdy and determined champion of all that were oppressed, and he made tireless war upon unjust laws: yet upon occasion, being offended, he could turn upon an earl, or even a duke, and give him a look that would make him tremble. Once, when his royal 'sister,' the grimly holy Lady Mary, set herself to reason with him against the wisdom of his course in pardoning so many people who would otherwise be jailed, or hanged, or burned, and reminded him that their august late father's prisons had sometimes contained as high as sixty thousand convicts at one time, and that during his admirable reign he had delivered seventy-two thousand thieves and robbers over to death by the executioner,* the boy was filled with generous indignation, and commanded her to go to her closet, and beseech God to take away the stone that was in her breast, and give her a human heart.

Did Tom Canty never feel troubled about the poor little rightful prince who had treated him so kindly, and flown out with such hot zeal to avenge him upon the insolent sentinel at the palace gate? Yes; his first royal days and nights were pretty well sprinkled with painful thoughts about the lost prince, and with sincere longings for his return, and happy restoration to his native rights and splendours. But as time wore on, and the prince did not come, Tom's mind became more and more occupied with his new and enchanting experiences, and by little and little the vanished monarch faded almost out of his thoughts; and finally, when he did intrude upon them at intervals, he was become an unwelcome spectre, for he made Tom feel guilty and ashamed.

Tom's poor mother and sisters travelled the same road out of his mind. At

* Hume's England.

first he pined for them, sorrowed for them, longed to see them, but later, the thought of their coming some day in their rags and dirt, and betraying him with their kisses, and pulling him down from his lofty place, and dragging him back to penury and degradation and the slums, made him shudder. At last they ceased to trouble his thoughts almost wholly. And he was content, even glad: for, whenever their mournful and accusing faces did rise before him now, they made him feel more despicable than the worms that crawl.

At midnight of the 19th of February, Tom Canty was sinking to sleep in his rich bed in the palace, guarded by his loyal vassals, and surrounded by the pomps of royalty, a happy boy; for tomorrow was the day appointed for his solemn crowning as King of England. At that same hour, Edward, the true king, hungry and thirsty, soiled and draggled, worn with travel, and clothed in rags and shreds—his share of the results of the riot—was wedged in among a crowd of people who were watching with deep interest certain hurrying gangs of workmen who streamed in and out of Westminster Abbey, busy as ants: they were making the last preparation for the royal coronation.

31

The Recognition Procession

When Tom Canty awoke the next morning, the air was heavy with a thunderous murmur: all the distances were charged with it. It was music to him; for it meant that the English world was out in its strength to give loyal welcome to the great day.

Presently Tom found himself once more the chief figure in a wonderful floating pageant on the Thames; for by ancient custom the 'recognition procession' through London must start from the Tower, and he was bound thither.

When he arrived there, the sides of the venerable fortress seemed suddenly rent in a thousand places, and from every rent leaped a red tongue of flame and a white gush of smoke; a deafening explosion followed, which drowned the shoutings of the multitude, and made the ground tremble; the flame-jets, the smoke, and the explosions, were repeated over and over again with marvellous celerity, so that in a few moments the old Tower disappeared in the vast fog of its own smoke, all but the very top of the tall pile called the White Tower; this, with its banners, stood out above the dense bank of vapour as a mountain-peak projects above a cloud-rack.

Tom Canty, splendidly arrayed, mounted a prancing war-steed, whose rich trappings almost reached to the ground; his 'uncle,' the Lord Protector Somerset, similarly mounted, took place in his rear; the King's Guard formed in single ranks on either side, clad in burnished armour; after the Protector followed a seemingly interminable procession of resplendent nobles attended by their vassals; after these came the lord mayor and the aldermanic body, in crimson velvet robes, and with their gold chains across their breasts; and after these the officers and members of all the guilds of London, in rich raiment, and bearing the showy banners of the several corporations. Also in the procession, as a special guard of honour through the city, was the Ancient and Honourable Artillery Company—an organisation already three hundred years old at that time, and the only military body in England possessing the privilege (which it still possesses in our day) of holding itself independent of the commands of Parliament. It was a brilliant spectacle, and was hailed with acclamations all along the line, as it took its stately way through the packed multitudes of citizens. The chronicler says, 'The King, as he entered the city, was received by the people with prayers, welcomings, cries, and tender words, and all signs which argue an earnest love of subjects toward their sovereign; and the King, by holding up his glad countenance to such as stood afar off, and most tender language to those that stood nigh his Grace, showed himself no less thankful to receive the people's goodwill than they to offer it. To all that wished him well, he gave thanks. To such as bade "God save his Grace," he said in return, "God save you all!" and added that "he thanked them with all his heart." Wonderfully transported were the people with the loving answers and gestures of their King.'

In Fenchurch Street a 'fair child, in costly apparel,' stood on a stage to welcome his Majesty to the city. The last verse of his greeting was in these words—

'Welcome, O King! as much as hearts can think;
Welcome, again, as much as tongue can tell—
Welcome to joyous tongues, and hearts that will not shrink:
God thee preserve, we pray, and wish thee ever well.'

The people burst forth in a glad shout, repeating with one voice what the child had said. Tom Canty gazed abroad over the surging sea of eager faces, and his heart swelled with exultation; and he felt that the one thing worth living for in this world was to be a king, and a nation's idol. Presently he caught sight, at a distance, of a couple of his ragged Offal Court comrades—one of them the lord high admiral in his late mimic court, the other the first lord of the bedchamber in the same pretentious fiction; and his pride swelled higher than ever. Oh, if they could only recognize him now! What unspeakable glory it would be, if they could recognize him, and realise that the derided mock king of the slums and back alleys was become a real King, with illustrious dukes and princes for his humble menials, and the English world at his feet! But he had to deny himself, and choke down his desire, for such a recognition might cost more than it would come to: so he turned away his head, and left the two soiled lads to go on with their shoutings and glad adulations, unsuspicious of whom it was they were lavishing them upon.

Every now and then rose the cry, "A largess! a largess!" and Tom responded by scattering a handful of bright new coins abroad for the multitude to scramble for.

The chronicler says, "At the upper end of Gracechurch Street, before the sign of the Eagle, the city had erected a gorgeous arch, beneath which was a stage, which stretched from one side of the street to the other. This was an historical pageant, representing the King's immediate progenitors. There sat Elizabeth of York in the midst of an immense white rose, whose petals formed elaborate furbelows around her; by her side was Henry VII, issuing out of a vast red rose, disposed in the same manner: the hands of the royal pair were locked together, and the wedding-ring ostentatiously displayed. From the red and white roses proceeded a stem, which reached up to a second stage, occupied by Henry VIII, issuing from a red and white rose, with the effigy of the new King's mother, Jane Seymour, represented by his side. One branch sprang from this pair, which mounted to a third stage, where sat the effigy of Edward VI himself, enthroned in royal majesty; and the whole pageant was framed with wreaths of roses, red and white."

This quaint and gaudy spectacle so wrought upon the rejoicing people, that their acclamations utterly smothered the small voice of the child whose business it was to explain the thing in eulogistic rhymes. But Tom Canty was not sorry; for this loyal uproar was sweeter music to him than any poetry, no matter what its quality might be. Whithersoever Tom turned his happy young face, the people recognized the exactness of his effigy's likeness to himself, the flesh and blood counterpart; and new whirlwinds of applause burst forth.

The great pageant moved on, and still on, under one triumphal arch after another, and past a bewildering succession of spectacular and symbolical tableaux, each of which typified and exalted some virtue, or talent, or merit, of the little King's. 'Throughout the whole of Cheapside, from every penthouse and window, hung banners and streamers; and the richest carpets, stuffs, and cloth-of-gold tapestried the streets—specimens of the great wealth of the stores within; and the splendour of this thoroughfare was equalled in the other streets, and in some even surpassed.'

"And all these wonders and these marvels are to welcome me—me!" murmured Tom Canty.

The mock King's cheeks were flushed with excitement, his eyes were flashing, his senses swam in a delirium of pleasure. At this point, just as he was raising his hand to fling another rich largess, he caught sight of a pale, astounded face, which was strained forward out of the second rank of the crowd, its intense eyes riveted upon him. A sickening consternation struck through him; he recognized his mother! and up flew his hand, palm outward, before his eyes—that old involuntary gesture, born of a forgotten episode, and perpetuated by habit. In an instant more she had torn her way out of the press, and past the guards, and was at his side. She embraced his leg, she covered it with kisses, she cried, "O my child, my darling!" lifting toward him a face that was transfigured with joy and love. The same instant an officer of the King's Guard snatched her away with a curse, and sent her reeling back whence she came with a vigorous impulse from his strong arm. The words "I do not know you, woman!" were falling from Tom Canty's lips when this piteous thing occurred; but it smote him to the heart to see her treated so; and as she turned for a last glimpse of him, whilst the crowd was swallowing her from his sight, she seemed so wounded, so broken-hearted, that a shame fell upon him which consumed his pride to ashes, and withered his stolen royalty. His grandeurs were stricken valueless: they seemed to fall away from him like rotten rags.

The procession moved on, and still on, through ever augmenting splendours and ever augmenting tempests of welcome; but to Tom Canty they were as if they had not been. He neither saw nor heard. Royalty had lost its grace and sweetness; its pomps were become a reproach. Remorse was eating his heart out. He said, "Would God I were free of my captivity!"

He had unconsciously dropped back into the phraseology of the first days of his compulsory greatness.

The shining pageant still went winding like a radiant and interminable serpent down the crooked lanes of the quaint old city, and through the huzzaing hosts; but still the King rode with bowed head and vacant eyes, seeing only his mother's face and that wounded look in it.

"Largess, largess!" The cry fell upon an unheeding ear.

"Long live Edward of England!" It seemed as if the earth shook with the explosion; but there was no response from the King. He heard it only as one hears the thunder of the surf when it is blown to the ear out of a great distance, for it was smothered under another sound which was still nearer, in his own breast, in his accusing conscience—a voice which kept repeating those shameful words, "I do not know you, woman!"

The words smote upon the King's soul as the strokes of a funeral bell smite upon the soul of a surviving friend when they remind him of secret treacheries suffered at his hands by him that is gone.

New glories were unfolded at every turning; new wonders, new marvels, sprang into view; the pent clamours of waiting batteries were released; new raptures poured from the throats of the waiting multitudes: but the King gave no sign, and the accusing voice that went moaning through his comfortless breast was all the sound he heard.

By and by the gladness in the faces of the populace changed a little, and became touched with a something like solicitude or anxiety: an abatement in the volume of the applause was observable too. The Lord Protector was quick to notice these things: he was as quick to detect the cause. He spurred to the King's side, bent low in his saddle, uncovered, and said—

"My liege, it is an ill time for dreaming. The people observe thy downcast head, thy clouded mien, and they take it for an omen. Be advised: unveil the sun of royalty, and let it shine upon these boding vapours, and disperse them. Lift up thy face, and smile upon the people."

So saying, the Duke scattered a handful of coins to right and left, then retired to his place. The mock King did mechanically as he had been bidden. His smile had no heart in it, but few eyes were near enough or sharp enough to detect that. The noddings of his plumed head as he saluted his subjects were full of grace and graciousness; the largess which he delivered from his hand was royally liberal: so the people's anxiety vanished, and the acclamations burst forth again in as mighty a volume as before.

Still once more, a little before the progress was ended, the Duke was obliged to ride forward, and make remonstrance. He whispered—

"O dread sovereign! shake off these fatal humours; the eyes of the world are upon thee." Then he added with sharp annoyance, "Perdition catch that crazy pauper! 'twas she that hath disturbed your Highness."

The gorgeous figure turned a lustreless eye upon the Duke, and said in a dead voice—

"She was my mother!"

"My God!" groaned the Protector as he reined his horse backward to his post, "the omen was pregnant with prophecy. He is gone mad again!"

32

Coronation Day

Let us go backward a few hours, and place ourselves in Westminster Abbey, at four o'clock in the morning of this memorable Coronation Day. We are not without company; for although it is still night, we find the torch-lighted galleries already filling up with people who are well content to sit still and wait seven or eight hours till the time shall come for them to see what they may not hope to see twice in their lives—the coronation of a King. Yes, London and Westminster have been astir ever since the warning guns boomed at three o'clock, and already crowds of untitled rich folk who have bought the privilege of trying to find sitting room in the galleries are flocking in at the entrances reserved for their sort.

The hours drag along tediously enough. All stir has ceased for some time, for every gallery has long ago been packed. We may sit, now, and look and think at our leisure. We have glimpses, here and there and yonder, through the dim cathedral twilight, of portions of many galleries and balconies, wedged full with other people, the other portions of these galleries and balconies being cut off from sight by intervening pillars and architectural projections. We have in view the whole of the great north transept—empty, and waiting for England's privileged ones. We see also the ample area or platform, carpeted with rich stuffs, whereon the throne stands. The throne occupies the centre of the platform, and is raised above it upon an elevation of four steps. Within the seat of the throne is enclosed a rough flat rock—the stone of Scone—which many generations of Scottish kings sat on to be crowned, and so it in time became holy enough to answer a like purpose for English monarchs. Both the throne and its footstool are covered with cloth of gold.

Stillness reigns, the torches blink dully, the time drags heavily. But at last the lagging daylight asserts itself, the torches are extinguished, and a mellow radiance suffuses the great spaces. All features of the noble building are distinct now, but soft and dreamy, for the sun is lightly veiled with clouds.

At seven o'clock the first break in the drowsy monotony occurs; for on the stroke of this hour the first peeress enters the transept, clothed like Solomon for splendour, and is conducted to her appointed place by an official clad in satins and velvets, whilst a duplicate of him gathers up the lady's long train, follows after, and, when the lady is seated, arranges the train across her lap for her. He then places her footstool according to her desire, after which he puts her coronet where it will be convenient to her hand when the time for the simultaneous coroneting of the nobles shall arrive.

By this time the peeresses are flowing in in a glittering stream, and the satin-clad officials are flitting and glinting everywhere, seating them and making them comfortable. The scene is animated enough now. There is stir and life, and shifting colour everywhere. After a time, quiet reigns again; for the peeresses are all come and are all in their places, a solid acre or such a matter, of human flowers, resplendent in variegated colours, and frosted like a Milky Way with diamonds. There are all ages here: brown, wrinkled, white-haired dowagers who are able to go back, and still back, down the stream of time, and recall the crowning of Richard III. and the troublous days of that old forgotten age; and there are handsome middle-aged dames; and lovely and gracious young matrons; and gentle and beautiful young girls, with beaming eyes and fresh complexions, who may possibly put on their jewelled coronets awkwardly when the great time comes; for the matter will be new to them, and their excitement will be a sore hindrance. Still, this may not happen, for the hair of all these ladies has been arranged with a special view to the swift and successful lodging of the crown in its place when the signal comes.

We have seen that this massed array of peeresses is sown thick with diamonds, and we also see that it is a marvellous spectacle—but now we are about to be astonished in earnest. About nine, the clouds suddenly break away and a shaft of sunshine cleaves the mellow atmosphere, and drifts slowly along the ranks of ladies; and every rank it touches flames into a dazzling splendour of many-coloured fires, and we tingle to our finger-tips with the electric thrill that is shot through us by the surprise and the beauty of the spectacle! Presently a special envoy from some distant corner of the Orient, marching with the general body of foreign ambassadors, crosses this bar of sunshine, and we catch our breath, the glory that streams and flashes and palpitates about him is so overpowering; for he is crusted from head to heel with gems, and his slightest movement showers a dancing radiance all around him.

Let us change the tense for convenience. The time drifted along—one hour—two hours—two hours and a half; then the deep booming of artillery told that the King and his grand procession had arrived at last; so the waiting multitude rejoiced. All knew that a further delay must follow, for the King must be prepared and robed for the solemn ceremony; but this delay would be pleasantly occupied by the assembling of the peers of the realm in their stately robes. These were conducted ceremoniously to their seats, and their coronets placed conveniently at hand; and meanwhile the multitude in the galleries were alive with interest, for most of them were beholding for the first time, dukes, earls, and barons, whose names had been historical for five hundred years. When all were finally seated, the spectacle from the galleries and all coigns of vantage was complete; a gorgeous one to look upon and to remember.

Now the robed and mitered great heads of the church, and their attendants, filed in upon the platform and took their appointed places; these were followed by the Lord Protector and other great officials, and these again by a steel-clad detachment of the Guard.

There was a waiting pause; then, at a signal, a triumphant peal of music burst forth, and Tom Canty, clothed in a long robe of cloth of gold, appeared at a door, and stepped upon the platform. The entire multitude rose, and the ceremony of the Recognition ensued.

Then a noble anthem swept the Abbey with its rich waves of sound; and thus heralded and welcomed, Tom Canty was conducted to the throne. The ancient ceremonies went on, with impressive solemnity, whilst the audience gazed; and as they drew nearer and nearer to completion, Tom Canty grew pale, and still paler, and a deep and steadily deepening woe and despondency settled down upon his spirits and upon his remorseful heart.

At last the final act was at hand. The Archbishop of Canterbury lifted up the crown of England from its cushion and held it out over the trembling mock-King's head. In the same instant a rainbow-radiance flashed along the spacious transept; for with one impulse every individual in the great concourse of nobles lifted a coronet and poised it over his or her head—and paused in that attitude.

A deep hush pervaded the Abbey. At this impressive moment, a startling apparition intruded upon the scene—an apparition observed by none in the absorbed multitude, until it suddenly appeared, moving up the great central aisle. It was a boy, bareheaded, ill shod, and clothed in coarse plebeian garments that were falling to rags. He raised his hand with a solemnity which ill comported with his soiled and sorry aspect, and delivered this note of warning—

"I forbid you to set the crown of England upon that forfeited head. I am the King!"

In an instant several indignant hands were laid upon the boy; but in the same instant Tom Canty, in his regal vestments, made a swift step forward, and cried out in a ringing voice—

"Loose him and forbear! He *is* the King!"

A sort of panic of astonishment swept the assemblage, and they partly rose in their places and stared in a bewildered way at one another and at the chief figures in this scene, like persons who wondered whether they were awake and in their senses, or asleep and dreaming. The Lord Protector was as amazed as the rest, but quickly recovered himself, and exclaimed in a voice of authority—

"Mind not his Majesty, his malady is upon him again—seize the vagabond!"

He would have been obeyed, but the mock-King stamped his foot and cried out—

"On your peril! Touch him not, he is the King!"

The hands were withheld; a paralysis fell upon the house; no one moved, no one spoke; indeed, no one knew how to act or what to say, in so strange and surprising an emergency. While all minds were struggling to right themselves, the boy still moved steadily forward, with high port and confident mien; he had never halted from the beginning; and while the tangled minds still floundered helplessly, he stepped upon the platform, and the mock-King ran with a glad face to meet him; and fell on his knees before him and said—

"Oh, my lord the King, let poor Tom Canty be first to swear fealty to thee, and say, 'Put on thy crown and enter into thine own again!'"

"And fell on his knees before him"

The Lord Protector's eye fell sternly upon the newcomer's face; but straightway the sternness vanished away, and gave place to an expression of wondering surprise. This thing happened also to the other great officers. They glanced at each other, and retreated a step by a common and unconscious impulse. The thought in each mind was the same: "What a strange resemblance!"

The Lord Protector reflected a moment or two in perplexity, then he said, with grave respectfulness—

"By your favour, sir, I desire to ask certain questions which—"

"I will answer them, my lord."

The Duke asked him many questions about the Court, the late King, the prince, the princesses—the boy answered them correctly and without hesitating. He described the rooms of state in the palace, the late King's apartments, and those of the Prince of Wales.

It was strange; it was wonderful; yes, it was unaccountable—so all said that heard it. The tide was beginning to turn, and Tom Canty's hopes to run high, when the Lord Protector shook his head and said—

"It is true it is most wonderful—but it is no more than our lord the King likewise can do." This remark, and this reference to himself as still the King, saddened Tom Canty, and he felt his hopes crumbling from under him. "These are not *proofs*," added the Protector.

The tide was turning very fast now, very fast indeed—but in the wrong direction; it was leaving poor Tom Canty stranded on the throne, and sweeping the other out to sea. The Lord Protector communed with himself—shook his head—the thought forced itself upon him, "It is perilous to the State and to us all, to entertain so fateful a riddle as this; it could divide the nation and undermine the throne." He turned and said—

"Sir Thomas, arrest this—No, hold!" His face lighted, and he confronted the ragged candidate with this question—

"Where lieth the Great Seal? Answer me this truly, and the riddle is unriddled; for only he that was Prince of Wales *can* so answer! On so trivial a thing hang a throne and a dynasty!"

It was a lucky thought, a happy thought. That it was so considered by the great officials was manifested by the silent applause that shot from eye to eye around their circle in the form of bright approving glances. Yes, none but the true prince could dissolve the stubborn mystery of the vanished Great Seal—this forlorn little impostor had been taught his lesson well, but here his teachings must fail, for his teacher himself could not answer *that* question—ah, very good, very good indeed; now we shall be rid of this troublesome and perilous business in short order! And so they nodded invisibly and smiled inwardly with satisfaction, and looked to see this foolish lad stricken with a palsy of guilty confusion. How surprised they were, then, to see nothing of the sort happen—how they marvelled to hear him answer up promptly, in a confident and untroubled voice, and say—

"There is nought in this riddle that is difficult." Then, without so much as a by-your-leave to anybody, he turned and gave this command, with the easy manner of one accustomed to doing such things: "My Lord St. John, go you to my private cabinet in the palace—for none knoweth the place better than you—and, close down to the floor, in the left corner remotest from the door that opens from the ante-chamber, you shall find in the wall a brazen nail-head; press upon it and a little jewel-closet will fly open which not even you do know of—no, nor any soul else in all the world but me and the trusty artisan that did contrive it for me. The first thing that falleth under your eye will be the Great Seal—fetch it hither."

All the company wondered at this speech, and wondered still more to see the little mendicant pick out this peer without hesitancy or apparent fear of mistake, and call him by name with such a placidly convincing air of having known him all his life. The peer was almost surprised into obeying. He even made a movement as if to go, but quickly recovered his tranquil attitude and confessed his blunder with a blush. Tom Canty turned upon him and said, sharply—

"Why dost thou hesitate? Hast not heard the King's command? Go!"

The Lord St. John made a deep obeisance—and it was observed that it was a significantly cautious and non-committal one, it not being delivered at either of the kings, but at the neutral ground about halfway between the two—and took his leave.

Now began a movement of the gorgeous particles of that official group which was slow, scarcely perceptible, and yet steady and persistent—a movement such as is observed in a kaleidoscope that is turned slowly, whereby the components of one splendid cluster fall away and join themselves to another—a movement which, little by little, in the present case, dissolved the glittering crowd that stood about Tom Canty and clustered it together again in the neighbourhood of the newcomer. Tom Canty stood almost alone. Now ensued a brief season of deep suspense and waiting—during which even the few faint hearts still remaining near Tom Canty gradually scraped together courage enough to glide, one by one, over to the majority. So at last Tom Canty, in his royal robes and jewels, stood wholly alone and isolated from the world, a conspicuous figure, occupying an eloquent vacancy.

Now the Lord St. John was seen returning. As he advanced up the mid-aisle the interest was so intense that the low murmur of conversation in the great assemblage died out and was succeeded by a profound hush, a breathless stillness, through which his footfalls pulsed with a dull and distant sound. Every eye was fastened upon him as he moved along. He reached the platform, paused a moment, then moved toward Tom Canty with a deep obeisance, and said—

"Sire, the Seal is not there!"

A mob does not melt away from the presence of a plague-patient with more haste than the band of pallid and terrified courtiers melted away from the presence of the shabby little claimant of the Crown. In a moment he stood all alone, without friend or supporter, a target upon which was concentrated a bitter fire of scornful and angry looks. The Lord Protector called out fiercely—

"Cast the beggar into the street, and scourge him through the town—the paltry knave is worth no more consideration!"

Officers of the guard sprang forward to obey, but Tom Canty waved them off and said—

"Back! Whoso touches him perils his life!"

The Lord Protector was perplexed in the last degree. He said to the Lord St. John—

"Searched you well?—but it boots not to ask that. It doth seem passing strange. Little things, trifles, slip out of one's ken, and one does not think it matter for surprise; but how so bulky a thing as the Seal of England can vanish away and no man be able to get track of it again—a massy golden disk—"

Tom Canty, with beaming eyes, sprang forward and shouted—

"Hold, that is enough! Was it round?—and thick?—and had it letters and devices graved upon it?—yes? Oh, *now* I know what this Great Seal is that there's been such worry and pother about. An' ye had described it to me, ye could have had it three weeks ago. Right well I know where it lies; but it was not I that put it there—first."

"Who, then, my liege?" asked the Lord Protector.

"He that stands there—the rightful King of England. And he shall tell you himself where it lies—then you will believe he knew it of his own knowledge. Bethink thee, my King—spur thy memory—it was the last, the very *last* thing thou didst that day before thou didst rush forth from the palace, clothed in my rags, to punish the soldier that insulted me."

"Bethink thee, my king"

A silence ensued, undisturbed by a movement or a whisper, and all eyes were fixed upon the newcomer, who stood, with bent head and corrugated brow, groping in his memory among a thronging multitude of valueless recollections for one single little elusive fact, which, found, would seat him upon a throne—unfound, would leave him as he was, for good and all—a pauper and an outcast. Moment after moment passed—the moments built themselves into minutes—still the boy struggled silently on, and gave no sign. But at last he heaved a sigh, shook his head slowly, and said, with a trembling lip and in a despondent voice—

"I call the scene back—all of it—but the Seal hath no place in it." He paused, then looked up, and said with gentle dignity, "My lords and gentlemen, if ye will rob your rightful sovereign of his own for lack of this evidence which he is not able to furnish, I may not stay ye, being powerless. But—"

"Oh, folly, oh, madness, my King!" cried Tom Canty, in a panic, "wait!—think! Do not give up!—the cause is not lost! Nor *shall* be, neither! List to what I say—follow every word—I am going to bring that morning back again, every hap just as it happened. We talked—I told you of my sisters, Nan and Bet—ah, yes, you remember that; and about mine old grandam—and the rough games of the lads of Offal Court—yes, you remember these things also; very well, follow me still, you shall recall everything. You gave me food and drink, and did with princely courtesy send away the servants, so that my low breeding might not shame me before them—ah, yes, this also you remember."

As Tom checked off his details, and the other boy nodded his head in recognition of them, the great audience and the officials stared in puzzled wonderment; the tale sounded like true history, yet how could this impossible conjunction between a prince and a beggar-boy have come about? Never was a company of people so perplexed, so interested, and so stupefied, before.

"For a jest, my prince, we did exchange garments. Then we stood before a mirror; and so alike were we that both said it seemed as if there had been no change made—yes, you remember that. Then you noticed that the soldier had hurt my hand—look! here it is, I cannot yet even write with it, the fingers are so stiff. At this your Highness sprang up, vowing vengeance upon that soldier, and ran towards the door—you passed a table—that thing you call the Seal lay on that table—you snatched it up and looked eagerly about, as if for a place to hide it—your eye caught sight of—"

"There, 'tis sufficient!—and the good God be thanked!" exclaimed the ragged claimant, in a mighty excitement. "Go, my good St. John—in an arm-piece of the Milanese armour that hangs on the wall, thou'lt find the Seal!"

"Right, my King! right!" cried Tom Canty; "*Now* the sceptre of England is thine own; and it were better for him that would dispute it that he had been born dumb! Go, my Lord St. John, give thy feet wings!"

The whole assemblage was on its feet now, and well-nigh out of its mind with uneasiness, apprehension, and consuming excitement. On the floor and on the platform a deafening buzz of frantic conversation burst forth, and for some time nobody knew anything or heard anything or was interested in anything but what his neighbour was shouting into his ear, or he was shouting into his neighbour's ear. Time—nobody knew how much of it—swept by unheeded and unnoted. At last a sudden hush fell upon the house, and in the same moment St. John appeared upon the platform, and held the Great Seal aloft in his hand. Then such a shout went up—

"Long live the true King!"

For five minutes the air quaked with shouts and the crash of musical instruments, and was white with a storm of waving handkerchiefs; and through it all a ragged lad, the most conspicuous figure in England, stood, flushed and happy and proud, in the centre of the spacious platform, with the great vassals of the kingdom kneeling around him.

Then all rose, and Tom Canty cried out—

"Now, O my King, take these regal garments back, and give poor Tom, thy servant, his shreds and remnants again."

The Lord Protector spoke up—

"Let the small varlet be stripped and flung into the Tower."

But the new King, the true King, said—

"I will not have it so. But for him I had not got my crown again—none shall lay a hand upon him to harm him. And as for thee, my good uncle, my

Lord Protector, this conduct of thine is not grateful toward this poor lad, for I hear he hath made thee a duke"—the Protector blushed—"yet he was not a king; wherefore what is thy fine title worth now? Tomorrow you shall sue to me, *through him*, for its confirmation, else no duke, but a simple earl, shalt thou remain."

Under this rebuke, his Grace the Duke of Somerset retired a little from the front for the moment. The King turned to Tom, and said kindly—"My poor boy, how was it that you could remember where I hid the Seal when I could not remember it myself?"

"Ah, my King, that was easy, since I used it divers days."

"Used it—yet could not explain where it was?"

"I did not know it was *that* they wanted. They did not describe it, your Majesty."

"Then how used you it?"

The red blood began to steal up into Tom's cheeks, and he dropped his eyes and was silent.

"Speak up, good lad, and fear nothing," said the King. "How used you the Great Seal of England?"

Tom stammered a moment, in a pathetic confusion, then got it out—

"To crack nuts with!"

Poor child, the avalanche of laughter that greeted this nearly swept him off his feet. But if a doubt remained in any mind that Tom Canty was not the King of England and familiar with the august appurtenances of royalty, this reply disposed of it utterly.

Meantime the sumptuous robe of state had been removed from Tom's shoulders to the King's, whose rags were effectually hidden from sight under it. Then the coronation ceremonies were resumed; the true King was anointed and the crown set upon his head, whilst cannon thundered the news to the city, and all London seemed to rock with applause.

33

Edward as King

Miles Hendon was picturesque enough before he got into the riot on London Bridge—he was more so when he got out of it. He had but little money when he got in, none at all when he got out. The pickpockets had stripped him of his last farthing.

But no matter, so he found his boy. Being a soldier, he did not go at his task in a random way, but set to work, first of all, to arrange his campaign.

What would the boy naturally do? Where would he naturally go? Well—argued Miles—he would naturally go to his former haunts, for that is the instinct of unsound minds, when homeless and forsaken, as well as of sound ones. Whereabouts were his former haunts? His rags, taken together with the low villain who seemed to know him and who even claimed to be his father, indicated that his home was in one or another of the poorest and meanest districts of London. Would the search for him be difficult, or long? No, it was likely to be easy and brief. He would not hunt for the boy, he would hunt for a crowd; in the centre of a big crowd or a little one, sooner or later, he should find his poor little friend, sure; and the mangy mob would be entertaining itself with pestering and aggravating the boy, who would be proclaiming himself King, as usual. Then Miles Hendon would cripple some of those people, and carry off his little ward, and comfort and cheer him with loving words, and the two would never be separated any more.

So Miles started on his quest. Hour after hour he tramped through back alleys and squalid streets, seeking groups and crowds, and finding no end of them, but never any sign of the boy. This greatly surprised him, but did not discourage him. To his notion, there was nothing the matter with his plan of campaign; the only miscalculation about it was that the campaign was becoming a lengthy one, whereas he had expected it to be short.

When daylight arrived, at last, he had made many a mile, and canvassed many a crowd, but the only result was that he was tolerably tired, rather hungry and very sleepy. He wanted some breakfast, but there was no way to get it. To beg for it did not occur to him; as to pawning his sword, he would as soon have thought of parting with his honour; he could spare some of his clothes—yes, but one could as easily find a customer for a disease as for such clothes.

At noon he was still tramping—among the rabble which followed after the royal procession, now; for he argued that this regal display would attract his little lunatic powerfully. He followed the pageant through all its devious windings about London, and all the way to Westminster and the Abbey. He drifted here and there amongst the multitudes that were massed in the vicinity for a weary long time, baffled and perplexed, and finally wandered off, thinking, and trying to contrive some way to better his plan of campaign. By and by, when he came to himself out of his musings, he discovered that the town was far behind him and that the day was growing old. He was near the river, and in the country; it was a region of fine rural seats—not the sort of district to welcome clothes like his.

It was not at all cold; so he stretched himself on the ground in the lee of a hedge to rest and think. Drowsiness presently began to settle upon his senses; the faint and far-off boom of cannon was wafted to his ear, and he said to himself, "The new King is crowned," and straightway fell asleep. He had not slept or rested, before, for more than thirty hours. He did not wake again until near the middle of the next morning.

He got up, lame, stiff, and half famished, washed himself in the river, stayed his stomach with a pint or two of water, and trudged off toward Westminster, grumbling at himself for having wasted so much time. Hunger helped him to a new plan, now; he would try to get speech with old Sir Humphrey Marlow and borrow a few marks, and—but that was enough of a plan for the present; it would be time enough to enlarge it when this first stage should be accomplished.

Toward eleven o'clock he approached the palace; and although a host of showy people were about him, moving in the same direction, he was not inconspicuous—his costume took care of that. He watched these people's faces narrowly, hoping to find a charitable one whose possessor might be willing to carry his name to the old lieutenant—as to trying to get into the palace himself, that was simply out of the question.

Presently our whipping-boy passed him, then wheeled about and scanned his figure well, saying to himself, "An' that is not the very vagabond his Majesty is in such a worry about, then am I an ass—though belike I was that before. He answereth the description to a rag—that God should make two such would be to cheapen miracles by wasteful repetition. I would I could contrive an excuse to speak with him."

Miles Hendon saved him the trouble; for he turned about, then, as a man generally will when somebody mesmerises him by gazing hard at him from behind; and observing a strong interest in the boy's eyes, he stepped toward him and said—

"You have just come out from the palace; do you belong there?"

"Yes, your worship."

"Know you Sir Humphrey Marlow?"

The boy started, and said to himself, "Lord! mine old departed father!" Then he answered aloud, "Right well, your worship."

"Good—is he within?"

"Yes," said the boy; and added, to himself, "within his grave."

"Might I crave your favour to carry my name to him, and say I beg to say a word in his ear?"

"I will dispatch the business right willingly, fair sir."

"Then say Miles Hendon, son of Sir Richard, is here without—I shall be greatly bounden to you, my good lad."

The boy looked disappointed. "The King did not name him so," he said to himself; "but it mattereth not, this is his twin brother, and can give his Majesty news of t'other Sir-Odds-and-Ends, I warrant." So he said to Miles, "Step in there a moment, good sir, and wait till I bring you word."

Hendon retired to the place indicated—it was a recess sunk in the palace wall, with a stone bench in it—a shelter for sentinels in bad weather. He had hardly seated himself when some halberdiers, in charge of an officer, passed by. The officer saw him, halted his men, and commanded Hendon to come forth. He obeyed, and was promptly arrested as a suspicious character prowling within the precincts of the palace. Things began to look ugly. Poor Miles was going to explain, but the officer roughly silenced him, and ordered his men to disarm him and search him.

"God of his mercy grant that they find somewhat," said poor Miles; "I have searched enow, and failed, yet is my need greater than theirs."

Nothing was found but a document. The officer tore it open, and Hendon smiled when he recognized the 'pot-hooks' made by his lost little friend that black day at Hendon Hall. The officer's face grew dark as he read the English paragraph, and Miles blenched to the opposite colour as he listened.

"Another new claimant of the Crown!" cried the officer. "Verily they breed like rabbits, today. Seize the rascal, men, and see ye keep him fast whilst I convey this precious paper within and send it to the King."

He hurried away, leaving the prisoner in the grip of the halberdiers.

"Now is my evil luck ended at last," muttered Hendon, "for I shall dangle at a rope's end for a certainty, by reason of that bit of writing. And what will become of my poor lad!—ah, only the good God knoweth."

By and by he saw the officer coming again, in a great hurry; so he plucked his courage together, purposing to meet his trouble as became a man. The officer ordered the men to loose the prisoner and return his sword to him; then bowed respectfully, and said—

"Please you, sir, to follow me."

Hendon followed, saying to himself, "An' I were not travelling to death and judgment, and so must needs economise in sin, I would throttle this knave for his mock courtesy."

The two traversed a populous court, and arrived at the grand entrance of the palace, where the officer, with another bow, delivered Hendon into the hands of a gorgeous official, who received him with profound respect and led him forward through a great hall, lined on both sides with rows of splendid flunkeys (who made reverential obeisance as the two passed along, but fell into death-throes of silent laughter at our stately scarecrow the moment his back was turned), and up a broad staircase, among flocks of fine folk, and finally conducted him into a vast room, clove a passage for him through the assembled nobility of England, then made a bow, reminded him to take his hat off, and left him standing in the middle of the room, a mark for all eyes, for plenty of indignant frowns, and for a sufficiency of amused and derisive smiles.

Miles Hendon was entirely bewildered. There sat the young King, under a canopy of state, five steps away, with his head bent down and aside, speaking with a sort of human bird of paradise—a duke, maybe. Hendon observed to himself that it was hard enough to be sentenced to death in the full vigour of life, without having this peculiarly public humiliation added. He wished the King would hurry about it—some of the gaudy people near by were becoming pretty offensive. At this moment the King raised his head slightly, and Hendon caught a good view of his face. The sight nearly took his breath away!—He stood gazing at the fair young face like one transfixed; then presently ejaculated—

"Lo, the Lord of the Kingdom of Dreams and Shadows on his throne!"

He muttered some broken sentences, still gazing and marvelling; then turned his eyes around and about, scanning the gorgeous throng and the splendid saloon, murmuring, "But these are *real*—verily these are *real*—surely it is not a dream."

He stared at the King again—and thought, "*Is* it a dream . . . or *is* he the veritable Sovereign of England, and not the friendless poor Tom o' Bedlam I took him for—who shall solve me this riddle?"

A sudden idea flashed in his eye, and he strode to the wall, gathered up a chair, brought it back, planted it on the floor, and sat down in it!

A buzz of indignation broke out, a rough hand was laid upon him and a voice exclaimed—

"Up, thou mannerless clown! Wouldst sit in the presence of the King?"

The disturbance attracted his Majesty's attention, who stretched forth his hand and cried out—

"Touch him not, it is his right!"

The throng fell back, stupefied. The King went on—

"Learn ye all, ladies, lords, and gentlemen, that this is my trusty and well-beloved servant, Miles Hendon, who interposed his good sword and saved his prince from bodily harm and possible death—and for this he is a knight, by the King's voice. Also learn, that for a higher service, in that he saved his sovereign stripes and shame, taking these upon himself, he is a peer of England, Earl of Kent, and shall have gold and lands meet for the dignity. More—the privilege which he hath just exercised is his by royal grant; for we have ordained that the chiefs of his line shall have and hold the right to sit in the presence of the Majesty of England henceforth, age after age, so long as the crown shall endure. Molest him not."

Two persons, who, through delay, had only arrived from the country during this morning, and had now been in this room only five minutes, stood listening to these words and looking at the King, then at the scarecrow, then at the King again, in a sort of torpid bewilderment. These were Sir Hugh and the Lady Edith. But the new Earl did not see them. He was still staring at the monarch, in a dazed way, and muttering—

"Oh, body o' me! *This* my pauper! This my lunatic! This is he whom *I* would show what grandeur was, in my house of seventy rooms and seven-and-twenty servants! This is he who had never known aught but rags for raiment, kicks for comfort, and offal for diet! This is he whom *I* adopted and would make respectable! Would God I had a bag to hide my head in!"

Then his manners suddenly came back to him, and he dropped upon his knees, with his hands between the King's, and swore allegiance and did homage for his lands and titles. Then he rose and stood respectfully aside, a mark still for all eyes—and much envy, too.

Now the King discovered Sir Hugh, and spoke out with wrathful voice and kindling eye—

"Strip this robber of his false show and stolen estates, and put him under lock and key till I have need of him."

The late Sir Hugh was led away.

There was a stir at the other end of the room, now; the assemblage fell apart, and Tom Canty, quaintly but richly clothed, marched down, between these living walls, preceded by an usher. He knelt before the King, who said—

"I have learned the story of these past few weeks, and am well pleased with thee. Thou hast governed the realm with right royal gentleness and mercy. Thou hast found thy mother and thy sisters again? Good; they shall be cared for—and thy father shall hang, if thou desire it and the law consent. Know, all ye that hear my voice, that from this day, they that abide in the shelter of Christ's Hospital and share the King's bounty shall have their minds and hearts fed, as well as their baser parts; and this boy shall dwell there, and hold the chief place in its honourable body of governors, during life. And for that he hath been a king, it is meet that other than common observance shall be his due; wherefore note this his dress of state, for by it he shall be known, and none shall copy it; and wheresoever he shall come, it shall remind the people that he hath been royal, in his time, and none shall deny him his due of reverence or fail to give him salutation. He hath the throne's protection, he hath the crown's support, he shall be known and called by the honourable title of the King's Ward."

The proud and happy Tom Canty rose and kissed the King's hand, and was conducted from the presence. He did not waste any time, but flew to his mother, to tell her and Nan and Bet all about it and get them to help him enjoy the great news.

Conclusion

Justice and Retribution

When the mysteries were all cleared up, it came out, by confession of Hugh Hendon, that his wife had repudiated Miles by his command, that day at Hendon Hall—a command assisted and supported by the perfectly trustworthy promise that if she did not deny that he was Miles Hendon, and stand firmly to it, he would have her life; whereupon she said, "Take it!"—she did not value it—and she would not repudiate Miles; then the husband said he would spare her life but have Miles assassinated! This was a different matter; so she gave her word and kept it.

Hugh was not prosecuted for his threats or for stealing his brother's estates and title, because the wife and brother would not testify against him—and the former would not have been allowed to do it, even if she had wanted to. Hugh deserted his wife and went over to the continent, where he presently died; and by and by the Earl of Kent married his relict. There were grand times and rejoicings at Hendon village when the couple paid their first visit to the Hall.

Tom Canty's father was never heard of again.

The King sought out the farmer who had been branded and sold as a slave, and reclaimed him from his evil life with the Ruffler's gang, and put him in the way of a comfortable livelihood.

He also took that old lawyer out of prison and remitted his fine. He provided good homes for the daughters of the two Baptist women whom he saw burned at the stake, and roundly punished the official who laid the undeserved stripes upon Miles Hendon's back.

He saved from the gallows the boy who had captured the stray falcon, and also the woman who had stolen a remnant of cloth from a weaver; but he was too late to save the man who had been convicted of killing a deer in the royal forest.

He showed favour to the justice who had pitied him when he was supposed to have stolen a pig, and he had the gratification of seeing him grow in the public esteem and become a great and honoured man.

As long as the King lived he was fond of telling the story of his adventures, all through, from the hour that the sentinel cuffed him away from the palace gate till the final midnight when he deftly mixed himself into a gang of hurrying workmen and so slipped into the Abbey and climbed up and hid himself in the Confessor's tomb, and then slept so long, next day, that he came within one of missing the Coronation altogether. He said that the frequent rehearsing of the precious lesson kept him strong in his purpose to make its teachings yield benefits to his people; and so, whilst his life was spared he should continue to tell the story, and thus keep its sorrowful spectacles fresh in his memory and the springs of pity replenished in his heart.

Miles Hendon and Tom Canty were favourites of the King, all through his brief reign, and his sincere mourners when he died. The good Earl of Kent had too much sense to abuse his peculiar privilege; but he exercised it twice after the instance we have seen of it before he was called from this world—once at the accession of Queen Mary, and once at the accession of Queen Elizabeth. A descendant of his exercised it at the accession of James I. Before this one's son chose to use the privilege, near a quarter of a century had elapsed, and the "privilege of the Kents" had faded out of most people's memories; so, when the Kent of that day appeared before Charles I. and his court and sat down in the sovereign's presence to assert and perpetuate the right of his house, there was a fine stir indeed! But the matter was soon explained, and the right confirmed. The last Earl of the line fell in the wars of the Commonwealth fighting for the King, and the odd privilege ended with him.

Tom Canty lived to be a very old man, a handsome, white-haired old fellow, of grave and benignant aspect. As long as he lasted he was honoured; and he was also reverenced, for his striking and peculiar costume kept the people reminded that "in his time he had been royal;" so, wherever he appeared the crowd fell apart, making way for him, and whispering, one to another, "Doff thy hat, it is the King's Ward!"—and so they saluted, and got his kindly smile in return—and they valued it, too, for his was an honourable history.

Yes, King Edward VI lived only a few years, poor boy, but he lived them worthily. More than once, when some great dignitary, some gilded vassal of the crown, made argument against his leniency, and urged that some law which he was bent upon amending was gentle enough for its purpose, and wrought no suffering or oppression which any one need mightily mind, the young King turned the mournful eloquence of his great compassionate eyes upon him and answered—

"What dost *thou* know of suffering and oppression? I and my people know, but not thou."

The reign of Edward VI was a singularly merciful one for those harsh times. Now that we are taking leave of him, let us try to keep this in our minds, to his credit.

GENERAL NOTE One hears much about the 'hideous Blue Laws of Connecticut,' and is accustomed to shudder piously when they are mentioned. There are people in America—and even in England!—who imagine that they were a very monument of malignity, pitilessness, and inhumanity; whereas in reality they were about the first *sweeping departure from judicial atrocity* which the 'civilised' world had seen. This humane and kindly Blue Law Code, of two hundred and forty years ago, stands all by itself, with ages of bloody law on the further side of it, and a century and three-quarters of bloody English law on *this* side of it.

There has never been a time—under the Blue Laws or any other—when above *fourteen* crimes were punishable by death in Connecticut. But in England, within the memory of men who are still hale in body and mind, *two hundred and twenty-three* crimes were punishable by death!* These facts are worth knowing—and worth thinking about, too.

---

* See Dr. J. Hammond Trumbull's Blue Laws, True and False, p. 11.

The Adventures of Huckleberry Finn (1884)

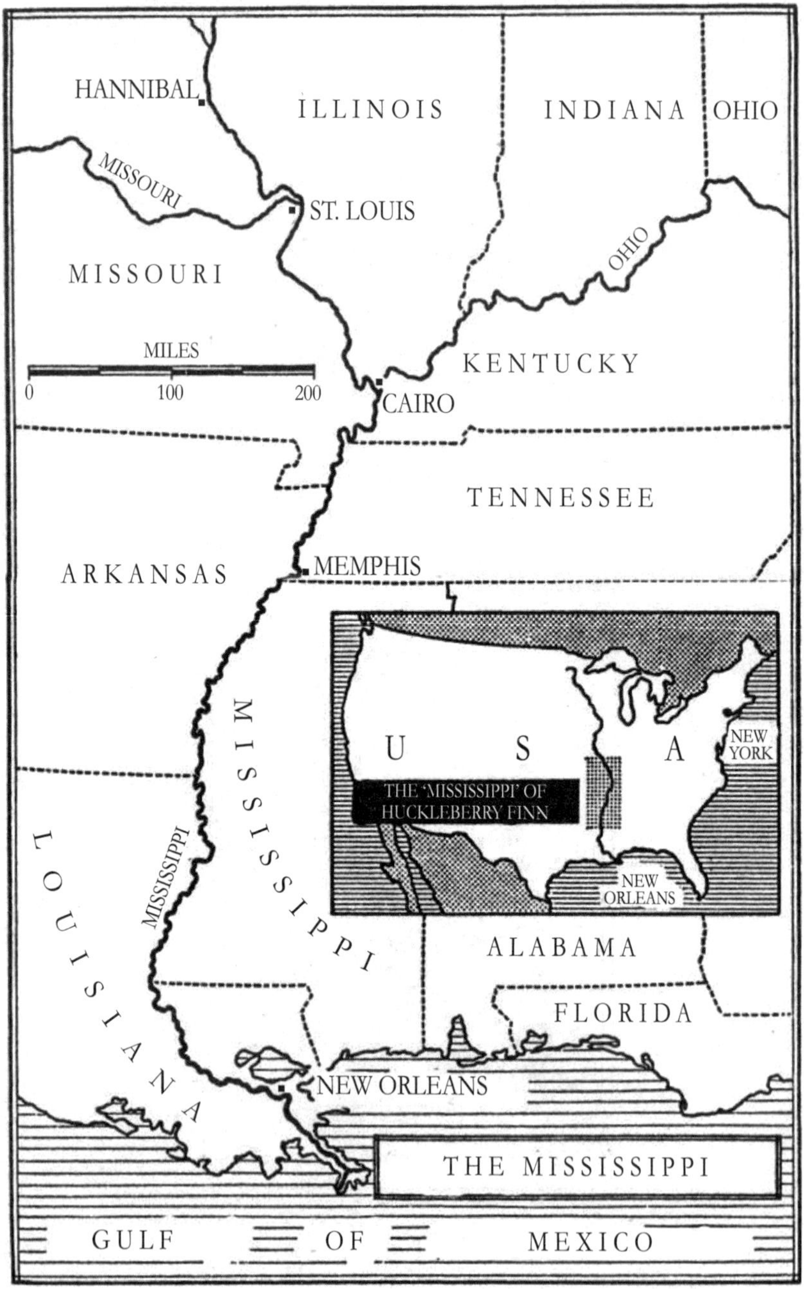
HANNIBAL
ILLINOIS
INDIANA
OHIO
MISSOURI
ST. LOUIS
OHIO
MISSOURI
MILES
0
100
200
KENTUCKY
CAIRO
TENNESSEE
ARKANSAS
MEMPHIS
U S A
NEW YORK
THE 'MISSISSIPPI' OF HUCKLEBERRY FINN
NEW ORLEANS
MISSISSIPPI
LOUISIANA
MISSISSIPPI
ALABAMA
FLORIDA
NEW ORLEANS
THE MISSISSIPPI
GULF OF MEXICO

NOTICE

Persons attempting to find a motive in this narrative will be prosecuted; persons attempting to find a moral in it will be banished; persons attempting to find a plot in it will be shot.

By Order of The Author

Per G. G., Chief of Ordnance

EXPLANATORY

In this book a number of dialects are used, to wit: the Missouri Negro dialect; the extremest form of the backwoods South-Western dialect; the ordinary 'Pike-Country' dialect; and four modified varieties of this last. The shadings have not been done in a haphazard fashion, or by guess-work; but painstakingly, and with the trustworthy guidance and support of personal familiarity with these several forms of speech.

I make this explanation for the reason that without it many readers would suppose that all these characters were trying to talk alike and not succeeding.

The Author

1

You don't know about me without you have read a book by the name of *The Adventures of Tom Sawyer*; but that ain't no matter. That book was made by Mr. Mark Twain, and he told the truth, mainly. There was things which he stretched, but mainly he told the truth. That is nothing. I never seen anybody but lied one time or another, without it was Aunt Polly, or the widow, or maybe Mary. Aunt Polly—Tom's Aunt Polly, she is—and Mary, and the Widow Douglas is all told about in that book, which is mostly a true book, with some stretchers, as I said before.

Now the way that the book winds up is this: Tom and me found the money that the robbers hid in the cave, and it made us rich. We got six thousand dollars apiece—all gold. It was an awful sight of money when it was piled up. Well, Judge Thatcher he took it and put it out at interest, and it fetched us a dollar a day apiece all the year round—more than a body could tell what to do with. The Widow Douglas she took me for her son, and allowed she would sivilize me; but it was rough living in the house all the time, considering how dismal regular and decent the widow was in all her ways; and so when I couldn't stand it no longer I lit out. I got into my old rags and my sugar-hogshead again, and was free and satisfied. But Tom Sawyer he hunted me up and said he was going to start a band of robbers, and I might join if I would go back to the widow and be respectable. So I went back.

The widow she cried over me, and called me a poor lost lamb, and she called me a lot of other names, too, but she never meant no harm by it. She put me in them new clothes again, and I couldn't do nothing but sweat and sweat, and feel all cramped up. Well, then, the old thing commenced again. The widow rung a bell for supper, and you had to come to time. When you got to the table you couldn't go right to eating, but you had to wait for the widow to tuck down her head and grumble a little over the victuals, though there warn't really anything the matter with them—that is, nothing only everything was cooked by itself. In a barrel of odds and ends it is different; things get mixed up, and the juice kind of swaps around, and the things go better.

After supper she got out her book and learned me about Moses and the Bulrushers, and I was in a sweat to find out all about him; but by and by she let it out that Moses had been dead a considerable long time; so then I didn't care no more about him, because I don't take no stock in dead people.

Learning about Moses and the "Bulrushers"

Pretty soon I wanted to smoke, and asked the widow to let me. But she wouldn't. She said it was a mean practice and wasn't clean, and I must try to not do it any more. That is just the way with some people. They get down on a thing when they don't know nothing about it. Here she was a-bothering about Moses, which was no kin to her, and no use to anybody, being gone, you see, yet finding a power of fault with me for doing a thing that had some good in it. And she took snuff, too; of course that was all right, because she done it herself.

Her sister, Miss Watson, a tolerable slim old maid, with goggles on, had just come to live with her, and took a set at me now with a spelling-book. She worked me middling hard for about an hour, and then the widow made her ease up. I couldn't stood it much longer. Then for an hour it was deadly dull, and I was fidgety. Miss Watson would say, "Don't put your feet up there, Huckleberry;" and "Don't scrunch up like that, Huckleberry—set up straight;" and pretty soon she would say, "Don't gap and stretch like that, Huckleberry—why don't you try to behave?" Then she told me all about the bad place, and I said I wished I was there. She got mad then, but I didn't mean no harm. All I wanted was to go somewheres; all I wanted was a change, I warn't particular. She said it was wicked to say what I said; said she wouldn't say it for the whole world; she was going to live so as to go to the good place. Well, I couldn't see no advantage in going where she was going, so I made up my mind I wouldn't try for it. But I never said so, because it would only make trouble, and wouldn't do no good.

Now she had got a start, and she went on and told me all about the good place. She said all a body would have to do there was to go around all day long with a harp and sing, forever and ever. So I didn't think much of it. But I never said so. I asked her if she reckoned Tom Sawyer would go there, and she said not by a considerable sight. I was glad about that, because I wanted him and me to be together.

Miss Watson she kept pecking at me, and it got tiresome and lonesome. By and by they fetched the niggers in and had prayers, and then everybody was off to bed. I went up to my room with a piece of candle, and put it on the table. Then I set down in a chair by the window and tried to think of something cheerful, but it warn't no use. I felt so lonesome I most wished I was dead. The stars were shining, and the leaves rustled in the woods ever so mournful; and I heard an owl, away off, who-whooing about somebody that was dead, and a whippowill* and a dog crying about somebody that was going to die; and the wind was trying to whisper something to me, and I couldn't make out what it was, and so it made the cold shivers run over me. Then away out in the woods I heard that kind of a sound that a ghost makes when it wants to tell about something that's on its mind and can't make itself understood, and so can't rest easy in its grave, and has to go about that way every night grieving. I got so down-hearted and scared I did wish I had some company. Pretty soon a spider went crawling up my shoulder, and I flipped it off and it lit in the candle; and before I could budge it was all shriveled up. I didn't need anybody to tell me that that was an awful bad sign and would

* Echoic name for American Goatsucker bird.

fetch me some bad luck, so I was scared and most shook the clothes off of me. I got up and turned around in my tracks three times and crossed my breast every time; and then I tied up a little lock of my hair with a thread to keep witches away. But I hadn't no confidence. You do that when you've lost a horseshoe that you've found, instead of nailing it up over the door, but I hadn't ever heard anybody say it was any way to keep off bad luck when you'd killed a spider.

I set down again, a-shaking all over, and got out my pipe for a smoke; for the house was all as still as death now, and so the widow wouldn't know. Well, after a long time I heard the clock away off in the town go boom—boom—boom—twelve licks; and all still again—stiller than ever. Pretty soon I heard a twig snap down in the dark amongst the trees—something was a stirring. I set still and listened. Directly I could just barely hear a *"me-yow! me-yow!"* down there. That was good! Says I, *"me-yow! me-yow!"* as soft as I could, and then I put out the light and scrambled out of the window on to the shed. Then I slipped down to the ground and crawled in among the trees, and, sure enough, there was Tom Sawyer waiting for me.

Huck Stealing Away

2

We went tiptoeing along a path amongst the trees back towards the end of the widow's garden, stooping down so as the branches wouldn't scrape our heads. When we was passing by the kitchen I fell over a root and made a noise. We scrouched down and laid still. Miss Watson's big nigger, named Jim, was setting in the kitchen door; we could see him pretty clear, because there was a light behind him. He got up and stretched his neck out about a minute, listening. Then he says:

"Who dah?"

He listened some more; then he come tiptoeing down and stood right between us; we could a touched him, nearly. Well, likely it was minutes and minutes that there warn't a sound, and we all there so close together. There was a place on my ankle that got to itching, but I dasn't scratch it; and then my ear begun to itch; and next my back, right between my shoulders. Seemed like I'd die if I couldn't scratch. Well, I've noticed that thing plenty times since. If you are with the quality, or at a funeral, or trying to go to sleep when you ain't sleepy—if you are anywheres where it won't do for you to scratch, why you will itch all over in upwards of a thousand places. Pretty soon Jim says:

"Say, who is you? Whar is you? Dog my cats ef I didn' hear sumf'n. Well, I know what I's gwyne to do: I's gwyne to set down here and listen tell I hears it agin."

So he set down on the ground betwixt me and Tom. He leaned his back up against a tree, and stretched his legs out till one of them most touched one of mine. My nose begun to itch. It itched till the tears come into my eyes. But I dasn't scratch. Then it begun to itch on the inside. Next I got to itching underneath. I didn't know how I was going to set still. This miserableness went on as much as six or seven minutes; but it seemed a sight longer than that. I was itching in eleven different places now. I reckoned I couldn't stand it more'n a minute longer, but I set my teeth hard and got ready to try. Just then Jim begun to breathe heavy; next he begun to snore—and then I was pretty soon comfortable again.

Tom he made a sign to me—kind of a little noise with his mouth—and we went creeping away on our hands and knees. When we was ten foot off Tom whispered to me, and wanted to tie Jim to the tree for fun. But I said no; he might wake and make a disturbance, and then they'd find out I warn't in. Then Tom said he hadn't got candles enough, and he would slip in the kitchen and get some more. I didn't want him to try. I said Jim might wake up and come. But Tom wanted to resk it; so we slid in there and got three candles, and Tom laid five cents on the table for pay. Then we got out, and I was in a sweat to get away; but nothing would do Tom but he must crawl to where Jim was, on his hands and knees, and play something on him. I waited, and it seemed a good while, everything was so still and lonesome.

As soon as Tom was back we cut along the path, around the garden fence, and by and by fetched up on the steep top of the hill the other side of the house. Tom said he slipped Jim's hat off of his head and hung it on a limb right over him, and Jim stirred a little, but he didn't wake. Afterwards Jim said the witches be witched him and put him in a trance, and rode him all over the State, and then set him under the trees again, and hung his hat on a limb to show who done it. And next time Jim told it he said they rode him down to New Orleans; and, after that, every time he told it he spread it more and more, till by and by he said they rode him all over the world, and tired him most to death, and his back was all over saddle-boils. Jim was monstrous proud about it, and he got so he wouldn't hardly notice the other niggers. Niggers would come miles to hear Jim tell about it, and he was more looked up to than any nigger in that country. Strange niggers would stand with their mouths open and look him all over, same as if he was a wonder. Niggers is always talking about witches in the dark by the kitchen fire; but whenever one was talking and letting on to know all about such things, Jim would happen in and say, "Hm! What you know 'bout witches?" and that nigger was corked up and had to take a back seat. Jim always kept that five-center piece round his neck with a string, and said it was a charm the devil give to him with his own hands, and told him he could cure anybody with it and fetch witches whenever he wanted to just by saying something to it; but he never told what it was he said to it. Niggers would come from all around there and give Jim anything they had, just for a sight of that five-center piece; but they wouldn't touch it, because the devil had had his hands on it. Jim was most ruined for a servant, because he got stuck up on account of having seen the devil and been rode by witches.

Well, when Tom and me got to the edge of the hilltop we looked away down into the village and could see three or four lights twinkling, where there was sick folks, maybe; and the stars over us was sparkling ever so fine; and down by the village was the river, a whole mile broad, and awful still and grand. We went down the hill and found Jo Harper and Ben Rogers, and two or three more of the boys, hid in the old tanyard. So we unhitched a skiff and pulled down the river two mile and a half, to the big scar on the hillside, and went ashore.

We went to a clump of bushes, and Tom made everybody swear to keep the secret, and then showed them a hole in the hill, right in the thickest part of the bushes. Then we lit the candles, and crawled in on our hands and knees. We went about two hundred yards, and then the cave opened up. Tom poked about amongst the passages, and pretty soon ducked under a wall where you wouldn't a noticed that there was a hole. We went along a narrow place and got into a kind of room, all damp and sweaty and cold, and there we stopped. Tom says:

"Now, we'll start this band of robbers and call it Tom Sawyer's Gang. Everybody that wants to join has got to take an oath, and write his name in blood."

Tom Sawyer's Band of Robbers

Everybody was willing. So Tom got out a sheet of paper that he had wrote the oath on, and read it. It swore every boy to stick to the band, and never tell any of the secrets; and if anybody done anything to any boy in the band, whichever boy was ordered to kill that person and his family must do it, and he mustn't eat and he mustn't sleep till he had killed them and hacked a cross in their breasts, which was the sign of the band. And nobody that didn't belong to the band could use that mark, and if he did he must be sued; and if he done it again he must be killed. And if anybody that belonged to the band told the secrets, he must have his throat cut, and then have his carcass burnt up and the ashes scattered all around, and his name blotted off of the list with blood and never mentioned again by the gang, but have a curse put on it and be forgot forever.

Everybody said it was a real beautiful oath, and asked Tom if he got it out of his own head. He said, some of it, but the rest was out of pirate-books and robber-books, and every gang that was high-toned had it.

Some thought it would be good to kill the *families* of boys that told the secrets. Tom said it was a good idea, so he took a pencil and wrote it in. Then Ben Rogers says:

"Here's Huck Finn, he hain't got no family; what you going to do 'bout him?"

"Well, hain't he got a father?" says Tom Sawyer.

"Yes, he's got a father, but you can't never find him these days. He used to lay drunk with the hogs in the tanyard, but he hain't been seen in these parts for a year or more."

They talked it over, and they was going to rule me out, because they said every boy must have a family or somebody to kill, or else it wouldn't be fair and square for the others. Well, nobody could think of anything to do—everybody was stumped, and set still. I was most ready to cry; but all at once I thought of a way, and so I offered them Miss Watson—they could kill her. Everybody said:

"Oh, she'll do. That's all right. Huck can come in."

Then they all stuck a pin in their fingers to get blood to sign with, and I made my mark on the paper.

"Now," says Ben Rogers, "what's the line of business of this Gang?"

"Nothing only robbery and murder," Tom said.

"But who are we going to rob?—houses, or cattle, or—"

"Stuff! stealing cattle and such things ain't robbery; it's burglary," says Tom Sawyer. "We ain't burglars. That ain't no sort of style. We are highwaymen. We stop stages and carriages on the road, with masks on, and kill the people and take their watches and money."

"Must we always kill the people?"

"Oh, certainly. It's best. Some authorities think different, but mostly it's considered best to kill them—except some that you bring to the cave here, and keep them till they're ransomed."

"Ransomed? What's that?"

"I don't know. But that's what they do. I've seen it in books; and so of course that's what we've got to do."

"But how can we do it if we don't know what it is?"

"Why, blame it all, we've *got* to do it. Don't I tell you it's in the books? Do you want to go to doing different from what's in the books, and get things all muddled up?"

"Oh, that's all very fine to *say*, Tom Sawyer, but how in the nation are these fellows going to be ransomed if we don't know how to do it to them?—that's the thing I want to get at. Now, what do you reckon it is?"

"Well, I don't know. But per'aps if we keep them till they're ransomed, it means that we keep them till they're dead."

"Now, that's something *like*. That'll answer. Why couldn't you said that before? We'll keep them till they're ransomed to death; and a bothersome lot they'll be, too—eating up everything, and always trying to get loose."

"How you talk, Ben Rogers. How can they get loose when there's a guard over them, ready to shoot them down if they move a peg?"

"A guard! Well, that *is* good. So somebody's got to set up all night and never get any sleep, just so as to watch them. I think that's foolishness. Why can't a body take a club and ransom them as soon as they get here?"

"Because it ain't in the books so—that's why. Now, Ben Rogers, do you want to do things regular, or don't you?—that's the idea. Don't you reckon that the people that made the books knows what's the correct thing to do? Do you reckon *you* can learn 'em anything? Not by a good deal. No, sir, we'll just go on and ransom them in the regular way."

"All right. I don't mind; but I say it's a fool way, anyhow. Say, do we kill the women, too?"

"Well, Ben Rogers, if I was as ignorant as you I wouldn't let on. Kill the women? No; nobody ever saw anything in the books like that. You fetch them to the cave, and you're always as polite as pie to them; and by and by they fall in love with you, and never want to go home any more."

"Well, if that's the way I'm agreed, but I don't take no stock in it. Mighty soon we'll have the cave so cluttered up with women, and fellows waiting to be ransomed, that there won't be no place for the robbers. But go ahead, I ain't got nothing to say."

Little Tommy Barnes was asleep now, and when they waked him up he was scared, and cried, and said he wanted to go home to his ma, and didn't want to be a robber any more.

So they all made fun of him, and called him cry-baby, and that made him mad, and he said he would go straight and tell all the secrets. But Tom give him five cents to keep quiet, and said we would all go home and meet next week, and rob somebody and kill some people.

Ben Rogers said he couldn't get out much, only Sundays, and so he wanted to begin next Sunday; but all the boys said it would be wicked to do it on Sunday, and that settled the thing. They agreed to get together and fix a day as soon as they could, and then we elected Tom Sawyer first captain and Jo Harper second captain of the Gang, and so started home.

I clumb up the shed and crept into my window just before day was breaking. My new clothes was all greased up and clayey, and I was dog-tired.

3

Well, I got a good going-over in the morning from old Miss Watson on account of my clothes; but the widow she didn't scold, but only cleaned off the grease and clay, and looked so sorry that I thought I would behave awhile if I could. Then Miss Watson she took me in the closet and prayed, but nothing come of it. She told me to pray every day, and whatever I asked for I would get it. But it warn't so. I tried it. Once I got a fish-line, but no hooks. It warn't any good to me without hooks. I tried for the hooks three or four times, but somehow I couldn't make it work. By and by, one day, I asked Miss Watson to try for me, but she said I was a fool. She never told me why, and I couldn't make it out no way.

I set down one time back in the woods, and had a long think about it. I says to myself, if a body can get anything they pray for, why don't Deacon Winn get back the money he lost on pork? Why can't the widow get back her silver snuffbox that was stole? Why can't Miss Watson fat up? No, says I to my self, there ain't nothing in it. I went and told the widow about it, and she said the thing a body could get by praying for it was "spiritual gifts." This was too many for me, but she told me what she meant—I must help other people, and do everything I could for other people, and look out for them all the time, and never think about myself. This was including Miss Watson, as I took it. I went out in the woods and turned it over in my mind a long time, but I couldn't see no advantage about it—except for the other people; so at last I reckoned I wouldn't worry about it any more, but just let it go. Sometimes the widow would take me one side and talk about Providence in a way to make a body's mouth water; but maybe next day Miss Watson would take hold and knock it all down again. I judged I could see that there was two Providences, and a poor chap would stand considerable show with the widow's Providence, but if Miss Watson's got him there warn't no help for him any more. I thought it all out, and reckoned I would belong to the widow's if he wanted me, though I couldn't make out how he was a-going to be any better off then than what he was before, seeing I was so ignorant, and so kind of low-down and ornery.

Pap he hadn't been seen for more than a year, and that was comfortable for me; I didn't want to see him no more. He used to always whale me when he was sober and could get his hands on me; though I used to take to the woods most of the time when he was around. Well, about this time he was found in the river drownded, about twelve mile above town, so people said. They judged it was him, anyway; said this drownded man was just his size, and was ragged, and had uncommon long hair, which was all like pap; but they couldn't make nothing out of the face, because it had been in the water so long it warn't much like a face at all. They said he was floating on his back in the water. They took him and buried him on the bank. But I warn't comfortable long, because I happened to think of something. I knowed mighty well that a drownded man don't float on his back, but on his face. So I knowed, then, that this warn't pap, but a woman dressed up in a man's clothes. So I was uncomfortable again. I judged the old man would turn up again by and by, though I wished he wouldn't.

We played robber now and then about a month, and then I resigned. All the boys did. We hadn't robbed nobody, hadn't killed any people, but only just pretended. We used to hop out of the woods and go charging down on hog-drivers and women in carts taking garden stuff to market, but we never hived any of them. Tom Sawyer called the hogs "ingots," and he called the turnips and stuff "julery," and we would go to the cave and powwow over what we had done, and how many people we had killed and marked. But I couldn't see no profit in it. One time Tom sent a boy to run about town with a blazing stick, which he called a slogan (which was the sign for the Gang to get together), and then he said he had got secret news by his spies that next day a whole parcel of Spanish merchants and rich A-rabs was going to camp in Cave Hollow with two hundred elephants, and six hundred camels, and over a thousand "sumter" mules,* all loaded down with di'monds, and they didn't have only a guard of four hundred soldiers, and so we would lay in ambuscade, as he called it, and kill the lot and scoop the things. He said we must slick up our swords and guns, and get ready. He never could go after even a turnip-cart but he must have the swords and guns all scoured up for it, though they was only lath and broomsticks, and you might scour at them till you rotted, and then they warn't worth a mouthful of ashes more

* Sumpter-mules, i.e. pack-mules.

than what they was before. I didn't believe we could lick such a crowd of Spaniards and A-rabs, but I wanted to see the camels and elephants, so I was on hand next day, Saturday, in the ambuscade; and when we got the word we rushed out of the woods and down the hill. But there warn't no Spaniards and A-rabs, and there warn't no camels nor no elephants. It warn't anything but a Sunday-school picnic, and only a primer-class at that. We busted it up, and chased the children up the hollow; but we never got anything but some doughnuts and jam, though Ben Rogers got a rag doll, and Jo Harper got a hymn book and a tract; and then the teacher charged in, and made us drop everything and cut.

The Robbers Dispersed

I didn't see no di'monds, and I told Tom Sawyer so. He said there was loads of them there, anyway; and he said there was A-rabs there, too, and elephants and things. I said, why couldn't we see them, then? He said if I warn't so ignorant, but had read a book called Don Quixote, I would know without asking. He said it was all done by enchantment. He said there was hundreds of soldiers there, and elephants and treasure, and so on, but we had enemies which he called magicians; and they had turned the whole thing into an infant Sunday-school, just out of spite. I said, all right; then the thing for us to do was to go for the magicians. Tom Sawyer said I was a numskull.

"Why," said he, "a magician could call up a lot of genies, and they would hash you up like nothing before you could say Jack Robinson. They are as tall as a tree and as big around as a church."

"Well," I says, "s'pose we got some genies to help *us*—can't we lick the other crowd then?"

"How you going to get them?"

"I don't know. How do *they* get them?"

"Why, they rub an old tin lamp or an iron ring, and then the genies come tearing in, with the thunder and lightning a-ripping around and the smoke a-rolling, and everything they're told to do they up and do it. They don't think nothing of pulling a shot-tower up by the roots, and belting a Sunday-school superintendent over the head with it—or any other man."

"Who makes them tear around so?"

"Why, whoever rubs the lamp or the ring. They belong to whoever rubs the lamp or the ring, and they've got to do whatever he says. If he tells them to build a palace forty miles long out of di'monds, and fill it full of chewing-gum, or whatever you want, and fetch an emperor's daughter from China for you to marry, they've got to do it—and they've got to do it before sun-up next morning, too. And more: they've got to waltz that palace around over the country wherever you want it, you understand."

"Well," says I, "I think they are a pack of flat-heads for not keeping the palace themselves 'stead of fooling them away like that. And what's more—if I was one of them I would see a man in Jericho before I would drop my business and come to him for the rubbing of an old tin lamp."

"How you talk, Huck Finn. Why, you'd *have* to come when he rubbed it, whether you wanted to or not."

"What! and I as high as a tree and as big as a church? All right, then; I *would* come; but I lay I'd make that man climb the highest tree there was in the country."

"Shucks, it ain't no use to talk to you, Huck Finn. You don't seem to know anything, somehow—perfect saphead."

I thought all this over for two or three days, and then I reckoned I would see if there was anything in it. I got an old tin lamp and an iron ring, and went out in the woods and rubbed and rubbed till I sweat like an Injun, calculating to build a palace and sell it; but it warn't no use, none of the genies come. So then I judged that all that stuff was only just one of Tom Sawyer's lies. I reckoned he believed in the A-rabs and the elephants, but as for me I think different. It had all the marks of a Sunday-school.

4

Well, three or four months run along, and it was well into the winter now. I had been to school most all the time and could spell and read and write just a little, and could say the multiplication table up to six times seven is thirty-five, and I don't reckon I could ever get any further than that if I was to live forever. I don't take no stock in mathematics, anyway.

At first I hated the school, but by and by I got so I could stand it. Whenever I got uncommon tired I played hookey, and the hiding I got next day done me good and cheered me up. So the longer I went to school the easier it got to be. I was getting sort of used to the widow's ways, too, and they warn't so raspy on me. Living in a house and sleeping in a bed pulled on me pretty tight mostly, but before the cold weather I used to slide out and sleep in the woods sometimes, and so that was a rest to me. I liked the old ways best, but I was getting so I liked the new ones, too, a little bit. The widow said I was coming along slow but sure, and doing very satisfactory. She said she warn't ashamed of me.

One morning I happened to turn over the salt-cellar at breakfast. I reached for some of it as quick as I could to throw over my left shoulder and keep off the bad luck, but Miss Watson was in ahead of me, and crossed me off. She says, "Take your hands away, Huckleberry; what a mess you are always making!" The widow put in a good word for me, but that warn't going to keep off the bad luck, I knowed that well enough. I started out, after breakfast, feeling worried and shaky, and wondering where it was going to fall on me, and what it was going to be. There is ways to keep off some kinds of bad luck, but this wasn't one of them kind; so I never tried to do anything, but just poked along low-spirited and on the watch-out.

I went down to the front garden and clumb over the stile where you go through the high board fence. There was an inch of new snow on the ground, and I seen somebody's tracks. They had come up from the quarry and stood around the stile a while, and then went on around the garden fence. It was funny they hadn't come in, after standing around so. I couldn't make it out. It was very curious, somehow. I was going to follow around, but I stooped down to look at the tracks first. I didn't notice anything at first, but next I did. There was a cross in the left boot-heel made with big nails, to keep off the devil.

I was up in a second and shinning down the hill. I looked over my shoulder every now and then, but I didn't see nobody. I was at Judge Thatcher's as quick as I could get there. He said:

"Why, my boy, you are all out of breath. Did you come for your interest?"

"No, sir," I says; "is there some for me?"

"Oh, yes, a half-yearly is in last night—over a hundred and fifty dollars. Quite a fortune for you. You had better let me invest it along with your six thousand, because if you take it you'll spend it."

"No, sir," I says, "I don't want to spend it. I don't want it at all—nor the six thousand, nuther. I want you to take it; I want to give it to you—the six thousand and all."

He looked surprised. He couldn't seem to make it out. He says:

"Why, what can you mean, my boy?"

I says, "Don't you ask me no questions about it, please. You'll take it—won't you?"

He says:

"Well, I'm puzzled. Is something the matter?"

"Please take it," says I, "and don't ask me nothing—then I won't have to tell no lies."

He studied a while, and then he says:

"Oho-o! I think I see. You want to *sell* all your property to me—not give it. That's the correct idea."

Then he wrote something on a paper and read it over, and says:

"There; you see it says 'for a consideration.' That means I have bought it of you and paid you for it. Here's a dollar for you. Now you sign it."

So I signed it, and left.

Miss Watson's nigger, Jim, had a hair-ball as big as your fist, which had been took out of the fourth stomach of an ox, and he used to do magic with it. He said there was a spirit inside of it, and it knowed everything. So I went to him that night and told him pap was here again, for I found his tracks in the snow. What I wanted to know was, what he was going to do, and was he going to stay? Jim got out his hair-ball and said something over it, and then he held it up and dropped it on the floor. It fell pretty solid, and only rolled about an inch. Jim tried it again, and then another time, and it acted just the same. Jim got down on his knees, and put his ear against it and listened. But it warn't no use; he said it wouldn't talk. He said sometimes it wouldn't talk without money. I told him I had an old slick counterfeit quarter that warn't no good because the brass showed through the silver a little, and it wouldn't pass nohow, even if the brass didn't show, because it was so slick it felt greasy, and so that would tell on it every time.

(I reckoned I wouldn't say nothing about the dollar I got from the judge.) I said it was pretty bad money, but maybe the hair-ball would take it, because maybe it wouldn't know the difference. Jim smelt it and bit it and rubbed it, and said he would manage so the hair-ball would think it was good. He said he would split open a raw Irish potato and stick the quarter in between and keep it there all night, and next morning you couldn't see no brass, and it wouldn't feel greasy no more, and so anybody in town would take it in a minute, let alone a hair-ball. Well, I knowed a potato would do that before, but I had forgot it.

Jim Listening

Jim put the quarter under the hair-ball, and got down and listened again. This time he said the hair-ball was all right. He said it would tell my whole fortune if I wanted it to. I says, go on. So the hair-ball talked to Jim, and Jim told it to me. He says:

"Yo' ole father doan' know yit what he's a-gwyne to do. Sometimes he spec he'll go 'way, en den agin he spec he'll stay. De bes' way is to res' easy en let de ole man take his own way. Dey's two angels hoverin' roun' 'bout him. One uv 'em is white en shiny, en t'other one is black. De white one gits him to go right a little while, den de black one sail in en bust it all up. A body can't tell yit which one gwyne to fetch him at de las'. But you is all right. You gwyne to have considable trouble in yo' life, en considable joy. Sometimes you gwyne to git hurt, en sometimes you gwyne to git sick; but every time you's gwyne to git well agin. Dey's two gals flyin' 'bout you in yo' life. One uv 'em's light en t'other one is dark. One is rich en t'other is po'. You's gwyne to marry de po' one fust en de rich one by en by. You wants to keep 'way fum de water as much as you kin, en don't run no resk, 'kase it's down in de bills dat you's gwyne to git hung."

When I lit my candle and went up to my room that night there sat pap his own self!

5

I had shut the door to. Then I turned around and there he was. I used to be scared of him all the time, he tanned me so much. I reckoned I was scared now, too; but in a minute I see I was mistaken—that is, after the first jolt, as you may say, when my breath sort of hitched, he being so unexpected; but right away after I see I warn't scared of him worth bothring about.

He was most fifty, and he looked it. His hair was long and tangled and greasy, and hung down, and you could see his eyes shining through like he was behind vines. It was all black, no grey; so was his long, mixed-up whiskers. There warn't no colour in his face, where his face showed; it was white; not like another man's white, but a white to make a body sick, a white to make a body's flesh crawl—a tree-toad white, a fish-belly white. As for his clothes—just rags, that was all. He had one ankle resting on t'other knee; the boot on that foot was busted, and two of his toes stuck through, and he worked them now and then. His hat was laying on the floor—an old black slouch with the top caved in, like a lid.

I stood a-looking at him; he set there a-looking at me, with his chair tilted back a little. I set the candle down. I noticed the window was up; so he had clumb in by the shed. He kept a-looking me all over. By and by he says:

"Starchy clothes—very. You think you're a good deal of a big-bug, *don't* you?"

"Maybe I am, maybe I ain't," I says.

"Don't you give me none o' your lip," says he. "You've put on considerable many frills since I been away. I'll take you down a peg before I get done with you. You're educated, too, they say—can read and write. You think you're better'n your father, now, don't you, because he can't? *I'll* take it out of you.

Who told you you might meddle with such hifalut'n foolishness, hey?—who told you you could?"

"The widow. She told me."

"The widow, hey?—and who told the widow she could put in her shovel about a thing that ain't none of her business?"

"Nobody never told her."

"Well, I'll learn her how to meddle. And looky here—you drop that school, you hear? I'll learn people to bring up a boy to put on airs over his own father and let on to be better'n what *he* is. You lemme catch you fooling around that school again, you hear? Your mother couldn't read, and she couldn't write, nuther, before she died. None of the family couldn't before *they* died. *I* can't; and here you're a-swelling yourself up like this. I ain't the man to stand it—you hear? Say, lemme hear you read."

I took up a book and begun something about General Washington and the wars. When I'd read about a half a minute, he fetched the book a whack with his hand and knocked it across the house. He says:

"It's so. You can do it. I had my doubts when you told me. Now looky here; you stop that putting on frills. I won't have it. I'll lay for you, my smarty; and if I catch you about that school I'll tan you good. First you know you'll get religion, too. I never see such a son."

He took up a little blue and yaller picture of some cows and a boy, and says:

"What's this?"

"It's something they give me for learning my lessons good."

He tore it up, and says:

"I'll give you something better—I'll give you a cowhide."

He set there a-mumbling and a-growling a minute, and then he says:

"*Ain't* you a sweet-scented dandy, though? A bed; and bedclothes; and a look'n'-glass; and a piece of carpet on the floor—and your own father got to sleep with the hogs in the tanyard. I never see such a son. I bet I'll take some o' these frills out o' you before I'm done with you. Why, there ain't no end to your airs—they say you're rich. Hey?—how's that?"

Huck and his Father

"They lie—that's how."

"Looky here—mind how you talk to me; I'm a-standing about all I can stand now—so don't gimme no sass. I've been in town two days, and I hain't heard nothing but about you bein' rich. I heard about it away down the river, too. That's why I come. You git me that money tomorrow—I want it."

"I hain't got no money."

"It's a lie. Judge Thatcher's got it. You git it. I want it."

"I hain't got no money, I tell you. You ask Judge Thatcher; he'll tell you the same."

"All right. I'll ask him; and I'll make him pungle,* too, or I'll know the reason why. Say, how much you got in your pocket? I want it."

"I hain't got only a dollar, and I want that to—"

"It don't make no difference what you want it for—you just shell it out."

He took it and bit it to see if it was good, and then he said he was going down town to get some whisky; said he hadn't had a drink all day. When he had got out on the shed he put his head in again, and cussed me for putting on frills and trying to be better than him; and when I reckoned he was gone he come back and put his head in again, and told me to mind about that school, because he was going to lay for me and lick me if I didn't drop that.

Next day he was drunk, and he went to Judge Thatcher's and bullyragged him, and tried to make him give up the money; but he couldn't, and then he swore he'd make the law force him.

The judge and the widow went to law to get the court to take me away from him and let one of them be my guardian; but it was a new judge that had just come, and he didn't know the old man; so he said courts mustn't interfere and separate families if they could help it; said he'd druther not take a child away from its father. So Judge Thatcher and the widow had to quit on the business.

That pleased the old man till he couldn't rest. He said he'd cowhide me till I was black and blue if I didn't raise some money for him. I borrowed three dollars from Judge Thatcher, and pap took it and got drunk, and went a-blowing around and cussing and whooping and carrying on; and he kept it up all over town, with a tin pan, till most midnight; then they jailed him, and next day they had him before court, and jailed him again for a week. But he said *he* was satisfied; said he was boss of his son, and he'd make it warm for *him*.

When he got out the new judge said he was a-going to make a man of him. So he took him to his own house, and dressed him up clean and nice, and had him to breakfast and dinner and supper with the family, and was

* Pay.

just old pie to him, so to speak. And after supper he talked to him about temperance and such things till the old man cried, and said he'd been a fool, and fooled away his life; but now he was a-going to turn over a new leaf and be a man nobody wouldn't be ashamed of, and he hoped the judge would help him and not look down on him. The judge said he could hug him for them words; so he cried, and his wife she cried again; pap said he'd been a man that had always been misunderstood before, and the judge said he believed it. The old man said that what a man wanted that was down was sympathy, and the judge said it was so; so they cried again. And when it was bedtime the old man rose up and held out his hand, and says:

"Look at it, gentlemen and ladies all; take a-hold of it; shake it. There's a hand that was the hand of a hog; but it ain't so no more; it's the hand of a man that's started in on a new life, and'll die before he'll go back. You mark them words—don't forget I said them. It's a clean hand now; shake it—don't be afeard."

Reforming the Drunkard

So they shook it, one after the other, all around, and cried. The judge's wife she kissed it. Then the old man he signed a pledge—made his mark. The judge said it was the holiest time on record, or something like that. Then they tucked the old man into a beautiful room, which was the spare room, and in the night some time he got powerful thirsty and clumb out on to the porch-roof and slid down a stanchion and traded his new coat for a jug of forty-rod,* and clumb back again and had a good old time; and

* Whisky, powerful enough to throw a man forty rods.

towards daylight he crawled out again, drunk as a fiddler, and rolled off the porch and broke his left arm in two places, and was most froze to death when somebody found him after sun-up. And when they come to look at that spare room they had to take soundings before they could navigate it.

The judge he felt kind of sore. He said he reckoned a body could reform the old man with a shotgun, maybe, but he didn't know no other way.

6

Well, pretty soon the old man was up and around again, and then he went for Judge Thatcher in the courts to make him give up that money, and he went for me, too, for not stopping school. He catched me a couple of times and thrashed me, but I went to school just the same, and dodged him or outrun him most of the time. I didn't want to go to school much before, but I reckoned I'd go now to spite pap. That law trial was a slow business—appeared like they warn't ever going to get started on it; so every now and then I'd borrow two or three dollars off of the judge for him, to keep from getting a cowhiding. Every time he got money he got drunk; and every time he got drunk he raised Cain around town; and every time he raised Cain he got jailed. He was just suited—this kind of thing was right in his line.

He got to hanging around the widow's too much and so she told him at last that if he didn't quit using around there she would make trouble for him. Well, *wasn't* he mad? He said he would show who was Huck Finn's boss. So he watched out for me one day in the spring, and catched me, and took me up the river about three mile in a skiff, and crossed over to the Illinois shore where it was woody and there warn't no houses but an old log hut in a place where the timber was so thick you couldn't find it if you didn't know where it was.

He kept me with him all the time, and I never got a chance to run off. We lived in that old cabin, and he always locked the door and put the key under his head nights. He had a gun which he had stole, I reckon, and we fished and hunted, and that was what we lived on. Every little while he locked me in and went down to the store, three miles, to the ferry, and traded fish and game for whisky, and fetched it home and got drunk and had a good time, and licked me. The widow she found out where I was by and by, and she sent a man over to try to get hold of me; but pap drove him off with the gun, and it warn't long after that till I was used to being where I was, and liked it—all but the cowhide part.

It was kind of lazy and jolly, laying off comfortable all day, smoking and fishing, and no books nor study. Two months or more run along, and my clothes got to be all rags and dirt, and I didn't see how I'd ever got to like it so well at the widow's, where you had to wash, and eat on a plate, and comb up, and go to bed and get up regular, and be forever bothering over a book, and have old Miss Watson pecking at you all the time. I didn't want to go back no more. I had stopped cussing, because the widow didn't like it; but now I took to it again because pap hadn't no objections. It was pretty good times up in the woods there, take it all around.

Solid Comfort

But by and by pap got too handy with his hick'ry, and I couldn't stand it. I was all over welts. He got to going away so much, too, and locking me in. Once he locked me in and was gone three days. It was dreadful lonesome. I judged he had got drownded, and I wasn't ever going to get out any more. I was scared. I made up my mind I would fix up some way to leave there. I had tried to get out of that cabin many a time, but I couldn't find no way. There warn't a window to it big enough for a dog to get through. I couldn't get up the chimbly; it was too narrow. The door was thick, solid oak slabs. Pap was pretty careful not to leave a knife or anything in the cabin when he was away; I reckon I had hunted the place over as much as a hundred times; well, I was most all the time at it, because it was about the only way to put in the time. But this time I found something at last; I found an old rusty wood-saw without any handle; it was laid in between a rafter and the clapboards of the roof. I greased it up and went to work. There was an old horse-blanket nailed against the logs at the far end of the cabin behind the table, to keep the wind from blowing through the chinks and putting the candle out. I got under the table and raised the blanket, and went to work to saw a section of the big bottom log out—big enough to let me through. Well, it was a good long job, but I was getting towards the end of it when I heard pap's gun in the woods. I got rid of the signs of my work, and dropped the blanket and hid my saw, and pretty soon pap come in.

Pap warn't in a good humour—so he was his natural self. He said he was down town, and everything was going wrong. His lawyer said he reckoned he would win his lawsuit and get the money if they ever got started on the trial; but then there was ways to put it off a long time, and Judge Thatcher knowed how to do it. And he said people allowed there'd be another trial to get me away from him and give me to the widow for my guardian, and they guessed it would win this time. This shook me up considerable, because I didn't want to go back to the widow's any more and be so cramped up and sivilized, as they called it. Then the old man got to cussing, and cussed everything and everybody he could think of, and then cussed them all over again to make sure he hadn't skipped any, and after that he polished off with a kind of a general cuss all round, including a considerable parcel of people which he didn't know the names of, and so called them what's-his-name when he got to them, and went right along with his cussing.

He said he would like to see the widow get me. He said he would watch out, and if they tried to come any such game on him he knowed of a place six or seven mile off to stow me in, where they might hunt till they dropped and they couldn't find me. That made me pretty uneasy again, but only for a minute; I reckoned I wouldn't stay on hand till he got that chance.

The old man made me go to the skiff and fetch the things he had got. There was a fifty-pound sack of corn meal, and a side of bacon, ammunition, and a four-gallon jug of whisky, and an old book and two newspapers for wadding, besides some tow. I toted up a load, and went back and set down on the bow of the skiff to rest. I thought it all over, and I reckoned I would walk off with the gun and some lines, and take to the woods when I run away. I guessed I wouldn't stay in one place, but just tramp right across the country, mostly night times, and hunt and fish to keep alive, and so get so far away that the old man nor the widow couldn't ever find me any more. I judged I would saw out and leave that night if pap got drunk enough, and I reckoned he would. I got so full of it I didn't notice how long I was staying till the old man hollered and asked me whether I was asleep or drownded.

I got the things all up to the cabin, and then it was about dark. While I was cooking supper the old man took a swig or two and got sort of warmed up, and went to ripping again. He had been drunk over in town, and laid in the gutter all night, and he was a sight to look at. A body would a thought he was Adam—he was just all mud. Whenever his liquor begun to work he most always went for the govment, this time he says:

"Call this a govment! why, just look at it and see what it's like. Here's the law a-standing ready to take a man's son away from him—a man's own son, which he has had all the trouble and all the anxiety and all the expense of raising. Yes, just as that man has got that son raised at last, and ready to go to work and begin to do suthin' for *him* and give him a rest, the law up and goes for him. And they call *that* govment! That ain't all, nuther. The law backs that old Judge Thatcher up and helps him to keep me out o' my property. Here's what the law does: The law takes a man worth six thousand dollars and up'ards, and jams him into an old trap of a cabin like this, and lets him go round in clothes that ain't fitten for a hog. They call that govment! A man can't get his rights in a govment like this. Sometimes I've a mighty notion to just leave the country for good and all. Yes, and I *told* 'em so; I told old Thatcher so to his face. Lots of 'em heard me, and can tell what I said. Says I, for two cents I'd leave the blamed country and never come a-near it agin. Them's the very words. I says look at my hat—if you call it a hat—but the lid raises up and the rest of it goes down till it's below my chin, and then it ain't rightly a hat at all, but more like my head was shoved up through a jint o' stove-pipe. Look at it, says I—such a hat for me to wear—one of the wealthiest men in this town if I could git my rights.

"Oh, yes, this is a wonderful govment, wonderful. Why, looky here. There was a free nigger there from Ohio—a mulatter, most as white as a white man. He had the whitest shirt on you ever see, too, and the shiniest hat; and there ain't a man in that town that's got as fine clothes as what he had; and he had a gold watch and chain, and a silver-headed cane—the awfulest old grey-headed nabob in the State. And what do you think? They said he was a p'fessor in a college, and could talk all kinds of languages, and knowed everything. And that ain't the wust. They said he could *vote* when he was at home. Well, that let me out. Thinks I, what is the country a-coming to? It was 'lection day, and I was just about to go and vote myself if I warn't too drunk to get there; but when they told me there was a State in this country where they'd let that nigger vote, I drawed out. I says I'll never vote agin. Them's the very words I said; they all heard me; and the country may rot for all me—I'll never vote agin as long as I live. And to see the cool way of that nigger—why, he wouldn't a give me the road if I hadn't shoved him out o' the way. I says to the people, why ain't this nigger put up at auction and sold?—that's what I want to know. And what do you reckon they said? Why, they said he couldn't be sold till he'd been in the State six months, and he hadn't been there that long yet. There, now—that's a specimen. They call that a govment that can't sell a free nigger till he's been in the State six months. Here's a govment that calls itself a govment, and lets on to be a govment, and thinks it is a govment, and yet's got to set stock-still for six whole months before it can take a hold of a prowling, thieving, infernal, white-shirted free nigger, and—"

Pap was agoing on so he never noticed where his old limber legs was taking him to, so he went head over heels over the tub of salt pork and barked both shins, and the rest of his speech was all the hottest kind of language—mostly hove at the nigger and the govment, though he give the tub some, too, all along, here and there. He hopped around the cabin considerable, first on one leg and then on the other, holding first one shin and then the other one, and at last he let out with his left foot all of a sudden and fetched the tub a rattling kick. But it warn't good judgment, because that was the boot that had a couple of his toes leaking out of the front end of it; so now he raised a howl that fairly made a body's hair raise, and down he went in the dirt, and rolled there, and held his toes; and the cussing he done then laid over anything he had ever done previous. He said so his own self afterwards. He had heard old Sowberry Hagan in his best days, and he said it laid over him, too; but I reckon that was sort of piling it on, maybe.

After supper pap took the jug, and said he had enough whisky there for two drunks and one delirium tremens. That was always his word. I judged he would be blind drunk in about an hour, and then I would steal the key, or saw myself out, one or t'other. He drank and drank, and tumbled down on his blankets by and by; but luck didn't run my way. He didn't go sound asleep, but was uneasy. He groaned and moaned and thrashed around this way and that for a long time. At last I got so sleepy I couldn't keep my eyes open all I could do, and so before I knowed what I was about I was sound asleep, and the candle burning.

I don't know how long I was asleep, but all of a sudden there was an awful scream and I was up. There was pap looking wild, and skipping around every which way and yelling about snakes. He said they was crawling up his legs; and then he would give a jump and scream, and say one had bit him on the cheek—but I couldn't see no snakes. He started and run round and round the cabin, hollering "Take him off! take him off! he's biting me on the neck!" I never see a man look so wild in the eyes. Pretty soon he was all fagged out, and fell down panting; then he rolled over and over wonderful fast, kicking things every which way, and striking and grabbing at the air with his hands, and screaming and saying there was devils a-hold of him. He wore out by and by, and laid still a while, moaning. Then he laid stiller, and didn't make a sound. I could hear the owls and the wolves away off in the woods, and it seemed terrible still. He was laying over by the corner. By and by he raised up part way and listened, with his head to one side. He says, very low:

"Tramp—tramp—tramp; that's the dead; tramp—tramp—tramp; they're coming after me; but I won't go. Oh, they're here! don't touch me—don't! hands off—they're cold; let go. Oh, let a poor devil alone!"

Then he went down on all fours and crawled off, begging them to let him alone, and he rolled himself up in his blanket and wallowed in under the old pine table, still a-begging; and then he went to crying. I could hear him through the blanket.

By and by he rolled out and jumped up on his feet looking wild, and he see me and went for me. He chased me round and round the place with a clasp-knife, calling me the Angel of Death, and saying he would kill me, and then I couldn't come for him no more. I begged, and told him I was only Huck; but he laughed *such* a screechy laugh, and roared and cussed, and kept on chasing me up. Once when I turned short and dodged under his arm he made a grab and got me by the jacket between my shoulders, and I thought I was gone; but I slid out of the jacket quick as lightning, and saved myself. Pretty soon he was all tired out, and dropped down with his back against the door, and said he would rest a minute and then kill me. He put his knife under him, and said he would sleep and get strong, and then he would see who was who.

So he dozed off pretty soon. By and by I got the old split-bottom chair and clumb up as easy as I could, not to make any noise, and got down the gun. I slipped the ramrod down it to make sure it was loaded, then I laid it across the turnip barrel, pointing towards pap, and set down behind it to wait for him to stir. And how slow and still the time did drag along.

7

"Git up! What you 'bout?"

I opened my eyes and looked around, trying to make out where I was. It was after sun-up, and I had been sound asleep. Pap was standing over me looking sour and sick, too. He says:

"What you doin' with this gun?"

I judged he didn't know nothing about what he had been doing, so I says:

"Somebody tried to get in, so I was laying for him."

"Why didn't you roust me out?"

"Well, I tried to, but I couldn't; I couldn't budge you."

"Well, all right. Don't stand there palavering all day, but out with you and see if there's a fish on the lines for breakfast. I'll be along in a minute."

He unlocked the door, and I cleared out up the river-bank. I noticed some pieces of limbs and such things floating down, and a sprinkling of bark; so I knowed the river had begun to rise. I reckoned I would have great times now if I was over at the town. The June rise used to be always luck for me; because as soon as that rise begins here comes cordwood floating down, and pieces of log rafts—sometimes a dozen logs together; so all you have to do is to catch them and sell them to the wood-yards and the sawmill.

I went along up the bank with one eye out for pap and t'other one out for what the rise might fetch along. Well, all at once here comes a canoe; just a beauty, too, about thirteen or fourteen foot long, riding high like a duck. I shot head-first off of the bank like a frog, clothes and all on, and struck out for the canoe. I just expected there'd be somebody laying down in it, because people often done that to fool folks, and when a chap had pulled a skiff out most to it they'd raise up and laugh at him. But it warn't so this time. It was a drift-canoe sure enough, and I clumb in and paddled her ashore. Thinks I, the old man will be glad when he sees this—she's worth ten dollars. But when I got to shore pap wasn't in sight yet, and as I was running her into a little creek like a gully, all hung over with vines and willows, I struck another idea: I judged I'd hide her good, and then, 'stead of taking to the woods when I run off, I'd go down the river about fifty mile and camp in one place for good, and not have such a rough time tramping on foot.

The Shanty

It was pretty close to the shanty, and I thought I heard the old man coming all the time; but I got her hid; and then I out and looked around a bunch of willows, and there was the old man down the path a piece just drawing a bead on a bird with his gun. So he hadn't seen anything.

When he got along I was hard at it taking up a "trot" line.* He abused me a little for being so slow; but I told him I fell in the river, and that was what made me so long. I knowed he would see I was wet, and then he would be asking questions. We got five catfish off the lines and went home.

While we laid off after breakfast to sleep up, both of us being about wore out, I got to thinking that if I could fix up some way to keep pap and the widow from trying to follow me, it would be a certainer thing than trusting to luck to get far enough off before they missed me; you see, all kinds of things might happen. Well, I didn't see no way for a while, but by and by pap raised up a minute to drink another barrel of water, and he says:

"Another time a man comes a-prowling round here you roust me out, you hear? That man warn't here for no good. I'd a shot him. Next time you roust me out, you hear?"

Then he dropped down and went to sleep again; but what he had been saying give me the very idea I wanted. I says to myself, I can fix it now so nobody won't think of following me.

* A fishing-line suspended across a stream with several hooks hanging from it.

About twelve o'clock we turned out and went along up the bank. The river was coming up pretty fast, and lots of driftwood going by on the rise. By and by along comes part of a log raft—nine logs fast together. We went out with the skiff and towed it ashore. Then we had dinner. Anybody but pap would a waited and seen the day through, so as to catch more stuff; but that warn't pap's style. Nine logs was enough for one time; he must shove right over to town and sell. So he locked me in and took the skiff, and started off towing the raft about half-past three. I judged he wouldn't come back that night. I waited till I reckoned he had got a good start; then I out with my saw, and went to work on that log again. Before he was t'other side of the river I was out of the hole; him and his raft was just a speck on the water away off yonder.

I took the sack of corn meal and took it to where the canoe was hid, and shoved the vines and branches apart and put it in; then I done the same with the side of bacon; then the whisky-jug. I took all the coffee and sugar there was, and all the ammunition; I took the wadding; I took the bucket and gourd; I took a dipper and a tin cup, and my old saw and two blankets, and the skillet and the coffee-pot. I took fish-lines and matches and other things—everything that was worth a cent. I cleaned out the place. I wanted an axe, but there wasn't any, only the one out at the woodpile, and I knowed why I was going to leave that. I fetched out the gun, and now I was done.

I had wore the ground a good deal crawling out of the hole and dragging out so many things. So I fixed that as good as I could from the outside by scattering dust on the place, which covered up the smoothness and the sawdust. Then I fixed the piece of log back into its place, and put two rocks under it and one against it to hold it there, for it was bent up at that place and didn't quite touch ground. If you stood four or five foot away and didn't know it was sawed, you wouldn't never notice it; and besides, this was the back of the cabin, and it warn't likely anybody would go fooling around there.

It was all grass clear to the canoe, so I hadn't left a track. I followed around to see. I stood on the bank and looked out over the river. All safe. So I took the gun and went up a piece into the woods, and was hunting around for some birds when I see a wild pig; hogs soon went wild in them bottoms after they had got away from the prairie farms. I shot this fellow and took him into camp.

I took the axe and smashed in the door. I beat it and hacked it considerable a-doing it. I fetched the pig in, and took him back nearly to the table and hacked into his throat with the axe, and laid him down on the ground to bleed; I say ground because it was ground—hard packed, and no boards.

Well, next I took an old sack and put a lot of big rocks in it—all I could drag—and I started it from the pig, and dragged it to the door and through the woods down to the river and dumped it in, and down it sunk, out of sight. You could easy see that something had been dragged over the ground. I did wish Tom Sawyer was there; I knowed he would take an interest in this kind of business, and throw in the fancy touches. Nobody could spread himself like Tom Sawyer in such a thing as that.

Well, last I pulled out some of my hair, and blooded the axe good, and stuck it on the back side, and slung the axe in the corner. Then I took up the pig and held him to my breast with my jacket (so he couldn't drip) till I got a good piece below the house and then dumped him into the river. Now I thought of something else. So I went and got the bag of meal and my old saw out of the canoe, and fetched them to the house. I took the bag to where it used to stand, and ripped a hole in the bottom of it with the saw, for there warn't no knives and forks on the place—pap done everything with his clasp-knife about the cooking. Then I carried the sack about a hundred yards across the grass and through the willows east of the house, to a shallow lake that was five mile wide and full of rushes—and ducks too, you might say, in the season. There was a slough or a creek leading out of it on the other side that went miles away, I don't know where, but it didn't go to the river. The meal sifted out and made a little track all the way to the lake. I dropped pap's whetstone there too, so as to look like it had been done by accident. Then I tied up the rip in the meal sack with a string, so it wouldn't leak no more, and took it and my saw to the canoe again.

It was about dark now; so I dropped the canoe down the river under some willows that hung over the bank, and waited for the moon to rise. I made fast to a willow; then I took a bite to eat, and by and by laid down in the canoe to smoke a pipe and lay out a plan. I says to myself, they'll follow the track of that sackful of rocks to the shore and then drag the river for me. And they'll follow that meal track to the lake and go browsing down the creek that leads out of it to find the robbers that killed me and took the things. They won't ever hunt the river for anything but my dead carcass. They'll soon get tired of that, and won't bother no more about me. All right; I can stop anywhere I want to. Jackson's Island is good enough for me; I know that island pretty well, and nobody ever comes there. And then I can paddle over to town nights, and slink around and pick up things I want. Jackson's Island's the place.

I was pretty tired, and the first thing I knowed I was asleep. When I woke up I didn't know where I was for a minute. I set up and looked around, a little scared. Then I remembered. The river looked miles and miles across.

The moon was so bright I could a counted the drift logs that went a-slipping along, black and still, hundreds of yards out from shore. Everything was dead quiet, and it looked late, and *smelt* late. You know what I mean—I don't know the words to put it in.

I took a good gap and a stretch, and was just going to unhitch and start when I heard a sound away over the water. I listened. Pretty soon I made it out. It was that dull kind of a regular sound that comes from oars working in rowlocks when it's a still night. I peeped out through the willow branches, and there it was—a skiff, away across the water. I couldn't tell how many was in it. It kept a-coming, and when it was abreast of me I see there warn't but one man in it. Think's I, maybe it's pap, though I warn't expecting him. He dropped below me with the current, and by and by he came a-swinging up shore in the easy water, and he went by so close I could a reached out the gun and touched him. Well, it *was* pap, sure enough—and sober, too, by the way he laid his oars.

I didn't lose no time. The next minute I was a-spinning down stream soft but quick in the shade of the bank. I made two mile and a half, and then struck out a quarter of a mile or more towards the middle of the river, because pretty soon I would be passing the ferry landing, and people might see me and hail me. I got out amongst the driftwood, and then laid down in the bottom of the canoe and let her float.

Taking a Rest

I laid there, and had a good rest and a smoke out of my pipe, looking away into the sky; not a cloud in it. The sky looks ever so deep when you lay down on your back in the moonshine; I never knowed it before. And how far a body can hear on the water such nights! I heard people talking at the ferry landing. I heard what they said, too—every word of it. One man said it was getting towards the long days and the short nights now. T'other one said *this* warn't one of the short ones, he reckoned—and then they laughed, and he said it over again, and they laughed again; then they waked up another fellow and told him, and laughed, but he didn't laugh; he ripped out something brisk, and said let him alone. The first fellow said he 'lowed to tell it to his old woman—she would think it was pretty good; but he said that warn't nothing to some things he had said in his time. I heard one man say it was nearly three o'clock, and he hoped daylight wouldn't wait more than about a week longer. After that the talk got further and further away, and I couldn't make out the words any more; but I could hear the mumble, and now and then a laugh, too, but it seemed a long ways off.

I was away below the ferry now. I rose up, and there was Jackson's Island, about two mile and a half down stream, heavy timbered and standing up out of the middle of the river, big and dark and solid, like a steamboat without any lights. There warn't any signs of the bar at the head—it was all under water now.

It didn't take me long to get there. I shot past the head at a ripping rate, the current was so swift, and then I got into the dead water and landed on the side towards the Illinois shore. I run the canoe into a deep dent in the bank that I knowed about; I had to part the willow branches to get in; and when I made fast nobody could a seen the canoe from the outside.

I went up and set down on a log at the head of the island, and looked out on the big river and the black driftwood and away over to the town, three mile away, where there was three or four lights twinkling. A monstrous big lumber-raft was about a mile up stream, coming along down, with a lantern in the middle of it. I watched it come creeping down, and when it was most abreast of where I stood I heard a man say, "Stern oars, there! heave her head to stabboard!" I heard that just as plain as if the man was by my side.

There was a little grey in the sky now; so I stepped into the woods, and laid down for a nap before breakfast.

8

The sun was up so high when I waked that I judged it was after eight o'clock. I laid there in the grass and the cool shade thinking about things, and feeling rested and ruther comfortable and satisfied. I could see the sun out at one or two holes, but mostly it was big trees all about, and gloomy in there amongst them. There was freckled places on the ground where the light sifted down through the leaves, and the freckled places swapped about a little, showing there was a little breeze up there. A couple of squirrels set on a limb and jabbered at me very friendly.

I was powerful lazy and comfortable—didn't want to get up and cook breakfast. Well, I was dozing off again when I thinks I hears a deep sound of "boom!" away up the river. I rouses up, and rests on my elbow and listens; pretty soon I hears it again. I hopped up, and went and looked out at a hole in the leaves, and I see a bunch of smoke laying on the water a long ways up—about abreast the ferry. And there was the ferryboat full of people floating along down. I knowed what was the matter now. "Boom!" I see the white smoke squirt out of the ferryboat's side. You see, they was firing cannon over the water, trying to make my carcass come to the top.

I was pretty hungry, but it warn't going to do for me to start a fire, because they might see the smoke. So I set there and watched the cannon-smoke and listened to the boom. The river was a mile wide there, and it always looks pretty on a summer morning—so I was having a good enough time seeing them hunt for my remainders if I only had a bite to eat. Well, then I happened to think how they always put quicksilver in loaves of bread and float them off, because they always go right to the drownded carcass and stop there. So, says I, I'll keep a lookout, and if any of them's floating around after me I'll give them a show. I changed to the Illinois edge of the island to see what luck I could have, and I warn't disappointed. A big double loaf come along, and I most got it with a long stick, but my foot slipped and she floated out further. Of course I was where the current set in the closest to the shore—I knowed enough for that. But by and by along comes another one, and this time I won. I took out the plug and shook out the little dab of quicksilver, and set my teeth in. It was "baker's bread"—what the quality eat; none of your low-down corn-pone.

I got a good place amongst the leaves, and set there on a log, munching the bread and watching the ferry-boat, and very well satisfied. And then something struck me. I says, now I reckon the widow or the parson or somebody prayed that this bread would find me, and here it has gone and done it. So there ain't no doubt but there is something in that thing—that is, there's something in it when a body like the widow or the parson prays, but it don't work for me, and I reckon it don't work for only just the right kind.

I lit a pipe and had a good long smoke, and went on watching. The ferryboat was floating with the current, and I allowed I'd have a chance to see who was aboard when she come along, because she would come in close, where the bread did. When she'd got pretty well along down towards me, I put out my pipe and went to where I fished out the bread, and laid down behind a log on the bank in a little open place. Where the log forked I could peep through.

By and by she come along, and she drifted in so close that they could a run out a plank and walked ashore. Most everybody was on the boat. Pap, and Judge Thatcher, and Bessie Thatcher, and Jo Harper, and Tom Sawyer, and his old Aunt Polly, and Sid and Mary, and plenty more. Everybody was talking about the murder, but the captain broke in and says:

"Look sharp, now; the current sets in the closest here, and maybe he's washed ashore and got tangled amongst the brush at the water's edge. I hope so, anyway."

I didn't hope so. They all crowded up and leaned over the rails, nearly in my face, and kept still, watching with all their might. I could see them first-rate, but they couldn't see me. Then the captain sung out:

"Stand away!" and the cannon let off such a blast right before me that it made me deef with the noise and pretty near blind with the smoke, and I judged I was gone. If they'd a had some bullets in, I reckon they'd a got the corpse they was after. Well, I see I warn't hurt, thanks to goodness. The boat floated on and went out of sight around the shoulder of the island. I could hear the booming now and then, further and further off, and by and by, after an hour, I didn't hear it no more. The island was three mile long. I judged they had got to the foot, and was giving it up. But they didn't yet a while. They turned around the foot of the island and started up the channel on the Missouri side, under steam, and booming once in a while as they went. I crossed over to that side and watched them. When they got abreast the head of the island they quit shooting and dropped over to the Missouri shore and went home to the town.

I knowed I was all right now. Nobody else would come a-hunting after me. I got my traps out of the canoe and made me a nice camp in the thick woods. I made a kind of a tent out of my blankets to put my things under so the rain couldn't get at them. I catched a catfish and haggled him open with my saw, and towards sundown I started my camp fire and had supper. Then I set out a line to catch some fish for breakfast.

When it was dark I set by my camp fire smoking, and feeling pretty well satisfied; but by and by it got sort of lonesome, and so I went and set on the bank and listened to the current swashing along, and counted the stars and drift logs and rafts that come down, and then went to bed; there ain't no better way to put in time when you are lonesome; you can't stay so, you soon get over it.

And so for three days and nights. No difference—just the same thing. But the next day I went exploring around down through the island. I was boss of it; it all belonged to me, so to say, and I wanted to know all about it; but mainly I wanted to put in the time. I found plenty strawberries, ripe and prime; and green summer grapes, and green razberries; and the green blackberries was just beginning to show. They would all come handy by and by, I judged.

Well, I went fooling along in the deep woods till I judged I warn't far from the foot of the island. I had my gun along, but I hadn't shot nothing; it was for protection; thought I would kill some game nigh home. About this time I mighty near stepped on a good-sized snake, and it went sliding off through the grass and flowers, and I after it, trying to get a shot at it. I clipped along, and all of a sudden I bounded right on to the ashes of a camp fire that was still smoking.

My heart jumped up amongst my lungs. I never waited for to look further, but uncocked my gun and went sneaking back on my tiptoes as fast as ever I could. Every now and then I stopped a second amongst the thick leaves and listened, but my breath come so hard I couldn't hear nothing else. I slunk along another piece further, then listened again; and so on, and so on. If I see a stump, I took it for a man; if I trod on a stick and broke it, it made me feel like a person had cut one of my breaths in two and I only got half, and the short half, too.

When I got to camp I warn't feeling very brash, there warn't much sand in my craw;* but I says, this ain't no time to be fooling around. So I got all my traps into my canoe again so as to have them out of sight, and I put out the fire and scattered the ashes around to look like an old last year's camp, and then clumb a tree.

I reckon I was up in the tree two hours; but I didn't see nothing, I didn't hear nothing—I only *thought* I heard and seen as much as a thousand things.

* Crop of a bird or stomach of a man.

Well, I couldn't stay up there forever; so at last I got down, but I kept in the thick woods and on the lookout all the time. All I could get to eat was berries and what was left over from breakfast.

By the time it was night I was pretty hungry. So when it was good and dark I slid out from shore before moonrise and paddled over to the Illinois bank—about a quarter of a mile. I went out in the woods and cooked a supper, and I had about made up my mind I would stay there all night when I hear a *plunkety-plunk, plunkety-plunk*, and says to myself, horses coming; and next I hear people's voices. I got everything into the canoe as quick as I could, and then went creeping through the woods to see what I could find out. I hadn't got far when I hear a man say:

"We better camp here if we can find a good place; the horses is about beat out. Let's look around."

I didn't wait, but shoved out and paddled away easy. I tied up in the old place, and reckoned I would sleep in the canoe.

I didn't sleep much. I couldn't, somehow, for thinking. And every time I waked up I thought somebody had me by the neck. So the sleep didn't do me no good. By and by I says to myself, I can't live this way; I'm a-going to find out who it is that's here on the island with me; I'll find it out or bust. Well, I felt better right off.

So I took my paddle and slid out from shore just a step or two, and then let the canoe drop along down amongst the shadows. The moon was shining, and outside of the shadows it made it most as light as day. I poked along well on to an hour, everything still as rocks and sound asleep. Well, by this time I was most down to the foot of the island. A little ripply, cool breeze begun to blow, and that was as good as saying the night was about done. I give her a turn with the paddle and brung her nose to shore; then I got my gun and slipped out and into the edge of the woods. I sat down there on a log, and looked out through the leaves. I see the moon go off watch, and the darkness begin to blanket the river. But in a little while I see a pale streak over the treetops, and knowed the day was coming. So I took my gun and slipped off towards where I had run across that camp fire, stopping every minute or two to listen. But I hadn't no luck somehow; I couldn't seem to find the place. But by and by, sure enough, I catched a glimpse of fire away through the trees. I went for it, cautious and slow. By and by I was close enough to have a look, and there laid a man on the ground. It most give me the fan-tods.* He had a blanket around his head, and his head was nearly in the fire. I set there behind a clump of bushes, in about six foot of him, and

* Literally, hallucinations experienced in *delirium tremens*.

kept my eyes on him steady. It was getting grey daylight now. Pretty soon he gapped and stretched himself and hove off the blanket, and it was Miss Watson's Jim! I bet I was glad to see him. I says:

"Hello, Jim!" and skipped out.

He bounced up and stared at me wild. Then he drops down on his knees, and puts his hands together and says:

"Doan' hurt me—don't! I hain't ever done no harm to a ghos'. I alwuz liked dead people, en done all I could for 'em. You go en git in de river agin, whah you b'longs, en doan' do nuffn to Ole Jim, 'at 'uz awluz yo' fren'."

Jim and the Ghost

Well, I warn't long making him understand I warn't dead. I was ever so glad to see Jim. I warn't lonesome now. I told him I warn't afraid of *him* telling the people where I was. I talked along, but he only set there and looked at me; never said nothing. Then I says:

"It's good daylight. Le's get breakfast. Make up your camp fire good."

"What's de use er makin' up de camp fire to cook strawbries en sich truck? But you got a gun, hain't you? Den we kin git sumfn better den strawbries."

"Strawberries and such truck," I says. "Is that what you live on?"

"I couldn' git nuffn else," he says.

"Why, how long you been on the island, Jim?"

"I come heah de night arter you's killed."

"What, all that time?"

"Yes—indeedy."

"And ain't you had nothing but that kind of rubbage to eat?"

"No, sah—nuffn else."

"Well, you must be most starved, ain't you?"

"I reck'n I could eat a hoss. I think I could. How long you ben on de islan'?"

"Since the night I got killed."

"No! W'y, what has you lived on? But you got a gun. Oh, yes, you got a gun. Dat's good. Now you kill sumfn en I'll make up de fire."

So we went over to where the canoe was, and while he built a fire in a grassy open place amongst the trees, I fetched meal and bacon and coffee, and coffee-pot and frying pan, and sugar and tin cups, and the nigger was set back considerable, because he reckoned it was all done with witchcraft. I catched a good big catfish, too, and Jim cleaned him with his knife, and fried him.

When breakfast was ready we lolled on the grass and eat it smoking hot. Jim laid it in with all his might, for he was most about starved. Then when we had got pretty well stuffed, we laid off and lazied.

By and by Jim says:

"But looky here, Huck, who wuz it dat 'uz killed in dat shanty ef it warn't you?"

Then I told him the whole thing, and he said it was smart. He said Tom Sawyer couldn't get up no better plan than what I had. Then I says:

"How do you come to be here, Jim, and how'd you get here?" He looked pretty uneasy, and didn't say nothing for a minute. Then he says:

"Maybe I better not tell."

"Why, Jim?"

"Well, dey's reasons. But you wouldn' tell on me ef I uz to tell you, would you, Huck?"

"Blamed if I would, Jim."

"Well, I b'lieve you, Huck. I—*I run off*."

"Jim!"

"But mind, you said you wouldn' tell—you know you said you wouldn' tell, Huck."

"Well, I did. I said I wouldn't, and I'll stick to it. Honest *injun*, I will. People would call me a low-down Abolitionist and despise me for keeping mum—but that don't make no difference. I ain't a-going to tell, and I ain't a-going back there, anyways. So, now, le's know all about it."

"Well, you see, it 'uz dis way. Ole missus—dat's Miss Watson—she pecks on me all de time, en treats me pooty rough, but she awluz said she wouldn' sell me down to Orleans. But I noticed dey wuz a nigger trader roun' de place considable lately, en I begin to git oneasy. Well, one night I creeps to de do' pooty late, en de do' warn't quite shet, en I hear old missus tell de widder she gwyne to sell me down to Orleans, but she didn' want to, but she could git eight hund'd dollars for me, en it 'uz sich a big stack o' money she couldn' resis'. De widder she try to git her to say she wouldn' do it, but I never waited to hear de res'. I lit out mighty quick, I tell you.

"I tuck out en shin down de hill, en 'spec to steal a skift 'long de sho' som'ers 'bove de town, but dey wuz people a-stirring yit, so I hid in de ole tumble-down cooper-shop on de bank to wait for everybody to go 'way. Well, I wuz dah all night. Dey wuz somebody roun' all de time. 'Long 'bout six in de mawnin' skifts begin to go by, en 'bout eight er nine every skift dat went 'long wuz talkin' 'bout how yo' pap come over to de town en say you's killed. Dese las' skifts wuz full o' ladies en genlmen a-goin' over for to see de place. Sometimes dey'd pull up at de sho' en take a res' b'fo' dey started acrost, so by de talk I got to know all 'bout de killin'. I 'uz powerful sorry you's killed, Huck, but I ain't no mo' now.

"I laid dah under de shavin's all day. I 'uz hungry, but I warn't afeard; bekase I knowed ole missus en de widder wuz goin' to start to de camp-meet'n' right arter breakfas' en be gone all day, en dey knows I goes off wid de cattle 'bout daylight, so dey wouldn' 'spec to see me roun' de place, en so dey wouldn' miss me tell arter dark in de evenin'. De yuther servants wouldn' miss me, kase dey'd shin out en take holiday soon as de ole folks 'uz out'n de way.

"Well, when it come dark I tuck out up de river road, en went 'bout two mile er more to whah dey warn't no houses. I'd made up my mine 'bout what I's agwyne to do. You see, ef I kep' on tryin' to git away afoot, de dogs 'ud track me; ef I stole a skift to cross over, dey'd miss dat skift, you see, en dey'd know 'bout whah I'd lan' on de yuther side, en whah to pick up my track. So I says, a raff is what I's arter; it doan' *make* no track.

"I see a light a-comin' roun' de p'int bymeby, so I wade' in en shove' a log ahead o' me en swum more'n half way acrost de river, en got in 'mongst de drift-wood, en kep' my head down low, en kinder swum agin de current tell de raff come along. Den I swum to de stern uv it en tuck a-holt. It clouded up en 'uz pooty dark for a little while. So I clumb up en laid down on de planks. De men 'uz all 'way yonder in de middle, whah de lantern wuz. De river wuz a-risin', en dey wuz a good current; so I reck'n'd 'at by fo' in de mawnin' I'd be twenty-five mile down de river, en den I'd slip in jis b'fo' daylight en swim asho', en take to de woods on de Illinois side.

"But I didn' have no luck. When we 'uz mos' down to de head er de islan' a man begin to come aft wid de lantern, I see it warn't no use fer to wait, so I slid overboard en struck out fer de islan'. Well, I had a notion I could lan' mos' anywhers, but I couldn't—bank too bluff. I 'uz mos' to de foot er de islan' b'fo' I found' a good place. I went into de woods en jedged I wouldn' fool wid raffs no mo', long as dey move de lantern roun' so. I had my pipe en a plug er dog-leg,* en some matches in my cap, en dey warn't wet, so I 'uz all right."

"And so you ain't had no meat nor bread to eat all this time? Why didn't you get mud-turkles?"†

"How you gwyne to git 'm? You can't slip up on um en grab um; en how's a body gwyne to hit um wid a rock? How could a body do it in de night? En I warn't gwyne to show mysef on de bank in de daytime."

"Well, that's so. You've had to keep in the woods all the time, of course. Did you hear 'em shooting the cannon?"

"Oh, yes. I knowed dey was arter you. I see um go by heah—watched um thoo de bushes."

Some young birds come along, flying a yard or two at a time and lighting. Jim said it was a sign it was going to rain. He said it was a sign when young chickens flew that way, and so he reckoned it was the same way when young birds done it. I was going to catch some of them, but Jim wouldn't let me. He said it was death. He said his father laid mighty sick once, and some of them catched a bird, and his old granny said his father would die, and he did.

And Jim said you mustn't count the things you are going to cook for dinner, because that would bring bad luck. The same if you shook the tablecloth after sundown. And he said if a man owned a beehive and that man died, the bees must be told about it before sun-up next morning, or else the bees would all weaken down and quit work and die. Jim said bees wouldn't sting idiots; but I didn't believe that, because I had tried them lots of times myself, and they wouldn't sting me.

I had heard about some of these things before, but not all of them. Jim knowed all kinds of signs. He said he knowed most everything. I said it looked to me like all the signs was about bad luck, and so I asked him if there warn't any good-luck signs. He says:

"Mighty few—an' *dey* ain't no use to a body. What you want to know when good luck's a-comin' for? Want to keep it off?" And he said: "Ef you's got hairy arms en a hairy breas', it's a sign dat you's agwyne to be rich. Well, dey's some use in a sign like dat, 'kase it's so fur ahead. You see, maybe you's got to be po' a long time fust, en so you might git discourage' en kill yo'sef 'f you didn' know by de sign dat you gwyne to be rich bymeby."

* Slang for cheap tabacco.

† Mud-turtles.

"Have you got hairy arms and a hairy breast, Jim?"

"What's de use to ax dat question? Don't you see I has?"

"Well, are you rich?"

"No, but I ben rich wunst, and gwyne to be rich agin. Wunst I had foteen dollars, but I tuck to specalat'n', en got busted out."

"What did you speculate in, Jim?"

"Well, fust I tackled stock."

"What kind of stock?"

"Why, live stock—cattle, you know. I put ten dollars in a cow. But I ain' gwyne to resk no mo' money in stock. De cow up 'n' died on my han's."

"So you lost the ten dollars."

"No, I didn't lose it all. I on'y los' 'bout nine of it. I sole de hide en taller* for a dollar en ten cents."

"You had five dollars and ten cents left. Did you speculate any more?"

"Yes. You know that one-laigged nigger dat b'longs to old Misto Bradish? Well, he sot up a bank, en say anybody dat put in a dollar would git fo' dollars mo' at de en' er de year. Well, all de niggers went in, but dey didn't have much. I wuz de on'y one dat had much. So I stuck out for mo' dan fo' dollars, en I said 'f I didn' git it I'd start a bank mysef. Well, o' course dat nigger want' to keep me out er de business, bekase he says dey warn't business 'nough for two banks, so he say I could put in my five dollars en he pay me thirty-five at de en' er de year.

"So I done it. Den I reck'n'd I'd inves' de thirty-five dollars right off en keep things a-movin'. Dey wuz a nigger name' Bob, dat had ketched a wood-flat,† en his marster didn' know it; en I bought it off'n him en told him to take de thirty-five dollars when de en' er de year come; but somebody stole de wood-flat dat night, en nex day de one-laigged nigger say de bank's busted. So dey didn' none uv us git no money."

"What did you do with the ten cents, Jim?"

"Well, I 'uz gwyne to spen' it, but I had a dream, en de dream tole me to give it to a nigger name' Balum—Balum's Ass dey call him for short; he's one er dem chuckleheads, you know. But he's lucky, dey say, en I see I warn't lucky. De dream say let Balum inves' de ten cents en he'd make a raise for me. Well, Balum he tuck de money, en when he wuz in church he hear de preacher say dat whoever give to de po' len' to de Lord, en boun' to git his money back a hund'd times. So Balum he tuck en give de ten cents to de po', en laid low to see what wuz gwyne to come of it."

---

* Tallow, i.e. the fat of an animal.

† A flat-bottomed boat for transporting wood.

"Well, what did come of it, Jim?"

"Nuffn never come of it. I couldn' manage to k'leck dat money no way; en Balum he couldn'. I ain' gwyne to len' no mo' money 'dout I see de security. Boun' to git yo' money back a hund'd times, de preacher says! Ef I could git de ten *cents* back, I'd call it squah, en be glad er de chanst."

"Well, it's all right anyway, Jim, long as you're going to be rich again some time or other."

"Yes; en I's rich now, come to look at it. I owns mysef, en I's wuth eight hund'd dollars. I wisht I had de money, I wouldn' want no mo'."

9

I wanted to go and look at a place right about the middle of the island that I'd found when I was exploring; so we started and soon got to it, because the island was only three miles long and a quarter of a mile wide.

This place was a tolerable long, steep hill or ridge about forty foot high. We had a rough time getting to the top, the sides was so steep and the bushes so thick. We tramped and clumb around all over it, and by and by found a good big cavern in the rock, most up to the top on the side towards Illinois. The cavern was as big as two or three rooms bunched together, and Jim could stand up straight in it. It was cool in there. Jim was for putting our traps in there right away, but I said we didn't want to be climbing up and down there all the time.

Jim said if we had the canoe hid in a good place, and had all the traps in the cavern, we could rush there if anybody was to come to the island, and they would never find us without dogs. And, besides, he said them little birds had said it was going to rain, and did I want the things to get wet?

So we went back and got the canoe, and paddled up abreast the cavern, and lugged all the traps up there. Then we hunted up a place close by to hide the canoe in, amongst the thick willows. We took some fish off of the lines and set them again, and begun to get ready for dinner.

The door of the cavern was big enough to roll a hogshead in, and on one side of the door the floor stuck out a little bit, and was flat and a good place to build a fire on. So we built it there and cooked dinner.

We spread the blankets inside for a carpet, and eat our dinner in there.

We put all the other things handy at the back of the cavern. Pretty soon it darkened up, and begun to thunder and lighten; so the birds was right about it. Directly it begun to rain, and it rained like all fury, too, and I never see the wind blow so. It was one of these regular summer storms. It would get so dark that it looked all blue-black outside, and lovely; and the rain would thrash along by so thick that the trees off a little ways looked dim and spider-webby; and here would come a blast of wind that would bend the trees down and turn up the pale underside of the leaves; and then a perfect ripper of a gust would follow along and set the branches to tossing their arms as if they was just wild; and next, when it was just about the bluest and blackest—*FST*! it was as bright as glory, and you'd have a little glimpse of tree-tops a-plunging about away off yonder in the storm, hundreds of yards further than you could see before; dark as sin again in a second, and now you'd hear the thunder let go with an awful crash, and then go rumbling, grumbling, tumbling, down the sky towards the under side of the world, like rolling empty barrels down stairs—where it's long stairs and they bounce a good deal, you know.

"Jim, this is nice," I says. "I wouldn't want to be nowhere else but here. Pass me along another hunk of fish and some hot corn-bread."

"Well, you wouldn't a ben here 'f it hadn't a ben for Jim. You'd a ben down dah in de woods widout any dinner, en gittn' mos' drownded, too; dat you would, honey. Chickens knows when it's gwyne to rain, en so do de birds, chile."

The river went on raising and raising for ten or twelve days, till at last it was over the banks. The water was three or four foot deep on the island in the low places and on the Illinois bottom. On that side it was a good many miles wide, but on the Missouri side it was the same old distance across—a half a mile—because the Missouri shore was just a wall of high bluffs.

Daytimes we paddled all over the island in the canoe, It was mighty cool and shady in the deep woods, even if the sun was blazing outside. We went winding in and out amongst the trees, and sometimes the vines hung so thick we had to back away and go some other way. Well, on every old broken-down tree you could see rabbits and snakes and such things; and when the island had been overflowed a day or two they got so tame, on account of being hungry, that you could paddle right up and put your hand on them if you wanted to; but not the snakes and turtles—they would slide off in the water. The ridge our cavern was in was full of them. We could a had pets enough if we'd wanted them.

One night we catched a little section of a lumber raft—nice pine planks. It was twelve foot wide and about fifteen or sixteen foot long, and the top stood above water six or seven inches—a solid, level floor. We could see saw-logs go by in the daylight sometimes, but we let them go; we didn't show ourselves in daylight.

Another night when we was up at the head of the island, just before daylight, here comes a frame-house down, on the west side. She was a two-storey, and tilted over considerable. We paddled out and got aboard—clumb in at an upstairs window. But it was too dark to see yet, so we made the canoe fast and set in her to wait for daylight.

The light begun to come before we got to the foot of the island. Then we looked in at the window. We could make out a bed, and a table, and two old chairs, and lots of things around about on the floor, and there was clothes hanging against the wall. There was something laying on the floor in the far corner that looked like a man. So Jim says:

"Hello, you!"

But it didn't budge. So I hollered again, and then Jim says:

"De man ain't asleep—he's dead. You hold still—I'll go en see."

He went, and bent down and looked, and says:

"It's a dead man. Yes, indeedy; naked, too. He's ben shot in de back. I reck'n he's ben dead two er three days. Come in, Huck, but doan' look at his face—it's too gashly."

Jim sees a Dead Man

I didn't look at him at all. Jim throwed some old rags over him, but he needn't done it; I didn't want to see him. There was heaps of old greasy cards scattered around over the floor, and old whisky bottles, and a couple of masks made out of black cloth; and all over the walls was the ignorantest kind of words and pictures made with charcoal. There was two old dirty calico dresses, and a sun-bonnet, and some women's underclothes hanging against the wall, and some men's clothing, too. We put the lot into the canoe—it might come good. There was a boy's old speckled straw hat on the floor; I took that, too. And there was a bottle that had had milk in it, and it had a rag stopper for a baby to suck. We would a took the bottle, but it was broke. There was a seedy old chest, and an old hair trunk with the hinges broke. They stood open, but there warn't nothing left in them that was any account. The way things was scattered about we reckoned the people left in a hurry, and warn't fixed so as to carry off most of their stuff.

We got an old tin lantern, and a butcher-knife without any handle, and a bran-new Barlow knife* worth two bits in any store, and a lot of tallow candles, and a tin candlestick, and a gourd, and a tin cup, and a ratty old bed-quilt off the bed, and a reticule with needles and pins and beeswax and buttons and thread and all such truck in it, and a hatchet and some nails, and a fishline as thick as my little finger with some monstrous hooks on it, and a roll of buckskin, and a leather dog-collar, and a horseshoe, and some vials of medicine that didn't have no label on them; and just as we was leaving I found a tolerable good curry-comb, and Jim he found a ratty old fiddle-bow, and a wooden leg. The straps was broke off of it, but, barring that, it was a good enough leg, though it was too long for me and not long enough for Jim, and we couldn't find the other one, though we hunted all around.

And so, take it all around, we made a good haul. When we was ready to shove off we was a quarter of a mile below the island, and it was pretty broad day; so I made Jim lay down in the canoe and cover up with the quilt, because if he set up people could tell he was a nigger a good ways off. I paddled over to the Illinois shore, and drifted down most a half a mile doing it. I crept up the dead water under the bank, and hadn't no accidents and didn't see nobody. We got home all safe.

* A jack-knife with only one blade, named after maker.

10

After breakfast I wanted to talk about the dead man and guess out how he come to be killed, but Jim didn't want to. He said it would fetch bad luck; and besides, he said, he might come and ha'nt us; he said a man that warn't buried was more likely to go a-ha'nting around than one that was planted and comfortable. That sounded pretty reasonable, so I didn't say no more; but I couldn't keep from studying over it and wishing I knowed who shot the man, and what they done it for.

We rummaged the clothes we'd got, and found eight dollars in silver sewed up in the lining of an old blanket overcoat. Jim said he reckoned the people in that house stole the coat, because if they'd a knowed the money was there they wouldn't a left it. I said I reckoned they killed him, too; but Jim didn't want to talk about that. I says:

"Now you think it's bad luck; but what did you say when I fetched in the snake-skin that I found on the top of the ridge day before yesterday? You said it was the worst bad luck in the world to touch a snake-skin with my hands. Well, here's your bad luck! We've raked in all this truck and eight dollars besides. I wish we could have some bad luck like this every day, Jim."

"Never you mind, honey, never you mind. Don't you git too peart. It's a-comin'. Mind I tell you, it's a-comin'."

It did come, too. It was a Tuesday that we had that talk. Well, after dinner Friday we was laying around in the grass at the upper end of the ridge, and got out of tobacco. I went to the cavern to get some, and found a rattlesnake in there. I killed him, and curled him up on the foot of Jim's blanket, ever so natural, thinking there'd be some fun when Jim found him there. Well, by night I forgot all about the snake, and when Jim flung himself down on the blanket while I struck a light the snake's mate was there, and bit him.

He jumped up yelling, and the first thing the light showed was the varmint curled up and ready for another spring. I laid him out in a second with a stick, and Jim grabbed pap's whisky-jug and begun to pour it down.

He was barefooted, and the snake bit him right on the heel. That all comes of my being such a fool as to not remember that wherever you leave a dead snake its mate always comes there and curls around it. Jim told me to chop off the snake's head and throw it away, and then skin the body and roast a piece of it. I done it, and he eat it and said it would help cure him. He made me take off the rattles and tie them around his wrist, too. He said that that would help. Then I slid out quiet and throwed the snakes clear away amongst the bushes; for I warn't going to let Jim find out it was all my fault, not if I could help it.

Jim sucked and sucked at the jug, and now and then he got out of his head and pitched around and yelled; but every time he come to himself he went to sucking at the jug again. His foot swelled up pretty big, and so did his leg; but by and by the drunk begun to come, and so I judged he was all right; but I'd druther been bit with a snake than pap's whisky.

Jim was laid up for four days and nights. Then the swelling was all gone and he was around again. I made up my mind I wouldn't ever take a-holt of a snake-skin again with my hands, now that I see what had come of it. Jim said he reckoned I would believe him next time. And he said that handling a snake-skin was such awful bad luck that maybe we hadn't got to the end of it yet. He said he druther see the new moon over his left shoulder as much as a thousand times than take up a snake-skin in his hand. Well, I was getting to feel that way myself, though I've always reckoned that looking at the new moon over your left shoulder is one of the carelessest and foolishest things a body can do. Old Hank Bunker done it once, and bragged about it; and in less than two years he got drunk and fell off of the shot-tower, and spread himself out so that he was just a kind of a layer, as you may say; and they slid him edgeways between two barn doors for a coffin, and buried him so, so they say, but I didn't see it. Pap told me. But anyway it all come of looking at the moon that way, like a fool.

Well, the days went along, and the river went down between its banks again; and about the first thing we done was to bait one of the big hooks with a skinned rabbit and set it and catch a catfish that was as big as a man, being six foot two inches long, and weighed over two hundred pounds. We couldn't handle him, of course; he would a flung us into Illinois. We just set there and watched him rip and tear around till he drownded. We found a brass button in his stomach and a round ball, and lots of rubbage. We split the ball open with the hatchet, and there was a spool in it. Jim said he'd had it there a long time, to coat it over so and make a ball of it. It was as big a fish as was ever catched in the Mississippi, I reckon. Jim said he hadn't ever seen a bigger one. He would a been worth a good deal over at the village. They peddle out such a fish as that by the pound in the market-house there; everybody buys some of him; his meat's as white as snow and makes a good fry.

Next morning I said it was getting slow and dull, and I wanted to get a stirring up some way. I said I reckoned I would slip over the river and find out what was going on. Jim liked that notion; but he said I must go in the dark and look sharp. Then he studied it over and said, couldn't I put on some of them old things and dress up like a girl? That was a good notion, too. So we shortened up one of the calico gowns, and I turned up my trouser-legs to my knees and got into it. Jim hitched it behind with the hooks, and it was a fair fit. I put on the sun-bonnet and tied it under my chin, and then for a body to look in and see my face was like looking down a joint of stove-pipe. Jim said nobody would know me, even in the daytime, hardly. I practiced around all day to get the hang of the things, and by and by I could do pretty well in them, only Jim said I didn't walk like a girl; and he said I must quit pulling up my gown to get at my britches-pocket. I took notice, and done better.

"A Fair Fit"

I started up the Illinois shore in the canoe just after dark.

I started across to the town from a little below the ferry-landing, and the drift of the current fetched me in at the bottom of the town. I tied up and started along the bank. There was a light burning in a little shanty that hadn't been lived in for a long time, and I wondered who had took up quarters there. I slipped up and peeped in at the window. There was a woman about forty year old in there knitting by a candle that was on a pine table. I didn't know her face; she was a stranger, for you couldn't start a face in that town that I didn't know. Now this was lucky, because I was weakening; I was getting afraid I had come; people might know my voice and find me out. But if this woman had been in such a little town two days she could tell me all I wanted to know; so I knocked at the door, and made up my mind I wouldn't forget I was a girl.

11

"Come in," says the woman, and I did. She says:

"Take a cheer."

I done it. She looked me all over with her little shiny eyes, and says:

"What might your name be?"

"Sarah Williams."

"Where 'bouts do you live? In this neighbourhood?'

"No'm. In Hookerville, seven mile below. I've walked all the way and I'm all tired out."

"Hungry, too, I reckon. I'll find you something."

"No'm, I ain't hungry. I was so hungry I had to stop two miles below here at a farm; so I ain't hungry no more. It's what makes me so late. My mother's down sick, and out of money and everything, and I come to tell my uncle Abner Moore. He lives at the upper end of the town, she says. I hain't ever been here before. Do you know him?"

"No; but I don't know everybody yet. I haven't lived here quite two weeks. It's a considerable ways to the upper end of the town. You better stay here all night. Take off your bonnet."

"No," I says; "I'll rest a while, I reckon, and go on. I ain't afeared of the dark."

She said she wouldn't let me go by myself, but her husband would be in by and by, maybe in a hour and a half, and she'd send him along with me. Then she got to talking about her husband, and about her relations up the river, and her relations down the river, and about how much better off they used to was, and how they didn't know but they'd made a mistake coming to our town, instead of letting well alone—and so on and so on, till I was afeard I had made a mistake coming to her to find out what was going on in the town; but by and by she dropped on to pap and the murder, and then I was pretty willing to let her clatter right along. She told about me and Tom Sawyer finding the six thousand dollars (only she got it ten) and all about pap and what a hard lot he was, and what a hard lot I was, and at last she got down to where I was murdered. I says:

"Who done it? We've heard considerable about these goings on down in Hookerville, but we don't know who 'twas that killed Huck Finn."

"Well, I reckon there's a right smart chance of people *here* that'd like to know who killed him. Some think old Finn done it himself."

"No—is that so?"

"Most everybody thought it at first. He'll never know how nigh he come to getting lynched. But before night they changed around and judged it was done by a runaway nigger named Jim."

"Why *he*—"

I stopped. I reckoned I better keep still. She run on, and never noticed I had put in at all:

"The nigger run off the very night Huck Finn was killed. So there's a reward out for him—three hundred dollars. And there's a reward out for old Finn, too—two hundred dollars. You see, he come to town the morning after the murder, and told about it, and was out with 'em on the ferryboat hunt, and right away after he up and left. Before night they wanted to lynch him, but he was gone, you see. Well, next day they found out the nigger was gone; they found out he hadn't ben seen sence ten o'clock the night the murder was done. So then they put it on him, you see; and while they was full of it, next day, back comes old Finn, and went boo-hooing to Judge Thatcher to get money to hunt for the nigger all over Illinois with. The judge gave him some, and that evening he got drunk, and was around till after midnight with a couple of mighty hard-looking strangers, and then went off with them. Well, he hain't come back sence, and they ain't looking for him back till this thing blows over a little, for people thinks now that he killed his boy and fixed things so folks would think robbers done it, and then he'd get Huck's money without having to bother a long time with a lawsuit. People do say he warn't any too good to do it. Oh, he's sly, I reckon. If he don't come back for a year he'll be all right. You can't prove anything on him, you know; everything will be quieted down then, and he'll walk in Huck's money as easy as nothing."

"Yes, I reckon so, 'm. I don't see nothing in the way of it. Has everybody quit thinking the nigger done it?"

"Oh, no, not everybody. A good many thinks he done it. But they'll get the nigger pretty soon now, and maybe they can scare it out of him."

"Why, are they after him yet?"

"Well, you're innocent, ain't you! Does three hundred dollars lay around every day for people to pick up? Some folks think the nigger ain't far from here. I'm one of them—but I hain't talked it around. A few days ago I was talking with an old couple that lives next door in the log shanty, and they happened to say hardly anybody ever goes to that island over yonder that they call Jackson's Island. Don't anybody live there? says I. No, nobody, says they. I didn't say any more, but I done some thinking. I was pretty near certain I'd seen smoke over there, about the head of the island, a day or two before that, so I says to myself, like as not that nigger's hiding over there; anyway, says I, it's worth the trouble to give the place a hunt. I hain't seen any smoke sence, so I reckon maybe he's gone, if it was him; but husband's going over to see—him and another man. He was gone up the river; but he got back today, and I told him as soon as he got here two hours ago."

I had got so uneasy I couldn't set still. I had to do something with my hands; so I took up a needle off of the table and went to threading it. My hands shook, and I was making a bad job of it. When the woman stopped talking I looked up, and she was looking at me pretty curious and smiling a little. I put down the needle and thread, and let on to be interested—and I was, too—and says:

"Three hundred dollars is a power of money. I wish my mother could get it. Is your husband going over there tonight?"

"Oh, yes. He went up-town with the man I was telling you of, to get a boat and see if they could borrow another gun. They'll go over after midnight."

"Couldn't they see better if they was to wait till daytime?"

"Yes. And couldn't the nigger see better, too? After midnight he'll likely be asleep, and they can slip around through the woods and hunt up his camp fire all the better for the dark, if he's got one."

"I didn't think of that."

The woman kept looking at me pretty curious, and I didn't feel a bit comfortable. Pretty soon she says:

"What did you say your name was, honey?"

"M—Mary Williams."

Somehow it didn't seem to me that I said it was Mary before, so I didn't look up—seemed to me I said it was Sarah; so I felt sort of cornered, and was afeared maybe I was looking it, too. I wished the woman would say something more; the longer she set still the uneasier I was. But now she says:

"Honey, I thought you said it was Sarah when you first come in?"

"Oh, yes'm, I did. Sarah Mary Williams. Sarah's my first name. Some calls me Sarah, some calls me Mary."

"Oh, that's the way of it?"

"Yes'm."

I was feeling better then, but I wished I was out of there, anyway. I couldn't look up yet.

Well, the woman fell to talking about how hard times was, and how poor they had to live, and how the rats was as free as if they owned the place, and so forth and so on, and then I got easy again. She was right about the rats. You'd see one stick his nose out of a hole in the corner every little while. She said she had to have things handy to throw at them when she was alone, or they wouldn't give her no peace. She showed me a bar of lead twisted up into a knot, and said she was a good shot with it generally, but she'd wrenched her arm a day or two ago, and didn't know whether she could throw true now. But she watched for a chance, and directly banged away at a rat; but she missed him wide, and said "Ouch!" it hurt her arm so. Then she told me to try for the next one. I wanted to be getting away before the old man got back, but of course I didn't let on. I got the thing, and the first rat that showed his nose I let drive, and if he'd a stayed where he was he'd a been a tolerable sick rat. She said that was first-rate, and she reckoned I would hive the next one. She went and got the lump of lead and fetched it back, and brought along a hank of yarn which she wanted me to help her with. I held up my two hands and she put the hank over them, and went on talking about her and her husband's matters. But she broke off to say:

"Keep your eye on the rats. You better have the lead in your lap, handy."

So she dropped the lump into my lap just at that moment, and I clapped my legs together on it and she went on talking. But only about a minute. Then she took off the hank and looked me straight in the face, and very pleasant, and says:

"Come, now, what's your real name?"

"Wh—what, mum?"

"What's your real name? Is it Bill, or Tom, or Bob?—or what is it?"

I reckon I shook like a leaf, and I didn't know hardly what to do. But I says:

"Please to don't poke fun at a poor girl like me, mum. If I'm in the way here, I'll—"

"No, you won't. Set down and stay where you are. I ain't going to hurt you, and I ain't going to tell on you, nuther. You just tell me your secret, and trust me. I'll keep it; and, what's more, I'll help you. So'll my old man if you want him to. You see, you're a runaway 'prentice, that's all. It ain't anything. There ain't no harm in it. You've been treated bad, and you made up your mind to cut. Bless you, child, I wouldn't tell on you. Tell me all about it now, that's a good boy."

So I said it wouldn't be no use to try to play it any longer, and I would just make a clean breast and tell her everything, but she musn't go back on her promise. Then I told her my father and mother was dead, and the law had bound me out to a mean old farmer in the country thirty mile back from the river, and he treated me so bad I couldn't stand it no longer; he went away to be gone a couple of days, and so I took my chance and stole some of his daughter's old clothes and cleared out, and I had been three nights coming the thirty miles. I traveled nights, and hid daytimes and slept, and the bag of bread and meat I carried from home lasted me all the way, and I had a-plenty. I said I believed my uncle Abner Moore would take care of me, and so that was why I struck out for this town of Goshen.

"Goshen, child? This ain't Goshen. This is St. Petersburg. Goshen's ten mile further up the river. Who told you this was Goshen?"

"Why, a man I met at daybreak this morning, just as I was going to turn into the woods for my regular sleep. He told me when the roads forked I must take the right hand, and five mile would fetch me to Goshen."

"He was drunk, I reckon. He told you just exactly wrong."

"Well, he did act like he was drunk, but it ain't no matter now. I got to be moving along. I'll fetch Goshen before daylight."

"Hold on a minute. I'll put you up a snack to eat. You might want it."

So she put me up a snack, and says:

"Say, when a cow's laying down, which end of her gets up first? Answer up prompt now—don't stop to study over it. Which end gets up first?"

"The hind end, mum."

"Well, then, a horse?"

"The for'rard end, mum."

"Which side of a tree does the moss grow on?"

"North side."

"If fifteen cows is browsing on a hillside, how many of them eats with their heads pointed the same direction?"

"The whole fifteen, mum."

"Well, I reckon you *have* lived in the country. I thought maybe you was trying to hocus me again. What's your real name, now?"

"George Peters, mum."

"Well, try to remember it, George. Don't forget and tell me it's Elexander before you go, and then get out by saying it's George Elexander when I catch you. And don't go about women in that old calico. You do a girl tolerable poor, but you might fool men, maybe. Bless you, child, when you set out to thread a needle don't hold the thread still and fetch the needle up to it; hold the needle still and poke the thread at it; that's the way a woman most always does, but a man always does t'other way. And when you throw at a rat or anything, hitch yourself up a tiptoe and fetch your hand up over your head as awkward as you can, and miss your rat about six or seven foot. Throw stiff-armed from the shoulder, like there was a pivot there for it to turn on, like a girl; not from the wrist and elbow, with your arm out to one side, like a boy.

And, mind you, when a girl tries to catch anything in her lap she throws her knees apart; she don't clap them together, the way you did when you catched the lump of lead. Why, I spotted you for a boy when you was threading the needle; and I contrived the other things just to make certain. Now trot along to your uncle, Sarah Mary Williams George Elexander Peters, and if you get into trouble you send word to Mrs. Judith Loftus, which is me, and I'll do what I can to get you out of it. Keep the river road all the way, and next time you tramp take shoes and socks with you. The river road's a rocky one, and your feet'll be in a condition when you get to Goshen, I reckon."

I went up the bank about fifty yards, and then I doubled on my tracks and slipped back to where my canoe was, a good piece below the house. I jumped in, and was off in a hurry. I went up-stream far enough to make the head of the island, and then started across. I took off the sun-bonnet, for I didn't want no blinders on then. When I was about the middle I heard the clock begin to strike, so I stops and listens; the sound come faint over the water but clear—eleven. When I struck the head of the island I never waited to blow, though I was most winded, but I shoved right into the timber where my old camp used to be, and started a good fire there on a high and dry spot.

Then I jumped in the canoe and dug out for our place, a mile and a half below, as hard as I could go. I landed, and slopped through the timber and up the ridge and into the cavern. There Jim laid, sound asleep on the ground. I roused him out and says:

"Git up and hump yourself, Jim! There ain't a minute to lose. They're after us!"

Jim never asked no questions, he never said a word; but the way he worked for the next half an hour showed about how he was scared. By that time everything we had in the world was on our raft, and she was ready to be shoved out from the willow cove where she was hid. We put out the camp fire at the cavern the first thing, and didn't show a candle outside after that.

I took the canoe out from the shore a little piece, and took a look; but if there was a boat around I couldn't see it, for stars and shadows ain't good to see by. Then we got out the raft and slipped along down in the shade, past the foot of the island dead still—never saying a word.

12

It must a been close on to one o'clock when we got below the island at last, and the raft did seem to go mighty slow. If a boat was to come along we was going to take to the canoe and break for the Illinois shore; and it was well a boat didn't come, for we hadn't ever thought to put the gun in the canoe, or a fishing-line, or anything to eat. We was in ruther too much of a sweat to think of so many things. It warn't good judgment to put *everything* on the raft.

If the men went to the island I just expect they found the camp fire I built, and watched it all night for Jim to come. Anyways, they stayed away from us, and if my building the fire never fooled them it warn't no fault of mine. I played it as low down on them as I could.

When the first streak of day began to show we tied up to a towhead in a big bend on the Illinois side, and hacked off cottonwood branches with the hatchet, and covered up the raft with them so she looked like there had been a cave-in in the bank there. A tow-head is a sandbar that has cottonwoods on it as thick as harrow-teeth.

We had mountains on the Missouri shore and heavy timber on the Illinois side, and the channel was down the Missouri shore at that place, so we warn't afraid of anybody running across us. We laid there all day, and watched the rafts and steamboats spin down the Missouri shore, and up-bound steamboats fight the big river in the middle. I told Jim all about the time I had jabbering with that woman; and Jim said she was a smart one, and if she was to start after us herself she wouldn't set down and watch a camp fire—no, sir, she'd fetch a dog. Well, then, I said, why couldn't she tell her husband to fetch a dog? Jim said he bet she did think of it by the time the men was ready to start, and he believed they must a gone up-town to get a dog and so they lost all that time, or else we wouldn't be here on a towhead sixteen or seventeen mile below the village—no, indeedy, we would be in that same old town again. So I said I didn't care what was the reason they didn't get us as long as they didn't.

When it was beginning to come on dark we poked our heads out of the cottonwood thicket, and looked up and down and across; nothing in sight; so Jim took up some of the top planks of the raft and built a snug wigwam to get under in blazing weather and rainy, and to keep the things dry. Jim made a floor for the wigwam, and raised it a foot or more above the level of the raft, so now the blankets and all the traps was out of reach of steamboat waves. Right in the middle of the wigwam we made a layer of dirt about five or six inches deep with a frame around it for to hold it to its place; this was to build a fire on in sloppy weather or chilly; the wigwam would keep it from being seen. We made an extra steering-oar, too, because one of the others might get broke on a snag or something. We fixed up a short forked stick to hang the old lantern on, because we must always light the lantern whenever we see a steamboat coming down-stream, to keep from getting run over; but we wouldn't have to light it for up-stream boats unless we see we was in what they call a "crossing"; for the river was pretty high yet, very low banks being still a little under water; so up-bound boats didn't always run the channel, but hunted easy water.

This second night we run between seven and eight hours, with a current that was making over four mile an hour. We catched fish and talked, and we took a swim now and then to keep off sleepiness. It was kind of solemn, drifting down the big, still river, laying on our backs looking up at the stars, and we didn't ever feel like talking loud, and it warn't often that we laughed—only a little kind of a low chuckle. We had mighty good weather as a general thing, and nothing ever happened to us at all—that night, nor the next, nor the next.

Every night we passed towns, some of them away up on black hillsides, nothing but just a shiny bed of lights; not a house could you see. The fifth night we passed St. Louis, and it was like the whole world lit up. In St. Petersburg they used to say there was twenty or thirty thousand people in St. Louis, but I never believed it till I see that wonderful spread of lights at two o'clock that still night. There warn't a sound there; everybody was asleep.

Every night now I used to slip ashore towards ten o'clock at some little village, and buy ten or fifteen cents' worth of meal or bacon or other stuff to eat; and sometimes I lifted a chicken that warn't roosting comfortable, and took him along. Pap always said, take a chicken when you get a chance, because if you don't want him yourself you can easy find somebody that does, and a good deed ain't ever forgot. I never see pap when he didn't want the chicken himself, but that is what he used to say, anyway.

Mornings before daylight I slipped into cornfields and borrowed a watermelon, or a mushmelon, or a punkin, or some new corn, or things of that kind. Pap always said it warn't no harm to borrow things if you was meaning to pay them back some time; but the widow said it warn't anything but a soft name for stealing, and no decent body would do it. Jim said he reckoned the widow was partly right and pap was partly right; so the best way would be for us to pick out two or three things from the list and say we wouldn't borrow them any more—then he reckoned it wouldn't be no harm to borrow the others. So we talked it over all one night, drifting along down the river, trying to make up our minds whether to drop the watermelons, or the cantelopes, or the mushmelons, or what. But towards daylight we got it all settled satisfactory, and concluded to drop crabapples and p'simmons.* We warn't feeling just right before that, but it was all comfortable now. I was glad the way it come out, too, because crabapples ain't ever good, and the p'simmons wouldn't be ripe for two or three months yet.

We shot a water-fowl now and then that got up too early in the morning or didn't go to bed early enough in the evening. Take it all round, we lived pretty high.

The fifth night below St. Louis we had a big storm after midnight, with a power of thunder and lightning, and the rain poured down in a solid sheet. We stayed in the wigwam and let the raft take care of itself. When the lightning glared out we could see a big straight river ahead, and high, rocky bluffs on both sides. By and by says I, "Hel-*lo*, Jim, looky yonder!" It was a steamboat that had killed herself on a rock. We was drifting straight down for her. The lightning showed her very distinct. She was leaning over, with part of her upper deck above water, and you could see every little chimbly-guy clean and clear, and a chair by the big bell, with an old slouch hat hanging on the back of it, when the flashes come.

Well, it being away in the night and stormy, and all so mysterious-like, I felt just the way any other boy would a felt when I see that wreck laying there so mournful and lonesome in the middle of the river. I wanted to get aboard of her and slink around a little, and see what there was there. So I says:

"Le's land on her, Jim."

But Jim was dead against it at first. He says:

"I doan' want to go fool'n 'long er no wrack. We's doin' blame' well, en we better let blame' well alone, as de good book says. Like as not dey's a watchman on dat wrack."

"Watchman your grandmother," I says; "there ain't nothing to watch but the texas† and the pilot-house; and do you reckon anybody's going to resk his life for a texas and a pilot-house such a night as this, when it's likely to break up and wash off down the river any minute?" Jim couldn't say nothing to that, so he didn't try. "And besides," I says, "we might borrow something worth having out of the captain's stateroom. Seegars, I bet you—and cost five cents apiece, solid cash. Steamboat captains is always rich, and

* Persimmons, the fruit of the American Date-plum.

† The officers' cabin (the largest—hence 'texas') on the upper deck of a steamboat.

get sixty dollars a month, and *they* don't care a cent what a thing costs, you know, long as they want it. Stick a candle in your pocket; I can't rest, Jim, till we give her a rummaging. Do you reckon Tom Sawyer would ever go by this thing? Not for pie, he wouldn't. He'd call it an adventure—that's what he'd call it; and he'd land on that wreck if it was his last act. And wouldn't he throw style into it?—wouldn't he spread himself, nor nothing? Why, you'd think it was Christopher C'lumbus discovering Kingdom-Come. I wish Tom Sawyer *was* here."

Jim he grumbled a little, but give in. He said we mustn't talk any more than we could help, and then talk mighty low. The lightning showed us the wreck again just in time, and we fetched the stabboard derrick, and made fast there.

The deck was high out here. We went sneaking down the slope of it to labboard,* in the dark, towards the texas, feeling our way slow with our feet, and spreading our hands out to fend off the guys, for it was so dark we couldn't see no sign of them. Pretty soon we struck the forward end of the skylight, and clumb on to it; and the next step fetched us in front of the captain's door, which was open, and by Jimminy, away down through the texas-hall we see a light! and all in the same second we seem to hear low voices in yonder!

Jim whispered and said he was feeling powerful sick, and told me to come along. I says, all right, and was going to start for the raft; but just then I heard a voice wail out and say:

"Oh, please don't, boys; I swear I won't ever tell!"

Another voice said, pretty loud:

"It's a lie, Jim Turner. You've acted this way before. You always want more'n your share of the truck, and you've always got it, too, because you've swore 't if you didn't you'd tell. But this time you've said it jest one time too many. You're the meanest, treacherousest hound in this country."

By this time Jim was gone for the raft. I was just a-biling with curiosity; and I says to myself, Tom Sawyer wouldn't back out now, and so I won't either; I'm a-going to see what's going on here. So I dropped on my hands and knees in the little passage, and crept aft in the dark till there warn't but one stateroom betwixt me and the cross-hall of the texas. Then in there I see a man stretched on the floor and tied hand and foot, and two men standing over him, and one of them had a dim lantern in his hand, and the other one had a pistol. This one kept pointing the pistol at the man's head on the floor, and saying:

"I'd *like* to! And I orter, too—a mean skunk!"

* Larboard = port, i.e. left-hand of ship looking towards bows.

"Please don't, Bill"

The man on the floor would shrivel up and say, "Oh, please don't, Bill; I hain't ever goin' to tell."

And every time he said that the man with the lantern would laugh and say:

"'Deed you *ain't!* You never said no truer thing 'n that, you bet you." And once he said: "Hear him beg! and yit if we hadn't got the best of him and tied him he'd a killed us both. And what *for*? Jist for noth'n. Jist because we stood on our *rights*—that's what for. But I lay you ain't a-goin' to threaten nobody any more, Jim Turner. Put *up* that pistol, Bill."

Bill says:

"I don't want to, Jake Packard. I'm for killin' him—and didn't he kill old Hatfield jist the same way—and don't he deserve it?"

"But I don't *want* him killed, and I've got my reasons for it."

"Bless yo' heart for them words, Jake Packard! I'll never forgit you long's I live!" says the man on the floor, sort of blubbering.

Packard didn't take no notice of that, but hung up his lantern on a nail and started towards where I was there in the dark, and motioned Bill to come. I crawfished* as fast as I could about two yards, but the boat slanted so that I couldn't make very good time; so to keep from getting run over and catched I crawled into a stateroom on the upper side. The man came a-pawing along in the dark, and when Packard got to my stateroom, he says:

* Crawled backwards.

"Here—come in here."

And in he come, and Bill after him. But before they got in I was up in the upper berth, cornered, and sorry I come. Then they stood there, with their hands on the ledge of the berth, and talked. I couldn't see them, but I could tell where they was by the whisky they'd been having. I was glad I didn't drink whisky; but it wouldn't made much difference anyway, because most of the time they couldn't a treed* me because I didn't breathe. I was too scared. And, besides, a body *couldn't* breathe and hear such talk. They talked low and earnest. Bill wanted to kill Turner. He says:

"He's said he'll tell, and he will. If we was to give both our shares to him *now* it wouldn't make no difference after the row and the way we've served him. Shore's you're born, he'll turn State's evidence; now you hear *me*. I'm for putting him out of his troubles."

"So'm I," says Packard, very quiet.

"Blame it, I'd sorter begun to think you wasn't. Well, then, that's all right. Le's go and do it."

"Hold on a minute; I hain't had my say yit. You listen to me. Shooting's good, but there's quieter ways if the thing's *got* to be done. But what I say is this: it ain't good sense to go court'n around after a halter if you can git at what you're up to in some way that's jist as good and at the same time don't bring you into no resks. Ain't that so?"

"You bet it is. But how you goin' to manage it this time?"

"Well, my idea is this: we'll rustle around and gather up whatever pickins we've overlooked in the staterooms, and shove for shore and hide the truck. Then we'll wait. Now I say it ain't a-goin' to be more'n two hours befo' this wrack breaks up and washes off down the river. See? He'll be drownded, and won't have nobody to blame for it but his own self. I reckon that's a considerble sight better 'n killin' of him. I'm unfavourable to killin' a man as long as you can git aroun' it; it ain't good sense, it ain't good morals. Ain't I right?"

"Yes, I reck'n you are. But s'pose she *don't* break up and wash off?"

"Well, we can wait the two hours anyway and see, can't we?"

"All right, then; come along."

So they started, and I lit out, all in a cold sweat, and scrambled forward. It was dark as pitch there; but I said, in a kind of a coarse whisper, "Jim!" and he answered up, right at my elbow, with a sort of a moan, and I says:

"Quick, Jim, it ain't no time for fooling around and moaning; there's a gang of murderers in yonder, and if we don't hunt up their boat and set

---

* Caught (as up a tree).

her drifting down the river so these fellows can't get away from the wreck there's one of 'em going to be in a bad fix. But if we find their boat we can put *all* of 'em in a bad fix—for the sheriff 'll get 'em. Quick—hurry! I'll hunt the labboard side, you hunt the stabboard. You start at the raft, and—"

"Oh, my lordy, lordy! *raf*? Dey ain' no raf' no mo'; she done broke loose en gone I—en here we is!"

13

Well, I catched my breath and most fainted. Shut up on a wreck with such a gang as that! But it warn't no time to be sentimentering. We'd *got* to find that boat now—had to have it for ourselves. So we went a-quaking and shaking down the stabboard side, and slow work it was, too—seemed a week before we got to the stern. No sign of a boat. Jim said he didn't believe he could go any further—so scared he hadn't hardly any strength left, he said. But I said, come on, if we get left on this wreck we are in a fix, sure. So on we prowled again. We struck for the stern of the texas, and found it, and then scrabbled along forwards on the skylight, hanging on from shutter to shutter, for the edge of the skylight was in the water. When we got pretty close to the cross-hall door there was the skiff, sure enough! I could just barely see her. I felt ever so thankful. In another second I would a been aboard of her, but just then the door opened. One of the men stuck his head out only about a couple of foot from me, and I thought I was gone; but he jerked it in again, and says:

"Heave that blame lantern out o' sight, Bill!"

He flung a bag of something into the boat, and then got in himself and set down. It was Packard. Then Bill *he* come out and got in. Packard says, in a low voice:

"All ready—shove off!"

I couldn't hardly hang on to the shutters, I was so weak. But Bill says:

"Hold on—'d you go through him?"

"No. Didn't you?"

"No. So he's got his share o' the cash yet."

"Well, then, come along; no use to take truck and leave money."

"Say, won't he suspicion what we're up to?"

"Maybe he won't. But we got to have it anyway. Come along."

So they got out and went in.

The door slammed to because it was on the careened side;* and in a half second I was in the boat, and Jim come tumbling after me. I out with my knife and cut the rope, and away we went!

We didn't touch an oar, and we didn't speak nor whisper, nor hardly even breathe. We went gliding swift along, dead silent, past the tip of the paddle-box, and past the stern; then in a second or two more we was a hundred yards below the wreck, and the darkness soaked her up, every last sign of her, and we was safe, and knowed it.

When we was three or four hundred yards down-stream we see the lantern show like a little spark at the texas door for a second, and we knowed by that that the rascals had missed their boat, and was beginning to understand that they was in just as much trouble now as Jim Turner was.

Then Jim manned the oars, and we took out after our raft. Now was the first time that I begun to worry about the men—I reckon I hadn't had time to before. I begun to think how dreadful it was, even for murderers, to be in such a fix. I says to myself, there ain't no telling but I might come to be a murderer myself yet, and then how would I like it? So says I to Jim:

"The first light we see we'll land a hundred yards below it or above it, in a place where it's a good hiding place for you and the skiff, and then I'll go and fix up some kind of a yarn, and get somebody to go for that gang and get them out of their scrape, so they can be hung when their time comes."

But that idea was a failure; for pretty soon it begun to storm again, and this time worse than ever. The rain poured down, and never a light showed; everybody in bed, I reckon. We boomed along down the river, watching for lights and watching for our raft. After a long time the rain let up, but the clouds stayed, and the lightning kept whimpering, and by and by a flash showed us a black thing ahead, floating, and we made for it.

It was the raft, and mighty glad was we to get aboard of it again. We seen a light now away down to the right, on shore. So I said I would go for it. The skiff was half full of plunder which that gang had stole there on the wreck. We hustled it on to the raft in a pile, and I told Jim to float along down, and show a light when he judged he had gone about two mile, and keep it burning till I come; then I manned my oars and shoved for the light. As I got down towards it three or four more showed—up on a hillside. It was a village. I closed in above the shore light, and laid on my oars and floated. As I went by I see it was a lantern hanging on the jackstaff of a double-hull ferryboat. I skimmed around for the watchman, a-wondering whereabouts

* The side of the wrecked steamboat turned over out of the water.

he slept; and by and by I found him roosting on the bitts* forward, with his head down between his knees. I gave his shoulder two or three little shoves, and begun to cry.

He stirred up in a kind of a startlish way; but when he see it was only me he took a good gap and stretch, and then he says:

"Hello, what's up?"

"Hello, what's up? Don't cry, bub. What's the trouble?"

I says:

"Pap, and mam, and sis, and—"

Then I broke down. He says:

"Oh, dang it now, *don't* take on so; we all has to have our troubles, and this 'n 'll come out all right. What's the matter with 'em?"

"They're—they're—are you the watchman of the boat?"

"Yes," he says, kind of pretty-well-satisfied like. "I'm the captain and the owner and the mate and the pilot and watchman and head deck-hand; and sometimes I'm the freight and passengers. I ain't as rich as old Jim Hornback, and I can't be so blame' generous and good to Tom, Dick, and Harry as what he is, and slam around money the way he does; but I've told him a many a time 't I wouldn't trade places with him; for, says I, a sailor's life's the life for me, and I'm derned if *I'd* live two mile out o' town, where there ain't nothing ever goin' on, not for all his spondulicks† and as much more on top of it. Says I—"

I broke in and says:

"They're in an awful peck of trouble, and—"

"*Who* is?"

"Why, pap and mam and sis and Miss Hooker; and if you'd take your ferryboat and go up there—"

"Up where? Where are they?"

"On the wreck."

"What wreck?"

* Posts fastened in pairs in deck of ship for securing cables and ropes.

† Money.

"Why, there ain't but one."

"What, you don't mean the Walter Scott?"

"Yes."

"Good land! what are they doin' *there*, for gracious sakes?"

"Well, they didn't go there a-purpose."

"I bet they didn't! Why, great goodness, there ain't no chance for 'em if they don't git off mighty quick! Why, how in the nation did they ever git into such a scrape?"

"Easy enough. Miss Hooker was a-visiting up there to the town—"

"Yes, Booth's Landing—go on."

"She was a-visiting there at Booth's Landing, and just in the edge of the evening she started over with her nigger woman in the horse-ferry to stay all night at her friend's house, Miss What-you-may-call-her I disremember her name—and they lost their steering-oar, and swung around and went a-floating down, stern first, about two mile, and saddle-baggsed on the wreck, and the ferryman and the nigger woman and the horses was all lost, but Miss Hooker she made a grab and got aboard the wreck. Well, about an hour after dark we come along down in our trading-scow,* and it was so dark we didn't notice the wreck till we was right on it; and so *we* saddle-baggsed; but all of us was saved but Bill Whipple—and oh, he *was* the best cretur!—I most wish 't it had been me, I do."

"My George! It's the beatenest thing I ever struck. And *then* what did you all do?"

"Well, we hollered and took on, but it's so wide there we couldn't make nobody hear. So pap said somebody got to get ashore and get help somehow. I was the only one that could swim, so I made a dash for it, and Miss Hooker she said if I didn't strike help sooner, come here and hunt up her uncle, and he'd fix the thing. I made the land about a mile below, and been fooling along ever since, trying to get people to do something, but they said, 'What, in such a night and such a current? There ain't no sense in it; go for the steam ferry.' Now if you'll go and—"

"By Jackson, I'd *like* to, and, blame it, I don't know but I will; but who in the dingnation's a-going' to *pay* for it? Do you reckon your pap—"

"Why *that's* all right. Miss Hooker she tole me, *particular*, that her uncle Hornback—"

"Great guns! is *he* her uncle? Looky here, you break for that light over yonder-way, and turn out west when you git there, and about a quarter of a mile out you'll come to the tavern; tell 'em to dart you out to Jim Hornback's,

---

* River-boat for carrying cargo.

and he'll foot the bill. And don't you fool around any, because he'll want to know the news. Tell him I'll have his niece all safe before he can get to town. Hump yourself, now; I'm a-going up around the corner here to roust out my engineer."

I struck for the light, but as soon as he turned the corner I went back and got into my skiff and bailed her out, and then pulled up shore in the easy water about six hundred yards, and tucked myself in among some woodboats; for I couldn't rest easy till I could see the ferryboat start. But take it all around, I was feeling ruther comfortable on accounts of taking all this trouble for that gang, for not many would a done it. I wished the widow knowed about it. I judged she would be proud of me for helping these rapscallions, because rapscallions and dead beats is the kind the widow and good people takes the most interest in.

Well, before long here comes the wreck, dim and dusky, sliding along down! A kind of cold shiver went through me, and then I struck out for her. She was very deep, and I see in a minute there warn't much chance for anybody being alive in her. I pulled all around her and hollered a little, but there wasn't any answer; all dead still. I felt a little bit heavy-hearted about the gang, but not much, for I reckoned if they could stand it I could.

Then here comes the ferryboat; so I shoved for the middle of the river on a long down-stream slant; and when I judged I was out of eye-reach I laid on my oars, and looked back and see her go and smell around the wreck for Miss Hooker's remainders, because the captain would know her uncle Hornback would want them; and then pretty soon the ferryboat give it up and went for the shore, and I laid into my work and went a-booming down the river.

It did seem a powerful long time before Jim's light showed up; and when it did show it looked like it was a thousand mile off. By the time I got there the sky was beginning to get a little grey in the east; so we struck for an island, and hid the raft, and sunk the skiff, and turned in and slept like dead people.

14

By and by, when we got up, we turned over the truck the gang had stole off of the wreck, and found boots, and blankets, and clothes, and all sorts of other things, and a lot of books, and a spyglass, and three boxes of seegars. We hadn't ever been this rich before in neither of our lives. The seegars was prime. We laid off all the afternoon in the woods talking, and me reading the books, and having a general good time. I told Jim all about what happened inside the wreck and at the ferryboat, and I said these kinds of things was adventures; but he said he didn't want no more adventures. He said that when I went in the texas and he crawled back to get on the raft and found her gone he nearly died, because he judged it was all up with *him* anyway it could be fixed; for if he didn't get saved he would get drownded; and if he did get saved, whoever saved him would send him back home so as to get the reward, and then Miss Watson would sell him South, sure. Well, he was right; he was most always right; he had an uncommon level head for a nigger.

I read considerable to Jim about kings and dukes and earls and such, and how gaudy they dressed, and how much style they put on, and called each other your majesty, and your grace, and your lordship, and so on, 'stead of mister; and Jim's eyes bugged out, and he was interested. He says:

"I didn' know dey was so many un um. I hain't hearn 'bout none un um, skasely, but ole King Sollermun, onless you counts dem kings dat's in a pack er k'yards. How much do a king git?"

"Get?" I says; "why, they get a thousand dollars a month if they want it; they can have just as much as they want; everything belongs to them."

"*Ain'* dat gay? En what dey got to do, Huck?"

"*They* don't do nothing! Why, how you talk! They just set around."

"No; is dat so?"

"Of course it is. They just set around—except, maybe, when there's a war; then they go to the war. But other times they just lazy around; or go hawking—just hawking and sp—Sh!—d' you hear a noise?"

We skipped out and looked; but it warn't nothing but the flutter of a steamboat's wheel away down, coming around the point; so we come back.

"Yes," says I, "and other times, when things is dull, they fuss with the parlyment; and if everybody don't go just so he whacks their heads off. But mostly they hang round the harem."

"Roun' de which?"

"Harem."

"What's de harem?"

"The place where he keeps his wives. Don't you know about the harem? Solomon had one; he had about a million wives."

"Why, yes, dat's so; I—I'd done forgot it. A harem's a bo'd'n-house, I reck'n. Mos' likely dey has rackety times in de nussery. En I reck'n de wives quarrels considable; en dat 'crease de racket. Yit dey say Sollermun de wises' man dat ever live'. I doan' take no stock in dat. Bekase why: would a wise man want to live in de mids' er sich a blim-blammin' all de time? No—'deed he wouldn't. A wise man 'ud take en buil' a biler-factry; en den he could shet *down* de biler-factry when he want to res'."

"Well, but he *was* the wisest man, anyway; because the widow she told me so, her own self."

"I doan k'yer what de widder say, he *warn't* no wise man nuther. He had some er de dad-fetchedes'* ways I ever see. Does you know 'bout dat chile dat he 'uz gwyne to chop in two?"

"Yes, the widow told me all about it."

"*Well*, den! Warn' dat de beatenes' notion in de worl'? You jes' take en look at it a minute. Dah's de stump, dah—dat's one er de women; heah's you—dat's de yuther one; I's Sollermun; en dish yer dollar bill's de chile. Bofe un you claims it. What does I do? Does I shin aroun' mongs' de neighbours en fine out which un you de bill *do* b'long to, en han' it over to de right one, all safe en soun', de way dat anybody dat had any gumption would? No; I take en whack de bill in *two*, en give half un it to you, en de yuther half to de yuther woman. Dat's de way Sollermun was gwyne to do wid de chile. Now I want to ast you: what's de use er dat half a bill?—can't buy noth'n wid it. En what use is a half a chile? I wouldn' give a dern for a million un um."

"But hang it, Jim, you've clean missed the point—blame it, you've missed it a thousand mile."

"Who? Me? Go 'long. Doan' talk to me 'bout yo' pints. I reck'n I knows sense when I sees it; en dey ain' no sense in sich doin's as dat. De 'spute warn't 'bout a half a chile, de 'spute was 'bout a whole chile; en de man dat think he kin settle a 'spute 'bout a whole chile wid a half a chile doan' know enough to come in out'n de rain. Doan' talk to me 'bout Sollermun, Huck, I knows him by de back."

"But I tell you you don't get the point."

"Blame de point! I reck'n I knows what I knows. En mine you, de *real*

* Goddamned

pint is down furder—it's down deeper. It lays in de way Sollermun was raised. You take a man dat's got on'y one or two chillen; is dat man gwyne to be waseful o' chillen? No, he ain't; he can't 'ford it. *He* know how to value 'em. But you take a man dat's got 'bout five million chillen runnin' roun' de house, en it's diffunt. *He* as soon chop a chile in two as a cat. Dey's plenty mo'. A chile er two, mo' er less, warn't no consekens to Sollermun, dad fatch him!"

I never see such a nigger. If he got a notion in his head once, there warn't no getting it out again. He was the most down on Solomon of any nigger I ever see. So I went to talking about other kings, and let Solomon slide. I told about Louis Sixteenth that got his head cut off in France long time ago; and about his little boy the dolphin, that would a been a king, but they took and shut him up in jail, and some say he died there.

"Po' little chap."

"But some says he got out and got away, and come to America."

"Dat's good! But he'll be pooty lonesome—dey ain' no kings here, is dey, Huck?"

"No."

"Den he cain't git no situation. What he gwyne to do?"

"Well, I don't know. Some of them gets on the police, and some of them learns people how to talk French."

"Why, Huck, doan' de French people talk de same way we does?"

"*No*, Jim; you couldn't understand a word they said—not a single word."

"Well, now, I be ding-busted! How do dat come?"

"I don't know; but it's so. I got some of their jabber out of a book. S'pose a man was to come to you and say Polly-voo-franzy—what would you think?"

"I wouldn' think nuff'n; I'd take en bust him over de head—dat is, if he warn't white. I wouldn't 'low no nigger to call me dat."

"Shucks, it ain't calling you anything. It's only saying, do you know how to talk French?"

"Well, den, why couldn't he *say* it?"

"Why, he *is* a-saying it. That's a Frenchman's *way* of saying it."

"Well, it's a blame ridicklous way, en I doan' want to hear no mo' 'bout it. Dey ain' no sense in it."

"Looky here, Jim; does a cat talk like we do?"

"No, a cat don't."

"Well, does a cow?"

"No, a cow don't, nuther."

"Does a cat talk like a cow, or a cow talk like a cat?"

"No, dey don't."

"It's natural and right for 'em to talk different from each other, ain't it?"

"Course."

"And ain't it natural and right for a cat and a cow to talk different from *us*?"

"Why, mos' sholy it is."

"Well, then, why ain't it natural and right for a *Frenchman* to talk different from us? You answer me that."

"Is a cat a man, Huck?"

"No."

"Well, den, dey ain't no sense in a cat talkin' like a man. Is a cow a man?—er is a cow a cat?"

"No, she ain't either of them."

"Well, den, she ain't got no business to talk like either one er the yuther of 'em. Is a Frenchman a man?"

"Yes."

"*Well*, den! Dad blame it, why doan' he *talk* like a man? You answer me *dat*!"

I see it warn't no use wasting words—you can't learn a nigger to argue. So I quit.

15

We judged that three nights more would fetch us to Cairo, at the bottom of Illinois, where the Ohio River comes in, and that was what we was after. We would sell the raft and get on a steamboat and go way up the Ohio amongst the free States, and then be out of trouble.

Well, the second night a fog begun to come on, and we made for a towhead* to tie to, for it wouldn't do to try to run in a fog; but when I paddled ahead in the canoe, with the line to make fast, there warn't anything but little saplings to tie to. I passed the line around one of them right on the edge of the cut bank, but there was a stiff current, and the raft come booming down so lively she tore it out by the roots and away she went. I see

* See third paragraph, p. 412.

the fog closing down, and it made me so sick and scared I couldn't budge for most a half a minute it seemed to me—and then there warn't no raft in sight; you couldn't see twenty yards. I jumped into the canoe and run back to the stern, and grabbed the paddle and set her back a stroke. But she didn't come. I was in such a hurry I hadn't untied her. I got up and tried to untie her, but I was so excited my hands shook so I couldn't hardly do anything with them.

As soon as I got started I took out after the raft, hot and heavy, right down the towhead. That was all right as far as it went, but the towhead warn't sixty yards long, and the minute I flew by the foot of it I shot out into the solid white fog, and hadn't no more idea which way I was going than a dead man.

Thinks I, it won't do to paddle; first I know I'll run into the bank or a towhead or something; I got to set still and float, and yet it's mighty fidgety business to have to hold your hands still at such a time. I whooped and listened. Away down there somewheres I hears a small whoop, and up comes my spirits. I went tearing after it, listening sharp to hear it again. The next time it come I see I warn't heading for it, but heading away to the right of it. And the next time I was heading away to the left of it—and not gaining on it much either, for I was flying around, this way and that and t'other, but it was going straight ahead all the time.

I did wish the fool would think to beat a tin pan, and beat it all the time, but he never did, and it was the still places between the whoops that was making the trouble for me. Well, I fought along, and directly I hears the whoop *behind* me. I was tangled good now. That was somebody else's whoop, or else I was turned around.

I throwed the paddle down. I heard the whoop again; it was behind me yet, but in a different place; it kept coming, and kept changing its place, and I kept answering, till by and by it was in front of me again, and I knowed the current had swung the canoe's head down-stream, and I was all right if that was Jim and not some other raftsman hollering. I couldn't tell nothing about voices in a fog, for nothing don't look natural nor sound natural in a fog.

The whooping went on, and in about a minute I come a-booming down on a cut bank with smoky ghosts of big trees on it, and the current throwed me off to the left and shot by, amongst a lot of snags that fairly roared, the currrent was tearing by them so swift.

In another second or two it was solid white and still again. I set perfectly still then, listening to my heart thump, and I reckon I didn't draw a breath while it thumped a hundred.

I just give up then. I knowed what the matter was. That cut bank was an island, and Jim had gone down t'other side of it. It warn't no towhead that you could float by in ten minutes. It had the big timber of a regular island; it might be five or six miles long and more than half a mile wide.

I kept quiet, with my ears cocked, about fifteen minutes, I reckon. I was floating along, of course, four or five miles an hour; but you don't ever think of that. No, you *feel* like you are laying dead still on the water; and if a little glimpse of a snag slips by you don't think to yourself how fast *you're* going, but you catch your breath and think, my! how that snag's tearing along. If you think it ain't dismal and lonesome out in a fog that way by yourself in the night, you try it once—you'll see.

Among the snags

Next, for about a half an hour, I whoops now and then; at last I hears the answer a long ways off, and tries to follow it, but I couldn't do it, and directly I judged I'd got into a nest of towheads, for I had little dim glimpses of them on both sides of me—sometimes just a narrow channel between, and some that I couldn't see I knowed was there because I'd hear the wash of the current against the old dead brush and trash that hung over the banks. Well, I warn't long loosing the whoops down amongst the towheads; and I only tried to chase them a little while, anyway, because it was worse than chasing a Jack-o'-lantern. You never knowed a sound dodge around so, and swap places so quick and so much.

I had to claw away from the bank pretty lively four or five times, to keep from knocking the islands out of the river; and so I judged the raft must be butting into the bank every now and then, or else it would get further ahead and clear out of hearing—it was floating a little faster than what I was.

Well, I seemed to be in the open river again by and by, but I couldn't hear no sign of a whoop nowheres. I reckoned Jim had fetched up on a snag, maybe, and it was all up with him. I was good and tired, so I laid down in the canoe and said I wouldn't bother no more. I didn't want to go to sleep, of course; but I was so sleepy I couldn't help it; so I thought I would take jest one little cat-nap.

But I reckon it was more than a cat-nap, for when I waked up the stars was shining bright, the fog was all gone, and I was spinning down a big bend stern first. First I didn't know where I was; I thought I was dreaming; and when things began to come back to me they seemed to come up dim out of last week.

It was a monstrous big river here, with the tallest and the thickest kind of timber on both banks; just a solid wall, as well as I could see by the stars. I looked away down-stream, and seen a black speck on the water. I took after it; but when I got to it it warn't nothing but a couple of sawlogs made fast together. Then I see another speck, and chased that; then another, and this time I was right. It was the raft.

When I got to it Jim was setting there with his head down between his knees, asleep, with his right arm hanging over the steering-oar. The other oar was smashed off, and the raft was littered up with leaves and branches and dirt. So she'd had a rough time.

I made fast and laid down under Jim's nose on the raft, and began to gap, and stretch my fists out against Jim, and says:

"Hello, Jim, have I been asleep? Why didn't you stir me up?"

"Goodness gracious, is dat you, Huck? En you ain' dead—you ain' drownded—you's back agin? It's too good for true, honey, it's too good for true. Lemme look at you chile, lemme feel o' you. No, you ain' dead! you's back agin, 'live en soun', jis de same ole Huck—de same ole Huck, thanks to goodness!"

"What's the matter with you, Jim? You been a-drinking?"

"Drinkin'? Has I ben a-drinkin'? Has I had a chance to be a-drinkin'?"

"Well, then, what makes you talk so wild?"

"How does I talk wild?"

"*How*? Why, hain't you been talking about my coming back, and all that stuff, as if I'd been gone away?"

"Huck—Huck Finn, you look me in de eye; look me in de eye. *Hain't* you ben gone away?"

"Gone away? Why, what in the nation do you mean? I hain't been gone anywheres. Where would I go to?"

"Well, looky here, boss, dey's sumf'n wrong, dey is. Is I *me*, or who *is* I? Is I heah, or whah *is* I? Now dat's what I wants to know."

"Well, I think you're here, plain enough, but I think you're a tangle-headed old fool, Jim."

"I is, is I? Well, you answer me dis: Didn't you tote out de line in de canoe fer to make fas' to de tow-head?"

"No, I didn't. What tow-head? I hain't see no tow-head."

"You hain't seen no towhead? Looky here, didn't de line pull loose en de raf' go a-hummin' down de river, en leave you en de canoe behine in de fog?"

"What fog?"

"Why, de fog!—de fog dat's been aroun' all night. En didn't you whoop, en didn't I whoop, tell we got mix' up in de islands en one un us got los' en t'other one was jis' as good as los', 'kase he didn' know whah he wuz? En didn't I bust up agin a lot er dem islands en have a turrible time en mos' git drownded? Now ain' dat so, boss—ain't it so? You answer me dat."

"Well, this is too many for me, Jim. I hain't seen no fog, nor no islands, nor no troubles, nor nothing. I been setting here talking with you all night till you went to sleep about ten minutes ago, and I reckon I done the same. You couldn't a got drunk in that time, so of course you've been dreaming."

"Dad fetch it, how is I gwyne to dream all dat in ten minutes?"

"Well, hang it all, you did dream it, because there didn't any of it happen."

"But, Huck, it's all jis' as plain to me as—"

"It don't make no difference how plain it is; there ain't nothing in it. I know, because I've been here all the time."

Jim didn't say nothing for about five minutes, but set there studying over it. Then he says:

"Well, den, I reck'n I did dream it, Huck; but dog my cats ef it ain't de powerfullest dream I ever see. En I hain't ever had no dream b'fo' dat's tired me like dis one."

"Oh, well, that's all right, because a dream does tire a body like everything sometimes. But this one was a staving* dream; tell me all about it, Jim."

So Jim went to work and told me the whole thing right through, just as it happened, only he painted it up considerable. Then he said he must start in

* Wonderful, marvellous, etc.

and "'terpret" it, because it was sent for a warning. He said the first towhead stood for a man that would try to do us some good, but the current was another man that would get us away from him. The whoops was warnings that would come to us every now and then, and if we didn't try hard to make out to understand them they'd just take us into bad luck, 'stead of keeping us out of it. The lot of towheads was troubles we was going to get into with quarrelsome people and all kinds of mean folks, but if we minded our business and didn't talk back and aggravate them, we would pull through and get out of the fog and into the big clear river, which was the free States, and wouldn't have no more trouble.

It had clouded up pretty dark just after I got on to the raft, but it was clearing up again now.

"Oh, well, that's all interpreted well enough as far as it goes, Jim," I says; "but what does *these* things stand for?"

It was the leaves and rubbish on the raft and the smashed oar. You could see them first-rate now.

Jim looked at the trash, and then looked at me, and back at the trash again. He had got the dream fixed so strong in his head that he couldn't seem to shake it loose and get the facts back into its place again right away. But when he did get the thing straightened around he looked at me steady without ever smiling, and says:

"What do dey stan' for? I'se gwyne to tell you. When I got all wore out wid work, en wid de callin' for you, en went to sleep, my heart wuz mos' broke bekase you wuz los', en I didn' k'yer no' mo' what become er me en de raf'. En when I wake up en fine you back agin, all safe en soun', de tears come, en I could a got down on my knees en kiss yo' foot, I's so thankful. En all you wuz thinkin' 'bout wuz how you could make a fool uv ole Jim wid a lie. Dat truck dah is *trash*; en trash is what people is dat puts dirt on de head er dey fren's en makes 'em ashamed."

Then he got up slow and walked to the wigwam, and went in there without saying anything but that. But that was enough. It made me feel so mean I could almost kissed *his* foot to get him to take it back.

It was fifteen minutes before I could work myself up to go and humble myself to a nigger; but I done it, and I warn't ever sorry for it afterwards, neither. I didn't do him no more mean tricks, and I wouldn't done that one if I'd a knowed it would make him feel that way.

16

We slept most all day, and started out at night, a little ways behind a monstrous long raft that was as long going by as a procession. She had four long sweeps* at each end, so we judged she carried as many as thirty men, likely. She had five big wigwams aboard, wide apart, and an open camp fire in the middle, and a tall flag-pole at each end. There was a power of style about her. It *amounted* to something being a raftsman on such a craft as that.

We went drifting down into a big bend, and the night clouded up and got hot. The river was very wide, and was walled with solid timber on both sides; you couldn't see a break in it hardly ever, or a light. We talked about Cairo, and wondered whether we would know it when we got to it. I said likely we wouldn't, because I had heard say there warn't but about a dozen houses there, and if they didn't happen to have them lit up, how was we going to know we was passing a town? Jim said if the two big rivers joined together there, that would show. But I said maybe we might think we was passing the foot of an island and coming into the same old river again. That disturbed Jim—and me too. So the question was, what to do? I said, paddle ashore the first time a light showed, and tell them pap was behind, coming along with a trading-scow, and was a green hand at the business, and wanted to know how far it was to Cairo. Jim thought it was a good idea, so we took a smoke on it and waited.

There warn't nothing to do now but to look out sharp for the town, and not pass it without seeing it. He said he'd be mighty sure to see it, because he'd be a free man the minute he seen it, but if he missed it he'd be in a slave country again and no more show for freedom. Every little while he jumps up and says:

"Dah she is?"

But it warn't. It was Jack-o'-lanterns, or lightning bugs; so he set down again, and went to watching, same as before. Jim said it made him all over trembly and feverish to be so close to freedom. Well, I can tell you it made me all over trembly and feverish, too, to hear him, because I begun to get it through my head that he *was* most free—and who was to blame for it? Why, *me*. I couldn't get that out of my conscience, no how nor no way. It got to troubling me so I couldn't rest; I couldn't stay still in one place. It hadn't

* Especially long oars.

ever come home to me before, what this thing was that I was doing. But now it did; and it stayed with me, and scorched me more and more. I tried to make out to myself that I warn't to blame, because I didn't run Jim off from his rightful owner; but it warn't no use, conscience up and says, every time, "But you knowed he was running for his freedom, and you could a paddled ashore and told somebody." That was so—I couldn't get around that noway. That was where it pinched. Conscience says to me, "What had poor Miss Watson done to you that you could see her nigger go off right under your eyes and never say one single word? What did that poor old woman do to you that you could treat her so mean? Why, she tried to learn you your book, she tried to learn you your manners, she tried to be good to you every way she knowed how. *That's* what she done."

I got to feeling so mean and so miserable I most wished I was dead. I fidgeted up and down the raft, abusing myself to myself, and Jim was fidgeting up and down past me. We neither of us could keep still. Every time he danced around and says, "Dah's Cairo!" it went through me like a shot, and I thought if it *was* Cairo I reckoned I would die of miserableness.

Jim talked out loud all the time while I was talking to myself. He was saying how the first thing he would do when he got to a free State he would go to saving up money and never spend a single cent, and when he got enough he would buy his wife, which was owned on a farm close to where Miss Watson lived; and then they would both work to buy the two children, and if their master wouldn't sell them, they'd get an Ab'litionist to go and steal them.

It most froze me to hear such talk. He wouldn't ever dared to talk such talk in his life before. Just see what a difference it made in him the minute he judged he was about free. It was according to the old saying, "Give a nigger an inch and he'll take an ell." Thinks I, this is what comes of my not thinking. Here was this nigger, which I had as good as helped to run away, coming right out flat-footed and saying he would steal his children—children that belonged to a man I didn't even know; a man that hadn't ever done me no harm.

I was sorry to hear Jim say that, it was such a lowering of him. My conscience got to stirring me up hotter than ever, until at last I says to it, "Let up on me—it ain't too late yet—I'll paddle ashore at the first light and tell." I felt easy and happy and light as a feather right off. All my troubles was gone. I went to looking out sharp for a light, and sort of singing to myself. By and by one showed. Jim sings out:

"We's safe, Huck, we's safe! Jump up and crack yo' heels! Dat's de good ole Cairo at las', I jis knows it!"

I says:

"I'll take the canoe and go and see, Jim. It mightn't be, you know."

He jumped and got the canoe ready, and put his old coat in the bottom for me to set on, and give me the paddle; and as I shoved off, he says:

"Pooty soon I'll be a-shout'n' for joy, en I'll say, it's all on accounts o' Huck; I's a free man, en I couldn't ever ben free ef it hadn' ben for Huck; Huck done it. Jim won't ever forgit you, Huck; you's de bes' fren' Jim's ever had; en you's de *only* fren' ole Jim's got now."

I was paddling off, all in a sweat to tell on him; but when he says this, it seemed to kind of take the tuck all out of me. I went along slow then, and I warn't right down certain whether I was glad I started or whether I warn't. When I was fifty yards off, Jim says:

"Dah you goes, de ole true Huck; de on'y white genlman dat ever kep' his promise to ole Jim."

Well, I just felt sick. But I says, I *got* to do it—I can't get *out* of it. Right then along comes a skiff with two men in it with guns, and they stopped and I stopped. One of them says:

"What's that yonder?"

"A piece of a raft," I says.

"Do you belong on it?"

"Yes, sir."

"Any men on it?"

"Only one, sir."

"Well, there's five niggers run off tonight up yonder, above the head of the bend. Is your man white or black?"

I didn't answer up prompt. I tried to, but the words wouldn't come. I tried for a second or two to brace up and out with it, but I warn't man enough—hadn't the spunk of a rabbit. I see I was weakening; so I just give up trying, and up and says:

"He's white."

"I reckon we'll go and see for ourselves."

"I wish you would," says I, "because it's pap that's there, and maybe you'd help me tow the raft ashore where the light is. He's sick—and so is mam and Mary Ann."

"Oh, the devil! we're in a hurry, boy. But I s'pose we've got to. Come, buckle to your paddle, and let's get along."

I buckled to my paddle and they laid to their oars. When we had made a stroke or two, I says:

"Pap'll be mighty much obleeged to you, I can tell you. Everybody goes away when I want them to help me tow the raft ashore, and I can't do it by myself."

"Well, that's infernal mean. Odd, too. Say, boy, what's the matter with your father?"

"It's the—a—the—well, it ain't anything much."

They stopped pulling. It warn't but a mighty little ways to the raft now. One says:

"Boy, that's a lie. What *is* the matter with your pap? Answer up square now, and it'll be the better for you."

"Boy, that's a lie"

"I will, sir, I will, honest—but don't leave us, please. It's the—the—Gentlemen, if you'll only pull ahead, and let me heave you the headline, you won't have to come a-near the raft—please do."

"Set her back, John, set her back!" says one. They backed water. "Keep away, boy—keep to looard. Confound it, I just expect the wind has blowed it to us. Your pap's got the small-pox, and you know it precious well. Why didn't you come out and say so? Do you want to spread it all over?"

"Well," says I, a-blubbering, "I've told everybody before, and they just went away and left us."

"Poor devil, there's something in that. We are right down sorry for you, but we—well, hang it, we don't want the small-pox, you see. Look here, I'll tell you what to do. Don't you try to land by yourself, or you'll smash everything to pieces. You float along down about twenty miles, and you'll come to a town on the left-hand side of the river. It will be long after sun-up then, and when you ask for help you tell them your folks are all down with chills and fever. Don't be a fool again, and let people guess what is the matter. Now we're trying to do you a kindness; so you just put twenty miles between us, that's a good boy. It wouldn't do any good to land yonder where the light is—it's only a wood-yard. Say, I reckon your father's poor, and I'm bound to say he's in pretty hard luck. Here, I'll put a twenty-dollar gold piece on this board, and you get it when it floats by. I feel mighty mean to leave you; but my kingdom! it won't do to fool with small-pox, don't you see?"

"Hold on, Parker," says the other man, "here's a twenty to put on the board for me. Goodbye, boy; you do as Mr. Parker told you, and you'll be all right."

"That's so, my boy—goodbye, goodbye. If you see any runaway niggers you get help and nab them, and you can make some money by it."

"Goodbye, sir," says I; "I won't let no runaway niggers get by me if I can help it."

They went off and I got aboard the raft, feeling bad and low, because I knowed very well I had done wrong, and I see it warn't no use for me to try to learn to do right; a body that don't get *started* right when he's little ain't got no show—when the pinch comes there ain't nothing to back him up and keep him to his work, and so he gets beat. Then I thought a minute, and says to myself, hold on; s'pose you'd a done right and give Jim up, would you felt better than what you do now? No, says I, I'd feel bad—I'd feel just the same way I do now. Well, then, says I, what's the use you learning to do right when it's troublesome to do right and ain't no trouble to do wrong, and the wages is just the same? I was stuck. I couldn't answer that. So I reckoned I wouldn't bother no more about it, but after this always do whichever come handiest at the time.

I went into the wigwam; Jim warn't there. I looked all around; he warn't anywhere. I says:

"Jim!"

"Here I is, Huck. Is dey out o' sight yit? Don't talk loud."

He was in the river under the stern oar, with just his nose out. I told him they were out of sight, so he come aboard. He says:

"I was a-listenin' to all de talk, en I slips into de river en was gwyne to shove for sho' if dey come aboard. Den I was gwyne to swim to de raf' agin when dey was gone. But lawsy, how you did fool 'em, Huck! Dat *wuz* de smartes' dodge! I tell you, chile, I'spec it save' ole Jim—ole Jim ain't going to forgit you for dat, honey."

Then we talked about the money. It was a pretty good raise—twenty dollars apiece. Jim said we could take deck passage on a steamboat now, and the money would last us as far as we wanted to go in the free States. He said twenty mile more warn't far for the raft to go, but he wished we was already there.

Towards daybreak we tied up, and Jim was mighty particular about hiding the raft good. Then he worked all day fixing things in bundles, and getting all ready to quit rafting.

That night about ten we hove in sight of the lights of a town away down in a left-hand bend.

I went off in the canoe to ask about it. Pretty soon I found a man out in the river with a skiff, setting a trot-line. I ranged up and says:

"Mister, is that town Cairo?"

"Cairo? no. You must be a blame' fool."

"What town is it, mister?"

"If you want to know, go and find out. If you stay here botherin' around me for about a half a minute longer you'll get something you won't want."

I paddled to the raft. Jim was awful disappointed, but I said never mind, Cairo would be the next place, I reckoned.

We passed another town before daylight, and I was going out again; but it was high ground, so I didn't go. No high ground about Cairo, Jim said. I had forgot it. We laid up for the day on a towhead tolerable close to the left-hand bank. I begun to suspicion something. So did Jim. I says:

"Maybe we went by Cairo in the fog that night."

He says:

"Doan' le's talk about it, Huck. Po' niggers can't have no luck. I awluz 'spected dat rattlesnake-skin warn't done wid its work."

"I wish I'd never seen that snake-skin, Jim—I do wish I'd never laid eyes on it."

"It ain't yo' fault, Huck; you didn' know. Don't you blame yo'self 'bout it."

When it was daylight, here was the clear Ohio water inshore, sure enough, and outside was the old regular Muddy! So it was all up with Cairo.

We talked it all over. It wouldn't do to take to the shore; we couldn't take the raft up the stream, of course. There warn't no way but to wait for dark, and start back in the canoe and take the chances. So we slept all day amongst the cottonwood thicket, so as to be fresh for the work, and when we went back to the raft about dark the canoe was gone!

We didn't say a word for a good while. There warn't anything to say. We both knowed well enough it was some more work of the rattlesnake-skin; so what was the use to talk about it? It would only look like we was finding fault, and that would be bound to fetch more bad luck—and keep on fetching it, too, till we knowed enough to keep still.

By and by we talked about what we better do, and found there warn't no way but just to go along down with the raft till we got a chance to buy a canoe to go back in. We warn't going to borrow it when there warn't anybody around, the way pap would do, for that might set people after us.

So we shoved out after dark on the raft.

Anybody that don't believe yet that it's foolishness to handle a snake-skin, after all that that snake-skin done for us, will believe it now if they read on and see what more it done for us.

The place to buy canoes is off of rafts laying up at shore. But we didn't see no rafts laying up; so we went along during three hours and more. Well, the night got grey and ruther thick, which is the next meanest thing to fog. You can't tell the shape of the river, and you can't see no distance. It got to be very late and still, and then along comes a steamboat up the river. We lit the lantern, and judged she would see it. Up-stream boats didn't generally come close to us; they go out and follow the bars and hunt for easy water under the reefs; but nights like this they bull right up the channel against the whole river.

We could hear her pounding along, but we didn't see her good till she was close. She aimed right for us. Often they do that and try to see how close they can come without touching; sometimes the wheel bites off a sweep, and then the pilot sticks his head out and laughs, and thinks he's mighty smart. Well, here she comes, and we said she was going to try and shave us; but she didn't seem to be sheering off a bit. She was a big one, and she was coming in a hurry, too, looking like a black cloud with rows of glow-worms around it; but all of a sudden she bulged out, big and scary, with a long row of wide-open furnace doors shining like red-hot teeth, and her monstrous bows and guards hanging right over us. There was a yell at us, and a jingling of bells to stop the engines, a powwow of cussing, and whistling of steam—and as Jim went overboard on one side and I on the other, she come smashing straight through the raft.

I dived—and I aimed to find the bottom, too, for a thirty-foot wheel had got to go over me, and I wanted it to have plenty of room. I could always stay under water a minute; this time I reckon I stayed under a minute and a half. Then I bounced for the top in a hurry, for I was nearly busting. I popped out to my armpits and blowed the water out of my nose, and puffed a bit. Of course there was a booming current; and of course that boat started her engines again ten seconds after she stopped them, for they never cared much for raftsmen; so now she was churning along up the river, out of sight in the thick weather, though I could hear her.

I sung out for Jim about a dozen times, but I didn't get any answer; so I grabbed a plank that touched me while I was "treading water," and struck out for shore, shoving it ahead of me. But I made out to see that the drift of the current was towards the left-hand shore, which meant that I was in a crossing; so I changed off and went that way.

It was one of these long, slanting, two-mile crossings; so I was a good long time in getting over. I made a safe landing, and clumb up the bank. I couldn't see but a little ways, but I went poking along over rough ground for a quarter of a mile or more, and then I run across a big old-fashioned double log-house before I noticed it. I was going to rush by and get away, but a lot of dogs jumped out and went to howling and barking at me, and I knowed better than to move another peg.

17

In about a minute somebody spoke out of a window without putting his head out, and says:

"Be done, boys! Who's there?"

I says:

"It's me."

"Who's me?"

"George Jackson, sir."

"What do you want?"

"I don't want nothing, sir. I only want to go along by, but the dogs won't let me."

"What are you prowling around here this time of night for—hey?"

"I warn't prowling around, sir, I fell overboard off of the steamboat."

"Oh, you did, did you? Strike a light there, somebody. What did you say your name was?"

"George Jackson, sir. I'm only a boy."

"Look here, if you're telling the truth you needn't be afraid—nobody'll hurt you. But don't try to budge; stand right where you are. Rouse out Bob and Tom, some of you, and fetch the guns. George Jackson, is there anybody with you?"

"No, sir, nobody."

I heard the people stirring around in the house now, and see a light. The man sung out:

"Snatch that light away, Betsy, you old fool—ain't you got any sense? Put it on the floor behind the front door. Bob, if you and Tom are ready, take your places."

"All ready."

"Now, George Jackson, do you know the Shepherdsons?"

"No, sir; I never heard of them."

"Well, that may be so, and it mayn't. Now, all ready. Step forward, George Jackson. And mind, don't you hurry—come mighty slow. If there's anybody with you, let him keep back—if he shows himself he'll be shot. Come along now. Come slow; push the door open yourself—just enough to squeeze in, d' you hear?"

I didn't hurry; I couldn't if I'd a wanted to. I took one slow step at a time and there warn't a sound, only I thought I could hear my heart. The dogs were as still as the humans, but they followed a little behind me. When I got to the three log doorsteps I heard them unlocking and unbarring and unbolting. I put my hand on the door and pushed it a little and a little more till somebody said, "There, that's enough—put your head in." I done it, but I judged they would take it off.

The candle was on the floor, and there they all was, looking at me, and me at them, for about a quarter of a minute: Three big men with guns pointed at me, which made me wince, I tell you; the oldest, grey and about sixty, the other two thirty or more—all of them fine and handsome—and the sweetest old grey-headed lady, and back of her two young women which I couldn't see right well. The old gentleman says:

"There; I reckon it's all right. Come in."

As soon as I was in the old gentleman he locked the door and barred it and bolted it, and told the young men to come in with their guns, and they all went in a big parlour that had a new rag carpet on the floor, and got together in a corner that was out of the range of the front windows—there warn't none on the side. They held the candle, and took a good look at me, and all said, "Why, *he* ain't a Shepherdson—no, there ain't any Shepherdson about him." Then the old man said he hoped I wouldn't mind being searched for arms, because he didn't mean no harm by it—it was only to make sure. So he didn't pry into my pockets, but only felt outside with his hands, and said it was all right. He told me to make myself easy and at home, and tell all about myself; but the old lady says:

"Why, bless you, Saul, the poor thing's as wet as he can be; and don't you reckon it may be he's hungry?"

"True for you, Rachel—I forgot."

So the old lady says:

"Betsy" (this was a nigger woman), "you fly around and get him something to eat as quick as you can, poor thing; and one of you girls go and wake up Buck and tell him—oh, here he is himself. Buck, take this little stranger and get the wet clothes off from him and dress him up in some of yours that's dry."

Buck looked about as old as me—thirteen or fourteen or along there, though he was a little bigger than me. He hadn't on anything but a shirt, and he was very frowzy-headed. He came in gaping and digging one fist into his eyes, and he was dragging a gun along with the other one. He says:

"Ain't they no Shepherdsons around?"

They said, no, 'twas a false alarm.

"Well," he says, "if they'd a ben some, I reckon I'd a got one."

They all laughed, and Bob says:

"Why, Buck, they might have scalped us all, you've been so slow in coming."

"Well, nobody come after me, and it ain't right I'm always kept down; I don't get no show."

"Never mind, Buck, my boy," says the old man, "you'll have show enough, all in good time, don't you fret about that. Go 'long with you now, and do as your mother told you."

When we got upstairs to his room he got me a coarse shirt and a roundabout* and pants of his, and I put them on. While I was at it he asked me what my name was, but before I could tell him he started to tell me about a bluejay and a young rabbit he had catched in the woods day before yesterday, and he asked me where Moses was when the candle went out. I said I didn't know; I hadn't heard about it before, no way.

"Well, guess," he says.

"How'm I going to guess," says I, "when I never heard tell of it before?"

"But you can guess, can't you? It's just as easy."

"*Which* candle?" I says.

"Why, any candle," he says.

"I don't know where he was," says I; "where was he?"

"Why, he was in the *dark*! That's where he was!"

"Well, if you knowed where he was, what did you ask me for?"

"Why, blame it, it's a riddle, don't you see? Say, how long are you going to stay here? You got to stay always. We can just have booming times—they don't have no school now. Do you own a dog? I've got a dog—and he'll go in the river and bring out chips that you throw in. Do you like to comb up Sundays, and all that kind of foolishness? You bet I don't, but ma she makes me. Confound these ole britches! I reckon I'd better put 'em on, but I'd ruther not, it's so warm. Are you all ready? All right. Come along, old hoss."

* A short jacket.

Cold corn-pone,* cold corn-beef, butter and buttermilk—that is what they had for me down there, and there ain't nothing better that ever I've come across yet. Buck and his ma and all of them smoked cob pipes, except the nigger woman, which was gone, and the two young women. They all smoked and talked, and I eat and talked. The young women had quilts around them, and their hair down their backs. They all asked me questions, and I told them how pap and me and all the family was living on a little farm down at the bottom of Arkansaw, and my sister Mary Ann run off and got married and never was heard of no more, and Bill went to hunt them and he warn't heard of no more, and Tom and Mort died, and then there warn't nobody but just me and pap left, and he was just trimmed down to nothing, on account of his troubles; so when he died I took what there was left, because the farm didn't belong to us, and started up the river, deck passage, and fell overboard; and that was how I come to be here. So they said I could have a home there as long as I wanted it. Then it was most daylight and everybody went to bed, and I went to bed with Buck, and when I waked up in the morning, drat it all, I had forgot what my name was. So I laid there about an hour trying to think, and when Buck waked up I says:

"Can you spell, Buck?"

"Yes," he says.

"I bet you can't spell my name," says I.

"I bet you what you dare I can," says he.

"All right," says I, "go ahead."

"G-e-o-r-g-e J-a-x-o-n—there now," he says.

"Well," says I, "you done it, but I didn't think you could. It ain't no slouch of a name to spell—right off without studying."

I set it down, private, because somebody might want *me* to spell it next, and so I wanted to be handy with it and rattle it off like I was used to it.

It was a mighty nice family, and a mighty nice house, too. I hadn't seen no house out in the country before that was so nice and had so much style. It didn't have an iron latch on the front door, nor a wooden one with a buckskin string, but a brass knob to turn, the same as houses in town. There warn't no bed in the parlour, nor a sign of a bed; but heaps of parlours in towns has beds in them. There was a big fireplace that was bricked on the bottom, and the bricks was kept clean and red by pouring water on them and scrubbing them with another brick; sometimes they wash them over with red water-paint that they call Spanish-brown, same as they do in town. They had big brass dog-irons that could hold up a saw-log. There was a clock

* Any bread made from maize. Originally, North American Indian.

on the middle of the mantelpiece, with a picture of a town painted on the bottom half of the glass front, and a round place in the middle of it for the sun, and you could see the pendulum swinging behind it. It was beautiful to hear that clock tick; and sometimes when one of these peddlers had been along and scoured her up and got her in good shape, she would start in and strike a hundred and fifty before she got tuckered out. They wouldn't took any money for her.

Well, there was a big outlandish parrot on each side of the clock, made out of something like chalk, and painted up gaudy. By one of the parrots was a cat made of crockery, and a crockery dog by the other; and when you pressed down on them they squeaked, but didn't open their mouths nor look different nor interested. They squeaked through underneath. There was a couple of big wild-turkey-wing fans spread out behind those things. On the table in the middle of the room was a kind of a lovely crockery basket that had apples and oranges and peaches and grapes piled up in it, which was much redder and yellower and prettier than real ones is, but they warn't real because you could see where pieces had got chipped off and showed the white chalk, or whatever it was, underneath.

This table had a cover made out of beautiful oilcloth, with a red and blue spread-eagle painted on it, and a painted border all around. It come all the way from Philadelphia, they said. There was some books, too, piled up perfectly exact, on each corner of the table. One was a big family Bible full of pictures. One was Pilgrim's Progress, about a man that left his family, it didn't say why. I read considerable in it now and then. The statements was interesting, but tough. Another was Friendship's Offering, full of beautiful stuff and poetry; but I didn't read the poetry. Another was Henry Clay's Speeches, and another was Dr. Gunn's Family Medicine, which told you all about what to do if a body was sick or dead. There was a hymn book, and a lot of other books. And there was nice split-bottom chairs, and perfectly sound, too—not bagged down in the middle and busted, like an old basket.

They had pictures hung on the walls—mainly Washingtons and Lafayettes, and battles, and Highland Marys, and one called "Signing the Declaration." There was some that they called crayons, which one of the daughters which was dead made her own self when she was only fifteen years old. They was different from any pictures I ever see before—blacker, mostly, than is common. One was a woman in a slim black dress, belted small under the armpits, with bulges like a cabbage in the middle of the sleeves, and a large black scoop-shovel bonnet with a black veil, and white slim ankles crossed about with black tape, and very wee black slippers, like a chisel, and she was leaning pensive on a tombstone on her right elbow, under a weeping willow, and her other hand hanging down her side holding a white handkerchief and a reticule, and underneath the picture it said "Shall I Never See Thee More Alas." Another one was a young lady with her hair all combed up straight to the top of her head, and knotted there in front of a comb like a chair-back, and she was crying into a handkerchief and had a dead bird laying on its back in her other hand with its heels up, and underneath the picture it said "I Shall Never Hear Thy Sweet Chirrup More Alas." There was one where a young lady was at a window looking up at the moon, and tears running down her cheeks; and she had an open letter in one hand with black sealing wax showing on one edge of it, and she was mashing a locket with a chain to it against her mouth, and underneath the picture it said "And Art Thou Gone Yes Thou Art Gone Alas." These was all nice pictures, I reckon, but I didn't somehow seem to take to them, because if ever I was down a little they always give me the fan-tods. Everybody was sorry she died, because she had laid out a lot more of these pictures to do, and a body could see by what she had done what they had lost. But I reckoned that with her disposition she was having a better time in the graveyard. She was at work on what they said was her greatest picture when she took sick, and every day and every night it was her prayer to be allowed to live till she got it done, but she never got the chance. It was a picture of a young woman in a long white gown, standing on the rail of a bridge all ready to jump off, with her hair all down her back, and looking up to the moon, with the tears running down her face, and she had two arms folded across her breast, and two arms stretched out in front, and two more reaching up towards the moon—and the idea was to see which pair would look best, and then scratch out all the other arms; but, as I was saying, she died before she got her mind made up, and now they kept this picture over the head of the bed in her room, and every time her birthday come they hung flowers on it. Other times it was hid with a little curtain. The young woman in the picture had a kind of a nice sweet face, but there was so many arms it made her look too spidery, seemed to me.

This young girl kept a scrap-book when she was alive, and used to paste obituaries and accidents and cases of patient suffering in it out of the *Presbyterian Observer*, and write poetry after them out of her own head. It was very good poetry. This is what she wrote about a boy by the name of Stephen Dowling Bots that fell down a well and was drownded:

ODE TO STEPHEN DOWLING BOTS, DEC'D

And did young Stephen sicken,
And did young Stephen die?

And did the sad hearts thicken,
And did the mourners cry?
No; such was not the fate of
Young Stephen Dowling Bots;
Though sad hearts round him thickened,
'Twas not from sickness' shots.
No whooping-cough did rack his frame,
Nor measles drear with spots;
Not these impaired the sacred name
Of Stephen Dowling Bots.
Despised love struck not with woe
That head of curly knots,
Nor stomach troubles laid him low,
Young Stephen Dowling Bots.
O no. Then list with tearful eye,
Whilst I his fate do tell.
His soul did from this cold world fly
By falling down a well.
They got him out and emptied him;
Alas it was too late;
His spirit was gone for to sport aloft
In the realms of the good and great.

If Emmeline Grangerford could make poetry like that before she was fourteen, there ain't no telling what she could a done by and by. Buck said she could rattle off poetry like nothing. She didn't ever have to stop to think. He said she would slap down a line, and if she couldn't find anything to rhyme with it would just scratch it out and slap down another one, and go ahead. She warn't particular; she could write about anything you choose to give her to write about just so it was sadful. Every time a man died, or a woman died, or a child died, she would be on hand with her "tribute" before he was cold. She called them tributes. The neighbours said it was the doctor first, then Emmeline, then the undertaker—the undertaker never got in ahead of Emmeline but once, and then she hung fire on a rhyme for the dead person's name, which was Whistler. She warn't ever the same after that; she never complained, but she kinder pined away and did not live long. Poor thing, many's the time I made myself go up to the little room that used to be hers and get out her poor old scrap-book and read in it when her pictures had been aggravating me and I had soured on her a little. I liked all that family, dead ones and all, and warn't going to let anything come between us. Poor Emmeline made poetry about all the dead people when she was alive, and it didn't seem right that there warn't nobody to make some about her now she was gone; so I tried to sweat out a verse or two myself, but I couldn't seem to make it go somehow. They kept Emmeline's room trim and nice, and all the things fixed in it just the way she liked to have them when she was alive, and nobody ever slept there. The old lady took care of the room herself, though there was plenty of niggers, and she sewed there a good deal and read her Bible there mostly.

Well, as I was saying about the parlour, there was beautiful curtains on the windows: white, with pictures painted on them of castles with vines all down the walls, and cattle coming down to drink. There was a little old piano, too, that had tin pans in it, I reckon, and nothing was ever so lovely as to hear the young ladies sing "The Last Link is Broken" and play "The Battle of Prague" on it. The walls of all the rooms was plastered, and most had carpets on the floors, and the whole house was whitewashed on the outside.

It was a double house, and the big open place betwixt them was roofed and floored, and sometimes the table was set there in the middle of the day, and it was a cool, comfortable place. Nothing couldn't be better. And warn't the cooking good, and just bushels of it too!

18

Col. Grangerford was a gentleman, you see. He was a gentleman all over; and so was his family. He was well born, as the saying is, and that's worth as much in a man as it is in a horse, so the Widow Douglas said, and nobody ever denied that she was of the first aristocracy in our town; and pap he always said it, too, though he warn't no more quality than a mudcat* himself. Col. Grangerford was very tall and very slim, and had a darkish-paly complexion, not a sign of red in it anywheres; he was clean shaved every morning all over his thin face, and he had the thinnest kind of lips, and the thinnest kind of nostrils, and a high nose, and heavy eyebrows, and the blackest kind of eyes, sunk so deep back that they seemed like they was looking out of caverns at you, as you may say. His forehead was high, and his hair was black and

* A species of cat-fish.

straight and hung to his shoulders. His hands was long and thin, and every day of his life he put on a clean shirt and a full suit from head to foot made out of linen so white it hurt your eyes to look at it; and on Sundays he wore a blue tail-coat with brass buttons on it. He carried a mahogany cane with a silver head to it. There warn't no frivolishness about him, not a bit, and he warn't ever loud. He was as kind as he could be—you could feel that, you know, and so you had confidence. Sometimes he smiled, and it was good to see; but when he straightened himself up like a liberty-pole,* and the lightning begun to flicker out from under his eyebrows, you wanted to climb a tree first, and find out what the matter was afterwards. He didn't ever have to tell anybody to mind their manners—everybody was always good-mannered where he was. Everybody loved to have him around, too; he was sunshine most always—I mean he made it seem like good weather. When he turned into a cloudbank it was awful dark for half a minute, and that was enough; there wouldn't nothing go wrong again for a week.

When him and the old lady come down in the morning all the family got up out of their chairs and give them good day, and didn't set down again till they had set down. Then Tom and Bob went to the sideboard where the decanter was, and mixed a glass of bitters and handed it to him, and he held it in his hand and waited till Tom's and Bob's was mixed, and then they bowed and said, "Our duty to you, sir, and madam;" and *they* bowed the least bit in the world and said thank you, and so they drank, all three, and Bob and Tom poured a spoonful of water on the sugar and the mite of whisky or apple brandy in the bottom of their tumblers, and give it to me and Buck, and we drank to the old people too.

Bob was the oldest and Tom next—tall, beautiful men with very broad shoulders and brown faces, and long black hair and black eyes. They dressed in white linen from head to foot, like the old gentleman, and wore broad Panama hats.

Then there was Miss Charlotte; she was twenty-five, and tall and proud and grand, but as good as she could be when she warn't stirred up; but when she was she had a look that would make you wilt in your tracks, like her father. She was beautiful.

So was her sister, Miss Sophia, but it was a different kind. She was gentle and sweet like a dove, and she was only twenty.

Each person had their own nigger to wait on them—Buck too. My nigger had a monstrous easy time, because I warn't used to having anybody do anything for me, but Buck's was on the jump most of the time.

---

* A tall pole with a Phrygian Cap hoisted on it.

This was all there was of the family now, but there used to be more—three sons; they got killed; and Emmeline that died.

The old gentleman owned a lot of farms and over a hundred niggers. Sometimes a stack of people would come there, horseback, from ten or fifteen mile around, and stay five or six days, and have such junketings round about and on the river, and dances and picnics in the woods daytimes, and balls at the house nights. These people was mostly kinfolks of the family. The men brought their guns with them. It was a handsome lot of quality, I tell you.

There was another clan of aristocracy around there—five or six families—mostly of the name of Shepherdson. They was as high-toned and well born and rich and grand as the tribe of Grangerfords. The Shepherdsons and Grangerfords used the same steamboat landing, which was about two mile above our house; so sometimes when I went up there with a lot of our folks I used to see a lot of the Shepherdsons there on their fine horses.

One day Buck and me was away out in the woods hunting, and heard a horse coming. We was crossing the road. Buck says:

"Quick! Jump for the woods!"

We done it, and then peeped down the woods through the leaves. Pretty soon a splendid young man come galloping down the road, setting his horse easy and looking like a soldier. He had his gun across his pommel. I had seen him before. It was young Harney Shepherdson. I heard Buck's gun go off at my ear, and Harney's hat tumbled off from his head. He grabbed his gun and rode straight to the place where we was hid. But we didn't wait. We started through the woods on a run. The woods warn't thick, so I looked over my shoulder to dodge the bullet, and twice I seen Harney cover Buck with his gun; and then he rode away the way he come—to get his hat, I reckon, but I couldn't see. We never stopped running till we got home. The old gentleman's eyes blazed a minute—'twas pleasure, mainly, I judged—then his face sort of smoothed down, and he says, kind of gentle:

"I don't like that shooting from behind a bush. Why didn't you step into the road, my boy?"

"The Shepherdsons don't, father. They always take advantage."

Miss Charlotte she held her head up like a queen while Buck was telling his tale, and her nostrils spread and her eyes snapped. The two young men looked dark, but never said nothing. Miss Sophia she turned pale, but the colour come back when she found the man warn't hurt.

Soon as I could get Buck down by the corn-cribs under the trees by ourselves, I says:

"Did you want to kill him, Buck?"

"Well, I bet I did."

"What did he do to you?"

"Him? He never done nothing to me."

"Well, then, what did you want to kill him for?"

"Why, nothing—only it's on account of the feud."

"What's a feud?"

"Why, where was you raised? Don't you know what a feud is?"

"Never heard of it before—tell me about it."

"Well," says Buck, "a feud is this way: A man has a quarrel with another man, and kills him; then that other man's brother kills *him*; then the other brothers, on both sides, goes for one another; then the *cousins* chip in—and by and by everybody's killed off, and there ain't no more feud. But it's kind of slow, and takes a long time."

"Has this one been going on long, Buck?"

"Well, I should *reckon*! It started thirty year ago, or som'ers along there. There was trouble 'bout something, and then a lawsuit to settle it; and the suit went agin one of the men, and so he up and shot the man that won the suit—which he would naturally do, of course. Anybody would."

"What was the trouble about, Buck?—land?"

"I reckon maybe—I don't know."

"Well, who done the shooting? Was it a Grangerford or a Shepherdson?"

"Laws, how do I know? It was so long ago."

"Don't anybody know?"

"Oh, yes, pa knows, I reckon, and some of the other old people; but they don't know now what the row was about in the first place."

"Has there been many killed, Buck?"

"Yes; right smart chance of funerals. But they don't always kill. Pa's got a few buckshot in him; but he don't mind it 'cuz he don't weigh much, anyway. Bob's been carved up some with a bowie, and Tom's been hurt once or twice."

"Has anybody been killed this year, Buck?"

"Yes; we got one and they got one. 'Bout three months ago my cousin Bud, fourteen year old, was riding through the woods on t'other side of the river, and didn't have no weapon with him, which was blame' foolishness, and in a lonesome place he hears a horse a-coming behind him, and sees old Baldy Shepherdson a-linkin' after him with his gun in his hand and his white hair a-flying in the wind; and 'stead of jumping off and taking to the brush, Bud 'lowed he could out-run him; so they had it, nip and tuck, for five mile or more, the old man a-gaining all the time; so at last Bud seen it warn't any use, so he stopped and faced around so as to have the bullet holes in front, you know, and the old man he rode up and shot him down. But he didn't git much chance to enjoy his luck, for inside of a week our folks laid *him* out."

"I reckon that old man was a coward, Buck."

"I reckon he *warn't* a coward. Not by a blame' sight. There ain't a coward amongst them Shepherdsons—not a one. And there ain't no cowards amongst the Grangerfords either. Why, that old man kep' up his end in a fight one day for half an hour against three Grangerfords, and come out winner. They was all a-horseback; he lit off of his horse and got behind a little woodpile, and kep' his horse before him to stop the bullets; but the Grangerfords stayed on their horses and capered around the old man, and peppered away at him, and he peppered away at them. Him and his horse both went home pretty leaky and crippled, but the Grangerfords had to be *fetched* home—and one of 'em was dead, and another died the next day. No, sir; if a body's out hunting for cowards he don't want to fool away any time amongst them Shepherdsons, becuz they don't breed any of that *kind*."

Next Sunday we all went to church, about three mile, everybody a-horseback. The men took their guns along, so did Buck, and kept them between their knees or stood them handy against the wall. The Shepherdsons done the same. It was pretty ornery preaching—all about brotherly love, and such-like tiresomeness; but everybody said it was a good sermon, and they all talked it over going home, and had such a powerful lot to say about faith and good works and free grace and preforeordestination, and I don't know what all, that it did seem to me to be one of the roughest Sundays I had run across yet.

About an hour after dinner everybody was dozing around, some in their chairs and some in their rooms, and it got to be pretty dull. Buck and a dog was stretched out on the grass in the sun sound asleep. I went up to our room, and judged I would take a nap myself. I found that sweet Miss Sophia standing in her door, which was next to ours, and she took me in her room and shut the door very soft, and asked me if I liked her, and I said I did; and she asked me if I would do something for her and not tell anybody, and I said I would. Then she said she'd forgot her Testament, and left it in the seat at church between two other books, and would I slip out quiet and go there and fetch it to her, and not say nothing to nobody. I said I would. So I slid out and slipped off up the road, and there warn't anybody at the church, except maybe a hog or two, for there warn't any lock on the door, and hogs likes a puncheon floor* in summer-time because it's cool. If you notice, most folks don't go to church only when they've got to; but a hog is different.

---

* A floor made of coarse, roughly-dressed timber.

Says I to myself, something's up; it ain't natural for a girl to be in such a sweat about a Testament. So I give it a shake, and out drops a little piece of paper with *"Half-Past Two"* wrote on it with a pencil. I ransacked it, but couldn't find anything else. I couldn't make anything out of that, so I put the paper in the book again, and when I got home and upstairs there was Miss Sophia in her door waiting for me. She pulled me in and shut the door; then she looked in the Testament till she found the paper, and as soon as she read it she looked glad; and before a body could think she grabbed me and give me a squeeze, and said I was the best boy in the world, and not to tell anybody. She was mighty red in the face for a minute, and her eyes lighted up, and it made her powerful pretty. I was a good deal astonished, but when I got my breath I asked her what the paper was about, and she asked me if I had read it, and I said no, and she asked me if I could read writing, and I told her "no, only coarse-hand,"* and then she said the paper warn't anything but a book-mark to keep her place, and I might go and play now.

I went off down to the river, studying over this thing, and pretty soon I noticed that my nigger was following along behind. When we was out of sight of the house he looked back and around a second, and then comes a-running, and says:

"Mars Jawge, if you'll come down into de swamp I'll show you a whole stack o' water-moccasins."†

Thinks I, that's mighty curious; he said that yesterday. He oughter know a body don't love water-moccasins enough to go around hunting for them. What is he up to, anyway? So I says:

"All right; trot ahead."

I followed a half a mile; then he struck out over the swamp, and waded ankle deep as much as another half-mile. We come to a little flat piece of land which was dry and very thick with trees and bushes and vines, and he says:

"You shove right in dah jist a few steps, Mars Jawge; dah's whah dey is. I's seed 'm befo'; I don't k'yer to see 'em no mo'."

Then he slopped right along and went away, and pretty soon the trees hid him. I poked into the place a-ways and come to a little open patch as big as a bedroom all hung around with vines, and found a man laying there asleep—and, by jings, it was my old Jim!

I waked him up, and I reckoned it was going to be a grand surprise to him to see me again, but it warn't. He nearly cried he was so glad, but he

* Printing.

† Species of venomous snake.

warn't surprised. Said he swum along behind me that night, and heard me yell every time, but dasn't answer, because he didn't want nobody to pick *him* up and take him into slavery again. Says he:

"I got hurt a little, en couldn't swim fas', so I wuz a considable ways behine you towards de las'; when you landed I reck'ned I could ketch up wid you on de lan' 'dout havin' to shout at you, but when I see dat house I begin to go slow. I 'uz off too fur to hear what dey say to you—I wuz 'fraid o' de dogs; but when it 'uz all quiet agin I knowed you's in de house, so I struck out for de woods to wait for day. Early in de mawnin' some er de niggers come along, gwyne to de fields, en dey tuk me en showed me dis place, whah de dogs can't track me on accounts o' de water, en dey brings me truck to eat every night, en tells me how you's a-gitt'n along."

"Why didn't you tell my Jack to fetch me here sooner, Jim?"

"Well, 'twarn't no use to 'sturb you, Huck, tell we could do sumfn—but we's all right now. I ben a-buyin' pots en pans en vittles, as I got a chanst, en a-patchin' up de raf' nights when—"

"*What* raft, Jim?"

"Our ole raf'."

"You mean to say our old raft warn't smashed all to flinders?"

"No, she warn't. She was tore up a good deal—one en' of her was; but dey warn't no great harm done, on'y our traps was mos' all los'. Ef we hadn' dive' so deep en swum so fur under water, en de night hadn' ben so dark, en we warn't so sk'yerd, en ben sich punkin-heads, as de sayin' is, we'd a seed de raf'. But it's jis' as well we didn't, 'kase now she's all fixed up agin mos' as good as new, en we's got a new lot o' stuff, in de place o' what 'uz los'."

"Why, how did you get hold of the raft again, Jim—did you catch her?"

"How I gwyne to ketch her en I out in de woods? No; some er de niggers foun' her ketched on a snag along heah in de ben', en dey hid her in a crick 'mongst de willows, en dey wuz so much jawin' 'bout which un 'um she b'long to de mos' dat I come to heah 'bout it pooty soon, so I ups en settles de trouble by tellin' 'um she don't b'long to none uv um, but to you en me; en I ast 'm if dey gwyne to grab a young white genlman's propaty, en git a hid'n for it? Den I gin 'm ten cents apiece, en dey 'uz mighty well satisfied, en wisht some mo' raf's 'ud come along en make 'm rich agin. Dey's mighty good to me, dese niggers is, en whatever I wants 'm to do fur me I doan' have to ast 'm twice, honey. Dat Jack's a good nigger, en pooty smart."

"Yes, he is. He ain't ever told me you was here; told me to come, and he'd show me a lot of water-moccasins. If anything happens *he* ain't mixed up in it. He can say he never seen us together, and it 'll be the truth."

I don't want to talk much about the next day. I reckon I'll cut it pretty short. I waked up about dawn, and was a-going to turn over and go to sleep again when I noticed how still it was—didn't seem to be anybody stirring. That warn't usual. Next I noticed that Buck was up and gone. Well, I gets up, a-wondering, and goes down stairs—nobody around; everything as still as a mouse. Just the same outside. Thinks I, what does it mean? Down by the wood-pile I comes across my Jack, and says:

"What's it all about?"

Says he:

"Don't you know, Mars Jawge?"

"No," says I, "I don't."

"Well, den, Miss Sophia's run off! 'deed she has. She run off in de night some time—nobody don't know jis' when; run off to get married to dat young Harney Shepherdson, you know—leastways, so dey 'spec. De fambly foun' it out 'bout half an hour ago—maybe a little mo'—en' I *tell* you dey warn't no time los'. Sich another hurryin' up guns en hosses *you* never see! De women folks has gone for to stir up de relations, en ole Mars Saul en de boys tuck dey guns en rode up de river road for to try to ketch dat young man en kill him 'fo' he kin git acrost de river wid Miss Sophia. I reck'n dey's gwyne to be mighty rough times."

"Buck went off 'thout waking me up."

"Well, I reck'n he *did!* Dey warn't gwyne to mix you up in it. Mars Buck he loaded up his gun en 'lowed he's gwyne to fetch home a Shepherdson or bust. Well, dey'll be plenty un 'm dah, I reck'n, en you bet you he'll fetch one ef he gits a chanst."

I took up the river road as hard as I could put. By and by I begin to hear guns a good ways off. When I come in sight of the log store and the woodpile where the steamboats lands I worked along under the trees and brush till I got to a good place, and then I clumb up into the forks of a cottonwood that was out of reach, and watched. There was a wood-rank four foot high a little ways in front of the tree, and first I was going to hide behind that; but maybe it was luckier I didn't.

There was four or five men cavorting around on their horses in the open place before the log store, cussing and yelling, and trying to get at a couple of young chaps that was behind the wood-rank alongside of the steamboat landing; but they couldn't come it. Every time one of them showed himself on the river side of the woodpile he got shot at. The two boys was squatting back to back behind the pile, so they could watch both ways.

By and by the men stopped cavorting around and yelling. They started riding towards the store; then up gets one of the boys, draws a steady bead over the wood-rank, and drops one of them out of his saddle. All the men jumped off of their horses and grabbed the hurt one and started to carry him to the store; and that minute the two boys started on the run. They got half way to the tree I was in before the men noticed. Then the men see them, and jumped on their horses and took out after them. They gained on the boys, but it didn't do no good, the boys had too good a start; they got to the woodpile that was in front of my tree, and slipped in behind it, and so they had the bulge on the men again. One of the boys was Buck, and the other was a slim young chap about nineteen years old.

The men ripped around awhile, and then rode away. As soon as they was out of sight I sung out to Buck and told him. He didn't know what to make of my voice coming out of the tree at first. He was awful surprised. He told me to watch out sharp and let him know when the men come in sight again; said they was up to some devilment or other—wouldn't be gone long. I wished I was out of that tree, but I dasn't come down. Buck begun to cry and rip, and 'lowed that him and his cousin Joe (that was the other young chap) would make up for this day yet. He said his father and his two brothers was killed, and two or three of the enemy. Said the Shepherdsons laid for them in ambush. Buck said his father and brothers ought to waited for their relations—the Shepherdsons was too strong for them. I asked him what was become of young Harney and Miss Sophia. He said they'd got across the river and was safe. I was glad of that; but the way Buck did take on because he didn't manage to kill Harney that day he shot at him—I hain't ever heard anything like it.

All of a sudden, bang! bang! bang! goes three or four guns—the men had slipped around through the woods and come in from behind without their horses! The boys jumped for the river—both of them hurt—and as they swum down the current the men run along the bank shooting at them and singing out, "Kill them, kill them!" It made me so sick I most fell out of the tree. I ain't a-going to tell *all* that happened—it would make me sick again if I was to do that. I wished I hadn't ever come ashore that night to see such things. I ain't ever going to get shut of them—lots of times I dream about them.

I stayed in the tree till it begun to get dark, afraid to come down. Sometimes I heard guns away off in the woods; and twice I seen little gangs of men gallop past the log store with guns; so I reckoned the trouble was still a-going on. I was mighty downhearted; so I made up my mind I wouldn't ever go anear that house again, because I reckoned I was to blame, somehow. I judged that that piece of paper meant that Miss Sophia was to meet Harney somewheres at half-past two and run off; and I judged I ought to told her father about that paper and the curious way she acted, and then maybe he would a locked her up, and this awful mess wouldn't ever happened.

When I got down out of the tree I crept along down the river bank a piece, and found the two bodies laying in the edge of the water, and tugged at them till I got them ashore; then I covered up their faces, and got away as quick as I could. I cried a little when I was covering up Buck's face, for he was mighty good to me.

It was just dark now. I never went near the house, but struck through the woods and made for the swamp. Jim warn't on his island, so I tramped off in a hurry for the crick, and crowded through the willows, red-hot to jump aboard and get out of that awful country. The raft was gone! My souls, but I was scared! I couldn't get my breath for most a minute. Then I raised a yell. A voice not twenty-five foot from me says:

"Good lan'! is dat you, honey? Doan' make no noise."

It was Jim's voice—nothing ever sounded so good before. I run along the bank a piece and got aboard, and Jim he grabbed me and hugged me, he was so glad to see me. He says:

"Laws bless you, chile, I 'uz right down sho' you's dead agin. Jack's been heah; he say he reck'n you's ben shot, kase you didn' come home no mo'; so I's jes' dis minute a startin' de raf' down towards de mouf er de crick, so's to be all ready for to shove out en leave soon as Jack comes agin en tells me for certain you *is* dead. Lawsy, I's mighty glad to git you back again, honey."

I says:

"All right—that's mighty good; they won't find me, and they'll think I've been killed, and floated down the river—there's something up there that 'll help them think so—so don't you lose no time, Jim, but just shove off for the big water as fast as ever you can."

I never felt easy till the raft was two mile below there and out in the middle of the Mississippi. Then we hung up our signal lantern, and judged that we was free and safe once more. I hadn't had a bite to eat since yesterday, so Jim he got out some corn-dodgers* and buttermilk, and pork and cabbage and greens—there ain't nothing in the world so good when it's cooked right—and whilst I eat my supper we talked and had a good time. I was powerful glad to get away from the feuds, and so was Jim to get away from the swamp. We said there warn't no home like a raft, after all. Other places do seem so cramped up and smothery, but a raft don't. You feel mighty free and easy and comfortable on a raft.

---

* Hard-baked corn cakes.

19

Two or three days and nights went by; I reckon I might say they swum by, they slid along so quiet and smooth and lovely. Here is the way we put in the time. It was a monstrous big river down there—sometimes a mile and a half wide; we run nights, and laid up and hid daytimes; soon as night was most gone we stopped navigating and tied up—nearly always in the dead water under a towhead; and then cut young cottonwoods and willows, and hid the raft with them. Then we set out the lines. Next we slid into the river and had a swim, so as to freshen up and cool off; then we set down on the sandy bottom where the water was about knee deep, and watched the daylight come. Not a sound anywheres—perfectly still—just like the whole world was asleep, only sometimes the bullfrogs a-cluttering, maybe. The first thing to see, looking away over the water, was a kind of dull line—that was the woods on t'other side; you couldn't make nothing else out; then a pale place in the sky; then more paleness spreading around; then the river softened up away off, and warn't black any more, but grey; you could see little dark spots drifting along ever so far away—trading scows, and such things; and long black streaks—rafts; sometimes you could hear a sweep screaking; or jumbled up voices, it was so still, and sounds come so far; and by and by you could see a streak on the water which you know by the look of the streak that there's a snag there in a swift current which breaks on it and makes that streak look that way; and you see the mist curl up off of the water, and the east reddens up, and the river, and you make out a log-cabin in the edge of the woods, away on the bank on t'other side of the river, being a woodyard, likely, and piled by them cheats so you can throw a dog through it anywheres; then the nice breeze springs up, and comes fanning you from over there, so cool and fresh and sweet to smell on account of the woods and the flowers; but sometimes not that way, because they've left dead fish laying around, gars* and such, and they do get pretty rank; and next you've got the full day, and everything smiling in the sun, and the song-birds just going it!

A little smoke couldn't be noticed now, so we would take some fish off of the lines and cook up a hot breakfast. And afterwards we would watch

* A fish of the Pike family.

the lonesomeness of the river, and kind of lazy along, and by and by lazy off to sleep. Wake up by and by, and look to see what done it, and maybe see a steamboat coughing along up-stream, so far off towards the other side you couldn't tell nothing about her only whether she was a stern-wheel or side-wheel; then for about an hour there wouldn't be nothing to hear nor nothing to see—just solid lonesomeness. Next you'd see a raft sliding by, away off yonder, and maybe a galoot* on it chopping, because they're most always doing it on a raft; you'd see the axe flash and come down—you don't hear nothing; you see that axe go up again, and by the time it's above the man's head then you hear the *k'chunk*!—it had took all that time to come over the water. So we would put in the day, lazying around, listening to the stillness. Once there was a thick fog, and the rafts and things that went by was beating tin pans so the steamboats wouldn't run over them. A scow or a raft went by so close we could hear them talking and cussing and laughing—heard them plain; but we couldn't see no sign of them; it made you feel crawly; it was like spirits carrying on that way in the air. Jim said he believed it was spirits; but I says:

"No; spirits wouldn't say, 'Dern the dern fog.'"

Soon as it was night out we shoved; when we got her out to about the middle we let her alone, and let her float wherever the current wanted her to; then we lit the pipes, and dangled our legs in the water, and talked about all kinds of things—we was always naked, day and night, whenever the mosquitoes would let us—the new clothes Buck's folks made for me was too good to be comfortable, and besides I didn't go much on clothes, nohow.

Sometimes we'd have that whole river all to ourselves for the longest time. Yonder was the banks and the islands, across the water; and maybe a spark—which was a candle in a cabin window; and sometimes on the water you could see a spark or two—on a raft or a scow, you know; and maybe you could hear a fiddle or a song coming over from one of them crafts. It's lovely to live on a raft. We had the sky up there, all speckled with stars, and we used to lay on our backs and look up at them, and discuss about whether they was made or only just happened. Jim he allowed they was made, but I allowed they happened; I judged it would have took too long to *make* so many. Jim said the moon could a *laid* them; well, that looked kind of reasonable, so I didn't say nothing against it, because I've seen a frog lay most as many, so of course it could be done. We used to watch the stars that fell, too, and see them streak down. Jim allowed they'd got spoiled and was hove out of the nest.

* A young, unfledged sailor.

Once or twice of a night we would see a steamboat slipping along in the dark, and now and then she would belch a whole world of sparks up out of her chimbleys, and they would rain down in the river and look awful pretty; then she would turn a corner and her lights would wink out and her powwow shut off and leave the river still again; and by and by her waves would get to us, a long time after she was gone, and joggle the raft a bit, and after that you wouldn't hear nothing for you couldn't tell how long, except maybe frogs or something.

After midnight the people on shore went to bed, and then for two or three hours the shores was black—no more sparks in the cabin windows. These sparks was our clock—the first one that showed again meant morning was coming, so we hunted a place to hide and tie up right away.

One morning about daybreak I found a canoe and crossed over a chute* to the main shore—it was only two hundred yards—and paddled about a mile up a crick amongst the cypress woods, to see if I couldn't get some berries. Just as I was passing a place where a kind of a cowpath crossed the crick, here comes a couple of men tearing up the path as tight as they could foot it. I thought I was a goner, for whenever anybody was after anybody I judged it was *me*—or maybe Jim. I was about to dig out from there in a hurry, but they was pretty close to me then, and sung out and begged me to save their lives—said they hadn't been doing nothing, and was being chased for it—said there was men and dogs a-coming. They wanted to jump right in, but I says:

"Don't you do it. I don't hear the dogs and horses yet; you've got time to crowd through the brush and get up the crick a little ways; then you take to the water and wade down to me and get in—that'll throw the dogs off the scent."

They done it, and soon as they was aboard I lit out for our towhead, and in about five or ten minutes we heard the dogs and the men away off, shouting. We heard them come along towards the crick, but couldn't see them; they seemed to stop and fool around a while; then, as we got further and further away all the time, we couldn't hardly hear them at all; by the time we had left a mile of woods behind us and struck the river, everything was quiet, and we paddled over to the towhead and hid in the cottonwoods and was safe.

One of these fellows was about seventy or upwards, and had a bald head and very grey whiskers. He had an old battered-up slouch hat on, and a greasy blue woollen shirt, and ragged old blue jeans britches stuffed into

---

* A narrow channel with a swift current leading towards the shore.

his boot-tops, and home-knit galluses—no, he only had one. He had an old long-tailed blue jeans coat with slick brass buttons flung over his arm, and both of them had big, fat, ratty-looking carpet-bags.

The other fellow was about thirty, and dressed about as ornery. After breakfast we all laid off and talked, and the first thing that come out was that these chaps didn't know one another.

"What got you into trouble?" says the baldhead to t'other chap.

"Well, I'd been selling an article to take the tartar off the teeth—and it does take it off, too, and generally the enamel along with it—but I stayed about one night longer than I ought to, and was just in the act of sliding out when I ran across you on the trail this side of town, and you told me they were coming, and begged me to help you to get off. So I told you I was expecting trouble myself, and would scatter out *with* you. That's the whole yarn—what's yourn?

"Well, I'd ben a-running' a little temperance revival thar 'bout a week, and was the pet of the women folks, big and little, for I was makin' it mighty warm for the rummies, I *tell* you, and takin' as much as five or six dollars a night—ten cents a head, children and niggers free—and business a-growin' all the time, when somehow or another a little report got around last night that I had a way of puttin' in my time with a private jug on the sly. A nigger rousted me out this mornin', and told me the people was getherin' on the quiet with their dogs and horses, and they'd be along pretty soon and give me 'bout half an hour's start, and then run me down if they could; and if they got me they'd tar and feather me and ride me on a rail, sure. I didn't wait for no breakfast—I warn't hungry."

"Old man," said the young one, "I reckon we might double-team it together; what do you think?"

"I ain't undisposed. What's your line—mainly?"

"Jour printer* by trade; do a little in patent medicines; theater-actor—tragedy, you know; take a turn to mesmerism and phrenology when there's a chance; teach singing-geography school for a change; sling a lecture sometimes—oh, I do lots of things—most anything that comes handy, so it ain't work. What's your lay?"

"I've done considerble in the doctoring way in my time. Layin' on o' hands is my best holt—for cancer and paralysis, and sich things; and I k'n tell a fortune pretty good when I've got somebody along to find out the facts for me. Preachin's my line, too, and workin' camp-meetin's, and missionaryin' around."

---

* Journeyman printer.

Nobody never said anything for a while; then the young man hove a sigh and says:

"Alas!"

"What 're you alassin' about?" says the bald-head.

"To think I should have lived to be leading such a life, and be degraded down into such company." And he begun to wipe the corner of his eye with a rag.

"Dern your skin, ain't the company good enough for you?" says the baldhead, pretty pert and uppish.

"Yes, it *is* good enough for me; it's as good as I deserve; for who fetched me so low when I was so high? I did myself. I don't blame *you*, gentlemen—far from it; I don't blame anybody. I deserve it all. Let the cold world do its worst; one thing I know—there's a grave somewhere for me. The world may go on just as it's always done, and take everything from me—loved ones, property, everything; but it can't take that. Some day I'll lie down in it and forget it all, and my poor broken heart will be at rest." He went on a-wiping.

"Drot your pore broken heart," says the baldhead; "what are you heaving your pore broken heart at *us* f'r? *we* hain't done nothing."

"No, I know you haven't. I ain't blaming you, gentlemen. I brought myself down—yes, I did it myself. It's right I should suffer—perfectly right—I don't make any moan."

"Brought you down from whar? Whar was you brought down from?"

"Ah, you would not believe me; the world never believes—let it pass—'tis no matter. The secret of my birth—"

"The secret of your birth! Do you mean to say—"

"Gentlemen," says the young man, very solemn, "I will reveal it to you, for I feel I may have confidence in you. By rights I am a duke!"

Jim's eyes bugged out when he heard that; and I reckon mine did, too. Then the baldhead says: "No! you can't mean it?"

"Yes. My great-grandfather, eldest son of the Duke of Bridgewater, fled to this country about the end of the last century, to breathe the pure air of freedom; married here, and died, leaving a son, his own father dying about the same time. The second son of the late duke seized the titles and estates—the infant real duke was ignored. I am the lineal descendant of that infant—I am the rightful Duke of Bridgewater; and here am I, forlorn, torn from my high estate, hunted of men, despised by the cold world, ragged, worn, heart-broken, and degraded to the companionship of felons on a raft!"

Jim pitied him ever so much, and so did I. We tried to comfort him, but he said it warn't much use, he couldn't be much comforted; said if we was a mind to acknowledge him, that would do him more good than most anything else; so we said we would, if he would tell us how. He said we ought to bow when we spoke to him, and say "Your Grace," or "My Lord," or "Your Lordship"—and he wouldn't mind it if we called him plain "Bridgewater," which, he said, was a title anyway, and not a name; and one of us ought to wait on him at dinner, and do any little thing for him he wanted done.

Well, that was all easy, so we done it. All through dinner Jim stood around and waited on him, and says, "Will yo' Grace have some o' dis or some o' dat?" and so on, and a body could see it was mighty pleasing to him.

But the old man got pretty silent by and by—didn't have much to say, and didn't look pretty comfortable over all that petting that was going on around that duke. He seemed to have something on his mind. So, along in the afternoon, he says:

"Looky here, Bilgewater," he says, "I'm nation sorry for you, but you ain't the only person that's had troubles like that."

"No?"

"No you ain't. You ain't the only person that's ben snaked down wrongfully out'n a high place."

"Alas!"

"No, you ain't the only person that's had a secret of his birth." And, by jings, *he* begins to cry.

"Hold! What do you mean?"

"Bilgewater, kin I trust you?" says the old man, still sort of sobbing.

"To the bitter death!" He took the old man by the hand and squeezed it, and says, "That secret of your being: speak!"

"Bilgewater, I am the late Dauphin!"

You bet you, Jim and me stared this time. Then the duke says:

"You are what?"

"Yes, my friend, it is too true—your eyes is lookin' at this very moment on the pore disappeared Dauphin, Looy the Seventeen, son of Looy the Sixteen and Marry Antonette."

"You! At your age! No! You mean you're the late Charlemagne; you must be six or seven hundred years old, at the very least."

"Trouble has done it, Bilgewater, trouble has done it; trouble has brung these grey hairs and this premature balditude. Yes, gentlemen, you see before you, in blue jeans and misery, the wanderin', exiled, trampled-on, and sufferin' rightful King of France."

Well, he cried and took on so that me and Jim didn't know hardly what to do, we was so sorry—and so glad and proud we'd got him with us, too. So we set in, like we done before with the duke, and tried to comfort *him*. But he said it warn't no use, nothing but to be dead and done with it all could do him any good; though he said it often made him feel easier and better for a while if people treated him according to his rights, and got down on one knee to speak to him, and always called him "Your Majesty," and waited on him first at meals, and didn't set down in his presence till he asked them. So Jim and me set to majestying him, and doing this and that and t'other for him, and standing up till he told us we might set down. This done him heaps of good, and so he got cheerful and comfortable. But the duke kind of soured on him, and didn't look a bit satisfied with the way things was going; still, the king acted real friendly towards him, and said the duke's great-grandfather and all the other Dukes of Bilgewater was a good deal thought of by *his* father, and was allowed to come to the palace considerable; but the duke stayed huffy a good while, till by and by the king says:

"Like as not we got to be together a blamed long time on this h-yer raft, Bilgewater, and so what's the use o' your bein' sour? It 'll only make things oncomfortable. It ain't my fault I warn't born a duke, it ain't your fault you warn't born a king—so what's the use to worry? Make the best o' things the way you find 'em, says I—that's my motto. This ain't no bad thing that we've struck here—plenty grub and an easy life—come, give us your hand, duke, and le's all be friends."

The duke done it, and Jim and me was pretty glad to see it. It took away all the uncomfortableness and we felt mighty good over it, because it would a been a miserable business to have any unfriendliness on the raft; for what you want, above all things, on a raft, is for everybody to be satisfied, and feel right and kind towards the others.

It didn't take me long to make up my mind that these liars warn't no kings nor dukes at all, but just low-down humbugs and frauds. But I never said nothing, never let on; kept it to myself; it's the best way; then you don't have no quarrels, and don't get into no trouble. If they wanted us to call them kings and dukes, I hadn't no objections, 'long as it would keep peace in the family; and it warn't no use to tell Jim, so I didn't tell him. If I never learnt nothing else out of pap, I learnt that the best way to get along with his kind of people is to let them have their own way.

20

They asked us considerable many questions; wanted to know what we covered up the raft that way for, and laid by in the daytime instead of running—was Jim a runaway nigger? Says I:

"Goodness sakes! would a runaway nigger run *south*?"

No, they allowed he wouldn't. I had to account for things some way, so I says:

"My folks was living in Pike County, in Missouri, where I was born, and they all died off but me and pa and my brother Ike. Pa, he 'lowed he'd break up and go down and live with Uncle Ben, who's got a little one-horse place on the river, forty-four mile below Orleans. Pa was pretty poor, and had some debts; so when he'd squared up there warn't nothing left but sixteen dollars and our nigger, Jim. That warn't enough to take us fourteen hundred mile, deck passage nor no other way. Well, when the river rose pa had a streak of luck one day; he ketched this piece of a raft; so we reckoned we'd go down to Orleans on it. Pa's luck didn't hold out; a steamboat run over the forrard corner of the raft one night, and we all went overboard and dove under the wheel; Jim and me come up all right, but pa was drunk, and Ike was only four years old, so they never come up no more. Well, for the next day or two we had considerable trouble, because people was always coming out in skiffs and trying to take Jim away from me, saying they believed he was a runaway nigger. We don't run daytimes no more now; nights they don't bother us."

The duke says:

"Leave me alone to cipher out a way so we can run in the daytime if we want to. I'll think the thing over—I'll invent a plan that'll fix it. We'll let it alone for today, because of course we don't want to go by that town yonder in daylight—it mightn't be healthy."

Towards night it begun to darken up and look like rain; the heat lightning was squirting around low down in the sky, and the leaves was beginning to shiver—it was going to be pretty ugly, it was easy to see that. So the duke and the king went to overhauling our wigwam, to see what the beds was like. My bed was a straw tick better than Jim's, which was a corn-shuck tick;* there's always cobs around about in a shuck tick, and they poke

* Mattress composed of outer husks of maize.

into you and hurt; and when you roll over the dry shucks sound like you was rolling over in a pile of dead leaves; it makes such a rustling that you wake up. Well, the duke allowed he would take my bed; but the king allowed he wouldn't. He says:

"I should a reckoned the difference in rank would a sejested to you that a corn-shuck bed warn't just fitten for me to sleep on. Your Grace 'll take the shuck bed yourself."

Jim and me was in a sweat again for a minute, being afraid there was going to be some more trouble amongst them; so we was pretty glad when the duke says:

"'Tis my fate to be always ground into the mire under the iron heel of oppression. Misfortune has broken my once haughty spirit; I yield, I submit; 'tis my fate. I am alone in the world—let me suffer; can bear it."

We got away as soon as it was good and dark. The king told us to stand well out towards the middle of the river, and not show a light till we got a long ways below the town. We come in sight of the little bunch of lights by and by—that was the town, you know—and slid by, about a half a mile out, all right. When we was three-quarters of a mile below we hoisted up our signal lantern; and about ten o'clock it come on to rain and blow and thunder and lighten like everything; so the king told us to both stay on watch till the weather got better; then him and the duke crawled into the wigwam and turned in for the night. It was my watch below till twelve, but I wouldn't a turned in anyway if I'd had a bed, because a body don't see such a storm as that every day in the week, not by a long sight. My souls, how the wind did scream along! And every second or two there'd come a glare that lit up the white-caps for a half a mile around, and you'd see the islands looking dusty through the rain, and the trees thrashing around in the wind; then comes a H-WHACK!—bum! bum! bumble-umble-um-bum-bum-bum-bum—and the thunder would go rumbling and grumbling away, and quit—and then RIP comes another flash and another sockdolager.* The waves most washed me off the raft sometimes, but I hadn't any clothes on, and didn't mind. We didn't have no trouble about snags; the lightning was glaring and flittering around so constant that we could see them plenty soon enough to throw her head this way or that and miss them.

I had the middle watch, you know, but I was pretty sleepy by that time, so Jim he said he would stand the first half of it for me; he was always mighty good that way, Jim was. I crawled into the wigwam, but the king and the

* Literally, a knock-out blow.

duke had their legs sprawled around so there warn't no show for me; so I laid outside—I didn't mind the rain, because it was warm, and the waves warn't running so high now. About two they come up again, though, and Jim was going to call me; but he changed his mind, because he reckoned they warn't high enough yet to do any harm; but he was mistaken about that, for pretty soon all of a sudden along comes a regular ripper and washed me overboard. It most killed Jim a-laughing. He was the easiest nigger to laugh that ever was, anyway.

I took the watch, and Jim he laid down and snored away; and by and by the storm let up for good and all; and the first cabin-light that showed I rousted him out, and we slid the raft into hiding quarters for the day.

The king got out an old ratty deck of cards after breakfast, and him and the duke played seven-up a while, five cents a game. Then they got tired of it, and allowed they would "lay out a campaign," as they called it. The duke went down into his carpet-bag, and fetched up a lot of little printed bills and read them out loud. One bill said, "The celebrated Dr. Armand de Montalban, of Paris," would "lecture on the Science of Phrenology" at such and such a place, on the blank day of blank, at ten cents admission, and "furnish charts of character at twenty-five cents apiece." The duke said that was *him*. In another bill he was the "world-renowned Shakespearian tragedian, Garrick the Younger, of Drury Lane, London." In other bills he had a lot of other names and done other wonderful things, like finding water and gold with a "divining-rod," "dissipating witch spells," and so on. By and by he says:

"But the histrionic muse is the darling. Have you ever trod the boards, Royalty?"

"No," says the king.

"You shall, then, before you're three days older, Fallen Grandeur," says the duke. "The first good town we come to we'll hire a hall and do the sword fight in Richard III. and the balcony scene in Romeo and Juliet. How does that strike you?"

"I'm in, up to the hub, for anything that will pay, Bilgewater; but, you see, I don't know nothing about play-actin', and hain't ever seen much of it. I was too small when pap used to have 'em at the palace. Do you reckon you can learn me?"

"Easy!"

"All right. I'm jist a-freezn' for something fresh, anyway. Le's commence right away."

So the duke he told him all about who Romeo was and who Juliet was, and said he was used to being Romeo, so the king could be Juliet.

"But if Juliet's such a young gal, duke, my peeled head and my white whiskers is goin' to look oncommon odd on her, maybe."

"No, don't you worry; these country jakes won't ever think of that. Besides, you know, you'll be in costume, and that makes all the difference in the world; Juliet's in a balcony, enjoying the moonlight before she goes to bed, and she's got on her night-gown and her ruffled nightcap. Here are the costumes for the parts."

He got out two or three curtain-calico suits, which he said was meedyevil armor for Richard III. and t'other chap, and a long white cotton nightshirt and a ruffled nightcap to match. The king was satisfied; so the duke got out his book and read the parts over in the most splendid spread-eagle way, prancing around and acting at the same time, to show how it had got to be done; then he give the book to the king and told him to get his part by heart.

There was a little one-horse town about three mile down the bend, and after dinner the duke said he had ciphered out his idea about how to run in daylight without it being dangersome for Jim; so he allowed he would go down to the town and fix that thing. The king allowed he would go, too, and see if he couldn't strike something. We was out of coffee, so Jim said I better go along with them in the canoe and get some.

When we got there there warn't nobody stirring; streets empty, and perfectly dead and still, like Sunday. We found a sick nigger sunning himself in a back yard, and he said everybody that warn't too young or too sick or too old was gone to camp-meeting, about two mile back in the woods. The king got the directions, and allowed he'd go and work that camp-meeting for all it was worth, and I might go, too.

The duke said what he was after was a printing-office. We found it; a little bit of a concern, up over a carpenter shop—carpenters and printers all gone to the meeting, and no doors locked. It was a dirty, littered-up place, and had ink marks, and handbills with pictures of horses and runaway niggers on them, all over the walls. The duke shed his coat and said he was all right now. So me and the king lit out for the camp-meeting.

We got there in about a half an hour fairly dripping, for it was a most awful hot day. There was as much as a thousand people there from twenty mile around. The woods was full of teams and wagons, hitched everywheres, feeding out of the wagon-troughs and stomping to keep off the flies. There was sheds made out of poles and roofed over with branches, where they had lemonade and gingerbread to sell, and piles of watermelons and green corn and such-like truck.

The preaching was going on under the same kinds of sheds, only they was bigger and held crowds of people. The benches was made out of outside slabs of logs, with holes bored in the round side to drive sticks into for legs. They didn't have no backs. The preachers had high platforms to stand on at one end of the sheds. The women had on sun-bonnets; and some had linsey-woolsey frocks, some gingham ones, and a few of the young ones had on calico. Some of the young men was barefooted, and some of the children didn't have on any clothes but just a tow-linen shirt. Some of the old women was knitting, and some of the young folks was courting on the sly.

"Courting on the sly"

The first shed we come to the preacher was lining out a hymn. He lined out two lines, everybody sung it, and it was kind of grand to hear it, there was so many of them and they done it in such a rousing way; then he lined out two more for them to sing—and so on. The people woke up more and more, and sung louder and louder; and towards the end some begun to groan, and some begun to shout. Then the preacher begun to preach, and begun in earnest, too; and went weaving first to one side of the platform and then the other, and then a-leaning down over the front of it, with his arms and his body going all the time, and shouting his words out with all his might; and every now and then he would hold up his Bible and spread it open, and kind of pass it around this way and that, shouting, "It's the brazen serpent in the wilderness! Look upon it and live!" And people would shout

out, "Glory!—A-a-*men*!" And so he went on, and the people groaning and crying and saying amen:

"Oh, come to the mourners' bench! come, black with sin! (*Amen*!) come, sick and sore! (*Amen*!) come, lame and halt and blind! (*Amen*!) come, pore and needy, sunk in shame! (*A-A-Men*!) come, all that's worn and soiled and suffering!—come with a broken spirit! come with a contrite heart! come in your rags and sin and dirt! the waters that cleanse is free, the door of heaven stands open—oh, enter in and be at rest!" (*A-A-Men*! *Glory, Glory Hallelujah*!)

And so on. You couldn't make out what the preacher said any more, on account of the shouting and crying. Folks got up everywheres in the crowd, and worked their way just by main strength to the mourners' bench, with the tears running down their faces; and when all the mourners had got up there to the front benches in a crowd, they sung and shouted and flung themselves down on the straw, just crazy and wild.

Well, the first I knowed the king got a-going, and you could hear him over everybody; and next he went a-charging up on to the platform, and the preacher he begged him to speak to the people, and he done it. He told them he was a pirate—been a pirate for thirty years out in the Indian Ocean—and his crew was thinned out considerable last spring in a fight, and he was home now to take out some fresh men, and thanks to goodness he'd been robbed last night and put ashore off of a steamboat without a cent, and he was glad of it; it was the blessedest thing that ever happened to him, because he was a changed man now, and happy for the first time in his life; and, poor as he was, he was going to start right off and work his way back to the Indian Ocean, and put in the rest of his life trying to turn the pirates into the true path; for he could do it better than anybody else, being acquainted with all pirate crews in that ocean; and though it would take him a long time to get there without money, he would get there anyway, and every time he convinced a pirate he would say to him, "Don't you thank me, don't you give me no credit; it all belongs to them dear people in Pokeville camp-meeting, natural brothers and benefactors of the race, and that dear preacher there, the truest friend a pirate ever had!"

And then he busted into tears, and so did everybody. Then somebody sings out, "Take up a collection for him, take up a collection!" Well, a half a dozen made a jump to do it, but somebody sings out, "Let *him* pass the hat around!" Then everybody said it, the preacher too.

So the king went all through the crowd with his hat swabbing his eyes, and blessing the people and praising them and thanking them for being so good to the poor pirates away off there; and every little while the prettiest kind of girls, with the tears running down their cheeks, would up and ask him would he let them kiss him for to remember him by; and he always done it; and some of them he hugged and kissed as many as five or six times—and he was invited to stay a week; and everybody wanted him to live in their houses, and said they'd think it was an honour; but he said as this was the last day of the camp-meeting he couldn't do no good, and besides he was in a sweat to get to the Indian Ocean right off and go to work on the pirates.

When we got back to the raft and he come to count up he found he had collected eighty-seven dollars and seventy-five cents. And then he had fetched away a three-gallon jug of whisky, too, that he found under a wagon when he was starting home through the woods. The king said, take it all around, it laid over any day he'd ever put in in the missionarying line. He said it warn't no use talking, heathens don't amount to shucks alongside of pirates to work a camp-meeting with.

The duke was thinking *he'd* been doing pretty well till the king come to show up, but after that he didn't think so so much. He had set up and printed off two little jobs for farmers in that printing-office—horse bills—and took the money, four dollars. And he had got in ten dollars' worth of advertisements for the paper, which he said he would put in for four dollars if they would pay in advance—so they done it. The price of the paper was two dollars a year, but he took in three subscriptions for half a dollar apiece on condition of them paying him in advance; they were going to pay in cordwood* and onions as usual, but he said he had just bought the concern and knocked down the price as low as he could afford it, and was going to run it for cash. He set up a little piece of poetry, which he made, himself, out of his own head—three verses—kind of sweet and saddish—the name of it was, "Yes, crush, cold world, this breaking heart"—and he left that all set up and ready to print in the paper, and didn't charge nothing for it. Well, he took in nine dollars and a half, and said he'd done a pretty square day's work for it.

Then he showed us another little job he'd printed and hadn't charged for, because it was for us. It had a picture of a runaway nigger with a bundle on a stick over his shoulder, and "$200 reward" under it. The reading was all about Jim, and just described him to a dot. It said he run away from St. Jacques' plantation, forty mile below New Orleans, last winter, and likely went north, and whoever would catch him and send him back he could have the reward and expenses.

"Now," says the duke, "after tonight we can run in the daytime if we

---

* Wood cut into lengths for fuel.

want to. Whenever we see anybody coming we can tie Jim hand and foot with a rope, and lay him in the wigwam and show this handbill and say we captured him up the river, and were too poor to travel on a steamboat, so we got this little raft on credit from our friends and are going down to get the reward. Handcuffs and chains would look still better on Jim, but it wouldn't go well with the story of us being so poor. Too much like jewellery. Ropes are the correct thing—we must preserve the unities, as we say on the boards."

We all said the duke was pretty smart, and there couldn't be no trouble about running daytimes. We judged we could make miles enough that night to get out of the reach of the powwow we reckoned the duke's work in the printing office was going to make in that little town; then we could boom right along if we wanted to.

We laid low and kept still, and never shoved out till nearly ten o'clock; then we slid by, pretty wide away from the town, and didn't hoist our lantern till we was clear out of sight of it.

When Jim called me to take the watch at four in the morning, he says:

"Huck, does you reck'n we gwyne to run acrost any mo' kings on dis trip?"

"No," I says, "I reckon not."

"Well," says he, "dat's all right, den. I doan' mine one er two kings, but dat's enough. Dis one's powerful drunk, en de duke ain' much better."

I found Jim had been trying to get him to talk French, so he could hear what it was like; but he said he had been in this country so long, and had so much trouble, he'd forgot it.

21

It was after sun-up now, but we went right on and didn't tie up. The king and the duke turned out by and by looking pretty rusty; but after they'd jumped overboard and took a swim it chippered them up a good deal. After breakfast the king he took a seat on the corner of the raft, and pulled off his boots and rolled up his britches, and let his legs dangle in the water, so as to be comfortable, and lit his pipe, and went to getting his Romeo and Juliet by heart. When he had got it pretty good him and the duke begun to practice it together. The duke had to learn him over and over again how to say every speech; and he made him sigh, and put his hand on his heart, and after a while he said he done it pretty well; "only," he says, "you mustn't bellow out *Romeo*! that way, like a bull—you must say it soft and sick and languishy, so—R-o-o-meo! that is the idea; for Juliet's a dear sweet mere child of a girl, you know, and she doesn't bray like a jackass."

Well, next they got out a couple of long swords that the duke made out of oak laths, and begun to practice the sword fight—the duke called himself Richard III.; and the way they laid on and pranced around the raft was grand to see. But by and by the king tripped and fell overboard, and after that they took a rest, and had a talk about all kinds of adventures they'd had in other times along the river.

After dinner the duke says:

"Well, Capet, we'll want to make this a first-class show, you know, so I guess we'll add a little more to it. We want a little something to answer encores with, anyway."

"What's onkores, Bilgewater?"

The duke told him, and then says:

"I'll answer by doing the Highland fling or the sailor's hornpipe; and you—well, let me see—oh, I've got it—you can do Hamlet's soliloquy."

"Hamlet's which?"

"Hamlet's soliloquy, you know; the most celebrated thing in Shakespeare. Ah, it's sublime, sublime! Always fetches the house. I haven't got it in the book—I've only got one volume—but I reckon I can piece it out from memory. I'll just walk up and down a minute, and see if I can call it back from recollection's vaults."

So he went to marching up and down, thinking, and frowning horrible every now and then; then he would hoist up his eyebrows; next he would squeeze his hand on his forehead and stagger back and kind of moan; next he would sigh, and next he'd let on to drop a tear. It was beautiful to see him. By and by he got it. He told us to give attention. Then he strikes a most noble attitude, with one leg shoved forwards, and his arms stretched away up, and his head tilted back, looking up at the sky; and then he begins to rip and rave and grit his teeth; and after that, all through his speech, he howled, and spread around, and swelled up his chest, and just knocked the spots out of any acting ever I see before. This is the speech—I learned it, easy enough, while he was learning it to the king:

To be, or not to be; that is the bare bodkin
That makes calamity of so long life;

For who would fardels bear, till Birnam Wood do come to Dunsinane,
But that the fear of something after death
Murders the innocent sleep,
Great nature's second course,
And makes us rather sling the arrows of outrageous fortune
Than fly to others that we know not of.
There's the respect must give us pause:
Wake Duncan with thy knocking! I would thou couldst;
For who would bear the whips and scorns of time,
The oppressor's wrong, the proud man's contumely,
The law's delay, and the quietus which his pangs might take.
In the dead waste and middle of the night, when churchyards yawn
In customary suits of solemn black,
But that the undiscovered country from whose bourne no traveler returns,
Breathes forth contagion on the world,
And thus the native hue of resolution, like the poor cat i' the adage,
Is sicklied o'er with care.
And all the clouds that lowered o'er our housetops,
With this regard their currents turn awry,
And lose the name of action.
Tis a consummation devoutly to be wished. But soft you, the fair Ophelia:
Ope not thy ponderous and marble jaws.
But get thee to a nunnery—go!

Well, the old man he liked that speech, and he mighty soon got it so he could do it first rate. It seemed like he was just born for it; and when he had his hand in and was excited, it was perfectly lovely the way he would rip and tear and rair up behind when he was getting it off.

The first chance we got, the duke he had some show bills printed; and after that, for two or three days as we floated along, the raft was a most uncommon lively place, for there warn't nothing but sword-fighting and rehearsing—as the duke called it—going on all the time. One morning, when we was pretty well down the State of Arkansaw, we come in sight of a little one-horse town in a big bend; so we tied up about three-quarters of a mile above it, in the mouth of a crick which was shut in like a tunnel by the cypress trees, and all of us but Jim took the canoe and went down there to see if there was any chance in that place for our show.

We struck it mighty lucky; there was going to be a circus there that afternoon, and the country people was already beginning to come in, in all kinds of old shackly wagons, and on horses. The circus would leave before night, so our show would have a pretty good chance. The duke he hired the court house, and we went around and stuck up our bills. They read like this:

Shaksperean Revival!!!
Wonderful Attraction!
For One Night Only! The world renowned tragedians,
David Garrick the younger, of Drury Lane Theatre, London,
and
Edmund Kean the elder, of the Royal Haymarket Theatre, Whitechapel, Pudding Lane, Piccadilly, London, and the Royal Continental Theatres, in their sublime Shaksperean Spectacle entitled The Balcony Scene in Romeo and Juliet!!!
Romeo...................................... Mr. Garrick.
Juliet...................................... Mr. Kean.
Assisted by the whole strength of the company!
New costumes, new scenery, new appointments!
Also:
The thrilling, masterly, and blood-curdling
Broad-sword conflict In Richard III!!!
Richard III................................ Mr. Garrick.
Richmond.................................. Mr. Kean.
also:
(by special request,)
Hamlet's Immortal Soliloquy!!
By the Illustrious Kean!
Done by him 300 consecutive nights in Paris!
For One Night Only,
On account of imperative European engagements!
Admission 25 cents; children and servants, 10 cents.

Then we went loafing around the town. The stores and houses was most all old shackly dried-up frame concerns that hadn't ever been painted; they was set up three or four foot above ground on stilts, so as to be out of reach of the water when the river was overflowed. The houses had little gardens around them, but they didn't seem to raise hardly anything in them but jimpson weeds, and sunflowers, and ash-piles, and old curled-up boots and shoes, and pieces of bottles, and rags, and played-out tin-ware. The fences was made of different kinds of boards, nailed on at different times; and they leaned every which-way, and had gates that didn't generally have but one hinge—a leather one. Some of the fences had been whitewashed, some time or another, but the duke said it was in Clumbus's time, like enough. There was generally hogs in the garden, and people driving them out.

All the stores was along one street. They had white domestic awnings in front, and the country people hitched their horses to the awning-posts. There was empty dry goods boxes under the awnings, and loafers roosting on them all day long, whittling them with their Barlow knives;* and chawing tobacco, and gaping and yawning and stretching—a mighty ornery lot. They generally had on yellow straw hats most as wide as an umbrella, but didn't wear no coats nor waistcoats, they called one another Bill, and Buck, and Hank, and Joe, and Andy, and talked lazy and drawly, and used considerable many cuss words. There was as many as one loafer leaning up against every awning-post, and he most always had his hands in his britches-pockets, except when he fetched them out to lend a chaw of tobacco or scratch. What a body was hearing amongst them all the time was:

"Gimme a chaw 'v tobacker, Hank."
"Cain't; I hain't got but one chaw left. Ask Bill."

Maybe Bill he gives him a chaw; maybe he lies and says he ain't got none. Some of them kinds of loafers never has a cent in the world, nor a chaw of tobacco of their own. They get all their chawing by borrowing; they say to a fellow, "I wisht you'd len' me a chaw, Jack, I jist this minute give Ben Thompson the last chaw I had"—which is a lie pretty much everytime; it don't fool nobody but a stranger; but Jack ain't no stranger, so he says:

"*You* give him a chaw, did you? So did your sister's cat's grandmother. You pay me back the chaws you've awready borry'd off'n me, Lafe Buckner, then I'll loan you one or two ton of it, and won't charge you no back intrust, nuther."

"Well, I *did* pay you back some of it wunst."

"Yes, you did—'bout six chaws. You borry'd store tobacker and paid back nigger-head."

Store tobacco is flat black plug, but these fellows mostly chaws the natural leaf twisted. When they borrow a chaw they don't generally cut it off with a knife, but set the plug in between their teeth, and gnaw with their teeth and tug at the plug with their hands till they get it in two; then sometimes the one that owns the tobacco looks mournful at it when it's handed back, and says, sarcastic:

---

* See Note, p. 402.

"Here, gimme the *chaw*, and you take the *plug*."

All the streets and lanes was just mud; they warn't nothing else *but* mud—mud as black as tar and nigh about a foot deep in some places, and two or three inches deep in *all* the places. The hogs loafed and grunted around everywheres. You'd see a muddy sow and a litter of pigs come lazying along the street and whollop herself right down in the way, where folks had to walk around her, and she'd stretch out and shut her eyes and wave her ears whilst the pigs was milking her, and look as happy as if she was on salary. And pretty soon you'd hear a loafer sing out, "Hi! *so* boy! sick him, Tige!" and away the sow would go, squealing most horrible, with a dog or two swinging to each ear, and three or four dozen more a-coming; and then you would see all the loafers get up and watch the thing out of sight, and laugh at the fun and look grateful for the noise. Then they'd settle back again till there was a dog fight. There couldn't anything wake them up all over, and make them happy all over, like a dog fight—unless it might be putting turpentine on a stray dog and setting fire to him, or tying a tin pan to his tail and see him run himself to death.

On the river front some of the houses was sticking out over the bank, and they was bowed and bent, and about ready to tumble in. The people had moved out of them. The bank was caved away under one corner of some others, and that corner was hanging over. People lived in them yet, but it was dangersome, because sometimes a strip of land as wide as a house caves in at a time. Sometimes a belt of land a quarter of a mile deep will start in and cave along and cave along till it all caves into the river in one summer. Such a town as that has to be always moving back, and back, and back, because the river's always gnawing at it.

The nearer it got to noon that day the thicker and thicker was the wagons and horses in the streets, and more coming all the time. Families fetched their dinners with them from the country, and eat them in the wagons. There was considerable whisky drinking going on, and I seen three fights. By and by somebody sings out:

"Here comes old Boggs!—in from the country for his little old monthly drunk; here he comes, boys!"

All the loafers looked glad; I reckoned they was used to having fun out of Boggs. One of them says:

"Wonder who he's a-gwyne to chaw up this time. If he'd a-chawed up all the men he's ben a-gwyne to chaw up in the last twenty year he'd have considerable ruputation now."

Another one says, "I wisht old Boggs 'd threaten me, 'cuz then I'd know I warn't gwyne to die for a thousan' year."

Boggs comes a-tearing along on his horse, whooping and yelling like an Injun, and singing out:

"Cler the track, thar. I'm on the waw-path, and the price uv coffins is a-gwyne to raise."

He was drunk, and weaving about in his saddle; he was over fifty year old, and had a very red face. Everybody yelled at him and laughed at him and sassed him, and he sassed back, and said he'd attend to them and lay them out in their regular turns, but he couldn't wait now because he'd come to town to kill old Colonel Sherburn, and his motto was, "Meat first, and spoon vittles to top off on."

He see me, and rode up and says:

"Whar'd you come f'm, boy? You prepared to die?"

Then he rode on. I was scared, but a man says:

"He don't mean nothing; he's always a-carryin' on like that when he's drunk. He's the best naturedest old fool in Arkansaw—never hurt nobody, drunk nor sober."

Boggs rode up before the biggest store in town, and bent his head down so he could see under the curtain of the awning and yells:

"Come out here, Sherburn! Come out and meet the man you've swindled. You're the houn' I'm after, and I'm a-gwyne to have you, too!"

And so he went on, calling Sherburn everything he could lay his tongue to, and the whole street packed with people listening and laughing and going on. By and by a proud-looking man about fifty-five—and he was a heap the best dressed man in that town, too—steps out of the store, and the crowd drops back on each side to let him come. He says to Boggs, mighty ca'm and slow—he says:

"I'm tired of this, but I'll endure it till one o'clock. Till one o'clock, mind—no longer. If you open your mouth against me only once after that time you can't travel so far but I will find you."

Then he turns and goes in. The crowd looked mighty sober; nobody stirred, and there warn't no more laughing. Boggs rode off blackguarding Sherburn as loud as he could yell, all down the street; and pretty soon back he comes and stops before the store, still keeping it up. Some men crowded around him and tried to get him to shut up, but he wouldn't; they told him it would be one o'clock in about fifteen minutes, and so he *must* go home—he must go right away. But it didn't do no good. He cussed away with all his might, and throwed his hat down in the mud and rode over it, and pretty soon away he went a-raging down the street again, with his grey hair a-flying. Everybody that could get a chance at him tried their best to coax him off of his horse so they could lock him up and get him sober; but it warn't no use—up the street he would tear again, and give Sherburn another cussing. By and by somebody says:

"Go for his daughter!—quick, go for his daughter; sometimes he'll listen to her. If anybody can persuade him, she can."

So somebody started on a run. I walked down street a ways and stopped. In about five or ten minutes here comes Boggs again, but not on his horse. He was a-reeling across the street towards me, bare-headed, with a friend on both sides of him a-holt of his arms and hurrying him along. He was quiet, and looked uneasy; and he warn't hanging back any, but was doing some of the hurrying himself. Somebody sings out:

"Boggs!"

I looked over there to see who said it, and it was that Colonel Sherburn. He was standing perfectly still in the street, and had a pistol raised in his right hand—not aiming it, but holding it out with the barrel tilted up towards the sky. The same second I see a young girl coming on the run, and two men with her. Boggs and the men turned round to see who called him, and when they see the pistol the men jumped to one side, and the pistol-barrel come down slow and steady to a level—both barrels cocked. Boggs throws up both of his hands and says, "O Lord, don't shoot!" Bang! goes the first shot, and he staggers back, clawing at the air—bang! goes the second one, and he tumbles backwards on to the ground, heavy and solid, with his arms spread out. That young girl screamed out and comes rushing, and down she throws herself on her father, crying, and saying, "Oh, he's killed him, he's killed him!" The crowd closed up around them, and shouldered and jammed one another, with their necks stretched, trying to see, and people on the inside trying to shove them back and shouting, "Back, back! give him air, give him air!"

Colonel Sherburn he tossed his pistol on to the ground, and turned around on his heels and walked off.

They took Boggs to a little drug store, the crowd pressing around just the same, and the whole town following, and I rushed and got a good place at the window, where I was close to him and could see in. They laid him on the floor and put one large Bible under his head, and opened another one and spread it on his breast; but they tore open his shirt first, and I seen where one of the bullets went in. He made about a dozen long gasps, his breast lifting the Bible up when he drawed in his breath, and letting it down again when he breathed it out—and after that he laid still; he was dead. Then they pulled his daughter away from him, screaming and crying, and took her off. She was about sixteen, and very sweet and gentle looking, but awful pale and scared.

Well, pretty soon the whole town was there, squirming and scrouging and pushing and shoving to get at the window and have a look, but people that had the places wouldn't give them up, and folks behind them was saying all the time, "Say, now, you've looked enough, you fellows; 'tain't right and 'tain't fair for you to stay thar all the time, and never give nobody a chance; other folks has their rights as well as you."

There was considerable jawing back, so I slid out, thinking maybe there was going to be trouble. The streets was full, and everybody was excited. Everybody that seen the shooting was telling how it happened, and there was a big crowd packed around each one of these fellows, stretching their necks and listening. One long, lanky man, with long hair and a big white fur stovepipe hat on the back of his head, and a crooked-handled cane, marked out the places on the ground where Boggs stood and where Sherburn stood, and the people following him around from one place to t'other and watching everything he done, and bobbing their heads to show they understood, and stooping a little and resting their hands on their thighs to watch him mark the places on the ground with his cane; and then he stood up straight and stiff where Sherburn had stood, frowning and having his hat-brim down over his eyes, and sung out, "Boggs!" and then fetched his cane down slow to a level, and says "Bang!" staggered backwards, says "Bang!" again, and fell down flat on his back. The people that had seen the thing said he done it perfect; said it was just exactly the way it all happened. Then as much as a dozen people got out their bottles and treated him.

Well, by and by somebody said Sherburn ought to be lynched. In about a minute everybody was saying it; so away they went, mad and yelling, and snatching down every clothes-line they come to to do the hanging with.

22

They swarmed up towards Sherburn's house, a-whooping and raging like Injuns, and everything had to clear the way or get run over and tromped to mush, and it was awful to see. Children was heeling it ahead of the mob, screaming and trying to get out of the way; and every window along the road was full of women's heads, and there was nigger boys in every tree, and bucks and wenches looking over every fence; and as soon as the mob would get nearly to them they would break and skaddle back out of reach. Lots of the women and girls was crying and taking on, scared most to death.

They swarmed up in front of Sherburn's palings as thick as they could jam together, and you couldn't hear yourself think for the noise. It was a little twenty-foot yard. Some sung out "Tear down the fence! tear down the fence!" Then there was a racket of ripping and tearing and smashing, and down she goes, and the front wall of the crowd begins to roll in like a wave.

Just then Sherburn steps out on to the roof of his little front porch, with a double-barrel gun in his hand, and takes his stand, perfectly ca'm and deliberate, not saying a word. The racket stopped, and the wave sucked back.

Sherburn never said a word—just stood there, looking down. The stillness was awful creepy and uncomfortable. Sherburn run his eye slow along the crowd; and wherever it struck the people tried a little to out-gaze him, but they couldn't; they dropped their eyes and looked sneaky. Then pretty soon Sherburn sort of laughed; not the pleasant kind, but the kind that makes you feel like when you are eating bread that's got sand in it.

Then he says, slow and scornful:

"The idea of *you* lynching anybody! It's amusing. The idea of you thinking you had pluck enough to lynch a *man*! Because you're brave enough to tar and feather poor friendless cast-out women that come along here, did that make you think you had grit enough to lay your hands on a *man*? Why, a *man's* safe in the hands of ten thousand of your kind—as long as it's daytime and you're not behind him.

"Do I know you? I know you clear through. I was born and raised in the South, and I've lived in the North; so I know the average all around. The average man's a coward. In the North he lets anybody walk over him that wants to, and goes home and prays for a humble spirit to bear it. In the South one man all by himself, has stopped a stage full of men in the daytime, and robbed the lot. Your newspapers call you a brave people so much that you think you are braver than any other people—whereas you're just *as* brave, and no braver. Why don't your juries hang murderers? Because they're afraid the man's friends will shoot them in the back, in the dark—and it's just what they *would* do.

"So they always acquit; and then a *man* goes in the night, with a hundred masked cowards at his back and lynches the rascal. Your mistake is, that you didn't bring a man with you; that's one mistake, and the other is that you didn't come in the dark and fetch your masks. You brought *part* of a man—Buck Harkness, there—and if you hadn't had him to start you, you'd a taken it out in blowing.

"You didn't want to come. The average man don't like trouble and danger.

You don't like trouble and danger. But if only *half* a man—like Buck Harkness, there—shouts 'Lynch him! lynch him!' you're afraid to back down—afraid you'll be found out to be what you are—*cowards*—and so you raise a yell, and hang yourselves on to that half-a-man's coat-tail, and come raging up here, swearing what big things you're going to do. The pitifulest thing out is a mob; that's what an army is—a mob; they don't fight with courage that's born in them, but with courage that's borrowed from their mass, and from their officers. But a mob without any *man* at the head of it is *beneath* pitifulness. Now the thing for *you* to do is to droop your tails and go home and crawl in a hole. If any real lynching's going to be done it will be done in the dark, Southern fashion; and when they come they'll bring their masks, and fetch a *man* along. Now *leave*—and take your half-a-man with you"—tossing his gun up across his left arm and cocking it when he says this.

The crowd washed back sudden, and then broke all apart, and went tearing off every which way, and Buck Harkness he heeled it after them, looking tolerable cheap. I could a stayed if I wanted to, but I didn't want to.

I went to the circus and loafed around the back side till the watchman went by, and then dived in under the tent. I had my twenty-dollar gold piece and some other money, but I reckoned I better save it, because there ain't no telling how soon you are going to need it, away from home and amongst strangers that way. You can't be too careful. I ain't opposed to spending money on circuses when there ain't no other way, but there ain't no use in *wasting* it on them.

It was a real bully circus. It was the splendidest sight that ever was when they all come riding in, two and two, a gentleman and lady, side by side, the men just in their drawers and undershirts, and no shoes nor stirrups, and resting their hands on their thighs easy and comfortable—there must a been twenty of them—and every lady with a lovely complexion, and perfectly beautiful, and looking just like a gang of real sure-enough queens, and dressed in clothes that cost millions of dollars, and just littered with diamonds. It was a powerful fine sight; I never see anything so lovely. And then one by one they got up and stood, and went a-weaving around the ring so gentle and wavy and graceful, the men looking ever so tall and airy and straight, with their heads bobbing and skimming along, away up there under the tent-roof, and every lady's rose-leafy dress flapping soft and silky around her hips, and she looking like the most loveliest parasol.

And then faster and faster they went, all of them dancing, first one foot out in the air and then the other, the horses leaning more and more, and the ringmaster going round and round the center-pole, cracking his whip and shouting "Hi!—hi!" and the clown cracking jokes behind him; and by and by all hands dropped the reins, and every lady put her knuckles on her hips and every gentleman folded his arms, and then how the horses did lean over and hump themselves! And so one after the other they all skipped off into the ring, and made the sweetest bow I ever see, and then scampered out, and everybody clapped their hands and went just about wild.

Well, all through the circus they done the most astonishing things; and all the time that clown carried on so it most killed the people. The ringmaster couldn't ever say a word to him but he was back at him quick as a wink with the funniest things a body ever said; and how he ever *could* think of so many of them, and so sudden and so pat, was what I couldn't noway understand. Why, I couldn't a thought of them in a year. And by and by a drunk man tried to get into the ring—said he wanted to ride; said he could ride as well as anybody that ever was. They argued and tried to keep him out, but he wouldn't listen, and the whole show come to a standstill. Then the people begun to holler at him and make fun of him, and that made him mad, and he begun to rip and tear; so that stirred up the people, and a lot of men begun to pile down off of the benches and swarm towards the ring, saying, "Knock him down! throw him out!" and one or two women begun to scream. So, then, the ringmaster he made a little speech, and said he hoped there wouldn't be no disturbance, and if the man would promise he wouldn't make no more trouble he would let him ride if he thought he could stay on the horse. So everybody laughed and said all right, and the man got on. The minute he was on, the horse begun to rip and tear and jump and cavort around, with two circus men hanging on to his bridle trying to hold him, and the drunk man hanging on to his neck, and his heels flying in the air every jump, and the whole crowd of people standing up shouting and laughing till tears rolled down. And at last, sure enough, all the circus men could do, the horse broke loose, and away he went like the very nation, round and round the ring, with that sot laying down on him and hanging to his neck, with first one leg hanging most to the ground on one side, and then t'other one on t'other side, and the people just crazy. It warn't funny to me, though; I was all of a tremble to see his danger. But pretty soon he struggled up astraddle and grabbed the bridle, a-reeling this way and that; and the next minute he sprung up and dropped the bridle and stood! and the horse a-going like a house afire too. He just stood up there, a-sailing around as easy and comfortable as if he warn't ever drunk in his life—and then he begun to pull off his clothes and sling them. He shed them so thick they kind of clogged up the air, and altogether he shed seventeen suits. And, then, there he was, slim and handsome, and dressed the gaudiest and prettiest you ever saw, and he lit into that horse with his whip and made him fairly hum—and finally skipped off, and made his bow and danced off to the dressing room, and everybody just a-howling with pleasure and astonishment.

Then the ringmaster he see how he had been fooled, and he *was* the sickest ringmaster you ever see, I reckon. Why, it was one of his own men! He had got up that joke all out of his own head, and never let on to nobody. Well, I felt sheepish enough to be took in so, but I wouldn't a been in that ringmaster's place, not for a thousand dollars. I don't know; there may be bullier circuses than what that one was, but I never struck them yet. Anyways, it was plenty good enough for *me*; and wherever I run across it, it can have all of *my* custom every time.

Well, that night we had *our* show; but there warn't only about twelve people there—just enough to pay expenses. And they laughed all the time, and that made the duke mad; and everybody left, anyway, before the show was over, but one boy which was asleep. So the duke said these Arkansaw lunkheads couldn't come up to Shakespeare; what they wanted was low comedy—and maybe something ruther worse than low comedy, he reckoned. He said he could size their style. So next morning he got some big sheets of wrapping paper and some black paint, and drawed off some handbills, and stuck them up all over the village. The bills said:

AT THE COURT HOUSE!
FOR 3 NIGHTS ONLY!
The World-Renowned Tragedians
DAVID GARRICK THE YOUNGER!
AND
EDMUND KEAN THE ELDER!
Of the London and Continental Theatres,
In their Thrilling Tragedy of
THE KING'S CAMELOPARD
OR
THE ROYAL NONESUCH!!!
Admission 50 cents.

Then at the bottom was the biggest line of all – which said:

LADIES AND CHILDREN NOT ADMITTED.

'There,' says he, 'if that line don't fetch them, I don't know Arkansaw!'

23

Well, all day him and the king was hard at it, rigging up a stage and a curtain and a row of candles for footlights; and that night the house was jam full of men in no time. When the place couldn't hold no more, the duke he quit tending door and went around the back way and come on to the stage and stood up before the curtain and made a little speech, and praised up this tragedy, and said it was the most thrillingest one that ever was; and so he went on a-bragging about the tragedy, and about Edmund Kean the Elder, which was to play the main principal part in it; and at last when he'd got everybody's expectations up high enough, he rolled up the curtain, and the next minute the king come a-prancing out on all fours, naked; and he was painted all over, ring-streaked-and-striped, all sorts of colours, as splendid as a rainbow. And—but never mind the rest of his outfit; it was just wild, but it was awful funny. The people most killed themselves laughing; and when the king got done capering and capered off behind the scenes, they roared and clapped and stormed and haw-hawed till he come back and done it over again, and after that they made him do it another time. Well, it would make a cow laugh to see the shines that old idiot cut.

Then the duke he lets the curtain down, and bows to the people, and says the great tragedy will be performed only two nights more, on accounts of pressing London engagements, where the seats is all sold already for it in Drury Lane; and then he makes them another bow, and says if he has succeeded in pleasing them and instructing them, he will be deeply obleeged if they will mention it to their friends and get them to come and see it.

Twenty people sings out:

"What, is it over? Is that *all*?"

The duke says yes. Then there was a fine time. Everybody sings out, "Sold!" and rose up mad, and was a-going for that stage and them tragedians. But a big, fine looking man jumps up on a bench and shouts:

"Hold on! Just a word, gentlemen." They stopped to listen. "We are sold—mighty badly sold. But we don't want to be the laughing stock of this whole town, I reckon, and never hear the last of this thing as long as we live. *No.* What we want is to go out of here quiet, and talk this show up, and sell the *rest* of the town! Then we'll all be in the same boat. Ain't that sensible?"

("You bet it is!—the jedge is right!" everybody sings out.) "All right, then—not a word about any sell. Go along home, and advise everybody to come and see the tragedy."

Next day you couldn't hear nothing around that town but how splendid that show was. House was jammed again that night, and we sold this crowd the same way. When me and the king and the duke got home to the raft we all had a supper; and by and by, about midnight, they made Jim and me back her out and float her down the middle of the river, and fetch her in and hide her about two mile below town.

The third night the house was crammed again—and they warn't newcomers this time, but people that was at the show the other two nights. I stood by the duke at the door, and I see that every man that went in had his pockets bulging, or something muffled up under his coat—and I see it warn't no perfumery, neither, not by a long sight. I smelt sickly eggs by the barrel, and rotten cabbages, and such things; and if I know the signs of a dead cat being around, and I bet I do, there was sixty-four of them went in. I shoved in there for a minute, but it was too various for me; I couldn't stand it. Well, when the place couldn't hold no more people the duke he give a fellow a quarter and told him to tend door for him a minute, and then he started around for the stage door, I after him; but the minute we turned the corner and was in the dark he says:

"Walk fast now till you get away from the houses, and then shin for the raft like the dickens was after you!"

I done it, and he done the same. We struck the raft at the same time, and in less than two seconds we was gliding down stream, all dark and still, and edging towards the middle of the river, nobody saying a word. I reckoned the poor king was in for a gaudy time of it with the audience, but nothing of the sort; pretty soon he crawls out from under the wigwam, and says:

"Well, how'd the old thing pan out this time, duke?"

He hadn't been up-town at all.

We never showed a light till we was about ten mile below the village. Then we lit up and had a supper, and the king and the duke fairly laughed their bones loose over the way they'd served them people. The duke says:

"Greenhorns, flatheads! I knew the first house would keep mum and let the rest of the town get roped in; and I knew they'd lay for us the third night, and consider it was *their* turn now. Well, it *is* their turn, and I'd give something to know how much they'd take for it. I *would* just like to know how they're putting in their opportunity. They can turn it into a picnic if they want to—they brought plenty provisions."

Them rapscallions took in four hundred and sixty-five dollars in that three nights. I never see money hauled in by the wagon-load like that before.

By and by, when they was asleep and snoring, Jim says:

"Don't it s'prise you de way dem kings carries on, Huck?"

Their Pockets Bulged

"No," I says, "it don't."

"Why don't it, Huck?"

"Well, it don't, because it's in the breed. I reckon they're all alike."

"But, Huck, dese kings o' ourn is reglar rapscallions; dat's jist what dey is; dey's reglar rapscallions."

"Well, that's what I'm a-saying; all kings is mostly rapscallions, as fur as I can make out."

"Is dat so?"

"You read about them once—you'll see. Look at Henry the Eight; this 'n 's a Sunday-school Superintendent to *him*. And look at Charles Second, and Louis Fourteen, and Louis Fifteen, and James Second, and Edward Second, and Richard Third, and forty more; besides all them Saxon heptarchies that used to rip around so in old times and raise Cain. My, you ought to seen old Henry the Eight when he was in bloom. He *was* a blossom. He used to marry a new wife every day, and chop off her head next morning. And he would do it just as indifferent as if he was ordering up eggs. 'Fetch up Nell Gwynn,' he says. They fetch her up. Next morning, 'Chop off her head!' And they chop it off. 'Fetch up Jane Shore,' he says; and up she comes, Next morning, 'Chop off her head'—and they chop it off. 'Ring up Fair Rosamun.' Fair Rosamun answers the bell. Next morning, 'Chop off her head.' And he made every one of them tell him a tale every night; and he kept that up till he had hogged a thousand and one tales that way, and then he put them all in a book, and called it Domesday Book—which was a good name and stated the case. You don't know kings, Jim, but I know them; and this old rip of ourn is one of the cleanest I've struck in history. Well, Henry he takes a notion he wants to get up some trouble with this country. How does he go at it—give notice?—give the country a show? No. All of a sudden he heaves all the tea in Boston Harbor overboard, and whacks out a declaration of independence, and dares them to come on. That was *his* style—he never give anybody a chance. He had suspicions of his father, the Duke of Wellington. Well, what did he do? Ask him to show up? No—drownded him in a butt of mamsey, like a cat. S'pose people left money laying around where he was—what did he do? He collared it. S'pose he contracted to do a thing, and you paid him, and didn't set down there and see that he done it—what did he do? He always done the other thing. S'pose he opened his mouth—what then? If he didn't shut it up powerful quick he'd lose a lie every time. That's the kind of a bug Henry was; and if we'd a had him along 'stead of our kings he'd a fooled that town a heap worse than ourn done. I don't say that ourn is lambs, because they ain't, when you come right down to the cold facts; but they ain't nothing to *that* old ram, anyway. All I say is, kings is kings, and you got to make allowances. Take them all around, they're a mighty ornery lot. It's the way they're raised."

"But dis one do *smell* so like de nation, Huck."

"Well, they all do, Jim. We can't help the way a king smells; history don't tell no way."

"Now de duke, he's a tolerble likely man in some ways."

"Yes, a duke's different. But not very different. This one's a middling hard lot for a duke. When he's drunk there ain't no near-sighted man could tell him from a king."

"Well, anyways, I doan' hanker for no mo' un um, Huck. Dese is all I kin stan'."

"It's the way I feel, too, Jim. But we've got them on our hands, and we got to remember what they are, and make allowances. Sometimes I wish we could hear of a country that's out of kings."

What was the use to tell Jim these warn't real kings and dukes? It wouldn't a done no good; and, besides, it was just as I said: you couldn't tell them from the real kind.

I went to sleep, and Jim didn't call me when it was my turn. He often done that. When I waked up just at daybreak he was sitting there with his head down betwixt his knees, moaning and mourning to himself. I didn't take notice nor let on. I knowed what it was about. He was thinking about his wife and his children, away up yonder, and he was low and homesick; because he hadn't ever been away from home before in his life; and I do believe he cared just as much for his people as white folks does for their'n. It don't seem natural, but I reckon it's so. He was often moaning and mourning that way nights, when he judged I was asleep, and saying, "Po' little 'Lizabeth! po' little Johnny! it's mighty hard; I spec' I ain't ever gwyne to see you no mo', no mo'!" He was a mighty good nigger, Jim was.

But this time I somehow got to talking to him about his wife and young ones; and by and by he says:

"What makes me feel so bad dis time 'uz bekase I hear sumpn over yonder on de bank like a whack, er a slam, while ago, en it mine me er de time I treat my little 'Lizabeth so ornery. She warn't on'y 'bout fo' year ole, en she tuck de sk'yarlet fever, en had a powful rough spell; but she got well, en one day she was a-stannin' aroun', en I says to her, I says:

"'Shet de do'.'

"She never done it; jis' stood dah, kiner smilin' up at me. It make me mad; en I says agin, mighty loud, I says:

"'Doan' you hear me? Shet de do'!'

"She jis stood de same way, kiner smilin' up. I was a-bilin'! I says:

"'I lay I *make* you mine!'

"En wid dat I fetch' her a slap side de head dat sont her a-sprawlin'. Den I went into de yuther room, en 'uz gone 'bout ten minutes; en when I come back dah was dat do' a-stannin' open *yit*, en dat chile stannin' mos' right in it, a-lookin' down and mournin', en de tears runnin' down. My, but I *wuz* mad! I was a-gwyne for de chile, but jis' den—it was a do' dat open innerds—jis' den, 'long come de wind en slam it to, behine de chile, ker-BLAM!—en my lan', de chile never move'! My breff mos' hop outer me; en I feel so—so—I doan' know HOW I feel. I crope out, all a-tremblin', en crope aroun' en open de do' easy en slow, en poke my head in behine de chile, sof' en still, en all uv a sudden I says POW! jis' as loud as I could yell. *She never budge!* Oh, Huck, I bust out a-cryin' en grab her up in my arms, en say, 'Oh, de po' little thing! De Lord God Amighty fogive po' ole Jim, kaze he never gwyne to fogive hisself as long's he live!' Oh, she was plumb deef en dumb, Huck, plumb deef en dumb—en I'd ben a-treat'n her so!"

24

Next day, towards night, we laid up under a little willow towhead out in the middle, where there was a village on each side of the river, and the duke and the king begun to lay out a plan for working them towns. Jim he spoke to the duke, and said he hoped it wouldn't take but a few hours, because it got mighty heavy and tiresome to him when he had to lay all day in the wigwam tied with the rope. You see, when we left him all alone we had to tie him, because if anybody happened on to him all by himself and not tied it wouldn't look much like he was a runaway nigger, you know. So the duke said it *was* kind of hard to have to lay roped all day, and he'd cipher out some way to get around it.

He was uncommon bright, the duke was, and he soon struck it. He dressed Jim up in King Lear's outfit—it was a long curtain-calico gown, and a white horse-hair wig and whiskers; and then he took his theater paint and painted Jim's face and hands and ears and neck all over a dead, dull, solid blue, like a man that's been drownded nine days. Blamed if he warn't the horriblest looking outrage I ever see. Then the duke took and wrote out a sign on a shingle* so:

Sick Arab—but harmless when not out of his head.

And he nailed that shingle to a lath, and stood the lath up four or five foot in front of the wigwam. Jim was satisfied. He said it was a sight better than lying tied a couple of years every day, and trembling all over every time there was a sound. The duke told him to make himself free and easy, and if anybody ever come meddling around, he must hop out of the wigwam, and carry on a little, and fetch a howl or two like a wild beast, and he reckoned they would light out and leave him alone. Which was sound enough judgment; but you take the average man, and he wouldn't wait for him to howl. Why, he didn't only look like he was dead, he looked considerable more than that.

These rapscallions wanted to try the Nonesuch again, because there was so much money in it, but they judged it wouldn't be safe, because maybe the news might a worked along down by this time. They couldn't hit no project that suited exactly; so at last the duke said he reckoned he'd lay off and work his brains an hour or two and see if he couldn't put up something on the Arkansaw village; and the king he allowed he would drop over to t'other village without any plan, but just trust in Providence to lead him the profitable way—meaning the devil, I reckon. We had all bought store clothes where we stopped last; and now the king put his'n on, and he told me to put mine on. I done it, of course. The king's duds was all black, and he did look real swell and starchy. I never knowed how clothes could change a body before. Why, before, he looked like the orneriest old rip that ever was; but now, when he'd take off his new white beaver and make a bow and do a smile, he looked that grand and good and pious that you'd say he had walked right out of the ark, and maybe was old Leviticus himself. Jim cleaned up the canoe, and I got my paddle ready. There was a big steamboat laying at

* American for small signboard.

the shore away up under the point, about three mile above the town—been there a couple of hours, taking on freight. Says the king:

"Seein' how I'm dressed, I reckon maybe I better arrive down from St. Louis or Cincinnati, or some other big place. Go for the steamboat, Huckleberry; we'll come down to the village on her."

I didn't have to be ordered twice to go and take a steamboat ride. I fetched the shore a half a mile above the village, and then went scooting along the bluff bank in the easy water. Pretty soon we come to a nice innocent-looking young country jake setting on a log swabbing the sweat off of his face, for it was powerful warm weather; and he had a couple of big carpet-bags by him.

"Run her nose in shore," says the king. I done it. "Wher' you bound for, young man?"

"For the steamboat; going to Orleans."

"Git aboard," says the king. "Hold on a minute, my servant 'll he'p you with them bags. Jump out and he'p the gentleman, Adolphus"—meaning me, I see.

I done so, and then we all three started on again. The young chap was mighty thankful; said it was tough work toting his baggage such weather. He asked the king where he was going, and the king told him he'd come down the river and landed at the other village this morning, and now he was going up a few mile to see an old friend on a farm up there. The young fellow says:

"When I first see you I says to myself, 'It's Mr. Wilks, sure, and he come mighty near getting here in time.' But then I says again, 'No, I reckon it ain't him, or else he wouldn't be paddling up the river.' You *ain't* him, are you?"

"No, my name's Blodgett—Elexander Blodgett—*Reverend* Elexander Blodgett, I s'pose I must say, as I'm one o' the Lord's poor servants. But still I'm jist as able to be sorry for Mr. Wilks for not arriving in time, all the same, if he's missed anything by it—which I hope he hasn't."

"Well, he don't miss any property by it, because he'll get that all right; but he's missed seeing his brother Peter die—which he mayn't mind, nobody can tell as to that—but his brother would a give anything in this world to see *him* before he died; never talked about nothing else all these three weeks; hadn't seen him since they was boys together—and hadn't ever seen his brother William at all—that's the deef and dumb one—William ain't more than thirty or thirty-five. Peter and George were the only ones that come out here; George was the married brother; him and his wife both died last year. Harvey and William's the only ones that's left now; and, as I was saying, they haven't got here in time."

"Did anybody send 'em word?"

"Oh, yes; a month or two ago, when Peter was first took; because Peter said then that he sorter felt like he warn't going to get well this time. You see, he was pretty old, and George's g'yirls was too young to be much company for him, except Mary Jane, the red-headed one; and so he was kinder lonesome after George and his wife died, and didn't seem to care much to live. He most desperately wanted to see Harvey—and William, too, for that matter—because he was one of them kind that can't bear to make a will. He left a letter behind for Harvey, and said he'd told in it where his money was hid, and how he wanted the rest of the property divided up so George's g'yirls would be all right—for George didn't leave nothing. And that letter was all they could get him to put a pen to."

"Why do you reckon Harvey don't come? Wher' does he live?"

"Oh, he lives in England—Sheffield—preaches there—hasn't ever been in this country. He hasn't had any too much time—and besides he mightn't a got the letter at all, you know."

"Too bad, too bad he couldn't a lived to see his brothers, poor soul. You going to Orleans, you say?"

"Yes, but that ain't only a part of it. I'm going in a ship, next Wednesday, for Ryo Janeero, where my uncle lives."

"It's a pretty long journey. But it'll be lovely; wisht I was a-going. Is Mary Jane the oldest? How old is the others?"

"Mary Jane's nineteen, Susan's fifteen, and Joanna's about fourteen—that's the one that gives herself to good works and has a hare-lip."

"Poor things! to be left alone in the cold world so."

"Well, they could be worse off. Old Peter had friends, and they ain't going to let them come to no harm. There's Hobson, the Babtis' preacher; and Deacon Lot Hovey, and Ben Rucker, and Abner Shackleford, and Levi Bell, the lawyer; and Dr. Robinson, and their wives, and the widow Bartley, and—well, there's a lot of them; but these are the ones that Peter was thickest with, and used to write about sometimes, when he wrote home; so Harvey 'll know where to look for friends when he gets here."

Well, the old man went on asking questions till he just fairly emptied that young fellow. Blamed if he didn't inquire about everybody and everything in that blessed town, and all about the Wilkses; and about Peter's business—which was a tanner; and about George's—which was a carpenter; and about Harvey's—which was a dissentering minister; and so on, and so on. Then he says:

"What did you want to walk all the way up to the steamboat for?"

"Because she's a big Orleans boat, and I was afeard she mightn't stop there. When they're deep they won't stop for a hail. A Cincinnati boat will, but this is a St. Louis one."

"Was Peter Wilks well off?"

"Oh, yes, pretty well off. He had houses and land, and it's reckoned he left three or four thousand in cash hid up som'ers."

"When did you say he died?"

"I didn't say, but it was last night."

"Funeral tomorrow, likely?"

"Yes, 'bout the middle of the day."

"Well, it's all terrible sad; but we've all got to go, one time or another. So what we want to do is to be prepared; then we're all right."

"Yes, sir, it's the best way. Ma used to always say that."

When we struck the boat she was about done loading, and pretty soon she got off. The king never said nothing about going aboard, so I lost my ride, after all. When the boat was gone the king made me paddle up another mile to a lonesome place, and then he got ashore and says:

"Now hustle back, right off, and fetch the duke up here, and the new carpet-bags. And if he's gone over to t'other side, go over there and git him. And tell him to git himself up regardless. Shove along, now."

I see what *he* was up to; but I never said nothing, of course. When I got back with the duke we hid the canoe, and then they set down on a log, and the king told him everything, just like the young fellow had said it—every last word of it. And all the time he was a-doing it he tried to talk like an Englishman; and he done it pretty well, too, for a slouch. I can't imitate him, and so I ain't a-going to try to; but he really done it pretty good. Then he says:

"How are you on the deef and dumb, Bilgewater?"

The duke said, leave him alone for that; said he had played a deef and dumb person on the histronic boards. So then they waited for a steamboat.

About the middle of the afternoon a couple of little boats come along, but they didn't come from high enough up the river; but at last there was a big one, and they hailed her. She sent out her yawl, and we went aboard, and she was from Cincinnati; and when they found we only wanted to go four or five mile they was booming mad, and gave us a cussing, and said they wouldn't land us. But the king was ca'm. He says:

"If gentlemen kin afford to pay a dollar a mile apiece to be took on and put off in a yawl, a steamboat kin afford to carry 'em, can't it?"

So they softened down and said it was all right; and when we got to the village they yawled us ashore. About two dozen men flocked down when they see the yawl a-coming, and when the king says:

"Kin any of you gentlemen tell me wher' Mr. Peter Wilks lives?" they give a glance at one another, and nodded their heads, as much as to say, "What d' I tell you?" Then one of them says, kind of soft and gentle:

"I'm sorry sir, but the best we can do is to tell you where he *did* live yesterday evening."

Sudden as winking the ornery old cretur went an to smash, and fell up against the man, and put his chin on his shoulder, and cried down his back, and says:

"Alas, alas, our poor brother—gone, and we never got to see him; oh, it's too, too hard!"

Then he turns around, blubbering, and makes a lot of idiotic signs to the duke on his hands, and blamed if he didn't drop a carpet-bag and bust out a-crying. If they warn't the beatenest lot, them two frauds, that ever I struck.

Well, the men gathered around and sympathized with them, and said all sorts of kind things to them, and carried their carpet-bags up the hill for them, and let them lean on them and cry, and told the king all about his brother's last moments, and the king he told it all over again on his hands to the duke, and both of them took on about that dead tanner like they'd lost the twelve disciples. Well, if ever I struck anything like it, I'm a nigger. It was enough to make a body ashamed of the human race.

25

The news was all over town in two minutes, and you could see the people tearing down on the run from every which way, some of them putting on their coats as they come. Pretty soon we was in the middle of a crowd, and the noise of the tramping was like a soldier march. The windows and dooryards was full; and every minute somebody would say, over a fence:

"Is it *them*?"

And somebody trotting along with the gang would answer back and say:

"You bet it is."

When we got to the house the street in front of it was packed, and the three girls was standing in the door. Mary Jane *was* red-headed, but that don't make no difference, she was most awful beautiful, and her face and her eyes was all lit up like glory, she was so glad her uncles was come. The king he spread his arms, and Mary Jane she jumped for them, and the hare-lip jumped for the duke, and there they had it! Everybody most, leastways women, cried for joy to see them meet again at last and have such good times.

Then the king he hunched the duke private—I see him do it—and then he looked around and see the coffin, over in the corner on two chairs; so then him and the duke, with a hand across each other's shoulder, and t'other hand to their eyes, walked slow and solemn over there, everybody dropping back to give them room, and all the talk and noise stopping, people saying "Sh!" and all the men taking their hats off and drooping their heads, so you could a heard a pin fall. And when they got there they bent over and looked in the coffin, and took one sight, and then they bust out a-crying so you could a heard them to Orleans, most; and then they put their arms around each other's necks, and hung their chins over each other's shoulders; and then for three minutes, or maybe four, I never see two men leak the way they done. And, mind you, everybody was doing the same; and the place was that damp I never see anything like it. Then one of them got on one side of the coffin, and t'other on t'other side, and they kneeled down and rested their foreheads on the coffin, and let on to pray all to themselves. Well, when it come to that it worked the crowd like you never see anything like it, and everybody broke down and went to sobbing right out loud—the poor girls, too; and every woman, nearly, went up to the girls, without saying a word, and kissed them, solemn, on the forehead, and then put their hand on their head, and looked up towards the sky, with the tears running down, and then busted out and went off sobbing and swabbing, and give the next woman a show. I never see anything so disgusting.

Well, by and by the king he gets up and comes forward a little, and works himself up and slobbers out a speech, all full of tears and flapdoodle about its being a sore trial for him and his poor brother to lose the diseased, and to miss seeing diseased alive after the long journey of four thousand mile, but it's a trial that's sweetened and sanctified to us by this dear sympathy and these holy tears, and so he thanks them out of his heart and out of his brother's heart, because out of their mouths they can't, words being too weak and cold, and all that kind of rot and slush, till it was just sickening; and then he blubbers out a pious goody-goody Amen, and turns himself loose and goes to crying fit to bust.

And the minute the words were out of his mouth somebody over in the crowd struck up the doxolojer, and everybody joined in with all their might, and it just warmed you up and made you feel as good as church letting out.

Music is a good thing; and after all that soul-butter and hogwash I never see it freshen up things so, and sound so honest and bully.

Then the king begins to work his jaw again, and says how him and his nieces would be glad if a few of the main principal friends of the family would take supper here with them this evening, and help set up with the ashes of the diseased; and says if his poor brother laying yonder could speak he knows who he would name, for they was names that was very dear to him, and mentioned often in his letters; and so he will name the same, to wit, as follows, vizz.:—Rev. Mr. Hobson, and Deacon Lot Hovey, and Mr. Ben Rucker, and Abner Shackleford, and Levi Bell, and Dr. Robinson, and their wives, and the widow Bartley.

Rev. Hobson and Dr. Robinson was down to the end of the town a-hunting together—that is, I mean the doctor was shipping a sick man to t'other world, and the preacher was pinting him right. Lawyer Bell was away up to Louisville on business. But the rest was on hand, and so they all come and shook hands with the king and thanked him and talked to him; and then they shook hands with the duke and didn't say nothing, but just kept a-smiling and bobbing their heads like a passel of sapheads whilst he made all sorts of signs with his hands and said "Goo-goo—goo-goo-goo" all the time, like a baby that can't talk.

So the king he blattered along, and managed to inquire about pretty much everybody and dog in town, by his name, and mentioned all sorts of little things that happened one time or another in the town, or to George's family, or to Peter. And he always let on that Peter wrote him the things; but that was a lie: he got every blessed one of them out of that young flathead that we canoed up to the steamboat.

Then Mary Jane she fetched the letter her father left behind, and the king he read it out loud and cried over it. It give the dwelling-house and three thousand dollars, gold, to the girls; and it give the tanyard (which was doing a good business), along with some other houses and land (worth about seven thousand), and three thousand dollars in gold to Harvey and William, and told where the six thousand cash was hid down cellar. So these two frauds said they'd go and fetch it up, and have everything square and above-board; and told me to come with a candle. We shut the cellar door behind us, and when they found the bag they spilt it out on the floor, and it was a lovely sight, all them yaller-boys. My, the way the king's eyes did shine! He slaps the duke on the shoulder and says:

"Oh, *this* ain't bully nor noth'n! Oh, no, I reckon not! Why, *bully*, it beats the Nonesuch, *don't* it?"

The duke allowed it did. They pawed the yaller-boys, and sifted them through their fingers and let them jingle down on the floor; and the king says:

"It ain't no use talkin'; bein' brothers to a rich dead man and representatives of furrin heirs that's got left is the line for you and me, Bilge. Thish yer comes of trust'n to Providence. It's the best way, in the long run. I've tried 'em all, and ther' ain't no better way."

Most everybody would a been satisfied with the pile, and took it on trust; but no, they must count it. So they counts it, and it comes out four hundred and fifteen dollars short. Says the king:

"Dern him, I wonder what he done with that four hundred and fifteen dollars?"

They worried over that awhile, and ransacked all around for it. Then the duke says:

"Well, he was a pretty sick man, and likely he made a mistake—I reckon that's the way of it. The best way's to let it go, and keep still about it. We can spare it."

"Oh, shucks, yes, we can *spare* it. I don't k'yer noth'n 'bout that—it's the *count* I'm thinkin' about. We want to be awful square and open and above-board here, you know. We want to lug this h-yer money up stairs and count it before everybody—then ther' ain't noth'n suspicious. But when the dead man says ther's six thous'n dollars, you know, we don't want to—"

"Hold on," says the duke. "Le's make up the deffisit," and he begun to haul out yaller-boys out of his pocket.

"It's a most amaz'n' good idea, duke—you *have* got a rattlin' clever head on you," says the king. "Blest if the old Nonesuch ain't a heppin' us out agin," and *he* begun to haul out yaller-jackets and stack them up.

It most busted them, but they made up the six thousand clean and clear.

"Say," says the duke, "I got another idea. Le's go up stairs and count this money, and then take and *give it to the girls*."

"Good land, duke, lemme hug you! It's the most dazzling idea 'at ever a man struck. You have cert'nly got the most astonishin' head I ever see. Oh, this is the boss dodge, ther' ain't no mistake 'bout it. Let 'em fetch along their suspicions now if they want to—this 'll lay 'em out."

When we got upstairs everybody gethered around the table, and the king he counted it and stacked it up, three hundred dollars in a pile—twenty elegant little piles. Everybody looked hungry at it, and licked their chops. Then they raked it into the bag again, and I see the king begin to swell himself up for another speech. He says:

"Friends all, my poor brother that lays yonder has done generous by them that's left behind in the vale of sorrers. He has done generous by these yer poor little lambs that he loved and sheltered, and that's left fatherless and motherless. Yes, and we that knowed him knows that he would a done *more* generous by 'em if he hadn't ben afeard o' woundin' his dear William and me. Now, *wouldn't* he? Ther' ain't no question 'bout it in *my* mind. Well, then, what kind o' brothers would it be that 'd stand in his way at sech a time? And what kind o' uncles would it be that 'd rob—yes, *rob*—sech poor sweet lambs as these 'at he loved so at sech a time? If I know William—and I *think* I do—he—well, I'll jest ask him." He turns around and begins to make a lot of signs to the duke with his hands, and the duke he looks at him stupid and leather-headed a while; then all of a sudden he seems to catch his meaning, and jumps for the king, goo-gooing with all his might for joy, and hugs him about fifteen times before he lets up. Then the king says, "I knowed it; I reckon *that 'll* convince anybody the way *he* feels about it. Here, Mary Jane, Susan, Joanner, take the money—take it *all*. It's the gift of him that lays yonder, cold but joyful."

Mary Jane she went for him, Susan and the hare-lip went for the duke, and then such another hugging and kissing I never see yet. And everybody crowded up with the tears in their eyes, and most shook the hands off of them frauds, saying all the time:

"You *dear* good souls!—how *lovely*!—how *could* you!"

Well, then, pretty soon all hands got to talking about the diseased again, and how good he was, and what a loss he was, and all that; and before long a big iron-jawed man worked himself in there from outside, and stood a-listening and looking, and not saying anything; and nobody saying anything to him either, because the king was talking and they was all busy listening. The king was saying—in the middle of something he'd started in on—

"—they bein' partickler friends o' the diseased. That's why they're invited here this evenin'; but tomorrow we want *all* to come—everybody; for he respected everybody, he liked everybody, and so it's fitten that his funeral orgies sh'd be public."

And so he went a-mooning on and on, liking to hear himself talk, and every little while he fetched in his funeral orgies again, till the duke he couldn't stand it no more; so he writes on a little scrap of paper, "*Obsequies*, you old fool," and folds it up, and goes to goo-gooing and reaching it over people's heads to him. The king he reads it and puts it in his pocket, and says:

"Poor William, afflicted as he is, his *heart's* aluz right. Asks me to invite everybody to come to the funeral—wants me to make 'em all welcome. But he needn't a worried—it was jest what I was at."

Then he weaves along again, perfectly ca'm, and goes to dropping in his funeral orgies again every now and then, just like he done before. And when he done it the third time he says:

"I say orgies, not because it's the common term, because it ain't—obsequies bein' the common term—but because orgies is the right term. Obsequies ain't used in England no more now—it's gone out. We say orgies now in England. Orgies is better, because it means the thing you're after more exact. It's a word that's made up out'n the Greek *orgo*, outside, open, abroad; and the Hebrew *jeesum*, to plant, cover up; hence in *ter*. So, you see, funeral orgies is an open er public funeral."

He was the *worst* I ever struck. Well, the iron-jawed man he laughed right in his face. Everybody was shocked. Everybody says, "Why, *doctor*!" and Abner Shackleford says:

"Why, Robinson, hain't you heard the news? This is Harvey Wilks."

The king he smiled eager, and shoved out his flapper, and says:

"Is it my poor brother's dear good friend and physician? I—"

"Keep your hands off of me!" says the doctor. "*You* talk like an Englishman, *don't* you? It's the worst imitation I ever heard. *You* Peter Wilks's brother! You're a fraud, that's what you are!"

Well, how they all took on! They crowded around the doctor and tried to quiet him down, and tried to explain to him and tell him how Harvey 'd showed in forty ways that he *was* Harvey, and knowed everybody by name, and the names of the very dogs, and begged and *begged* him not to hurt Harvey's feelings and the poor girl's feelings, and all that. But it warn't no use; he stormed right along, and said any man that pretended to be an Englishman and couldn't imitate the lingo no better than what he did was a fraud and a liar. The poor girls was hanging to the king and crying; and all of a sudden the doctor ups and turns on *them*. He says:

"I was your father's friend, and I'm your friend; and I warn you as a friend, and an honest one that wants to protect you and keep you out of harm and trouble, to turn your backs on that scoundrel and have nothing to do with him, the ignorant tramp, with his idiotic Greek and Hebrew, as he calls it. He is the thinnest kind of an impostor—has come here with a lot of empty names and facts which he picked up somewheres, and you take them for *proofs*, and are helped to fool yourselves by these foolish friends here, who ought to know better. Mary Jane Wilks, you know me for your friend, and for your unselfish friend, too. Now listen to me; turn this pitiful rascal out—I *beg* you to do it. Will you?"

Mary Jane straightened herself up, and my, but she was handsome! She says:

"*Here* is my answer." She hove up the bag of money and put it in the king's hands, and says, "Take this six thousand dollars, and invest for me and my sisters any way you want to, and don't give us no receipt for it."

Then she put her arm around the king on one side, and Susan and the hare-lip done the same on the other. Everybody clapped their hands and stomped on the floor like a perfect storm, whilst the king held up his head and smiled proud. The doctor says:

"All right; I wash *my* hands of the matter. But I warn you all that a time 's coming when you're going to feel sick whenever you think of this day." And away he went.

"All right, doctor," says the king, kinder mocking him; "we'll try and get 'em to send for you;" which made them all laugh, and they said it was a prime good hit.

26

Well, when they was all gone the king he asks Mary Jane how they was off for spare rooms, and she said she had one spare room, which would do for Uncle William, and she'd give her own room to Uncle Harvey, which was a little bigger, and she would turn into the room with her sisters and sleep on a cot; and up garret was a little cubby, with a pallet in it. The king said the cubby would do for his valley—meaning me.

So Mary Jane took us up, and she showed them their rooms, which was plain but nice. She said she'd have her frocks and a lot of other traps took out of her room if they was in Uncle Harvey's way, but he said they warn't. The frocks was hung along the wall, and before them was a curtain made out of calico that hung down to the floor. There was an old hair trunk in one corner, and a guitar-box in another, and all sorts of little knickknacks and jimcracks around, like girls brisken up a room with. The king said it was all the more homely and more pleasanter for these fixings, and so don't disturb them. The duke's room was pretty small, but plenty good enough, and so was my cubby.

That night they had a big supper, and all them men and women was there, and I stood behind the king and the duke's chairs and waited on them, and the niggers waited on the rest. Mary Jane she set at the head of the table, with Susan alongside of her, and said how bad the biscuits was, and how mean the preserves was, and how ornery and tough the fried chickens was—and all that kind of rot, the way women always do for to force out compliments; and the people all knowed everything was tiptop, and said so—said "How *do* you get biscuits to brown so nice?" and "Where, for the land's sake, *did* you get these amaz'n pickles?" and all that kind of humbug talky-talk, just the way people always does at a supper, you know.

And when it was all done me and the hare-lip had supper in the kitchen off of the leavings, whilst the others was helping the niggers clean up the things. The hare-lip she got to pumping me about England, and blest if I didn't think the ice was getting mighty thin sometimes. She says:

"Did you ever see the king?"

"Who? William Fourth? Well, I bet I have—he goes to our church." I knowed he was dead years ago, but I never let on. So when I says he goes to our church, she says:

"What—regular?"

"Yes—regular. His pew's right over opposite ourn—on t'other side the pulpit."

"I thought he lived in London?"

"Well, he does. Where *would* he live?"

"But I thought *you* lived in Sheffield?"

I see I was up a stump. I had to let on to get choked with a chicken bone, so as to get time to think how to get down again. Then I says:

"I mean he goes to our church regular when he's in Sheffield. That's only in the summer time, when he comes there to take the sea baths."

"Why, how you talk—Sheffield ain't on the sea."

"Well, who said it was?"

"Why, you did."

"I *didn't* nuther."

"You did!"

"I didn't."

"You did."

"I never said nothing of the kind."

"Well, what *did* you say, then?"

"Said he come to take the sea *baths*—that's what I said."

"Well, then, how's he going to take the sea baths if it ain't on the sea?"

"Looky here," I says; "did you ever see any Congress-water?"

"Yes."

"Well, did you have to go to Congress to get it?"

"Why, no."

"Well, neither does William Fourth have to go to the sea to get a sea bath."

"How does he get it, then?"

"Gets it the way people down here gets Congress-water—in barrels. There in the palace at Sheffield they've got furnaces, and he wants his water hot. They can't bile that amount of water away off there at the sea. They haven't got no conveniences for it."

"Oh, I see, now. You might a said that in the first place and saved time."

When she said that I see I was out of the woods again, and so I was comfortable and glad. Next, she says:

"Do you go to church, too?"

"Yes—regular."

"Where do you set?"

"Why, in our pew."

"*Whose* pew?"

"Why, *ourn*—your Uncle Harvey's."

"His'n? What does *he* want with a pew?"

"Wants it to set in. What did you *reckon* he wanted with it?"

"Why, I thought he'd be in the pulpit."

Rot him, I forgot he was a preacher. I see I was up a stump again, so I played another chicken bone and got another think. Then I says:

"Blame it, do you suppose there ain't but one preacher to a church?"

"Why, what do they want with more?"

"What!—to preach before a king? I never did see such a girl as you. They don't have no less than seventeen."

"Seventeen! My land! Why, I wouldn't set out such a string as that, not if I *never* got to glory. It must take 'em a week."

"Shucks, they don't *all* of 'em preach the same day—only *one* of 'em."

"Well, then, what does the rest of 'em do?"

"Oh, nothing much. Loll around, pass the plate—and one thing or another. But mainly they don't do nothing."

"Well, then, what are they *for*?"

"Why, they're for *style*. Don't you know nothing?"

"Well, I don't *want* to know no such foolishness as that. How is servants treated in England? Do they treat 'em better 'n we treat our niggers?"

"*No*! A servant ain't nobody there. They treat them worse than dogs."

"Don't they give 'em holidays, the way we do, Christmas and New Year's week, and Fourth of July?"

"Oh, just listen! A body could tell *you* hain't ever been to England by that. Why, Hare-l—why, Joanna, they never see a holiday from year's end to year's end; never go to the circus, nor theater, nor nigger shows, nor nowheres."

"Nor church?"

"Nor church."

"But *you* always went to church."

Well, I was gone up again. I forgot I was the old man's servant. But next minute I whirled in on a kind of an explanation how a valley was different from a common servant and *had* to go to church whether he wanted to or not, and set with the family, on account of its being the law. But I didn't do it pretty good, and when I got done I see she warn't satisfied. She says:

"Honest injun, now, hain't you been telling me a lot of lies?"

"Honest injun," says I.

"None of it at all?"

"None of it at all. Not a lie in it," says I.

"Lay your hand on this book and say it."

I see it warn't nothing but a dictionary, so I laid my hand on it and said it. So then she looked a little better satisfied, and says:

"Well, then, I'll believe some of it; but I hope to gracious if I'll believe the rest."

"What is it you won't believe, Joe?" says Mary Jane, stepping in with Susan behind her. "It ain't right nor kind for you to talk so to him, and him a stranger and so far from his people. How would you like to be treated so?"

"That's always your way, Maim—always sailing in to help somebody before they're hurt. I hain't done nothing to him. He's told some stretchers, I reckon, and I said I wouldn't swallow it all; and that's every bit and grain I *did* say. I reckon he can stand a little thing like that, can't he?"

"I don't care whether 'twas little or whether 'twas big; he's here in our house and a stranger, and it wasn't good of you to say it. If you was in his place it would make you feel ashamed; and so you oughtn't to say a thing to another person that will make *them* feel ashamed."

"Why, Mam, he said—"

"It don't make no difference what he *said*—that ain't the thing. The thing is for you to treat him *kind*, and not be saying things to make him remember he ain't in his own country and amongst his own folks."

I says to myself, *this* is a girl that I'm letting that old reptile rob her of her money!

Then Susan *she* waltzed in; and if you'll believe me, she did give Hare-lip hark from the tomb!

Says I to myself, and this is *another* one that I'm letting him rob her of her money!

Then Mary Jane she took another inning, and went in sweet and lovely again—which was her way; but when she got done there warn't hardly anything left o' poor Hare lip. So she hollered.

"All right, then," says the other girls; "you just ask his pardon."

She done it, too; and she done it beautiful. She done it so beautiful it was good to hear; and I wished I could tell her a thousand lies, so she could do it again.

I says to myself, this is *another* one that I'm letting him rob her of her money. And when she got through they all jest laid theirselves out to make me feel at home and know I was amongst friends. I felt so ornery and low down and mean that I says to myself, my mind's made up; I'll hive that money for them or bust.

So then I lit out—for bed, I said, meaning some time or another. When I got by myself I went to thinking the thing over. I says to myself, shall I go to that doctor, private, and blow on these frauds? No—that won't do. He might tell who told him; then the king and the duke would make it warm for me. Shall I go, private, and tell Mary Jane? No—I dasn't do it. Her face would give them a hint, sure; they've got the money, and they'd slide right out and get away with it. If she was to fetch in help I'd get mixed up in the business before it was done with, I judge. No; there ain't no good way but one. I got to steal that money, somehow; and I got to steal it some way that they won't suspicion that I done it. They've got a good thing here, and they ain't a-going to leave till they've played this family and this town for all they're worth, so I'll find a chance time enough. I'll steal it and hide it; and by and by, when I'm away down the river, I'll write a letter and tell Mary Jane where it's hid. But I better hive it tonight if I can, because the doctor maybe hasn't let up as much as he lets on he has; he might scare them out of here yet.

So, thinks I, I'll go and search them rooms. Upstairs the hall was dark, but I found the duke's room, and started to paw around it with my hands; but I recollected it wouldn't be much like the king to let anybody else take care of that money but his own self; so then I went to his room and begun to paw around there. But I see I couldn't do nothing without a candle, and I dasn't light one, of course. So I judged I'd got to do the other thing—lay for them and eavesdrop. About that time I hears their footsteps coming, and was going to skip under the bed; I reached for it, but it wasn't where I thought it would be; but I touched the curtain that hid Mary Jane's frocks, so I jumped in behind that and snuggled in amongst the gowns, and stood there perfectly still.

They come in and shut the door; and the first thing the duke done was to get down and look under the bed. Then I was glad I hadn't found the bed when I wanted it. And yet, you know, it's kind of natural to hide under the bed when you are up to anything private. They sets down then, and the king says:

"Well, what is it? And cut it middlin' short, because it's better for us to be down there a-whoopin' up the mournin' than up here givin' 'em a chance to talk us over."

"Well, this is it, Capet. I ain't easy; I ain't comfortable. That doctor lays on my mind. I wanted to know your plans. I've got a notion, and I think it's a sound one."

"What is it, duke?"

"That we better glide out of this before three in the morning, and clip it down the river with what we've got. Specially, seeing we got it so easy—*given* back to us, flung at our heads, as you may say, when of course we allowed to have to steal it back. I'm for knocking off and lighting out."

That made me feel pretty bad. About an hour or two ago it would a been a little different, but now it made me feel bad and disappointed, The king rips out and says:

"What! And not sell out the rest o' the property? March off like a passel of fools and leave eight or nine thous'n' dollars' worth o' property layin' around jest sufferin' to be scooped in?—and all good, salable stuff, too."

The duke he grumbled; said the bag of gold was enough, and he didn't want to go no deeper—didn't want to rob a lot of orphans of *everything* they had.

"Why, how you talk!" says the king. "We sha'n't rob 'em of nothing at all but jest this money. The people that *buys* the property is the suff'rers; because as soon 's it's found out 'at we didn't own it—which won't be long after we've slid—the sale won't be valid, and it 'll all go back to the estate. These yer orphans 'll git their house back agin, and that's enough for *them*; they're young and spry, and k'n easy earn a livin'. *they* ain't a-goin to suffer. Why, jest think—there's thous'n's and thous'n's that ain't nigh so well off. Bless you, *they* ain't got noth'n' to complain of."

Well, the king he talked him blind; so at last he give in, and said all right, but said he believed it was blamed foolishness to stay, and that doctor hanging over them. But the king says:

"Cuss the doctor! What do we k'yer for *him*? Hain't we got all the fools in town on our side? And ain't that a big enough majority in any town?"

So they got ready to go down stairs again. The duke says:

"I don't think we put that money in a good place."

That cheered me up. I'd begun to think I warn't going to get a hint of no kind to help me. The king says:

"Why?"

"Because Mary Jane 'll be in mourning from this out; and first you know the nigger that does up the rooms will get an order to box these duds up and put 'em away; and do you reckon a nigger can run across money and not borrow some of it?"

"Your head's level agin, duke," says the king; and he comes a-fumbling under the curtain two or three foot from where I was. I stuck tight to the wall and kept mighty still, though quivery; and I wondered what them fellows would say to me if they catched me; and I tried to think what I'd better do if they did catch me. But the king he got the bag before I could think more than about a half a thought, and he never suspicioned I was around. They took and shoved the bag through a rip in the straw tick that was under the feather-bed, and crammed it in a foot or two amongst the straw and said it was all right now, because a nigger only makes up the feather-bed, and don't turn over the straw tick only about twice a year, and so it warn't in no danger of getting stole now.

Huck takes the money

But I knowed better. I had it out of there before they was halfway down stairs. I groped along up to my cubby, and hid it there till I could get a chance to do better. I judged I better hide it outside of the house somewheres, because if they missed it they would give the house a good ransacking: I knowed that very well. Then I turned in, with my clothes all on; but I couldn't a gone to sleep if I'd a wanted to, I was in such a sweat to get through with the business. By and by I heard the king and the duke come up; so I rolled off my pallet and laid with my chin at the top of my ladder, and waited to see if anything was going to happen. But nothing did.

So I held on till all the late sounds had quit and the early ones hadn't begun yet; and then I slipped down the ladder.

27

I crept to their doors and listened; they was snoring. So I tiptoed along, and got down stairs all right. There warn't a sound anywheres. I peeped through a crack of the dining-room door, and see the men that was watching the corpse all sound asleep on their chairs. The door was open into the parlour, where the corpse was laying, and there was a candle in both rooms. I passed along, and the parlour door was open; but I see there warn't nobody in there but the remainders of Peter; so I shoved on by; but the front door was locked, and the key wasn't there. Just then I heard somebody coming down the stairs, back behind me. I run in the parlour and took a swift look around, and the only place I see to hide the bag was in the coffin. The lid was shoved along about a foot, showing the dead man's face down in there, with a wet cloth over it, and his shroud on. I tucked the money-bag in under the lid, just down beyond where his hands was crossed, which made me creep, they was so cold, and then I run back across the room and in behind the door.

The person coming was Mary Jane. She went to the coffin, very soft, and kneeled down and looked in; then she put up her handkerchief, and I see she begun to cry, though I couldn't hear her, and her back was to me. I slid out, and as I passed the dining room I thought I'd make sure them watchers hadn't seen me; so I looked through the crack, and everything was all right. They hadn't stirred.

I slipped up to bed, feeling ruther blue, on accounts of the thing playing out that way after I had took so much trouble and run so much resk about it. Says I, if it could stay where it is, all right; because when we get down the river a hundred mile or two I could write back to Mary Jane, and she could dig him up again and get it; but that ain't the thing that's going to happen; the thing that's going to happen is, the money 'll be found when they come to screw on the lid. Then the king 'll get it again, and it 'll be a long day before he gives anybody another chance to smouch it from him. Of course I *wanted* to slide down and get it out of there, but I dasn't try it. Every minute it was getting earlier now, and pretty soon some of them watchers would begin to stir, and I might get catched—catched with six thousand dollars in my hands that nobody hadn't hired me to take care of. I don't wish to be mixed up in no such business as that, I says to myself.

When I got down stairs in the morning the parlour was shut up, and the watchers was gone. There warn't nobody around but the family and the widow Bartley and our tribe. I watched their faces to see if anything had been happening, but I couldn't tell.

Towards the middle of the day the undertaker come with his man, and they set the coffin in the middle of the room on a couple of chairs, and then set all our chairs in rows, and borrowed more from the neighbours till the hall and the parlour and the dining room was full. I see the coffin lid was the way it was before, but I dasn't go to look in under it, with folks around.

Then the people begun to flock in, and the beats and the girls took seats in the front row at the head of the coffin, and for a half an hour the people filed around slow, in single rank, and looked down at the dead man's face a minute, and some dropped in a tear, and it was all very still and solemn, only the girls and the beats holding handkerchiefs to their eyes and keeping their heads bent, and sobbing a little. There warn't no other sound but the scraping of the feet on the floor and blowing noses—because people always blows them more at a funeral than they do at other places except church.

When the place was packed full the undertaker he slid around in his black gloves with his softy soothering ways, putting on the last touches, and getting people and things all shipshape and comfortable, and making no more sound than a cat. He never spoke; he moved people around, he squeezed in late ones, he opened up passageways, and done it with nods, and signs with his hands. Then he took his place over against the wall. He was the softest, glidingest, stealthiest man I ever see; and there warn't no more smile to him than there is to a ham.

They had borrowed a melodeum*—a sick one; and when everything was ready a young woman set down and worked it, and it was pretty skreeky and colicky, and everybody joined in and sung, and Peter was the only one that had a good thing, according to my notion. Then the Reverend Hobson

* A wind-instrument with keyboard, the bellows being worked by foot-pedals.

opened up, slow and solemn, and begun to talk; and straight off the most outrageous row busted out in the cellar a body ever heard; it was only one dog, but he made a most powerful racket, and he kept it up right along; the parson he had to stand there, over the coffin, and wait—you couldn't hear yourself think. It was right down awkward, and nobody didn't seem to know what to do. But pretty soon they see that long-legged undertaker make a sign to the preacher as much as to say, "Don't you worry—just depend on me." Then he stooped down and begun to glide along the wall, just his shoulders showing over the people's heads. So he glided along, and the powwow and racket getting more and more outrageous all the time; and at last, when he had gone around two sides of the room, he disappears down cellar. Then in about two seconds we heard a whack, and the dog he finished up with a most amazing howl or two, and then everything was dead still, and the parson begun his solemn talk where he left off. In a minute or two here comes this undertaker's back and shoulders gliding along the wall again; and so he glided and glided around three sides of the room, and then rose up, and shaded his mouth with his hands, and stretched his neck out towards the preacher, over the people's heads, and says, in a kind of a coarse whisper, "*He had a rat*!" Then he drooped down and glided along the wall again to his place. You could see it was a great satisfaction to the people, because naturally they wanted to know. A little thing like that don't cost nothing, and it's just the little things that makes a man to be looked up to and liked. There warn't no more popular man in town than what that undertaker was.

Well, the funeral sermon was very good, but pison long and tiresome; and then the king he shoved in and got off some of his usual rubbage, and at last the job was through, and the undertaker begun to sneak up on the coffin with his screw-driver. I was in a sweat then, and watched him pretty keen. But he never meddled at all; just slid the lid along as soft as mush, and screwed it down tight and fast. So there I was! I didn't know whether the money was in there or not. So, says I, s'pose somebody has hogged that bag on the sly?—now how do I know whether to write to Mary Jane or not? S'pose she dug him up and didn't find nothing, what would she think of me? Blame it, I says, I might get hunted up and jailed; I'd better lay low and keep dark, and not write at all; the thing's awful mixed now; trying to better it, I've worsened it a hundred times, and I wish to goodness I'd just let it alone, dad fetch the whole business!

They buried him, and we come back home, and I went to watching faces again—I couldn't help it, and I couldn't rest easy. But nothing come of it; the faces didn't tell me nothing.

The king he visited around in the evening, and sweetened everybody up, and made himself ever so friendly; and he give out the idea that his congregation over in England would be in a sweat about him, so he must hurry and settle up the estate right away and leave for home. He was very sorry he was so pushed, and so was everybody; they wished he could stay longer, but they said they could see it couldn't be done. And he said of course him and William would take the girls home with them; and that pleased everybody too, because then the girls would be well fixed and amongst their own relations; and it pleased the girls, too—tickled them so they clean forgot they ever had a trouble in the world; and told him to sell out as quick as he wanted to, they would be ready. Them poor things was that glad and happy it made my heart ache to see them getting fooled and lied to so, but I didn't see no safe way for me to chip in and change the general tune.

Well, blamed if the king didn't bill the house and the niggers and all the property for auction straight off—sale two days after the funeral; but anybody could buy private beforehand if they wanted to.

So the next day after the funeral, along about noon-time, the girls' joy got the first jolt. A couple of nigger traders come along, and the king sold them the niggers reasonable, for three-day drafts as they called it, and away they went, the two sons up the river to Memphis, and their mother down the river to Orleans. I thought them poor girls and them niggers would break their hearts for grief; they cried around each other, and took on so it most made me down sick to see it. The girls said they hadn't ever dreamed of seeing the family separated or sold away from the town. I can't ever get it out of my memory, the sight of them poor miserable girls and niggers hanging around each other's necks and crying; and I reckon I couldn't a stood it all, but would a had to bust out and tell on our gang if I hadn't knowed the sale warn't no account and the niggers would be back home in a week or two.

The thing made a big stir in the town, too, and a good many come out flatfooted and said it was scandalous to separate the mother and the children that way. It injured the frauds some; but the old fool he bulled right along, spite of all the duke could say or do, and I tell you the duke was powerful uneasy.

Next day was auction day. About broad day in the morning the king and the duke come up in the garret and woke me up, and I see by their look that there was trouble. The king says:

"Was you in my room night before last?"

"No, your majesty"—which was the way I always called him when nobody but our gang warn't around.

"Was you in there yisterday er last night?"

"No, your majesty."

"Honour bright, now—no lies."

"Honour bright, your majesty, I'm telling you the truth. I hain't been a-near your room since Miss Mary Jane took you and the duke and showed it to you."

"Was you in my room?"

The duke says:

"Have you seen anybody else go in there?"

"No, your grace, not as I remember, I believe."

"Stop and think."

I studied awhile and see my chance; then I says:

"Well, I see the niggers go in there several times."

Both of them gave a little jump, and looked like they hadn't ever expected it, and then like they *had*. Then the duke says:

"What, all of them?"

"No—leastways, not all at once—that is, I don't think I ever see them all come *out* at once but just one time."

"Hello! When was that?"

"It was the day we had the funeral. In the morning. It warn't early, because I overslept. I was just starting down the ladder, and I see them."

"Well, go on, *go* on! What did they do? How'd they act?"

"They didn't do nothing. And they didn't act anyway much, as fur as I see. They tiptoed away; so I seen, easy enough, that they'd shoved in there to do up your majesty's room, or something, s'posing you was up; and found you *warn't* up, and so they was hoping to slide out of the way of trouble without waking you up, if they hadn't already waked you up."

"Great guns, *this* is a go!" says the king; and both of them looked pretty sick and tolerable silly. They stood there a-thinking and scratching their heads a minute, and the duke he bust into a kind of a little raspy chuckle, and says:

"It does beat all how neat the niggers played their hand. They let on to be *sorry* they was going out of this region! And I believed they *was* sorry, and so did you, and so did everybody. Don't ever tell *me* any more that a nigger ain't got any histrionic talent. Why, the way they played that thing it would fool *anybody*. In my opinion, there's a fortune in 'em. If I had capital and a theater, I wouldn't want a better lay-out than that—and here we've gone and sold 'em for a song. Yes, and ain't privileged to sing the song yet. Say, where *is* that song—that draft?"

"In the bank for to be collected. Where *would* it be?"

"Well, *that's* all right then, thank goodness."

Says I, kind of timid-like:

"Is something gone wrong?"

The king whirls on me and rips out:

"None o' your business! You keep your head shet, and mind y'r own affairs—if you got any. Long as you're in this town don't you forgit *that*—you hear?" Then he says to the duke, "We got to jest swaller it and say noth'n': mum's the word for *us*."

As they was starting down the ladder the duke he chuckles again, and says:

"Quick sales *and* small profits! It's a good business—yes."

The king snarls around on him and says:

"I was trying to do for the best in sellin' 'em out so quick. If the profits has turned out to be none, lackin' considable, and none to carry, is it my fault any more'n it's yourn?"

"Well, *they'd* be in this house yet and we *wouldn't* if I could a got my advice listened to."

The king sassed back as much as was safe for him, and then swapped around and lit into *me* again. He give me down the banks for not coming and *telling* him I see the niggers come out of his room acting that way—said any fool would a *knowed* something was up. And then waltzed in and cussed *himself* awhile, and said it all come of him not laying late and taking his natural rest that morning, and he'd be blamed if he'd ever do it again. So they went off a-jawing; and I felt dreadful glad I'd worked it all off on to the niggers, and yet hadn't done the niggers no harm by it.

28

By and by it was getting-up time. So I come down the ladder and started for downstairs; but as I come to the girls' room the door was open, and I see Mary Jane setting by her old hair trunk, which was open and she'd been packing things in it—getting ready to go to England. But she had stopped now with a folded gown in her lap, and had her face in her hands, crying. I felt awful bad to see it; of course anybody would. I went in there and says:

"Miss Mary Jane, you can't a-bear to see people in trouble, and I can't—most always. Tell me about it."

So she done it. And it was the niggers—I just expected it. She said the beautiful trip to England was most about spoiled for her; she didn't know *how* she was ever going to be happy there, knowing the mother and the children warn't ever going to see each other no more—and then busted out bitterer than ever, and flung up her hands, and says:

"Oh, dear, dear, to think they ain't *ever* going to see each other any more!"

"But they *will*—and inside of two weeks—and I *know* it!" says I.

Laws, it was out before I could think! And before I could budge she throws her arms around my neck and told me to say it *again*, say it *again*, say it *again*!

I see I had spoke too sudden and said too much, and was in a close place. I asked her to let me think a minute; and she set there, very impatient and excited and handsome, but looking kind of happy and eased-up, like a person that's had a tooth pulled out. So I went to studying it out. I says to myself, I reckon a body that ups and tells the truth when he is in a tight place is taking considerable many resks, though I ain't had no experience, and can't say for certain; but it looks so to me, anyway; and yet here's a case where I'm blest if it don't look to me like the truth is better and actuly *safer* than a lie. I must lay it by in my mind, and think it over some time or other, it's so kind of strange and unregular. I never see nothing like it. Well, I says to myself at last, I'm a-going to chance it; I'll up and tell the truth this time, though it does seem most like setting down on a kag of powder and touching it off just to see where you'll go to. Then I says:

"Miss Mary Jane, is there any place out of town a little ways where you could go and stay three or four days?"

"Yes; Mr. Lothrop's. Why?"

"Never mind why yet. If I'll tell you how I know the niggers will see each other again inside of two weeks—here in this house—and *prove* how I know it—will you go to Mr. Lothrop's and stay four days?"

"Four days!" she says; "I'll stay a year!"

"All right," I says, "I don't want nothing more out of *you* than just your word—I druther have it than another man's kiss-the-Bible." She smiled and reddened up very sweet, and I says, "If you don't mind it, I'll shut the door—and bolt it."

Then I come back and set down again, and says:

"Don't you holler. Just set still and take it like a man. I got to tell the truth, and you want to brace up, Miss Mary, because it's a bad kind, and going to be hard to take, but there ain't no help for it. These uncles of yourn ain't no uncles at all; they're a couple of frauds—regular dead-beats. There, now we're over the worst of it, you can stand the rest middling easy."

It jolted her up like everything, of course; but I was over the shoal water now, so I went right along, her eyes a-blazing higher and higher all the time, and told her every blame thing, from where we first struck that young fool going up to the steamboat, clear through to where she flung herself on to the king's breast at the front door and he kissed her sixteen or seventeen times—and then up she jumps, with her face afire like sunset, and says:

"The brute! Come, don't waste a minute—not a *second*—we'll have them tarred and feathered, and flung in the river!"

Says I:

"Cert'nly. But do you mean *before* you go to Mr. Lothrop's, or—"

"Oh," she says, "what am I *thinking* about!" she says, and set right down again. "Don't mind what I said—please don't—you *won't,* now, *will* you?" Laying her silky hand on mine in that kind of a way that I said I would die first. "I never thought, I was so stirred up," she says; "now go on, and I won't do so any more. You tell me what to do, and whatever you say I'll do it."

"Well," I says, "it's a rough gang, them two frauds, and I'm fixed so I got to travel with them a while longer, whether I want to or not—I druther not tell you why; and if you was to blow on them this town would get me out of their claws, and I'd be all right; but there'd be another person that you don't know about who'd be in big trouble. Well, we got to save *him*, hain't we? Of course. Well, then, we won't blow on them."

Saying them words put a good idea in my head. I see how maybe I could get me and Jim rid of the frauds; get them jailed here, and then leave. But I didn't want to run the raft in the daytime without anybody aboard to answer questions but me; so I didn't want the plan to begin working till pretty late tonight. I says:

"Miss Mary Jane, I'll tell you what we'll do, and you won't have to stay at Mr. Lothrop's so long, nuther. How fur is it?"

"A little short of four miles—right out in the country, back here."

"Well, that 'll answer. Now you go along out there, and lay low till nine or half-past tonight, and then get them to fetch you home again—tell them you've thought of something. If you get here before eleven put a candle in this window, and if I don't turn up wait *till* eleven, and *then* if I don't turn up it means I'm gone, and out of the way, and safe. Then you come out and spread the news around, and get these beats jailed."

"Good," she says, "I'll do it."

"And if it just happens so that I don't get away, but get took up along with them, you must up and say I told you the whole thing beforehand, and you must stand by me all you can."

"Stand by you! indeed I will. They sha'n't touch a hair of your head!" she says, and I see her nostrils spread and her eyes snap when she said it, too.

"If I get away I sha'n't be here," I says, "to prove these rapscallions ain't your uncles, and I couldn't do it if I *was* here. I could swear they was beats and bummers, that's all, though that's worth something. Well, there's others can do that better than what I can, and they're people that ain't going to be doubted as quick as I'd be. I'll tell you how to find them. Gimme a pencil and a piece of paper. There— *'Royal Nonesuch, Bricksville.'* Put it away, and don't lose it. When the court wants to find out something about these two, let them send up to Bricksville and say they've got the men that played the Royal Nonesuch, and ask for some witnesses—why, you'll have that entire town down here before you can hardly wink, Miss Mary. And they'll come a-biling, too."

I judged we had got everything fixed about right now. So I says:

"Just let the auction go right along, and don't worry. Nobody don't have to pay for the things they buy till a whole day after the auction on accounts of the short notice, and they ain't going out of this till they get that money; and the way we've fixed it the sale ain't going to count, and they ain't going to get no money. It's just like the way it was with the niggers—it warn't no sale, and the niggers will be back before long. Why, they can't collect the money for the *niggers* yet—they're in the worst kind of a fix, Miss Mary."

"Well," she says, "I'll run down to breakfast now, and then I'll start straight for Mr. Lothrop's."

"'Deed, *that* ain't the ticket, Miss Mary Jane," I says, "by no manner of means; go *before* breakfast."

"Why?"

"What did you reckon I wanted you to go at all for, Miss Mary?"

"Well, I never thought—and come to think, I don't know. What was it?"

"Why, it's because you ain't one of these leather-face people. I don't want no better book than what your face is. A body can set down and read it off like coarse print. Do you reckon you can go and face your uncles when they come to kiss you good morning, and never—"

"There, there, don't! Yes, I'll go before breakfast—I'll be glad to. And leave my sisters with them?"

"Yes; never mind about them. They've got to stand it yet a while. They might suspicion something if all of you was to go. I don't want you to see them, nor your sisters, nor nobody in this town; if a neighbour was to ask how is your uncles this morning your face would tell something. No, you go right along, Miss Mary Jane, and I'll fix it with all of them. I'll tell Miss Susan to give your love to your uncles and say you've went away for a few hours for to get a little rest and change, or to see a friend, and you'll be back tonight or early in the morning."

"Gone to see a friend is all right, but I won't have my love given to them."

"Well, then, it sha'n't be." It was well enough to tell *her* so—no harm in it. It was only a little thing to do, and no trouble; and it's the little things that smooths people's roads the most, down here below; it would make Mary Jane comfortable, and it wouldn't cost nothing. Then I says: "There's one more thing—that bag of money."

"Well, they've got that; and it makes me feel pretty silly to think *how* they got it."

"No, you're out, there. They hain't got it."

"Why, who's got it?"

"I wish I knowed, but I don't. I *had* it, because I stole it from them; and I stole it to give to you; and I know where I hid it, but I'm afraid it ain't there no more. I'm awful sorry, Miss Mary Jane, I'm just as sorry as I can be; but I done the best I could; I did honest. I come nigh getting caught, and I had to shove it into the first place I come to, and run—and it warn't a good place."

"Oh, stop blaming yourself—it's too bad to do it, and I won't allow it—you couldn't help it; it wasn't your fault. Where did you hide it?"

I didn't want to set her to thinking about her troubles again; and I couldn't seem to get my mouth to tell her what would make her see that corpse laying in the coffin with that bag of money on his stomach. So for a minute I didn't say nothing; then I says:

"I'd ruther not *tell* you where I put it, Miss Mary Jane, if you don't mind letting me off; but I'll write it for you on a piece of paper, and you can read it along the road to Mr. Lothrop's, if you want to. Do you reckon that 'll do?"

"Oh, yes."

So I wrote: "I put it in the coffin. It was in there when you was crying there, away in the night. I was behind the door, and I was mighty sorry for you, Miss Mary Jane."

It made my eyes water a little to remember her crying there all by herself in the night, and them devils laying there right under her own roof, shaming her and robbing her; and when I folded it up and give it to her I see the water come into her eyes, too; and she shook me by the hand, hard, and says:

"*Good*bye. I'm going to do everything just as you've told me; and if I don't ever see you again, I sha'n't ever forget you and I'll think of you a many and a many a time, and I'll *pray* for you, too!"—and she was gone.

Pray for me! I reckoned if she knowed me she'd take a job that was more nearer her size. But I bet she done it, just the same—she was just that kind. She had the grit to pray for Judus if she took the notion—there warn't no back-down to her, I judge. You may say what you want to, but in my opinion she had more sand in her than any girl I ever see; in my opinion she was just full of sand. It sounds like flattery, but it ain't no flattery. And when it comes to beauty—and goodness, too—she lays over them all. I hain't ever seen her since that time that I see her go out of that door; no, I hain't ever seen her since, but I reckon I've thought of her a many and a many a million times, and of her saying she would pray for me; and if ever I'd a thought it would do any good for me to pray for *her*, blamed if I wouldn't a done it or bust.

Well, Mary Jane she lit out the back way, I reckon; because nobody see her go. When I struck Susan and the hare-lip, I says:

"What's the name of them people over on t'other side of the river that you all goes to see sometimes?"

They says:

"There's several; but it's the Proctors, mainly."

"That's the name," I says; "I most forgot it. Well, Miss Mary Jane she told me to tell you she's gone over there in a dreadful hurry—one of them's sick."

"Which one?"

"I don't know; leastways, I kinder forget; but I thinks it's—"

"Sakes alive, I hope it ain't *Hanner*?"

"I'm sorry to say it," I says, "but Hanner's the very one."

"My goodness, and she so well only last week! Is she took bad?"

"It ain't no name for it. They set up with her all night, Miss Mary Jane said, and they don't think she'll last many hours."

"Only think of that, now! What's the matter with her?"

I couldn't think of anything reasonable, right off that way, so I says:

"Mumps."

"Mumps your granny! They don't set up with people that's got the mumps."

"They don't, don't they? You better bet they do with *these* mumps. These mumps is different. It's a new kind, Miss Mary Jane said."

"How's it a new kind?"

"Because it's mixed up with other things."

"What other things?"

"Well, measles, and whooping-cough, and erysiplas, and consumption, and yaller janders, and brain-fever, and I don't know what all."

"My land! And they call it the *mumps*?"

"That's what Miss Mary Jane said."

"Well, what in the nation do they call it the *mumps* for?"

"Why, because it *is* the mumps. That's what it starts with."

"Well, ther' ain't no sense in it. A body might stump his toe, and take pison, and fall down the well, and break his neck, and bust his brains out, and somebody come along and ask what killed him, and some numskull up and say, 'Why, he stumped his *toe*.' Would ther' be any sense in that? *No*. And ther' ain't no sense in *this*, nuther. Is it ketching?"

"Is it *ketching*? Why, how you talk. Is a *harrow* catching—in the dark? If you don't hitch on to one tooth, you're bound to on another, ain't you? And you can't get away with that tooth without fetching the whole harrow along, can you? Well, these kind of mumps is a kind of a harrow, as you may say—and it ain't no slouch of a harrow, nuther, you come to get it hitched on good."

"Well, it's awful, I think," says the hare-lip. "I'll go to Uncle Harvey and—"

"Oh, yes," I says, "I *would*. Of *course* I would. I wouldn't lose no time."

"Well, why wouldn't you?"

"Just look at it a minute, and maybe you can see. Hain't your uncles obleegd to get along home to England as fast as they can? And do you reckon they'd be mean enough to go off and leave you to go all that journey by yourselves? *you* know they'll wait for you. So fur, so good. Your uncle Harvey's a preacher, ain't he? Very well, then; is a *preacher* going to deceive a steamboat clerk? is he going to deceive a *ship clerk?*—so as to get them to let Miss Mary Jane go aboard? Now *you* know he ain't. What *will* he do, then? Why, he'll say, 'It's a great pity, but my church matters has got to get along the best way they can; for my niece has been exposed to the dreadful pluribus-unum mumps, and so it's my bounden duty to set down here and wait the three months it takes to show on her if she's got it.' But never mind, if you think it's best to tell your uncle Harvey—"

"Shucks, and stay fooling around here when we could all be having good times in England whilst we was waiting to find out whether Mary Jane's got it or not? Why, you talk like a muggins."

"Well, anyway, maybe you'd better tell some of the neighbours."

"Listen at that, now. You do beat all for natural stupidness. Can't you *see* that *they'd* go and tell? Ther' ain't no way but just to not tell anybody at *all*."

"Well, maybe you're right—yes, I judge you *are* right."

"But I reckon we ought to tell Uncle Harvey she's gone out a while, anyway, so he won't be uneasy about her?"

"Yes, Miss Mary Jane she wanted you to do that. She says, 'Tell them to give Uncle Harvey and William my love and a kiss, and say I've run over the river to see Mr.'—Mr.—what *is* the name of that rich family your uncle Peter used to think so much of?—I mean the one that—"

"Why, you must mean the Apthorps, ain't it?"

"Of course; bother them kind of names, a body can't ever seem to remember them, half the time, somehow. Yes, she said, say she has run over for to ask the Apthorps to be sure and come to the auction and buy this house, because she allowed her uncle Peter would ruther they had it than anybody else; and she's going to stick to them till they say they'll come, and then, if she ain't too tired, she's coming home; and if she is, she'll be home in the morning anyway. She said, don't say nothing about the Proctors, but only about the Apthorps—which 'll be perfectly true, because she is going there to speak about their buying the house; I know it, because she told me so herself."

"All right," they said, and cleared out to lay for their uncles, and give them the love and the kisses, and tell them the message.

Everything was all right now. The girls wouldn't say nothing because they wanted to go to England; and the king and the duke would ruther Mary Jane was off working for the auction than around in reach of Doctor Robinson. I felt very good; I judged I had done it pretty neat—I reckoned Tom Sawyer couldn't a done it no neater himself. Of course he would a throwed more style into it, but I can't do that very handy, not being brung up to it.

Well, they held the auction in the public square, along towards the end of the afternoon, and it strung along, and strung along, and the old man he was on hand and looking his level pisonest, up there longside of the auctioneer, and chipping in a little Scripture now and then, or a little goody-

goody saying of some kind, and the duke he was around goo-gooing for sympathy all he knowed how, and just spreading himself generally.

But by and by the thing dragged through, and everything was sold—everything but a little old trifling lot in the graveyard. So they'd got to work that off—I never see such a girafft as the king was for wanting to swallow *everything.* Well, whilst they was at it a steamboat landed, and in about two minutes up comes a crowd a-whooping and yelling and laughing and carrying on, and singing out:

"*Here's* your opposition line! here's your two sets o' heirs to old Peter Wilks—and you pays your money and you takes your choice!"

29

They was fetching a very nice-looking old gentleman along, and a nice-looking younger one, with his right arm in a sling. And, my souls, how the people yelled and laughed, and kept it up. But I didn't see no joke about it, and I judged it would strain the duke and the king some to see any. I reckoned they'd turn pale. But no, nary a pale did *they* turn. The duke he never let on he suspicioned what was up, but just went a goo-gooing around, happy and satisfied, like a jug that's googling out buttermilk; and as for the king, he just gazed and gazed down sorrowful on them newcomers like it give him the stomach-ache in his very heart to think there could be such frauds and rascals in the world. Oh, he done it admirable. Lots of the principal people gethered around the king, to let him see they was on his side. That old gentleman that had just come looked all puzzled to death. Pretty soon he begun to speak, and I see straight off he pronounced *like* an Englishman—not the king's way, though the king's *was* pretty good for an imitation. I can't give the old gent's words, nor I can't imitate him; but he turned around to the crowd, and says, about like this:

"This is a surprise to me which I wasn't looking for; and I'll acknowledge, candid and frank, I ain't very well fixed to meet it and answer it; for my brother and me has had misfortunes; he's broke his arm, and our baggage got put off at a town above here last night in the night by a mistake. I am Peter Wilks' brother Harvey, and this is his brother William, which can't hear nor speak—and can't even make signs to amount to much, now't he's only got one hand to work them with. We are who we say we are; and in a day or two, when I get the baggage, I can prove it. But up till then I won't say nothing more, but go to the hotel and wait."

So him and the new dummy started off; and the king he laughs, and blethers out:

"Broke his arm—*very* likely, *ain't* it?—and very convenient, too, for a fraud that's got to make signs, and ain't learnt how. Lost their baggage! That's *mighty* good!—and mighty ingenious—under the *circumstances*!"

So he laughed again; and so did everybody else, except three or four, or maybe half a dozen. One of these was that doctor; another one was a sharp-looking gentleman, with a carpet-bag of the old-fashioned kind made out of carpet-stuff, that had just come off of the steamboat and was talking to him in a low voice, and glancing towards the king now and then and nodding their heads—it was Levi Bell, the lawyer that was gone up to Louisville; and another one was a big rough husky that come along and listened to all the old gentleman said, and was listening to the king now. And when the king got done this husky up and says:

"Say, looky here; if you are Harvey Wilks, when'd you come to this town?"

"The day before the funeral, friend," says the king.

"But what time o' day?"

"In the evenin'—'bout an hour er two before sundown."

"*How'd* you come?"

"I come down on the Susan Powell from Cincinnati."

"Well, then, how'd you come to be up at the Pint in the *mornin'*—in a canoe?"

"I warn't up at the Pint in the mornin'."

"It's a lie."

Several of them jumped for him and begged him not to talk that way to an old man and a preacher.

"Preacher be hanged, he's a fraud and a liar. He was up at the Pint that mornin'. I live up there, don't I? Well, I was up there, and he was up there. I see him there. He come in a canoe, along with Tim Collins and a boy."

The doctor he up and says: "Would you know the boy again if you was to see him, Hines?"

"I reckon I would, but I don't know. Why, yonder he is, now. I know him perfectly easy."

It was me he pointed at. The doctor says:

"Neighbours, I don't know whether the new couple is frauds or not; but if *these* two ain't frauds, I am an idiot, that's all. I think it's our duty to see that they don't get away from here till we've looked into this thing. Come along, Hines; come along, the rest of you. We'll take these fellows to the tavern and affront them with t'other couple, and I reckon we'll find out *something* before we get through."

It was nuts for the crowd, though maybe not for the king's friends; so we all started. It was about sundown. The doctor he led me along by the hand, and was plenty kind enough, but he never let go my hand.

The Doctor leads Huck

We all got in a big room in the hotel, and lit up some candles, and fetched in the new couple. First, the doctor says:

"I don't wish to be too hard on these two men, but I think they're frauds, and they may have complices that we don't know nothing about. If they have, won't the complices get away with that bag of gold Peter Wilks left? It ain't unlikely. If these men ain't frauds, they won't object to sending for that money and letting us keep it till they prove they're all right—ain't that so?"

Everybody agreed to that. So I judged they had our gang in a pretty tight place right at the outstart. But the king he only looked sorrowful, and says:

"Gentlemen, I wish the money was there, for I ain't got no disposition to throw anything in the way of a fair, open, out-and-out investigation o' this misable business; but, alas, the money ain't there; you k'n send and see, if you want to."

"Where is it, then?"

"Well, when my niece give it to me to keep for her I took and hid it inside o' the straw tick o' my bed, not wishin' to bank it for the few days we'd be here, and considerin' the bed a safe place, we not bein' used to niggers, and suppos'n' 'em honest, like servants in England. The niggers stole it the very next mornin' after I had went down stairs; and when I sold 'em I hadn't missed the money yit, so they got clean away with it. My servant here k'n tell you 'bout it, gentlemen."

The doctor and several said "Shucks!" and I see nobody didn't altogether believe him. One man asked me if I see the niggers steal it. I said no, but I see them sneaking out of the room and hustling away, and I never thought nothing, only I reckoned they was afraid they had waked up my master and was trying to get away before he made trouble with them. That was all they asked me. Then the doctor whirls on me and says:

"Are *you* English, too?"

I says yes; and him and some others laughed, and said, "Stuff!"

Well, then they sailed in on the general investigation, and there we had it, up and down, hour in, hour out, and nobody never said a word about supper, nor ever seemed to think about it—and so they kept it up, and kept it up; and it *was* the worst mixed-up thing you ever see. They made the king tell his yarn, and they made the old gentleman tell his'n; and anybody but a lot of prejudiced chuckleheads would a *seen* that the old gentleman was spinning truth and t'other one lies. And by and by they had me up to tell what I knowed. The king he give me a left-handed look out of the corner of his eye, and so I knowed enough to talk on the right side. I begun to tell about Sheffield, and how we lived there, and all about the English Wilkses, and so on; but I didn't get pretty fur till the doctor begun to laugh; and Levi Bell, the lawyer, says:

"Set down, my boy; I wouldn't strain myself if I was you. I reckon you ain't used to lying, it don't seem to come handy; what you want is practice. You do it pretty awkward."

I didn't care nothing for the compliment, but I was glad to be let off, anyway.

The doctor he started to say something, and turns and says:

"If you'd been in town at first, Levi Bell—"

The king broke in and reached out his hand, and says:

"Why, is this my poor dead brother's old friend that he's wrote so often about?"

The lawyer and him shook hands, and the lawyer smiled and looked pleased, and they talked right along awhile, and then got to one side and talked low; and at last the lawyer speaks up and says:

"That 'll fix it. I'll take the order and send it, along with your brother's, and then they'll know it's all right."

So they got some paper and a pen, and the king he set down and twisted his head to one side, and chawed his tongue, and scrawled off something; and then they give the pen to the duke—and then for the first time the duke looked sick. But he took the pen and wrote. So then the lawyer turns to the new old gentleman and says:

"You and your brother please write a line or two and sign your names."

The old gentleman wrote, but nobody couldn't read it. The lawyer looked powerful astonished, and says:

"Well, it beats *me*"—and snaked a lot of old letters out of his pocket, and examined them, and then examined the old man's writing, and then *them* again; and then says: "These old letters is from Harvey Wilks; and here's *these* two handwritings, and anybody can see they didn't write them" (the king and the duke looked sold and foolish, I tell you, to see how the lawyer had took them in), "and here's *this* old gentleman's hand writing, and anybody can tell, easy enough, *he* didn't write them—fact is, the scratches he makes ain't properly *writing* at all. Now, here's some letters from—"

The new old gentleman says:

"If you please, let me explain. Nobody can read my hand but my brother there—so he copies for me. It's *his* hand you've got there, not mine."

"Well!" says the lawyer, "this *is* a state of things. I've got some of William's letters, too; so if you'll get him to write a line or so we can com—"

"He *can't* write with his left hand," says the old gentleman. "If he could use his right hand, you would see that he wrote his own letters and mine too. Look at both, please—they're by the same hand."

The lawyer done it, and says:

"I believe it's so—and if it ain't so, there's a heap stronger resemblance than I'd noticed before, anyway. Well, well, well! I thought we was right on the track of a solution, but it's gone to grass, partly. But anyway, one thing is proved—*these* two ain't either of 'em Wilkses"—and he wagged his head towards the king and the duke.

Well, what do you think? That muleheaded old fool wouldn't give in *then*! Indeed he wouldn't. Said it warn't no fair test. Said his brother William was the cussedest joker in the world, and hadn't tried to write—*he* see William was going to play one of his jokes the minute he put the pen to paper. And so he warmed up and went warbling and warbling right along till he was actuly beginning to believe what he was saying *himself*; but pretty soon the new gentleman broke in, and says:

"I've thought of something. Is there anybody here that helped to lay out my br—helped to lay out the late Peter Wilks for burying?"

"Yes," says somebody, "me and Ab Turner done it. We're both here."

Then the old man turns towards the king, and says:

"Perhaps this gentleman can tell me what was tattooed on his breast?"

Blamed if the king didn't have to brace up mighty quick, or he'd a squshed down like a bluff bank that the river has cut under, it took him so sudden; and, mind you, it was a thing that was calculated to make most *anybody* sqush to get fetched such a solid one as that without any notice, because how was *he* going to know what was tattooed on the man? He whitened a little; he couldn't help it; and it was mighty still in there, and everybody bending a little forwards and gazing at him. Says I to myself, *now* he'll throw up the sponge—there ain't no more use. Well, did he? A body can't hardly believe it, but he didn't. I reckon he thought he'd keep the thing up till he tired them people out, so they'd thin out, and him and the duke could break loose and get away. Anyway, he set there, and pretty soon he begun to smile, and says:

"Mf! It's a *very* tough question, *ain't* it! *yes*, sir, I k'n tell you what's tattooed on his breast. It's jest a small, thin, blue arrow—that's what it is; and if you don't look clost, you can't see it. *now* what do you say—hey?"

Well, I never see anything like that old blister for clean out-and-out cheek.

The new old gentleman turns brisk towards Ab Turner and his pard, and his eye lights up like he judged he'd got the king *this* time, and says:

"There—you've heard what he said! Was there any such mark on Peter Wilks' breast?"

Both of them spoke up and says:

"We didn't see no such mark."

"Good!" says the old gentleman. "Now, what you *did* see on his breast was a small dim P, and a B (which is an initial he dropped when he was young), and a W, with dashes between them, so: P—B—W"—and he marked them that way on a piece of paper. "Come, ain't that what you saw?"

Both of them spoke up again, and says:

"No, we *didn't*. We never seen any marks at all."

Well, everybody *was* in a state of mind now, and they sings out:

"The whole *bilin*' of 'm 's frauds! Le's duck 'em! le's drown 'em! le's ride 'em on a rail!" and everybody was whooping at once, and there was a rattling powwow. But the lawyer he jumps on the table and yells, and says:

"Gentlemen—gentle*men!* Hear me just a word—just a *single* word—if you *please*! There's one way yet—let's go and dig up the corpse and look."

That took them.

"Hooray!" they all shouted, and was starting right off; but the lawyer and the doctor sung out:

"Hold on, hold on! Collar all these four men and the boy, and fetch *them* along, too!"

"We'll do it!" they all shouted; "and if we don't find them marks we'll lynch the whole gang!"

I *was* scared, now, I tell you. But there warn't no getting away, you know. They gripped us all, and marched us right along, straight for the graveyard, which was a mile and a half down the river, and the whole town at our heels, for we made noise enough, and it was only nine in the evening.

As we went by our house I wished I hadn't sent Mary Jane out of town; because now if I could tip her the wink she'd light out and save me, and blow on our dead-beats.

Well, we swarmed along down the river road, just carrying on like wildcats; and to make it more scary the sky was darking up, and the lightning beginning to wink and flitter, and the wind to shiver amongst the leaves. This was the most awful trouble and most dangersome I ever was in; and I was kinder stunned; everything was going so different from what I had allowed for; stead of being fixed so I could take my own time if I wanted to, and see all the fun, and have Mary Jane at my back to save me and set me free when the close-fit come, here was nothing in the world betwixt me and sudden death but just them tattoo-marks. If they didn't find them—

I couldn't bear to think about it; and yet, somehow, I couldn't think about nothing else. It got darker and darker, and it was a beautiful time to give the crowd the slip; but that big husky had me by the wrist—Hines—and a body might as well try to give Goliar* the slip. He dragged me right along, he was so excited, and I had to run to keep up.

When they got there they swarmed into the graveyard and washed over it like an overflow. And when they got to the grave they found they had about a hundred times as many shovels as they wanted, but nobody hadn't thought to fetch a lantern. But they sailed into digging anyway by the flicker of the lightning, and sent a man to the nearest house, a half a mile off, to borrow one.

So they dug and dug like everything; and it got awful dark, and the rain started, and the wind swished and swushed along, and the lightning come brisker and brisker, and the thunder boomed; but them people never took no notice of it, they was so full of this business; and one minute you could

* Goliath.

see everything and every face in that big crowd, and the shovelfuls of dirt sailing up out of the grave, and the next second the dark wiped it all out, and you couldn't see nothing at all.

At last they got out the coffin and begun to unscrew the lid, and then such another crowding and shouldering and shoving as there was, to scrouge in and get a sight, you never see; and in the dark, that way, it was awful. Hines he hurt my wrist dreadful pulling and tugging so, and I reckon he clean forgot I was in the world, he was so excited and panting.

All of a sudden the lightning let go a perfect sluice of white glare, and somebody sings out:

"By the living jingo, here's the bag of gold on his breast!"

Hines let out a whoop, like everybody else, and dropped my wrist and give a big surge to bust his way in and get a look, and the way I lit out and shinned for the road in the dark there ain't nobody can tell.

I had the road all to myself, and I fairly flew—leastways, I had it all to myself except the solid dark, and the now-and-then glares, and the buzzing of the rain, and the thrashing of the wind, and the splitting of the thunder; and sure as you are born I did clip it along!

When I struck the town I see there warn't nobody out in the storm, so I never hunted for no back streets, but humped it straight through the main one; and when I begun to get towards our house I aimed my eye and set it. No light there; the house all dark—which made me feel sorry and disappointed, I didn't know why. But at last, just as I was sailing by, *flash* comes the light in Mary Jane's window! and my heart swelled up sudden, like to bust; and the same second the house and all was behind me in the dark, and wasn't ever going to be before me no more in this world. She *was* the best girl I ever see, and had the most sand.

The minute I was far enough above the town to see I could make the towhead, I begun to look sharp for a boat to borrow, and the first time the lightning showed me one that wasn't chained I snatched it and shoved. It was a canoe, and warn't fastened with nothing but a rope. The towhead was a rattling big distance off, away out there in the middle of the river, but I didn't lose no time; and when I struck the raft at last I was so fagged I would a just laid down to blow and gasp if I could afforded it. But I didn't. As I sprung aboard I sung out:

"Out with you, Jim, and set her loose! Glory be to goodness, we're shut of them!"

Jim lit out, and was a-coming for me with both arms spread, he was so full of joy; but when I glimpsed him in the lightning my heart shot up in my mouth and I went overboard backwards; for I forgot he was old King Lear and a drownded A-rab all in one, and it most scared the livers and lights out of me. But Jim fished me out, and was going to hug me and bless me, and so on, he was so glad I was back and we was shut of the king and the duke, but I says:

"Not now; have it for breakfast, have it for breakfast! Cut loose and let her slide!"

So in two seconds away we went a-sliding down the river, and it *did* seem so good to be free again and all by ourselves on the big river, and nobody to bother us. I had to skip around a bit, and jump up and crack my heels a few times—I couldn't help it; but about the third crack I noticed a sound that I knowed mighty well, and held my breath and listened and waited; and sure enough, when the next flash busted out over the water, here they come!—and just a-laying to their oars and making their skiff hum! It was the king and the duke.

So I wilted right down on to the planks then, and give up; and it was all I could do to keep from crying.

30

When they got aboard the king went for me, and shook me by the collar, and says:

"Tryin' to give us the slip, was ye, you pup! Tired of our company, hey?"

I says:

"No, your majesty, we warn't—*please* don't, your majesty!"

"Quick, then, and tell us what *was* your idea, or I'll shake the insides out o' you!"

"Honest, I'll tell you everything just as it happened, your majesty. The man that had a-holt of me was very good to me, and kept saying he had a boy about as big as me that died last year, and he was sorry to see a boy in such a dangerous fix; and when they was all took by surprise by finding the gold, and made a rush for the coffin, he lets go of me and whispers, 'Heel it now, or they'll hang ye, sure!' and I lit out. It didn't seem no good for *me* to stay—I couldn't do nothing, and I didn't want to be hung if I could get away. So I never stopped running till I found the canoe; and when I got here I told Jim to hurry, or they'd catch me and hang me yet, and said I was afeard you and the duke wasn't alive now, and I was awful sorry, and so was Jim, and was awful glad when we see you coming; you may ask Jim if I didn't."

Jim said it was so; and the king told him to shut up, and said, "Oh, yes, it's *mighty* likely!" and shook me up again, and said he reckoned he'd drownd me. But the duke says:

"Leggo the boy, you old idiot! Would *you* a done any different? Did you inquire around for *him* when you got loose? I don't remember it."

So the king let go of me, and begun to cuss that town and everybody in it. But the duke says:

"You better a blame' sight give *yourself* a good cussing, for you're the one that's entitled to it most. You hain't done a thing from the start that had any sense in it, except coming out so cool and cheeky with that imaginary blue-arrow mark. That *was* bright—it was right down bully; and it was the thing that saved us. For if it hadn't been for that they'd a jailed us till them Englishmen's baggage come—and then—the penitentiary, you bet! But that trick took 'em to the graveyard, and the gold done us a still bigger kindness; for if the excited fools hadn't let go all holts and made that rush to get a look we'd a slept in our cravats tonight—cravats warranted to *wear*, too—longer than *we'd* need 'em."

They was still a minute—thinking; then the king says, kind of absent-minded like:

"Mf! And we reckoned the *niggers* stole it!"

That made me squirm!

"Yes," says the duke, kinder slow and deliberate and sarcastic, "*we* did."

After about a half a minute the king drawls out:

"Leastways, I did."

The duke says, the same way:

"On the contrary, I did."

The king kind of ruffles up, and says:

"Looky here, Bilgewater, what'r you referrin' to?"

The duke says, pretty brisk:

"When it comes to that, maybe you'll let me ask, what was *you* referring to?"

"Shucks!" says the king, very sarcastic; "but I don't know—maybe you was asleep, and didn't know what you was about."

The duke bristles up now, and says:

"Oh, let *up* on this cussed nonsense; do you take me for a blame' fool? Don't you reckon I know who hid that money in that coffin?"

"*Yes*, sir! I know you *do* know, because you done it yourself!"

"It's a lie!"—and the duke went for him. The king sings out:

"Take y'r hands off!—leggo my throat!—I take it all back!"

The duke says:

"Well, you just own up, first, that you *did* hide that money there, intending to give me the slip one of these days, and come back and dig it up, and have it all to yourself."

"Wait jest a minute, duke—answer me this one question, honest and fair; if you didn't put the money there, say it, and I'll b'lieve you, and take back everything I said."

"You old scoundrel, I didn't, and you know I didn't. There, now!"

"Well, then, I b'lieve you. But answer me only jest this one more—now *don't* git mad; didn't you have it in your mind to hook the money and hide it?"

The duke never said nothing for a little bit; then he says:

"Well, I don't care if I *did*, I didn't *do* it, anyway. But you not only had it in mind to do it, but you *done* it."

"I wisht I never die if I done it, duke, and that's honest. I won't say I warn't goin' to do it, because I *was*; but you—I mean somebody—got in ahead o' me."

"It's a lie! You done it, and you got to *say* you done it, or—"

The king began to gurgle, and then he gasps out:

"'Nough!—I *own up!*"

I was very glad to hear him say that; it made me feel much more easier than what I was feeling before. So the duke took his hands off and says:

"If you ever deny it again I'll drown you. It's *well* for you to set there and blubber like a baby—it's fitten for you, after the way you've acted. I never see such an old ostrich for wanting to gobble everything—and I a-trusting you all the time, like you was my own father. You ought to been ashamed of yourself to stand by and hear it saddled on to a lot of poor niggers, and you never say a word for 'em. It makes me feel ridiculous to think I was soft enough to *believe* that rubbage. Cuss you, I can see now why you was so anxious to make up the deffisit—you wanted to get what money I'd got out of the Nonesuch and one thing or another, and scoop it *all*!"

The king says, timid, and still a-snuffling:

"Why, duke, it was you that said make up the deffisit; it warn't me."

"Dry up! I don't want to hear no more out of you!" says the duke. "And *now* you see what you GOT by it. They've got all their own money back, and all of *ourn* but a shekel or two *besides*. G'long to bed, and don't you deffersit *me* no more deffersits, long 's *you* live!"

So the king sneaked into the wigwam and took to his bottle for comfort, and before long the duke tackled HIS bottle; and so in about a half an hour they was as thick as thieves again, and the tighter they got the lovinger they got, and went off a-snoring in each other's arms. They both got powerful mellow, but I noticed the king didn't get mellow enough to forget to remember to not deny about hiding the money-bag again. That made me feel easy and satisfied. Of course when they got to snoring we had a long gabble, and I told Jim everything.

31

We dasn't stop again at any town for days and days; kept right along down the river. We was down south in the warm weather now, and a mighty long ways from home. We begun to come to trees with Spanish moss on them, hanging down from the limbs like long, grey beards. It was the first I ever see it growing, and it made the woods look solemn and dismal. So now the frauds reckoned they was out of danger, and they begun to work the villages again.

First they done a lecture on temperance; but they didn't make enough for them both to get drunk on. Then in another village they started a dancing-school; but they didn't know no more how to dance than a kangaroo does; so the first prance they made the general public jumped in and pranced them out of town. Another time they tried to go at yellocution; but they didn't yellocute long till the audience got up and give them a solid good cussing, and made them skip out. They tackled missionarying, and mesmerizing, and doctoring, and telling fortunes, and a little of everything; but they couldn't seem to have no luck. So at last they got just about dead broke, and laid around the raft as she floated along, thinking and thinking, and never saying nothing, by the half a day at a time, and dreadful blue and desperate.

And at last they took a change and begun to lay their heads together in the wigwam and talk low and confidential two or three hours at a time. Jim and me got uneasy. We didn't like the look of it. We judged they was studying up some kind of worse deviltry than ever. We turned it over and over, and at last we made up our minds they was going to break into somebody's house or store, or was going into the counterfeit-money business, or something. So then we was pretty scared, and made up an agreement that we wouldn't have nothing in the world to do with such actions, and if we ever got the least show we would give them the cold shake and clear out and leave them behind. Well, early one morning we hid the raft in a good, safe place about two mile below a little bit of a shabby village named Pikesville, and the king he went ashore and told us all to stay hid whilst he went up to town and smelt around to see if anybody had got any wind of the Royal Nonesuch there yet. ("House to rob, you *mean*," says I to myself; "and when you get through robbing it you'll come back here and wonder what has become of me and Jim and the raft—and you'll have to take it out in wondering.") And he said if he warn't back by midday the duke and me would know it was all right, and we was to come along.

So we stayed where we was. The duke he fretted and sweated around, and was in a mighty sour way. He scolded us for everything, and we couldn't seem to do nothing right; he found fault with every little thing. Something was a-brewing, sure. I was good and glad when midday come and no king; we could have a change, anyway—and maybe a chance for *the* change on top of it. So me and the duke went up to the village, and hunted around there for the king, and by and by we found him in the back room of a little low doggery,* very tight, and a lot of loafers bullyragging him for sport, and he a-cussing and a-threatening with all his might, and so tight he couldn't walk, and couldn't do nothing to them. The duke he begun to abuse him for an old fool, and the king begun to sass back, and the minute they was fairly at it I lit out and shook the reefs out of my hind legs, and spun down the river road like a deer, for I see our chance; and I made up my mind that it would be a long day before they ever see me and Jim again. I got down there all out of breath but loaded up with joy, and sung out:

"Set her loose, Jim! we're all right now!"

But there warn't no answer, and nobody come out of the wigwam. Jim was gone! I set up a shout—and then another—and then another one; and run this way and that in the woods, whooping and screeching; but it warn't no use—old Jim was gone. Then I set down and cried; I couldn't help it. But I couldn't set still long. Pretty soon I went out on the road, trying to think what I better do, and I run across a boy walking, and asked him if he'd seen a strange nigger dressed so and so, and he says:

"Yes."

"Whereabouts?" says I.

"Down to Silas Phelps' place, two mile below here. He's a runaway nigger, and they've got him. Was you looking for him?"

"You bet I ain't! I run across him in the woods about an hour or two ago, and he said if I hollered he'd cut my livers out—and told me to lay

* A low drinking saloon.

down and stay where I was; and I done it. Been there ever since; afeard to come out."

"Well," he says, "you needn't be afeard no more, becuz they've got him. He run off f'm down South, som'ers."

"It's a good job they got him."

"Well, I *reckon*! There's two hunderd dollars reward on him. It's like picking up money out'n the road."

"Yes, it is—and I could a had it if I'd been big enough; I see him *first*. Who nailed him?"

"It was an old fellow—a stranger—and he sold out his chance in him for forty dollars, becuz he's got to go up the river and can't wait. Think o' that, now! You bet *I'd* wait, if it was seven year."

"That's me, every time," says I. "But maybe his chance ain't worth no more than that, if he'll sell it so cheap. Maybe there's something ain't straight about it."

"But it *is*, though—straight as a string. I see the handbill myself. It tells all about him, to a dot—paints him like a picture, and tells the plantation he's frum, below Newr *leans*. No-sirree-*bob*, they ain't no trouble 'bout *that* speculation, you bet you. Say, gimme a chaw tobacker, won't ye?"

I didn't have none, so he left. I went to the raft, and set down in the wigwam to think. But I couldn't come to nothing. I thought till I wore my head sore, but I couldn't see no way out of the trouble. After all this long journey, and after all we'd done for them scoundrels, here it was all come to nothing, everything all busted up and ruined, because they could have the heart to serve Jim such a trick as that, and make him a slave again all his life, and amongst strangers, too, for forty dirty dollars.

Once I said to myself it would be a thousand times better for Jim to be a slave at home where his family was, as long as he'd *got* to be a slave, and so I'd better write a letter to Tom Sawyer and tell him to tell Miss Watson where he was. But I soon give up that notion for two things: she'd be mad and disgusted at his rascality and ungratefulness for leaving her, and so she'd sell him straight down the river again; and if she didn't, everybody naturally despises an ungrateful nigger, and they'd make Jim feel it all the time, and so he'd feel ornery and disgraced. And then think of *me*! It would get all around that Huck Finn helped a nigger to get his freedom; and if I was ever to see anybody from that town again I'd be ready to get down and lick his boots for shame. That's just the way: a person does a low-down thing, and then he don't want to take no consequences of it. Thinks as long as he can hide it, it ain't no disgrace. That was my fix exactly. The more I studied about this the more my conscience went to grinding me, and the more wicked and low-down and ornery I got to feeling. And at last, when it hit me all of a sudden that here was the plain hand of Providence slapping me in the face and letting me know my wickedness was being watched all the time from up there in heaven, whilst I was stealing a poor old woman's nigger that hadn't ever done me no harm, and now was showing me there's One that's always on the lookout, and ain't a-going to allow no such miserable doings to go only just so fur and no further, I most dropped in my tracks I was so scared. Well, I tried the best I could to kinder soften it up somehow for myself by saying I was brung up wicked, and so I warn't so much to blame; but something inside of me kept saying, "There was the Sunday-school, you could a gone to it; and if you'd a done it they'd a learnt you there that people that acts as I'd been acting about that nigger goes to everlasting fire."

It made me shiver. And I about made up my mind to pray, and see if I couldn't try to quit being the kind of a boy I was and be better. So I kneeled down. But the words wouldn't come. Why wouldn't they? It warn't no use to try and hide it from Him. Nor from *me*, neither. I knowed very well why they wouldn't come. It was because my heart warn't right; it was because I warn't square; it was because I was playing double. I was letting *on* to give up sin, but away inside of me I was holding on to the biggest one of all. I was trying to make my mouth *say* I would do the right thing and the clean thing, and go and write to that nigger's owner and tell where he was; but deep down in me I knowed it was a lie, and He knowed it. You can't pray a lie—I found that out.

So I was full of trouble, full as I could be; and didn't know what to do. At last I had an idea; and I says, I'll go and write the letter—and then see if I can pray. Why, it was astonishing, the way I felt as light as a feather right straight off, and my troubles all gone. So I got a piece of paper and a pencil, all glad and excited, and set down and wrote:

Thinking

> Miss Watson, your runaway nigger Jim is down here two mile below Pikesville, and Mr. Phelps has got him and he will give him up for the reward if you send.
>
> *Huck Finn*

I felt good and all washed clean of sin for the first time I had ever felt so in my life, and I knowed I could pray now. But I didn't do it straight off, but laid the paper down and set there thinking—thinking how good it was all this happened so, and how near I come to being lost and going to hell. And went on thinking. And got to thinking over our trip down the river; and I see Jim before me all the time: in the day and in the night-time, sometimes moonlight, sometimes storms, and we a-floating along, talking and singing and laughing. But somehow I couldn't seem to strike no places to harden me against him, but only the other kind. I'd see him standing my watch on top of his'n, 'stead of calling me, so I could go on sleeping; and see him how glad he was when I come back out of the fog; and when I come to him again in the swamp, up there where the feud was; and such-like times; and would always call me honey, and pet me and do everything he could think of for me, and how good he always was; and at last I struck the time I saved him by telling the men we had small-pox aboard, and he was so grateful, and said I was the best friend old Jim ever had in the world, and the *only* one he's got now; and then I happened to look around and see that paper.

It was a close place. I took it up, and held it in my hand. I was a-trembling, because I'd got to decide, forever, betwixt two things, and I knowed it. I studied a minute, sort of holding my breath, and then says to myself:

"All right, then, I'll *go* to hell"—and tore it up.

It was awful thoughts and awful words, but they was said. And I let them stay said; and never thought no more about reforming. I shoved the whole thing out of my head, and said I would take up wickedness again, which was in my line, being brung up to it, and the other warn't. And for a starter I would go to work and steal Jim out of slavery again; and if I could think up anything worse, I would do that, too; because as long as I was in, and in for good, I might as well go the whole hog.

Then I set to thinking over how to get at it, and turned over some considerable many ways in my mind; and at last fixed up a plan that suited me. So then I took the bearings of a woody island that was down the river a piece, and as soon as it was fairly dark I crept out with my raft and went for it, and hid it there, and then turned in. I slept the night through, and got up before it was light, and had my breakfast, and put on my store clothes, and tied up some others and one thing or another in a bundle, and took the canoe and cleared for shore. I landed below where I judged was Phelps's place, and hid my bundle in the woods, and then filled up the canoe with water, and loaded rocks into her and sunk her where I could find her again when I wanted her, about a quarter of a mile below a little steam sawmill that was on the bank.

Then I struck up the road, and when I passed the mill I see a sign on it, "Phelps's Sawmill," and when I come to the farmhouses, two or three hundred yards further along, I kept my eyes peeled, but didn't see nobody around, though it was good daylight now. But I didn't mind, because I didn't want to see nobody just yet—I only wanted to get the lay of the land. According to my plan, I was going to turn up there from the village, not from below. So I just took a look, and shoved along, straight for town. Well, the very first man I see when I got there was the duke. He was sticking up a bill for the Royal Nonesuch—three-night performance—like that other time. They had the cheek, them frauds! I was right on him before I could shirk. He looked astonished, and says:

"Hel-*lo*! Where'd *you* come from?" Then he says, kind of glad and eager, "Where's the raft?—got her in a good place?"

I says:

"Why, that's just what I was going to ask your grace."

Then he didn't look so joyful, and says:

"What was your idea for asking *me*?" he says.

"Well," I says, "when I see the king in that doggery yesterday I says to myself, we can't get him home for hours, till he's soberer; so I went a-loafing around town to put in the time and wait. A man up and offered me ten cents to help him pull a skiff over the river and back to fetch a sheep, and so I went along; but when we was dragging him to the boat, and the man left me a-holt of the rope and went behind him to shove him along, he was too strong for me and jerked loose and run, and we after him. We didn't have no dog, and so we had to chase him all over the country till we tired him out. We never got him till dark; then we fetched him over, and I started down for the raft. When I got there and see it was gone, I says to myself, 'They've got into trouble and had to leave; and they've took my nigger, which is the only nigger I've got in the world, and now I'm in a strange country, and ain't got no property no more, nor nothing, and no way to make my living;' so I set down and cried. I slept in the woods all night. But what *did* become of the raft, then?—and Jim—poor Jim!"

"Blamed if I know—that is, what's become of the raft. That old fool had made a trade and got forty dollars, and when we found him in the doggery the loafers had matched half-dollars with him and got every cent but what he'd spent for whisky; and when I got him home late last night and found the raft gone, we said, 'That little rascal has stole our raft and shook us, and run off down the river.'"

"I wouldn't shake my *nigger*, would I?—the only nigger I had in the world, and the only property."

"We never thought of that. Fact is, I reckon we'd come to consider him *our* nigger; yes, we did consider him so—goodness knows we had trouble enough for him. So when we see the raft was gone and we flat broke, there warn't anything for it but to try the Royal Nonesuch another shake. And I've pegged along ever since, dry as a powder-horn. Where's that ten cents? Give it here."

I had considerable money, so I give him ten cents, but begged him to spend it for something to eat, and give me some, because it was all the money I had, and I hadn't had nothing to eat since yesterday. He never said nothing. The next minute he whirls on me and says:

"Do you reckon that nigger would blow on us? We'd skin him if he done that!"

"How can he blow? Hain't he run off?"

"No! That old fool sold him, and never divided with me, and the money's gone."

"*Sold* him?" I says, and begun to cry; "why, he was *my* nigger, and that was my money. Where is he?—I want my nigger."

"Well, you can't *get* your nigger, that's all—so dry up your blubbering. Looky here—do you think *you'd* venture to blow on us? Blamed if I think I'd trust you. Why, if you *was* to blow on us—"

He stopped, but I never see the duke look so ugly out of his eyes before. I went on a-whimpering, and says:

"I don't want to blow on nobody; and I ain't got no time to blow, nohow. I got to turn out and find my nigger."

He looked kinder bothered, and stood there with his bills fluttering on his arm, thinking, and wrinkling up his forehead. At last he says:

"I'll tell you something. We got to be here three days. If you'll promise you won't blow, and won't let the nigger blow, I'll tell you where to find him."

So I promised, and he says:

"A farmer by the name of Silas Ph—" and then he stopped. You see, he started to tell me the truth; but when he stopped that way, and begun to study and think again, I reckoned he was changing his mind. And so he was. He wouldn't trust me; he wanted to make sure of having me out of the way the whole three days. So pretty soon he says: "The man that bought him is named Abram Foster—Abram G. Foster—and he lives forty mile back here in the country, on the road to Lafayette."

"All right," I says, "I can walk it in three days. And I'll start this very afternoon."

"No you wont, you'll start *now*; and don't you lose any time about it, neither, nor do any gabbling by the way. Just keep a tight tongue in your head and move right along, and then you won't get into trouble with *us*, d'ye hear?"

That was the order I wanted, and that was the one I played for. I wanted to be left free to work my plans.

"So clear out," he says; "and you can tell Mr. Foster whatever you want to. Maybe you can get him to believe that Jim *is* your nigger—some idiots don't require documents—leastways I've heard there's such down South here. And when you tell him the handbill and the reward's bogus, maybe he'll believe you when you explain to him what the idea was for getting 'em out. Go 'long now, and tell him anything you want to; but mind you don't work your jaw any *between* here and there."

Striking for the Back Country

So I left, and struck for the back country. I didn't look around, but I kinder felt like he was watching me. But I knowed I could tire him out at that. I went straight out in the country as much as a mile before I stopped; then I doubled back through the woods towards Phelps'. I reckoned I better start in on my plan straight off without fooling around, because I wanted to stop Jim's mouth till these fellows could get away. I didn't want no trouble with their kind. I'd seen all I wanted to of them, and wanted to get entirely shut of them.

32

When I got there it was all still and Sunday-like, and hot and sunshiny; the hands was gone to the fields; and there was them kind of faint dronings of bugs and flies in the air that makes it seem so lonesome and like everybody's dead and gone; and if a breeze fans along and quivers the leaves it makes you feel mournful, because you feel like it's spirits whispering—spirits that's been dead ever so many years—and you always think they're talking about *you.* As a general thing it makes a body wish *he* was dead, too, and done with it all.

Phelps' was one of these little one-horse cotton plantations, and they all look alike. A rail fence round a two-acre yard; a stile made out of logs sawed off and upended in steps, like barrels of a different length, to climb over the fence with, and for the women to stand on when they are going to jump on to a horse; some sickly grass-patches in the big yard, but mostly it was bare and smooth, like an old hat with the nap rubbed off; big double log-house for the white folks—hewed logs, with the chinks stopped up with mud or mortar, and these mud-stripes been whitewashed some time or another; round-log kitchen, with a big broad, open but roofed passage joining it to the house; log smoke-house back of the kitchen; three little log nigger-cabins in a row t'other side the smoke-house; one little hut all by itself away down against the back fence, and some outbuildings down a piece the other side; ash-hopper and big kettle to bile soap in by the little hut; bench by the kitchen door, with bucket of water and a gourd; hound asleep there in the sun; more hounds asleep round about; about three shade trees away off in a corner; some currant bushes and gooseberry bushes in one place by the fence; outside of the fence a garden and a watermelon patch; then the cotton fields begins, and after the fields the woods.

I went around and clumb over the back stile by the ash-hopper, and started for the kitchen. When I got a little ways I heard the dim hum of a spinning-wheel wailing along up and sinking along down again; and then I knowed for certain I wished I was dead—for that *is* the lonesomest sound in the whole world.

I went right along, not fixing up any particular plan, but just trusting to Providence to put the right words in my mouth when the time come; for I'd noticed that Providence always did put the right words in my mouth if I left it alone.

When I got halfway, first one hound and then another got up and went for me, and of course I stopped and faced them, and kept still. And such another powwow as they made! In a quarter of a minute I was a kind of a hub of a wheel, as you may say—spokes made out of dogs—circle of fifteen of them packed together around me, with their necks and noses stretched up towards me, a-barking and howling; and more a-coming; you could see them sailing over fences and around corners from everywheres.

A nigger woman come tearing out of the kitchen with a rolling-pin in her hand, singing out, "Begone *you* Tige! you Spot! begone sah!" and she fetched first one and then another of them a clip and sent them howling, and then the rest followed; and the next second half of them come back, wagging their tails around me, and making friends with me. There ain't no harm in a hound, nohow.

And behind the woman comes a little nigger girl and two little nigger boys without anything on but tow-linen shirts, and they hung on to their mother's gown, and peeped out from behind her at me, bashful, the way they always do. And here comes the white woman running from the house, about forty-five or fifty year old, bareheaded, and her spinning-stick in her hand; and behind her comes her little white children, acting the same way the little niggers was doing. She was smiling all over so she could hardly stand—and says:

"It's *you*, at last!—*ain't* it?"

I out with a "Yes'm" before I thought.

She hugged him tight

She grabbed me and hugged me tight; and then gripped me by both hands and shook and shook; and the tears come in her eyes, and run down over; and she couldn't seem to hug and shake enough, and kept saying, "You don't look as much like your mother as I reckoned you would; but law sakes, I don't care for that, I'm so glad to see you! Dear, dear, it does seem like I could eat you up! Children, it's your cousin Tom!—tell him howdy."

But they ducked their heads, and put their fingers in their mouths, and hid behind her. So she run on:

"Lize, hurry up and get him a hot breakfast right away—or did you get your breakfast on the boat?"

I said I had got it on the boat. So then she started for the house, leading me by the hand, and the children tagging after. When we got there she set me down in a split-bottomed chair, and set herself down on a little low stool in front of me, holding both of my hands, and says:

"Now I can have a *good* look at you; and, laws-a-me, I've been hungry for it a many and a many a time, all these long years, and it's come at last! We been expecting you a couple of days and more. What kep' you?—boat get aground?"

"Yes'm—she—"

"Don't say yes'm—say Aunt Sally. Where'd she get aground?"

I didn't rightly know what to say, because I didn't know whether the boat would be coming up the river or down. But I go a good deal on instinct; and my instinct said she would be coming up—from down towards Orleans. That didn't help me much, though; for I didn't know the names of bars down that way. I see I'd got to invent a bar, or forget the name of the one we got aground on—or—Now I struck an idea, and fetched it out:

"It warn't the grounding—that didn't keep us back but a little. We blowed out a cylinder-head."

"Good gracious! anybody hurt?"

"No'm. Killed a nigger."

"Well, it's lucky; because sometimes people do get hurt. Two years ago last Christmas your uncle Silas was coming up from Newrleans on the old *Lally Rook*, and she blowed out a cylinder-head and crippled a man. And I think he died afterwards. He was a Baptist. Your uncle Silas knowed a family in Baton Rouge that knowed his people very well. Yes, I remember now, he *did* die. Mortification set in, and they had to amputate him. But it didn't save him. Yes, it was mortification—that was it. He turned blue all over, and died in the hope of a glorious resurrection. They say he was a sight to look at. Your uncle's been up to the town every day to fetch you. And he's gone again, not more'n an hour ago; he'll be back any minute now. You must a met him on the road, didn't you?—oldish man, with a—"

"No, I didn't see nobody, Aunt Sally. The boat landed just at daylight, and I left my baggage on the wharf-boat and went looking around the town and out a piece in the country, to put in the time and not get here too soon; and so I come down the back way."

"Who'd you give the baggage to?"

"Nobody."

"Why, child, it 'll be stole!"

"Not where I hid it I reckon it won't," I says.

"How'd you get your breakfast so early on the boat?"

It was kinder thin ice, but I says:

"The captain see me standing around, and told me I better have something to eat before I went ashore; so he took me in the texas to the officers' lunch, and give me all I wanted."

I was getting so uneasy I couldn't listen good. I had my mind on the children all the time; I wanted to get them out to one side and pump them a little, and find out who I was. But I couldn't get no show, Mrs. Phelps kept it up and run on so. Pretty soon she made the cold chills streak all down my back, because she says:

"But here we're a-running on this way, and you hain't told me a word about Sis, nor any of them. Now I'll rest my works a little, and you start up yourn; just tell me *everything*—tell me all about 'm all every one of 'm; and how they are, and what they're doing, and what they told you to tell me; and every last thing you can think of."

Well, I see I was up a stump—and up it good. Providence had stood by me this fur all right, but I was hard and tight aground now. I see it warn't a bit of use to try to go ahead—I'd got to throw up my hand. So I says to myself, here's another place where I got to resk the truth. I opened my mouth to begin; but she grabbed me and hustled me in behind the bed, and says:

"Here he comes! Stick your head down lower—there, that'll do; you can't be seen now. Don't you let on you're here. I'll play a joke on him. Children, don't you say a word."

I see I was in a fix now. But it warn't no use to worry; there warn't nothing to do but just hold still, and try and be ready to stand from under when the lightning struck.

I had just one little glimpse of the old gentleman when he come in; then the bed hid him. Mrs. Phelps she jumps for him, and says:

"Has he come?"

"No," says her husband.

"Good-*ness* gracious!" she says, "what in the warld can have become of him?"

"I can't imagine," says the old gentleman; "and I must say it makes me dreadful uneasy."

"Uneasy!" she says; "I'm ready to go distracted! He *must* a come; and you've missed him along the road. I *know* it's so—something tells me so."

"Why, Sally, I *couldn't* miss him along the road—*you* know that."

"But oh, dear, dear, what *will* Sis say! He must a come! You must a missed him. He—"

"Oh, don't distress me any more'n I'm already distressed. I don't know what in the world to make of it. I'm at my wit's end, and I don't mind acknowledging 't I'm right down scared. But there's no hope that he's come; for he *couldn't* come and me miss him. Sally, it's terrible—just terrible—something's happened to the boat, sure!"

"Why, Silas! Look yonder!—up the road!—ain't that somebody coming?"

He sprung to the window at the head of the bed, and that give Mrs. Phelps the chance she wanted. She stooped down quick at the foot of the bed and give me a pull, and out I come; and when he turned back from the window there she stood, a-beaming and a-smiling like a house afire, and I standing pretty meek and sweaty alongside. The old gentleman stared, and says:

"Why, who's that?"

"Who do you reckon 't is?"

"I hain't no idea. Who *is* it?"

"It's *Tom Sawyer!*"

By jings, I most slumped through the floor! But there warn't no time to swap knives; the old man grabbed me by the hand and shook, and kept on shaking; and all the time how the woman did dance around and laugh and cry; and then how they both did fire off questions about Sid, and Mary, and the rest of the tribe.

But if they was joyful, it warn't nothing to what I was; for it was like being born again, I was so glad to find out who I was. Well, they froze to me for two hours; and at last, when my chin was so tired it couldn't hardly go any more, I had told them more about my family—I mean the Sawyer family—than ever happened to any six Sawyer families. And I explained all about how we blowed out a cylinder-head at the mouth of White River, and it took us three days to fix it. Which was all right, and worked first-rate; because *they* didn't know but what it would take three days to fix it. If I'd a called it a bolthead it would a done just as well.

Now I was feeling pretty comfortable all down one side, and pretty uncomfortable all up the other. Being Tom Sawyer was easy and comfortable, and it stayed easy and comfortable till by and by I hear a steamboat coughing along down the river. Then I says to myself, s'pose Tom Sawyer comes down on that boat? And s'pose he steps in here any minute, and sings out my name before I can throw him a wink to keep quiet? Well, I couldn't *have* it that way; it wouldn't do at all. I must go up the road and waylay him. So I told the folks I reckoned I would go up to the town and fetch down my baggage. The old gentleman was for going along with me, but I said no, I could drive the horse myself, and I druther he wouldn't take no trouble about me.

33

So I started for town in the wagon, and when I was halfway I see a wagon coming, and sure enough it was Tom Sawyer, and I stopped and waited till he come along. I says "Hold on!" and it stopped alongside, and his mouth opened up like a trunk, and stayed so; and he swallowed two or three times like a person that's got a dry throat, and then says:

"I hain't ever done you no harm. You know that. So, then, what you want to come back and ha'nt *me* for?"

I says:

"I hain't come back—I hain't been *gone*."

When he heard my voice it righted him up some, but he warn't quite satisfied yet. He says:

"Don't you play nothing on me, because I wouldn't on you. Honest injun now, you ain't a ghost?"

"Honest injun, I ain't," I says.

"Well—I—I—well, that ought to settle it, of course; but I can't somehow seem to understand it no way. Looky here, warn't you ever murdered *at all?*"

"No. I warn't ever murdered at all—I played it on them. You come in here and feel of me if you don't believe me."

So he done it; and it satisfied him; and he was that glad to see me again he didn't know what to do. And he wanted to know all about it right off, because it was a grand adventure, and mysterious, and so it hit him where he lived. But I said, leave it alone till by and by; and told his driver to wait, and we drove off a little piece, and I told him the kind of a fix I was in, and what did he reckon we better do? He said, let him alone a minute, and don't disturb him. So he thought and thought, and pretty soon he says:

"It's all right; I've got it. Take my trunk in your wagon, and let on it's your'n; and you turn back and fool along slow, so as to get to the house about the time you ought to; and I'll go towards town a piece, and take a fresh start, and get there a quarter or a half an hour after you; and you needn't let on to know me at first."

I says:

"All right; but wait a minute. There's one more thing—a thing that *nobody* don't know but me. And that is, there's a nigger here that I'm a-trying to steal out of slavery, and his name is *Jim*—old Miss Watson's Jim."

He says:

"What! Why, Jim is—"

He stopped and went to studying. I says:

"I know what you'll say. You'll say it's dirty, low-down business; but what if it is? I'm low down; and I'm a-going to steal him, and I want you keep mum and not let on. Will you?"

His eye lit up, and he says:

"I'll *help* you steal him!"

Well, I let go all holts then, like I was shot. It was the most astonishing speech I ever heard—and I'm bound to say Tom Sawyer fell considerable in my estimation. Only I couldn't believe it. Tom Sawyer a *nigger-stealer!*

"Oh, shucks!" I says; "you're joking."

"I ain't joking, either."

"Well, then," I says, "joking or no joking, if you hear anything said about a runaway nigger, don't forget to remember that *you* don't know nothing about him, and I don't know nothing about him."

Then we took the trunk and put it in my wagon, and he drove off his way and I drove mine. But of course I forgot all about driving slow on accounts of being glad and full of thinking; so I got home a heap too quick for that length of a trip. The old gentleman was at the door, and he says:

"Why, this is wonderful! Whoever would a thought it was in that mare to do it? I wish we'd a timed her. And she hain't sweated a hair—not a hair. It's wonderful. Why, I wouldn't take a hundred dollars for that horse now—I wouldn't, honest; and yet I'd a sold her for fifteen before, and thought 'twas all she was worth."

That's all he said. He was the innocentest, best old soul I ever see. But it warn't surprising; because he warn't only just a farmer, he was a preacher, too, and had a little one-horse log church down back of the plantation, which he built it himself at his own expense, for a church and schoolhouse, and never charged nothing for his preaching, and it was worth it, too. There was plenty other farmer-preachers like that, and done the same way, down South.

In about half an hour Tom's wagon drove up to the front stile, and Aunt Sally she see it through the window, because it was only about fifty yards, and says:

"Why, there's somebody come! I wonder who 'tis? Why, I do believe it's a stranger. Jimmy" (that's one of the children) "run and tell Lize to put on another plate for dinner."

Everybody made a rush for the front door, because, of course, a stranger don't come *every* year, and so he lays over the yaller-fever, for interest, when he does come. Tom was over the stile and starting for the house; the wagon was spinning up the road for the village, and we was all bunched in the front door. Tom had his store clothes on, and an audience—and that was always nuts for Tom Sawyer. In them circumstances it warn't no trouble to him to throw in an amount of style that was suitable. He warn't a boy to meeky along up that yard like a sheep; no, he come ca'm and important, like the ram. When he got a-front of us he lifts his hat ever so gracious and dainty, like it was the lid of a box that had butterflies asleep in it and he didn't want to disturb them, and says:

"Mr. Archibald Nichols, I presume?"

"No, my boy," says the old gentleman, "I'm sorry to say 't your driver has deceived you; Nichols's place is down a matter of three mile more. Come in, come in."

Tom he took a look back over his shoulder, and says, "Too late—he's out of sight."

"Yes, he's gone, my son, and you must come in and eat your dinner with us; and then we'll hitch up and take you down to Nichols's."

"Oh, I *can't* make you so much trouble; I couldn't think of it. I'll walk—I don't mind the distance."

"But we won't *let* you walk—it wouldn't be Southern hospitality to do it. Come right in."

"Oh, *do*," says Aunt Sally; "it ain't a bit of trouble to us, not a bit in the world. You must stay. It's a long, dusty three mile, and we can't let you walk. And, besides, I've already told 'em to put on another plate when I see you coming; so you mustn't disappoint us. Come right in and make yourself at home."

So Tom he thanked them very hearty and handsome, and let himself be persuaded, and come in; and when he was in he said he was a stranger from Hicksville, Ohio, and his name was William Thompson—and he made another bow.

Well, he run on, and on, and on, making up stuff about Hicksville and everybody in it he could invent, and I getting a little nervious, and wondering how this was going to help me out of my scrape; and at last, still talking along, he reached over and kissed Aunt Sally right on the mouth, and then settled back again in his chair comfortable, and was going on talking; but she jumped up and wiped it off with the back of her hand, and says:

"You owdacious puppy!"

He looked kind of hurt, and says:

"I'm surprised at you, m'am."

"You're s'rp—Why, what do you reckon I am? I've a good notion to take and—Say, what do you mean by kissing me?"

He looked kind of humble, and says:

"I didn't mean nothing, m'am. I didn't mean no harm. I—I—thought you'd like it."

"Why, you born fool!" She took up the spinning stick, and it looked like it was all she could do to keep from giving him a crack with it. "What made you think I'd like it?"

"Well, I don't know. Only, they—they—told me you would."

"*They* told you I would. Whoever told you's *another* lunatic. I never heard the beat of it. Who's *they*?"

"Why, everybody. They all said so, m'am."

It was all she could do to hold in; and her eyes snapped, and her fingers worked like she wanted to scratch him; and she says:

"Who's 'everybody'? Out with their names, or ther'll be an idiot short."

He got up and looked distressed, and fumbled his hat, and says:

"I'm sorry, and I warn't expecting it. They told me to. They all told me to. They all said, kiss her; and said she'd like it. They all said it—every one of them. But I'm sorry, m'am, and I won't do it no more—I won't, honest."

"You won't, won't you? Well, I sh'd *reckon* you won't!"

"No'm, I'm honest about it; I won't ever do it again—till you ask me."

"Till I *ask* you! Well, I never see the beat of it in my born days! I lay you'll be the Methusalem-numskull of creation before ever I ask you—or the likes of you."

"Well," he says, "it does surprise me so. I can't make it out, somehow. They said you would, and I thought you would. But—" He stopped and looked around slow, like he wished he could run across a friendly eye somewheres, and fetched up on the old gentleman's, and says, "Didn't *you* think she'd like me to kiss her, sir?"

"Why, no; I—I—well, no, I b'lieve I didn't."

Then he looks on around the same way to me, and says:

"Tom, didn't *you* think Aunt Sally 'd open out her arms and say, 'Sid Sawyer—'"

"My land!" she says, breaking in and jumping for him, "you impudent young rascal, to fool a body so—" and was going to hug him, but he fended her off, and says:

"No, not till you've asked me first."

So she didn't lose no time, but asked him; and hugged him and kissed him over and over again, and then turned him over to the old man, and he took what was left. And after they got a little quiet again she says:

"Why, dear me, I never see such a surprise. We warn't looking for *you* at all, but only Tom. Sis never wrote to me about anybody coming but him."

"It's because it warn't *intended* for any of us to come but Tom," he says; "but I begged and begged, and at the last minute she let me come, too; so, coming down the river, me and Tom thought it would be a first-rate surprise for him to come here to the house first, and for me to by and by tag along and drop in, and let on to be a stranger. But it was a mistake, Aunt Sally. This ain't no healthy place for a stranger to come."

"No—not impudent whelps, Sid. You ought to had your jaws boxed; I hain't been so put out since I don't know when. But I don't care, I don't mind the terms—I'd be willing to stand a thousand such jokes to have you here. Well, to think of that performance! I don't deny it, I was most putrified with astonishment when you give me that smack."

A pretty long Blessing

We had dinner out in that broad open passage betwixt the house and the kitchen; and there was things enough on that table for seven families—

and all hot, too; none of your flabby, tough meat that's laid in a cupboard in a damp cellar all night and tastes like a hunk of old cold cannibal in the morning. Uncle Silas he asked a pretty long blessing over it, but it was worth it; and it didn't cool it a bit, neither, the way I've seen them kind of interruptions do lots of times.

There was a considerable good deal of talk all the afternoon, and me and Tom was on the lookout all the time; but it warn't no use, they didn't happen to say nothing about any runaway nigger, and we was afraid to try to work up to it. But at supper, at night, one of the little boys says:

"Pa, mayn't Tom and Sid and me go to the show?"

"No," says the old man, "I reckon there ain't going to be any; and you couldn't go if there was; because the runaway nigger told Burton and me all about that scandalous show, and Burton said he would tell the people; so I reckon they've drove the owdacious loafers out of town before this time."

So there it was!—but I couldn't help it. Tom and me was to sleep in the same room and bed; so, being tired, we bid goodnight and went up to bed right after supper, and clumb out of the window and down the lightning-rod, and shoved for the town; for I didn't believe anybody was going to give the king and the duke a hint, and so if I didn't hurry up and give them one they'd get into trouble sure.

On the road Tom he told me all about how it was reckoned I was murdered, and how pap disappeared pretty soon, and didn't come back no more, and what a stir there was when Jim run away; and I told Tom all about our Royal Nonesuch rapscallions, and as much of the raft voyage as I had time to; and as we struck into the town and up through the the middle of it—it was as much as half-after eight, then—here comes a raging rush of people with torches, and an awful whooping and yelling, and banging tin pans and blowing horns; and we jumped to one side to let them go by; and as they went by I see they had the king and the duke astraddle of a rail—that is, I knowed it *was* the king and the duke, though they was all over tar and feathers, and didn't look like nothing in the world that was human—just looked like a couple of monstrous big soldier-plumes. Well, it made me sick to see it; and I was sorry for them poor pitiful rascals, it seemed like I couldn't ever feel any hardness against them any more in the world. It was a dreadful thing to see. Human beings *can* be awful cruel to one another.

We see we was too late—couldn't do no good. We asked some stragglers about it, and they said everybody went to the show looking very innocent; and laid low and kept dark till the poor old king was in the middle of his cavortings on the stage; then somebody give a signal, and the house rose up and went for them.

So we poked along back home, and I warn't feeling so brash as I was before, but kind of ornery, and humble, and to blame, somehow—though I hadn't done nothing. But that's always the way; it don't make no difference whether you do right or wrong, a person's conscience ain't got no sense, and just goes for him anyway. If I had a yaller dog that didn't know no more than a person's conscience does I would pison him. It takes up more room than all the rest of a person's insides, and yet ain't no good, nohow. Tom Sawyer he says the same.

34

We stopped talking, and got to thinking.

By and by Tom says:

"Looky here, Huck, what fools we are to not think of it before! I bet I know where Jim is."

"No! Where?"

"In that hut down by the ash-hopper. Why, looky here. When we was at dinner, didn't you see a nigger man go in there with some vittles?"

"Yes."

"What did you think the vittles was for?"

"For a dog."

"So 'd I. Well, it wasn't for a dog."

"Why?"

"Because part of it was watermelon."

"So it was—I noticed it. Well, it does beat all that I never thought about a dog not eating watermelon. It shows how a body can see and don't see at the same time."

"Well, the nigger unlocked the padlock when he went in, and he locked it again when he came out. He fetched uncle a key about the time we got up from table—same key, I bet. Watermelon shows man, lock shows prisoner; and it ain't likely there's two prisoners on such a little plantation, and where the people's all so kind and good. Jim's the prisoner. All right—I'm glad we found it out detective fashion; I wouldn't give shucks for any other way. Now you work your mind, and study out a plan to steal Jim, and I will study out one, too; and we'll take the one we like the best."

What a head for just a boy to have! If I had Tom Sawyer's head I wouldn't trade it off to be a duke, nor mate of a steamboat, nor clown in a circus, nor nothing I can think of. I went to thinking out a plan, but only just to be doing something; I knowed very well where the right plan was going to come from. Pretty soon Tom says:

"Ready?"

"Yes," I says.

"All right—bring it out."

"My plan is this," I says. "We can easy find out if it's Jim in there. Then get up my canoe tomorrow night, and fetch my raft over from the island. Then the first dark night that comes steal the key out of the old man's britches after he goes to bed, and shove off down the river on the raft with Jim, hiding daytimes and running nights, the way me and Jim used to do before. Wouldn't that plan work?"

"*Work*? Why, cert'nly it would work, like rats a-fighting. But it's too blame' simple; there ain't nothing *to* it. What's the good of a plan that ain't no more trouble than that? It's as mild as goose-milk. Why, Huck, it wouldn't make no more talk than breaking into a soap factory."

I never said nothing, because I warn't expecting nothing different; but I knowed mighty well that whenever he got *his* plan ready it wouldn't have none of them objections to it.

And it didn't. He told me what it was, and I see in a minute it was worth fifteen of mine for style, and would make Jim just as free a man as mine would, and maybe get us all killed besides. So I was satisfied, and said we would waltz in on it. I needn't tell what it was here, because I knowed it wouldn't stay the way, it was. I knowed he would be changing it around every which way as we went along, and heaving in new bullinesses wherever he got a chance. And that is what he done.

Well, one thing was dead sure, and that was that Tom Sawyer was in earnest, and was actuly going to help steal that nigger out of slavery. That was the thing that was too many for me. Here was a boy that was respectable and well brung up; and had a character to lose; and folks at home that had characters; and he was bright and not leather-headed; and knowing and not ignorant; and not mean, but kind; and yet here he was, without any more pride, or rightness, or feeling, than to stoop to this business, and make himself a shame, and his family a shame, before everybody. I *couldn't* understand it no way at all. It was outrageous, and I knowed I ought to just up and tell him so; and so be his true friend, and let him quit the thing right where he was and save himself. And I *did* start to tell him; but he shut me up, and says:

"Don't you reckon I know what I'm about? Don't I generally know what I'm about?"

"Yes."

"Didn't I *say* I was going to help steal the nigger?"

"Yes."

"*Well*, then."

That's all he said, and that's all I said. It warn't no use to say any more; because when he said he'd do a thing, he always done it. But I couldn't make out how he was willing to go into this thing; so I just let it go, and never bothered no more about it. If he was bound to have it so, I couldn't help it.

When we got home the house was all dark and still; so we went on down to the hut by the ash-hopper for to examine it. We went through the yard so as to see what the hounds would do. They knowed us, and didn't make no more noise than country dogs is always doing when anything comes by in the night. When we got to the cabin we took a look at the front and the two sides; and on the side I warn't acquainted with—which was the north side—we found a square window-hole, up tolerable high, with just one stout board nailed across it. I says:

"Here's the ticket. This hole's big enough for Jim to get through if we wrench off the board."

Tom says:

"It's as simple as tit-tat-toe, three-in-a-row, and as easy as playing hooky. I should *hope* we can find a way that's a little more complicated than *that*, Huck Finn."

"Well, then," I says, "how 'll it do to saw him out, the way I done before I was murdered that time?"

"That's more *like*," he says. "It's real mysterious, and troublesome, and good," he says; "but I bet we can find a way that's twice as long. There ain't no hurry; le's keep on looking around."

Betwixt the hut and the fence, on the back side, was a lean-to that joined the hut at the eaves, and was made out of plank. It was as long as the hut, but narrow—only about six foot wide. The door to it was at the south end, and was padlocked. Tom he went to the soap-kettle and searched around, and fetched back the iron thing they lift the lid with; so he took it and prized out one of the staples. The chain fell down, and we opened the door and went in, and shut it, and struck a match, and see the shed was only built against a cabin and hadn't no connection with it; and there warn't no floor to the shed, nor nothing in it but some old rusty played-out hoes and spades and picks and a crippled plow. The match went out, and so did we, and shoved in the staple again, and the door was locked as good as ever. Tom was joyful. He says;

"Now we're all right. We'll *dig* him out. It 'll take about a week!"

Then we started for the house, and I went in the back door—you only have to pull a buckskin latch-string, they don't fasten the doors—but that warn't romantical enough for Tom Sawyer; no way would do him but he must climb up the lightning-rod. But after he got up half way about three times, and missed fire and fell every time, and the last time most busted his brains out, he thought he'd got to give it up; but after he was rested he allowed he would give her one more turn for luck, and this time he made the trip.

In the morning we was up at break of day, and down to the nigger cabins to pet the dogs and make friends with the nigger that fed Jim—if it *was* Jim that was being fed. The niggers was just getting through breakfast and starting for the fields; and Jim's nigger was piling up a tin pan with bread and meat and things; and whilst the others was leaving, the key come from the house.

This nigger had a good-natured, chuckle-headed face, and his wool was all tied up in little bunches with thread. That was to keep witches off. He said the witches was pestering him awful these nights, and making him see all kinds of strange things, and hear all kinds of strange words and noises, and he didn't believe he was ever witched so long before in his life. He got so worked up, and got to running on so about his troubles, he forgot all about what he'd been a-going to do. So Tom says:

"What's the vittles for? Going to feed the dogs?"

The nigger kind of smiled around gradually over his face, like when you heave a brickbat in a mud-puddle, and he says:

"Yes, Mars Sid, A dog. Cur'us dog, too. Does you want to go en look at 'im?"

"Yes."

I hunched Tom, and whispers:

"You going, right here in the daybreak? *that* warn't the plan."

"No, it warn't; but it's the plan *now*."

So, drat him, we went along, but I didn't like it much. When we got in we couldn't hardly see anything, it was so dark; but Jim was there, sure enough, and could see us; and he sings out:

"Why, *Huck*! En good *lan*'! ain' dat Misto Tom?"

I just knowed how it would be; I just expected it. I didn't know nothing to do; and if I had I couldn't a done it, because that nigger busted in and says:

"Why, de gracious sakes! do he know you genlmen?"

We could see pretty well now. Tom he looked at the nigger, steady and kind of wondering, and says:

"Does *who* know us?"

"Why, dis-yer runaway nigger."

"I don't reckon he does; but what put that into your head?"

"What *put* it dar? Didn' he jis' dis minute sing out like he knowed you?"

Tom says, in a puzzled-up kind of way:

"Well, that's mighty curious. *Who* sung out? *when* did he sing out? *what* did he sing out?" And turns to me, perfectly ca'm, and says, "Did *you* hear anybody sing out?"

Of course there warn't nothing to be said but the one thing; so I says:

"No; I ain't heard nobody say nothing."

Then he turns to Jim, and looks him over like he never see him before, and says:

"Did you sing out?"

"No, sah," says Jim; "I hain't said nothing, sah."

"Not a word?"

"No, sah, I hain't said a word."

"Did you ever see us before?"

"No, sah; not as I knows on."

So Tom turns to the nigger, which was looking wild and distressed, and says, kind of severe:

"What do you reckon's the matter with you, anyway? What made you think somebody sung out?"

"Oh, it's de dad-blame' witches, sah, en I wisht I was dead, I do. Dey's awluz at it, sah, en dey do mos' kill me, dey sk'yers me so. Please to don't tell nobody 'bout it sah, er ole Mars Silas he'll scole me; 'kase he say dey *ain't* no witches. I jis' wish to goodness he was heah now—*den* what would he say! I jis' bet he couldn' fine no way to git aroun' it *dis* time. But it's awluz jis' so; people dat's *sot*, stays sot; dey won't look into noth'n'en fine it out f'r deyselves, en when *you* fine it out en tell um 'bout it, dey doan' b'lieve you."

Tom give him a dime, and said we wouldn't tell nobody; and told him to buy some more thread to tie up his wool with; and then looks at Jim, and says:

"I wonder if Uncle Silas is going to hang this nigger. If I was to catch a nigger that was ungrateful enough to run away, I wouldn't give him up, I'd hang him." And whilst the nigger stepped to the door to look at the dime and bite it to see if it was good, he whispers to Jim and says:

"Don't ever let on to know us. And if you hear any digging going on nights, it's us; we're going to set you free."

Jim only had time to grab us by the hand and squeeze it; then the nigger come back, and we said we'd come again some time if the nigger wanted us to; and he said he would, more particular if it was dark, because the witches went for him mostly in the dark, and it was good to have folks around then.

35

It would be most an hour yet till breakfast, so we left and struck down into the woods; because Tom said we got to have *some* light to see how to dig by, and a lantern makes too much, and might get us into trouble; what we must have was a lot of them rotten chunks that's called fox-fire,* and just makes a soft kind of a glow when you lay them in a dark place. We fetched an armful and hid it in the weeds, and set down to rest, and Tom says, kind of dissatisfied:

"Blame it, this whole thing is just as easy and awkward as it can be. And so it makes it so rotten difficult to get up a difficult plan. There ain't no watchman to be drugged—now there *ought* to be a watchman. There ain't even a dog to give a sleeping-mixture to. And there's Jim chained by one leg, with a ten-foot chain, to the leg of his bed: why, all you got to do is to lift up the bedstead and slip off the chain. And Uncle Silas he trusts everybody; sends the key to the punkin-headed nigger, and don't send nobody to watch the nigger. Jim could a got out of that window-hole before this, only there wouldn't be no use trying to travel with a ten-foot chain on his leg. Why, drat it, Huck, it's the stupidest arrangement I ever see. You got to invent *all* the difficulties. Well, we can't help it; we got to do the best we can with the materials we've got. Anyhow, there's one thing—there's more honour in getting him out through a lot of difficulties and dangers, where there warn't one of them furnished to you by the people who it was their duty to furnish them, and you had to contrive them all out of your own head. Now look at just that one thing of the lantern. When you come down to the cold facts, we simply got to *let on* that a lantern's resky. Why, we could work with a torchlight procession if we wanted to, I believe. Now, whilst I think of it, we got to hunt up something to make a saw out of the first chance we get."

* Phosphorescent light emitted by decayed timber.

"What do we want of a saw?"

"What do we *want* of it? Hain't we got to saw the leg of Jim's bed off, so as to get the chain loose?"

"Why, you just said a body could lift up the bedstead and slip the chain off."

"Well, if that ain't just like you, Huck Finn. You *can* get up the infant-schooliest ways of going at a thing. Why, hain't you ever read any books at all?—Baron Trenck, nor Casanova, nor Benvenuto Chelleeny, nor Henri IV., nor none of them heroes? Who ever heard of getting a prisoner loose in such an old-maidy way as that? No; the way all the best authorities does is to saw the bed-leg in two, and leave it just so, and swallow the sawdust, so it can't be found, and put some dirt and grease around the sawed place so the very keenest seneskal can't see no sign of it's being sawed, and thinks the bed-leg is perfectly sound. Then, the night you're ready, fetch the leg a kick, down she goes; slip off your chain, and there you are. Nothing to do but hitch your rope ladder to the battlements, shin down it, break your leg in the moat—because a rope ladder is nineteen foot too short, you know—and there's your horses and your trusty vassles, and they scoop you up and fling you across a saddle, and away you go to your native Langudoc, or Navarre, or wherever it is. It's gaudy, Huck. I wish there was a moat to this cabin. If we get time, the night of the escape, we'll dig one."

I says:

"What do we want of a moat when we're going to snake him out from under the cabin?"

But he never heard me. He had forgot me and everything else. He had his chin in his hand, thinking. Pretty soon he sighs and shakes his head; then sighs again, and says:

"No, it wouldn't do—there ain't necessity enough for it."

"For what?" I says.

"Why, to saw Jim's leg off," he says.

"Good land!" I says; "why, there ain't *no* necessity for it. And what would you want to saw his leg off for, anyway?"

"Well, some of the best authorities has done it. They couldn't get the chain off, so they just cut their hand off and shoved. And a leg would be better still. But we got to let that go. There ain't necessity enough in this case; and, besides, Jim's a nigger, and wouldn't understand the reasons for it, and how it's the custom in Europe; so we'll let it go. But there's one thing—he can have a rope ladder; we can tear up our sheets and make him a rope ladder easy enough. And we can send it to him in a pie; it's mostly done that way. And I've et worse pies."

"Why, Tom Sawyer, how you talk," I says; "Jim ain't got no use for a rope ladder."

"He *has* got use for it. How *you* talk, you better say; you don't know nothing about it. He's *got* to have a rope ladder; they all do."

"What in the nation can he *do* with it?"

"*Do* with it? He can hide it in his bed, can't he?" That's what they all do; and *he's* got to, too. Huck, you don't ever seem to want to do anything that's regular; you want to be starting something fresh all the time. S'pose he *don't* do nothing with it? ain't it there in his bed, for a clew, after he's gone? and don't you reckon they'll want clews? Of course they will. And you wouldn't leave them any? That would be a *pretty* howdy-do, *wouldn't* it! I never heard of such a thing."

"Well," I says, "if it's in the regulations, and he's got to have it, all right, let him have it; because I don't wish to go back on no regulations; but there's one thing, Tom Sawyer—if we go to tearing up our sheets to make Jim a rope ladder, we're going to get into trouble with Aunt Sally, just as sure as you're born. Now, the way I look at it, a hickry-bark ladder don't cost nothing, and don't waste nothing, and is just as good to load up a pie with, and hide in a straw tick, as any rag ladder you can start; and as for Jim, he ain't had no experience, and so he don't care what kind of a—"

"Oh, shucks, Huck Finn, if I was as ignorant as you I'd keep still—that's what I'D do. Who ever heard of a state prisoner escaping by a hickry-bark ladder? Why, it's perfectly ridiculous."

"Well, all right, Tom, fix it your own way; but if you'll take my advice, you'll let me borrow a sheet off of the clothesline."

He said that would do. And that gave him another idea, and he says:

"Borrow a shirt, too."

"What do we want of a shirt, Tom?"

"Want it for Jim to keep a journal on."

"Journal your granny—*Jim* can't write."

"S'pose he *can't* write—he can make marks on the shirt, can't he, if we make him a pen out of an old pewter spoon or a piece of an old iron barrel-hoop?"

"Why, Tom, we can pull a feather out of a goose and make him a better one; and quicker, too."

"*Prisoners* don't have geese running around the donjon-keep to pull pens out of, you muggins. They *always* make their pens out of the hardest, toughest, troublesomest piece of old brass candlestick or something like that they can get their hands on; and it takes them weeks and weeks and months and months to file it out, too, because they've got to do it by rubbing it on the wall. *They* wouldn't use a goose-quill if they had it. It ain't regular."

"Well, then, what'll we make him the ink out of?"

"Many makes it out of iron-rust and tears; but that's the common sort and women; the best authorities uses their own blood. Jim can do that; and when he wants to send any little common ordinary mysterious message to let the world know where he's captivated, he can write it on the bottom of a tin plate with a fork and throw it out of the window. The Iron Mask always done that, and it's a blame' good way, too."

"Jim ain't got no tin plates. They feed him in a pan."

"That ain't nothing; we can get him some."

"Can't nobody *read* his plates."

"That ain't got anything to *do* with it, Huck Finn. All *he's* got to do is to write on the plate and throw it out. You don't *have* to be able to read it. Why, half the time you can't read anything a prisoner writes on a tin plate, or anywhere else."

"Well, then, what's the sense in wasting the plates?"

"Why, blame it all, it ain't the *prisoner's* plates."

"But it's *somebody's* plates, ain't it?"

"Well, spos'n it is? What does the *prisoner* care whose—"

He broke off there, because we heard the breakfast-horn blowing. So we cleared out for the house.

The Breakfast-Horn

Along during the morning I borrowed a sheet and a white shirt off of the clothes-line; and I found an old sack and put them in it, and we went down and got the fox-fire, and put that in too. I called it borrowing, because that was what pap always called it; but Tom said it warn't borrowing, it was stealing. He said we was representing prisoners; and prisoners don't care how they get a thing so they get it, and nobody don't blame them for it, either. It ain't no crime in a prisoner to steal the thing he needs to get away with, Tom said; it's his right; and so, as long as we was representing a prisoner, we had a perfect right to steal anything on this place we had the least use for to get ourselves out of prison with. He said if we warn't prisoners it would be a very different thing, and nobody but a mean, ornery person would steal when he warn't a prisoner. So we allowed we would steal everything there was that come handy. And yet he made a mighty fuss, one day, after that, when I stole a watermelon out of the nigger-patch and eat it; and he made me go and give the niggers a dime without telling them what it was for. Tom said that what he meant was, we could steal anything we *needed*. Well, I says, I needed the watermelon. But he said I didn't need it to get out of prison with; there's where the difference was. He said if I'd a wanted it to hide a knife in, and smuggle it to Jim to kill the seneskal with, it would a been all right. So I let it go at that, though I couldn't see no advantage in my representing a prisoner if I got to set down and chaw over a lot of gold-leaf distinctions like that every time I see a chance to hog a watermelon.

Well, as I was saying, we waited that morning till everybody was settled down to business, and nobody in sight around the yard; then Tom he carried the sack into the lean-to whilst I stood off a piece to keep watch. By and by he come out, and we went and set down on the woodpile to talk. He says:

"Everything's all right now except tools; and that's easy fixed."

"Tools?" I says.

"Yes."

"Tools for what?"

"Why, to dig with. We ain't a-going to *gnaw* him out, are we?"

"Ain't them old crippled picks and things in there good enough to dig a nigger out with?" I says.

He turns on me, looking pitying enough to make a body cry, and says:

"Huck Finn, did you *ever* hear of a prisoner having picks and shovels, and all the modern conveniences in his wardrobe to dig himself out with? Now I want to ask you—if you got any reasonableness in you at all—what kind of a show would *that* give him to be a hero? Why, they might as well lend him the key and done with it. Picks and shovels—why, they wouldn't furnish 'em to a king."

"Well, then," I says, "if we don't want the picks and shovels, what do we want?"

"A couple of case-knives."

"To dig the foundations out from under that cabin with?"

"Yes."

"Confound it, it's foolish, Tom."

"It don't make no difference how foolish it is, it's the *right* way—and it's the regular way. And there ain't no *other* way, that ever I heard of, and I've read all the books that gives any information about these things. They always dig out with a case-knife—and not through dirt, mind you; generally it's through solid rock. And it takes them weeks and weeks and weeks, and for ever and ever. Why, look at one of them prisoners in the bottom dungeon of the Castle Deef, in the harbor of Marseilles, that dug himself out that way; how long was *he* at it, you reckon?"

"I don't know."

"Well, guess."

"I don't know. A month and a half."

"*Thirty-seven year*—and he come out in China. *That's* the kind. I wish the bottom of *this* fortress was solid rock."

"*Jim* don't know nobody in China."

"What's *that* got to do with it? Neither did that other fellow. But you're always a-wandering off on a side issue. Why can't you stick to the main point?"

"All right—I don't care where he comes out, so he *comes* out; and Jim don't, either, I reckon. But there's one thing, anyway—Jim's too old to be dug out with a case-knife. He won't last."

"Yes he will *last*, too. You don't reckon it's going to take thirty-seven years to dig out through a *dirt* foundation, do you?"

"How long will it take, Tom?"

"Well, we can't resk being as long as we ought to, because it mayn't take very long for Uncle Silas to hear from down there by New Orleans. He'll hear Jim ain't from there. Then his next move will be to advertise Jim, or something like that. So we can't resk being as long digging him out as we ought to. By rights I reckon we ought to be a couple of years; but we can't. Things being so uncertain, what I recommend is this: that we really dig right in, as quick as we can; and after that, we can *let on*, to ourselves, that we was at it thirty-seven years. Then we can snatch him out and rush him away the first time there's an alarm. Yes, I reckon that 'll be the best way."

"Now, there's *sense* in that," I says. "Letting on don't cost nothing; letting on ain't no trouble; and if it's any object, I don't mind letting on we was at it a hundred and fifty year. It wouldn't strain me none, after I got my hand in. So I'll mosey along now, and smouch a couple of case-knives."

Smouching the Knives

"Smouch three," he says; "we want one to make a saw out of."

"Tom, if it ain't unregular and irreligious to sejest it," I says, "there's an old rusty saw-blade around yonder sticking under the weather-boarding behind the smoke-house."

He looked kind of weary and discouraged-like, and says:

"It ain't no use to try to learn you nothing, Huck. Run along and smouch the knives—three of them." So I done it.

36

As soon as we reckoned everybody was asleep that night we went down the lightning-rod, and shut ourselves up in the lean-to, and got out our pile of fox-fire, and went to work. We cleared everything out of the way, about four or five foot along the middle of the bottom log. Tom said he was right behind Jim's bed now, and we'd dig in under it, and when we got through there couldn't nobody in the cabin ever know there was any hole there, because Jim's counter-pin hung down most to the ground, and you'd have to raise it up and look under to see the hole. So we dug and dug with the case-knives till most midnight; and then we was dog-tired, and our hands was blistered, and yet you couldn't see we'd done anything hardly. At last I says:

"This ain't no thirty-seven year job; this is a thirty-eight year job, Tom Sawyer."

He never said nothing. But he sighed, and pretty soon he stopped digging, and then for a good little while I knowed that he was thinking. Then he says:

"It ain't no use, Huck, it ain't a-going to work. If we was prisoners it would, because then we'd have as many years as we wanted, and no hurry; and we wouldn't get but a few minutes to dig, every day, while they was changing watches, and so our hands wouldn't get blistered, and we could keep it up right along, year in and year out, and do it right, and the way it ought to be done. But *we* can't fool along; we got to rush; we ain't got no time to spare. If we was to put in another night this way we'd have to knock off for a week to let our hands get well—couldn't touch a case-knife with them sooner."

"Well, then, what we going to do, Tom?"

"I'll tell you. It ain't right, and it ain't moral, and I wouldn't like it to get out; but there ain't only just the one way: we got to dig him out with the picks, and *let on* it's case-knives."

"*Now* you're *talking*!" I says; "your head gets leveler and leveler all the time, Tom Sawyer," I says. "Picks is the thing, moral or no moral; and as for me, I don't care shucks for the morality of it, nohow. When I start in to steal a nigger, or a watermelon, or a Sunday-school book, I ain't no ways particular how it's done so it's done. What I want is my nigger; or what I want is my watermelon; or what I want is my Sunday-school book; and if a pick's the handiest thing, that's the thing I'm a-going to dig that nigger or that watermelon or that Sunday-school book out with; and I don't give a dead rat what the authorities thinks about it nuther."

"Well," he says, "there's excuse for picks and letting-on in a case like this; if it warn't so, I wouldn't approve of it, nor I wouldn't stand by and see the rules broke—because right is right, and wrong is wrong, and a body ain't got no business doing wrong when he ain't ignorant and knows better. It might answer for *you* to dig Jim out with a pick, *without* any letting on, because you don't know no better; but it wouldn't for me, because I do know better. Gimme a case-knife."

He had his own by him, but I handed him mine. He flung it down, and says:

"Gimme a *case-knife*."

I didn't know just what to do—but then I thought. I scratched around amongst the old tools, and got a pickaxe and give it to him, and he took it and went to work, and never said a word.

He was always just that particular. Full of principle.

So then I got a shovel, and then we picked and shoveled, turn about, and made the fur fly. We stuck to it about a half an hour, which was as long as we could stand up; but we had a good deal of a hole to show for it. When I got up stairs I looked out at the window and see Tom doing his level best with the lightning-rod, but he couldn't come it, his hands was so sore. At last he says:

"It ain't no use, it can't be done. What you reckon I better do? Can't you think of no way?"

"Yes," I says, "but I reckon it ain't regular. Come up the stairs, and let on it's a lightning-rod."

So he done it.

Stealing spoons

Next day Tom stole a pewter spoon and a brass candlestick in the house, for to make some pens for Jim out of, and six tallow candles; and I hung around the nigger cabins and laid for a chance, and stole three tin plates. Tom says it wasn't enough; but I said nobody wouldn't ever see the plates that Jim throwed out, because they'd fall in the dog-fennel and jimpson weeds under the window-hole—then we could tote them back and he could use them over again. So Tom was satisfied. Then he says:

"Now, the thing to study out is, how to get the things to Jim."

"Take them in through the hole," I says, "when we get it done."

He only just looked scornful, and said something about nobody ever heard of such an idiotic idea, and then he went to studying. By and by he said he had ciphered out two or three ways, but there warn't no need to decide on any of them yet. Said we'd got to post Jim first.

That night we went down the lightning-rod a little after ten, and took one of the candles along, and listened under the window-hole, and heard Jim snoring; so we pitched it in, and it didn't wake him. Then we whirled in with the pick and shovel, and in about two hours and a half the job was done. We crept in under Jim's bed and into the cabin, and pawed around and found the candle and lit it, and stood over Jim awhile, and found him looking hearty and healthy, and then we woke him up gentle and gradual. He was so glad to see us he most cried; and called us honey, and all the pet names he could think of; and was for having us hunt up a cold-chisel to cut the chain off of his leg with right away, and clearing out without losing any time. But Tom he showed him how unregular it would be, and set down and told him all about our plans, and how we could alter them in a minute any time there was an alarm; and not to be the least afraid, because we would see he got away, *sure*. So Jim he said it was all right, and we set there and talked over old times awhile, and then Tom asked a lot of questions, and when Jim told him Uncle Silas come in every day or two to pray with him, and Aunt Sally come in to see if he was comfortable and had plenty to eat, and both of them was kind as they could be, Tom says:

"*Now* I know how to fix it. We'll send you some things by them."

I said, "Don't do nothing of the kind; it's one of the most jackass ideas I ever struck;" but he never paid no attention to me; went right on. It was his way when he'd got his plans set.

So he told Jim how we'd have to smuggle in the rope-ladder pie and other large things by Nat, the nigger that fed him, and he must be on the lookout, and not be surprised, and not let Nat see him open them; and we would put small things in uncle's coat-pockets and he must steal them out; and we would tie things to aunt's apron-strings or put them in her apron-pocket, if we got a chance; and told him what they would be and what they was for. And told him how to keep a journal on the shirt with his blood, and all that. He told him everything. Jim he couldn't see no sense in the most of it, but he allowed we was white folks and knowed better than him; so he was satisfied, and said he would do it all just as Tom said.

Jim had plenty corn-cob pipes and tobacco; so we had a right down good sociable time; then we crawled out through the hole, and so home to bed, with hands that looked like they'd been chawed. Tom was in high spirits. He said it was the best fun he ever had in his life, and the most intellectural;

and said if he only could see his way to it we would keep it up all the rest of our lives and leave Jim to our children to get out; for he believed Jim would come to like it better and better the more he got used to it. He said that in that way it could be strung out to as much as eighty year, and would be the best time on record. And he said it would make us all celebrated that had a hand in it.

In the morning we went out to the woodpile and chopped up the brass candlestick into handy sizes, and Tom put them and the pewter spoon in his pocket. Then we went to the nigger cabins, and while I got Nat's notice off, Tom shoved a piece of candlestick into the middle of a corn-pone that was in Jim's pan, and we went along with Nat to see how it would work, and it just worked noble; when Jim bit into it it most mashed all his teeth out; and there warn't ever anything could a worked better. Tom said so himself. Jim he never let on but what it was only just a piece of rock or something like that that's always getting into bread, you know; but after that he never bit into nothing but what he jabbed his fork into it in three or four places first.

And whilst we was a-standing there in the dimmish light, here comes a couple of the hounds bulging in from under Jim's bed; and they kept on piling in till there was eleven of them, and there warn't hardly room in there to get your breath. By jings, we forgot to fasten that lean-to door! The nigger Nat he only just hollered "Witches" once, and keeled over on to the floor amongst the dogs, and begun to groan like he was dying. Tom jerked the door open and flung out a slab of Jim's meat, and the dogs went for it, and in two seconds he was out himself and back again and shut the door, and I knowed he'd fixed the other door too. Then he went to work on the nigger, coaxing him and petting him, and asking him if he'd been imagining he saw something again. He raised up, and blinked his eyes around, and says:

"Mars Sid, you'll say I's a fool, but if I didn't b'lieve I see most a million dogs, er devils, er some'n, I wisht I may die right heah in dese tracks. I did, mos' sholy. Mars Sid, I *felt* um—I *felt* um, sah; dey was all over me. Dad fetch it, I jis' wisht I could git my han's on one er dem witches jis' wunst—on'y jis' wunst—it's all I'd ast. But mos'ly I wisht dey'd lemme 'lone, I does."

Tom says:

"Well, I tell you what I think. What makes them come here just at this runaway nigger's breakfast-time? It's because they're hungry; that's the reason. You make them a witch pie; that's the thing for *you* to do."

Tom advises a Witch Pie

"But my lan', Mars Sid, how's I gwyne to make 'm a witch pie? I doan' know how to make it. I hain't ever hearn er sich a thing b'fo'."

"Well, then, I'll have to make it myself."

"Will you do it, honey?—will you? I'll wusshup de groun' und' yo' foot, I will!"

"All right, I'll do it, seeing it's you, and you've been good to us and showed us the runaway nigger. But you got to be mighty careful. When we come around, you turn your back; and then whatever we've put in the pan, don't you let on you see it at all. And don't you look when Jim unloads the pan—something might happen, I don't know what. And above all, don't you *handle* the witch-things."

"*Hannel 'M*, Mars Sid? What *is* you a-talkin' 'bout? I wouldn' lay de weight er my finger on um, not f'r ten hund'd thous'n billion dollars, I wouldn't."

37

That was all fixed. So then we went away and went to the rubbage-pile in the back yard, where they keep the old boots, and rags, and pieces of bottles, and wore-out tin things, and all such truck, and scratched around and found an old tin washpan, and stopped up the holes as well as we could, to bake the pie in, and took it down cellar and stole it full of flour and started for breakfast, and found a couple of shingle-nails* that Tom said would be handy for a prisoner to scrabble his name and sorrows on the dungeon walls with, and dropped one of them in Aunt Sally's apron-pocket which was hanging on a chair, and t'other we stuck in the band of Uncle Silas's hat, which was on the bureau, because we heard the children say their pa and ma was going to the runaway nigger's house this morning, and then went to breakfast, and Tom dropped the pewter spoon in Uncle Silas's coat-pocket, and Aunt Sally wasn't come yet, so we had to wait a little while.

And when she come she was hot and red and cross, and couldn't hardly wait for the blessing; and then she went to sluicing out coffee with one hand and cracking the handiest child's head with her thimble with the other, and says:

"I've hunted high and I've hunted low, and it does beat all what *has* become of your other shirt."

My heart fell down amongst my lungs and livers and things, and a hard piece of corn-crust started down my throat after it and got met on the road with a cough, and was shot across the table, and took one of the children in the eye and curled him up like a fishing-worm, and let a cry out of him the size of a warwhoop, and Tom he turned kinder blue around the gills, and it all amounted to a considerable state of things for about a quarter of a minute or as much as that, and I would a sold out for half price if there was a bidder. But after that we was all right again—it was the sudden surprise of it that knocked us so kind of cold. Uncle Silas he says:

"It's most uncommon curious, I can't understand it. I know perfectly well I took it *off*, because—"

"Because you hain't got but one *on*. Just *listen* at the man! I know you took it off, and know it by a better way than your wool-gethering memory,

---

* See Note, p. 488.

too, because it was on the clo's-line yesterday—I see it there myself. But it's gone, that's the long and the short of it, and you'll just have to change to a red flann'l one till I can get time to make a new one. And it 'll be the third I've made in two years. It just keeps a body on the jump to keep you in shirts; and whatever you do manage to *do* with 'm all is more'n I can make out. A body 'd think you *would* learn to take some sort of care of 'em at your time of life."

"I know it, Sally, and I do try all I can. But it oughtn't to be altogether my fault, because, you know, I don't see them nor have nothing to do with them except when they're on me; and I don't believe I've ever lost one of them *off* of me."

"Well, it ain't *your* fault if you haven't, Silas; you'd a done it if you could, I reckon. And the shirt ain't all that's gone, nuther. Ther's a spoon gone; and *that* ain't all. There was ten, and now ther's only nine. The calf got the shirt, I reckon, but the calf never took the spoon, *that's* certain."

"Why, what else is gone, Sally?"

"Ther's six *candles* gone—that's what. The rats could a got the candles, and I reckon they did; I wonder they don't walk off with the whole place, the way you're always going to stop their holes and don't do it; and if they warn't fools they'd sleep in your hair, Silas—*you'd* never find it out; but you can't lay the *spoon* on the rats, and that I know."

"Well, Sally, I'm in fault, and I acknowledge it; I've been remiss; but I won't let tomorrow go by without stopping up them holes."

"Oh, I wouldn't hurry; next year 'll do. Matilda Angelina Araminta *Phelps!*"

Whack comes the thimble, and the child snatches her claws out of the sugar-bowl without fooling around any. Just then the nigger woman steps on to the passage, and says:

"Missus, dey's a sheet gone."

"A *sheet* gone! Well, for the land's sake!"

"I'll stop up them holes today," says Uncle Silas, looking sorrowful.

"Oh, *do* shet up!—s'pose the rats took the *sheet*? *where's* it gone, Lize?"

"Clah to goodness I hain't no notion, Miss' Sally. She wuz on de clo'sline yistiddy, but she done gone: she ain' dah no mo' now."

"I reckon the world *is* coming to an end. I *never* see the beat of it in all my born days. A shirt, and a sheet, and a spoon, and six can—"

"Missus," comes a young yaller wench, "dey's a brass cannelstick miss'n."

"Cler out from here, you hussy, er I'll take a skillet* to ye!"

Well, she was just a-biling. I begun to lay for a chance; I reckoned I

* A large boiling-pan.

would sneak out and go for the woods till the weather moderated. She kept a-raging right along, running her insurrection all by herself, and everybody else mighty meek and quiet; and at last Uncle Silas, looking kind of foolish, fishes up that spoon out of his pocket. She stopped, with her mouth open and her hands up; and as for me, I wished I was in Jeruslem or somewheres. But not long, because she says:

"It's *just* as I expected. So you had it in your pocket all the time; and like as not you've got the other things there, too. How'd it get there?"

"I reely don't know, Sally," he says, kind of apologizing, "or you know I would tell. I was a-studying over my text in Acts Seventeen before breakfast, and I reckon I put it in there, not noticing, meaning to put my Testament in, and it must be so, because my Testament ain't in; but I'll go and see; and if the Testament is where I had it, I'll know I didn't put it in, and that will show that I laid the Testament down and took up the spoon, and—"

"Oh, for the land's sake! Give a body a rest! Go 'long now, the whole kit and biling of ye; and don't come nigh me again till I've got back my peace of mind."

I'd a heard her if she'd a said it to herself, let alone speaking it out; and I'd a got up and obeyed her if I'd a been dead. As we was passing through the setting room the old man he took up his hat, and the shingle-nail fell out on the floor, and he just merely picked it up and laid it on the mantel-shelf, and never said nothing, and went out. Tom see him do it, and remembered about the spoon, and says:

"Well, it ain't no use to send things by *him* no more, he ain't reliable." Then he says: "But he done us a good turn with the spoon, anyway, without knowing it, and so we'll go and do him one without *him* knowing it—stop up his rat-holes."

There was a noble good lot of them down cellar, and it took us a whole hour, but we done the job tight and good and shipshape. Then we heard steps on the stairs, and blowed out our light and hid; and here comes the old man, with a candle in one hand and a bundle of stuff in t'other, looking as absent-minded as year before last. He went a mooning around, first to one rat-hole and then another, till he'd been to them all. Then he stood about five minutes, picking tallow-drip off of his candle and thinking. Then he turns off slow and dreamy towards the stairs, saying:

"Well, for the life of me I can't remember when I done it. I could show her now that I warn't to blame on account of the rats. But never mind—let it go. I reckon it wouldn't do no good."

And so he went on a-mumbling up stairs, and then we left. He was a mighty nice old man. And always is.

Tom was a good deal bothered about what to do for a spoon, but he said we'd got to have it; so he took a think. When he had ciphered it out he told me how we was to do; then we went and waited around the spoon-basket till we see Aunt Sally coming, and then Tom went to counting the spoons and laying them out to one side, and I slid one of them up my sleeve, and Tom says:

"Why, Aunt Sally, there ain't but nine spoons *yet.*"

She says:

"Go 'long to your play, and don't bother me. I know better, I counted 'm myself."

"Well, I've counted them twice, Aunty, and I can't make but nine."

She looked out of all patience, but of course she come to count—anybody would.

"I declare to gracious ther' *ain't* but nine!" she says. "Why, what in the world—plague *take* the things, I'll count 'm again."

So I slipped back the one I had, and when she got done counting, she says:

"Hang the troublesome rubbage, ther's *ten* now!" and she looked huffy and bothered both. But Tom says:

"Why, Aunty, I don't think there's ten."

"You numskull, didn't you see me *count 'm?*"

"I know, but—"

"Well, I'll count 'm *again.*"

So I smouched one, and they come out nine, same as the other time. Well, she *was* in a tearing way—just a-trembling all over, she was so mad. But she counted and counted till she got that addled she'd start to count in the basket for a spoon sometimes; and so, three times they come out right, and three times they come out wrong. Then she grabbed up the basket and slammed it across the house and knocked the cat galley-west;* and she said cle'r out and let her have some peace, and if we come bothering around her again betwixt that and dinner she'd skin us. So we had the odd spoon, and dropped it in her apron-pocket whilst she was a-giving us our sailing orders, and Jim got it all right, along with her shingle nail, before noon. We was very well satisfied with this business, and Tom allowed it was worth twice the trouble it took, because he said *now* she couldn't ever count them spoons twice alike again to save her life; and wouldn't believe she'd counted them right if she *did*; and said that after she'd about counted her head off for the next three days he judged she'd give it up and offer to kill anybody that wanted her to ever count them any more.

---

* Head over heels.

So we put the sheet back on the line that night, and stole one out of her closet; and kept on putting it back and stealing it again for a couple of days till she didn't know how many sheets she had any more, and she didn't *care*, and warn't a-going to bullyrag the rest of her soul out about it, and wouldn't count them again not to save her life; she druther die first.

So we was all right now, as to the shirt and the sheet and the spoon and the candles, by the help of the calf and the rats and the mixed-up counting; and as to the candlestick, it warn't no consequence, it would blow over by and by.

But that pie was a job; we had no end of trouble with that pie. We fixed it up away down in the woods, and cooked it there; and we got it done at last, and very satisfactory, too; but not all in one day; and we had to use up three wash-pans full of flour before we got through, and we got burnt pretty much all over, in places, and eyes put out with the smoke; because, you see, we didn't want nothing but a crust, and we couldn't prop it up right, and she would always cave in. But of course we thought of the right way at last—which was to cook the ladder, too, in the pie. So then we laid in with Jim the second night, and tore up the sheet all in little strings and twisted them together, and long before daylight we had a lovely rope that you could a hung a person with. We let on it took nine months to make it.

And in the forenoon we took it down to the woods, but it wouldn't go into the pie. Being made of a whole sheet, that way, there was rope enough for forty pies if we'd a wanted them, and plenty left over for soup, or sausage, or anything you choose. We could a had a whole dinner.

But we didn't need it. All we needed was just enough for the pie, and so we throwed the rest away. We didn't cook none of the pies in the wash-pan—afraid the solder would melt; but Uncle Silas he had a noble brass warming-pan which he thought considerable of, because it belonged to one of his ancesters with a long wooden handle that come over from England with William the Conqueror in the *Mayflower* or one of them early ships and was hid away up garret with a lot of other old pots and things that was valuable, not on account of being any account, because they warn't, but on account of them being relicts, you know, and we snaked her out, private, and took her down there, but she failed on the first pies, because we didn't know how, but she come up smiling on the last one. We took and lined her with dough, and set her in the coals, and loaded her up with rag rope, and put on a dough roof, and shut down the lid, and put hot embers on top, and stood off five foot, with the long handle, cool and comfortable, and in fifteen minutes she turned out a pie that was a satisfaction to look at. But the person that et it would want to fetch a couple of kags of toothpicks along, for if that rope ladder wouldn't cramp him down to business I don't know nothing what I'm talking about, and lay him in enough stomach-ache to last him till next time, too.

Nat didn't look when we put the witch pie in Jim's pan; and we put the three tin plates in the bottom of the pan under the vittles; and so Jim got everything all right, and as soon as he was by himself he busted into the pie and hid the rope ladder inside of his straw tick, and scratched some marks on a tin plate and throwed it out of the window-hole.

38

Making them pens was a distressid tough job, and so was the saw; and Jim allowed the inscription was going to be the toughest of all. That's the one which the prisoner has to scrabble on the wall. But he had to have it; Tom said he'd *got* to; there warn't no case of a state prisoner not scrabbling his inscription to leave behind, and his coat of arms.

"Look at Lady Jane Grey," he says; "look at Gilford Dudley; look at old Northumberland! Why, Huck, s'pose it *is* considerble trouble?—what you going to do?—how you going to get around it? Jim's *got* to do his inscription and coat of arms. They all do."

Jim says:

"Why, Mars Tom, I hain't got no coat o' arm; I hain't got nuffn but dish yer ole shirt, en you knows I got to keep de journal on dat."

"Oh, you don't understand, Jim; a coat of arms is very different."

"Well," I says, "Jim's right, anyway, when he says he ain't got no coat of arms, because he hain't."

"I reckon I knowed that," Tom says, "but you bet he'll have one before he goes out of this—because he's going out *right*, and there ain't going to be no flaws in his record."

So whilst me and Jim filed away at the pens on a brickbat apiece, Jim a-making his'n out of the brass and I making mine out of the spoon, Tom set to work to think out the coat of arms. By and by he said he'd struck so many good ones he didn't hardly know which to take, but there was one which he reckoned he'd decide on. He says:

"On the scutcheon we'll have a bend *or* in the dexter base, a saltire *murrey* in the fess, with a dog, couchant, for common charge, and under his foot a chain embattled, for slavery, with a chevron *vert* in a chief engrailed, and three invected lines on a field *azure*, with the nombril points rampant on a dancette indented; crest, a runaway nigger, *sable*, with his bundle over his shoulder on a bar sinister; and a couple of gules for supporters, which is you and me; motto, *Maggiore Fretta, Minore Otto.* Got it out of a book—means the more haste the less speed."

"Geewhillikins," I says, "but what does the rest of it mean?"

"We ain't got no time to bother over that," he says; "we got to dig in like all git-out."

"Well, anyway," I says, "what's *some* of it? What's a fess?"

"A fess—a fess is—*you* don't need to know what a fess is. I'll show him how to make it when he gets to it."

"Shucks, Tom," I says, "I think you might tell a person. What's a bar sinister?"

"Oh, I don't know. But he's got to have it. All the nobility does."

That was just his way. If it didn't suit him to explain a thing to you, he wouldn't do it. You might pump at him a week, it wouldn't make no difference.

He'd got all that coat of arms business fixed, so now he started in to finish up the rest of that part of the work, which was to plan out a mournful inscription—said Jim got to have one, like they all done. He made up a lot, and wrote them out on a paper, and read them off, so:

1. *Here a captive heart busted.*

2. *Here a poor prisoner, forsook by the world and friends, fretted his sorrowful life.*

3. *Here a lonely heart broke, and a worn spirit went to its rest, after thirty-seven years of solitary captivity.*

4. *Here, homeless and friendless, after thirty-seven years of bitter captivity, perished a noble stranger, natural son of Louis XIV.*

Tom's voice trembled whilst he was reading them, and he most broke down. When he got done he couldn't no way make up his mind which one for Jim to scrabble on to the wall, they was all so good; but at last he allowed he would let him scrabble them all on. Jim said it would take him a year to scrabble such a lot of truck on to the logs with a nail, and he didn't know how to make letters, besides; but Tom said he would block them out for him, and then he wouldn't have nothing to do but just follow the lines. Then pretty soon he says:

"Come to think, the logs ain't a-going to do; they don't have log walls in a dungeon: we got to dig the inscriptions into a rock. We'll fetch a rock."

Jim said the rock was worse than the logs; he said it would take him such a pison long time to dig them into a rock he wouldn't ever get out. But Tom said he would let me help him do it. Then he took a look to see how me and Jim was getting along with the pens. It was most pesky tedious hard work and slow, and didn't give my hands no show to get well of the sores, and we didn't seem to make no headway, hardly; so Tom says:

"I know how to fix it. We got to have a rock for the coat of arms and mournful inscriptions, and we can kill two birds with that same rock. There's a gaudy big grindstone down at the mill, and we'll smouch it, and carve the things on it, and file out the pens and the saw on it, too."

It warn't no slouch of an idea; and it warn't no slouch of a grindstone nuther; but we allowed we'd tackle it. It warn't quite midnight yet, so we cleared out for the mill, leaving Jim at work. We smouched the grindstone, and set out to roll her home, but it was a most nation tough job. Sometimes, do what we could, we couldn't keep her from falling over, and she come mighty near mashing us every time. Tom said she was going to get one of us, sure, before we got through. We got her half way; and then we was plumb played out, and most drownded with sweat. We see it warn't no use; we got to go and fetch Jim. So he raised up his bed and slid the chain off of the bed-leg, and wrapt it round and round his neck, and we crawled out through our hole and down there, and Jim and me laid into that grindstone and walked her along like nothing; and Tom superintended. He could out-superintend any boy I ever see. He knowed how to do everything.

Our hole was pretty big, but it warn't big enough to get the grindstone through; but Jim he took the pick and soon made it big enough. Then Tom marked out them things on it with the nail, and set Jim to work on them, with the nail for a chisel and an iron bolt from the rubbage in the lean-to for a hammer, and told him to work till the rest of his candle quit on him, and then he could go to bed, and hide the grindstone under his straw tick and sleep on it. Then we helped him fix his chain back on the bed-leg, and was ready for bed ourselves. But Tom thought of something, and says:

"You got any spiders in here, Jim?"

"No, sah, thanks to goodness I hain't, Mars Tom."

"All right, we'll get you some."

"But bless you, honey, I doan' *want* none. I's afeard un um. I jis' 's soon have rattlesnakes aroun'."

Tom thought a minute or two, and says:

"It's a good idea. And I reckon it's been done. It *must* a been done; it stands to reason. Yes, it's a prime good idea. Where could you keep it?"

"Keep what, Mars Tom?"

"Why, a rattlesnake."

"De goodness gracious alive, Mars Tom! Why, if dey was a rattlesnake to come in heah I'd take en bust right out thoo dat log wall, I would, wid my head."

"Why, Jim, you wouldn't be afraid of it after a little. You could tame it."

"*Tame* it!"

"Yes—easy enough. Every animal is grateful for kindness and petting, and they wouldn't *think* of hurting a person that pets them. Any book will tell you that. You try—that's all I ask; just try for two or three days. Why, you can get him so, in a little while, that he'll love you; and sleep with you; and won't stay away from you a minute; and will let you wrap him round your neck and put his head in your mouth."

"*Please*, Mars Tom—*doan*' talk so! I can't *stan*' it! He'd *let* me shove his head in my mouf—fer a favour, hain't it? I lay he'd wait a pow'ful long time 'fo' I *ast* him. En mo' en dat, I doan' *want* him to sleep wid me."

"Jim, don't act so foolish. A prisoner's *got* to have some kind of a dumb pet, and if a rattlesnake hain't ever been tried, why, there's more glory to be gained in your being the first to ever try it than any other way you could ever think of to save your life."

"Why, Mars Tom, I doan' *want* no sich glory. Snake take 'n bite Jim's chin off, den *whah* is de glory? No, sah, I doan' want no sich doin's."

"Blame it, can't you *try*? I only *want* you to try—you needn't keep it up if it don't work."

"But de trouble all *done* ef de snake bite me while I's a tryin' him. Mars Tom, I's willin' to tackle mos' anything 'at ain't onreasonable, but ef you en Huck fetches a rattlesnake in heah for me to tame, I's gwyne to *leave*, dat's *shore*."

"Well, then, let it go, let it go, if you're so bull-headed about it. We can get you some garter-snakes, and you can tie some buttons on their tails, and let on they're rattlesnakes, and I reckon that 'll have to do."

"I k'n stan' *dem*, Mars Tom, but blame' 'f I couldn' get along widout um, I tell you dat. I never knowed b'fo' 't was so much bother and trouble to be a prisoner."

"Well, it *always* is when it's done right. You got any rats around here?"

"No, sah, I hain't seed none."

"Well, we'll get you some rats."

"Why, Mars Tom, I doan' *want* no rats. Dey's de dadblamedest creturs to 'sturb a body, en rustle roun' over 'im, en bite his feet, when he's tryin' to sleep, I ever see. No, sah, gimme g'yarter-snakes, 'f I's got to have 'm, but doan' gimme no rats; I hain' got no use f'r um, skasely."

"But, Jim, you *got* to have 'em—they all do. So don't make no more fuss about it. Prisoners ain't ever without rats. There ain't no instance of it. And they train them, and pet them, and learn them tricks, and they get to be as sociable as flies. But you got to play music to them. You got anything to play music on?"

"I ain' got nuffn but a coase comb en a piece o' paper, en a juice-harp; but I reck'n dey wouldn' take no stock in a juice-harp."

"Yes they would *they* don't care what kind of music 'tis. A jews-harp's plenty good enough for a rat. All animals like music—in a prison they dote on it. Specially, painful music; and you can't get no other kind out of a jews-harp. It always interests them; they come out to see what's the matter with you. Yes, you're all right; you're fixed very well. You want to set on your bed nights before you go to sleep, and early in the mornings, and play your jews-harp; play 'The Last Link is Broken'—that's the thing that 'll scoop a rat quicker 'n anything else; and when you've played about two minutes you'll see all the rats, and the snakes, and spiders, and things begin to feel worried about you, and come. And they'll just fairly swarm over you, and have a noble good time."

"Yes, *dey* will, I reck'n, Mars Tom, but what kine er time is *Jim* havin'? Blest if I kin see de pint. But I'll do it ef I got to. I reck'n I better keep de animals satisfied, en not have no trouble in de house."

Tom waited to think it over, and see if there wasn't nothing else; and pretty soon he says:

"Oh, there's one thing I forgot. Could you raise a flower here, do you reckon?"

"I doan know but maybe I could, Mars Tom; but it's tolable dark in heah, en I ain' got no use f'r no flower, nohow, en she'd be a pow'ful sight o' trouble."

"Well, you try it, anyway. Some other prisoners has done it."

"One er dem big cat-tail-lookin' mullen-stalks* would grow in heah, Mars Tom, I reck'n, but she wouldn't be wuth half de trouble she'd coss."

"Don't you believe it. We'll fetch you a little one and you plant it in the corner over there, and raise it. And don't call it mullen, call it Pitchiola—that's its right name when it's in a prison. And you want to water it with your tears."

"Why, I got plenty spring water, Mars Tom."

"You don't *want* spring water; you want to water it with your tears. It's the way they always do."

---

* The Mullen (usually 'mullein') is a plant of the *verbascum* family, of which the foxglove grows wild in N. America.

"Why, Mars Tom, I lay I kin raise one er dem mullen-stalks twyste wid spring water whiles another man's a *start'n* one wid tears."

"That ain't the idea. You *got* to do it with tears."

"She'll die on my han's, Mars Tom, she sholy will; kase I doan' skasely ever cry."

So Tom was stumped. But he studied it over, and then said Jim would have to worry along the best he could with an onion. He promised he would go to the nigger cabins and drop one, private, in Jim's coffee-pot, in the morning. Jim said he would "jis' 's soon have tobacker in his coffee;" and found so much fault with it, and with the work and bother of raising the mullen, and jews-harping the rats, and petting and flattering up the snakes and spiders and things, on top of all the other work he had to do on pens, and inscriptions, and journals, and things, which made it more trouble and worry and responsibility to be a prisoner than anything he ever undertook, that Tom most lost all patience with him; and said he was just loadened down with more gaudier chances than a prisoner ever had in the world to make a name for himself, and yet he didn't know enough to appreciate them, and they was just about wasted on him. So Jim he was sorry, and said he wouldn't behave so no more, and then me and Tom shoved for bed.

39

In the morning we went up to the village and bought a wire rat-trap and fetched it down, and unstopped the best rat-hole, and in about an hour we had fifteen of the bulliest kind of ones; and then we took it and put it in a safe place under Aunt Sally's bed. But while we was gone for spiders little Thomas Franklin Benjamin Jefferson Elexander Phelps found it there, and opened the door of it to see if the rats would come out, and they did; and Aunt Sally she come in, and when we got back she was a-standing on top of the bed raising Cain, and the rats was doing what they could to keep off the dull times for her. So she took and dusted us both with the hickry, and we was as much as two hours catching another fifteen or sixteen, drat that meddlesome cub, and they warn't the likeliest, nuther, because the first haul was the pick of the flock. I never see a likelier lot of rats than what that first haul was.

We got a splendid stock of sorted spiders, and bugs, and frogs, and caterpillars, and one thing or another; and we like to got a hornet's nest, but we didn't. The family was at home. We didn't give it right up, but stayed with them as long as we could; because we allowed we'd tire them out or they'd got to tire us out, and they done it. Then we got allycumpain and rubbed on the places, and was pretty near all right again, but couldn't set down convenient. And so we went for the snakes, and grabbed a couple of dozen garters and house-snakes, and put them in a bag, and put it in our room, and by that time it was supper-time, and a rattling good honest day's work: and hungry?—oh, no, I reckon not! And there warn't a blessed snake up there when we went back—we didn't half tie the sack, and they worked out somehow, and left. But it didn't matter much, because they was still on the premises somewheres. So we judged we could get some of them again. No, there warn't no real scarcity of snakes about the house for a considerable spell. You'd see them dripping from the rafters and places every now and then; and they generally landed in your plate, or down the back of your neck, and most of the time where you didn't want them. Well, they was handsome and striped, and there warn't no harm in a million of them; but that never made no difference to Aunt Sally; she despised snakes, be the breed what they might, and she couldn't stand them no way you could fix it; and every time one of them flopped down on her, it didn't make no difference what she was doing, she would just lay that work down and light out. I never see such a woman. And you could hear her whoop to Jericho. You couldn't get her to take a-holt of one of them with the tongs. And if she turned over and found one in bed she would scramble out and lift a howl that you would think the house was afire. She disturbed the old man so that he said he could most wish there hadn't ever been no snakes created. Why, after every last snake had been gone clear out of the house for as much as a week Aunt Sally warn't over it yet; she warn't near over it; when she was setting thinking about something you could touch her on the back of her neck with a feather and she would jump right out of her stockings. It was very curious. But Tom said all women was just so. He said they was made that way for some reason or other.

We got a licking every time one of our snakes come in her way, and she allowed these lickings warn't nothing to what she would do if we ever loaded up the place again with them. I didn't mind the lickings, because they didn't amount to nothing; but I minded the trouble we had to lay in another lot. But we got them laid in, and all the other things; and you never see a cabin as blithesome as Jim's was when they'd all swarm out for music and go for him. Jim didn't like the spiders, and the spiders didn't like Jim; and so they'd lay for him, and make it mighty warm for him. And he said that between the rats and the snakes and the grindstone there warn't no room in bed for him, skasely; and when there was, a body couldn't sleep, it was so lively, and it was always lively, he said, because *they* never all slept at one time, but took turn about, so when the snakes was asleep the rats was on deck, and when the rats turned in the snakes come on watch, so he always had one gang under him, in his way, and t'other gang having a circus over him, and if he got up to hunt a new place the spiders would take a chance at him as he crossed over. He said if he ever got out this time he wouldn't ever be a prisoner again, not for a salary.

Well, by the end of three weeks everything was in pretty good shape. The shirt was sent in early, in a pie, and every time a rat bit Jim he would get up and write a little in his journal whilst the ink was fresh; the pens was made, the inscriptions and so on was all carved on the grindstone; the bed-leg was sawed in two, and we had et up the sawdust, and it give us a most amazing stomach-ache. We reckoned we was all going to die, but didn't. It was the most undigestible sawdust I ever see; and Tom said the same.

Sawdust Diet

But as I was saying, we'd got all the work done now, at last; and we was all pretty much fagged out, too, but mainly Jim. The old man had wrote a couple of times to the plantation below Orleans to come and get their runaway nigger, but hadn't got no answer, because there warn't no such plantation; so he allowed he would advertise Jim in the St. Louis and New

Orleans papers; and when he mentioned the St. Louis ones it give me the cold shivers, and I see we hadn't no time to lose. So Tom said, now for the nonnamous letters.

"What's them?" I says.

"Warnings to the people that something is up. Sometimes it's done one way, sometimes another. But there's always somebody spying around that gives notice to the governor of the castle. When Louis XVI. was going to light out of the Tooleries, a servant-girl done it. It's a very good way, and so is the nonnamous letters. We'll use them both. And it's usual for the prisoner's mother to change clothes with him, and she stays in, and he slides out in her clothes. We'll do that, too."

"But looky here, Tom, what do we want to *warn* anybody for that something's up? Let them find it out for themselves—it's their lookout."

"Yes, I know; but you can't depend on them. It's the way they've acted from the very start—left us to do *everything*. They're so confiding and mullet-headed they don't take notice of nothing at all. So if we don't *give* them notice there won't be nobody nor nothing to interfere with us, and so after all our hard work and trouble this escape 'll go off perfectly flat; won't amount to nothing—won't be nothing *to* it."

"Well, as for me, Tom, that's the way I'd like."

"Shucks!" he says, and looked disgusted. So I says:

"But I ain't going to make no complaint. Any way that suits you suits me. What you going to do about the servant-girl?"

"You'll be her. You slide in, in the middle of the night, and hook that yaller girl's frock."

"Why, Tom, that 'll make trouble next morning; because, of course, she prob'bly hain't got any but that one."

"I know; but you don't want it but fifteen minutes, to carry the nonnamous letter and shove it under the front door."

"All right, then, I'll do it; but I could carry it just as handy in my own togs."

"You wouldn't look like a servant-girl *then*, would you?"

"No, but there won't be nobody to see what I look like, *anyway*."

"That ain't got nothing to do with it. The thing for us to do is just to do our *duty*, and not worry about whether anybody *sees* us do it or not. Hain't you got no principle at all?"

"All right, I ain't saying nothing; I'm the servant-girl. Who's Jim's mother?"

"I'm his mother. I'll hook a gown from Aunt Sally."

"Well, then, you'll have to stay in the cabin when me and Jim leaves."

"Not much. I'll stuff Jim's clothes full of straw and lay it on his bed to represent his mother in disguise, and Jim 'll take the nigger woman's gown off of me and wear it, and we'll all evade together. When a prisoner of style escapes it's called an evasion. It's always called so when a king escapes, f'rinstance. And the same with a king's son; it don't make no difference whether he's a natural one or an unnatural one."

So Tom he wrote the nonnamous letter, and I smouched the yaller wench's frock that night, and put it on, and shoved it under the front door, the way Tom told me to. It said:

Beware. Trouble is brewing. Keep a sharp lookout.
Unknown Friend.

Trouble is Brewing

Next night we stuck a picture, which Tom drawed in blood, of a skull and crossbones on the front door; and next night another one of a coffin on the back door. I never see a family in such a sweat. They couldn't a been worse scared if the place had a been full of ghosts laying for them behind everything and under the beds and shivering through the air. If a door banged, Aunt Sally she jumped and said "ouch!" if anything fell, she jumped and said "ouch!" if you happened to touch her, when she warn't noticing, she done the same; she couldn't face noway and be satisfied, because she allowed there was something behind her every time—so she was always a-whirling around sudden, and saying "ouch," and before she'd got two-thirds around she'd whirl back again, and say it again; and she was afraid to go to bed, but she dasn't set up. So the thing was working very well, Tom said; he said he never see a thing work more satisfactory. He said it showed it was done right.

So he said, now for the grand bulge! So the very next morning at the streak of dawn we got another letter ready, and was wondering what we better do with it, because we heard them say at supper they was going to have a nigger on watch at both doors all night. Tom he went down the lightning-rod to spy around; and the nigger at the back door was asleep, and he stuck it in the back of his neck and come back. This letter said:

> *Don't betray me, I wish to be your friend. There is a desprate gang of cutthroats from over in the Indian Territory going to steal your runaway nigger tonight, and they have been trying to scare you so as you will stay in the house and not bother them. I am one of the gang, but have got religgion and wish to quit it and lead an honest life again, and will betray the helish design. They will sneak down from northards, along the fence, at midnight exact, with a false key, and go in the nigger's cabin to get him. I am to be off a piece and blow a tin horn if I see any danger; but stead of that I will baa like a sheep soon as they get in and not blow at all; then whilst they are getting his chains loose, you slip there and lock them in, and can kill them at your leasure. Don't do anything but just the way I am telling you, if you do they will suspicion something and raise whoop-jamboreehoo. I do not wish any reward but to know I have done the right thing.*
>
> Unknown Friend.

40

We was feeling pretty good after breakfast, and took my canoe and went over the river a-fishing, with a lunch, and had a good time, and took a look at the raft and found her all right, and got home late to supper, and found them in such a sweat and worry they didn't know which end they was standing on, and made us go right off to bed the minute we was done supper, and wouldn't tell us what the trouble was, and never let on a word about the new letter, but didn't need to, because we knowed as much about it as anybody did, and as soon as we was half up stairs and her back was turned we slid for the cellar cupboard and loaded up a good lunch and took it up to our room and went to bed, and got up about half-past eleven, and Tom put on Aunt Sally's dress that he stole and was going to start with the lunch, but says:

"Where's the butter?"

"I laid out a hunk of it," I says, "on a piece of a corn-pone."

"Well, you *left* it laid out, then—it ain't here."

"We can get along without it," I says.

"We can get along *with* it, too," he says; "just you slide down cellar and fetch it. And then mosey right down the lightning-rod and come along. I'll go and stuff the straw into Jim's clothes to represent his mother in disguise, and be ready to *baa* like a sheep and shove soon as you get there."

So out he went, and down cellar went I. The hunk of butter, big as a person's fist, was where I had left it, so I took up the slab of corn-pone with it on, and blowed out my light, and started up stairs very stealthy, and got up to the main floor all right, but here comes Aunt Sally with a candle, and I clapped the truck in my hat, and clapped my hat on my head, and the next second she see me; and she says:

"You been down cellar?"

"Yes'm."

"What you been doing down there?"

"Noth'n."

"*Noth'n!*"

"No'm."

"Well, then, what possessed you to go down there this time of night?"

"I don't know 'm."

"You don't *know*? Don't answer me that way. Tom, I want to know what you been *doing* down there."

"I hain't been doing a single thing, Aunt Sally, I hope to gracious if I have."

I reckoned she'd let me go now, and as a general thing she would; but I s'pose there was so many strange things going on she was just in a sweat about every little thing that warn't yard-stick straight; so she says, very decided:

"You just march into that setting room and stay there till I come. You been up to something you no business to, and I lay I'll find out what it is before I'M done with you."

So she went away as I opened the door and walked into the setting room. My, but there was a crowd there! Fifteen farmers, and every one of them had a gun. I was most powerful sick, and slunk to a chair and set down. They was setting around, some of them talking a little, in a low voice, and all of them fidgety and uneasy, but trying to look like they warn't; but I knowed they was, because they was always taking off their hats, and putting them on, and scratching their heads, and changing their seats, and fumbling with their buttons. I warn't easy myself, but I didn't take my hat off, all the same.

I did wish Aunt Sally would come, and get done with me, and lick me, if she wanted to, and let me get away and tell Tom how we'd overdone this thing, and what a thundering hornet's-nest we'd got ourselves into, so we could stop fooling around straight off, and clear out with Jim before these rips got out of patience and come for us.

At last she come and begun to ask me questions, but I *couldn't* answer them straight, I didn't know which end of me was up; because these men was in such a fidget now that some was wanting to start right NOW and lay for them desperadoes, and saying it warn't but a few minutes to midnight; and others was trying to get them to hold on and wait for the sheep-signal; and here was Aunty pegging away at the questions, and me a-shaking all over and ready to sink down in my tracks I was that scared; and the place getting hotter and hotter, and the butter beginning to melt and run down my neck and behind my ears; and pretty soon, when one of them says, "I'M for going and getting in the cabin *first* and right *now*, and catching them when they come," I most dropped; and a streak of butter come a-trickling down my forehead, and Aunt Sally she see it, and turns white as a sheet, and says:

"For the land's sake, what *is* the matter with the child? He's got the brain-fever as shore as you're born, and they're oozing out!"

And everybody runs to see, and she snatches off my hat, and out comes the bread and what was left of the butter, and she grabbed me, and hugged me, and says:

"Oh, what a turn you did give me! and how glad and grateful I am it ain't no worse; for luck's against us, and it never rains but it pours, and when I see that truck I thought we'd lost you, for I knowed by the colour and all it was just like your brains would be if—Dear, dear, whyd'nt you *tell* me that was what you'd been down there for, I wouldn't a cared. Now cler out to bed, and don't lemme see no more of you till morning!"

I was up stairs in a second, and down the lightning-rod in another one, and shinning through the dark for the lean-to. I couldn't hardly get my words out, I was so anxious; but I told Tom as quick as I could we must jump for it now, and not a minute to lose—the house full of men, yonder, with guns!

His eyes just blazed; and he says:

"No!—is that so? *ain't* it bully! Why, Huck, if it was to do over again, I bet I could fetch two hundred! If we could put it off till—"

"Hurry! *Hurry*!" I says. "Where's Jim?"

"Right at your elbow; if you reach out your arm you can touch him. He's dressed, and everything's ready. Now we'll slide out and give the sheep-signal."

But then we heard the tramp of men coming to the door, and heard them begin to fumble with the pad-lock, and heard a man say:

"I *told* you we'd be too soon; they haven't come—the door is locked. Here, I'll lock some of you into the cabin, and you lay for 'em in the dark and kill 'em when they come; and the rest scatter around a piece, and listen if you can hear 'em coming."

So in they come, but couldn't see us in the dark, and most trod on us whilst we was hustling to get under the bed. But we got under all right, and out through the hole, swift but soft—Jim first, me next, and Tom last, which was according to Tom's orders. Now we were in the lean-to, and heard trampings close by outside. So we crept to the door, and Tom stopped us there and put his eye to the crack, but couldn't make out nothing, it was so dark; and whispered and said he would listen for the steps to get further, and when he nudged us Jim must glide out first, and him last. So he set his ear to the crack and listened, and listened, and listened, and the steps a-scraping around out there all the time; and at last he nudged us, and we slid out, and stooped down, not breathing, and not making the least noise, and slipped stealthy towards the fence in Injun file, and got to it all right, and me and Jim over it; but Tom's britches catched fast on a splinter on the top rail, and then he hear the steps coming, so he had to pull loose, which snapped the splinter and made a noise; and as he dropped in our tracks and started somebody sings out:

"Who's that? Answer, or I'll shoot!"

But we didn't answer; we just unfurled our heels and shoved. Then there was a rush, and a *Bang, Bang, Bang!* and the bullets fairly whizzed around us! We heard them sing out:

"Here they are! They've broke for the river! After 'em, boys, and turn loose the dogs!"

So here they come, full tilt. We could hear them because they wore boots and yelled, but we didn't wear no boots and didn't yell. We was in the path to the mill; and when they got pretty close on to us we dodged into the bush and let them go by, and then dropped in behind them. They'd had all the dogs shut up, so they wouldn't scare off the robbers; but by this time somebody had let them loose, and here they come, making powwow enough for a million; but they was our dogs; so we stopped in our tracks till they catched up; and when they see it warn't nobody but us, and no excitement to offer them, they only just said howdy, and tore right ahead towards the shouting and clattering; and then we up-steam again, and whizzed along after them till we was nearly to the mill, and then struck up through the bush to where my canoe was tied, and hopped in and pulled for dear life towards the middle of the river, but didn't make no more noise than we was obleeged to. Then we struck out, easy and comfortable, for the island where my raft was; and we could hear them yelling and barking at each other all up and down the bank, till we was so far away the sounds got dim and died out. And when we stepped on to the raft I says:

"*Now*, old Jim, you're a free man again, and I bet you won't ever be a slave no more."

"En a mighty good job it wuz, too, Huck. It 'uz planned beautiful, en it 'uz done beautiful; en dey ain't *nobody* kin git up a plan dat's mo' mixed-up en splendid den what dat one wuz."

We was all glad as we could be, but Tom was the gladdest of all because he had a bullet in the calf of his leg.

When me and Jim heard that we didn't feel so brash as what we did before. It was hurting him considerable, and bleeding; so we laid him in the wigwam and tore up one of the duke's shirts for to bandage him, but he says:

"Gimme the rags; I can do it myself. Don't stop now; don't fool around here, and the evasion booming along so handsome; man the sweeps, and set her loose! Boys, we done it elegant!—'deed we did. I wish *we'd* a had the handling of Louis XVI., there wouldn't a been no 'Son of Saint Louis, ascend to heaven!' wrote down in *his* biography; no, sir, we'd a whooped him over the *border*—that's what we'd a done with *him*—and done it just as slick as nothing at all, too. Man the sweeps—man the sweeps!"

But me and Jim was consulting—and thinking. And after we'd thought a minute, I says:

"Say it, Jim."

So he says:

"Well, den, dis is de way it look to me, Huck. Ef it wuz *him* dat 'uz bein' sot free, en one er de boys wuz to git shot, would he say, 'Go on en save me, nemmine 'bout a doctor f'r to save dis one?' Is dat like Mars Tom Sawyer? Would he say dat? You *bet* he wouldn't! *well*, den, is *Jim* gywne to say it? No, sah—I doan' budge a step out'n dis place 'dout a *doctor*, not if it's forty year!"

I knowed he was white inside, and I reckoned he'd say what he did say—so it was all right now, and I told Tom I was a-going for a doctor. He raised considerable row about it, but me and Jim stuck to it and wouldn't budge; so he was for crawling out and setting the raft loose himself; but we wouldn't let him. Then he give us a piece of his mind, but it didn't do no good.

So when he sees me getting the canoe ready, he says:

"Well, then, if you're bound to go, I'll tell you the way to do when you get to the village. Shut the door and blindfold the doctor tight and fast, and make him swear to be silent as the grave, and put a purse full of gold in his hand, and then take and lead him all around the back alleys and everywheres in the dark, and then fetch him here in the canoe, in a roundabout way amongst the islands, and search him and take his chalk away from him, and don't give it back to him till you get him back to the village, or else he will chalk this raft so he can find it again. It's the way they all do."

So I said I would, and left, and Jim was to hide in the woods when he see the doctor coming till he was gone again.

41

The doctor was an old man; a very nice, kind-looking old man when I got him up. I told him me and my brother was over on Spanish Island hunting yesterday afternoon, and camped on a piece of a raft we found, and about midnight he must a kicked his gun in his dreams, for it went off and shot him in the leg, and we wanted him to go over there and fix it and not say nothing about it, nor let anybody know, because we wanted to come home this evening and surprise the folks.

"Who is your folks?" he says.

"The Phelpses, down yonder."

"Oh," he says. And after a minute, he says: "How'd you say he got shot?"

"He had a dream," I says, "and it shot him."

"Singular dream," he says.

So he lit up his lantern, and got his saddle-bags, and we started. But when he sees the canoe he didn't like the look of her—said she was big enough for one, but didn't look pretty safe for two. I says:

"Oh, you needn't be afeard, sir, she carried the three of us easy enough."

"What three?"

"Why, me and Sid, and—and—and *the guns*; that's what I mean."

"Oh," he says.

But he put his foot on the gunnel and rocked her, and shook his head, and said he reckoned he'd look around for a bigger one. But they was all locked and chained; so he took my canoe, and said for me to wait till he come back, or I could hunt around further, or maybe I better go down home and get them ready for the surprise if I wanted to. But I said I didn't; so I told him just how to find the raft, and then he started.

I struck an idea pretty soon. I says to myself, spos'n he can't fix that leg just in three shakes of a sheep's tail, as the saying is? spos'n it takes him three or four days? What are we going to do?—lay around there till he lets the cat out of the bag? No, sir; I know what *I'll* do. I'll wait, and when he comes back if he says he's got to go any more I'll get down there, too, if I swim; and we'll take and tie him, and keep him, and shove out down the river; and when Tom's done with him we'll give him what it's worth, or all we got, and then let him get ashore.

So then I crept into a lumber-pile to get some sleep; and next time I waked up the sun was away up over my head! I shot out and went for the doctor's house, but they told me he'd gone away in the night some time or other, and warn't back yet. Well, thinks I, that looks powerful bad for Tom, and I'll dig out for the island right off. So away I shoved, and turned the corner, and nearly rammed my head into Uncle Silas's stomach! He says:

"Why, *Tom!* Where you been all this time, you rascal?"

Uncle Silas in danger

"I hain't been nowheres," I says, "only just hunting for the runaway nigger—me and Sid."

"Why, where ever did you go?" he says. "Your aunt's been mighty uneasy."

"She needn't," I says, "because we was all right. We followed the men and the dogs, but they outrun us, and we lost them; but we thought we heard them on the water, so we got a canoe and took out after them and crossed over, but couldn't find nothing of them; so we cruised along up-shore till we got kind of tired and beat out; and tied up the canoe and went to sleep, and never waked up till about an hour ago; then we paddled over here to hear the news, and Sid's at the post-office to see what he can hear, and I'm a-branching out to get something to eat for us, and then we're going home."

So then we went to the post-office to get "Sid"; but just as I suspicioned, he warn't there; so the old man he got a letter out of the office, and we waited awhile longer, but Sid didn't come; so the old man said, come along, let Sid foot it home, or canoe it, when he got done fooling around—but we would ride. I couldn't get him to let me stay and wait for Sid; and he said there warn't no use in it, and I must come along, and let Aunt Sally see we was all right.

When we got home Aunt Sally was that glad to see me she laughed and cried both, and hugged me, and give me one of them lickings of hern that don't amount to shucks, and said she'd serve Sid the same when he come.

And the place was plum full of farmers and farmers' wives, to dinner; and such another clack a body never heard. Old Mrs. Hotchkiss was the worst; her tongue was a-going all the time. She says:

"Well, Sister Phelps, I've ransacked that-air cabin over, an' I b'lieve the nigger was crazy. I says to Sister Damrell—didn't I, Sister Damrell?—s'I, he's crazy, s'I—them's the very words I said. You all hearn me: he's crazy, s'I; everything shows it, s'I. Look at that-air grindstone, s'I; want to tell *me*'t any cretur 't's in his right mind 's a goin' to scrabble all them crazy things onto a grindstone, s'I? Here sich 'n' sich a person busted his heart; 'n' here so 'n' so pegged along for thirty-seven year, 'n' all that—natcherl son o' Louis somebody, 'n' sich everlast'n rubbage. He's plumb crazy, s'I; it's what I says in the fust place, it's what I says in the middle, 'n' it's what I says last 'n' all the time—the nigger's crazy—crazy 's Nebokoodneezer, s'I."

"An' look at that-air ladder made out'n rags, Sister Hotchkiss," says old Mrs. Damrell; "what in the name o' goodness *could* he ever want of—"

"The very words I was a-sayin' no longer ago th'n this minute to Sister Utterback, 'n' she'll tell you so herself. Sh-she, look at that—air rag ladder, sh-she; 'n' s'I, yes, *look* at it, s'I—what *could* he a-wanted of it, s'I. Sh-she, Sister Hotchkiss, sh-she—"

"But how in the nation'd they ever *git* that grindstone *in* there, *anyway*? 'n' who dug that-air *hole*? 'n' who—"

"My very *words*, Brer Penrod! I was a-sayin'—pass that-air sasser o' m'lasses, won't ye?—I was a-sayin' to Sister Dunlap, jist this minute, how *did* they git that grindstone in there, s'I. Without *help*, mind you—'thout *help*! *that's* wher 'tis. Don't tell *me*, s'I; there *wuz* help, s'I; 'n' ther' wuz a *plenty* help, too, s'I; ther's ben a *dozen* a-helpin' that nigger, 'n' I lay I'd skin every last nigger on this place but *I'd* find out who done it, s'I; 'n' moreover, s'I—"

"A *dozen* says you!—*forty* couldn't a done every thing that's been done. Look at them case-knife saws and things, how tedious they've been made; look at that bed-leg sawed off with 'm, a week's work for six men; look at that nigger made out'n straw on the bed; and look at—"

"You may *well* say it, Brer Hightower! It's jist as I was a-sayin' to Brer Phelps, his own self. S'e, what do *you* think of it, Sister Hotchkiss, s'e? Think o' what, Brer Phelps, s'I? Think o' that bed-leg sawed off that a way, s'e? *think* of it, s'I? I lay it never sawed *itself* off, s'I—somebody *sawed* it, s'I; that's my opinion, take it or leave it, it mayn't be no 'count, s'I, but sich as 't is, it's my opinion, s'I, 'n' if any body k'n start a better one, s'I, let him *do* it, s'I, that's all. I says to Sister Dunlap, s'I—"

"Why, dog my cats, they must a ben a house-full o' niggers in there every night for four weeks to a done all that work, Sister Phelps. Look at that shirt—every last inch of it kivered over with secret African writ'n done with blood! Must a ben a raft uv 'm at it right along, all the time, amost. Why, I'd give two dollars to have it read to me; 'n' as for the niggers that wrote it, I 'low I'd take 'n' lash 'm t'll—"

"People to *help* him, Brother Marples! Well, I reckon you'd *think* so if you'd a been in this house for a while back. Why, they've stole everything they could lay their hands on—and we a-watching all the time, mind you. They stole that shirt right off o' the line! and as for that sheet they made the rag ladder out of, ther' ain't no telling how many times they *didn't* steal that; and flour, and candles, and candlesticks, and spoons, and the old warming-pan, and most a thousand things that I disremember now, and my new calico dress; and me and Silas and my Sid and Tom on the constant watch day *and* night, as I was a-telling you, and not a one of us could catch hide nor hair nor sight nor sound of them; and here at the last minute, lo and behold you, they slides right in under our noses and fools us, and not only fools *us* but the Injun Territory robbers too, and actuly gets *away* with that nigger safe and sound, and that with sixteen men and twenty-two dogs right on their very heels at that very time! I tell you, it just bangs anything I ever *heard* of. Why, *sperits* couldn't a done better and been no smarter. And I reckon they must a *been* sperits—because, *you* know our dogs, and ther' ain't no better; well, them dogs never even got on the *track* of 'm once! You explain *that* to me if you can!—*any* of you!"

"Well, it does beat—"

"Laws alive, I never—"

"So help me, I wouldn't a be—"

"*House*-thieves as well as—"

"Goodnessgracioussakes, I'd a ben afeard to live in sich a—"

"'Fraid to *live*!—why, I was that scared I dasn't hardly go to bed, or get up, or lay down, or *set* down, Sister Ridgeway. Why, they'd steal the very—why, goodness sakes, you can guess what kind of a fluster I was in by the time midnight come last night. I hope to gracious if I warn't afraid they'd steal some o' the family! I was just to that pass I didn't have no reasoning faculties no more. It looks foolish enough *now*, in the daytime; but I says to myself, there's my two poor boys asleep, 'way up stairs in that lonesome room, and I declare to goodness I was that uneasy 't I crep' up there and locked 'em in! I *did*. And anybody would. Because, you know, when you get scared that way, and it keeps running on, and getting worse and worse all the time, and your wits gets to addling, and you get to doing all sorts o' wild things, and by and by you think to yourself, spos'n I was a boy, and was away up there, and the door ain't locked, and you—" She stopped, looking kind of wondering, and then she turned her head around slow, and when her eye lit on me—I got up and took a walk.

Says I to myself, I can explain better how we come to not be in that room this morning if I go out to one side and study over it a little. So I done it. But I dasn't go fur, or she'd a sent for me. And when it was late in the day the people all went, and then I come in and told her the noise and shooting waked up me and "Sid," and the door was locked, and we wanted to see the fun, so we went down the lightning-rod, and both of us got hurt a little, and we didn't never want to try *that* no more. And then I went on and told her all what I told Uncle Silas before; and then she said she'd forgive us, and maybe it was all right enough anyway, and about what a body might expect of boys, for all boys was a pretty harum-scarum lot as fur as she could see; and so, as long as no harm hadn't come of it, she judged she better put in her time being grateful we was alive and well and she had us still, stead of fretting over what was past and done. So then she kissed me, and patted me on the head, and dropped into a kind of a brown study; and pretty soon jumps up, and says:

"Why, lawsamercy, it's most night, and Sid not come yet! What *has* become of that boy?"

I see my chance; so I skips up and says:

"I'll run right up to town and get him," I says.

"No you won't," she says. "You'll stay right wher' you are; *one's* enough to be lost at a time. If he ain't here to supper, your uncle 'll go."

Well, he warn't there to supper; so right after supper uncle went.

He come back about ten a little bit uneasy; hadn't run across Tom's track. Aunt Sally was a good *deal* uneasy; but Uncle Silas he said there warn't no occasion to be—boys will be boys, he said, and you'll see this one turn up in the morning all sound and right. So she had to be satisfied. But she said she'd set up for him a while anyway, and keep a light burning so he could see it.

Aunt Sally talks to Huck

And then when I went up to bed she come up with me and fetched her candle, and tucked me in, and mothered me so good I felt mean, and like I couldn't look her in the face; and she set down on the bed and talked with me a long time, and said what a splendid boy Sid was, and didn't seem to want to ever stop talking about him; and kept asking me every now and then if I reckoned he could a got lost, or hurt, or maybe drownded, and might be laying at this minute somewheres suffering or dead, and she not by him to help him, and so the tears would drip down silent, and I would tell her that Sid was all right, and would be home in the morning, sure; and she would squeeze my hand, or maybe kiss me, and tell me to say it again, and keep on saying it, because it done her good, and she was in so much trouble.

And when she was going away she looked down in my eyes so steady and gentle, and says:

"The door ain't going to be locked, Tom, and there's the window and the rod; but you'll be good, *won't* you? And you won't go? For *my* sake."

Laws knows I *wanted* to go bad enough to see about Tom, and was all intending to go; but after that I wouldn't a went, not for kingdoms.

But she was on my mind and Tom was on my mind, so I slept very restless. And twice I went down the rod away in the night, and slipped around front, and see her setting there by her candle in the window with her eyes towards the road and the tears in them; and I wished I could do something for her, but I couldn't, only to swear that I wouldn't never do nothing to grieve her any more. And the third time I waked up at dawn, and slid down, and she was there yet, and her candle was most out, and her old grey head was resting on her hand, and she was asleep.

42

The old man was uptown again before breakfast, but couldn't get no track of Tom; and both of them set at the table thinking, and not saying nothing, and looking mournful, and their coffee getting cold, and not eating anything. And by and by the old man says:

"Did I give you the letter?"

"What letter?"

"The one I got yesterday out of the post-office."

"No, you didn't give me no letter."

"Well, I must a forgot it."

So he rummaged his pockets, and then went off somewheres where he had laid it down, and fetched it, and give it to her. She says:

"Why, it's from St. Petersburg—it's from Sis."

I allowed another walk would do me good; but I couldn't stir. But before she could break it open she dropped it and run—for she see something. And so did I. It was Tom Sawyer on a mattress; and that old doctor; and Jim, in *her* calico dress, with his hands tied behind him; and a lot of people. I hid the letter behind the first thing that come handy, and rushed. She flung herself at Tom, crying, and says:

"Oh, he's dead, he's dead, I know he's dead!"

And Tom he turned his head a little, and muttered something or other, which showed he warn't in his right mind; then she flung up her hands, and says:

"He's alive, thank God! And that's enough!" and she snatched a kiss of him, and flew for the house to get the bed ready, and scattering orders right and left at the niggers and everybody else, as fast as her tongue could go, every jump of the way.

I followed the men to see what they was going to do with Jim; and the old doctor and Uncle Silas followed after Tom into the house. The men was very huffy, and some of them wanted to hang Jim for an example to all the other niggers around there, so they wouldn't be trying to run away like Jim done, and making such a raft of trouble, and keeping a whole family scared most to death for days and nights. But the others said, don't do it, it wouldn't answer at all; he ain't our nigger, and his owner would turn up and make us pay for him, sure. So that cooled them down a little, because the people that's always the most anxious for to hang a nigger that hain't done just right is always the very ones that ain't the most anxious to pay for him when they've got their satisfaction out of him.

They cussed Jim considerble, though, and give him a cuff or two side the head once in a while, but Jim never said nothing, and he never let on to know me, and they took him to the same cabin, and put his own clothes on him, and chained him again, and not to no bed-leg this time, but to a big staple drove into the bottom log, and chained his hands, too, and both legs, and said he warn't to have nothing but bread and water to eat after this till his owner come, or he was sold at auction because he didn't come in a certain length of time, and filled up our hole, and said a couple of farmers with guns must stand watch around about the cabin every night, and a bulldog tied to the door in the daytime; and about this time they was through with the job and was tapering off with a kind of general goodbye cussing, and then the old doctor comes and takes a look, and says:

"Don't be no rougher on him than you're obleeged to, because he ain't a bad nigger. When I got to where I found the boy I see I couldn't cut the bullet out without some help, and he warn't in no condition for me to leave to go and get help; and he got a little worse and a little worse, and after a long time he went out of his head, and wouldn't let me come a-nigh him any more, and said if I chalked his raft he'd kill me, and no end of wild foolishness like that, and I see I couldn't do anything at all with him; so I says, I got to have *help* somehow; and the minute I says it out crawls this nigger from somewheres and says he'll help, and he done it, too, and done it very well. Of course I judged he must be a runaway nigger, and there I *was*! and there I had to stick right straight along all the rest of the day and all night. It was a fix, I tell you! I had a couple of patients with the chills, and of course I'd of liked to run up to town and see them, but I dasn't, because the nigger might get away, and then I'd be to blame; and yet never a skiff come close enough for me to hail. So there I had to stick plumb until daylight this morning; and I never see a nigger that was a better nuss or faithfuller, and yet he was risking his freedom to do it, and was all tired out, too, and I see plain enough he'd been worked main hard lately. I liked the nigger for that; I tell you, gentlemen, a nigger like that is worth a thousand dollars—and kind treatment, too. I had everything I needed, and the boy was doing as well there as he would a done at home—better, maybe, because it was so quiet; but there I *was*, with both of 'm on my hands, and there I had to stick till about dawn this morning; then some men in a skiff come by, and as good luck would have it the nigger was setting by the pallet with his head propped on his knees sound asleep; so I motioned them in quiet, and they slipped up on him and grabbed him and tied him before he knowed what he was about, and we never had no trouble. And the boy being in a kind of a flighty sleep, too, we muffled the oars and hitched the raft on, and towed her over very nice and quiet, and the nigger never made the least row nor said a word from the start. He ain't no bad nigger, gentlemen; that's what I think about him."

Somebody says:

"Well, it sounds very good, doctor, I'm obleeged to say."

Then the others softened up a little, too, and I was mighty thankful to that old doctor for doing Jim that good turn; and I was glad it was according to my judgment of him, too; because I thought he had a good heart in him and was a good man the first time I see him. Then they all agreed that Jim had acted very well, and was deserving to have some notice took of it, and reward. So every one of them promised, right out and hearty, that they wouldn't cuss him no more.

Then they come out and locked him up. I hoped they was going to say he could have one or two of the chains took off, because they was rotten heavy, or could have meat and greens with his bread and water; but they didn't think of it, and I reckoned it warn't best for me to mix in, but I judged I'd get the doctor's yarn to Aunt Sally somehow or other as soon as I'd got through the breakers that was laying just ahead of me—explanations, I mean, of how I forgot to mention about Sid being shot when I was telling how him and me put in that dratted night paddling around hunting the runaway nigger.

But I had plenty time. Aunt Sally she stuck to the sickroom all day and all night, and every time I see Uncle Silas mooning around I dodged him.

Next morning I heard Tom was a good deal better, and they said Aunt Sally was gone to get a nap. So I slips to the sickroom, and if I found him awake I reckoned we could put up a yarn for the family that would wash. But he was sleeping, and sleeping very peaceful, too; and pale, not fire-faced the way he was when he come. So I set down and laid for him to wake. In about half an hour Aunt Sally comes gliding in, and there I was, up a stump again! She motioned me to be still, and set down by me, and begun to whisper, and said we could all be joyful now, because all the symptoms was first-rate, and he'd been sleeping like that for ever so long, and looking better and peacefuller all the time, and ten to one he'd wake up in his right mind.

So we set there watching, and by and by he stirs a bit, and opened his eyes very natural, and takes a look, and says:

"Hello!—why, I'm at *home*! How's that? Where's the raft?"

"It's all right," I says.

"And *Jim*?"

"The same," I says, but couldn't say it pretty brash. But he never noticed, but says:

"Good! Splendid! *Now* we're all right and safe! Did you tell Aunty?"

I was going to say yes; but she chipped in and says:

"About what, Sid?"

"Why, about the way the whole thing was done."

"What whole thing?"

"Why, *the* whole thing. There ain't but one; how we set the runaway nigger free—me and Tom."

"Good land! Set the run—What *is* the child talking about! Dear, dear, out of his head again!"

"*No*, I ain't out of my *head*; I know all what I'm talking about. We *did* set him free—me and Tom. We laid out to do it, and we *done* it. And we done it elegant, too." He'd got a start, and she never checked him up, just set and stared and stared, and let him clip along, and I see it warn't no use for *me* to put in. "Why, Aunty, it cost us a power of work—weeks of it—hours and hours, every night, whilst you was all asleep. And we had to steal candles, and the sheet, and the shirt, and your dress, and spoons, and tin plates, and case-knives, and the warming-pan, and the grindstone, and flour, and just no end of things, and you can't think what work it was to make the saws, and pens, and inscriptions, and one thing or another, and you can't think *half* the fun it was. And we had to make up the pictures of coffins and things, and nonnamous letters from the robbers, and get up and down the lightning-rod, and dig the hole into the cabin, and made the rope ladder and send it in cooked up in a pie, and send in spoons and things to work with in your apron pocket—"

"Mercy sakes!"

"—and load up the cabin with rats and snakes and so on, for company for Jim; and then you kept Tom here so long with the butter in his hat that you come near spiling the whole business, because the men come before we was out of the cabin, and we had to rush, and they heard us and let drive at us, and I got my share, and we dodged out of the path and let them go by, and when the dogs come they warn't interested in us, but went for the most noise, and we got our canoe, and made for the raft, and was all safe, and Jim was a free man, and we done it all by ourselves, and *wasn't* it bully, Aunty!"

"Well, I never heard the likes of it in all my born days! So it was *you*, you little rapscallions, that's been making all this trouble, and turned everybody's wits clean inside out and scared us all most to death. I've as good a notion as ever I had in my life to take it out o' you this very minute. To think, here I've been, night after night, a—*you* just get well once, you young scamp, and I lay I'll tan the Old Harry out o' both o' ye!"

But Tom, he *was* so proud and joyful, he just *couldn't* hold in, and his tongue just *went* it—she a-chipping in, and spitting fire all along, and both of them going it at once, like a cat convention; and she says:

"*Well*, you get all the enjoyment you can out of it *now*, for mind I tell you if I catch you meddling with him again—"

"Meddling with *who*?" Tom says, dropping his smile and looking surprised.

"With *who*? Why, the runaway nigger, of course. Who'd you reckon?"

Tom looks at me very grave, and says:

"Tom, didn't you just tell me he was all right? Hasn't he got away?"

"*Him*?" says Aunt Sally; "the runaway nigger? 'Deed he hasn't. They've got him back, safe and sound, and he's in that cabin again, on bread and water, and loaded down with chains, till he's claimed or sold!"

Tom rose square up in bed, with his eye hot, and his nostrils opening and shutting like gills, and sings out to me:

"They hain't no *right* to shut him up! SHOVE!—and don't you lose a minute. Turn him loose! he ain't no slave; he's as free as any cretur that walks this earth!"

"What *does* the child mean?"

"I mean every word I *say*, Aunt Sally, and if somebody don't go, *I'll* go. I've knowed him all his life, and so has Tom, there. Old Miss Watson died two months ago, and she was ashamed she ever was going to sell him down the river, and *said* so; and she set him free in her will."

"Then what on earth did *you* want to set him free for, seeing he was already free?"

"Well, that *is* a question, I must say; and just like women! Why, I wanted the *adventure* of it; and I'd a waded neck-deep in blood to—goodness alive, *Aunt Polly!*"

If she warn't standing right there, just inside the door, looking as sweet and contented as an angel half full of pie, I wish I may never!

Aunt Sally jumped for her, and most hugged the head off of her, and cried over her, and I found a good enough place for me under the bed, for it was getting pretty sultry for us, seemed to me. And I peeped out, and in a little while Tom's Aunt Polly shook herself loose and stood there looking across at Tom over her spectacles—kind of grinding him into the earth, you know. And then she says:

"Yes, you *better* turn y'r head away—I would if I was you, Tom."

"Oh, deary me!" says Aunt Sally; "*Is* he changed so? Why, that ain't *Tom*, it's Sid; Tom's—Tom's—why, where is Tom? He was here a minute ago."

"You mean where's Huck *Finn*—that's what you mean! I reckon I hain't raised such a scamp as my Tom all these years not to know him when I *see* him. That *would* be a pretty howdy-do. Come out from under that bed, Huck Finn."

So I done it. But not feeling brash.

Aunt Sally she was one of the mixed-upest-looking persons I ever see—except one, and that was Uncle Silas, when he come in and they told it all to him. It kind of made him drunk, as you may say, and he didn't know nothing at all the rest of the day, and preached a prayer-meeting sermon that night that gave him a rattling ruputation, because the oldest man in the world couldn't a understood it. So Tom's Aunt Polly, she told all about who I was, and what; and I had to up and tell how I was in such a tight place that when Mrs. Phelps took me for Tom Sawyer—she chipped in and says, "Oh, go on and call me Aunt Sally, I'm used to it now, and 'tain't no need to change"—that when Aunt Sally took me for Tom Sawyer I had to stand it—there warn't no other way, and I knowed he wouldn't mind, because it would be nuts for him, being a mystery, and he'd make an adventure out of it, and be perfectly satisfied. And so it turned out, and he let on to be Sid, and made things as soft as he could for me.

And his Aunt Polly she said Tom was right about old Miss Watson setting Jim free in her will; and so, sure enough, Tom Sawyer had gone and took all that trouble and bother to set a free nigger free! and I couldn't ever understand before, until that minute and that talk, how he *could* help a body set a nigger free with his bringing-up.

Well, Aunt Polly she said that when Aunt Sally wrote to her that Tom and *Sid* had come all right and safe, she says to herself:

"Look at that, now! I might have expected it, letting him go off that way without anybody to watch him. So now I got to go and trapse all the way down the river, eleven hundred mile, and find out what that creetur's up to *this* time, as long as I couldn't seem to get any answer out of you about it."

"Why, I never heard nothing from you," says Aunt Sally.

"Well, I wonder! Why, I wrote you twice to ask you what you could mean by Sid being here."

"Well, I never got 'em, Sis."

Aunt Polly she turns around slow and severe, and says:

"You, Tom!"

"Well—*what*?" he says, kind of pettish.

"Don't you what *me*, you impudent thing—hand out them letters."

"What letters?"

"*Them* letters. I be bound, if I have to take a-holt of you I'll—"

"They're in the trunk. There, now. And they're just the same as they was when I got them out of the office. I hain't looked into them, I hain't touched them. But I knowed they'd make trouble, and I thought if you warn't in no hurry, I'd—"

"Well, you *do* need skinning, there ain't no mistake about it. And I wrote another one to tell you I was coming; and I s'pose he—"

"No, it come yesterday; I hain't read it yet, but *it's* all right, I've got that one."

I wanted to offer to bet two dollars she hadn't, but I reckoned maybe it was just as safe to not to. So I never said nothing.

THE LAST

The first time I catched Tom private I asked him what was his idea, time of the evasion?—what it was he'd planned to do if the evasion worked all right and he managed to set a nigger free that was already free before? And he said, what he had planned in his head from the start, if we got Jim out all safe, was for us to run him down the river on the raft, and have adventures plumb to the mouth of the river, and then tell him about his being free, and take him back up home on a steamboat, in style, and pay him for his lost time, and write word ahead and get out all the niggers around, and have them waltz him into town with a torchlight procession and a brass-band,

and then he would be a hero, and so would we. But I reckoned it was about as well the way it was.

We had Jim out of the chains in no time, and when Aunt Polly and Uncle Silas and Aunt Sally found out how good he helped the doctor nurse Tom, they made a heap of fuss over him, and fixed him up prime, and give him all he wanted to eat, and a good time, and nothing to do. And we had him up to the sickroom, and had a high talk; and Tom give Jim forty dollars for being prisoner for us so patient, and doing it up so good, and Jim was pleased most to death, and busted out, and says:

"*Dah*, now, Huck, what I tell you?—what I tell you up dah on Jackson islan'? I *tole* you I got a hairy breas', en what's de sign un it; en I *tole* you I ben rich wunst, en gwineter to be rich *agin*; en it's come true; en heah she is! *dah*, now! doan' talk to *me*—signs is *signs*, mine I tell you; en I knowed jis' 's well 'at I 'uz gwineter be rich agin as I's a-stannin' heah dis minute!"

And then Tom he talked along and talked along, and says, le's all three slide out of here one of these nights and get an outfit, and go for howling adventures amongst the Injuns, over in the Territory, for a couple of weeks or two; and I says, all right, that suits me, but I ain't got no money for to buy the outfit, and I reckon I couldn't get none from home, because it's likely pap's been back before now, and got it all away from Judge Thatcher and drunk it up.

"No, he hain't," Tom says; "it's all there yet—six thousand dollars and more; and your pap hain't ever been back since. Hadn't when I come away, anyhow."

Jim says, kind of solemn:

"He ain't a-comin' back no mo', Huck."

I says:

"Why, Jim?"

"Nemmine why, Huck—but he ain't comin' back no mo."

But I kept at him; so at last he says:

"Doan' you 'member de house dat was float'n down de river, en dey wuz a man in dah, kivered up, en I went in en unkivered him and didn' let you come in? Well, den, you kin git yo' money when you wants it, kase dat wuz him."

Tom's most well now, and got his bullet around his neck on a watch-guard for a watch, and is always seeing what time it is, and so there ain't nothing more to write about, and I am rotten glad of it, because if I'd a knowed what a trouble it was to make a book I wouldn't a tackled it, and ain't a-going to no more. But I reckon I got to light out for the Territory ahead of the rest, because Aunt Sally she's going to adopt me and sivilize me, and I can't stand it. I been there before.

THE END. YOURS TRULY, *HUCK FINN*

A Connecticut Yankee in King Arthur's Court

(1889)

Preface

The ungentle laws and customs touched upon in this tale are historical, and the episodes which are used to illustrate them are also historical. It is not pretended that these laws and customs existed in England in the sixth century; no, it is only pretended that inasmuch as they existed in the English and other civilizations of far later times, it is safe to consider that it is no libel upon the sixth century to suppose them to have been in practice in that day also. One is quite justified in inferring that whatever one of these laws or customs was lacking in that remote time, its place was competently filled by a worse one.

The question as to whether there is such a thing as divine right of kings is not settled in this book. It was found too difficult. That the executive head of a nation should be a person of lofty character and extraordinary ability, was manifest and indisputable; that none but the Deity could select that head unerringly, was also manifest and indisputable; that the Deity ought to make that selection, then, was likewise manifest and indisputable; consequently, that He does make it, as claimed, was an unavoidable deduction. I mean, until the author of this book encountered the Pompadour, and Lady Castlemaine, and some other executive heads of that kind; these were found so difficult to work into the scheme, that it was judged better to take the other tack in this book (which must be issued this fall), and then go into training and settle the question in another book. It is, of course, a thing which ought to be settled, and I am not going to have anything particular to do next winter anyway.

MARK TWAIN

HARTFORD, July 21, 1889

A Word of Explanation

It was in Warwick Castle that I came across the curious stranger whom I am going to talk about. He attracted me by three things: his candid simplicity, his marvelous familiarity with ancient armor, and the restfulness of his company—for he did all the talking. We fell together, as modest people will, in the tail of the herd that was being shown through, and he at once began to say things which interested me. As he talked along, softly, pleasantly, flowingly, he seemed to drift away imperceptibly out of this world and time, and into some remote era and old forgotten country; and so he gradually wove such a spell about me that I seemed to move among the spectres and shadows and dust and mold of a grey antiquity, holding speech with a relic of it! Exactly as I would speak of my nearest personal friends or enemies, or my most familiar neighbours, he spoke of Sir Bedivere, Sir Bors de Ganis, Sir Launcelot of the Lake, Sir Galahad, and all the other great names of the Table Round—and how old, old, unspeakably old and faded and dry and musty and ancient he came to look as he went on! Presently he turned to me and said, just as one might speak of the weather, or any other common matter—

"You know about transmigration of souls; do you know about transposition of epochs—and bodies?"

I said I had not heard of it. He was so little interested—just as when people speak of the weather—that he did not notice whether I made him any answer or not. There was half a moment of silence, immediately interrupted by the droning voice of the salaried cicerone:

"Ancient hauberk, date of the sixth century, time of King Arthur and the Round Table; said to have belonged to the knight Sir Sagramor le Desirous; observe the round hole through the chain-mail in the left breast; can't be accounted for; supposed to have been done with a bullet since invention of firearms—perhaps maliciously by Cromwell's soldiers."

My acquaintance smiled—not a modern smile, but one that must have gone out of general use many, many centuries ago—and muttered apparently to himself:

"Wit ye well, *I saw it done.*" Then, after a pause, added: "I did it myself."

By the time I had recovered from the electric surprise of this remark, he was gone.

All that evening I sat by my fire at the Warwick Arms, steeped in a dream of the olden time, while the rain beat upon the windows, and the wind roared about the eaves and corners. From time to time I dipped into old Sir Thomas Malory's enchanting book, and fed at its rich feast of prodigies and adventures, breathed in the fragrance of its obsolete names, and dreamed again. Midnight being come at length, I read another tale, for a nightcap—this which here follows, to wit:

How Sir Launcelot slew two giants, and made a castle free

Anon withal came there upon him two great giants, well armed, all save the heads, with two horrible clubs in their hands. Sir Launcelot put his shield afore him, and put the stroke away of the one giant, and with his sword he clave his head asunder. When his fellow saw that, he ran away as he were wood, for fear of the horrible strokes, and Sir Launcelot after him with all his might, and smote him on the shoulder, and clave him to the middle. Then Sir Launcelot went into the hall, and there came afore him three score ladies and damsels, and all kneeled unto him, and thanked God and him of their deliverance. For, sir, said they, the most part of us have been here this seven year their prisoners, and we have worked all manner of silk works for our meat, and we are all great gentle-women born, and blessed be the time, knight, that ever thou wert born; for thou hast done the most worship that ever did knight in the world, that will we bear record, and we all pray you to tell us your name, that we may tell our friends who delivered us out of prison. Fair damsels, he said, my name is Sir Launcelot du Lake. And so he departed from them and betaught them unto God. And then he mounted upon his horse, and rode into many strange and wild*

* demented

countries, and through many waters and valleys, and evil was he lodged. And at the last by fortune him happened against a night to come to a fair courtelage, and therein he found an old gentle-woman that lodged him with a good-will, and there he had good cheer for him and his horse. And when time was, his host brought him into a fair garret over the gate to his bed. There Sir Launcelot unarmed him, and set his harness by him, and went to bed, and anon he fell on sleep. So, soon after there came one on horseback, and knocked at the gate in great haste. And when Sir Launcelot heard this he rose up, and looked out at the window, and saw by the moonlight three knights come riding after that one man, and all three lashed on him at once with swords, and that one knight turned on them knightly again and defended him. Truly, said Sir Launcelot, yonder one knight shall I help, for it were shame for me to see three knights on one, and if he be slain I am partner of his death. And therewith he took his harness and went out at a window by a sheet down to the four knights, and then Sir Launcelot said on high, Turn you knights unto me, and leave your fighting with that knight. And then they all three left Sir Kay, and turned unto Sir Launcelot, and there began great battle, for they alight all three, and strake many strokes at Sir Launcelot, and assailed him on every side. Then Sir Kay dressed him for to have holpen Sir Launcelot. Nay, sir, said he, I will none of your help, therefore as ye will have my help let me alone with them. Sir Kay for the pleasure of the knight suffered him for to do his will, and so stood aside. And then anon within six strokes Sir Launcelot had stricken them to the earth.

And then they all three cried, Sir Knight, we yield us unto you as man of might matchless. As to that, said Sir Launcelot, I will not take your yielding unto me, but so that ye yield you unto Sir Kay the seneschal, on that covenant I will save your lives and else not. Fair knight, said they, that were we loath to do; for as for Sir Kay we chased him hither, and had overcome him had ye not been; therefore, to yield us unto him it were no reason. Well, as to that, said Sir Launcelot, advise you well, for ye may choose whether ye will die or live, for an ye be yielden, it shall be unto Sir Kay. Fair knight, then they said, in saving our lives we will do as thou commandest us. Then shall ye, said Sir Launcelot, on Whitsunday next coming go unto the court of King Arthur, and there shall ye yield you unto Queen Guenever, and put you all three in her grace and mercy, and say that Sir Kay sent you thither to be her prisoners. On the morn Sir Launcelot arose early, and left Sir Kay sleeping; and Sir Launcelot took Sir Kay's armor and his shield and armed him, and so he went to the stable and took his horse, and took his leave of his host, and so he departed. Then soon after arose Sir Kay and missed Sir Launcelot; and then he espied that he had his armor and his horse. Now by my faith I know well that he will grieve some of the court of King Arthur; for on him knights will be bold, and deem that it is I, and that will beguile them; and because of his armor and shield I am sure I shall ride in peace. And then soon after departed Sir Kay, and thanked his host.

As I laid the book down there was a knock at the door, and my stranger came in. I gave him a pipe and a chair, and made him welcome. I also comforted him with a hot Scotch whisky; gave him another one; then still another—hoping always for his story. After a fourth persuader, he drifted into it himself, in a quite simple and natural way:

The Stranger's History

I am an American. I was born and reared in Hartford, in the State of Connecticut—anyway, just over the river, in the country. So I am a Yankee of the Yankees—and practical; yes, and nearly barren of sentiment, I suppose—or poetry, in other words. My father was a blacksmith, my uncle was a horse doctor, and I was both, along at first. Then I went over to the great arms factory and learned my real trade; learned all there was to it; learned to make everything: guns, revolvers, cannon, boilers, engines, all sorts of labour-saving machinery. Why, I could make anything a body wanted—anything in the world, it didn't make any difference what; and if there wasn't any quick new-fangled way to make a thing, I could invent one—and do it as easy as rolling off a log. I became head superintendent; had a couple of thousand men under me.

Well, a man like that is a man that is full of fight—that goes without saying. With a couple of thousand rough men under one, one has plenty of that sort of amusement. I had, anyway. At last I met my match, and I got my dose. It was during a misunderstanding conducted with crowbars with a fellow we used to call Hercules. He laid me out with a crusher alongside the head that made everything crack, and seemed to spring every joint in my skull and made it overlap its neighbour. Then the world went out in darkness, and I didn't feel anything more, and didn't know anything at all—at least for a while.

When I came to again, I was sitting under an oak tree, on the grass, with a whole beautiful and broad country landscape all to myself—nearly. Not entirely; for there was a fellow on a horse, looking down at me—a fellow fresh out of a picture-book. He was in old-time iron armor from head to heel, with a helmet on his head the shape of a nail-keg with slits in it; and he had a shield, and a sword, and a prodigious spear; and his horse had armor on, too, and a steel horn projecting from his forehead, and gorgeous red and green silk trappings that hung down all around him like a bed-quilt, nearly to the ground.

"Fair sir, will ye just?" said this fellow.

"Will I which?"

"Will ye try a passage of arms for land or lady or for—"

"What are you giving me?" I said. "Get along back to your circus, or I'll report you."

Now what does this man do but fall back a couple of hundred yards and then come rushing at me as hard as he could tear, with his nail-keg bent down nearly to his horse's neck and his long spear pointed straight ahead. I saw he meant business, so I was up the tree when he arrived.

He allowed that I was his property, the captive of his spear. There was argument on his side—and the bulk of the advantage—so I judged it best to humour him. We fixed up an agreement whereby I was to go with him and he was not to hurt me. I came down, and we started away, I walking by the side of his horse. We marched comfortably along, through glades and over brooks which I could not remember to have seen before—which puzzled me and made me wonder—and yet we did not come to any circus or sign of a circus. So I gave up the idea of a circus, and concluded he was from an asylum. But we never came to an asylum—so I was up a stump, as you may say. I asked him how far we were from Hartford. He said he had never heard of the place; which I took to be a lie, but allowed it to go at that. At the end of an hour we saw a far-away town sleeping in a valley by a winding river; and beyond it on a hill, a vast grey fortress, with towers and turrets, the first I had ever seen out of a picture.

"Bridgeport?" said I, pointing.

"Camelot," said he.

My stranger had been showing signs of sleepiness. He caught himself nodding, now, and smiled one of those pathetic, obsolete smiles of his, and said:

"I find I can't go on; but come with me, I've got it all written out, and you can read it if you like."

In his chamber, he said: "First, I kept a journal; then by and by, after years, I took the journal and turned it into a book. How long ago that was!"

He handed me his manuscript, and pointed out the place where I should begin:

"Begin here—I've already told you what goes before." He was steeped in drowsiness by this time. As I went out at his door I heard him murmur sleepily: "Give you good den, fair sir."

I sat down by my fire and examined my treasure. The first part of it—the great bulk of it—was parchment, and yellow with age. I scanned a leaf particularly and saw that it was a palimpsest. Under the old dim writing of the Yankee historian appeared traces of a penmanship which was older and dimmer still—Latin words and sentences: fragments from old monkish legends, evidently. I turned to the place indicated by my stranger and began to read—as follows.

The Tale of the Lost Land

1

Camelot

"Camelot—Camelot," said I to myself. "I don't seem to remember hearing of it before. Name of the asylum, likely."

It was a soft, reposeful summer landscape, as lovely as a dream, and as lonesome as Sunday. The air was full of the smell of flowers, and the buzzing of insects, and the twittering of birds, and there were no people, no wagons, there was no stir of life, nothing going on. The road was mainly a winding path with hoof-prints in it, and now and then a faint trace of wheels on either side in the grass—wheels that apparently had a tire as broad as one's hand.

Presently a fair slip of a girl, about ten years old, with a cataract of golden hair streaming down over her shoulders, came along. Around her head she wore a hoop of flame-red poppies. It was as sweet an outfit as ever I saw, what there was of it. She walked indolently along, with a mind at rest, its peace reflected in her innocent face. The circus man paid no attention to her; didn't even seem to see her. And she—she was no more startled at his fantastic make-up than if she was used to his like every day of her life. She was going by as indifferently as she might have gone by a couple of cows; but when she happened to notice me, *then* there was a change! Up went her hands, and she was turned to stone; her mouth dropped open, her eyes stared wide and timorously, she was the picture of astonished curiosity touched with fear. And there she stood gazing, in a sort of stupefied fascination, till we turned a corner of the wood and were lost to her view. That she should be startled at me instead of at the other man, was too many for me; I couldn't make head or tail of it. And that she should seem to consider me a spectacle, and totally overlook her own merits in that respect, was another puzzling thing, and a display of magnanimity, too, that was surprising in one so young. There was food for thought here. I moved along as one in a dream.

As we approached the town, signs of life began to appear. At intervals we passed a wretched cabin, with a thatched roof, and about it small fields and garden patches in an indifferent state of cultivation. There were people, too; brawny men, with long, coarse, uncombed hair that hung down over their faces and made them look like animals. They and the women, as a rule, wore a coarse tow-linen robe that came well below the knee, and a rude sort of sandal, and many wore an iron collar. The small boys and girls were always naked; but nobody seemed to know it. All of these people stared at me, talked about me, ran into the huts and fetched out their families to gape at me; but nobody ever noticed that other fellow, except to make him humble salutation and get no response for their pains.

In the town were some substantial windowless houses of stone scattered among a wilderness of thatched cabins; the streets were mere crooked alleys, and unpaved; troops of dogs and nude children played in the sun and made life and noise; hogs roamed and rooted contentedly about, and one of them lay in a reeking wallow in the middle of the main thoroughfare and suckled her family. Presently there was a distant blare of military music; it came nearer, still nearer, and soon a noble cavalcade wound into view, glorious with plumed helmets and flashing mail and flaunting banners and rich doublets and horse-cloths and gilded spearheads; and through the muck and swine, and naked brats, and joyous dogs, and shabby huts, it took its gallant way, and in its wake we followed.

Followed through one winding alley and then another—and climbing, always climbing—till at last we gained the breezy height where the huge castle stood. There was an exchange of bugle blasts; then a parley from the walls, where men-at-arms, in hauberk and morion, marched back and forth with halberd at shoulder under flapping banners with the rude figure of a dragon displayed upon them; and then the great gates were flung open, the drawbridge was lowered, and the head of the cavalcade swept forward under the frowning arches; and we, following, soon found ourselves in a great paved court, with towers and turrets stretching up into the blue air on all the four sides; and all about us the dismount was going on, and much greeting and ceremony, and running to and fro, and a gay display of moving and intermingling colours, and an altogether pleasant stir and noise and confusion.

2

King Arthur's Court

The moment I got a chance I slipped aside privately and touched an ancient common looking man on the shoulder and said, in an insinuating, confidential way:

"Friend, do me a kindness. Do you belong to the asylum, or are you just on a visit or something like that?"

He looked me over stupidly, and said:

"Marry, fair sir, me seemeth—"

"That will do," I said; "I reckon you are a patient."

I moved away, cogitating, and at the same time keeping an eye out for any chance passenger in his right mind that might come along and give me some light. I judged I had found one, presently; so I drew him aside and said in his ear:

"If I could see the head keeper a minute—only just a minute—"

"Prithee do not let me."

"Let you *what*?"

"*Hinder* me, then, if the word please thee better. Then he went on to say he was an under-cook and could not stop to gossip, though he would like it another time; for it would comfort his very liver to know where I got my clothes. As he started away he pointed and said yonder was one who was idle enough for my purpose, and was seeking me besides, no doubt. This was an airy slim boy in shrimp-coloured tights that made him look like a forked carrot, the rest of his gear was blue silk and dainty laces and ruffles; and he had long yellow curls, and wore a plumed pink satin cap tilted complacently over his ear. By his look, he was good-natured; by his gait, he was satisfied with himself. He was pretty enough to frame. He arrived, looked me over with a smiling and impudent curiosity; said he had come for me, and informed me that he was a page.

"Go 'long," I said; "you ain't more than a paragraph."

"Go 'long," I said; "You ain't more than a paragraph"

It was pretty severe, but I was nettled. However, it never phazed him; he didn't appear to know he was hurt. He began to talk and laugh, in happy, thoughtless, boyish fashion, as we walked along, and made himself old friends with me at once; asked me all sorts of questions about myself and about my clothes, but never waited for an answer—always chattered straight ahead, as if he didn't know he had asked a question and wasn't expecting any reply, until at last he happened to mention that he was born in the beginning of the year 513.

It made the cold chills creep over me! I stopped and said, a little faintly:

"Maybe I didn't hear you just right. Say it again—and say it slow. What year was it?"

"513."

"513! You don't look it! Come, my boy, I am a stranger and friendless; be honest and honourable with me. Are you in your right mind?"

He said he was.

"Are these other people in their right minds?"

He said they were.

"And this isn't an asylum? I mean, it isn't a place where they cure crazy people?"

He said it wasn't.

"Well, then," I said, "either I am a lunatic, or something just as awful has happened. Now tell me, honest and true, where am I?"

"*In King Arthur's Court.*"

I waited a minute, to let that idea shudder its way home, and then said:

"And according to your notions, what year is it now?"

"528—nineteenth of June."

I felt a mournful sinking at the heart, and muttered: "I shall never see my friends again—never, never again. They will not be born for more than thirteen hundred years yet."

I seemed to believe the boy, I didn't know why. *Something* in me seemed to believe him—my consciousness, as you may say; but my reason didn't. My reason straightway began to clamor; that was natural. I didn't know how to go about satisfying it, because I knew that the testimony of men wouldn't serve—my reason would say they were lunatics, and throw out their evidence. But all of a sudden I stumbled on the very thing, just by luck. I knew that the only total eclipse of the sun in the first half of the sixth century occurred on the 21st of June, A.D. 528, O.S., and began at 3 minutes after 12 noon. I also knew that no total eclipse of the sun was due in what to *me* was the present year—i.e., 1879. So, if I could keep my anxiety and curiosity from eating the heart out of me for forty-eight hours, I should then find out for certain whether this boy was telling me the truth or not.

Wherefore, being a practical Connecticut man, I now shoved this whole problem clear out of my mind till its appointed day and hour should come, in order that I might turn all my attention to the circumstances of the present moment, and be alert and ready to make the most out of them that could be made. One thing at a time, is my motto—and just play that thing for all it is worth, even if it's only two pair and a jack. I made up my mind to two things: if it was still the nineteenth century and I was among lunatics and couldn't get away, I would presently boss that asylum or know the reason why; and if, on the other hand, it was really the sixth century, all right, I didn't want any softer thing: I would boss the whole country inside of three months; for I judged I would have the start of the best-educated man in the kingdom by a matter of thirteen hundred years and upward. I'm not a man to waste time after my mind's made up and there's work on hand; so I said to the page:

"Now, Clarence, my boy—if that might happen to be your name—I'll get you to post me up a little if you don't mind. What is the name of that apparition that brought me here?"

"My master and thine? That is the good knight and great lord Sir Kay the Seneschal, foster brother to our liege the king."

"Very good; go on, tell me everything."

He made a long story of it; but the part that had immediate interest for me was this: He said I was Sir Kay's prisoner, and that in the due course of custom I would be flung into a dungeon and left there on scant commons until my friends ransomed me—unless I chanced to rot, first. I saw that the last chance had the best show, but I didn't waste any bother about that; time was too precious. The page said, further, that dinner was about ended in the great hall by this time, and that as soon as the sociability and the heavy drinking should begin, Sir Kay would have me in and exhibit me before King Arthur and his illustrious knights seated at the Table Round, and would brag about his exploit in capturing me, and would probably exaggerate the facts a little, but it wouldn't be good form for me to correct him, and not over safe, either; and when I was done being exhibited, then ho for the dungeon; but he, Clarence, would find a way to come and see me every now and then, and cheer me up, and help me get word to my friends.

Get word to my friends! I thanked him; I couldn't do less; and about this time a lackey came to say I was wanted; so Clarence led me in and took me off to one side and sat down by me.

Well, it was a curious kind of spectacle, and interesting. It was an immense place, and rather naked—yes, and full of loud contrasts. It was very, very lofty; so lofty that the banners depending from the arched beams and girders away up there floated in a sort of twilight; there was a stone-railed gallery at each end, high up, with musicians in the one, and women, clothed in stunning colours, in the other. The floor was of big stone flags laid in black and white squares, rather battered by age and use, and needing repair. As to ornament, there wasn't any, strictly speaking; though on the walls hung some huge tapestries which were probably taxed as works of art; battle-pieces, they were, with horses shaped like those which children cut out of paper or create in gingerbread; with men on them in scale armor whose scales are represented by round holes—so that the man's coat looks as if it had been done with a biscuit-punch. There was a fireplace big enough to camp in; and its projecting sides and hood, of carved and pillared stonework, had the look of a cathedral door. Along the walls stood men-at-arms, in breastplate and morion, with halberds for their only weapon—rigid as statues; and that is what they looked like.

In the middle of this groined and vaulted public square was an oaken table which they called the Table Round. It was as large as a circus ring; and around it sat a great company of men dressed in such various and splendid colours that it hurt one's eyes to look at them. They wore their plumed hats, right along, except that whenever one addressed himself directly to the king, he lifted his hat a trifle just as he was beginning his remark.

Mainly they were drinking—from entire ox horns; but a few were still munching bread or gnawing beef bones. There was about an average of two dogs to one man; and these sat in expectant attitudes till a spent bone was flung to them, and then they went for it by brigades and divisions, with a rush, and there ensued a fight which filled the prospect with a tumultuous chaos of plunging heads and bodies and flashing tails, and the storm of howlings and barkings deafened all speech for the time; but that was no matter, for the dog-fight was always a bigger interest anyway; the men rose, sometimes, to observe it the better and bet on it, and the ladies and the musicians stretched themselves out over their balusters with the same object; and all broke into delighted ejaculations from time to time. In the end, the winning dog stretched himself out comfortably with his bone between his paws, and proceeded to growl over it, and gnaw it, and grease the floor with it, just as fifty others were already doing; and the rest of the court resumed their previous industries and entertainments.

As a rule, the speech and behavior of these people were gracious and courtly; and I noticed that they were good and serious listeners when anybody was telling anything—I mean in a dog-fightless interval. And plainly, too, they were a childlike and innocent lot; telling lies of the stateliest pattern with a most gentle and winning naivety, and ready and willing to listen to anybody else's lie, and believe it, too. It was hard to associate them with anything cruel or dreadful; and yet they dealt in tales of blood and suffering with a guileless relish that made me almost forget to shudder.

I was not the only prisoner present. There were twenty or more. Poor devils, many of them were maimed, hacked, carved, in a frightful way; and their hair, their faces, their clothing, were caked with black and stiffened drenchings of blood. They were suffering sharp physical pain, of course; and weariness, and hunger and thirst, no doubt; and at least none had given them the comfort of a wash, or even the poor charity of a lotion for their wounds; yet you never heard them utter a moan or a groan, or saw them show any sign of restlessness, or any disposition to complain. The thought was forced upon me: "The rascals—*they* have served other people so in their day; it being their own turn, now, they were not expecting any better treatment than this; so their philosophical bearing is not an outcome of mental training, intellectual fortitude, reasoning; it is mere animal training; they are white Indians."

3

Knights of the Table Round

Mainly the Round Table talk was monologues—narrative accounts of the adventures in which these prisoners were captured and their friends and backers killed and stripped of their steeds and armor. As a general thing—as far as I could make out—these murderous adventures were not forays undertaken to avenge injuries, nor to settle old disputes or sudden fallings out; no, as a rule they were simply duels between strangers—duels between people who had never even been introduced to each other, and between whom existed no cause of offense whatever. Many a time I had seen a couple of boys, strangers, meet by chance, and say simultaneously, "I can lick you," and go at it on the spot; but I had always imagined until now that that sort of thing belonged to children only, and was a sign and mark of childhood; but here were these big boobies sticking to it and taking pride in it clear up into full age and beyond. Yet there was something very engaging about these great simple-hearted creatures, something attractive and lovable. There did not seem to be brains enough in the entire nursery, so to speak, to bait a fish-hook with; but you didn't seem to mind that, after a little, because you soon saw that brains were not needed in a society like that, and indeed would have marred it, hindered it, spoiled its symmetry—perhaps rendered its existence impossible.

There was a fine manliness observable in almost every face; and in some a certain loftiness and sweetness that rebuked your belittling criticisms and stilled them. A most noble benignity and purity reposed in the countenance of him they called Sir Galahad, and likewise in the king's also; and there was majesty and greatness in the giant frame and high bearing of Sir Launcelot of the Lake.

There was presently an incident which centered the general interest upon this Sir Launcelot. At a sign from a sort of master of ceremonies, six or eight of the prisoners rose and came forward in a body and knelt on the floor and lifted up their hands toward the ladies' gallery and begged the grace of a word with the queen. The most conspicuously situated lady in that massed flower-bed of feminine show and finery inclined her head by way of assent, and then the spokesman of the prisoners delivered himself and his fellows into her hands for free pardon, ransom, captivity, or death, as she in her good pleasure might elect; and this, as he said, he was doing by command of Sir Kay the Seneschal, whose prisoners they were, he having vanquished them by his single might and prowess in sturdy conflict in the field.

Surprise and astonishment flashed from face to face all over the house; the queen's gratified smile faded out at the name of Sir Kay, and she looked disappointed; and the page whispered in my ear with an accent and manner expressive of extravagant derision—

"Sir *Kay*, forsooth! Oh, call me pet names, dearest, call me a marine! In twice a thousand years shall the unholy invention of man labour at odds to beget the fellow to this majestic lie!"

Every eye was fastened with severe inquiry upon Sir Kay. But he was equal to the occasion. He got up and played his hand like a major—and took every trick. He said he would state the case exactly according to the facts; he would tell the simple straightforward tale, without comment of his own; "and then," said he, "if ye find glory and honour due, ye will give it unto him who is the mightiest man of his hands that ever bare shield or strake with sword in the ranks of Christian battle—even him that sitteth there!" and he pointed to Sir Launcelot. Ah, he fetched them; it was a rattling good stroke. Then he went on and told how Sir Launcelot, seeking adventures, some brief time gone by, killed seven giants at one sweep of his sword, and set a hundred and forty-two captive maidens free; and then went further, still seeking adventures, and found him (Sir Kay) fighting a desperate fight against nine foreign knights, and straightway took the battle solely into his own hands, and conquered the nine; and that night Sir Launcelot rose quietly, and dressed him in Sir Kay's armor and took Sir Kay's horse and gat him away into distant lands, and vanquished sixteen knights in one pitched battle and thirty-four in another; and all these and the former nine he made to swear that about Whitsuntide they would ride to Arthur's court and yield them to Queen Guenever's hands as captives of Sir Kay the Seneschal, spoil of his knightly prowess; and now here were these half-dozen, and the rest would be along as soon as they might be healed of their desperate wounds.

Well, it was touching to see the queen blush and smile, and look embarrassed and happy, and fling furtive glances at Sir Launcelot that would have got him shot in Arkansas, to a dead certainty.

Everybody praised the valor and magnanimity of Sir Launcelot; and as for me, I was perfectly amazed, that one man, all by himself, should have been able to beat down and capture such battalions of practiced fighters. I said as much to Clarence; but this mocking featherhead only said:

"An Sir Kay had had time to get another skin of sour wine into him, ye had seen the accompt doubled."

I looked at the boy in sorrow; and as I looked I saw the cloud of a deep despondency settle upon his countenance. I followed the direction of his eye, and saw that a very old and white-bearded man, clothed in a flowing black gown, had risen and was standing at the table upon unsteady legs, and feebly swaying his ancient head and surveying the company with his watery and wandering eye. The same suffering look that was in the page's face was observable in all the faces around—the look of dumb creatures who know that they must endure and make no moan.

"Marry, we shall have it again," sighed the boy; "that same old weary tale that he hath told a thousand times in the same words, and that he *will* tell till he dieth, every time he hath gotten his barrel full and feeleth his exaggeration-mill a-working. Would God I had died or I saw this day!"

"Who is it?"

"Merlin, the mighty liar and magician, perdition singe him for the weariness he worketh with his one tale! But that men fear him for that he hath the storms and the lightnings and all the devils that be in hell at his beck and call, they would have dug his entrails out these many years ago to get at that tale and squelch it. He telleth it always in the third person, making believe he is too modest to glorify himself—maledictions light upon him, misfortune be his dole! Good friend, prithee call me for evensong."

The boy nestled himself upon my shoulder and pretended to go to sleep. The old man began his tale; and presently the lad was asleep in reality; so also were the dogs, and the court, the lackeys, and the files of men-at-arms. The droning voice droned on; a soft snoring arose on all sides and supported it like a deep and subdued accompaniment of wind instruments. Some heads were bowed upon folded arms, some lay back with open mouths that issued unconscious music; the flies buzzed and bit, unmolested, the rats swarmed softly out from a hundred holes, and pattered about, and made themselves at home everywhere; and one of them sat up like a squirrel on the king's head and held a bit of cheese in its hands and nibbled it, and dribbled the crumbs in the king's face with naive and impudent irreverence. It was a tranquil scene, and restful to the weary eye and the jaded spirit.

This was the old man's tale. He said:

"Right so the king and Merlin departed, and went until an hermit that was a good man and a great leech. So the hermit searched all his wounds and gave him good salves; so the king was there three days, and then were his wounds well amended that he might ride and go, and so departed. And as they rode, Arthur said, I have no sword. No force,* said Merlin, hereby is a sword that shall be yours and I may. So they rode till they came to a lake, the which was a fair water and broad, and in the midst of the lake Arthur was ware of an arm clothed in white samite, that held a fair sword in that hand. Lo, said Merlin, yonder is that sword that I spake of. With that they saw a damsel going upon the lake. What damsel is that? said Arthur. That is the Lady of the lake, said Merlin; and within that lake is a rock, and therein is as fair a place as any on earth, and richly beseen, and this damsel will come to you anon, and then speak ye fair to her that she will give you that sword. Anon withal came the damsel unto Arthur and saluted him, and he her again. Damsel, said Arthur, what sword is that, that yonder the arm holdeth above the water? I would it were mine, for I have no sword. Sir Arthur King, said the damsel, that sword is mine, and if ye will give me a gift when I ask it you, ye shall have it. By my faith, said Arthur, I will give you what gift ye will ask. Well, said the damsel, go ye into yonder barge and row yourself to the sword, and take it and the scabbard with you, and I will ask my gift when I see my time. So Sir Arthur and Merlin alight, and tied their horses to two trees, and so they went into the ship, and when they

* No matter— M.T.

came to the sword that the hand held, Sir Arthur took it up by the handles, and took it with him.

And the arm and the hand went under the water; and so they came unto the land and rode forth. And then Sir Arthur saw a rich pavilion. What signifieth yonder pavilion? It is the knight's pavilion, said Merlin, that ye fought with last, Sir Pellinore, but he is out, he is not there; he hath ado with a knight of yours, that hight Egglame, and they have fought together, but at the last Egglame fled, and else he had been dead, and he hath chased him even to Carlion, and we shall meet with him anon in the highway. That is well said, said Arthur, now have I a sword, now will I wage battle with him, and be avenged on him. Sir, ye shall not so, said Merlin, for the knight is weary of fighting and chasing, so that ye shall have no worship to have ado with him; also, he will not lightly be matched of one knight living; and therefore it is my counsel, let him pass, for he shall do you good service in short time, and his sons, after his days. Also ye shall see that day in short space ye shall be right glad to give him your sister to wed. When I see him, I will do as ye advise me, said Arthur. Then Sir Arthur looked on the sword, and liked it passing well. Whether liketh you better, said Merlin, the sword or the scabbard? Me liketh better the sword, said Arthur. Ye are more unwise, said Merlin, for the scabbard is worth ten of the sword, for while ye have the scabbard upon you ye shall never lose no blood, be ye never so sore wounded; therefore, keep well the scabbard always with you. So they rode into Carlion, and by the way they met with Sir Pellinore; but Merlin had done such a craft that Pellinore saw not Arthur, and he passed by without any words. I marvel, said Arthur, that the knight would not speak. Sir, said Merlin, he saw you not; for and he had seen you ye had not lightly departed. So they came unto Carlion, whereof his knights were passing glad. And when they heard of his adventures they marveled that he would jeopard his person so alone. But all men of worship said it was merry to be under such a chieftain that would put his person in adventure as other poor knights did."

4

Sir Dinadan the Humorist

It seemed to me that this quaint lie was most simply and beautifully told; but then I had heard it only once, and that makes a difference; it was pleasant to the others when it was fresh, no doubt.

Sir Dinadan the Humorist was the first to awake, and he soon roused the rest with a practical joke of a sufficiently poor quality. He tied some metal mugs to a dog's tail and turned him loose, and he tore around and around the place in a frenzy of fright, with all the other dogs bellowing after him and battering and crashing against everything that came in their way and making altogether a chaos of confusion and a most deafening din and turmoil; at which every man and woman of the multitude laughed till the tears flowed, and some fell out of their chairs and wallowed on the floor in ecstasy. It was just like so many children. Sir Dinadan was so proud of his exploit that he could not keep from telling over and over again, to weariness, how the immortal idea happened to occur to him; and as is the way with humorists of his breed, he was still laughing at it after everybody else had got through.

He was so set up that he concluded to make a speech—of course a humorous speech. I think I never heard so many old played-out jokes strung together in my life. He was worse than the minstrels, worse than the clown in the circus. It seemed peculiarly sad to sit here, thirteen hundred years before I was born, and listen again to poor, flat, worm-eaten jokes that had given me the dry gripes when I was a boy thirteen hundred years afterwards. It about convinced me that there isn't any such thing as a new joke possible. Everybody laughed at these antiquities—but then they always do; I had noticed that, centuries later. However, of course the scoffer didn't laugh—I mean the boy. No, he scoffed; there wasn't anything he wouldn't scoff at. He said the most of Sir Dinadan's jokes were rotten and the rest were petrified. I said "petrified" was good; as I believed, myself, that the only right way to classify the majestic ages of some of those jokes was by geologic periods. But that neat idea hit the boy in a blank place, for geology hadn't been invented yet. However, I made a note of the remark, and calculated to educate the commonwealth up to it if I pulled through. It is no use to throw a good thing away merely because the market isn't ripe yet.

Now Sir Kay arose and began to fire up on his history-mill with me for fuel. It was time for me to feel serious, and I did. Sir Kay told how he had encountered me in a far land of barbarians, who all wore the same ridiculous garb that I did—a garb that was a work of enchantment, and intended to make the wearer secure from hurt by human hands. However he had nullified the force of the enchantment by prayer, and had killed my thirteen knights in a three hours' battle, and taken me prisoner, sparing my life in order that so strange a curiosity as I was might be exhibited to the wonder and admiration of the king and the court. He spoke of me all the time, in the blandest way, as "this prodigious giant," and "this horrible sky-towering monster," and "this tusked and taloned man-devouring ogre", and everybody took in all this bosh in the naivest way, and never smiled or seemed to notice that there was any discrepancy between these watered statistics and me. He said that in trying to escape from him I sprang into the top of a tree two hundred cubits high at a single bound, but he dislodged me with a stone the size of a cow, which "all-to brast" the most of my bones, and then swore me to appear at Arthur's court for sentence. He ended by condemning me to die at noon on the 21st; and was so little concerned about it that he stopped to yawn before he named the date.

I was in a dismal state by this time; indeed, I was hardly enough in my right mind to keep the run of a dispute that sprung up as to how I had better be killed, the possibility of the killing being doubted by some, because of the enchantment in my clothes. And yet it was nothing but an ordinary suit of fifteen-dollar slop-shops. Still, I was sane enough to notice this detail, to wit: many of the terms used in the most matter-of-fact way by this great assemblage of the first ladies and gentlemen in the land would have made a Comanche blush.

Indelicacy is too mild a term to convey the idea. However, I had read "Tom Jones," and "Roderick Random," and other books of that kind, and knew that the highest and first ladies and gentlemen in England had remained little or no cleaner in their talk, and in the morals and conduct which such talk implies, clear up to a hundred years ago; in fact clear into our own nineteenth century—in which century, broadly speaking, the earliest samples of the real lady and real gentleman discoverable in English history—or in European history, for that matter—may be said to have made their appearance. Suppose Sir Walter, instead of putting the conversations into the mouths of his characters, had allowed the characters to speak for themselves? We should have had talk from Rebecca and Ivanhoe and the soft lady Rowena which would embarrass a tramp in our day. However, to the unconsciously indelicate all things are delicate. King Arthur's people were not aware that they were indecent and I had presence of mind enough not to mention it.

They were so troubled about my enchanted clothes that they were mightily relieved, at last, when old Merlin swept the difficulty away for them with a common-sense hint. He asked them why they were so dull—why didn't it occur to them to strip me. In half a minute I was as naked as a pair of tongs! And dear, dear, to think of it: I was the only embarrassed person there. Everybody discussed me; and did it as unconcernedly as if I had been a cabbage. Queen Guenever was as naively interested as the rest, and said she had never seen anybody with legs just like mine before. It was the only compliment I got—if it was a compliment.

Finally I was carried off in one direction, and my perilous clothes in another. I was shoved into a dark and narrow cell in a dungeon, with some scant remnants for dinner, some moldy straw for a bed, and no end of rats for company.

5

An Inspiration

I was so tired that even my fears were not able to keep me awake long.

When I next came to myself, I seemed to have been asleep a very long time. My first thought was, "Well, what an astonishing dream I've had! I reckon I've waked only just in time to keep from being hanged or drowned or burned or something. . . . I'll nap again till the whistle blows, and then I'll go down to the arms factory and have it out with Hercules."

But just then I heard the harsh music of rusty chains and bolts, a light flashed in my eyes, and that butterfly, Clarence, stood before me! I gasped with surprise; my breath almost got away from me.

"What!" I said, "you here yet? Go along with the rest of the dream! scatter!"

But he only laughed, in his light-hearted way, and fell to making fun of my sorry plight.

"All right," I said resignedly, "let the dream go on; I'm in no hurry."

"Prithee what dream?"

"What dream? Why, the dream that I am in Arthur's court—a person who never existed; and that I am talking to you, who are nothing but a work of the imagination."

"Oh, la, indeed! and is it a dream that you're to be burned tomorrow? Ho-ho—answer me that!"

The shock that went through me was distressing. I now began to reason that my situation was in the last degree serious, dream or no dream; for I knew by past experience of the lifelike intensity of dreams, that to be burned to death, even in a dream, would be very far from being a jest, and was a thing to be avoided, by any means, fair or foul, that I could contrive. So I said beseechingly:

"Ah, Clarence, good boy, only friend I've got—for you *are* my friend, aren't you?—don't fail me; help me to devise some way of escaping from this place!"

"Now do but hear thyself! Escape? Why, man, the corridors are in guard and keep of men-at-arms."

"No doubt, no doubt. But how many, Clarence? Not many, I hope?"

"Full a score. One may not hope to escape." After a pause—hesitatingly: "and there be other reasons—and weightier."

"Other ones? What are they?"

"Well, they say—oh, but I daren't, indeed daren't!"

"Why, poor lad, what is the matter? Why do you blench? Why do you tremble so?"

"Oh, in sooth, there is need! I do want to tell you, but—"

"Come, come, be brave, be a man—speak out, there's a good lad!"

He hesitated, pulled one way by desire, the other way by fear; then he stole to the door and peeped out, listening; and finally crept close to me and put his mouth to my ear and told me his fearful news in a whisper, and with all the cowering apprehension of one who was venturing upon awful ground and speaking of things whose very mention might be freighted with death.

"Merlin, in his malice, has woven a spell about this dungeon, and there bides not the man in these kingdoms that would be desperate enough to essay to cross its lines with you! Now God pity me, I have told it! Ah, be kind to me, be merciful to a poor boy who means thee well; for an thou betray me I am lost!"

I laughed the only really refreshing laugh I had had for some time; and shouted:

"Merlin has wrought a spell! *Merlin*, forsooth! That cheap old humbug, that maundering old ass? Bosh, pure bosh, the silliest bosh in the world! Why, it does seem to me that of all the childish, idiotic, chuckle-headed, chicken-livered superstitions that ev—oh, damn Merlin!"

But Clarence had slumped to his knees before I had half finished, and he was like to go out of his mind with fright.

"Oh, beware! These are awful words! Any moment these walls may crumble upon us if you say such things. Oh call them back before it is too late!"

Now this strange exhibition gave me a good idea and set me to thinking. If everybody about here was so honestly and sincerely afraid of Merlin's pretended magic as Clarence was, certainly a superior man like me ought to be shrewd enough to contrive some way to take advantage of such a state of things. I went on thinking, and worked out a plan. Then I said:

"Get up. Pull yourself together; look me in the eye. Do you know why I laughed?"

"No—but for our blessed Lady's sake, do it no more."

"Well, I'll tell you why I laughed. Because I'm a magician myself."

"Thou!" The boy recoiled a step, and caught his breath, for the thing hit him rather sudden; but the aspect which he took on was very, very respectful. I took quick note of that; it indicated that a humbug didn't need to have a reputation in this asylum; people stood ready to take him at his word, without that. I resumed.

"I've known Merlin seven hundred years, and he—"

"Seven hun—"

"Don't interrupt me. He has died and come alive again thirteen times, and traveled under a new name every time: Smith, Jones, Robinson, Jackson, Peters, Haskins, Merlin—a new alias every time he turns up. I knew him in Egypt three hundred years ago; I knew him in India five hundred years ago—he is always blethering around in my way, everywhere I go; he makes me tired. He don't amount to shucks, as a magician; knows some of the old common tricks, but has never got beyond the rudiments, and never will. He is well enough for the provinces—one-night stands and that sort of thing, you know—but dear me, *he* oughtn't to set up for an expert—anyway not where there's a real artist. Now look here, Clarence, I am going to stand your friend, right along, and in return you must be mine. I want you to do me a favour. I want you to get word to the king that I am a magician myself—and the Supreme Grand High-yu-Muck-amuck and head of the tribe, at that;

and I want him to be made to understand that I am just quietly arranging a little calamity here that will make the fur fly in these realms if Sir Kay's project is carried out and any harm comes to me. Will you get that to the king for me?"

The poor boy was in such a state that he could hardly answer me. It was pitiful to see a creature so terrified, so unnerved, so demoralized. But he promised everything; and on my side he made me promise over and over again that I would remain his friend, and never turn against him or cast any enchantments upon him. Then he worked his way out, staying himself with his hand along the wall, like a sick person.

Presently this thought occurred to me: how heedless I have been! When the boy gets calm, he will wonder why a great magician like me should have begged a boy like him to help me get out of this place; he will put this and that together, and will see that I am a humbug.

I worried over that heedless blunder for an hour, and called myself a great many hard names, meantime. But finally it occurred to me all of a sudden that these animals didn't reason; that *they* never put this and that together; that all their talk showed that they didn't know a discrepancy when they saw it. I was at rest, then.

But as soon as one is at rest, in this world, off he goes on something else to worry about. It occurred to me that I had made another blunder: I had sent the boy off to alarm his betters with a threat—I intending to invent a calamity at my leisure; now the people who are the readiest and eagerest and willingest to swallow miracles are the very ones who are hungriest to see you perform them; suppose I should be called on for a sample? Suppose I should be asked to name my calamity? Yes, I had made a blunder; I ought to have invented my calamity first. "What shall I do? what can I say, to gain a little time?" I was in trouble again; in the deepest kind of trouble . . .

"There's a footstep!—they're coming. If I had only just a moment to think. . . . Good, I've got it. I'm all right."

You see, it was the eclipse. It came into my mind in the nick of time, how Columbus, or Cortez, or one of those people, played an eclipse as a saving trump once, on some savages, and I saw my chance. I could play it myself, now, and it wouldn't be any plagiarism, either, because I should get it in nearly a thousand years ahead of those parties.

Clarence came in, subdued, distressed, and said:

"I hasted the message to our liege the king, and straightway he had me to his presence. He was frighted even to the marrow, and was minded to give order for your instant enlargement, and that you be clothed in fine raiment and lodged as befitted one so great; but then came Merlin and spoiled all; for he persuaded the king that you are mad, and know not whereof you speak; and said your threat is but foolishness and idle vaporing. They disputed long, but in the end, Merlin, scoffing, said, 'Wherefore hath he not *named* his brave calamity? Verily it is because he cannot.' This thrust did in a most sudden sort close the king's mouth, and he could offer naught to turn the argument; and so, reluctant, and full loth to do you the discourtesy, he yet prayeth you to consider his perplexed case, as noting how the matter stands, and name the calamity—if so be you have determined the nature of it and the time of its coming. Oh, prithee delay not; to delay at such a time were to double and treble the perils that already compass thee about. Oh, be thou wise—name the calamity!"

I allowed silence to accumulate while I got my impressiveness together, and then said:

"How long have I been shut up in this hole?"

"Ye were shut up when yesterday was well spent. It is 9 of the morning now."

"No! Then I have slept well, sure enough. Nine in the morning now! And yet it is the very complexion of midnight, to a shade. This is the 20th, then?"

"The 20th—yes."

"And I am to be burned alive tomorrow." The boy shuddered.

"At what hour?"

"At high noon."

"Now then, I will tell you what to say." I paused, and stood over that cowering lad a whole minute in awful silence; then, in a voice deep, measured, charged with doom, I began, and rose by dramatically graded stages to my colossal climax, which I delivered in as sublime and noble a way as ever I did such a thing in my life: "Go back and tell the king that at that hour I will smother the whole world in the dead blackness of midnight; I will blot out the sun, and he shall never shine again; the fruits of the earth shall rot for lack of light and warmth, and the peoples of the earth shall famish and die, to the last man!"

I had to carry the boy out myself, he sunk into such a collapse. I handed him over to the soldiers, and went back.

6

The Eclipse

In the stillness and the darkness, realization soon began to supplement knowledge. The mere knowledge of a fact is pale; but when you come to *realize* your fact, it takes on colour. It is all the difference between hearing of a man being stabbed to the heart, and seeing it done. In the stillness and the darkness, the knowledge that I was in deadly danger took to itself deeper and deeper meaning all the time; a something which was realization crept inch by inch through my veins and turned me cold.

But it is a blessed provision of nature that at times like these, as soon as a man's mercury has got down to a certain point there comes a revulsion, and he rallies. Hope springs up, and cheerfulness along with it, and then he is in good shape to do something for himself, if anything can be done. When my rally came, it came with a bound. I said to myself that my eclipse would be sure to save me, and make me the greatest man in the kingdom besides; and straightway my mercury went up to the top of the tube, and my solicitudes all vanished. I was as happy a man as there was in the world. I was even impatient for tomorrow to come, I so wanted to gather in that great triumph and be the center of all the nation's wonder and reverence. Besides, in a business way it would be the making of me; I knew that.

Meantime there was one thing which had got pushed into the background of my mind. That was the half-conviction that when the nature of my proposed calamity should be reported to those superstitious people, it would have such an effect that they would want to compromise. So, by and by when I heard footsteps coming, that thought was recalled to me, and I said to myself, "As sure as anything, it's the compromise. Well, if it is good, all right, I will accept; but if it isn't, I mean to stand my ground and play my hand for all it is worth."

The door opened, and some men-at-arms appeared. The leader said:

"The stake is ready. Come!"

The stake! The strength went out of me, and I almost fell down. It is hard to get one's breath at such a time, such lumps come into one's throat, and such gaspings; but as soon as I could speak, I said:

"But this is a mistake—the execution is tomorrow."

"Order changed; been set forward a day. Haste thee!"

I was lost. There was no help for me. I was dazed, stupefied; I had no command over myself, I only wandered purposely about, like one out of his mind; so the soldiers took hold of me, and pulled me along with them, out of the cell and along the maze of underground corridors, and finally into the fierce glare of daylight and the upper world. As we stepped into the vast enclosed court of the castle I got a shock; for the first thing I saw was the stake, standing in the center, and near it the piled fagots and a monk. On all four sides of the court the seated multitudes rose rank above rank, forming sloping terraces that were rich with colour. The King and the Queen sat in their thrones, the most conspicuous figures there, of course.

To note all this, occupied but a second. The next second Clarence had slipped from some place of concealment and was pouring news into my ear, his eyes beaming with triumph and gladness. He said:

"'Tis through *me* the change was wrought! And main hard have I worked to do it, too. But when I revealed to them the calamity in store, and saw how mighty was the terror it did engender, then saw I also that this was the time to strike! Wherefore I diligently pretended, unto this and that and the other one, that your power against the sun could not reach its full until the morrow; and so if any would save the sun and the world, you must be slain today, while your enchantments are but in the weaving and lack potency. Odsbodikins, it was but a dull lie, a most indifferent invention, but you should have seen them seize it and swallow it, in the frenzy of their fright, as it were salvation sent from heaven; and all the while was I laughing in my sleeve the one moment, to see them so cheaply deceived, and glorifying God the next, that He was content to let the meanest of His creatures be His instrument to the saving of thy life. Ah how happy has the matter sped! You will not need to do the sun a *real* hurt—ah, forget not that, on your soul forget it not! Only make a little darkness—only the littlest little darkness, mind, and cease with that. It will be sufficient. They will see that I spoke falsely—being ignorant, as they will fancy—and with the falling of the first shadow of that darkness you shall see them go mad with fear; and they will set you free and make you great! Go to thy triumph, now! But remember—ah, good friend, I implore thee remember my supplication, and do the blessed sun no hurt. For *my* sake, thy true friend."

I choked out some words through my grief and misery; as much as to say I would spare the sun; for which the lad's eyes paid me back with such deep and loving gratitude that I had not the heart to tell him his good-hearted foolishness had ruined me and sent me to my death.

As the soldiers assisted me across the court the stillness was so profound that if I had been blindfold I should have supposed I was in a solitude instead of walled in by four thousand people. There was not a movement perceptible in those masses of humanity; they were as rigid as stone images, and as pale; and dread sat upon every countenance. This hush continued while I was being chained to the stake; it still continued while the fagots were carefully and tediously piled about my ankles, my knees, my thighs, my body. Then there was a pause, and a deeper hush, if possible, and a man knelt down at my feet with a blazing torch; the multitude strained forward, gazing, and parting slightly from their seats without knowing it; the monk raised his hands above my head, and his eyes toward the blue sky, and began some words in Latin; in this attitude he droned on and on, a little while, and then stopped. I waited two or three moments; then looked up; he was standing there petrified. With a common impulse the multitude rose slowly up and stared into the sky. I followed their eyes, as sure as guns, there was my eclipse beginning! The life went boiling through my veins; I was a new man! The rim of black spread slowly into the sun's disk, my heart beat higher and higher, and still the assemblage and the priest stared into the sky, motionless. I knew that this gaze would be turned upon me, next. When it was, I was ready. I was in one of the most grand attitudes I ever struck, with my arm stretched up pointing to the sun. It was a noble effect. You could *see* the shudder sweep the mass like a wave. Two shouts rang out, one close upon the heels of the other:

"Apply the torch!"

"I forbid it!"

The one was from Merlin, the other from the king. Merlin started from his place—to apply the torch himself, I judged. I said:

"Stay where you are. If any man moves—even the king—before I give him leave, I will blast him with thunder, I will consume him with lightnings!"

The multitude sank meekly into their seats, and I was just expecting they would. Merlin hesitated a moment or two, and I was on pins and needles during that little while. Then he sat down, and I took a good breath; for I knew I was master of the situation now. The King said:

"Be merciful, fair sir, and essay no further in this perilous matter, lest disaster follow. It was reported to us that your powers could not attain unto their full strength until the morrow; but—"

"Your Majesty thinks the report may have been a lie? It *was* a lie."

That made an immense effect; up went appealing hands everywhere, and the king was assailed with a storm of supplications that I might be bought off at any price, and the calamity stayed. The King was eager to comply. He said:

"Name any terms, reverend sir, even to the halving of my kingdom; but banish this calamity, spare the sun!"

My fortune was made. I would have taken him up in a minute, but I couldn't stop an eclipse; the thing was out of the question. So I asked time to consider. The King said:

"How long—ah, how long, good sir? Be merciful; look, it groweth darker, moment by moment. Prithee how long?"

"Not long. Half an hour—maybe an hour."

There were a thousand pathetic protests, but I couldn't shorten up any, for I couldn't remember how long a total eclipse lasts. I was in a puzzled condition, anyway, and wanted to think. Something was wrong about that eclipse, and the fact was very unsettling. If this wasn't the one I was after, how was I to tell whether this was the sixth century, or nothing but a dream? Dear me, if I could only prove it was the latter! Here was a glad new hope. If the boy was right about the date, and this was surely the 20th, it *wasn't* the sixth century. I reached for the monk's sleeve, in considerable excitement, and asked him what day of the month it was.

Hang him, he said it was the *twenty-first*! It made me turn cold to hear him. I begged him not to make any mistake about it; but he was sure; he knew it was the 21st. So, that feather-headed boy had botched things again! The time of the day was right for the eclipse; I had seen that for myself, in the beginning, by the dial that was near by. Yes, I was in King Arthur's court, and I might as well make the most out of it I could.

The darkness was steadily growing, the people becoming more and more distressed. I now said:

"I have reflected, Sir King. For a lesson, I will let this darkness proceed, and spread night in the world; but whether I blot out the sun for good, or restore it, shall rest with you. These are the terms, to wit: You shall remain king over all your dominions, and receive all the glories and honours that belong to the kingship; but you shall appoint me your perpetual minister and executive, and give me for my services one per cent of such actual increase of revenue over and above its present amount as I may succeed in creating for the state. If I can't live on that, I sha'n't ask anybody to give me a lift. Is it satisfactory?"

There was a prodigious roar of applause, and out of the midst of it the king's voice rose, saying:

"Away with his bonds, and set him free! and do him homage, high and low, rich and poor, for he is become the king's right hand, is clothed with power and authority, and his seat is upon the highest step of the throne! Now sweep away this creeping night, and bring the light and cheer again, that all the world may bless thee."

But I said:

"That a common man should be shamed before the world, is nothing; but it were dishonour to the *King* if any that saw his minister naked should not also see him delivered from his shame. If I might ask that my clothes be brought again—"

"They are not meet," the King broke in. "Fetch raiment of another sort; clothe him like a prince!"

My idea worked. I wanted to keep things as they were till the eclipse was total, otherwise they would be trying again to get me to dismiss the darkness, and of course I couldn't do it. Sending for the clothes gained some delay, but not enough. So I had to make another excuse. I said it would be but natural if the king should change his mind and repent to some extent of what he had done under excitement; therefore I would let the darkness grow a while, and if at the end of a reasonable time the king had kept his mind the same, the darkness should be dismissed. Neither the King nor anybody else was satisfied with that arrangement, but I had to stick to my point.

It grew darker and darker and blacker and blacker, while I struggled with those awkward sixth-century clothes. It got to be pitch dark, at last, and the multitude groaned with horror to feel the cold uncanny night breezes fan through the place and see the stars come out and twinkle in the sky. At last the eclipse was total, and I was very glad of it, but everybody else was in misery; which was quite natural. I said:

"The King, by his silence, still stands to the terms." Then I lifted up my hands—stood just so a moment—then I said, with the most awful solemnity: "Let the enchantment dissolve and pass harmless away!"

There was no response, for a moment, in that deep darkness and that graveyard hush. But when the silver rim of the sun pushed itself out, a moment or two later, the assemblage broke loose with a vast shout and came pouring down like a deluge to smother me with blessings and gratitude; and Clarence was not the last of the wash, to be sure.

7

Merlin's Tower

Inasmuch as I was now the second personage in the Kingdom, as far as political power and authority were concerned, much was made of me. My raiment was of silks and velvets and cloth of gold, and by consequence was very showy, also uncomfortable. But habit would soon reconcile me to my clothes; I was aware of that. I was given the choicest suite of apartments in the castle, after the King's. They were aglow with loud-coloured silken hangings, but the stone floors had nothing but rushes on them for a carpet, and they were misfit rushes at that, being not all of one breed. As for conveniences, properly speaking, there weren't any. I mean *little* conveniences; it is the little conveniences that make the real comfort of life. The big oaken chairs, graced with rude carvings, were well enough, but that was the stopping place. There was no soap, no matches, no looking glass—except a metal one, about as powerful as a pail of water. And not a chromo. I had been used to chromos for years, and I saw now that without my suspecting it a passion for art had got worked into the fabric of my being, and was become a part of me.

"There was no soap, no matches, no looking glass"

It made me homesick to look around over this proud and gaudy but heartless barrenness and remember that in our house in East Hartford, all unpretending as it was, you couldn't go into a room but you would find an insurance-chromo, or at least a three-colour God-Bless-Our-Home over the door; and in the parlour we had nine. But here, even in my grand room of state, there wasn't anything in the nature of a picture except a thing the size of a bed-quilt, which was either woven or knitted (it had darned places in it), and nothing in it was the right colour or the right shape; and as for proportions, even Raphael himself couldn't have botched them more formidably, after all his practice on those nightmares they call his "celebrated Hampton Court cartoons." Raphael was a bird. We had several of his chromos; one was his "Miraculous Draught of Fishes," where he puts in a miracle of his own—puts three men into a canoe which wouldn't have held a dog without upsetting. I always admired to study R.'s art, it was so fresh and unconventional.

There wasn't even a bell or a speaking-tube in the castle. I had a great many servants, and those that were on duty lolled in the anteroom; and when I wanted one of them I had to go and call for him. There was no gas, there were no candles; a bronze dish half full of boarding-house butter with a blazing rag floating in it was the thing that produced what was regarded as light. A lot of these hung along the walls and modified the dark, just toned it down enough to make it dismal. If you went out at night, your servants carried torches. There were no books, pens, paper or ink, and no glass in the openings they believed to be windows. It is a little thing—glass is—until it is absent, then it becomes a big thing. But perhaps the worst of all was, that there wasn't any sugar, coffee, tea, or tobacco. I saw that I was just another Robinson Crusoe cast away on an uninhabited island, with no society but some more or less tame animals, and if I wanted to make life bearable I must do as he did—invent, contrive, create, reorganize things; set brain and hand to work, and keep them busy. Well, that was in my line.

One thing troubled me along at first—the immense interest which people took in me. Apparently the whole nation wanted a look at me. It soon transpired that the eclipse had scared the British world almost to death; that while it lasted the whole country, from one end to the other, was in a pitiable state of panic, and the churches, hermitages, and monkeries overflowed with praying and weeping poor creatures who thought the end of the world was come. Then had followed the news that the producer of this awful event was a stranger, a mighty magician at Arthur's Court; that he could have blown out the sun like a candle, and was just going to do it when his mercy was purchased, and he then dissolved his enchantments, and was now recognized and honoured as the man who had by his unaided might saved the globe from destruction and its peoples from extinction. Now if you consider that everybody believed that, and not only believed it, but never even dreamed of doubting it, you will easily understand that there was not a person in all Britain that would not have walked fifty miles to get a sight of me. Of course I was all the talk—all other subjects were dropped;

even the king became suddenly a person of minor interest and notoriety. Within twenty-four hours the delegations began to arrive, and from that time onward for a fortnight they kept coming. The village was crowded, and all the countryside. I had to go out a dozen times a day and show myself to these reverent and awe-stricken multitudes.

"The reverent and awe-stricken multitudes."

It came to be a great burden, as to time and trouble, but of course it was at the same time compensatingly agreeable to be so celebrated and such a center of homage. It turned Brer Merlin green with envy and spite, which was a great satisfaction to me. But there was one thing I couldn't understand—nobody had asked for an autograph. I spoke to Clarence about it. By George! I had to explain to him what it was. Then he said nobody in the country could read or write but a few dozen priests. Land! think of that.

There was another thing that troubled me a little. Those multitudes presently began to agitate for another miracle. That was natural. To be able to carry back to their far homes the boast that they had seen the man who could command the sun, riding in the heavens, and be obeyed, would make them great in the eyes of their neighbours, and envied by them all; but to be able to also say they had seen him work a miracle themselves—why, people would come a distance to see *them.* The pressure got to be pretty strong. There was going to be an eclipse of the moon, and I knew the date and hour, but it was too far away. Two years. I would have given a good deal for license to hurry it up and use it now when there was a big market for it. It seemed a great pity to have it wasted so, and come lagging along at a time when a body wouldn't have any use for it, as like as not. If it had been booked for only a month away, I could have sold it short; but, as matters stood, I couldn't seem to cipher out any way to make it do me any good, so I gave up trying. Next, Clarence found that old Merlin was making himself busy on the sly among those people. He was spreading a report that I was a humbug, and that the reason I didn't accommodate the people with a miracle was because I couldn't. I saw that I must do something. I presently thought out a plan.

By my authority as executive I threw Merlin into prison—the same cell I had occupied myself. Then I gave public notice by herald and trumpet that I should be busy with affairs of state for a fortnight, but about the end of that time I would take a moment's leisure and blow up Merlin's stone tower by fires from heaven; in the meantime, whoso listened to evil reports about me, let him beware. Furthermore, I would perform but this one miracle at this time, and no more; if it failed to satisfy and any murmured, I would turn the murmurers into horses, and make them useful. Quiet ensued.

I took Clarence into my confidence, to a certain degree, and we went to work privately. I told him that this was a sort of miracle that required a trifle of preparation, and that it would be sudden death to ever talk about these preparations to anybody. That made his mouth safe enough. Clandestinely we made a few bushels of first-rate blasting powder, and I superintended my armorers while they constructed a lightning-rod and some wires. This old stone tower was very massive—and rather ruinous, too, for it was Roman, and four hundred years old. Yes, and handsome, after a rude fashion, and clothed with ivy from base to summit, as with a shirt of scale mail. It stood on a lonely eminence, in good view from the castle, and about half a mile away.

Working by night, we stowed the powder in the tower—dug stones out, on the inside, and buried the powder in the walls themselves, which were fifteen feet thick at the base. We put in a peck at a time, in a dozen places. We could have blown up the Tower of London with these charges. When the thirteenth night was come we put up our lightning-rod, bedded it in one of the batches of powder, and ran wires from it to the other batches. Everybody had shunned that locality from the day of my proclamation, but on the morning of the fourteenth I thought best to warn the people, through the heralds, to keep clear away—a quarter of a mile away. Then added, by command, that at some time during the twenty-four hours I would consummate the miracle, but would first give a brief notice; by flags on the castle towers if in the daytime, by torch-baskets in the same places if at night.

Thunder-showers had been tolerably frequent of late, and I was not much afraid of a failure; still, I shouldn't have cared for a delay of a day or two; I should have explained that I was busy with affairs of state yet, and the people must wait.

Of course, we had a blazing sunny day—almost the first one without a cloud for three weeks; things always happen so. I kept secluded, and watched the weather. Clarence dropped in from time to time and said the public excitement was growing and growing all the time, and the whole country filling up with human masses as far as one could see from the battlements. At last the wind sprang up and a cloud appeared—in the right quarter, too, and just at nightfall. For a little while I watched that distant cloud spread and blacken, then I judged it was time for me to appear. I ordered the torch-baskets to be lit, and Merlin liberated and sent to me. A quarter of an hour later I ascended the parapet and there found the king and the court assembled and gazing off in the darkness toward Merlin's Tower. Already the darkness was so heavy that one could not see far; these people and the old turrets, being partly in deep shadow and partly in the red glow from the great torch-baskets overhead, made a good deal of a picture.

Merlin arrived in a gloomy mood. I said:

"You wanted to burn me alive when I had not done you any harm, and latterly you have been trying to injure my professional reputation. Therefore I am going to call down fire and blow up your tower, but it is only fair to give you a chance; now if you think you can break my enchantments and ward off the fires, step to the bat, it's your innings."

"I can, fair sir, and I will. Doubt it not."

He drew an imaginary circle on the stones of the roof, and burnt a pinch of powder in it, which sent up a small cloud of aromatic smoke, whereat everybody fell back and began to cross themselves and get uncomfortable. Then he began to mutter and make passes in the air with his hands. He worked himself up slowly and gradually into a sort of frenzy, and got to thrashing around with his arms like the sails of a windmill. By this time the storm had about reached us; the gusts of wind were flaring the torches and making the shadows swash about, the first heavy drops of rain were falling, the world abroad was black as pitch, the lightning began to wink fitfully. Of course, my rod would be loading itself now. In fact, things were imminent. So I said:

"You have had time enough. I have given you every advantage, and not interfered. It is plain your magic is weak. It is only fair that I begin now."

I made about three passes in the air, and then there was an awful crash and that old tower leaped into the sky in chunks, along with a vast volcanic fountain of fire that turned night to noonday, and showed a thousand acres of human beings groveling on the ground in a general collapse of consternation. Well, it rained mortar and masonry the rest of the week. This was the report; but probably the facts would have modified it.

It was an effective miracle. The great bothersome temporary population vanished. There were a good many thousand tracks in the mud the next morning, but they were all outward bound. If I had advertised another miracle I couldn't have raised an audience with a sheriff.

Merlin's stock was flat. The king wanted to stop his wages; he even wanted to banish him, but I interfered. I said he would be useful to work the weather, and attend to small matters like that, and I would give him a lift now and then when his poor little parlour-magic soured on him. There wasn't a rag of his tower left, but I had the government rebuild it for him, and advised him to take boarders; but he was too high-toned for that. And as for being grateful, he never even said thank you. He was a rather hard lot, take him how you might; but then you couldn't fairly expect a man to be sweet that had been set back so.

8

The Boss

To be vested with enormous authority is a fine thing; but to have the on-looking world consent to it is a finer. The tower episode solidified my power, and made it impregnable. If any were perchance disposed to be jealous and critical before that, they experienced a change of heart, now. There was not any one in the kingdom who would have considered it good judgment to meddle with my matters.

I was fast getting adjusted to my situation and circumstances. For a time, I used to wake up, mornings, and smile at my "dream," and listen for the Colt's factory whistle; but that sort of thing played itself out, gradually, and at last I was fully able to realize that I was actually living in the sixth century, and in Arthur's court, not a lunatic asylum. After that, I was just as much at home in that century as I could have been in any other; and as for preference, I wouldn't have traded it for the twentieth. Look at the opportunities here for a man of knowledge, brains, pluck, and enterprise to sail in and grow up with the country. The grandest field that ever was; and all my own; not a competitor; not a man who wasn't a baby to me in acquirements and capacities; whereas, what would I amount to in the twentieth century? I should be foreman of a factory, that is about all; and could drag a seine down street any day and catch a hundred better men than myself.

What a jump I had made! I couldn't keep from thinking about it, and contemplating it, just as one does who has struck oil. There was nothing back of me that could approach it, unless it might be Joseph's case; and Joseph's only approached it, it didn't equal it, quite. For it stands to reason that as Joseph's splendid financial ingenuities advantaged nobody but the king, the general public must have regarded him with a good deal of disfavour, whereas I had done my entire public a kindness in sparing the sun, and was popular by reason of it.

I was no shadow of a King; I was the substance; the King himself was the shadow. My power was colossal; and it was not a mere name, as such things have generally been, it was the genuine article. I stood here, at the very spring and source of the second great period of the world's history; and could see the trickling stream of that history gather and deepen and broaden, and roll its mighty tides down the far centuries; and I could note the upspringing of adventurers like myself in the shelter of its long array of thrones: De Montforts, Gavestons, Mortimers, Villierses; the war-making, campaign-directing wantons of France, and Charles the Second's scepter-wielding drabs; but nowhere in the procession was my full-sized fellow visible. I was a Unique; and glad to know that that fact could not be dislodged or challenged for thirteen centuries and a half, for sure. Yes, in power I was equal to the king. At the same time there was another power that was a trifle stronger than both of us put together. That was the Church. I do not wish to disguise that fact. I couldn't, if I wanted to. But never mind about that, now; it will show up, in its proper place, later on. It didn't cause me any trouble in the beginning—at least any of consequence.

Well, it was a curious country, and full of interest. And the people! They were the quaintest and simplest and trustingest race; why, they were nothing but rabbits. It was pitiful for a person born in a wholesome free atmosphere to listen to their humble and hearty outpourings of loyalty toward their king and Church and nobility; as if they had any more occasion to love and honour king and Church and noble than a slave has to love and honour the lash, or a dog has to love and honour the stranger that kicks him! Why, dear me, *any* kind of royalty, howsoever modified, *any* kind of aristocracy, howsoever pruned, is rightly an insult; but if you are born and brought up under that sort of arrangement you probably never find it out for yourself, and don't believe it when somebody else tells you. It is enough to make a body ashamed of his race to think of the sort of froth that has always occupied its thrones without shadow of right or reason, and the seventh-rate people that have always figured as its aristocracies—a company of monarchs and nobles who, as a rule, would have achieved only poverty and obscurity if left, like their betters, to their own exertions.

The most of King Arthur's British nation were slaves, pure and simple, and bore that name, and wore the iron collar on their necks; and the rest were slaves in fact, but without the name; they imagined themselves men and freemen, and called themselves so. The truth was, the nation as a body was in the world for one object, and one only: to grovel before king and Church and noble; to slave for them, sweat blood for them, starve that they might be fed, work that they might play, drink misery to the dregs that they might be happy, go naked that they might wear silks and jewels, pay taxes that they might be spared from paying them, be familiar all their lives with the degrading language and postures of adulation that they might walk in pride and think themselves the gods of this world. And for all this, the thanks they got were cuffs and contempt; and so poor-spirited were they that they took even this sort of attention as an honour.

Inherited ideas are a curious thing, and interesting to observe and examine. I had mine, the King and his people had theirs. In both cases they flowed in ruts worn deep by time and habit, and the man who should have proposed to divert them by reason and argument would have had a long contract on his hands. For instance, those people had inherited the idea that all men without title and a long pedigree, whether they had great natural gifts and acquirements or hadn't, were creatures of no more consideration than so many animals, bugs, insects; whereas I had inherited the idea that human daws who can consent to masquerade in the peacock-shams of inherited dignities and unearned titles, are of no good but to be laughed at. The way I was looked upon was odd, but it was natural. You know how the keeper and the public regard the elephant in the menagerie: well, that is the idea. They are full of admiration of his vast bulk and his prodigious strength; they speak with pride of the fact that he can do a hundred marvels which are far and away beyond their own powers; and they speak with the same pride of the fact that in his wrath he is able to drive a thousand men before him. But does that make him one of *them*? No; the raggedest tramp in the pit would smile at the idea. He couldn't comprehend it; couldn't take it in; couldn't in any remote way conceive of it. Well, to the king, the nobles, and all the nation, down to the very slaves and tramps, I was just that kind of an elephant, and nothing more. I was admired, also feared; but it was as an animal is admired and feared. The animal is not reverenced, neither was I; I was not even respected. I had no pedigree, no inherited title; so in the King's and nobles' eyes I was mere dirt; the people regarded me with wonder and awe, but there was no reverence mixed with it; through the force of inherited ideas they were not able to conceive of anything being entitled to that except pedigree and lordship. There you see the hand of that awful power, the Roman Catholic Church. In two or three little centuries it had converted a nation of men to a nation of worms. Before the day of the Church's supremacy in the world, men were men, and held their heads up, and had a man's pride and spirit and independence; and what of greatness and position a person got, he got mainly by achievement, not by birth. But then the Church came to the front, with an axe to grind; and she was wise, subtle, and knew more than one way to skin a cat—or a nation; she invented "divine right of kings," and propped it all around, brick by brick, with the Beatitudes—wrenching them from their good purpose to make them fortify an evil one; she preached (to the commoner) humility, obedience to superiors, the beauty of self-sacrifice; she preached (to the commoner) meekness under insult; preached (still to the commoner, always to the commoner) patience, meanness of spirit, non-resistance under oppression; and she introduced heritable ranks and aristocracies, and taught all the Christian populations of the earth to bow down to them and worship them.

Even down to my birth-century that poison was still in the blood of Christendom, and the best of English commoners was still content to see his inferiors impudently continuing to hold a number of positions, such as lordships and the throne, to which the grotesque laws of his country did not allow him to aspire; in fact, he was not merely contented with this strange condition of things, he was even able to persuade himself that he was proud of it. It seems to show that there isn't anything you can't stand, if you are only born and bred to it. Of course that taint, that reverence for rank and title, had been in our American blood, too—I know that; but when I left America it had disappeared—at least to all intents and purposes. The remnant of it was restricted to the dudes and dudesses. When a disease has worked its way down to that level, it may fairly be said to be out of the system.

But to return to my anomalous position in King Arthur's kingdom. Here I was, a giant among pigmies, a man among children, a master intelligence among intellectual moles: by all rational measurement the one and only actually great man in that whole British world; and yet there and then, just as in the remote England of my birth-time, the sheep-witted earl who could claim long descent from a King's leman, acquired at second-hand from the slums of London, was a better man than I was. Such a personage was fawned upon in Arthur's realm and reverently looked up to by everybody, even though his dispositions were as mean as his intelligence, and his morals as base as his lineage. There were times when *he* could sit down in the King's presence, but I couldn't. I could have got a title easily enough, and that would have raised me a large step in everybody's eyes; even in the King's, the giver of it. But I didn't ask for it; and I declined it when it was offered. I couldn't have enjoyed such a thing with my notions; and it wouldn't have been fair, anyway, because as far back as I could go, our tribe had always been short of the bar sinister. I couldn't have felt really and satisfactorily fine and proud and set-up over any title except one that should come from the nation itself, the only legitimate source; and such an one I hoped to win; and in the course of years of honest and honourable endeavor, I did win it and did wear it with a high and clean pride. This title fell casually from the lips of a blacksmith, one day, in a village, was caught up as a happy thought and tossed from mouth to mouth with a laugh and an affirmative vote; in ten days it had swept the kingdom, and was become as familiar as the King's name. I was never known by any other designation afterward, whether in the nation's talk or in grave debate upon matters of state at the council-board of the sovereign. This title, translated into modern speech, would be THE BOSS. Elected by the nation. That suited me. And it was a pretty high title. There were very few *the's*, and I was one of them. If you spoke of the duke, or the earl, or the bishop, how could anybody tell which one you meant? But if you spoke of The King or The Queen or The Boss, it was different.

Well, I liked the King, and *as* King I respected him—respected the office; at least respected it as much as I was capable of respecting any unearned supremacy; but as *men* I looked down upon him and his nobles—privately. And he and they liked me, and respected my office; but as an animal, without birth or sham title, they looked down upon me—and were not particularly private about it, either. I didn't charge for my opinion about them, and they didn't charge for their opinion about me: the account was square, the books balanced, everybody was satisfied.

9

The Tournament

They were always having grand tournaments there at Camelot; and very stirring and picturesque and ridiculous human bull-fights they were, too, but just a little wearisome to the practical mind. However, I was generally on hand—for two reasons: a man must not hold himself aloof from the things which his friends and his community have at heart if he would be liked—especially as a statesman; and both as business man and statesman I wanted to study the tournament and see if I couldn't invent an improvement on it. That reminds me to remark, in passing, that the very first official thing I did, in my administration—and it was on the very first day of it, too—was to start a patent office; for I knew that a country without a patent office and good patent laws was just a crab, and couldn't travel any way but sideways or backways.

Things ran along, a tournament nearly every week; and now and then the boys used to want me to take a hand—I mean Sir Launcelot and the rest—but I said I would by and by; no hurry yet, and too much government machinery to oil up and set to rights and start a-going.

We had one tournament which was continued from day to day during more than a week, and as many as five hundred knights took part in it, from first to last. They were weeks gathering. They came on horseback from everywhere; from the very ends of the country, and even from beyond the sea; and many brought ladies, and all brought squires and troops of servants. It was a most gaudy and gorgeous crowd, as to costumery, and very characteristic of the country and the time, in the way of high animal spirits, innocent indecencies of language, and happy-hearted indifference to morals. It was fight or look on, all day and every day; and sing, gamble, dance, carouse half the night every night. They had a most noble good time. You never saw such people. Those banks of beautiful ladies, shining in their barbaric splendours, would see a knight sprawl from his horse in the lists with a lance-shaft the thickness of your ankle clean through him and the blood spouting, and instead of fainting they would clap their hands and crowd each other for a better view; only sometimes one would dive into her handkerchief, and look ostentatiously broken-hearted, and then you could lay two to one that there was a scandal there somewhere and she was afraid the public hadn't found it out.

The noise at night would have been annoying to me ordinarily, but I didn't mind it in the present circumstances, because it kept me from hearing the quacks detaching legs and arms from the day's cripples. They ruined an uncommon good old cross-cut saw for me, and broke the saw-buck, too, but I let it pass. And as for my axe—well, I made up my mind that the next time I lent an axe to a surgeon I would pick my century.

I not only watched this tournament from day to day, but detailed an intelligent priest from my Department of Public Morals and Agriculture, and ordered him to report it; for it was my purpose by and by, when I should have gotten the people along far enough, to start a newspaper. The first thing you want in a new country, is a patent office; then work up your school system; and after that, out with your paper. A newspaper has its faults, and plenty of them, but no matter, it's hark from the tomb for a dead nation, and don't you forget it. You can't resurrect a dead nation without it; there isn't any way. So I wanted to sample things, and be finding out what sort of reporter-material I might be able to rake together out of the sixth century when I should come to need it.

Well, the priest did very well, considering. He got in all the details, and that is a good thing in a local item: you see, he had kept books for the undertaker-department of his church when he was younger, and there, you know, the money's in the details; the more details, the more swag: bearers, mutes, candles, prayers—everything counts; and if the bereaved don't buy prayers enough you mark up your candles with a forked pencil, and your bill shows up all right. And he had a good knack at getting in the complimentary thing here and there about a knight that was likely to advertise—no, I mean a knight that had influence; and he also had a neat gift of exaggeration, for in his time he had kept door for a pious hermit who lived in a sty and worked miracles.

Of course this novice's report lacked whoop and crash and lurid description, and therefore wanted the true ring; but its antique wording was quaint and sweet and simple, and full of the fragrances and flavors of the time, and these little merits made up in a measure for its more important lacks. Here is an extract from it:

> *Then Sir Brian de les Isles and Grummore Grummorsum, knights of the castle, encountered with Sir Aglovale and Sir Tor, and Sir Tor smote down Sir Grummore Grummorsum*

to the earth. Then came Sir Carados of the dolorous tower, and Sir Turquine, knights of the castle, and there encountered with them Sir Percivale de Galis and Sir Lamorak de Galis, that were two brethren, and there encountered Sir Percivale with Sir Carados, and either brake their spears unto their hands, and then Sir Turquine with Sir Lamorak, and either of them smote down other, horse and all, to the earth, and either parties rescued other and horsed them again. And Sir Arnold, and Sir Gauter, knights of the castle, encountered with Sir Brandiles and Sir Kay, and these four knights encountered mightily, and brake their spears to their hands. Then came Sir Pertolope from the castle, and there encountered with him Sir Lionel, and there Sir Pertolope the green knight smote down Sir Lionel, brother to Sir Launcelot. All this was marked by noble heralds, who bare him best, and their names. Then Sir Bleobaris brake his spear upon Sir Gareth, but of that stroke Sir Bleobaris fell to the earth. When Sir Galihodin saw that, he bad Sir Gareth keep him, and Sir Gareth smote him to the earth. Then Sir Galihud gat a spear to avenge his brother, and in the same wise Sir Gareth served him, and Sir Dinadan and his brother La Cote Male Taile, and Sir Sagramore le Disirous, and Sir Dodinas le Savage; all these he bare down with one spear. When King Aswisance of Ireland saw Sir Gareth fare so he marvelled what he might be, that one time seemed green, and another time, at his again coming, he seemed blue. And thus at every course that he rode to and fro he changed his colour, so that there might neither king nor knight have ready cognizance of him. Then Sir Agwisance the King of Ireland encountered with Sir Gareth, and there Sir Gareth smote him from his horse, saddle and all. And then came King Carados of Scotland, and Sir Gareth smote him down horse and man. And in the same wise he served King Uriens of the land of Gore. And then there came in Sir Bagdemagus, and Sir Gareth smote him down horse and man to the earth. And Bagdemagus's son Meliganus brake a spear upon Sir Gareth mightily and knightly. And then Sir

Galahault the noble prince cried on high, Knight with the many colours, well hast thou justed; now make thee ready that I may just with thee. Sir Gareth heard him, and he gat a great spear, and so they encountered together, and there the prince brake his spear; but Sir Gareth smote him upon the left side of the helm, that he reeled here and there, and he had fallen down had not his men recovered him. Truly, said King Arthur, that knight with the many colours is a good knight. Wherefore the king called unto him Sir Launcelot, and prayed him to encounter with that knight. Sir, said Launcelot, I may as well find in my heart for to forbear him at this time, for he hath had travail enough this day, and when a good knight doth so well upon some day, it is no good knight's part to let him of his worship, and, namely, when he seeth a knight hath done so great labour; for peradventure, said Sir Launcelot, his quarrel is here this day, and peradventure he is best beloved with this lady of all that be here, for I see well he paineth himself and enforceth him to do great deeds, and therefore, said Sir Launcelot, as for me, this day he shall have the honour; though it lay in my power to put him from it, I would not.

There was an unpleasant little episode that day, which for reasons of state I struck out of my priest's report. You will have noticed that Garry was doing some great fighting in the engagement. When I say Garry I mean Sir Gareth. Garry was my private pet name for him; it suggests that I had a deep affection for him, and that was the case. But it was a private pet name only, and never spoken aloud to any one, much less to him; being a noble, he would not have endured a familiarity like that from me. Well, to proceed: I sat in the private box set apart for me as the King's minister. While Sir Dinadan was waiting for his turn to enter the lists, he came in there and sat down and began to talk; for he was always making up to me, because I was a stranger and he liked to have a fresh market for his jokes, the most of them having reached that stage of wear where the teller has to do the laughing himself while the other person looks sick. I had always responded to his efforts as well as I could, and felt a very deep and real kindness for him, too, for the reason that if by malice of fate he knew the one particular anecdote which I had heard oftenest and had most hated and most loathed all my life, he had at least spared it me. It was one which I had heard attributed to every humorous person who had ever stood on American soil, from Columbus down to Artemus Ward. It was about a humorous lecturer who flooded an ignorant audience with the killingest jokes for an hour and never got a laugh; and then when he was leaving, some grey simpletons wrung him gratefully by the hand and said it had been the funniest thing they had ever heard, and "it was all they could do to keep from laughin' right out in meetin'." That anecdote never saw the day that it was worth the telling; and yet I had sat under the telling of it hundreds and thousands and millions and billions of times, and cried and cursed all the way through. Then who can hope to know what my feelings were, to hear this armor-plated ass start in on it again, in the murky twilight of tradition, before the dawn of history, while even Lactantius might be referred to as "the late Lactantius," and the Crusades wouldn't be born for five hundred years yet? Just as he finished, the call-boy came; so, haw-hawing like a demon, he went rattling and clanking out like a crate of loose castings, and I knew nothing more. It was some minutes before I came to, and then I opened my eyes just in time to see Sir Gareth fetch him an awful welt, and I unconsciously out with the prayer, "I hope to gracious he's killed!" But by ill-luck, before I had got half through with the words, Sir Gareth crashed into Sir Sagramor le Desirous and sent him thundering over his horse's crupper, and Sir Sagramor caught my remark and thought I meant it for *him*.

Well, whenever one of those people got a thing into his head, there was no getting it out again. I knew that, so I saved my breath, and offered no explanations. As soon as Sir Sagramor got well, he notified me that there was a little account to settle between us, and he named a day three or four years in the future; place of settlement, the lists where the offense had been given. I said I would be ready when he got back. You see, he was going for the Holy Grail. The boys all took a flier at the Holy Grail now and then. It was a several years' cruise. They always put in the long absence snooping around, in the most conscientious way, though none of them had any idea where the Holy Grail really was, and I don't think any of them actually expected to find it, or would have known what to do with it if he *had* run across it. You see, it was just the Northwest Passage of that day, as you may say; that was all. Every year expeditions went out holy grailing, and next year relief expeditions went out to hunt for *them*. There was worlds of reputation in it, but no money. Why, they actually wanted *me* to put in! Well, I should smile.

10

Beginnings of Civilization

The Round Table soon heard of the challenge, and of course it was a good deal discussed, for such things interested the boys. The king thought I ought now to set forth in quest of adventures, so that I might gain renown and be the more worthy to meet Sir Sagramor when the several years should have rolled away. I excused myself for the present; I said it would take me three or four years yet to get things well fixed up and going smoothly; then I should be ready; all the chances were that at the end of that time Sir Sagramor would still be out grailing, so no valuable time would be lost by the postponement; I should then have been in office six or seven years, and I believed my system and machinery would be so well developed that I could take a holiday without its working any harm.

I was pretty well satisfied with what I had already accomplished. In various quiet nooks and corners I had the beginnings of all sorts of industries under way—nuclei of future vast factories, the iron and steel missionaries of my future civilization. In these were gathered together the brightest young minds I could find, and I kept agents out raking the country for more, all the time. I was training a crowd of ignorant folk into experts—experts in every sort of handiwork and scientific calling. These nurseries of mine went smoothly and privately along undisturbed in their obscure country retreats, for nobody was allowed to come into their precincts without a special permit—for I was afraid of the Church.

I had started a teacher-factory and a lot of Sunday-schools the first thing; as a result, I now had an admirable system of graded schools in full blast in those places, and also a complete variety of Protestant congregations all in a prosperous and growing condition. Everybody could be any kind of a Christian he wanted to; there was perfect freedom in that matter. But I confined public religious teaching to the churches and the Sunday-schools, permitting nothing of it in my other educational buildings. I could have given my own sect the preference and made everybody a Presbyterian without any trouble, but that would have been to affront a law of human nature: spiritual wants and instincts are as various in the human family as are physical appetites, complexions, and features, and a man is only at his best, morally, when he is equipped with the religious garment whose colour and shape and size most nicely accommodate themselves to the spiritual complexion, angularities, and stature of the individual who wears it; and, besides, I was afraid of a united Church; it makes a mighty power, the mightiest conceivable, and then when it by and by gets into selfish hands, as it is always bound to do, it means death to human liberty and paralysis to human thought.

All mines were royal property, and there were a good many of them. They had formerly been worked as savages always work mines—holes grubbed in the earth and the mineral brought up in sacks of hide by hand, at the rate of a ton a day; but I had begun to put the mining on a scientific basis as early as I could.

Yes, I had made pretty handsome progress when Sir Sagramor's challenge struck me.

Four years rolled by—and then! Well, you would never imagine it in the world. Unlimited power is the ideal thing when it is in safe hands. The despotism of heaven is the one absolutely perfect government. An earthly despotism would be the absolutely perfect earthly government, if the conditions were the same, namely, the despot the perfectest individual of the human race, and his lease of life perpetual. But as a perishable perfect man must die, and leave his despotism in the hands of an imperfect successor, an earthly despotism is not merely a bad form of government, it is the worst form that is possible.

My works showed what a despot could do with the resources of a kingdom at his command. Unsuspected by this dark land, I had the civilization of the nineteenth century booming under its very nose! It was fenced away from the public view, but there it was, a gigantic and unassailable fact—and to be heard from, yet, if I lived and had luck. There it was, as sure a fact and as substantial a fact as any serene volcano, standing innocent with its smokeless summit in the blue sky and giving no sign of the rising hell in its bowels. My schools and churches were children four years before; they were grown-up now; my shops of that day were vast factories now; where I had a dozen trained men then, I had a thousand now; where I had one brilliant expert then, I had fifty now. I stood with my hand on the cock, so to speak, ready to turn it on and flood the midnight world with light at any moment. But I was not going to do the thing in that sudden way. It was not my policy. The people could not have stood it; and, moreover, I should have had the Established Roman Catholic Church on my back in a minute.

No, I had been going cautiously all the while. I had had confidential agents trickling through the country some time, whose office was to undermine knighthood by imperceptible degrees, and to gnaw a little at this and that and the other superstition, and so prepare the way gradually for a better order of things. I was turning on my light one-candle-power at a time, and meant to continue to do so.

I had scattered some branch schools secretly about the kingdom, and they were doing very well. I meant to work this racket more and more, as time wore on, if nothing occurred to frighten me. One of my deepest secrets was my West Point—my military academy. I kept that most jealously out of sight; and I did the same with my naval academy which I had established at a remote seaport. Both were prospering to my satisfaction.

Clarence was twenty-two now, and was my head executive, my right hand. He was a darling; he was equal to anything; there wasn't anything he couldn't turn his hand to. Of late I had been training him for journalism, for the time seemed about right for a start in the newspaper line; nothing big, but just a small weekly for experimental circulation in my civilization-nurseries. He took to it like a duck; there was an editor concealed in him, sure. Already he had doubled himself in one way; he talked sixth century and wrote nineteenth. His journalistic style was climbing, steadily; it was already up to the back settlement Alabama mark, and couldn't be told from the editorial output of that region either by matter or flavor.

We had another large departure on hand, too. This was a telegraph and a telephone; our first venture in this line. These wires were for private service only, as yet, and must be kept private until a riper day should come. We had a gang of men on the road, working mainly by night. They were stringing ground wires; we were afraid to put up poles, for they would attract too much inquiry. Ground wires were good enough, in both instances, for my wires were protected by an insulation of my own invention which was perfect. My men had orders to strike across country, avoiding roads, and establishing connection with any considerable towns whose lights betrayed their presence, and leaving experts in charge. Nobody could tell you how to find any place in the kingdom, for nobody ever went intentionally to any place, but only struck it by accident in his wanderings, and then generally left it without thinking to inquire what its name was. At one time and another we had sent out topographical expeditions to survey and map the kingdom, but the priests had always interfered and raised trouble. So we had given the thing up, for the present; it would be poor wisdom to antagonize the Church.

As for the general condition of the country, it was as it had been when I arrived in it, to all intents and purposes. I had made changes, but they were necessarily slight, and they were not noticeable. Thus far, I had not even meddled with taxation, outside of the taxes which provided the royal revenues. I had systematized those, and put the service on an effective and righteous basis. As a result, these revenues were already quadrupled, and yet the burden was so much more equably distributed than before, that all the kingdom felt a sense of relief, and the praises of my administration were hearty and general.

Personally, I struck an interruption, now, but I did not mind it, it could not have happened at a better time. Earlier it could have annoyed me, but now everything was in good hands and swimming right along. The king had reminded me several times, of late, that the postponement I had asked for, four years before, had about run out now. It was a hint that I ought to be starting out to seek adventures and get up a reputation of a size to make me worthy of the honour of breaking a lance with Sir Sagramor, who was still out grailing, but was being hunted for by various relief expeditions, and might be found any year, now. So you see I was expecting this interruption; it did not take me by surprise.

11

The Yankee in Search of Adventures

There never was such a country for wandering liars; and they were of both sexes. Hardly a month went by without one of these tramps arriving; and generally loaded with a tale about some princess or other wanting help to get her out of some far-away castle where she was held in captivity by a lawless scoundrel, usually a giant. Now you would think that the first thing the king would do after listening to such a novelette from an entire stranger, would be to ask for credentials—yes, and a pointer or two as to locality of castle, best route to it, and so on. But nobody ever thought of so simple and common-sense a thing at that. No, everybody swallowed these people's lies whole, and never asked a question of any sort or about anything. Well, one day when I was not around, one of these people came along—it was a she one, this time—and told a tale of the usual pattern. Her mistress was a captive in a vast and gloomy castle, along with forty-four other young and beautiful girls, pretty much all of them princesses; they had been languishing in that cruel captivity for twenty-six years; the masters of the castle were three stupendous brothers, each with four arms and one eye—the eye in the center of the forehead, and as big as a fruit. Sort of fruit not mentioned; their usual slovenliness in statistics.

Would you believe it? The king and the whole Round Table were in raptures over this preposterous opportunity for adventure. Every knight of the Table jumped for the chance, and begged for it; but to their vexation and chagrin the king conferred it upon me, who had not asked for it at all.

By an effort, I contained my joy when Clarence brought me the news. But he—he could not contain his. His mouth gushed delight and gratitude in a steady discharge—delight in my good fortune, gratitude to the king for this splendid mark of his favour for me. He could keep neither his legs nor his body still, but pirouetted about the place in an airy ecstasy of happiness.

On my side, I could have cursed the kindness that conferred upon me this benefaction, but I kept my vexation under the surface for policy's sake, and did what I could to let on to be glad. Indeed, I *said* I was glad. And in a way it was true; I was as glad as a person is when he is scalped.

Well, one must make the best of things, and not waste time with useless fretting, but get down to business and see what can be done. In all lies there is wheat among the chaff; I must get at the wheat in this case: so I sent for the girl and she came. She was a comely enough creature, and soft and modest, but, if signs went for anything, she didn't know as much as a lady's watch. I said:

"My dear, have you been questioned as to particulars?"

She said she hadn't.

"Well, I didn't expect you had, but I thought I would ask, to make sure; it's the way I've been raised. Now you mustn't take it unkindly if I remind you that as we don't know you, we must go a little slow. You may be all right, of course, and we'll hope that you are; but to take it for granted isn't business. *You* understand that. I'm obliged to ask you a few questions; just answer up fair and square, and don't be afraid. Where do you live, when you are at home?"

"In the land of Moder, fair sir."

"Land of Moder. I don't remember hearing of it before. Parents living?"

"As to that, I know not if they be yet on live, sith it is many years that I have lain shut up in the castle."

"Your name, please?"

"I hight the Demoiselle Alisande la Carteloise, an it please you."

"Do you know anybody here who can identify you?"

"That were not likely, fair lord, I being come hither now for the first time."

"Have you brought any letters—any documents—any proofs that you are trustworthy and truthful?"

"Of a surety, no; and wherefore should I? Have I not a tongue, and cannot I say all that myself?"

"But *your* saying it, you know, and somebody else's saying it, is different."

"Different? How might that be? I fear me I do not understand."

"Don't *understand*? Land of—why, you see—you see—why, great Scott, can't you understand a little thing like that? Can't you understand the difference between your—*why* do you look so innocent and idiotic!"

"Great Scott, can't you understand a little thing like that?"

"I? In truth I know not, but an it were the will of God."

"Yes, yes, I reckon that's about the size of it. Don't mind my seeming excited; I'm not. Let us change the subject. Now as to this castle, with forty-five princesses in it, and three ogres at the head of it, tell me—where is this harem?"

"Harem?"

"The *castle*, you understand; where is the castle?"

"Oh, as to that, it is great, and strong, and well beseen, and lieth in a far country. Yes, it is many leagues."

"*How* many?"

"Ah, fair sir, it were woundily hard to tell, they are so many, and do so lap the one upon the other, and being made all in the same image and tincted with the same colour, one may not know the one league from its fellow, nor how to count them except they be taken apart, and ye wit well it were God's work to do that, being not within man's capacity; for ye will note—"

"Hold on, hold on, never mind about the distance; *whereabouts* does the castle lie? What's the direction from here?"

"Ah, please you sir, it hath no direction from here; by reason that the road lieth not straight, but turneth evermore; wherefore the direction of its place abideth not, but is some time under the one sky and anon under another, whereso if ye be minded that it is in the east, and wend thitherward, ye shall observe that the way of the road doth yet again turn upon itself by the space of half a circle, and this marvel happing again and yet again and still again, it will grieve you that you had thought by vanities of the mind to thwart and bring to naught the will of Him that giveth not a castle a direction from a place except it pleaseth Him, and if it please Him not, will the rather that even all castles and all directions thereunto vanish out of the earth, leaving the places wherein they tarried desolate and vacant, so warning His creatures that where He will He will, and where He will not He—"

"Oh, that's all right, that's all right, give us a rest; never mind about the direction, *hang* the direction—I beg pardon, I beg a thousand pardons, I am not well today; pay no attention when I soliloquize, it is an old habit, an old, bad habit, and hard to get rid of when one's digestion is all disordered with eating food that was raised forever and ever before he was born; good land! a man can't keep his functions regular on spring chickens thirteen hundred years old. But come—never mind about that; let's—have you got such a thing as a map of that region about you? Now a good map—"

"Is it peradventure that manner of thing which of late the unbelievers have brought from over the great seas, which, being boiled in oil, and an onion and salt added thereto, doth—"

"What, a map? What are you talking about? Don't you know what a map is? There, there, never mind, don't explain, I hate explanations; they fog a thing up so that you can't tell anything about it. Run along, dear; good day; show her the way, Clarence."

Oh, well, it was reasonably plain, now, why these donkeys didn't prospect these liars for details. It may be that this girl had a fact in her somewhere, but I don't believe you could have sluiced it out with a hydraulic; nor got it with the earlier forms of blasting, even; it was a case for dynamite. Why, she was a perfect ass; and yet the King and his knights had listened to her as if she had been a leaf out of the gospel. It kind of sizes up the whole party. And think of the simple ways of this court: this wandering wench hadn't any more trouble to get access to the King in his palace than she would have had to get into the poorhouse in my day and country. In fact, he was glad to see her, glad to hear her tale; with that adventure of hers to offer, she was as welcome as a corpse is to a coroner.

Just as I was ending-up these reflections, Clarence came back. I remarked upon the barren result of my efforts with the girl; hadn't got hold of a single point that could help me to find the castle. The youth looked a little surprised, or puzzled, or something, and intimated that he had been wondering to himself what I had wanted to ask the girl all those questions for.

"Why, great guns," I said, "don't I want to find the castle? And how else would I go about it?"

"La, sweet your worship, one may lightly answer that, I ween. She will go with thee. They always do. She will ride with thee."

"Ride with me? Nonsense!"

"But of a truth she will. She will ride with thee. Thou shalt see."

"What? She browse around the hills and scour the woods with me—alone—and I as good as engaged to be married? Why, it's scandalous. Think how it would look."

My, the dear face that rose before me! The boy was eager to know all about this tender matter. I swore him to secrecy and then whispered her name—"Puss Flanagan." He looked disappointed, and said he didn't remember the countess. How natural it was for the little courtier to give her a rank. He asked me where she lived.

"In East Har—" I came to myself and stopped, a little confused; then I said, "Never mind, now; I'll tell you some time."

And might he see her? Would I let him see her some day?

It was but a little thing to promise—thirteen hundred years or so—and he so eager; so I said Yes. But I sighed; I couldn't help it. And yet there was no sense in sighing, for she wasn't born yet. But that is the way we are made: we don't reason, where we feel; we just feel.

My expedition was all the talk that day and that night, and the boys were very good to me, and made much of me, and seemed to have forgotten their vexation and disappointment, and come to be as anxious for me to hive those ogres and set those ripe old virgins loose as if it were themselves that had the contract. Well, they *were* good children—but just children, that is all. And they gave me no end of points about how to scout for giants, and how to scoop them in; and they told me all sorts of charms against enchantments, and gave me salves and other rubbish to put on my wounds. But it never occurred to one of them to reflect that if I was such a wonderful necromancer as I was pretending to be, I ought not to need salves or instructions, or charms against enchantments, and, least of all, arms and armor, on a foray of any kind—even against fire-spouting dragons, and devils hot from perdition, let alone such poor adversaries as these I was after, these commonplace ogres of the back settlements.

I was to have an early breakfast, and start at dawn, for that was the usual way; but I had the demon's own time with my armor, and this delayed me a little. It is troublesome to get into, and there is so much detail. First you wrap a layer or two of blanket around your body, for a sort of cushion and to keep off the cold iron; then you put on your sleeves and shirt of chain mail—these are made of small steel links woven together, and they form a fabric so flexible that if you toss your shirt onto the floor, it slumps into a pile like a peck of wet fish-net; it is very heavy and is nearly the uncomfortablest material in the world for a night shirt, yet plenty used it for that—tax collectors, and reformers, and one-horse kings with a defective title, and those sorts of people; then you put on your shoes—flat-boats roofed over with interleaving bands of steel—and screw your clumsy spurs into the heels. Next you buckle your greaves on your legs, and your cuisses on your thighs; then come your backplate and your breastplate, and you begin to feel crowded; then you hitch onto the breastplate the half-petticoat of broad overlapping bands of steel which hangs down in front but is scolloped out behind so you can sit down, and isn't any real improvement on an inverted coal scuttle, either for looks or for wear, or to wipe your hands on; next you belt on your sword; then you put your stove-pipe joints onto your arms, your iron gauntlets onto your hands, your iron rat-trap onto your head, with a rag of steel web hitched onto it to hang over the back of your neck—and there you are, snug as a candle in a candle-mould. This is no time to dance. Well, a man that is packed away like that is a nut that isn't worth the cracking, there is so little of the meat, when you get down to it, by comparison with the shell.

The boys helped me, or I never could have got in. Just as we finished, Sir Bedivere happened in, and I saw that as like as not I hadn't chosen the most convenient outfit for a long trip. How stately he looked; and tall and broad and grand. He had on his head a conical steel casque that only came down to his ears, and for visor had only a narrow steel bar that extended down to his upper lip and protected his nose; and all the rest of him, from neck to heel, was flexible chain mail, trousers and all. But pretty much all of him was hidden under his outside garment, which of course was of chain mail, as I said, and hung straight from his shoulders to his ankles; and from his middle to the bottom, both before and behind, was divided, so that he could ride and let the skirts hang down on each side. He was going grailing, and it was just the outfit for it, too. I would have given a good deal for that ulster, but it was too late now to be fooling around. The sun was just up, the king and the court were all on hand to see me off and wish me luck; so it wouldn't be etiquette for me to tarry. You don't get on your horse yourself; no, if you tried it you would get disappointed. They carry you out, just as they carry a sun-struck man to the drug store, and put you on, and help get you to rights, and fix your feet in the stirrups; and all the while you do feel so strange and stuffy and like somebody else—like somebody that has been married on a sudden, or struck by lightning, or something like that, and hasn't quite fetched around yet, and is sort of numb, and can't just get his bearings. Then they stood up the mast they called a spear, in its socket by my left foot, and I gripped it with my hand; lastly they hung my shield around my neck, and I was all complete and ready to up anchor and get to sea. Everybody was as good to me as they could be, and a maid of honour gave me the stirrup-cup her own self. There was nothing more to do now, but for that damsel to get up behind me on a pillion, which she did, and put an arm or so around me to hold on.

"And so we started"

And so we started, and everybody gave us a goodbye and waved their handkerchiefs or helmets. And everybody we met, going down the hill and through the village was respectful to us, except some shabby little boys on the outskirts. They said:

"Oh, what a guy!" And hove clods at us.

In my experience boys are the same in all ages. They don't respect anything, they don't care for anything or anybody. They say "Go up, baldhead" to the prophet going his unoffending way in the grey of antiquity; they sass me in the holy gloom of the Middle Ages; and I had seen them act the same way in Buchanan's administration; I remember, because I was there and helped. The prophet had his bears and settled with his boys; and I wanted to get down and settle with mine, but it wouldn't answer, because I couldn't have got up again. I hate a country without a derrick.

12

Slow Torture

Straight off, we were in the country. It was most lovely and pleasant in those sylvan solitudes in the early cool morning in the first freshness of autumn. From hilltops we saw fair green valleys lying spread out below, with streams winding through them, and island groves of trees here and there, and huge lonely oaks scattered about and casting black blots of shade; and beyond the valleys we saw the ranges of hills, blue with haze, stretching away in billowy perspective to the horizon, with at wide intervals a dim fleck of white or grey on a wave-summit, which we knew was a castle. We crossed broad natural lawns sparkling with dew, and we moved like spirits, the cushioned turf giving out no sound of footfall; we dreamed along through glades in a mist of green light that got its tint from the sun-drenched roof of leaves overhead, and by our feet the clearest and coldest of runlets went frisking and gossiping over its reefs and making a sort of whispering music, comfortable to hear; and at times we left the world behind and entered into the solemn great deeps and rich gloom of the forest, where furtive wild things whisked and scurried by and were gone before you could even get your eye on the place where the noise was; and where only the earliest birds were turning out and getting to business with a song here and a quarrel yonder and a mysterious far-off hammering and drumming for worms on a tree trunk away somewhere in the impenetrable remotenesses of the woods. And by and by out we would swing again into the glare.

About the third or fourth or fifth time that we swung out into the glare—it was along there somewhere, a couple of hours or so after sun-up—it wasn't as pleasant as it had been. It was beginning to get hot. This was quite noticeable. We had a very long pull, after that, without any shade. Now it is curious how progressively little frets grow and multiply after they once get a start. Things which I didn't mind at all, at first, I began to mind now—and more and more, too, all the time. The first ten or fifteen times I wanted my handkerchief I didn't seem to care; I got along, and said never mind, it isn't any matter, and dropped it out of my mind. But now it was different; I wanted it all the time; it was nag, nag, nag, right along, and no rest; I couldn't get it out of my mind; and so at last I lost my temper and said hang a man that would make a suit of armor without any pockets in it. You see I had my handkerchief in my helmet; and some other things; but it was that kind of a helmet that you can't take off by yourself. That hadn't occurred to me when I put it there; and in fact I didn't know it. I supposed it would be particularly convenient there. And so now, the thought of its being there, so handy and close by, and yet not get-at-able, made it all the worse and the harder to bear. Yes, the thing that you can't get is the thing that you want, mainly; every one has noticed that. Well, it took my mind off from everything else; took it clear off, and centered it in my helmet; and mile after mile, there it stayed, imagining the handkerchief, picturing the handkerchief; and it was bitter and aggravating to have the salt sweat keep trickling down into my eyes, and I couldn't get at it. It seems like a little thing, on paper, but it was not a little thing at all; it was the most real kind of misery. I would not say it if it was not so. I made up my mind that I would carry along a reticule next time, let it look how it might, and people say what they would. Of course these iron dudes of the Round Table would think it was scandalous, and maybe raise Sheol about it, but as for me, give me comfort first, and style afterwards. So we jogged along, and now and then we struck a stretch of dust, and it would tumble up in clouds and get into my nose and make me sneeze and cry; and of course I said things I oughtn't to have said, I don't deny that. I am not better than others.

We couldn't seem to meet anybody in this lonesome Britain, not even an ogre; and, in the mood I was in then, it was well for the ogre; that is, an ogre with a handkerchief. Most knights would have thought of nothing but getting his armor; but so I got his bandanna, he could keep his hardware, for all of me.

Meantime, it was getting hotter and hotter in there. You see, the sun was beating down and warming up the iron more and more all the time. Well, when you are hot, that way, every little thing irritates you. When I trotted, I rattled like a crate of dishes, and that annoyed me; and moreover I couldn't seem to stand that shield slatting and banging, now about my breast, now around my back; and if I dropped into a walk my joints creaked and screeched in that wearisome way that a wheelbarrow does, and as we didn't create any breeze at that gait, I was like to get fried in that stove; and besides, the quieter you went the heavier the iron settled down on you and the more and more tons you seemed to weigh every minute. And you had to be always changing hands, and passing your spear over to the other foot, it got so irksome for one hand to hold it long at a time.

Well, you know, when you perspire that way, in rivers, there comes a time when you—when you—well, when you itch. You are inside, your hands are outside; so there you are; nothing but iron between. It is not a light thing, let it sound as it may. First it is one place; then another; then some more; and it goes on spreading and spreading, and at last the territory is all occupied, and nobody can imagine what you feel like, nor how unpleasant it is. And when it had got to the worst, and it seemed to me that I could not stand anything more, a fly got in through the bars and settled on my nose, and the bars were stuck and wouldn't work, and I couldn't get the visor up; and I could only shake my head, which was baking hot by this time, and the fly—well, you know how a fly acts when he has got a certainty—he only minded the shaking enough to change from nose to lip, and lip to ear, and buzz and buzz all around in there, and keep on lighting and biting, in a way that a person, already so distressed as I was, simply could not stand. So I gave in, and got Alisande to unship the helmet and relieve me of it. Then she emptied the conveniences out of it and fetched it full of water, and I drank and then stood up, and she poured the rest down inside the armor. One cannot think how refreshing it was. She continued to fetch and pour until I was well soaked and thoroughly comfortable.

"She continued to fetch and pour until I was well soaked"

It was good to have a rest—and peace. But nothing is quite perfect in this life, at any time. I had made a pipe a while back, and also some pretty fair tobacco; not the real thing, but what some of the Indians use: the inside bark of the willow, dried. These comforts had been in the helmet, and now I had them again, but no matches.

Gradually, as the time wore along, one annoying fact was borne in upon my understanding—that we were weather-bound. An armed novice cannot mount his horse without help and plenty of it. Sandy was not enough; not enough for me, anyway. We had to wait until somebody should come along. Waiting, in silence, would have been agreeable enough, for I was full of matter for reflection, and wanted to give it a chance to work. I wanted to try and think out how it was that rational or even half-rational men could ever have learned to wear armor, considering its inconveniences; and how they had managed to keep up such a fashion for generations when it was plain that what I had suffered today they had had to suffer all the days of their lives. I wanted to think that out; and moreover I wanted to think out some way to reform this evil and persuade the people to let the foolish fashion die out; but thinking was out of the question in the circumstances. You couldn't think, where Sandy was.

She was a quite biddable creature and good-hearted, but she had a flow of talk that was as steady as a mill, and made your head sore like the drays and wagons in a city. If she had had a cork she would have been a comfort. But you can't cork that kind; they would die. Her clack was going all day, and you would think something would surely happen to her works, by and by; but no, they never got out of order; and she never had to slack up for words. She could grind, and pump, and churn, and buzz by the week, and never stop to oil up or blow out. And yet the result was just nothing but wind. She never had any ideas, any more than a fog has. She was a perfect blatherskite; I mean for jaw, jaw, jaw, talk, talk, talk, jabber, jabber, jabber; but just as good as she could be. I hadn't minded her mill that morning, on account of having that hornets' nest of other troubles; but more than once in the afternoon I had to say:

"Take a rest, child; the way you are using up all the domestic air, the kingdom will have to go to importing it by tomorrow, and it's a low enough treasury without that."

13

Freemen

Yes, it is strange how little a while at a time a person can be contented. Only a little while back, when I was riding and suffering, what a heaven this peace, this rest, this sweet serenity in this secluded shady nook by this purling stream would have seemed, where I could keep perfectly comfortable all the time by pouring a dipper of water into my armor now and then; yet already I was getting dissatisfied; partly because I could not light my pipe—for, although I had long ago started a match factory, I had forgotten to bring matches with me—and partly because we had nothing to eat. Here was another illustration of the childlike improvidence of this age and people. A man in armor always trusted to chance for his food on a journey, and would have been scandalized at the idea of hanging a basket of sandwiches on his spear. There was probably not a knight of all the Round Table combination who would not rather have died than been caught carrying such a thing as that on his flagstaff. And yet there could not be anything more sensible. It had been my intention to smuggle a couple of sandwiches into my helmet, but I was interrupted in the act, and had to make an excuse and lay them aside, and a dog got them.

Night approached, and with it a storm. The darkness came on fast. We must camp, of course. I found a good shelter for the demoiselle under a rock, and went off and found another for myself. But I was obliged to remain in my armor, because I could not get it off by myself and yet could not allow Alisande to help, because it would have seemed so like undressing before folk. It would not have amounted to that in reality, because I had clothes on underneath; but the prejudices of one's breeding are not gotten rid of just at a jump, and I knew that when it came to stripping off that bob-tailed iron petticoat I should be embarrassed.

With the storm came a change of weather; and the stronger the wind blew, and the wilder the rain lashed around, the colder and colder it got. Pretty soon, various kinds of bugs and ants and worms and things began to flock in out of the wet and crawl down inside my armor to get warm; and while some of them behaved well enough, and snuggled up amongst my clothes and got quiet, the majority were of a restless, uncomfortable sort, and never stayed still, but went on prowling and hunting for they did not know what; especially the ants, which went tickling along in wearisome procession from one end of me to the other by the hour, and are a kind of creatures which I never wish to sleep with again. It would be my advice to persons situated in this way, to not roll or thrash around, because this excites the interest of all the different sorts of animals and makes every last one of them want to turn out and see what is going on, and this makes things worse than they were before, and of course makes you objurgate harder, too, if you can. Still, if one did not roll and thrash around he would die; so perhaps it is as well to do one way as the other; there is no real choice. Even after I was frozen solid I could still distinguish that tickling, just as a corpse does when he is taking electric treatment. I said I would never wear armor after this trip.

All those trying hours whilst I was frozen and yet was in a living fire, as you may say, on account of that swarm of crawlers, that same unanswerable question kept circling and circling through my tired head: How do people stand this miserable armor? How have they managed to stand it all these generations? How can they sleep at night for dreading the tortures of next day?

When the morning came at last, I was in a bad enough plight: seedy, drowsy, fagged, from want of sleep; weary from thrashing around, famished from long fasting; pining for a bath, and to get rid of the animals; and crippled with rheumatism. And how had it fared with the nobly born, the titled aristocrat, the Demoiselle Alisande la Carteloise? Why, she was as fresh as a squirrel; she had slept like the dead; and as for a bath, probably neither she nor any other noble in the land had ever had one, and so she was not missing it. Measured by modern standards, they were merely modified savages, those people. This noble lady showed no impatience to get to breakfast—and that smacks of the savage, too. On their journeys those Britons were used to long fasts, and knew how to bear them; and also how to freight up against probable fasts before starting, after the style of the Indian and the anaconda. As like as not, Sandy was loaded for a three-day stretch.

We were off before sunrise, Sandy riding and I limping along behind. In half an hour we came upon a group of ragged poor creatures who had assembled to mend the thing which was regarded as a road. They were as humble as animals to me; and when I proposed to breakfast with them, they were so flattered, so overwhelmed by this extraordinary condescension of mine that at first they were not able to believe that I was in earnest. My lady put up her scornful lip and withdrew to one side; she said in their hearing that she would as soon think of eating with the other cattle—a remark which embarrassed these poor devils merely because it referred to them, and not because it insulted or offended them, for it didn't. And yet they were not slaves, not chattels. By a sarcasm of law and phrase they were freemen. Seven-tenths of the free population of the country were of just their class and degree: small "independent" farmers, artisans, etc.; which is to say, they were the nation, the actual Nation; they were about all of it that was useful, or worth saving, or really respect-worthy, and to subtract them would have been to subtract the Nation and leave behind some dregs, some refuse, in the shape of a king, nobility and gentry, idle, unproductive, acquainted mainly with the arts of wasting and destroying, and of no sort of use or value in any rationally constructed world.

"By a sarcasm of law and phrase they were freemen"

And yet, by ingenious contrivance, this gilded minority, instead of being in the tail of the procession where it belonged, was marching head up and banners flying, at the other end of it; had elected itself to be the Nation, and these innumerable clams had permitted it so long that they had come at last to accept it as a truth; and not only that, but to believe it right and as it should be. The priests had told their fathers and themselves that this ironical state of things was ordained of God; and so, not reflecting upon how unlike God it would be to amuse himself with sarcasms, and especially such poor transparent ones as this, they had dropped the matter there and become respectfully quiet.

The talk of these meek people had a strange enough sound in a formerly American ear. They were freemen, but they could not leave the estates of their lord or their bishop without his permission; they could not prepare their own bread, but must have their corn ground and their bread baked at his mill and his bakery, and pay roundly for the same; they could not sell a piece of their own property without paying him a handsome percentage of the proceeds, nor buy a piece of somebody else's without remembering him in cash for the privilege; they had to harvest his grain for him gratis, and be ready to come at a moment's notice, leaving their own crop to destruction by the threatened storm; they had to let him plant fruit trees in their fields, and then keep their indignation to themselves when his heedless fruit-gatherers trampled the grain around the trees; they had to smother their anger when his hunting parties galloped through their fields laying waste the result of their patient toil; they were not allowed to keep doves themselves, and when the swarms from my lord's dovecote settled on their crops they must not lose their temper and kill a bird, for awful would the penalty be; when the harvest was at last gathered, then came the procession of robbers to levy their blackmail upon it: first the Church carted off its fat tenth, then the king's commissioner took his twentieth, then my lord's people made a mighty inroad upon the remainder; after which, the skinned freeman had liberty to bestow the remnant in his barn, in case it was worth the trouble; there were taxes, and taxes, and taxes, and more taxes, and taxes again, and yet other taxes—upon this free and independent pauper, but none upon his lord the baron or the bishop, none upon the wasteful nobility or the all-devouring Church; if the baron would sleep unvexed, the freeman must sit up all night after his day's work and whip the ponds to keep the frogs quiet; if the freeman's daughter—but no, that last infamy of monarchical government is unprintable; and finally, if the freeman, grown desperate with his tortures, found his life unendurable under such conditions, and sacrificed it and fled to death for mercy and refuge, the gentle Church condemned him to eternal fire, the gentle law buried him at midnight at the cross-roads with a stake through his back, and his master the baron or the bishop confiscated all his property and turned his widow and his orphans out of doors.

And here were these freemen assembled in the early morning to work on their lord the bishop's road three days each—gratis; every head of a family, and every son of a family, three days each, gratis, and a day or so added for their servants. Why, it was like reading about France and the French, before the ever memorable and blessed Revolution, which swept a thousand years of such villany away in one swift tidal-wave of blood—one: a settlement of that hoary debt in the proportion of half a drop of blood for each hogshead of it that had been pressed by slow tortures out of that people in the weary stretch of ten centuries of wrong and shame and misery the like of which was not to be mated but in hell. There were two "Reigns of Terror," if we would but remember it and consider it; the one wrought murder in hot passion, the other in heartless cold blood; the one lasted mere months, the other had lasted a thousand years; the one inflicted death upon ten thousand persons, the other upon a hundred millions; but our shudders are all for the "horrors" of the minor Terror, the momentary Terror, so to speak; whereas, what is the horror of swift death by the axe, compared with lifelong death from hunger, cold, insult, cruelty, and heartbreak? What is swift death by lightning compared with death by slow fire at the stake? A city cemetery could contain the coffins filled by that brief Terror which we have all been so diligently taught to shiver at and mourn over; but all France could hardly contain the coffins filled by that older and real Terror—that unspeakably bitter and awful Terror which none of us has been taught to see in its vastness or pity as it deserves.

These poor ostensible freemen who were sharing their breakfast and their talk with me, were as full of humble reverence for their king and Church and nobility as their worst enemy could desire. There was something pitifully ludicrous about it. I asked them if they supposed a nation of people ever existed, who, with a free vote in every man's hand, would elect that a single family and its descendants should reign over it forever, whether gifted or boobies, to the exclusion of all other families—including the voter's; and would also elect that a certain hundred families should be raised to dizzy summits of rank, and clothed on with offensive transmissible glories and privileges to the exclusion of the rest of the nation's families—*including his own.*

They all looked unhit, and said they didn't know; that they had never thought about it before, and it hadn't ever occurred to them that a nation could be so situated that every man *could* have a say in the government. I said I had seen one—and that it would last until it had an Established Church. Again they were all unhit—at first. But presently one man looked up and asked me to state that proposition again; and state it slowly, so it could soak into his understanding. I did it; and after a little he had the idea, and he brought his fist down and said *he* didn't believe a nation where every man had a vote would voluntarily get down in the mud and dirt in any such way; and that to steal from a nation its will and preference must be a crime and the first of all crimes. I said to myself:

"This one's a man. If I were backed by enough of his sort, I would make a strike for the welfare of this country, and try to prove myself its loyalest citizen by making a wholesome change in its system of government."

You see my kind of loyalty was loyalty to one's country, not to its institutions or its office-holders. The country is the real thing, the substantial thing, the eternal thing; it is the thing to watch over, and care for, and be loyal to; institutions are extraneous, they are its mere clothing, and clothing can wear out, become ragged, cease to be comfortable, cease to protect the body from winter, disease, and death. To be loyal to rags, to shout for rags, to worship rags, to die for rags—that is a loyalty of unreason, it is pure animal; it belongs to monarchy, was invented by monarchy; let monarchy keep it. I was from Connecticut, whose Constitution declares "that all political power is inherent in the people, and all free governments are founded on their authority and instituted for their benefit; and that they have *at all times* an undeniable and indefeasible right to *alter their form of government* in such a manner as they may think expedient."

Under that gospel, the citizen who thinks he sees that the

commonwealth's political clothes are worn out, and yet holds his peace and does not agitate for a new suit, is disloyal; he is a traitor. That he may be the only one who thinks he sees this decay, does not excuse him; it is his duty to agitate anyway, and it is the duty of the others to vote him down if they do not see the matter as he does.

And now here I was, in a country where a right to say how the country should be governed was restricted to six persons in each thousand of its population. For the nine hundred and ninety-four to express dissatisfaction with the regnant system and propose to change it, would have made the whole six shudder as one man, it would have been so disloyal, so dishonourable, such putrid black treason. So to speak, I was become a stockholder in a corporation where nine hundred and ninety-four of the members furnished all the money and did all the work, and the other six elected themselves a permanent board of direction and took all the dividends. It seemed to me that what the nine hundred and ninety-four dupes needed was a new deal. The thing that would have best suited the circus side of my nature would have been to resign the Boss-ship and get up an insurrection and turn it into a revolution; but I knew that the Jack Cade or the Wat Tyler who tries such a thing without first educating his materials up to revolution grade is almost absolutely certain to get left. I had never been accustomed to getting left, even if I do say it myself. Wherefore, the "deal" which had been for some time working into shape in my mind was of a quite different pattern from the Cade-Tyler sort.

So I did not talk blood and insurrection to that man there who sat munching black bread with that abused and mistaught herd of human sheep, but took him aside and talked matter of another sort to him. After I had finished, I got him to lend me a little ink from his veins; and with this and a sliver I wrote on a piece of bark—

Put him in the Man-factory—

and gave it to him, and said:

"Take it to the palace at Camelot and give it into the hands of Amyas le Poulet, whom I call Clarence, and he will understand."

"He is a priest, then," said the man, and some of the enthusiasm went out of his face.

"How—a priest? Didn't I tell you that no chattel of the Church, no bond-slave of pope or bishop can enter my Man-Factory? Didn't I tell you that *you* couldn't enter unless your religion, whatever it might be, was your own free property?"

"Marry, it is so, and for that I was glad; wherefore it liked me not, and bred in me a cold doubt, to hear of this priest being there."

"But he isn't a priest, I tell you."

The man looked far from satisfied. He said:

"He is not a priest, and yet can read?"

"He is not a priest and yet can read—yes, and write, too, for that matter. I taught him myself." The man's face cleared. "And it is the first thing that you yourself will be taught in that Factory—"

"I? I would give blood out of my heart to know that art. Why, I will be your slave, your—"

"No you won't, you won't be anybody's slave. Take your family and go along. Your lord the bishop will confiscate your small property, but no matter. Clarence will fix you all right."

14

"Defend Thee, Lord"

I paid three pennies for my breakfast, and a most extravagant price it was, too, seeing that one could have breakfasted a dozen persons for that money; but I was feeling good by this time, and I had always been a kind of spendthrift anyway; and then these people had wanted to give me the food for nothing, scant as their provision was, and so it was a grateful pleasure to emphasize my appreciation and sincere thankfulness with a good big financial lift where the money would do so much more good than it would in my helmet, where, these pennies being made of iron and not stinted in weight, my half-dollar's worth was a good deal of a burden to me. I spent money rather too freely in those days, it is true; but one reason for it was that I hadn't got the proportions of things entirely adjusted, even yet, after so long a sojourn in Britain—hadn't got along to where I was able to absolutely realize that a penny in Arthur's land and a couple of dollars in Connecticut were about one and the same thing: just twins, as you may say, in purchasing power. If my start from Camelot could have been delayed a very few days I could have paid these people in beautiful new coins from our own mint, and that would have pleased me; and them, too, not less. I had adopted the American values exclusively. In a week or two now, cents, nickels, dimes, quarters, and half-dollars, and also a trifle of gold, would be trickling in thin but steady streams all through the commercial veins of the kingdom, and I looked to see this new blood freshen up its life.

The farmers were bound to throw in something, to sort of offset my liberality, whether I would or no; so I let them give me a flint and steel; and as soon as they had comfortably bestowed Sandy and me on our horse, I lit my pipe. When the first blast of smoke shot out through the bars of my helmet, all those people broke for the woods, and Sandy went over backwards and struck the ground with a dull thud. They thought I was one of those fire-belching dragons they had heard so much about from knights and other professional liars. I had infinite trouble to persuade those people to venture back within explaining distance. Then I told them that this was only a bit of enchantment which would work harm to none but my enemies. And I promised, with my hand on my heart, that if all who felt no enmity toward me would come forward and pass before me they should see that only those who remained behind would be struck dead. The procession moved with a good deal of promptness. There were no casualties to report, for nobody had curiosity enough to remain behind to see what would happen.

I lost some time, now, for these big children, their fears gone, became so ravished with wonder over my awe-compelling fireworks that I had to stay there and smoke a couple of pipes out before they would let me go. Still the delay was not wholly unproductive, for it took all that time to get Sandy thoroughly wonted to the new thing, she being so close to it, you know. It plugged up her conversation mill, too, for a considerable while, and that was a gain. But above all other benefits accruing, I had learned something. I was ready for any giant or any ogre that might come along, now.

We tarried with a holy hermit, that night, and my opportunity came about the middle of the next afternoon. We were crossing a vast meadow by way of short-cut, and I was musing absently, hearing nothing, seeing nothing, when Sandy suddenly interrupted a remark which she had begun that morning, with the cry:

"Defend thee, lord!—peril of life is toward!"

And she slipped down from the horse and ran a little way and stood. I looked up and saw, far off in the shade of a tree, half a dozen armed knights and their squires; and straightway there was bustle among them and tightening of saddle-girths for the mount. My pipe was ready and would have been lit, if I had not been lost in thinking about how to banish oppression from this land and restore to all its people their stolen rights and manhood without disobliging anybody. I lit up at once, and by the time I had got a good head of reserved steam on, here they came. All together, too; none of those chivalrous magnanimities which one reads so much about—one courtly rascal at a time, and the rest standing by to see fair play. No, they came in a body, they came with a whirr and a rush, they came like a volley from a battery; came with heads low down, plumes streaming out behind, lances advanced at a level. It was a handsome sight, a beautiful sight—for a man up a tree. I laid my lance in rest and waited, with my heart beating, till the iron wave was just ready to break over me, then spouted a column of white smoke through the bars of my helmet. You should have seen the wave go to pieces and scatter! This was a finer sight than the other one.

But these people stopped, two or three hundred yards away, and this troubled me. My satisfaction collapsed, and fear came; I judged I was a lost man. But Sandy was radiant; and was going to be eloquent—but I stopped her, and told her my magic had miscarried, somehow or other, and she must mount, with all dispatch, and we must ride for life. No, she wouldn't. She said that my enchantment had disabled those knights; they were not riding on, because they couldn't; wait, they would drop out of their saddles presently, and we would get their horses and harness. I could not deceive such trusting simplicity, so I said it was a mistake; that when my fireworks killed at all, they killed instantly; no, the men would not die, there was something wrong about my apparatus, I couldn't tell what; but we must hurry and get away, for those people would attack us again, in a minute. Sandy laughed, and said:

"Lack-a-day, sir, they be not of that breed! Sir Launcelot will give battle to dragons, and will abide by them, and will assail them again, and yet again, and still again, until he do conquer and destroy them; and so likewise will Sir Pellinore and Sir Aglovale and Sir Carados, and mayhap others, but there be none else that will venture it, let the idle say what the idle will. And, la, as to yonder base rufflers, think ye they have not their fill, but yet desire more?"

"Well, then, what are they waiting for? Why don't they leave? Nobody's hindering. Good land, I'm willing to let bygones be bygones, I'm sure."

"Leave, is it? Oh, give thyself easement as to that. They dream not of it, no, not they. They wait to yield them."

"Come—really, is that 'sooth'—as you people say? If they want to, why don't they?"

"It would like them much; but an ye wot how dragons are esteemed, ye would not hold them blamable. They fear to come."

"Well, then, suppose I go to them instead, and—"

"Ah, wit ye well they would not abide your coming. I will go."

And she did. She was a handy person to have along on a raid. I would have considered this a doubtful errand, myself. I presently saw the knights riding away, and Sandy coming back. That was a relief. I judged she had somehow failed to get the first innings—I mean in the conversation; otherwise the interview wouldn't have been so short. But it turned out that she had managed the business well; in fact, admirably. She said that when she told those people I was The Boss, it hit them where they lived: "smote them sore with fear and dread" was her word; and then they were ready to put up with anything she might require. So she swore them to appear at Arthur's court within two days and yield them, with horse and harness, and be my knights henceforth, and subject to my command. How much better she managed that thing than I should have done it myself! She was a daisy.

15

Sandy's Tale

"And so I'm proprietor of some knights," said I, as we rode off. "Who would ever have supposed that I should live to list up assets of that sort. I sha'n't know what to do with them; unless I raffle them off. How many of them are there, Sandy?"

"Seven, please you, sir, and their squires."

"It is a good haul. Who are they? Where do they hang out?"

"Where do they hang out?"

"Yes, where do they live?"

"Ah, I understood thee not. That will I tell eftsoons." Then she said musingly, and softly, turning the words daintily over her tongue: "Hang they out—hang they out—where hang—where do they hang out; eh, right so; where do they hang out. Of a truth the phrase hath a fair and winsome grace, and is prettily worded withal. I will repeat it anon and anon in mine idlesse, whereby I may peradventure learn it. Where do they hang out. Even so! already it falleth trippingly from my tongue, and forasmuch as—"

"Don't forget the cowboys, Sandy."

"Cowboys?"

"Yes; the knights, you know: You were going to tell me about them. A while back, you remember. Figuratively speaking, game's called."

"Game—"

"Yes, yes, yes! Go to the bat. I mean, get to work on your statistics, and don't burn so much kindling getting your fire started. Tell me about the knights."

"I will well, and lightly will begin. So they two departed and rode into a great forest. And—"

"Great Scott!"

You see, I recognized my mistake at once. I had set her works a-going; it was my own fault; she would be thirty days getting down to those facts. And she generally began without a preface and finished without a result. If you interrupted her she would either go right along without noticing, or answer with a couple of words, and go back and say the sentence over again. So, interruptions only did harm; and yet I had to interrupt, and interrupt pretty frequently, too, in order to save my life; a person would die if he let her monotony drip on him right along all day.

"Great Scott!" I said in my distress. She went right back and began over again:

"So they two departed and rode into a great forest. And—"

"*Which* two?"

"Sir Gawaine and Sir Uwaine. And so they came to an abbey of monks, and there were well lodged. So on the morn they heard their masses in the abbey, and so they rode forth till they came to a great forest; then was Sir Gawaine ware in a valley by a turret, of twelve fair damsels, and two knights armed on great horses, and the damsels went to and fro by a tree. And then was Sir Gawaine ware how there hung a white shield on that tree, and ever as the damsels came by it they spit upon it, and some threw mire upon the shield—"

"Now, if I hadn't seen the like myself in this country, Sandy, I wouldn't believe it. But I've seen it, and I can just see those creatures now, parading before that shield and acting like that. The women here do certainly act like all possessed. Yes, and I mean your best, too, society's very choicest brands. The humblest hello-girl along ten thousand miles of wire could teach gentleness, patience, modesty, manners, to the highest duchess in Arthur's land."

"Hello-girl?"

"Yes, but don't you ask me to explain; it's a new kind of a girl; they don't have them here; one often speaks sharply to them when they are not the least in fault, and he can't get over feeling sorry for it and ashamed of himself in thirteen hundred years, it's such shabby mean conduct and so unprovoked;

the fact is, no gentleman ever does it—though I—well, I myself, if I've got to confess—"

"Peradventure she—"

"Never mind her; never mind her; I tell you I couldn't ever explain her so you would understand."

"Even so be it, sith ye are so minded. Then Sir Gawaine and Sir Uwaine went and saluted them, and asked them why they did that despite to the shield. Sirs, said the damsels, we shall tell you. There is a knight in this country that owneth this white shield, and he is a passing good man of his hands, but he hateth all ladies and gentlewomen, and therefore we do all this despite to the shield. I will say you, said Sir Gawaine, it beseemeth evil a good knight to despise all ladies and gentlewomen, and peradventure though he hate you he hath some cause, and peradventure he loveth in some other places ladies and gentlewomen, and to be loved again, and he such a man of prowess as ye speak of—"

"Man of prowess—yes, that is the man to please them, Sandy. Man of brains—that is a thing they never think of. Tom Sayers—John Heenan—John L. Sullivan—pity but you could be here. You would have your legs under the Round Table and a 'Sir' in front of your names within the twenty-four hours; and you could bring about a new distribution of the married princesses and duchesses of the Court in another twenty-four. The fact is, it is just a sort of polished-up court of Comanches, and there isn't a squaw in it who doesn't stand ready at the dropping of a hat to desert to the buck with the biggest string of scalps at his belt."

"—and he be such a man of prowess as ye speak of, said Sir Gawaine. Now, what is his name? Sir, said they, his name is Marhaus the king's son of Ireland."

"Son of the king of Ireland, you mean; the other form doesn't mean anything. And look out and hold on tight, now, we must jump this gully. . . . There, we are all right now. This horse belongs in the circus; he is born before his time."

"I know him well, said Sir Uwaine, he is a passing good knight as any is on live."

"*On live.* If you've got a fault in the world, Sandy, it is that you are a shade too archaic. But it isn't any matter."

"—for I saw him once proved at a justs where many knights were gathered, and that time there might no man withstand him. Ah, said Sir Gawaine, damsels, methinketh ye are to blame, for it is to suppose he that hung that shield there will not be long therefrom, and then may those knights match him on horseback, and that is more your worship than thus; for I will abide no longer to see a knight's shield dishonoured. And therewith Sir Uwaine and Sir Gawaine departed a little from them, and then were they ware where Sir Marhaus came riding on a great horse straight toward them. And when the twelve damsels saw Sir Marhaus they fled into the turret as they were wild, so that some of them fell by the way. Then the one of the knights of the tower dressed his shield, and said on high, Sir Marhaus defend thee. And so they ran together that the knight brake his spear on Marhaus, and Sir Marhaus smote him so hard that he brake his neck and the horse's back—"

"Well, that is just the trouble about this state of things, it ruins so many horses."

"That saw the other knight of the turret, and dressed him toward Marhaus, and they went so eagerly together, that the knight of the turret was soon smitten down, horse and man, stark dead—"

"*Another* horse gone; I tell you it is a custom that ought to be broken up. I don't see how people with any feeling can applaud and support it."

"So these two knights came together with great random—"

I saw that I had been asleep and missed a chapter, but I didn't say anything. I judged that the Irish knight was in trouble with the visitors by this time, and this turned out to be the case.

"—that Sir Uwaine smote Sir Marhaus that his spear brast in pieces on the shield, and Sir Marhaus smote him so sore that horse and man he bare to the earth, and hurt Sir Uwaine on the left side—"

"The truth is, Alisande, these archaics are a little *too* simple; the vocabulary is too limited, and so, by consequence, descriptions suffer in the matter of variety; they run too much to level Saharas of fact, and not enough to picturesque detail; this throws about them a certain air of the monotonous; in fact the fights are all alike: a couple of people come together with great random—random is a good word, and so is exegesis, for that matter, and so is holocaust, and defalcation, and usufruct and a hundred others, but land! a body ought to discriminate—they come together with great random, and a spear is brast, and one party brake his shield and the other one goes down, horse and man, over his horse-tail and brake his neck, and then the next candidate comes randoming in, and brast *his* spear, and the other man brast his shield, and down *he* goes, horse and man, over his horse-tail, and brake *his* neck, and then there's another elected, and another and another and still another, till the material is all used up; and when you come to figure up results, you can't tell one fight from another, nor who whipped; and as a *picture*, of living, raging, roaring battle, sho! why, it's pale and noiseless—just ghosts scuffling in a fog. Dear me, what would this barren vocabulary get out of the mightiest spectacle?—the burning of Rome in Nero's time, for instance? Why, it would merely say, 'Town burned down; no insurance; boy brast a window, fireman brake his neck!' Why, *that* ain't a picture!"

It was a good deal of a lecture, I thought, but it didn't disturb Sandy, didn't turn a feather; her steam soared steadily up again, the minute I took off the lid:

"Then Sir Marhaus turned his horse and rode toward Gawaine with his spear. And when Sir Gawaine saw that, he dressed his shield, and they aventred their spears, and they came together with all the might of their horses, that either knight smote other so hard in the midst of their shields, but Sir Gawaine's spear brake—"

"I knew it would."

—"but Sir Marhaus's spear held; and therewith Sir Gawaine and his horse rushed down to the earth—"

"Just so—and brake his back."

—"and lightly Sir Gawaine rose upon his feet and pulled out his sword, and dressed him toward Sir Marhaus on foot, and therewith either came unto other eagerly, and smote together with their swords, that their shields flew in cantels, and they bruised their helms and their hauberks, and wounded either other. But Sir Gawaine, fro it passed nine of the clock, waxed by the space of three hours ever stronger and stronger and thrice his might was increased. All this espied Sir Marhaus, and had great wonder how his might increased, and so they wounded other passing sore; and then when it was come noon—"

The pelting sing-song of it carried me forward to scenes and sounds of my boyhood days:

"N-e-e-ew Haven! ten minutes for refreshments—knductr'll strike the gong-bell two minutes before train leaves—passengers for the Shore-line please take seats in the rear k'yar, this k'yar don't go no furder—*ahh* -pls, *aw* -rnjz, b'*nan* ners, *s-a-n-d*'ches, p—op-corn!"

"—and waxed past noon and drew toward evensong. Sir Gawaine's strength feebled and waxed passing faint, that unnethes he might dure any longer, and Sir Marhaus was then bigger and bigger—"

"Which strained his armor, of course; and yet little would one of these people mind a small thing like that."

"—and so, Sir Knight, said Sir Marhaus, I have well felt that ye are a passing good knight, and a marvellous man of might as ever I felt any, while it lasteth, and our quarrels are not great, and therefore it were a pity to do you hurt, for I feel you are passing feeble. Ah, said Sir Gawaine, gentle knight, ye say the word that I should say. And therewith they took off their helms and either kissed other, and there they swore together either to love other as brethren—"

But I lost the thread there, and dozed off to slumber, thinking about what a pity it was that men with such superb strength—strength enabling them to stand up cased in cruelly burdensome iron and drenched with perspiration, and hack and batter and bang each other for six hours on a stretch—should not have been born at a time when they could put it to some useful purpose. Take a jackass, for instance: a jackass has that kind of strength, and puts it to a useful purpose, and is valuable to this world because he is a jackass; but a nobleman is not valuable because he is a jackass. It is a mixture that is always ineffectual, and should never have been attempted in the first place. And yet, once you start a mistake, the trouble is done and you never know what is going to come of it.

When I came to myself again and began to listen, I perceived that I had lost another chapter, and that Alisande had wandered a long way off with her people.

"And so they rode and came into a deep valley full of stones, and thereby they saw a fair stream of water; above thereby was the head of the stream, a fair fountain, and three damsels sitting thereby. In this country, said Sir Marhaus, came never knight since it was christened, but he found strange adventures—"

"This is not good form, Alisande. Sir Marhaus the king's son of Ireland talks like all the rest; you ought to give him a brogue, or at least a characteristic expletive; by this means one would recognize him as soon as he spoke, without his ever being named. It is a common literary device with the great authors. You should make him say, 'In this country, be jabers, came never knight since it was christened, but he found strange adventures, be jabers.' You see how much better that sounds."

"—came never knight but he found strange adventures, be jabers. Of a truth it doth indeed, fair lord, albeit 'tis passing hard to say, though peradventure that will not tarry but better speed with usage. And then they rode to the damsels, and either saluted other, and the eldest had a garland of gold about her head, and she was threescore winter of age or more—"

"The *damsel* was?"

"Even so, dear lord—and her hair was white under the garland—"

"Celluloid teeth, nine dollars a set, as like as not—the loose-fit kind, that go up and down like a portcullis when you eat, and fall out when you laugh."

"The second damsel was of thirty winter of age, with a circlet of gold about her head. The third damsel was but fifteen year of age—"

Billows of thought came rolling over my soul, and the voice faded out of my hearing!

Fifteen! Break—my heart! oh, my lost darling! Just her age who was so gentle, and lovely, and all the world to me, and whom I shall never see again! How the thought of her carries me back over wide seas of memory to a vague dim time, a happy time, so many, many centuries hence, when I used to wake in the soft summer mornings, out of sweet dreams of her, and say "Hello, Central!" just to hear her dear voice come melting back to me with a "Hello, Hank!" that was music of the spheres to my enchanted ear. She got three dollars a week, but she was worth it.

I could not follow Alisande's further explanation of who our captured knights were, now—I mean in case she should ever get to explaining who they were. My interest was gone, my thoughts were far away, and sad. By fitful glimpses of the drifting tale, caught here and there and now and then, I merely noted in a vague way that each of these three knights took one of these three damsels up behind him on his horse, and one rode north, another east, the other south, to seek adventures, and meet again and lie, after a year and a day. A year and a day—and without baggage. It was of a piece with the general simplicity of the country.

The sun was now setting. It was about three in the afternoon when Alisande had begun to tell me who the cowboys were; so she had made pretty good progress with it—for her. She would arrive some time or other, no doubt, but she was not a person who could be hurried.

We were approaching a castle which stood on high ground; a huge, strong, venerable structure, whose grey towers and battlements were charmingly draped with ivy, and whose whole majestic mass was drenched with splendours flung from the sinking sun. It was the largest castle we had seen, and so I thought it might be the one we were after, but Sandy said no. She did not know who owned it; she said she had passed it without calling, when she went down to Camelot.

16

Morgan Le Fay

If knights errant were to be believed, not all castles were desirable places to seek hospitality in. As a matter of fact, knights errant were *not* persons to be believed—that is, measured by modern standards of veracity; yet, measured by the standards of their own time, and scaled accordingly, you got the truth. It was very simple: you discounted a statement ninety-seven per cent; the rest was fact. Now after making this allowance, the truth remained that if I could find out something about a castle before ringing the door-bell—I mean hailing the warders—it was the sensible thing to do. So I was pleased when I saw in the distance a horseman making the bottom turn of the road that wound down from this castle.

As we approached each other, I saw that he wore a plumed helmet, and seemed to be otherwise clothed in steel, but bore a curious addition also—a stiff square garment like a herald's tabard. However, I had to smile at my own forgetfulness when I got nearer and read this sign on his tabard:

"*Persimmon's Soap—All the Prime-Donna Use It.*"

That was a little idea of my own, and had several wholesome purposes in view toward the civilizing and uplifting of this nation. In the first place, it was a furtive, underhand blow at this nonsense of knight errantry, though nobody suspected that but me. I had started a number of these people out—the bravest knights I could get—each sandwiched between bulletin boards bearing one device or another, and I judged that by and by when they got to be numerous enough they would begin to look ridiculous; and then, even the steel-clad ass that *hadn't* any board would himself begin to look ridiculous because he was out of the fashion.

Secondly, these missionaries would gradually, and without creating suspicion or exciting alarm, introduce a rudimentary cleanliness among the nobility, and from them it would work down to the people, if the priests could be kept quiet. This would undermine the Church. I mean would be a step toward that. Next, education—next, freedom—and then she would begin to crumble. It being my conviction that any Established Church is an established crime, an established slave-pen, I had no scruples, but was willing to assail it in any way or with any weapon that promised to hurt it. Why, in my own former day—in remote centuries not yet stirring in the womb of time—there were old Englishmen who imagined that they had been born in a free country: a "free" country with the Corporation Act and the Test still in force in it—timbers propped against men's liberties and dishonoured consciences to shore up an Established Anachronism with.

My missionaries were taught to spell out the gilt signs on their tabards—the showy gilding was a neat idea, I could have got the king to wear a bulletin board for the sake of that barbaric splendour—they were to spell out these signs and then explain to the lords and ladies what soap was; and if the lords and ladies were afraid of it, get them to try it on a dog. The missionary's next move was to get the family together and try it on himself; he was to stop at no experiment, however desperate, that could convince the nobility that soap was harmless; if any final doubt remained, he must catch a hermit—the woods were full of them; saints they called themselves, and saints they were believed to be. They were unspeakably holy, and worked miracles, and everybody stood in awe of them. If a hermit could survive a wash, and that failed to convince a duke, give him up, let him alone.

Whenever my missionaries overcame a knight errant on the road they washed him, and when he got well they swore him to go and get a bulletin board and disseminate soap and civilization the rest of his days. As a consequence the workers in the field were increasing by degrees, and the reform was steadily spreading. My soap factory felt the strain early. At first I had only two hands; but before I had left home I was already employing fifteen, and running night and day; and the atmospheric result was getting so pronounced that the King went sort of fainting and gasping around and said he did not believe he could stand it much longer, and Sir Launcelot got so that he did hardly anything but walk up and down the roof and swear, although I told him it was worse up there than anywhere else, but he said he wanted plenty of air; and he was always complaining that a palace was no place for a soap factory anyway, and said if a man was to start one in his house he would be damned if he wouldn't strangle him. There were ladies present, too, but much these people ever cared for that; they would swear before children, if the wind was their way when the factory was going.

This missionary knight's name was La Cote Male Taile, and he said that this castle was the abode of Morgan le Fay, sister of King Arthur, and wife of King Uriens, monarch of a realm about as big as the District of Columbia—you could stand in the middle of it and throw bricks into the next kingdom. "Kings" and "Kingdoms" were as thick in Britain as they had been in little Palestine in Joshua's time, when people had to sleep with their knees pulled up because they couldn't stretch out without a passport.

La Cote was much depressed, for he had scored here the worst failure of his campaign. He had not worked off a cake; yet he had tried all the tricks of the trade, even to the washing of a hermit; but the hermit died. This was, indeed, a bad failure, for this animal would now be dubbed a martyr, and would take his place among the saints of the Roman calendar. Thus made he his moan, this poor Sir La Cote Male Taile, and sorrowed passing sore. And so my heart bled for him, and I was moved to comfort and stay him. Wherefore I said:

"Forbear to grieve, fair knight, for this is not a defeat. We have brains, you and I; and for such as have brains there are no defeats, but only victories. Observe how we will turn this seeming disaster into an advertisement; an advertisement for our soap; and the biggest one, to draw, that was ever thought of; an advertisement that will transform that Mount Washington defeat into a Matterhorn victory. We will put on your bulletin board, '*Patronized by the elect.*' How does that strike you?"

"Verily, it is wonderly bethought!"

"Well, a body is bound to admit that for just a modest little one-line ad, it's a corker."

So the poor colporteur's griefs vanished away. He was a brave fellow, and had done mighty feats of arms in his time. His chief celebrity rested upon the events of an excursion like this one of mine, which he had once made with a damsel named Maledisant, who was as handy with her tongue as was Sandy, though in a different way, for her tongue churned forth only railings and insult, whereas Sandy's music was of a kindlier sort. I knew his story well, and so I knew how to interpret the compassion that was in his face when he bade me farewell. He supposed I was having a bitter hard time of it.

Sandy and I discussed his story, as we rode along, and she said that La Cote's bad luck had begun with the very beginning of that trip; for the king's fool had overthrown him on the first day, and in such cases it was customary for the girl to desert to the conqueror, but Maledisant didn't do it; and also persisted afterward in sticking to him, after all his defeats. But, said I, suppose the victor should decline to accept his spoil? She said that that wouldn't answer—he must. He couldn't decline; it wouldn't be regular. I made a note of that. If Sandy's music got to be too burdensome, some time, I would let a knight defeat me, on the chance that she would desert to him.

In due time we were challenged by the warders, from the castle walls, and after a parley admitted. I have nothing pleasant to tell about that visit. But it was not a disappointment, for I knew Mrs. le Fay by reputation, and was not expecting anything pleasant. She was held in awe by the whole realm, for she had made everybody believe she was a great sorceress. All her ways were wicked, all her instincts devilish. She was loaded to the eyelids with cold malice. All her history was black with crime; and among her crimes murder was common. I was most curious to see her; as curious as I could have been to see Satan. To my surprise she was beautiful; black thoughts had failed to make her expression repulsive, age had failed to wrinkle her satin skin or mar its bloomy freshness. She could have passed for old Uriens' granddaughter, she could have been mistaken for sister to her own son.

As soon as we were fairly within the castle gates we were ordered into her presence. King Uriens was there, a kind-faced old man with a subdued look; and also the son, Sir Uwaine le Blanchemains, in whom I was, of course, interested on account of the tradition that he had once done battle with thirty knights, and also on account of his trip with Sir Gawaine and Sir Marhaus, which Sandy had been aging me with. But Morgan was the main attraction, the conspicuous personality here; she was head chief of this household, that was plain. She caused us to be seated, and then she began, with all manner of pretty graces and graciousnesses, to ask me questions. Dear me, it was like a bird or a flute, or something, talking. I felt persuaded that this woman must have been misrepresented, lied about. She trilled along, and trilled along, and presently a handsome young page, clothed like the rainbow, and as easy and undulatory of movement as a wave, came with something on a golden salver, and, kneeling to present it to her, overdid his graces and lost his balance, and so fell lightly against her knee. She slipped a dirk into him in as matter-of-course a way as another person would have harpooned a rat!

Poor child! he slumped to the floor, twisted his silken limbs in one great straining contortion of pain, and was dead. Out of the old king was wrung an involuntary "O-h!" of compassion. The look he got, made him cut it suddenly short and not put any more hyphens in it. Sir Uwaine, at a sign from his mother, went to the anteroom and called some servants, and meanwhile madame went rippling sweetly along with her talk.

I saw that she was a good housekeeper, for while she talked she kept a corner of her eye on the servants to see that they made no balks in handling the body and getting it out; when they came with fresh clean towels, she sent back for the other kind; and when they had finished wiping the floor and were going, she indicated a crimson fleck the size of a tear which their duller eyes had overlooked. It was plain to me that La Cote Male Taile had failed to see the mistress of the house. Often, how louder and clearer than any tongue, does dumb circumstantial evidence speak.

Morgan le Fay rippled along as musically as ever. Marvellous woman. And what a glance she had: when it fell in reproof upon those servants, they shrunk and quailed as timid people do when the lightning flashes out of a cloud. I could have got the habit myself. It was the same with that poor old Brer Uriens; he was always on the ragged edge of apprehension; she could not even turn toward him but he winced.

In the midst of the talk I let drop a complimentary word about King Arthur, forgetting for the moment how this woman hated her brother. That one little compliment was enough. She clouded up like storm; she called for her guards, and said:

"Hale me these varlets to the dungeons."

That struck cold on my ears, for her dungeons had a reputation. Nothing occurred to me to say—or do. But not so with Sandy. As the guard laid a hand upon me, she piped up with the tranquilest confidence, and said:

"God's wounds, dost thou covet destruction, thou maniac? It is The Boss!"

Now what a happy idea that was!—and so simple; yet it would never have occurred to me. I was born modest; not all over, but in spots; and this was one of the spots.

The effect upon madame was electrical. It cleared her countenance and brought back her smiles and all her persuasive graces and blandishments; but nevertheless she was not able to entirely cover up with them the fact that she was in a ghastly fright. She said:

"La, but do list to thine handmaid! as if one gifted with powers like to mine might say the thing which I have said unto one who has vanquished Merlin, and not be jesting. By mine enchantments I foresaw your coming, and by them I knew you when you entered here. I did but play this little jest with hope to surprise you into some display of your art, as not doubting you would blast the guards with occult fires, consuming them to ashes on the spot, a marvel much beyond mine own ability, yet one which I have long been childishly curious to see."

The guards were less curious, and got out as soon as they got permission.

17

A Royal Banquet

Madame, seeing me pacific and unresentful, no doubt judged that I was deceived by her excuse; for her fright dissolved away, and she was soon so importunate to have me give an exhibition and kill somebody, that the thing grew to be embarrassing. However, to my relief she was presently interrupted by the call to prayers. I will say this much for the nobility: that, tyrannical, murderous, rapacious, and morally rotten as they were, they were deeply and enthusiastically religious. Nothing could divert them from the regular and faithful performance of the pieties enjoined by the Church. More than once I had seen a noble who had gotten his enemy at a disadvantage, stop to pray before cutting his throat; more than once I had seen a noble, after ambushing and dispatching his enemy, retire to the nearest wayside shrine and humbly give thanks, without even waiting to rob the body. There was to be nothing finer or sweeter in the life of even Benvenuto Cellini, that rough-hewn saint, ten centuries later. All the nobles of Britain, with their families, attended divine service morning and night daily, in their private chapels, and even the worst of them had family worship five or six times a day besides. The credit of this belonged entirely to the Church. Although I was no friend to that Catholic Church, I was obliged to admit this. And often, in spite of me, I found myself saying, "What would this country be without the Church?"

After prayers we had dinner in a great banqueting hall which was lighted by hundreds of grease-jets, and everything was as fine and lavish and rudely splendid as might become the royal degree of the hosts. At the head of the hall, on a dais, was the table of the king, queen, and their son, Prince Uwaine. Stretching down the hall from this, was the general table, on the floor. At this, above the salt, sat the visiting nobles and the grown members of their families, of both sexes—the resident Court, in effect—sixty-one persons; below the salt sat minor officers of the household, with their principal subordinates: altogether a hundred and eighteen persons sitting, and about as many liveried servants standing behind their chairs, or serving in one capacity or another. It was a very fine show. In a gallery a band with cymbals, horns, harps, and other horrors, opened the proceedings with what seemed to be the crude first-draft or original agony of the wail known to later centuries as "In the Sweet Bye and Bye." It was new, and ought to have been rehearsed a little more. For some reason or other the queen had the composer hanged, after dinner.

After this music, the priest who stood behind the royal table said a noble long grace in ostensible Latin. Then the battalion of waiters broke away from their posts, and darted, rushed, flew, fetched and carried, and the mighty feeding began; no words anywhere, but absorbing attention to business. The rows of chops opened and shut in vast unison, and the sound of it was like to the muffled burr of subterranean machinery.

The havoc continued an hour and a half, and unimaginable was the destruction of substantials. Of the chief feature of the feast—the huge wild boar that lay stretched out so portly and imposing at the start—nothing was left but the semblance of a hoop-skirt; and he was but the type and symbol of what had happened to all the other dishes.

With the pastries and so on, the heavy drinking began—and the talk. Gallon after gallon of wine and mead disappeared, and everybody got comfortable, then happy, then sparklingly joyous—both sexes—and by and by pretty noisy. Men told anecdotes that were terrific to hear, but nobody blushed; and when the nub was sprung, the assemblage let go with a horse-laugh that shook the fortress. Ladies answered back with historiettes that would almost have made Queen Margaret of Navarre or even the great Elizabeth of England hide behind a handkerchief, but nobody hid here, but only laughed—howled, you may say. In pretty much all of these dreadful stories, ecclesiastics were the hardy heroes, but that didn't worry the chaplain any, he had his laugh with the rest; more than that, upon invitation he roared out a song which was of as daring a sort as any that was sung that night.

By midnight everybody was fagged out, and sore with laughing; and, as a rule, drunk: some weepingly, some affectionately, some hilariously, some quarrelsomely, some dead and under the table. Of the ladies, the worst spectacle was a lovely young duchess, whose wedding-eve this was; and indeed she was a spectacle, sure enough. Just as she was she could have sat in advance for the portrait of the young daughter of the Regent d'Orleans, at the famous dinner whence she was carried, foul-mouthed, intoxicated, and helpless, to her bed, in the lost and lamented days of the Ancient Regime.

Suddenly, even while the priest was lifting his hands, and all conscious heads were bowed in reverent expectation of the coming blessing, there appeared under the arch of the far-off door at the bottom of the hall an old and bent and white-haired lady, leaning upon a crutch-stick; and she lifted the stick and pointed it toward the queen and cried out:

"The wrath and curse of God fall upon you, woman without pity, who have slain mine innocent grandchild and made desolate this old heart that had nor chick, nor friend nor stay nor comfort in all this world but him!"

Everybody crossed himself in a grisly fright, for a curse was an awful thing to those people; but the queen rose up majestic, with the death-light in her eye, and flung back this ruthless command:

"Lay hands on her! To the stake with her!"

The guards left their posts to obey. It was a shame; it was a cruel thing to see. What could be done? Sandy gave me a look; I knew she had another inspiration. I said:

"Do what you choose."

She was up and facing toward the queen in a moment. She indicated me, and said:

"Madame, *he* saith this may not be. Recall the commandment, or he will dissolve the castle and it shall vanish away like the instable fabric of a dream!"

Confound it, what a crazy contract to pledge a person to! What if the queen—

But my consternation subsided there, and my panic passed off; for the queen, all in a collapse, made no show of resistance but gave a countermanding sign and sunk into her seat. When she reached it she was sober. So were many of the others. The assemblage rose, whiffed ceremony to the winds, and rushed for the door like a mob; overturning chairs, smashing crockery, tugging, struggling, shouldering, crowding—anything to get out before I should change my mind and puff the castle into the measureless dim vacancies of space. Well, well, well, they *were* a superstitious lot. It is all a body can do to conceive of it.

The poor queen was so scared and humbled that she was even afraid to hang the composer without first consulting me. I was very sorry for her—indeed, any one would have been, for she was really suffering; so I was willing to do anything that was reasonable, and had no desire to carry things to wanton extremities. I therefore considered the matter thoughtfully, and ended by having the musicians ordered into our presence to play that Sweet Bye and Bye again, which they did. Then I saw that she was right, and gave her permission to hang the whole band. This little relaxation of sternness had a good effect upon the queen. A statesman gains little by the arbitrary exercise of iron-clad authority upon all occasions that offer, for this wounds the just pride of his subordinates, and thus tends to undermine his strength. A little concession, now and then, where it can do no harm, is the wiser policy.

Now that the queen was at ease in her mind once more, and measurably happy, her wine naturally began to assert itself again, and it got a little the start of her. I mean it set her music going—her silver bell of a tongue. Dear me, she was a master talker. It would not become me to suggest that it was pretty late and that I was a tired man and very sleepy. I wished I had gone off to bed when I had the chance. Now I must stick it out; there was no other way. So she tinkled along and along, in the otherwise profound and ghostly hush of the sleeping castle, until by and by there came, as if from deep down under us, a far-away sound, as of a muffled shriek—with an expression of agony about it that made my flesh crawl. The queen stopped, and her eyes lighted with pleasure; she tilted her graceful head as a bird does when it listens. The sound bored its way up through the stillness again.

"What is it?" I said.

"It is truly a stubborn soul, and endureth long. It is many hours now."

"Endureth what?"

"The rack. Come—ye shall see a blithe sight. An he yield not his secret now, ye shall see him torn asunder."

What a silky smooth hellion she was; and so composed and serene, when the cords all down my legs were hurting in sympathy with that man's pain. Conducted by mailed guards bearing flaring torches, we tramped along echoing corridors, and down stone stairways dank and dripping, and smelling of mould and ages of imprisoned night—a chill, uncanny journey and a long one, and not made the shorter or the cheerier by the sorceress's talk, which was about this sufferer and his crime. He had been accused by an anonymous informer, of having killed a stag in the royal preserves. I said:

"Anonymous testimony isn't just the right thing, your Highness. It were fairer to confront the accused with the accuser."

"I had not thought of that, it being but of small consequence. But an I would, I could not, for that the accuser came masked by night, and told the forester, and straightway got him hence again, and so the forester knoweth him not."

"Then is this Unknown the only person who saw the stag killed?"

"Marry, *no* man *saw* the killing, but this Unknown saw this hardy wretch near to the spot where the stag lay, and came with right loyal zeal and betrayed him to the forester."

"So the Unknown was near the dead stag, too? Isn't it just possible that he did the killing himself? His loyal zeal—in a mask—looks just a shade suspicious. But what is your highness's idea for racking the prisoner? Where is the profit?"

"He will not confess, else; and then were his soul lost. For his crime his life is forfeited by the law—and of a surety will I see that he payeth it!—but it were peril to my own soul to let him die unconfessed and unabsolved. Nay, I were a fool to fling me into hell for *his* accommodation."

"But, your Highness, suppose he has nothing to confess?"

"As to that, we shall see, anon. An I rack him to death and he confess not, it will peradventure show that he had indeed naught to confess—ye will grant that that is sooth? Then shall I not be damned for an unconfessed man that had naught to confess—wherefore, I shall be safe."

It was the stubborn unreasoning of the time. It was useless to argue with her. Arguments have no chance against petrified training; they wear it as little as the waves wear a cliff. And her training was everybody's. The brightest intellect in the land would not have been able to see that her position was defective.

As we entered the rack-cell I caught a picture that will not go from me; I wish it would. A native young giant of thirty or thereabouts lay stretched upon the frame on his back, with his wrists and ankles tied to ropes which led over windlasses at either end. There was no colour in him; his features were contorted and set, and sweat-drops stood upon his forehead. A priest bent over him on each side; the executioner stood by; guards were on duty; smoking torches stood in sockets along the walls; in a corner crouched a poor young creature, her face drawn with anguish, a half-wild and hunted look in her eyes, and in her lap lay a little child asleep. Just as we stepped across the threshold the executioner gave his machine a slight turn, which wrung a cry from both the prisoner and the woman; but I shouted, and the executioner released the strain without waiting to see who spoke. I could not let this horror go on; it would have killed me to see it. I asked the queen to let me clear the place and speak to the prisoner privately; and when she was going to object I spoke in a low voice and said I did not want to make a scene before her servants, but I must have my way; for I was King Arthur's representative, and was speaking in his name. She saw she had to yield. I asked her to indorse me to these people, and then leave me. It was not pleasant for her, but she took the pill; and even went further than I was meaning to require. I only wanted the backing of her own authority; but she said:

"Ye will do in all things as this lord shall command. It is The Boss."

It was certainly a good word to conjure with: you could see it by the squirming of these rats. The queen's guards fell into line, and she and they marched away, with their torch-bearers, and woke the echoes of the cavernous tunnels with the measured beat of their retreating footfalls. I had the prisoner taken from the rack and placed upon his bed, and medicaments applied to his hurts, and wine given him to drink. The woman crept near and looked on, eagerly, lovingly, but timorously—like one who fears a repulse; indeed, she tried furtively to touch the man's forehead, and jumped back, the picture of fright, when I turned unconsciously toward her. It was pitiful to see.

"Lord," I said, "stroke him, lass, if you want to. Do anything you're a mind to; don't mind me."

Why, her eyes were as grateful as an animal's, when you do it a kindness that it understands. The baby was out of her way and she had her cheek against the man's in a minute and her hands fondling his hair, and her happy tears running down. The man revived and caressed his wife with his eyes, which was all he could do. I judged I might clear the den, now, and I did; cleared it of all but the family and myself. Then I said:

"Now, my friend, tell me your side of this matter; I know the other side."

The man moved his head in sign of refusal. But the woman looked pleased—as it seemed to me—pleased with my suggestion. I went on—

"You know of me?"

"Yes. All do, in Arthur's realms."

"If my reputation has come to you right and straight, you should not be afraid to speak."

The woman broke in, eagerly:

"Ah, fair my lord, do thou persuade him! Thou canst an thou wilt. Ah, he suffereth so; and it is for me—for *me*! And how can I bear it? I would I might see him die—a sweet, swift death; oh, my Hugo, I cannot bear this one!"

And she fell to sobbing and grovelling about my feet, and still imploring. Imploring what? The man's death? I could not quite get the bearings of the thing. But Hugo interrupted her and said:

"Peace! Ye wit not what ye ask. Shall I starve whom I love, to win a gentle death? I wend thou knewest me better."

"Well," I said, "I can't quite make this out. It is a puzzle. Now—"

"Ah, dear my lord, an ye will but persuade him! Consider how these his tortures wound me! Oh, and he will not speak!—whereas, the healing, the solace that lie in a blessed swift death—"

"What *are* you maundering about? He's going out from here a free man and whole—he's not going to die."

The man's white face lit up, and the woman flung herself at me in a most surprising explosion of joy, and cried out:

"He is saved!—for it is the king's word by the mouth of the king's servant—Arthur, the king whose word is gold!"

"Well, then you do believe I can be trusted, after all. Why didn't you before?"

"Who doubted? Not I, indeed; and not she."

"Well, why wouldn't you tell me your story, then?"

"Ye had made no promise; else had it been otherwise."

"I see, I see. . . . And yet I believe I don't quite see, after all. You stood the torture and refused to confess; which shows plain enough to even the dullest understanding that you had nothing to confess—"

"I, my lord? How so? It was I that killed the deer!"

"You *did*? Oh, dear, this is the most mixed-up business that ever—"

"Dear lord, I begged him on my knees to confess, but—"

"You *did*! It gets thicker and thicker. What did you want him to do that for?"

"Sith it would bring him a quick death and save him all this cruel pain."

"Well—yes, there is reason in that. But *he* didn't want the quick death."

"He? Why, of a surety he *did*."

"Well, then, why in the world *didn't* he confess?"

"Ah, sweet sir, and leave my wife and chick without bread and shelter?"

"Oh, heart of gold, now I see it! The bitter law takes the convicted man's estate and beggars his widow and his orphans. They could torture you to death, but without conviction or confession they could not rob your wife and baby. You stood by them like a man; and *you*—true wife and the woman that you are—you would have bought him release from torture at cost to yourself of slow starvation and death—well, it humbles a body to think what your sex can do when it comes to self-sacrifice. I'll book you both for my colony; you'll like it there; it's a Factory where I'm going to turn groping and grubbing automata into *men*."

18

In the Queen's Dungeons

Well, I arranged all that; and I had the man sent to his home. I had a great desire to rack the executioner; not because he was a good, painstaking and painsgiving official—for surely it was not to his discredit that he performed his functions well—but to pay him back for wantonly cuffing and otherwise distressing that young woman. The priests told me about this, and were generously hot to have him punished. Something of this disagreeable sort was turning up every now and then. I mean, episodes that showed that not all priests were frauds and self-seekers, but that many, even the great majority, of these that were down on the ground among the common people, were sincere and right-hearted, and devoted to the alleviation of human troubles and sufferings. Well, it was a thing which could not be helped, so I seldom fretted about it, and never many minutes at a time; it has never been my way to bother much about things which you can't cure. But I did not like it, for it was just the sort of thing to keep people reconciled to an Established Church. We *must* have a religion—it goes without saying—but my idea is, to have it cut up into forty free sects, so that they will police each other, as had been the case in the United States in my time. Concentration of power in a political machine is bad; and an Established Church is only a political machine; it was invented for that; it is nursed, cradled, preserved for that; it is an enemy to human liberty, and does no good which it could not better do in a split-up and scattered condition. That wasn't law; it wasn't gospel: it was only an opinion—my opinion, and I was only a man, one man: so it wasn't worth any more than the pope's—or any less, for that matter.

Well, I couldn't rack the executioner, neither would I overlook the just complaint of the priests. The man must be punished somehow or other, so I degraded him from his office and made him leader of the band—the new one that was to be started. He begged hard, and said he couldn't play—a plausible excuse, but too thin; there wasn't a musician in the country that could.

The queen was a good deal outraged, next morning when she found she was going to have neither Hugo's life nor his property. But I told her she must bear this cross; that while by law and custom she certainly was entitled to both the man's life and his property, there were extenuating circumstances, and so in Arthur the King's name I had pardoned him. The deer was ravaging the man's fields, and he had killed it in sudden passion, and not for gain; and he had carried it into the royal forest in the hope that that might make detection of the misdoer impossible. Confound her, I couldn't make her see that sudden passion is an extenuating circumstance in the killing of venison—or of a person—so I gave it up and let her sulk it out. I *did* think I was going to make her see it by remarking that her own sudden passion in the case of the page modified that crime.

"Crime!" she exclaimed. "How thou talkest! Crime, forsooth! Man, I am going to *pay* for him!"

Oh, it was no use to waste sense on her. Training—training is everything; training is all there is *to* a person. We speak of nature; it is folly; there is no such thing as nature; what we call by that misleading name is merely heredity and training. We have no thoughts of our own, no opinions of our own; they are transmitted to us, trained into us. All that is original in us, and therefore fairly creditable or discreditable to us, can be covered up and hidden by the point of a cambric needle, all the rest being atoms contributed by, and inherited from, a procession of ancestors that stretches back a billion years to the Adam-clam or grasshopper or monkey from whom our race has been so tediously and ostentatiously and unprofitably developed. And as for me, all that I think about in this plodding sad pilgrimage, this pathetic drift between the eternities, is to look out and humbly live a pure and high and blameless life, and save that one microscopic atom in me that is truly *me*: the rest may land in Sheol and welcome for all I care.

No, confound her, her intellect was good, she had brains enough, but her training made her an ass—that is, from a many-centuries-later point of view. To kill the page was no crime—it was her right; and upon her right she stood, serenely and unconscious of offense. She was a result of generations of training in the unexamined and unassailed belief that the law which permitted her to kill a subject when she chose was a perfectly right and righteous one.

Well, we must give even Satan his due. She deserved a compliment for one thing; and I tried to pay it, but the words stuck in my throat. She had a right to kill the boy, but she was in no wise obliged to pay for him. That was law for some other people, but not for her. She knew quite well that she was doing a large and generous thing to pay for that lad, and that I ought in common fairness to come out with something handsome about it, but I couldn't—my mouth refused. I couldn't help seeing, in my fancy, that poor old grandma with the broken heart, and that fair young creature lying butchered, his little silken pomps and vanities laced with his golden blood. How could she *pay* for him! *Whom* could she pay? And so, well knowing that this woman, trained as she had been, deserved praise, even adulation, I was yet not able to utter it, trained as I had been. The best I could do was to fish up a compliment from outside, so to speak—and the pity of it was, that it was true:

"Madame, your people will adore you for this."

Quite true, but I meant to hang her for it some day if I lived. Some of those laws were too bad, altogether too bad. A master might kill his slave for nothing—for mere spite, malice, or to pass the time—just as we have seen that the crowned head could do it with *his* slave, that is to say, anybody. A gentleman could kill a free commoner, and pay for him—cash or garden-truck. A noble could kill a noble without expense, as far as the law was concerned, but reprisals in kind were to be expected. *Any* body could kill *some* body, except the commoner and the slave; these had no privileges. If they killed, it was murder, and the law wouldn't stand murder. It made short work of the experimenter—and of his family, too, if he murdered somebody who belonged up among the ornamental ranks. If a commoner gave a noble even so much as a Damiens-scratch which didn't kill or even hurt, he got Damiens' dose for it just the same; they pulled him to rags and tatters with horses, and all the world came to see the show, and crack jokes, and have a good time; and some of the performances of the best people present were as tough, and as properly unprintable, as any that have been printed by the pleasant Casanova in his chapter about the dismemberment of Louis XV's poor awkward enemy.

The Church, The King, The Nobleman, and The Freeman

I had had enough of this grisly place by this time, and wanted to leave, but I couldn't, because I had something on my mind that my conscience kept prodding me about, and wouldn't let me forget. If I had the remaking of man, he wouldn't have any conscience. It is one of the most disagreeable things connected with a person; and although it certainly does a great deal of good, it cannot be said to pay, in the long run; it would be much better to have less good and more comfort. Still, this is only my opinion, and I am only one man; others, with less experience, may think differently. They have a right to their view. I only stand to this: I have noticed my conscience for many years, and I know it is more trouble and bother to me than anything else I started with. I suppose that in the beginning I prized it, because we prize anything that is ours; and yet how foolish it was to think so. If we look at it in another way, we see how absurd it is: if I had an anvil in me would I prize it? Of course not. And yet when you come to think, there is no real difference between a conscience and an anvil—I mean for comfort. I have noticed it a thousand times. And you could dissolve an anvil with acids, when you couldn't stand it any longer; but there isn't any way that you can work off a conscience—at least so it will stay worked off; not that I know of, anyway.

There was something I wanted to do before leaving, but it was a disagreeable matter, and I hated to go at it. Well, it bothered me all the morning. I could have mentioned it to the old king, but what would be the use?—he was but an extinct volcano; he had been active in his time, but his fire was out, this good while, he was only a stately ash-pile now; gentle enough, and kindly enough for my purpose, without doubt, but not usable. He was nothing, this so-called King: the queen was the only power there. And she was a Vesuvius. As a favour, she might consent to warm a flock of sparrows for you, but then she might take that very opportunity to turn herself loose and bury a city. However, I reflected that as often as any other way, when you are expecting the worst, you get something that is not so bad, after all.

So I braced up and placed my matter before her royal Highness. I said I had been having a general jail-delivery at Camelot and among neighbouring castles, and with her permission I would like to examine her collection, her bric-a-brac—that is to say, her prisoners. She resisted; but I was expecting that. But she finally consented. I was expecting that, too, but not so soon. That about ended my discomfort. She called her guards and torches, and we went down into the dungeons. These were down under the castle's foundations, and mainly were small cells hollowed out of the living rock. Some of these cells had no light at all. In one of them was a woman, in foul rags, who sat on the ground, and would not answer a question or speak a word, but only looked up at us once or twice, through a cobweb of tangled hair, as if to see what casual thing it might be that was disturbing with sound and light the meaningless dull dream that was become her life; after that, she sat bowed, with her dirt-caked fingers idly interlocked in her lap, and gave no further sign. This poor rack of bones was a woman of middle age, apparently; but only apparently; she had been there nine years, and was eighteen when she entered. She was a commoner, and had been sent here on her bridal night by Sir Breuse Sance Pite, a neighbouring lord whose vassal her father was, and to which said lord she had refused what has since been called *le droit du seigneur*, and, moreover, had opposed violence to violence and spilt half a gill of his almost sacred blood. The young husband had interfered at that point, believing the bride's life in danger, and had flung the noble out into the midst of the humble and trembling wedding guests, in the parlour, and left him there astonished at this strange treatment, and implacably embittered against both bride and groom. The said lord being cramped for dungeon-room had asked the queen to accommodate his two criminals, and here in her bastile they had been ever since; hither, indeed, they had come before their crime was an hour old, and had never seen each other since. Here they were, kenneled like toads in the same rock; they had passed nine pitch dark years within fifty feet of each other, yet neither knew whether the other was alive or not. All the first years, their only question had been—asked with beseechings and tears that might have moved stones, in time, perhaps, but hearts are not stones: "Is he alive?" "Is she alive?" But they had never got an answer; and at last that question was not asked any more—or any other.

I wanted to see the man, after hearing all this. He was thirty-four years old, and looked sixty. He sat upon a squared block of stone, with his head bent down, his forearms resting on his knees, his long hair hanging like a fringe before his face, and he was muttering to himself. He raised his chin and looked us slowly over, in a listless dull way, blinking with the distress of the torchlight, then dropped his head and fell to muttering again and took no further notice of us. There were some pathetically suggestive dumb witnesses present. On his wrists and ankles were cicatrices, old smooth scars, and fastened to the stone on which he sat was a chain with manacles and fetters attached; but this apparatus lay idle on the ground, and was thick with rust. Chains cease to be needed after the spirit has gone out of a prisoner.

I could not rouse the man; so I said we would take him to her, and see—to the bride who was the fairest thing in the earth to him, once—

roses, pearls, and dew made flesh, for him; a wonder-work, the master-work of nature: with eyes like no other eyes, and voice like no other voice, and a freshness, and lithe young grace, and beauty, that belonged properly to the creatures of dreams—as he thought—and to no other. The sight of her would set his stagnant blood leaping; the sight of her—

But it was a disappointment. They sat together on the ground and looked dimly wondering into each other's faces a while, with a sort of weak animal curiosity; then forgot each other's presence, and dropped their eyes, and you saw that they were away again and wandering in some far land of dreams and shadows that we know nothing about.

I had them taken out and sent to their friends. The queen did not like it much. Not that she felt any personal interest in the matter, but she thought it disrespectful to Sir Breuse Sance Pite. However, I assured her that if he found he couldn't stand it I would fix him so that he could.

I set forty-seven prisoners loose out of those awful rat-holes, and left only one in captivity. He was a lord, and had killed another lord, a sort of kinsman of the queen. That other lord had ambushed him to assassinate him, but this fellow had got the best of him and cut his throat. However, it was not for that that I left him jailed, but for maliciously destroying the only public well in one of his wretched villages. The queen was bound to hang him for killing her kinsman, but I would not allow it: it was no crime to kill an assassin. But I said I was willing to let her hang him for destroying the well; so she concluded to put up with that, as it was better than nothing.

Dear me, for what trifling offenses the most of those forty-seven men and women were shut up there! Indeed, some were there for no distinct offense at all, but only to gratify somebody's spite; and not always the queen's by any means, but a friend's. The newest prisoner's crime was a mere remark which he had made. He said he believed that men were about all alike, and one man as good as another, barring clothes. He said he believed that if you were to strip the nation naked and send a stranger through the crowd, he couldn't tell the King from a quack doctor, nor a duke from a hotel clerk. Apparently here was a man whose brains had not been reduced to an ineffectual mush by idiotic training. I set him loose and sent him to the Factory.

Some of the cells carved in the living rock were just behind the face of the precipice, and in each of these an arrow-slit had been pierced outward to the daylight, and so the captive had a thin ray from the blessed sun for his comfort. The case of one of these poor fellows was particularly hard. From his dusky swallow's hole high up in that vast wall of native rock he could peer out through the arrow-slit and see his own home off yonder in the valley; and for twenty-two years he had watched it, with heartache and longing, through that crack. He could see the lights shine there at night, and in the daytime he could see figures go in and come out—his wife and children, some of them, no doubt, though he could not make out at that distance. In the course of years he noted festivities there, and tried to rejoice, and wondered if they were weddings or what they might be. And he noted funerals; and they wrung his heart. He could make out the coffin, but he could not determine its size, and so could not tell whether it was wife or child. He could see the procession form, with priests and mourners, and move solemnly away, bearing the secret with them. He had left behind him five children and a wife; and in nineteen years he had seen five funerals issue, and none of them humble enough in pomp to denote a servant. So he had lost five of his treasures; there must still be one remaining—one now infinitely, unspeakably precious—but *which* one? wife, or child? That was the question that tortured him, by night and by day, asleep and awake. Well, to have an interest, of some sort, and half a ray of light, when you are in a dungeon, is a great support to the body and preserver of the intellect. This man was in pretty good condition yet. By the time he had finished telling me his distressful tale, I was in the same state of mind that you would have been in yourself, if you have got average human curiosity; that is to say, I was as burning up as he was to find out which member of the family it was that was left. So I took him over home myself; and an amazing kind of a surprise party it was, too—typhoons and cyclones of frantic joy, and whole Niagaras of happy tears; and by George! we found the aforetime young matron greying toward the imminent verge of her half century, and the babies all men and women, and some of them married and experimenting familywise themselves—for not a soul of the tribe was dead! Conceive of the ingenious devilishness of that queen: she had a special hatred for this prisoner, and she had *invented* all those funerals herself, to scorch his heart with; and the sublimest stroke of genius of the whole thing was leaving the family-invoice a funeral *short*, so as to let him wear his poor old soul out guessing.

But for me, he never would have got out. Morgan le Fay hated him with her whole heart, and she never would have softened toward him. And yet his crime was committed more in thoughtlessness than deliberate depravity. He had said she had red hair. Well, she had; but that was no way to speak of it. When red-headed people are above a certain social grade their hair is auburn.

Consider it: among these forty-seven captives there were five whose names, offenses, and dates of incarceration were no longer known! One woman and four men—all bent, and wrinkled, and mind-extinguished patriarchs. They themselves had long ago forgotten these details; at any rate they had mere vague theories about them, nothing definite and nothing that they repeated twice in the same way. The succession of priests whose office it had been to pray daily with the captives and remind them that God had put them there, for some wise purpose or other, and teach them that patience, humbleness, and submission to oppression was what He loved to see in parties of a subordinate rank, had traditions about these poor old human ruins, but nothing more. These traditions went but little way, for they concerned the length of the incarceration only, and not the names of the offenses. And even by the help of tradition the only thing that could be proven was that none of the five had seen daylight for thirty-five years: how much longer this privation has lasted was not guessable. The King and the Queen knew nothing about these poor creatures, except that they were heirlooms, assets inherited, along with the throne, from the former firm. Nothing of their history had been transmitted with their persons, and so the inheriting owners had considered them of no value, and had felt no interest in them. I said to the queen:

"Then why in the world didn't you set them free?"

The question was a puzzler. She didn't know *why* she hadn't, the thing had never come up in her mind. So here she was, forecasting the veritable history of future prisoners of the Castle d'If, without knowing it. It seemed plain to me now, that with her training, those inherited prisoners were merely property—nothing more, nothing less. Well, when we inherit property, it does not occur to us to throw it away, even when we do not value it.

When I brought my procession of human bats up into the open world and the glare of the afternoon sun—previously blindfolding them, in charity for eyes so long untortured by light—they were a spectacle to look at. Skeletons, scarecrows, goblins, pathetic frights, every one; legitimatest possible children of Monarchy by the Grace of God and the Established Church. I muttered absently:

"I *wish* I could photograph them!"

You have seen that kind of people who will never let on that they don't know the meaning of a new big word. The more ignorant they are, the more pitifully certain they are to pretend you haven't shot over their heads. The queen was just one of that sort, and was always making the stupidest blunders by reason of it. She hesitated a moment; then her face brightened up with sudden comprehension, and she said she would do it for me.

I thought to myself: She? why what can she know about photography? But it was a poor time to be thinking. When I looked around, she was moving on the procession with an axe!

Well, she certainly was a curious one, was Morgan le Fay. I have seen a good many kinds of women in my time, but she laid over them all for variety. And how sharply characteristic of her this episode was. She had no more idea than a horse of how to photograph a procession; but being in doubt, it was just like her to try to do it with an axe.

19

Knight Errantry as a Trade

Sandy and I were on the road again, next morning, bright and early. It was so good to open up one's lungs and take in whole luscious barrels-ful of the blessed God's untainted, dew-fashioned, woodland-scented air once more, after suffocating body and mind for two days and nights in the moral and physical stenches of that intolerable old buzzard-roost! I mean, for me: of course the place was all right and agreeable enough for Sandy, for she had been used to high life all her days.

Poor girl, her jaws had had a wearisome rest now for a while, and I was expecting to get the consequences. I was right; but she had stood by me most helpfully in the castle, and had mightily supported and reinforced me with gigantic foolishnesses which were worth more for the occasion than wisdoms double their size; so I thought she had earned a right to work her mill for a while, if she wanted to, and I felt not a pang when she started it up:

"Now turn we unto Sir Marhaus that rode with the damsel of thirty winter of age southward—"

"Are you going to see if you can work up another half-stretch on the trail of the cowboys, Sandy?"

"Even so, fair my lord."

"Go ahead, then. I won't interrupt this time, if I can help it. Begin over again; start fair, and shake out all your reefs, and I will load my pipe and give good attention."

"Now turn we unto Sir Marhaus that rode with the damsel of thirty winter of age southward. And so they came into a deep forest, and by fortune they were nighted, and rode along in a deep way, and at the last they came into a courtelage where abode the duke of South Marches, and there they asked harbour. And on the morn the duke sent unto Sir Marhaus, and bad him make him ready. And so Sir Marhaus arose and armed him, and there was a mass sung afore him, and he brake his fast, and so mounted on horseback in the court of the castle, there they should do the battle. So there was the duke already on horseback, clean armed, and his six sons by him, and every each had a spear in his hand, and so they encountered, whereas the duke and his two sons brake their spears upon him, but Sir Marhaus held up his spear and touched none of them. Then came the four sons by couples, and two of them brake their spears, and so did the other two. And all this while Sir Marhaus touched them not. Then Sir Marhaus ran to the duke, and smote him with his spear that horse and man fell to the earth. And so he served his sons. And then Sir Marhaus alight down, and bad the duke yield him or else he would slay him. And then some of his sons recovered, and would have set upon Sir Marhaus. Then Sir Marhaus said to the duke, Cease thy sons, or else I will do the uttermost to you all. When the duke saw he might not escape the death, he cried to his sons, and charged them to yield them to Sir Marhaus. And they kneeled all down and put the pommels of their swords to the knight, and so he received them. And then they holp up their father, and so by their common assent promised unto Sir Marhaus never to be foes unto King Arthur, and thereupon at Whitsuntide after, to come he and his sons, and put them in the king's grace.*

"Even so standeth the history, fair Sir Boss. Now ye shall wit that that very duke and his six sons are they whom but few days past you also did overcome and send to Arthur's court!"

"Why, Sandy, you can't mean it!"

"An I speak not sooth, let it be the worse for me."

"Well, well, well—now who would ever have thought it? One whole duke and six dukelets; why, Sandy, it was an elegant haul. Knight errantry is a most chuckle-headed trade, and it is tedious hard work, too, but I begin to see that there *is* money in it, after all, if you have luck. Not that I would ever engage in it as a business, for I wouldn't. No sound and legitimate business can be established on a basis of speculation. A successful whirl in the knight-errantry line—now what is it when you blow away the nonsense and come down to the cold facts? It's just a corner in pork, that's all, and you can't make anything else out of it. You're rich—yes—suddenly rich—for about a day, maybe a week; then somebody corners the market on *you*, and down goes your bucket-shop; ain't that so, Sandy?"

* The story is borrowed, language and all, from the Morte d'Arthur.—M.T.

"Whethersoever it be that my mind miscarrieth, bewraying simple language in such sort that the words do seem to come endlong and overthwart—"

"There's no use in beating about the bush and trying to get around it that way, Sandy, it's *so*, just as I say. I *know* it's so. And, moreover, when you come right down to the bedrock, knight errantry is *worse* than pork; for whatever happens, the pork's left, and so somebody's benefited anyway; but when the market breaks, in a knight-errantry whirl, and every knight in the pool passes in his checks, what have you got for assets? Just a rubbish-pile of battered corpses and a barrel or two of busted hardware. Can you call *those* assets? Give me pork, every time. Am I right?"

"Ah, peradventure my head being distraught by the manifold matters whereunto the confusions of these but late adventured haps and fortunings whereby not I alone nor you alone, but every each of us, meseemeth—"

"No, it's not your head, Sandy. Your head's all right, as far as it goes, but you don't know business; that's where the trouble is. It unfits you to argue about business, and you're wrong to be always trying. However, that aside, it was a good haul, anyway, and will breed a handsome crop of reputation in Arthur's court. And speaking of the cowboys, what a curious country this is for women and men that never get old. Now there's Morgan le Fay, as fresh and young as a Vassar pullet, to all appearances, and here is this old duke of the South Marches still slashing away with sword and lance at his time of life, after raising such a family as he has raised. As I understand it, Sir Gawaine killed seven of his sons, and still he had six left for Sir Marhaus and me to take into camp. And then there was that damsel of sixty winter of age still excursioning around in her frosty bloom—How old are you, Sandy?"

It was the first time I ever struck a still place in her. The mill had shut down for repairs, or something.

20

The Ogre's Castle

Between six and nine we made ten miles, which was plenty for a horse carrying triple—man, woman, and armor; then we stopped for a long nooning under some trees by a limpid brook.

Right so came by and by a knight riding; and as he drew near he made dolorous moan, and by the words of it I perceived that he was cursing and swearing; yet nevertheless was I glad of his coming, for that I saw he bore a bulletin board whereon in letters all of shining gold was writ:

"USE PETERSON'S PROPHYLACTIC TOOTH-BRUSH—ALL THE GO."

I was glad of his coming, for even by this token I knew him for knight of mine. It was Sir Madok de la Montaine, a burly great fellow whose chief distinction was that he had come within an ace of sending Sir Launcelot down over his horse-tail once. He was never long in a stranger's presence without finding some pretext or other to let out that great fact. But there was another fact of nearly the same size, which he never pushed upon anybody unasked, and yet never withheld when asked: that was, that the reason he didn't quite succeed was, that he was interrupted and sent down over horse-tail himself. This innocent vast lubber did not see any particular difference between the two facts. I liked him, for he was earnest in his work, and very valuable. And he was so fine to look at, with his broad mailed shoulders, and the grand leonine set of his plumed head, and his big shield with its quaint device of a gauntleted hand clutching a prophylactic tooth-brush, with motto: "Try Noyoudont." This was a tooth-wash that I was introducing.

He was aweary, he said, and indeed he looked it; but he would not alight. He said he was after the stove-polish man; and with this he broke out cursing and swearing anew. The bulletin-boarder referred to was Sir Ossaise of Surluse, a brave knight, and of considerable celebrity on account of his having tried conclusions in a tournament once, with no less a Mogul than Sir Gaheris himself—although not successfully. He was of a light and laughing disposition, and to him nothing in this world was serious. It was for this reason that I had chosen him to work up a stove-polish sentiment. There were no stoves yet, and so there could be nothing serious about stove-polish. All that the agent needed to do was to deftly and by degrees prepare the public for the great change, and have them established in predilections toward neatness against the time when the stove should appear upon the stage.

Sir Madok was very bitter, and brake out anew with cursings. He said he had cursed his soul to rags; and yet he would not get down from his horse, neither would he take any rest, or listen to any comfort, until he should have found Sir Ossaise and settled this account. It appeared, by what I could piece together of the unprofane fragments of his statement, that he had chanced upon Sir Ossaise at dawn of the morning, and been told that if he would make a short cut across the fields and swamps and broken hills and glades, he could head off a company of travelers who would be rare customers for prophylactics and tooth-wash. With characteristic zeal Sir Madok had plunged away at once upon this quest, and after three hours of awful crosslot riding had overhauled his game. And behold, it was the five patriarchs that had been released from the dungeons the evening before! Poor old creatures, it was all of twenty years since any one of them had known what it was to be equipped with any remaining snag or remnant of a tooth.

"Blank-blank-blank him," said Sir Madok, "an I do not stove-polish him an I may find him, leave it to me; for never no knight that hight Ossaise or aught else may do me this disservice and bide on live, an I may find him, the which I have thereunto sworn a great oath this day."

And with these words and others, he lightly took his spear and gat him thence. In the middle of the afternoon we came upon one of those very patriarchs ourselves, in the edge of a poor village. He was basking in the love of relatives and friends whom he had not seen for fifty years; and about him and caressing him were also descendants of his own body whom he had never seen at all till now; but to him these were all strangers, his memory was gone, his mind was stagnant. It seemed incredible that a man could outlast half a century shut up in a dark hole like a rat, but here were his old wife and some old comrades to testify to it. They could remember him as he was in the freshness and strength of his young manhood, when he kissed his child and delivered it to its mother's hands and went away into that long oblivion. The people at the castle could not tell within half a generation the length of time the man had been shut up there for his unrecorded and forgotten offense; but this old wife knew; and so did her old child, who stood there among her married sons and daughters trying to realize a father who had been to her a name, a thought, a formless image, a tradition, all her life, and now was suddenly concreted into actual flesh and blood and set before her face.

It was a curious situation; yet it is not on that account that I have made room for it here, but on account of a thing which seemed to me still more curious. To wit, that this dreadful matter brought from these downtrodden people no outburst of rage against these oppressors. They had been heritors and subjects of cruelty and outrage so long that nothing could have startled them but a kindness. Yes, here was a curious revelation, indeed, of the depth to which this people had been sunk in slavery. Their entire being was reduced to a monotonous dead level of patience, resignation, dumb uncomplaining acceptance of whatever might befall them in this life. Their very imagination was dead. When you can say that of a man, he has struck bottom, I reckon; there is no lower deep for him.

I rather wished I had gone some other road. This was not the sort of experience for a statesman to encounter who was planning out a peaceful revolution in his mind. For it could not help bringing up the unget-aroundable fact that, all gentle cant and philosophizing to the contrary notwithstanding, no people in the world ever did achieve their freedom by goody-goody talk and moral suasion: it being immutable law that all revolutions that will succeed must *begin* in blood, whatever may answer afterward. If history teaches anything, it teaches that. What this folk needed, then, was a Reign of Terror and a guillotine, and I was the wrong man for them.

Two days later, toward noon, Sandy began to show signs of excitement and feverish expectancy. She said we were approaching the ogre's castle. I was surprised into an uncomfortable shock. The object of our quest had gradually dropped out of my mind; this sudden resurrection of it made it seem quite a real and startling thing for a moment, and roused up in me a smart interest. Sandy's excitement increased every moment; and so did mine, for that sort of thing is catching. My heart got to thumping. You can't reason with your heart; it has its own laws, and thumps about things which the intellect scorns. Presently, when Sandy slid from the horse, motioned me to stop, and went creeping stealthily, with her head bent nearly to her knees, toward a row of bushes that bordered a declivity, the thumpings grew stronger and quicker. And they kept it up while she was gaining her ambush and getting her glimpse over the declivity; and also while I was creeping to her side on my knees. Her eyes were burning now, as she pointed with her finger, and said in a panting whisper:

"The castle! The castle! Lo, where it looms!"

What a welcome disappointment I experienced! I said:

"Castle? It is nothing but a pigsty; a pigsty with a wattled fence around it."

She looked surprised and distressed. The animation faded out of her face; and during many moments she was lost in thought and silent. Then:

"It was not enchanted aforetime," she said in a musing fashion, as if to herself. "And how strange is this marvel, and how awful—that to the one perception it is enchanted and dight in a base and shameful aspect; yet to the perception of the other it is not enchanted, hath suffered no change, but stands firm and stately still, girt with its moat and waving its banners in the blue air from its towers. And God shield us, how it pricks the heart to see again these gracious captives, and the sorrow deepened in their sweet faces! We have tarried along, and are to blame."

I saw my cue. The castle was enchanted to *me*, not to her. It would be wasted time to try to argue her out of her delusion, it couldn't be done; I must just humour it. So I said:

"This is a common case—the enchanting of a thing to one eye and leaving it in its proper form to another. You have heard of it before, Sandy, though you haven't happened to experience it. But no harm is done. In fact, it is lucky the way it is. If these ladies were hogs to everybody and to themselves, it would be necessary to break the enchantment, and that might be impossible if one failed to find out the particular process of the enchantment. And hazardous, too; for in attempting a disenchantment without the true key, you are liable to err, and turn your hogs into dogs, and the dogs into cats, the cats into rats, and so on, and end by reducing your materials to nothing finally, or to an odourless gas which you can't follow—which, of course, amounts to the same thing. But here, by good luck, no one's eyes but mine are under the enchantment, and so it is of no consequence to dissolve it. These ladies remain ladies to you, and to themselves, and to everybody else; and at the same time they will suffer in no way from my delusion, for when I know that an ostensible hog is a lady, that is enough for me, I know how to treat her."

"Thanks, oh, sweet my lord, thou talkest like an angel. And I know that thou wilt deliver them, for that thou art minded to great deeds and art as strong a knight of your hands and as brave to will and to do, as any that is on live."

"I will not leave a princess in the sty, Sandy. Are those three yonder that to my disordered eyes are starveling swineherds—"

"The ogres, Are *they* changed also? It is most wonderful. Now am I fearful; for how canst thou strike with sure aim when five of their nine cubits of stature are to thee invisible? Ah, go warily, fair sir; this is a mightier emprise than I wend."

"You be easy, Sandy. All I need to know is, how *much* of an ogre is invisible; then I know how to locate his vitals. Don't you be afraid, I will make short work of these bunco-steerers. Stay where you are."

I left Sandy kneeling there, corpse-faced but plucky and hopeful, and rode down to the pigsty, and struck up a trade with the swineherds. I won their gratitude by buying out all the hogs at the lump sum of sixteen pennies, which was rather above latest quotations. I was just in time; for the Church, the lord of the manor, and the rest of the tax-gatherers would have been along next day and swept off pretty much all the stock, leaving the swineherds very short of hogs and Sandy out of princesses. But now the tax people could be paid in cash, and there would be a stake left besides. One of the men had ten children; and he said that last year when a priest came and of his ten pigs took the fattest one for tithes, the wife burst out upon him, and offered him a child and said:

"Thou beast without bowels of mercy, why leave me my child, yet rob me of the wherewithal to feed it?"

How curious. The same thing had happened in the Wales of my day, under this same old Established Church, which was supposed by many to have changed its nature when it changed its disguise.

I sent the three men away, and then opened the sty gate and beckoned Sandy to come—which she did; and not leisurely, but with the rush of a prairie fire. And when I saw her fling herself upon those hogs, with tears of joy running down her cheeks, and strain them to her heart, and kiss them, and caress them, and call them reverently by grand princely names, I was ashamed of her, ashamed of the human race.

We had to drive those hogs home—ten miles; and no ladies were ever more fickle-minded or contrary. They would stay in no road, no path; they broke out through the brush on all sides, and flowed away in all directions, over rocks, and hills, and the roughest places they could find. And they must not be struck, or roughly accosted; Sandy could not bear to see them treated in ways unbecoming their rank. The troublesomest old sow of the lot had to be called my Lady, and your Highness, like the rest. It is annoying and difficult to scour around after hogs, in armor. There was one small countess, with an iron ring in her snout and hardly any hair on her back, that was the devil for perversity. She gave me a race of an hour, over all sorts of country, and then we were right where we had started from, having made not a rod of real progress. I seized her at last by the tail, and brought her along squealing. When I overtook Sandy she was horrified, and said it was in the last degree indelicate to drag a countess by her train.

We got the hogs home just at dark—most of them. The princess Nerovens de Morganore was missing, and two of her ladies in waiting: namely, Miss Angela Bohun, and the Demoiselle Elaine Courtemains, the former of these two being a young black sow with a white star in her forehead, and the latter a brown one with thin legs and a slight limp in the forward shank on the starboard side—a couple of the tryingest blisters to drive that I ever saw. Also among the missing were several mere baronesses—and I wanted them to stay missing; but no, all that sausage-meat had to be found; so servants were sent out with torches to scour the woods and hills to that end.

Of course, the whole drove was housed in the house, and, great guns!—well, I never saw anything like it. Nor ever heard anything like it. And never smelt anything like it. It was like an insurrection in a gasometer.

21

The Pilgrims

When I did get to bed at last I was unspeakably tired; the stretching out, and the relaxing of the long-tense muscles, how luxurious, how delicious! but that was as far as I could get—sleep was out of the question for the present. The ripping and tearing and squealing of the nobility up and down the halls and corridors was pandemonium come again, and kept me broad awake. Being awake, my thoughts were busy, of course; and mainly they busied themselves with Sandy's curious delusion. Here she was, as sane a person as the kingdom could produce; and yet, from my point of view she was acting like a crazy woman. My land, the power of training! of influence! of education! It can bring a body up to believe anything. I had to put myself in Sandy's place to realize that she was not a lunatic. Yes, and put her in mine, to demonstrate how easy it is to seem a lunatic to a person who has not been taught as you have been taught. If I had told Sandy I had seen a wagon, uninfluenced by enchantment, spin along fifty miles an hour; had seen a man, unequipped with magic powers, get into a basket and soar out of sight among the clouds; and had listened, without any necromancer's help, to the conversation of a person who was several hundred miles away, Sandy would not merely have supposed me to be crazy, she would have thought she knew it. Everybody around her believed in enchantments; nobody had any doubts; to doubt that a castle could be turned into a sty, and its occupants into hogs, would have been the same as my doubting among Connecticut people the actuality of the telephone and its wonders—and in both cases would be absolute proof of a diseased mind, an unsettled reason. Yes, Sandy was sane; that must be admitted. If I also would be sane—to Sandy—I must keep my superstitions about unenchanted and unmiraculous locomotives, balloons, and telephones, to myself. Also, I believed that the world was not flat, and hadn't pillars under it to support it, nor a canopy over it to turn off a universe of water that occupied all space above; but as I was the only person in the kingdom afflicted with such impious and criminal opinions, I recognized that it would be good wisdom to keep quiet about this matter, too, if I did not wish to be suddenly shunned and forsaken by everybody as a madman.

The next morning Sandy assembled the swine in the dining room and gave them their breakfast, waiting upon them personally and manifesting in every way the deep reverence which the natives of her island, ancient and modern, have always felt for rank, let its outward casket and the mental and moral contents be what they may. I could have eaten with the hogs if I had had birth approaching my lofty official rank; but I hadn't, and so accepted the unavoidable slight and made no complaint. Sandy and I had our breakfast at the second table. The family were not at home. I said:

"How many are in the family, Sandy, and where do they keep themselves?"

"Family?"

"Yes."

"Which family, good my lord?"

"Why, this family; your own family."

"Sooth to say, I understand you not. I have no family."

"No family? Why, Sandy, isn't this your home?"

"Now how indeed might that be? I have no home."

"Well, then, whose house is this?"

"Ah, wit you well I would tell you an I knew myself."

"Come—you don't even know these people? Then who invited us here?"

"None invited us. We but came; that is all."

"Why, woman, this is a most extraordinary performance. The effrontery of it is beyond admiration. We blandly march into a man's house, and cram it full of the only really valuable nobility the sun has yet discovered in the earth, and then it turns out that we don't even know the man's name. How did you ever venture to take this extravagant liberty? I supposed, of course, it was your home. What will the man say?"

"What will he say? Forsooth what can he say but give thanks?"

"Thanks for what?"

Her face was filled with a puzzled surprise:

"Verily, thou troublest mine understanding with strange words. Do ye dream that one of his estate is like to have the honour twice in his life to entertain company such as we have brought to grace his house withal?"

"Well, no—when you come to that. No, it's an even bet that this is the first time he has had a treat like this."

"Then let him be thankful, and manifest the same by grateful speech and due humility; he were a dog, else, and the heir and ancestor of dogs."

To my mind, the situation was uncomfortable. It might become more so. It might be a good idea to muster the hogs and move on. So I said:

"The day is wasting, Sandy. It is time to get the nobility together and be moving."

"Wherefore, fair sir and Boss?"

"We want to take them to their home, don't we?"

"La, but list to him! They be of all the regions of the earth! Each must hie to her own home; wend you we might do all these journeys in one so brief life as He hath appointed that created life, and thereto death likewise with help of Adam, who by sin done through persuasion of his helpmeet, she being wrought upon and bewrayed by the beguilements of the great enemy of man, that serpent hight Satan, aforetime consecrated and set apart unto that evil work by overmastering spite and envy begotten in his heart through fell ambitions that did blight and mildew a nature erst so white and pure whenso it hove with the shining multitudes its brethren-born in glade and shade of that fair heaven wherein all such as native be to that rich estate and—"

"Great Scott!"

"My lord?"

"Well, you know we haven't got time for this sort of thing. Don't you see, we could distribute these people around the earth in less time than it is going to take you to explain that we can't. We mustn't talk now, we must act. You want to be careful; you mustn't let your mill get the start of you that way, at a time like this. To business now—and sharp's the word. Who is to take the aristocracy home?"

"Even their friends. These will come for them from the far parts of the earth."

This was lightning from a clear sky, for unexpectedness; and the relief of it was like pardon to a prisoner. She would remain to deliver the goods, of course.

"Well, then, Sandy, as our enterprise is handsomely and successfully ended, I will go home and report; and if ever another one—"

"I also am ready; I will go with thee."

This was recalling the pardon.

"How? You will go with me? Why should you?"

"Will I be traitor to my knight, dost think? That were dishonour. I may not part from thee until in knightly encounter in the field some overmatching champion shall fairly win and fairly wear me. I were to blame an I thought that that might ever hap."

"Elected for the long term," I sighed to myself. "I may as well make the best of it." So then I spoke up and said:

"All right; let us make a start."

While she was gone to cry her farewells over the pork, I gave that whole peerage away to the servants. And I asked them to take a duster and dust around a little where the nobilities had mainly lodged and promenaded; but they considered that that would be hardly worth while, and would moreover be a rather grave departure from custom, and therefore likely to make talk. A departure from custom—that settled it; it was a nation capable of committing any crime but that. The servants said they would follow the fashion, a fashion grown sacred through immemorial observance; they would scatter fresh rushes in all the rooms and halls, and then the evidence of the aristocratic visitation would be no longer visible. It was a kind of satire on Nature: it was the scientific method, the geologic method; it deposited the history of the family in a stratified record; and the antiquary could dig through it and tell by the remains of each period what changes of diet the family had introduced successively for a hundred years.

The first thing we struck that day was a procession of pilgrims. It was not going our way, but we joined it, nevertheless; for it was hourly being borne in upon me now, that if I would govern this country wisely, I must be posted in the details of its life, and not at second hand, but by personal observation and scrutiny.

This company of pilgrims resembled Chaucer's in this: that it had in it a sample of about all the upper occupations and professions the country could show, and a corresponding variety of costume. There were young men and old men, young women and old women, lively folk and grave folk. They rode upon mules and horses, and there was not a side-saddle in the party; for this specialty was to remain unknown in England for nine hundred years yet.

It was a pleasant, friendly, sociable herd; pious, happy, merry and full of unconscious coarsenesses and innocent indecencies. What they regarded as the merry tale went the continual round and caused no more embarrassment than it would have caused in the best English society twelve centuries later. Practical jokes worthy of the English wits of the first quarter of the far-off nineteenth century were sprung here and there and yonder along the line, and compelled the delightedest applause; and sometimes when a bright remark was made at one end of the procession and started on its travels toward the other, you could note its progress all the way by the sparkling spray of laughter it threw off from its bows as it plowed along; and also by the blushes of the mules in its wake.

Sandy knew the goal and purpose of this pilgrimage, and she posted me. She said:

"They journey to the Valley of Holiness, for to be blessed of the godly hermits and drink of the miraculous waters and be cleansed from sin."

"Where is this watering place?"

"It lieth a two-day journey hence, by the borders of the land that hight the Cuckoo Kingdom."

"Tell me about it. Is it a celebrated place?"

"Oh, of a truth, yes. There be none more so. Of old time there lived there an abbot and his monks. Belike were none in the world more holy than these; for they gave themselves to study of pious books, and spoke not the one to the other, or indeed to any, and ate decayed herbs and naught thereto, and slept hard, and prayed much, and washed never; also they wore the same garment until it fell from their bodies through age and decay. Right so came they to be known of all the world by reason of these holy austerities, and visited by rich and poor, and reverenced."

"Proceed."

"But always there was lack of water there. Whereas, upon a time, the holy abbot prayed, and for answer a great stream of clear water burst forth by miracle in a desert place. Now were the fickle monks tempted of the Fiend, and they wrought with their abbot unceasingly by beggings and beseechings that he would construct a bath; and when he was become aweary and might not resist more, he said have ye your will, then, and granted that they asked. Now mark thou what 'tis to forsake the ways of purity the which He loveth, and wanton with such as be worldly and an offense. These monks did enter into the bath and come thence washed as white as snow; and lo, in that moment His sign appeared, in miraculous rebuke! for His insulted waters ceased to flow, and utterly vanished away."

"They fared mildly, Sandy, considering how that kind of crime is regarded in this country."

"Belike; but it was their first sin; and they had been of perfect life for long, and differing in naught from the angels. Prayers, tears, torturings of the flesh, all was vain to beguile that water to flow again. Even processions; even burnt-offerings; even votive candles to the Virgin, did fail every each of them; and all in the land did marvel."

"How odd to find that even this industry has its financial panics, and at times sees its assignats and greenbacks languish to zero, and everything come to a standstill. Go on, Sandy."

"And so upon a time, after year and day, the good abbot made humble surrender and destroyed the bath. And behold, His anger was in that moment appeased, and the waters gushed richly forth again, and even unto this day they have not ceased to flow in that generous measure."

"Then I take it nobody has washed since."

"He that would essay it could have his halter free; yes, and swiftly would he need it, too."

"The community has prospered since?"

"Even from that very day. The fame of the miracle went abroad into all lands. From every land came monks to join; they came even as the fishes come, in shoals; and the monastery added building to building, and yet others to these, and so spread wide its arms and took them in. And nuns came, also; and more again, and yet more; and built over against the monastery on the yon side of the vale, and added building to building, until mighty was that nunnery. And these were friendly unto those, and they joined their loving labours together, and together they built a fair great foundling asylum midway of the valley between."

"You spoke of some hermits, Sandy."

"These have gathered there from the ends of the earth. A hermit thriveth best where there be multitudes of pilgrims. Ye shall not find no hermit of no sort wanting. If any shall mention a hermit of a kind he thinketh new and not to be found but in some far strange land, let him but scratch among the holes and caves and swamps that line that Valley of Holiness, and whatsoever be his breed, it skills not, he shall find a sample of it there."

I closed up alongside of a burly fellow with a fat good-humoured face, purposing to make myself agreeable and pick up some further crumbs of fact; but I had hardly more than scraped acquaintance with him when he began eagerly and awkwardly to lead up, in the immemorial way, to that same old anecdote—the one Sir Dinadan told me, what time I got into trouble with Sir Sagramor and was challenged of him on account of it. I excused myself and dropped to the rear of the procession, sad at heart, willing to go hence from this troubled life, this vale of tears, this brief day of broken rest, of cloud and storm, of weary struggle and monotonous defeat; and yet shrinking from the change, as remembering how long eternity is, and how many have wended thither who know that anecdote.

Early in the afternoon we overtook another procession of pilgrims; but in this one was no merriment, no jokes, no laughter, no playful ways, nor any happy giddiness, whether of youth or age. Yet both were here, both age and youth; grey old men and women, strong men and women of middle age, young husbands, young wives, little boys and girls, and three babies at the breast. Even the children were smileless; there was not a face among all these half a hundred people but was cast down, and bore that set expression of hopelessness which is bred of long and hard trials and old acquaintance with despair. They were slaves. Chains led from their fettered feet and their manacled hands to a sole-leather belt about their waists; and all except the children were also linked together in a file six feet apart, by a single chain which led from collar to collar all down the line. They were on foot, and had tramped three hundred miles in eighteen days, upon the cheapest odds and ends of food, and stingy rations of that. They had slept in these chains every night, bundled together like swine. They had upon their bodies some poor rags, but they could not be said to be clothed. Their irons had chafed the skin from their ankles and made sores which were ulcerated and wormy. Their naked feet were torn, and none walked without a limp. Originally there had been a hundred of these unfortunates, but about half had been sold on the trip. The trader in charge of them rode a horse and carried a whip with a short handle and a long heavy lash divided into several knotted tails at the end. With this whip he cut the shoulders of any that tottered from weariness and pain, and straightened them up. He did not speak; the whip conveyed his desire without that. None of these poor creatures looked up as we rode along by; they showed no consciousness of our presence. And they made no sound but one; that was the dull and awful clank of their chains from end to end of the long file, as forty-three burdened feet rose and fell in unison. The file moved in a cloud of its own making.

All these faces were grey with a coating of dust. One has seen the like of this coating upon furniture in unoccupied houses, and has written his idle thought in it with his finger. I was reminded of this when I noticed the faces of some of those women, young mothers carrying babes that were near to death and freedom, how a something in their hearts was written in the dust upon their faces, plain to see, and lord, how plain to read! for it was the track of tears. One of these young mothers was but a girl, and it hurt me to the heart to read that writing, and reflect that it was come up out of the breast of such a child, a breast that ought not to know trouble yet, but only the gladness of the morning of life; and no doubt—

She reeled just then, giddy with fatigue, and down came the lash and flicked a flake of skin from her naked shoulder. It stung me as if I had been hit instead. The master halted the file and jumped from his horse. He stormed and swore at this girl, and said she had made annoyance enough with her laziness, and as this was the last chance he should have, he would settle the account now. She dropped on her knees and put up her hands and began to beg, and cry, and implore, in a passion of terror, but the master gave no attention. He snatched the child from her, and then made the men-slaves who were chained before and behind her throw her on the ground and hold her there and expose her body; and then he laid on with his lash like a madman till her back was flayed, she shrieking and struggling the while piteously. One of the men who was holding her turned away his face, and for this humanity he was reviled and flogged.

All our pilgrims looked on and commented—on the expert way in which the whip was handled. They were too much hardened by lifelong everyday familiarity with slavery to notice that there was anything else in the exhibition that invited comment. This was what slavery could do, in the way of ossifying what one may call the superior lobe of human feeling; for these pilgrims were kind-hearted people, and they would not have allowed that man to treat a horse like that.

I wanted to stop the whole thing and set the slaves free, but that would not do. I must not interfere too much and get myself a name for riding over the country's laws and the citizen's rights roughshod. If I lived and prospered I would be the death of slavery, that I was resolved upon; but I would try to fix it so that when I became its executioner it should be by command of the nation.

Just here was the wayside shop of a smith; and now arrived a landed proprietor who had bought this girl a few miles back, deliverable here where her irons could be taken off. They were removed; then there was a squabble between the gentleman and the dealer as to which should pay the blacksmith. The moment the girl was delivered from her irons, she flung herself, all tears and frantic sobbings, into the arms of the slave who had turned away his face when she was whipped. He strained her to his breast, and smothered her face and the child's with kisses, and washed them with the rain of his tears. I suspected. I inquired. Yes, I was right; it was husband and wife. They had to be torn apart by force; the girl had to be dragged away, and she struggled and fought and shrieked like one gone mad till a turn of the road hid her from sight; and even after that, we could still make out the fading plaint of those receding shrieks. And the husband and father, with his wife and child gone, never to be seen by him again in life?—well, the look of him one might not bear at all, and so I turned away; but I knew I should never get his picture out of my mind again, and there it is to this day, to wring my heartstrings whenever I think of it.

We put up at the inn in a village just at nightfall, and when I rose next morning and looked abroad, I was ware where a knight came riding in the golden glory of the new day, and recognized him for knight of mine—Sir Ozana le Cure Hardy. He was in the gentlemen's furnishing line, and his missionarying specialty was plug hats. He was clothed all in steel, in the beautifulest armor of the time—up to where his helmet ought to have been; but he hadn't any helmet, he wore a shiny stove-pipe hat, and was ridiculous a spectacle as one might want to see. It was another of my surreptitious schemes for extinguishing knighthood by making it grotesque and absurd. Sir Ozana's saddle was hung about with leather hat boxes, and every time he overcame a wandering knight he swore him into my service and fitted him with a plug and made him wear it. I dressed and ran down to welcome Sir Ozana and get his news.

"How is trade?" I asked.

"Ye will note that I have but these four left; yet were they sixteen whenas I got me from Camelot."

"Why, you have certainly done nobly, Sir Ozana. Where have you been foraging of late?"

"I am but now come from the Valley of Holiness, please you sir."

"I am pointed for that place myself. Is there anything stirring in the monkery, more than common?"

"By the mass ye may not question it!. . . . Give him good feed, boy, and stint it not, an thou valuest thy crown; so get ye lightly to the stable and do even as I bid. . . . Sir, it is parlous news I bring, and—be these pilgrims? Then ye may not do better, good folk, than gather and hear the tale I have to tell, sith it concerneth you, forasmuch as ye go to find that ye will not find, and seek that ye will seek in vain, my life being hostage for my word, and my word and message being these, namely: That a hap has happened whereof the like has not been seen no more but once this two hundred years, which was the first and last time that that said misfortune strake the holy valley in that form by commandment of the Most High whereto by reasons just and causes thereunto contributing, wherein the matter—"

"The miraculous fount hath ceased to flow!" This shout burst from twenty pilgrim mouths at once.

"Ye say well, good people. I was verging to it, even when ye spake."

"Has somebody been washing again?"

"Nay, it is suspected, but none believe it. It is thought to be some other sin, but none wit what."

"How are they feeling about the calamity?"

"None may describe it in words. The fount is these nine days dry. The prayers that did begin then, and the lamentations in sackcloth and ashes, and the holy processions, none of these have ceased nor night nor day; and so the monks and the nuns and the foundlings be all exhausted, and do hang up prayers writ upon parchment, sith that no strength is left in man to lift up voice. And at last they sent for thee, Sir Boss, to try magic and enchantment; and if you could not come, then was the messenger to fetch Merlin, and he is there these three days now, and saith he will fetch that water though he burst the globe and wreck its kingdoms to accomplish it; and right bravely doth he work his magic and call upon his hellions to hie them hither and help, but not a whiff of moisture hath he started yet, even so much as might qualify as mist upon a copper mirror an ye count not the barrel of sweat he sweateth betwixt sun and sun over the dire labours of his task; and if ye—"

Breakfast was ready. As soon as it was over I showed to Sir Ozana these words which I had written on the inside of his hat: "*Chemical Department, Laboratory extension, Section G. Pxxp. Send two of first size, two of No. 3, and six of No. 4, together with the proper complementary details—and two of my trained assistants.*" And I said:

"Now get you to Camelot as fast as you can fly, brave knight, and show the writing to Clarence, and tell him to have these required matters in the Valley of Holiness with all possible dispatch."

"I will well, Sir Boss," and he was off.

22

The Holy Fountain

The pilgrims were human beings. Otherwise they would have acted differently. They had come a long and difficult journey, and now when the journey was nearly finished, and they learned that the main thing they had come for had ceased to exist, they didn't do as horses or cats or angle-worms would probably have done—turn back and get at something profitable—no, anxious as they had before been to see the miraculous fountain, they were as much as forty times as anxious now to see the place where it had used to be. There is no accounting for human beings.

We made good time; and a couple of hours before sunset we stood upon the high confines of the Valley of Holiness, and our eyes swept it from end to end and noted its features. That is, its large features. These were the three masses of buildings. They were distant and isolated temporalities shrunken to toy constructions in the lonely waste of what seemed a desert—and was. Such a scene is always mournful, it is so impressively still, and looks so steeped in death. But there was a sound here which interrupted the stillness only to add to its mournfulness; this was the faint far sound of tolling bells which floated fitfully to us on the passing breeze, and so faintly, so softly, that we hardly knew whether we heard it with our ears or with our spirits.

We reached the monastery before dark, and there the males were given lodging, but the women were sent over to the nunnery. The bells were close at hand now, and their solemn booming smote upon the ear like a message of doom. A superstitious despair possessed the heart of every monk and published itself in his ghastly face. Everywhere, these black-robed, soft-sandaled, tallow-visaged spectres appeared, flitted about and disappeared, noiseless as the creatures of a troubled dream, and as uncanny.

The old abbot's joy to see me was pathetic. Even to tears; but he did the shedding himself. He said:

"Delay not, son, but get to thy saving work. An we bring not the water back again, and soon, we are ruined, and the good work of two hundred years must end. And see thou do it with enchantments that be holy, for the Church will not endure that work in her cause be done by devil's magic."

"When I work, Father, be sure there will be no devil's work connected with it. I shall use no arts that come of the devil, and no elements not created by the hand of God. But is Merlin working strictly on pious lines?"

"Ah, he said he would, my son, he said he would, and took oath to make his promise good."

"Well, in that case, let him proceed."

"But surely you will not sit idle by, but help?"

"It will not answer to mix methods, Father; neither would it be professional courtesy. Two of a trade must not underbid each other. We might as well cut rates and be done with it; it would arrive at that in the end. Merlin has the contract; no other magician can touch it till he throws it up."

"But I will take it from him; it is a terrible emergency and the act is thereby justified. And if it were not so, who will give law to the Church? The Church giveth law to all; and what she wills to do, that she may do, hurt whom it may. I will take it from him; you shall begin upon the moment."

"It may not be, Father. No doubt, as you say, where power is supreme, one can do as one likes and suffer no injury; but we poor magicians are not so situated. Merlin is a very good magician in a small way, and has quite a neat provincial reputation. He is struggling along, doing the best he can, and it would not be etiquette for me to take his job until he himself abandons it."

The abbot's face lighted.

"Ah, that is simple. There are ways to persuade him to abandon it."

"No-no, Father, it skills not, as these people say. If he were persuaded against his will, he would load that well with a malicious enchantment which would balk me until I found out its secret. It might take a month. I could set up a little enchantment of mine which I call the telephone, and he could not find out its secret in a hundred years. Yes, you perceive, he might block me for a month. Would you like to risk a month in a dry time like this?"

"A month! The mere thought of it maketh me to shudder. Have it thy way, my son. But my heart is heavy with this disappointment. Leave me, and let me wear my spirit with weariness and waiting, even as I have done these ten long days, counterfeiting thus the thing that is called rest, the prone body making outward sign of repose where inwardly is none."

Of course, it would have been best, all round, for Merlin to waive etiquette and quit and call it half a day, since he would never be able to start that water, for he was a true magician of the time; which is to say, the big miracles, the ones that gave him his reputation, always had the luck to be performed when nobody but Merlin was present; he couldn't start this well with all this crowd around to see; a crowd was as bad for a magician's miracle in that day as it was for a spiritualist's miracle in mine; there was sure to be some skeptic on hand to turn up the gas at the crucial moment and spoil everything. But I did not want Merlin to retire from the job until I was ready to take hold of it effectively myself; and I could not do that until I got my things from Camelot, and that would take two or three days.

My presence gave the monks hope, and cheered them up a good deal; insomuch that they ate a square meal that night for the first time in ten days. As soon as their stomachs had been properly reinforced with food, their spirits began to rise fast; when the mead began to go round they rose faster. By the time everybody was half-seas over, the holy community was in good shape to make a night of it; so we stayed by the board and put it through on that line. Matters got to be very jolly. Good old questionable stories were told that made the tears run down and cavernous mouths stand wide and the round bellies shake with laughter; and questionable songs were bellowed out in a mighty chorus that drowned the boom of the tolling bells.

At last I ventured a story myself; and vast was the success of it. Not right off, of course, for the native of those islands does not, as a rule, dissolve upon the early applications of a humorous thing; but the fifth time I told it, they began to crack in places; the eight time I told it, they began to crumble; at the twelfth repetition they fell apart in chunks; and at the fifteenth they disintegrated, and I got a broom and swept them up. This language is figurative. Those islanders—well, they are slow pay at first, in the matter of return for your investment of effort, but in the end they make the pay of all other nations poor and small by contrast.

I was at the well next day betimes. Merlin was there, enchanting away like a beaver, but not raising the moisture. He was not in a pleasant humour; and every time I hinted that perhaps this contract was a shade too hefty for a novice he unlimbered his tongue and cursed like a bishop—French bishop of the Regency days, I mean.

Matters were about as I expected to find them. The "fountain" was an ordinary well, it had been dug in the ordinary way, and stoned up in the ordinary way. There was no miracle about it. Even the lie that had created its reputation was not miraculous; I could have told it myself, with one hand tied behind me. The well was in a dark chamber which stood in the center of a cut-stone chapel, whose walls were hung with pious pictures of a workmanship that would have made a chromo feel good; pictures historically commemorative of curative miracles which had been achieved by the waters when nobody was looking. That is, nobody but angels; they are always on deck when there is a miracle to the fore—so as to get put in the picture, perhaps. Angels are as fond of that as a fire company; look at the old masters.

The well-chamber was dimly lighted by lamps; the water was drawn with a windlass and chain by monks, and poured into troughs which delivered it into stone reservoirs outside in the chapel—when there was water to draw, I mean—and none but monks could enter the well-chamber. I entered it, for I had temporary authority to do so, by courtesy of my professional brother and subordinate. But he hadn't entered it himself. He did everything by incantations; he never worked his intellect. If he had stepped in there and used his eyes, instead of his disordered mind, he could have cured the well by natural means, and then turned it into a miracle in the customary way; but no, he was an old numskull, a magician who believed in his own magic; and no magician can thrive who is handicapped with a superstition like that.

I had an idea that the well had sprung a leak; that some of the wall stones near the bottom had fallen and exposed fissures that allowed the water to escape. I measured the chain—98 feet. Then I called in a couple of monks, locked the door, took a candle, and made them lower me in the bucket. When the chain was all paid out, the candle confirmed my suspicion; a considerable section of the wall was gone, exposing a good big fissure.

I almost regretted that my theory about the well's trouble was correct, because I had another one that had a showy point or two about it for a miracle. I remembered that in America, many centuries later, when an oil well ceased to flow, they used to blast it out with a dynamite torpedo. If I should find this well dry and no explanation of it, I could astonish these people most nobly by having a person of no especial value drop a dynamite bomb into it. It was my idea to appoint Merlin. However, it was plain that there was no occasion for the bomb. One cannot have everything the way he would like it. A man has no business to be depressed by a disappointment, anyway; he ought to make up his mind to get even. That is what I did. I said to myself, I am in no hurry, I can wait; that bomb will come good yet. And it did, too.

When I was above ground again, I turned out the monks, and let down a fish-line; the well was a hundred and fifty feet deep, and there was forty-one feet of water in it. I called in a monk and asked:

"How deep is the well?"

"That, sir, I wit not, having never been told."

"How does the water usually stand in it?"

"Near to the top, these two centuries, as the testimony goeth, brought down to us through our predecessors."

It was true—as to recent times at least—for there was witness to it, and better witness than a monk; only about twenty or thirty feet of the chain showed wear and use, the rest of it was unworn and rusty. What had happened when the well gave out that other time? Without doubt some practical person had come along and mended the leak, and then had come up and told the abbot he had discovered by divination that if the sinful bath were destroyed the well would flow again. The leak had befallen again now, and these children would have prayed, and processioned, and tolled their bells for heavenly succor till they all dried up and blew away, and no innocent of them all would ever have thought to drop a fish-line into the well or go down in it and find out what was really the matter. Old habit of mind is one of the toughest things to get away from in the world. It transmits itself like physical form and feature; and for a man, in those days, to have had an idea that his ancestors hadn't had, would have brought him under suspicion of being illegitimate. I said to the monk:

"It is a difficult miracle to restore water in a dry well, but we will try, if my brother Merlin fails. Brother Merlin is a very passable artist, but only in the parlour-magic line, and he may not succeed; in fact, is not likely to succeed. But that should be nothing to his discredit; the man that can do *this* kind of miracle knows enough to keep hotel."

"Hotel? I mind not to have heard—"

"Of hotel? It's what you call hostel. The man that can do this miracle can keep hostel. I can do this miracle; I shall do this miracle; yet I do not try to conceal from you that it is a miracle to tax the occult powers to the last strain."

"None knoweth that truth better than the brotherhood, indeed; for it is of record that aforetime it was parlous difficult and took a year. Natheless, God send you good success, and to that end will we pray."

As a matter of business it was a good idea to get the notion around that the thing was difficult. Many a small thing has been made large by the right kind of advertising. That monk was filled up with the difficulty of this enterprise; he would fill up the others. In two days the solicitude would be booming.

On my way home at noon, I met Sandy. She had been sampling the hermits. I said:

"I would like to do that myself. This is Wednesday. Is there a matinee?"

"A which, please you, sir?"

"Matinee. Do they keep open afternoons?"

"Who?"

"The hermits, of course."

"Keep open?"

"Yes, keep open. Isn't that plain enough? Do they knock off at noon?"

"Knock off?"

"Knock off?—yes, knock off. What is the matter with knock off? I never saw such a dunderhead; can't you understand anything at all? In plain terms, do they shut up shop, draw the game, bank the fires—"

"Shut up shop, draw—"

"There, never mind, let it go; you make me tired. You can't seem to understand the simplest thing."

"I would I might please thee, sir, and it is to me dole and sorrow that I fail, albeit sith I am but a simple damsel and taught of none, being from the cradle unbaptized in those deep waters of learning that do anoint with a sovereignty him that partaketh of that most noble sacrament, investing him with reverend state to the mental eye of the humble mortal who, by bar and lack of that great consecration seeth in his own unlearned estate but a symbol of that other sort of lack and loss which men do publish to the pitying eye with sackcloth trappings whereon the ashes of grief do lie bepowdered and bestrewn, and so, when such shall in the darkness of his mind encounter these golden phrases of high mystery, these shut-up-shops, and draw-the-game, and bank-the-fires, it is but by the grace of God that he burst not for envy of the mind that can beget, and tongue that can deliver so great and mellow-sounding miracles of speech, and if there do ensue confusion in that humbler mind, and failure to divine the meanings of these wonders, then if so be this miscomprehension is not vain but sooth and true, wit ye well it is the very substance of worshipful dear homage and may not lightly be misprized, nor had been, an ye had noted this complexion of mood and mind and understood that that I would I could not, and that I could not I might not, nor yet nor might *nor* could, nor might-not nor could-not, might be by advantage turned to the desired *would*, and so I pray you mercy of my fault, and that ye will of your kindness and your charity forgive it, good my master and most dear lord."

I couldn't make it all out—that is, the details—but I got the general idea; and enough of it, too, to be ashamed. It was not fair to spring those nineteenth century technicalities upon the untutored infant of the sixth and then rail at her because she couldn't get their drift; and when she was making the honest best drive at it she could, too, and no fault of hers that she couldn't fetch the home plate; and so I apologized. Then we meandered pleasantly away toward the hermit holes in sociable converse together, and better friends than ever.

I was gradually coming to have a mysterious and shuddery reverence for this girl; nowadays whenever she pulled out from the station and got her train fairly started on one of those horizonless transcontinental sentences of hers, it was borne in upon me that I was standing in the awful presence of the Mother of the German Language. I was so impressed with this, that sometimes when she began to empty one of these sentences on me I unconsciously took the very attitude of reverence, and stood uncovered; and if words had been water, I had been drowned, sure. She had exactly the German way; whatever was in her mind to be delivered, whether a mere remark, or a sermon, or a cyclopedia, or the history of a war, she would get it into a single sentence or die. Whenever the literary German dives into a sentence, that is the last you are going to see of him till he emerges on the other side of his Atlantic with his verb in his mouth.

We drifted from hermit to hermit all the afternoon. It was a most strange menagerie. The chief emulation among them seemed to be, to see which could manage to be the uncleanest and most prosperous with vermin. Their manner and attitudes were the last expression of complacent self-righteousness. It was one anchorite's pride to lie naked in the mud and let the insects bite him and blister him unmolested; it was another's to lean against a rock, all day long, conspicuous to the admiration of the throng of pilgrims and pray; it was another's to go naked and crawl around on all fours; it was another's to drag about with him, year in and year out, eighty pounds of iron; it was another's to never lie down when he slept, but to stand among the thorn-bushes and snore when there were pilgrims around to look; a woman, who had the white hair of age, and no other apparel, was black from crown to heel with forty-seven years of holy abstinence from water. Groups of gazing pilgrims stood around all and every of these strange objects, lost in reverent wonder, and envious of the fleckless sanctity which these pious austerities had won for them from an exacting heaven.

By and by we went to see one of the supremely great ones. He was a mighty celebrity; his fame had penetrated all Christendom; the noble and the renowned journeyed from the remotest lands on the globe to pay him reverence. His stand was in the center of the widest part of the valley; and it took all that space to hold his crowds.

His stand was a pillar sixty feet high, with a broad platform on the top of it. He was now doing what he had been doing every day for twenty years up there—bowing his body ceaselessly and rapidly almost to his feet. It was his way of praying. I timed him with a stop watch, and he made 1,244 revolutions in 24 minutes and 46 seconds. It seemed a pity to have all this power going to waste. It was one of the most useful motions in mechanics, the pedal movement; so I made a note in my memorandum book, purposing some day to apply a system of elastic cords to him and run a sewing machine with it. I afterward carried out that scheme, and got five years' good service out of him; in which time he turned out upward of eighteen thousand first-rate tow-linen shirts, which was ten a day. I worked him Sundays and all; he was going, Sundays, the same as week days, and it was no use to waste the power. These shirts cost me nothing but just the mere trifle for the materials—I furnished those myself, it would not have been right to make him do that—and they sold like smoke to pilgrims at a dollar and a half apiece, which was the price of fifty cows or a blooded race horse in Arthurdom. They were regarded as a perfect protection against sin, and advertised as such by my knights everywhere, with the paint-pot and stencil-plate; insomuch that there was not a cliff or a bowlder or a dead wall in England but you could read on it at a mile distance:

"*Buy the only genuine St. Stylite; patronized by the Nobility. Patent applied for.*"

There was more money in the business than one knew what to do with. As it extended, I brought out a line of goods suitable for kings, and a nobby thing for duchesses and that sort, with ruffles down the forehatch and the running-gear clewed up with a featherstitch to leeward and then hauled aft with a back-stay and triced up with a half-turn in the standing rigging forward of the weather-gaskets. Yes, it was a daisy.

But about that time I noticed that the motive power had taken to standing on one leg, and I found that there was something the matter with the other one; so I stocked the business and unloaded, taking Sir Bors de Ganis into camp financially along with certain of his friends; for the works stopped within a year, and the good saint got him to his rest. But he had earned it. I can say that for him.

When I saw him that first time—however, his personal condition will not quite bear description here. You can read it in the Lives of the Saints.*

[*All the details concerning the hermits, in this chapter, are from Lecky—but greatly modified. This book not being a history but only a tale, the majority of the historian's frank details were too strong for reproduction in it.—*Editor*]

23

Restoration of the Fountain

Saturday noon I went to the well and looked on a while. Merlin was still burning smoke-powders, and pawing the air, and muttering gibberish as hard as ever, but looking pretty down-hearted, for of course he had not started even a perspiration in that well yet. Finally I said:

"How does the thing promise by this time, partner?"

"Behold, I am even now busied with trial of the powerfulest enchantment known to the princes of the occult arts in the lands of the East; an it fail me, naught can avail. Peace, until I finish."

He raised a smoke this time that darkened all the region, and must have made matters uncomfortable for the hermits, for the wind was their way, and it rolled down over their dens in a dense and billowy fog. He poured out volumes of speech to match, and contorted his body and sawed the air with his hands in a most extraordinary way. At the end of twenty minutes he dropped down panting, and about exhausted. Now arrived the abbot and several hundred monks and nuns, and behind them a multitude of pilgrims and a couple of acres of foundlings, all drawn by the prodigious smoke, and all in a grand state of excitement. The abbot inquired anxiously for results. Merlin said:

"If any labour of mortal might break the spell that binds these waters, this which I have but just essayed had done it. It has failed; whereby I do now know that that which I had feared is a truth established; the sign of this failure is, that the most potent spirit known to the magicians of the East, and whose name none may utter and live, has laid his spell upon this well. The mortal does not breathe, nor ever will, who can penetrate the secret of that spell, and without that secret none can break it. The water will flow no more forever, good Father. I have done what man could. Suffer me to go."

Of course this threw the abbot into a good deal of a consternation. He turned to me with the signs of it in his face, and said:

"Ye have heard him. Is it true?"

"Part of it is."

"Not all, then, not all! What part is true?"

"That that spirit with the Russian name has put his spell upon the well."

"God's wounds, then are we ruined!"

"Possibly."

"But not certainly? Ye mean, not certainly?"

"That is it."

"Wherefore, ye also mean that when he saith none can break the spell—"

"Yes, when he says that, he says what isn't necessarily true. There are conditions under which an effort to break it may have some chance—that is, some small, some trifling chance—of success."

"The conditions—"

"Oh, they are nothing difficult. Only these: I want the well and the surroundings for the space of half a mile, entirely to myself from sunset today until I remove the ban—and nobody allowed to cross the ground but by my authority."

"Are these all?"

"Yes."

"And you have no fear to try?"

"Oh, none. One may fail, of course; and one may also succeed. One can try, and I am ready to chance it. I have my conditions?"

"These and all others ye may name. I will issue commandment to that effect."

"Wait," said Merlin, with an evil smile. "Ye wit that he that would break this spell must know that spirit's name?"

"Yes, I know his name."

"And wit you also that to know it skills not of itself, but ye must likewise pronounce it? Ha-ha! Knew ye that?"

"Yes, I knew that, too."

"You had that knowledge! Art a fool? Are ye minded to utter that name and die?"

"Utter it? Why certainly. I would utter it if it was Welsh."

"Ye are even a dead man, then; and I go to tell Arthur."

"That's all right. Take your gripsack and get along. The thing for *you* to do is to go home and work the weather, John W. Merlin."

It was a home shot, and it made him wince; for he was the worst weather-failure in the kingdom. Whenever he ordered up the danger-signals along the coast there was a week's dead calm, sure, and every time he prophesied fair weather it rained brickbats. But I kept him in the weather bureau right along, to undermine his reputation. However, that shot raised his bile, and instead of starting home to report my death, he said he would remain and enjoy it.

My two experts arrived in the evening, and pretty well fagged, for they had traveled double tides. They had pack-mules along, and had brought everything I needed—tools, pump, lead pipe, Greek fire, sheaves of big rockets, roman candles, coloured fire sprays, electric apparatus, and a lot of sundries—everything necessary for the stateliest kind of a miracle. They got their supper and a nap, and about midnight we sallied out through a solitude so wholly vacant and complete that it quite overpassed the required conditions. We took possession of the well and its surroundings. My boys were experts in all sorts of things, from the stoning up of a well to the constructing of a mathematical instrument. An hour before sunrise we had that leak mended in shipshape fashion, and the water began to rise. Then we stowed our fireworks in the chapel, locked up the place, and went home to bed.

Before the noon mass was over, we were at the well again; for there was a deal to do yet, and I was determined to spring the miracle before midnight, for business reasons: for whereas a miracle worked for the Church on a weekday is worth a good deal, it is worth six times as much if you get it in on a Sunday. In nine hours the water had risen to its customary level—that is to say, it was within twenty-three feet of the top. We put in a little iron pump, one of the first turned out by my works near the capital; we bored into a stone reservoir which stood against the outer wall of the well-chamber and inserted a section of lead pipe that was long enough to reach to the door of the chapel and project beyond the threshold, where the gushing water would be visible to the two hundred and fifty acres of people I was intending should be present on the flat plain in front of this little holy hillock at the proper time.

We knocked the head out of an empty hogshead and hoisted this hogshead to the flat roof of the chapel, where we clamped it down fast, poured in gunpowder till it lay loosely an inch deep on the bottom, then we stood up rockets in the hogshead as thick as they could loosely stand, all the different breeds of rockets there are; and they made a portly and imposing sheaf, I can tell you. We grounded the wire of a pocket electrical battery in that powder, we placed a whole magazine of Greek fire on each corner of the roof—blue on one corner, green on another, red on another, and purple on the last—and grounded a wire in each.

About two hundred yards off, in the flat, we built a pen of scantlings, about four feet high, and laid planks on it, and so made a platform. We covered it with swell tapestries borrowed for the occasion, and topped it off with the abbot's own throne. When you are going to do a miracle for an ignorant race, you want to get in every detail that will count; you want to make all the properties impressive to the public eye; you want to make matters comfortable for your head guest; then you can turn yourself loose and play your effects for all they are worth. I know the value of these things, for I know human nature. You can't throw too much style into a miracle. It costs trouble, and work, and sometimes money; but it pays in the end. Well, we brought the wires to the ground at the chapel, and then brought them under the ground to the platform, and hid the batteries there. We put a rope fence a hundred feet square around the platform to keep off the common multitude, and that finished the work. My idea was, doors open at 10:30, performance to begin at 11:25 sharp. I wished I could charge admission, but of course that wouldn't answer. I instructed my boys to be in the chapel as early as 10, before anybody was around, and be ready to man the pumps at the proper time, and make the fur fly. Then we went home to supper.

The news of the disaster to the well had traveled far by this time; and now for two or three days a steady avalanche of people had been pouring into the valley. The lower end of the valley was become one huge camp; we should have a good house, no question about that. Criers went the rounds early in the evening and announced the coming attempt, which put every pulse up to fever heat. They gave notice that the abbot and his official suite would move in state and occupy the platform at 10:30, up to which time all the region which was under my ban must be clear; the bells would then cease from tolling, and this sign should be permission to the multitudes to close in and take their places.

I was at the platform and all ready to do the honours when the abbot's solemn procession hove in sight—which it did not do till it was nearly to the rope fence, because it was a starless black night and no torches permitted. With it came Merlin, and took a front seat on the platform; he was as good as his word for once. One could not see the multitudes banked together beyond the ban, but they were there, just the same. The moment the bells stopped, those banked masses broke and poured over the line like a vast black wave, and for as much as a half hour it continued to flow, and then it solidified itself, and you could have walked upon a pavement of human heads to—well, miles.

"BGWJJILLIGKKK!!"

We had a solemn stage-wait, now, for about twenty minutes—a thing I had counted on for effect; it is always good to let your audience have a chance to work up its expectancy. At length, out of the silence a noble Latin chant—men's voices—broke and swelled up and rolled away into the night, a majestic tide of melody. I had put that up, too, and it was one of the best effects I ever invented. When it was finished I stood up on the platform and extended my hands abroad, for two minutes, with my face uplifted—

that always produces a dead hush—and then slowly pronounced this ghastly word with a kind of awfulness which caused hundreds to tremble, and many women to faint:

"**Constantinopolitanischerdudelsackspfeifenmachersgesellschafft!**"

Just as I was moaning out the closing hunks of that word, I touched off one of my electric connections and all that murky world of people stood revealed in a hideous blue glare! It was immense—that effect! Lots of people shrieked, women curled up and quit in every direction, foundlings collapsed by platoons. The abbot and the monks crossed themselves nimbly and their lips fluttered with agitated prayers. Merlin held his grip, but he was astonished clear down to his corns; he had never seen anything to begin with that, before. Now was the time to pile in the effects. I lifted my hands and groaned out this word—as it were in agony:

"**Nihilistendynamittheaterkaestchenssprengungsattentaetsversuchungen!**"

—and turned on the red fire! You should have heard that Atlantic of people moan and howl when that crimson hell joined the blue! After sixty seconds I shouted:

"**Transvaaltruppentropentransporttrampelthiertreibertrauungsthraenentragoedie!**"

—and lit up the green fire! After waiting only forty seconds this time, I spread my arms abroad and thundered out the devastating syllables of this word of words:

"**Mekkamuselmannenmassenmenchenmoerdermohrenmuttermarmor-monumentenmacher!**"

—and whirled on the purple glare! There they were, all going at once, red, blue, green, purple!—four furious volcanoes pouring vast clouds of radiant smoke aloft, and spreading a blinding rainbowed noonday to the furthest confines of that valley. In the distance one could see that fellow on the pillar standing rigid against the background of sky, his seesaw stopped for the first time in twenty years. I knew the boys were at the pump now and ready. So I said to the abbot:

"The time is come, Father. I am about to pronounce the dread name and command the spell to dissolve. You want to brace up, and take hold of something." Then I shouted to the people: "Behold, in another minute the spell will be broken, or no mortal can break it. If it break, all will know it, for you will see the sacred water gush from the chapel door!"

I stood a few moments, to let the hearers have a chance to spread my announcement to those who couldn't hear, and so convey it to the furthest ranks, then I made a grand exhibition of extra posturing and gesturing, and shouted:

"Lo, I command the fell spirit that possesses the holy fountain to now disgorge into the skies all the infernal fires that still remain in him, and straightway dissolve his spell and flee hence to the pit, there to lie bound a thousand years. By his own dread name I command it—BGWJJILLIGKKK!"

Then I touched off the hogshead of rockets, and a vast fountain of dazzling lances of fire vomited itself toward the zenith with a hissing rush, and burst in mid-sky into a storm of flashing jewels! One mighty groan of terror started up from the massed people—then suddenly broke into a wild hosannah of joy—for there, fair and plain in the uncanny glare, they saw the freed water leaping forth! The old abbot could not speak a word, for tears and the chokings in his throat; without utterance of any sort, he folded me in his arms and mashed me. It was more eloquent than speech. And harder to get over, too, in a country where there were really no doctors that were worth a damaged nickel.

You should have seen those acres of people throw themselves down in that water and kiss it; kiss it, and pet it, and fondle it, and talk to it as if it were alive, and welcome it back with the dear names they gave their darlings, just as if it had been a friend who was long gone away and lost, and was come home again. Yes, it was pretty to see, and made me think more of them than I had done before.

I sent Merlin home on a shutter. He had caved in and gone down like a landslide when I pronounced that fearful name, and had never come to since. He never had heard that name before—neither had I—but to him it was the right one. Any jumble would have been the right one. He admitted, afterward, that that spirit's own mother could not have pronounced that name better than I did. He never could understand how I survived it, and I didn't tell him. It is only young magicians that give away a secret like that. Merlin spent three months working enchantments to try to find out the deep trick of how to pronounce that name and outlive it. But he didn't arrive.

When I started to the chapel, the populace uncovered and fell back reverently to make a wide way for me, as if I had been some kind of a superior being—and I was. I was aware of that. I took along a night shift of monks, and taught them the mystery of the pump, and set them to work, for it was plain that a good part of the people out there were going to sit up with the water all night, consequently it was but right that they should have all they wanted of it. To those monks that pump was a good deal of a miracle itself, and they were full of wonder over it; and of admiration, too, of the exceeding effectiveness of its performance.

It was a great night, an immense night. There was reputation in it. I could hardly get to sleep for glorying over it.

24

A Rival Magician

My influence in the Valley of Holiness was something prodigious now. It seemed worth while to try to turn it to some valuable account. The thought came to me the next morning, and was suggested by my seeing one of my knights who was in the soap line come riding in. According to history, the monks of this place two centuries before had been worldly minded enough to want to wash. It might be that there was a leaven of this unrighteousness still remaining. So I sounded a Brother:

"Wouldn't you like a bath?"

He shuddered at the thought—the thought of the peril of it to the well—but he said with feeling:

"One needs not to ask that of a poor body who has not known that blessed refreshment sith that he was a boy. Would God I might wash me! but it may not be, fair sir, tempt me not; it is forbidden."

And then he sighed in such a sorrowful way that I was resolved he should have at least one layer of his real estate removed, if it sized up my whole influence and bankrupted the pile. So I went to the abbot and asked for a permit for this Brother. He blenched at the idea—I don't mean that you could see him blench, for of course you couldn't see it without you scraped him, and I didn't care enough about it to scrape him, but I knew the blench was there, just the same, and within a book-cover's thickness of the surface, too—blenched, and trembled. He said:

"Ah, son, ask aught else thou wilt, and it is thine, and freely granted out of a grateful heart—but this, oh, this! Would you drive away the blessed water again?"

"No, Father, I will not drive it away. I have mysterious knowledge which teaches me that there was an error that other time when it was thought the institution of the bath banished the fountain." A large interest began to show up in the old man's face. "My knowledge informs me that the bath was innocent of that misfortune, which was caused by quite another sort of sin."

"These are brave words—but—but right welcome, if they be true."

"They are true, indeed. Let me build the bath again, Father. Let me build it again, and the fountain shall flow forever."

"You promise this?—you promise it? Say the word—say you promise it!"

"I do promise it."

"Then will I have the first bath myself! Go—get ye to your work. Tarry not, tarry not, but go."

I and my boys were at work, straight off. The ruins of the old bath were there yet in the basement of the monastery, not a stone missing. They had been left just so, all these lifetimes, and avoided with a pious fear, as things accursed. In two days we had it all done and the water in—a spacious pool of clear pure water that a body could swim in. It was running water, too. It came in, and went out, through the ancient pipes. The old abbot kept his word, and was the first to try it. He went down black and shaky, leaving the whole black community above troubled and worried and full of bodings; but he came back white and joyful, and the game was made! another triumph scored.

It was a good campaign that we made in that Valley of Holiness, and I was very well satisfied, and ready to move on now, but I struck a disappointment. I caught a heavy cold, and it started up an old lurking rheumatism of mine. Of course the rheumatism hunted up my weakest place and located itself there. This was the place where the abbot put his arms about me and mashed me, what time he was moved to testify his gratitude to me with an embrace.

When at last I got out, I was a shadow. But everybody was full of attentions and kindnesses, and these brought cheer back into my life, and were the right medicine to help a convalescent swiftly up toward health and strength again; so I gained fast.

Sandy was worn out with nursing; so I made up my mind to turn out and go a cruise alone, leaving her at the nunnery to rest up. My idea was to disguise myself as a freeman of peasant degree and wander through the country a week or two on foot. This would give me a chance to eat and lodge with the lowliest and poorest class of free citizens on equal terms. There was no other way to inform myself perfectly of their everyday life and the operation of the laws upon it. If I went among them as a gentleman, there would be restraints and conventionalities which would shut me out from their private joys and troubles, and I should get no further than the outside shell.

One morning I was out on a long walk to get up muscle for my trip, and had climbed the ridge which bordered the northern extremity of the valley, when I came upon an artificial opening in the face of a low precipice, and recognized it by its location as a hermitage which had often been pointed out to me from a distance as the den of a hermit of high renown for dirt and austerity. I knew he had lately been offered a situation in the Great Sahara, where lions and sandflies made the hermit-life peculiarly attractive and difficult, and had gone to Africa to take possession, so I thought I would look in and see how the atmosphere of this den agreed with its reputation.

My surprise was great: the place was newly swept and scoured. Then there was another surprise. Back in the gloom of the cavern I heard the clink of a little bell, and then this exclamation:

"*Hello Central! Is this you, Camelot?*—Behold, thou mayst glad thy heart an thou hast faith to believe the wonderful when that it cometh in unexpected guise and maketh itself manifest in impossible places—here standeth in the flesh his mightiness The Boss, and with thine own ears shall ye hear him speak!"

Now what a radical reversal of things this was; what a jumbling together of extravagant incongruities; what a fantastic conjunction of opposites and irreconcilables—the home of the bogus miracle become the home of a real one, the den of a mediaeval hermit turned into a telephone office!

The telephone clerk stepped into the light, and I recognized one of my young fellows. I said:

"How long has this office been established here, Ulfius?"

"But since midnight, fair Sir Boss, an it please you. We saw many lights in the valley, and so judged it well to make a station, for that where so many lights be needs must they indicate a town of goodly size."

"Quite right. It isn't a town in the customary sense, but it's a good stand, anyway. Do you know where you are?"

"Of that I have had no time to make inquiry; for whenas my comradeship moved hence upon their labours, leaving me in charge, I got me to needed rest, purposing to inquire when I waked, and report the place's name to Camelot for record."

"Well, this is the Valley of Holiness."

It didn't take; I mean, he didn't start at the name, as I had supposed he would. He merely said:

"I will so report it."

"Why, the surrounding regions are filled with the noise of late wonders that have happened here! You didn't hear of them?"

"Ah, ye will remember we move by night, and avoid speech with all. We learn naught but that we get by the telephone from Camelot."

"Why *they* know all about this thing. Haven't they told you anything about the great miracle of the restoration of a holy fountain?"

"Oh, *that*? Indeed yes. But the name of *this* valley doth woundily differ from the name of *that* one; indeed to differ wider were not pos—"

"What was that name, then?"

"The Valley of Hellishness."

"*That* explains it. Confound a telephone, anyway. It is the very demon for conveying similarities of sound that are miracles of divergence from similarity of sense. But no matter, you know the name of the place now. Call up Camelot."

He did it, and had Clarence sent for. It was good to hear my boy's voice again. It was like being home. After some affectionate interchanges, and some account of my late illness, I said:

"What is new?"

"The king and queen and many of the court do start even in this hour, to go to your valley to pay pious homage to the waters ye have restored, and cleanse themselves of sin, and see the place where the infernal spirit spouted true hell-flames to the clouds—an ye listen sharply ye may hear me wink and hear me likewise smile a smile, sith 'twas I that made selection of those flames from out our stock and sent them by your order."

"Does the king know the way to this place?"

"The king?—no, nor to any other in his realms, mayhap; but the lads that holp you with your miracle will be his guide and lead the way, and appoint the places for rests at noons and sleeps at night."

"This will bring them here—when?"

"Mid-afternoon, or later, the third day."

"Anything else in the way of news?"

"The king hath begun the raising of the standing army ye suggested to him; one regiment is complete and officered."

"The mischief! I wanted a main hand in that myself. There is only one body of men in the kingdom that are fitted to officer a regular army."

"Yes—and now ye will marvel to know there's not so much as one West Pointer in that regiment."

"What are you talking about? Are you in earnest?"

"It is truly as I have said."

"Why, this makes me uneasy. Who were chosen, and what was the method? Competitive examination?"

"Indeed, I know naught of the method. I but know this—these officers be all of noble family, and are born—what is it you call it?—chuckleheads."

"There's something wrong, Clarence."

"Comfort yourself, then; for two candidates for a lieutenancy do travel hence with the king—young nobles both—and if you but wait where you are you will hear them questioned."

"That is news to the purpose. I will get one West Pointer in, anyway. Mount a man and send him to that school with a message; let him kill horses, if necessary, but he must be there before sunset tonight and say—"

"There is no need. I have laid a ground wire to the school. Prithee let me connect you with it."

It sounded good! In this atmosphere of telephones and lightning communication with distant regions, I was breathing the breath of life again after long suffocation. I realized, then, what a creepy, dull, inanimate horror this land had been to me all these years, and how I had been in such a stifled condition of mind as to have grown used to it almost beyond the power to notice it.

I gave my order to the superintendent of the Academy personally. I also asked him to bring me some paper and a fountain pen and a box or so of safety matches. I was getting tired of doing without these conveniences. I could have them now, as I wasn't going to wear armor any more at present, and therefore could get at my pockets.

When I got back to the monastery, I found a thing of interest going on. The abbot and his monks were assembled in the great hall, observing with childish wonder and faith the performances of a new magician, a fresh arrival. His dress was the extreme of the fantastic; as showy and foolish as the sort of thing an Indian medicine-man wears. He was mowing, and mumbling, and gesticulating, and drawing mystical figures in the air and on the floor—the regular thing, you know. He was a celebrity from Asia—so he said, and that was enough. That sort of evidence was as good as gold, and passed current everywhere.

How easy and cheap it was to be a great magician on this fellow's terms. His specialty was to tell you what any individual on the face of the globe was doing at the moment; and what he had done at any time in the past, and what he would do at any time in the future. He asked if any would like to know what the Emperor of the East was doing now? The sparkling eyes and the delighted rubbing of hands made eloquent answer—this reverend crowd *would* like to know what that monarch was at, just as this moment. The fraud went through some more mummery, and then made grave announcement:

"The high and mighty Emperor of the East doth at this moment put money in the palm of a holy begging friar—one, two, three pieces, and they be all of silver."

A buzz of admiring exclamations broke out, all around:

"It is marvellous!" "Wonderful!" "What study, what labour, to have acquired a so amazing power as this!"

Would they like to know what the Supreme Lord of Inde was doing? Yes. He told them what the Supreme Lord of Inde was doing. Then he told them what the Sultan of Egypt was at; also what the King of the Remote Seas was about. And so on and so on; and with each new marvel the astonishment at his accuracy rose higher and higher. They thought he must surely strike an uncertain place sometime; but no, he never had to hesitate, he always knew, and always with unerring precision. I saw that if this thing went on I should lose my supremacy, this fellow would capture my following, I should be left out in the cold. I must put a cog in his wheel, and do it right away, too. I said:

"If I might ask, I should very greatly like to know what a certain person is doing."

"Speak, and freely. I will tell you."

"It will be difficult—perhaps impossible."

"My art knoweth not that word. The more difficult it is, the more certainly will I reveal it to you."

You see, I was working up the interest. It was getting pretty high, too; you could see that by the craning necks all around, and the half-suspended breathing. So now I climaxed it:

"If you make no mistake—if you tell me truly what I want to know—I will give you two hundred silver pennies."

"The fortune is mine! I will tell you what you would know."

"Then tell me what I am doing with my right hand."

"Ah-h!" There was a general gasp of surprise. It had not occurred to anybody in the crowd—that simple trick of inquiring about somebody who wasn't ten thousand miles away. The magician was hit hard; it was an emergency that had never happened in his experience before, and it corked him; he didn't know how to meet it. He looked stunned, confused; he couldn't say a word. "Come," I said, "what are you waiting for? Is it possible you can answer up, right off, and tell what anybody on the other side of the earth is doing, and yet can't tell what a person is doing who isn't three yards from you? Persons behind me know what I am doing with my right hand—they will indorse you if you tell correctly." He was still dumb. "Very well, I'll tell you why you don't speak up and tell; it is because you don't know. *You* a magician! Good friends, this tramp is a mere fraud and liar."

This distressed the monks and terrified them. They were not used to hearing these awful beings called names, and they did not know what might be the consequence. There was a dead silence now; superstitious bodings were in every mind. The magician began to pull his wits together, and when he presently smiled an easy, nonchalant smile, it spread a mighty relief around; for it indicated that his mood was not destructive. He said:

"It hath struck me speechless, the frivolity of this person's speech. Let all know, if perchance there be any who know it not, that enchanters of my degree deign not to concern themselves with the doings of any but Kings, Princes, Emperors, them that be born in the purple and them only. Had ye asked me what Arthur the great king is doing, it were another matter, and I had told ye; but the doings of a subject interest me not."

"Oh, I misunderstood you. I thought you said 'anybody,' and so I supposed 'anybody' included—well, anybody; that is, everybody."

"It doth—anybody that is of lofty birth; and the better if he be royal."

"That, it meseemeth, might well be," said the abbot, who saw his opportunity to smooth things and avert disaster, "for it were not likely that so wonderful a gift as this would be conferred for the revelation of the concerns of lesser beings than such as be born near to the summits of greatness. Our Arthur the king—"

"Would you know of him?" broke in the enchanter.

"Most gladly, yea, and gratefully."

Everybody was full of awe and interest again right away, the incorrigible idiots. They watched the incantations absorbingly, and looked at me with a "There, now, what can you say to that?" air, when the announcement came:

"The king is weary with the chase, and lieth in his palace these two hours sleeping a dreamless sleep."

"God's benison upon him!" said the abbot, and crossed himself; "may that sleep be to the refreshment of his body and his soul."

"And so it might be, if he were sleeping," I said, "but the king is not sleeping, the king rides."

Here was trouble again—a conflict of authority. Nobody knew which of us to believe; I still had some reputation left. The magician's scorn was stirred, and he said:

"Lo, I have seen many wonderful soothsayers and prophets and magicians in my life days, but none before that could sit idle and see to the heart of things with never an incantation to help."

"You have lived in the woods, and lost much by it. I use incantations myself, as this good brotherhood are aware—but only on occasions of moment."

When it comes to sarcasming, I reckon I know how to keep my end up. That jab made this fellow squirm. The abbot inquired after the queen and the court, and got this information:

"They be all on sleep, being overcome by fatigue, like as to the king."

I said:

"That is merely another lie. Half of them are about their amusements, the queen and the other half are not sleeping, they ride. Now perhaps you can spread yourself a little, and tell us where the king and queen and all that are this moment riding with them are going?"

"They sleep now, as I said; but on the morrow they will ride, for they go a journey toward the sea."

"And where will they be the day after tomorrow at vespers?"

"Far to the north of Camelot, and half their journey will be done."

"That is another lie, by the space of a hundred and fifty miles. Their journey will not be merely half done, it will be all done, and they will be *here*, in this valley."

That was a noble shot! It set the abbot and the monks in a whirl of excitement, and it rocked the enchanter to his base. I followed the thing right up:

"If the king does not arrive, I will have myself ridden on a rail: if he does I will ride you on a rail instead."

Next day I went up to the telephone office and found that the king had passed through two towns that were on the line. I spotted his progress on the succeeding day in the same way. I kept these matters to myself. The third day's reports showed that if he kept up his gait he would arrive by four in the afternoon. There was still no sign anywhere of interest in his coming; there seemed to be no preparations making to receive him in state; a strange thing, truly. Only one thing could explain this: that other magician had been cutting under me, sure. This was true. I asked a friend of mine, a monk, about it, and he said, yes, the magician had tried some further enchantments and found out that the court had concluded to make no journey at all, but stay at home. Think of that! Observe how much a reputation was worth in such a country. These people had seen me do the very showiest bit of magic in history, and the only one within their memory that had a positive value, and yet here they were, ready to take up with an adventurer who could offer no evidence of his powers but his mere unproven word.

The false prophet going to meet the King

However, it was not good politics to let the king come without any fuss and feathers at all, so I went down and drummed up a procession of pilgrims and smoked out a batch of hermits and started them out at two o'clock to meet him. And that was the sort of state he arrived in. The abbot was helpless with rage and humiliation when I brought him out on a balcony and showed him the head of the state marching in and never a monk on hand to offer him welcome, and no stir of life or clang of joy-bell to glad his spirit. He took one look and then flew to rouse out his forces. The next minute the bells were dinning furiously, and the various buildings were vomiting monks and nuns, who went swarming in a rush toward the coming procession; and with them went that magician—and he was on a rail, too, by the abbot's order; and his reputation was in the mud, and mine was in the sky again. Yes, a man can keep his trademark current in such a country, but he can't sit around and do it; he has got to be on deck and attending to business right along.

25

A Competitive Examination

When the king traveled for change of air, or made a progress, or visited a distant noble whom he wished to bankrupt with the cost of his keep, part of the administration moved with him. It was a fashion of the time. The Commission charged with the examination of candidates for posts in the army came with the king to the Valley, whereas they could have transacted their business just as well at home. And although this expedition was strictly a holiday excursion for the king, he kept some of his business functions going just the same. He touched for the evil, as usual; he held court in the gate at sunrise and tried cases, for he was himself Chief Justice of the King's Bench.

He shone very well in this latter office. He was a wise and humane judge, and he clearly did his honest best and fairest—according to his lights. That is a large reservation. His lights—I mean his rearing—often coloured his decisions. Whenever there was a dispute between a noble or gentleman and a person of lower degree, the king's leanings and sympathies were for the former class always, whether he suspected it or not. It was impossible that this should be otherwise. The blunting effects of slavery upon the slaveholder's moral perceptions are known and conceded, the world over; and a privileged class, an aristocracy, is but a band of slaveholders under another name. This has a harsh sound, and yet should not be offensive to any—even to the noble himself—unless the fact itself be an offense: for the statement simply formulates a fact. The repulsive feature of slavery is the *thing*, not its name. One needs but to hear an aristocrat speak of the classes that are below him to recognize—and in but indifferently modified measure—the very air and tone of the actual slaveholder; and behind these are the slaveholder's spirit, the slaveholder's blunted feeling. They are the result of the same cause in both cases: the possessor's old and inbred custom of regarding himself as a superior being. The king's judgments wrought frequent injustices, but it was merely the fault of his training, his natural and unalterable sympathies. He was as unfitted for a judgeship as would be the average mother for the position of milk-distributor to starving children in famine-time; her own children would fare a shade better than the rest.

One very curious case came before the king. A young girl, an orphan, who had a considerable estate, married a fine young fellow who had nothing. The girl's property was within a seigniory held by the Church. The bishop of the diocese, an arrogant scion of the great nobility, claimed the girl's estate on the ground that she had married privately, and thus had cheated the Church out of one of its rights as lord of the seigniory—the one heretofore referred to as *le droit du seigneur.* The penalty of refusal or avoidance was confiscation. The girl's defense was, that the lordship of the seigniory was vested in the bishop, and the particular right here involved was not transferable, but must be exercised by the lord himself or stand vacated; and that an older law, of the Church itself, strictly barred the bishop from exercising it. It was a very odd case, indeed.

It reminded me of something I had read in my youth about the ingenious way in which the aldermen of London raised the money that built the Mansion House. A person who had not taken the Sacrament according to the Anglican rite could not stand as a candidate for sheriff of London. Thus Dissenters were ineligible; they could not run if asked, they could not serve if elected. The aldermen, who without any question were Yankees in disguise, hit upon this neat device: they passed a by-law imposing a fine of L400 upon any one who should refuse to be a candidate for sheriff, and a fine of L600 upon any person who, after being elected sheriff, refused to serve. Then they went to work and elected a lot of Dissenters, one after another, and kept it up until they had collected L15,000 in fines; and there stands the stately Mansion House to this day, to keep the blushing citizen in mind of a long past and lamented day when a band of Yankees slipped into London and played games of the sort that has given their race a unique and shady reputation among all truly good and holy peoples that be in the earth.

The girl's case seemed strong to me; the bishop's case was just as strong. I did not see how the king was going to get out of this hole. But he got out. I append his decision:

"Truly I find small difficulty here, the matter being even a child's affair for simpleness. An the young bride had conveyed notice, as in duty bound, to her feudal lord and proper master and protector the bishop, she had suffered no loss, for the said bishop could have got a dispensation making him, for temporary conveniency, eligible to the exercise of his said right, and thus would she have kept all she had. Whereas, failing in her first duty, she hath by that failure failed in all; for whoso, clinging to a rope, severeth it above his hands, must fall; it being no defense to claim that the rest of the rope is sound, neither any deliverance from his peril, as he shall find. Pardy, the woman's case is rotten at the source. It is the decree of the court that she forfeit to the said lord bishop all her goods, even to the last farthing that she doth possess, and be thereto mulcted in the costs. Next!"

Here was a tragic end to a beautiful honeymoon not yet three months old. Poor young creatures! They had lived these three months lapped to the lips in worldly comforts. These clothes and trinkets they were wearing were as fine and dainty as the shrewdest stretch of the sumptuary laws allowed to people of their degree; and in these pretty clothes, she crying on his shoulder, and he trying to comfort her with hopeful words set to the music of despair, they went from the judgment seat out into the world homeless, bedless, breadless; why, the very beggars by the roadsides were not so poor as they.

Well, the king was out of the hole; and on terms satisfactory to the Church and the rest of the aristocracy, no doubt. Men write many fine and plausible arguments in support of monarchy, but the fact remains that where every man in a State has a vote, brutal laws are impossible. Arthur's people were of course poor material for a republic, because they had been debased so long by monarchy; and yet even they would have been intelligent enough to make short work of that law which the king had just been administering if it had been submitted to their full and free vote. There is a phrase which has grown so common in the world's mouth that it has come to seem to have sense and meaning—the sense and meaning implied when it is used; that is the phrase which refers to this or that or the other nation as possibly being "capable of self-government"; and the implied sense of it is, that there has been a nation somewhere, some time or other which *wasn't* capable of it—wasn't as able to govern itself as some self-appointed specialists were or would be to govern it. The master minds of all nations, in all ages, have sprung in affluent multitude from the mass of the nation, and from the mass of the nation only—not from its privileged classes; and so, no matter what the nation's intellectual grade was; whether high or low, the bulk of its ability was in the long ranks of its nameless and its poor, and so it never saw the day that it had not the material in abundance whereby to govern itself. Which is to assert an always self-proven fact: that even the best governed and most free and most enlightened monarchy is still behind the best condition attainable by its people; and that the same is true of kindred governments of lower grades, all the way down to the lowest.

King Arthur had hurried up the army business altogether beyond my calculations. I had not supposed he would move in the matter while I was away; and so I had not mapped out a scheme for determining the merits of officers; I had only remarked that it would be wise to submit every candidate to a sharp and searching examination; and privately I meant to put together a list of military qualifications that nobody could answer to but my West Pointers. That ought to have been attended to before I left; for the king was so taken with the idea of a standing army that he couldn't wait but must get about it at once, and get up as good a scheme of examination as he could invent out of his own head.

I was impatient to see what this was; and to show, too, how much more admirable was the one which I should display to the Examining Board. I intimated this, gently, to the king, and it fired his curiosity. When the Board was assembled, I followed him in; and behind us came the candidates. One of these candidates was a bright young West Pointer of mine, and with him were a couple of my West Point professors.

When I saw the Board, I did not know whether to cry or to laugh. The head of it was the officer known to later centuries as Norroy King-at-Arms! The two other members were chiefs of bureaus in his department; and all three were priests, of course; all officials who had to know how to read and write were priests.

My candidate was called first, out of courtesy to me, and the head of the Board opened on him with official solemnity:

"Name?"

"Mal-ease."

"Son of?"

"Webster."

"Webster—Webster. H'm—I—my memory faileth to recall the name. Condition?"

"Weaver."

"Weaver!—God keep us!"

The king was staggered, from his summit to his foundations; one clerk fainted, and the others came near it. The chairman pulled himself together, and said indignantly:

"It is sufficient. Get you hence."

But I appealed to the king. I begged that my candidate might be examined. The king was willing, but the Board, who were all well-born folk, implored the king to spare them the indignity of examining the weaver's son. I knew they didn't know enough to examine him anyway, so I joined my prayers to theirs and the king turned the duty over to my professors. I had had a blackboard prepared, and it was put up now, and the circus began. It was beautiful to hear the lad lay out the science of war, and wallow in details of battle and siege, of supply, transportation, mining and countermining, grand tactics, big strategy and little strategy, signal service, infantry, cavalry, artillery, and all about siege guns, field guns, gatling guns, rifled guns, smooth bores, musket practice, revolver practice—and not a solitary word of it all could these catfish make head or tail of, you understand—and it was handsome to see him chalk off mathematical nightmares on the blackboard that would stump the angels themselves, and do it like nothing, too—all about eclipses, and comets, and solstices, and constellations, and mean time, and sidereal time, and dinner time, and bedtime, and every other imaginable thing above the clouds or under them that you could harry or bullyrag an enemy with and make him wish he hadn't come—and when the boy made his military salute and stood aside at last, I was proud enough to hug him, and all those other people were so dazed they looked partly petrified, partly drunk, and wholly caught out and snowed under. I judged that the cake was ours, and by a large majority.

Education is a great thing. This was the same youth who had come to West Point so ignorant that when I asked him, "If a general officer should have a horse shot under him on the field of battle, what ought he to do?" answered up naively and said:

"Get up and brush himself."

One of the young nobles was called up now. I thought I would question him a little myself. I said:

"Can your lordship read?"

His face flushed indignantly, and he fired this at me:

"Takest me for a clerk? I trow I am not of a blood that—"

"Answer the question!"

He crowded his wrath down and made out to answer "No."

"Can you write?"

He wanted to resent this, too, but I said:

"You will confine yourself to the questions, and make no comments. You are not here to air your blood or your graces, and nothing of the sort will be permitted. Can you write?"

"No."

"Do you know the multiplication table?"

"I wit not what ye refer to."

"How much is 9 times 6?"

"It is a mystery that is hidden from me by reason that the emergency requiring the fathoming of it hath not in my life-days occurred, and so, not having no need to know this thing, I abide barren of the knowledge."

"If A trade a barrel of onions to B, worth 2 pence the bushel, in exchange for a sheep worth 4 pence and a dog worth a penny, and C kill the dog before delivery, because bitten by the same, who mistook him for D, what sum is still due to A from B, and which party pays for the dog, C or

D, and who gets the money? If A, is the penny sufficient, or may he claim consequential damages in the form of additional money to represent the possible profit which might have inured from the dog, and classifiable as earned increment, that is to say, usufruct?"

"Verily, in the all-wise and unknowable providence of God, who moveth in mysterious ways his wonders to perform, have I never heard the fellow to this question for confusion of the mind and congestion of the ducts of thought. Wherefore I beseech you let the dog and the onions and these people of the strange and godless names work out their several salvations from their piteous and wonderful difficulties without help of mine, for indeed their trouble is sufficient as it is, whereas an I tried to help I should but damage their cause the more and yet mayhap not live myself to see the desolation wrought."

"What do you know of the laws of attraction and gravitation?"

"If there be such, mayhap his grace the king did promulgate them whilst that I lay sick about the beginning of the year and thereby failed to hear his proclamation."

"What do you know of the science of optics?"

"I know of governors of places, and seneschals of castles, and sheriffs of counties, and many like small offices and titles of honour, but him you call the Science of Optics I have not heard of before; peradventure it is a new dignity."

"Yes, in this country."

Try to conceive of this mollusk gravely applying for an official position, of any kind under the sun! Why, he had all the earmarks of a typewriter copyist, if you leave out the disposition to contribute uninvited emendations of your grammar and punctuation. It was unaccountable that he didn't attempt a little help of that sort out of his majestic supply of incapacity for the job. But that didn't prove that he hadn't material in him for the disposition, it only proved that he wasn't a typewriter copyist yet. After nagging him a little more, I let the professors loose on him and they turned him inside out, on the line of scientific war, and found him empty, of course. He knew somewhat about the warfare of the time—bushwhacking around for ogres, and bull-fights in the tournament ring, and such things—but otherwise he was empty and useless. Then we took the other young noble in hand, and he was the first one's twin, for ignorance and incapacity. I delivered them into the hands of the chairman of the Board with the comfortable consciousness that their cake was dough. They were examined in the previous order of precedence.

"Name, so please you?"

"Pertipole, son of Sir Pertipole, Baron of Barley Mash."

"Grandfather?"

"Also Sir Pertipole, Baron of Barley Mash."

"Great-grandfather?"

"The same name and title."

"Great-great-grandfather?"

"We had none, worshipful sir, the line failing before it had reached so far back."

"It mattereth not. It is a good four generations, and fulfilleth the requirements of the rule."

"Fulfills what rule?" I asked.

"The rule requiring four generations of nobility or else the candidate is not eligible."

"A man not eligible for a lieutenancy in the army unless he can prove four generations of noble descent?"

"Even so; neither lieutenant nor any other officer may be commissioned without that qualification."

"Oh, come, this is an astonishing thing. What good is such a qualification as that?"

"What good? It is a hardy question, fair sir and Boss, since it doth go far to impugn the wisdom of even our holy Mother Church herself."

"As how?"

"For that she hath established the self-same rule regarding saints. By her law none may be canonized until he hath lain dead four generations."

"I see, I see—it is the same thing. It is wonderful. In the one case a man lies dead-alive four generations—mummified in ignorance and sloth—and that qualifies him to command live people, and take their weal and woe into his impotent hands; and in the other case, a man lies bedded with death and worms four generations, and that qualifies him for office in the celestial camp. Does the king's grace approve of this strange law?"

The king said:

"Why, truly I see naught about it that is strange. All places of honour and of profit do belong, by natural right, to them that be of noble blood, and so these dignities in the army are their property and would be so without this or any rule. The rule is but to mark a limit. Its purpose is to keep out too recent blood, which would bring into contempt these offices, and men of lofty lineage would turn their backs and scorn to take them. I were to blame an I permitted this calamity. *You* can permit it an you are minded so to do, for you have the delegated authority, but that the king should do it were a most strange madness and not comprehensible to any."

"I yield. Proceed, sir Chief of the Herald's College."

The chairman resumed as follows:

"By what illustrious achievement for the honour of the Throne and State did the founder of your great line lift himself to the sacred dignity of the British nobility?"

"He built a brewery."

"Sire, the Board finds this candidate perfect in all the requirements and qualifications for military command, and doth hold his case open for decision after due examination of his competitor."

The competitor came forward and proved exactly four generations of nobility himself. So there was a tie in military qualifications that far.

He stood aside a moment, and Sir Pertipole was questioned further:

"Of what condition was the wife of the founder of your line?"

"She came of the highest landed gentry, yet she was not noble; she was gracious and pure and charitable, of a blameless life and character, insomuch that in these regards was she peer of the best lady in the land."

"That will do. Stand down." He called up the competing lordling again, and asked: "What was the rank and condition of the great-grandmother who conferred British nobility upon your great house?"

"She was a king's leman and did climb to that splendid eminence by her own unholpen merit from the sewer where she was born."

"Ah, this, indeed, is true nobility, this is the right and perfect intermixture. The lieutenancy is yours, fair lord. Hold it not in contempt; it is the humble step which will lead to grandeurs more worthy of the splendour of an origin like to thine."

I was down in the bottomless pit of humiliation. I had promised myself an easy and zenith-scouring triumph, and this was the outcome!

I was almost ashamed to look my poor disappointed cadet in the face. I told him to go home and be patient, this wasn't the end.

I had a private audience with the king, and made a proposition. I said it was quite right to officer that regiment with nobilities, and he couldn't have done a wiser thing. It would also be a good idea to add five hundred officers to it; in fact, add as many officers as there were nobles and relatives of nobles in the country, even if there should finally be five times as many officers as privates in it; and thus make it the crack regiment, the envied regiment, the King's Own regiment, and entitled to fight on its own hook and in its own way, and go whither it would and come when it pleased, in time of war, and be utterly swell and independent. This would make that regiment the heart's desire of all the nobility, and they would all be satisfied and happy. Then we would make up the rest of the standing army out of commonplace materials, and officer it with nobodies, as was proper—nobodies selected on a basis of mere efficiency—and we would make this regiment toe the line, allow it no aristocratic freedom from restraint, and force it to do all the work and persistent hammering, to the end that whenever the King's Own was tired and wanted to go off for a change and rummage around amongst ogres and have a good time, it could go without uneasiness, knowing that matters were in safe hands behind it, and business going to be continued at the old stand, same as usual. The king was charmed with the idea.

When I noticed that, it gave me a valuable notion. I thought I saw my way out of an old and stubborn difficulty at last. You see, the royalties of the Pendragon stock were a long-lived race and very fruitful. Whenever a child was born to any of these—and it was pretty often—there was wild joy in the nation's mouth, and piteous sorrow in the nation's heart. The joy was questionable, but the grief was honest. Because the event meant another call for a Royal Grant. Long was the list of these royalties, and they were a heavy and steadily increasing burden upon the treasury and a menace to the crown. Yet Arthur could not believe this latter fact, and he would not listen to any of my various projects for substituting something in the place of the royal grants. If I could have persuaded him to now and then provide a support for one of these outlying scions from his own pocket, I could have made a grand to-do over it, and it would have had a good effect with the nation; but no, he wouldn't hear of such a thing. He had something like a religious passion for royal grant; he seemed to look upon it as a sort of sacred swag, and one could not irritate him in any way so quickly and so surely as by an attack upon that venerable institution. If I ventured to cautiously hint that there was not another respectable family in England that would humble itself to hold out the hat—however, that is as far as I ever got; he always cut me short there, and peremptorily, too.

But I believed I saw my chance at last. I would form this crack regiment out of officers alone—not a single private. Half of it should consist of nobles, who should fill all the places up to Major General, and serve gratis and pay their own expenses; and they would be glad to do this when they should learn that the rest of the regiment would consist exclusively of princes of the blood. These princes of the blood should range in rank from Lieutenant General up to Field Marshal, and be gorgeously salaried and equipped and fed by the state. Moreover—and this was the master stroke—it should be decreed that these princely grandees should be always addressed by a stunningly gaudy and awe-compelling title (which I would presently invent), and they and they only in all England should be so addressed. Finally, all princes of the blood should have free choice; join that regiment, get that great title, and renounce the royal grant, or stay out and receive a grant. Neatest touch of all: unborn but imminent princes of the blood could be *born* into the regiment, and start fair, with good wages and a permanent situation, upon due notice from the parents.

All the boys would join, I was sure of that; so, all existing grants would be relinquished; that the newly born would always join was equally certain. Within sixty days that quaint and bizarre anomaly, the Royal Grant, would cease to be a living fact, and take its place among the curiosities of the past.

26

The First Newspaper

When I told the king I was going out disguised as a petty freeman to scour the country and familiarize myself with the humbler life of the people, he was all afire with the novelty of the thing in a minute, and was bound to take a chance in the adventure himself—nothing should stop him—he would drop everything and go along—it was the prettiest idea he had run across for many a day. He wanted to glide out the back way and start at once; but I showed him that that wouldn't answer. You see, he was billed for the king's-evil—to touch for it, I mean—and it wouldn't be right to disappoint the house and it wouldn't make a delay worth considering, anyway, it was only a one-night stand. And I thought he ought to tell the queen he was going away. He clouded up at that and looked sad. I was sorry I had spoken, especially when he said mournfully:

"Thou forgettest that Launcelot is here; and where Launcelot is, she noteth not the going forth of the king, nor what day he returneth."

Of course, I changed the Subject. Yes, Guenever was beautiful, it is true, but take her all around she was pretty slack. I never meddled in these matters, they weren't my affair, but I did hate to see the way things were going on, and I don't mind saying that much. Many's the time she had asked me, "Sir Boss, hast seen Sir Launcelot about?" but if ever she went fretting around for the king I didn't happen to be around at the time.

There was a very good layout for the king's-evil business—very tidy and creditable. The king sat under a canopy of state; about him were clustered a large body of the clergy in full canonicals. Conspicuous, both for location and personal outfit, stood Marinel, a hermit of the quack-doctor species, to introduce the sick. All abroad over the spacious floor, and clear down to the doors, in a thick jumble, lay or sat the scrofulous, under a strong light. It was as good as a tableau; in fact, it had all the look of being gotten up for that, though it wasn't. There were eight hundred sick people present. The work was slow; it lacked the interest of novelty for me, because I had seen the ceremonies before; the thing soon became tedious, but the proprieties required me to stick it out. The doctor was there for the reason that in all such crowds there were many people who only imagined something was the matter with them, and many who were consciously sound but wanted the immortal honour of fleshly contact with a king, and yet others who pretended to illness in order to get the piece of coin that went with the touch. Up to this time this coin had been a wee little gold piece worth about a third of a dollar. When you consider how much that amount of money would buy, in that age and country, and how usual it was to be scrofulous, when not dead, you would understand that the annual king's-evil appropriation was just the River and Harbor bill of that government for the grip it took on the treasury and the chance it afforded for skinning the surplus. So I had privately concluded to touch the treasury itself for the king's-evil. I covered six-sevenths of the appropriation into the treasury a week before starting from Camelot on my adventures, and ordered that the other seventh be inflated into five-cent nickels and delivered into the hands of the head clerk of the King's Evil Department; a nickel to take the place of each gold coin, you see, and do its work for it. It might strain the nickel some, but I judged it could stand it. As a rule, I do not approve of watering stock, but I considered it square enough in this case, for it was just a gift, anyway. Of course, you can water a gift as much as you want to; and I generally do. The old gold and silver coins of the country were of ancient and unknown origin, as a rule, but some of them were Roman; they were ill-shapen, and seldom rounder than a moon that is a week past the full; they were hammered, not minted, and they were so worn with use that the devices upon them were as illegible as blisters, and looked like them. I judged that a sharp, bright new nickel, with a first-rate likeness of the king on one side of it and Guenever on the other, and a blooming pious motto, would take the tuck out of scrofula as handy as a nobler coin and please the scrofulous fancy more; and I was right. This batch was the first it was tried on, and it worked to a charm. The saving in expense was a notable economy. You will see that by these figures: We touched a trifle over 700 of the 800 patients; at former rates, this would have cost the government about $240; at the new rate we pulled through for about $35, thus saving upward of $200 at one swoop. To appreciate the full magnitude of this stroke, consider these other figures: the annual expenses of a national government amount to the equivalent of a contribution of three days' average wages of every individual of the population, counting every individual as if he were a man. If you take a nation of 60,000,000, where average wages are $2 per day, three days' wages taken from each individual will provide $360,000,000 and pay the government's expenses. In my day, in my own country, this money was collected from imposts, and the citizen imagined that the foreign importer paid it, and it made him comfortable to think so; whereas, in fact, it was paid by the American people, and was so equally and exactly distributed among them that the annual cost to the 100-millionaire and the annual cost to the sucking child of the day-labourer was precisely the same—each paid $6. Nothing could be equaller than that, I reckon. Well, Scotland and Ireland were tributary to Arthur, and the united populations of the British Islands amounted to something less than 1,000,000. A mechanic's average wage was 3 cents a day, when he paid his own keep. By this rule the national government's expenses were $90,000 a year, or about $250 a day. Thus, by the substitution of nickels for gold on a king's-evil day, I not only injured no one, dissatisfied no one, but pleased all concerned and saved four-fifths of that day's national expense into the bargain—a saving which would have been the equivalent of $800,000 in my day in America. In making this substitution I had drawn upon the wisdom of a very remote source—the wisdom of my boyhood—for the true statesman does not despise any wisdom, howsoever lowly may be its origin: in my boyhood I had always saved my pennies and contributed buttons to the foreign missionary cause. The buttons would answer the ignorant savage as well as the coin, the coin would answer me better than the buttons; all hands were happy and nobody hurt.

Marinel took the patients as they came. He examined the candidate; if he couldn't qualify he was warned off; if he could he was passed along to the king. A priest pronounced the words, "They shall lay their hands on the sick, and they shall recover." Then the king stroked the ulcers, while the reading continued; finally, the patient graduated and got his nickel—the king hanging it around his neck himself—and was dismissed. Would you think that that would cure? It certainly did. Any mummery will cure if the patient's faith is strong in it. Up by Astolat there was a chapel where the Virgin had once appeared to a girl who used to herd geese around there—

the girl said so herself—and they built the chapel upon that spot and hung a picture in it representing the occurrence—a picture which you would think it dangerous for a sick person to approach; whereas, on the contrary, thousands of the lame and the sick came and prayed before it every year and went away whole and sound; and even the well could look upon it and live. Of course, when I was told these things I did not believe them; but when I went there and saw them I had to succumb. I saw the cures effected myself; and they were real cures and not questionable. I saw cripples whom I had seen around Camelot for years on crutches, arrive and pray before that picture, and put down their crutches and walk off without a limp. There were piles of crutches there which had been left by such people as a testimony.

In other places people operated on a patient's mind, without saying a word to him, and cured him. In others, experts assembled patients in a room and prayed over them, and appealed to their faith, and those patients went away cured. Wherever you find a king who can't cure the king's-evil you can be sure that the most valuable superstition that supports his throne—the subject's belief in the divine appointment of his sovereign—has passed away. In my youth the monarchs of England had ceased to touch for the evil, but there was no occasion for this diffidence: they could have cured it forty-nine times in fifty.

Well, when the priest had been droning for three hours, and the good king polishing the evidences, and the sick were still pressing forward as plenty as ever, I got to feeling intolerably bored. I was sitting by an open window not far from the canopy of state. For the five hundredth time a patient stood forward to have his repulsivenesses stroked; again those words were being droned out: "they shall lay their hands on the sick"—when outside there rang clear as a clarion a note that enchanted my soul and tumbled thirteen worthless centuries about my ears: "Camelot *Weekly Hosannah and Literary Volcano!*—latest irruption—only two cents—all about the big miracle in the Valley of Holiness!" One greater than kings had arrived—the newsboy. But I was the only person in all that throng who knew the meaning of this mighty birth, and what this imperial magician was come into the world to do.

I dropped a nickel out of the window and got my paper; the Adam-newsboy of the world went around the corner to get my change; is around the corner yet. It was delicious to see a newspaper again, yet I was conscious of a secret shock when my eye fell upon the first batch of display headlines. I had lived in a clammy atmosphere of reverence, respect, deference, so long that they sent a quivery little cold wave through me:

HIGH TIMES IN THE VALLEY OF HOLINESS!

THE WATER-MORKSCORKED!

BRER MERLIN WORKS HIS ARTS, BUT GETS LEFT!

But t he Boss scores on his first Innings!

The Miraculous Well Uncorked amid awful outbursts of

INFERNAL FIRE AND SMOKE ANDTHUNDER!

THE BUZZARD-ROOST ASTONISHED!

UNPARALLELED REJOIBINGS!

—and so on, and so on. Yes, it was too loud. Once I could have enjoyed it and seen nothing out of the way about it, but now its note was discordant. It was good Arkansas journalism, but this was not Arkansas. Moreover, the next to the last line was calculated to give offense to the hermits, and perhaps lose us their advertising. Indeed, there was too lightsome a tone of flippancy all through the paper. It was plain I had undergone a considerable change without noticing it. I found myself unpleasantly affected by pert little irreverences which would have seemed but proper and airy graces of speech at an earlier period of my life. There was an abundance of the following breed of items, and they discomforted me:

LOCAL SMOKE AND CINDERS.

Sir Launcelot met up with old King Agrivance of Ireland unexpectedly last weok over on the moor south of Sir Balmoral le Merveilleuse's hog dasture. The widow has been notified.

Expedition No. 3 will start adout the first of mext month on a search f8r Sir Sagramour le Desirous. It is in com-and of the renowned Knight of the Red Lawns, assissted by Sir Persant of Inde, who is compete9t. intelligent, courte-ous, and in every way a brick, and fur-tHer assisted by Sir Palamides the Sara-cen, who is no huckleberry hinself. This is no pic-nic, these boys mean busine&s.
The readers of the Hosannah will re-gret to learn that the hadndsome and popular Sir Charolais of Gaul, who dur-ing his four weeks' stay at the Bull and Halibut, this city, has won every heart by his polished manners and elegant cPnversation, will pUll out today for home. Give us another call, Charley!
The bdsiness end of the funeral of the late Sir Dalliance the duke's son of Cornwall, killed in an encounter with the Giant of the Knotted Bludgeon last Tuesday on the borders of the Plain of Enchantment was in the hands of the ever affable and efficient Mumble, prince of un3ertakers, then whom there exists none by whom it were a more satisfying pleasure to have the last sad offices performed. Give him a trial.
The cordial thanks of the Hosannah office are due, from editor down to devil, to the ever courteous and thought-ful Lord High Stew d of the Palace's Third Assistant V t for several sau-ceTs of ice crEam a quality calculated to make the ey of the recipients hu-mid with grt ude; and it done it.
When this administration wants to chalk up a desirable name for early

promotion, the Hosannah would like a chance to sudgest.
The Demoiselle Irene Dewlap, of South Astolat, is visiting her uncle, the popular host of the Cattlemen's Boarding Ho&se, Liver Lane, this city.
Young Barker the bellows-mender is hoMe again, and looks much improved by his vacation round-up among the outlying smithies. See his ad.

Of course it was good enough journalism for a beginning; I knew that quite well, and yet it was somehow disappointing. The "Court Circular" pleased me better; indeed, its simple and dignified respectfulness was a distinct refreshment to me after all those disgraceful familiarities. But even it could have been improved. Do what one may, there is no getting an air of variety into a court circular, I acknowledge that. There is a profound monotonousness about its facts that baffles and defeats one's sincerest efforts to make them sparkle and enthuse. The best way to manage—in fact, the only sensible way—is to disguise repetitiousness of fact under variety of form: skin your fact each time and lay on a new cuticle of words. It deceives the eye; you think it is a new fact; it gives you the idea that the court is carrying on like everything; this excites you, and you drain the whole column, with a good appetite, and perhaps never notice that it's a barrel of soup made out of a single bean. Clarence's way was good, it was simple, it was dignified, it was direct and business-like; all I say is, it was not the best way:

However, take the paper by and large, I was vastly pleased with it. Little crudities of a mechanical sort were observable here and there, but there were not enough of them to amount to anything, and it was good enough Arkansas proofreading, anyhow, and better than was needed in Arthur's day and realm. As a rule, the grammar was leaky and the construction more or less lame; but I did not much mind these things. They are common defects of my own, and one mustn't criticise other people on grounds where he can't stand perpendicular himself.

I was hungry enough for literature to want to take down the whole paper at this one meal, but I got only a few bites, and then had to postpone, because the monks around me besieged me so with eager questions: What is this curious thing? What is it for? Is it a handkerchief?—saddle blanket?—part of a shirt? What is it made of? How thin it is, and how dainty and frail; and how it rattles. Will it wear, do you think, and won't the rain injure it? Is it writing that appears on it, or is it only ornamentation? They suspected it was writing, because those among them who knew how to read Latin and had a smattering of Greek, recognized some of the letters, but they could make nothing out of the result as a whole. I put my information in the simplest form I could:

"It is a public journal; I will explain what that is, another time. It is not cloth, it is made of paper; some time I will explain what paper is. The lines on it are reading matter; and not written by hand, but printed; by and by I will explain what printing is. A thousand of these sheets have been made, all exactly like this, in every minute detail—they can't be told apart." Then they all broke out with exclamations of surprise and admiration:

"A thousand! Verily a mighty work—a year's work for many men."

"No—merely a day's work for a man and a boy."

They crossed themselves, and whiffed out a protective prayer or two.

"Ah-h—a miracle, a wonder! Dark work of enchantment."

I let it go at that. Then I read in a low voice, to as many as could crowd their shaven heads within hearing distance, part of the account of the miracle of the restoration of the well, and was accompanied by astonished and reverent ejaculations all through: "Ah-h-h!" "How true!" "Amazing, amazing!" "These be the very haps as they happened, in marvellous exactness!" And might they take this strange thing in their hands, and feel of it and examine it?—they would be very careful. Yes. So they took it, handling it as cautiously and devoutly as if it had been some holy thing come from some supernatural region; and gently felt of its texture, caressed its pleasant smooth surface with lingering touch, and scanned the mysterious characters with fascinated eyes. These grouped bent heads, these charmed faces, these speaking eyes—how beautiful to me! For was not this my darling, and was not all this mute wonder and interest and homage a most eloquent tribute and unforced compliment to it? I knew, then, how a mother feels when women, whether strangers or friends, take her new baby, and close themselves about it with one eager impulse, and bend their heads over it in a tranced adoration that makes all the rest of the universe vanish out of their consciousness and be as if it were not, for that time. I knew how she feels, and that there is no other satisfied ambition, whether of king, conqueror, or poet, that ever reaches halfway to that serene far summit or yields half so divine a contentment.

During all the rest of the séance my paper traveled from group to group all up and down and about that huge hall, and my happy eye was upon it always, and I sat motionless, steeped in satisfaction, drunk with enjoyment. Yes, this was heaven; I was tasting it once, if I might never taste it more.

27

The Yankee and the King Travel Incognito

About bedtime I took the king to my private quarters to cut his hair and help him get the hang of the lowly raiment he was to wear. The high classes wore their hair banged across the forehead but hanging to the shoulders the rest of the way around, whereas the lowest ranks of commoners were banged fore and aft both; the slaves were bangless, and allowed their hair free growth. So I inverted a bowl over his head and cut away all the locks that hung below it. I also trimmed his whiskers and mustache until they were only about a half-inch long; and tried to do it inartistically, and succeeded. It was a villainous disfigurement. When he got his lubberly sandals on, and his long robe of coarse brown linen cloth, which hung straight from his neck to his ankle-bones, he was no longer the comeliest man in his kingdom, but one of the unhandsomest and most commonplace and unattractive. We were dressed and barbered alike, and could pass for small farmers, or farm bailiffs, or shepherds, or carters; yes, or for village artisans, if we chose, our costume being in effect universal among the poor, because of its strength and cheapness. I don't mean that it was really cheap to a very poor person, but I do mean that it was the cheapest material there was for male attire—manufactured material, you understand.

We slipped away an hour before dawn, and by broad sun-up had made eight or ten miles, and were in the midst of a sparsely settled country. I had a pretty heavy knapsack; it was laden with provisions—provisions for the king to taper down on, till he could take to the coarse fare of the country without damage.

I found a comfortable seat for the king by the roadside, and then gave him a morsel or two to stay his stomach with. Then I said I would find some water for him, and strolled away. Part of my project was to get out of sight and sit down and rest a little myself. It had always been my custom to stand when in his presence; even at the council board, except upon those rare occasions when the sitting was a very long one, extending over hours; then I had a trifling little backless thing which was like a reversed culvert and was as comfortable as the toothache. I didn't want to break him in suddenly, but do it by degrees. We should have to sit together now when in company, or people would notice; but it would not be good politics for me to be playing equality with him when there was no necessity for it.

I found the water some three hundred yards away, and had been resting about twenty minutes, when I heard voices. That is all right, I thought—peasants going to work; nobody else likely to be stirring this early. But the next moment these comers jingled into sight around a turn of the road—smartly clad people of quality, with luggage-mules and servants in their train! I was off like a shot, through the bushes, by the shortest cut. For a while it did seem that these people would pass the king before I could get to him; but desperation gives you wings, you know, and I canted my body forward, inflated my breast, and held my breath and flew. I arrived. And in plenty good enough time, too.

"Pardon, my king, but it's no time for ceremony—jump! Jump to your feet—some quality are coming!"

"Is that a marvel? Let them come."

"But my liege! You must not be seen sitting. Rise!—and stand in humble posture while they pass. You are a peasant, you know."

"True—I had forgot it, so lost was I in planning of a huge war with Gaul"—he was up by this time, but a farm could have got up quicker, if there was any kind of a boom in real estate—"and right-so a thought came randoming overthwart this majestic dream the which—"

"A humbler attitude, my lord the king—and quick! Duck your head!—more!—still more!—droop it!"

He did his honest best, but lord, it was no great things. He looked as humble as the leaning tower at Pisa. It is the most you could say of it. Indeed, it was such a thundering poor success that it raised wondering scowls all along the line, and a gorgeous flunkey at the tail end of it raised his whip; but I jumped in time and was under it when it fell; and under cover of the volley of coarse laughter which followed, I spoke up sharply and warned the king to take no notice. He mastered himself for the moment, but it was a sore tax; he wanted to eat up the procession. I said:

"It would end our adventures at the very start; and we, being without weapons, could do nothing with that armed gang. If we are going to succeed in our emprise, we must not only look the peasant but act the peasant."

"It is wisdom; none can gainsay it. Let us go on, Sir Boss. I will take note and learn, and do the best I may."

He kept his word. He did the best he could, but I've seen better. If you have ever seen an active, heedless, enterprising child going diligently out of one mischief and into another all day long, and an anxious mother at its heels all the while, and just saving it by a hair from drowning itself or breaking its neck with each new experiment, you've seen the king and me.

If I could have foreseen what the thing was going to be like, I should have said, No, if anybody wants to make his living exhibiting a king as a peasant, let him take the layout; I can do better with a menagerie, and last longer. And yet, during the first three days I never allowed him to enter a hut or other dwelling. If he could pass muster anywhere during his early novitiate it would be in small inns and on the road; so to these places we confined ourselves. Yes, he certainly did the best he could, but what of that? He didn't improve a bit that I could see.

He was always frightening me, always breaking out with fresh astonishers, in new and unexpected places. Toward evening on the second day, what does he do but blandly fetch out a dirk from inside his robe!

"Great guns, my liege, where did you get that?"

"From a smuggler at the inn, yester eve."

"What in the world possessed you to buy it?"

"We have escaped divers dangers by wit—thy wit—but I have bethought me that it were but prudence if I bore a weapon, too. Thine might fail thee in some pinch."

"But people of our condition are not allowed to carry arms. What would a lord say—yes, or any other person of whatever condition—if he caught an upstart peasant with a dagger on his person?"

It was a lucky thing for us that nobody came along just then. I persuaded him to throw the dirk away; and it was as easy as persuading a child to give up some bright fresh new way of killing itself. We walked along, silent and thinking. Finally the king said:

"When ye know that I meditate a thing inconvenient, or that hath a peril in it, why do you not warn me to cease from that project?"

It was a startling question, and a puzzler. I didn't quite know how to take hold of it, or what to say, and so, of course, I ended by saying the natural thing:

"But, sire, how can I know what your thoughts are?"

The king stopped dead in his tracks, and stared at me.

"I believed thou wert greater than Merlin; and truly in magic thou art. But prophecy is greater than magic. Merlin is a prophet."

I saw I had made a blunder. I must get back my lost ground. After a deep reflection and careful planning, I said:

"Sire, I have been misunderstood. I will explain. There are two kinds of prophecy. One is the gift to foretell things that are but a little way off, the other is the gift to foretell things that are whole ages and centuries away. Which is the mightier gift, do you think?"

"Oh, the last, most surely!"

"True. Does Merlin possess it?"

"Partly, yes. He foretold mysteries about my birth and future kingship that were twenty years away."

"Has he ever gone beyond that?"

"He would not claim more, I think."

"It is probably his limit. All prophets have their limit. The limit of some of the great prophets has been a hundred years."

"These are few, I ween."

"There have been two still greater ones, whose limit was four hundred and six hundred years, and one whose limit compassed even seven hundred and twenty."

"Gramercy, it is marvellous!"

"But what are these in comparison with me? They are nothing."

"What? Canst thou truly look beyond even so vast a stretch of time as—"

"Seven hundred years? My liege, as clear as the vision of an eagle does my prophetic eye penetrate and lay bare the future of this world for nearly thirteen centuries and a half!"

My land, you should have seen the king's eyes spread slowly open, and lift the earth's entire atmosphere as much as an inch! That settled Brer Merlin. One never had any occasion to prove his facts, with these people; all he had to do was to state them. It never occurred to anybody to doubt the statement.

"Now, then," I continued, "I *could* work both kinds of prophecy—the long and the short—if I chose to take the trouble to keep in practice; but I seldom exercise any but the long kind, because the other is beneath my dignity. It is properer to Merlin's sort—stump-tail prophets, as we call them in the profession. Of course, I whet up now and then and flirt out a minor prophecy, but not often—hardly ever, in fact. You will remember that there was great talk, when you reached the Valley of Holiness, about my having prophesied your coming and the very hour of your arrival, two or three days beforehand."

"Indeed, yes, I mind it now."

"Well, I could have done it as much as forty times easier, and piled on a thousand times more detail into the bargain, if it had been five hundred years away instead of two or three days."

"How amazing that it should be so!"

"Yes, a genuine expert can always foretell a thing that is five hundred years away easier than he can a thing that's only five hundred seconds off."

"And yet in reason it should clearly be the other way; it should be five hundred times as easy to foretell the last as the first, for, indeed, it is so close by that one uninspired might almost see it. In truth, the law of prophecy doth contradict the likelihoods, most strangely making the difficult easy, and the easy difficult."

It was a wise head. A peasant's cap was no safe disguise for it; you could know it for a king's under a diving-bell, if you could hear it work its intellect.

I had a new trade now, and plenty of business in it. The king was as hungry to find out everything that was going to happen during the next thirteen centuries as if he were expecting to live in them. From that time out, I prophesied myself bald-headed trying to supply the demand. I have done some indiscreet things in my day, but this thing of playing myself for a prophet was the worst. Still, it had its ameliorations. A prophet doesn't have to have any brains. They are good to have, of course, for the ordinary exigencies of life, but they are no use in professional work. It is the restfulest vocation there is. When the spirit of prophecy comes upon you, you merely take your intellect and lay it off in a cool place for a rest, and unship your jaw and leave it alone; it will work itself: the result is prophecy.

Every day a knight errant or so came along, and the sight of them fired the king's martial spirit every time. He would have forgotten himself, sure, and said something to them in a style a suspicious shade or so above his ostensible degree, and so I always got him well out of the road in time. Then he would stand and look with all his eyes; and a proud light would flash from them, and his nostrils would inflate like a war-horse's, and I knew he was longing for a brush with them. But about noon of the third day I had stopped in the road to take a precaution which had been suggested by the whip-stroke that had fallen to my share two days before; a precaution which I had afterward decided to leave untaken, I was so loath to institute it; but now I had just had a fresh reminder: while striding heedlessly along, with jaw spread and intellect at rest, for I was prophesying, I stubbed my toe and fell sprawling. I was so pale I couldn't think for a moment; then I got softly and carefully up and unstrapped my knapsack. I had that dynamite bomb in it, done up in wool in a box. It was a good thing to have along; the time would come when I could do a valuable miracle with it, maybe, but it was a nervous thing to have about me, and I didn't like to ask the king to carry it. Yet I must either throw it away or think up some safe way to get along with its society. I got it out and slipped it into my scrip, and just then here came a couple of knights. The king stood, stately as a statue, gazing toward them—had forgotten himself again, of course—and before I could get a word of warning out, it was time for him to skip, and well that he did it, too. He supposed they would turn aside. Turn aside to avoid trampling peasant dirt under foot? When had he ever turned aside himself—or ever had the chance to do it, if a peasant saw him or any other noble knight in time to judiciously save him the trouble? The knights paid no attention to the king at all; it was his place to look out himself, and if he hadn't skipped he would have been placidly ridden down, and laughed at besides.

The king was in a flaming fury, and launched out his challenge and epithets with a most royal vigor. The knights were some little distance by now. They halted, greatly surprised, and turned in their saddles and looked back, as if wondering if it might be worth while to bother with such scum as we. Then they wheeled and started for us. Not a moment must be lost. I started for *them*. I passed them at a rattling gait, and as I went by I flung out a hair-lifting soul-scorching thirteen-jointed insult which made the king's effort poor and cheap by comparison. I got it out of the nineteenth century where they know how. They had such headway that they were nearly to the king before they could check up; then, frantic with rage, they stood up their horses on their hind hoofs and whirled them around, and the next moment here they came, breast to breast. I was seventy yards off, then, and scrambling up a great bowlder at the roadside. When they were within thirty yards of me they let their long lances droop to a level, depressed their mailed heads, and so, with their horse-hair plumes streaming straight out behind, most gallant to see, this lightning express came tearing for me! When they were within fifteen yards, I sent that bomb with a sure aim, and it struck the ground just under the horses' noses.

Another Miracle

Yes, it was a neat thing, very neat and pretty see. It resembled a steamboat explosion on the Mississippi; and during the next fifteen minutes we stood under a steady drizzle of microscopic fragments of knights and hardware and horse-flesh. say we, for the king joined the audience, of course, as soon as he had got his breath again. There was a hole there which would afford steady work for all the people in that region for some years to come—in trying to explain it, I mean; as for filling it up, that service would be comparatively prompt, and would fall to the lot of a select few—peasants of that seignory; and they wouldn't get anything for it, either.

But I explained it to the king myself. I said it was done with a dynamite bomb. This information did him no damage, because it left him as intelligent as he was before. However, it was a noble miracle, in his eyes, and was another settler for Merlin. I thought it well enough to explain that this was a miracle of so rare a sort that it couldn't be done except when the atmospheric conditions were just right. Otherwise he would be encoring it every time we had a good subject, and that would be inconvenient, because I hadn't any more bombs along.

28

Drilling the King

On the morning of the fourth day, when it was just sunrise, and we had been tramping an hour in the chill dawn, I came to a resolution: the king *must* be drilled; things could not go on so, he must be taken in hand and deliberately and conscientiously drilled, or we couldn't ever venture to enter a dwelling; the very cats would know this masquerader for a humbug and no peasant. So I called a halt and said:

"Sire, as between clothes and countenance, you are all right, there is no discrepancy; but as between your clothes and your bearing, you are all wrong, there is a most noticeable discrepancy. Your soldierly stride, your lordly port—these will not do. You stand too straight, your looks are too high, too confident. The cares of a kingdom do not stoop the shoulders, they do not droop the chin, they do not depress the high level of the eye-glance, they do not put doubt and fear in the heart and hang out the signs of them in slouching body and unsure step. It is the sordid cares of the lowly born that do these things. You must learn the trick; you must imitate the trademarks of poverty, misery, oppression, insult, and the other several and common inhumanities that sap the manliness out of a man and make him a loyal and proper and approved subject and a satisfaction to his masters, or the very infants will know you for better than your disguise, and we shall go to pieces at the first hut we stop at. Pray try to walk like this."

The king took careful note, and then tried an imitation.

"Pretty fair—pretty fair. Chin a little lower, please—there, very good. Eyes too high; pray don't look at the horizon, look at the ground, ten steps in front of you. Ah—that is better, that is very good. Wait, please; you betray too much vigor, too much decision; you want more of a shamble. Look at me, please—this is what I mean. . . . Now you are getting it; that is the idea—at least, it sort of approaches it. . . . Yes, that is pretty fair. *But!* There is a great big something wanting, I don't quite know what it is. Please walk thirty yards, so that I can get a perspective on the thing. . . . Now, then—your head's right, speed's right, shoulders right, eyes right, chin right, gait, carriage, general style right—everything's right! And yet the fact remains, the aggregate's wrong. The account don't balance. Do it again, please. . . . *Now* I think I begin to see what it is. Yes, I've struck it. You see, the genuine spiritlessness is wanting; that's what's the trouble. It's all *amateur*—mechanical details all right, almost to a hair; everything about the delusion perfect, except that it don't delude."

"What, then, must one do, to prevail?"

"Let me think . . . I can't seem to quite get at it. In fact, there isn't anything that can right the matter but practice. This is a good place for it: roots and stony ground to break up your stately gait, a region not liable to interruption, only one field and one hut in sight, and they so far away that nobody could see us from there. It will be well to move a little off the road and put in the whole day drilling you, sire."

After the drill had gone on a little while, I said:

"Now, sire, imagine that we are at the door of the hut yonder, and the family are before us. Proceed, please—accost the head of the house."

The king unconsciously straightened up like a monument, and said, with frozen austerity:

"Varlet, bring a seat; and serve to me what cheer ye have."

"Ah, your grace, that is not well done."

"In what lacketh it?"

"These people do not call *each other* varlets."

"Nay, is that true?"

"Yes; only those above them call them so."

"Then must I try again. I will call him villein."

"No-no; for he may be a freeman."

"Ah—so. Then peradventure I should call him goodman."

"That would answer, your grace, but it would be still better if you said friend, or brother."

"Brother!—to dirt like that?"

"Ah, but *we* are pretending to be dirt like that, too."

"It is even true. I will say it. Brother, bring a seat, and thereto what cheer ye have, withal. Now 'tis right."

"Not quite, not wholly right. You have asked for one, not *us*—for one, not both; food for one, a seat for one."

The king looked puzzled—he wasn't a very heavy weight, intellectually. His head was an hourglass; it could stow an idea, but it had to do it a grain at a time, not the whole idea at once.

"Would *you* have a seat also—and sit?"

"If I did not sit, the man would perceive that we were only pretending to be equals—and playing the deception pretty poorly, too."

"It is well and truly said! How wonderful is truth, come it in whatsoever unexpected form it may! Yes, he must bring out seats and food for both, and in serving us present not ewer and napkin with more show of respect to the one than to the other."

"And there is even yet a detail that needs correcting. He must bring nothing outside; we will go in—in among the dirt, and possibly other repulsive things—and take the food with the household, and after the fashion of the house, and all on equal terms, except the man be of the serf class; and finally, there will be no ewer and no napkin, whether he be serf or free. Please walk again, my liege. There—it is better—it is the best yet; but not perfect. The shoulders have known no ignobler burden than iron mail, and they will not stoop."

"Give me, then, the bag. I will learn the spirit that goeth with burdens that have not honour. It is the spirit that stoopeth the shoulders, I ween, and not the weight; for armor is heavy, yet it is a proud burden, and a man standeth straight in it. . . . Nay, but me no buts, offer me no objections. I will have the thing. Strap it upon my back."

He was complete now with that knapsack on, and looked as little like a king as any man I had ever seen. But it was an obstinate pair of shoulders; they could not seem to learn the trick of stooping with any sort of deceptive naturalness. The drill went on, I prompting and correcting:

"Now, make believe you are in debt, and eaten up by relentless creditors; you are out of work—which is horse-shoeing, let us say—and can get none; and your wife is sick, your children are crying because they are hungry—"

And so on, and so on. I drilled him as representing in turn all sorts of people out of luck and suffering dire privations and misfortunes. But lord, it was only just words, words—they meant nothing in the world to him, I might just as well have whistled. Words realize nothing, vivify nothing to you, unless you have suffered in your own person the thing which the words try to describe. There are wise people who talk ever so knowingly and complacently about "the working classes," and satisfy themselves that a day's hard intellectual work is very much harder than a day's hard manual toil, and is righteously entitled to much bigger pay. Why, they really think that, you know, because they know all about the one, but haven't tried the other. But I know all about both; and so far as I am concerned, there isn't money enough in the universe to hire me to swing a pickaxe thirty days, but I will do the hardest kind of intellectual work for just as near nothing as you can cipher it down—and I will be satisfied, too.

Intellectual "work" is misnamed; it is a pleasure, a dissipation, and is its own highest reward. The poorest paid architect, engineer, general, author, sculptor, painter, lecturer, advocate, legislator, actor, preacher, singer is constructively in heaven when he is at work; and as for the musician with the fiddle-bow in his hand who sits in the midst of a great orchestra with the ebbing and flowing tides of divine sound washing over him—why, certainly, he is at work, if you wish to call it that, but lord, it's a sarcasm just the same. The law of work does seem utterly unfair—but there it is, and nothing can change it: the higher the pay in enjoyment the worker gets out of it, the higher shall be his pay in cash, also. And it's also the very law of those transparent swindles, transmissible nobility and kingship.

29

The Smallpox Hut

When we arrived at that hut at mid-afternoon, we saw no signs of life about it. The field near by had been denuded of its crop some time before, and had a skinned look, so exhaustively had it been harvested and gleaned. Fences, sheds, everything had a ruined look, and were eloquent of poverty. No animal was around anywhere, no living thing in sight. The stillness was awful, it was like the stillness of death. The cabin was a one-storey one, whose thatch was black with age, and ragged from lack of repair.

The door stood a trifle ajar. We approached it stealthily—on tiptoe and at half-breath—for that is the way one's feeling makes him do, at such a time. The king knocked. We waited. No answer. Knocked again. No answer. I pushed the door softly open and looked in. I made out some dim forms, and a woman started up from the ground and stared at me, as one does who is wakened from sleep. Presently she found her voice:

"Have mercy!" she pleaded. "All is taken, nothing is left."

"I have not come to take anything, poor woman."

"You are not a priest?"

"No."

"Nor come not from the lord of the manor?"

"No, I am a stranger."

"Oh, then, for the fear of God, who visits with misery and death such as be harmless, tarry not here, but fly! This place is under his curse—and his Church's."

"Let me come in and help you—you are sick and in trouble."

I was better used to the dim light now. I could see her hollow eyes fixed upon me. I could see how emaciated she was.

"I tell you the place is under the Church's ban. Save yourself—and go, before some straggler see thee here, and report it."

"Give yourself no trouble about me; I don't care anything for the Church's curse. Let me help you."

"Now all good spirits—if there be any such—bless thee for that word. Would God I had a sup of water!—but hold, hold, forget I said it, and fly; for there is that here that even he that feareth not the Church must fear: this disease whereof we die. Leave us, thou brave, good stranger, and take with thee such whole and sincere blessing as them that be accursed can give."

But before this I had picked up a wooden bowl and was rushing past the king on my way to the brook. It was ten yards away. When I got back and entered, the king was within, and was opening the shutter that closed the window-hole, to let in air and light. The place was full of a foul stench. I put the bowl to the woman's lips, and as she gripped it with her eager talons the shutter came open and a strong light flooded her face. Smallpox!

I sprang to the king, and said in his ear:

"Out of the door on the instant, sire! the woman is dying of that disease that wasted the skirts of Camelot two years ago."

He did not budge.

"Of a truth I shall remain—and likewise help."

I whispered again:

"King, it must not be. You must go."

"Ye mean well, and ye speak not unwisely. But it were shame that a king should know fear, and shame that belted knight should withhold his hand where be such as need succor. Peace, I will not go. It is you who must go. The Church's ban is not upon me, but it forbiddeth you to be here, and she will deal with you with a heavy hand an word come to her of your trespass."

It was a desperate place for him to be in, and might cost him his life, but it was no use to argue with him. If he considered his knightly honour at stake here, that was the end of argument; he would stay, and nothing could prevent it; I was aware of that. And so I dropped the subject. The woman spoke:

"Fair sir, of your kindness will ye climb the ladder there, and bring me news of what ye find? Be not afraid to report, for times can come when even a mother's heart is past breaking—being already broken."

"Abide," said the king, "and give the woman to eat. I will go." And he put down the knapsack.

I turned to start, but the king had already started. He halted, and looked down upon a man who lay in a dim light, and had not noticed us thus far, or spoken.

"Is it your husband?" the king asked.

"Yes."

"Is he asleep?"

"God be thanked for that one charity, yes—these three hours. Where shall I pay to the full, my gratitude! for my heart is bursting with it for that sleep he sleepeth now."

I said:

"We will be careful. We will not wake him."

"Ah, no, that ye will not, for he is dead."

"Dead?"

"Yes, what triumph it is to know it! None can harm him, none insult him more. He is in heaven now, and happy; or if not there, he bides in hell and is content; for in that place he will find neither abbot nor yet bishop. We were boy and girl together; we were man and wife these five and twenty years, and never separated till this day. Think how long that is to love and suffer together. This morning was he out of his mind, and in his fancy we were boy and girl again and wandering in the happy fields; and so in that innocent glad converse wandered he far and farther, still lightly gossiping, and entered into those other fields we know not of, and was shut away from mortal sight. And so there was no parting, for in his fancy I went with him; he knew not but I went with him, my hand in his—my young soft hand, not this withered claw. Ah, yes, to go, and know it not; to separate and know it not; how could one go peace—fuller than that? It was his reward for a cruel life patiently borne."

There was a slight noise from the direction of the dim corner where the ladder was. It was the king descending. I could see that he was bearing something in one arm, and assisting himself with the other. He came forward into the light; upon his breast lay a slender girl of fifteen. She was but half conscious; she was dying of smallpox. Here was heroism at its last and loftiest possibility, its utmost summit; this was challenging death in the open field unarmed, with all the odds against the challenger, no reward set upon the contest, and no admiring world in silks and cloth of gold to gaze and applaud; and yet the king's bearing was as serenely brave as it had always been in those cheaper contests where knight meets knight in equal fight and clothed in protecting steel. He was great now; sublimely great. The rude statues of his ancestors in his palace should have an addition—I would see to that; and it would not be a mailed king killing a giant or a dragon, like the rest, it would be a king in commoner's garb bearing death in his arms that a peasant mother might look her last upon her child and be comforted.

He laid the girl down by her mother, who poured out endearments and caresses from an overflowing heart, and one could detect a flickering faint light of response in the child's eyes, but that was all. The mother hung over her, kissing her, petting her, and imploring her to speak, but the lips only moved and no sound came. I snatched my liquor flask from my knapsack, but the woman forbade me, and said:

"No—she does not suffer; it is better so. It might bring her back to life. None that be so good and kind as ye are would do her that cruel hurt. For look you—what is left to live for? Her brothers are gone, her father is gone, her mother goeth, the Church's curse is upon her, and none may shelter or befriend her even though she lay perishing in the road. She is desolate. I have not asked you, good heart, if her sister be still on live, here overhead; I had no need; ye had gone back, else, and not left the poor thing forsaken—"

"She lieth at peace," interrupted the king, in a subdued voice.

"I would not change it. How rich is this day in happiness! Ah, my Annis, thou shalt join thy sister soon—thou'rt on thy way, and these be merciful friends that will not hinder."

And so she fell to murmuring and cooing over the girl again, and softly stroking her face and hair, and kissing her and calling her by endearing names; but there was scarcely sign of response now in the glazing eyes. I saw tears well from the king's eyes, and trickle down his face. The woman noticed them, too, and said:

"Ah, I know that sign: thou'st a wife at home, poor soul, and you and she have gone hungry to bed, many's the time, that the little ones might have your crust; you know what poverty is, and the daily insults of your betters, and the heavy hand of the Church and the king."

The king winced under this accidental home-shot, but kept still; he was learning his part; and he was playing it well, too, for a pretty dull beginner. I struck up a diversion. I offered the woman food and liquor, but she refused both. She would allow nothing to come between her and the release of death. Then I slipped away and brought the dead child from aloft, and laid it by her. This broke her down again, and there was another scene that was full of heartbreak. By and by I made another diversion, and beguiled her to sketch her story.

"Ye know it well yourselves, having suffered it—for truly none of our condition in Britain escape it. It is the old, weary tale. We fought and struggled and succeeded; meaning by success, that we lived and did not die; more than that is not to be claimed. No troubles came that we could not outlive, till this year brought them; then came they all at once, as one might say, and overwhelmed us. Years ago the lord of the manor planted certain fruit trees on our farm; in the best part of it, too—a grievous wrong and shame—"

"But it was his right," interrupted the king.

"None denieth that, indeed; an the law mean anything, what is the lord's is his, and what is mine is his also. Our farm was ours by lease, therefore 'twas likewise his, to do with it as he would. Some little time ago, three of those trees were found hewn down. Our three grown sons ran frightened to report the crime. Well, in his lordship's dungeon there they lie, who saith there shall they lie and rot till they confess. They have naught to confess, being innocent, wherefore there will they remain until they die.

Ye know that right well, I ween. Think how this left us; a man, a woman and two children, to gather a crop that was planted by so much greater force, yes, and protect it night and day from pigeons and prowling animals that be sacred and must not be hurt by any of our sort. When my lord's crop was nearly ready for the harvest, so also was ours; when his bell rang to call us to his fields to harvest his crop for nothing, he would not allow that I and my two girls should count for our three captive sons, but for only two of them; so, for the lacking one were we daily fined. All this time our own crop was perishing through neglect; and so both the priest and his lordship fined us because their shares of it were suffering through damage. In the end the fines ate up our crop—and they took it all; they took it all and made us harvest it for them, without pay or food, and we starving. Then the worst came when I, being out of my mind with hunger and loss of my boys, and grief to see my husband and my little maids in rags and misery and despair, uttered a deep blasphemy—oh! a thousand of them!—against the Church and the Church's ways. It was ten days ago. I had fallen sick with this disease, and it was to the priest I said the words, for he was come to chide me for lack of due humility under the chastening hand of God. He carried my trespass to his betters; I was stubborn; wherefore, presently upon my head and upon all heads that were dear to me, fell the curse of Rome.

"Since that day we are avoided, shunned with horror. None has come near this hut to know whether we live or not. The rest of us were taken down. Then I roused me and got up, as wife and mother will. It was little they could have eaten in any case; it was less than little they had to eat. But there was water, and I gave them that. How they craved it! and how they blessed it! But the end came yesterday; my strength broke down. Yesterday was the last time I ever saw my husband and this youngest child alive. I have lain here all these hours—these ages, ye may say—listening, listening for any sound up there that—"

She gave a sharp quick glance at her eldest daughter, then cried out, "Oh, my darling!" and feebly gathered the stiffening form to her sheltering arms. She had recognized the death rattle.

30

The Tragedy of the Manor-house

At midnight all was over, and we sat in the presence of four corpses. We covered them with such rags as we could find, and started away, fastening the door behind us. Their home must be these people's grave, for they could not have Christian burial, or be admitted to consecrated ground. They were as dogs, wild beasts, lepers, and no soul that valued its hope of eternal life would throw it away by meddling in any sort with these rebuked and smitten outcasts.

We had not moved four steps when I caught a sound as of footsteps upon gravel. My heart flew to my throat. We must not be seen coming from that house. I plucked at the king's robe and we drew back and took shelter behind the corner of the cabin.

"Now we are safe," I said, "but it was a close call—so to speak. If the night had been lighter he might have seen us, no doubt, he seemed to be so near."

"Mayhap it is but a beast and not a man at all."

"True. But man or beast, it will be wise to stay here a minute and let it get by and out of the way."

"Hark! It cometh hither."

True again. The step was coming toward us—straight toward the hut. It must be a beast, then, and we might as well have saved our trepidation. I was going to step out, but the king laid his hand upon my arm. There was a moment of silence, then we heard a soft knock on the cabin door. It made me shiver. Presently the knock was repeated, and then we heard these words in a guarded voice:

"Mother! Father! Open—we have got free, and we bring news to pale your cheeks but glad your hearts; and we may not tarry, but must fly! And—but they answer not. Mother! father!—"

I drew the king toward the other end of the hut and whispered:

"Come—now we can get to the road."

The king hesitated, was going to demur; but just then we heard the door give way, and knew that those desolate men were in the presence of their dead.

"Come, my liege! in a moment they will strike a light, and then will follow that which it would break your heart to hear."

He did not hesitate this time. The moment we were in the road I ran; and after a moment he threw dignity aside and followed. I did not want to think of what was happening in the hut—I couldn't bear it; I wanted to drive it out of my mind; so I struck into the first subject that lay under that one in my mind:

"I have had the disease those people died of, and so have nothing to fear; but if you have not had it also—"

He broke in upon me to say he was in trouble, and it was his conscience that was troubling him:

"These young men have got free, they say—but *how*? It is not likely that their lord hath set them free."

"Oh, no, I make no doubt they escaped."

"That is my trouble; I have a fear that this is so, and your suspicion doth confirm it, you having the same fear."

"I should not call it by that name though. I do suspect that they escaped, but if they did, I am not sorry, certainly."

"I am not sorry, I *think*—but—"

"What is it? What is there for one to be troubled about?"

"*If* they did escape, then are we bound in duty to lay hands upon them and deliver them again to their lord; for it is not seemly that one of his quality should suffer a so insolent and high-handed outrage from persons of their base degree."

There it was again. He could see only one side of it. He was born so, educated so, his veins were full of ancestral blood that was rotten with this sort of unconscious brutality, brought down by inheritance from a long procession of hearts that had each done its share toward poisoning the stream. To imprison these men without proof, and starve their kindred, was no harm, for they were merely peasants and subject to the will and pleasure of their lord, no matter what fearful form it might take; but for these men to break out of unjust captivity was insult and outrage, and a thing not to be countenanced by any conscientious person who knew his duty to his sacred caste.

I worked more than half an hour before I got him to change the subject—and even then an outside matter did it for me. This was a something which caught our eyes as we struck the summit of a small hill—a red glow, a good way off.

"That's a fire," said I.

Fires interested me considerably, because I was getting a good deal of an insurance business started, and was also training some horses and building some steam fire-engines, with an eye to a paid fire department by and by. The priests opposed both my fire and life insurance, on the ground that it was an insolent attempt to hinder the decrees of God; and if you pointed out that they did not hinder the decrees in the least, but only modified the hard consequences of them if you took out policies and had luck, they retorted that that was gambling against the decrees of God, and was just as bad. So they managed to damage those industries more or less, but I got even on my accident business. As a rule, a knight is a lummux, and some times even a labrick, and hence open to pretty poor arguments when they come glibly from a superstition-monger, but even *he* could see the practical side of a thing once in a while; and so of late you couldn't clean up a tournament and pile the result without finding one of my accident-tickets in every helmet.

The Fire

We stood there awhile, in the thick darkness and stillness, looking toward the red blur in the distance, and trying to make out the meaning of a far-away murmur that rose and fell fitfully on the night. Sometimes it swelled up and for a moment seemed less remote; but when we were hopefully expecting it to betray its cause and nature, it dulled and sank again, carrying its mystery with it. We started down the hill in its direction, and the winding road plunged us at once into almost solid darkness—darkness that was packed and crammed in between two tall forest walls. We groped along down for half a mile, perhaps, that murmur growing more and more distinct all the time. The coming storm threatening more and more, with now and then a little shiver of wind, a faint show of lightning, and dull grumblings of distant thunder. I was in the lead. I ran against something—a soft heavy something which gave, slightly, to the impulse of my weight; at the same moment the lightning glared out, and within a foot of my face was the writhing face of a man who was hanging from the limb of a tree! That is, it seemed to be writhing, but it was not. It was a gruesome sight. Straightway there was an ear-splitting explosion of thunder, and the bottom of heaven fell out; the rain poured down in a deluge. No matter, we must try to cut this man down, on the chance that there might be life in him yet, mustn't we? The lightning came quick and sharp now, and the place was alternately noonday and midnight. One moment the man would be hanging before me in an intense light, and the next he was blotted out again in the darkness. I told the king we must cut him down. The king at once objected.

"If he hanged himself, he was willing to lose his property to his lord; so let him be. If others hanged him, belike they had the right—let him hang."

"But—"

"But me no buts, but even leave him as he is. And for yet another reason. When the lightning cometh again—there, look abroad."

Two others hanging, within fifty yards of us!

"It is not weather meet for doing useless courtesies unto dead folk. They are past thanking you. Come—it is unprofitable to tarry here."

There was reason in what he said, so we moved on. Within the next mile we counted six more hanging forms by the blaze of the lightning, and altogether it was a grisly excursion. That murmur was a murmur no longer, it was a roar; a roar of men's voices. A man came flying by now, dimly through the darkness, and other men chasing him. They disappeared. Presently another case of the kind occurred, and then another and another. Then a sudden turn of the road brought us in sight of that fire—it was a large manor-house, and little or nothing was left of it—and everywhere men were flying and other men raging after them in pursuit.

I warned the king that this was not a safe place for strangers. We would better get away from the light, until matters should improve. We stepped back a little, and hid in the edge of the wood. From this hiding place we saw both men and women hunted by the mob. The fearful work went on until nearly dawn. Then, the fire being out and the storm spent, the voices and flying footsteps presently ceased, and darkness and stillness reigned again.

We ventured out, and hurried cautiously away; and although we were worn out and sleepy, we kept on until we had put this place some miles behind us. Then we asked hospitality at the hut of a charcoal burner, and got what was to be had. A woman was up and about, but the man was still asleep, on a straw shake-down, on the clay floor. The woman seemed uneasy until I explained that we were travelers and had lost our way and been wandering in the woods all night. She became talkative, then, and asked if we had heard of the terrible goings-on at the manor-house of Abblasoure. Yes, we had heard of them, but what we wanted now was rest and sleep. The king broke in:

"Sell us the house and take yourselves away, for we be perilous company, being late come from people that died of the Spotted Death."

It was good of him, but unnecessary. One of the commonest decorations of the nation was the waffle-iron face. I had early noticed that the woman and her husband were both so decorated. She made us entirely welcome, and had no fears; and plainly she was immensely impressed by the king's proposition; for, of course, it was a good deal of an event in her life to run across a person of the king's humble appearance who was ready to buy a man's house for the sake of a night's lodging. It gave her a large respect for us, and she strained the lean possibilities of her hovel to the utmost to make us comfortable.

We slept till far into the afternoon, and then got up hungry enough to make cotter fare quite palatable to the king, the more particularly as it was scant in quantity. And also in variety; it consisted solely of onions, salt, and the national black bread made out of horse-feed. The woman told us about the affair of the evening before. At ten or eleven at night, when everybody was in bed, the manor-house burst into flames. The countryside swarmed to the rescue, and the family were saved, with one exception, the master. He did not appear. Everybody was frantic over this loss, and two brave yeomen sacrificed their lives in ransacking the burning house seeking that valuable personage. But after a while he was found—what was left of him—which was his corpse. It was in a copse three hundred yards away, bound, gagged, stabbed in a dozen places.

Who had done this? Suspicion fell upon a humble family in the neighbourhood who had been lately treated with peculiar harshness by the baron; and from these people the suspicion easily extended itself to their relatives and familiars. A suspicion was enough; my lord's liveried retainers proclaimed an instant crusade against these people, and were promptly joined by the community in general. The woman's husband had been active with the mob, and had not returned home until nearly dawn. He was gone now to find out what the general result had been. While we were still talking he came back from his quest. His report was revolting enough. Eighteen persons hanged or butchered, and two yeomen and thirteen prisoners lost in the fire.

"And how many prisoners were there altogether in the vaults?"

"Thirteen."

"Then every one of them was lost?"

"Yes, all."

"But the people arrived in time to save the family; how is it they could save none of the prisoners?"

The man looked puzzled, and said:

"Would one unlock the vaults at such a time? Marry, some would have escaped."

"Then you mean that nobody *did* unlock them?"

"None went near them, either to lock or unlock. It standeth to reason that the bolts were fast; wherefore it was only needful to establish a watch, so that if any broke the bonds he might not escape, but be taken. None were taken."

"Natheless, three did escape," said the king, "and ye will do well to publish it and set justice upon their track, for these murthered the baron and fired the house."

I was just expecting he would come out with that. For a moment the man and his wife showed an eager interest in this news and an impatience to go out and spread it; then a sudden something else betrayed itself in their faces, and they began to ask questions. I answered the questions myself, and narrowly watched the effects produced. I was soon satisfied that the knowledge of who these three prisoners were had somehow changed the atmosphere; that our hosts' continued eagerness to go and spread the news was now only pretended and not real. The king did not notice the change, and I was glad of that. I worked the conversation around toward other details of the night's proceedings, and noted that these people were relieved to have it take that direction.

The painful thing observable about all this business was the alacrity with which this oppressed community had turned their cruel hands against their own class in the interest of the common oppressor. This man and woman seemed to feel that in a quarrel between a person of their own class and his lord, it was the natural and proper and rightful thing for that poor devil's whole caste to side with the master and fight his battle for him, without ever stopping to inquire into the rights or wrongs of the matter. This man had been out helping to hang his neighbours, and had done his work with zeal, and yet was aware that there was nothing against them but a mere suspicion, with nothing back of it describable as evidence, still neither he nor his wife seemed to see anything horrible about it.

This was depressing—to a man with the dream of a republic in his head. It reminded me of a time thirteen centuries away, when the "poor whites" of our South who were always despised and frequently insulted by the slave-lords around them, and who owed their base condition simply to the presence of slavery in their midst, were yet pusillanimously ready to side with the slave-lords in all political moves for the upholding and perpetuating of slavery, and did also finally shoulder their muskets and pour out their lives in an effort to prevent the destruction of that very institution which degraded them. And there was only one redeeming feature connected with that pitiful piece of history; and that was, that secretly the "poor white" did detest the slave-lord, and did feel his own shame. That feeling was not brought to the surface, but the fact that it was there and could have been brought out, under favouring circumstances, was something—in fact, it was enough; for it showed that a man is at bottom a man, after all, even if it doesn't show on the outside.

Well, as it turned out, this charcoal burner was just the twin of the Southern "poor white" of the far future. The king presently showed impatience, and said:

"An ye prattle here all the day, justice will miscarry. Think ye the criminals will abide in their father's house? They are fleeing, they are not waiting. You should look to it that a party of horse be set upon their track."

The woman paled slightly, but quite perceptibly, and the man looked flustered and irresolute. I said:

"Come, friend, I will walk a little way with you, and explain which direction I think they would try to take. If they were merely resisters of the gabelle or some kindred absurdity I would try to protect them from capture; but when men murder a person of high degree and likewise burn his house, that is another matter."

The last remark was for the king—to quiet him. On the road the man pulled his resolution together, and began the march with a steady gait, but there was no eagerness in it. By and by I said:

"What relation were these men to you—cousins?"

He turned as white as his layer of charcoal would let him, and stopped, trembling.

"Ah, my God, how know ye that?"

"I didn't know it; it was a chance guess."

"Poor lads, they are lost. And good lads they were, too."

"Were you actually going yonder to tell on them?"

He didn't quite know how to take that; but he said, hesitatingly:

"Ye-s."

"Then I think you are a damned scoundrel!"

It made him as glad as if I had called him an angel.

"Say the good words again, brother! for surely ye mean that ye would not betray me an I failed of my duty."

"Duty? There is no duty in the matter, except the duty to keep still and let those men get away. They've done a righteous deed."

He looked pleased; pleased, and touched with apprehension at the same time. He looked up and down the road to see that no one was coming, and then said in a cautious voice:

"From what land come you, brother, that you speak such perilous words, and seem not to be afraid?"

"They are not perilous words when spoken to one of my own caste, I take it. You would not tell anybody I said them?"

"I? I would be drawn asunder by wild horses first."

"Well, then, let me say my say. I have no fears of your repeating it. I think devil's work has been done last night upon those innocent poor people. That old baron got only what he deserved. If I had my way, all his kind should have the same luck."

Fear and depression vanished from the man's manner, and gratefulness and a brave animation took their place:

"Even though you be a spy, and your words a trap for my undoing, yet are they such refreshment that to hear them again and others like to them, I would go to the gallows happy, as having had one good feast at least in a starved life. And I will say my say now, and ye may report it if ye be so minded. I helped to hang my neighbours for that it were peril to my own life to show lack of zeal in the master's cause; the others helped for none other reason. All rejoice today that he is dead, but all do go about seemingly sorrowing, and shedding the hypocrite's tear, for in that lies safety. I have said the words, I have said the words! the only ones that have ever tasted good in my mouth, and the reward of that taste is sufficient. Lead on, an ye will, be it even to the scaffold, for I am ready."

There it was, you see. A man is a man, at bottom. Whole ages of abuse and oppression cannot crush the manhood clear out of him. Whoever thinks it a mistake is himself mistaken. Yes, there is plenty good enough material for a republic in the most degraded people that ever existed—even the Russians; plenty of manhood in them—even in the Germans—if one could but force it out of its timid and suspicious privacy, to overthrow and trample in the mud any throne that ever was set up and any nobility that ever supported it. We should see certain things yet, let us hope and believe. First, a modified monarchy, till Arthur's days were done, then the destruction of the throne, nobility abolished, every member of it bound out to some useful trade, universal suffrage instituted, and the whole government placed in the hands of the men and women of the nation there to remain. Yes, there was no occasion to give up my dream yet a while.

31

Marco

We strolled along in a sufficiently indolent fashion now, and talked. We must dispose of about the amount of time it ought to take to go to the little hamlet of Abblasoure and put justice on the track of those murderers and get back home again. And meantime I had an auxiliary interest which had never paled yet, never lost its novelty for me since I had been in Arthur's kingdom: the behavior—born of nice and exact subdivisions of caste—of chance passers-by toward each other. Toward the shaven monk who trudged along with his cowl tilted back and the sweat washing down his fat jowls, the coal-burner was deeply reverent; to the gentleman he was abject; with the small farmer and the free mechanic he was cordial and gossipy; and when a slave passed by with a countenance respectfully lowered, this chap's nose was in the air—he couldn't even see him. Well, there are times when one would like to hang the whole human race and finish the farce.

"Presently we struck an incident"

Presently we struck an incident. A small mob of half-naked boys and girls came tearing out of the woods, scared and shrieking. The eldest among them were not more than twelve or fourteen years old. They implored help, but they were so beside themselves that we couldn't make out what the matter was. However, we plunged into the wood, they skurrying in the lead, and the trouble was quickly revealed: they had hanged a little fellow with a bark rope, and he was kicking and struggling, in the process of choking to death. We rescued him, and fetched him around. It was some more human nature; the admiring little folk imitating their elders; they were playing mob, and had achieved a success which promised to be a good deal more serious than they had bargained for.

It was not a dull excursion for me. I managed to put in the time very well. I made various acquaintanceships, and in my quality of stranger was able to ask as many questions as I wanted to. A thing which naturally interested me, as a statesman, was the matter of wages. I picked up what I could under that head during the afternoon. A man who hasn't had much experience, and doesn't think, is apt to measure a nation's prosperity or lack of prosperity by the mere size of the prevailing wages; if the wages be high, the nation is prosperous; if low, it isn't. Which is an error. It isn't what sum you get, it's how much you can buy with it, that's the important thing; and it's that that tells whether your wages are high in fact or only high in name. I could remember how it was in the time of our great civil war in the nineteenth century. In the North a carpenter got three dollars a day, gold valuation; in the South he got fifty—payable in Confederate shinplasters worth a dollar a bushel. In the North a suit of overalls cost three dollars—a day's wages; in the South it cost seventy-five—which was two days' wages. Other things were in proportion. Consequently, wages were twice as high in the North as they were in the South, because the one wage had that much more purchasing power than the other had.

Yes, I made various acquaintances in the hamlet and a thing that gratified me a good deal was to find our new coins in circulation—lots of milrays, lots of mills, lots of cents, a good many nickels, and some silver; all this among the artisans and commonalty generally; yes, and even some gold—but that was at the bank, that is to say, the goldsmith's. I dropped in there while Marco, the son of Marco, was haggling with a shopkeeper over a quarter of a pound of salt, and asked for change for a twenty-dollar gold piece. They furnished it—that is, after they had chewed the piece, and rung it on the counter, and tried acid on it, and asked me where I got it, and who I was, and where I was from, and where I was going to, and when I expected to get there, and perhaps a couple of hundred more questions; and when they got aground, I went right on and furnished them a lot of information voluntarily; told them I owned a dog, and his name was Watch, and my first wife was a Free Will Baptist, and her grandfather was a Prohibitionist, and I used to know a man who had two thumbs on each hand and a wart on the inside of his upper lip, and died in the hope of a glorious resurrection, and so on, and so on, and so on, till even that hungry village questioner began to look satisfied, and also a shade put out; but he had to respect a man of my financial strength, and so he didn't give me any lip, but I noticed he took it out of his underlings, which was a perfectly natural thing to do. Yes, they changed my twenty, but I judged it strained the bank a little, which was a thing to be expected, for it was the same as walking into a paltry village store in the nineteenth century and requiring the boss of it to change a two thousand-dollar bill for you all of a sudden. He could do it, maybe; but at the same time he would wonder how a small farmer happened to be carrying so much money around in his pocket; which was probably this goldsmith's thought, too; for he followed me to the door and stood there gazing after me with reverent admiration.

Our new money was not only handsomely circulating, but its language was already glibly in use; that is to say, people had dropped the names of the former moneys, and spoke of things as being worth so many dollars or cents or mills or milrays now. It was very gratifying. We were progressing, that was sure.

I got to know several master mechanics, but about the most interesting fellow among them was the blacksmith, Dowley. He was a live man and a brisk talker, and had two journeymen and three apprentices, and was doing a raging business. In fact, he was getting rich, hand over fist, and was vastly respected. Marco was very proud of having such a man for a friend. He had taken me there ostensibly to let me see the big establishment which bought so much of his charcoal, but really to let me see what easy and almost familiar terms he was on with this great man. Dowley and I fraternized at once; I had had just such picked men, splendid fellows, under me in the Colt Arms Factory. I was bound to see more of him, so I invited him to come out to Marco's Sunday, and dine with us. Marco was appalled, and held his breath; and when the grandee accepted, he was so grateful that he almost forgot to be astonished at the condescension.

Marco's joy was exuberant—but only for a moment; then he grew thoughtful, then sad; and when he heard me tell Dowley I should have Dickon, the boss mason, and Smug, the boss wheelwright, out there, too, the coal-dust on his face turned to chalk, and he lost his grip. But I knew what was the matter with him; it was the expense. He saw ruin before him;

he judged that his financial days were numbered. However, on our way to invite the others, I said:

"You must allow me to have these friends come; and you must also allow me to pay the costs."

His face cleared, and he said with spirit:

"But not all of it, not all of it. Ye cannot well bear a burden like to this alone."

I stopped him, and said:

"Now let's understand each other on the spot, old friend. I am only a farm bailiff, it is true; but I am not poor, nevertheless. I have been very fortunate this year—you would be astonished to know how I have thriven. I tell you the honest truth when I say I could squander away as many as a dozen feasts like this and never care *that* for the expense!" and I snapped my fingers. I could see myself rise a foot at a time in Marco's estimation, and when I fetched out those last words I was become a very tower for style and altitude. "So you see, you must let me have my way. You can't contribute a cent to this orgy, that's *settled*."

"It's grand and good of you—"

"No, it isn't. You've opened your house to Jones and me in the most generous way; Jones was remarking upon it today, just before you came back from the village; for although he wouldn't be likely to say such a thing to you—because Jones isn't a talker, and is diffident in society—he has a good heart and a grateful, and knows how to appreciate it when he is well treated; yes, you and your wife have been very hospitable toward us—"

"Ah, brother, 'tis nothing—*such* hospitality!"

"But it *is* something; the best a man has, freely given, is always something, and is as good as a prince can do, and ranks right along beside it—for even a prince can but do his best. And so we'll shop around and get up this layout now, and don't you worry about the expense. I'm one of the worst spendthrifts that ever was born. Why, do you know, sometimes in a single week I spend—but never mind about that—you'd never believe it anyway."

And so we went gadding along, dropping in here and there, pricing things, and gossiping with the shopkeepers about the riot, and now and then running across pathetic reminders of it, in the persons of shunned and tearful and houseless remnants of families whose homes had been taken from them and their parents butchered or hanged. The raiment of Marco and his wife was of coarse tow-linen and linsey-woolsey respectively, and resembled township maps, it being made up pretty exclusively of patches which had been added, township by township, in the course of five or six years, until hardly a hand's-breadth of the original garments was surviving and present. Now I wanted to fit these people out with new suits, on account of that swell company, and I didn't know just how to get at it—with delicacy, until at last it struck me that as I had already been liberal in inventing wordy gratitude for the king, it would be just the thing to back it up with evidence of a substantial sort; so I said:

"And Marco, there's another thing which you must permit—out of kindness for Jones—because you wouldn't want to offend him. He was very anxious to testify his appreciation in some way, but he is so diffident he couldn't venture it himself, and so he begged me to buy some little things and give them to you and Dame Phyllis and let him pay for them without your ever knowing they came from him—you know how a delicate person feels about that sort of thing—and so I said I would, and we would keep mum. Well, his idea was, a new outfit of clothes for you both—"

"Oh, it is wastefulness! It may not be, brother, it may not be. Consider the vastness of the sum—"

"Hang the vastness of the sum! Try to keep quiet for a moment, and see how it would seem; a body can't get in a word edgeways, you talk so much. You ought to cure that, Marco; it isn't good form, you know, and it will grow on you if you don't check it. Yes, we'll step in here now and price this man's stuff—and don't forget to remember to not let on to Jones that you know he had anything to do with it. You can't think how curiously sensitive and proud he is. He's a farmer—pretty fairly well-to-do farmer—and I'm his bailiff; *but*—the imagination of that man! Why, sometimes when he forgets himself and gets to blowing off, you'd think he was one of the swells of the earth; and you might listen to him a hundred years and never take him for a farmer—especially if he talked agriculture. He *thinks* he's a Sheol of a farmer; thinks he's old Grayback from Wayback; but between you and me privately he don't know as much about farming as he does about running a kingdom—still, whatever he talks about, you want to drop your underjaw and listen, the same as if you had never heard such incredible wisdom in all your life before, and were afraid you might die before you got enough of it. That will please Jones."

It tickled Marco to the marrow to hear about such an odd character; but it also prepared him for accidents; and in my experience when you travel with a king who is letting on to be something else and can't remember it more than about half the time, you can't take too many precautions.

This was the best store we had come across yet; it had everything in it, in small quantities, from anvils and dry goods all the way down to fish and pinchbeck jewellery. I concluded I would bunch my whole invoice right here, and not go pricing around any more. So I got rid of Marco, by sending him off to invite the mason and the wheelwright, which left the field free to me. For I never care to do a thing in a quiet way; it's got to be theatrical or I don't take any interest in it. I showed up money enough, in a careless way, to corral the shopkeeper's respect, and then I wrote down a list of the things I wanted, and handed it to him to see if he could read it. He could, and was proud to show that he could. He said he had been educated by a priest, and could both read and write. He ran it through, and remarked with satisfaction that it was a pretty heavy bill. Well, and so it was, for a little concern like that. I was not only providing a swell dinner, but some odds and ends of extras. I ordered that the things be carted out and delivered at the dwelling of Marco, the son of Marco, by Saturday evening, and send me the bill at dinner-time Sunday. He said I could depend upon his promptness and exactitude, it was the rule of the house. He also observed that he would throw in a couple of miller-guns for the Marcos gratis—that everybody was using them now. He had a mighty opinion of that clever device. I said:

"And please fill them up to the middle mark, too; and add that to the bill."

He would, with pleasure. He filled them, and I took them with me. I couldn't venture to tell him that the miller-gun was a little invention of my own, and that I had officially ordered that every shopkeeper in the kingdom keep them on hand and sell them at government price—which was the merest trifle, and the shopkeeper got that, not the government. We furnished them for nothing.

The king had hardly missed us when we got back at nightfall. He had early dropped again into his dream of a grand invasion of Gaul with the whole strength of his kingdom at his back, and the afternoon had slipped away without his ever coming to himself again.

32

Dowley's Humiliation

Well, when that cargo arrived toward sunset, Saturday afternoon, I had my hands full to keep the Marcos from fainting. They were sure Jones and I were ruined past help, and they blamed themselves as accessories to this bankruptcy. You see, in addition to the dinner-materials, which called for a sufficiently round sum, I had bought a lot of extras for the future comfort of the family: for instance, a big lot of wheat, a delicacy as rare to the tables of their class as was ice-cream to a hermit's; also a sizeable deal dinner-table; also two entire pounds of salt, which was another piece of extravagance in those people's eyes; also crockery, stools, the clothes, a small cask of beer, and so on. I instructed the Marcos to keep quiet about this sumptuousness, so as to give me a chance to surprise the guests and show off a little. Concerning the new clothes, the simple couple were like children; they were up and down, all night, to see if it wasn't nearly daylight, so that they could put them on, and they were into them at last as much as an hour before dawn was due. Then their pleasure—not to say delirium—was so fresh and novel and inspiring that the sight of it paid me well for the interruptions which my sleep had suffered. The king had slept just as usual—like the dead. The Marcos could not thank him for their clothes, that being forbidden; but they tried every way they could think of to make him see how grateful they were. Which all went for nothing: he didn't notice any change.

It turned out to be one of those rich and rare fall days which is just a June day toned down to a degree where it is heaven to be out of doors. Toward noon the guests arrived, and we assembled under a great tree and were soon as sociable as old acquaintances. Even the king's reserve melted a little, though it was some little trouble to him to adjust himself to the name of Jones along at first. I had asked him to try to not forget that he was a farmer; but I had also considered it prudent to ask him to let the thing stand at that, and not elaborate it any. Because he was just the kind of person you could depend on to spoil a little thing like that if you didn't warn him, his tongue was so handy, and his spirit so willing, and his information so uncertain.

Dowley was in fine feather, and I early got him started, and then adroitly worked him around onto his own history for a text and himself for a hero, and then it was good to sit there and hear him hum. Self-made man, you know. They know how to talk. They do deserve more credit than any other breed of men, yes, that is true; and they are among the very first to find it out, too. He told how he had begun life an orphan lad without money and without friends able to help him; how he had lived as the slaves of the meanest master lived; how his day's work was from sixteen to eighteen hours long, and yielded him only enough black bread to keep him in a half-fed condition; how his faithful endeavors finally attracted the attention of a good blacksmith, who came near knocking him dead with kindness by suddenly offering, when he was totally unprepared, to take him as his bound apprentice for nine years and give him board and clothes and teach him the trade—or "mystery" as Dowley called it. That was his first great rise, his first gorgeous stroke of fortune; and you saw that he couldn't yet speak of it without a sort of eloquent wonder and delight that such a gilded promotion should have fallen to the lot of a common human being. He got no new clothing during his apprenticeship, but on his graduation day his master tricked him out in spang-new tow-linens and made him feel unspeakably rich and fine.

"I remember me of that day!" the wheelwright sang out, with enthusiasm.

"And I likewise!" cried the mason. "I would not believe they were thine own; in faith I could not."

"Nor other!" shouted Dowley, with sparkling eyes. "I was like to lose my character, the neighbours wending I had mayhap been stealing. It was a great day, a great day; one forgetteth not days like that."

Yes, and his master was a fine man, and prosperous, and always had a great feast of meat twice in the year, and with it white bread, true wheaten bread; in fact, lived like a lord, so to speak. And in time Dowley succeeded to the business and married the daughter.

"And now consider what is come to pass," said he, impressively. "Two times in every month there is fresh meat upon my table." He made a pause here, to let that fact sink home, then added—"and eight times salt meat."

"It is even true," said the wheelwright, with bated breath.

"I know it of mine own knowledge," said the mason, in the same reverent fashion.

"On my table appeareth white bread every Sunday in the year," added the master smith, with solemnity. "I leave it to your own consciences, friends, if this is not also true?"

"By my head, yes," cried the mason.

"I can testify it—and I do," said the wheelwright.

"And as to furniture, ye shall say yourselves what mine equipment is." He waved his hand in fine gesture of granting frank and unhampered freedom of speech, and added: "Speak as ye are moved; speak as ye would speak; an I were not here."

"Ye have five stools, and of the sweetest workmanship at that, albeit your family is but three," said the wheelwright, with deep respect.

"And six wooden goblets, and six platters of wood and two of pewter to eat and drink from withal," said the mason, impressively. "And I say it as knowing God is my judge, and we tarry not here alway, but must answer at the last day for the things said in the body, be they false or be they sooth."

"Now ye know what manner of man I am, brother Jones," said the smith, with a fine and friendly condescension, "and doubtless ye would look to find me a man jealous of his due of respect and but sparing of outgo to strangers till their rating and quality be assured, but trouble yourself not, as concerning that; wit ye well ye shall find me a man that regardeth not these matters but is willing to receive any he as his fellow and equal that carrieth a right heart in his body, be his worldly estate howsoever modest. And in token of it, here is my hand; and I say with my own mouth we are equals—equals"—and he smiled around on the company with the satisfaction of a god who is doing the handsome and gracious thing and is quite well aware of it.

The king took the hand with a poorly disguised reluctance, and let go of it as willingly as a lady lets go of a fish; all of which had a good effect, for it was mistaken for an embarrassment natural to one who was being called upon by greatness.

The dame brought out the table now, and set it under the tree. It caused a visible stir of surprise, it being brand new and a sumptuous article of deal. But the surprise rose higher still when the dame, with a body oozing easy indifference at every pore, but eyes that gave it all away by absolutely flaming with vanity, slowly unfolded an actual simon-pure tablecloth and spread it. That was a notch above even the blacksmith's domestic grandeurs, and it hit him hard; you could see it. But Marco was in Paradise; you could see that, too. Then the dame brought two fine new stools—whew! that was a sensation; it was visible in the eyes of every guest. Then she brought two more—as calmly as she could. Sensation again—with awed murmurs. Again she brought two—walking on air, she was so proud. The guests were petrified, and the mason muttered:

"There is that about earthly pomps which doth ever move to reverence."

As the dame turned away, Marco couldn't help slapping on the climax while the thing was hot; so he said with what was meant for a languid composure but was a poor imitation of it:

"These suffice; leave the rest."

So there were more yet! It was a fine effect. I couldn't have played the hand better myself.

From this out, the madam piled up the surprises with a rush that fired the general astonishment up to a hundred and fifty in the shade, and at the same time paralyzed expression of it down to gasped "Oh's" and "Ah's," and mute upliftings of hands and eyes. She fetched crockery—new, and plenty of it; new wooden goblets and other table furniture; and beer, fish, chicken, a goose, eggs, roast beef, roast mutton, a ham, a small roast pig, and a wealth of genuine white wheaten bread. Take it by and large, that spread laid everything far and away in the shade that ever that crowd had seen before. And while they sat there just simply stupefied with wonder and awe, I sort of waved my hand as if by accident, and the storekeeper's son emerged from space and said he had come to collect.

"That's all right," I said, indifferently. "What is the amount? Give us the items."

Then he read off this bill, while those three amazed men listened, and serene waves of satisfaction rolled over my soul and alternate waves of terror and admiration surged over Marco's:

He ceased. There was a pale and awful silence. Not a limb stirred. Not a nostril betrayed the passage of breath.

"Is that all?" I asked, in a voice of the most perfect calmness.

"All, fair sir, save that certain matters of light moment are placed together under a head hight sundries. If it would like you, I will sepa—"

"It is of no consequence," I said, accompanying the words with a gesture of the most utter indifference; "give me the grand total, please."

The clerk leaned against the tree to stay himself, and said:

"Thirty-nine thousand one hundred and fifty milrays!"

The wheelwright fell off his stool, the others grabbed the table to save themselves, and there was a deep and general ejaculation of:

"God be with us in the day of disaster!"

The clerk hastened to say:

"My father chargeth me to say he cannot honourably require you to pay it all at this time, and therefore only prayeth you—"

I paid no more heed than if it were the idle breeze, but, with an air of indifference amounting almost to weariness, got out my money and tossed four dollars on to the table. Ah, you should have seen them stare!

The clerk was astonished and charmed. He asked me to retain one of the dollars as security, until he could go to town and—I interrupted:

"What, and fetch back nine cents? Nonsense! Take the whole. Keep the change."

There was an amazed murmur to this effect:

"Verily this being is *made* of money! He throweth it away even as if it were dirt."

The blacksmith was a crushed man.

The clerk took his money and reeled away drunk with fortune. I said to Marco and his wife:

"Good folk, here is a little trifle for you"—handing the miller-guns as if it were a matter of no consequence, though each of them contained fifteen cents in solid cash; and while the poor creatures went to pieces with astonishment and gratitude, I turned to the others and said as calmly as one would ask the time of day:

"Well, if we are all ready, I judge the dinner is. Come, fall to."

Ah, well, it was immense; yes, it was a daisy. I don't know that I ever put a situation together better, or got happier spectacular effects out of the materials available. The blacksmith—well, he was simply mashed. Land! I wouldn't have felt what that man was feeling, for anything in the world. Here he had been blowing and bragging about his grand meat-feast twice a year, and his fresh meat twice a month, and his salt meat twice a week, and his white bread every Sunday the year round—all for a family of three; the entire cost for the year not above 69.2.6 (sixty-nine cents, two mills and six milrays), and all of a sudden here comes along a man who slashes out nearly four dollars on a single blow-out; and not only that, but acts as if it made him tired to handle such small sums. Yes, Dowley was a good deal wilted, and shrunk-up and collapsed; he had the aspect of a bladder-balloon that's been stepped on by a cow.

33

Sixth Century Political Economy

However, I made a dead set at him, and before the first third of the dinner was reached, I had him happy again. It was easy to do—in a country of ranks and castes. You see, in a country where they have ranks and castes, a man isn't ever a man, he is only part of a man, he can't ever get his full growth. You prove your superiority over him in station, or rank, or fortune, and that's the end of it—he knuckles down. You can't insult him after that. No, I don't mean quite that; of course you *can* insult him, I only mean it's difficult; and so, unless you've got a lot of useless time on your hands it doesn't pay to try. I had the smith's reverence now, because I was apparently immensely prosperous and rich; I could have had his adoration if I had had some little gimcrack title of nobility. And not only his, but any commoner's in the land, though he were the mightiest production of all the ages, in intellect, worth, and character, and I bankrupt in all three. This was to remain so, as long as England should exist in the earth. With the spirit of prophecy upon me, I could look into the future and see her erect statues and monuments to her unspeakable Georges and other royal and noble clothes-horses, and leave unhonoured the creators of this world—after God—Gutenberg, Watt, Arkwright, Whitney, Morse, Stephenson, Bell.

The king got his cargo aboard, and then, the talk not turning upon battle, conquest, or iron-clad duel, he dulled down to drowsiness and went off to take a nap. Mrs. Marco cleared the table, placed the beer keg handy, and went away to eat her dinner of leavings in humble privacy, and the rest of us soon drifted into matters near and dear to the hearts of our sort—business and wages, of course. At a first glance, things appeared to be exceeding prosperous in this little tributary kingdom—whose lord was King Bagdemagus—as compared with the state of things in my own region. They had the "protection" system in full force here, whereas we were working along down toward free-trade, by easy stages, and were now about half way. Before long, Dowley and I were doing all the talking, the others hungrily listening. Dowley warmed to his work, snuffed an advantage in the air, and began to put questions which he considered pretty awkward ones for me, and they did have something of that look:

"In your country, brother, what is the wage of a master bailiff, master hind, carter, shepherd, swineherd?"

"Twenty-five milrays a day; that is to say, a quarter of a cent."

The smith's face beamed with joy. He said:

"With us they are allowed the double of it! And what may a mechanic get—carpenter, dauber, mason, painter, blacksmith, wheelwright, and the like?"

"On the average, fifty milrays; half a cent a day."

"Ho-ho! With us they are allowed a hundred! With us any good mechanic is allowed a cent a day! I count out the tailor, but not the others—they are all allowed a cent a day, and in driving times they get more—yes, up to a hundred and ten and even fifteen milrays a day. I've paid a hundred and fifteen myself, within the week. 'Rah for protection—to Sheol with free-trade!"

And his face shone upon the company like a sunburst. But I didn't scare at all. I rigged up my pile-driver, and allowed myself fifteen minutes to drive him into the earth—drive him *all* in—drive him in till not even the curve of his skull should show above ground. Here is the way I started in on him. I asked:

"What do you pay a pound for salt?"

"A hundred milrays."

"We pay forty. What do you pay for beef and mutton—when you buy it?" That was a neat hit; it made the colour come.

"It varieth somewhat, but not much; one may say seventy-five milrays the pound."

"*We* pay thirty-three. What do you pay for eggs?"

"Fifty milrays the dozen."

"We pay twenty. What do you pay for beer?"

"It costeth us eight and one-half milrays the pint."

"We get it for four; twenty-five bottles for a cent. What do you pay for wheat?"

"At the rate of nine hundred milrays the bushel."

"We pay four hundred. What do you pay for a man's tow-linen suit?"

"Thirteen cents."

"We pay six. What do you pay for a stuff gown for the wife of the labourer or the mechanic?"

"We pay eight cents, four mills."

"Well, observe the difference: you pay eight cents and four mills, we pay only four cents." I prepared now to sock it to him. I said: "Look here, dear friend, *what's become of your high wages you were bragging so about a few minutes ago?*"—and I looked around on the company with placid satisfaction, for I had slipped up on him gradually and tied him hand and foot, you see, without his ever noticing that he was being tied at all. "What's become of those noble high wages of yours?—I seem to have knocked the stuffing all out of them, it appears to me."

But if you will believe me, he merely looked surprised, that is all! he didn't grasp the situation at all, didn't know he had walked into a trap, didn't discover that he was *in* a trap. I could have shot him, from sheer vexation. With cloudy eye and a struggling intellect he fetched this out:

"Marry, I seem not to understand. It is *proved* that our wages be double thine; how then may it be that thou'st knocked therefrom the stuffing?—an miscall not the wonderly word, this being the first time under grace and providence of God it hath been granted me to hear it."

Well, I was stunned; partly with this unlooked-for stupidity on his part, and partly because his fellows so manifestly sided with him and were of his mind—if you might call it mind. My position was simple enough, plain enough; how could it ever be simplified more? However, I must try:

"Why, look here, brother Dowley, don't you see? Your wages are merely higher than ours in *name*, not in *fact*."

"Hear him! They are the *double*—ye have confessed it yourself."

"Yes-yes, I don't deny that at all. But that's got nothing to do with it; the *amount* of the wages in mere coins, with meaningless names attached to them to know them by, has got nothing to do with it. The thing is, how much can you *buy* with your wages?—that's the idea. While it is true that with you a good mechanic is allowed about three dollars and a half a year, and with us only about a dollar and seventy-five—"

"There—ye're confessing it again, ye're confessing it again!"

"Confound it, I've never denied it, I tell you! What I say is this. With us *half* a dollar buys more than a *dollar* buys with you—and *therefore* it stands to reason and the commonest kind of common-sense, that our wages are *higher* than yours."

He looked dazed, and said, despairingly:

"Verily, I cannot make it out. Ye've just said ours are the higher, and with the same breath ye take it back."

"Oh, great Scott, isn't it possible to get such a simple thing through your head? Now look here—let me illustrate. We pay four cents for a woman's stuff gown, you pay 8.4.0, which is four mills more than *double*. What do you allow a labouring woman who works on a farm?"

"Two mills a day."

"Very good; we allow but half as much; we pay her only a tenth of a cent a day; and—"

"Again ye're conf—"

"Wait! Now, you see, the thing is very simple; this time you'll understand it. For instance, it takes your woman 42 days to earn her gown, at 2 mills a day—7 weeks' work; but ours earns hers in forty days—two days *short* of 7 weeks. Your woman has a gown, and her whole seven weeks wages are gone; ours has a gown, and two days' wages left, to buy something else with. There—*now* you understand it!"

He looked—well, he merely looked dubious, it's the most I can say; so did the others. I waited—to let the thing work. Dowley spoke at last—and betrayed the fact that he actually hadn't gotten away from his rooted and grounded superstitions yet. He said, with a trifle of hesitancy:

"But—but—ye cannot fail to grant that two mills a day is better than one."

Shucks! Well, of course, I hated to give it up. So I chanced another flyer:

"Let us suppose a case. Suppose one of your journeymen goes out and buys the following articles:

1 pound of salt;
1 dozen eggs;
1 dozen pints of beer;
1 bushel of wheat;
1 tow-linen suit;
5 pounds of beef;
5 pounds of mutton.

"The lot will cost him 32 cents. It takes him 32 working days to earn the money—5 weeks and 2 days. Let him come to us and work 32 days at *half* the wages; he can buy all those things for a shade under 14 1/2 cents; they will cost him a shade under 29 days' work, and he will have about half a week's wages over. Carry it through the year; he would save nearly a week's wages every two months, *your* man nothing; thus saving five or six weeks' wages in a year, your man not a cent. *Now* I reckon you understand that 'high wages' and 'low wages' are phrases that don't mean anything in the world until you find out which of them will *buy* the most!"

It was a crusher.

But, alas! it didn't crush. No, I had to give it up. What those people valued was *high wages*; it didn't seem to be a matter of any consequence to them whether the high wages would buy anything or not. They stood for "protection," and swore by it, which was reasonable enough, because interested parties had gulled them into the notion that it was protection which had created their high wages. I proved to them that in a quarter of a century their wages had advanced but 30 per cent., while the cost of living had gone up 100; and that with us, in a shorter time, wages had advanced 40 per cent. while the cost of living had gone steadily down. But it didn't do any good. Nothing could unseat their strange beliefs.

Well, I was smarting under a sense of defeat. Undeserved defeat, but what of that? That didn't soften the smart any. And to think of the circumstances! the first statesman of the age, the capablest man, the best-informed man in the entire world, the loftiest uncrowned head that had moved through the clouds of any political firmament for centuries, sitting here apparently defeated in argument by an ignorant country blacksmith! And I could see that those others were sorry for me—which made me blush till I could smell my whiskers scorching. Put yourself in my place; feel as mean as I did, as ashamed as I felt—wouldn't *you* have struck below the belt to get even? Yes, you would; it is simply human nature. Well, that is what I did. I am not trying to justify it; I'm only saying that I was mad, and *anybody* would have done it.

Well, when I make up my mind to hit a man, I don't plan out a love-tap; no, that isn't my way; as long as I'm going to hit him at all, I'm going to hit him a lifter. And I don't jump at him all of a sudden, and risk making a blundering halfway business of it; no, I get away off yonder to one side, and work up on him gradually, so that he never suspects that I'm going to hit him at all; and by and by, all in a flash, he's flat on his back, and he can't tell for the life of him how it all happened. That is the way I went for brother Dowley. I started to talking lazy and comfortable, as if I was just talking to pass the time; and the oldest man in the world couldn't have taken the bearings of my starting place and guessed where I was going to fetch up:

"Boys, there's a good many curious things about law, and custom, and usage, and all that sort of thing, when you come to look at it; yes, and about the drift and progress of human opinion and movement, too. There are written laws—they perish; but there are also unwritten laws—*they* are eternal. Take the unwritten law of wages: it says they've got to advance, little by little, straight through the centuries. And notice how it works. We know what wages are now, here and there and yonder; we strike an average, and say that's the wages of today. We know what the wages were a hundred years ago, and what they were two hundred years ago; that's as far back as we can get, but it suffices to give us the law of progress, the measure and rate of the periodical augmentation; and so, without a document to help us, we can come pretty close to determining what the wages were three and four and five hundred years ago. Good, so far. Do we stop there? No. We stop looking backward; we face around and apply the law to the future. My friends, I can tell you what people's wages are going to be at any date in the future you want to know, for hundreds and hundreds of years."

"What, goodman, what!"

"Yes. In seven hundred years wages will have risen to six times what they are now, here in your region, and farm hands will be allowed 3 cents a day, and mechanics 6."

"I would't I might die now and live then!" interrupted Smug, the wheelwright, with a fine avaricious glow in his eye.

"And that isn't all; they'll get their board besides—such as it is: it won't bloat them. Two hundred and fifty years later—pay attention now—a mechanic's wages will be—mind you, this is law, not guesswork; a mechanic's wages will then be *twenty* cents a day!"

There was a general gasp of awed astonishment, Dickon the mason murmured, with raised eyes and hands:

"More than three weeks' pay for one day's work!"

"Riches!—of a truth, yes, riches!" muttered Marco, his breath coming quick and short, with excitement.

"Wages will keep on rising, little by little, little by little, as steadily as a tree grows, and at the end of three hundred and forty years more there'll be at least *one* country where the mechanic's average wage will be *two hundred* cents a day!"

It knocked them absolutely dumb! Not a man of them could get his breath for upwards of two minutes. Then the coal-burner said prayerfully:

"Might I but live to see it!"

"It is the income of an earl!" said Smug.

"An earl, say ye?" said Dowley; "ye could say more than that and speak no lie; there's no earl in the realm of Bagdemagus that hath an income like to that. Income of an earl—mf! it's the income of an angel!"

"Now, then, that is what is going to happen as regards wages. In that remote day, that man will earn, with *one* week's work, that bill of goods which it takes you upwards of *fifty* weeks to earn now. Some other pretty surprising things are going to happen, too. Brother Dowley, who is it that determines, every spring, what the particular wage of each kind of mechanic, labourer, and servant shall be for that year?"

"Sometimes the courts, sometimes the town council; but most of all, the magistrate. Ye may say, in general terms, it is the magistrate that fixes the wages."

"Doesn't ask any of those poor devils to *help* him fix their wages for them, does he?"

"Hm! That *were* an idea! The master that's to pay him the money is the one that's rightly concerned in that matter, ye will notice."

"Yes—but I thought the other man might have some little trifle at stake in it, too; and even his wife and children, poor creatures. The masters are these: nobles, rich men, the prosperous generally. These few, who do no work, determine what pay the vast hive shall have who *do* work. You see? They're a 'combine'—a trade union, to coin a new phrase—who band themselves together to force their lowly brother to take what they choose to give. Thirteen hundred years hence—so says the unwritten law—the 'combine' will be the other way, and then how these fine people's posterity will fume and fret and grit their teeth over the insolent tyranny of trade unions! Yes, indeed! the magistrate will tranquilly arrange the wages from now clear away down into the nineteenth century; and then all of a sudden the wage-earner will consider that a couple of thousand years or so is enough of this one-sided sort of thing; and he will rise up and take a hand in fixing his wages himself. Ah, he will have a long and bitter account of wrong and humiliation to settle."

"Do ye believe—"

"That he actually will help to fix his own wages? Yes, indeed. And he will be strong and able, then."

"Brave times, brave times, of a truth!" sneered the prosperous smith.

"Oh—and there's another detail. In that day, a master may hire a man for only just one day, or one week, or one month at a time, if he wants to."

"What?"

"It's true. Moreover, a magistrate won't be able to force a man to work for a master a whole year on a stretch whether the man wants to or not."

"Will there be *no* law or sense in that day?"

"Both of them, Dowley. In that day a man will be his own property, not the property of magistrate and master. And he can leave town whenever he wants to, if the wages don't suit him!—and they can't put him in the pillory for it."

"Perdition catch such an age!" shouted Dowley, in strong indignation. "An age of dogs, an age barren of reverence for superiors and respect for authority! The pillory—"

"Oh, wait, brother; say no good word for that institution. I think the pillory ought to be abolished."

"A most strange idea. Why?"

"Well, I'll tell you why. Is a man ever put in the pillory for a capital crime?"

"No."

"Is it right to condemn a man to a slight punishment for a small offense and then kill him?"

There was no answer. I had scored my first point! For the first time, the smith wasn't up and ready. The company noticed it. Good effect.

"You don't answer, brother. You were about to glorify the pillory a while ago, and shed some pity on a future age that isn't going to use it. I think the pillory ought to be abolished. What usually happens when a poor fellow is put in the pillory for some little offense that didn't amount to anything in the world? The mob try to have some fun with him, don't they?"

"Yes."

"They begin by clodding him; and they laugh themselves to pieces to see him try to dodge one clod and get hit with another?"

"Yes."

"Then they throw dead cats at him, don't they?"

"Yes."

"Well, then, suppose he has a few personal enemies in that mob and here and there a man or a woman with a secret grudge against him—and suppose especially that he is unpopular in the community, for his pride, or his prosperity, or one thing or another—stones and bricks take the place of clods and cats presently, don't they?"

"There is no doubt of it."

"As a rule he is crippled for life, isn't he?—jaws broken, teeth smashed out?—or legs mutilated, gangrened, presently cut off?—or an eye knocked out, maybe both eyes?"

"It is true, God knoweth it."

"And if he is unpopular he can depend on *dying*, right there in the stocks, can't he?"

"He surely can! One may not deny it."

"I take it none of *you* are unpopular—by reason of pride or insolence, or conspicuous prosperity, or any of those things that excite envy and malice among the base scum of a village? *You* wouldn't think it much of a risk to take a chance in the stocks?"

Dowley winced, visibly. I judged he was hit. But he didn't betray it by any spoken word. As for the others, they spoke out plainly, and with strong feeling. They said they had seen enough of the stocks to know what a man's chance in them was, and they would never consent to enter them if they could compromise on a quick death by hanging.

"Well, to change the subject—for I think I've established my point that the stocks ought to be abolished. I think some of our laws are pretty unfair. For instance, if I do a thing which ought to deliver me to the stocks, and you know I did it and yet keep still and don't report me, *you* will get the stocks if anybody informs on you."

"Ah, but that would serve you but right," said Dowley, "for you *must* inform. So saith the law."

The others coincided.

"Well, all right, let it go, since you vote me down. But there's one thing which certainly isn't fair. The magistrate fixes a mechanic's wage at one cent a day, for instance. The law says that if any master shall venture, even under utmost press of business, to pay anything *over* that cent a day, even for a single day, he shall be both fined and pilloried for it; and whoever knows he did it and doesn't inform, they also shall be fined and pilloried. Now it seems to me unfair, Dowley, and a deadly peril to all of us, that because you thoughtlessly confessed, a while ago, that within a week you have paid a cent and fifteen mil—"

Oh, I tell *you* it was a smasher! You ought to have seen them to go to pieces, the whole gang. I had just slipped up on poor smiling and complacent Dowley so nice and easy and softly, that he never suspected anything was going to happen till the blow came crashing down and knocked him all to rags.

A fine effect. In fact, as fine as any I ever produced, with so little time to work it up in.

But I saw in a moment that I had overdone the thing a little. I was expecting to scare them, but I wasn't expecting to scare them to death. They were mighty near it, though. You see they had been a whole lifetime learning to appreciate the pillory; and to have that thing staring them in the face, and every one of them distinctly at the mercy of me, a stranger, if I chose to go and report—well, it was awful, and they couldn't seem to recover from the shock, they couldn't seem to pull themselves together. Pale, shaky, dumb, pitiful? Why, they weren't any better than so many dead men. It was very uncomfortable. Of course, I thought they would appeal to me to keep mum, and then we would shake hands, and take a drink all round, and laugh it off, and there an end. But no; you see I was an unknown person, among a cruelly oppressed and suspicious people, a people always accustomed to having advantage taken of their helplessness, and never expecting just or kind treatment from any but their own families and very closest intimates. Appeal to *me* to be gentle, to be fair, to be generous? Of course, they wanted to, but they couldn't dare.

34

The Yankee and the King Sold as Slaves

Well, what had I better do? Nothing in a hurry, sure. I must get up a diversion; anything to employ me while I could think, and while these poor fellows could have a chance to come to life again. There sat Marco, petrified in the act of trying to get the hang of his miller-gun—turned to stone, just in the attitude he was in when my pile-driver fell, the toy still gripped in his unconscious fingers. So I took it from him and proposed to explain its mystery. Mystery! a simple little thing like that; and yet it was mysterious enough, for that race and that age.

I never saw such an awkward people, with machinery; you see, they were totally unused to it. The miller-gun was a little double-barreled tube of toughened glass, with a neat little trick of a spring to it, which upon pressure would let a shot escape. But the shot wouldn't hurt anybody, it would only drop into your hand. In the gun were two sizes—wee mustard-seed shot, and another sort that were several times larger. They were money. The mustard-seed shot represented milrays, the larger ones mills. So the gun was a purse; and very handy, too; you could pay out money in the dark with it, with accuracy; and you could carry it in your mouth; or in your vest pocket, if you had one. I made them of several sizes—one size so large that it would carry the equivalent of a dollar. Using shot for money was a good thing for the government; the metal cost nothing, and the money couldn't be counterfeited, for I was the only person in the kingdom who knew how to manage a shot tower. "Paying the shot" soon came to be a common phrase. Yes, and I knew it would still be passing men's lips, away down in the nineteenth century, yet none would suspect how and when it originated.

The king joined us, about this time, mightily refreshed by his nap, and feeling good. Anything could make me nervous now, I was so uneasy—for our lives were in danger; and so it worried me to detect a complacent something in the king's eye which seemed to indicate that he had been loading himself up for a performance of some kind or other; confound it, why must he go and choose such a time as this?

I was right. He began, straight off, in the most innocently artful, and transparent, and lubberly way, to lead up to the subject of agriculture. The cold sweat broke out all over me. I wanted to whisper in his ear, "Man, we are in awful danger! every moment is worth a principality till we get back these men's confidence; *don't* waste any of this golden time." But of course I couldn't do it. Whisper to him? It would look as if we were conspiring. So I had to sit there and look calm and pleasant while the king stood over that dynamite mine and mooned along about his damned onions and things. At first the tumult of my own thoughts, summoned by the danger-signal and swarming to the rescue from every quarter of my skull, kept up such a hurrah and confusion and fifing and drumming that I couldn't take in a word; but presently when my mob of gathering plans began to crystallize and fall into position and form line of battle, a sort of order and quiet ensued and I caught the boom of the king's batteries, as if out of remote distance:

"—were not the best way, methinks, albeit it is not to be denied that authorities differ as concerning this point, some contending that the onion is but an unwholesome berry when stricken early from the tree—"

The audience showed signs of life, and sought each other's eyes in a surprised and troubled way.

"—whileas others do yet maintain, with much show of reason, that this is not of necessity the case, instancing that plums and other like cereals do be always dug in the unripe state—"

The audience exhibited distinct distress; yes, and also fear.

"—yet are they clearly wholesome, the more especially when one doth assuage the asperities of their nature by admixture of the tranquilizing juice of the wayward cabbage—"

The wild light of terror began to glow in these men's eyes, and one of them muttered, "These be errors, every one—God hath surely smitten the mind of this farmer." I was in miserable apprehension; I sat upon thorns.

"—and further instancing the known truth that in the case of animals, the young, which may be called the green fruit of the creature, is the better, all confessing that when a goat is ripe, his fur doth heat and sore engame his flesh, the which defect, taken in connection with his several rancid habits, and fulsome appetites, and godless attitudes of mind, and bilious quality of morals—"

They rose and went for him! With a fierce shout, "The one would betray us, the other is mad! Kill them! Kill them!" they flung themselves upon us. What joy flamed up in the king's eye! He might be lame in agriculture, but this kind of thing was just in his line. He had been fasting long, he was hungry for a fight. He hit the blacksmith a crack under the jaw that lifted him clear off his feet and stretched him flat on his back. "St. George for Britain!" and he downed the wheelwright. The mason was big, but I laid him out like nothing. The three gathered themselves up and came again; went down again; came again; and kept on repeating this, with native British pluck, until they were battered to jelly, reeling with exhaustion, and so blind that they couldn't tell us from each other; and yet they kept right on, hammering away with what might was left in them. Hammering each other—for we stepped aside and looked on while they rolled, and struggled, and gouged, and pounded, and bit, with the strict and wordless attention to business of so many bulldogs. We looked on without apprehension, for they were fast getting past ability to go for help against us, and the arena was far enough from the public road to be safe from intrusion.

Well, while they were gradually playing out, it suddenly occurred to me to wonder what had become of Marco. I looked around; he was nowhere to be seen. Oh, but this was ominous! I pulled the king's sleeve, and we glided away and rushed for the hut. No Marco there, no Phyllis there! They had gone to the road for help, sure. I told the king to give his heels wings, and I would explain later. We made good time across the open ground, and as we darted into the shelter of the wood I glanced back and saw a mob of excited peasants swarm into view, with Marco and his wife at their head. They were making a world of noise, but that couldn't hurt anybody; the wood was dense, and as soon as we were well into its depths we would take to a tree and let them whistle. Ah, but then came another sound—dogs! Yes, that was quite another matter. It magnified our contract—we must find running water.

We tore along at a good gait, and soon left the sounds far behind and modified to a murmur. We struck a stream and darted into it. We waded swiftly down it, in the dim forest light, for as much as three hundred yards, and then came across an oak with a great bough sticking out over the water. We climbed up on this bough, and began to work our way along it to the body of the tree; now we began to hear those sounds more plainly; so the mob had struck our trail. For a while the sounds approached pretty fast. And then for another while they didn't. No doubt the dogs had found the place where we had entered the stream, and were now waltzing up and down the shores trying to pick up the trail again.

When we were snugly lodged in the tree and curtained with foliage, the king was satisfied, but I was doubtful. I believed we could crawl along a branch and get into the next tree, and I judged it worth while to try. We tried it, and made a success of it, though the king slipped, at the junction, and came near failing to connect. We got comfortable lodgment and satisfactory concealment among the foliage, and then we had nothing to do but listen to the hunt.

Presently we heard it coming—and coming on the jump, too; yes, and down both sides of the stream. Louder—louder—next minute it swelled swiftly up into a roar of shoutings, barkings, tramplings, and swept by like a cyclone.

"I was afraid that the overhanging branch would suggest something to them," said I, "but I don't mind the disappointment. Come, my liege, it were well that we make good use of our time. We've flanked them. Dark is coming on, presently. If we can cross the stream and get a good start, and borrow a couple of horses from somebody's pasture to use for a few hours, we shall be safe enough."

We started down, and got nearly to the lowest limb, when we seemed to hear the hunt returning. We stopped to listen.

"Yes," said I, "they're baffled, they've given it up, they're on their way home. We will climb back to our roost again, and let them go by."

So we climbed back. The king listened a moment and said:

"They still search—I wit the sign. We did best to abide."

He was right. He knew more about hunting than I did. The noise approached steadily, but not with a rush. The king said:

"They reason that we were advantaged by no parlous start of them, and being on foot are as yet no mighty way from where we took the water."

"Yes, sire, that is about it, I am afraid, though I was hoping better things."

The noise drew nearer and nearer, and soon the van was drifting under us, on both sides of the water. A voice called a halt from the other bank, and said:

"An they were so minded, they could get to yon tree by this branch that overhangs, and yet not touch ground. Ye will do well to send a man up it."

"Marry, that we will do!"

I was obliged to admire my cuteness in foreseeing this very thing and swapping trees to beat it. But, don't you know, there are some things that can beat smartness and foresight? Awkwardness and stupidity can. The best swordsman in the world doesn't need to fear the second best swordsman in the world; no, the person for him to be afraid of is some ignorant antagonist who has never had a sword in his hand before; he doesn't do the thing he ought to do, and so the expert isn't prepared for him; he does the thing he ought not to do; and often it catches the expert out and ends him on the spot. Well, how could I, with all my gifts, make any valuable preparation against a near-sighted, cross-eyed, pudding-headed clown who would aim himself at the wrong tree and hit the right one? And that is what he did. He went for the wrong tree, which was, of course, the right one by mistake, and up he started.

Matters were serious now. We remained still, and awaited developments. The peasant toiled his difficult way up. The king raised himself up and stood; he made a leg ready, and when the comer's head arrived in reach of it there was a dull thud, and down went the man floundering to the ground. There was a wild outbreak of anger below, and the mob swarmed in from all around, and there we were treed, and prisoners. Another man started up; the bridging bough was detected, and a volunteer started up the tree that furnished the bridge. The king ordered me to play Horatius and keep the bridge. For a while the enemy came thick and fast; but no matter, the head man of each procession always got a buffet that dislodged him as soon as he came in reach. The king's spirits rose, his joy was limitless. He said that if nothing occurred to mar the prospect we should have a beautiful night, for on this line of tactics we could hold the tree against the whole countryside.

However, the mob soon came to that conclusion themselves; wherefore they called off the assault and began to debate other plans. They had no weapons, but there were plenty of stones, and stones might answer. We had no objections. A stone might possibly penetrate to us once in a while, but it wasn't very likely; we were well protected by boughs and foliage, and were not visible from any good aiming point. If they would but waste half an hour in stone-throwing, the dark would come to our help. We were feeling very well satisfied. We could smile; almost laugh.

But we didn't; which was just as well, for we should have been interrupted. Before the stones had been raging through the leaves and bouncing from the boughs fifteen minutes, we began to notice a smell. A couple of sniffs of it was enough of an explanation—it was smoke! Our game was up at last. We recognized that. When smoke invites you, you have to come. They raised their pile of dry brush and damp weeds higher and higher, and when they saw the thick cloud begin to roll up and smother the tree, they broke out in a storm of joy-clamors. I got enough breath to say:

"Proceed, my liege; after you is manners."

The king gasped:

"Follow me down, and then back thyself against one side of the trunk, and leave me the other. Then will we fight. Let each pile his dead according to his own fashion and taste."

Then he descended, barking and coughing, and I followed. I struck the ground an instant after him; we sprang to our appointed places, and began to give and take with all our might. The powwow and racket were prodigious;

it was a tempest of riot and confusion and thick-falling blows. Suddenly some horsemen tore into the midst of the crowd, and a voice shouted:

"Hold—or ye are dead men!"

How good it sounded! The owner of the voice bore all the marks of a gentleman: picturesque and costly raiment, the aspect of command, a hard countenance, with complexion and features marred by dissipation. The mob fell humbly back, like so many spaniels. The gentleman inspected us critically, then said sharply to the peasants:

"What are ye doing to these people?"

"They be madmen, worshipful sir, that have come wandering we know not whence, and—"

"Ye know not whence? Do ye pretend ye know them not?"

"Most honoured sir, we speak but the truth. They are strangers and unknown to any in this region; and they be the most violent and bloodthirsty madmen that ever—"

"Peace! Ye know not what ye say. They are not mad. Who are ye? And whence are ye? Explain."

"We are but peaceful strangers, sir," I said, "and travelling upon our own concerns. We are from a far country, and unacquainted here. We have purposed no harm; and yet but for your brave interference and protection these people would have killed us. As you have divined, sir, we are not mad; neither are we violent or bloodthirsty."

The gentleman turned to his retinue and said calmly: "Lash me these animals to their kennels!"

The mob vanished in an instant; and after them plunged the horsemen, laying about them with their whips and pitilessly riding down such as were witless enough to keep the road instead of taking to the bush. The shrieks and supplications presently died away in the distance, and soon the horsemen began to straggle back. Meantime the gentleman had been questioning us more closely, but had dug no particulars out of us. We were lavish of recognition of the service he was doing us, but we revealed nothing more than that we were friendless strangers from a far country. When the escort were all returned, the gentleman said to one of his servants:

"Bring the led-horses and mount these people."

"Yes, my lord."

We were placed toward the rear, among the servants. We traveled pretty fast, and finally drew rein some time after dark at a roadside inn some ten or twelve miles from the scene of our troubles. My lord went immediately to his room, after ordering his supper, and we saw no more of him. At dawn in the morning we breakfasted and made ready to start.

My lord's chief attendant sauntered forward at that moment with indolent grace, and said:

"Ye have said ye should continue upon this road, which is our direction likewise; wherefore my lord, the earl Grip, hath given commandment that ye retain the horses and ride, and that certain of us ride with ye a twenty mile to a fair town that hight Cambenet, whenso ye shall be out of peril."

We could do nothing less than express our thanks and accept the offer. We jogged along, six in the party, at a moderate and comfortable gait, and in conversation learned that my lord Grip was a very great personage in his own region, which lay a day's journey beyond Cambenet. We loitered to such a degree that it was near the middle of the forenoon when we entered the market square of the town. We dismounted, and left our thanks once more for my lord, and then approached a crowd assembled in the center of the square, to see what might be the object of interest. It was the remnant of that old peregrinating band of slaves! So they had been dragging their chains about, all this weary time. That poor husband was gone, and also many others; and some few purchases had been added to the gang. The king was not interested, and wanted to move along, but I was absorbed, and full of pity. I could not take my eyes away from these worn and wasted wrecks of humanity. There they sat, grounded upon the ground, silent, uncomplaining, with bowed heads, a pathetic sight. And by hideous contrast, a redundant orator was making a speech to another gathering not thirty steps away, in fulsome laudation of "our glorious British liberties!"

I was boiling. I had forgotten I was a plebeian, I was remembering I was a man. Cost what it might, I would mount that rostrum and—

Click! the king and I were handcuffed together! Our companions, those servants, had done it; my lord Grip stood looking on. The king burst out in a fury, and said:

"What meaneth this ill-mannered jest?"

My lord merely said to his head miscreant, coolly:

"Put up the slaves and sell them!"

Slaves! The word had a new sound—and how unspeakably awful! The king lifted his manacles and brought them down with a deadly force; but my lord was out of the way when they arrived. A dozen of the rascal's servants sprang forward, and in a moment we were helpless, with our hands bound behind us. We so loudly and so earnestly proclaimed ourselves freemen, that we got the interested attention of that liberty-mouthing orator and his patriotic crowd, and they gathered about us and assumed a very determined attitude. The orator said:

"If, indeed, ye are freemen, ye have nought to fear—the God-given liberties of Britain are about ye for your shield and shelter! (Applause.) Ye shall soon see. Bring forth your proofs."

"What proofs?"

"Proof that ye are freemen."

Ah—I remembered! I came to myself; I said nothing. But the king stormed out:

"Thou'rt insane, man. It were better, and more in reason, that this thief and scoundrel here prove that we are *not* freemen."

You see, he knew his own laws just as other people so often know the laws; by words, not by effects. They take a *meaning*, and get to be very vivid, when you come to apply them to yourself.

All hands shook their heads and looked disappointed; some turned away, no longer interested. The orator said—and this time in the tones of business, not of sentiment:

"An ye do not know your country's laws, it were time ye learned them. Ye are strangers to us; ye will not deny that. Ye may be freemen, we do not deny that; but also ye may be slaves. The law is clear: it doth not require the claimant to prove ye are slaves, it requireth you to prove ye are *not*."

I said:

"Dear sir, give us only time to send to Astolat; or give us only time to send to the Valley of Holiness—"

"Peace, good man, these are extraordinary requests, and you may not hope to have them granted. It would cost much time, and would unwarrantably inconvenience your master—"

"*Master*, idiot!" stormed the king. "I have no master, I myself am the m—"

"Silence, for God's sake!"

I got the words out in time to stop the king. We were in trouble enough already; it could not help us any to give these people the notion that we were lunatics.

There is no use in stringing out the details. The earl put us up and sold us at auction. This same infernal law had existed in our own South in my own time, more than thirteen hundred years later, and under it hundreds of freemen who could not prove that they were freemen had been sold into lifelong slavery without the circumstance making any particular impression upon me; but the minute law and the auction block came into my personal experience, a thing which had been merely improper before became suddenly hellish. Well, that's the way we are made.

Yes, we were sold at auction, like swine. In a big town and an active market we should have brought a good price; but this place was utterly stagnant and so we sold at a figure which makes me ashamed, every time I think of it. The King of England brought seven dollars, and his prime minister nine; whereas the king was easily worth twelve dollars and I as easily worth fifteen. But that is the way things always go; if you force a sale on a dull market, I don't care what the property is, you are going to make a poor business of it, and you can make up your mind to it. If the earl had had wit enough to—

However, there is no occasion for my working my sympathies up on his account. Let him go, for the present; I took his number, so to speak.

The slave dealer bought us both, and hitched us onto that long chain of his, and we constituted the rear of his procession. We took up our line of march and passed out of Cambenet at noon; and it seemed to me unaccountably strange and odd that the King of England and his chief minister, marching manacled and fettered and yoked, in a slave convoy, could move by all manner of idle men and women, and under windows where sat the sweet and the lovely, and yet never attract a curious eye, never provoke a single remark. Dear, dear, it only shows that there is nothing diviner about a king than there is about a tramp, after all. He is just a cheap and hollow artificiality when you don't know he is a king. But reveal his quality, and dear me it takes your very breath away to look at him. I reckon we are all fools. Born so, no doubt.

35

A Pitiful Incident

It's a world of surprises. The king brooded; this was natural. What would he brood about, should you say? Why, about the prodigious nature of his fall, of course—from the loftiest place in the world to the lowest; from the most illustrious station in the world to the obscurest; from the grandest vocation among men to the basest. No, I take my oath that the thing that graveled him most, to start with, was not this, but the price he had fetched! He couldn't seem to get over that seven dollars. Well, it stunned me so, when I first found it out, that I couldn't believe it; it didn't seem natural.

But as soon as my mental sight cleared and I got a right focus on it, I saw I was mistaken; it *was* natural. For this reason: a king is a mere artificiality, and so a king's feelings, like the impulses of an automatic doll, are mere artificialities; but as a man, he is a reality, and his feelings, as a man, are real, not phantoms. It shames the average man to be valued below his own estimate of his worth, and the king certainly wasn't anything more than an average man, if he was up that high.

Confound him, he wearied me with arguments to show that in anything like a fair market he would have fetched twenty-five dollars, sure—a thing which was plainly nonsense, and full or the baldest conceit; I wasn't worth it myself. But it was tender ground for me to argue on. In fact, I had to simply shirk argument and do the diplomatic instead. I had to throw conscience aside, and brazenly concede that he ought to have brought twenty-five dollars; whereas I was quite well aware that in all the ages, the world had never seen a king that was worth half the money, and during the next thirteen centuries wouldn't see one that was worth the fourth of it. Yes, he tired me. If he began to talk about the crops; or about the recent weather; or about the condition of politics; or about dogs, or cats, or morals, or theology—no matter what—I sighed, for I knew what was coming; he was going to get out of it a palliation of that tiresome seven-dollar sale. Wherever we halted where there was a crowd, he would give me a look which said plainly: "if that thing could be tried over again now, with this kind of folk, you would see a different result." Well, when he was first sold, it secretly tickled me to see him go for seven dollars; but before he was done with his sweating and worrying I wished he had fetched a hundred. The thing never got a chance to die, for every day, at one place or another, possible purchasers looked us over, and, as often as any other way, their comment on the king was something like this:

"Here's a two-dollar-and-a-half chump with a thirty-dollar style. Pity but style was marketable."

At last this sort of remark produced an evil result. Our owner was a practical person and he perceived that this defect must be mended if he hoped to find a purchaser for the king. So he went to work to take the style out of his sacred majesty. I could have given the man some valuable advice, but I didn't; you mustn't volunteer advice to a slave-driver unless you want to damage the cause you are arguing for. I had found it a sufficiently difficult job to reduce the king's style to a peasant's style, even when he was a willing and anxious pupil; now then, to undertake to reduce the king's style to a slave's style—and by force—go to! it was a stately contract. Never mind the details—it will save me trouble to let you imagine them. I will only remark that at the end of a week there was plenty of evidence that lash and club and fist had done their work well; the king's body was a sight to see—and to weep over; but his spirit?—why, it wasn't even phased. Even that dull clod of a slave-driver was able to see that there can be such a thing as a slave who will remain a man till he dies; whose bones you can break, but whose manhood you can't. This man found that from his first effort down to his latest, he couldn't ever come within reach of the king, but the king was ready to plunge for him, and did it. So he gave up at last, and left the king in possession of his style unimpaired. The fact is, the king was a good deal more than a king, he was a man; and when a man is a man, you can't knock it out of him.

We had a rough time for a month, tramping to and fro in the earth, and suffering. And what Englishman was the most interested in the slavery question by that time? His grace the king! Yes; from being the most indifferent, he was become the most interested. He was become the bitterest hater of the institution I had ever heard talk. And so I ventured to ask once more a question which I had asked years before and had gotten such a sharp answer that I had not thought it prudent to meddle in the matter further. Would he abolish slavery?

His answer was as sharp as before, but it was music this time; I shouldn't ever wish to hear pleasanter, though the profanity was not good, being awkwardly put together, and with the crash-word almost in the middle instead of at the end, where, of course, it ought to have been.

I was ready and willing to get free now; I hadn't wanted to get free any sooner. No, I cannot quite say that. I had wanted to, but I had not been willing to take desperate chances, and had always dissuaded the king from them. But now—ah, it was a new atmosphere! Liberty would be worth any cost that might be put upon it now. I set about a plan, and was straightway charmed with it. It would require time, yes, and patience, too, a great deal of both. One could invent quicker ways, and fully as sure ones; but none that would be as picturesque as this; none that could be made so dramatic. And so I was not going to give this one up. It might delay us months, but no matter, I would carry it out or break something.

Now and then we had an adventure. One night we were overtaken by a snow-storm while still a mile from the village we were making for. Almost instantly we were shut up as in a fog, the driving snow was so thick. You couldn't see a thing, and we were soon lost. The slave-driver lashed us desperately, for he saw ruin before him, but his lashings only made matters worse, for they drove us further from the road and from likelihood of succor. So we had to stop at last and slump down in the snow where we were. The storm continued until toward midnight, then ceased. By this time two of our feebler men and three of our women were dead, and others past moving and threatened with death. Our master was nearly beside himself. He stirred up the living, and made us stand, jump, slap ourselves, to restore our circulation, and he helped as well as he could with his whip.

Now came a diversion. We heard shrieks and yells, and soon a woman came running and crying; and seeing our group, she flung herself into our midst and begged for protection. A mob of people came tearing after her, some with torches, and they said she was a witch who had caused several cows to die by a strange disease, and practiced her arts by help of a devil in the form of a black cat. This poor woman had been stoned until she hardly looked human, she was so battered and bloody. The mob wanted to burn her.

Well, now, what do you suppose our master did? When we closed around this poor creature to shelter her, he saw his chance. He said, burn her here, or they shouldn't have her at all. Imagine that! They were willing. They fastened her to a post; they brought wood and piled it about her; they applied the torch while she shrieked and pleaded and strained her two young daughters to her breast; and our brute, with a heart solely for business, lashed us into position about the stake and warmed us into life and commercial value by the same fire which took away the innocent life of that poor harmless mother. That was the sort of master we had. I took *his* number. That snow-storm cost him nine of his flock; and he was more brutal to us than ever, after that, for many days together, he was so enraged over his loss.

We had adventures all along. One day we ran into a procession. And such a procession! All the riffraff of the kingdom seemed to be comprehended in it; and all drunk at that. In the van was a cart with a coffin in it, and on the coffin sat a comely young girl of about eighteen suckling a baby, which she squeezed to her breast in a passion of love every little while, and every little while wiped from its face the tears which her eyes rained down upon it; and always the foolish little thing smiled up at her, happy and content, kneading her breast with its dimpled fat hand, which she patted and fondled right over her breaking heart.

Men and women, boys and girls, trotted along beside or after the cart, hooting, shouting profane and ribald remarks, singing snatches of foul song, skipping, dancing—a very holiday of hellions, a sickening sight. We had struck a suburb of London, outside the walls, and this was a sample of one sort of London society. Our master secured a good place for us near the gallows. A priest was in attendance, and he helped the girl climb up, and said comforting words to her, and made the under-sheriff provide a stool for her. Then he stood there by her on the gallows, and for a moment looked down upon the mass of upturned faces at his feet, then out over the solid pavement of heads that stretched away on every side occupying the vacancies far and near, and then began to tell the story of the case. And there was pity in his voice—how seldom a sound that was in that ignorant and savage land! I remember every detail of what he said, except the words he said it in; and so I change it into my own words:

"A sample of one sort of London Society"

"Law is intended to mete out justice. Sometimes it fails. This cannot be helped. We can only grieve, and be resigned, and pray for the soul of him who falls unfairly by the arm of the law, and that his fellows may be few. A law sends this poor young thing to death—and it is right. But another law had placed her where she must commit her crime or starve with her child—and before God that law is responsible for both her crime and her ignominious death!

"A little while ago this young thing, this child of eighteen years, was as happy a wife and mother as any in England; and her lips were blithe with song, which is the native speech of glad and innocent hearts. Her young husband was as happy as she; for he was doing his whole duty, he worked early and late at his handicraft, his bread was honest bread well and fairly earned, he was prospering, he was furnishing shelter and sustenance to his family, he was adding his mite to the wealth of the nation. By consent of a treacherous law, instant destruction fell upon this holy home and swept it away! That young husband was waylaid and impressed, and sent to sea. The wife knew nothing of it. She sought him everywhere, she moved the hardest hearts with the supplications of her tears, the broken eloquence of her despair. Weeks dragged by, she watching, waiting, hoping, her mind going slowly to wreck under the burden of her misery. Little by little all her small possessions went for food. When she could no longer pay her rent, they turned her out of doors. She begged, while she had strength; when she was starving at last, and her milk failing, she stole a piece of linen cloth of the value of a fourth part of a cent, thinking to sell it and save her child. But she was seen by the owner of the cloth. She was put in jail and brought to trial. The man testified to the facts. A plea was made for her, and her sorrowful story was told in her behalf. She spoke, too, by permission, and said she did steal the cloth, but that her mind was so disordered of late by trouble that when she was overborne with hunger all acts, criminal or other, swam meaningless through her brain and she knew nothing rightly, except that she was so hungry! For a moment all were touched, and there was disposition to deal mercifully with her, seeing that she was so young and friendless, and her case so piteous, and the law that robbed her of her support to blame as being the first and only cause of her transgression; but the prosecuting officer replied that whereas these things were all true, and most pitiful as well, still there was much small theft in these days, and mistimed mercy here would be a danger to property—oh, my God, is there no property in ruined homes, and orphaned babes, and broken hearts that British law holds precious!—and so he must require sentence.

"When the judge put on his black cap, the owner of the stolen linen rose trembling up, his lip quivering, his face as grey as ashes; and when the awful words came, he cried out, 'Oh, poor child, poor child, I did not know it was death!' and fell as a tree falls. When they lifted him up his reason was gone; before the sun was set, he had taken his own life. A kindly man; a man whose heart was right, at bottom; add his murder to this that is to be now done here; and charge them both where they belong—to the rulers and the bitter laws of Britain. The time is come, my child; let me pray over thee—not *for* thee, dear abused poor heart and innocent, but for them that be guilty of thy ruin and death, who need it more."

After his prayer they put the noose around the young girl's neck, and they had great trouble to adjust the knot under her ear, because she was devouring the baby all the time, wildly kissing it, and snatching it to her face and her breast, and drenching it with tears, and half moaning, half shrieking all the while, and the baby crowing, and laughing, and kicking its feet with delight over what it took for romp and play. Even the hangman couldn't stand it, but turned away. When all was ready the priest gently pulled and tugged and forced the child out of the mother's arms, and stepped quickly out of her reach; but she clasped her hands, and made a wild spring toward him, with a shriek; but the rope—and the under-sheriff—held her short. Then she went on her knees and stretched out her hands and cried:

"One more kiss—oh, my God, one more, one more—it is the dying that begs it!"

She got it; she almost smothered the little thing. And when they got it away again, she cried out:

"Oh, my child, my darling, it will die! It has no home, it has no father, no friend, no mother—"

"It has them all!" said that good priest. "All these will I be to it till I die."

You should have seen her face then! Gratitude? Lord, what do you want with words to express that? Words are only painted fire; a look is the fire itself. She gave that look, and carried it away to the treasury of heaven, where all things that are divine belong.

36

An Encounter in the Dark

London—to a slave—was a sufficiently interesting place. It was merely a great big village; and mainly mud and thatch. The streets were muddy, crooked, unpaved. The populace was an ever flocking and drifting swarm of rags, and splendours, of nodding plumes and shining armor. The king had a palace there; he saw the outside of it. It made him sigh; yes, and swear a little, in a poor juvenile sixth century way. We saw knights and grandees whom we knew, but they didn't know us in our rags and dirt and raw welts and bruises, and wouldn't have recognized us if we had hailed them, nor stopped to answer, either, it being unlawful to speak with slaves on a chain. Sandy passed within ten yards of me on a mule—hunting for me, I imagined. But the thing which clean broke my heart was something which happened in front of our old barrack in a square, while we were enduring the spectacle of a man being boiled to death in oil for counterfeiting pennies. It was the sight of a newsboy—and I couldn't get at him! Still, I had one comfort—here was proof that Clarence was still alive and banging away. I meant to be with him before long; the thought was full of cheer.

I had one little glimpse of another thing, one day, which gave me a great uplift. It was a wire stretching from housetop to housetop. Telegraph or telephone, sure. I did very much wish I had a little piece of it. It was just what I needed, in order to carry out my project of escape. My idea was to get loose some night, along with the king, then gag and bind our master, change clothes with him, batter him into the aspect of a stranger, hitch him to the slave-chain, assume possession of the property, march to Camelot, and—

But you get my idea; you see what a stunning dramatic surprise I would wind up with at the palace. It was all feasible, if I could only get hold of a slender piece of iron which I could shape into a lock-pick. I could then undo the lumbering padlocks with which our chains were fastened, whenever I might choose. But I never had any luck; no such thing ever happened to fall in my way. However, my chance came at last. A gentleman who had come twice before to dicker for me, without result, or indeed any approach to a result, came again. I was far from expecting ever to belong to him, for the price asked for me from the time I was first enslaved was exorbitant, and always provoked either anger or derision, yet my master stuck stubbornly to it—twenty-two dollars. He wouldn't bate a cent. The king was greatly admired, because of his grand physique, but his kingly style was against him, and he wasn't salable; nobody wanted that kind of a slave. I considered myself safe from parting from him because of my extravagant price. No, I was not expecting to ever belong to this gentleman whom I have spoken of, but he had something which I expected would belong to me eventually, if he would but visit us often enough. It was a steel thing with a long pin to it, with which his long cloth outside garment was fastened together in front. There were three of them. He had disappointed me twice, because he did not come quite close enough to me to make my project entirely safe; but this time I succeeded; I captured the lower clasp of the three, and when he missed it he thought he had lost it on the way.

I had a chance to be glad about a minute, then straightway a chance to be sad again. For when the purchase was about to fail, as usual, the master suddenly spoke up and said what would be worded thus—in modern English:

"I'll tell you what I'll do. I'm tired supporting these two for no good. Give me twenty-two dollars for this one, and I'll throw the other one in."

The king couldn't get his breath, he was in such a fury. He began to choke and gag, and meantime the master and the gentleman moved away discussing.

"An ye will keep the offer open—"

"'Tis open till the morrow at this hour."

"Then I will answer you at that time," said the gentleman, and disappeared, the master following him.

I had a time of it to cool the king down, but I managed it. I whispered in his ear, to this effect:

"Your grace *will* go for nothing, but after another fashion. And so shall I. Tonight we shall both be free."

"Ah! How is that?"

"With this thing which I have stolen, I will unlock these locks and cast off these chains tonight. When he comes about nine-thirty to inspect us for the night, we will seize him, gag him, batter him, and early in the morning we will march out of this town, proprietors of this caravan of slaves."

That was as far as I went, but the king was charmed and satisfied. That evening we waited patiently for our fellow-slaves to get to sleep and signify it by the usual sign, for you must not take many chances on those poor fellows if you can avoid it. It is best to keep your own secrets. No doubt they fidgeted only about as usual, but it didn't seem so to me. It seemed to me that they were going to be forever getting down to their regular snoring. As the time dragged on I got nervously afraid we shouldn't have enough of it left for our needs; so I made several premature attempts, and merely delayed things by it; for I couldn't seem to touch a padlock, there in the dark, without starting a rattle out of it which interrupted somebody's sleep and made him turn over and wake some more of the gang.

But finally I did get my last iron off, and was a free man once more. I took a good breath of relief, and reached for the king's irons. Too late! in comes the master, with a light in one hand and his heavy walking-staff in the other. I snuggled close among the wallow of snorers, to conceal as nearly as possible that I was naked of irons; and I kept a sharp lookout and prepared to spring for my man the moment he should bend over me.

But he didn't approach. He stopped, gazed absently toward our dusky mass a minute, evidently thinking about something else; then set down his light, moved musingly toward the door, and before a body could imagine what he was going to do, he was out of the door and had closed it behind him.

"Quick!" said the king. "Fetch him back!"

Of course, it was the thing to do, and I was up and out in a moment. But, dear me, there were no lamps in those days, and it was a dark night. But I glimpsed a dim figure a few steps away. I darted for it, threw myself upon it, and then there was a state of things and lively! We fought and scuffled and struggled, and drew a crowd in no time. They took an immense interest in the fight and encouraged us all they could, and, in fact, couldn't have been pleasanter or more cordial if it had been their own fight. Then a tremendous row broke out behind us, and as much as half of our audience left us, with a rush, to invest some sympathy in that. Lanterns began to swing in all directions; it was the watch gathering from far and near. Presently a halberd fell across my back, as a reminder, and I knew what it meant. I was in custody. So was my adversary. We were marched off toward prison, one on each side of the watchman. Here was disaster, here was a fine scheme gone to sudden destruction! I tried to imagine what would happen when the master should discover that it was I who had been fighting him; and what would happen if they jailed us together in the general apartment for brawlers and petty law-breakers, as was the custom; and what might—

Just then my antagonist turned his face around in my direction, the freckled light from the watchman's tin lantern fell on it, and, by George, he was the wrong man!

37

An Awful Predicament

Sleep? It was impossible. It would naturally have been impossible in that noisome cavern of a jail, with its mangy crowd of drunken, quarrelsome, and song-singing rapscallions. But the thing that made sleep all the more a thing not to be dreamed of, was my racking impatience to get out of this place and find out the whole size of what might have happened yonder in the slave-quarters in consequence of that intolerable miscarriage of mine.

It was a long night, but the morning got around at last. I made a full and frank explanation to the court. I said I was a slave, the property of the great Earl Grip, who had arrived just after dark at the Tabard inn in the village on the other side of the water, and had stopped there over night, by compulsion, he being taken deadly sick with a strange and sudden disorder. I had been ordered to cross to the city in all haste and bring the best physician; I was doing my best; naturally I was running with all my might; the night was dark, I ran against this common person here, who seized me by the throat and began to pummel me, although I told him my errand, and implored him, for the sake of the great earl my master's mortal peril—

The common person interrupted and said it was a lie; and was going to explain how I rushed upon him and attacked him without a word—

"Silence, sirrah!" from the court. "Take him hence and give him a few stripes whereby to teach him how to treat the servant of a nobleman after a different fashion another time. Go!"

Then the court begged my pardon, and hoped I would not fail to tell his lordship it was in no wise the court's fault that this high-handed thing had happened. I said I would make it all right, and so took my leave. Took it just in time, too; he was starting to ask me why I didn't fetch out these facts the moment I was arrested. I said I would if I had thought of it—which was true—but that I was so battered by that man that all my wit was knocked out of me—and so forth and so on, and got myself away, still mumbling.

I didn't wait for breakfast. No grass grew under my feet. I was soon at the slave quarters. Empty—everybody gone! That is, everybody except one body—the slave-master's. It lay there all battered to pulp; and all about were the evidences of a terrific fight. There was a rude board coffin on a cart at the door, and workmen, assisted by the police, were thinning a road through the gaping crowd in order that they might bring it in.

I picked out a man humble enough in life to condescend to talk with one so shabby as I, and got his account of the matter.

"There were sixteen slaves here. They rose against their master in the night, and thou seest how it ended."

"Yes. How did it begin?"

"There was no witness but the slaves. They said the slave that was most valuable got free of his bonds and escaped in some strange way—by magic arts 'twas thought, by reason that he had no key, and the locks were neither broke nor in any wise injured. When the master discovered his loss, he was mad with despair, and threw himself upon his people with his heavy stick, who resisted and brake his back and in other and divers ways did give him hurts that brought him swiftly to his end."

"This is dreadful. It will go hard with the slaves, no doubt, upon the trial."

"Marry, the trial is over."

"Over!"

"Would they be a week, think you—and the matter so simple? They were not the half of a quarter of an hour at it."

"Why, I don't see how they could determine which were the guilty ones in so short a time."

"*Which* ones? Indeed, they considered not particulars like to that. They condemned them in a body. Wit ye not the law?—which men say the Romans left behind them here when they went—that if one slave killeth his master all the slaves of that man must die for it."

"True. I had forgotten. And when will these die?"

"Belike within a four and twenty hours; albeit some say they will wait a pair of days more, if peradventure they may find the missing one meantime."

The missing one! It made me feel uncomfortable.

"Is it likely they will find him?"

"Before the day is spent—yes. They seek him everywhere. They stand at the gates of the town, with certain of the slaves who will discover him to them if he cometh, and none can pass out but he will be first examined."

"Might one see the place where the rest are confined?"

"The outside of it—yes. The inside of it—but ye will not want to see that."

I took the address of that prison for future reference and then sauntered off. At the first second-hand clothing shop I came to, up a back street, I got a rough rig suitable for a common seaman who might be going on a cold voyage, and bound up my face with a liberal bandage, saying I had a toothache. This concealed my worst bruises. It was a transformation. I no longer resembled my former self. Then I struck out for that wire, found it and followed it to its den. It was a little room over a butcher's shop—which meant that business wasn't very brisk in the telegraphic line. The young chap in charge was drowsing at his table. I locked the door and put the vast key in my bosom. This alarmed the young fellow, and he was going to make a noise; but I said:

"Save your wind; if you open your mouth you are dead, sure. Tackle your instrument. Lively, now! Call Camelot."

"This doth amaze me! How should such as you know aught of such matters as—"

"Call Camelot! I am a desperate man. Call Camelot, or get away from the instrument and I will do it myself."

"What—you?"

"Yes—certainly. Stop gabbling. Call the palace."

He made the call.

"Now, then, call Clarence."

"Clarence *who*?"

"Never mind Clarence who. Say you want Clarence; you'll get an answer."

He did so. We waited five nerve-straining minutes—ten minutes—how long it did seem!—and then came a click that was as familiar to me as a human voice; for Clarence had been my own pupil.

"Now, my lad, vacate! They would have known *my* touch, maybe, and so your call was surest; but I'm all right now."

He vacated the place and cocked his ear to listen—but it didn't win. I used a cipher. I didn't waste any time in sociabilities with Clarence, but squared away for business, straight-off—thus:

"The king is here and in danger. We were captured and brought here as slaves. We should not be able to prove our identity—and the fact is, I am not in a position to try. Send a telegram for the palace here which will carry conviction with it."

His answer came straight back:

"They don't know anything about the telegraph; they haven't had any experience yet, the line to London is so new. Better not venture that. They might hang you. Think up something else."

Might hang us! Little he knew how closely he was crowding the facts. I couldn't think up anything for the moment. Then an idea struck me, and I started it along:

"Send five hundred picked knights with Launcelot in the lead; and send them on the jump. Let them enter by the southwest gate, and look out for the man with a white cloth around his right arm."

The answer was prompt:

"They shall start in half an hour."

"All right, Clarence; now tell this lad here that I'm a friend of yours and a dead-head; and that he must be discreet and say nothing about this visit of mine."

The instrument began to talk to the youth and I hurried away. I fell to ciphering. In half an hour it would be nine o'clock. Knights and horses in heavy armor couldn't travel very fast. These would make the best time they could, and now that the ground was in good condition, and no snow or mud, they would probably make a seven-mile gait; they would have to change horses a couple of times; they would arrive about six, or a little after; it would still be plenty light enough; they would see the white cloth which I should tie around my right arm, and I would take command. We would surround that prison and have the king out in no time. It would be showy and picturesque enough, all things considered, though I would have preferred noonday, on account of the more theatrical aspect the thing would have.

Now, then, in order to increase the strings to my bow, I thought I would look up some of those people whom I had formerly recognized, and make myself known. That would help us out of our scrape, without the knights. But I must proceed cautiously, for it was a risky business. I must get into sumptuous raiment, and it wouldn't do to run and jump into it. No, I must work up to it by degrees, buying suit after suit of clothes, in shops wide apart, and getting a little finer article with each change, until I should finally reach silk and velvet, and be ready for my project. So I started.

But the scheme fell through like scat! The first corner I turned, I came plump upon one of our slaves, snooping around with a watchman. I coughed at the moment, and he gave me a sudden look that bit right into my marrow. I judge he thought he had heard that cough before. I turned immediately into a shop and worked along down the counter, pricing things and watching out of the corner of my eye. Those people had stopped, and were talking together and looking in at the door. I made up my mind to get out the back way, if there was a back way, and I asked the shopwoman if I could step out there and look for the escaped slave, who was believed to be in hiding back there somewhere, and said I was an officer in disguise, and my pard was yonder at the door with one of the murderers in charge, and would she be good enough to step there and tell him he needn't wait, but had better go at once to the further end of the back alley and be ready to head him off when I rousted him out.

She was blazing with eagerness to see one of those already celebrated murderers, and she started on the errand at once. I slipped out the back way, locked the door behind me, put the key in my pocket and started off, chuckling to myself and comfortable.

Well, I had gone and spoiled it again, made another mistake. A double one, in fact. There were plenty of ways to get rid of that officer by some simple and plausible device, but no, I must pick out a picturesque one; it is the crying defect of my character. And then, I had ordered my procedure upon what the officer, being human, would *naturally* do; whereas when you are least expecting it, a man will now and then go and do the very thing which it's *not* natural for him to do. The natural thing for the officer to do, in this case, was to follow straight on my heels; he would find a stout oaken door, securely locked, between him and me; before he could break it down, I should be far away and engaged in slipping into a succession of baffling disguises which would soon get me into a sort of raiment which was a surer protection from meddling law-dogs in Britain than any amount of mere innocence and purity of character. But instead of doing the natural thing, the officer took me at my word, and followed my instructions. And so, as I came trotting out of that cul-de-sac, full of satisfaction with my own cleverness, he turned the corner and I walked right into his handcuffs. If I had known it was a cul-de-sac—however, there isn't any excusing a blunder like that, let it go. Charge it up to profit and loss.

Of course, I was indignant, and swore I had just come ashore from a long voyage, and all that sort of thing—just to see, you know, if it would deceive that slave. But it didn't. He knew me. Then I reproached him for betraying me. He was more surprised than hurt. He stretched his eyes wide, and said:

"What, wouldst have me let thee, of all men, escape and not hang with us, when thou'rt the very *cause* of our hanging? Go to!"

"Go to" was their way of saying "I should smile!" or "I like that!" Queer talkers, those people.

Well, there was a sort of bastard justice in his view of the case, and so I dropped the matter. When you can't cure a disaster by argument, what is the use to argue? It isn't my way. So I only said:

"You're not going to be hanged. None of us are."

Both men laughed, and the slave said:

"Ye have not ranked as a fool—before. You might better keep your reputation, seeing the strain would not be for long."

"It will stand it, I reckon. Before tomorrow we shall be out of prison, and free to go where we will, besides."

The witty officer lifted at his left ear with his thumb, made a rasping noise in his throat, and said:

"Out of prison—yes—ye say true. And free likewise to go where ye will, so ye wander not out of his grace the Devil's sultry realm."

I kept my temper, and said, indifferently:

"Now I suppose you really think we are going to hang within a day or two."

"I thought it not many minutes ago, for so the thing was decided and proclaimed."

"Ah, then you've changed your mind, is that it?"

"Even that. I only *thought*, then; I *know*, now."

I felt sarcastical, so I said:

"Oh, sapient servant of the law, condescend to tell us, then, what you *know*."

"That ye will all be hanged *today*, at mid-afternoon! Oho! that shot hit home! Lean upon me."

The fact is I did need to lean upon somebody. My knights couldn't arrive in time. They would be as much as three hours too late. Nothing in the world could save the King of England; nor me, which was more important. More important, not merely to me, but to the nation—the only nation on earth standing ready to blossom into civilization. I was sick. I said no more, there wasn't anything to say. I knew what the man meant; that if the missing slave was found, the postponement would be revoked, the execution take place today. Well, the missing slave was found.

38

Sir Launcelot and Knights to the Rescue

Nearing four in the afternoon. The scene was just outside the walls of London. A cool, comfortable, superb day, with a brilliant sun; the kind of day to make one want to live, not die. The multitude was prodigious and far-reaching; and yet we fifteen poor devils hadn't a friend in it. There was something painful in that thought, look at it how you might. There we sat, on our tall scaffold, the butt of the hate and mockery of all those enemies. We were being made a holiday spectacle. They had built a sort of grand stand for the nobility and gentry, and these were there in full force, with their ladies. We recognized a good many of them.

The crowd got a brief and unexpected dash of diversion out of the king. The moment we were freed of our bonds he sprang up, in his fantastic rags, with face bruised out of all recognition, and proclaimed himself Arthur, King of Britain, and denounced the awful penalties of treason upon every soul there present if hair of his sacred head were touched. It startled and surprised him to hear them break into a vast roar of laughter. It wounded his dignity, and he locked himself up in silence. Then, although the crowd begged him to go on, and tried to provoke him to it by catcalls, jeers, and shouts of:

"Let him speak! The king! The king! his humble subjects hunger and thirst for words of wisdom out of the mouth of their master his Serene and Sacred Raggedness!"

But it went for nothing. He put on all his majesty and sat under this rain of contempt and insult unmoved. He certainly was great in his way. Absently, I had taken off my white bandage and wound it about my right arm. When the crowd noticed this, they began upon me. They said:

"Doubtless this sailor-man is his minister—observe his costly badge of office!"

I let them go on until they got tired, and then I said:

"Yes, I am his minister, The Boss; and tomorrow you will hear that from Camelot which—"

I got no further. They drowned me out with joyous derision. But presently there was silence; for the sheriffs of London, in their official robes, with their subordinates, began to make a stir which indicated that business was about to begin. In the hush which followed, our crime was recited, the death warrant read, then everybody uncovered while a priest uttered a prayer.

Then a slave was blindfolded; the hangman unslung his rope. There lay the smooth road below us, we upon one side of it, the banked multitude wailing its other side—a good clear road, and kept free by the police—how good it would be to see my five hundred horsemen come tearing down it! But no, it was out of the possibilities. I followed its receding thread out into the distance—not a horseman on it, or sign of one.

There was a jerk, and the slave hung dangling; dangling and hideously squirming, for his limbs were not tied.

A second rope was unslung, in a moment another slave was dangling.

In a minute a third slave was struggling in the air. It was dreadful. I turned away my head a moment, and when I turned back I missed the king! They were blindfolding him! I was paralyzed; I couldn't move, I was choking, my tongue was petrified. They finished blindfolding him, they led him under the rope. I couldn't shake off that clinging impotence. But when I saw them put the noose around his neck, then everything let go in me and I made a spring to the rescue—and as I made it I shot one more glance abroad—by George! here they came, a-tilting!—five hundred mailed and belted knights on bicycles!

The grandest sight that ever was seen. Lord, how the plumes streamed, how the sun flamed and flashed from the endless procession of webby wheels!

I waved my right arm as Launcelot swept in—he recognized my rag—I tore away noose and bandage, and shouted:

"On your knees, every rascal of you, and salute the king! Who fails shall sup in hell tonight!"

I always use that high style when I'm climaxing an effect. Well, it was noble to see Launcelot and the boys swarm up onto that scaffold and heave sheriffs and such overboard. And it was fine to see that astonished multitude go down on their knees and beg their lives of the king they had just been deriding and insulting. And as he stood apart there, receiving this homage in rags, I thought to myself, well, really there is something peculiarly grand about the gait and bearing of a king, after all.

I was immensely satisfied. Take the whole situation all around, it was one of the gaudiest effects I ever instigated.

And presently up comes Clarence, his own self! and winks, and says, very modernly:

"Good deal of a surprise, wasn't it? I knew you'd like it. I've had the boys practicing this long time, privately; and just hungry for a chance to show off."

39

The Yankee's Fight with the Knights

Home again, at Camelot. A morning or two later I found the paper, damp from the press, by my plate at the breakfast table. I turned to the advertising columns, knowing I should find something of personal interest to me there. It was this:

DE PAR LE ROI.

Know that the great lord and illustrious Knight, SIR SAGRAMOR LE DESIROUS having condescended to meet the King's Minister, Hank Morgan, the which is surnamed The Boss, for satisfgction of offence anciently given, these wilL engage in the lists by Camelot about the fourth hour of the morning of the sixteenth day of this next succeeding month. The battle will be a l outrance, sith the said offence was of a deadly sort, admitting of no commmon Position.

Clarence's editorial reference to this affair was to this effect:

> *It will be observed, by a gl7nce at our advertising columns, that the community is to be favoured with a treat of unusual interest in the tournament line. The n ames of the artists are warrant of good enterTemment. The box-office will be open at noon of the 13th; admission 3 cents, reserved seatsh 5; proceeds to go to the hospital fund The royal pair and all the Court will be present. With these exceptions, and the press and the clergy, the free list is strictly susPended. Parties are hereby warned against buying tickets of speculators; they will not be good at the door. Everybody knows and likes The Boss, everybody knows and likes Sir Sag.; come, let us give the lads a good send-off. ReMember, the proceeds go to a great and free charity, and one whose broad begevolence stretches out its helping hand, warm with the blood of a loving heart, to all that suffer, regardless of race, creed, condition or colour—the only charity yet established in the earth which has no politico-religious stop-cock on its compassion, but says Here flows the stream, let* ALL *come and drink! Turn out, all hands! fetch along your dou3hnuts and your gum-drops and have a good time. Pie for sale on the grounds, and rocks to crack it with; and ciRcus-lemonade—three drops of lime juice to a barrel of water.*
>
> *N.B. This is the first tournament under the new law, whidh allow each*

combatant to use any weapon he may prefer. You may want to make a note of that.

Up to the day set, there was no talk in all Britain of anything but this combat. All other topics sank into insignificance and passed out of men's thoughts and interest. It was not because a tournament was a great matter, it was not because Sir Sagramor had found the Holy Grail, for he had not, but had failed; it was not because the second (official) personage in the kingdom was one of the duellists; no, all these features were commonplace. Yet there was abundant reason for the extraordinary interest which this coming fight was creating. It was born of the fact that all the nation knew that this was not to be a duel between mere men, so to speak, but a duel between two mighty magicians; a duel not of muscle but of mind, not of human skill but of superhuman art and craft; a final struggle for supremacy between the two master enchanters of the age. It was realized that the most prodigious achievements of the most renowned knights could not be worthy of comparison with a spectacle like this; they could be but child's play, contrasted with this mysterious and awful battle of the gods. Yes, all the world knew it was going to be in reality a duel between Merlin and me, a measuring of his magic powers against mine. It was known that Merlin had been busy whole days and nights together, imbuing Sir Sagramor's arms and armor with supernal powers of offense and defense, and that he had procured for him from the spirits of the air a fleecy veil which would render the wearer invisible to his antagonist while still visible to other men. Against Sir Sagramor, so weaponed and protected, a thousand knights could accomplish nothing; against him no known enchantments could prevail. These facts were sure; regarding them there was no doubt, no reason for doubt. There was but one question: might there be still other enchantments, *unknown* to Merlin, which could render Sir Sagramor's veil transparent to me, and make his enchanted mail vulnerable to my weapons? This was the one thing to be decided in the lists. Until then the world must remain in suspense.

So the world thought there was a vast matter at stake here, and the world was right, but it was not the one they had in their minds. No, a far vaster one was upon the cast of this die: *the life of knight errantry.* I was a champion, it was true, but not the champion of the frivolous black arts, I was the champion of hard unsentimental common-sense and reason. I was entering the lists to either destroy knight errantry or be its victim.

Vast as the show-grounds were, there were no vacant spaces in them outside of the lists, at ten o'clock on the morning of the 16th. The mammoth grand-stand was clothed in flags, streamers, and rich tapestries, and packed with several acres of small-fry tributary kings, their suites, and the British aristocracy; with our own royal gang in the chief place, and each and every individual a flashing prism of gaudy silks and velvets—well, I never saw anything to begin with it but a fight between an Upper Mississippi sunset and the aurora borealis. The huge camp of beflagged and gay-coloured tents at one end of the lists, with a stiff-standing sentinel at every door and a shining shield hanging by him for challenge, was another fine sight. You see, every knight was there who had any ambition or any caste feeling; for my feeling toward their order was not much of a secret, and so here was their chance. If I won my fight with Sir Sagramor, others would have the right to call me out as long as I might be willing to respond.

Down at our end there were but two tents; one for me, and another for my servants. At the appointed hour the king made a sign, and the heralds, in their tabards, appeared and made proclamation, naming the combatants and stating the cause of quarrel. There was a pause, then a ringing bugle-blast, which was the signal for us to come forth. All the multitude caught their breath, and an eager curiosity flashed into every face.

Out from his tent rode great Sir Sagramor, an imposing tower of iron, stately and rigid, his huge spear standing upright in its socket and grasped in his strong hand, his grand horse's face and breast cased in steel, his body clothed in rich trappings that almost dragged the ground—oh, a most noble picture. A great shout went up, of welcome and admiration.

And then out I came. But I didn't get any shout. There was a wondering and eloquent silence for a moment, then a great wave of laughter began to sweep along that human sea, but a warning bugle-blast cut its career short. I was in the simplest and comfortablest of gymnast costumes—flesh-coloured tights from neck to heel, with blue silk puffings about my loins, and bareheaded. My horse was not above medium size, but he was alert, slender-limbed, muscled with watch-springs, and just a greyhound to go. He was a beauty, glossy as silk, and naked as he was when he was born, except for bridle and ranger-saddle.

The iron tower and the gorgeous bed-quilt came cumbrously but gracefully pirouetting down the lists, and we tripped lightly up to meet them. We halted; the tower saluted, I responded; then we wheeled and rode side by side to the grand-stand and faced our king and queen, to whom we made obeisance. The queen exclaimed:

"Alack, Sir Boss, wilt fight naked, and without lance or sword or—"

But the king checked her and made her understand, with a polite phrase or two, that this was none of her business. The bugles rang again; and we separated and rode to the ends of the lists, and took position. Now old Merlin stepped into view and cast a dainty web of gossamer threads over Sir Sagramor which turned him into Hamlet's ghost; the king made a sign, the bugles blew, Sir Sagramor laid his great lance in rest, and the next moment here he came thundering down the course with his veil flying out behind, and I went whistling through the air like an arrow to meet him—cocking my ear the while, as if noting the invisible knight's position and progress by hearing, not sight. A chorus of encouraging shouts burst out for him, and one brave voice flung out a heartening word for me—said:

"Go it, slim Jim!"

It was an even bet that Clarence had procured that favour for me—and furnished the language, too. When that formidable lance-point was within a yard and a half of my breast I twitched my horse aside without an effort, and the big knight swept by, scoring a blank. I got plenty of applause that time. We turned, braced up, and down we came again. Another blank for the knight, a roar of applause for me. This same thing was repeated once more; and it fetched such a whirlwind of applause that Sir Sagramor lost his temper, and at once changed his tactics and set himself the task of chasing me down. Why, he hadn't any show in the world at that; it was a game of tag, with all the advantage on my side; I whirled out of his path with ease whenever I chose, and once I slapped him on the back as I went to the rear. Finally I took the chase into my own hands; and after that, turn, or twist, or do what he would, he was never able to get behind me again; he found himself always in front at the end of his maneuver. So he gave up that business and retired to his end of the lists. His temper was clear gone now, and he forgot himself and flung an insult at me which disposed of mine. I slipped my lasso from the horn of my saddle, and grasped the coil in my right hand. This time you should have seen him come!—it was a business trip, sure; by his gait there was blood in his eye. I was sitting my horse at ease, and swinging the great loop of my lasso in wide circles about my head; the moment he was under way, I started for him; when the space between us had narrowed to forty feet, I sent the snaky spirals of the rope a-cleaving through the air, then darted aside and faced about and brought my trained animal to a halt with all his feet braced under him for a surge. The next moment the rope sprang taut and yanked Sir Sagramor out of the saddle! Great Scott, but there was a sensation!

"Great Scott, but there was a sensation!"

Unquestionably, the popular thing in this world is novelty. These people had never seen anything of that cowboy business before, and it carried them clear off their feet with delight. From all around and everywhere, the shout went up:

"Encore! encore!"

I wondered where they got the word, but there was no time to cipher on philological matters, because the whole knight-errantry hive was just humming now, and my prospect for trade couldn't have been better. The moment my lasso was released and Sir Sagramor had been assisted to his tent, I hauled in the slack, took my station and began to swing my loop around my head again. I was sure to have use for it as soon as they could elect a successor for Sir Sagramor, and that couldn't take long where there were so many hungry candidates. Indeed, they elected one straight off—Sir Hervis de Revel.

Bzz! Here he came, like a house afire; I dodged: he passed like a flash, with my horse-hair coils settling around his neck; a second or so later, *fst*! his saddle was empty.

I got another encore; and another, and another, and still another. When I had snaked five men out, things began to look serious to the ironclads, and they stopped and consulted together. As a result, they decided that it was time to waive etiquette and send their greatest and best against me. To the astonishment of that little world, I lassoed Sir Lamorak de Galis, and after him Sir Galahad. So you see there was simply nothing to be done now, but play their right bower—bring out the superbest of the superb, the mightiest of the mighty, the great Sir Launcelot himself!

A proud moment for me? I should think so. Yonder was Arthur, King of Britain; yonder was Guenever; yes, and whole tribes of little provincial kings and kinglets; and in the tented camp yonder, renowned knights from many lands; and likewise the selectest body known to chivalry, the Knights of the Table Round, the most illustrious in Christendom; and biggest fact of all, the very sun of their shining system was yonder couching his lance, the focal point of forty thousand adoring eyes; and all by myself, here was I laying for him. Across my mind flitted the dear image of a certain hello-girl of West Hartford, and I wished she could see me now. In that moment, down came the Invincible, with the rush of a whirlwind—the courtly world rose to its feet and bent forward—the fateful coils went circling through the air, and before you could wink I was towing Sir Launcelot across the field on his back, and kissing my hand to the storm of waving kerchiefs and the thunder-crash of applause that greeted me!

Said I to myself, as I coiled my lariat and hung it on my saddle-horn, and sat there drunk with glory, "The victory is perfect—no other will venture against me—knight errantry is dead." Now imagine my astonishment—and everybody else's, too—to hear the peculiar bugle-call which announces that another competitor is about to enter the lists! There was a mystery here; I couldn't account for this thing. Next, I noticed Merlin gliding away from me; and then I noticed that my lasso was gone! The old sleight-of-hand expert had stolen it, sure, and slipped it under his robe.

The bugle blew again. I looked, and down came Sagramor riding again, with his dust brushed off and his veil nicely re-arranged. I trotted up to meet him, and pretended to find him by the sound of his horse's hoofs. He said:

"Thou'rt quick of ear, but it will not save thee from this!" and he touched the hilt of his great sword. "An ye are not able to see it, because of the influence of the veil, know that it is no cumbrous lance, but a sword—and I ween ye will not be able to avoid it."

His visor was up; there was death in his smile. I should never be able to dodge his sword, that was plain. Somebody was going to die this time. If he got the drop on me, I could name the corpse. We rode forward together, and saluted the royalties. This time the king was disturbed. He said:

"Where is thy strange weapon?"

"It is stolen, sire."

"Hast another at hand?"

"No, sire, I brought only the one."

Then Merlin mixed in:

"He brought but the one because there was but the one to bring. There exists none other but that one. It belongeth to the king of the Demons of the Sea. This man is a pretender, and ignorant, else he had known that that weapon can be used in but eight bouts only, and then it vanisheth away to its home under the sea."

"Then is he weaponless," said the king. "Sir Sagramore, ye will grant him leave to borrow."

"And I will lend!" said Sir Launcelot, limping up. "He is as brave a knight of his hands as any that be on live, and he shall have mine."

He put his hand on his sword to draw it, but Sir Sagramor said:

"Stay, it may not be. He shall fight with his own weapons; it was his privilege to choose them and bring them. If he has erred, on his head be it."

"Knight!" said the king. "Thou'rt overwrought with passion; it disorders thy mind. Wouldst kill a naked man?"

"An he do it, he shall answer it to me," said Sir Launcelot.

"I will answer it to any he that desireth!" retorted Sir Sagramor hotly.

Merlin broke in, rubbing his hands and smiling his low-downest smile of malicious gratification:

"'Tis well said, right well said! And 'tis enough of parleying, let my lord the king deliver the battle signal."

The king had to yield. The bugle made proclamation, and we turned apart and rode to our stations. There we stood, a hundred yards apart, facing each other, rigid and motionless, like horsed statues. And so we remained, in a soundless hush, as much as a full minute, everybody gazing, nobody stirring. It seemed as if the king could not take heart to give the signal. But at last he lifted his hand, the clear note of the bugle followed, Sir Sagramor's long blade described a flashing curve in the air, and it was superb to see him come. I sat still. On he came. I did not move. People got so excited that they shouted to me:

"Fly, fly! Save thyself! This is murther!"

I never budged so much as an inch till that thundering apparition had got within fifteen paces of me; then I snatched a dragoon revolver out of my holster, there was a flash and a roar, and the revolver was back in the holster before anybody could tell what had happened.

Here was a riderless horse plunging by, and yonder lay Sir Sagramor, stone dead.

The people that ran to him were stricken dumb to find that the life was actually gone out of the man and no reason for it visible, no hurt upon his body, nothing like a wound. There was a hole through the breast of his chain-mail, but they attached no importance to a little thing like that; and as a bullet wound there produces but little blood, none came in sight because of the clothing and swaddlings under the armor. The body was dragged over to let the king and the swells look down upon it. They were stupefied with astonishment naturally. I was requested to come and explain the miracle. But I remained in my tracks, like a statue, and said:

"If it is a command, I will come, but my lord the king knows that I am where the laws of combat require me to remain while any desire to come against me."

I waited. Nobody challenged. Then I said:

"If there are any who doubt that this field is well and fairly won, I do not wait for them to challenge me, I challenge them."

"It is a gallant offer," said the king, "and well beseems you. Whom will you name first?"

"I name none, I challenge all! Here I stand, and dare the chivalry of England to come against me—not by individuals, but in mass!"

"What!" shouted a score of knights.

"You have heard the challenge. Take it, or I proclaim you recreant knights and vanquished, every one!"

It was a "bluff" you know. At such a time it is sound judgment to put on a bold face and play your hand for a hundred times what it is worth; forty-nine times out of fifty nobody dares to "call," and you rake in the chips. But just this once—well, things looked squally! In just no time, five hundred knights were scrambling into their saddles, and before you could wink a widely scattering drove were under way and clattering down upon me. I snatched both revolvers from the holsters and began to measure distances and calculate chances.

Bang! One saddle empty. Bang! another one. Bang—bang, and I bagged two. Well, it was nip and tuck with us, and I knew it. If I spent the eleventh shot without convincing these people, the twelfth man would kill me, sure. And so I never did feel so happy as I did when my ninth downed its man and I detected the wavering in the crowd which is premonitory of panic. An instant lost now could knock out my last chance. But I didn't lose it. I raised both revolvers and pointed them—the halted host stood their ground just about one good square moment, then broke and fled.

The day was mine. Knight errantry was a doomed institution. The march of civilization was begun. How did I feel? Ah, you never could imagine it.

And Brer Merlin? His stock was flat again. Somehow, every time the magic of fol-de-rol tried conclusions with the magic of science, the magic of fol-de-rol got left.

40

Three Years Later

When I broke the back of knight errantry that time, I no longer felt obliged to work in secret. So, the very next day I exposed my hidden schools, my mines, and my vast system of clandestine factories and workshops to an astonished world. That is to say, I exposed the nineteenth century to the inspection of the sixth.

Well, it is always a good plan to follow up an advantage promptly. The knights were temporarily down, but if I would keep them so I must just simply paralyze them—nothing short of that would answer. You see, I was "bluffing" that last time in the field; it would be natural for them to work around to that conclusion, if I gave them a chance. So I must not give them time; and I didn't.

I renewed my challenge, engraved it on brass, posted it up where any priest could read it to them, and also kept it standing in the advertising columns of the paper.

I not only renewed it, but added to its proportions. I said, name the day, and I would take fifty assistants and stand up *against the massed chivalry of the whole earth and destroy it.*

I was not bluffing this time. I meant what I said; I could do what I promised. There wasn't any way to misunderstand the language of that challenge. Even the dullest of the chivalry perceived that this was a plain case of "put up, or shut up." They were wise and did the latter. In all the next three years they gave me no trouble worth mentioning.

Consider the three years sped. Now look around on England. A happy and prosperous country, and strangely altered. Schools everywhere, and several colleges; a number of pretty good newspapers. Even authorship was taking a start; Sir Dinadan the Humorist was first in the field, with a volume of grey-headed jokes which I had been familiar with during thirteen centuries. If he had left out that old rancid one about the lecturer I wouldn't have said anything; but I couldn't stand that one. I suppressed the book and hanged the author.

Slavery was dead and gone; all men were equal before the law; taxation had been equalized. The telegraph, the telephone, the phonograph, the typewriter, the sewing-machine, and all the thousand willing and handy servants of steam and electricity were working their way into favour. We had a steamboat or two on the Thames, we had steam warships, and the beginnings of a steam commercial marine; I was getting ready to send out an expedition to discover America.

We were building several lines of railway, and our line from Camelot to London was already finished and in operation. I was shrewd enough to make all offices connected with the passenger service places of high and distinguished honour. My idea was to attract the chivalry and nobility, and make them useful and keep them out of mischief. The plan worked very well, the competition for the places was hot. The conductor of the 4.33 express was a duke; there wasn't a passenger conductor on the line below the degree of earl. They were good men, every one, but they had two defects which I couldn't cure, and so had to wink at: they wouldn't lay aside their armor, and they would "knock down" fare—I mean rob the company.

There was hardly a knight in all the land who wasn't in some useful employment. They were going from end to end of the country in all manner of useful missionary capacities; their penchant for wandering, and their experience in it, made them altogether the most effective spreaders of civilization we had. They went clothed in steel and equipped with sword and lance and battle-axe, and if they couldn't persuade a person to try a sewing-machine on the installment plan, or a melodeon, or a barbed-wire fence, or a prohibition journal, or any of the other thousand and one things they canvassed for, they removed him and passed on.

I was very happy. Things were working steadily toward a secretly longed-for point. You see, I had two schemes in my head which were the vastest of all my projects. The one was to overthrow the Catholic Church and set up the Protestant faith on its ruins—not as an Established Church, but a go-as-you-please one; and the other project was to get a decree issued by and by, commanding that upon Arthur's death unlimited suffrage should be introduced, and given to men and women alike—at any rate to all men, wise or unwise, and to all mothers who at middle age should be found to know nearly as much as their sons at twenty-one. Arthur was good for thirty years yet, he being about my own age—that is to say, forty—and I believed that in that time I could easily have the active part of the population of that day ready and eager for an event which should be the first of its kind in the history of the world—a rounded and complete governmental revolution without bloodshed. The result to be a republic. Well, I may as well confess, though I do feel ashamed when I think of it: I was beginning to have a base hankering to be its first president myself. Yes, there was more or less human nature in me; I found that out.

Clarence was with me as concerned the revolution, but in a modified way. His idea was a republic, without privileged orders, but with a hereditary royal family at the head of it instead of an elective chief magistrate. He believed that no nation that had ever known the joy of worshiping a royal family could ever be robbed of it and not fade away and die of melancholy. I urged that kings were dangerous. He said, then have cats. He was sure that a royal family of cats would answer every purpose. They would be as useful as any other royal family, they would know as much, they would have the same virtues and the same treacheries, the same disposition to get up shindies with other royal cats, they would be laughably vain and absurd and never know it, they would be wholly inexpensive; finally, they would have as sound a divine right as any other royal house, and "Tom VII, or Tom XI, or Tom XIV by the grace of God King," would sound as well as it would when applied to the ordinary royal tomcat with tights on. "And as a rule," said he, in his neat modern English, "the character of these cats would be considerably above the character of the average king, and this would be an immense moral advantage to the nation, for the reason that a nation always models its morals after its monarch's. The worship of royalty being founded in unreason, these graceful and harmless cats would easily become as sacred as any other royalties, and indeed more so, because it would presently be noticed that they hanged nobody, beheaded nobody, imprisoned nobody, inflicted no cruelties or injustices of any sort, and so must be worthy of a deeper love and reverence than the customary human king, and would certainly get it. The eyes of the whole harried world would soon be fixed upon this humane and gentle system, and royal butchers would presently begin to disappear; their subjects would fill the vacancies with catlings from our own royal house; we should become a factory; we should supply the thrones of the world; within forty years all Europe would be governed by cats, and we should furnish the cats. The reign of universal peace would begin then, to end no more forever. . . . *Me-e-e-yow-ow-ow-ow—fzt!—wow!*"

Hang him, I supposed he was in earnest, and was beginning to be persuaded by him, until he exploded that cat-howl and startled me almost out of my clothes. But he never could be in earnest. He didn't know what it was. He had pictured a distinct and perfectly rational and feasible improvement upon constitutional monarchy, but he was too feather-headed to know it, or care anything about it, either. I was going to give him a scolding, but Sandy came flying in at that moment, wild with terror, and so choked with sobs that for a minute she could not get her voice. I ran and took her in my arms, and lavished caresses upon her and said, beseechingly:

"Speak, darling, speak! What is it?"

Her head fell limp upon my bosom, and she gasped, almost inaudibly:

"*Hello-Central!*"

"Quick!" I shouted to Clarence; "telephone the king's homeopath to come!"

In two minutes I was kneeling by the child's crib, and Sandy was dispatching servants here, there, and everywhere, all over the palace. I took in the situation almost at a glance—membranous croup! I bent down and whispered:

"Wake up, sweetheart! Hello-Central."

She opened her soft eyes languidly, and made out to say:

"Papa."

That was a comfort. She was far from dead yet. I sent for preparations of sulphur, I rousted out the croup-kettle myself; for I don't sit down and wait for doctors when Sandy or the child is sick. I knew how to nurse both of them, and had had experience. This little chap had lived in my arms a good part of its small life, and often I could soothe away its troubles and get it to laugh through the tear-dews on its eye-lashes when even its mother couldn't.

Sir Launcelot, in his richest armor, came striding along the great hall now on his way to the stock-board; he was president of the stock-board, and occupied the Siege Perilous, which he had bought of Sir Galahad; for the stock-board consisted of the Knights of the Round Table, and they used the Round Table for business purposes now. Seats at it were worth—well, you would never believe the figure, so it is no use to state it. Sir Launcelot was a bear, and he had put up a corner in one of the new lines, and was just getting ready to squeeze the shorts today; but what of that? He was the same old Launcelot, and when he glanced in as he was passing the door and found out that his pet was sick, that was enough for him; bulls and bears might fight it out their own way for all him, he would come right in here and stand by little Hello-Central for all he was worth. And that was what he did. He shied his helmet into the corner, and in half a minute he had a new wick in the alcohol lamp and was firing up on the croup-kettle. By this time Sandy had built a blanket canopy over the crib, and everything was ready.

Sir Launcelot got up steam, he and I loaded up the kettle with unslaked lime and carbolic acid, with a touch of lactic acid added thereto, then filled the thing up with water and inserted the steam-spout under the canopy. Everything was shipshape now, and we sat down on either side of the crib to stand our watch. Sandy was so grateful and so comforted that she charged a couple of church-wardens with willow-bark and sumach-tobacco for us, and told us to smoke as much as we pleased, it couldn't get under the canopy, and she was used to smoke, being the first lady in the land who had ever seen a cloud blown. Well, there couldn't be a more contented or comfortable sight than Sir Launcelot in his noble armor sitting in gracious serenity at the end of a yard of snowy church-warden. He was a beautiful man, a lovely man, and was just intended to make a wife and children happy. But, of course Guenever—however, it's no use to cry over what's done and can't be helped.

Well, he stood watch-and-watch with me, right straight through, for three days and nights, till the child was out of danger; then he took her up in his great arms and kissed her, with his plumes falling about her golden head, then laid her softly in Sandy's lap again and took his stately way down the vast hall, between the ranks of admiring men-at-arms and menials, and so disappeared. And no instinct warned me that I should never look upon him again in this world! Lord, what a world of heartbreak it is.

The doctors said we must take the child away, if we would coax her back to health and strength again. And she must have sea-air. So we took a man-of-war, and a suite of two hundred and sixty persons, and went cruising about, and after a fortnight of this we stepped ashore on the French coast, and the doctors thought it would be a good idea to make something of a stay there. The little king of that region offered us his hospitalities, and we were glad to accept. If he had had as many conveniences as he lacked, we should have been plenty comfortable enough; even as it was, we made out very well, in his queer old castle, by the help of comforts and luxuries from the ship.

At the end of a month I sent the vessel home for fresh supplies, and for news. We expected her back in three or four days. She would bring me, along with other news, the result of a certain experiment which I had been starting. It was a project of mine to replace the tournament with something which might furnish an escape for the extra steam of the chivalry, keep those bucks entertained and out of mischief, and at the same time preserve the best thing in them, which was their hardy spirit of emulation. I had had a choice band of them in private training for some time, and the date was now arriving for their first public effort.

This experiment was baseball. In order to give the thing vogue from the start, and place it out of the reach of criticism, I chose my nines by rank, not capacity. There wasn't a knight in either team who wasn't a sceptered sovereign. As for material of this sort, there was a glut of it always around Arthur. You couldn't throw a brick in any direction and not cripple a king. Of course, I couldn't get these people to leave off their armor; they wouldn't do that when they bathed. They consented to differentiate the armor so that a body could tell one team from the other, but that was the most they would do. So, one of the teams wore chain-mail ulsters, and the other wore plate-armor made of my new Bessemer steel. Their practice in the field was the most fantastic thing I ever saw. Being ball-proof, they never skipped out of the way, but stood still and took the result; when a Bessemer was at the bat and a ball hit him, it would bound a hundred and fifty yards sometimes. And when a man was running, and threw himself on his stomach to slide to his base, it was like an iron-clad coming into port. At first I appointed men of no rank to act as umpires, but I had to discontinue that. These people were no easier to please than other nines. The umpire's first decision was usually his last; they broke him in two with a bat, and his friends toted him home on a shutter. When it was noticed that no umpire ever survived a game, umpiring got to be unpopular. So I was obliged to appoint somebody whose rank and lofty position under the government would protect him.

Here are the names of the nines:

Bessemers	Ulsters
King Arthur.	Emperor Lucius.
King Lot of Lothian.	King Logris.
King of Northgalis.	King Marhalt of Ireland.
King Marsil.	King Morganore.
King of Little Britain.	King Mark of Cornwall.
King Labor.	King Nentres of Garlot.
King Pellam of Listengese.	King Meliodas of Liones.
King Bagdemagus.	King of the Lake.
King Tolleme la Feintes.	The Sowdan of Syria.
□mpire□ Clarence.	

The first public game would certainly draw fifty thousand people; and for solid fun would be worth going around the world to see. □verything would be favourable; it was balmy and beautiful spring weather now, and □ ature was all tailored out in her new clothes.

41

The Interdict

However, my attention was suddenly snatched from such matters; our child began to lose ground again, and we had to go to sitting up with her, her case became so serious. We couldn't bear to allow anybody to help in this service, so we two stood watch-and-watch, day in and day out. Ah, Sandy, what a right heart she had, how simple, and genuine, and good she was! She was a flawless wife and mother; and yet I had married her for no other particular reasons, except that by the customs of chivalry she was my property until some knight should win her from me in the field. She had hunted Britain over for me; had found me at the hanging-bout outside of London, and had straightway resumed her old place at my side in the placidest way and as of right. I was a New Englander, and in my opinion this sort of partnership would compromise her, sooner or later. She couldn't see how, but I cut argument short and we had a wedding.

Now I didn't know I was drawing a prize, yet that was what I did draw. Within the twelvemonth I became her worshiper; and ours was the dearest and perfectest comradeship that ever was. People talk about beautiful friendships between two persons of the same sex. What is the best of that sort, as compared with the friendship of man and wife, where the best impulses and highest ideals of both are the same? There is no place for comparison between the two friendships; the one is earthly, the other divine.

In my dreams, along at first, I still wandered thirteen centuries away, and my unsatisfied spirit went calling and harking all up and down the unreplying vacancies of a vanished world. Many a time Sandy heard that imploring cry come from my lips in my sleep. With a grand magnanimity she saddled that cry of mine upon our child, conceiving it to be the name of some lost darling of mine. It touched me to tears, and it also nearly knocked me off my feet, too, when she smiled up in my face for an earned reward, and played her quaint and pretty surprise upon me:

"The name of one who was dear to thee is here preserved, here made holy, and the music of it will abide alway in our ears. Now thou'lt kiss me, as knowing the name I have given the child."

But I didn't know it, all the same. I hadn't an idea in the world; but it would have been cruel to confess it and spoil her pretty game; so I never let on, but said:

"Yes, I know, sweetheart—how dear and good it is of you, too! But I want to hear these lips of yours, which are also mine, utter it first—then its music will be perfect."

Pleased to the marrow, she murmured:

"*Hello-Central!*"

"Hello-Central!"

I didn't laugh—I am always thankful for that—but the strain ruptured every cartilage in me, and for weeks afterward I could hear my bones clack when I walked. She never found out her mistake. The first time she heard that form of salute used at the telephone she was surprised, and not pleased; but I told her I had given order for it: that henceforth and forever the telephone must always be invoked with that reverent formality, in perpetual honour and remembrance of my lost friend and her small namesake. This was not true. But it answered.

Well, during two weeks and a half we watched by the crib, and in our deep solicitude we were unconscious of any world outside of that sickroom. Then our reward came: the center of the universe turned the corner and began to mend. Grateful? It isn't the term. There *isn't* any term for it. You know that yourself, if you've watched your child through the Valley of the Shadow and seen it come back to life and sweep night out of the earth with one all-illuminating smile that you could cover with your hand.

Why, we were back in this world in one instant! Then we looked the same startled thought into each other's eyes at the same moment; more than two weeks gone, and that ship not back yet!

In another minute I appeared in the presence of my train. They had been steeped in troubled bodings all this time—their faces showed it. I called an escort and we galloped five miles to a hilltop overlooking the sea. Where was my great commerce that so lately had made these glistening expanses populous and beautiful with its white-winged flocks? Vanished, every one! Not a sail, from verge to verge, not a smoke-bank—just a dead and empty solitude, in place of all that brisk and breezy life.

I went swiftly back, saying not a word to anybody. I told Sandy this ghastly news. We could imagine no explanation that would begin to explain. Had there been an invasion? an earthquake? a pestilence? Had the nation been swept out of existence? But guessing was profitless. I must go—at once. I borrowed the king's navy—a "ship" no bigger than a steam launch—and was soon ready.

The parting—ah, yes, that was hard. As I was devouring the child with last kisses, it brisked up and jabbered out its vocabulary!—the first time in more than two weeks, and it made fools of us for joy. The darling mispronunciations of childhood!—dear me, there's no music that can touch it; and how one grieves when it wastes away and dissolves into correctness, knowing it will never visit his bereaved ear again. Well, how good it was to be able to carry that gracious memory away with me!

I approached England the next morning, with the wide highway of salt water all to myself. There were ships in the harbor, at Dover, but they were naked as to sails, and there was no sign of life about them. It was Sunday; yet at Canterbury the streets were empty; strangest of all, there was not even a priest in sight, and no stroke of a bell fell upon my ear. The mournfulness of death was everywhere. I couldn't understand it. At last, in the further edge of that town I saw a small funeral procession—just a family and a few friends following a coffin—no priest; a funeral without bell, book, or candle; there was a church there close at hand, but they passed it by weeping, and did not enter it; I glanced up at the belfry, and there hung the bell, shrouded in black, and its tongue tied back. Now I knew! Now I understood the stupendous calamity that had overtaken England. Invasion? Invasion is a triviality to it. It was the *Interdict*!

I asked no questions; I didn't need to ask any. The Church had struck; the thing for me to do was to get into a disguise, and go warily. One of my servants gave me a suit of clothes, and when we were safe beyond the town I put them on, and from that time I traveled alone; I could not risk the embarrassment of company.

A miserable journey. A desolate silence everywhere. Even in London itself. Traffic had ceased; men did not talk or laugh, or go in groups, or even in couples; they moved aimlessly about, each man by himself, with his head down, and woe and terror at his heart. The Tower showed recent war-scars. Verily, much had been happening.

Of course, I meant to take the train for Camelot. Train! Why, the station was as vacant as a cavern. I moved on. The journey to Camelot was a repetition of what I had already seen. The Monday and the Tuesday differed in no way from the Sunday. I arrived far in the night. From being the best electric-lighted town in the kingdom and the most like a recumbent sun of anything you ever saw, it was become simply a blot—a blot upon darkness—that is to say, it was darker and solider than the rest of the darkness, and so you could see it a little better; it made me feel as if maybe it was symbolical—a sort of sign that the Church was going to *keep* the upper hand now, and snuff out all my beautiful civilization just like that. I found no life stirring in the somber streets. I groped my way with a heavy heart. The vast castle loomed black upon the hilltop, not a spark visible about it. The drawbridge was down, the great gate stood wide, I entered without challenge, my own heels making the only sound I heard—and it was sepulchral enough, in those huge vacant courts.

42

War!

I found Clarence alone in his quarters, drowned in melancholy; and in place of the electric light, he had reinstituted the ancient rag-lamp, and sat there in a grisly twilight with all curtains drawn tight. He sprang up and rushed for me eagerly, saying:

"Oh, it's worth a billion milrays to look upon a live person again!"

He knew me as easily as if I hadn't been disguised at all. Which frightened me; one may easily believe that.

"Quick, now, tell me the meaning of this fearful disaster," I said. "How did it come about?"

"Well, if there hadn't been any Queen Guenever, it wouldn't have come so early; but it would have come, anyway. It would have come on your own account by and by; by luck, it happened to come on the queen's."

"*And* Sir Launcelot's?"

"Just so."

"Give me the details."

"I reckon you will grant that during some years there has been only one pair of eyes in these kingdoms that has not been looking steadily askance at the queen and Sir Launcelot—"

"Yes, King Arthur's."

"—and only one heart that was without suspicion—"

"Yes—the king's; a heart that isn't capable of thinking evil of a friend."

"Well, the king might have gone on, still happy and unsuspecting, to the end of his days, but for one of your modern improvements—the stock-board. When you left, three miles of the London, Canterbury and Dover were ready for the rails, and also ready and ripe for manipulation in the stock-market. It was wildcat, and everybody knew it. The stock was for sale at a give-away. What does Sir Launcelot do, but—"

"Yes, I know; he quietly picked up nearly all of it for a song; then he bought about twice as much more, deliverable upon call; and he was about to call when I left."

"Very well, he did call. The boys couldn't deliver. Oh, he had them—

and he just settled his grip and squeezed them. They were laughing in their sleeves over their smartness in selling stock to him at 15 and 16 and along there that wasn't worth 10. Well, when they had laughed long enough on that side of their mouths, they rested-up that side by shifting the laugh to the other side. That was when they compromised with the Invincible at 283!"

"Good land!"

"He skinned them alive, and they deserved it—anyway, the whole kingdom rejoiced. Well, among the flayed were Sir Agravaine and Sir Mordred, nephews to the king. End of the first act. Act second, scene first, an apartment in Carlisle castle, where the court had gone for a few days' hunting. Persons present, the whole tribe of the king's nephews. Mordred and Agravaine propose to call the guileless Arthur's attention to Guenever and Sir Launcelot. Sir Gawaine, Sir Gareth, and Sir Gaheris will have nothing to do with it. A dispute ensues, with loud talk; in the midst of it enter the king. Mordred and Agravaine spring their devastating tale upon him. *Tableau.* A trap is laid for Launcelot, by the king's command, and Sir Launcelot walks into it. He made it sufficiently uncomfortable for the ambushed witnesses—to wit, Mordred, Agravaine, and twelve knights of lesser rank, for he killed every one of them but Mordred; but of course that couldn't straighten matters between Launcelot and the king, and didn't."

"Oh, dear, only one thing could result—I see that. War, and the knights of the realm divided into a king's party and a Sir Launcelot's party."

"Yes—that was the way of it. The king sent the queen to the stake, proposing to purify her with fire. Launcelot and his knights rescued her, and in doing it slew certain good old friends of yours and mine—in fact, some of the best we ever had; to wit, Sir Belias le Orgulous, Sir Segwarides, Sir Griflet le Fils de Dieu, Sir Brandiles, Sir Aglovale—"

"Oh, you tear out my heartstrings."

"—wait, I'm not done yet—Sir Tor, Sir Gauter, Sir Gillimer—"

"The very best man in my subordinate nine. What a handy right-fielder he was!"

"—Sir Reynold's three brothers, Sir Damus, Sir Priamus, Sir Kay the Stranger—"

"My peerless short-stop! I've seen him catch a daisy-cutter in his teeth. Come, I can't stand this!"

"—Sir Driant, Sir Lambegus, Sir Herminde, Sir Pertilope, Sir Perimones, and—whom do you think?"

"Rush! Go on."

"Sir Gaheris, and Sir Gareth—both!"

"Oh, incredible! Their love for Launcelot was indestructible."

"Well, it was an accident. They were simply onlookers; they were unarmed, and were merely there to witness the queen's punishment. Sir Launcelot smote down whoever came in the way of his blind fury, and he killed these without noticing who they were. Here is an instantaneous photograph one of our boys got of the battle; it's for sale on every news-stand. There—the figures nearest the queen are Sir Launcelot with his sword up, and Sir Gareth gasping his latest breath. You can catch the agony in the queen's face through the curling smoke. It's a rattling battle-picture."

"Indeed, it is. We must take good care of it; its historical value is incalculable. Go on."

"Well, the rest of the tale is just war, pure and simple. Launcelot retreated to his town and castle of Joyous Gard, and gathered there a great following of knights. The king, with a great host, went there, and there was desperate fighting during several days, and, as a result, all the plain around was paved with corpses and cast-iron. Then the Church patched up a peace between Arthur and Launcelot and the queen and everybody—everybody but Sir Gawaine. He was bitter about the slaying of his brothers, Gareth and Gaheris, and would not be appeased. He notified Launcelot to get him thence, and make swift preparation, and look to be soon attacked. So Launcelot sailed to his Duchy of Guienne with his following, and Gawaine soon followed with an army, and he beguiled Arthur to go with him. Arthur left the kingdom in Sir Mordred's hands until you should return—"

"Ah—a king's customary wisdom!"

"Yes. Sir Mordred set himself at once to work to make his kingship permanent. He was going to marry Guenever, as a first move; but she fled and shut herself up in the Tower of London. Mordred attacked; the Bishop of Canterbury dropped down on him with the Interdict. The king returned; Mordred fought him at Dover, at Canterbury, and again at Barham Down. Then there was talk of peace and a composition. Terms, Mordred to have Cornwall and Kent during Arthur's life, and the whole kingdom afterward."

"Well, upon my word! My dream of a republic to *be* a dream, and so remain."

"Yes. The two armies lay near Salisbury. Gawaine—Gawaine's head is at Dover Castle, he fell in the fight there—Gawaine appeared to Arthur in a dream, at least his ghost did, and warned him to refrain from conflict for a month, let the delay cost what it might. But battle was precipitated by an accident. Arthur had given order that if a sword was raised during the consultation over the proposed treaty with Mordred, sound the trumpet and fall on! for he had no confidence in Mordred. Mordred had given a similar order to *his* people. Well, by and by an adder bit a knight's heel; the knight forgot all about the order, and made a slash at the adder with his sword. Inside of half a minute those two prodigious hosts came together with a crash! They butchered away all day. Then the king—however, we have started something fresh since you left—our paper has."

"No? What is that?"

"War correspondence!"

"Why, that's good."

"Yes, the paper was booming right along, for the Interdict made no impression, got no grip, while the war lasted. I had war correspondents with both armies. I will finish that battle by reading you what one of the boys says:

> *'Then the king looked about him, and then was he ware of all his host and of all his good knights were left no more on live but two knights, that was Sir Lucan de Butlere, and his brother Sir Bedivere: and they were full sore wounded. Jesu mercy, said the king, where are all my noble knights becomen? Alas that ever I should see this doleful day. For now, said Arthur, I am come to mine end. But would to God that I wist where were that traitor Sir Mordred, that hath caused all this mischief. Then was King Arthur ware where Sir Mordred leaned upon his sword among a great heap of dead men. Now give me my spear, said Arthur unto Sir Lucan, for yonder I have espied the traitor that all this woe hath wrought. Sir, let him be, said Sir Lucan, for he is unhappy; and if ye pass this unhappy day, ye shall be right well revenged upon him. Good lord, remember ye of your night's dream, and what the spirit of Sir Gawaine told you this night, yet God of his great goodness hath preserved you hitherto. Therefore, for God's sake, my lord, leave off by this. For blessed be God ye have won the field: for here we be three on live, and with Sir Mordred is none on live. And if ye leave off now, this wicked day of destiny is past. Tide me death, betide me life, saith the king, now I see him yonder alone, he shall never escape mine hands, for at a better avail shall I never have him. God speed you well,*

said Sir Bedivere. Then the king gat his spear in both his hands, and ran toward Sir Mordred crying, Traitor, now is thy death day come. And when Sir Mordred heard Sir Arthur, he ran until him with his sword drawn in his hand. And then King Arthur smote Sir Mordred under the shield, with a foin of his spear throughout the body more than a fathom. And when Sir Mordred felt that he had his death's wound, he thrust himself, with the might that he had, up to the butt of King Arthur's spear. And right so he smote his father Arthur with his sword holden in both his hands, on the side of the head, that the sword pierced the helmet and the brain-pan, and therewithal Sir Mordred fell stark dead to the earth. And the noble Arthur fell in a swoon to the earth, and there he swooned oft-times—'"

"That is a good piece of war correspondence, Clarence; you are a first-rate newspaper man. Well—is the king all right? Did he get well?"

"Poor soul, no. He is dead."

I was utterly stunned; it had not seemed to me that any wound could be mortal to him.

"And the queen, Clarence?"

"She is a nun, in Almesbury."

"What changes! and in such a short while. It is inconceivable. What next, I wonder?"

"I can tell you what next."

"Well?"

"Stake our lives and stand by them!"

"What do you mean by that?"

"The Church is master now. The Interdict included you with Mordred; it is not to be removed while you remain alive. The clans are gathering. The Church has gathered all the knights that are left alive, and as soon as you are discovered we shall have business on our hands."

"Stuff! With our deadly scientific war-material; with our hosts of trained—"

"Save your breath—we haven't sixty faithful left!"

"What are you saying? Our schools, our colleges, our vast workshops, our—"

"When those knights come, those establishments will empty themselves and go over to the enemy. Did you think you had educated the superstition out of those people?"

"I certainly did think it."

"Well, then, you may unthink it. They stood every strain easily—until the Interdict. Since then, they merely put on a bold outside—at heart they are quaking. Make up your mind to it—when the armies come, the mask will fall."

"It's hard news. We are lost. They will turn our own science against us."

"No they won't."

"Why?"

"Because I and a handful of the faithful have blocked that game. I'll tell you what I've done, and what moved me to it. Smart as you are, the Church was smarter. It was the Church that sent you cruising—through her servants, the doctors."

"Clarence!"

"It is the truth. I know it. Every officer of your ship was the Church's picked servant, and so was every man of the crew."

"Oh, come!"

"It is just as I tell you. I did not find out these things at once, but I found them out finally. Did you send me verbal information, by the commander of the ship, to the effect that upon his return to you, with supplies, you were going to leave Cadiz—"

"Cadiz! I haven't been at Cadiz at all!"

"—going to leave Cadiz and cruise in distant seas indefinitely, for the health of your family? Did you send me that word?"

"Of course not. I would have written, wouldn't I?"

"Naturally. I was troubled and suspicious. When the commander sailed again I managed to ship a spy with him. I have never heard of vessel or spy since. I gave myself two weeks to hear from you in. Then I resolved to send a ship to Cadiz. There was a reason why I didn't."

"What was that?"

"Our navy had suddenly and mysteriously disappeared! Also, as suddenly and as mysteriously, the railway and telegraph and telephone service ceased, the men all deserted, poles were cut down, the Church laid a ban upon the electric light! I had to be up and doing—and straight off. Your life was safe—nobody in these kingdoms but Merlin would venture to touch such a magician as you without ten thousand men at his back—I had nothing to think of but how to put preparations in the best trim against your coming. I felt safe myself—nobody would be anxious to touch a pet of yours. So this is what I did. From our various works I selected all the men—boys I mean—

whose faithfulness under whatsoever pressure I could swear to, and I called them together secretly and gave them their instructions. There are fifty-two of them; none younger than fourteen, and none above seventeen years old."

"Why did you select boys?"

"Because all the others were born in an atmosphere of superstition and reared in it. It is in their blood and bones. We imagined we had educated it out of them; they thought so, too; the Interdict woke them up like a thunderclap! It revealed them to themselves, and it revealed them to me, too. With boys it was different. Such as have been under our training from seven to ten years have had no acquaintance with the Church's terrors, and it was among these that I found my fifty-two. As a next move, I paid a private visit to that old cave of Merlin's—not the small one—the big one—"

"Yes, the one where we secretly established our first great electric plant when I was projecting a miracle."

"Just so. And as that miracle hadn't become necessary then, I thought it might be a good idea to utilize the plant now. I've provisioned the cave for a siege—"

"A good idea, a first-rate idea."

"I think so. I placed four of my boys there as a guard—inside, and out of sight. Nobody was to be hurt—while outside; but any attempt to enter—well, we said just let anybody try it! Then I went out into the hills and uncovered and cut the secret wires which connected your bedroom with the wires that go to the dynamite deposits under all our vast factories, mills, workshops, magazines, etc., and about midnight I and my boys turned out and connected that wire with the cave, and nobody but you and I suspects where the other end of it goes to. We laid it under ground, of course, and it was all finished in a couple of hours or so. We sha'n't have to leave our fortress now when we want to blow up our civilization."

"It was the right move—and the natural one; military necessity, in the changed condition of things. Well, what changes *have* come! We expected to be besieged in the palace some time or other, but—however, go on."

"Next, we built a wire fence."

"Wire fence?"

"Yes. You dropped the hint of it yourself, two or three years ago."

"Oh, I remember—the time the Church tried her strength against us the first time, and presently thought it wise to wait for a hopefuller season. Well, how have you arranged the fence?"

"I start twelve immensely strong wires—naked, not insulated—from a big dynamo in the cave—dynamo with no brushes except a positive and a negative one—"

"Yes, that's right."

"The wires go out from the cave and fence in a circle of level ground a hundred yards in diameter; they make twelve independent fences, ten feet apart—that is to say, twelve circles within circles—and their ends come into the cave again."

"Right; go on."

"The fences are fastened to heavy oaken posts only three feet apart, and these posts are sunk five feet in the ground."

"That is good and strong."

"Yes. The wires have no ground-connection outside of the cave. They go out from the positive brush of the dynamo; there is a ground-connection through the negative brush; the other ends of the wire return to the cave, and each is grounded independently."

"No, no, that won't do!"

"Why?"

"It's too expensive—uses up force for nothing. You don't want any ground-connection except the one through the negative brush. The other end of every wire must be brought back into the cave and fastened independently, and *without* any ground-connection. Now, then, observe the economy of it. A cavalry charge hurls itself against the fence; you are using no power, you are spending no money, for there is only one ground-connection till those horses come against the wire; the moment they touch it they form a connection with the negative brush *through the ground*, and drop dead. Don't you see?—you are using no energy until it is needed; your lightning is there, and ready, like the load in a gun; but it isn't costing you a cent till you touch it off. Oh, yes, the single ground-connection—"

"Of course! I don't know how I overlooked that. It's not only cheaper, but it's more effectual than the other way, for if wires break or get tangled, no harm is done."

"No, especially if we have a telltale in the cave and disconnect the broken wire. Well, go on. The gatlings?"

"Yes—that's arranged. In the center of the inner circle, on a spacious platform six feet high, I've grouped a battery of thirteen gatling guns, and provided plenty of ammunition."

"That's it. They command every approach, and when the Church's knights arrive, there's going to be music. The brow of the precipice over the cave—"

"I've got a wire fence there, and a gatling. They won't drop any rocks down on us."

"Well, and the glass-cylinder dynamite torpedoes?"

"That's attended to. It's the prettiest garden that was ever planted. It's a belt forty feet wide, and goes around the outer fence—distance between it and the fence one hundred yards—kind of neutral ground that space is. There isn't a single square yard of that whole belt but is equipped with a torpedo. We laid them on the surface of the ground, and sprinkled a layer of sand over them. It's an innocent looking garden, but you let a man start in to hoe it once, and you'll see."

"You tested the torpedoes?"

"Well, I was going to, but—"

"But what? Why, it's an immense oversight not to apply a—"

"Test? Yes, I know; but they're all right; I laid a few in the public road beyond our lines and they've been tested."

"Oh, that alters the case. Who did it?"

"A Church committee."

"How kind!"

"Yes. They came to command us to make submission. You see they didn't really come to test the torpedoes; that was merely an incident."

"Did the committee make a report?"

"Yes, they made one. You could have heard it a mile."

"Unanimous?"

"That was the nature of it. After that I put up some signs, for the protection of future committees, and we have had no intruders since."

"Clarence, you've done a world of work, and done it perfectly."

"We had plenty of time for it; there wasn't any occasion for hurry."

We sat silent awhile, thinking. Then my mind was made up, and I said:

"Yes, everything is ready; everything is shipshape, no detail is wanting. I know what to do now."

"So do I; sit down and wait."

"No, *sir*! rise up and *strike*!"

"Do you mean it?"

"Yes, indeed! The *de*fensive isn't in my line, and the *of*fensive is. That is, when I hold a fair hand—two-thirds as good a hand as the enemy. Oh, yes, we'll rise up and strike; that's our game."

"A hundred to one you are right. When does the performance begin?"

"*Now!* We'll proclaim the Republic."

"Well, that *will* precipitate things, sure enough!"

"It will make them buzz, I tell you! England will be a hornets' nest before noon tomorrow, if the Church's hand hasn't lost its cunning—and we know it hasn't. Now you write and I'll dictate thus:

"PROCLAMATION

"BE IT KNOWN UNTO ALL. Whereas the king having died and left no heir, it becomes my duty to continue the executive authority vested in me, until a government shall have been created and set in motion. The monarchy has lapsed, it no longer exists. By consequence, all political power has reverted to its original source, the people of the nation. With the monarchy, its several adjuncts died also; wherefore there is no longer a nobility, no longer a privileged class, no longer an Established Church; all men are become exactly equal; they are upon one common level, and religion is free. A Republic is hereby proclaimed, as being the natural estate of a nation when other authority has ceased. It is the duty of the British people to meet together immediately, and by their votes elect representatives and deliver into their hands the government."

I signed it "The Boss," and dated it from Merlin's Cave. Clarence said—

"Why, that tells where we are, and invites them to call right away."

"That is the idea. We *strike*—by the Proclamation—then it's their innings. Now have the thing set up and printed and posted, right off; that is, give the order; then, if you've got a couple of bicycles handy at the foot of the hill, ho for Merlin's Cave!"

"I shall be ready in ten minutes. What a cyclone there is going to be tomorrow when this piece of paper gets to work! . . . It's a pleasant old palace, this is; I wonder if we shall ever again—but never mind about that."

43

The Battle of the Sand Belt

In Merlin's Cave—Clarence and I and fifty-two fresh, bright, well-educated, clean-minded young British boys. At dawn I sent an order to the factories and to all our great works to stop operations and remove all life to a safe distance, as everything was going to be blown up by secret mines, "*and no telling at what moment—therefore, vacate at once.*" These people knew me, and had confidence in my word. They would clear out without waiting to part their hair, and I could take my own time about dating the explosion. You couldn't hire one of them to go back during the century, if the explosion was still impending.

We had a week of waiting. It was not dull for me, because I was writing all the time. During the first three days, I finished turning my old diary into this narrative form; it only required a chapter or so to bring it down to date. The rest of the week I took up in writing letters to my wife. It was always my habit to write to Sandy every day, whenever we were separate, and now I kept up the habit for love of it, and of her, though I couldn't do anything with the letters, of course, after I had written them. But it put in the time, you see, and was almost like talking; it was almost as if I was saying, "Sandy, if you and Hello-Central were here in the cave, instead of only your photographs, what good times we could have!" And then, you know, I could imagine the baby goo-gooing something out in reply, with its fists in its mouth and itself stretched across its mother's lap on its back, and she a-laughing and admiring and worshipping, and now and then tickling under the baby's chin to set it cackling, and then maybe throwing in a word of answer to me herself—and so on and so on—well, don't you know, I could sit there in the cave with my pen, and keep it up, that way, by the hour with them. Why, it was almost like having us all together again.

I had spies out every night, of course, to get news. Every report made things look more and more impressive. The hosts were gathering, gathering; down all the roads and paths of England the knights were riding, and priests rode with them, to hearten these original Crusaders, this being the Church's war. All the nobilities, big and little, were on their way, and all the gentry.

This was all as was expected. We should thin out this sort of folk to such a degree that the people would have nothing to do but just step to the front with their republic and—

Ah, what a donkey I was! Toward the end of the week I began to get this large and disenchanting fact through my head: that the mass of the nation had swung their caps and shouted for the republic for about one day, and there an end! The Church, the nobles, and the gentry then turned one grand, all-disapproving frown upon them and shriveled them into sheep! From that moment the sheep had begun to gather to the fold—that is to say, the camps—and offer their valueless lives and their valuable wool to the "righteous cause." Why, even the very men who had lately been slaves were in the "righteous cause," and glorifying it, praying for it, sentimentally slabbering over it, just like all the other commoners. Imagine such human muck as this; conceive of this folly!

Yes, it was now "Death to the Republic!" everywhere—not a dissenting voice. All England was marching against us! Truly, this was more than I had bargained for.

I watched my fifty-two boys narrowly; watched their faces, their walk, their unconscious attitudes: for all these are a language—a language given us purposely that it may betray us in times of emergency, when we have secrets which we want to keep. I knew that that thought would keep saying itself over and over again in their minds and hearts, *All England is marching against us!* and ever more strenuously imploring attention with each repetition, ever more sharply realizing itself to their imaginations, until even in their sleep they would find no rest from it, but hear the vague and flitting creatures of the dreams say, *All England—All England!—is marching against you!* I knew all this would happen; I knew that ultimately the pressure would become so great that it would compel utterance; therefore, I must be ready with an answer at that time—an answer well chosen and tranquilizing.

I was right. The time came. They *had* to speak. Poor lads, it was pitiful to see, they were so pale, so worn, so troubled. At first their spokesman could hardly find voice or words; but he presently got both. This is what he said—and he put it in the neat modern English taught him in my schools:

"We have tried to forget what we are—English boys! We have tried to put reason before sentiment, duty before love; our minds approve, but our hearts reproach us. While apparently it was only the nobility, only the gentry, only the twenty-five or thirty thousand knights left alive out of the late wars, we were of one mind, and undisturbed by any troubling doubt; each and every one of these fifty-two lads who stand here before you, said, 'They have chosen—it is their affair.' But think!—the matter is altered—*All*

England is marching against us! Oh, sir, consider!—reflect!—these people are our people, they are bone of our bone, flesh of our flesh, we love them—do not ask us to destroy our nation!"

Well, it shows the value of looking ahead, and being ready for a thing when it happens. If I hadn't foreseen this thing and been fixed, that boy would have had me!—I couldn't have said a word. But I was fixed. I said:

"My boys, your hearts are in the right place, you have thought the worthy thought, you have done the worthy thing. You are English boys, you will remain English boys, and you will keep that name unsmirched. Give yourselves no further concern, let your minds be at peace. Consider this: while all England is marching against us, who is in the van? Who, by the commonest rules of war, will march in the front? Answer me."

"The mounted host of mailed knights."

"True. They are thirty thousand strong. Acres deep they will march. Now, observe: none but *they* will ever strike the sand-belt! Then there will be an episode! Immediately after, the civilian multitude in the rear will retire, to meet business engagements elsewhere. None but nobles and gentry are knights, and *none but these* will remain to dance to our music after that episode. It is absolutely true that we shall have to fight nobody but these thirty thousand knights. Now speak, and it shall be as you decide. Shall we avoid the battle, retire from the field?"

"No!!!"

The shout was unanimous and hearty.

"Are you—are you—well, afraid of these thirty thousand knights?"

That joke brought out a good laugh, the boys' troubles vanished away, and they went gaily to their posts. Ah, they were a darling fifty-two! As pretty as girls, too.

I was ready for the enemy now. Let the approaching big day come along—it would find us on deck.

The big day arrived on time. At dawn the sentry on watch in the corral came into the cave and reported a moving black mass under the horizon, and a faint sound which he thought to be military music. Breakfast was just ready; we sat down and ate it.

This over, I made the boys a little speech, and then sent out a detail to man the battery, with Clarence in command of it.

The sun rose presently and sent its unobstructed splendours over the land, and we saw a prodigious host moving slowly toward us, with the steady drift and aligned front of a wave of the sea. Nearer and nearer it came, and more and more sublimely imposing became its aspect; yes, all England was there, apparently. Soon we could see the innumerable banners fluttering, and then the sun struck the sea of armor and set it all aflash. Yes, it was a fine sight; I hadn't ever seen anything to beat it.

At last we could make out details. All the front ranks, no telling how many acres deep, were horsemen—plumed knights in armor. Suddenly we heard the blare of trumpets; the slow walk burst into a gallop, and then—well, it was wonderful to see! Down swept that vast horse-shoe wave—it approached the sand-belt—my breath stood still; nearer, nearer—the strip of green turf beyond the yellow belt grew narrow—narrower still—became a mere ribbon in front of the horses—then disappeared under their hoofs. Great Scott! Why, the whole front of that host shot into the sky with a thunder-crash, and became a whirling tempest of rags and fragments; and along the ground lay a thick wall of smoke that hid what was left of the multitude from our sight.

Time for the second step in the plan of campaign! I touched a button, and shook the bones of England loose from her spine!

In that explosion all our noble civilization-factories went up in the air and disappeared from the earth. It was a pity, but it was necessary. We could not afford to let the enemy turn our own weapons against us.

Now ensued one of the dullest quarter-hours I had ever endured. We waited in a silent solitude enclosed by our circles of wire, and by a circle of heavy smoke outside of these. We couldn't see over the wall of smoke, and we couldn't see through it. But at last it began to shred away lazily, and by the end of another quarter-hour the land was clear and our curiosity was enabled to satisfy itself. No living creature was in sight! We now perceived that additions had been made to our defenses. The dynamite had dug a ditch more than a hundred feet wide, all around us, and cast up an embankment some twenty-five feet high on both borders of it. As to destruction of life, it was amazing. Moreover, it was beyond estimate. Of course, we could not *count* the dead, because they did not exist as individuals, but merely as homogeneous protoplasm, with alloys of iron and buttons.

No life was in sight, but necessarily there must have been some wounded in the rear ranks, who were carried off the field under cover of the wall of smoke; there would be sickness among the others—there always is, after an episode like that. But there would be no reinforcements; this was the last stand of the chivalry of England; it was all that was left of the order, after the recent annihilating wars. So I felt quite safe in believing that the utmost force that could for the future be brought against us would be but small; that is, of knights. I therefore issued a congratulatory proclamation to my army in these words:

> SOLDIERS, CHAMPIONS OF HUMAN LIBERTY AND EQUALITY:
>
> *Your General congratulates you! In the pride of his strength and the vanity of his renown, an arrogant enemy came against you. You were ready. The conflict was brief; on your side, glorious. This mighty victory, having been achieved utterly without loss, stands without example in history. So long as the planets shall continue to move in their orbits, the Battle Of The Sand-Belt will not perish out of the memories of men.*
> *THE BOSS.*

I read it well, and the applause I got was very gratifying to me. I then wound up with these remarks:

"The war with the English nation, as a nation, is at an end. The nation has retired from the field and the war. Before it can be persuaded to return, war will have ceased. This campaign is the only one that is going to be fought. It will be brief—the briefest in history. Also the most destructive to life, considered from the standpoint of proportion of casualties to numbers engaged. We are done with the nation; henceforth we deal only with the knights. English knights can be killed, but they cannot be conquered. We know what is before us. While one of these men remains alive, our task is not finished, the war is not ended. We will kill them all." [Loud and long continued applause.]

I picketed the great embankments thrown up around our lines by the dynamite explosion—merely a lookout of a couple of boys to announce the enemy when he should appear again.

Next, I sent an engineer and forty men to a point just beyond our lines on the south, to turn a mountain brook that was there, and bring it within our lines and under our command, arranging it in such a way that I could make instant use of it in an emergency. The forty men were divided into two shifts of twenty each, and were to relieve each other every two hours. In ten hours the work was accomplished.

It was nightfall now, and I withdrew my pickets. The one who had had the northern outlook reported a camp in sight, but visible with the glass only. He also reported that a few knights had been feeling their way toward us, and had driven some cattle across our lines, but that the knights themselves had not come very near. That was what I had been expecting. They were feeling us, you see; they wanted to know if we were going to play that red terror on them again. They would grow bolder in the night, perhaps. I believed I knew what project they would attempt, because it was plainly the thing I would attempt myself if I were in their places and as ignorant as they were. I mentioned it to Clarence.

"I think you are right," said he; "it is the obvious thing for them to try."

"Well, then," I said, "if they do it they are doomed."

"Certainly."

"They won't have the slightest show in the world."

"Of course they won't."

"It's dreadful, Clarence. It seems an awful pity."

The thing disturbed me so that I couldn't get any peace of mind for thinking of it and worrying over it. So, at last, to quiet my conscience, I framed this message to the knights:

> *TO THE HONOURABLE THE COMMANDER OF THE INSURGENT CHIVALRY OF ENGLAND: YOU fight in vain. We know your strength—if one may call it by that name. We know that at the utmost you cannot bring against us above five and twenty thousand knights. Therefore, you have no chance—none whatever. Reflect: we are well equipped, well fortified, we number 54. Fifty-four what? Men? No, minds—the capablest in the world; a force against which*

mere animal might may no more hope to prevail than may the idle waves of the sea hope to prevail against the granite barriers of England. Be advised. We offer you your lives; for the sake of your families, do not reject the gift. We offer you this chance, and it is the last: throw down your arms; surrender unconditionally to the Republic, and all will be forgiven.
(Signed) THE BOSS.

I read it to Clarence, and said I proposed to send it by a flag of truce. He laughed the sarcastic laugh he was born with, and said:

"Somehow it seems impossible for you to ever fully realize what these nobilities are. Now let us save a little time and trouble. Consider me the commander of the knights yonder. Now, then, you are the flag of truce; approach and deliver me your message, and I will give you your answer."

I humoured the idea. I came forward under an imaginary guard of the enemy's soldiers, produced my paper, and read it through. For answer, Clarence struck the paper out of my hand, pursed up a scornful lip and said with lofty disdain:

"Dismember me this animal, and return him in a basket to the base-born knave who sent him; other answer have I none!"

How empty is theory in presence of fact! And this was just fact, and nothing else. It was the thing that would have happened, there was no getting around that. I tore up the paper and granted my mistimed sentimentalities a permanent rest.

Then, to business. I tested the electric signals from the gatling platform to the cave, and made sure that they were all right; I tested and retested those which commanded the fences—these were signals whereby I could break and renew the electric current in each fence independently of the others at will. I placed the brook-connection under the guard and authority of three of my best boys, who would alternate in two-hour watches all night and promptly obey my signal, if I should have occasion to give it—three revolver-shots in quick succession. Sentry-duty was discarded for the night, and the corral left empty of life; I ordered that quiet be maintained in the cave, and the electric lights turned down to a glimmer.

As soon as it was good and dark, I shut off the current from all the fences, and then groped my way out to the embankment bordering our side of the great dynamite ditch. I crept to the top of it and lay there on the slant of the muck to watch. But it was too dark to see anything. As for sounds, there were none. The stillness was death-like. True, there were the usual night-sounds of the country—the whir of night-birds, the buzzing of insects, the barking of distant dogs, the mellow lowing of far-off kine—but these didn't seem to break the stillness, they only intensified it, and added a grucsome melancholy to it into the bargain.

I presently gave up looking, the night shut down so black, but I kept my ears strained to catch the least suspicious sound, for I judged I had only to wait, and I shouldn't be disappointed. However, I had to wait a long time. At last I caught what you may call in distinct glimpses of sound—dulled metallic sound. I pricked up my ears, then, and held my breath, for this was the sort of thing I had been waiting for. This sound thickened, and approached—from toward the north. Presently, I heard it at my own level—the ridge-top of the opposite embankment, a hundred feet or more away. Then I seemed to see a row of black dots appear along that ridge—human heads? I couldn't tell; it mightn't be anything at all; you can't depend on your eyes when your imagination is out of focus. However, the question was soon settled. I heard that metallic noise descending into the great ditch. It augmented fast, it spread all along, and it unmistakably furnished me this fact: an armed host was taking up its quarters in the ditch. Yes, these people were arranging a little surprise party for us. We could expect entertainment about dawn, possibly earlier.

I groped my way back to the corral now; I had seen enough. I went to the platform and signaled to turn the current on to the two inner fences. Then I went into the cave, and found everything satisfactory there—nobody awake but the working-watch. I woke Clarence and told him the great ditch was filling up with men, and that I believed all the knights were coming for us in a body. It was my notion that as soon as dawn approached we could expect the ditch's ambuscaded thousands to swarm up over the embankment and make an assault, and be followed immediately by the rest of their army.

Clarence said:

"They will be wanting to send a scout or two in the dark to make preliminary observations. Why not take the lightning off the outer fences, and give them a chance?"

"I've already done it, Clarence. Did you ever know me to be inhospitable?"

"No, you are a good heart. I want to go and—"

"Be a reception committee? I will go, too."

We crossed the corral and lay down together between the two inside fences. Even the dim light of the cave had disordered our eyesight somewhat, but the focus straightway began to regulate itself and soon it was adjusted for present circumstances. We had had to feel our way before, but we could make out to see the fence posts now. We started a whispered conversation, but suddenly Clarence broke off and said:

"What is that?"

"What is what?"

"That thing yonder."

"What thing—where?"

"There beyond you a little piece—dark something—a dull shape of some kind—against the second fence."

I gazed and he gazed. I said:

"Could it be a man, Clarence?"

"No, I think not. If you notice, it looks a lit—why, it *is* a man!—leaning on the fence."

"I certainly believe it is; let us go and see."

We crept along on our hands and knees until we were pretty close, and then looked up. Yes, it was a man—a dim great figure in armor, standing erect, with both hands on the upper wire—and, of course, there was a smell of burning flesh. Poor fellow, dead as a door-nail, and never knew what hurt him. He stood there like a statue—no motion about him, except that his plumes swished about a little in the night wind. We rose up and looked in through the bars of his visor, but couldn't make out whether we knew him or not—features too dim and shadowed.

We heard muffled sounds approaching, and we sank down to the ground where we were. We made out another knight vaguely; he was coming very stealthily, and feeling his way. He was near enough now for us to see him put out a hand, find an upper wire, then bend and step under it and over the lower one. Now he arrived at the first knight—and started slightly when he discovered him. He stood a moment—no doubt wondering why the other one didn't move on; then he said, in a low voice, "Why dreamest thou here, good Sir Mar—" then he laid his hand on the corpse's shoulder—and just uttered a little soft moan and sunk down dead. Killed by a dead man, you see—killed by a dead friend, in fact. There was something awful about it.

These early birds came scattering along after each other, about one every five minutes in our vicinity, during half an hour. They brought no armor of offense but their swords; as a rule, they carried the sword ready in the hand, and put it forward and found the wires with it. We would now and then see a blue spark when the knight that caused it was so far away as to be invisible to us; but we knew what had happened, all the same; poor fellow, he had touched a charged wire with his sword and been electrocuted. We had brief intervals of grim stillness, interrupted with piteous regularity by the clash made by the falling of an iron-clad; and this sort of thing was going on, right along, and was very creepy there in the dark and lonesomeness.

We concluded to make a tour between the inner fences. We elected to walk upright, for convenience's sake; we argued that if discerned, we should be taken for friends rather than enemies, and in any case we should be out of reach of swords, and these gentry did not seem to have any spears along. Well, it was a curious trip. Everywhere dead men were lying outside the second fence—not plainly visible, but still visible; and we counted fifteen of those pathetic statues—dead knights standing with their hands on the upper wire.

One thing seemed to be sufficiently demonstrated: our current was so tremendous that it killed before the victim could cry out. Pretty soon we detected a muffled and heavy sound, and next moment we guessed what it was. It was a surprise in force coming! whispered Clarence to go and wake the army, and notify it to wait in silence in the cave for further orders. He was soon back, and we stood by the inner fence and watched the silent lightning do its awful work upon that swarming host. One could make out but little of detail; but he could note that a black mass was piling itself up beyond the second fence. That swelling bulk was dead men! Our camp was enclosed with a solid wall of the dead—a bulwark, a breastwork, of corpses, you may say. One terrible thing about this thing was the absence of human voices; there were no cheers, no war cries; being intent upon a surprise, these men moved as noiselessly as they could; and always when the front rank was near enough to their goal to make it proper for them to begin to get a shout ready, of course they struck the fatal line and went down without testifying.

I sent a current through the third fence now; and almost immediately through the fourth and fifth, so quickly were the gaps filled up. I believed the time was come now for my climax; I believed that that whole army was in our trap. Anyway, it was high time to find out. So I touched a button and set fifty electric suns aflame on the top of our precipice.

Land, what a sight! We were enclosed in three walls of dead men! All the other fences were pretty nearly filled with the living, who were stealthily working their way forward through the wires. The sudden glare paralyzed this host, petrified them, you may say, with astonishment; there was just one instant for me to utilize their immobility in, and I didn't lose the chance. You see, in another instant they would have recovered their faculties, then they'd have burst into a cheer and made a rush, and my wires would have gone down before it; but that lost instant lost them their opportunity forever; while even that slight fragment of time was still unspent, I shot the current through all the fences and struck the whole host dead in their tracks! *There* was a groan you could *hear*! It voiced the death-pang of eleven thousand men. It swelled out on the night with awful pathos.

A glance showed that the rest of the enemy—perhaps ten thousand strong—were between us and the encircling ditch, and pressing forward to the assault. Consequently we had them *all!* and had them past help. Time for the last act of the tragedy. I fired the three appointed revolver shots—which meant:

"Turn on the water!"

There was a sudden rush and roar, and in a minute the mountain brook was raging through the big ditch and creating a river a hundred feet wide and twenty-five deep.

"Stand to your guns, men! Open fire!"

The thirteen gatlings began to vomit death into the fated ten thousand. They halted, they stood their ground a moment against that withering deluge of fire, then they broke, faced about and swept toward the ditch like chaff before a gale. A full fourth part of their force never reached the top of the lofty embankment; the three-fourths reached it and plunged over—to death by drowning.

Within ten short minutes after we had opened fire, armed resistance was totally annihilated, the campaign was ended, we fifty-four were masters of England. Twenty-five thousand men lay dead around us.

But how treacherous is fortune! In a little while—say an hour—happened a thing, by my own fault, which—but I have no heart to write that. Let the record end here.

44

A Postscript by Clarence

I, Clarence, must write it for him. He proposed that we two go out and see if any help could be accorded the wounded. I was strenuous against the project. I said that if there were many, we could do but little for them; and it would not be wise for us to trust ourselves among them, anyway. But he could seldom be turned from a purpose once formed; so we shut off the electric current from the fences, took an escort along, climbed over the enclosing ramparts of dead knights, and moved out upon the field. The first wounded mall who appealed for help was sitting with his back against a dead comrade. When The Boss bent over him and spoke to him, the man recognized him and stabbed him. That knight was Sir Meliagraunce, as I found out by tearing off his helmet. He will not ask for help any more.

We carried The Boss to the cave and gave his wound, which was not very serious, the best care we could. In this service we had the help of Merlin, though we did not know it. He was disguised as a woman, and appeared to be a simple old peasant goodwife. In this disguise, with brown-stained face and smooth shaven, he had appeared a few days after The Boss was hurt and offered to cook for us, saying her people had gone off to join certain new camps which the enemy were forming, and that she was starving. The Boss had been getting along very well, and had amused himself with finishing up his record.

We were glad to have this woman, for we were short handed. We were in a trap, you see—a trap of our own making. If we stayed where we were, our dead would kill us; if we moved out of our defenses, we should no longer be invincible. We had conquered; in turn we were conquered. The Boss recognized this; we all recognized it. If we could go to one of those new camps and patch up some kind of terms with the enemy—yes, but The Boss could not go, and neither could I, for I was among the first that were made sick by the poisonous air bred by those dead thousands. Others were taken down, and still others. Tomorrow—

Tomorrow. It is here. And with it the end. About midnight I awoke, and saw that hag making curious passes in the air about The Boss's head and face, and wondered what it meant. Everybody but the dynamo-watch lay steeped in sleep; there was no sound. The woman ceased from her mysterious foolery, and started tip-toeing toward the door. I called out:

"Stop! What have you been doing?"

She halted, and said with an accent of malicious satisfaction:

"Ye were conquerors; ye are conquered! These others are perishing—you also. Ye shall all die in this place—every one—except *him.* He sleepeth now—and shall sleep thirteen centuries. I am Merlin!"

Then such a delirium of silly laughter overtook him that he reeled about like a drunken man, and presently fetched up against one of our wires. His mouth is spread open yet; apparently he is still laughing. I suppose the face will retain that petrified laugh until the corpse turns to dust.

The Boss has never stirred—sleeps like a stone. If he does not wake today we shall understand what kind of a sleep it is, and his body will then be borne to a place in one of the remote recesses of the cave where none will ever find it to desecrate it. As for the rest of us—well, it is agreed that if any one of us ever escapes alive from this place, he will write the fact here, and loyally hide this Manuscript with The Boss, our dear good chief, whose property it is, be he alive or dead.

THE END OF THE MANUSCRIPT

FINAL P.S. BY M.T.

The dawn was come when I laid the Manuscript aside. The rain had almost ceased, the world was grey and sad, the exhausted storm was sighing and sobbing itself to rest. I went to the stranger's room, and listened at his door, which was slightly ajar. I could hear his voice, and so I knocked. There was no answer, but I still heard the voice. I peeped in. The man lay on his back in bed, talking brokenly but with spirit, and punctuating with his arms, which he thrashed about, restlessly, as sick people do in delirium. I slipped in softly and bent over him. His mutterings and ejaculations went on. I spoke—merely a word, to call his attention. His glassy eyes and his ashy face were alight in an instant with pleasure, gratitude, gladness, welcome:

"Oh, Sandy, you are come at last—how I have longed for you! Sit by me—do not leave me—never leave me again, Sandy, never again. Where is your hand?—give it me, dear, let me hold it—there—now all is well, all is peace, and I am happy again—*we* are happy again, isn't it so, Sandy? You are so dim, so vague, you are but a mist, a cloud, but you are *here*, and that is blessedness sufficient; and I have your hand; don't take it away—it is for only a little while, I shall not require it long. . . . Was that the child? . . . Hello-Central! . . . she doesn't answer. Asleep, perhaps? Bring her when she wakes, and let me touch her hands, her face, her hair, and tell her goodbye. . . . Sandy! Yes, you are there. I lost myself a moment, and I thought you were gone. . . . Have I been sick long? It must be so; it seems months to me. And such dreams! such strange and awful dreams, Sandy! Dreams that were as real as reality—delirium, of course, but *so* real! Why, I thought the king was dead, I thought you were in Gaul and couldn't get home, I thought there was a revolution; in the fantastic frenzy of these dreams, I thought that Clarence and I and a handful of my cadets fought and exterminated the whole chivalry of England! But even that was not the strangest. I seemed to be a creature out of a remote unborn age, centuries hence, and even *that* was as real as the rest! Yes, I seemed to have flown back out of that age into this of ours, and then forward to it again, and was set down, a stranger and forlorn in that strange England, with an abyss of thirteen centuries yawning between me and you! between me and my home and my friends! between me and all that is dear to me, all that could make life worth the living! It was awful—awfuller than you can ever imagine, Sandy. Ah, watch by me, Sandy—stay by me every moment—*don't* let me go out of my mind again; death is nothing, let it come, but not with those dreams, not with the torture of those hideous dreams—I cannot endure *that* again. . . . Sandy? . . ."

He lay muttering incoherently some little time; then for a time he lay silent, and apparently sinking away toward death. Presently his fingers began to pick busily at the coverlet, and by that sign I knew that his end was at hand with the first suggestion of the death rattle in his throat he started up slightly, and seemed to listen: then he said:

"A bugle? . . . It is the king! The drawbridge, there! Man the battlements!—turn out the—"

He was getting up his last "effect"; but he never finished it.

The Tragedy of Pudd'nhead Wilson (1894)

A Whisper to the Reader

> There is no character, howsoever good and fine, but it can be destroyed by ridicule, howsoever poor and witless. Observe the ass, for instance: his character is about perfect, he is the choicest spirit among all the humbler animals, yet see what ridicule has brought him to. Instead of feeling complimented when we are called an ass, we are left in doubt.—*Pudd'nhead Wilson's Calendar*

A person who is ignorant of legal matters is always liable to make mistakes when he tries to photograph a court scene with his pen; and so I was not willing to let the law chapters in this book go to press without first subjecting them to rigid and exhausting revision and correction by a trained barrister—if that is what they are called. These chapters are right, now, in every detail, for they were rewritten under the immediate eye of William Hicks, who studied law part of a while in southwest Missouri thirty-five years ago and then came over here to Florence for his health and is still helping for exercise and board in Macaroni Vermicelli's horse-feed shed which is up the back alley as you turn around the corner out of the Piazza del Duomo just beyond the house where that stone that Dante used to sit on six hundred years ago is let into the wall when he let on to be watching them build Giotto's campanile and yet always got tired looking as soon as Beatrice passed along on her way to get a chunk of chestnut cake to defend herself with in case of a Ghibelline outbreak before she got to school, at the same old stand where they sell the same old cake to this day and it is just as light and good as it was then, too, and this is not flattery, far from it. He was a little rusty on his law, but he rubbed up for this book, and those two or three legal chapters are right and straight, now. He told me so himself.

Given under my hand this second day of January, 1893, at the Villa Viviani, village of Settignano, three miles back of Florence, on the hills—the same certainly affording the most charming view to be found on this planet, and with it the most dreamlike and enchanting sunsets to be found in any planet or even in any solar system—and given, too, in the swell room of the house, with the busts of Cerretani senators and other grandees of this line looking approvingly down upon me as they used to look down upon Dante, and mutely asking me to adopt them into my family, which I do with pleasure, for my remotest ancestors are but spring chickens compared with these robed and stately antiques, and it will be a great and satisfying lift for me, that six hundred years will.

MARK TWAIN

1

Pudd'nhead Wins His Name

Tell the truth or trump—but get the trick.—*Pudd'nhead Wilson's Calendar*

The scene of this chronicle is the town of Dawson's Landing, on the Missouri side of the Mississippi, half a day's journey, per steamboat, below St. Louis.

In 1830 it was a snug little collection of modest one- and two-storey frame dwellings whose whitewashed exteriors were almost concealed from sight by climbing tangles of rose-vines, honeysuckles, and morning glories. Each of these pretty homes had a garden in front fenced with white palings and opulently stocked with hollyhocks, marigolds, touch-me-nots, prince's-feathers and other old-fashioned flowers; while on the windowsills of the houses stood wooden boxes containing moss-rose plants and terracotta pots in which grew a breed of geranium whose spread of intensely red blossoms accented the prevailing pink tint of the rose-clad house-front like an explosion of flame. When there was room on the ledge outside of the pots and boxes for a cat, the cat was there—in sunny weather—stretched at full length, asleep and blissful, with her furry belly to the sun and a paw curved over her nose. Then that house was complete, and its contentment and peace were made manifest to the world by this symbol, whose testimony is infallible. A home without a cat—and a well-fed, well-petted and properly revered cat—may be a perfect home, perhaps, but how can it prove title?

All along the streets, on both sides, at the outer edge of the brick sidewalks, stood locust-trees with trunks protected by wooden boxing, and these furnished shade for summer and a sweet fragrance in spring when the clusters of buds came forth. The main street, one block back from the river, and running parallel with it, was the sole business street. It was six blocks long, and in each block two or three brick stores three stories high towered above interjected bunches of little frame shops. Swinging signs creaked in the wind, the street's whole length. The candy-striped pole which indicates nobility proud and ancient along the palace-bordered canals of Venice, indicated merely the humble barber shop along the main street of Dawson's Landing. On a chief corner stood a lofty unpainted pole wreathed from top to bottom with tin pots and pans and cups, the chief tinmonger's noisy notice to the world (when the wind blew) that his shop was on hand for business at that corner.

The hamlet's front was washed by the clear waters of the great river; its body stretched itself rearward up a gentle incline; its most rearward border fringed itself out and scattered its houses about the base-line of the hills; the hills rose high, inclosing the town in a half-moon curve, clothed with forests from foot to summit.

Steamboats passed up and down every hour or so. Those belonging to the little Cairo line and the little Memphis line always stopped; the big Orleans liners stopped for hails only, or to land passengers or freight; and this was the case also with the great flotilla of "transients." These latter came out of a dozen rivers—the Illinois, the Missouri, the Upper Mississippi, the Ohio, the Monongahela, the Tennessee, the Red River, the White River, and so on; and were bound every whither and stocked with every imaginable comfort or necessity which the Mississippi's communities could want, from the frosty Falls of St. Anthony down through nine climates to torrid New Orleans.

Dawson's Landing was a slaveholding town, with a rich slave-worked grain and pork country back of it. The town was sleepy and comfortable and contented. It was fifty years old, and was growing slowly—very slowly, in fact, but still it was growing.

The chief citizen was York Leicester Driscoll, about forty years old, judge of the county court. He was very proud of his old Virginian ancestry, and in his hospitalities and his rather formal and stately manners he kept up its traditions. He was fine and just and generous. To be a gentleman—a gentleman without stain or blemish—was his only religion, and to it he was always faithful. He was respected, esteemed and beloved by all the community. He was well off, and was gradually adding to his store. He and his wife were very nearly happy, but not quite, for they had no children. The longing for the treasure of a child had grown stronger and stronger as the years slipped away, but the blessing never came—and was never to come.

With this pair lived the Judge's widowed sister, Mrs. Rachel Pratt, and she also was childless—childless, and sorrowful for that reason, and not to be comforted. The women were good and commonplace people, and did their duty and had their reward in clear consciences and the community's approbation. They were Presbyterians, the Judge was a freethinker.

Pembroke Howard, lawyer and bachelor, aged about forty, was another old Virginian grandee with proved descent from the First Families. He was a fine, brave, majestic creature, a gentleman according to the nicest requirements of the Virginia rule, a devoted Presbyterian, an authority on the "code," and a man always courteously ready to stand up before you in the field if any act or word of his had seemed doubtful or suspicious to you, and explain it with any weapon you might prefer from brad-awls to artillery. He was very popular with the people, and was the Judge's dearest friend.

Then there was Colonel Cecil Burleigh Essex, another F. F. V. of formidable caliber—however, with him we have no concern.

Percy Northumberland Driscoll, brother to the Judge, and younger than he by five years, was a married man, and had had children around his hearthstone; but they were attacked in detail by measles, croup and scarlet fever, and this had given the doctor a chance with his effective antediluvian methods; so the cradles were empty. He was a prosperous man, with a good head for speculations, and his fortune was growing. On the 1st of February, 1830, two boy babes were born in his house: one to him, the other to one of his slave girls, Roxana by name. Roxana was twenty years old. She was up and around the same day, with her hands full, for she was tending both babies.

Mrs. Percy Driscoll died within the week. Roxy remained in charge of the children. She had her own way, for Mr. Driscoll soon absorbed himself in his speculations and left her to her own devices.

In that same month of February, Dawson's Landing gained a new citizen. This was Mr. David Wilson, a young fellow of Scotch parentage. He had wandered to this remote region from his birthplace in the interior of the State of New York, to seek his fortune. He was twenty-five years old, college-bred, and had finished a post-college course in an Eastern law school a couple of years before.

He was a homely, freckled, sandy-haired young fellow, with an intelligent blue eye that had frankness and comradeship in it and a covert twinkle of a pleasant sort. But for an unfortunate remark of his, he would no doubt have entered at once upon a successful career at Dawson's Landing. But he made his fatal remark the first day he spent in the village, and it "gaged" him. He had just made the acquaintance of a group of citizens when an invisible dog began to yelp and snarl and howl and make himself very comprehensively disagreeable, whereupon young Wilson said, much as one who is thinking aloud—

"I wish I owned half of that dog."

"Why?" somebody asked.

"Because I would kill my half."

The group searched his face with curiosity, with anxiety even, but found no light there, no expression that they could read. They fell away from him as from something uncanny, and went into privacy to discuss him. One said:

"'Pears to be a fool."

"'Pears?" said another. "*Is,* I reckon you better say."

"Said he wished he owned *half* of the dog, the idiot," said a third. "What did he reckon would become of the other half if he killed his half? Do you reckon he thought it would live?"

"Why, he must have thought it, unless he *is* the downrightest fool in the world; because if he hadn't thought it, he would have wanted to own the whole dog, knowing that if he killed his half and the other half died, he would be responsible for that half just the same as if he had killed that half instead of his own. Don't it look that way to you, gents?"

"Yes, it does. If he owned one half of the general dog, it would be so; if he owned one end of the dog and another person owned the other end, it would be so, just the same; particularly in the first case, because if you kill one half of a general dog, there ain't any man that can tell whose half it was, but if he owned one end of the dog, maybe he could kill his end of it and—"

"No, he couldn't either; he couldn't and not be responsible if the other end died, which it would. In my opinion the man ain't in his right mind."

"In my opinion he hain't *got* any mind."

No. 3 said: "Well, he's a lummox, anyway."

"That's what he is," said No. 4, "he's a labrick—just a Simon-pure labrick, if ever there was one."

"Yes, sir, he's a dam fool, that's the way I put him up," said No. 5. "Anybody can think different that wants to, but those are my sentiments."

"I'm with you, gentlemen," said No. 6. "Perfect jackass—yes, and it ain't going too far to say he is a pudd'nhead. If he ain't a pudd'nhead, I ain't no judge, that's all."

Mr. Wilson stood elected. The incident was told all over the town, and gravely discussed by everybody. Within a week he had lost his first name; Pudd'nhead took its place. In time he came to be liked, and well liked too; but by that time the nickname had got well stuck on, and it stayed. That first day's verdict made him a fool, and he was not able to get it set aside, or even modified. The nickname soon ceased to carry any harsh or unfriendly feeling with it, but it held its place, and was to continue to hold its place for twenty long years.

2

Driscoll Spares His Slaves

Adam was but human—this explains it all. He did not want the apple for the apple's sake, he wanted it only because it was forbidden. The mistake was in not forbidding the serpent; then he would have eaten the serpent.—*Pudd'nhead Wilson's Calendar*

Pudd'nhead Wilson had a trifle of money when he arrived, and he bought a small house on the extreme western verge of the town. Between it and Judge Driscoll's house there was only a grassy yard, with a paling fence dividing the properties in the middle. He hired a small office down in the town and hung out a tin sign with these words on it:

DAVID WILSON.
ATTORNEY AND COUNSELOR-AT-LAW.
SURVEYING, CONVEYANCING, ETC.

But his deadly remark had ruined his chance—at least in the law. No clients came. He took down his sign, after a while, and put it up on his own house with the law features knocked out of it. It offered his services now in the humble capacities of land-surveyor and expert accountant. Now and then he got a job of surveying to do, and now and then a merchant got him to straighten out his books. With Scotch patience and pluck he resolved to live down his reputation and work his way into the legal field yet. Poor fellow, he could not foresee that it was going to take him such a weary long time to do it.

He had a rich abundance of idle time, but it never hung heavy on his hands, for he interested himself in every new thing that was born into the universe of ideas, and studied it and experimented upon it at his house. One of his pet fads was palmistry. To another one he gave no name, neither would he explain to anybody what its purpose was, but merely said it was an amusement. In fact he had found that his fads added to his reputation as a pudd'nhead; therefore he was growing chary of being too communicative about them. The fad without a name was one which dealt with people's finger-marks. He carried in his coat pocket a shallow box with grooves in it, and in the grooves strips of glass five inches long and three inches wide. Along the lower edge of each strip was pasted a slip of white paper. He asked people to pass their hands through their hair (thus collecting upon them a thin coating of the natural oil) and then make a thumb-mark on a glass strip, following it with the mark of the ball of each finger in succession. Under this row of faint grease-prints he would write a record on the strip of white paper—thus:

John Smith, *right hand*—

and add the day of the month and the year, then take Smith's left hand on another glass strip, and add name and date and the words "left hand." The strips were now returned to the grooved box, and took their place among what Wilson called his "records."

He often studied his records, examining and poring over them with absorbing interest until far into the night; but what he found there—if he found anything—he revealed to no one. Sometimes he copied on paper the involved and delicate pattern left by the ball of a finger, and then vastly enlarged it with a pantograph so that he could examine its web of curving lines with ease and convenience.

One sweltering afternoon—it was the first day of July, 1830—he was at work over a set of tangled account-books in his workroom, which looked westward over a stretch of vacant lots, when a conversation outside disturbed him. It was carried on in yells, which showed that the people engaged in it were not close together:

"Say, Roxy, how does yo' baby come on?" This from the distant voice.

"Fust-rate; how does *you* come on, Jasper?" This yell was from close by.

"Oh, I's middlin'; hain't got noth'n' to complain of. I's gwine to come a-court'n' you bimeby, Roxy."

"*You* is, you black mud-cat! Yah—yah—yah! I got somep'n' better to do den 'sociat'n' wid niggers as black as you is. Is ole Miss Cooper's Nancy done give you de mitten?" Roxy followed this sally with another discharge of care-free laughter.

"You's jealous, Roxy, dat's what's de matter wid *you*, you hussy—yah—yah—yah! Dat's de time I got you!"

"Oh, yes, *you* got me, hain't you. 'Clah to goodness if dat conceit o' yo'n strikes in, Jasper, it gwine to kill you sho'. If you b'longed to me I'd sell you down de river 'fo' you git too fur gone. Fust time I runs acrost yo' marster, I's gwine to tell him so."

This idle and aimless jabber went on and on, both parties enjoying the friendly duel and each well satisfied with his own share of the wit exchanged—for wit they considered it.

Wilson stepped to the window to observe the combatants; he could not work while their chatter continued. Over in the vacant lots was Jasper, young, coal-black and of magnificent build, sitting on a wheelbarrow in the pelting sun—at work, supposably, whereas he was in fact only preparing for it by taking an hour's rest before beginning. In front of Wilson's porch stood Roxy, with a local handmade baby-wagon, in which sat her two charges—one at each end and facing each other. From Roxy's manner of speech, a stranger would have expected her to be black, but she was not. Only one sixteenth of her was black, and that sixteenth did not show. She was of majestic form and stature, her attitudes were imposing and statuesque, and her gestures and movements distinguished by a noble and stately grace. Her complexion was very fair, with the rosy glow of vigorous health in the cheeks, her face was full of character and expression, her eyes were brown and liquid, and she had a heavy suit of fine soft hair which was also brown, but the fact was not apparent because her head was bound about with a checkered handkerchief and the hair was concealed under it. Her face was shapely, intelligent and comely—even beautiful. She had an easy, independent carriage—when she was among her own caste—and a high and "sassy" way, withal; but of course she was meek and humble enough where white people were.

To all intents and purposes Roxy was as white as anybody, but the one sixteenth of her which was black outvoted the other fifteen parts and made her a negro. She was a slave, and salable as such. Her child was thirty-one parts white, and he, too, was a slave, and by a fiction of law and custom a negro. He had blue eyes and flaxen curls like his white comrade, but even the father of the white child was able to tell the children apart—little as he had commerce with them—by their clothes: for the white babe wore ruffled soft muslin and a coral necklace, while the other wore merely a coarse tow-linen shirt which barely reached to its knees, and no jewellery.

The white child's name was Thomas à Becket Driscoll, the other's name was Valet de Chambre: no surname—slaves hadn't the privilege. Roxana had heard that phrase somewhere, the fine sound of it had pleased her ear, and as she had supposed it was a name, she loaded it on to her darling. It soon got shorted to "Chambers," of course.

Wilson knew Roxy by sight, and when the duel of wit began to play out, he stepped outside to gather in a record or two. Jasper went to work energetically, at once, perceiving that his leisure was observed. Wilson inspected the children and asked—

"How old are they, Roxy?"

"Bofe de same age, sir—five months. Bawn de fust o' Feb'uary."

"They're handsome little chaps. One's just as handsome as the other, too."

A delighted smile exposed the girl's white teeth, and she said:

"Bless yo' soul, Misto Wilson, it's pow'ful nice o' you to say dat, 'ca'se one of 'em ain't on'y a nigger. Mighty prime little nigger, *I* al'ays says, but dat's 'ca'se it's mine, o' course."

"How do you tell them apart, Roxy, when they haven't any clothes on?"

Roxy laughed a laugh proportioned to her size, and said:

"Oh, *I* kin tell 'em 'part, Misto Wilson, but I bet Marse Percy couldn't, not to save his life."

Wilson chatted along for awhile, and presently got Roxy's fingerprints for his collection—right hand and left—on a couple of his glass strips; then labeled and dated them, and took the "records" of both children, and labeled and dated them also.

Two months later, on the 3d of September, he took this trio of finger-marks again. He liked to have a "series," two or three "takings" at intervals during the period of childhood, these to be followed by others at intervals of several years.

The next day—that is to say, on the 4th of September—something occurred which profoundly impressed Roxana. Mr. Driscoll missed another small sum of money—which is a way of saying that this was not a new thing, but had happened before. In truth it had happened three times before. Driscoll's patience was exhausted. He was a fairly humane man toward slaves and other animals; he was an exceedingly humane man toward the erring of his own race. Theft he could not abide, and plainly there was a thief in his house. Necessarily the thief must be one of his negroes. Sharp measures must be taken. He called his servants before him. There were three of these, besides Roxy: a man, a woman, and a boy twelve years old. They were not related. Mr. Driscoll said:

"You have all been warned before. It has done no good. This time I will teach you a lesson. I will sell the thief. Which of you is the guilty one?"

They all shuddered at the threat, for here they had a good home, and a new one was likely to be a change for the worse. The denial was general. None had stolen anything—not money, anyway—a little sugar, or cake, or honey, or something like that, that "Marse Percy wouldn't mind or miss," but not money—never a cent of money. They were eloquent in their protestations, but Mr. Driscoll was not moved by them. He answered each in turn with a stern "Name the thief!"

The truth was, all were guilty but Roxana; she suspected that the others were guilty, but she did not know them to be so. She was horrified to think how near she had come to being guilty herself; she had been saved in the nick of time by a revival in the coloured Methodist Church, a fortnight before, at which time and place she "got religion." The very next day after that gracious experience, while her change of style was fresh upon her and she was vain of her purified condition, her master left a couple dollars lying unprotected on his desk, and she happened upon that temptation when she was polishing around with a dust-rag. She looked at the money awhile with a steady rising resentment, then she burst out with—

"Dad blame dat revival, I wisht it had 'a' be'n put off till tomorrow!"

Then she covered the tempter with a book, and another member of the kitchen cabinet got it. She made this sacrifice as a matter of religious etiquette; as a thing necessary just now, but by no means to be wrested into a precedent; no, a week or two would limber up her piety, then she would be rational again, and the next two dollars that got left out in the cold would find a comforter—and she could name the comforter.

Was she bad? Was she worse than the general run of her race? No. They had an unfair show in the battle of life, and they held it no sin to take military advantage of the enemy—in a small way; in a small way, but not in a large one. They would smouch provisions from the pantry whenever they got a chance; or a brass thimble, or a cake of wax, or an emery-bag, or a paper of needles, or a silver spoon, or a dollar bill, or small articles of clothing, or any other property of light value; and so far were they from considering such reprisals sinful, that they would go to church and shout and pray the loudest and sincerest with their plunder in their pockets. A farm smoke-house had to be kept heavily padlocked, for even the coloured deacon himself could not resist a ham when Providence showed him in a dream, or otherwise, where such a thing hung lonesome and longed for some one to love. But with a hundred hanging before him the deacon would not take two—that is, on the same night. On frosty nights the humane negro prowler would warm the end of a plank and put it up under the cold claws of chickens roosting in a tree; a drowsy hen would step on to the comfortable board, softly clucking her gratitude, and the prowler would dump her into his bag, and later into his stomach, perfectly sure that in taking this trifle from the man who daily robbed him of an inestimable treasure—his liberty—he was not committing any sin that God would remember against him in the Last Great Day.

"Name the thief!"

For the fourth time Mr. Driscoll had said it, and always in the same hard tone. And now he added these words of awful import:

"I give you one minute"—he took out his watch. "If at the end of that time you have not confessed, I will not only sell all four of you, *but*—I will sell you DOWN THE RIVER!"

It was equivalent to condemning them to hell! No Missouri negro doubted this. Roxy reeled in her tracks and the colour vanished out of her face; the others dropped to their knees as if they had been shot; tears gushed from their eyes, their supplicating hands went up, and three answers came in the one instant:

"I done it!"

"I done it!"

"I done it!—have mercy, marster—Lord have mercy on us po' niggers!"

"Very good," said the master, putting up his watch, "I will sell you *here* though you don't deserve it. You ought to be sold down the river."

The culprits flung themselves prone, in an ecstasy of gratitude, and kissed his feet, declaring that they would never forget his goodness and never cease to pray for him as long as they lived. They were sincere, for like a god he had stretched forth his mighty hand and closed the gates of hell against them. He knew, himself, that he had done a noble and gracious thing, and was privately well pleased with his magnanimity; and that night he set the incident down in his diary, so that his son might read it in after years, and be thereby moved to deeds of gentleness and humanity himself.

3

Roxy Plays a Shrewd Trick

> Whoever has lived long enough to find out what life is, knows how deep a debt of gratitude we owe to Adam, the first great benefactor of our race. He brought death into the world.—*Pudd'nhead Wilson's Calendar*

Percy Driscoll slept well the night he saved his house-minions from going down the river, but no wink of sleep visited Roxy's eyes. A profound terror had taken possession of her. Her child could grow up and be sold down the river! The thought crazed her with horror. If she dozed and lost herself for a moment, the next moment she was on her feet flying to her child's cradle to see if it was still there. Then she would gather it to her heart and pour out her love upon it in a frenzy of kisses, moaning, crying, and saying, "Dey sha'n't, oh, dey *sha'n't!*—yo' po' mammy will kill you fust!"

Once, when she was tucking it back in its cradle again, the other child nestled in its sleep and attracted her attention. She went and stood over it a long time communing with herself:

"What has my po' baby done, dat he couldn't have yo' luck? He hain't done noth'n'. God was good to you; why warn't he good to him? Dey can't sell *you* down de river. I hates yo' pappy; he hain't got no heart—for niggers he hain't, anyways. I hates him, en I could kill him!" She paused awhile, thinking; then she burst into wild sobbings again, and turned away, saying, "Oh, I got to kill my chile, dey ain't no yuther way—killin' *him* wouldn't save de chile fum goin' down de river. Oh, I got to do it, yo' po' mammy's got to kill you to save you, honey"—she gathered her baby to her bosom, now, and began to smother it with caresses—"Mammy's got to kill you—how *kin* I do it! But yo' mammy ain't gwine to desert you—no, no; *dah*, don't cry—she gwine *wid* you, she gwine to kill herself too. Come along, honey, come along wid mammy; we gwine to jump in de river, den de troubles o' dis worl' is all over—dey don't sell po' niggers down the river over *yonder*."

She started toward the door, crooning to the child and hushing it; midway she stopped, suddenly. She had caught sight of her new Sunday gown—a cheap curtain-calico thing, a conflagration of gaudy colours and fantastic figures. She surveyed it wistfully, longingly.

"Hain't ever wore it yet," she said, "en it's jist lovely." Then she nodded her head in response to a pleasant idea, and added, "No, I ain't gwine to be fished out, wid everybody lookin' at me, in dis mis'able ole linsey-woolsey."

She put down the child and made the change. She looked in the glass and was astonished at her beauty. She resolved to make her death-toilet perfect. She took off her handkerchief-turban and dressed her glossy wealth of hair "like white folks"; she added some odds and ends of rather lurid ribbon and a spray of atrocious artificial flowers; finally she threw over her shoulders a fluffy thing called a "cloud" in that day, which was of a blazing red complexion. Then she was ready for the tomb.

She gathered up her baby once more; but when her eye fell upon its miserably short little grey tow-linen shirt and noted the contrast between its pauper shabbiness and her own volcanic irruption of infernal splendours, her mother-heart was touched, and she was ashamed.

"No, dolling, mammy ain't gwine to treat you so. De angels is gwine to 'mire you jist as much as dey does yo' mammy. Ain't gwine to have 'em putt'n' dey han's up 'fo' dey eyes en sayin' to David en Goliah en dem yuther prophets, 'Dat chile is dress' too indelicate fo' dis place.'"

By this time she had stripped off the shirt. Now she clothed the naked little creature in one of Thomas à Becket's snowy long baby-gowns, with its bright blue bows and dainty flummery of ruffles.

"Dah—now you's fixed." She propped the child in a chair and stood off to inspect it. Straightway her eyes began to widen with astonishment and admiration, and she clapped her hands and cried out, "Why, it do beat all!—I *never* knowed you was so lovely. Marse Tommy ain't a bit puttier—not a single bit."

She stepped over and glanced at the other infant; she flung a glance back at her own; then one more at the heir of the house. Now a strange light dawned in her eyes, and in a moment she was lost in thought. She seemed in a trance; when she came out of it she muttered, "When I 'uz a-washin' 'em in de tub, yistiddy, his own pappy asked me which of 'em was his'n."

She began to move about like one in a dream. She undressed Thomas à Becket, stripping him of everything, and put the tow-linen shirt on him. She put his coral necklace on her own child's neck. Then she placed the children side by side, and after earnest inspection she muttered—

"Now who would b'lieve clo'es could do de like o' dat? Dog my cats if it ain't all *I* kin do to tell t'other fum which, let alone his pappy."

She put her cub in Tommy's elegant cradle and said—

"You's young Marse *Tom* fum dis out, en I got to practise and git used to 'memberin' to call you dat, honey, or I's gwine to make a mistake some time en git us bofe into trouble. Dah—now you lay still en don't fret no mo', Marse Tom—oh, thank de good Lord in heaven, you's saved, you's saved!—dey ain't no man kin ever sell mammy's po' little honey down de river now!"

She put the heir of the house in her own child's unpainted pine cradle, and said, contemplating its slumbering form uneasily—

"I's sorry for you, honey; I's sorry, God knows I is—but what *kin* I do, what *could* I do? Yo' pappy would sell him to somebody, some time, en den he'd go down de river, sho', en I couldn't, couldn't, *couldn't* stan' it."

She flung herself on her bed and began to think and toss, toss and think. By and by she sat suddenly upright, for a comforting thought had flown through her worried mind—

"'Tain't no sin—*white* folks has done it! It ain't no sin, glory to goodness it ain't no sin! *Dey's* done it—yes, en dey was de biggest quality in de whole bilin', too—*kings!*"

She began to muse; she was trying to gather out of her memory the dim particulars of some tale she had heard some time or other. At last she said—

"Now I's got it; now I 'member. It was dat ole nigger preacher dat tole it, de time he come over here fum Illinois en preached in de nigger church. He said dey ain't nobody kin save his own self—can't do it by faith, can't do it by works, can't do it no way at all. Free grace is de *on'y* way, en dat don't come fum nobody but jis' de Lord; en *he* kin give it to anybody he please, saint or sinner—*he* don't kyer. He do jis' as he's a mineter. He s'lect out anybody dat suit him, en put another one in his place, and make de fust one happy forever en leave t'other one to burn wid Satan. De preacher said it was jist like dey done in Englan' one time, long time ago. De queen she lef' her baby layin' aroun' one day, en went out callin'; en one o' de niggers roun'-'bout de place dat was 'mos' white, she come in en see de chile layin' aroun', en tuck en put her own chile's clo'es on de queen's chile, en put de queen's chile's clo'es on her own chile, en den lef' her own chile layin' aroun' en tuck en toted de queen's chile home to de nigger-quarter, en nobody ever foun' it out, en her chile was de king bimeby, en sole de queen's chile down de river one time when dey had to settle up de estate. Dah, now—de preacher said it his own self, en it ain't no sin, 'ca'se white folks done it. *Dey* done it—yes, *dey* done it; en not on'y jis' common white folks nuther, but de biggest quality dey is in de whole bilin'. Oh, I's *so* glad I 'member 'bout dat!"

She got up light-hearted and happy, and went to the cradles and spent what was left of the night "practising." She would give her own child a light pat and say humbly, "Lay still, Marse Tom," then give the real Tom a pat and say with severity, "Lay *still*, Chambers!—does you want me to take somep'n' *to* you?"

As she progressed with her practice, she was surprised to see how steadily and surely the awe which had kept her tongue reverent and her manner humble toward her young master was transferring itself to her speech and manner toward the usurper, and how similarly handy she was becoming in transferring her motherly curtness of speech and peremptoriness of manner to the unlucky heir of the ancient house of Driscoll.

She took occasional rests from practising, and absorbed herself in calculating her chances.

"Dey'll sell dese niggers today fo' stealin' de money, den dey'll buy some mo' dat don't know de chillen—so *dat's* all right. When I takes de chillen out to git de air, de minute I's roun' de corner I's gwine to gaum dey mouths all roun' wid jam, den dey can't *nobody* notice dey's changed. Yes, I gwineter do dat till I's safe, if it's a year.

"Dey ain't but one man dat I's afeard of, en dat's dat Pudd'nhead Wilson. Dey calls him a pudd'nhead, en says he's a fool. My lan', dat man ain't no mo' fool den I is! He's de smartes' man in dis town, less'n it's Jedge Driscoll or maybe Pem Howard. Blame dat man, he worries me wid dem ornery glasses o' hisn; *I* b'lieve he's a witch. But nemmine, I's gwine to happen aroun' dah one o' dese days en let on dat I reckon he wants to print de chillen's fingers ag'in; en if *he* don't notice dey's changed, I bound dey ain't nobody gwine to notice it, en den I's safe, sho'. But I reckon I'll tote along a hoss-shoe to keep off de witch-work."

The new negroes gave Roxy no trouble, of course. The master gave her none, for one of his speculations was in jeopardy, and his mind was so occupied that he hardly saw the children when he looked at them, and all Roxy had to do was to get them both into a gale of laughter when he came about; then their faces were mainly cavities exposing gums, and he was gone again before the spasm passed and the little creatures resumed a human aspect.

Within a few days the fate of the speculation became so dubious that Mr. Percy went away with his brother the Judge, to see what could be done with it. It was a land speculation as usual, and it had gotten complicated with a lawsuit. The men were gone seven weeks. Before they got back Roxy had paid her visit to Wilson, and was satisfied. Wilson took the fingerprints, labeled them with the names and with the date—October the first—put them carefully away and continued his chat with Roxy, who seemed very anxious that he should admire the great advance in flesh and beauty which the babies had made since he took their fingerprints a month before. He complimented their improvement to her contentment; and as they were without any disguise of jam or other stain, she trembled all the while and was miserably frightened lest at any moment he—

But he didn't. He discovered nothing; and she went home jubilant, and dropped all concern about the matter permanently out of her mind.

4

The Ways of the Changelings

> Adam and Eve had many advantages, but the principal one was, that they escaped teething.—*Pudd'nhead Wilson's Calendar.*
> There is this trouble about special providences—namely, there is so often a doubt as to which party was intended to be the beneficiary. In the case of the children, the bears and the prophet, the bears got more real satisfaction out of the episode than the prophet did, because they got the children.—*Pudd'nhead Wilson's Calendar*

This history must henceforth accommodate itself to the change which Roxana has consummated, and call the real heir "Chambers" and the usurping little slave "Thomas à Becket"—shortening this latter name to "Tom," for daily use, as the people about him did.

"Tom" was a bad baby, from the very beginning of his usurpation. He would cry for nothing; he would burst into storms of devilish temper without notice, and let go scream after scream and squall after squall, then climax the thing with "holding his breath"—that frightful specialty of the teething nursling, in the throes of which the creature exhausts its lungs, then is convulsed with noiseless squirmings and twistings and kickings in the effort to get its breath, while the lips turn blue and the mouth stands wide and rigid, offering for inspection one wee tooth set in the lower rim of a hoop of red gums; and when the appalling stillness has endured until one is sure the lost breath will never return, a nurse comes flying, and dashes water in the child's face, and—presto! the lungs fill, and instantly discharge a shriek, or a yell, or a howl which bursts the listening ear and surprises the owner of it into saying words which would not go well with a halo if he had one. The baby Tom would claw anybody who came within reach of his nails, and pound anybody he could reach with his rattle. He would scream for water until he got it, and then throw cup and all on the floor and scream for more. He was indulged in all his caprices, howsoever troublesome and exasperating they might be; he was allowed to eat anything he wanted, particularly things that would give him the stomach-ache.

When he got to be old enough to begin to toddle about and say broken words and get an idea of what his hands were for, he was a more consummate pest than ever. Roxy got no rest while he was awake. He would call for anything and everything he saw, simply saying "Awnt it!" (want it), which was a command. When it was brought, he said in a frenzy, and motioning it away with his hands, "Don't awnt it! don't awnt it!" and the moment it was gone he set up frantic yells of "Awnt it! awnt it! awnt it!" and Roxy had to give wings to her heels to get that thing back to him again before he could get time to carry out his intention of going into convulsions about it.

What he preferred above all other things was the tongs. This was because his "father" had forbidden him to have them lest he break windows and furniture with them. The moment Roxy's back was turned he would toddle to the presence of the tongs and say "Like it!" and cock his eye to one side to see if Roxy was observing; then, "Awnt it!" and cock his eye again; then, "Hab it!" with another furtive glance; and finally, "Take it!"—and the prize was his. The next moment the heavy implement was raised aloft; the next, there was a crash and a squall, and the cat was off on three legs to meet an engagement; Roxy would arrive just as the lamp or a window went to irremediable smash.

Tom got all the petting, Chambers got none. Tom got all the delicacies, Chambers got mush and milk, and clabber without sugar. In consequence Tom was a sickly child and Chambers wasn't. Tom was "fractious," as Roxy called it, and overbearing; Chambers was meek and docile.

With all her splendid common sense and practical everyday ability, Roxy was a doting fool of a mother. She was this toward her child—and she was also more than this: by the fiction created by herself, he was become her master; the necessity of recognizing this relation outwardly and of perfecting herself in the forms required to express the recognition, had moved her to such diligence and faithfulness in practicing these forms that this exercise soon concreted itself into habit; it became automatic and unconscious; then a natural result followed: deceptions intended solely for others gradually grew practically into self-deceptions as well; the mock reverence became real reverence, the mock obsequiousness real obsequiousness, the mock homage real homage; the little counterfeit rift of separation between imitation-slave and imitation-master widened and widened, and became an abyss, and a very real one—and on one side of it stood Roxy, the dupe of her own deceptions, and on the other stood her child, no longer a usurper to her, but her accepted and recognized master. He was her darling, her master, and her deity all in one, and in her worship of him she forgot who she was and what he had been.

In babyhood Tom cuffed and banged and scratched Chambers unrebuked, and Chambers early learned that between meekly bearing it and resenting it, the advantage all lay with the former policy. The few times that his persecutions had moved him beyond control and made him fight back had cost him very dear at headquarters; not at the hands of Roxy, for if she ever went beyond scolding him sharply for "forgitt'n' who his young marster was," she at least never extended her punishment beyond a box on the ear. No, Percy Driscoll was the person. He told Chambers that under no provocation whatever was he privileged to lift his hand against his little master. Chambers overstepped the line three times, and got three such convincing canings from the man who was his father and didn't know it, that he took Tom's cruelties in all humility after that, and made no more experiments.

Outside of the house the two boys were together all through their boyhood. Chambers was strong beyond his years, and a good fighter; strong because he was coarsely fed and hard worked about the house, and a good fighter because Tom furnished him plenty of practice—on white boys whom he hated and was afraid of. Chambers was his constant bodyguard, to and from school; he was present on the playground at recess to protect his charge. He fought himself into such a formidable reputation, by and by, that Tom could have changed clothes with him, and "ridden in peace," like Sir Kay in Launcelot's armor.

He was good at games of skill, too. Tom staked him with marbles to play "keeps" with, and then took all the winnings away from him. In the winter season Chambers was on hand, in Tom's worn-out clothes, with "holy" red mittens, and "holy" shoes, and pants "holy" at the knees and seat, to drag a sled up the hill for Tom, warmly clad, to ride down on; but he never got a ride himself. He built snow men and snow fortifications under Tom's directions. He was Tom's patient target when Tom wanted to do some snowballing, but the target couldn't fire back. Chambers carried Tom's skates to the river and strapped them on him, then trotted around after him on the ice, so as to be on hand when wanted; but he wasn't ever asked to try the skates himself.

In summer the pet pastime of the boys of Dawson's Landing was to steal apples, peaches, and melons from the farmers' fruit-wagons—mainly on account of the risk they ran of getting their heads laid open with the butt of the farmer's whip. Tom was a distinguished adept at these thefts—by proxy. Chambers did his stealing, and got the peach-stones, apple-cores, and melon-rinds for his share.

Tom always made Chambers go in swimming with him, and stay by him as a protection. When Tom had had enough, he would slip out and tie knots in Chambers's shirt, dip the knots in the water and make them hard to undo, then dress himself and sit by and laugh while the naked shiverer tugged at the stubborn knots with his teeth.

Tom did his humble comrade these various ill turns partly out of native viciousness, and partly because he hated him for his superiorities of physique and pluck, and for his manifold cleverness. Tom couldn't dive, for it gave him splitting headaches. Chambers could dive without inconvenience, and was fond of doing it. He excited so much admiration, one day, among a crowd of white boys, by throwing back somersaults from the stern of a canoe, that it wearied Tom's spirit, and at last he shoved the canoe underneath Chambers while he was in the air—so he came down on his head in the canoe-bottom; and while he lay unconscious, several of Tom's ancient adversaries saw that their long-desired opportunity was come, and they gave the false heir such a drubbing that with Chambers's best help he was hardly able to drag himself home afterward.

When the boys were fifteen and upward, Tom was "showing off" in the river one day, when he was taken with a cramp, and shouted for help. It was a common trick with the boys—particularly if a stranger was present—to pretend a cramp and howl for help; then when the stranger came tearing hand over hand to the rescue, the howler would go on struggling and howling till he was close at hand, then replace the howl with a sarcastic smile and swim blandly away, while the town boys assailed the dupe with a volley of jeers and laughter. Tom had never tried this joke as yet, but was supposed to be trying it now, so the boys held warily back; but Chambers believed his master was in earnest, therefore he swam out, and arrived in time, unfortunately, and saved his life.

This was the last feather. Tom had managed to endure everything else, but to have to remain publicly and permanently under such an obligation as this to a nigger, and to this nigger of all niggers—this was too much. He heaped insults upon Chambers for "pretending" to think he was in earnest in calling for help, and said that anybody but a blockheaded nigger would have known he was funning and left him alone.

Tom's enemies were in strong force here, so they came out with their opinions quite freely. They laughed at him, and called him coward, liar, sneak, and other sorts of pet names, and told him they meant to call Chambers by a new name after this, and make it common in the town—"Tom Driscoll's niggerpappy,"—to signify that he had had a second birth into this life, and that Chambers was the author of his new being. Tom grew frantic under these taunts, and shouted—

"Knock their heads off, Chambers! knock their heads off! What do you stand there with your hands in your pockets for?"

Chambers expostulated, and said, "But, Marse Tom, dey's too many of 'em—dey's—"

"Do you hear me?"

"Please, Marse Tom, don't make me! Dey's so many of 'em dat—"

Tom sprang at him and drove his pocket-knife into him two or three times before the boys could snatch him away and give the wounded lad a chance to escape. He was considerably hurt, but not seriously. If the blade had been a little longer his career would have ended there.

Tom had long ago taught Roxy "her place." It had been many a day now since she had ventured a caress or a fondling epithet in his quarter. Such things, from a "nigger," were repulsive to him, and she had been warned to keep her distance and remember who she was. She saw her darling gradually cease from being her son, she saw *that* detail perish utterly; all that was left was master—master, pure and simple, and it was not a gentle mastership, either. She saw herself sink from the sublime height of motherhood to the somber depths of unmodified slavery. The abyss of separation between her and her boy was complete. She was merely his chattel, now, his convenience, his dog, his cringing and helpless slave, the humble and unresisting victim of his capricious temper and vicious nature.

Sometimes she could not go to sleep, even when worn out with fatigue, because her rage boiled so high over the day's experiences with her boy. She would mumble and mutter to herself—

"He struck me, en I warn't no way to blame—struck me in de face, right before folks. En he's al'ays callin' me nigger-wench, en hussy, en all dem mean names, when I's doin' de very bes' I kin. Oh, Lord, I done so much for him—I lift' him away up to what he is—en dis is what I git for it."

Sometimes when some outrage of peculiar offensiveness stung her to the heart, she would plan schemes of vengeance and revel in the fancied spectacle of his exposure to the world as an imposter and a slave; but in the midst of these joys fear would strike her: she had made him too strong; she could prove nothing, and—heavens, she might get sold down the river for her pains! So her schemes always went for nothing, and she laid them aside in impotent rage against the fates, and against herself for playing the fool on that fatal September day in not providing herself with a witness for use in the day when such a thing might be needed for the appeasing of her vengeance-hungry heart.

And yet the moment Tom happened to be good to her, and kind—and this occurred every now and then—all her sore places were healed, and she was happy; happy and proud, for this was her son, her nigger son, lording it among the whites and securely avenging their crimes against her race.

There were two grand funerals in Dawson's Landing that fall—the fall of 1845. One was that of Colonel Cecil Burleigh Essex, the other that of Percy Driscoll.

On his death-bed Driscoll set Roxy free and delivered his idolized ostensible son solemnly into the keeping of his brother, the Judge and his wife. Those childless people were glad to get him. Childless people are not difficult to please.

Judge Driscoll had gone privately to his brother, a month before, and bought Chambers. He had heard that Tom had been trying to get his father to sell the boy down the river, and he wanted to prevent the scandal—for public sentiment did not approve of that way of treating family servants for light cause or for no cause.

Percy Driscoll had worn himself out in trying to save his great speculative landed estate, and had died without succeeding. He was hardly in his grave before the boom collapsed and left his hitherto envied young devil of an heir a pauper. But that was nothing; his uncle told him he should be his heir and have all his fortune when he died; so Tom was comforted.

Roxy had no home, now; so she resolved to go around and say goodbye to her friends and then clear out and see the world—that is to say, she would go chambermaiding on a steamboat, the darling ambition of her race and sex.

Her last call was on the black giant, Jasper. She found him chopping Pudd'nhead Wilson's winter provision of wood.

Wilson was chatting with him when Roxy arrived. He asked her how she could bear to go off chambermaiding and leave her boys; and chaffingly offered to copy off a series of their fingerprints, reaching up to their twelfth year, for her to remember them by; but she sobered in a moment, wondering if he suspected anything; then she said she believed she didn't want them. Wilson said to himself, "The drop of black blood in her is superstitious; she thinks there's some devilry, some witch-business about my glass mystery somewhere; she used to come here with an old horseshoe in her hand; it could have been an accident, but I doubt it."

5

The Twins Thrill Dawson's Landing

Training is everything. The peach was once a bitter almond; cauliflower is nothing but cabbage with a college education.—*Pudd'nhead Wilson's Calendar*

Remark of Dr. Baldwin's, concerning upstarts: We don't care to eat toadstools that think they are truffles.—*Pudd'nhead Wilson's Calendar*

Mrs. York Driscoll enjoyed two years of bliss with that prize, Tom—bliss that was troubled a little at times, it is true, but bliss nevertheless; then she died, and her husband and his childless sister, Mrs. Pratt, continued the bliss-business at the old stand. Tom was petted and indulged and spoiled to his entire content—or nearly that; this went on till he was nineteen, then he was sent to Yale. He was handsomely equipped with "conditions," but otherwise he was not an object of distinction there. He remained at Yale two years, and then threw up the struggle. He came home with his manners a good deal improved; he had lost his surliness and brusqueness, and was rather pleasantly soft and smooth, now; he was furtively, and sometimes openly, ironical of speech, and given to gently touching people on the raw, but he did it with a good-natured semiconscious air that carried it off safely, and kept him from getting into trouble. He was as indolent as ever and showed no very strenuous desire to hunt up an occupation. People argued from this that he preferred to be supported by his uncle until his uncle's shoes should become vacant. He brought back one or two new habits with him, one of which he rather openly practised—tippling—but concealed another which was gambling. It would not do to gamble where his uncle could hear of it; he knew that quite well.

Tom's Eastern polish was not popular among the young people. They could have endured it, perhaps, if Tom had stopped there; but he wore gloves, and that they couldn't stand, and wouldn't; so he was mainly without society. He brought home with him a suit of clothes of such exquisite style and cut and fashion—Eastern fashion, city fashion—that it filled everybody with anguish and was regarded as a peculiarly wanton affront. He enjoyed the feeling which he was exciting, and paraded the town serene and happy all day; but the young fellows set a tailor to work that night, and when Tom started out on his parade next morning he found the old deformed negro bell-ringer straddling along in his wake tricked out in a flamboyant curtain-calico exaggeration of his finery, and imitating his fancy Eastern graces as well as he could.

Tom surrendered, and after that clothed himself in the local fashion. But the dull country town was tiresome to him, since his acquaintanceship with livelier regions, and it grew daily more and more so. He began to make little trips to St. Louis for refreshment. There he found companionship to suit him, and pleasures to his taste, along with more freedom, in some particulars, than he could have at home. So, during the next two years his visits to the city grew in frequency and his tarryings there grew steadily longer in duration.

He was getting into deep waters. He was taking chances, privately, which might get him into trouble some day—in fact, *did.*

Judge Driscoll had retired from the bench and from all business activities in 1850, and had now been comfortably idle three years. He was president of the Freethinkers' Society, and Pudd'nhead Wilson was the other member. The society's weekly discussions were now the old lawyer's main interest in life. Pudd'nhead was still toiling in obscurity at the bottom of the ladder, under the blight of that unlucky remark which he had let fall twenty-three years before about the dog.

Judge Driscoll was his friend, and claimed that he had a mind above the average, but that was regarded as one of the Judge's whims, and it failed to modify the public opinion. Or rather, that was one of the reasons why it failed, but there was another and better one. If the Judge had stopped with bare assertion, it would have had a good deal of effect; but he made the mistake of trying to prove his position. For some years Wilson had been privately at work on a whimsical almanac, for his amusement—a calendar, with a little dab of ostensible philosophy, usually in ironical form, appended to each date; and the Judge thought that these quips and fancies of Wilson's were neatly turned and cute; so he carried a handful of them around, one day, and read them to some of the chief citizens. But irony was not for those people; their mental vision was not focussed for it. They read those playful trifles in the solidest earnest, and decided without hesitancy that if there had ever been any doubt that Dave Wilson was a pudd'nhead—which there hadn't—this revelation removed that doubt for good and all. That is just the way in this world; an enemy can partly ruin a man, but it takes a good-natured injudicious friend to complete the thing and make it perfect. After this the Judge felt tenderer than ever toward Wilson, and surer than ever that his calendar had merit.

Judge Driscoll could be a freethinker and still hold his place in society because he was the person of most consequence in the community, and therefore could venture to go his own way and follow out his own notions. The other member of his pet organization was allowed the like liberty because he was a cipher in the estimation of the public, and nobody attached any importance to what he thought or did. He was liked, he was welcome enough all around, but he simply didn't count for anything.

The widow Cooper—affectionately called "aunt Patsy" by everybody—lived in a snug and comely cottage with her daughter Rowena, who was nineteen, romantic, amiable, and very pretty, but otherwise of no consequence. Rowena had a couple of young brothers—also of no consequence.

The widow had a large spare room which she let to a lodger, with board, when she could find one, but this room had been empty for a year now, to her sorrow. Her income was only sufficient for the family support, and she needed the lodging-money for trifling luxuries. But now, at last, on a flaming June day, she found herself happy; her tedious wait was ended; her year-worn advertisement had been answered; and not by a village applicant, oh, no!—this letter was from away off yonder in the dim great world to the North: it was from St. Louis. She sat on her porch gazing out with unseeing eyes upon the shining reaches of the mighty Mississippi, her thoughts steeped in her good fortune. Indeed, it was specially good fortune, for she was to have two lodgers instead of one.

She had read the letter to the family, and Rowena had danced away to see to the cleaning and airing of the room by the slave woman Nancy, and the boys had rushed abroad in the town to spread the great news, for it was matter of public interest, and the public would wonder and not be pleased if not informed. Presently Rowena returned, all ablush with joyous excitement, and begged for a re-reading of the letter. It was framed thus:

Honoured Madam: My brother and I have seen your advertisement, by chance, and beg leave to take the room you offer. We are twenty-four years of age and twins. We are Italians by birth, but have lived long in the various countries of Europe, and several years in the United States. Our names are Luigi and Angelo Capello. You desire but one guest; but dear Madam, if you will allow us to pay for two, we will not incommode you. We shall be down Thursday.

"Italians! How romantic! Just think, ma—there's never been one in this town, and everybody will be dying to see them, and they're all *ours*! Think of that!"

"Yes, I reckon they'll make a grand stir."

"Oh, indeed they will. The whole town will be on its head! Think—they've been in Europe and everywhere! There's never been a traveler in this town before. Ma, I shouldn't wonder if they've seen kings!"

"Well, a body can't tell, but they'll make stir enough, without that."

"Yes, that's of course. Luigi—Angelo. They're lovely names; and so grand and foreign—not like Jones and Robinson and such. Thursday they are coming, and this is only Tuesday; it's a cruel long time to wait. Here comes Judge Driscoll in at the gate. He's heard about it. I'll go and open the door."

The Judge was full of congratulations and curiosity. The letter was read and discussed. Soon Justice Robinson arrived with more congratulations, and there was a new reading and a new discussion. This was the beginning. Neighbour after neighbour, of both sexes, followed, and the procession drifted in and out all day and evening and all Wednesday and Thursday. The letter was read and re-read until it was nearly worn out; everybody admired its courtly and gracious tone, and smooth and practised style, everybody was sympathetic and excited, and the Coopers were steeped in happiness all the while.

The boats were very uncertain in low water, in these primitive times. This time the Thursday boat had not arrived at ten at night—so the people had waited at the landing all day for nothing; they were driven to their homes by a heavy storm without having had a view of the illustrious foreigners.

Eleven o'clock came; and the Cooper house was the only one in the town that still had lights burning. The rain and thunder were booming yet, and the anxious family were still waiting, still hoping. At last there was a knock at the door and the family jumped to open it. Two negro men entered, each carrying a trunk, and proceeded upstairs toward the guest room. Then entered the twins—the handsomest, the best dressed, the most distinguished-looking pair of young fellows the West had ever seen. One was a little fairer than the other, but otherwise they were exact duplicates.

6

Swimming in Glory

Let us endeavor so to live that when we come to die even the undertaker will be sorry.—*Pudd'nhead Wilson's Calendar*
Habit is habit, and not to be flung out of the window by any man, but coaxed downstairs a step at a time.—*Pudd'nhead Wilson's Calendar*

At breakfast in the morning the twins' charm of manner and easy and polished bearing made speedy conquest of the family's good graces. All constraint and formality quickly disappeared, and the friendliest feeling succeeded. Aunt Patsy called them by their Christian names almost from the beginning. She was full of the keenest curiosity about them, and showed it; they responded by talking about themselves, which pleased her greatly. It presently appeared that in their early youth they had known poverty and hardship. As the talk wandered along the old lady watched for the right place to drop in a question or two concerning that matter, and when she found it she said to the blond twin who was now doing the biographies in his turn while the brunette one rested—

"If it ain't asking what I ought not to ask, Mr. Angelo, how did you come to be so friendless and in such trouble when you were little? Do you mind telling? But don't if you do."

"Oh, we don't mind it at all, madam; in our case it was merely misfortune, and nobody's fault. Our parents were well to do, there in Italy, and we were their only child. We were of the old Florentine nobility"—Rowena's heart gave a great bound, her nostrils expanded, and a fine light played in her eyes—"and when the war broke out my father was on the losing side and had to fly for his life. His estates were confiscated, his personal property seized, and there we were, in Germany, strangers, friendless, and in fact paupers. My brother and I were ten years old, and well educated for that age, very studious, very fond of our books, and well grounded in the German, French, Spanish, and English languages. Also, we were marvellous musical prodigies—if you will allow me to say it, it being only the truth.

"Our father survived his misfortunes only a month, our mother soon followed him, and we were alone in the world. Our parents could have made themselves comfortable by exhibiting us as a show, and they had many and large offers; but the thought revolted their pride, and they said they would starve and die first. But what they wouldn't consent to do we had to do without the formality of consent. We were seized for the debts occasioned by their illness and their funerals, and placed among the attractions of a cheap museum in Berlin to earn the liquidation money. It took us two years to get out of that slavery. We traveled all about Germany receiving no wages, and not even our keep. We had to be exhibited for nothing, and beg our bread.

"Well, madam, the rest is not of much consequence. When we escaped from that slavery at twelve years of age, we were in some respects men. Experience had taught us some valuable things; among others, how to take care of ourselves, how to avoid and defeat sharks and sharpers, and how to conduct our own business for our own profit and without other people's help. We traveled everywhere—years and years—picking up smatterings of strange tongues, familiarizing ourselves with strange sights and strange customs, accumulating an education of a wide and varied and curious sort. It was a pleasant life. We went to Venice—to London, Paris, Russia, India, China, Japan—"

At this point Nancy the slave woman thrust her head in at the door and exclaimed:

"Ole Missus, de house is plum' jam full o' people, en dey's jes a-spi'lin' to see de gen'lmen!" She indicated the twins with a nod of her head, and tucked it back out of sight again.

It was a proud occasion for the widow, and she promised herself high satisfaction in showing off her fine foreign birds before her neighbours and friends—simple folk who had hardly ever seen a foreigner of any kind, and never one of any distinction or style. Yet her feeling was moderate indeed when contrasted with Rowena's. Rowena was in the clouds, she walked on air; this was to be the greatest day, the most romantic episode, in the colourless history of that dull country town. She was to be familiarly near the source of its glory and feel the full flood of it pour over her and about her; the other girls could only gaze and envy, not partake.

The widow was ready, Rowena was ready, so also were the foreigners.

The party moved along the hall, the twins in advance, and entered the open parlour door, whence issued a low hum of conversation. The twins took a position near the door, the widow stood at Luigi's side, Rowena stood beside Angelo, and the march-past and the introductions began. The widow was all smiles and contentment. She received the procession and passed it on to Rowena.

"Good mornin', Sister Cooper"—hand-shake.

"Good morning, Brother Higgins—Count Luigi Capello, Mr. Higgins"—hand-shake, followed by a devouring stare and "I'm glad to see ye," on the part of Higgins, and a courteous inclination of the head and a pleasant "Most happy!" on the part of Count Luigi.

"Good mornin', Roweny"—hand-shake.

"Good morning, Mr. Higgins—present you to Count Angelo Capello." Hand-shake, admiring stare, "Glad to see ye,"—courteous nod, smily "Most happy!" and Higgins passes on.

None of these visitors was at ease, but, being honest people, they didn't pretend to be. None of them had ever seen a person bearing a title of nobility before, and none had been expecting to see one now, consequently the title came upon them as a kind of pile-driving surprise and caught them unprepared. A few tried to rise to the emergency, and got out an awkward "My lord," or "Your lordship," or something of that sort, but the great majority were overwhelmed by the unaccustomed word and its dim and awful associations with gilded courts and stately ceremony and anointed kingship, so they only fumbled through the hand-shake and passed on, speechless. Now and then, as happens at all receptions everywhere, a more than ordinary friendly soul blocked the procession and kept it waiting while he inquired how the brothers liked the village, and how long they were going to stay, and if their families were well, and dragged in the weather, and hoped it would get cooler soon, and all that sort of thing, so as to be able to say, when they got home, "I had quite a long talk with them"; but nobody did or said anything of a regrettable kind, and so the great affair went through to the end in a creditable and satisfactory fashion.

General conversation followed, and the twins drifted about from group to group, talking easily and fluently and winning approval, compelling admiration and achieving favour from all. The widow followed their conquering march with a proud eye, and every now and then Rowena said to herself with deep satisfaction, "And to think they are ours—all ours!"

There were no idle moments for mother or daughter. Eager inquiries concerning the twins were pouring into their enchanted ears all the time; each was the constant center of a group of breathless listeners; each recognized that she knew now for the first time the real meaning of that great word Glory, and perceived the stupendous value of it, and understood why men in all ages had been willing to throw away meaner happinesses, treasure, life itself, to get a taste of its sublime and supreme joy. Napoleon and all his kind stood accounted for—and justified.

When Rowena had at last done all her duty by the people in the parlour, she went upstairs to satisfy the longings of an overflow-meeting there, for the parlour was not big enough to hold all the comers. Again she was besieged by eager questioners and again she swam in sunset seas of glory. When the forenoon was nearly gone, she recognized with a pang that this most splendid episode of her life was almost over, that nothing could prolong it, that nothing quite its equal could ever fall to her fortune again. But never mind, it was sufficient unto itself, the grand occasion had moved on an ascending scale from the start, and was a noble and memorable success. If the twins could but do some crowning act, now, to climax it, something unusual, something startling, something to concentrate upon themselves the company's loftiest admiration, something in the nature of an electric surprise—

Here a prodigious slam-banging broke out below, and everybody rushed down to see. It was the twins knocking out a classic four-handed piece on the piano, in great style. Rowena was satisfied—satisfied down to the bottom of her heart.

The young strangers were kept long at the piano. The villagers were astonished and enchanted with the magnificence of their performance, and could not bear to have them stop. All the music that they had ever heard before seemed spiritless prentice-work and barren of grace or charm when compared with these intoxicating floods of melodious sound. They realized that for once in their lives they were hearing masters.

7

The Unknown Nymph

> One of the most striking differences between a cat and a lie is that a cat has only nine lives.—*Pudd'nhead Wilson's Calendar*

The company broke up reluctantly, and drifted toward their several homes, chatting with vivacity, and all agreeing that it would be many a long day before Dawson's Landing would see the equal of this one again. The twins had accepted several invitations while the reception was in progress, and had also volunteered to play some duets at an amateur entertainment for the benefit of a local charity. Society was eager to receive them to its bosom. Judge Driscoll had the good fortune to secure them for an immediate drive, and to be the first to display them in public. They entered his buggy with him, and were paraded down the main street, everybody flocking to the windows and sidewalks to see.

The Judge showed the strangers the new graveyard, and the jail, and where the richest man lived, and the Freemasons' hall, and the Methodist church, and the Presbyterian church, and where the Baptist church was going to be when they got some money to build it with, and showed them the town hall and the slaughterhouse, and got out the independent fire company in uniform and had them put out an imaginary fire; then he let them inspect the muskets of the militia company, and poured out an exhaustless stream of enthusiasm over all these splendours, and seemed very well satisfied with the responses he got, for the twins admired his admiration, and paid him back the best they could, though they could have done better if some fifteen or sixteen hundred thousand previous experiences of this sort in various countries had not already rubbed off a considerable part of the novelty of it.

The Judge laid himself out hospitably to make them have a good time, and if there was a defect anywhere it was not his fault. He told them a good many humorous anecdotes, and always forgot the nub, but they were always able to furnish it, for these yarns were of a pretty early vintage, and they had had many a rejuvenating pull at them before. And he told them all about his several dignities, and how he had held this and that and the other place of honour or profit, and had once been to the legislature, and was now president of the Society of Freethinkers. He said the society had been in existence four years, and already had two members, and was firmly established. He would call for the brothers in the evening if they would like to attend a meeting of it.

Accordingly he called for them, and on the way he told them all about Pudd'nhead Wilson, in order that they might get a favourable impression of him in advance and be prepared to like him. This scheme succeeded—the favourable impression was achieved. Later it was confirmed and solidified when Wilson proposed that out of courtesy to the strangers the usual topics be put aside and the hour be devoted to conversation upon ordinary subjects and the cultivation of friendly relations and good-fellowship—a proposition which was put to vote and carried.

The hour passed quickly away in lively talk, and when it was ended the lonesome and neglected Wilson was richer by two friends than he had been when it began. He invited the twins to look in at his lodgings, presently, after disposing of an intervening engagement, and they accepted with pleasure.

Toward the middle of the evening they found themselves on the road to his house. Pudd'nhead was at home waiting for them and putting in his time puzzling over a thing which had come under his notice that morning. The matter was this: He happened to be up very early—at dawn, in fact; and he crossed the hall which divided his cottage through the center, and entered a room to get something there. The window of the room had no curtains, for that side of the house had long been unoccupied, and through this window he caught sight of something which surprised and interested him. It was a young woman—a young woman where properly no young woman belonged; for she was in Judge Driscoll's house, and in the bedroom over the Judge's private study or sitting room. This was young Tom Driscoll's bedroom. He and the Judge, the Judge's widowed sister Mrs. Pratt and three negro servants were the only people who belonged in the house. Who, then, might this young lady be? The two houses were separated by an ordinary yard, with a low fence running back through its middle from the street in front to the lane in the rear. The distance was not great, and Wilson was able to see the girl very well, the window-shades of the room she was in being up, and the window also. The girl had on a neat and trim summer dress, patterned in broad stripes of pink and white, and her bonnet was equipped with a pink veil. She was practising steps, gaits and attitudes, apparently; she was doing the thing gracefully, and was very much absorbed in her work. Who could she be, and how came she to be in young Tom Driscoll's room?

Wilson had quickly chosen a position from which he could watch the girl without running much risk of being seen by her, and he remained there hoping she would raise her veil and betray her face. But she disappointed him. After a matter of twenty minutes she disappeared, and although he stayed at his post half an hour longer, she came no more.

Toward noon he dropped in at the Judge's and talked with Mrs. Pratt about the great event of the day, the levee of the distinguished foreigners at Aunt Patsy Cooper's. He asked after her nephew Tom, and she said he was on his way home, and that she was expecting him to arrive a little before night; and added that she and the Judge were gratified to gather from his letters that he was conducting himself very nicely and creditably—at which Wilson winked to himself privately. Wilson did not ask if there was a newcomer in the house, but he asked questions that would have brought light-throwing answers as to that matter if Mrs. Pratt had had any light to throw; so he went away satisfied that he knew of things that were going on in her house of which she herself was not aware.

He was now waiting for the twins, and still puzzling over the problem of who that girl might be, and how she happened to be in that young fellow's room at daybreak in the morning.

8

Marse Tom Tramples His Chance

The holy passion of Friendship is of so sweet and steady and loyal and enduring a nature that it will last through a whole lifetime, if not asked to lend money.—*Pudd'nhead Wilson's Calendar*

Consider well the proportions of things. It is better to be a young June-bug than an old bird of paradise.—*Pudd'nhead Wilson's Calendar*

It is necessary now, to hunt up Roxy.

At the time she was set free and went away chambermaiding, she was thirty-five. She got a berth as second chambermaid on a Cincinnati boat in the New Orleans trade, the *Grand Mogul.* A couple of trips made her wonted and easy-going at the work, and infatuated her with the stir and adventure and independence of steamboat life. Then she was promoted and became head chambermaid. She was a favourite with the officers, and exceedingly proud of their joking and friendly way with her.

During eight years she served three parts of the year on that boat, and the winters on a Vicksburg packet. But now for two months she had had rheumatism in her arms, and was obliged to let the wash-tub alone. So she resigned. But she was well fixed—rich, as she would have described it; for she had lived a steady life, and had banked four dollars every month in New Orleans as a provision for her old age. She said in the start that she had "put shoes on one bar'footed nigger to tromple on her with," and that one mistake like that was enough; she would be independent of the human race thenceforth forevermore if hard work and economy could accomplish it. When the boat touched the levee at New Orleans she bade goodbye to her comrades on the *Grand Mogul* and moved her kit ashore.

But she was back in a hour. The bank had gone to smash and carried her four hundred dollars with it. She was a pauper, and homeless. Also disabled bodily, at least for the present. The officers were full of sympathy for her in her trouble, and made up a little purse for her. She resolved to go to her birthplace; she had friends there among the negroes, and the unfortunate always help the unfortunate, she was well aware of that; those lowly comrades of her youth would not let her starve.

She took the little local packet at Cairo, and now she was on the home-stretch. Time had worn away her bitterness against her son, and she was able to think of him with serenity. She put the vile side of him out of her mind, and dwelt only on recollections of his occasional acts of kindness to her. She gilded and otherwise decorated these, and made them very pleasant to contemplate. She began to long to see him. She would go and fawn upon him, slave-like—for this would have to be her attitude, of course—and maybe she would find that time had modified him, and that he would be glad to see his long-forgotten old nurse and treat her gently. That would be lovely; that would make her forget her woes and her poverty.

Her poverty! That thought inspired her to add another castle to her dream: maybe he would give her a trifle now and then—maybe a dollar, once a month, say; any little thing like that would help, oh, ever so much.

By the time she reached Dawson's Landing she was her old self again; her blues were gone, she was in high feather. She would get along, surely; there were many kitchens where the servants would share their meals with her, and also steal sugar and apples and other dainties for her to carry home—or give her a chance to pilfer them herself, which would answer just as well. And there was the church. She was a more rabid and devoted Methodist than ever, and her piety was no sham, but was strong and sincere. Yes, with plenty of creature comforts and her old place in the amen-corner in her possession again, she would be perfectly happy and at peace thenceforward to the end.

She went to Judge Driscoll's kitchen first of all. She was received there in great form and with vast enthusiasm. Her wonderful travels, and the strange countries she had seen and the adventures she had had, made her a marvel, and a heroine of romance. The negroes hung enchanted upon the great story of her experiences, interrupting her all along with eager questions, with laughter, exclamations of delight and expressions of applause; and she was obliged to confess to herself that if there was anything better in this world than steamboating, it was the glory to be got by telling about it. The audience loaded her stomach with their dinners, and then stole the pantry bare to load up her basket.

Tom was in St. Louis. The servants said he had spent the best part of his time there during the previous two years. Roxy came every day, and had many talks about the family and its affairs. Once she asked why Tom was away so much. The ostensible "Chambers" said:

"De fac' is, ole marster kin git along better when young marster's away den he kin when he's in de town; yes, en he love him better, too; so he gives him fifty dollahs a month—"

"No, is dat so? Chambers, you's a-jokin', ain't you?"

"'Clah to goodness I ain't, mammy; Marse Tom tole me so his own self. But nemmine, 't ain't enough."

"My lan', what de reason 't ain't enough?"

"Well, I's gwine to tell you, if you gimme a chanst, mammy. De reason it ain't enough is 'ca'se Marse Tom gambles."

Roxy threw up her hands in astonishment and Chambers went on—

"Ole marster found it out, 'ca'se he had to pay two hundred dollahs for Marse Tom's gamblin' debts, en dat's true, mammy, jes as dead certain as you's bawn."

"Two—hund'd—dollahs! Why, what is you talkin' 'bout? Two—hund'd—dollahs. Sakes alive, it's 'mos' enough to buy a tol'able good second-hand nigger wid. En you ain't lyin', honey?—you wouldn't lie to yo' ole mammy?"

"It's God's own truth, jes as I tell you—two hund'd dollahs—I wisht I may never stir outen my tracks if it ain't so. En, oh, my lan', ole Marse was jes a-hoppin'! he was b'ilin' mad, I tell you! He tuck 'n' dissenhurrit him."

He licked his chops with relish after that stately word. Roxy struggled with it a moment, then gave it up and said—

"Dissen*whiched* him?"

"Dissenhurrit him."

"What's dat? What do it mean?"

"Means he bu'sted de will."

"Bu's—ted de will! He wouldn't *ever* treat him so! Take it back, you mis'able imitation nigger dat I bore in sorrow en tribbilation."

Roxy's pet castle—an occasional dollar from Tom's pocket—was tumbling to ruin before her eyes. She could not abide such a disaster as that; she couldn't endure the thought of it. Her remark amused Chambers:

"Yah-yah-yah! jes listen to dat! If I's imitation, what is you? Bofe of us is imitation *white*—dat's what we is—en pow'ful good imitation, too—yah-yah-yah!—we don't 'mount to noth'n as imitation *niggers*; en as for—"

"Shet up yo' foolin', 'fo' I knock you side de head, en tell me 'bout de will. Tell me 'tain't bu'sted—do, honey, en I'll never forgit you."

"Well, *'tain't*—'ca'se dey's a new one made, en Marse Tom's all right ag'in. But what is you in sich a sweat 'bout it for, mammy? 'Tain't none o' your business I don't reckon."

"'Tain't none o' my business? Whose business is it den, I'd like to know? Wuz I his mother tell he was fifteen years old, or wusn't I?—you answer me dat. En you speck I could see him turned out po' en ornery on de worl' en never care noth'n' 'bout it? I reckon if you'd ever be'n a mother yo'self, Valet de Chambers, you wouldn't talk sich foolishness as dat."

"Well, den, ole Marse forgive him en fixed up de will ag'in—do dat satisfy you?"

Yes, she was satisfied now, and quite happy and sentimental over it. She kept coming daily, and at last she was told that Tom had come home. She began to tremble with emotion, and straightway sent to beg him to let his "po' ole nigger mammy have jes one sight of him en die for joy."

Tom was stretched at his lazy ease on a sofa when Chambers brought the petition. Time had not modified his ancient detestation of the humble drudge and protector of his boyhood; it was still bitter and uncompromising. He sat up and bent a severe gaze upon the fair face of the young fellow whose name he was unconsciously using and whose family rights he was enjoying. He maintained the gaze until the victim of it had become satisfactorily pallid with terror, then he said—

"What does the old rip want with me?"

The petition was meekly repeated.

"Who gave you permission to come and disturb me with the social attentions of niggers?"

Tom had risen. The other young man was trembling now, visibly. He saw what was coming, and bent his head sideways, and put up his left arm to shield it. Tom rained cuffs upon the head and its shield, saying no word: the victim received each blow with a beseeching, "Please, Marse Tom!—oh, please, Marse Tom!" Seven blows—then Tom said, "Face the door—march!" He followed behind with one, two, three solid kicks. The last one helped the pure-white slave over the door-sill, and he limped away mopping his eyes with his old ragged sleeve. Tom shouted after him, "Send her in!"

Then he flung himself panting on the sofa again, and rasped out the remark, "He arrived just at the right moment; I was full to the brim with bitter thinkings, and nobody to take it out of. How refreshing it was! I feel better."

Tom's mother entered now, closing the door behind her, and approached her son with all the wheedling and supplicating servilities that fear and interest can impart to the words and attitudes of the born slave. She stopped a yard from her boy and made two or three admiring exclamations over his manly stature and general handsomeness, and Tom put an arm under his head and hoisted a leg over the sofa-back in order to look properly indifferent.

"My lan', how you is growed, honey! 'Clah to goodness, I wouldn't a-knowed you, Marse Tom! 'deed I wouldn't! Look at me good; does you 'member old Roxy?—does you know yo' old nigger mammy, honey? Well, now, I kin lay down en die in peace, 'ca'se I'se seed—"

"Cut it short—it, cut it short! What is it you want?"

"You heah dat? Jes the same old Marse Tom, al'ays so gay and funnin' wid de ole mammy. I 'uz jes as shore—"

"Cut it short, I tell you, and get along! What do you want?"

This was a bitter disappointment. Roxy had for so many days nourished and fondled and petted her notion that Tom would be glad to see his old nurse, and would make her proud and happy to the marrow with a cordial word or two, that it took two rebuffs to convince her that he was not funning, and that her beautiful dream was a fond and foolish vanity, a shabby and pitiful mistake. She was hurt to the heart, and so ashamed that for a moment she did not quite know what to do or how to act. Then her breast began to heave, the tears came, and in her forlornness she was moved to try that other dream of hers—an appeal to her boy's charity; and so, upon the impulse, and without reflection, she offered her supplication:

"Oh, Marse Tom, de po' ole mammy is in sich hard luck dese days; en she's kinder crippled in de arms en can't work, en if you could gimme a dollah—on'y jes one little dol—"

Tom was on his feet so suddenly that the supplicant was startled into a jump herself.

"A dollar!—give you a dollar! I've a notion to strangle you! Is *that* your errand here? Clear out! and be quick about it!"

Roxy backed slowly toward the door. When she was halfway she stopped, and said mournfully:

"Marse Tom, I nussed you when you was a little baby, en I raised you all by myself tell you was 'most a young man; en now you is young en rich, en I is po' en gitt'n ole, en I come heah b'lievin' dat you would he'p de ole mammy 'long down de little road dat's lef' 'twix' her en de grave, en—"

Tom relished this tune less than any that had preceded it, for it began to wake up a sort of echo in his conscience; so he interrupted and said with decision, though without asperity, that he was not in a situation to help her, and wasn't going to do it.

"Ain't you ever gwine to he'p me, Marse Tom?"

"No! Now go away and don't bother me any more."

Roxy's head was down, in an attitude of humility. But now the fires of her old wrongs flamed up in her breast and began to burn fiercely. She raised her head slowly, till it was well up, and at the same time her great frame unconsciously assumed an erect and masterful attitude, with all the majesty and grace of her vanished youth in it. She raised her finger and punctuated with it:

"You has said de word. You has had yo' chance, en you has trompled it under yo' foot. When you git another one, you'll git down on yo' knees en *beg* for it!"

A cold chill went to Tom's heart, he didn't know why; for he did not reflect that such words, from such an incongruous source, and so solemnly delivered, could not easily fail of that effect. However, he did the natural thing: he replied with bluster and mockery:

"*You'll* give me a chance—*you*! Perhaps I'd better get down on my knees now! But in case I don't—just for argument's sake—what's going to happen, pray?"

"Dis is what is gwine to happen. I's gwine as straight to yo' uncle as I kin walk, en tell him every las' thing I knows 'bout you."

Tom's cheek blenched, and she saw it. Disturbing thoughts began to chase each other through his head. "How can she know? And yet she must have found out—she looks it. I've had the will back only three months, and am already deep in debt again, and moving heaven and earth to save myself from exposure and destruction, with a reasonably fair show of getting the thing covered up if I'm let alone, and now this fiend has gone and found me out somehow or other. I wonder how much she knows? Oh, oh, oh, it's enough to break a body's heart! But I've got to humour her—there's no other way."

Then he worked up a rather sickly sample of a gay laugh and a hollow chipperness of manner, and said:

"Well, well, Roxy dear, old friends like you and me mustn't quarrel. Here's your dollar—now tell me what you know."

He held out the wild-cat bill; she stood as she was, and made no movement. It was her turn to scorn persuasive foolery, now, and she did not waste it. She said, with a grim implacability in voice and manner which made Tom almost realize that even a former slave can remember for ten minutes insults and injuries returned for compliments and flatteries received, and can also enjoy taking revenge for them when the opportunity offers:

"What does I know? I'll tell you what I knows. I knows enough to bu'st dat will to flinders—en more, mind you, *more!*"

Tom was aghast.

"More?" he said. "What do you call more? Where's there any room for more?"

Roxy laughed a mocking laugh, and said scoffingly, with a toss of her head, and her hands on her hips—

"Yes!—oh, I reckon! *Co'se* you'd like to know—wid yo' po' little ole rag dollah. What you reckon I's gwine to tell *you* for?—you ain't got no money. I's gwine to tell yo' uncle—en I'll do it dis minute, too—he'll gimme *five* dollahs for de news, en mighty glad, too."

She swung herself around disdainfully, and started away. Tom was in a panic. He seized her skirts, and implored her to wait. She turned and said, loftily—

"Look-a-heah, what 'uz it I tole you?"

"You—you—I don't remember anything. What was it you told me?"

"I tole you dat de next time I give you a chance you'd git down on yo' knees en beg for it."

Tom was stupefied for a moment. He was panting with excitement. Then he said:

"Oh, Roxy, you wouldn't require your young master to do such a horrible thing. You can't mean it."

"I'll let you know mighty quick whether I means it or not! You call me names, en as good as spit on me when I comes here po' en ornery en 'umble, to praise you for bein' growed up so fine en handsome, en tell you how I used to nuss you en tend you en watch you when you 'uz sick en hadn't no mother but me in de whole worl', en beg you to give de po' ole nigger a dollah for to git her som'n' to eat, en you call me names—*names*, dad blame you! Yassir, I gives you jes one chance mo', and dat's *now*, en it las' on'y a half a second—you hear?"

Tom slumped to his knees and began to beg, saying—

"You see, I'm begging, and it's honest begging, too! Now tell me, Roxy, tell me."

The heir of two centuries of unatoned insult and outrage looked down on him and seemed to drink in deep draughts of satisfaction. Then she said—

"Fine nice young white gen'l'man kneelin' down to a nigger-wench! I's wanted to see dat jes once befo' I's called. Now, Gabr'el, blow de hawn, I's ready . . . Git up!"

Tom did it. He said, humbly—

"Now, Roxy, don't punish me any more. I deserved what I've got, but be good and let me off with that. Don't go to uncle. Tell me—I'll give you the five dollars."

"Yes, I bet you will; en you won't stop dah, nuther. But I ain't gwine to tell you heah—"

"Good gracious, no!"

"Is you 'feared o' de ha'nted house?"

"N-no."

"Well, den, you come to de ha'nted house 'bout ten or 'leven tonight, en climb up de ladder, 'ca'se de sta'r-steps is broke down, en you'll find me. I's a-roostin' in de ha'nted house 'ca'se I can't 'ford to roos' nowhers' else." She started toward the door, but stopped and said, "Gimme de dollah bill!" He gave it to her. She examined it and said, "H'm—like enough de bank's bu'sted." She started again, but halted again. "Has you got any whisky?"

"Yes, a little."

"Fetch it!"

He ran to his room overhead and brought down a bottle which was two-thirds full. She tilted it up and took a drink. Her eyes sparkled with satisfaction, and she tucked the bottle under her shawl, saying, "It's prime. I'll take it along."

Tom humbly held the door for her, and she marched out as grim and erect as a grenadier.

9

Tom Practises Sycophancy

Why is it that we rejoice at a birth and grieve at a funeral? It is because we are not the person involved.—*Pudd'nhead Wilson's Calendar*

It is easy to find fault, if one has that disposition. There was once a man who, not being able to find any other fault with his coal, complained that there were too many prehistoric toads in it.—*Pudd'nhead Wilson's Calendar.*

Tom flung himself on the sofa, and put his throbbing head in his hands, and rested his elbows on his knees. He rocked himself back and forth and moaned.

"I've knelt to a nigger wench!" he muttered. "I thought I had struck the deepest depths of degradation before, but oh, dear, it was nothing to this. . . . Well, there is one consolation, such as it is—I've struck bottom this time; there's nothing lower."

But that was a hasty conclusion.

At ten that night he climbed the ladder in the haunted house, pale, weak and wretched. Roxy was standing in the door of one of the rooms, waiting, for she had heard him.

This was a two-storey log house which had acquired the reputation a few years before of being haunted, and that was the end of its usefulness. Nobody would live in it afterward, or go near it by night, and most people even gave it a wide berth in the daytime. As it had no competition, it was called *the* haunted house. It was getting crazy and ruinous, now, from long neglect. It stood three hundred yards beyond Pudd'nhead Wilson's house, with nothing between but vacancy. It was the last house in the town at that end.

Tom followed Roxy into the room. She had a pile of clean straw in the corner for a bed, some cheap but well-kept clothing was hanging on the wall, there was a tin lantern freckling the floor with little spots of light, and there were various soap-and-candle boxes scattered about, which served for chairs. The two sat down. Roxy said—

"Now den, I'll tell you straight off, en I'll begin to k'leck de money later on; I ain't in no hurry. What does you reckon I's gwine to tell you?"

"Well, you—you—oh, Roxy, don't make it too hard for me! Come right out and tell me you've found out somehow what a shape I'm in on account of dissipation and foolishness."

"Disposition en foolishness! *No* sir, dat ain't it. Dat jist ain't nothin' at all, 'longside o' what *I* knows."

Tom stared at her, and said—

"Why, Roxy, what do you mean?"

She rose, and gloomed above him like a Fate.

"I means dis—en it's de Lord's truth. You ain't no more kin to ole Marse Driscoll den I is!—*dat's* what I means!" and her eyes flamed with triumph.

"What!"

"Yassir, en *dat* ain't all! You's a *nigger!—bawn* a nigger en a *slave!*—en you's a nigger en a slave dis minute; en if I opens my mouf ole Marse Driscoll'll sell you down de river befo' you is two days older den what you is now!"

"It's a thundering lie, you miserable old blatherskite!"

"It ain't no lie, nuther. It's jes de truth, en nothin' *but* de truth, so he'p me. Yassir—you's my *son*—"

"You devil!"

"En dat po' boy dat you's be'n a-kickin' en a-cuffin' today is Percy Driscoll's son en yo' *marster*—"

"You beast!"

"En *his* name's Tom Driscoll, en *yo'* name's Valet de Chambers, en you ain't *got* no fambly name, beca'se niggers don't *have* em!"

Tom sprang up and seized a billet of wood and raised it; but his mother only laughed at him, and said—

"Set down, you pup! Does you think you kin skyer me? It ain't in you, nor de likes of you. I reckon you'd shoot me in de back, maybe, if you got a chance, for dat's jist yo' style—*I* knows you, throo en throo—but I don't mind gitt'n killed, beca'se all dis is down in writin' en it's in safe hands, too, en de man dat's got it knows whah to look for de right man when I gits killed. Oh, bless yo' soul, if you puts yo' mother up for as big a fool as *you* is, you's pow'ful mistaken, I kin tell you! Now den, you set still en behave yo'self; en don't you git up ag'in till I tell you!"

Tom fretted and chafed awhile in a whirlwind of disorganizing sensations and emotions, and finally said, with something like settled conviction—

"The whole thing is moonshine; now then, go ahead and do your worst; I'm done with you."

Roxy made no answer. She took the lantern and started toward the door. Tom was in a cold panic in a moment.

"Come back, come back!" he wailed. "I didn't mean it, Roxy; I take it all back, and I'll never say it again! Please come back, Roxy!"

The woman stood a moment, then she said gravely:

"Dat's one thing you's got to stop, Valet de Chambers. You can't call me *Roxy*, same as if you was my equal. Chillen don't speak to dey mammies like dat. You'll call me ma or mammy, dat's what you'll call me—leastways when dey ain't nobody aroun'. *Say* it!"

It cost Tom a struggle, but he got it out.

"Dat's all right. Don't you ever forgit it ag'in, if you knows what's good for you. Now den, you has said you wouldn't ever call it lies en moonshine ag'in. I'll tell you dis, for a warnin': if you ever does say it ag'in, it's de *las'* time you'll ever say it to me; I'll tramp as straight to de Judge as I kin walk, en tell him who you is, en *prove* it. Does you b'lieve me when I says dat?"

"Oh," groaned Tom, "I more than believe it; I *know* it."

Roxy knew her conquest was complete. She could have proved nothing to anybody, and her threat about the writings was a lie; but she knew the person she was dealing with, and had made both statements without any doubt as to the effect they would produce.

She went and sat down on her candle-box, and the pride and pomp of her victorious attitude made it a throne. She said—

"Now den, Chambers, we's gwine to talk business, en dey ain't gwine to be no mo' foolishness. In de fust place, you gits fifty dollahs a month; you's gwine to han' over half of it to yo' ma. Plank it out!"

But Tom had only six dollars in the world. He gave her that, and promised to start fair on next month's pension.

"Chambers, how much is you in debt?"

Tom shuddered, and said—

"Nearly three hundred dollars."

"How is you gwine to pay it?"

Tom groaned out—"Oh, I don't know; don't ask me such awful questions."

But she stuck to her point until she wearied a confession out of him: he had been prowling about in disguise, stealing small valuables from private houses; in fact, he made a good deal of a raid on his fellow-villagers a fortnight before, when he was supposed to be in St. Louis; but he doubted if he had sent away enough stuff to realize the required amount, and was afraid to make a further venture in the present excited state of the town. His mother approved of his conduct, and offered to help, but this frightened him. He tremblingly ventured to say that if she would retire from the town he should feel better and safer, and could hold his head higher—and was going on to make an argument, but she interrupted and surprised him pleasantly by saying she was ready; it didn't make any difference to her where she stayed, so that she got her share of the pension regularly. She said she would not go far, and would call at the haunted house once a month for her money. Then she said—

"I don't hate you so much now, but I've hated you a many a year—and anybody would. Didn't I change you off, en give you a good fambly en a good name, en made you a white gen'l'man en rich, wid store clothes on—en what did I git for it? You despised me all de time, en was al'ays sayin' mean hard things to me befo' folks, en wouldn't ever let me forgit I's a nigger—en—en—"

She fell to sobbing, and broke down. Tom said—"But you know I didn't know you were my mother; and besides—"

"Well, nemmine 'bout dat, now; let it go. I's gwine to fo'git it." Then she added fiercely, "En don't ever make me remember it ag'in, or you'll be sorry, *I* tell you."

When they were parting, Tom said, in the most persuasive way he could command—

"Ma, would you mind telling me who was my father?"

He had supposed he was asking an embarrassing question. He was mistaken. Roxy drew herself up with a proud toss of her head, and said—

"Does I mine tellin' you? No, dat I don't! You ain't got no 'casion to be shame' o' yo' father, *I* kin tell you. He wuz de highest quality in dis whole town—ole Virginny stock. Fust famblies, he wuz. Jes as good stock as de Driscolls en de Howards, de bes' day dey ever seed." She put on a little prouder air, if possible, and added impressively: "Does you 'member Cunnel Cecil Burleigh Essex, dat died de same year yo' young Marse Tom Driscoll's pappy died, en all de Masons en Odd Fellers en Churches turned out en give him de bigges' funeral dis town ever seed? Dat's de man."

Under the inspiration of her soaring complacency the departed graces of her earlier days returned to her, and her bearing took to itself a dignity and state that might have passed for queenly if her surroundings had been a little more in keeping with it.

"Dey ain't another nigger in dis town dat's as high-bawn as you is. Now den, go 'long! En jes you hold yo' head up as high as you want to—you has de right, en dat I kin swah."

10

The Nymph Revealed

> All say, "How hard it is that we have to die"—a strange complaint to come from the mouths of people who have had to live.—*Pudd'nhead Wilson's Calendar*
>
> When angry, count four; when very angry, swear.—*Pudd'nhead Wilson's Calendar*

Every now and then, after Tom went to bed, he had sudden wakings out of his sleep, and his first thought was, "Oh, joy, it was all a dream!" Then he laid himself heavily down again, with a groan and the muttered words, "A nigger! I am a nigger! Oh, I wish I was dead!"

He woke at dawn with one more repetition of this horror, and then he resolved to meddle no more with that treacherous sleep. He began to think. Sufficiently bitter thinkings they were. They wandered along something after this fashion:

"Why were niggers *and* whites made? What crime did the uncreated first nigger commit that the curse of birth was decreed for him? And why is this awful difference made between white and black? . . . How hard the nigger's fate seems, this morning!—yet until last night such a thought never entered my head."

He sighed and groaned an hour or more away. Then "Chambers" came humbly in to say that breakfast was nearly ready. "Tom" blushed scarlet to see this aristocratic white youth cringe to him, a nigger, and call him "Young Marster." He said roughly—

"Get out of my sight!" and when the youth was gone, he muttered, "He has done me no harm, poor wretch, but he is an eyesore to me now, for he is Driscoll the young gentleman, and I am a—oh, I wish I was dead!"

A gigantic irruption, like that of Krakatoa a few years ago, with the accompanying earthquakes, tidal waves, and clouds of volcanic dust, changes the face of the surrounding landscape beyond recognition, bringing down the high lands, elevating the low, making fair lakes where deserts had been, and deserts where green prairies had smiled before. The tremendous catastrophe which had befallen Tom had changed his moral landscape in much the same way. Some of his low places he found lifted to ideals, some of his ideals had sunk to the valleys, and lay there with the sackcloth and ashes of pumice-stone and sulphur on their ruined heads.

For days he wandered in lonely places, thinking, thinking, thinking—trying to get his bearings. It was new work. If he met a friend, he found that the habit of a lifetime had in some mysterious way vanished—his arm hung limp, instead of involuntarily extending the hand for a shake. It was the "nigger" in him asserting its humility, and he blushed and was abashed. And the "nigger" in him was surprised when the white friend put out his hand for a shake with him. He found the "nigger" in him involuntarily giving the road, on the sidewalk, to a white rowdy and loafer. When Rowena, the dearest thing his heart knew, the idol of his secret worship, invited him in, the "nigger" in him made an embarrassed excuse and was afraid to enter and sit with the dread white folks on equal terms. The "nigger" in him went shrinking and skulking here and there and yonder, and fancying it saw suspicion and maybe detection in all faces, tones, and gestures. So strange and uncharacteristic was Tom's conduct that people noticed it, and turned to look after him when he passed on; and when he glanced back—as he could not help doing, in spite of his best resistance—and caught that puzzled expression in a person's face, it gave him a sick feeling, and he took himself out of view as quickly as he could. He presently came to have a hunted sense and a hunted look, and then he fled away to the hill-tops and the solitudes. He said to himself that the curse of Ham was upon him.

He dreaded his meals; the "nigger" in him was ashamed to sit at the white folks' table, and feared discovery all the time; and once when Judge Driscoll said, "What's the matter with you? You look as meek as a nigger," he felt as secret murderers are said to feel when the accuser says, "Thou art the man!" Tom said he was not well, and left the table.

His ostensible "aunt's" solicitudes and endearments were become a terror to him, and he avoided them.

And all the time, hatred of his ostensible "uncle" was steadily growing in his heart; for he said to himself, "He is white; and I am his chattel, his property, his goods, and he can sell me, just as he could his dog."

For as much as a week after this, Tom imagined that his character had undergone a pretty radical change. But that was because he did not know himself.

In several ways his opinions were totally changed, and would never go back to what they were before, but the main structure of his character was not changed, and could not be changed. One or two very important features of it were altered, and in time effects would result from this, if opportunity offered—effects of a quite serious nature, too. Under the influence of a great mental and moral upheaval his character and habits had taken on the appearance of complete change, but after a while with the subsidence of the storm both began to settle toward their former places. He dropped gradually back into his old frivolous and easy-going ways and conditions of feeling and manner of speech, and no familiar of his could have detected anything in him that differentiated him from the weak and careless Tom of other days.

The theft-raid which he had made upon the village turned out better than he had ventured to hope. It produced the sum necessary to pay his gaming-debts, and saved him from exposure to his uncle and another smashing of the will. He and his mother learned to like each other fairly well. She couldn't love him, as yet, because there "warn't nothing *to* him," as she expressed it, but her nature needed something or somebody to rule over, and he was better than nothing. Her strong character and aggressive and commanding ways compelled Tom's admiration in spite of the fact that he got more illustrations of them than he needed for his comfort. However, as a rule her conversation was made up of racy tattle about the privacies of the chief families of the town (for she went harvesting among their kitchens every time she came to the village), and Tom enjoyed this. It was just in his line. She always collected her half of his pension punctually, and he was always at the haunted house to have a chat with her on these occasions. Every now and then she paid him a visit there on between-days also.

Occasionally he would run up to St. Louis for a few weeks, and at last temptation caught him again. He won a lot of money, but lost it, and with it a deal more besides, which he promised to raise as soon as possible.

For this purpose he projected a new raid on his town. He never meddled with any other town, for he was afraid to venture into houses whose ins and outs he did not know and the habits of whose households he was not acquainted with. He arrived at the haunted house in disguise on the Wednesday before the advent of the twins—after writing his aunt Pratt that he would not arrive until two days after—and lay in hiding there with his mother until toward daylight Friday morning, when he went to his uncle's house and entered by the back way with his own key, and slipped up to his room, where he could have the use of the mirror and toilet articles. He had a suit of girl's clothes with him in a bundle as a disguise for his raid, and was wearing a suit of his mother's clothing, with black gloves and veil. By dawn he was tricked out for his raid, but he caught a glimpse of Pudd'nhead Wilson through the window over the way, and knew that Pudd'nhead had caught a glimpse of him. So he entertained Wilson with some airs and graces and attitudes for a while, then stepped out of sight and resumed the other disguise, and by and by went down and out the back way and started down town to reconnoiter the scene of his intended labours.

But he was ill at ease. He had changed back to Roxy's dress, with the stoop of age added to the disguise, so that Wilson would not bother himself about a humble old woman leaving a neighbour's house by the back way in the early morning, in case he was still spying. But supposing Wilson had seen him leave, and had thought it suspicious, and had also followed him? The thought made Tom cold. He gave up the raid for the day, and hurried back to the haunted house by the obscurest route he knew. His mother was gone; but she came back, by and by, with the news of the grand reception at Patsy Cooper's, and soon persuaded him that the opportunity was like a special providence, it was so inviting and perfect. So he went raiding, after all, and made a nice success of it while everybody was gone to Patsy Cooper's. Success gave him nerve and even actual intrepidity; insomuch, indeed, that after he had conveyed his harvest to his mother in a back alley, he went to the reception himself, and added several of the valuables of that house to his takings.

After this long digression we have now arrived once more at the point where Pudd'nhead Wilson, while waiting for the arrival of the twins on that same Friday evening, sat puzzling over the strange apparition of that morning—a girl in young Tom Driscoll's bedroom; fretting, and guessing, and puzzling over it, and wondering who the shameless creature might be.

11

Pudd'nhead's Startling Discovery

> There are three infallible ways of pleasing an author, and the three form a rising scale of compliment: 1, to tell him you have read one of his books; 2, to tell him you have read all of his books; 3, to ask him to let you read the manuscript of his forthcoming book. No. 1 admits you to his respect; No. 2 admits you to his admiration; No. 3 carries you clear into his heart.—*Pudd'nhead Wilson's Calendar*
>
> As to the Adjective: when in doubt, strike it out.—*Pudd'nhead Wilson's Calendar*

The twins arrived presently, and talk began. It flowed along chattily and sociably, and under its influence the new friendship gathered ease and strength. Wilson got out his Calendar, by request, and read a passage or two from it, which the twins praised quite cordially. This pleased the author so much that he complied gladly when they asked him to lend them a batch of the work to read at home. In the course of their wide travels they had found out that there are three sure ways of pleasing an author; they were now working the best of the three.

There was an interruption, now. Young Tom Driscoll appeared, and joined the party. He pretended to be seeing the distinguished strangers for the first time when they rose to shake hands; but this was only a blind, as he had already had a glimpse of them, at the reception, while robbing the house. The twins made mental note that he was smooth-faced and rather handsome, and smooth and undulatory in his movements—graceful, in fact. Angelo thought he had a good eye; Luigi thought there was something veiled and sly about it. Angelo thought he had a pleasant free-and-easy way of talking; Luigi thought it was more so than was agreeable. Angelo thought he was a sufficiently nice young man; Luigi reserved his decision. Tom's first contribution to the conversation was a question which he had put to Wilson a hundred times before. It was always cheerily and good-naturedly put, and always inflicted a little pang, for it touched a secret sore; but this time the pang was sharp, since strangers were present.

"Well, how does the law come on? Had a case yet?"

Wilson bit his lip, but answered, "No—not yet," with as much indifference as he could assume. Judge Driscoll had generously left the law feature out of the Wilson biography which he had furnished to the twins. Young Tom laughed pleasantly, and said:

"Wilson's a lawyer, gentlemen, but he doesn't practise now."

The sarcasm bit, but Wilson kept himself under control, and said without passion:

"I don't practise, it is true. It is true that I have never had a case, and have had to earn a poor living for twenty years as an expert accountant in a town where I can't get hold of a set of books to untangle as often as I should like. But it is also true that I did fit myself well for the practice of the law. By the time I was your age, Tom, I had chosen a profession, and was soon competent to enter upon it." Tom winced. "I never got a chance to try my hand at it, and I may never get a chance; and yet if I ever do get it I shall be found ready, for I have kept up my law-studies all these years."

"That's it; that's good grit! I like to see it. I've a notion to throw all my business your way. My business and your law-practice ought to make a pretty gay team, Dave," and the young fellow laughed again.

"If you will throw—" Wilson had thought of the girl in Tom's bedroom, and was going to say, "If you will throw the surreptitious and disreputable part of your business my way, it may amount to something;" but thought better of it and said, "However, this matter doesn't fit well in a general conversation."

"All right, we'll change the subject; I guess you were about to give me another dig, anyway, so I'm willing to change. How's the Awful Mystery flourishing these days? Wilson's got a scheme for driving plain window-glass out of the market by decorating it with greasy finger-marks, and getting rich by selling it at famine prices to the crowned heads over in Europe to outfit their palaces with. Fetch it out, Dave."

Wilson brought three of his glass strips, and said—

"I get the subject to pass the fingers of his right hand through his hair, so as to get a little coating of the natural oil on them, and then press the balls of them on the glass. A fine and delicate print of the lines in the skin results, and is permanent, if it doesn't come in contact with something able to rub it off. You begin, Tom."

"Why, I think you took my finger-marks once or twice before."

"Yes; but you were a little boy the last time, only about twelve years old."

"That's so. Of course I've changed entirely since then, and variety is what the crowned heads want, I guess."

He passed his fingers through his crop of short hair, and pressed them one at a time on the glass. Angelo made a print of his fingers on another glass, and Luigi followed with the third. Wilson marked the glasses with names and date, and put them away. Tom gave one of his little laughs, and said—

"I thought I wouldn't say anything, but if varicty is what you are after, you have wasted a piece of glass. The hand-print of one twin is the same as the hand-print of the fellow-twin."

"Well, it's done now, and I like to have them both, anyway," said Wilson, returning to his place.

"But look here, Dave," said Tom, "you used to tell people's fortunes, too, when you took their finger-marks. Dave's just an all-round genius—a genius of the first water, gentlemen; a great scientist running to seed here in this village, a prophet with the kind of honour that prophets generally get at home—for here they don't give shucks for his scientifics, and they call his skull a notion-factory—hey, Dave, ain't it so? But never mind; he'll make his mark some day—finger-mark, you know, he-he! But really, you want to let him take a shy at your palms once; it's worth twice the price of admission or your money's returned at the door. Why, he'll read your wrinkles as easy as a book, and not only tell you fifty or sixty things that's going to happen to you, but fifty or sixty thousand that ain't. Come, Dave, show thc gentlemen what an inspired Jack-at-all-science we've got in this town, and don't know it."

Wilson winced under this nagging and not very courteous chaff, and the twins suffered with him and for him. They rightly judged, now, that the best way to relieve him would be to take the thing in earnest and treat it with respect, ignoring Tom's rather overdone raillery; so Luigi said—

"We have seen something of palmistry in our wanderings, and know very well what astonishing things it can do. If it isn't a science, and one of the greatest of them, too, I don't know what its other name ought to be. In the Orient—"

Tom looked surprised and incredulous. He said—

"That juggling a science? But really, you ain't serious, are you?"

"Yes, entirely so. Four years ago we had our hands read out to us as if our palms had been covered with print."

"Well, do you mean to say there was actually anything in it?" asked Tom, his incredulity beginning to weaken a little.

"There was this much in it," said Angelo: "what was told us of our characters was minutely exact—we could not have bettered it ourselves. Next, two or three memorable things that had happened to us were laid bare—things which no one present but ourselves could have known about."

"Why, it's rank sorcery!" exclaimed Tom, who was now becoming very much interested. "And how did they make out with what was going to happen to you in the future?"

"On the whole, quite fairly," said Luigi. "Two or three of the most striking things foretold have happened since; much the most striking one of all happened within that same year. Some of the minor prophecies have come true; some of the minor and some of the major ones have not been fulfilled yet, and of course may never be: still, I should be more surprised if they failed to arrive than if they didn't."

Tom was entirely sobered, and profoundly impressed. He said, apologetically—

"Dave, I wasn't meaning to belittle that science; I was only chaffing—chattering, I reckon I'd better say. I wish you would look at their palms. Come, won't you?"

"Why certainly, if you want me to; but you know I've had no chance to become an expert, and don't claim to be one. When a past event is somewhat prominently recorded in the palm I can generally detect that, but minor ones often escape me—not always, of course, but often—but I haven't much confidence in myself when it comes to reading the future. I am talking as if palmistry was a daily study with me, but that is not so. I haven't examined half a dozen hands in the last half-dozen years; you see, the people got to joking about it, and I stopped to let the talk die down. I'll tell you what we'll do, Count Luigi: I'll make a try at your past, and if I have any success there—no, on the whole, I'll let the future alone; that's really the affair of an expert."

He took Luigi's hand. Tom said—

"Wait—don't look yet, Dave! Count Luigi, here's paper and pencil. Set down that thing that you said was the most striking one that was foretold to you, and happened less than a year afterward, and give it to me so I can see if Dave finds it in your hand."

Luigi wrote a line privately, and folded up the piece of paper, and handed it to Tom, saying—

"I'll tell you when to look at it, if he finds it."

Wilson began to study Luigi's palm, tracing life lines, heart lines, head lines, and so on, and noting carefully their relations with the cobweb of finer and more delicate marks and lines that enmeshed them on all sides; he felt of the fleshy cushion at the base of the thumb, and noted its shape; he felt of the fleshy side of the hand between the wrist and the base of the little finger, and noted its shape also; he painstakingly examined the fingers, observing their form, proportions, and natural manner of disposing themselves when in repose. All this process was watched by the three spectators with absorbing interest, their heads bent together over Luigi's palm, and nobody disturbing the stillness with a word. Wilson now entered upon a close survey of the palm again, and his revelations began.

He mapped out Luigi's character and disposition, his tastes, aversions, proclivities, ambitions, and eccentricities in a way which sometimes made Luigi wince and the others laugh, but both twins declared that the chart was artistically drawn and was correct.

Next, Wilson took up Luigi's history. He proceeded cautiously and with hesitation, now, moving his finger slowly along the great lines of the palm, and now and then halting it at a "star" or some such landmark, and examining that neighbourhood minutely. He proclaimed one or two past events, Luigi confirmed his correctness, and the search went on. Presently Wilson glanced up suddenly with a surprised expression—

"Here is a record of an incident which you would perhaps not wish me to—"

"Bring it out," said Luigi, good-naturedly; "I promise you it sha'n't embarrass me."

But Wilson still hesitated, and did not seem quite to know what to do. Then he said—

"I think it is too delicate a matter to—to—I believe I would rather write it or whisper it to you, and let you decide for yourself whether you want it talked out or not."

"That will answer," said Luigi; "write it."

Wilson wrote something on a slip of paper and handed it to Luigi, who read it to himself and said to Tom—

"Unfold your slip and read it, Mr. Driscoll."

Tom read:

"*It was prophesied that I would kill a man. It came true before the year was out.*"

Tom added, "Great Scott!"

Luigi handed Wilson's paper to Tom, and said—

"Now read this one."

Tom read:

"*You have killed some one, but whether man, woman or child, I do not make out.*"

"Cæsar's ghost!" commented Tom, with astonishment. "It beats anything that was ever heard of! Why, a man's own hand is his deadliest enemy! Just think of that—a man's own hand keeps a record of the deepest and fatalest secrets of his life, and is treacherously ready to expose him to any black-magic stranger that comes along. But what do you let a person look at your hand for, with that awful thing printed on it?"

"Oh," said Luigi, reposefully, "I don't mind it. I killed the man for good reasons, and I don't regret it."

"What were the reasons?"

"Well, he needed killing."

"I'll tell you why he did it, since he won't say himself," said Angelo, warmly. "He did it to save my life, that's what he did it for. So it was a noble act, and not a thing to be hid in the dark."

"So it was, so it was," said Wilson; "to do such a thing to save a brother's life is a great and fine action."

"Now come," said Luigi, "it is very pleasant to hear you say these things, but for unselfishness, or heroism, or magnanimity, the circumstances won't stand scrutiny. You overlook one detail; suppose I hadn't saved Angelo's life, what would have become of mine? If I had let the man kill him, wouldn't he have killed me, too? I saved my own life, you see."

"Yes, that is your way of talking," said Angelo, "but I know you—I don't believe you thought of yourself at all. I keep that weapon yet that Luigi killed the man with, and I'll show it to you sometime. That incident makes it interesting, and it had a history before it came into Luigi's hands which adds to its interest. It was given to Luigi by a great Indian prince, the Gaikowar of Baroda, and it had been in his family two or three centuries. It killed a good many disagreeable people who troubled that hearthstone at one time and another. It isn't much too look at, except that it isn't shaped like other knives, or dirks, or whatever it may be called—here, I'll draw it for you." He took a sheet of paper and made a rapid sketch. "There it is—a broad and murderous blade, with edges like a razor for sharpness. The devices engraved on it are the ciphers or names of its long line of possessors—I had Luigi's name added in Roman letters myself with our coat of arms, as you see. You notice what a curious handle the thing has. It is solid ivory, polished like a mirror, and is four or five inches long—round, and as thick as a large man's wrist, with the end squared off flat, for your thumb to rest on; for you grasp it, with your thumb resting on the blunt end—so—and lift it aloft and strike downward. The Gaikowar showed us how the thing was done when he gave it to Luigi, and before that night was ended Luigi had used the knife, and the Gaikowar was a man short by reason of it. The sheath is magnificently ornamented with gems of great value. You will find the sheath more worth looking at than the knife itself, of course."

Tom said to himself—

"It's lucky I came here. I would have sold that knife for a song; I supposed the jewels were glass."

"But go on; don't stop," said Wilson. "Our curiosity is up now, to hear about the homicide. Tell us about that."

"Well, briefly, the knife was to blame for that, all around. A native servant slipped into our room in the palace in the night, to kill us and steal the knife on account of the fortune incrusted on its sheath, without a doubt. Luigi had it under his pillow; we were in bed together. There was a dim night-light burning. I was asleep, but Luigi was awake, and he thought he detected a vague form nearing the bed. He slipped the knife out of the sheath and was ready, and unembarrassed by hampering bed-clothes, for the weather was hot and we hadn't any. Suddenly that native rose at the bedside, and bent over me with his right hand lifted and a dirk in it aimed at my throat; but Luigi grabbed his wrist, pulled him downward, and drove his own knife into the man's neck. That is the whole story."

Wilson and Tom drew deep breaths, and after some general chat about the tragedy, Pudd'nhead said, taking Tom's hand—

"Now, Tom, I've never had a look at your palms, as it happens; perhaps you've got some little questionable privacies that need—hel-lo!"

Tom had snatched away his hand, and was looking a good deal confused.

"Why, he's blushing!" said Luigi.

Tom darted an ugly look at him, and said sharply—

"Well, if I am, it ain't because I'm a murderer!" Luigi's dark face flushed, but before he could speak or move, Tom added with anxious haste: "Oh, I beg a thousand pardons. I didn't mean that; it was out before I thought, and I'm very, very sorry—you must forgive me!"

Wilson came to the rescue, and smoothed things down as well as he could; and in fact was entirely successful as far as the twins were concerned, for they felt sorrier for the affront put upon him by his guest's outburst of ill manners than for the insult offered to Luigi. But the success was not so pronounced with the offender. Tom tried to seem at his ease, and he went through the motions fairly well, but at bottom he felt resentful toward all the three witnesses of his exhibition; in fact, he felt so annoyed at them for having witnessed it and noticed it that he almost forgot to feel annoyed at himself for placing it before them. However, something presently happened which made him almost comfortable, and brought him nearly back to a state of charity and friendliness. This was a little spat between the twins; not much of a spat, but still a spat; and before they got far with it they were in a decided condition of irritation with each other. Tom was charmed; so pleased, indeed, that he cautiously did what he could to increase the irritation while pretending to be actuated by more respectable motives. By his help the fire got warmed up to the blazing-point, and he might have had the happiness of seeing the flames show up, in another moment, but for the interruption of a knock on the door—an interruption which fretted him as much as it gratified Wilson. Wilson opened the door.

The visitor was a good-natured, ignorant, energetic, middle-aged

Irishman named John Buckstone, who was a great politician in a small way, and always took a large share in public matters of every sort. One of the town's chief excitements, just now, was over the matter of rum. There was a strong rum party and a strong anti-rum party. Buckstone was training with the rum party, and he had been sent to hunt up the twins and invite them to attend a mass-meeting of that faction. He delivered his errand, and said the clans were already gathering in the big hall over the market-house. Luigi accepted the invitation cordially, Angelo less cordially, since he disliked crowds, and did not drink the powerful intoxicants of America. In fact, he was even a teetotaler sometimes—when it was judicious to be one.

The twins left with Buckstone, and Tom Driscoll joined company with them uninvited.

In the distance one could see a long wavering line of torches drifting down the main street, and could hear the throbbing of the bass drum, the clash of cymbals, the squeaking of a fife or two, and the faint roar of remote hurrahs. The tail-end of this procession was climbing the market-house stairs when the twins arrived in its neighbourhood; when they reached the hall it was full of people, torches, smoke, noise and enthusiasm. They were conducted to the platform by Buckstone—Tom Driscoll still following—and were delivered to the chairman in the midst of a prodigious explosion of welcome. When the noise had moderated a little, the chair proposed that "our illustrious guests be at once elected, by complimentary acclamation, to membership in our ever-glorious organization, the paradise of the free and the perdition of the slave."

This eloquent discharge opened the flood-gates of enthusiasm again, and the election was carried with thundering unanimity. Then arose a storm of cries:

"Wet them down! Wet them down! Give them a drink!"

Glasses of whisky were handed to the twins. Luigi waved his aloft, then brought it to his lips; but Angelo set his down. There was another storm of cries:

"What's the matter with the other one?" "What is the blond one going back on us for?" "Explain! Explain!"

The chairman inquired, and then reported—

"We have made an unfortunate mistake, gentlemen. I find that the Count Angelo Capello is opposed to our creed—is a teetotaler, in fact, and was not intending to apply for membership with us. He desires that we reconsider the vote by which he was elected. What is the pleasure of the house?"

There was a general burst of laughter, plentifully accented with whistlings and cat-calls, but the energetic use of the gavel presently restored something like order. Then a man spoke from the crowd, and said that while he was very sorry that the mistake had been made, it would not be possible to rectify it at the present meeting. According to the by-laws it must go over to the next regular meeting for action. He would not offer a motion, as none was required. He desired to apologize to the gentleman in the name of the house, and begged to assure him that as far as it might lie in the power of the Sons of Liberty, his temporary membership in the order would be made pleasant to him.

This speech was received with great applause, mixed with cries of—

"That's the talk!" "He's a good fellow, anyway, if he *is* a teetotaler!" "Drink his health!" "Give him a rouser, and no heeltaps!"

Glasses were handed around, and everybody on the platform drank Angelo's health, while the house bellowed forth in song:

For he's a jolly good fel-low,
For he's a jolly good fel-low,
For he's a jolly good fe-el-low—
Which nobody can deny.

Tom Driscoll drank. It was his second glass, for he had drunk Angelo's the moment that Angelo had set it down. The two drinks made him very merry—almost idiotically so—and he began to take a most lively and prominent part in the proceedings, particularly in the music and cat-calls and side-remarks.

The chairman was still standing at the front, the twins at his side. The extraordinarily close resemblance of the brothers to each other suggested a witticism to Tom Driscoll, and just as the chairman began a speech he skipped forward and said with an air of tipsy confidence to the audience—

"Boys, I move that he keeps still and lets this human philopena snip you out a speech."

The descriptive aptness of the phrase caught the house, and a mighty burst of laughter followed.

Luigi's southern blood leaped to the boiling-point in a moment under the sharp humiliation of this insult delivered in the presence of four hundred strangers. It was not in the young man's nature to let the matter pass, or to delay the squaring of the account. He took a couple of strides and halted behind the unsuspecting joker. Then he drew back and delivered a kick of such titanic vigor that it lifted Tom clear over the footlights and landed him on the heads of the front row of the Sons of Liberty.

Even a sober person does not like to have a human being emptied on him when he is not doing any harm; a person who is not sober cannot endure such an attention at all. The nest of Sons of Liberty that Driscoll landed in had not a sober bird in it; in fact there was probably not an entirely sober one in the auditorium. Driscoll was promptly and indignantly flung on to the heads of Sons in the next row, and these Sons passed him on toward the rear, and then immediately began to pummel the front-row Sons who had passed him to them. This course was strictly followed by bench after bench as Driscoll traveled in his tumultuous and airy flight toward the door; so he left behind him an ever lengthening wake of raging and plunging and fighting and swearing humanity. Down went group after group of torches, and presently above the deafening clatter of the gavel, roar of angry voices, and crash of succumbing benches, rose the paralyzing cry of "Fire!"

The fighting ceased instantly; the cursing ceased; for one distinctly defined moment there was a dead hush, a motionless calm, where the tempest had been; then with one impulse the multitude awoke to life and energy again, and went surging and struggling and swaying, this way and that, its outer edges melting away through windows and doors and gradually lessening the pressure and relieving the mass.

The fire-boys were never on hand so suddenly before; for there was no distance to go, this time, their quarters being in the rear end of the market-house. There was an engine company and a hook-and-ladder company. Half of each was composed of rummies and the other half of anti-rummies, after the moral and political share-and-share-alike fashion of the frontier town of the period. Enough anti-rummies were loafing in quarters to man the engine and the ladders. In two minutes they had their red shirts and helmets on—they never stirred officially in unofficial costume—and as the mass meeting overhead smashed through the long row of windows and poured out upon the roof of the arcade, the deliverers were ready for them with a powerful stream of water which washed some of them off the roof and nearly drowned the rest. But water was preferable to fire, and still the stampede from the windows continued, and still the pitiless drenching assailed it until the building was empty; then the fire-boys mounted to the hall and flooded it with water enough to annihilate forty times as much fire as there was there; for a village fire-company does not often get a chance to show off, and so when it does get a chance it makes the most of it. Such citizens of that village as were of a thoughtful and judicious temperament did not insure against fire; they insured against the fire-company.

12

The Shame of Judge Driscoll

Courage is resistance to fear, mastery of fear—not absence of fear. Except a creature be part coward it is not a compliment to say it is brave; it is merely a loose misapplication of the word. Consider the flea!—incomparably the bravest of all the creatures of God, if ignorance of fear were courage. Whether you are asleep or awake he will attack you, caring nothing for the fact that in bulk and strength you are to him as are the massed armies of the earth to a sucking child; he lives both day and night and all days and nights in the very lap of peril and the immediate presence of death, and yet is no more afraid than is the man who walks the streets of a city that was threatened by an earthquake ten centuries before. When we speak of Clive, Nelson, and Putnam as men who "didn't know what fear was," we ought always to add the flea—and put him at the head of the procession.—*Pudd'nhead Wilson's Calendar*

Judge Driscoll was in bed and asleep by ten o'clock on Friday night, and he was up and gone a-fishing before daylight in the morning with his friend Pembroke Howard. These two had been boys together in Virginia when that State still ranked as the chief and most imposing member of the Union, and they still coupled the proud and affectionate adjective "old" with her name when they spoke of her. In Missouri a recognized superiority attached to any person who hailed from Old Virginia; and this superiority was exalted to supremacy when a person of such nativity could also prove descent from the First Families of that great commonwealth. The Howards and Driscolls were of this aristocracy. In their eyes it was a nobility. It had its unwritten laws, and they were as clearly defined and as strict as any that could be found among the printed statutes of the land. The F. F. V. was born a gentleman; his highest duty in life was to watch over that great inheritance and keep it unsmirched. He must keep his honour spotless. Those laws were his chart; his course was marked out on it; if he swerved from it by so much as half a point of the compass it meant shipwreck to his honour; that is to say, degradation from his rank as a gentleman. These laws required certain things of him which his religion might forbid: then his religion must yield—the laws could not be relaxed to accommodate religions or anything else. Honour stood first; and the laws defined what it was and wherein it differed in certain details from honour as defined by church creeds and by the social laws and customs of some of the minor divisions of the globe that had got crowded out when the sacred boundaries of Virginia were staked out.

If Judge Driscoll was the recognized first citizen of Dawson's Landing, Pembroke Howard was easily its recognized second citizen. He was called "the great lawyer"—an earned title. He and Driscoll were of the same age—a year or two past sixty.

Although Driscoll was a freethinker and Howard a strong and determined Presbyterian, their warm intimacy suffered no impairment in consequence. They were men whose opinions were their own property and not subject to revision and amendment, suggestion or criticism, by anybody, even their friends.

The day's fishing finished, they came floating down stream in their skiff, talking national politics and other high matters, and presently met a skiff coming up from town, with a man in it who said:

"I reckon you know one of the new twins gave your nephew a kicking last night, Judge?"

"Did *what*?"

"Gave him a kicking."

The old Judge's lips paled, and his eyes began to flame. He choked with anger for a moment, then he got out what he was trying to say—

"Well—well—go on! Give me the details!"

The man did it. At the finish the Judge was silent a minute, turning over in his mind the shameful picture of Tom's flight over the footlights; then he said, as if musing aloud—"H'm—I don't understand it. I was asleep at home. He didn't wake me. Thought he was competent to manage his affair without my help, I reckon." His face lit up with pride and pleasure at that thought, and he said with a cheery complacency, "I like that—it's the true old blood—hey, Pembroke?"

Howard smiled an iron smile, and nodded his head approvingly. Then the news-bringer spoke again—

"But Tom beat the twin on the trial."

The Judge looked at the man wonderingly, and said—

"The trial? What trial?"

"Why, Tom had him up before Judge Robinson for assault and battery."

The old man shrank suddenly together like one who has received a death-stroke. Howard sprang for him as he sank forward in a swoon, and took him in his arms, and bedded him on his back in the boat. He sprinkled water in his face, and said to the startled visitor—

"Go, now—don't let him come to and find you here. You see what an effect your heedless speech has had; you ought to have been more considerate than to blurt out such a cruel piece of slander as that."

"I'm right down sorry I did it now, Mr. Howard, and I wouldn't have done it if I had thought: but it ain't slander; it's perfectly true, just as I told him."

He rowed away. Presently the old Judge came out of his faint and looked up piteously into the sympathetic face that was bent over him.

"Say it ain't true, Pembroke; tell me it ain't true!" he said in a weak voice.

There was nothing weak in the deep organ-tones that responded—

"You know it's a lie as well as I do, old friend. He is of the best blood of the Old Dominion."

"God bless you for saying it!" said the old gentleman, fervently. "Ah, Pembroke, it was such a blow!"

Howard stayed by his friend, and saw him home, and entered the house with him. It was dark, and past supper-time, but the Judge was not thinking of supper; he was eager to hear the slander refuted from headquarters, and as eager to have Howard hear it, too. Tom was sent for, and he came immediately. He was bruised and lame, and was not a happy-looking object. His uncle made him sit down, and said—

"We have been hearing about your adventure, Tom, with a handsome lie added to it for embellishment. Now pulverize that lie to dust! What measures have you taken? How does the thing stand?"

Tom answered guilelessly: "It don't stand at all; it's all over. I had him up in court and beat him. Pudd'nhead Wilson defended him—first case he ever had, and lost it. The judge fined the miserable hound five dollars for the assault."

Howard and the Judge sprang to their feet with the opening sentence—why, neither knew; then they stood gazing vacantly at each other. Howard stood a moment, then sat mournfully down without saying anything. The Judge's wrath began to kindle, and he burst out—

"You cur! You scum! You vermin! Do you mean to tell me that blood of my race has suffered a blow and crawled to a court of law about it? Answer me!"

Tom's head drooped, and he answered with an eloquent silence. His uncle stared at him with a mixed expression of amazement and shame and incredulity that was sorrowful to see. At last he said—

"Which of the twins was it?"

"Count Luigi."

"You have challenged him?"

"N—no," hesitated Tom, turning pale.

"You will challenge him tonight. Howard will carry it."

Tom began to turn sick, and to show it. He turned his hat round and round in his hand, his uncle glowering blacker and blacker upon him as the heavy seconds drifted by; then at last he began to stammer, and said piteously—

"Oh, please don't ask me to do it, uncle! He is a murderous devil—I never could—I—I'm afraid of him!"

Old Driscoll's mouth opened and closed three times before he could get it to perform its office; then he stormed out—

"A coward in my family! A Driscoll a coward! Oh, what have I done to deserve this infamy!" He tottered to his secretary in the corner repeating that lament again and again in heartbreaking tones, and got out of a drawer a paper, which he slowly tore to bits scattering the bits absently in his track as he walked up and down the room, still grieving and lamenting. At last he said—

"There it is, shreds and fragments once more—my will. Once more you have forced me to disinherit you, you base son of a most noble father! Leave my sight! Go—before I spit on you!"

The young man did not tarry. Then the Judge turned to Howard:

"You will be my second, old friend?"

"Of course."

"There is pen and paper. Draft the cartel, and lose no time."

"The Count shall have it in his hands in fifteen minutes," said Howard.

Tom was very heavy-hearted. His appetite was gone with his property and his self-respect. He went out the back way and wandered down the obscure lane grieving, and wondering if any course of future conduct, however discreet and carefully perfected and watched over, could win back his uncle's favour and persuade him to reconstruct once more that generous will which had just gone to ruin before his eyes. He finally concluded that it could. He said to himself that he had accomplished this sort of triumph once already, and that what had been done once could be done again. He would set about it. He would bend every energy to the task, and he would score that triumph once more, cost what it might to his convenience, limit as it might his frivolous and liberty-loving life.

"To begin," he said to himself, "I'll square up with the proceeds of my raid, and then gambling has got to be stopped—and stopped short off. It's the worst vice I've got—from my standpoint, anyway, because it's the one he can most easily find out, through the impatience of my creditors. He thought it expensive to have to pay two hundred dollars to them for me once. Expensive—*that!* Why, it cost me the whole of his fortune—but of course he never thought of that; some people can't think of any but their own side of a case. If he had known how deep I am in, now, the will would have gone to pot without waiting for a duel to help. Three hundred dollars! It's a pile! But he'll never hear of it, I'm thankful to say. The minute I've cleared it off, I'm safe; and I'll never touch a card again. Anyway, I won't while he lives, I make oath to that. I'm entering on my last reform—I know it—yes, and I'll win; but after that, if I ever slip again I'm gone."

13

Tom Stares at Ruin

> When I reflect upon the number of disagreeable people who I know have gone to a better world, I am moved to lead a different life.—*Pudd'nhead Wilson's Calendar*
>
> October. This is one of the peculiarly dangerous months to speculate in stocks in. The others are July, January, September, April, November, May, March, June, December, August, and February.—*Pudd'nhead Wilson's Calendar*

Thus mournfully communing with himself Tom moped along the lane past Pudd'nhead Wilson's house, and still on and on between fences inclosing vacant country on each hand till he neared the haunted house, then he came moping back again, with many sighs and heavy with trouble. He sorely wanted cheerful company. Rowena! His heart gave a bound at the thought, but the next thought quieted it—the detested twins would be there.

He was on the inhabited side of Wilson's house, and now as he approached it he noticed that the sitting room was lighted. This would do; others made him feel unwelcome sometimes, but Wilson never failed in courtesy toward him, and a kindly courtesy does at least save one's feelings, even if it is not professing to stand for a welcome. Wilson heard footsteps at his threshold, then the clearing of a throat.

"It's that fickle-tempered, dissipated young goose—poor devil, he find friends pretty scarce today, likely, after the disgrace of carrying a personal-assault case into a law-court."

A dejected knock. "Come in!"

Tom entered, and drooped into a chair, without saying anything. Wilson said kindly—

"Why, my boy, you look desolate. Don't take it so hard. Try and forget you have been kicked."

"Oh, dear," said Tom, wretchedly, "it's not that, Pudd'nhead—it's not that. It's a thousand times worse than that—oh, yes, a million times worse."

"Why, Tom, what do you mean? Has Rowena—"

"Flung me? No, but the old man has."

Wilson said to himself, "Aha!" and thought of the mysterious girl in the bedroom. "The Driscolls have been making discoveries!" Then he said aloud, gravely:

"Tom, there are some kinds of dissipation which—"

"Oh, shucks, this hasn't got anything to do with dissipation. He wanted me to challenge that derned Italian savage, and I wouldn't do it."

"Yes, of course he would do that," said Wilson in a meditative matter-of-course way, "but the thing that puzzled me was, why he didn't look to that last night, for one thing, and why he let you carry such a matter into a court of law at all, either before the duel or after it. It's no place for it. It was not like him. I couldn't understand it. How did it happen?"

"It happened because he didn't know anything about it. He was asleep when I got home last night."

"And you didn't wake him? Tom, is that possible?"

Tom was not getting much comfort here. He fidgeted a moment, then said:

"I didn't choose to tell him—that's all. He was going a-fishing before dawn, with Pembroke Howard, and if I got the twins into the common calaboose—and I thought sure I could—I never dreamed of their slipping out on a paltry fine for such an outrageous offense—well, once in the calaboose they would be disgraced, and uncle wouldn't want any duels with that sort of characters, and wouldn't allow any."

"Tom, I am ashamed of you! I don't see how you could treat your good old uncle so. I am a better friend of his than you are; for if I had known the circumstances I would have kept that case out of court until I got word to him and let him have a gentleman's chance."

"You would?" exclaimed Tom, with lively surprise. "And it your first case! And you know perfectly well there never would have *been* any case if he had got that chance, don't you? And you'd have finished your days a pauper nobody, instead of being an actually launched and recognized lawyer today. And you would really have done that, would you?"

"Certainly."

Tom looked at him a moment or two, then shook his head sorrowfully and said—

"I believe you—upon my word I do. I don't know why I do, but I do. Pudd'nhead Wilson, I think you're the biggest fool I ever saw."

"Thank you."

"Don't mention it."

"Well, he has been requiring you to fight the Italian and you have refused. You degenerate remnant of an honourable line! I'm thoroughly ashamed of you, Tom!"

"Oh, that's nothing! I don't care for anything, now that the will's torn up again."

"Tom, tell me squarely—didn't he find any fault with you for anything but those two things—carrying the case into court and refusing to fight?"

He watched the young fellow's face narrowly, but it was entirely reposeful, and so also was the voice that answered:

"No, he didn't find any other fault with me. If he had had any to find, he would have begun yesterday, for he was just in the humour for it. He drove that jack-pair around town and showed them the sights, and when he came home he couldn't find his father's old silver watch that don't keep time and he thinks so much of, and couldn't remember what he did with it three or four days ago when he saw it last, and so when I arrived he was all in a sweat about it, and when I suggested that it probably wasn't lost but stolen, it put him in a regular passion and he said I was a fool—which convinced me, without any trouble, that that was just what he was afraid *had* happened, himself, but did not want to believe it, because lost things stand a better chance of being found again than stolen ones."

"Whe-ew!" whistled Wilson; "score another on the list."

"Another what?"

"Another theft!"

"Theft?"

"Yes, theft. That watch isn't lost, it's stolen. There's been another raid on the town—and just the same old mysterious sort of thing that has happened once before, as you remember."

"You don't mean it!"

"It's as sure as you are born! Have you missed anything yourself?"

"No. That is, I did miss a silver pencil-case that Aunt Mary Pratt gave me last birthday—"

"You'll find it stolen—that's what you'll find."

"No, I sha'n't; for when I suggested theft about the watch and got such a rap, I went and examined my room, and the pencil-case was missing, but it was only mislaid, and I found it again."

"You are sure you missed nothing else?"

"Well, nothing of consequence. I missed a small plain gold ring worth two or three dollars, but that will turn up. I'll look again."

"In my opinion you'll not find it. There's been a raid, I tell you. Come *in!*"

Mr. Justice Robinson entered, followed by Buckstone and the town-constable, Jim Blake. They sat down, and after some wandering and aimless weather-conversation Wilson said—

"By the way, we've just added another to the list of thefts, maybe two. Judge Driscoll's old silver watch is gone, and Tom here has missed a gold ring."

"Well, it is a bad business," said the Justice, "and gets worse the further it goes. The Hankses, the Dobsons, the Pilligrews, the Ortons, the Grangers, the Hales, the Fullers, the Holcombs, in fact everybody that lives around about Patsy Cooper's has been robbed of little things like trinkets and teaspoons and such-like small valuables that are easily carried off. It's perfectly plain that the thief took advantage of the reception at Patsy Cooper's when all the neighbours were in her house and all their niggers hanging around her fence for a look at the show, to raid the vacant houses undisturbed. Patsy is miserable about it; miserable on account of the neighbours, and particularly miserable on account of her foreigners, of course; so miserable on their account that she hasn't any room to worry about her own little losses."

"It's the same old raider," said Wilson. "I suppose there isn't any doubt about that."

"Constable Blake doesn't think so."

"No, you're wrong there," said Blake; "the other times it was a man; there was plenty of signs of that, as we know, in the profession, though we never got hands on him; but this time it's a woman."

Wilson thought of the mysterious girl straight off. She was always in his mind now. But she failed him again. Blake continued:

"She's a stoop-shouldered old woman with a covered basket on her arm, in a black veil, dressed in mourning. I saw her going aboard the ferry-boat yesterday. Lives in Illinois, I reckon; but I don't care where she lives, I'm going to get her—she can make herself sure of that."

"What makes you think she's the thief?"

"Well, there ain't any other, for one thing; and for another, some nigger draymen that happened to be driving along saw her coming out of or going into houses, and told me so—and it just happens that they was *robbed* houses, every time."

It was granted that this was plenty good enough circumstantial evidence. A pensive silence followed, which lasted some moments, then Wilson said—

"There's one good thing, anyway. She can't either pawn or sell Count Luigi's costly Indian dagger."

"My!" said Tom, "is *that* gone?"

"Yes."

"Well, that was a haul! But why can't she pawn it or sell it?"

"Because when the twins went home from the Sons of Liberty meeting last night, news of the raid was sifting in from everywhere, and Aunt Patsy was in distress to know if they had lost anything. They found that the dagger was gone, and they notified the police and pawnbrokers everywhere. It was a great haul, yes, but the old woman won't get anything out of it, because she'll get caught."

"Did they offer a reward?" asked Buckstone.

"Yes; five hundred dollars for the knife, and five hundred more for the thief."

"What a leather-headed idea!" exclaimed the constable. "The thief da'sn't go near them, nor send anybody. Whoever goes is going to get himself nabbed, for their ain't any pawnbroker that's going to lose the chance to—"

If anybody had noticed Tom's face at that time, the grey-green colour of it might have provoked curiosity; but nobody did. He said to himself: "I'm gone! I never can square up; the rest of the plunder won't pawn or sell for half of the bill. Oh, I know it—I'm gone, I'm gone—and this time it's for good. Oh, this is awful—I don't know what to do, nor which way to turn!"

"Softly, softly," said Wilson to Blake. "I planned their scheme for them at midnight last night, and it was all finished up shipshape by two this morning. They'll get their dagger back, and then I'll explain to you how the thing was done."

There were strong signs of a general curiosity, and Buckstone said—

"Well, you have whetted us up pretty sharp, Wilson, and I'm free to say that if you don't mind telling us in confidence—"

"Oh, I'd as soon tell as not, Buckstone, but as long as the twins and I agreed to say nothing about it, we must let it stand so. But you can take my word for it you won't be kept waiting three days. Somebody will apply for that reward pretty promptly, and I'll show you the thief and the dagger both very soon afterward."

The constable was disappointed, and also perplexed. He said—

"It may all be—yes, and I hope it will, but I'm blamed if I can see my way through it. It's too many for yours truly."

The subject seemed about talked out. Nobody seemed to have anything further to offer. After a silence the justice of the peace informed Wilson that he and Buckstone and the constable had come as a committee, on the part of the Democratic party, to ask him to run for mayor—for the little town was about to become a city and the first charter election was approaching. It was the first attention which Wilson had ever received at the hands of any party; it was a sufficiently humble one, but it was a recognition of his début into the town's life and activities at last; it was a step upward, and he was deeply gratified. He accepted, and the committee departed, followed by young Tom.

14

Roxana Insists Upon Reform

> The true Southern watermelon is a boon apart, and not to be mentioned with commoner things. It is chief of this world's luxuries, king by the grace of God over all the fruits of the earth. When one has tasted it, he knows what the angels eat. It was not a Southern watermelon that Eve took: we know it because she repented.—*Pudd'nhead Wilson's Calendar*

About the time that Wilson was bowing the committee out, Pembroke Howard was entering the next house to report. He found the old Judge sitting grim and straight in his chair, waiting.

"Well, Howard—the news?"

"The best in the world."

"Accepts, does he?" and the light of battle gleamed joyously in the Judge's eye.

"Accepts? Why, he jumped at it."

"Did, did he? Now that's fine—that's very fine. I like that. When is it to be?"

"Now! Straight off! Tonight! An admirable fellow—admirable!"

"Admirable? He's a darling! Why, it's an honour as well as a pleasure to stand up before such a man. Come—off with you! Go and arrange everything—and give him my heartiest compliments. A rare fellow, indeed; an admirable fellow, as you have said!"

Howard hurried away, saying—

"I'll have him in the vacant stretch between Wilson's and the haunted house within the hour, and I'll bring my own pistols."

Judge Driscoll began to walk the floor in a state of pleased excitement; but presently he stopped, and began to think—began to think of Tom. Twice he moved toward the secretary, and twice he turned away again; but finally he said—

"This may be my last night in the world—I must not take the chance. He is worthless and unworthy, but it is largely my fault. He was entrusted to me by my brother on his dying bed, and I have indulged him to his hurt, instead of training him up severely, and making a man of him. I have violated my trust, and I must not add the sin of desertion to that. I have forgiven him once already, and would subject him to a long and hard trial before forgiving him again, if I could live; but I must not run that risk. No, I must restore the will. But if I survive the duel, I will hide it away, and he will not know, and I will not tell him until he reforms, and I see that his reformation is going to be permanent."

He re-drew the will, and his ostensible nephew was heir to a fortune again. As he was finishing his task, Tom, wearied with another brooding tramp, entered the house and went tiptoeing past the sitting-room door. He glanced in, and hurried on, for the sight of his uncle had nothing but terrors for him tonight. But his uncle was writing! That was unusual at this late hour. What could he be writing? A chill of anxiety settled down upon Tom's heart. Did that writing concern him? He was afraid so. He reflected that when ill luck begins, it does not come in sprinkles, but in showers. He said he would get a glimpse of that document or know the reason why. He heard some one coming, and stepped out of sight and hearing. It was Pembroke Howard. What could be hatching?

Howard said, with great satisfaction:

"Everything's right and ready. He's gone to the battle-ground with his second and the surgeon—also with his brother. I've arranged it all with Wilson—Wilson's his second. We are to have three shots apiece."

"Good! How is the moon?"

"Bright as day, nearly. Perfect, for the distance—fifteen yards. No wind—not a breath; hot and still."

"All good; all first-rate. Here, Pembroke, read this, and witness it."

Pembroke read and witnessed the will, then gave the old man's hand a hearty shake and said:

"Now that's right, York—but I knew you would do it. You couldn't leave that poor chap to fight along without means or profession, with certain defeat before him, and I knew you wouldn't, for his father's sake if not for his own."

"For his dead father's sake I couldn't, I know; for poor Percy—but you know what Percy was to me. But mind—Tom is not to know of this unless I fall tonight."

"I understand. I'll keep the secret."

The Judge put the will away, and the two started for the battle-ground. In another minute the will was in Tom's hands. His misery vanished, his feelings underwent a tremendous revulsion. He put the will carefully back in its place, and spread his mouth and swung his hat once, twice, three times around his head, in imitation of three rousing huzzas, no sound issuing from his lips. He fell to communing with himself excitedly and joyously, but every now and then he let off another volley of dumb hurrahs.

He said to himself: "I've got the fortune again, but I'll not let on that I know about it. And this time I'm going to hang on to it. I take no more risks. I'll gamble no more, I'll drink no more, because—well, because I'll not go where there is any of that sort of thing going on, again. It's the sure way, and the only sure way; I might have thought of that sooner—well, yes, if I had wanted to. But now—dear me, I've had a scare this time, and I'll take no more chances. Not a single chance more. Land! I persuaded myself this evening that I could fetch him around without any great amount of effort, but I've been getting more and more heavy-hearted and doubtful straight along, ever since. If he tells me about this thing, all right; but if he doesn't, I sha'n't let on. I—well, I'd like to tell Pudd'nhead Wilson, but—no, I'll think about that; perhaps I won't." He whirled off another dead huzza, and said, "I'm reformed, and this time I'll stay so, sure!"

He was about to close with a final grand silent demonstration, when he suddenly recollected that Wilson had put it out of his power to pawn or sell the Indian knife, and that he was once more in awful peril of exposure by his creditors for that reason. His joy collapsed utterly, and he turned away and moped toward the door moaning and lamenting over the bitterness of his luck. He dragged himself upstairs, and brooded in his room a long time disconsolate and forlorn, with Luigi's Indian knife for a text. At last he sighed and said:

"When I supposed these stones were glass and this ivory bone, the thing hadn't any interest for me because it hadn't any value, and couldn't help me out of my trouble. But now—why, now it is full of interest; yes, and of a sort to break a body's heart. It's a bag of gold that has turned to dirt and ashes in my hands. It could save me, and save me so easily, and yet I've got to go to ruin. It's like drowning with a life-preserver in my reach. All the hard luck comes to me, and all the good luck goes to other people—Pudd'nhead Wilson, for instance; even his career has got a sort of a little start at last, and what has he done to deserve it, I should like to know? Yes, he has opened his own road, but he isn't content with that, but must block mine. It's a sordid, selfish world, and I wish I was out of it." He allowed the light of the candle to play upon the jewels of the sheath, but the flashings and sparklings had no charm for his eye; they were only just so many pangs to his heart. "I must not say anything to Roxy about this thing," he said, "she is too daring. She would be for digging these stones out and selling them, and then—why, she would be arrested and the stones traced, and then—" The thought made him quake, and he hid the knife away, trembling all over and glancing furtively about, like a criminal who fancies that the accuser is already at hand.

Should he try to sleep? Oh, no, sleep was not for him; his trouble was too haunting, too afflicting for that. He must have somebody to mourn with. He would carry his despair to Roxy.

He had heard several distant gunshots, but that sort of thing was not uncommon, and they had made no impression upon him. He went out at the back door, and turned westward. He passed Wilson's house and proceeded along the lane, and presently saw several figures approaching Wilson's place through the vacant lots. These were the duelists returning from the fight; he thought he recognized them, but as he had no desire for white people's company, he stooped down behind the fence until they were out of his way.

Roxy was feeling fine. She said:

"Whah was you, child? Warn't you in it?"

"In what?"

"In de duel."

"Duel? Has there been a duel?"

"'Co'se dey has. De ole Jedge has be'n havin' a duel wid one o' dem twins."

"Great Scott!" Then he added to himself: "That's what made him remake the will; he thought he might get killed, and it softened him toward me. And that's what he and Howard were so busy about. . . . Oh dear, if the twin had only killed him, I should be out of my—"

"What is you mumblin' 'bout, Chambers? Whah was you? Didn't you know dey was gwyne to be a duel?"

"No, I didn't. The old man tried to get me to fight one with Count Luigi, but he didn't succeed, so I reckon he concluded to patch up the family honour himself."

He laughed at the idea, and went rambling on with a detailed account of his talk with the Judge, and how shocked and ashamed the Judge was to find that he had a coward in his family. He glanced up at last, and got a shock himself. Roxana's bosom was heaving with suppressed passion, and she was glowering down upon him with measureless contempt written in her face.

"En you refuse' to fight a man dat kicked you, 'stid o' jumpin' at de chance! En you ain't got no mo' feelin' den to come en tell me, dat fetched sich a po' low-down ornery rabbit into de worl'! Pah! it make me sick! It's de nigger in you, dat's what it is. Thirty-one parts o' you is white, en on'y one part nigger, en dat po' little one part is yo' *soul.* Tain't wuth savin'; tain't wuth totin' out on a shovel en throwin' in de gutter. You has disgraced yo' birth. What would yo' pa think o' you? It's enough to make him turn in his grave."

The last three sentences stung Tom into a fury, and he said to himself that if his father were only alive and in reach of assassination his mother would soon find that he had a very clear notion of the size of his indebtedness to that man, and was willing to pay it up in full, and would do it too, even at risk of his life; but he kept this thought to himself; that was safest in his mother's present state.

"Whatever has come o' yo' Essex blood? Dat's what I can't understan'. En it ain't on'y jist Essex blood dat's in you, not by a long sight—'deed it ain't! My great-great-great-gran'father en yo' great-great-great-great-gran'father was Ole Cap'n John Smith, de highest blood dat Ole Virginny ever turned out, en *his* great-great-gran'mother or somers along back dah, was Pocahontas de Injun queen, en her husbun' was a nigger king outen Africa—en yit here you is, a slinkin' outen a duel en disgracin' our whole line like a ornery low-down hound! Yes, it's de nigger in you!"

She sat down on her candle-box and fell into a reverie. Tom did not disturb her; he sometimes lacked prudence, but it was not in circumstances of this kind, Roxana's storm went gradually down, but it died hard, and even when it seemed to be quite gone, it would now and then break out in a distant rumble, so to speak, in the form of muttered ejaculations. One of these was, "Ain't nigger enough in him to show in his finger-nails, en dat takes mighty little—yit dey's enough to paint his soul."

Presently she muttered. "Yassir, enough to paint a whole thimbleful of 'em." At last her ramblings ceased altogether, and her countenance began to clear—a welcome sign to Tom, who had learned her moods, and knew she was on the threshold of good-humour, now. He noticed that from time to time she unconsciously carried her finger to the end of her nose. He looked closer and said:

"Why, mammy, the end of your nose is skinned. How did that come?"

She sent out the sort of whole-hearted peal of laughter which God had vouchsafed in its perfection to none but the happy angels in heaven and the bruised and broken black slave on the earth, and said:

"Dad fetch dat duel, I be'n in it myself."

"Gracious! did a bullet do that?"

"Yassir, you bet it did!"

"Well, I declare! Why, how did that happen?"

"Happened dis-away. I 'uz a-sett'n' here kinder dozin' in de dark, en *che-bang!* goes a gun, right out dah. I skips along out towards t'other end o' de house to see what's gwyne on, en stops by de ole winder on de side towards Pudd'nhead Wilson's house dat ain't got no sash in it—but dey ain't none of 'em got any sashes, fur as dat's concerned—en I stood dah in de dark en look out, en dar in de moonlight, right down under me 'uz one o' de twins a-cussin'—not much, but jist a-cussin' soft—it 'uz de brown one dat 'uz cussin', 'ca'se he 'uz hit in de shoulder. En Doctor Claypool he 'uz a-workin' at him, en Pudd'nhead Wilson he 'uz a-he'pin', en ole Jedge Driscoll en Pem Howard 'uz a-standin' out yonder a little piece waitin' for 'em to git ready agin. En treckly dey squared off en give de word, en *bang-bang* went de pistols, en de twin he say, 'Ouch!'—hit him on de han' dis time—en I hear dat same bullet go *spat!* ag'in, de logs under de winder; en de nex' time dey shoot, de twin say, 'Ouch!' ag'in, en I done it too, 'ca'se de bullet glance' on his cheek-bone en skip up here en glance on de side o' de winder en whiz right acrost my face en tuck de hide off'n my nose—why, if I'd 'a' be'n jist a inch or a inch en a half furder 't would 'a' tuck de whole nose en disfiggered me. Here's de bullet; I hunted her up."

"Did you stand there all the time?"

"Dat's a question to ask, ain't it? What else would I do? Does I git a chance to see a duel every day?"

"Why, you were right in range! Weren't you afraid?"

The woman gave a sniff of scorn.

"'Fraid! De Smith-Pocahontases ain't 'fraid o' nothin', let alone bullets."

"They've got pluck enough, I suppose; what they lack is judgment. *I* wouldn't have stood there."

"Nobody's accusin' you!"

"Did anybody else get hurt?"

"Yes, we all got hit 'cep' de blon' twin en de doctor en de seconds. De

Jedge didn't git hurt, but I hear Pudd'nhead say de bullet snip some o' his ha'r off."

"'George!" said Tom to himself, "to come so near being out of my trouble, and miss it by an inch. Oh dear, dear, he will live to find me out and sell me to some nigger-trader yet—yes, and he would do it in a minute." Then he said aloud, in a grave tone—

"Mother, we are in an awful fix."

Roxana caught her breath with a spasm, and said—

"Chile! What you hit a body so sudden for, like dat? What's be'n en gone en happen'?"

"Well, there's one thing I didn't tell you. When I wouldn't fight, he tore up the will again, and—"

Roxana's face turned a dead white, and she said—

"Now you's *done!*—done forever! Dat's de end. Bofe un us is gwyne to starve to—"

"Wait and hear me through, can't you! I reckon that when he resolved to fight, himself, he thought he might get killed and not have a chance to forgive me any more in this life, so he made the will again, and I've seen it, and it's all right. But—"

"Oh, thank goodness, den we's safe ag'in!—safe! en so what did you want to come here en talk sich dreadful—"

"Hold *on*, I tell you, and let me finish. The swag I gathered won't half square me up, and the first thing we know, my creditors—well, you know what'll happen."

Roxana dropped her chin, and told her son to leave her alone—she must think this matter out. Presently she said impressively:

"You got to go mighty keerful now, I tell you! En here's what you got to do. He didn't git killed, en if you gives him de least reason, he'll bust de will ag'in, en dat's de *las'* time, now you hear me! So—you's got to show him what you kin do in de nex' few days. You's got to be pison good, en let him see it; you got to do everything dat'll make him b'lieve in you, en you got to sweeten aroun' ole Aunt Pratt, too—she's pow'ful strong wid de Jedge, en de bes' frien' you got. Nex', you'll go 'long away to Sent Louis, en dat'll *keep* him in yo' favour. Den you go en make a bargain wid dem people. You tell 'em he ain't gwyne to live long—en dat's de fac', too—en tell 'em you'll pay 'em intrust, en big intrust, too—ten per—what you call it?"

"Ten per cent a month?"

"Dat's it. Den you take and sell yo' truck aroun', a little at a time, en pay de intrust. How long will it las'?"

"I think there's enough to pay the interest five or six months."

"Den you's all right. If he don't die in six months, dat don't make no diff'rence—Providence'll provide. You's gwyne to be safe—if you behaves." She bent an austere eye on him and added, "En you *is* gwyne to behave—does you know dat?"

He laughed and said he was going to try, anyway. She did not unbend. She said gravely:

"Tryin' ain't de thing. You's gwyne to *do* it. You ain't gwyne to steal a pin—'ca'se it ain't safe no mo'; en you ain't gwyne into no bad comp'ny—not even once, you understand; en you ain't gwyne to drink a drop—nary single drop; en you ain't gwyne to gamble one single gamble—not one! Dis ain't what you's gwyne to *try* to do, it's what you's gwyne to *do*. En I'll tell you how I knows it. Dis is how. I's gwyne to foller along to Sent Louis my own self; en you's gwyne to come to me every day o' yo' life, en I'll look you over; en if you fails in one single one o' dem things—jist *one*—I take my oath I'll come straight down to dis town en tell de Jedge you's a nigger en a slave—en *prove*it!" She paused to let her words sink home. Then she added, "Chambers, does you b'lieve me when I says dat?"

Tom was sober enough now. There was no levity in his voice when he answered:

"Yes, mother, I know, now, that I am reformed—and permanently. Permanently—and beyond the reach of any human temptation."

"Den g' long home en begin!"

15

The Robber Robbed

Nothing so needs reforming as other people's habits.—*Pudd'nhead Wilson's Calendar*

Behold, the fool saith, "Put not all thine eggs in the one basket"—which is but a manner of saying, "Scatter your money and your attention;" but the wise man saith, "Put all your eggs in the one basket and—watch that basket"—*Pudd'nhead Wilson's Calendar*

What a time of it Dawson's Landing was having! All its life it had been asleep, but now it hardly got a chance for a nod, so swiftly did big events and crashing surprises come along in one another's wake: Friday morning, first glimpse of Real Nobility, also grand reception at Aunt Patsy Cooper's, also great robber-raid; Friday evening, dramatic kicking of the heir of the chief citizen in presence of four hundred people; Saturday morning, emergence as practising lawyer of the long-submerged Pudd'nhead Wilson; Saturday night, duel between chief citizen and titled stranger.

The people took more pride in the duel than in all the other events put together, perhaps. It was a glory to their town to have such a thing happen there. In their eyes the principals had reached the summit of human honour. Everybody paid homage to their names; their praises were in all mouths. Even the duelists' subordinates came in for a handsome share of the public approbation: wherefore Pudd'nhead Wilson was suddenly become a man of consequence. When asked to run for the mayoralty Saturday night he was risking defeat, but Sunday morning found him a made man and his success assured.

The twins were prodigiously great, now; the town took them to its bosom with enthusiasm. Day after day, and night after night, they went dining and visiting from house to house, making friends, enlarging and solidifying their popularity, and charming and surprising all with their musical prodigies, and now and then heightening the effects with samples of what they could do in other directions, out of their stock of rare and curious accomplishments. They were so pleased that they gave the regulation thirty days' notice, the required preparation for citizenship, and resolved to finish their days in this pleasant place. That was the climax. The delighted community rose as one man and applauded; and when the twins were asked to stand for seats in the forthcoming aldermanic board, and consented, the public contentment was rounded and complete.

Tom Driscoll was not happy over these things; they sunk deep, and hurt all the way down. He hated the one twin for kicking him, and the other one for being the kicker's brother.

Now and then the people wondered why nothing was heard of the raider, or of the stolen knife or the other plunder, but nobody was able to throw any light on that matter. Nearly a week had drifted by, and still the thing remained a vexed mystery.

On Saturday Constable Blake and Pudd'nhead Wilson met on the street, and Tom Driscoll joined them in time to open their conversation for them. He said to Blake—"You are not looking well, Blake; you seem to be annoyed about something. Has anything gone wrong in the detective business? I believe you fairly and justifiably claim to have a pretty good reputation in that line, isn't it so?"—which made Blake feel good, and look it; but Tom added, "for a country detective"—which made Blake feel the other way, and not only look it, but betray it in his voice—

"Yes, sir, I *have* got a reputation; and it's as good as anybody's in the profession, too, country or no country."

"Oh, I beg pardon; I didn't mean any offense. What I started out to ask was only about the old woman that raided the town—the stoop-shouldered old woman, you know, that you said you were going to catch; and I knew you would, too, because you have the reputation of never boasting, and—well, you—you've caught the old woman?"

"D——— the old woman!"

"Why, sho! you don't mean to say you haven't caught her?"

"No; I haven't caught her. If anybody could have caught her, I could; but nobody couldn't, I don't care who he is."

"I am sorry, real sorry—for your sake; because, when it gets around that a detective has expressed himself so confidently, and then—"

"Don't you worry, that's all—don't you worry; and as for the town, the town needn't worry, either. She's my meat—make yourself easy about that. I'm on her track; I've got clues that—"

"That's good! Now if you could get an old veteran detective down from St. Louis to help you find out what the clues mean, and where they lead to, and then—"

"I'm plenty veteran enough myself, and I don't need anybody's help. I'll have her inside of a we—inside of a month. That I'll swear to!"

Tom said carelessly—

"I suppose that will answer—yes, that will answer. But I reckon she is pretty old, and old people don't often outlive the cautious pace of the professional detective when he has got his clues together and is out on his still-hunt."

Blake's dull face flushed under this gibe, but before he could set his retort in order Tom had turned to Wilson, and was saying, with placid indifference of manner and voice—

"Who got the reward, Pudd'nhead?"

Wilson winced slightly, and saw that his own turn was come.

"What reward?"

"Why, the reward for the thief, and the other one for the knife."

Wilson answered—and rather uncomfortably, to judge by his hesitating fashion of delivering himself—

"Well, the—well, in fact, nobody has claimed it yet."

Tom seemed surprised.

"Why, is that so?"

Wilson showed a trifle of irritation when he replied—

"Yes, it's so. And what of it?"

"Oh, nothing. Only I thought you had struck out a new idea, and invented a scheme that was going to revolutionize the time-worn and ineffectual methods of the—" He stopped, and turned to Blake, who was happy now that another had taken his place on the gridiron: "Blake, didn't you understand him to intimate that it wouldn't be necessary for you to hunt the old woman down?"

"B'George, he said he'd have thief and swag both inside of three days—he did, by hokey! and that's just about a week ago. Why, I said at the time that no thief and no thief's pal was going to try to pawn or sell a thing where he knowed the pawnbroker could get both rewards by taking *him* into camp *with* the swag. It was the blessedest idea that ever *I* struck!"

"You'd change your mind," said Wilson, with irritated bluntness, "if you knew the entire scheme instead of only part of it."

"Well," said the constable, pensively, "I had the idea that it wouldn't work, and up to now I'm right anyway."

"Very well, then, let it stand at that, and give it a further show. It has worked at least as well as your own methods, you perceive."

The constable hadn't anything handy to hit back with, so he discharged a discontented sniff, and said nothing.

After the night that Wilson had partly revealed his scheme at his house, Tom had tried for several days to guess out the secret of the rest of it, but had failed. Then it occurred to him to give Roxana's smarter head a chance at it. He made up a supposititious case, and laid it before her. She thought it over, and delivered her verdict upon it. Tom said to himself, "She's hit it, sure!" He thought he would test that verdict, now, and watch Wilson's face; so he said reflectively—

"Wilson, you're not a fool—a fact of recent discovery. Whatever your scheme was, it had sense in it, Blake's opinion to the contrary notwithstanding. I don't ask you to reveal it, but I will suppose a case—a case which will answer as a starting-point for the real thing I am going to come at, and that's all I want. You offered five hundred dollars for the knife, and five hundred for the thief. We will suppose, for argument's sake, that the first reward is *advertised* and the second offered by *private letter* to pawnbrokers and—"

Blake slapped his thigh, and cried out—

"By Jackson, he's got you, Pudd'nhead! Now why couldn't I or *any* fool have thought of that?"

Wilson said to himself, "Anybody with a reasonably good head would have thought of it. I am not surprised that Blake didn't detect it; I am only surprised that Tom did. There is more to him than I supposed." He said nothing aloud, and Tom went on:

"Very well. The thief would not suspect that there was a trap, and he would bring or send the knife, and say he bought it for a song, or found it in the road, or something like that, and try to collect the reward, and be arrested—wouldn't he?"

"Yes," said Wilson.

"I think so," said Tom. "There can't be any doubt of it. Have you ever seen that knife?"

"No."

"Has any friend of yours?"

"Not that I know of."

"Well, I begin to think I understand why your scheme failed."

"What do you mean, Tom? What are you driving at?" asked Wilson, with a dawning sense of discomfort.

"Why, that there *isn't* any such knife."

"Look here, Wilson," said Blake, "Tom Driscoll's right, for a thousand dollars—if I had it."

Wilson's blood warmed a little, and he wondered if he had been played upon by those strangers; it certainly had something of that look. But what could they gain by it? He threw out that suggestion. Tom replied:

"Gain? Oh, nothing that you would value, maybe. But they are strangers making their way in a new community. Is it nothing to them to appear as pets of an Oriental prince—at no expense? Is it nothing to them to be able to dazzle this poor little town with thousand-dollar rewards—at no expense? Wilson, there isn't any such knife, or your scheme would have fetched it to light. Or if there is any such knife, they've got it yet. I believe, myself, that they've seen such a knife, for Angelo pictured it out with his pencil too swiftly and handily for him to have been inventing it, and of course I can't swear that they've never had it; but this I'll go bail for—if they had it when they came to this town, they've got it yet."

Blake said—

"It looks mighty reasonable, the way Tom puts it; it most certainly does."

Tom responded, turning to leave—

"You find the old woman, Blake, and if she can't furnish the knife, go and search the twins!"

Tom sauntered away. Wilson felt a good deal depressed. He hardly knew what to think. He was loath to withdraw his faith from the twins, and was resolved not to do it on the present indecisive evidence; but—well, he would think, and then decide how to act.

"Blake, what do you think of this matter?"

"Well, Pudd'nhead, I'm bound to say I put it up the way Tom does. They hadn't the knife; or if they had it, they've got it yet."

The men parted. Wilson said to himself:

"I believe they had it; if it had been stolen, the scheme would have restored it, that is certain. And so I believe they've got it yet."

Tom had no purpose in his mind when he encountered those two men. When he began his talk he hoped to be able to gall them a little and get a trifle of malicious entertainment out of it. But when he left, he left in great spirits, for he perceived that just by pure luck and no troublesome labour he had accomplished several delightful things: he had touched both men on a raw spot and seen them squirm; he had modified Wilson's sweetness for the twins with one small bitter taste that he wouldn't be able to get out of his mouth right away; and, best of all, he had taken the hated twins down a peg with the community; for Blake would gossip around freely, after the manner of detectives, and within a week the town would be laughing at them in its sleeve for offering a gaudy reward for a bauble which they either never possessed or hadn't lost. Tom was very well satisfied with himself.

Tom's behavior at home had been perfect during the entire week. His uncle and aunt had seen nothing like it before. They could find no fault with him anywhere.

Saturday evening he said to the Judge—

"I've had something preying on my mind, uncle, and as I am going away, and might never see you again, I can't bear it any longer. I made you believe I was afraid to fight that Italian adventurer. I had to get out of it on some pretext or other, and maybe I chose badly, being taken unawares, but no honourable person could consent to meet him in the field, knowing what I knew about him."

"Indeed? What was that?"

"Count Luigi is a confessed assassin."

"Incredible!"

"It's perfectly true. Wilson detected it in his hand, by palmistry, and charged him with it, and cornered him up so close that he had to confess; but both twins begged us on their knees to keep the secret, and swore they would lead straight lives here; and it was all so pitiful that we gave our word of honour never to expose them while they kept that promise. You would have done it yourself, uncle."

"You are right, my boy; I would. A man's secret is still his own property, and sacred, when it has been surprised out of him like that. You did well, and I am proud of you." Then he added mournfully, "But I wish I could have been saved the shame of meeting an assassin on the field of honour."

"It couldn't be helped, uncle. If I had known you were going to challenge him I should have felt obliged to sacrifice my pledged word in order to stop it, but Wilson couldn't be expected to do otherwise than keep silent."

"Oh, no; Wilson did right, and is in no way to blame. Tom, Tom, you have lifted a heavy load from my heart; I was stung to the very soul when I seemed to have discovered that I had a coward in my family."

"You may imagine what it cost *me* to assume such a part, uncle."

"Oh, I know it, poor boy, I know it. And I can understand how much it has cost you to remain under that unjust stigma to this time. But it is all right now, and no harm is done. You have restored my comfort of mind, and with it your own; and both of us had suffered enough."

The old man sat awhile plunged in thought; then he looked up with a satisfied light in his eye, and said: "That this assassin should have put the affront upon me of letting me meet him on the field of honour as if he were a gentleman is a matter which I will presently settle—but not now. I will not shoot him until after election. I see a way to ruin them both before; I will attend to that first. Neither of them shall be elected, that I promise. You are sure that the fact that he is an assassin has not got abroad?"

"Perfectly certain of it, sir."

"It will be a good card. I will fling a hint at it from the stump on the polling-day. It will sweep the ground from under both of them."

"There's not a doubt of it. It will finish them."

"That and outside work among the voters will, to a certainty. I want you to come down here by and by and work privately among the rag-tag and bobtail. You shall spend money among them; I will furnish it."

Another point scored against the detested twins! Really it was a great day for Tom. He was encouraged to chance a parting shot, now, at the same target, and did it.

"You know that wonderful Indian knife that the twins have been making such a to-do about? Well, there's no track or trace of it yet; so the town is beginning to sneer and gossip and laugh. Half the people believe they never had any such knife, the other half believe they had it and have got it still. I've heard twenty people talking like that today."

Yes, Tom's blemishless week had restored him to the favour of his aunt and uncle.

His mother was satisfied with him, too. Privately, she believed she was coming to love him, but she did not say so. She told him to go along to St. Louis, now, and she would get ready and follow. Then she smashed her whisky bottle and said—

"Dah now! I's a-gwyne to make you walk as straight as a string, Chambers, en so I's bown' you ain't gwyne to git no bad example out o' yo' mammy. I tole you you couldn't go into no bad comp'ny. Well, you's gwyne into my comp'ny, en I's gwyne to fill de bill. Now, den, trot along, trot along!"

Tom went aboard one of the big transient boats that night with his heavy satchel of miscellaneous plunder, and slept the sleep of the unjust, which is serener and sounder than the other kind, as we know by the hanging-eve history of a million rascals. But when he got up in the morning, luck was against him again: A brother-thief had robbed him while he slept, and gone ashore at some intermediate landing.

16

Sold Down the River

> If you pick up a starving dog and make him prosperous, he will not bite you. This is the principal difference between a dog and a man.—*Pudd'nhead Wilson's Calendar*
>
> We know all about the habits of the ant, we know all about the habits of the bee, but we know nothing at all about the habits of the oyster. It seems almost certain that we have been choosing the wrong time for studying the oyster.—*Pudd'nhead Wilson's Calendar*

When Roxana arrived, she found her son in such despair and misery that her heart was touched and her motherhood rose up strong in her. He was ruined past hope, now; his destruction would be immediate and sure, and he would be an outcast and friendless. That was reason enough for a mother to love a child; so she loved him, and told him so. It made him wince, secretly—for she was a "nigger." That he was one himself was far from reconciling him to that despised race.

Roxana poured out endearments upon him, to which he responded uncomfortably, but as well as he could. And she tried to comfort him, but that was not possible. These intimacies quickly became horrible to him, and within the hour he began to try to get up courage enough to tell her so, and require that they be discontinued or very considerably modified. But he was afraid of her; and besides, there came a lull, now, for she had begun to think. She was trying to invent a saving plan. Finally she started up, and said she had found a way out. Tom was almost suffocated by the joy of this sudden good news. Roxana said:

"Here is de plan, en she'll win, sure. I's a nigger, en nobody ain't gwyne to doubt it dat hears me talk. I's wuth six hund'd dollahs. Take en sell me, en pay off dese gamblers."

Tom was dazed. He was not sure he had heard aright. He was dumb for a moment; then he said:

"Do you mean that you would be sold into slavery to save me?"

"Ain't you my chile? En does you know anything dat a mother won't do for her chile? Day ain't nothin' a white mother won't do for her chile. Who made 'em so? De Lord done it. En who made de niggers? De Lord made 'em. In de inside, mothers is all de same. De good Lord he made 'em so. I's gwyne to be sole into slavery, en in a year you's gwyne to buy yo' ole mammy free ag'in. I'll show you how. Dat's de plan."

Tom's hopes began to rise, and his spirits along with them. He said—

"It's lovely of you, mammy—it's just—"

"Say it ag'in! En keep on sayin' it! It's all de pay a body kin want in dis worl', en it's mo' den enough. Laws bless you, honey, when I's slavin' aroun', en dey 'buses me, if I knows you's a-sayin' dat, 'way off yonder somers, it'll heal up all de sore places, en I kin stan' 'em."

"I *do* say it again, mammy, and I'll keep on saying it, too. But how am I going to sell you? You're free, you know."

"Much diff'rence dat make! White folks ain't partic'lar. De law kin sell me now if dey tell me to leave de State in six months en I don't go. You draw up a paper—bill o' sale—en put it 'way off yonder, down in de middle o' Kaintuck somers, en sign some names to it, en say you'll sell me cheap 'ca'se you's hard up; you'll find you ain't gwyne to have no trouble. You take me up de country a piece, en sell me on a farm; dem people ain't gwyne to ask no questions if I's a bargain."

Tom forged a bill of sale and sold his mother to an Arkansas cotton-planter for a trifle over six hundred dollars. He did not want to commit this treachery, but luck threw the man in his way, and this saved him the necessity of going up country to hunt up a purchaser, with the added risk of having to answer a lot of questions, whereas this planter was so pleased with Roxy that he asked next to none at all. Besides, the planter insisted that Roxy wouldn't know where she was, at first, and that by the time she found out she would already have become contented. And Tom argued with himself that it was an immense advantage for Roxy to have a master who was so pleased with her, as this planter manifestly was. In almost no time his flowing reasonings carried him to the point of even half believing he was doing Roxy a splendid surreptitious service in selling her "down the river." And then he kept diligently saying to himself all the time: "It's for only a year. In a year I buy her free again; she'll keep that in mind, and it'll reconcile her." Yes; the little deception could do no harm, and everything would come out right and pleasant in the end, any way. By agreement, the conversation in Roxy's presence was all about the man's "upcountry" farm, and how pleasant a place it was, and how happy the slaves were there; so poor Roxy was entirely deceived; and easily, for she was not dreaming that her own son could be guilty of treason to a mother who, in voluntarily going into slavery—slavery of any kind, mild or severe, or of any duration, brief or long—was making a sacrifice for him compared with which death would have been a poor and commonplace one. She lavished tears and loving caresses upon him privately, and then went away with her owner—went away broken-hearted, and yet proud of what she was doing, and glad it was in her power to do it.

Tom squared his accounts, and resolved to keep to the very letter of his reform, and never to put that will in jeopardy again. He had three hundred dollars left. According to his mother's plan, he was to put that safely away, and add her half of his pension to it monthly. In one year this fund would buy her free again.

For a whole week he was not able to sleep well, so much the villainy which he had played upon his trusting mother preyed upon his rag of a conscience; but after that he began to get comfortable again, and was presently able to sleep like any other miscreant.

The boat bore Roxy away from St. Louis at four in the afternoon, and she stood on the lower guard abaft the paddle-box and watched Tom through a blur of tears until he melted into the throng of people and disappeared; then she looked no more, but sat there on a coil of cable crying till far into the night. When she went to her foul steerage-bunk at last, between the clashing engines, it was not to sleep, but only to wait for the morning, and, waiting, grieve.

It had been imagined that she "would not know," and would think she was travelling up stream. She! Why, she had been steamboating for years. At dawn she got up and went listlessly and sat down on the cable-coil again. She passed many a snag whose "break" could have told her a thing to break her heart, for it showed a current moving in the same direction that the boat was going; but her thoughts were elsewhere, and she did not notice. But at last the roar of a bigger and nearer break than usual brought her out of her torpor, and she looked up, and her practised eye fell upon that telltale rush of water. For one moment her petrified gaze fixed itself there. Then her head dropped upon her breast, and she said—

"Oh, de good Lord God have mercy on po' sinful me—*I's sole down de river!*"

17

The Judge Utters Dire Prophecy

> Even popularity can be overdone. In Rome, along at first, you are full of regrets that Michelangelo died; but by and by you only regret that you didn't see him do it.—*Pudd'nhead Wilson's Calendar*
>
> *July 4.* Statistics show that we lose more fools on this day than in all the other days of the year put together. This proves, by the number left in stock, that one Fourth of July per year is now inadequate, the country has grown so.—*Pudd'nhead Wilson's Calendar*

The summer weeks dragged by, and then the political campaign opened—opened in pretty warm fashion, and waxed hotter and hotter daily. The twins threw themselves into it with their whole heart, for their self-love was engaged. Their popularity, so general at first, had suffered afterward; mainly because they had been *too* popular, and so a natural reaction had followed. Besides, it had been diligently whispered around that it was curious—indeed, *very* curious—that that wonderful knife of theirs did not turn up—*if* it was so valuable, or *if* it had ever existed. And with the whisperings went chucklings and nudgings and winks, and such things have an effect. The twins considered that success in the election would reinstate them, and that defeat would work them irreparable damage. Therefore they worked hard, but not harder than Judge Driscoll and Tom worked against them in the closing days of the canvas. Tom's conduct had remained so letter-perfect during two whole months, now, that his uncle not only trusted him with money with which to persuade voters, but trusted him to go and get it himself out of the safe in the private sitting room.

The closing speech of the campaign was made by Judge Driscoll, and he made it against both of the foreigners. It was disastrously effective. He poured out rivers of ridicule upon them, and forced the big mass-meeting to laugh and applaud. He scoffed at them as adventurers, mountebanks, side-show riff-raff, dime museum freaks; he assailed their showy titles with measureless derision; he said they were back-alley barbers disguised as nobilities, peanut peddlers masquerading as gentlemen, organ-grinders bereft of their brother monkey. At last he stopped and stood still. He waited until the place had become absolutely silent and expectant, then he delivered his deadliest shot; delivered it with ice-cold seriousness and deliberation, with a significant emphasis upon the closing words: he said that he believed that the reward offered for the lost knife was humbug and buncombe, and that its owner would know where to find it whenever he should have occasion *to assassinate somebody.*

Then he stepped from the stand, leaving a startled and impressive hush behind him instead of the customary explosion of cheers and party cries.

The strange remark flew far and wide over the town and made an extraordinary sensation. Everybody was asking, "What could he mean by that?" And everybody went on asking that question, but in vain; for the Judge only said he knew what he was talking about, and stopped there; Tom said he hadn't any idea what his uncle meant, and Wilson, whenever he was asked what he thought it meant, parried the question by asking the questioner what *he* thought it meant.

Wilson was elected, the twins were defeated—crushed, in fact, and left forlorn and substantially friendless. Tom went back to St. Louis happy.

Dawson's Landing had a week of repose, now, and it needed it. But it was in an expectant state, for the air was full of rumors of a new duel. Judge Driscoll's election labours had prostrated him, but it was said that as soon as he was well enough to entertain a challenge he would get one from Count Luigi.

The brothers withdrew entirely from society, and nursed their humiliation in privacy. They avoided the people, and went out for exercise only late at night, when the streets were deserted.

18

Roxana Commands

Gratitude and treachery are merely the two extremities of the same procession. You have seen all of it that is worth staying for when the band and the gaudy officials have gone by.—*Pudd'nhead Wilson's Calendar*

Thanksgiving Day. Let all give humble, hearty, and sincere thanks, now, but the turkeys. In the island of Fiji they do not use turkeys; they use plumbers. It does not become you and me to sneer at Fiji.—*Pudd'nhead Wilson's Calendar.*

The Friday after the election was a rainy one in St. Louis. It rained all day long, and rained hard, apparently trying its best to wash that soot-blackened town white, but of course not succeeding. Toward midnight Tom Driscoll arrived at his lodgings from the theatre in the heavy downpour, and closed his umbrella and let himself in; but when he would have shut the door, he found that there was another person entering—doubtless another lodger; this person closed the door and tramped upstairs behind Tom. Tom found his door in the dark, and entered it and turned up the gas. When he faced about, lightly whistling, he saw the back of a man. The man was closing and locking his door for him. His whistle faded out and he felt uneasy. The man turned around, a wreck of shabby old clothes, sodden with rain and all a-drip, and showed a black face under an old slouch hat. Tom was frightened. He tried to order the man out, but the words refused to come, and the other man got the start. He said, in a low voice—

"Keep still—I's yo' mother!"

Tom sunk in a heap on a chair, and gasped out—

"It was mean of me, and base—I know it; but I meant it for the best, I did indeed—I can swear it."

Roxana stood awhile looking mutely down on him while he writhed in shame and went on incoherently babbling self-accusations mixed with pitiful attempts at explanation and palliation of his crime; then she seated herself and took off her hat, and her unkempt masses of long brown hair tumbled down about her shoulders.

"It ain't no fault o' yo'n dat dat ain't grey," she said sadly, noticing the hair.

"I know it, I know it! I'm a scoundrel. But I swear I meant it for the best. It was a mistake, of course, but I thought it was for the best, I truly did."

Roxana began to cry softly, and presently words began to find their way out between her sobs. They were uttered lamentingly, rather than angrily—

"Sell a pusson down de river—*down the river!*—for de bes'! I wouldn't treat a dog so! I is all broke down en wore out, now, en so I reckon it ain't in me to storm aroun' no mo', like I used to when I 'uz trompled on en 'bused. I don't know—but maybe it's so. Leastways, I's suffered so much dat mournin' seem to come mo' handy to me now den stormin'."

These words should have touched Tom Driscoll, but if they did, that effect was obliterated by a stronger one—one which removed the heavy weight of fear which lay upon him, and gave his crushed spirit a most grateful rebound, and filled all his small soul with a deep sense of relief. But he kept prudently still, and ventured no comment. There was a voiceless interval of some duration, now, in which no sounds were heard but the beating of the rain upon the panes, the sighing and complaining of the winds, and now and then a muffled sob from Roxana. The sobs became more and more infrequent, and at last ceased. Then the refugee began to talk again:

"Shet down dat light a little. More. More yit. A pusson dat is hunted don't like de light. Dah—dat'll do. I kin see whah you is, en dat's enough. I's gwine to tell you de tale, en cut it jes as short as I kin, en den I'll tell you what you's got to do. Dat man dat bought me ain't a bad man; he's good enough, as planters goes; en if he could 'a' had his way I'd 'a' be'n a house servant in his fambly en be'n comfortable: but his wife she was a Yank, en not right down good lookin', en she riz up agin me straight off; so den dey sent me out to de quarter 'mongst de common fiel' han's. Dat woman warn't satisfied even wid dat, but she worked up de overseer ag'in' me, she 'uz dat jealous en hateful; so de overseer he had me out befo' day in de mawnin's en worked me de whole long day as long as dey 'uz any light to see by; en many's de lashin's I got 'ca'se I couldn't come up to de work o' de stronges'. Dat overseer wuz a Yank, too, outen New Englan', en anybody down South kin tell you what dat mean. *Dey* knows how to work a nigger to death, en dey knows how to whale 'em, too—whale 'em till dey backs is welted like a washboard. 'Long at fust my marster say de good word for me to de overseer, but dat 'uz bad for me; for de mistis she fine it out, en arter dat I jist ketched it at every turn—dey warn't no mercy for me no mo'."

Tom's heart was fired—with fury against the planter's wife; and he said to himself, "But for that meddlesome fool, everything would have gone all right." He added a deep and bitter curse against her.

The expression of this sentiment was fiercely written in his face, and stood thus revealed to Roxana by a white glare of lightning which turned the somber dusk of the room into dazzling day at that moment. She was pleased—pleased and grateful; for did not that expression show that her child was capable of grieving for his mother's wrongs and of feeling resentment toward her persecutors?—a thing which she had been doubting. But her flash of happiness was only a flash, and went out again and left her spirit dark; for she said to herself, "He sole me down de river—he can't feel for a body long: dis'll pass en go." Then she took up her tale again.

"'Bout ten days ago I 'uz sayin' to myself dat I couldn't las' many mo' weeks I 'uz so wore out wid de awful work en de lashin's, en so downhearted en misable. En I didn't care no mo', nuther—life warn't wuth noth'n' to me, if I got to go on like dat. Well, when a body is in a frame o' mine like dat, what do a body care what a body do? Dey was a little sickly nigger wench 'bout ten year ole dat 'uz good to me, en hadn't no mammy, po' thing, en I loved her en she loved me; en she come out whah I 'uz workin 'en she had a roasted tater, en tried to slip it to me—robbin' herself, you see, 'ca'se she knowed de overseer didn't gimme enough to eat—en he ketched her at it, en give her a lick acrost de back wid his stick, which 'uz as thick as a broom-handle, en she drop' screamin' on de groun', en squirmin' en wallerin' aroun' in de dust like a spider dat's got crippled. I couldn't stan' it. All de hell-fire dat 'uz ever in my heart flame' up, en I snatch de stick outen his han' en laid him flat. He laid dah moanin' en cussin', en all out of his head, you know, en de niggers 'uz plumb sk'yred to death. Dey gathered roun' him to he'p him, en I jumped on his hoss en took out for de river as tight as I could go. I knowed what dey would do wid me. Soon as he got well he would start in en work me to death if marster let him; en if dey didn't do dat, they'd sell me furder down de river, en dat's de same thing. So I 'lowed to drown myself en git out o' my troubles. It 'uz gitt'n' towards dark. I 'uz at de river in two minutes. Den I see a canoe, en I says dey ain't no use to drown myself tell I got to; so I ties de hoss in de edge o' de timber en shove out down de river, keepin' in under de shelter o' de bluff bank en prayin' for de dark to shet down quick. I had a pow'ful good start, 'ca'se de big house 'uz three mile back f'om de river en on'y de work-mules to ride dah on, en on'y niggers to ride 'em, en *dey* warn't gwine to hurry—dey'd gimme all de chance dey could. Befo' a body could go to de house en back it would be long pas' dark, en dey couldn't track de hoss en fine out which way I went tell mawnin', en de niggers would tell 'em all de lies dey could 'bout it.

"Well, de dark come, en I went on a-spinnin' down de river. I paddled mo'n two hours, den I warn't worried no mo', so I quit paddlin, en floated down de current, considerin' what I 'uz gwine to do if I didn't have to drown myself. I made up some plans, en floated along, turnin' 'em over in my mine. Well, when it 'uz a little pas' midnight, as I reckoned, en I had come fifteen or twenty mile, I see de lights o' a steamboat layin' at de bank, whah dey warn't no town en no woodyard, en putty soon I ketched de shape o' de chimbly-tops ag'in' de stars, en den good gracious me, I 'most jumped out o' my skin for joy! It 'uz de *Gran' Mogul*—I 'uz chambermaid on her for eight seasons in de Cincinnati en Orleans trade. I slid 'long pas'—don't see nobody stirrin' nowhah—hear 'em a-hammerin' away in de engine room, den I knowed what de matter was—some o' de machinery's broke. I got asho' below de boat and turn' de canoe loose, den I goes 'long up, en dey 'uz jes one plank out, en I step' 'board de boat. It 'uz pow'ful hot, deckhan's en roustabouts 'uz sprawled aroun' asleep on de fo'cas'l', de second mate, Jim Bangs, he sot dah on de bitts wid his head down, asleep—'ca'se dat's de way de second mate stan' de cap'n's watch!—en de ole watchman, Billy Hatch, he 'uz a-noddin' on de companion way;—en I knowed 'em all; 'en, lan', but dey did look good! I says to myself, I wished old marster'd come along *now* en try to take me—bless yo' heart, I's 'mong frien's, I is. So I tromped right along 'mongst 'em, en went up on de b'iler deck en 'way back aft to de ladies' cabin guard, en sot down dah in de same cheer dat I'd sot in 'mos' a hund'd million times, I reckon; en it 'uz jist home ag'in, I tell you!

"In 'bout an hour I heard de ready-bell jingle, en den de racket begin. Putty soon I hear de gong strike. 'Set her back on de outside,' I says to myself—'I reckon I knows dat music!' I hear de gong ag'in. 'Come ahead on de inside,' I says. Gong ag'in. 'Stop de outside.' Gong ag'in. 'Come ahead on de outside—now we's pinted for Sent Louis, en I's outer de woods en ain't got to drown myself at all.' I knowed de *Mogul*'uz in de Sent Louis trade now, you see. It 'uz jes fair daylight when we passed our plantation, en I seed a gang o' niggers en white folks huntin' up en down de sho', en troublin' deyselves a good deal 'bout me; but I warn't troublin' myself none 'bout dem.

"'Bout dat time Sally Jackson, dat used to be my second chambermaid en 'uz head chambermaid now, she come out on de guard, en 'uz pow'ful glad to see me, en so 'uz all de officers; en I tole 'em I'd got kidnapped en sole down de river, en dey made me up twenty dollahs en give it to me, en Sally she rigged me out wid good clo'es, en when I got here I went straight to whah you used to wuz, en den I come to dis house, en dey say you's away but 'spected back every day; so I didn't dast to go down de river to Dawson's, 'ca'se I might miss you.

"Well, las' Monday I 'uz pass'n' by one o' dem places in Fourth street whah deh sticks up runaway-nigger bills, en he'ps to ketch 'em, en I seed my marster! I 'mos' flopped down on de groun', I felt so gone. He had his back to me, en 'uz talkin' to de man en givin' him some bills—nigger-bills, I reckon, en I'se de nigger. He's offerin' a reward—dat's it. Ain't I right, don't you reckon?"

Tom had been gradually sinking into a state of ghastly terror, and he said to himself, now: "I'm lost, no matter what turn things take! This man has said to me that he thinks there was something suspicious about that sale. He said he had a letter from a passenger on the *Grand Mogul* saying that Roxy came here on that boat and that everybody on board knew all about the case; so he says that her coming here instead of flying to a free State looks bad for me, and that if I don't find her for him, and that pretty soon, he will make trouble for me. I never believed that story; I couldn't believe she would be so dead to all motherly instincts as to come here, knowing the risk she would run of getting me into irremediable trouble. And after all, here she is! And I stupidly swore I would help him find her, thinking it was a perfectly safe thing to promise. If I venture to deliver her up, she—she—but how can I help myself? I've got to do that or pay the money, and where's the money to come from? I—I—well, I should think that if he would swear to treat her kindly hereafter—and she says, herself, that he is a good man—and if he would swear to never allow her to be overworked, or ill fed, or—"

A flash of lightning exposed Tom's pallid face, drawn and rigid with these worrying thoughts. Roxana spoke up sharply now, and there was apprehension in her voice—

"Turn up dat light! I want to see yo' face better. Dah now—lemme look at you. Chambers, you's as white as yo' shirt! Has you see dat man? Has he be'n to see you?"

"Ye-s."

"When?"

"Monday noon."

"Monday noon! Was he on my track?"

"He—well, he thought he was. That is, he hoped he was. This is the bill you saw." He took it out of his pocket.

"Read it to me!"

She was panting with excitement, and there was a dusky glow in her eyes that Tom could not translate with certainty, but there seemed to be something threatening about it. The handbill had the usual rude woodcut of a turbaned negro woman running, with the customary bundle on a stick over her shoulder, and the heading in bold type, "$100 Reward." Tom read the bill aloud—at least the part that described Roxana and named the master and his St. Louis address and the address of the Fourth-street agency; but he left out the item that applicants for the reward might also apply to Mr. Thomas Driscoll.

"Gimme de bill!"

Tom had folded it and was putting it in his pocket. He felt a chilly streak creeping down his back, but said as carelessly as he could—

"The bill? Why, it isn't any use to you, you can't read it. What do you want with it?"

"Gimme de bill!" Tom gave it to her, but with a reluctance which he could not entirely disguise. "Did you read it *all* to me?"

"Certainly I did."

"Hole up yo' han' en swah to it."

Tom did it. Roxana put the bill carefully away in her pocket, with her eyes fixed upon Tom's face all the while; then she said—

"Yo's lyin'!"

"What would I want to lie about it for?"

"I don't know—but you is. Dat's my opinion, anyways. But nemmine 'bout dat. When I seed dat man I 'uz dat sk'yerd dat I could sca'sely wobble home. Den I give a nigger man a dollar for dese clo'es, en I ain't be'n in a house sence, night ner day, till now. I blacked my face en laid hid in de cellar of a ole house dat's burnt down, daytimes, en robbed de sugar hogsheads en grain sacks on de wharf, nights, to git somethin' to eat, en never dast to try to buy noth'n', en I's 'mos' starved. En I never dast to come near dis place till dis rainy night, when dey ain't no people roun' sca'sely. But tonight I be'n a-stannin' in de dark alley ever sence night come, waitin' for you to go by. En here I is."

She fell to thinking. Presently she said—

"You seed dat man at noon, las' Monday?"

"Yes."

"I seed him de middle o' dat arternoon. He hunted you up, didn't he?"

"Yes."

"Did he give you de bill dat time?"

"No, he hadn't got it printed yet."

Roxana darted a suspicious glance at him.

"Did you he'p him fix up de bill?"

Tom cursed himself for making that stupid blunder, and tried to rectify it by saying he remembered, now, that it *was* at noon Monday that the man gave him the bill. Roxana said—

"You's lyin' ag'in, sho." Then she straightened up and raised her finger:

"Now den! I's gwine to ask you a question, en I wants to know how you's gwine to git aroun' it. You knowed he 'uz arter me; en if you run off, 'stid o' stayin' here to he'p him, he'd know dey 'uz somethin' wrong 'bout dis business, en den he would inquire 'bout you, en dat would take him to yo' uncle, en yo' uncle would read de bill en see dat you be'n sellin' a free nigger down de river, en you know *him*, I reckon! He'd t'ar up de will en kick you outen de house. Now, den, you answer me dis question: hain't you tole dat man dat I would be sho' to come here, en den you would fix it so he could set a trap en ketch me?"

Tom recognized that neither lies nor arguments could help him any longer—he was in a vise, with the screw turned on, and out of it there was no budging. His face began to take on an ugly look, and presently he said, with a snarl—

"Well, what could I do? You see, yourself, that I was in his grip and couldn't get out."

Roxy scorched him with a scornful gaze awhile, then she said—

"What could you do? You could be Judas to yo' own mother to save yo' wuthless hide! Would anybody b'lieve it? No—a dog couldn't! You is de low-downest orneriest hound dat was ever pup'd into dis worl'—en I's 'sponsible for it!"—and she spat on him.

He made no effort to resent this. Roxy reflected a moment, then she said—

"Now I'll tell you what you's gwine to do. You's gwine to give dat man de money dat you's got laid up, en make him wait till you kin go to de Judge en git de res' en buy me free agin."

"Thunder! what are you thinking of? Go and ask him for three hundred dollars and odd? What would I tell him I want with it, pray?"

Roxy's answer was delivered in a serene and level voice—

"You'll tell him you's sole me to pay yo' gamblin' debts en dat you lied to me en was a villain, en dat I 'quires you to git dat money en buy me back ag'in."

"Why, you've gone stark mad! He would tear the will to shreds in a minute—don't you know that?"

"Yes, I does."

"Then you don't believe I'm idiot enough to go to him, do you?"

"I don't b'lieve nothin' 'bout it—I *knows* you's a-goin'. I knows it 'ca'se you knows dat if you don't raise dat money I'll go to him myself, en den he'll sell *you* down de river, en you kin see how you like it!"

Tom rose, trembling and excited, and there was an evil light in his eye. He strode to the door and said he must get out of this suffocating place for a moment and clear his brain in the fresh air so that he could determine what to do. The door wouldn't open. Roxy smiled grimly, and said—

"I's got de key, honey—set down. You needn't cle'r up yo' brain none to fine out what you gwine to do—*I* knows what you's gwine to do." Tom sat down and began to pass his hands through his hair with a helpless and desperate air. Roxy said, "Is dat man in dis house?"

Tom glanced up with a surprised expression, and asked—

"What gave you such an idea?"

"You done it. Gwine out to cle'r yo' brain! In de fust place you ain't got none to cle'r, en in de second place yo' ornery eye tole on you. You's de low-downest hound dat ever—but I done tole you dat befo'. Now den, dis is Friday. You kin fix it up wid dat man, en tell him you's gwine away to git de res' o' de money, en dat you'll be back wid it nex' Tuesday, or maybe Wednesday. You understan'?"

Tom answered sullenly—

"Yes."

"En when you gits de new bill o' sale dat sells me to my own self, take en send it in de mail to Mr. Pudd'nhead Wilson, en write on de back dat he's to keep it tell I come. You understan'?"

"Yes."

"Dat's all den. Take yo' umbreller, en put on yo' hat."

"Why?"

"Beca'se you's gwine to see me home to de wharf. You see dis knife? I's toted it aroun' sence de day I seed dat man en bought dese clo'es en it. If he ketch me, I's gwine to kill myself wid it. Now start along, en go sof', en lead de way; en if you gives a sign in dis house, or if anybody comes up to you in de street, I's gwine to jam it right into you. Chambers, does you b'lieve me when I says dat?"

"It's no use to bother me with that question. I know your word's good."

"Yes, it's diff'rent from yo'n! Shet de light out en move along—here's de key."

They were not followed. Tom trembled every time a late straggler brushed by them on the street, and half expected to feel the cold steel in his back. Roxy was right at his heels and always in reach. After tramping a mile they reached a wide vacancy on the deserted wharves, and in this dark and rainy desert they parted.

As Tom trudged home his mind was full of dreary thoughts and wild plans; but at last he said to himself, wearily—

"There is but the one way out. I must follow her plan. But with a variation—I will not ask for the money and ruin myself; I will *rob* the old skinflint."

19

The Prophecy Realized

Few things are harder to put up with than the annoyance of a good example.—*Pudd'nhead Wilson's Calendar*
It were not best that we should all think alike; it is difference of opinion that makes horse-races.—*Pudd'nhead Wilson's Calendar*

Dawson's Landing was comfortably finishing its season of dull repose and waiting patiently for the duel. Count Luigi was waiting, too; but not patiently, rumor said. Sunday came, and Luigi insisted on having his challenge conveyed. Wilson carried it. Judge Driscoll declined to fight with an assassin—"that is," he added significantly, "in the field of honour."

Elsewhere, of course, he would be ready. Wilson tried to convince him that if he had been present himself when Angelo told about the homicide committed by Luigi, he would not have considered the act discreditable to Luigi; but the obstinate old man was not to be moved.

Wilson went back to his principal and reported the failure of his mission. Luigi was incensed, and asked how it could be that the old gentleman, who was by no means dull-witted, held his trifling nephew's evidence and inferences to be of more value than Wilson's. But Wilson laughed, and said—

"That is quite simple; that is easily explicable. I am not his doll—his baby—his infatuation: his nephew is. The Judge and his late wife never had any children. The Judge and his wife were past middle age when this treasure fell into their lap. One must make allowances for a parental instinct that has been starving for twenty-five or thirty years. It is famished, it is crazed with hunger by that time, and will be entirely satisfied with anything that comes handy; its taste is atrophied, it can't tell mud-cat from shad. A devil born to a young couple is measurably recognizable by them as a devil before long, but a devil adopted by an old couple is an angel to them, and remains so, through thick and thin. Tom is this old man's angel; he is infatuated with him. Tom can persuade him into things which other people can't—not all things; I don't mean that, but a good many—particularly one class of things: the things that create or abolish personal partialities or prejudices in the old man's mind. The old man liked both of you. Tom conceived a hatred for you. That was enough; it turned the old man around at once. The oldest and strongest friendship must go to the ground when one of these late-adopted darlings throws a brick at it."

"It's a curious philosophy," said Luigi.

"It ain't a philosophy at all—it's a fact. And there is something pathetic and beautiful about it, too. I think there is nothing more pathetic than to see one of these poor old childless couples taking a menagerie of yelping little worthless dogs to their hearts; and then adding some cursing and squawking parrots and a jackass-voiced macaw; and next a couple of hundred screeching song-birds, and presently some fetid guinea-pigs and rabbits, and a howling colony of cats. It is all a groping and ignorant effort to construct out of base metal and brass filings, so to speak, something to take the place of that golden treasure denied them by Nature, a child. But this is a digression. The unwritten law of this region requires you to kill Judge Driscoll on sight, and he and the community will expect that attention at your hands—though of course your own death by his bullet will answer every purpose. Look out for him! Are you heeled—that is, fixed?"

"Yes, he shall have his opportunity. If he attacks me I will respond."

As Wilson was leaving, he said—

"The Judge is still a little used up by his campaign work, and will not get out for a day or so; but when he does get out, you want to be on the alert."

About eleven at night the twins went out for exercise, and started on a long stroll in the veiled moonlight.

Tom Driscoll had landed at Hackett's Store, two miles below Dawson's, just about half an hour earlier, the only passenger for that lonely spot, and had walked up the shore road and entered Judge Driscoll's house without having encountered any one either on the road or under the roof.

He pulled down his window-blinds and lighted his candle. He laid off his coat and hat and began his preparations. He unlocked his trunk and got his suit of girl's clothes out from under the male attire in it, and laid it by. Then he blacked his face with burnt cork and put the cork in his pocket. His plan was, to slip down to his uncle's private sitting room below, pass into the bedroom, steal the safe-key from the old gentleman's clothes, and then go back and rob the safe. He took up his candle to start. His courage and confidence were high, up to this point, but both began to waver a little, now. Suppose he should make a noise, by some accident, and get caught—say, in the act of opening the safe? Perhaps it would be well to go armed. He took the Indian knife from its hiding place, and felt a pleasant return of his wandering courage. He slipped stealthily down the narrow stair, his hair rising and his pulses halting at the slightest creak. When he was halfway down, he was disturbed to perceive that the landing below was touched by a faint glow of light. What could that mean? Was his uncle still up? No, that was not likely; he must have left his night-taper there when he went to bed. Tom crept on down, pausing at every step to listen. He found the door standing open, and glanced in. What he saw pleased him beyond measure. His uncle was asleep on the sofa; on a small table at the head of the sofa a lamp was burning low, and by it stood the old man's small tin cash-box, closed. Near the box was a pile of banknotes and a piece of paper covered with figures in pencil. The safe-door was not open. Evidently the sleeper had wearied himself with work upon his finances, and was taking a rest.

Tom set his candle on the stairs, and began to make his way toward the pile of notes, stooping low as he went. When he was passing his uncle, the old man stirred in his sleep, and Tom stopped instantly—stopped, and softly drew the knife from its sheath, with his heart thumping, and his eyes fastened upon his benefactor's face. After a moment or two he ventured forward again—one step—reached for his prize and seized it, dropping the knife-sheath. Then he felt the old man's strong grip upon him, and a wild cry of "Help! help!" rang in his ear. Without hesitation he drove the knife home—and was free. Some of the notes escaped from his left hand and fell in the blood on the floor. He dropped the knife and snatched them up and started to fly; transferred them to his left hand, and seized the knife again, in his fright and confusion, but remembered himself and flung it from him, as being a dangerous witness to carry away with him.

He jumped for the stair-foot, and closed the door behind him; and as he snatched his candle and fled upward, the stillness of the night was broken by the sound of urgent footsteps approaching the house. In another moment he was in his room and the twins were standing aghast over the body of the murdered man!

Tom put on his coat, buttoned his hat under it, threw on his suit of girl's clothes, dropped the veil, blew out his light, locked the room door by which he had just entered, taking the key, passed through his other door into the back hall, locked that door and kept the key, then worked his way along in the dark and descended the back stairs. He was not expecting to meet anybody, for all interest was centered in the other part of the house, now; his calculation proved correct. By the time he was passing through the backyard, Mrs. Pratt, her servants, and a dozen half-dressed neighbours had joined the twins and the dead, and accessions were still arriving at the front door.

As Tom, quaking as with a palsy, passed out at the gate, three women came flying from the house on the opposite side of the lane. They rushed by him and in at the gate, asking him what the trouble was there, but not waiting for an answer. Tom said to himself, "Those old maids waited to dress—they did the same thing the night Stevens's house burned down next door." In a few minutes he was in the haunted house. He lighted a candle and took off his girl-clothes. There was blood on him all down his left side, and his right hand was red with the stains of the blood-soaked notes which he had crushed in it; but otherwise he was free from this sort of evidence. He cleansed his hand on the straw, and cleaned most of the smut from his face. Then he burned his male and female attire to ashes, scattered the ashes, and put on a disguise proper for a tramp. He blew out his light, went below, and was soon loafing down the river road with the intent to borrow and use one of Roxy's devices. He found a canoe and paddled off down-stream, setting the canoe adrift as dawn approached, and making his way by land to the next village, where he kept out of sight till a transient steamer came along, and then took deck passage for St. Louis. He was ill at ease until Dawson's Landing was behind him; then he said to himself, "All the detectives on earth couldn't trace me now; there's not a vestige of a clue left in the world; that homicide will take its place with the permanent mysteries, and people won't get done trying to guess out the secret of it for fifty years."

In St. Louis, next morning, he read this brief telegram in the papers—dated at Dawson's Landing:

Judge Driscoll, an old and respected citizen, was assassinated here about midnight by a profligate Italian nobleman or barber on account of a quarrel growing out of the recent election. The assassin will probably be lynched.

"One of the twins!" soliloquized Tom; "how lucky! It is the knife that has done him this grace. We never know when fortune is trying to favour us. I actually cursed Pudd'nhead Wilson in my heart for putting it out of my power to sell that knife. I take it back, now."

Tom was now rich and independent. He arranged with the planter, and mailed to Wilson the new bill of sale which sold Roxana to herself; then he telegraphed his Aunt Pratt:

Have seen the awful news in the papers and am almost prostrated with grief. Shall start by packet today. Try to bear up till I come.

When Wilson reached the house of mourning and had gathered such details as Mrs. Pratt and the rest of the crowd could tell him, he took command as mayor, and gave orders that nothing should be touched, but everything left as it was until Justice Robinson should arrive and take the proper measures as coroner. He cleared everybody out of the room but the twins and himself. The sheriff soon arrived and took the twins away to jail. Wilson told them to keep heart, and promised to do his best in their defense when the case should come to trial. Justice Robinson came presently, and with him Constable Blake. They examined the room thoroughly. They found the knife and the sheath. Wilson noticed that there were fingerprints on the knife-handle. That pleased him, for the twins had required the earliest comers to make a scrutiny of their hands and clothes, and neither these people nor Wilson himself had found any blood-stains upon them. Could there be a possibility that the twins had spoken the truth when they said they found the man dead when they ran into the house in answer to the cry for help? He thought of that mysterious girl at once. But this was not the sort of work for a girl to be engaged in. No matter; Tom Driscoll's room must be examined.

After the coroner's jury had viewed the body and its surroundings, Wilson suggested a search upstairs, and he went along. The jury forced an entrance to Tom's room, but found nothing, of course.

The coroner's jury found that the homicide was committed by Luigi, and that Angelo was accessory to it.

The town was bitter against the unfortunates, and for the first few days after the murder they were in constant danger of being lynched. The grand jury presently indicted Luigi for murder in the first degree, and Angelo as accessory before the fact. The twins were transferred from the city jail to the county prison to await trial.

Wilson examined the finger-marks on the knife-handle and said to himself, "Neither of the twins made those marks." Then manifestly there was another person concerned, either in his own interest or as hired assassin.

But who could it be? That, he must try to find out. The safe was not open, the cash-box was closed, and had three thousand dollars in it. Then robbery was not the motive, and revenge was. Where had the murdered man an enemy except Luigi? There was but that one person in the world with a deep grudge against him.

The mysterious girl! The girl was a great trial to Wilson. If the motive had been robbery, the girl might answer; but there wasn't any girl that would want to take this old man's life for revenge. He had no quarrels with girls; he was a gentleman.

Wilson had perfect tracings of the finger-marks of the knife-handle; and among his glass-records he had a great array of fingerprints of women and girls, collected during the last fifteen or eighteen years, but he scanned them in vain, they successfully withstood every test; among them were no duplicates of the prints on the knife.

The presence of the knife on the stage of the murder was a worrying circumstance for Wilson. A week previously he had as good as admitted to himself that he believed Luigi had possessed such a knife, and that he still possessed it notwithstanding his pretense that it had been stolen. And now here was the knife, and with it the twins. Half the town had said the twins were humbugging when they claimed that they had lost their knife, and now these people were joyful, and said, "I told you so!"

If their fingerprints had been on the handle—but it was useless to bother any further about that; the fingerprints on the handle were *not* theirs—that he knew perfectly.

Wilson refused to suspect Tom; for first, Tom couldn't murder anybody—he hadn't character enough; secondly, if he could murder a person he wouldn't select his doting benefactor and nearest relative; thirdly, self-interest was in the way; for while the uncle lived, Tom was sure of a free support and a chance to get the destroyed will revived again, but with the uncle gone, that chance was gone, too. It was true the will had really been revived, as was now discovered, but Tom could not have been aware of it, or he would have spoken of it, in his native talky, unsecretive way. Finally, Tom was in St. Louis when the murder was done, and got the news out of the morning journals, as was shown by his telegram to his aunt. These speculations were unemphasized sensations rather than articulated thoughts, for Wilson would have laughed at the idea of seriously connecting Tom with the murder.

Wilson regarded the case of the twins as desperate—in fact, about hopeless. For he argued that if a confederate was not found, an enlightened Missouri jury would hang them, sure; if a confederate was found, that would not improve the matter, but simply furnish one more person for the sheriff to hang. Nothing could save the twins but the discovery of a person who did the murder on his sole personal account—an undertaking which had all the aspect of the impossible. Still, the person who made the fingerprints must be sought. The twins might have no case *with* him, but they certainly would have none without him.

So Wilson mooned around, thinking, thinking, guessing, guessing, day and night, and arriving nowhere. Whenever he ran across a girl or a woman he was not acquainted with, he got her fingerprints, on one pretext or another; and they always cost him a sigh when he got home, for they never tallied with the finger-marks on the knife-handle.

As to the mysterious girl, Tom swore he knew no such girl, and did not remember ever seeing a girl wearing a dress like the one described by Wilson. He admitted that he did not always lock his room, and that sometimes the servants forgot to lock the house doors; still, in his opinion the girl must have made but few visits or she would have been discovered. When Wilson tried to connect her with the stealing-raid, and thought she might have been the old woman's confederate, if not the very thief herself disguised as an old woman, Tom seemed stuck, and also much interested, and said he would keep a sharp eye out for this person or persons, although he was afraid that she or they would be too smart to venture again into a town where everybody would now be on the watch for a good while to come.

Everybody was pitying Tom, he looked so quiet and sorrowful, and seemed to feel his great loss so deeply. He was playing a part, but it was not all a part. The picture of his alleged uncle, as he had last seen him, was before him in the dark pretty frequently, when he was awake, and called again in his dreams, when he was asleep. He wouldn't go into the room where the tragedy had happened. This charmed the doting Mrs. Pratt, who realized now, "as she had never done before," she said, what a sensitive and delicate nature her darling had, and how he adored his poor uncle.

20

The Murderer Chuckles

Even the clearest and most perfect circumstantial evidence is likely to be at fault, after all, and therefore ought to be received with great caution. Take the case of any pencil, sharpened by any woman: if you have witnesses, you will find she did it with a knife; but if you take simply the aspect of the pencil, you will say she did it with her teeth.—*Pudd'nhead Wilson's Calendar*

The weeks dragged along, no friend visiting the jailed twins but their counsel and Aunt Patsy Cooper, and the day of trial came at last—the heaviest day in Wilson's life; for with all his tireless diligence he had discovered no sign or trace of the missing confederate. "Confederate" was the term he had long ago privately accepted for that person—not as being unquestionably the right term, but as being at least possibly the right one, though he was never able to understand why the twins did not vanish and escape, as the confederate had done, instead of remaining by the murdered man and getting caught there.

The court house was crowded, of course, and would remain so to the finish, for not only in the town itself, but in the country for miles around, the trial was the one topic of conversation among the people. Mrs. Pratt, in deep mourning, and Tom with a weed on his hat, had seats near Pembroke Howard, the public prosecutor, and back of them sat a great array of friends of the family. The twins had but one friend present to keep their counsel in countenance, their poor old sorrowing landlady. She sat near Wilson, and looked her friendliest. In the "nigger corner" sat Chambers; also Roxy, with good clothes on, and her bill of sale in her pocket. It was her most precious possession, and she never parted with it, day or night. Tom had allowed her thirty-five dollars a month ever since he came into his property, and had said that he and she ought to be grateful to the twins for making them rich; but had roused such a temper in her by this speech that he did not repeat the argument afterward. She said the old Judge had treated her child a thousand times better than he deserved, and had never done her an unkindness in his life; so she hated these outlandish devils for killing him, and shouldn't ever sleep satisfied till she saw them hanged for it. She was here to watch the trial, now, and was going to lift up just one "hooraw" over it if the County Judge put her in jail a year for it. She gave her turbaned head a toss and said, "When dat verdic' comes, I's gwine to lif' dat *roof*, now, I *tell* you."

Pembroke Howard briefly sketched the State's case. He said he would show by a chain of circumstantial evidence without break or fault in it anywhere, that the principal prisoner at the bar committed the murder; that the motive was partly revenge, and partly a desire to take his own life out of jeopardy, and that his brother, by his presence, was a consenting accessory to the crime; a crime which was the basest known to the calendar of human misdeeds—assassination; that it was conceived by the blackest of hearts and consummated by the cowardliest of hands; a crime which had broken a loving sister's heart, blighted the happiness of a young nephew who was as dear as a son, brought inconsolable grief to many friends, and sorrow and loss to the whole community. The utmost penalty of the outraged law would be exacted, and upon the accused, now present at the bar, that penalty would unquestionably be executed. He would reserve further remark until his closing speech.

He was strongly moved, and so also was the whole house; Mrs. Pratt and several other women were weeping when he sat down, and many an eye that was full of hate was riveted upon the unhappy prisoners.

Witness after witness was called by the State, and questioned at length; but the cross-questioning was brief. Wilson knew they could furnish nothing valuable for his side. People were sorry for Pudd'nhead; his budding career would get hurt by this trial.

Several witnesses swore they heard Judge Driscoll say in his public speech that the twins would be able to find their lost knife again when they needed it to assassinate somebody with. This was not news, but now it was seen to have been sorrowfully prophetic, and a profound sensation quivered through the hushed courtroom when those dismal words were repeated.

The public prosecutor rose and said that it was within his knowledge, through a conversation held with Judge Driscoll on the last day of his life, that counsel for the defense had brought him a challenge from the person charged at this bar with murder; that he had refused to fight with a confessed assassin—"that is, on the field of honour," but had added significantly, that he would be ready for him elsewhere. Presumably the person here charged with murder was warned that he must kill or be killed the first time he should meet Judge Driscoll. If counsel for the defense chose to let the statement stand so, he would not call him to the witness stand. Mr. Wilson said he would offer no denial. [Murmurs in the house—"It is getting worse and worse for Wilson's case."]

Mrs. Pratt testified that she heard no outcry, and did not know what woke her up, unless it was the sound of rapid footsteps approaching the front door. She jumped up and ran out in the hall just as she was, and heard the footsteps flying up the front steps and then following behind her as she ran to the sitting room. There she found the accused standing over her murdered brother. [Here she broke down and sobbed. Sensation in the court.] Resuming, she said the persons entering behind her were Mr. Rogers and Mr. Buckstone.

Cross-examined by Wilson, she said the twins proclaimed their innocence; declared that they had been taking a walk, and had hurried to the house in response to a cry for help which was so loud and strong that they had heard it at a considerable distance; that they begged her and the gentlemen just mentioned to examine their hands and clothes—which was done, and no bloodstains found.

Confirmatory evidence followed from Rogers and Buckstone.

The finding of the knife was verified, the advertisement minutely describing it and offering a reward for it was put in evidence, and its exact correspondence with that description proved. Then followed a few minor details, and the case for the State was closed.

Wilson said that he had three witnesses, the Misses Clarkson, who would testify that they met a veiled young woman leaving Judge Driscoll's premises by the back gate a few minutes after the cries for help were heard, and that their evidence, taken with certain circumstantial evidence which he would call the court's attention to, would in his opinion convince the court that there was still one person concerned in this crime who had not yet been found, and also that a stay of proceedings ought to be granted, in justice to his clients, until that person should be discovered. As it was late, he would ask leave to defer the examination of his three witnesses until the next morning.

The crowd poured out of the place and went flocking away in excited groups and couples, talking the events of the session over with vivacity and consuming interest, and everybody seemed to have had a satisfactory and enjoyable day except the accused, their counsel, and their old-lady friend. There was no cheer among these, and no substantial hope.

In parting with the twins Aunt Patsy did attempt a goodnight with a gay pretense of hope and cheer in it, but broke down without finishing.

Absolutely secure as Tom considered himself to be, the opening solemnities of the trial had nevertheless oppressed him with a vague uneasiness, his being a nature sensitive to even the smallest alarms; but from the moment that the poverty and weakness of Wilson's case lay exposed to the court, he was comfortable once more, even jubilant. He left the courtroom sarcastically sorry for Wilson. "The Clarksons met an unknown woman in the back lane," he said to himself—"*that* is his case! I'll give him a century to find her in—a couple of them if he likes. A woman who doesn't exist any longer, and the clothes that gave her her sex burnt up and the ashes thrown away—oh, certainly, he'll find *her* easy enough!" This reflection set him to admiring, for the hundredth time, the shrewd ingenuities by which he had insured himself against detection—more, against even suspicion.

"Nearly always in cases like this there is some little detail or other overlooked, some wee little track or trace left behind, and detection follows; but here there's not even the faintest suggestion of a trace left. No more than a bird leaves when it flies through the air—yes, through the night, you may say. The man that can track a bird through the air in the dark and find that bird is the man to track me out and find the Judge's assassin—no other need apply. And that is the job that has been laid out for poor Pudd'nhead Wilson, of all people in the world! Lord, it will be pathetically funny to see him grubbing and groping after that woman that don't exist, and the right person sitting under his very nose all the time!" The more he thought the situation over, the more the humour of it struck him. Finally he said, "I'll never let him hear the last of that woman. Every time I catch him in company, to his dying day, I'll ask him in the guileless affectionate way that used to gravel him so when I inquired how his unborn law-business was coming along, 'Got on her track yet—hey, Pudd'nhead?'" He wanted to laugh, but that would not have answered; there were people about, and he was mourning for his uncle. He made up his mind that it would be good entertainment to look in on Wilson that night and watch him worry over his barren law-case and goad him with an exasperating word or two of sympathy and commiseration now and then.

Wilson wanted no supper, he had no appetite. He got out all the fingerprints of girls and women in his collection of records and pored gloomily over them an hour or more, trying to convince himself that that troublesome girl's marks were there somewhere and had been overlooked. But it was not so. He drew back his chair, clasped his hands over his head, and gave himself up to dull and arid musings.

Tom Driscoll dropped in, an hour after dark, and said with a pleasant laugh as he took a seat—

"Hello, we've gone back to the amusements of our days of neglect and obscurity for consolation, have we?" and he took up one of the glass strips and held it against the light to inspect it. "Come, cheer up, old man; there's no use in losing your grip and going back to this child's-play merely because this big sunspot is drifting across your shiny new disk. It'll pass, and you'll be all right again,"—and he laid the glass down. "Did you think you could win always?"

"Oh, no," said Wilson, with a sigh, "I didn't expect that, but I can't believe Luigi killed your uncle, and I feel very sorry for him. It makes me blue. And you would feel as I do, Tom, if you were not prejudiced against those young fellows."

"I don't know about that," and Tom's countenance darkened, for his memory reverted to his kicking; "I owe them no good will, considering the brunette one's treatment of me that night. Prejudice or no prejudice, Pudd'nhead, I don't like them, and when they get their deserts you're not going to find me sitting on the mourner's bench."

He took up another strip of glass, and exclaimed—

"Why, here's old Roxy's label! Are you going to ornament the royal palaces with nigger paw-marks, too? By the date here, I was seven months old when this was done, and she was nursing me and her little nigger cub. There's a line straight across her thumb-print. How comes that?" and Tom held out the piece of glass to Wilson.

"That is common," said the bored man, wearily. "Scar of a cut or a scratch, usually"—and he took the strip of glass indifferently, and raised it toward the lamp.

All the blood sunk suddenly out of his face; his hand quaked, and he gazed at the polished surface before him with the glassy stare of a corpse.

"Great Heavens, what's the matter with you, Wilson? Are you going to faint?"

Tom sprang for a glass of water and offered it, but Wilson shrank shuddering from him and said—

"No, no!—take it away!" His breast was rising and falling, and he moved his head about in a dull and wandering way, like a person who had been stunned. Presently he said, "I shall feel better when I get to bed; I have been overwrought today; yes, and over worked for many days."

"Then I'll leave you and let you to get to your rest. Goodnight, old man." But as Tom went out he couldn't deny himself a small parting gibe: "Don't take it so hard; a body can't win every time; you'll hang somebody yet."

Wilson muttered to himself, "It is no lie to say I am sorry I have to begin with you, miserable dog though you are!"

He braced himself up with a glass of cold whisky, and went to work again. He did not compare the new finger-marks unintentionally left by Tom a few minutes before on Roxy's glass with the tracings of the marks left on the knife-handle, there being no need for that (for his trained eye), but busied himself with another matter, muttering from time to time, "Idiot that I was!—Nothing but a *girl* would do me—a man in girl's clothes never occurred to me." First, he hunted out the plate containing the fingerprints made by Tom when he was twelve years old, and laid it by itself; then he brought forth the marks made by Tom's baby fingers when he was a suckling of seven months, and placed these two plates with the one containing this subject's newly (and unconsciously) made record.

"Now the series is complete," he said with satisfaction, and sat down to inspect these things and enjoy them.

But his enjoyment was brief. He stared a considerable time at the three strips, and seemed stupefied with astonishment. At last he put them down and said, "I can't make it out at all—hang it, the baby's don't tally with the others!"

He walked the floor for half an hour puzzling over his enigma, then he hunted out two other glass plates.

He sat down and puzzled over these things a good while, but kept muttering, "It's no use; I can't understand it. They don't tally right, and yet I'll swear the names and dates are right, and so of course they *ought* to tally. I never labeled one of these thing carelessly in my life. There is a most extraordinary mystery here."

He was tired out, now, and his brains were beginning to clog. He said he would sleep himself fresh, and then see what he could do with this riddle. He slept through a troubled and unrestful hour, then unconsciousness began to shred away, and presently he rose drowsily to a sitting posture. "Now what was that dream?" he said, trying to recall it; "what was that dream?—it seemed to unravel that puz—"

He landed in the middle of the floor at a bound, without finishing the sentence, and ran and turned up his light and seized his "records." He took a single swift glance at them and cried out—

"It's so! Heavens, what a revelation! And for twenty-three years no man has ever suspected it!"

21

Doom

> He is useless on top of the ground; he ought to be under it, inspiring the cabbages.—*Pudd'nhead Wilson's Calendar*
> *April 1.* This is the day upon which we are reminded of what we are on the other three hundred and sixty-four.—*Pudd'nhead Wilson's Calendar*

Wilson put on enough clothes for business purposes and went to work under a high pressure of steam. He was awake all over. All sense of weariness had been swept away by the invigorating refreshment of the great and hopeful discovery which he had made. He made fine and accurate reproductions of a number of his "records," and then enlarged them on a scale of ten to one with his pantograph. He did these pantograph enlargements on sheets of white cardboard, and made each individual line of the bewildering maze of whorls or curves or loops which constituted the "pattern," of a "record" stand out bold and black by reinforcing it with ink. To the untrained eye the collection of delicate originals made by the human finger on the glass plates looked about alike; but when enlarged ten times they resembled the markings of a block of wood that has been sawed across the grain, and the dullest eye could detect at a glance, and at a distance of many feet, that no two of the patterns were alike. When Wilson had at last finished his tedious and difficult work, he arranged its results according to a plan in which a progressive order and sequence was a principal feature; then he added to the batch several pantograph enlargements which he had made from time to time in bygone years.

The night was spent and the day well advanced, now. By the time he had snatched a trifle of breakfast it was nine o'clock, and the court was ready to begin its sitting. He was in his place twelve minutes later with his "records."

Tom Driscoll caught a slight glimpse of the records, and nudged his nearest friend and said, with a wink, "Pudd'nhead's got a rare eye to business—thinks that as long as he can't win his case it's at least a noble good chance to advertise his palace-window decorations without any expense." Wilson was informed that his witnesses had been delayed, but would arrive presently; but he rose and said he should probably not have occasion to make use of their testimony. [An amused murmur ran through the room—"It's a clean backdown! he gives up without hitting a lick!"] Wilson continued—"I have other testimony—and better. [This compelled interest, and evoked murmurs of surprise that had a detectable ingredient of disappointment in them.] If I seem to be springing this evidence upon the court, I offer as my justification for this, that I did not discover its existence until late last night, and have been engaged in examining and classifying it ever since, until half an hour ago. I shall offer it presently; but first I wish to say a few preliminary words.

"May it please the Court, the claim given the front place, the claim most persistently urged, the claim most strenuously and I may even say aggressively and defiantly insisted upon by the prosecution, is this—that the person whose hand left the blood-stained fingerprints upon the handle of the Indian knife is the person who committed the murder." Wilson paused, during several moments, to give impressiveness to what he was about to say, and then added tranquilly, "*We grant that claim.*"

It was an electrical surprise. No one was prepared for such an admission. A buzz of astonishment rose on all sides, and people were heard to intimate that the overworked lawyer had lost his mind. Even the veteran judge, accustomed as he was to legal ambushes and masked batteries in criminal procedure, was not sure that his ears were not deceiving him, and asked counsel what it was he had said. Howard's impassive face betrayed no sign, but his attitude and bearing lost something of their careless confidence for a moment. Wilson resumed:

"We not only grant that claim, but we welcome it and strongly endorse it. Leaving that matter for the present, we will now proceed to consider other points in the case which we propose to establish by evidence, and shall include that one in the chain in its proper place."

He had made up his mind to try a few hardy guesses, in mapping out his theory of the origin and motive of the murder—guesses designed to fill up gaps in it—guesses which could help if they hit, and would probably do no harm if they didn't.

"To my mind, certain circumstances of the case before the court seem to suggest a motive for the homicide quite different from the one insisted on by the State. It is my conviction that the motive was not revenge, but robbery. It has been urged that the presence of the accused brothers in that fatal room, just after notification that one of them must take the life of Judge Driscoll or lose his own the moment the parties should meet, clearly signifies that the natural instinct of self-preservation moved my clients to go there secretly and save Count Luigi by destroying his adversary.

"Then why did they stay there, after the deed was done? Mrs. Pratt had time, although she did not hear the cry for help, but woke up some moments later, to run to that room—and there she found these men standing and making no effort to escape. If they were guilty, they ought to have been running out of the house at the same time that she was running to that room. If they had had such a strong instinct toward self-preservation as to move them to kill that unarmed man, what had become of it now, when it should have been more alert than ever? Would any of us have remained there? Let us not slander our intelligence to that degree.

"Much stress has been laid upon the fact that the accused offered a very large reward for the knife with which this murder was done; that no thief came forward to claim that extraordinary reward; that the latter fact was good circumstantial evidence that the claim that the knife had been stolen was a vanity and a fraud; that these details taken in connection with the memorable and apparently prophetic speech of the deceased concerning that knife, and the final discovery of that very knife in the fatal room where no living person was found present with the slaughtered man but the owner of the knife and his brother, form an indestructible chain of evidence which fixes the crime upon those unfortunate strangers.

"But I shall presently ask to be sworn, and shall testify that there was a large reward offered for the *thief*, also; and it was offered secretly and not advertised; that this fact was indiscreetly mentioned—or at least tacitly admitted—in what was supposed to be safe circumstances, but may *not* have been. The thief may have been present himself. [Tom Driscoll had been looking at the speaker, but dropped his eyes at this point.] In that case he would retain the knife in his possession, not daring to offer it for sale, or for pledge in a pawn-shop. [There was a nodding of heads among the audience by way of admission that this was not a bad stroke.] I shall prove to the satisfaction of the jury that there *was* a person in Judge Driscoll's room several minutes before the accused entered it. [This produced a strong sensation; the last drowsy-head in the courtroom roused up, now, and made preparation to listen.] If it shall seem necessary, I will prove by the Misses Clarkson that they met a veiled person—ostensibly a woman—coming out of the back gate a few minutes after the cry for help was heard. This person was not a woman, but a man dressed in woman's clothes." Another sensation. Wilson had his eye on Tom when he hazarded this guess, to see what effect it would produce. He was satisfied with the result, and said to himself, "It was a success—he's hit!"

"The object of that person in that house was robbery, not murder. It is true that the safe was not open, but there was an ordinary tin cash-box on the table, with three thousand dollars in it. It is easily supposable that the thief was concealed in the house; that he knew of this box, and of its owner's habit of counting its contents and arranging his accounts at night—if he had that habit, which I do not assert, of course;—that he tried to take the box while its owner slept, but made a noise and was seized, and had to use the knife to save himself from capture; and that he fled without his booty because he heard help coming.

"I have now done with my theory, and will proceed to the evidences by which I propose to try to prove its soundness." Wilson took up several of his strips of glass. When the audience recognized these familiar mementoes of Pudd'nhead's old-time childish "puttering" and folly, the tense and funereal interest vanished out of their faces, and the house burst into volleys of relieving and refreshing laughter, and Tom chirked up and joined in the fun himself; but Wilson was apparently not disturbed. He arranged his records on the table before him, and said—

"I beg the indulgence of the court while I make a few remarks in explanation of some evidence which I am about to introduce, and which I shall presently ask to be allowed to verify under oath on the witness stand. Every human being carries with him from his cradle to his grave certain physical marks which do not change their character, and by which he can always be identified—and that without shade of doubt or question. These marks are his signature, his physiological autograph, so to speak, and this autograph can not be counterfeited, nor can he disguise it or hide it away, nor can it become illegible by the wear and mutations of time. This signature is not his face—age can change that beyond recognition; it is not his hair, for that can fall out; it is not his height, for duplicates of that exist; it is not his form, for duplicates of that exist also, whereas this signature is each man's very own—there is no duplicate of it among the swarming populations of the globe! [The audience were interested once more.]

"This autograph consists of the delicate lines or corrugations with which Nature marks the insides of the hands and the soles of the feet. If you will look at the balls of your fingers—you that have very sharp eyesight—you will observe that these dainty curving lines lie close together, like those that indicate the borders of oceans in maps, and that they form various clearly defined patterns, such as arches, circles, long curves, whorls, etc., and that these patterns differ on the different fingers. [Every man in the room had his hand up to the light, now, and his head canted to one side, and was minutely scrutinizing the balls of his fingers; there were whispered ejaculations of 'Why, it's so—I never noticed that before!'] The patterns on the right hand are not the same as those on the left. [Ejaculations of 'Why, that's so, too!'] Taken finger for finger, your patterns differ from your neighbour's. [Comparisons were made all over the house—even the judge and jury were absorbed in this curious work.] The patterns of a twin's right hand are not the same as those on his left. One twin's patterns are never the same as his fellow-twin's patterns—the jury will find that the patterns upon the finger-balls of the accused follow this rule. [An examination of the twins' hands was begun at once.] You have often heard of twins who were so exactly alike that when dressed alike their own parents could not tell them apart. Yet there was never a twin born into this world that did not carry from birth to death a sure identifier in this mysterious and marvellous natal autograph. That once known to you, his fellow-twin could never personate him and deceive you."

Wilson stopped and stood silent. Inattention dies a quick and sure death when a speaker does that. The stillness gives warning that something is coming. All palms and finger-balls went down, now, all slouching forms straightened, all heads came up, all eyes were fastened upon Wilson's face. He waited yet one, two, three moments, to let his pause complete and perfect its spell upon the house; then, when through the profound hush he could hear the ticking of the clock on the wall, he put out his hand and took the Indian knife by the blade and held it aloft where all could see the sinister spots upon its ivory handle; then he said, in a level and passionless voice—

"Upon this haft stands the assassin's natal autograph, written in the blood of that helpless and unoffending old man who loved you and whom you all loved. There is but one man in the whole earth whose hand can duplicate that crimson sign,"—he paused and raised his eyes to the pendulum swinging back and forth—"and please God we will produce that man in this room before the clock strikes noon!"

Stunned, distraught, unconscious of its own movement, the house half rose, as if expecting to see the murderer appear at the door, and a breeze of muttered ejaculations swept the place. "Order in the court!—sit down!" This from the sheriff. He was obeyed, and quiet reigned again. Wilson stole a glance at Tom, and said to himself, "He is flying signals of distress, now; even people who despise him are pitying him; they think this is a hard ordeal for a young fellow who has lost his benefactor by so cruel a stroke—and they are right." He resumed his speech:

"For more than twenty years I have amused my compulsory leisure with collecting these curious physical signatures in this town. At my house I have hundreds upon hundreds of them. Each and every one is labelled with name and date; not labelled the next day or even the next hour, but in the very minute that the impression was taken. When I go upon the witness stand I will repeat under oath the things which I am now saying. I have the fingerprints of the court, the sheriff, and every member of the jury. There is hardly a person in this room, white or black, whose natal signature I cannot produce, and not one of them can so disguise himself that I cannot pick him out from a multitude of his fellow-creatures and unerringly identify him by his hands. And if he and I should live to be a hundred I could still do it. [The interest of the audience was steadily deepening, now.]

"I have studied some of these signatures so much that I know them as well as the bank cashier knows the autograph of his oldest customer. While I turn my back now, I beg that several persons will be so good as to pass their fingers through their hair, and then press them upon one of the panes of the window near the jury, and that among them the accused may set *their* finger-marks. Also, I beg that these experimenters, or others, will set their finger-marks upon another pane, and add again the marks of the accused, but not placing them in the same order or relation to the other signatures as before—for, by one chance in a million, a person might happen upon the right marks by pure guess-work *once*, therefore I wish to be tested twice."

He turned his back, and the two panes were quickly covered with delicately-lined oval spots, but visible only to such persons as could get a dark background for them—the foliage of a tree, outside, for instance. Then, upon call, Wilson went to the window, made his examination, and said—

"This is Count Luigi's right hand; this one, three signatures below, is his left. Here is Count Angelo's right; down here is his left. Now for the other pane: here and here are Count Luigi's, here and here are his brother's." He faced about. "Am I right?"

A deafening explosion of applause was the answer. The Bench said—

"This certainly approaches the miraculous!"

Wilson turned to the window again and remarked, pointing with his finger—

"This is the signature of Mr. Justice Robinson. [Applause.] This, of Constable Blake. [Applause.] This, of John Mason, juryman. [Applause.] This, of the sheriff. [Applause.] I cannot name the others, but I have them all at home, named and dated, and could identify them all by my fingerprint records."

He moved to his place through a storm of applause—which the sheriff stopped, and also made the people sit down, for they were all standing and struggling to see, of course. Court, jury, sheriff, and everybody had been too absorbed in observing Wilson's performance to attend to the audience earlier.

"Now, then," said Wilson, "I have here the natal autographs of two children—thrown up to ten times the natural size by the pantograph, so that any one who can see at all can tell the markings apart at a glance. We will call the children *A* and *B*. Here are *A*'s finger-marks, taken at the age of five months. Here they are again, taken at seven months. [Tom started.] They are alike, you see. Here are *B*'s at five months, and also at seven months. They, too, exactly copy each other, but the patterns are quite different from *A*'s, you observe. I shall refer to these again presently, but we will turn them face down, now.

"Here, thrown up ten sizes, are the natal autographs of the two persons who are here before you accused of murdering Judge Driscoll. I made these pantograph copies last night, and will so swear when I go upon the witness stand. I ask the jury to compare them with the finger-marks of the accused upon the window panes, and tell the court if they are the same."

He passed a powerful magnifying-glass to the foreman.

One juryman after another took the cardboard and the glass and made the comparison. Then the foreman said to the judge—

"Your honour, we are all agreed that they are identical."

Wilson said to the foreman—

"Please turn that cardboard face down, and take this one, and compare it searchingly, by the magnifier, with the fatal signature upon the knife-handle, and report your finding to the court."

Again the jury made minute examinations, and again reported—

"We find them to be exactly identical, your honour."

Wilson turned toward the counsel for the prosecution, and there was a clearly recognizable note of warning in his voice when he said—

"May it please the court, the State has claimed, strenuously and persistently, that the blood-stained fingerprints upon that knife-handle were left there by the assassin of Judge Driscoll. You have heard us grant that claim, and welcome it." He turned to the jury: "Compare the fingerprints of the accused with the fingerprints left by the assassin—and report."

The comparison began. As it proceeded, all movement and all sound ceased, and the deep silence of an absorbed and waiting suspense settled upon the house; and when at last the words came—

"*They do not even resemble*," a thunder-crash of applause followed and the house sprang to its feet, but was quickly repressed by official force and brought to order again. Tom was altering his position every few minutes, now, but none of his changes brought repose nor any small trifle of comfort. When the house's attention was become fixed once more, Wilson said gravely, indicating the twins with a gesture—

"These men are innocent—I have no further concern with them. [Another outbreak of applause began, but was promptly checked.] We will now proceed to find the guilty. [Tom's eyes were starting from their sockets—yes, it was a cruel day for the bereaved youth, everybody thought.] We will return to the infant autographs of *A* and *B*. I will ask the jury to take these large pantograph facsimilies of *A*'s marked five months and seven months. Do they tally?"

The foreman responded—

"Perfectly."

"Now examine this pantograph, taken at eight months, and also marked *A*. Does it tally with the other two?"

The surprised response was—

"*No—they differ widely*!"

"You are quite right. Now take these two pantographs of *B*'s autograph, marked five months and seven months. Do they tally with each other?"

"Yes—perfectly."

"Take this third pantograph marked *B*, eight months. Does it tally with *B*'s other two?"

"*By no means*!"

"Do you know how to account for those strange discrepancies? I will tell you. For a purpose unknown to us, but probably a selfish one, somebody changed those children in the cradle."

This produced a vast sensation, naturally; Roxana was astonished at this admirable guess, but not disturbed by it. To guess the exchange was one thing, to guess who did it quite another. Pudd'nhead Wilson could do wonderful things, no doubt, but he couldn't do impossible ones. Safe? She was perfectly safe. She smiled privately.

"Between the ages of seven months and eight months those children were changed in the cradle"—he made one of his effect-collecting pauses, and added—"and the person who did it is in this house!"

Roxy's pulses stood still! The house was thrilled as with an electric shock, and the people half rose as if to seek a glimpse of the person who had made that exchange. Tom was growing limp; the life seemed oozing out of him. Wilson resumed:

"*A* was put into *B*'s cradle in the nursery; *B* was transferred to the kitchen and became a negro and a slave, [Sensation—confusion of angry ejaculations]—but within a quarter of an hour he will stand before you white and free! [Burst of applause, checked by the officers.] From seven months onward until now, *A* has still been a usurper, and in my finger-record he bears *B*'s name. Here is his pantograph at the age of twelve. Compare it with the assassin's signature upon the knife-handle. Do they tally?"

The foreman answered—

"*To the minutest detail!*"

Wilson said, solemnly—

"The murderer of your friend and mine—York Driscoll of the generous hand and the kindly spirit—sits in among you. Valet de Chambre, negro and slave—falsely called Thomas à Becket Driscoll—make upon the window the fingerprints that will hang you!"

Tom turned his ashen face imploring toward the speaker, made some impotent movements with his white lips, then slid limp and lifeless to the floor.

Wilson broke the awed silence with the words—

"There is no need. He has confessed."

Roxy flung herself upon her knees, covered her face with her hands, and out through her sobs the words struggled—

"De Lord have mercy on me, po' misable sinner dat I is!"

The clock struck twelve.

The court rose; the new prisoner, handcuffed, was removed.

Conclusion

> It is often the case that the man who can't tell a lie thinks he is the best judge of one.—*Pudd'nhead Wilson's Calendar*
>
> *October 12, the Discovery.* It was wonderful to find America, but it would have been more wonderful to miss it.—*Pudd'nhead Wilson's Calendar*

The town sat up all night to discuss the amazing events of the day and swap guesses as to when Tom's trial would begin. Troop after troop of citizens came to serenade Wilson, and require a speech, and shout themselves hoarse over every sentence that fell from his lips—for all his sentences were golden, now, all were marvellous. His long fight against hard luck and prejudice was ended; he was a made man for good.

And as each of these roaring gangs of enthusiasts marched away, some remorseful member of it was quite sure to raise his voice and say—

"And this is the man the likes of us have called a pudd'nhead for more than twenty years. He has resigned from that position, friends."

"Yes, but it isn't vacant—we're elected."

The twins were heroes of romance, now, and with rehabilitated reputations. But they were weary of Western adventure, and straightway retired to Europe.

Roxy's heart was broken. The young fellow upon whom she had inflicted twenty-three years of slavery continued the false heir's pension of thirty-five dollars a month to her, but her hurts were too deep for money to heal; the spirit in her eye was quenched, her martial bearing departed with it, and the voice of her laughter ceased in the land. In her church and its affairs she found her only solace.

The real heir suddenly found himself rich and free, but in a most embarrassing situation. He could neither read nor write, and his speech was the basest dialect of the negro quarter. His gait, his attitudes, his gestures, his bearing, his laugh—all were vulgar and uncouth; his manners were the manners of a slave. Money and fine clothes could not mend these defects or cover them up; they only made them the more glaring and the more pathetic. The poor fellow could not endure the terrors of the white man's parlour, and felt at home and at peace nowhere but in the kitchen. The family pew was a misery to him, yet he could nevermore enter into the solacing refuge of the "nigger gallery"—that was closed to him for good and all. But we cannot follow his curious fate further—that would be a long story.

The false heir made a full confession and was sentenced to imprisonment for life. But now a complication came up. The Percy Driscoll estate was in such a crippled shape when its owner died that it could pay only sixty per cent. of its great indebtedness, and was settled at that rate. But the creditors came forward, now, and complained that inasmuch as through an error for which *they* were in no way to blame the false heir was not inventoried at the time with the rest of the property, great wrong and loss had thereby been inflicted upon them. They rightly claimed that "Tom" was lawfully their property and had been so for eight years; that they had already lost sufficiently in being deprived of his services during that long period, and ought not to be required to add anything to that loss; that if he had been delivered up to them in the first place, they would have sold him and he could not have murdered Judge Driscoll; therefore it was not he that had really committed the murder, the guilt lay with the erroneous inventory. Everybody saw that there was reason in this. Everybody granted that if "Tom" were white and free it would be unquestionably right to punish him—it would be no loss to anybody; but to shut up a valuable slave for life—that was quite another matter.

As soon as the Governor understood the case, he pardoned Tom at once, and the creditors sold him down the river.